THE OXFORD COMPANION TO
Crime and Mystery Writing

THE OXFORD COMPANION TO

Crime and Mystery Writing

EDITOR IN CHIEF

Rosemary Herbert

EDITORS

Catherine Aird

John M. Reilly

CONSULTING EDITOR

Susan Oleksiw

New York   Oxford
OXFORD UNIVERSITY PRESS
1999

OXFORD UNIVERSITY PRESS

Oxford   New York

Athens   Auckland   Bangkok   Bogotá   Buenos Aires   Calcutta
Cape Town   Chennai   Dar es Salaam   Delhi   Florence   Hong Kong   Istanbul
Karachi   Kuala Lumpur   Madrid   Melbourne   Mexico City   Mumbai   Nairobi
Paris   São Paulo   Singapore   Taipei   Tokyo   Toronto   Warsaw

and associated companies in
Berlin   Ibadan

Library of Congress Cataloging-in-Publication Data

Herbert, Rosemary.
The Oxford companion to crime and mystery writing / Rosemary Herbert
p.   cm.
Includes bibliographical references and index.
ISBN 0-19-507239-1 (alk. paper)
1. Detective and mystery stories—Encyclopedias.
2. Crime in literature—Encyclopedias. I. Title.
PN3488.D4H37   1999
809.3'872'03—dc21   99-21182

1 3 5 7 9 8 6 4 2

Printed in the United States of America
on acid-free paper

Contents

Introduction

It was a cold and wintry afternoon in Oxford, England, when the editors of the then nascent volume which would come to be known as *The Oxford Companion to Crime and Mystery Writing* concluded the meeting that would lay the groundwork for this book. After brainstorming about overarching principles of *Companion* construction and individual topics to be included, the editors crammed themselves companionably into a single elevator while continuing to converse about the project that had brought them together. Although the elevator doors closed in the normal way, the passengers soon noticed that the elevator itself did not stop where they expected, but descended beyond their chosen floor. All conversation stopped as the doors opened upon a solid stone wall offering absolutely no egress. In unison came the cry "For the love of God, Montresor!"

This outcry, echoing the horrified plea of the victim who has been entombed behind a stone wall in Edgar Allan Poe's story "The Cask of Amontillado," was proof positive that the editors experiencing the nightmarish elevator ride shared a mental landscape distinguished by at least one landmark from the world of crime and mystery fiction. Realizing this, the group engaged in nervous laughter, which only reached a stage of true levity as the elevator doors closed themselves upon the masonry, the machine ascended, and the doors finally opened into a clean, well-lighted corridor.

It is not insignificant that these scholars of crime and mystery writing shared quotations, images, and a sense of play about a genre that demands intelligence, imagination, and active involvement from its readers. With the exception of the riddle, there is no form of writing that shares with the genre of crime and mystery writing its playful engagement of the intellect in the attempt to solve a puzzle. From the penny dreadful, which challenged seekers of sensation to discover the truth in a pattern of gory details; to the complex twentieth-century detective novel, which offers an intricate puzzle solved through the erudite application of arcane knowledge; to the crime novel, with its probing into the psyches of reliable and deviant characters alike, this broad-ranging genre offers readers an intellectual excitement unsurpassed by other forms of fiction. The genre includes works of many kinds in which crime is central to the theme, action, and especially plot structure of the narrative. These range from tales of detection in the forms of the short story or novel, to radio, stage, and film dramas, comic strips, computer games, and jigsaw puzzle and book combinations, all of which engage their users in participatory intellectual play.

The genre's reputation as a kind of intellectual recreation or game has drawn practitioners, aficionados, and detractors from all strata of society. Distinguished writers have included the British poet Cecil Day-Lewis, writing as Nicholas Blake; Oxford don J. I. M. Stewart, writing as Michael Innes; and American professor Carolyn Heilbrun, writing as Amanda Cross. Famous readers of the genre include Thomas De Quincey, who celebrated it in his essay "On Murder Considered as One of the Fine Arts"; the former poet laureate of England, W. H. Auden, who compared the form to classical tragedy in his essay "The Guilty Vicarage"; and Edmund Wilson, who disdained detective fiction in his critique "Who Cares Who Killed Roger Ackroyd?" Published as cheap penny dreadfuls, dime novels, railway novels, comic books, book club editions, and paperbacks, and in newspapers and magazines, crime and mystery writing has been successfully marketed to the masses as entertainment intended to puzzle. One of the most substantial subgenres of crime and mystery writing, the detective novel, famously fulfilled a grave need for escape reading when it was the reading matter of choice for Londoners who grabbed books provided free to them as they fled into the Underground system during the aerial bombardment of their city in World War II.

Despite the fact that influential people admit publicly to their admiration of crime writing, and although the enjoyment of crime and mystery writing can be traced back to thirteenth-century China, the validation of this genre as a legitimate area of study within academic institutions is a much more recent phenomenon. Only since the early 1970s has it been possible to enroll in college and university courses in literary history and analysis of the genre. Scholars have even begun to share information regarding their course syllabi and teaching techniques through the *Murder Is Academic* newsletter, edited by Professor B. J. Rahn of Hunter College, The City University of New York; on the Internet; and at academic conferences. This is not to mention the slew of articles that have appeared in the past decades for audiences devoted to a more or less serious study of crime and mystery writing.

Accompanying the development of the genre as a subject of academic discourse has been the publication of secondary and reference books. Much solid work has been accomplished in the area of biography, including traditional biographies and biographical dictionaries treating authors and characters in this genre. While *The Oxford Companion to Crime and Mystery Writing* includes biographical entries for 149 iconic authors in the genre, its contribution is not meant to be chiefly biographical. The volume's index also directs readers to information about hundreds of additional authors who are treated in the context of entries regarding settings, milieus, themes, character types, and aspects of craft with which they are associated. It is the treatment of authors in context that distinguishes this volume. Besides authors, the *Companion* also contains authoritative individual entries on 85 characters, listed under their last names, who may be regarded as giants or archetypes of the genre.

The determination of which authors and characters would receive individual entries in this book was made by the editors and advisory editors who selected those whom they deemed to be groundbreaking in their time, highly influential, or hugely memorable. Countless additional authors and characters who do not have entries may be found by consulting the comprehensive index, which will lead readers to favorite figures in a large variety of contexts. It is also possible to look up characters by type in articles that examine every prominent figure from that of the femme fatale to the county constable.

Like the field of authors' biography, the bibliography of crime and mystery writing is an area in which considerable work precedes this book, as is exemplified in Allen J. Hubin's *Crime Fiction: A Comprehensive Bibliography, 1749–1980*. Thanks to the information contained in Hubin's work and to countless hours spent by the editor-in-chief and fact checkers who are also librarians in the Harvard University library system, this *Companion* is unusually strong bibliographically. Most short stories, novels, essays, and articles mentioned in these pages are followed by parenthetical information supplying the earliest verifiable date of publication. Scholars and aficionados alike may find it instructive to know that certain stories were first printed in such publications as homely journals catering to "ladies" and "gentlemen," while others appeared in pulp magazines, and still others in "highbrow" literary publications.

Throughout this volume, the year of publication given for novels is that in which the first edition appeared in the writer's own country. And, as longtime readers of detective fiction know, title changes are not uncommon in this genre (especially when a work by an English author is published in both English and American editions); in such cases we have also included up to two variants of the title in question. While the intention here is to help readers to recognize books that they may have read under other titles, most of which were changed to eliminate national words or turns of phrase that foreigners would not recognize, this editorial policy serves to illuminate other rationales for the alteration of titles. The now famous example is Agatha Christie's 1939 novel, originally titled *Ten Little Niggers*, after an insensitive children's rhyme. When the publisher realized what the title conveyed, it was changed, in a 1940 edition, to *And Then There Were None*, which is the last line of the rhyme that gave the book its original title and which is used throughout the story as a key element of plot. A further complication—and clearly no improvement—was the publication in 1965 of a paperback edition of the book under the title *Ten Little Indians*.

In addition to the biographical dictionaries and bibliographies that are available today, many other secondary works about crime and mystery fiction reflect the enthusiasms of their authors, editors, and contributors. These vary considerably in mission, some succeeding as collections of curiosities aimed at devotees of certain characters or schools of writing, others—at the other end of the spectrum—pursuing heavily academic or earnestly polemical approaches to the analysis of text. *The Oxford Companion to Crime and Mystery Writing* addresses the still outstanding need for a single-volume reference work that will serve, as the title suggests, as a companion to the enjoyment or study of the crime and mystery genre. Its mission is to reflect the collective fervor of its editors and advisory editors for the genre rather than to propound any single enthusiasm. Designed for readers of the English language around the world, its focus is upon works of crime and mystery writing published in English.

A limited number of international writers whose first language is not English—such as the Belgian Georges Simenon and the Swedish writing team of Maj Sjöwall and Per Wahlöö—are accorded entries of their own, since their work, which has been readily available in English translation, has contributed to the development of the genre as a whole. Other international writers may receive attention in the context of their languages or national literatures, as is the case in "Europe, Crime and Mystery Writing in Continental: The Netherlands and Flanders." In the case of fiction published in languages other than English, titles are given, where possible, of the first edition in the author's own language, followed by parenthetical information regarding first publication in English. When our contributors choose to translate titles (for the purpose of adding to the reader's understanding of a title that has never been translated into English), that information is also contained in parentheses, but is not italicized.

It should be noted that the *Companion*'s coverage of works originally published in languages other than English is intended to enhance the reader's awareness of the international nature of the genre without presuming to be comprehensive, particularly regarding authors whose work may never have been published in English. In addition, while our articles "China, Crime and Mystery Writing in Greater" and "Japan, Crime and Mystery Writing in" show that narratives involving crime-solving judges long predate crime and mystery writing in English, the *Companion* largely looks at English-language crime and mystery writing from its development during the nineteenth century. Although some of our contributors cite classical myths and Bible stories as falling within the parameters of the genre, the coverage in this volume dates mostly from around the time of the publication of Edgar Allan Poe's "The Murders in the Rue Morgue" in 1841.

Within these parameters of time and language, *The Oxford Companion to Crime and Mystery Writing* is envisioned as a volume to turn to as a compendium of information regarding the literary history and craft of crime and mystery writing, an authoritative source on iconic authors and characters, an omnium-gatherum of curiosities, a single source to consult for points of information, and, especially, as pages to peruse at leisure in the interest of expanding and enriching one's knowledge and appreciation of the genre.

Any reader of crime and mystery fiction, whether pursuing academic expertise in the subject or simply seeking to enhance armchair enjoyment of the literature, is bound to welcome the composite entry "History of Crime and Mystery Writing," which offers a chronological survey of the development of the genre. Similarly, the reader who turns to the two-part "Gold Age Traditions" will be able to compare and contrast the manners in which British and American authors handled classic detective fiction generally written between the two world wars. Fans of hard-boiled fiction can peruse the composite entry on "Police Procedural." In this case the entry not only surveys American and British fiction of this type but includes a section citing international exemplars of the police procedural. In all of these entries, the reader who admires a particular form or style of crime and mystery writing will encounter familiar along with less-known authors and characters about whom they might like to read in works identified by our contributors. Readers who would like to learn more about a topic will also benefit from the suggestions for further reading at the end of many entries.

Numerous broad areas are covered in the *Companion*. They include literary history, which incorporates entries on time periods, national and regional traditions, subgenres and schools of writing, precursors and parameters of the genre, and particular geographic settings. The entries on parameters of the genre help to place crime and mystery writing within the context of popular forms of literature including the "Ghost Story," "Novel of Manners," "Potboiler," and "Sensation Novel." Another area of coverage concerns the craft of crime and mystery writing, which entails discussion of types of characters, crimes, milieus, themes, literary conventions, and components (like the use of the "Double Bluff" or the significance of "Fingerprints and Footprints") that often figure in crime and mystery writing. Included also are entries on criminal types such as the "Con Artist," "Gentleman Thief," and "Underworld Figure"; on sleuth types such as "Amateur Detective," "Country Constable," and "Private Eye"; and on the thematic treatment of topics ranging from "Alcohol and Alcoholism" to "Virtue." No book on this subject would be complete without discussion of some of the most engaging characteristics of this literature and its practitioners, including "Ingenuity," "Humor," and deftly exercised "Sleight of Hand."

The publishing history of the genre is outlined in articles such as "Pulp Magazines," "Paperbacks," and "Titles and Titling." Authorship, readership, and scholarship are addressed in "Syndicate Authors," "Audience Participation Activities," and in entries on various readers' and writers' organizations. Finally, the *Companion* links the literary history of the genre to the real world through articles on subjects including "Police History" and "Poisons, Unusual."

Using the *Companion*, readers may easily look up small points of information. For instance, the American reader who has never been quite certain what the CID is will learn that the acronym stands for the Criminal Investigation Department of London's Metropolitan Police, based at New Scotland Yard. The British reader, in turn, might enjoy discovering just what jurisdiction is covered by the FBI, or Federal Bureau of Investigation. These two entries reflect the volume's mission to span the Atlantic Ocean between the two great centers of crime and mystery writing in English, the United States and Britain—although writings from other English-speaking nations, including Canada, Australia, and New Zealand, are also addressed.

Other curiosities may pique the interest of a larger audience. The colorful term "red herring" may be recognized by many fans of the genre as referring to a false or misleading clue, but how many know that the word may be traced back to 1420? As the entry devoted to it explains, the term derives from the practice of dragging smoked herring across the path of hounds during foxhunts in order to throw the dogs off the scent. Word origins are worked into more expansive essays as well. In turning, for instance, to the survey of famous sleuths in detective fiction, the reader will learn that the term entered the English language as early as 1194, and first denoted the track rather than the tracker.

The tracking of information itself from one context to another is an important mission of this volume, one which should ensure that readers are lured from one entry to the next. For example, the reader who turns to the entry term "Murder" will find a definition of this capital crime, also known as homicide, and a discussion of why the crime is at the heart of so many detective novels. The "Murder" entry then will lead to an entry on "Taking of Life," which puts murder in the context of assassination, accidental killing, and suicide. The "Taking of Life" entry, in turn, leads to additional entries including a quirky compendium of lifeless bodies organized under the entry heading "Corpse."

As the above three entries illustrate, the mood of this volume ranges from deadly serious to irrepressibly vivacious, as does the literature of crime and mystery writing itself. As the editors who exited the renegade elevator at Oxford University Press will attest, just as the literature of crime and mystery often entertains while describing violent crime, this volume is designed to celebrate the playful side of an essentially entertaining literature while also satisfying the demand for solid scholarship in the genre.

USE OF THE COMPANION

The *Companion* is arranged alphabetically. Extensive cross-references guide the reader to related articles; these cross-references are of three types:

1) Within an entry, the first occurrence of a name, word, or phrase that has its own entry is marked with an asterisk (*).

2) When a topic is treated in another entry or a related topic is discussed elsewhere in the volume, the italicized words "see," "see also," or "please refer to" direct the reader to the appropriate entry term(s).

3) "Blind entries," or entry terms that have no accompanying text but are terms that readers might expect to find discussed, appear alphabetically in the volume and refer to the entries where the topics are actually treated. Thus the blind entry "Criminal Mastermind" refers readers to "Master Criminal."

Cross-references, including terms that are marked with asterisks and those used in blind entries, match the entry terms, with the exceptions of plurals and possessives. Therefore the asterisked terms "*clue" and "*clues" will lead the reader to the entry "Clues."

Real people and characters are alphabetized by last name, the former in capitals, the latter in ordinary bold type (e.g., Edgar Allan Poe under **POE, EDGAR ALLAN,** and The Chevalier C. Auguste Dupin under **Dupin, The Chevalier C. Auguste**). Each author is listed by the name under which he or she is best known in the crime and mystery field, even if that name is a pseudonym. Thus "Rhode, John" is the entry title for the article about Major Cecil John Charles Street, who produced much of his detective fiction under the Rhode pseudonym. Throughout the volume, any author who is not the subject of an entry is also referred to by the name he or she most commonly uses on works in this genre. In the case of authors who write mysteries under more than one name, the editors have chosen the name that they believe is most likely to come to mind for the most readers. In the case of Street/ Rhode, his second pseudonym, Miles Burton, is mentioned in the context of the Rhode entry. Authors and characters who are known by full names and nicknames are generally given entry titles under their full names. Blind entries will help to lead the reader who looks up the author sometimes known as Sapper to the entry for "McNeile, H(erman) C(yril)," and the reader who seeks the character known as the Thinking Machine will find a blind entry pointing the way to "Van Dusen, Professor Augustus S. F. X."

Abbreviations used in this volume include acronyms for organizations or police agencies, as well as for magazines that are heavily cited in these pages. A list of abbreviations follows:

AHMM *Alfred Hitchcock's Mystery Magazine*
AIEP Asociación Internacional de Escritores Policíacos (International Association of Crime Writers)
CADS *Crime and Detective Stories*
CIA   Central Intelligence Agency
CID   Criminal Investigation Department
CWA   Crime Writers Association
EQMM *Ellery Queen's Mystery Magazine*
FBI   Federal Bureau of Investigation
KGB   Komitet Gosudarstvennoy Bezopasnosti (Committee of State Security)
MWA   Mystery Writers of America

All entries are signed by their author(s), who are listed along with their affiliation(s) and title(s) of their article(s) in the Contributors section following the introduction.

ACKNOWLEDGMENTS

I wish to thank co-editors Catherine Aird and John M. Reilly for their invaluable contributions to the volume; Susan M. Oleksiw for her outstanding editorial work;

the advisory editors for their aid in shaping the volume; and our contributors for their expertise and ongoing support of the project. Boundless gratitude goes to Edward Gorey for his cover illustration. Edward D. Hoch, who made instant replies to a great variety of editorial queries, supplied incalculable support to the project. Gratitude must also be expressed for the fact-checking efforts of Lorraine Clairmont, Sarah Phillips, and Scott Williamson, who greatly enhanced the bibliographical strength of this book using the magnificent resources of the Harry Elkins Widener Memorial Library, the Houghton Library, and the Lamont Library at Harvard University.

Many people at Oxford University Press have been indispensable in the development and completion of this volume. They include Linda Halvorson, Nancy Toff, Ellen Satrom, Karen Fein, Karen Murphy, John Drexel, Ann Toback, Kathleen Lynch, and Russell Perreault. Additional friends of the project include Gina C. Guy of the Gotham Book Mart, Anna Lowi, Rebecca Eaton and Steven Ashley of WGBH Boston–Mystery!, and Peter X. Accardo, Christina Baum, Jean C. Behnke, Dana Bisbee, Joe Bourneuf, Margaret Byer, Mark Chapman, Eddie Doctoroff, Justine Du Hoffman, Dare Enriquez, Alea Henle, Robert H. Morehouse, Elaine M. Ober, Diana O'Neill, Eliza Partington, Daisy Partington, Janet Potter, Chris Rippen, Marion Schoon, Joyce Williams, and William C. Wyman, Jr.

As editor-in-chief, I dedicate my efforts to Susan Kron Moody, the companion of my childhood, and to Juliet Gazelle Herbert Partington I present this *Companion* of *her* childhood. I would also like to thank my mother, Barbara F. Herbert, and remember my late father, Robert D. Herbert, for their steadfast support of this project.

Rosemary Herbert
Newtonville, Massachusetts
March 1999

Contributors

Katherine Anne Ackley, *Professor of English, University of Wisconsin—Stevens Point*
Marriage; Mystery Writers of America

Robert C. S. Adey, *Book Collector, Writer, Anthologist, Colwall, England*
Impossible Crime; Locked Room Mystery; Short Story: The British Crime Short Story

Jack Adrian, *Author, Editor, North Malvern, England*
Strand Magazine, The

Catherine Aird, *Detective Novelist, Kent, England*
Allusion, Literary; Characterization; Clerical Sleuth; Conservative vs. Radical Worldview: Conservative Worldview; Country House Milieu; Europe, Crime and Mystery Writing in Continental: Introduction; Golden Age Forms: The Golden Age Novel; Pontificators, The; Trusted Figure as Criminal

Nadya Aisenberg, *Independent Scholar, Poet, Boston, Massachusetts*
Fairy Tale; Family; Resolution and Irresolution

Brian Aldiss, *Fellow, Royal Society of Literature, Green College, Oxford, England*
Science Fiction

Kathryn Alexander, *Technical Writer, Texas Engineering Extension Service, College Station, Texas*
Cadfael, Brother

Rupert Allason, *Author, London, England*
CID

L. M. Anderson, *Associate Professor of English, Virginia Polytechnic Institute and State University, Blacksburg, Virginia*
Revenge

Patricia Anderson-Boerger, *Reporter, The News-Sentinel, Fort Wayne, Indiana*
True Crime

Frankie Y. Bailey, *Associate Professor, School of Criminal Justice, State University of New York at Albany*
African American Sleuth; Crimes, Minor; Criminal Cases: Infamous American Criminal Cases; Johnson, Coffin Ed, and Grave Digger Jones; Linington, (Barbara) Elizabeth; Moto, Mr.; Police History: History of American Policing; Prejudice; Prisons: American Prisons; Racism; Urban Milieu

Chris Baldick, *Professor of English, Goldsmiths' College, University of London, England*
Gothic Novel

Elaine Bander, *English Department Faculty, Dawson College, Montreal, Quebec*
Setting

Burl Barer, *Walla Walla, Washington*
Saint, The

Robert Barnard, *Writer, Leeds, England*
Brand, Christianna; Dickens, Charles; Red Flags; Sleight of Hand

Melvyn Barnes, *Director of Libraries, Corporation of London, London, England*
Ball, John (Dudley, Jr.); Cole, G(eorge) D(ouglas) H(oward) and Margaret (Isabel Postgate); Creasey, John; Eberhart, Mignon G(ood); French, Inspector Joseph; Gethryn, Colonel Anthony Ruthven; Ghote, Inspector Ganesh Vinayak; Priestley, Dr. Lancelot; Reeder, Mr. J(ohn) G.; Wallace, (Richard Horatio) Edgar

Jacques Baudou, *Member, L'OULIPOPO, Author, Paris, France*
Leblanc, Maurice (Marie Émile); Lupin, Arsène; Sûreté

Mary Helen Becker, *Owner, Booked For Murder, Ltd., Madison, Wisconsin*
Mayo, Asey

Kate Begnal, *Associate Professor of English, Utah State University, Logan, Utah*
Theft

Ian Bell, *Head of English Department, University of Wales, Swansea*
Hansen, Joseph; Master Criminal; Raffles, A. J.; Wade, Henry; Wexford, Inspector

Bernard Benstock, *Professor of English, University of Miami, Coral Gables, Florida (deceased)*
Charles, Nick and Nora

Christopher Bentley, *Critic, Senior Lecturer in English (retired), University of Sydney, Australia*
Medical Milieu; Medical Sleuth

Jesse Berrett, *Instructor in History, San Francisco University High School, California*
Hammer, Mike; Macdonald, Ross; Voyeurism

Hans Bertens, *Professor of Comparative Literature, University of Utrecht, The Netherlands*
Drummond, Bulldog

T. J. Binyon, *Senior Research Fellow, Wadham College, Oxford, England*
Childers, (Robert) Erskine; Crofts, Freeman Wills; Dostoyevsky, Fyodor (Mikhaylovich); Gaboriau, Émile; Garve, Andrew; Gentleman Thief; McNeile, H(erman) C(yril); Oxford; Private Detective; Private Eye; Rhode, John; Sleuth; Superman Sleuth; Yates, Dornford

Dana Bisbee, *Writer, Boston, Massachusetts*
Bond, James; Christie, Agatha (Mary Clarissa); Greene, Graham; Sidekicks and Sleuthing Teams; Tibbs, Virgil; Vance, Philo; Van de Wetering, Janwillem

Richard Bleiler, *Humanities Reference Librarian, Homer Babbidge Library, University of Connecticut, Storrs*
Black Mask; Brown, Carter; Formula: Character; Serialization and Series Publication; Stribling, T(homas) S(igismund); Treat, Lawrence

Jan Blodgett, *College Archivist and Records Management Coordinator, Davidson College Library, Davidson, North Carolina*
Loyalty and Betrayal; Suspicion

K. Arne Blom, *Author, Lund, Sweden*
Europe, Crime and Mystery Writing in Continental: Nordic Countries

Clive Bloom, *Reader in English and American Studies, School of Humanities and Cultural Studies, Middlesex University, London, England*
Horror Fiction; Occult and Supernatural Literature

Michael Bowen, *Attorney-at-Law and Partner, Foley & Lardner, Milwaukee, Wisconsin*
Legal Systems: The U.S. Legal System

Timothy W. Boyd, *Junior Fellow, The Center for Hellenic Studies, Washington, D.C.*
Historical Figures in Crime and Mystery Writing: Royals, Politicians, and Statesmen; Period Mystery

Thomas Boyle, *Professor of English, Brooklyn College, Brooklyn, New York*
Newspaper Reports

Jon L. Breen, *Professor of English, Rio Hondo College, Whittier, California*
Alfred Hitchcock's Mystery Magazine; Biggers, Earl Derr; Block, Lawrence; Celebrity Crime and Mystery Writers; Ellery Queen's Mystery Magazine; Ellin, Stanley; Ghostwriters; Golden Age Traditions: The American Golden Age Tradition; Howdunit; Jury; Lawyer: The American Lawyer-Sleuth; Lawyer: Lawyers as Secondary Characters; Least Likely Suspect; Pastiche; Reference Works; Theatrical Milieu: Radio and Television Industry

Ray B. Browne, *Distinguished University Professor of Popular Culture, Bowling Green State University, Bowling Green, Ohio*
Australia, Crime and Mystery Writing in; Baantjer, A(lbert) C(ornelis); Bonaparte, Napoleon

Landon Burns, *Professor Emeritus of English, The Pennsylvania State University, State College, Pennsylvania*
Brandstetter, Dave; Goodwin, Archie; Wolfe, Nero

Rex Burns, *Professor of English, University of Colorado at Denver*
Black Mask School; Hard-Boiled Fiction; Shayne, Michael

Margaret Byer, *Graduate Student, Library and Information Science, Simmons College, Boston, Massachusetts*
Horse Racing Milieu

Marvin Carlson, *Sidney E. Cohn Distinguished Professor of Theater and Comparative Literature, Graduate Center, City University of New York*
Theater, the Crime and Mystery Genre in: British Theater; Theater, the Crime and Mystery Genre in: American Theater

Sarah Caudwell, *Barrister, Mystery Writer, London, England*
Banking and Financial Milieu; Rumpole, Horace; White-Collar Crime

Peter V. Cenci, *Assistant Professor of English, Essex Community College, Baltimore County, Maryland*
Christmas Crime; Expeditions; Innocence; Murderless Mystery; Plagiarism; Transportation, Modes of; Travel Milieu

Kathleen Chamberlain, *Associate Professor of English/Women's Studies, Emory & Henry College, Emory, Virginia*
Juvenile Mystery: Girls' Juvenile Mysteries; Keene, Carolyn

Kate Charles, *Crime Writer, Bedford, England*
Chivalry, Code of; Voice: Genteel Voice

Jean A. Coakley, *Associate Professor of English, Miami University, Oxford, Ohio*
Crispin, Edmund; Fashion and Design Milieu; Juvenile Sleuth: Girl Sleuth; Novel of Manners; Tey, Josephine

Paul Cobley, *Senior Lecturer in Communications, London Guildhall University, London, England*
Potboiler; Thriller: Psychological Thriller

Matthew Cohen, *Ph.D. Candidate in American Studies, The College of William and Mary, Williamsburg, Virginia*
Fleming, Ian

Michael Cohen, *Professor of English, Murray State University, Murray, Kentucky*
Atmosphere; Mason, A(lfred) E(dward) W(oodley); Shakespeare, William; Violent Entertainment, The Paradox of

Max Allan Collins, *President, M.A.C. Productions, Muscatine, Iowa*
Fiction Noir; Spillane, Mickey (Frank Morrison); Thompson, Jim

John D. Constable, *Senior Surgeon, Massachusetts General Hospital, Associate Clinical Professor of Surgery, Harvard Medical School, Boston, Massachusetts*
Watson, Dr. John H.

Michael Coren, *Broadcaster/Journalist, CFRB Radio and CTS Television, Toronto, Canada*
Brown, Father; Chesterton, G(ilbert) K(eith)

J. Randolph Cox, *Professor Emeritus and Reference Librarian, St. Olaf College, Northfield, Minnesota*
Accidental Sleuth; Carter, Nick; Coxe, George Harmon; Dime Novel; Gentleman Adventurer; Maigret, Inspector; Morrison, Arthur; Pathfinder Fiction; Pentecost, Hugh; Reeve, Arthur B(enjamin); Rohmer, Sax; Simenon, Georges; Slicks; Withers, Miss

Michael Cox, *Senior Commissioning Editor, Reference Books, Oxford University Press, Oxford, England*
Ghost Story

Patricia Craig, *Critic/Biographer, London, England*
Blake, Nicholas; Mitchell, Gladys (Maude Winifred)

Bill Crider, *Chair, Division of English and Fine Arts, Alvin Community College, Alvin, Texas*
Gault, William Campbell; Rural Milieu; Western, The

Jack Crowley, *Assistant Professor of Liberal Studies, Montana Tech of the University of Montana, Butte*
Chan, Charlie

Alzina Stone Dale, *Freelance Writer/Lecturer, Chicago, Illinois*
Heyer, Georgette; New York City; Peters, Ellis

J. Madison Davis, *Professor of Journalism, University of Oklahoma, Norman*
Francis, Dick

Mary Jean DeMarr, *Professor Emerita of English and Women's Studies, Indiana State University, Terre Haute*
Fen, Gervase

John T. Dizer, *Professor and Dean Emeritus, Mohawk Valley Community College, Utica, New York*
Juvenile Mystery: Boys' Juvenile Mysteries; Syndicate Authors

Susan Docherty
Anti-Semitism; Courtroom Milieu

Gregory Dowling, *Researcher of American Literature, University of Venice, Italy*
Europe, Crime and Mystery Writing in Continental: Italy

Bernard A. Drew, *Freelance Writer and Editor, Great Barrington, Massachusetts*
Adventurer and Adventuress; Royal Canadian Mounted Police

John Drexel, *Independent Scholar, Glen Ridge, New Jersey*
Morse, Inspector

Martin Edwards, *Crime Writer, Lymm, England*
Barnard, Robert; Berkeley, Anthony; Clues, Famous; Coroner; Crime Inspired by Fiction; England, State of; Golden Age Forms: The Golden Age Short Story; Guilt; Hare, Cyril; Hill, Reginald; Home Office, The; Impersonation; Justice; Kidnapping; Lawyer: The British Lawyer-Sleuth; Legal Systems: The English Legal System; Letters and Written Messages; MacDonald, Philip; Poets

as Crime Writers; Poirot, Hercule; Prodigal Son/Daughter; Regionalism: British; Victim; Villains and Villainy; Who-Was-Dun-In; Wills

Sue Feder, *Founder, Historical Mystery Appreciation Society; Editor/Publisher, Murder: Past Tense, Towson, Maryland*
FBI; Holiday Mysteries; Prohibition

Joseph J. Fink, *Professor of Marketing, Fairleigh Dickinson University, Teaneck, New Jersey*
Moriarty, Professor

Penelope Fitzgerald, *London, England*
Knox, Ronald A(rbuthnott)

Elizabeth Foxwell, *Mystery Writer and Editor, Alexandria, Virginia*
Hotel Milieu

Anthea Fraser, *Author, Former Secretary, Crime Writers Association, Hertfordshire, England*
Awards: British Awards

Mary P. Freier, *Coordinator of Instructional Services, Houston Cole Library, Jacksonville State University, Jacksonville, Alabama*
Had-I-but-Known; Rinehart, Mary Roberts

Helen S. Garson, *Professor Emeritus of English and American Studies, George Mason University, Fairfax, Virginia*
Pornography

Chris Gausden, *London, England*
Dover, Wilfred; Kramer, Lieutenant, and Sergeant Zondi; Oppenheim, E(dward) Phillips

David Geherin, *Professor of English, Eastern Michigan University, Ypsilanti*
Leonard, Elmore; McGee, Travis; Parker, Robert B(rown)

Michael C. Gerald, *Dean and Professor of Pharmacology, School of Pharmacy, University of Connecticut, Storrs*
Poisons and Poisoning

Jonathan Goodman, *Crime Historian, Honorary Secretary, OUR Society, London, England*
Criminal Cases: Infamous British Criminal Cases

Ron Goulart, *Writer, Weston, Connecticut*
Publishing, History of American Magazine; Pulp Magazines

Stephen Gray, *Professor of English (retired), Rand University, Johannesburg, South Africa*
Africa, Crime and Mystery Writing in

Martin Green, *Professor Emeritus of English Literature, Tufts University, Medford, Massachusetts*
Buchan, John

Douglas G. Greene, *Professor of History, Old Dominion University, Norfolk, Virginia*
Couples: Sleuth Couples; Puzzle

George Grella, *Professor of English and Film Studies, University of Rochester, Rochester, New York*
Conventions of the Genre: Overview; Ethics of Detectives

Jenny Grove, *Freelance Writer and Journalist, Surrey, England*
White-Collar Crime

W. M. Hagen, *Professor of English, Oklahoma Baptist University, Shawnee, Oklahoma*
Computer Detective Games

Jasmine Yong Hall, *Associate Professor of English, Elms College, Chicopee, Massachusetts*
Terror

Deborah E. Hamilton, *Assistant Professor of French, Augustana College, Rock Island, Illinois*
Europe, Crime and Mystery Writing in Continental: France and Belgium; Roman Policier

Margaret Broom Harp, *Associate Professor of French, University of Nevada, Las Vegas*
Gambling, Illegal

Carolyn G. Hart, *Author, Oklahoma City, Oklahoma*
Sisters in Crime

Patricia Hart
Europe, Crime and Mystery Writing in Continental: Spain

Barrie Hayne, *Professor of English, St. Michael's College, University of Toronto, Ontario, Canada*
Aristocratic Characters: Secondary Aristocratic Characters; Closed-World Settings and Open-World Settings; Collins, (William) Wilkie; Drood, Edwin; Eccentrics; Hanaud, Inspector; Island Milieu; Names and Naming of Characters; Spoof Scholarship; Theatrical Milieu: Motion Picture Industry; Titles and Titling

Michael G. Heenan, *Genealogist (retired), Canterbury, England*
Appleby, Sir John

Rosemary Herbert, *Mystery Book Review Columnist, Boston Herald, Boston, Massachusetts*
Academic Milieu; Adler, Irene; Aristocratic Characters: Aristocratic Sleuth; Canon, The; Daly, Carroll John; Christie, Agatha (Mary Clarissa); Daly, Elizabeth; Dexter, (Norman Colin); Gentleman Sleuth; Grafton, Sue; Gray, Cordelia; Hillerman, Tony; Holmes, Mycroft; Holmes, Sherlock; Humor; Japan, Crime and Mystery Writing in; Lathen, Emma; Mortimer, John (Clifford); Murder; Newgate Novel; Plainman Sleuth; Poison Pen Letters; Sports Milieu; Surrogate Detective; Suspense; Symons, Julian (Gustave); Theatrical Milieu: Legitimate Theater, Amateur Theater, and Touring Companies; Vane, Harriet; Van Gulik, Robert H(ans); Whitney, Phyllis A(yame); Williams, Race; Witness

Carolyn Higbie, *Associate Professor, Department of Classics, Harvard University, Cambridge, Massachusetts*
Historical Figures in Crime and Mystery Writing: Royals, Politicians, and Statesmen; Period Mystery

Edward D. Hoch, *Author, Rochester, New York*
Ciphers and Code; Digest-Sized Mystery Magazines; Dying Message; Hornung, E(rnest) W(illiam); Short Story: The American Crime Short Story; Stout, Rex (Todhunter); Waugh, Hillary (Baldwin)

Daniel Hoffman, *Poet in Residence and Felix E. Schelling Professor of English Emeritus, University of Pennsylvania, Philadelphia*
Poe, Edgar Allan

Wilson J. Hoffman, *Emeritus Pendleton Professor of History, Hiram College, Hiram, Ohio*
Great Depression, The; Greed

Martha Stoddard Holmes, *Assistant Professor of English, Plymouth State College, Plymouth, New Hampshire*
Zangwill, Israel

William Hood, *Author, Amagansett, New York*
CIA

Pierre L. Horn, *Professor of French, Wright State University, Dayton, Ohio*
Police Procedural: The International Police Procedural

Clark Howard, *Author, Palm Springs, California*
Hoch, Edward D(entinger)

Catherine E. Hoyser, *Associate Professor of English, Saint Joseph College, West Hartford, Connecticut*
Ethnicity; Historical Mystery

E. D. Huntley, *Professor of English, Appalachian State University, Boone, North Carolina*
Culinary Mystery

Peter Ibbotson, *Freelance Writer, Bournemouth, England*
Charteris, Leslie

Fred Isaac, *Freelance Writer and Librarian, Berkeley, California*
San Francisco

Dean James, *Manager, Murder By The Book, Writer, Houston, Texas*
Wentworth, Patricia

Louise Conley Jones, *Director, Fort Wayne Center, Concordia University, Fort Wayne, Indiana*
Suicide; Whydunit

H. R. F. Keating, *President, The Detection Club, London, England*
Brown, Fredric (William); Conventions of the Genre: Traditional Conventions; Golden Age Traditions: The British Golden Age Tradition; Ingenuity

George Kelley, *Professor of Business Administration, Erie Community College, Buffalo, New York*
Caper; Continental Op; Paperbacks; Terrorism and the Terrorist Procedural

Jeffrey Kinkley, *Professor of History, St. John's University, Jamaica, New York*
China, Crime and Mystery Writing in Greater

Margaret H. Kinsman, *Senior Lecturer in English, South Bank University, London, England*
Friendship

Kathleen Gregory Klein, *Professor of English, Southern Connecticut State University, New Haven*
Cross, Amanda; Females and Feminists; Gender; Milhone, Kinsey; Warshawski, V. I.

Joan G. Kotker, *English Faculty, Bellevue Community College, Bellevue, Washington*
Plot

John E. Kramer Jr., *Professor-Emeritus, Department of Sociology, State University of New York, College at Brockport*
Academic Milieu; Academic Sleuth

Henry Kratz, *Professor Emeritus of German, University of Tennessee, Knoxville*
Mason, Perry

Anne K. Krook, *Independent Scholar, Seattle, Washington*
Rape and Other Sex Crimes; Stalking; Taking of Life

Marvin Lachman, *Author and Reviewer, Santa Fe, New Mexico*
Chambrun, Pierre; Fell, Dr. Gideon; Gardner, Erle Stanley; Murdock, Kent; Musical Milieu; North, Mr. and Mrs.; Queen, Ellery: The Character; Readers, Distinguished; Regionalism: American; Thatcher, John Putnam

Larry N. Landrum, *Professor of English, Michigan State University, East Lansing*
Archer, Lew; Symbolism

Stephen Leadbeatter, *Senior Lecturer in Forensic Pathology, University of Wales College of Medicine, Cardiff*
Forensic Pathologist

A. Robert Lee, *Professor of American Literature, Nihon University, Tokyo*
Japan; Ethnic Sleuth

Anthony Lejeune, *Middlesex, England*
Advertising Milieu; Club Milieu

Jon Lellenberg, *Historian, Baker Street Irregulars, Literary Agent, The Conan Doyle Estate, Washington, D.C.*
Sherlockian Societies

Margaret Lewis, *Temporary Lecturer, University of Newcastle Upon Tyne, England*
Alleyn, Roderick; Marsh, (Edith) Ngaio; New Zealand, Crime and Mystery Writing in

Peter Lewis, *Emeritus Reader in English Studies, University of Durham, England*
Ambler, Eric; Interpol; Le Carré, John; MI5 and MI6; Spy Fiction

Dick Lochte, *Novelist, Critic, Columnist, Los Angeles, California*
Los Angeles

Joan Lock, *Freelance Writer, London, England*
Police History: History of British Policing; Prisons: British Prisons; Scotland Yard

John Loughery, *Art Critic, The Hudson Review, New York, New York*
Van Dine, S. S.

John Lutz, *Author, Webster Groves, Missouri*
Criminal Viewpoint

Andrew and Gina MacDonald
Political and Social Views, Authors

Gina MacDonald
Bagley, Desmond; Deighton, Len (Leonard Cyril)

Anne Scott MacLeod, *Professor, College of Library and Information Services, University of Maryland, College Park*
Drew, Nancy

Charlotte Macleod
Gardening

Michael Macmillan, *Member of the Council of the Law Society of Scotland, Ross-shire*
Legal Systems: The Scottish Legal System and the "Not Proven" Verdict

David Madden, *Novelist, Professor of English, Louisiana State University, Baton Rouge*
Cain, James M(allahan)

Jeffrey H. Mahan, *Associate Professor of Ministry, Media and Culture, Iliff School of Theology, Denver, Colorado*
Evil

Jessica Mann, *Writer, Cornwall, England*
Archaeological Milieu; Cambridge

Edward Marston, *Author, Critic, Former Chairman, The Crime Writers Association of Great Britain, Ashford, England*
Red Herrings; Sports Milieu

Harold Q. Masur, *Former President and General Counsel, Mystery Writers of America, Inc., Boca Raton, Florida*
Judge

Thomas Mavor, *English Instructor, Brother Martin High School, New Orleans, Louisiana*
Assault

John McAleer, *Professor of English, Boston College, Permanent Fellow, Durham University, England, Boston, Massachusetts*
Freeman, R(ichard) Austin

Frank D. McSherry Jr. *(deceased)*
Missing Persons

Tony Medawar, *London, England*
Radio: The Crime and Mystery Genre on British Radio; Television: The Crime and Mystery Genre on British Television

John Kennedy Melling, *Author, Critic, Broadcaster, London, England*
Forgery

John Michielsen, *Associate Professor of German, Brock University, St. Catherine's, Ontario, Canada*
Dürrenmatt, Friedrich

Dean A. Miller, *Emeritus Professor of History, The University of Rochester, Rochester, New York*
Class; Coincidence; Police Procedural: The British Police Procedural

Marcia Muller, *Author, Petaluma, California*
Chandler, Raymond

Stephen Murray, *United Kingdom*
Series Milieu; Technical Backgrounds

William Nadel, *Radio and Mystery Historian and Writer, New York, New York*
Radio: The Crime and Mystery Genre on American Radio

Robert Napier, *Civilian Employee, U.S. Air Force, Tacoma, Washington*
Armchair Detective, The

Ellen A. Nehr *(deceased)*
Doubleday Crime Club; Fans and Fan Organizations; Nosy Parker Sleuth; Taylor, Phoebe Atwood

Erica Noonan, *Journalist, Boston, Massachusetts*
Private Eye Writers of America

Nils Nordberg, *Radio Drama Producer, Norwegian Broadcasting Corporation, Oslo, Norway*
Beck, Martin

Albert F. Nussbaum *(deceased)*
Prison Writing

Maryann McLoughlin O'Donnell, *Assistant Professor of English Literature, Rowan University, Glassboro, New Jersey*
Americans in England

Michael Occleshaw, *Doctor, Kent, England*
KGB

Susan Oleksiw, *Writer, Editor, The Larcom Review, Beverly, Massachusetts*
Amateur Detective; Aristocratic Characters: Aristocratic Sleuth; Beef, Sergeant; Clerical Milieu: The British Clerical Milieu; Cozy Mystery; Dexter, (Norman) Colin; Genteel Woman Sleuth; Humor; Incidental Crime Writers; Lugg, Magersfontein; McClure, James; Poison Pen Letters; Secret Agent; Watson, Colin; Whodunit

LeRoy L. Panek, *Professor of English, Western Maryland College, Westminster, Maryland*
Bentley, E(dmund) C(lerihew); Ellroy, James

Lizabeth Paravisini-Gebert, *Professor of Caribbean Studies, Vassar College, Poughkeepsie, New York*
Chee, Jim, and Joe Leaphorn; Circus and Carnival Milieu; Native American Sleuth; Publishing Milieu; Visitors Abroad

Sara Paretsky, *Author, Founder, Sisters in Crime, Chicago, Illinois*
Independent Sleuth

B. A. Pike, *Writer, English Teacher (retired), London, England*
Allingham, Margery (Louise); Bailey, H(enry) C(hristopher); Bruce, Leo; Cathedral Close Milieu; Disability, Sleuth with a; Gilbert, Michael; Innes, Michael; Journalist Sleuth; Legal Procedural; Partnerships, Literary; Singletons; Spinster Sleuth

Bonnie C. Plummer, *Professor of English, Director of Freshman Writing, Eastern Kentucky University, Richmond*
Mean Streets Milieu; Spade, Sam

Janet L. Potter, *Associate Provost for Library and Information Services, State University of New York at Oneonta*
Library Milieu

K. D. Prince, *Former Teacher, Local Secondary and Technical Colleges, Canterbury, England*
Bradley, Mrs. Beatrice Adela Lestrange; Castang, Henri

B. J. Rahn, *Professor of English, Hunter College of the City University of New York*
Audience Participation Activities; "Butler Did It, The"; Elderly Sleuth; Motive; Poisons, Unusual; Regester, Seeley; Weapons, Unusual Murder; Who-Gets-Away-with-It

Helaine Razovsky, *Associate Professor of English, Northwestern State University of Louisiana, Natchitoches*
Bribery; Urbanism

Maureen T. Reddy, *Professor of English and Director of the Women's Studies Program, Rhode Island College, Providence*
Fansler, Kate; Muller, Marcia; Paretsky, Sara; Sexism

Robin Anne Reid, *Assistant Professor Of Literature and Languages, Texas A & M University, Commerce, Texas*
Suspense Novel

John M. Reilly, *Graduate Professor of English, Howard University, Washington, D.C.*
Archetypal Characters; Armstrong, Charlotte; Baxt, George; Belloc Lowndes, Marie Adelaide; Blood-and-Thunder Fiction; Bramah (Smith), Ernest; Canonization; Carrados, Max; Chase, James Hadley; Clark, Mary Higgins; Clues; Conservative vs. Radical Worldview: Radical Worldview; Conservative vs. Radical Worldview: Introduction; Conventions of the Genre: Overview; Conventions of the Genre: Hard-Boiled Conventions; Corpse; Corruption; Craft of Crime and Mystery Writing, The; Criminals, Types of; Criticism, Literary; Cuff, Sergeant; Davis, Dorothy Salisbury; Detective Novel; Deviance; Extortion; Femme Fatale; Formula: Plot; Freeling, Nicolas; Fu Manchu; Godwin, William; Great Detective, The; Hard-Boiled Sleuth; Heroic Romance; Heroism; History of Crime and Mystery Writing; Inverted Detective Story; Loner, Sleuth as; Males and the Male Image; Means, Motive, and Opportunity; Memoirs, Early Detective and Police; Menacing Characters; Milieu; Millar, Margaret (Ellis Sturm); Mosley, Walter; Motivation, Psychological; Mystery Story; Outcasts and Outsiders; Penny Dreadful; Police Procedural: Introduction; Pseudonyms; Publishing, History of Book; Realism, Conventions of; Rice, Craig; Scientific Sleuth; Settings, Geographical; Sex and Sexuality; Spenser; Stereotypes, Reversals of; Stock Characters; Suspects; Theory: Descriptive Theory; Theory: Prescriptive Theory; Thriller: Introduction; Thriller: Action Thriller; Underworld Figure; Van der Valk, Inspector; Violence; Voice: Overview; Voice: Hard-Boiled Voice; Wood, Mrs. Henry

Katherine M. Restaino, *Dean of Undergraduate Evening and Summer Sessions (retired), St. Peter's College, Jersey City, New Jersey*
Historical Figures in Crime and Mystery Writing: Celebrities

Barbara Reynolds, *Reader in Italian (retired), Cambridge, England*
Sayers, Dorothy L(eigh)

Nicholas Rhea
Country Constable; Fingerprints and Footprints

Georgia Rhoades, *Associate Professor of English, Appalachian State University, Boone, North Carolina*
Lesbian Characters and Perspectives; Porter, Joyce

Judith Rhodes, *Librarian, Leeds, England*
Art and Antiques Milieu; Farceurs; Robin Hood Criminal; Stewart, Mary

Betty Richardson, *Professor of English, Southern Illinois University, Edwardsville*
Mistaken Identity; Van Dusen, Professor Augustus S. F. X.; Vidocq, Eugène François

Steven Riddle, *Senior Editor, Harcourt Inc., Orlando, Florida*
Mayhem Parva

Priscilla Ridgway, *Former Executive Director, Mystery Writers of America, New York, New York*
Awards: North American Awards

Dieter Riegel, *Professor of German (retired), Bishop's University, Lennoxville, Quebec, Canada*
Europe, Crime and Mystery Writing in Continental: Germany

David Rife, *The John P. Graham Professor of English, Lycoming College, Williamsport, Pennsylvania*
Marlowe, Philip

Nigel Rigby, *Research Coordinator, National Maritime Museum, Greenwich, England*
Adventure Story; Pursuit

Chris Rippen, *Writer, Member, International Association of Crime Writers, The Netherlands*
Europe, Crime and Mystery Writing in Continental: The Netherlands and Flanders

Joan Warthling Roberts, *Professor of English, Buffalo State College, Buffalo, New York*
Green, Anna Katharine; Sensation Novel

Lucy Rollin, *Associate Professor of English, Clemson University, Clemson, South Carolina*
Nursery Rhymes

Vassily Rudich, *Visiting Professor of Classics, Yale University, New Haven, Connecticut*
Europe, Crime and Mystery Writing in Continental: Russia; Europe, Crime and Mystery Writing in Continental: Eastern Europe

Donald Rumbelow, *Writer/Lecturer, Former Chairman of the British Crime Writers' Association, London, England*
Old Bailey; Tower of London, The

Sharon A. Russell, *Professor of Communication and Women's Studies, Indiana State University, Terre Haute*
Animals

Marilyn Rye, *Assistant Professor of English, Fairleigh Dickinson University, Madison, New Jersey*
Child Abuse

Dale Salwak, *Professor of English, Citrus College, Glendora, California*
Con Artist; Disguise; Double Bluff; English Village Milieu; Individualism; Merrivale, Sir Henry

Donald G. Sandstrom *(deceased)*
Military Milieu

William Anthony Swithin Sarjeant, *Professor of Geological Sciences, University of Saskatchewan, Canada*
Arson; Organized Crime; Upfield, Arthur W(illiam)

George L. Scheper, *Professor of Humanities, Essex Community College, Baltimore County, Maryland*
Christmas Crime; Expeditions; Innocence; Murderless Mystery; Plagiarism; Transportation, Modes of; Travel Milieu

Philip Scowcroft, *Solicitor (retired), South York, England*
Alibi, Unbreakable; Aviation Milieu; Nautical Milieu: Ocean Liner and Ferry Milieu; Nautical Milieu: Boating and Sailing Milieu; Railway Milieu; Smuggling; Sports Milieu; "Time Is of the Essence"; Wimsey, Lord Peter

Mark Silver, *Instructor in Japanese, Colgate University, Hamilton, New York*
Japan, Crime and Mystery Writing in; Matsumoto Seicho

Amelia Simpson, *Freelance Writer, Washington, D.C.*
Latin America, Crime and Mystery Writing in

Christine R. Simpson, B.A.A.L.A. *(retired), Milton Keynes, England*
Marple, Miss Jane; Our Society; Satire

David Skene-Melvin, *Librarian (retired), Independent Scholar, Toronto, Canada*
Canada, Crime and Mystery Writing in; Starrett, (Charles) Vincent (Emerson)

Robert E. Skinner, *Librarian, Xavier University of Louisiana, Author, New Orleans, Louisiana*
Himes, Chester (Bomar); Mosley, Walter; Rawlins, Ezekiel "Easy"

Barbara Sloan-Hendershott, *Teacher of English Literature, York Community High School, Writer, Lecturer, Elmhurst, Illinois*
Addresses and Abodes, Famous; Ferrars, E. X.; London; Silver, Miss Maud; Suspicious Characters

Michele Slung, *Editor, Critic, Washington, D.C.*
Bluestocking Sleuth

Curtis C. Smith, *Provost, California University of Pennsylvania, California, Pennsylvania*
Future, Use of the

David N. Smith, *Vice-Dean, Harvard Law School, Cambridge, Massachusetts*
Voice: Wisecracking Voice

Richard Smyer, *Associate Professor Emeritus of English, University of Arizona, Tucson*
Escapism

Judy L. Solberg, *Government Documents Librarian and Subject Specialist, Gelman Library, George Washington University, Washington, D.C.*
Book Clubs

Marcia J. Songer, *Assistant Professor of English and Assistant Chair for Undergraduate Studies, East Tennessee State University, Johnson City*
Police Detective

William D. Spencer, *Writer, Minister, Presbyterian Church, South Hamilton, Massachusetts*
Clerical Milieu: The American Clerical Milieu

Michael Steed, *Honorary Lecturer in Politics & International Relations, University of Kent, Canterbury, England*
Braddon, Mary Elizabeth

Richard Steiger, *Professor of English, Murray State University, Murray, Kentucky*
Dupin, The Chevalier C. Auguste; Higgins, George V(incent); Woolrich, Cornell (George Hopley)

T. R. Steiner, *Professor Emeritus of English, University of California at Santa Barbara*
Alibi; Point of View, Narrative; Reasoning, Types of; Small, Rabbi David

John D. Stevens, *Professor of Communications Emeritus, University of Michigan, Ann Arbor*
McBain, Ed

Kate Stine, *Editor, Writer, Publishing Consultant, New York, New York*
Bookstores, Specialized

Gerald H. Strauss, *Professor Emeritus of English, Bloomsburg University, Bloomsburg, Pennsylvania*
Old Man in the Corner; Tragedy, Dramatic, Elements of in Crime and Mystery Writing

Cushing Strout, *Ernest I. White Professor (Emeritus) of American Studies and Humane Letters, Cornell University, Ithaca, New York*
War

Mary Rose Sullivan, *Professor Emerita of English, University of Colorado at Denver*
Armchair Detective; Du Maurier, Daphne; Futrelle, Jacques; Narrator as Criminal; Orczy, Baroness Emmuska; Rendell, Ruth; Virtue

Marion Swan, *Consultant Forensic Psychiatrist, Cleveland, England*
Serial Killers and Mass Murderers

Julian Symons, *Writer, Critic, London, England (deceased)*
Crime Novel; Crime Writers Association; Detection Club, The; Doyle, Arthur Conan; Hammett, Dashiell; Highsmith, Patricia; Keating, H(enry) R(eymond) F(itzwalter); Rules of the Game

Nancy Ellen Talburt, *Associate Vice Chancellor for Academic Affairs and Professor of English, University of Arkansas, Fayetteville, Arkansas*
Fortune, Reggie; Religion

Stefano Tani, *Associate Professor of Comparative Literature, Universita Degli Studi Di Verona, Facolta Di Lettere, Verona, Italy*
Truth, Quest for

William G. Tapply, *Professor of English, Clark University, Worcester, Massachusetts*
Great Outdoors, The

Julia Thorogood, *Lecturer, Workers' Educational Association, Eastern District, Cambridge, England*
Campion, Albert

John C. Tibbetts, *Assistant Professor of Theater and Film, University of Kansas, Lawrence*
Carr, John Dickson; Film; Juvenile Sleuth: Boy Sleuth; Psychic Sleuth; Queen, Ellery: The Writing Team; Television: The Crime and Mystery Genre on American Television; Thorndyke, Dr. John

James L. Traylor, *Independent Scholar, Meansville, Georgia*
Fiction Noir; Spillane, Mickey; Thompson, Jim

J. K. Van Dover, *Professor of English, Lincoln University, Oxford, Pennsylvania*
Industry Writers; Sjöwall, Maj, and Per Wahlöö

Lucy Walker, *Edinburgh, United Kingdom*
Chivalry, Code of; Voice: Genteel Voice

Donald C. Wall, *Professor of English Emeritus, Eastern Washington University, Cheney, Washington*
MacDonald, John D(ann); Police Procedural: The American Police Procedural

David C. Wallace, *Assistant Professor of General Education, Life University, Marietta, Georgia*
Gay Characters and Perspectives

Elizabeth M. Walter, *Editor (1973–93), Collins Crime Club, London, England*
Collins Crime Club

Priscilla L. Walton, *Professor of English, Carleton University, Ontario, Canada*
Antihero; Narrative Theory

Susan Ward, *Professor of English, St. Lawrence University, Canton, New York*
Naturalism

George F. Wedge, *Associate Professor of English Emeritus, University of Kansas, Lawrence (deceased)*
Alcohol and Alcoholism

Thomas Whissen, *Professor of English Emeritus, Wright State University, Dayton, Ohio*
Boucher, Anthony; Underworld

David Whittle, *Director of Music, Leicester Grammar School, Leicester, England*
Musical Milieu; Music and Song

Anna Wilson, *Lecturer, Department of American and Canadian Studies, Birmingham University, Birmingham, England*
Couples: Secondary Characters

Robin W. Winks, *Randolph W. Townsend Jr. Professor of History, Yale University, New Haven, Connecticut*
Dalgliesh, Adam; Household, Geoffrey; James, P(hyllis) D(orothy)

Paula M. Woods, *Lecturer in English, Baylor University, Waco, Texas*
Silly-Ass Sleuth

Donald A. Yates, *Professor Emeritus of Spanish American Literature, Michigan State University, East Lansing*
Abner, Uncle; Post, Melville Davisson

THE OXFORD COMPANION TO
Crime and Mystery Writing

ABDUCTION. *See* Kidnapping.

Abner, Uncle. One of six detectives created by Melville Davisson *Post, Uncle Abner is a squire in the western counties of Virginia in the time of Thomas Jefferson. A self-appointed protector and avenger, Uncle Abner harks back to a time when crime was not a social issue but rather a matter of violation of God's order. Nevertheless, he employs the ratiocinative techniques of a nineteenth-century detective in stories that Post crafted to exhibit the criminal mystery as the basis of *plot and narrative development. The career of Uncle Abner is related exclusively in short stories that enjoyed success in popular magazines and are collected in *Uncle Abner, Master of Mysteries* (1918). Three additional stories appear in *The Methods of Uncle Abner* (1974). All extant stories were reissued in 1977 in *The Complete Uncle Abner*.

[*See also* Locked Room Mystery; Rural Milieu.]
—Donald Yates

ABODES, FAMOUS. *See* Addresses and Abodes, Famous.

ACADEMIC MILIEU. Writers who set their mysteries in schools, colleges, and universities may portray the academic *milieu as an ordered environment, philosophically dedicated to lofty goals, which is disrupted by the intrusion of violence. In the work of such writers, the detective's goal is to restore order in an essentially good place. Some writers of crime and mystery fiction also look at the academic milieu as a place populated by faculty who do not live up to the noble goals that the academic life would seem to promise. In the work of these writers, any crime exacerbates already existing pettiness, personality clashes, professional jealousies, and competitiveness among the characters, while it is the mission of the *sleuth to solve the case through understanding the disordered state of affairs so as to get to the truth of the matter. Some detective fiction set in the academic world also focuses on students and the pressures that they experience.

The most memorable cluster of academic mysteries was published during the 1930s. Known as "dons' delights," these mostly British productions were generally set in prestigious institutions like the universities at *Oxford and *Cambridge, in fictionalized colleges within either of these two universities, or in a fictionalized university combination dubbed "Ox-

bridge." Generally written by authors who had experience of college life, either as students or as dons themselves, their *plots were built around the routines of academic life, while the characters were given definite places in the hierarchy of academe, and were endowed with the erudition and eccentricities that made them both memorable and capable of perpetrating crimes that require special knowledge.

In most dons' delights, the world of the senior common room and the faculty who have access to it are the focus, with students and staff playing more minor roles. At first this seems to be the case in Dorothy L. *Sayers's *Gaudy Night* (1935), set in "Shrewsbury College," a fictionalized version of the author's alma mater, Somerville College at Oxford University. At the novel's conclusion, however, the presumption that the murderer must come from the dominant social set—the faculty—is proven false. This book does epitomize the academic mystery in its focus on the routines and preoccupations of those who lead the academic life, and in its use of a *sleuth whose familiarity with the academic life is essential to solving the crime.

Cambridge is the setting for *The Cambridge Murders* (1945) by Glyn Daniel, a don at St. John's College who penned his first two novels under the pseudonym Dilwyn Rees. Here the scholarly life is as well described as is the geography and *atmosphere of the place. T. H. White, the author of the Arthurian saga *The Sword in the Stone* (1937), also chose Cambridge as the setting for his detective novel *Darkness at Pemberly* (1932).

Oxbridge is the scene of the crime in *Death at the President's Lodging* (1936; *Seven Suspects*), the first mystery by J. I. M. Stewart, who wrote it under the pseudonym Michael *Innes en route to taking up a teaching position in Adelaide, Australia. The novel is notable for its elegant use of language, inventive plot, and its relentlessly droll depictions of the faculty. A 1928 graduate of Oriel College, Oxford, Stewart was destined to become a don at Christ Church College, Oxford, for most of his academic career.

Another Oxford notable, John Masterman, was educated at Worcester College, Oxford and was a lecturer in history at Christ Church College before he directed much of Great Britain's counterintelligence effort during World War II as deputy director of MI5. He also served as provost at Worcester College and vice-chancellor of Oxford University. His novel *An Oxford Tragedy* (1933), which begins with the murder of an unpopular fellow in classics at St. Thomas College is rich with the atmosphere of common rooms and high tables. Typical of the dons' delight, as the action advances, many of the victim's faculty colleagues emerge as suspects.

This influence is still felt in later novels, including Helen Eustis's *The Horizontal Man* (1946), one of the best-known American college mysteries. While this novel incorporates detection and some lighthearted dialogue, it also takes a step forward from the classical murder-as-entertainment thrust of dons' delights to seriously probe the netherworld of psychological abnormality. While many other college mysteries written after the 1930s, including Robert *Barnard's *Death of an Old Goat* (1977) and Colin *Dexter's *Death Is Now My Neighbor* (1996), are firmly centered upon faculty rivalries, some memorable novels look at the pressures upon students, academic and social. Josephine *Tey's *Miss Pym Disposes* (1946) is a case in point. Set in Leys Physical Training College, an institution without the academic luster of Oxford or Cambridge, this novel convincingly depicts the lives of undergraduates. Other novels emphasizing the stresses inherent in student life include Simon Nash's *Dead of a Counterplot* (1962), Antonia Fraser's *Oxford Blood* (1985), and *The Student Body* (1998) by Faith Abiele, Julia Sullivan, Michael Francisco Melcher, and Bennett Singer writing under the joint pseudonym Jane Harvard. The latter centers on the activities of a student reporter who investigates a sex ring that trades on the cachet of the prestigious Harvard name.

Harvard University is also the scene of *Death in a Tenured Position* (1981), one of several mysteries by English literature professor Carolyn Heilbrun writing as Amanda *Cross. Cross's novels featuring Professor Kate *Fansler epitomize the academic mystery that also serves as an exploration of *gender issues on college and university campuses. Salient treatments of gender on campus in the context of crime writing include Valerie Miner's *Murder in the English Department* (1982), Nora Kelly's *In the Shadow of King's* (1984), and Joan Smith's *Don't Leave Me This Way* (1990).

The academic milieu includes not only institutions of higher learning but boarding schools, day schools, and institutions related to universities such as museums and an examination syndicate. Boys' schools form the setting in Nicholas *Blake's *A Question of Proof* (1935), Leo *Bruce's *Case with Ropes and Rings* (1940) and *Death at St. Asprey's School* (1967), Gladys *Mitchell's *Tom Brown's Body* (1949), Edmund *Crispin's *Love Lies Bleeding* (1948), Michael Underwood's *Victim of Circumstance* (1979), and Barnard's *Little Victims* (1983; *School for Murder*). Girls' schools figure in Agatha *Christie's *Cat among the Pigeons* (1959), Elizabeth Lemarchand's *Death of an Old Girl* (1967), Catherine Aird's *Some Die Eloquent* (1979), and Douglas Clark's *Golden Rain* (1980). University museums used as murder scenes seem to invite humorous treatment of the academic life, as is the case in Jane Langton's *Dead as a Dodo* (1996), set in the Oxford University Museum, and Alfred Alcorn's *Murder in the Museum of Man* (1997), which takes place in a fictional museum modeled on Harvard University's Museum of Natural History. A far graver approach to murder is seen in the Oxford Foreign Examinations Syndicate as portrayed by Dexter in *The Silent World of Nicholas Quinn* (1977), a novel in which the possibility of a leak of highly confidential examination materials is viewed with as much horror as is the act of murder.

[*See also* Academic Sleuth; Eccentrics.]

—Rosemary Herbert *and* John E. Kramer

ACADEMIC SLEUTH. Working in the *academic milieu, the academic *sleuth is a prevalent character type in crime and mystery fiction. By far the greatest number of academic sleuths have come from the ranks of higher education, but they can also be schoolteachers, college librarians, administrators, or students. When engaged in detective work, academic sleuths employ the sharp analytic skills they have developed through their scholarly pursuits, and their efforts are not always confined to on-campus crimes. As Robin Winks points out (introduction, *The Historian as Detective: Essays on Evidence*, 1968), the reasoning processes that facilitate productive academic research closely parallel the reasoning processes necessary for successful detection.

Academic sleuths are most commonly expert in English literature, but nearly all academic disciplines have their representatives. Among the more esoteric fields represented are Sanskrit (Anthony *Boucher's Professor John Ashwin) and agronomy (Charlotte MacLeod's Peter Shandy). Whatever his or her field of expertise, the academic sleuth has a body of information to draw on to enliven discussion, confound *suspects, and guide the investigation. For example, those who are professors of literature employ their esoteric knowledge and familiarity with literary *allusions to interpret *clues the police find impenetrable.

The first professorial sleuth to achieve widespread popularity was Professor Augustus S. F. X. *Van Dusen. Created by Jacques *Futrelle, Van Dusen is a master of all known sciences; his brain is so large that he wears size-eight hat. Thanks to his prodigious powers of deduction, Van Dusen is known as the Thinking Machine. A sometime member of the faculty at the fictional Hale University in New England, Van Dusen makes his debut in *The Chase of the Golden Plate* (1906).

Craig Kennedy was Van Dusen's immediate successor as the preeminent professor-detective. The creation of Arthur B. *Reeve, Kennedy is a professor of chemistry at a university in New York City that resembles Columbia University. Although proficient in logical deduction, Kennedy triumphs over evildoers largely by his talent for inventing scientific crime-fighting instruments such as a lie detector. Kennedy begins his literary life in *The Poisoned Pen* (1911), and his subsequent detection career focuses exclusively on off-campus crimes.

Of all professor-detectives, Dr. Lancelot *Priestley holds the distinction of bringing the largest number of criminals to justice. Created by John *Rhode, Priestley investigates crime off campus beginning with *The Paddington Mystery* (1925). Priestley, a mathematician, is less concerned with the human aspects of crimes than with the *puzzles they present. Depending principally on *Scotland Yard detectives to provide him with information, Priestley seldom leaves his *London home in the course of his ratiocination. Like Van Dusen, he does not suffer fools gladly; a man of independent means, he takes up detection after leaving a major British university following a succession of bitter quarrels with the administration.

Van Dusen, Kennedy, and Priestley are all *Great Detectives, and all three stand apart from the stream of ordinary life. Egocentric as well as intellectually arrogant, the academic sleuth became an appealing topic for satire. Among the most popular of the academic sleuths constructed as a satirical commentary on real-life professors was Gervase *Fen, an eccentric whose detection is often erratic and inefficient; his efforts are fueled more by his own high opinion of his sleuthing abilities than by any innate brilliance. The creation of Edmund *Crispin, Fen—a professor of English language and literature at the fictional St. Christopher's College, Oxford—is introduced in *The Case of the Gilded Fly* (1944; *Obsequies at Oxford*). A lean man of about forty, his hair plastered down with water, he owns a red sports car, which he drives badly, wears bizarre clothing, and offers pompous opinions on all forms and genres of literature, whether or not he has any significant familiarity with them. His brilliant mind and elite education are regularly contrasted with the matter-of-fact attitudes of people in nonacademic life. Although he is sometimes shown at St. Christopher's and some of his faculty colleagues appear in his stories, all of the tales are essentially off-campus mysteries.

In recent decades many professor detectives, including several women sleuths, have been depicted as appealingly human, even sympathetic figures. Dr. R. V. Davie, the creation of V. C. Clinton-Baddeley, is a wry septuagenarian fellow in classics at the fictional St. Nicholas's College, *Cambridge. He first appears in *Death's Bright Dart* (1967). Neither a detecting genius nor oppressively eccentric, Dr. Davie is a more congenial character than most of his colleagues: He is a man with friends who enjoys a wide range of activities and associations. In detection he is curious and astute rather than arrogant and pushy.

Women academics have played a large part in deepening and humanizing the character of the academic sleuth. Amanda *Cross's Kate *Fansler first appears in *In the Last Analysis* (1964). She is a serious-minded, thoroughly professional academician who must often juggle the demands of her teaching and research with detection. She leads the reader through the academic world as it is experienced by women: a place of discrimination, small-mindedness, and ambition. Joan Smith's Loretta Lawson is even more avowedly feminist and does not confine her detection to the campus. She works closely with a fellow professor and in *Don't Leave Me This Way* (1990) explores the life of a friend who comes to her for help and is later found murdered. With her close friendships, humane attitudes, and philosophical commitment to improving the life of women, Lawson is the diametric opposite of the earliest academic sleuths.

[*See also* Allusion, Literary; Eccentrics.]

• John E. Kramer Jr. and John E. Kramer III, *College Mystery Novels: An Annotated Bibliography, Including a Guide to Professorial Series-Character Sleuths* (1983). Rosemary DePaolo, "Scholastic Skullduggery," *Armchair Detective* 21, no. 3 (Summer 1988): 280–84. John E. Kramer Jr., "How to Become a Series-Character Professor-Detective," *Clues* 9, no. 2 (fall/winter 1988): 75–94. Lois Marchino, "The Female Sleuth in Academe," *Journal of Popular Culture* 23 (winter 1989): 89–100.   —John E. Kramer Jr.

ACCIDENTAL SLEUTH. "Accidental sleuth" is a term applied to the protagonist who is not a detective by avocation or profession, either amateur, private, or official, but who nonetheless assumes the role of *sleuth. Often a character falls into the role because of his or her proximity to the scene of the crime, whether as a guest in a country house that becomes a murder scene or as an unwilling bystander who observes a criminal act in the mean streets. Accidental sleuths are frequently related to or personally involved in the lives of other characters directly affected by crime. They may assume the role of detective contrary to personal preference, becoming what is known to readers as the detective in spite of him-or herself; or they may find themselves in the role of accidental sleuth with a mission, as is the case when a mother, for instance, feels her determination will serve to avenge or prevent a crime against her child where police efforts appear to be failing. Several of Mary Higgins *Clark's novels feature mothers who find themselves taking this role. There is notable tradition of accidental sleuthing in the *Had-I-But-Known school of writing, which generally features female characters whose chance encounters with crime, often in isolated settings, cause them to undertake amateur sleuthing in a way that parallels the official police investigation.

Individual characters whose repeated encounters with crime fill multiple books are generally not considered accidental sleuths. Agatha *Christie's Miss Jane *Marple, for instance, is an *amateur detective: she comes to be known for her sleuthing abilities and is often called in to help with perplexing crimes in her neighborhood. Characters whose professions regularly cause them to visit crime scenes—primarily journalists, photojournalists, doctors, and lawyers—fall into a closely related category. When these characters use their expertise to guide them in investigating crimes in tandem with, along parallel lines to, or especially in lieu of official investigators, they become *surrogate detectives.

One of the earliest recognized works in the crime and mystery genre features a character who illustrates how closely related the two categories are. In William Godwin's novel *Things as They Are; or, The Adventures of Caleb Williams* (1794; *Caleb Williams; The Adventures of Caleb Williams*), the secretary to Ferdinando Falkland finds that his position enables him first to suspect and then to prove the identity of a murderer. A more classic example of the purely accidental sleuth is Rachel Innes in Mary Roberts *Rinehart's early novel *The Circular Staircase* (1908). When this character rents a country house for the summer, her natural curiosity draws her into investigating the mysterious occurrences that arise. The unnamed protagonist of Daphne *du Maurier's *Rebecca* (1938) is another accidental sleuth, whose love for her brooding new husband drives her to penetrate the mystery surrounding his deceased first wife.

Writers who use accidental sleuths have an advantage over those who use amateur detectives, for readers may find it easy to identify with a protagonist who is an ordinary citizen caught up in a web of intrigue. The lack of fixed expectations regarding the character's expertise, courage, and personality also allows for greater depth of *characterization, more potential surprises, and sometimes a greater sense of jeopardy threatening the protagonist. For instance, in Josephine *Tey's *Miss Pym Disposes* (1946) the sleuth character develops from an observer into an active participant in the circumstances surrounding the crime. In Tey's *Brat Farrar* (1949; *Come and Kill Me*), the eponymous antihero finds himself investigating the circumstances surrounding the death of the youth he is impersonating in order to inherit the deceased's fortune, transforming him in the reader's eyes from an opportunist adventurer in to a sympathetic character who is himself in jeopardy.

[See also Adventure and Adventuress; Suspense]
—J. Randolph Cox

ADDRESSES AND ABODES, FAMOUS. Detective fiction is known for its world-famous *sleuths; many of them have homes that are equally vivid, inspiring devoted readers to visit their probable or known real locales. The most famous fictional address is perhaps 221B Baker Street, the *London address of Sherlock *Holmes and Dr. John H. *Watson, with its cozy rooms, familiar clutter, and violin. Although the residence is imaginary nearby businesses have received mail and visitors to that address for decades, and a Sherlock Holmes museum continues to attract business on Baker Street.

Patricia *Wentworth's indomitable spinster and *private eye, Miss Maud *Silver, lives in a snug little flat in the fictional Montague Mansions located near Baker Street. The curtains and the carpet are faded peacock blue; the walls are decorated with pictures that have Victorian themes like "The Soul's Awakening." The chairs are curly walnut, and every inch of table space bears a framed photograph of a former client.

Dorothy L. *Sayers deliberately cut Holmes's 221B Baker Street address in half when deciding on the address for Lord Peter *Wimsey's luxurious flat; he resides just across from Green Park at 110A Piccadilly. Wimsey's rooms are decorated in black and primrose, and the walls are lined with rare editions. A wood fire always seems to burn on a wide, old-fashioned hearth.

Margery *Allingham's Albert *Campion lives in the same district as Wimsey, in a flat located next to the fictional Bottle Street Police Station off Piccadilly. On the left side of the building a dirty yellow door leads to a stairway. At the top of the stairs a carved oak door bears a brass plaque engraved with the words "Albert Campion, Merchant Goods Dept." The flat itself is luxuriously and tastefully furnished. Included in the decor is a display of trophies from Campion's cases, including the Black Dudley dagger.

*New York brownstones are home to both Nero *Wolfe and Ellery *Queen. Rex *Stout's Wolfe lives somewhere on West Thirty-fifth Street, in a comfortable house with a marvelous kitchen and orchids growing on the roof. The house can be recognized by its front stoop with seven steps. Ellery *Queen's eponymous character lives on West Eighty-seventh Street between Amsterdam and Columbus Avenues, in a well-kept, old-fashioned brownstone located midblock. Its most easily identifiable characteristic is an elaborately carved oak front door.

The fictional village of St. Mary Mead, located about twenty-five miles from London and twelve from the coast, is the home of Agatha *Christie's Miss Jane *Marple. From her snug cottage with its well-tended, much-loved garden, Miss Marple keeps her eye on village goings-on. John *Mortimer knows well his model for Horace *Rumpole's legal chambers, at number 2 Equity Court in London's Inns of Court.

These and other writers have created evocative settings by drawing on elements of real places, but Daphne *du Maurier goes further. Manderley, the setting of the haunting thriller *Rebecca* (1938), is based on the brooding mansion called Menabilly, near the rugged Cornish coastline a few miles from the seaport town of Fowey; du Maurier lived in the house from 1943 to 1967. This was du Maurier's house of darkness, filled with secrets, long passages, and fear at the top of the stairs.

Few definite addresses are associated with *private eyes, whose eschewal of the domestic life places them in more generic abodes and offices. An exception is John D. *MacDonald's Travis *McGee, whose residence is a boat named "The Busted Flush," moored in Bahia Mar, Fort Lauderdale, Florida.

[See also Settings.]

• Alzina Stone Dale and Barbara Sloan Hendershott, *A Mystery Reader's Walking Guide: London* (1987). Dilys Winn, *Murder Ink: The Mystery Reader's Companion* (1977).

—Barbara Sloan-Hendershott

Adler, Irene. Although she appears in just one story in the Sherlock *Holmes Canon, Irene Adler is perhaps the most famous woman in detective fiction. The only woman to dupe Holmes, Adler is regarded by the *Great Detective as *"the* woman," who "eclipses and predominates the whole of her sex." Born in New Jersey in 1858, Adler is a contralto who has performed at La Scala and held the role of primadonna at the Imperial Opera of Warsaw. When she claims the attention of Holmes in "A Scandal in Bohemia" (*Strand*, July 1891), she has retired from the operatic stage as well as from the embrace of Wilhelm Gottsreich Sigismond von Ormstein, grand duke of Cassel-Felstein and hereditary king of Bohemia. The Bohemian king engages Holmes to secure a compromising photograph in which he is posed with Adler. Von Ormstein believes that his former paramour will use the photograph to ruin him when he marries another.

Described by Holmes as "the daintiest thing under a bonnet on this planet" and "a lovely woman, with a face that a man might die for," she is seen by the threatened grand duke as having "the face of the most beautiful of women and the mind of the most resolute of men." Indeed, Adler impulsively disguises herself as a man and tails Holmes to his own door after he literally tries to smoke out the photograph's secret hiding place. The Great Detective's scheme involves two uninvited visits to Adler's bijou villa in London. He first gains entry disguised as a loafer who has been injured in a scuffle, and subsequently presents himself as "an amiable and simple-minded clergyman." But despite Holmes's cleverness, Adler uses her "woman's wit" to remain a step ahead of the sleuth, marrying Godfrey Norton and fleeing with her new spouse—and the scandalous photograph—while rising in Holmes's regard to the point that he prefers to accept her portrait rather than the Bohemian's showy jeweled ring in payment for his services.

[See also Disguise; Females and Feminists; Femme Fatale.]
　　　　　　　　　　　　　　　　—Rosemary Herbert

ADVENTURER AND ADVENTURESS.

An adventurer is a thrill seeker who engages in dangerous and exciting experiences or a person who is willing to take risks to make (sometimes unscrupulous) gains. Courageous thrill seekers are frequently found in the pages of *spy fiction, with James *Bond as the prime exemplar. In crime and mystery fiction, the adventure seeker may be exemplified by military men in search of peacetime excitement; some *private eyes, especially of the hard-boiled school; well-heeled *gentlemen adventurers; and sometimes the British colonial. In fiction written toward the end of the nineteenth century and during the early twentieth century, the term "adventuress" was applied to spunky female characters who exhibited pluck and courage, or derogatorily to women who exercised their feminine wiles for financial gain. The term was similarly but less frequently applied to men who used their sexuality to advance a scheme. The more manipulative adventurer is personified in the *gentleman thief, the *femme fatale, the charmer or dandy, and sometimes the character playing the returning *prodigal, real or impersonated.

When the adventure seeker serves as *sleuth, the character may be independently wealthy or have apparently unlimited financial backing, allowing him or her to obey a personal code of honor. John D. *MacDonald's Travis *McGee, for instance, seems to derive as much altruistic satisfaction from restoring damaged psyches as he does from any financial reward. Stories about adventurer-sleuths are generally fast-paced, with action preferred over cerebration, as is the case in The Saint in New York (1935) when Leslie *Charteris's modern-day buccaneer, Simon Templar, allows himself to be taken prisoner before carrying out a promise to destroy his adversaries. Action is also the keynote of H. C. *McNeile's Bulldog *Drummond tales featuring a former British military officer who continues to right wrongs long after World War I is ended. A related character type is the corporate executive who, at the top of his career, needs to make a "killing" of a different sort to sate his appetite for thrills. The villainous businessman-adventurer is exemplified in David Ely's aptly named John Goforth in "The Sailing Club" (Cosmopolitan, Oct. 1962).

Adventurers of the cunning sort can be well-heeled, charming rogues like E. W. *Hornung's A. J. *Raffles, a *gentleman thief who uses his suavity and social connections to gain entrée into the posh premises he burglarizes. His adventures are recounted in The Amateur Cracksman (1899; Raffles, the Amateur Cracksman). John Kendrick Bangs's Mrs. A. J. Raffles similarly invades high society in twelve *pastiches collected in Mrs. Raffles (1905). Another man of means as adventurer is John *Creasey's the Honourable Richard Rollison, also known as "the Toff." Hubert Footner's determinedly unmarried detective, Madame Rosika Storey, moves in the glamorous world of Monte Carlo, where she is not above using vampish behavior in the process of procuring information. Adventurers may also operate in the underworld, as does Frank Packard's safecracker Jimmie Dale, who leaves behind a gray seal that becomes both his signature and his nom de crime.

Perhaps the most famous female character to be labeled with the term "adventuress" is proven not to be one of the gold-digging sort, although she lacks neither adventurousness nor cunning. Irene *Adler becomes the one person to dupe Sherlock *Holmes when she prevents the *Great Detective from succeeding in perpetrating a crime himself, the theft of a compromising photograph of the beautiful Adler and the hereditary king of Bohemia. Rather than scheming for gain, however, Adler is only protecting her own reputation in Arthur Conan *Doyle's "A Scandal in Bohemia" (Strand, July 1891).

Adventurers may be opportunists, as is the eponymous hero of Josephine *Tey's Brat Farrar (1949; Come and Kill Me), who, upon discovering that he is a convincing double for a dead man destined to inherit a fortune, cannot resist impersonating the deceased. Works about such accidental adventurers often become stories of complex characterization.

Peter O'Donnell's Modesty Blaise is a modern-day adventuress. A post-World War II orphan from the slums of Turkey and Persia, she rises to lead the criminal Network. In comfortable retirement, she and companion Willie Garvin tackle nasty villains on behalf of British Secret Service.

[See also Adventure Story; Archetypal Characters; Con Artist; Impersonation; Sex and Sexuality; Stereotypes, Reversals of.]

• Robert Sampson, Yesterday's Faces, 6 vols. (1983–93). Andy East, The Cold War File (1983).　　　—Bernard A. Drew

ADVENTURE STORY.

Adventure stories have been told for thousands of years, but within the wider and older tradition represented by The Odyssey, the Hindu epic the Mahabharata, and the Sumerian epic Gilgamesh, the European adventure story is descended from the knights' quests in medieval romances. Adventure stories reflect the collective fantasy of their age. In the fifteenth century "out there" was synonymous with empire; in the twentieth, outer space.

Romances followed a structure that encompassed themes of exile, physical challenge, and return of the hero or small group. Such adventuring is predominantly a male activity in fiction. During the challenge, good triumphs over evil. However, within that formula there is rarely a simple opposition of good and evil, for the villain often has a strength that the hero's society has temporarily lost, and the defeat of evil abroad is primarily the means to correct a weakness at home. A common theme traceable through *Gilgamesh*, the fourteenth-century romance *Sir Gawain and the Green Knight*, James Fenimore Cooper's *Leather-Stocking Tales* (1823–1841), and into the twentieth-century novels of Ernest Hemingway and John *Buchan, is that of an overcivilized society regaining contact with nature through the adventure of the individual. It is a central paradox of adventure stories that they reinforce the values of the home society by providing a temporary escape from the constraints of civilization. Adventure happens "out there," but its meaning is found at home.

Within the basic formula of exile and return are normally found a further series of motifs: the disruption of the ordered home society, a journey through a hostile natural world, an attempted seduction by a "savage princess," a talisman to protect the hero, a treasure, a faithful companion, a mysterious stranger, and a "savage king."

The adventurer falls into two main categories: the human and the superhuman. In the *Action Comics Superman* adventure stories, the hero is both the modest Clark Kent and the godlike Superman. A common type of hero is the renegade driven outside society. The outlaws Robin Hood and Dick Turpin, for example, are the holders of good in a corrupt society, and become the forerunners of renegade *private eyes like Raymond *Chandler's Philip *Marlowe. Constant exposure to evil can turn the adventurer bad; Kurtz in Joseph Conrad's anti-adventure *Heart of Darkness* (1902) is consumed by the savagery he has come to civilize.

Sir Gawain and the Green Knight contains three tests of Gawain's courage and three of his virtue, but the romance also incorporates elements of mystery in the identity of the Green Knight, who is both savage king and mysterious stranger. Mystery challenges the intellect and varies the pace of the action. In the early chapters of Edgar Allan *Poe's adventure story *The Narrative of Arthur Gordon Pym of Nantucket* (1838), the reader is entombed in the hold of the ship along with the hero and denied knowledge of the mysterious happenings in the outside world. Mystery provides an intellectual action during a period of enforced physical immobility.

Daniel Defoe's *Robinson Crusoe* (1719) and *Captain Singleton* (1720) were influential models that incorporated elements of the romance but substituted a mercantile for a chivalric ethos. Following the publication of Defoe's work, there were many reworkings of the survival-on-a-desert-island theme, in which the adventure was in the creation of arable land from the wilderness, with unfriendly natives threatening the new colony. From *Crusoe* onward, good and evil are increasingly seen in racial rather than moral terms. *Captain Singleton* is the model for the picaresque imperial adventure in which the journey into the wilderness forms the main motif. The adventure novels of Joseph Conrad, James Fenimore Cooper, Herman Melville, and H. Rider Haggard connect with this tradition.

Erskine *Childers's *The Riddle of the Sands* (1903), Buchan's *The Thirty-Nine Steps* (1915), and more recently the novels of John *le Carré and Len *Deighton incorporate adventure and mystery in the spy *thriller concerned with superpower rivalry rather than savagery, reflecting a concern to maintain international prestige. Detective stories and domestic thrillers, like those of Chandler and Dick *Francis, still draw heavily on the adventure formula and motifs for their pace and narrative structure. Adventure has adapted well to film, and the popularity of Steven Spielberg's fast-moving *Indiana Jones* trilogy is a tribute to the strength of the exile and return formula of medieval romances.

[*See also* Adventurer and Adventuress; Formula: Plot; Heroic Romance; Heroism.]

• John G. Cawelti, *Adventure, Mystery, and Romance: Formula Stories as Art and Popular Culture* (1976). Martin Green, *Dreams of Adventure, Deeds of Empire* (1979).

—Nigel Rigby

ADVERTISING MILIEU. As a *setting for a *mystery story, the advertising agency holds considerable advantages, providing a rich *milieu for symbolism and cynical fun in a relatively closed community of articulate characters. In *Before Midnight* (1955), where the agency is Nero *Wolfe's client, hiring him to deal with the potentially ruinous effect of a murder that interrupts a nationwide perfume ad contest, Rex *Stout portrays the directors individually as they visit Wolfe's old brownstone on West Thirty-fifth Street. The portraits are not flattering.

Julian *Symons, who worked briefly as a copywriter for the firm Rumble, Crowther and Nicholas (familiarly known as Rumble, Stumble and Bumble), used advertising agencies as the background for two novels: *A Man Called Jones* (1947) and *The Thirty-First of February* (1950). He paints a characteristically dark, acidulous picture.

While the advertising world, like many distinctive occupational environments, can serve as mere colorful background to the mystery, the best work in this subgenre is enriched by symbolic use of the business. Advertising's creation of false promises and its appeal to *greed and vanity are fertile ground for constructing parallel structures and themes. The undisputed classic work set in this milieu is *Murder Must Advertise* (1933), by Dorothy L. *Sayers, in which Lord Peter *Wimsey, lightly disguised as Mr. Death Bredon and looking "like Bertie Wooster in horn-rims," poses as a copywriter at a *London agency in order to investigate the suspicious death of his predecessor. Sayers herself spent nine years working for the firm of S. H. Benson, where she enjoyed playing with words and was appreciated by her colleagues.

Her account of agency life is shrewd, witty, affectionate, and authentic for its time.

The Benson agency always attracted literary employees. Marion Babson, who wrote two mystery novels about the public relations industry, *Cover-Up Story* (1971) and *Murder on Show* (1972; *Murder at the Cat Show*, 1989) once worked there, as did Paula Gosling and David Williams. Williams was managing director of a subsidiary company, which he bought and turned into one of Britain's top twenty agencies, David Williams and Ketchum. His novel *Advertise for Treasure* (1984), focusing on the takeover bid for a young London agency by a New York-based international one, deals authentically with the financial side of the business. Believing that the advertising process is valid, Williams also takes its pretensions seriously. His characters, speaking for him, go so far as to claim that advertisements do not lie.

[*See also* Milieu.]

• Barbara Reynolds, *Dorothy L. Sayers: Her Life and Soul* (1993).
—Anthony Lejeune

AFRICA, CRIME AND MYSTERY WRITING IN.
The first crime work written by a writer born or resident in an African country and set in modern Africa was published in London in 1900. *Kruger's Secret Service*, by One Who Was in It—the journalist Douglas Blackburn—reflects the newsworthy issues of the Anglo-Boer War. However, only after the Second World War does African crime and mystery writing get under way. In South African Donald Swanson's *Murder in the Game Reserve* (1950), the question is whether crafty rangers or wild beasts are responsible for the corpses strewn across the veld. And in Nigeria, Edmund Odili's *The Mystery of the Missing Sandals* (1953) is an early popular work.

A variant of the orthodox crime novel stems from Joseph Conrad's *Heart of Darkness* (1902), with its journey into the forbidding interior. Among examples of this type are Elspeth Huxley's *The Red Rock Wilderness* (1957), in which a young *sleuth seeks a mad biologist in French Equatorial Africa, and Justin Cartwright's *Interior* (1988). Many writers explore what Julian *Symons calls the "borderland between the crime story and the novel." One of the strands of Alan Paton's *Cry, the Beloved Country* (1948) follows the arrest and trial of a young black man wanted for robbery with violence. Doris Lessing's debut, *The Grass Is Singing* (1950), analyzes the polarized society of Southern Rhodesia (now Zimbabwe) in the form of the crime story. South African Herman Charles Bosman's noted short story "Unto Dust" (1949), about the frontier wars of dispossession, is also written as a murder mystery. Bosman's *Willemsdorp* (1977), like William Faulkner's *Intruder in the Dust* (1948), is organized as a *crime novel with a comic yet menacing *detective derived from Edgar Allan *Poe.

Works about the struggle for independence also use crime formulas. A. S. Mopeli-Paulus's *Blanket Boy's Moon* (with Peter Lanham, 1953) concerns a ritual murder in Basutoland (now Lesotho), leading to the execution of the anticolonial hero. In Portuguese Angola, José Luandino Vieira's novel *A Vida Verdadeira de Domingos* (1961; *The Real Life of Domingos Xavier*, 1978) follows the case of a worker arrested and tortured to death in a cover-up. The victimized criminal is also featured in three crucial works of literature. Al-Tayyib Salih's *Season of Migration to the North*, translated from the Arabic in 1969, concerns a Sudanese returnee from London confessing to serial killings; *Le Docker Noir* (1956; *Black Docker*), the first novel of the Senegalese Sembene Ousmane; and Lewis Nkosi's South African *Mating Birds* (1987). Bessie Head's *The Collector of Treasures* (1977), set in Botswana, concerns a woman who murders her husband. A *whydunit, the story explores how gender inequalities in a *rural world lead to prison.

*Violence is inexorable and inevitable in Alex La Guma's thriller about apartheid in South Africa, *Time of the Butcherbird* (1979). Andre Brink's political problem novels involve detention and trial of the protagonists with the expected revelations of injustice, by the dreaded security police in *A Dry White Season* (1980), and in the system of slavery in *A Chain of Voices* (1982).

Major writers in Kenya are Mwangi Ruheni (*The Mystery Smugglers*, 1975); Frank Saisi, whose *police procedural *The Bhang Syndicate* (1984) features the endearing Chief Inspector Kip, trained at Scotland Yard; and Marjorie Oludhe Macgoye, who wrote *Murder in Majengo* (1972). Ngugi wa Thiong'o uses a crime format in *Petals of Blood* (1977).

Many South African crime authors have achieved an international readership. Geoffrey Jenkins is a productive adventure writer whose early *Scent of the Sea* (1971; *The Hollow Sea*) is a pure mystery. Glynn Croudace wrote *Motives for Murder* in 1950 and Wessel Ebersohn writes variations on the crime novel in *A Lonely Place to Die* (1979) and *Store Up the Anger* (1980), based on the case of Steve Biko; both Ebersohn novels expose corrupt and unjust police methods. In addition to a series set in Britain, Alan Scholefield has written numerous works set in Africa, including *The Sea Cave* (1983). Prolific crime writer June Drummond's *Hidden Agenda* (1993) concerns a murder in a South African university English department. Her work is notable for its domestic detail, which in the hands of most overseas writers is merely exotic. In 1971 James *McClure, who has not lived in South Africa, his place of birth, since 1965, launched a series set in Trekkersburg, a thinly disguised Pietermaritzburg in Natal, with *The Steam Pig*. In addition to detective novels set in Britain, Gillian Slovo introduced the punchy South African Captain Gert Malan, unraveler of loyalty and lies within the liberation movement, in *The Betrayal* (1991). Two comic novels, both spoofs, appeared in South Africa in the early 1990s: *Time for Murder* (1990) by Wilfred Levitt and *Machado* (1990) by Johann de Waal, featuring a particularly slothful small-town investigator.

[*See also* African American Sleuth; Ethnic Sleuth; Visitors Abroad.]
—Stephen Gray

AFRICAN AMERICAN SLEUTH. In the twentieth century, African Americans began the mass migration that would transform them from a rural to an urban people. Although the African American writers who chronicled this transition examined the impact of crime on the black community, they did not typically write genre mystery fiction. Among those who did was Rudolph Fisher, whose *The Conjure-Man Dies* (1932), a classic mystery novel, features Harlem detective Perry Dart and Dr. John Archer. Twenty-five years later, expatriate Chester *Himes, living in France, created Coffin Ed *Johnson and Grave Digger Jones, who in policing a ghetto that has become a slum are both more cynical and more brutal than Perry Dart.

By the 1940s, African American police officers as minor characters included Detective Zilgitt in Ellery *Queen's *Cat of Many Tails* (1949) and Officer Connolly in Bart Spicer's *Blues for the Prince* (1950). But a significant step forward occurred with the publication of "Corollary" in the July 1948 issue of *Ellery Queen's Mystery Magazine*. Written by African American writer Hughes Allison, the story features Detective Joe Hill.

During the civil rights era, other sleuths were created. John *Ball's *In the Heat of the Night* (1965) featured Virgil *Tibbs, a Pasadena homicide detective. In marked contrast to George *Baxt's flamboyant homosexual detective Pharoah Love (*A Queer Kind of Death*, 1966) and his successor, the hip Satan Stagg (*Topsy and Evil*, 1968), Tibbs was conservative in dress and behavior. But he brought to his work a compassion rooted in his own struggles.

However, African American sleuths were becoming more assertive in demanding respect. As hard-boiled *private eyes, they also became more violent. This was linked to the *urban milieu in which *private eyes such as Ernest Tidyman's John Shaft, Percy Spurlock Parker's Bull Benson, and Kenn Davis's Carver Bascombe functioned. They followed in the footsteps of private eye Toussaint Marcus Moore, created by Ed Lacy in the 1950s.

In the 1990s, a group of African American mystery writers shaped their sleuths within the context of their own culture-based awareness of the social structure. Thus Walter *Mosley's Ezekiel "Easy" *Rawlins is a migrant from the South, financially secure, but still painfully aware of the precariousness of being black in 1940s *Los Angeles. And although Barbara Neely's eponymous sleuth in *Blanche on the Lam* (1992) lives in the New South, she too experiences a sense of jeopardy. As a domestic worker, Blanche conducts a murder investigation while dealing with issues of race, class, gender, and oppression.

Perhaps the one thing that sets African American sleuths apart from their European American counterparts is what W. E. B. DuBois once referred to as a "double consciousness." When the sleuths are fully realized as three-dimensional characters, the writers who create them present them as the products of a society in which they must develop a heightened sense of awareness that sometimes amounts to "cultural paranoia." This awareness serves them well in encounters not only with criminals but also with police officers and others, who may respond to them based on racial stereotypes.

However, in the tradition of the genre, African American private eyes also have their police contacts. And the client who comes through the door is sometimes white. Sometimes, as with Virginia Kelly, the lesbian investment counselor in Nikki Baker's *The Lavender House Murder* (1992), the case is one in which the sleuth is intimately involved. But on other occasions private eyes such as Clifford Mason's Joe Cinquez and Gar Anthony Haywood's Aaron Gunner turn to their kinship and friendship networks for information and resources. The sidekicks of these sleuths are varied and eccentric. Easy Rawlins has an uneasy relationship with "Mouse," who is as lethal as he is loyal. Richard Hilary's New Jersey-based private eye, Ezell "Easy" Barnes, has a sidekick named "Angel," who is a transvestite. The plot conventions are all there. What is different is how the African American sleuth interprets them.

[*See also* Ethnicity; Racism.]

• Stephen F. Soitos, *The Blues Detective: A Study of African American Detective Fiction* (1996). Paula L. Woods, ed., *Spooks, Spies, and Private Eyes: Black Mystery, Crime, and Suspense Fiction of the 20th Century* (1995).

—Frankie Y. Bailey

ALCOHOL AND ALCOHOLISM. In the construction of crime and mystery fiction, the portrayal of the use and abuse of alcohol may be significant. Alcohol itself may be depicted as a vehicle for poison, as a beverage that lends sophistication to an occasion, or as a drink that may conveniently either loosen up or cloud the recollections of witnesses. It is also used as a means of freeing the thought processes of some sleuths. The disease of alcoholism tends to be used more thematically, although the struggle to conquer the affliction of alcoholism may serve as a fine indicator of character.

Genevieve Knupfer's study of drinking in forty-six detective novels established alcohol use as a basis for a convention of characterization. In these works she found 667 mentions of alcohol, with two-thirds of the occasion connected to sociability, relaxation, or relief of stress. Rex *Stout's *Fer-de-Lance* (1934), one of the early works in the study, refers to Nero *Wolfe's consumption of six quarts of beer a day and his desire to cut back to five. The *Great Detective's habit is a feature in many novels and stories. Wolfe's purpose in drinking is to achieve relaxation, it is suggested: Like Colin *Dexter's Inspector *Morse, the *sleuth drinks "to think." Relief of stress is also the function of the bottle in Sam *Spade's desk drawer.

Why, how, and with whom one drinks becomes significant in a story because social drinking implies shared intimacy, often revealing questions of class and demonstrations of classiness. Displays of connoisseurship by Dorothy L. *Sayers's Lord Peter *Wimsey and Robert B. *Parker's *Spenser are both entertaining and informative. But a refined palate can also be fatal, as Fortunato learns in Edgar Allan *Poe's "The Cask of Amontillado" (*Godey's Lady's Book*, Nov. 1846).

Writers exploit the dangers of social drinking,

which include speaking incautiously or being outwitted by an opponent. Raymond *Chandler's Philip *Marlowe plies Jesse Florian with bonded bourbon in *Farewell, My Lovely* (1940). In Dashiell *Hammett's *Red Harvest* (1929), the *Continental Op tries gin to loosen Dinah Brand's tongue, but his plan backfires and he passes out at a key moment. Spade suffers similar defeat when Gutman doctors his drink in *The Maltese Falcon* (1930). In *The Glass Key* (1931), Ned Beaumont's intimate drinks with Eloise Mathews effectively block Shad O'Rory's plans. A later scene involving Beaumont and the sadistic Jeff Gardner, a masterful parody of social drinking, results in O'Rory's death.

The most serious danger in a social drink for fictional characters in this genre is that it provides the opportunity—with poison or drugs as the means—for *murder. A daiquiri serves as the vehicle for poison in Agatha *Christie's *The Mirror Crack'd from Side to Side* (1962; *The Mirror Crack'd*); a glass of Arak (a brandy-like rum) fulfills a similar function in Cornell *Woolrich's *The Bride Wore Black* (1940). In an original variation on drinking linked to murder, an observant suspect in Wolfe's *Fer-de-Lance* introduces a poisonous snake into the drawer where Wolfe keeps his bottle opener.

Despite the appearance of unhappy outcomes to social drinking, drunkenness is often viewed with a sense of humor. Drunks as comic figures are *stock characters. Although few are as attractive or sharp as Nick Charles in Hammett's *The Thin Man* (1934), perhaps the wittiest of detective novels, John J. Malone and the Justuses in the Craig *Rice series that begins with *8 Faces at 3* (1939; *Death at Three*) are comic inebriates. In Hammett, the point is social satire; in Rice, it is irrepressible fun.

The line between heavy drinking and alcohol addiction or alcoholism is indistinct in much fiction. If in *Red Harvest* the Continental Op loses control of his drinking, the lapse is case specific; in *The Dain Curse* (1929), he is back on track. Philip Marlowe may drink more—and for more private reasons—than Hammett's detectives, but like them he stays on the job and claims to see himself as objectively (and as cynically) as he sees anyone else.

Many secondary characters in detective novels are alcoholics. Marlowe spends a sympathetic morning drinking with Bill Chess, whose alcoholism and isolation make his home a safe hiding place for Muriel Chess, alias Mildred Haviland, in *The Lady in the Lake* (1943). In *The Long Goodbye* (1953), Marlowe drinks with Terry Lennox, an alcoholic he likes, and with Roger Wade, one he does not. Other secondary characters attempt to recover from alcoholism. Bill Sweeney, a newspaper reporter in Frederic *Brown's *The Screaming Mimi* (1949), desires Yolanda Land. Testing the hypothesis that "A guy can get anything he wants, if he wants it bad enough," he succeeds in staying sober until the last paragraph of the book. In Elmore *Leonard's *Unknown Man No. 89* (1977), the process server Jack Ryan and his quarry, Denise Leary, join forces at an Alcoholics Anonymous meeting, solve the crime, and lead sober lives together.

In Dexter's police procedurals set in Oxford, Morse drinks so heavily that in *The Wench Is Dead* (1989) he is hospitalized with an ulcer; yet after recovering, he makes a drinking companion of Nurse Maclean, just as he does of Sheila Williams in *The Jewel That Was Ours* (1991). In *Death Is Now My Neighbor* (1996), Morse is diagnosed as diabetic, a consequence of his drinking. John Harvey's Charlie Resnick police procedurals feature an alcoholic jazz musician, Ed Silver, who becomes sober by the end of *Cutting Edge* (1991), and an alcoholic film director, Harold Roy, in *Rough Treatment* (1990).

Four private eyes are themselves self-admitted alcoholics: James Crumley's Milo Milodragovitch and W. W. Sugrue, James Lee Burke's Dave Robicheaux, and Lawrence *Block's Matt Scudder. Crumley's novels offer remarkable bar scenes with sharp portraits of alcoholic patrons. By the end of *Dancing Bear* (1983), Milodragovitch has stopped drinking and appears ready to join Robicheaux and Scudder in sobriety. Robicheaux wants nothing more than a peaceful family life, but his sobriety is constantly tested as he is drawn into the criminal underworld of the Mississippi delta.

In the first four of thirteen Scudder novels, Block's hero drinks heavily. In *Eight Million Ways to Die* (1982), he struggles to stay sober after hospitalization and is able finally, in the last sentence of the book, to tell an AA group that "My name is Matt and I'm an alcoholic." In *When the Sacred Ginmill Closes* (1986), from his now sober point of view, Scudder reexamines three cases on which he worked simultaneously while he was still drinking. This novel presents the most penetrating study in the twentieth century of the private eye as recovering alcoholic.

[*See also* Characterization; Loner, Sleuth as; Poisons, Unusual; Prohibition.]

• Richard A. Filloy, "Of Drink and Detectives: The Genesis and Function of a Literary Convention," *Contemporary Drug Problems* 13, no. 2 (summer 1986): 249–71. Genevieve Knupfer, "The Use of Alcoholic Beverages as Portrayed in Popular Detective Fiction," *Contemporary Drug Problems* 20, no. 1 (spring 1993): 51–63.   —George F. Wedge

ALCOTT, LOUISA MAY. *See* Blood-and-Thunder Fiction; Bluestocking Sleuth.

Alfred Hitchcock's Mystery Magazine. One of the best and longest running digest-sized crime fiction periodicals, *Alfred Hitchcock's Mystery Magazine* (*AHMM*) first appeared with a December 1956 issue labeled Volume 1, Number 12, thus instantly creating eleven phantom issues to frustrate collectors. It appeared monthly until expanding to a thirteen-issues-per-year schedule in the 1980s. While including all varieties of crime fiction, the magazine specialized in the kind of ironic twist-in-the-tail story suited to half-hour presentation on the *Alfred Hitchcock Presents* television show, which antedated the magazine by a year. With Hitchcock's name and image as the main selling points, there was little emphasis on big-name writers, although many have appeared in the magazine's pages. Among the most prolific and typical *AHMM* contributors has been Henry Slesar, who also wrote extensively for the television series. Other notables have included Clark Howard, Jack Ritchie, C. B. Gilford, Donald Honig, John Lutz, Lawrence *Block, Bill Pronzini, James Holding, Richard Deming, Fletcher Flora, Edward D. *Hoch, Talmage Powell, Lawrence *Treat, and, in recent years, Brendan DuBois, Stephen Wasylyk, Doug Allyn, and Joseph *Hansen. Although Hitchcock signed a monthly editorial (which was more promotional than substantive) and posed for covers in the early years, and although the brief story introductions were implicitly attributed to him, the great film director never had any direct editorial connection with the magazine. The first editor was William Manners, successively succeeded by G. F. Goster, Ernest M. Hutter, and, when original publisher H.S.D. Publications sold the magazine to Davis Publications in 1976, Eleanor Sullivan, managing editor of *AHMM*'s new stablemate, *Ellery Queen's Mystery Magazine*. During the tenure of editor Cathleen Jordan, who took over in 1982, nonfiction features such as contests and book reviews have been developed, and more of an editorial personality has emerged. In 1992 the magazine was sold along with the other Davis fiction magazines to Bantam Doubleday Dell. In 1996, the Dell Magazines were sold to Penny Marketing.

[*See also* Digest-Sized Mystery Magazines.]

• Michael L. Cook, *Monthly Murders: A Checklist and Chronological Listing of Fiction in the Digest-Sized Mystery Magazines in the United States and England* (1982). David H. Doerrer, "Alfred Hitchcock's *Mystery Magazine*," in Michael L. Cook, ed., *Mystery, Detective, and Espionage Magazines* (1983).   —Jon L. Breen

ALIBI. The word "alibi" as a noun—from the Latin adverb *alibi*, meaning "elsewhere"—entered British legal discourse in the eighteenth century. The plea of alibi alleges that the accused is innocent because he or she was somewhere other than the scene of the crime at the time of its commission. Because an alibi provides the "perfect defense," an accused or suspected person is strongly motivated to produce one. This circumstance has created the notorious ambiguity of the alibi: Vitally important to those accused, it is routinely suspected by the police, juries, and readers of detective fiction.

The Golden Age of crime and mystery writing, between the two world wars, was the great era of fictional alibi. The making and breaking of alibis became a principal means to complicate detections. An early and notable instance of an elaborate and apparently impregnable alibi is that in Freeman Wills *Crofts's first novel *The Cask* (1920). This alibi depends largely on complicated railroad schedules, the first instance of their special attraction for Golden Age writers.

Detectives in the Golden Age refer continually to the notion of *means, motive, and opportunity. However strong a *suspect's *motive, a good alibi can cancel reasonable suspicion by convincing the reader that the character had no opportunity to commit the crime. Therefore, much narrative energy in *Golden Age forms is devoted to questioning the the places and times that may provide opportunity. Often maps and timetables must be constructed from bits of evidence, and many novels of this type even provide them graphically. Because all persons within the circle of investigation are to be suspected, a principal task of Golden Age detection, for both the detective and the reader, is to test every alibi.

The alibi was most notably developed in the novels of Agatha *Christie. Among her innumerable variations were alibis that manipulated not only time and place but also identity. She plays with time in *Evil Under the Sun* (1941), and with identity in *Murder in Three Acts* (1934; *Three Act Tragedy*). Some Christie alibis are, however, much more complex and bizarre. In *One, Two, Buckle My Shoe* (1940; *The Patriotic Murders, An Overdose of Death*), Christie manipulates time and identity while presenting solutions to two puzzling murders. The killer in *Lord Edgware Dies* (1933; *Thirteen at Dinner*) hires an actress to impersonate her at a dinner party while she commits the *murder. Christie even produces the seemingly perfect alibi of a possible suspect being dead: In *Ten Little Niggers* (1939; *And Then There Were None*), the last murders on Indian Island are committed after the actual murderer appears to have become yet another victim in a growing series. This paradoxical "alibi for a corpse" may be found again in the novel of that name by Elizabeth Lemarchand (1969) and even in legal writing on alibi.

Perhaps the most dazzling tour de force of Golden Age alibi is Dorothy L. *Sayers's Crofts-like production in *The Five Red Herrings* (1931; *Suspicious Characters*). Witnesses corroborate the alibi of a likely suspect that he was many miles from the scene of a murder. Nevertheless, Lord Peter *Wimsey eventually uncovers the murderer's ingenious device, his nearly impossible cross-country dash to the crime scene by train (as in *The Cask*), with the added garnish of bicycle and auto.

In the 1920s and 1930s, Raymond *Chandler and other hardboiled writers were questioning the need to construct complex alibis. It was Chandler's view that a writer striving for realism and the truth of crime could not be bothered with "the same old futzing around with timetables." Alibi has taken on increased importance, however, in some contemporary hardboiled novels. Sue *Grafton's debut mystery was even titled "*A*" *Is for Alibi* (1982). Ironically, in this novel alibi is rendered meaningless when the killer puts poison into a medicine that may be taken at any time. By contrast, in Grafton's "*I*" *Is for Innocent* (1992), alibi is crucial: To make his alibi, the most likely suspect establishes his distance from the crime scene by a transportation almost as implausible as its analogue in Crofts and Sayers. In Judith Van Gieson's *The Wolf Path* (1992), a suspect provides both his and his lady's alibis by revealing where and how they spent the night—no Golden Age mystification here to protect the lady's honor.

Many crimes in the period of supersonic travel and instant communication make alibi insignificant or irrelevant. The criminals are often multiple and nearly impossible to trace as in Stanislaw Lem's mock-hardboiled novel *Chain of Chance* (1976;

Katar). The time and space that once governed "opportunity" have been undermined; Golden Age fantasies of murder at a distance are realized every day through letter bombs and electronic triggers. No alibis are offered, and none would serve.

[*See also* Impersonation; Red Herrings; "Time Is of the Essence."]

• Howard Haycraft, *Murder for Pleasure: The Life and Times of the Detective Story* (1941). G. C. Ramsey, *Agatha Christie: Mistress of Mystery* (1967). R. N. Gooderson, *Alibi* (1977). H. R. F. Keating, *Writing Crime Fiction* (1986).

—T. R. Steiner

ALIBI, UNBREAKABLE. The phrase "unbreakable alibi" refers to a convention in crime fiction that was especially popular during the Golden Age of crime and mystery writing and is still used in the *whodunit. The term "alibi" from the Latin adverb *alibi*, meaning "elsewhere," refers to the defensive plea that the accused was somewhere other than the scene of the crime with which he is charged. The adjective "unbreakable" is used to underscore the challenge facing the detective in disproving the accused's assertion. In classic detective fiction, alibis may be offered by *suspects even before anyone is formally charged with a crime. In real life, an unbreakable alibi is one that stands up to police scrutiny or cross-examination in court when it is presented as a defense by an accused person. Such an alibi can be quite simple, often consisting of a person or persons swearing, truthfully or otherwise, that to their knowledge the accused was elsewhere at the time of the crime in question. If the deponent is believed, then the alibi is unbroken in a legal sense and the accused is acquitted. This type of alibi occurs in fiction, too, from time to time, but more memorable are those elaborate manufactured alibis involving the manipulation of clocks, railway timetables, and the like that were felt to be a worthy test of the *Great Detective's powers.

A convincing, unbreakable alibi is at the root of much fictional detection. A complicated alibi is not necessarily more unbreakable than an uncomplicated one, however. Lord Peter *Wimsey's comment about *ciphers and code in Dorothy L. *Sayers's *Have His Carcase* (1932) is applicable to alibis: "Any code," he pointed out, "ever coded can be decoded with pains and patience." The Chevalier C. Auguste *Dupin, Edgar Allan *Poe's detective introduced in "The Murders in the Rue Morgue" (1841; *Graham's Lady's and Gentleman's Magazine*, Apr. 1841), goes a step further when he says that the more outré a matter appears, the easier it is to solve.

Probably the best constructor of the more complicated alibis in Golden Age fiction was Freeman Wills *Crofts, whose novels often focus on the single line of investigation into the major suspect's alibi. The murderer may be clearly indicated, as he is in *The Sea Mystery* (1928), but Crofts maintains a high level of *suspense merely by working out exactly how the murder was committed and the *corpse disposed of. In his first work, *The Cask* (1920), a cask that eventually proves to contain a murdered body makes three rail and sea journeys: from Paris to London (via le

Havre), from London to Paris (via Calais), and again from Paris to London (via Rouen). The killer establishes an alibi by visiting Brussels at the same time he is supposed to be meeting and dispatching the cask in London. His alibi, worked by means of a second cask and the telephone, serves a double purpose. It not only diverts suspicion from him, but because it appears certain to the police that the body must have been put into the cask in London, it also throws suspicion on another, London-domiciled, suspect.

Some writers hang the unbreakable alibi on a single piece of crucial evidence. In Sayers's *The Five Red Herrings* (1931; *Suspicious Characters*), a painter in Galloway's artists' colony is killed by a fellow artist, who then tries to hide the time of the crime by transporting his victim miles away, painting a picture in the style of the deceased, and staging an accident to the body. He escapes by bicycle and then proceeds by train to Glasgow; his alibi rests on his producing a rail ticket to Glasgow by a different, slower route. The accurate time of his arrival is disguised from the investigators by forgery of the ticket punch marks he recalls thanks to his artist's memory for visual detail. The same trick in a simpler form, by means of a triangular clip simulated with nail scissors, is used in J. J. Connington's *The Two Tickets Puzzle* (1930; *The Two Ticket Puzzle*).

A more complicated—and in theory, more impenetrable—alibi can be devised if the murderer is not a singleton but a syndicate. The murderer in Sayers's *Have His Carcase* is a syndicate of three, two of whom are major participants in the crime. The position of each is, as Wimsey remarks, intended to be "really impregnable with double and triple lines of defence." Yet there are matters like weather and physical problems that no one can foresee. Moreover, more can go wrong with two or more participants, as is the case here and in A. E. W. Mason's *They Wouldn't Be Chessmen* (1935). In these and other novels with a syndicate standing in for the murderer, the focus on the behavior of several suspects can dilute the suspense and tension. Crofts's *Sir John Magill's Last Journey* (1930), which is alluded to along with Connington's *The Two Tickets Puzzle* and Sayers's *The Five Red Herrings* and is like the latter partly set in Galloway, has no fewer than four conspirators to build an elaborate alibi involving a motor boat and the Stranraer boat train. Perhaps the master of demolishing the unbreakable alibi in a dramatic manner is Erle Stanley *Gardner's lawyer-detective Perry *Mason.

[*See also* Railway Milieu; Red Herrings; "Time Is of the Essence."]

• William Bell, "Railway Timetables in *The Five Red Herrings*," *The Proceedings of the Dorothy L. Sayers Society 1986 Seminar*: 17–19. Reprinted in *Backtrack* (1990): 251–55. Philip L. Scowcroft, "The Five Red Herrings Filleted," *Ibid*: 2–15. Philip L. Scowcroft, "Railways and Alibis: The Work of Freeman Wills Crofts," in *Deadly Pleasures* 1, no. 4 (spring 1994): 20–21.

—Philip L. Scowcroft

Alleyn, Roderick. Inspector (later Superintendent) Roderick Alleyn is almost the *victim of his own elegance, entering Ngaio *Marsh's first detective novel in 1934 as tall, handsome, well dressed, and well connected: the sort who would "do" for house parties. With his brother a baronet and his mother Lady Alleyn of Danes Lodge, Alleyn retains his aristocratic sangfroid through thirty-two novels from 1934 to 1982, traveling to France, Italy, New Zealand, and South Africa in his pursuit of criminals. In that time he acquires a wife, the famous portrait painter Agatha Troy, and a son, Ricky. Alleyn ages little, but he and his reliable helper Inspector Fox become somewhat stranded in the police methods of the 1950s.

Marsh created Alleyn very much to suit her own world, naming him after the famous Elizabethan actor Edward Alleyn, and endowing him with her own love for William *Shakespeare and the stage. His marriage to Troy opens up a number of interesting plot possibilities, and even Marsh's penultimate novel, *Photo-Finish* (1980), which is set in New Zealand, has Troy's portrait commission at its heart. Troy is infinitely understanding, but distant, and her career is never subsidiary to that of her husband.

Comparisons between Alleyn and Lord Peter *Wimsey may have been inevitable in the early novels, but Alleyn soon proves to be a very different sort of character. He is no *gentleman amateur, but a serving police officer who is always seen as part of a team. Marsh describes him as "an attractive, civilized man with whom it would be pleasant to talk, but much less pleasant to fall out." Although his role as upholder of the law may sometimes create tensions with the wealthy and powerful circles which are his natural *milieu, Alleyn accepts no deviation from his sense of duty, no matter how well-mannered his investigative technique may be.

[*See also* Aristocratic Sleuth; New Zealand, Crime and Mystery Writing in; Police Detective; Sleuth.]

• Margaret Lewis, *Ngaio Marsh: A Life* (1991). Ngaio Marsh, *Black Beech and Honeydew* (1966; rev. ed. 1981).

—Margaret Lewis

ALLINGHAM, MARGERY (LOUISE) (1904–1966), English author, considered one of the great mystery writers of the Golden Age. Allingham published her first novel in 1928 and her last, posthumously, in 1968. She came of a writing family and was a published novelist before she was twenty. When she failed to complete a mainstream novel about her own 1920s generation, she turned with relief to the *mystery story, which she saw as a box with four sides: "a Killing, a Mystery, an Enquiry and a Conclusion with an Element of Satisfaction in it." She felt safe within the box, "at once a prison and a refuge," keeping her in line but allowing free play to her imagination.

The White Cottage Mystery was serialized in 1927 and appeared as a book the following year. An effective *whodunit with a daring solution, it is more interesting in some ways than *The Crime at Black Dudley* (1929; *The Black Dudley Murder*), which followed in 1929 and is much better known, less for its merit than because it introduces a "dubious" character known as Albert *Campion, a typical 1920s *silly-ass sleuth. From the first his foolish appearance and manner make it almost obligatory to underestimate

him, yet he proves unexpectedly resourceful and reliable when trouble starts. Over the years he matures into a figure of weight and authority.

The Crime at Black Dudley was written by what Allingham called the "plum pudding" method, whereby anything may be stirred into the mixture to enhance its richness. Three further novels were composed on the same principle, all lively and inventive, all set in rural Suffolk, all less concerned with methods of *murder than with precious objects and the struggle to possess them. *Mystery Mile* (1930) introduces Magersfontein *Lugg, Campion's lugubrious manservant, and *Sweet Danger* (1933; *The Fear Sign*; *Kingdom of Death*), the Lady Amanda Fitton, who after a long and eccentric courtship eventually becomes Campion's wife. *Police at the Funeral* (1931) marks a new stage in Campion's career and is notably accomplished in its more formal manner. Investigating murder in a grimly repressive *Cambridge household, he has perforce to behave himself, and though he lapses occasionally into calculated inanity, he never loses sight of the seriousness of his undertaking. He is, in fact, ready to grow up and take his place in the smart urban world of the 1930s.

Four novels feature aspects of contemporary culture and together form a distinctive group within the Canon. Each is set in a specific world with the mystery evolving from the particular preoccupations of those who inhabit it: art in *Death of a Ghost* (1934), books in *Flowers for the Judge* (1936; *Legacy in Blood*), musical theater in *Dancers in Mourning* (1937), and haute couture in *The Fashion in Shrouds* (1938). A lighter, shorter novel, *The Case of the Late Pig*, also appeared in 1937. Though based on an improbable premise unquestioningly accepted by all right-minded persons, it is a most engaging story, narrated by Campion himself with echoes of P. G. Wodehouse.

Campion does not appear in *Black Plumes* (1940), despite its wartime date set firmly in an opulent prewar world, but he makes a memorable return in *Traitor's Purse* (1941), contending with amnesia, an emotional crisis, and a secret vital to national security locked in his brain. *Coroner's Pidgin* (1945; *Pearls before Swine*) shows a segment of the smart set adapting to life in a Blitz-ravaged *London.

The postwar novels were less frequent, and each differs significantly from its immediate predecessor. *More Work for the Undertaker* (1948), fizzing with wit and fancy, introduces Charlie Luke, a young policeman with a "pile-driver personality." *The Tiger in the Smoke* (1952) is dark and disquieting, set in a fogbound London with a vicious killer at large. *The Beckoning Lady* (1955; *The Estate of the Beckoning Lady*) returns to rural Suffolk, enveloping even Luke in sunlit languor. *Hide My Eyes* (1958; *Tether's End*) charts the events of a memorable day in which a murderous psychopath learns that he, too, can be a *victim. *The China Governess* (1962) is a dense and intricate study of deception within a privileged family conditioned to denying the truth. *The Mind Readers* (1965) combines schoolboy daring with adult deceits in an exuberant *thriller about extrasensory perception. *Cargo of Eagles* (1968) takes Campion on a last exhilarating treasure-hunt. It was completed after her death by her husband, Youngman Carter.

Allingham remains among the most beguiling of mystery writers, for her warmth and humor, her eye for character, her vivid inventive powers, and her graceful, pointed style. She also adapted to a changing world and was not afraid to test her range, refining and deepening her fictions and exploring significant themes. Above all, she created a world that is indisputably her own.

[See also Art and Antiques Milieu; Aristocratic Sleuth; Cozy Mystery; Fashion and Design Milieu; Humor; Publishing Milieu; Theatrical Milieu.]

• B. A. Pike, Campion's Career: A Study of the Novels of Margery Allingham (1987). Richard Martin, Ink in Her Blood: The Life and Crime Fiction of Margery Allingham (1988). Julia Thorogood, Margery Allingham: A Biography (1991).

—B. A. Pike

ALLUSION, LITERARY. Quotations from and references to the works of authors famous in English literature have specific significance in three different aspects of detective fiction. The first is the use of a quotation for the title of the book. Lines to do with death and dying taken from the plays and sonnets of William *Shakespeare are among those that appear most commonly in this connection. Some examples are Put Out the Light (1985) and Naked Villainy (1987) by Sara Woods, all of whose titles come from Shakespeare, and Come to Dust by Emma Lathen (1968), while the title Full Fathom Five has been used by three authors—Hugh Sykes Davies (1956), Bart Davis (1987), and G. V. Galwey (1951). Excerpts from traditional nursery rhymes such as Agatha *Christie's One, Two, Buckle My Shoe (1940; The Patriotic Murders, 1941, An Overdose of Death, 1953), A Pocketful of Rye (1953), and Hickory Dickory Dock, (1955; Hickory, Dickory Death) are similarly popular.

An extension of this form of titling is the use of a pun that plays on a literary quotation, as in Don Among the Dead Men (1952), by C. E. Vulliamy; Tom Brown's Body (1949), by Gladys *Mitchell; and The Lady in the Lake (1943), by Raymond *Chandler.

A second aspect of literary allusion may be seen in the fuller quotation from both prose and verse to be found in the now slightly old-fashioned custom of chapter headings. This usage is probably best exemplified in the detective novels of Michael *Innes, Dorothy L. *Sayers, and Mitchell. It is possible that such extracts are merely a mild conceit employed to demonstrate wide reading, if not actual scholarship, on the part of the author; but, as in the studies on campanology that Sayers cites in The Nine Tailors (1934), they can also be used to give background information relevant to the narrative and to heighten the *atmosphere. In some instances, they also serve to highlight the action in the chapter they precede. However, only rarely do the chapter headings themselves presage actual *clues.

Third, the uses to which literary allusion are put within the detective story itself are diverse. An important function is that of simple *characterization, where felicitous quotations in the dialogue contribute to an aura of culture and scholarship on the part of the character. This is apparent in the urbane employment of this style of dialogue by fictional detectives such as Sayers's Lord Peter *Wimsey, Edmund *Crispin's Gervase *Fen, Mitchell's Beatrice Lestrange *Bradley, and P. D. *James's Adam *Dalgliesh. That this facility with quotation from the literary works of the great and good is perceived to be a virtuous characteristic is underlined by the observation that it is seldom shared by the murderer within the story.

The caliber of the quotation is usually both distinguished and pertinent. The character called Fairlight in Robert Robinson's Landscape with Dead Dons (1956) who "does not care much for Chaucer, or, indeed, for anyone writing prior to the nativity of Mr. T. S. Eliot" is quite unusual in this respect. Most of the literary allusions in the genre are relatively well known, and it may be assumed that the pleasure the reader undoubtedly derives from encountering them in an unexpected context is due partly to the quotation being reasonably familiar and partly to an appreciation of its appositeness to the situation in which it is delivered.

As with titles and chapter headings, it is unusual for a literary allusion to be highly germane to the *plot. An exception to this occurs in Brat Farrar (1949; Come and Kill Me), by Josephine *Tey, in which the eponymous hero mentions the biblical "pit in Dothan." The method of the murder in the book is exactly as described in Genesis.

The employment of a notable amount of literary allusion has become the hallmark of a certain category of somewhat mannered detective novels, most of which are set in the *academic milieu. In these, a penchant for literary allusion is not only a vehicle for the display of erudition on the part of the characters (and therefore the author), but also a considerable part of the entertainment, as in Crispin's The Moving Toyshop (1946). When two of the characters are temporarily imprisoned, they divert themselves (and the reader) by arguing over unreadable books. The tendency, though, of Patricia *Wentworth's Miss Maud *Silver to quote from Alfred, Lord Tennyson, tells the reader something about the detective herself.

Much more subtle is such usage in the writings of Nicholas *Blake, as in A Question of Proof (1935), and in Death of an Old Goat, by Robert *Barnard (1974), where the action concerns the study of English literature in an Australian university.

There are, too, stories that are set around specific works of literature. Among these are Christie's The Mirror Crack'd from Side to Side (1962; The Mirror Crack'd), which makes great play with Tennyson's Lady of Shalott; Belladonna, by Donald Thomas (1984; Mad Hatter Summer), a Lewis Carroll mystery; and Murder Being Once Done, by Ruth *Rendell (1972), which draws on Sir Thomas More's Utopia.

Extensions of the use of literary allusions may be found in Edward Candy's Words for Murder Perhaps (1971), where the victims are all namesakes of people celebrated in famous English elegies; and in Graves in Academe (1985), by Susan Kenney, in which the manner of all the killings mirror deaths made famous in English literature, from *Beowulf* to Chaucer to Milton.

"The Gate of Baghdad," in *Parker Pyne Investigates*, by Christie (1934), is a good example of the embodiment of the literary allusion in detective fiction. In this work the title, the mise-en-scene, and some of the plot are all set around selected verses that are taken from the works of James Elroy Flecker.

[*See also* Academic Sleuth; Poets as Crime Writers.]   —Catherine Aird

AMATEUR DETECTIVE. The first detective of the mystery genre was an amateur. In Edgar Allan *Poe's story "The Murders in the Rue Morgue" (1841; in *Graham's Lady's and Gentleman's Magazine*, Apr. 1841), the Chevalier C. Auguste *Dupin is the quintessential amateur detective: eccentric in his personal habits and brilliant in his deductions, smarter than the police and his adoring chronicler, moved to investigate by the intellectual challenge of the crime. This description remains in broad terms the definition of every amateur *sleuth that follows Dupin.

Early writers in the genre worked hard to make their series characters distinctive, and we may distribute amateur sleuths into several broad categories. After decades that saw the creation of overly cerebral and emotionally flat sleuths, E. C. *Bentley introduced Philip Trent in *Trent's Last Case* (1913; *The Woman in Black*), the first *silly-ass sleuth; his most famous successor is perhaps the early Albert *Campion, in *The Crime at Black Dudley* (1929; *The Black Dudley Murder*), by Margery *Allingham. Among the eccentrics are Agatha *Christie's Hercule *Poirot, the retired Belgian policeman with his egg-shaped head, waxed moustaches, and "little gray cells" introduced in *The Mysterious Affair at Styles* (1920). Philo *Vance, who first appears in *The Benson Murder Case* (1926) by S. S. *Van Dine, is a younger man who lectures insufferably on art and life while tailing after the police. Far more likable but just as eccentric is Gervase *Fen, Edmund *Crispin's *Oxford don introduced in *The Case of the Gilded Fly* (1944; *Obsequies at Oxford*, 1945), who prefers *murder to Milton and lives in a fey world.

"Little old ladies" capable of deceiving *suspects by their benign aspects were popular from the early years of the genre. Christie's Miss Jane *Marple in *The Murder at the Vicarage* (1930) knits and twitters but always sees through people's behavior, and Gladys *Mitchell's Mrs. Adela Beatrice Lestrange *Bradley is an alienist with a sometimes caustic personality, as seen in *The Saltmarsh Murders* (1932). In more recent years, writers have modified the character of the elderly female sleuth and made her more realistic. Dorothy Gilman's Mrs. Emily Pollifax, well into her sixties, answers the call of the government to track down stolen plutonium in Europe in *A Palm for Mrs. Pollifax* (1973), and Stefanie Matteson's Charlotte Graham, a once-famous actress now in her early sixties, visits friends and unravels crime in *Murder at the Spa* (1990). The amateur detective may be a cleric, as is G. K. *Chesterton's Father *Brown; an aristocrat, like Dorothy L. *Sayers's Lord Peter *Wimsey; a physician, such as Josephine Bell's Dr.

David Wintringham; a teacher, as is Leo *Bruce's Carolus Deene; or any other occupation and age.

Beginning with Poe's Dupin, the amateur sleuth has usually been smarter than the police and makes much of the stupidity of the officers of the law: Christie's Poirot is a fine example. It is also a convention that over time the police may come to respect the mental acuity of the amateur, as is the case with Miss Marple, and may even seek his or her advice, as they do with Crispin's Gervase Fen. The relationship between the amateur and the police has vexed many writers who preferred to solve the problem by establishing a *friendship between amateur and police, as Anthony Oliver does between Lizzie Thomas and retired police detective Inspector John Webber in *The Pew Group* (1980). Additional strategies include locating a relative among the police, like the character Ellery *Queen's father, who is a police detective, in *The Greek Coffin Mystery*, by Ellery *Queen (1932), or leading the amateur into an engagement and later marriage with an attorney, as Amanda *Cross does with Kate *Fansler and Reed Amherst in *Poetic Justice* (1970) or with a private detective as is the case with Annie Laurance and Max Darling in Carolyn G. Hart's *Honeymoon with Murder* (1988). Other amateur detectives remain on a precarious footing with the authorities. Faith Sibley Fairchild evokes polite but firm skepticism from the French police in *The Body in the Vestibule* by Katherine Hall Page (1992); Simon Brett's Charles Paris, an actor limping through his career, is barely tolerated by the police, whereas Brett's Mrs. Melita Pargeter, an elderly widow, has a clear view of the police from the opposite side of the line, thanks to her late husband, in *A Nice Class of Corpse* (1986). Frank Parrish's Dan Mallett, a poacher who has little good to say about the local police, groundskeepers, and anyone else in the middle class, often works against the police to clear himself of suspicion, as in *Fire in the Barley* (1977). Joyce *Porter's Honourable Constance Ethel Morrison-Burke is absolutely despised by the authorities in *A Meddler and Her Murder* (1972).

The sleuth moves among the *suspects as an equal, engaging in light conversation at parties or on holiday trips, listening intently with no hint of *suspicion, exploring possibilities without indicating who is the favored suspect; this ability to blend with the community under examination is in fact a considerable advantage of the amateur detective. In addition to these visits and polite queryings, detectives use a number of techniques to arrive at the correct solution. Some, like Page's Fairchild, merely follow their curiosity until the murderer reveals himself or herself; others, like Van Dine's Vance, apply psychology and make much of their method; and still others, such as R. Austin *Freeman's Dr. John *Thorndyke, rely on rigorous logic and evidence. For the most part, however, amateur detectives arrive at their conclusions by intuition and circumstantial evidence, as does Joan Hess's Claire Malloy. A good number arrive at erroneous conclusions; for instance, Anthony *Berkeley's Roger Sheringham raises false reasoning to an art form in *The Poisoned Chocolates Case* (1929).

It would be a mistake to assume that every amateur detective is the alter ego of his or her creator; many are as different from their creators as the writers can manage. And yet in many passages the reader senses that the sleuth speaks for the writer. Christie's Marple offers judgments on Americans, punishment for criminals, and the *class system that have parallels in her autobiography and interviews; Chesterton's Father Brown expounds on faith and doubt, sin and redemption in passages that clearly reflect the developing theology of his creator. Gwen Moffat's Melinda Pink casts an acute eye on the deadly consequences of foolish behavior in a harsh environment, reflecting her own experience as a highly regarded rock climber.

[*See also* Academic Sleuth; Aristocratic Sleuth; Eccentrics; Great Detective, The; Reasoning, Types of.]

• R. F. Stewart, *And Always a Detective: Chapters on the History of Detective Fiction* (1980). T. J. Binyon, *"Murder Will Out": The Detective in Fiction* (1989).   —Susan Oleksiw

AMBLER, ERIC (1909–1998), British author of some of the most accomplished and innovative modern thrillers. In the mid-1930s Ambler set out to redeem the then lowest form of popular fiction, the *thriller, by making it a vehicle for serious treatment of the European political situation, increasingly polarized between fascism and communism. Here as elsewhere his career ran parallel to that of Graham *Greene. In six novels between 1936 and 1940, Ambler revolutionized the thriller, bridging the gap between "popular" and "serious," "entertainment" and "literature." The first, *The Dark Frontier* (1936), burlesqued the formulaic, chauvinistic thrillers of the time and provides the basis for an alternative form of the genre, politically well to the Left. In the second and fourth, *Uncommon Danger* (1937; *Background to Danger)* and *Cause for Alarm* (1938), respectively, he retained standard thriller elements but substituted credible *antiheroes and realistic *settings for stereotypical heroes and fantasy situations. Between these two related antifascist novels with their sympathetic Soviet agents, Ambler published an original blend of detective story and spy novel, *Epitaph for a Spy* (1938). But it was with his fifth, *The Mask of Dimitrios* (1939; *A Coffin for Dimitrios*), that he produced a sophisticated classic of the genre and a decisive landmark in its history. Covering the interwar years in fragmented flashbacks, this novel is highly ambitious in its attempt to encapsulate the traumatic experience of Europe in the criminal career of Dimitrios himself, who symbolizes the destructive forces subverting civilization itself. This menace is also central to the most psychologically analytical of Ambler's early novels, *Journey into Fear* (1940).

Just as Ambler was achieving well-earned success and recognition, World War II brought his novelwriting career to a temporary standstill. His army service as a filmmaker led to prolific screenwriting work after the *war, very fruitfully in Britain until 1958 and less satisfactorily in Hollywood for the next ten years. The first of his twelve postwar novels, *Judgment on Deltchev* (1951), uses a thriller format to deal with the topical issue of the Stalinist show trials and is a seminal work in the history of Cold War literature. Ambler's subsequent novels are remarkable for their diversity and for his determination to explore new possibilities for the genre. Both *The Night-Comers* (1956; *State of Siege*) and *Passage of Arms* (1959) tackle the upheavals of decolonization in Southeast Asia, with an unexpected element of comedy appearing in the latter, book. Ambler took this potential further in *The Light of Day* (1962; *Topkapi*) a brilliantly inventive fusion of comedy and thriller. In *A Kind of Anger* (1964) Ambler for the first time made an intimate relationship between a man and a woman pivotal to a story of international political intrigue and *violence. *The Levanter* (1972) deals with the Palestinian problem; *Send No More Roses* (1977; *The Siege of the Villa Lipp*), with international white collar crime; and *The Care of Time* (1981), with the threat of chemical weapons. Technically, the most virtuosic of his postwar novels is *The Intercom Conspiracy* (1970; *Quiet Conspiracy*), in which a Cold War intelligence scam is narrated through a dossier-like assembly of letters, documents, and interviews, but the best is arguably the Greenean *Doctor Frigo* (1974), about political machiavellianism and the sinister maneuverings for power in the Caribbean and Latin America.

[*See also* Spy Fiction.]

• Eric Ambler, *Here Lies: An Autobiography* (1985). Peter Lewis, *Eric Ambler* (1990).   —Peter Lewis

AMERICANS IN ENGLAND. Throughout the literary history of crime and mystery fiction, a number of American authors have chosen to set all or some of their works in England. In some cases the authors may be indulging their love of England or a specific English city such as *London. Others combine a love of an English *setting with a penchant for writing historical fiction set there. Still others may be drawn to a *milieu that calls to mind classic English detective fiction. In addition, there are a number of especially convincing American writers who use English scenes with authority, since they have resided there for a significant number of years.

American-born John Dickson *Carr, who made his home in England for most of his adult life, is the best-known author to place his work in English settings. There is no doubt that his *puzzle-centered work was well suited to such traditional English environments as the *country house milieu, where predictable routines were useful to the making and breaking of *alibis and where quirky architectural features, like the folly, were likely places to discover *locked room mysteries. Carr, who was politically conservative, also valued the well-defined *class order that he found in British society. While he set a good deal of his work in his own day, he also used a period English setting in *The Hungry Goblin: A Victorian Detective Novel* (1972).

The most well-known American author of stories set in the English past is Lillian de la Torre, who termed herself a "histo-detector." She chose for her sleuth a fictionalized version of the eighteenth-century lexicographer Dr. Samuel Johnson and narrated his crime-solving escapades in the voice of a fictionalized James Boswell. These stories are collected in four volumes, beginning with *Dr. Sam Johnson: Detector* (1946) and concluding with *The Exploits of Dr. Sam Johnson: Detector* (1985). Another American to set her work in a period English setting is Elizabeth Peters in *The Murders of Richard III* (1974).

England is also the home of American author Martha Grimes's characters Richard Jury and Melrose Plant, who detect in a series of books titled after the quirky names of English pubs. Like Jury and Plant, Elizabeth George's Inspector Thomas Lynley and Sergeant Barbara Havers work out puzzles along with their personal lives in traditional English scenes darkened by the intrusion of *violence. Grimes and George, who do not reside in England, are wise to center their strengths in a believable English *atmosphere, since some British critics are understandably quick to point out where Americans go astray in portraying English life.

In fact, although still criticized for factual errors, Marion Babson, an American from Salem, Massachusetts, decided to set some of her work in England only after residing there for decades. Other Americans who have lived in England long enough to set their mysteries there with confidence are Zenith Jones Brown and Paula Gosling. Newer to the English scene, but still very capable, are Kate Charles and Deborah Crombie. Charles has a series of novels set in another traditional English setting, the *cathedral close milieu.

A contemporary American writer who uses classic English settings but populates them with a contemporary multiethnic mix is Gaylord Dold. His *Rude Boys* (1992) brings together *Old Bailey lawyers with Jamaican Rastafarians.

[*See also* Period Mystery.]

• William O. Aydelotte, "The Detective Story as a Historical Source," in *Dimensions of Detective Fiction*, ed. Larry N. Landrum, Pat Browne, Ray B. Browne (1976). George Grella, "Murder and Manners: The Formal Detective Novel," in *Dimensions of Detective Fiction*. LeRoy Panek, *Watteau's Shepherds: The Detective Novel in Britain, 1914–1940* (1979). Dennis Porter, *The Pursuit of Crime* (1981). Ernest Mandel, *Delightful Murder: A Social History of the Crime Story* (1984).
—Maryann McLoughlin O'Donnell

ANIMALS. Animals have long played an important role in the mystery genre. Closely connected with the origins of the genre, animals can be killers, *clues, detectives, and sidekicks; they can and in fact do take any role normally held by human beings. In the earliest mystery story, "The Murders in the Rue Morgue" (*Graham's Lady's and Gentleman's Magazine*, Apr. 1841) by Edgar Allan *Poe, the murderer is an orangutang kept as a pet. In "The Adventure of the Speckled Band" (*Strand*, Feb. 1892) by Arthur Conan *Doyle, the murderer is a swamp adder. More subtle is the use of an animal to provide a *clue. Perhaps the best known example is the dog who did not bark at night in Doyle's "Silver Blaze" (*Strand*, Dec. 1892; 1894).

Some animals, such as the frequently appearing cats in mysteries, have an evidently inherent attraction for writers and readers of mysteries. The many works of Dick *Francis concerning steeple chasing have made horses strong competitors to felines and canines.

Aside from the consuming interest we take in certain animals, though, there is also to be considered the utility they have for story-telling. Animals may set the *plot in motion by aiding in the discovery of a crime while they explore the natural world according to their own nature. In addition to their role as agents of death, wild animals may give a murderer the opportunity to conceal a crime, as in Freeman Wills *Crofts's *Antidote to Venom* (1938). Animals also serve as *witnesses to crimes. Though rarely able to identify the criminal clearly, their presence may cause the guilty to react and reveal culpability. In those rare cases in which they identify the criminal, they still must work with humans to resolve the situation; in Frances Fyfield's *Shadows on the Mirror* (1989) a dog aids a *victim at a vital moment. Animals may also serve as assistants; Lillian Jackson Braun's two Siamese cats have become crucial to their owner's sleuthing success in the *Cat Who . . .* series. Rita Mae Brown takes the notion of an animal assistant further by sharing authorship of a series initiated with *Wish You Were Here* (1990) with her tiger cat, Sneaky Pie Brown, a collaborator in detection but also contributor of animal conversation to the narratives. A hard-boiled variation of feline detection appears in the series by Carole Nelson Douglas pairing a tomcat named Midnight Louie with Las Vegas publicist Temple Barr.

Animals define the character of humans as good or evil. The owner of two Alsatians uses them to abuse his neighbors and the local nature trails in *Die Like a Dog* by Gwen Moffat (1982). The murderer who kills an animal as a prelude to human destruction becomes a totally unsympathetic character, as in H. R. F. *Keating's *Inspector Ghote Plays a Joker* (1969). In *The Deer Leap* (1985), Martha Grimes explores the character of one who would kill animals and one who would protect them.

Animals have also become the focus for exploring the conflict between the needs of human beings and the environment, between consumption and conservation. In such instances the *theft or abduction of an animal functions as a plot development as significant as *kidnapping or burglary. In *Roll Over and Play Dead* (1991) Joan Hess explores the dark side of medical research that sanctions the abduction and maltreatment of family pets. Karin McQuillan raises the question of preservation of nature in her series featuring Jazz Jasper; Africa and its wildlife are vivid background in *Deadly Safari* (1990) and other novels. The danger of using animals in fiction is that of falling into sentimentality or cuteness. Both McQuillan and Moffat avoid this, focusing instead on the needs and manners of the animals. In *Grizzly Trail* (1984) Moffat depicts the very real dangers of hiking in parts of Montana, the habitat of the grizzly bear; in *The Stone Hawk* (1989) the harsh realities of life in a remote corner of Utah form the backdrop for the murder of a child.

The expanding role of animals in mysteries may reflect growing concern for animal welfare and animal rights as well as a deepening understanding of the very nature of animals. They may have first appeared in mysteries as criminals and clues, but they have become more than plot devices. As humans see them more clearly, animals are finding new roles.

[See also Great Outdoors; Horse Racing Milieu; Sidekicks and Sleuthing Teams.]

—Sharon A. Russell

ANTIHERO denotes an antithetical character, often lacking in nobility, virtue, bravery, and morality, qualities generally associated with the traditional hero. There are famous examples of the antihero throughout literary history; these include Don Quixote, Tristram Shandy, and Willy Loman. However, this *archetypal character is quite prevalent in *formula fiction, particularly in crime writing.

From its early days, detective fiction has drawn on the antihero archetype, embodied in characters as notable (and noble) as Sherlock *Holmes and Lord Peter *Wimsey. Both Holmes and Wimsey are, in a conventional sense, virtuous and moral figures, but they are also social misfits, psychologically damaged or lacking in some way. Holmes, a cocaine addict, is alienated from society, and relies upon his friend, Dr. John H. *Watson, for a normative grounding in the world; Wimsey struggles to come to grips with the psychological trauma he suffered during the war, and often depends upon his butler, Mervyn Bunter, to enable him to function.

As detective fiction evolves as a genre, the figure of the antihero evolves along with it. Such authors as Graham *Greene and Patricia *Highsmith have been credited with transforming the detective antihero, who, in their hands, becomes less idiosyncratic and more degenerate. In works like Stamboul Train (1932; Orient Express), It's a Battlefield (1934), and Brighton Rock (1938), Greene focuses on unconventional and disillusioned social misfits, and in A Gun for Sale (1936; This Gun for Hire), his protagonist, James Raven, becomes a scapegoat for his society's sins. Because Raven's crimes result from poverty, A Gun for Sale is as much a social critique as a *murder mystery. Highsmith depicts a *gentleman thief and social deviant, Tom Ripley, who is introduced in The Talented Mr. Ripley (1955) and appears in a number of Highsmith texts. He is involved in a number of shady activities. In Ripley's Game (1974), Ripley is responsible for arranging and conducting the murders of several mafiosi. He is not condemned for his behavior, since the narrative delineates the Mafia hoods as the "real" villains, thus justifying Ripley's elimination of them. Despite the unconventional traits of the protagonist, Highsmith's novels, like Greene's, conform to a certain moral code, even if it is a code that is largely self-defined by the antihero. While both Ripley and Raven play fast and loose with certain aspects of law and order, they also uphold and abide by others.

The American hard-boiled tradition provides for more radical developments in this archetypal character. In *hard-boiled fiction, the protagonist is often as unsavory as the criminals. Lacking the moral impetus of the earlier detective antiheroes, hard-boiled protagonists, even in early exemplars of the mode, are solitary figures who do not hesitate to take the law into their own hands. Sam *Spade, in Dashiell *Hammett's The Maltese Falcon (1930), serves as a good example of the deviant antihero, for while he has some moral scruples (he cannot be bribed by the villains, for instance), he also shows little attachment to his murdered partner, Miles Archer, with whose wife he is having an affair. Nor does he hesitate to hand over his former bed partner, Brigid O'Shaughnessy, to the police. In Mickey *Spillane's I, the Jury (1947), Mike *Hammer's misogyny motivates his behavior and engenders much of the novel's gratuitous *violence.

Hard-boiled authors dramatize the blight pervading the social order, as exemplified by their antiheroes and the mean streets of the major urban centers through which they walk. Some of these novels encourage readers to identify with their distasteful protagonists and then prompt readers to analyze the affinities they feel with the characters. The texts thereby move to implicate readers in their social critique and suggest that we are all criminals in one way or another. Jim Thompson's The Killer Inside Me (1952), serves as a culmination of this trajectory of detective fiction, for it is narrated by a psychopathic killer. Readers are embroiled in the protagonist's murderous action because they experience it through him, and they are cast as accomplices to his crimes because the author manipulates them to identify with him and the enjoyment he finds in beating and killing women.

In the hands of contemporary authors who are consciously revising it, the representation of women in hard-boiled fiction gives rise to a new development in the antihero archetype. Writers like Sara *Paretsky, Sue *Grafton, and Liza Cody cast their female sleuths as hard-boiled detectives. These characters are generally moral and upstanding, but they are placed in an ambivalent position in the novels as a result of their gender. The female *private eyes disrupt and subvert traditional portrayals of women as *femmes fatales or as "good" female detectives like Miss Jane *Marple and Harriet *Vane. Rejecting the loner stance of the conventional hard-boiled private eye, the female protagonists function in communities on which they draw for support. Such variants on the hard-boiled female detective as Meg O'Brien's Jessica "Jesse" James—an alcoholic investigative reporter who is romantically involved with a Mafia leader— not only subvert the established rules of the genre underpinning feminine representations, but also provide further twists to the antihero archetype.

Through the use of the antihero, who is unscrupulous, unsavory, and often amoral, the detective genre queries conventional portrayals of *victims and victimizers and of crime and punishment. By implicating the reader in the actions of the protagonist through narrative point of view, the texts suggest that the divisions between law and justice, and truth and appearance, are not as simple as they may at first appear, and cause the reader to speculate on the nature of crime and criminality. Thus, these novels not only offer "deviant" perspectives, they also provide a venue through which readers can explore crucial social constructs and interrogate simplistic moral judgments.

[See also Characterization; Deviance; Formula: Character; Mean Streets Milieu; Sex and Sexuality.]

• Howard Haycraft, Murder for Pleasure: The Life and Times of the Detective Story (1968). John Cawelti, "The Study of Literary Formulas," in Detective Fiction: A Collection of Critical Essays, ed. Robin W. Winks (1980). R. F. Stewart, . . . And Always a Detective: Chapters on the History of Detective Fiction (1980). Kathleen Gregory Klein, The Woman Detective: Gender & Genre (1988). Peter J. Rabinowitz, " 'Reader, I Blew Him Away': Convention and Transgression in Sue Grafton," in Famous Last Words: Changes in Gender and Narrative Closure, ed. Alison Booth (1993).   —Priscilla L. Walton

ANTI-SEMITISM. Popular attitudes ranging from noble sentiments to bigoted views have always been especially prevalent in genre fiction. In crime and mystery fiction, a literature always designed to appeal to the masses, such attitudes may betray an author's prejudice, or they may be used by an enlightened writer to manipulate or inspire the reader. Anti-Semitism, like *racism and negative attitudes toward ethnic groups, has appeared in crime writing in the forms of casual, hostile slurs regarding Jewish characters and in the presentation of stereotyped characters. Sometimes those stereotypes are used by a writer who believes in them; other writers may manipulate the perceived prejudices of the reader by using stereotypes to cast *suspicion on characters who subsequently prove to be admirable members of society. Especially since the 1980s, anti-Semitism has been shown in detective fiction as an *evil to be faced head-on by *sleuths and others who stand firmly against it.

Works written during the Golden Age of the *detective novel often centered on the upper classes and the social elite, a category of *class that was often off-limits to Jews in the period between the two World Wars. Jewish characters were rare in such fiction. In his literary history of the genre, Bloody Murder: From the Detective Story to the Crime Novel: A History (1972; Mortal Consequences) Julian *Symons stated that it would have been "unthinkable" for writers at that time to have portrayed a Jewish detective "or a working class one aggressively conscious of his origins," since such figures would have seemed "incongruous" to them. Symons noted, however, that Jewish characters could be treated with "casual anti-Semistism" by the likes of Dorothy L. *Sayers, who gives her hero Lord Peter *Wimsey Jewish friends, only to have those friends fit stereotypes like dealing in jewelery and moneylending. In Whose Body? (1923) Sayers expects readers to believe that a naked man found dead in a bathtub can be identified as Jewish solely by his appearance.

Among writers of classic detective fiction during that period, Sayers was unusual in depicting Jews at all. Most American authors avoided them altogether. Some negative stereotypes do emerge, but Jewishness itself is used more to make a character seem "foreign" and suspicious than as a motivating factor for murder. An interesting example of an American evasion of *ethnicity can be seen in the retooling of Carolyn *Keene's Nancy *Drew series beginning in 1959. In the revised edition of The Case of the Broken Locket, the possibly Jewish name of a criminal couple, Sellerstein, is altered to one that may be presumed to be more gentile. The couple's name can be changed with ease because neither their religion nor their culture is germane to the *plot.

After the Golden Age period, more Jewish authors turned to writing detective fiction; but, as James Yaffe notes in his essay "Is This Any Job for a Nice Jewish Boy?" (A Synod of Sleuths: Essays on Judeo-Christian Detective Fiction, edited by Jon L. Breen and Martin H. Greenberg, 1990), those writers rarely ventured further than introducing detectives with Jewish names who occasionally used Yiddish expressions. Many were portrayed without allusion to their Jewish *religion or heritage at all. The pseudonymous team who called themselves Ellery *Queen were two Jewish cousins from Brooklyn, New York. They did not endow their series sleuth (also called Ellery *Queen) with any Jewish attributes.

A major change occurred when Harry Kemelman introduced Rabbi David *Small in Friday the Rabbi Slept Late (1964). Small applies Talmudic wisdom to solve crimes that usually occur within the community of the synagogue rather than as any result of outside threats or bigotry. Ten years later Andrew Bergman introduced his hard-boiled Jewish sleuth, Jacob "Jack" LeVine. This character deflates prejudice with wisecracks and courage as is the case in In the Big Kiss-Off of 1944 (1974). Here Bergman depicts a woman holding a gun on LeVine and remarking, "I can always tell a Jewboy. Always." LeVine replies, "The Germans could use you." Anti-Semitism is a significant theme in Hollywood and LeVine (1975) in which LeVine travels to Hollywood to help out a boyhood friend, a screenwriter who has been politically blacklisted. However, when Bergman has Humphrey Bogart get involved in the case, the possibility of serious discussion of anti-Semitism becomes lodged in the absurd.

During the 1980s and 1990s, Faye Kellerman regularly addressed the problem of anti-Semitism. Her series detective, Peter Decker, meets an orthodox Jew, Rina Lazarus, who plays a particularly important role in The Ritual Bath (1986) when she becomes a *victim of a hate crime. During this same period, best-selling *thrillers like Allan Folsom's The Day After Tomorrow (1994) posit a neo-Nazi world. Robert Harris's Fatherland (1992) depicts the evils of a society where Adolph Hitler never died.

[See also Ethnic Sleuth; Voice; Wisecracking Voice.]

—Susan Docherty

Appleby, Sir John. Created by Michael *Innes, John Appleby first appears as a young, well-educated and well-mannered inspector working out of Scotland Yard in Death at the President's Lodging (1936; Seven Suspects). He meets and woos Judith Raven in Appleby's End (1945), and they later have a son who first appears in *An Awkward Lie* (1971). Appleby rises in rank from inspector to end his official career as Sir John Appleby, commissioner of the Metropolitan Police. After retirement he continues to investigate, appearing in 38 books in all. Appleby has few distinctive physical traits: He is "remarkably young" and "quite plainly genteel" and has "lots of jaw, and that long upper lip." He recites poetry and discovers the murderer through luck, intuition, and rudimentary detection. Though a policeman throughout, Appleby defines the donnish mystery and the farce, presiding over a droll world in which villages are named Drool, Sneak, and Snarl. He lives in retirement in Long Dream Manor, in the Village of Long Dream.

[*See also* Allusion, Literary; Farceurs; Police Detective.]
—Michael G. Heenan

ARCHAEOLOGICAL MILIEU. Used so often that it can almost be said to constitute a subtype in mystery writing, the archaeological *milieu encompasses any site where professional or amateur workers are or have been excavating the artifacts, relics, or structures of an earlier culture or civilization. The milieu offers several benefits: an exotic or unusual *setting; an isolated or closed environment; a variety of characters, from professional archaeologists to day laborers; and different cultures through which to comment on contemporary life or historical events.

Among the earliest novels with archaeological settings are *John Macnab* (1925) by John *Buchan and *Murder in Mesopotamia* (1936) by Agatha *Christie, whose portrayals of life at an excavation camp draw on her own experiences with her archaeologist husband and reflect the high degree of accuracy usually found in stories with this setting. Elizabeth Peters, an Egyptologist, complements her exploration of the sites of ancient Egypt with the history and growth of archaeology as a science in her *period mystery series featuring a husband-and-wife team of Egyptologists, Amelia Peabody and Radcliff Emerson.

Many writers focus on the exotic details of the milieu, as Christie in *Death on the Nile* (1937), or rely on the threat to a single ancient object to supply the *suspense in the story, as Katherine Farrer in *The Cretan Counterfeit* (1954) and G. K. *Chesterton in "The Curse of the Golden Cross" in *The Incredulity of Father Brown* (1926). Still others make use of the most obvious features of the site, the ready-made tomb; John Trench in *Dishonoured Bones* (1953) and Stanley Casson in *Murder by Burial* (1938) are only two writers who place a *corpse where only ancient bones should lie. Still others find in this milieu opportunities to comment on the modern world. In Tony *Hillerman's *A Thief of Time* (1988), Sergeant Jim Chee discovers the bodies of two men who paid with their lives for despoiling an ancient burial ground; Hillerman goes on to explore the conflict between modern materialism and ancient beliefs. In Dermot Morrah's *The Mummy Case* (1933), three archaeologists jealously fight over the ownership of the "oldest royal mummy in the world," any thoughts of regard for an ancient culture trampled beneath their ambitions. A threat to a single object or group of ob-

jects can even represent the larger threat of one culture to another, an idea explored in Michael Pearce's *The Mamur Zapt and the Spoils of Egypt* (1995).

The most obvious choice for *amateur detective in this setting is the archaeologist, whose skills put him or her in the position to serve as surrogate sleuth. The detective's and archaeologist's professional techniques are similar; both involve the meticulous observation, collection, and analysis of material evidence. As R. G. Collingwood pointed out in *The Idea of History* (1946), the hero of a detective novel thinks very much like a historian when he or she builds a picture of how a crime was committed from the diverse clues uncovered in an investigation. Many of the most interesting archaeologist-detectives face circumstances based on their creators' experiences. For example, Sir Richard Cherrington, archaeologist and vice president of his Cambridge college, appears in *The Cambridge Murders* (published under the pseudonym Dilwyn Rees, 1945) and *Welcome Death* (1954) by distinguished archaeologist the Glyn Daniel. His former pupil Jessica *Mann follows the detective careers of archaeologists Professor Thea Crawford, introduced in *The Only Security* (1973; *Troublecross*), and Dr. Tamara Hoyland, introduced in *Funeral Sites* (1981). Elizabeth Peters's characters also belong here.

Archaeological settings may also appear as background, such as the destination of holiday trips or cruises; in Nicholas *Blake's *The Widow's Cruise* (1959) the sites of ancient Greece are the background for a modern-day drama of family passions.

[*See also* Settings, Geographical; Surrogate Detective; Visitors Abroad.]
—Jessica Mann

Archer, Lew. The featured character in most of Ross *Macdonald's detective fiction, Archer when first introduced is a rather stiff exemplar of the hard-boiled *sleuth. However, he becomes distinctive over the course of more than a dozen novels and a smattering of short stories. While Macdonald's detective fiction originated in the wake of Dashiell *Hammett and the *Black Mask* school, Archer can be seen as evolving into the prototypical figure of the Vietnam and Watergate years. He is "not the usual peeper," as one character observes in *The Far Side of the Dollar* (1965) and he becomes less so in the course of the series. He retains traits of the hard-boiled detective, such as durability in a violent world, when, in *Find a Victim* (1954), someone notices he has been injured and he replies, "I don't matter at the moment. I'll survive." But his principal *milieu, Santa Teresa (a thinly disguised Santa Barbara) is an elaboration of Raymond *Chandler's suburbia—one in which commercial competitiveness subsumes the most intimate social relations. Archer's occasional observations make clear his relation to this world. Comfortable surfaces cover histories of self-deception and the plastic morality of the marketplace. The older generations have hidden their failures and buried their atrocities, but not well enough or deeply enough to evade Archer. Quarreling adults and disoriented children are the telltale symptoms of the social chaos of which Archer becomes more a quiet moral center and less the focus of action. Macdonald himself identifies *The Galton Case* (1959) as the pivotal novel in which Archer's investigation takes a more psychological turn. Although Archer does not assume the role of the psychoanalyst, the *plots as well as the *settings and discourses demand a detective figure who becomes less prone to physical action and more to talk. Interrogations become less matters of intimidation and more the opportunity for participants to unburden their knowledge. Archer is mediator in this process, observing in *Sleeping Beauty* (1973) that "every witness has his own way of creeping up on the truth." This innovation requires a detective who displays more human qualities than the traditional hard-boiled detective while not appearing soft. Ultimately, as in *The Ivory Grin* (1952; *Marked for Murder*), Archer is the vehicle for moral distinctions that emerge in the language of the times: "It's not just the people you've killed. It's the human idea you've been butchering and boiling down and trying to burn away. You can't stand the human idea."

[*See also* Hard-Boiled Sleuth; Symbolism.]

—Larry Landrum

ARCHETYPAL CHARACTERS. "Archetype" has historically referred in common usage to an original pattern such as one used by an artisan as a model for reproduction. Adopted by the psychoanalyst Carl Jung as a key term in his theory of the psyche, where archetype denotes an inherited idea in the unconscious, the term gains the denotation of deeply seated images with universal appeal. The utility of archetypal elements for crime and mystery fiction is well illustrated by contrasting archetypal renditions of character to portrayals that are simply required by the story.

Hawk, companion and confidante of *Spenser in Robert B. *Parker's series of latter-day hard-boiled detective stories, apparently earns a substantial income as hired gun. That detail of character appears through veiled allusion in the texts. The traits emphasized by Parker about Hawk are his fidelity to a code of honor he shares with Spenser, efficiency in all the adventures he undertakes with Spenser, controlled *humor, an attractive and sexually appealing appearance and habits of dress, and his capability for warmth toward Susan Silverman, Spenser's beloved. Tony *Hillerman also introduces hit men into his narratives, Colton Wolf in *People of Darkness* (1980) and Eric Vaggans in *The Ghostway* (1984). There can be no doubt about the primary occupation and obsessions of Wolf and Vaggans, because Hillerman devises narrations that allow readers access to their subjective consciousness where their motivations and their perverted self-images are lucidly revealed.

Another contrast of characters suggests the scope of possible differences in *characterization. In the typical opening of short stories about Sherlock *Holmes, clients make their way to 221B Baker Street to recount a problem and to seek Holmes's assistance in its solution. The problems can be woeful or scandalous, the clients guarded or distraught. Once the problem is set, Arthur Conan *Doyle be-

comes free to take Holmes and his faithful companion Dr. John H. *Watson through an investigation that results in a full explanation to the client who reappears for the presentation. In *The Maltese Falcon* (1930) by Dashiell *Hammett, Sam *Spade, half of the detective partnership of Spade and Miles Archer, also receives an evidently upset woman, one Brigid O'Shaughnessy, who enlists Spade in her cause with her tale of woe. As the narrative proceeds, though, O'Shaughnessy is not sent to the wings. Readers discover that she is fully implicated in the greedy *plot to secure the historic black bird, ready to use wiles and a developed talent for emotional rhetoric to gain her ends. Indeed, even as Spade reasons that she used her seductive ways to lure Archer to his death, he falls for her and only shakes free by a remarkable exercise of will and the timely arrival of the police.

The well-developed character of Hawk and the barely sketched needy clients of Holmes have narrative utility. Without Hawk, the character of Spenser would lack a dimension. Without the clients in Baker Street, the Holmes plots would lack a neat beginning. These characters are limned in a realistic manner, that is, the authors present them with verisimilitude and create their behavior in terms of familiar probability. Moreover, these characters are like others who appear in detective and mystery fiction: Hawk echoes Dr. Watson himself and other sidekicks of the detective; the female clients come from the well-known type of "damsels in distress." In other words, these characters are derived by their creators from the stock of characters who have proven over the years to be useful for moving along a narrative.

Hillerman's killers and Brigid O'Shaughnessy are something else. In addition to the role they play in generating narrative motion, they carry the added value to the writer of introducing into the narratives resonances of deeply seated fears of *violence and sexuality conditioned into the preconscious minds of writers and readers by a lifetime of cultural instruction. They are archetypal characters. Bearing a surface resemblance to *stock characters in the sense that they can be portrayed in a realistic manner, and in the sense that like stock characters they may serve the function of expediting narration, archetypal characters evoke sensations beneath the realism of verisimilitude.

The categories of archetypal characters in crime and mystery fiction are complex. The character of *evil may come dressed in the guise of the *master criminal, such as Professor James *Moriarty or Sax *Rohmer's *Fu Manchu. In the instance of Moriarty the archetype calls upon a distrust of the person learned in arcane lore that also informs the portrayals of mad scientists, while Fu Manchu invests the archetypal figure with a prevalent *racism that allows for embodiment of the fear of conspiracy in the person of someone classed as "Other," other than WASP and, therefore, savage despite any veneer of "civilization," by which is meant white European civilization.

A deeply conditioned distrust of power yields the archetypal character of the political boss, like Laird Brunette in Raymond *Chandler's *Farewell, My Lovely* (1940). Fears about sexuality produce not only *femme fatale Brigid O'Shaughnessy, but also the gay characters in *The Maltese Falcon*—Joel Cairo, Gutman, and "the gunsel"—who introduce to the black bird conspiracy resonances of heterosexual uneasiness about sexual identity.

Archetypal characters abound in hard-boiled writing because the hard-boiled perspective carries the conviction that the establishment is corrupted in capitalist society. Assertion of that view gains reinforcement through the character of the doctor who deals in dope, the pillar of society who manages fraud, and the wealthy individual whose rapacity is manifest in arrogance and exploitation. In their role as stock characters, these types from hard-boiled literature move the plot along, while in their role as archetypal characters they become allegorical representations of a fallen world.

The archetypal characters resident in Golden Age detection fiction are considerably more benign. They include the *gentleman sleuth and the *Great Detective who call up from the subconscious images of protectors and saviors. In fact, the claim is possible that the closed world of Golden Age detective fiction where order is the norm and reason the prevalent attribute of mind constitutes a projection of a dream world, the location of salvific images of control wrested from the Freudian id.

Archetypal characters are collective products of culture and society. As such they cannot be created by a single writer. What a writer can do is take the archetypes she or he can feel certain float freely in their readers' minds, as they do in their own, clothe them in contemporary garb, and give them an individualized visage. And that is precisely how writers of crime and mystery fiction employ their skills at innovative characterization to award readers either the frisson or delight consequent to meeting an archetype.

• Maud Bodkin, *Archetypal Patterns in Poetry: Psychological Studies of Imagination* (1934). Northrop Frye, *Anatomy of Criticism* (1957). —John M. Reilly

ARISTOCRATIC CHARACTERS. *In crime and mystery fiction, aristocratic characters are most likely to be found in *detective novels and stories that follow the *Golden Age traditions, as well as in the *adventure story. This entry is divided into two parts, the first treating the upper class detective or aristocratic sleuth, and the second surveying aristocratic characters who succeed as secondary but memorable characters.*

Aristocratic Sleuth
Secondary Aristocratic Characters

For further information, please refer to Adventurer and Adventuress; Class.

ARISTOCRATIC SLEUTH

The aristocratic sleuth has been a mainstay of detective fiction since its inception, when Edgar Allan *Poe introduced his series character, the Chevalier C. Auguste *Dupin. Despite his poverty, Dupin comes "of an excellent family—indeed an illustrious family," but because Poe is more interested in his reasoning powers than his pedigree, we learn nothing more about Dupin's antecedents. In this Dupin contrasts with later aristocratic sleuths, whose personal lives and histories constitute part of their strong appeal.

Although drawn from a single *class, the aristocratic sleuth exhibits great variety. Baroness *Orczy introduced Lady Molly Robertson-Kirk in a series of short stories collected in 1910; this character brings "feminine tact" and "intuition" to *Scotland Yard, where, guarding a personal secret she heads the Female Department. Although she is a daughter of the earl of Flintshire, her title is no great factor in her success as a detective, which derives primarily from her being "ultra-feminine."

Beginning in the Golden Age, the aristocratic sleuth was typically an old and venerable family's younger son who had to find something to occupy his time, talents, and energy. As a detective, he had obvious advantages: he understood the code of the upper classes and had an entrée into high society. Such sleuths may have regarded setting off after a murderer, blackmailer, or terrorist as serious business, but personal danger could also be something of a lark. Although some writers quickly outgrew the silliness of this approach and endowed their characters with a measure of maturity and wisdom that substantiated their abilities to solve crimes, behind the success of every aristocratic detective was some measure of acknowledgment of the sheer force of class.

Perhaps the most famous aristocratic sleuths are three characters introduced during the Golden Age. Dorothy L. *Sayers endowed her character Lord Peter *Wimsey with a pedigree going back to William the Conqueror; this was examined at length by C. W. Scott-Giles in *The Wimsey Family: A Fragmentary History Compiled from Correspondence with Dorothy L. Sayers* (1977). As the younger son of a duke, Wimsey has wealth and position, which contribute immeasurably to his success in criminal investigations, especially among the upper classes. Margery *Allingham's creation Lord Rudolph K—— is also a venturesome younger son freed from responsibility by a stodgy elder brother. He goes much further than Wimsey by breaking with his family, disowning his identity, and adopting various noms de guerre, one of which, Albert *Campion, becomes his established name. The woman he eventually marries, the Lady Amanda Fitton, is a sister of the earl of Pontisbright, whose title is in abeyance until Campion ensures its restoration. Ngaio *Marsh's Roderick *Alleyn, a professional policeman, is the younger son of a baronet in the diplomatic corps. A natural aristocrat with a high degree of finish, Alleyn is in his element in *Death in a White Tie* (1938), in which he investigates blackmail and the death of a friend after a ball. The continuing contrast with his esteemed plebeian assistant, Detective Inspector Fox, enhances Alleyn's image, showing him to be egalitarian and likable.

Many writers adopted this form of sleuth. The Honorable Richard Rollison figures in a long series of lighthearted thrillers by John *Creasey and is better known as the Toff. He is "tall, immaculate, a perfect specimen" of the wealthy and leisured class, with a flat in Gresham Terrace and a manservant called Jolly. As both man-about-town and man of action, he is equally at home in the West End and the East End of London. More recently, Martha Grimes has paired her police detective Inspector Richard Jury with an aristocratic friend, Melrose Plant, who has declined his title (Lord Ardry, earl of Caverness); Elizabeth George joined her detective, Viscount Lynley, eighth earl of Asherton—known professionally as Inspector Thomas Lynley—with a working-class sergeant, Barbara Havers.

The aristocratic sleuth has not been as readily embraced in the United States; he or she may be distrusted by the authorities, face financial difficulties, or move more comfortably outside the upper class. S. S. *Van Dine's creation, Philo *Vance, is the complete "social aristocrat," both by "birth and instinct." Rich enough to indulge his passions, which briefly include the investigation of bizarre murders, he talks like a caricature of a clubman, swallowing syllables and (like Lord Peter *Wimsey) clippin' the ends of present participles. He displays his erudition plainly. Anthony Abbott follows the investigations of Police Commissioner Thatcher Colt, who though born to wealth and family position is unjustly derided by the popular press as a "flaneur" and a "dilettante in crime." More recently, Charlotte MacLeod created Sarah Helling (Bittersohn), who is of a financially declining family of Boston Brahmins; she escapes her slide into genteel poverty and her family by taking in paying guests, eventually marrying, and investigating crimes. Clarissa Watson's detective Persis Willum is the niece of a railroad heiress. Though the least affluent member of the Gull Harbor community, she nonetheless moves freely among the "old money, old property and upper class." A bridge between the British and American aristocratic worlds is Joyce Christmas's Lady Margaret Priam, who lives in New York and works in an antiques shop. The aristocrat who is never troubled by financial worries and changing society is a rarity in American crime fiction.

Just as the richest aristocratic sleuths are British, so too is the most biting satire of the form. Joyce *Porter's creation, the Honorable Constance Morrison-Burke, is the daughter of a viscount, wears only army surplus clothing, and is belligerent, dense, and offensive. She enters criminal investigation as an act of noblesse oblige (*Rather a Common Sort of Crime*, 1970), and detects by grilling everyone until even she can discern the truth. The police want nothing to do with her; nor does anyone else, save her near poverty-stricken companion, Miss Jones. In her stories of the Hon-Con, Porter plays on the absurdity of an idle rich playboy or matron being taken into the confidence of the police and allowed to examine evidence, interrogate *suspects, and generally interfere with serious government work.

[*See also* Bluestocking Sleuth; Club Milieu; Country House Milieu; Gentleman Sleuth.]

—Susan Oleksiw *and* Rosemary Herbert

SECONDARY ARISTOCRATIC CHARACTERS

The aristocrat as a secondary character in detective fiction has developed from formidable antagonist or authoritative presence to one brought down by democracy to the detective's and the reader's level. In *Bleak House* (1853), Sir Leicester Dedlock treats Inspector Bucket with aristocratic hauteur; in *The Moonstone* (1868), Julia, Lady Verinder, dismisses Sergeant *Cuff from the investigation when his suspicions settle upon her daughter, Rachel Verinder, as the thief; in *Monsieur Lecoq* (1880; *Monsieur Lecoq: The Detective's Dilemma*), and its sequel, the ducal criminal is beyond Lecoq's reach; and in Anna Katharine *Green's *The Leavenworth Case* (1878), Inspector Ebenezer Gryce needs an upper-class coadjutor to gain entrée into aristocratic circles. By the end of the century, however, Sherlock *Holmes is classless and can rebuke Lord Robert St. Simon, the duke of Holdernesse, and even the king of Bohemia, with equal freedom. In the twentieth century, there are few doors closed to the detective, who may even be an aristocrat himself.

Where respect for the aristocracy never seems to die is in the genre in which fiction adventure crosses with crime—notably, in the pages of William Le Queux, E. Phillips *Oppenheim, John *Buchan, Dornford *Yates, and "Sapper" (H. C. *McNeile). In the first two, the locale is cosmopolitan, and princes and counts abound. The other three are more often set in the *club milieu, where the aristocracy is homegrown. All five writers celebrate the leisured life of the upper *class before the Great War and just after; the enemy tends to be comprised of proletarian foreigners and democratic intellectuals. One novel of this period that inverts the stereotype is Roy Horniman's *Israel Rank* (1907), on which the film *Kind Hearts and Coronets* is based: Here a Jewish outsider systematically murders those who stand between him and a noble title; his victims are all as dull and pedestrian as a Yates bourgeois, and only the murderer has the wit and acumen usually reserved for the aristocracy.

In the world between the wars, Agatha *Christie, Dorothy L. *Sayers, and their school maintained the upper classes better than they did in reality themselves, and in the lilywhite, Podsnappian world of Golden Age detective fiction, the aristocrat continued—indeed continues—to flourish: in Michael *Innes through to Martha Grimes. It is worth noting that those actual members of the nobility who have written crime or detective fiction do not always put their characters in their own circles: Baroness *Orczy and John Bingham (Lord Clanmorris) look very much at the seamy side of society. The transatlantic upper crust, however—such as Elliott Roosevelt and Margaret Truman—are *bluestocking sleuths who do not stray far from their powerful circles.

Indeed, on the western side of the Atlantic can be found no titled aristocracy, but rather a plutocratic, frequently regional society, epitomized in the "East Side nabobs" of S. S. *Van Dine's *The Greene Murder Case* (1928). The American attitude toward the aristocracy is, from the beginning, skeptical. Before the 1920s, such writers as Anna Katharine *Green, Mary Roberts *Rinehart, and Carolyn Wells treat the upper classes, to which they themselves generally belonged, with Christian forbearance rather than Christian forelock-pulling. The hard-boiled writers begin the denigration, comic at first: General Sternwood in Raymond *Chandler's The Big Sleep (1939) is dehumanized; Philip *Marlowe is "calling on a million dollars." In Ross *Macdonald's The Chill (1964), Letitia Bradshaw is a monstrous grande dame.

At the apex of any aristocratic pyramid are the royals, who are rarely the subjects of detective fiction. However, they do appear: As well as the hereditary king of Bohemia, Sherlock *Holmes has to deal with the bank robber John Clay, whose grandfather was a royal duke, a fact Holmes treats with amusement. Much later, Antonia Fraser described the *kidnapping of a minor British princess in Your Royal Hostage (1987); Peter Dickinson had already brought abduction closer to the throne in King and Joker (1976). Peter Lovesey brought back Holmes's illustrious client, the Prince of Wales, as detective in the series beginning with Bertie and the Tinman (1987). With the future Edward the Seventh as a *private eye, aristocracy can yield nothing further to democracy.

[See also Aristocratic Characters, article on Aristocratic Sleuth; Club Milieu; Gentleman Sleuth.]

• Richard Usborne, Clubland Heroes: A Nostalgic Study of Some Recurrent Characters in the Romantic Fiction of Dornford Yates, John Buchan, and Sapper (1953). Colin Watson, Snobbery With Violence: Crime Stories and Their Audience (1971).
—Barrie Hayne

ARMCHAIR DETECTIVE is a phrase that describes a type of fictional detective who solves crimes solely on the basis of secondhand information, rather than through personal observation of evidence. The first example of armchair detecting can be found in the work of Edgar Allan *Poe. In "The Mystery of Marie Rogèt" (Snowden's Lady's Companion, Nov. 1842), the Chevalier C. Auguste *Dupin, working wholly from newspaper accounts, arrives at the correct explanation for a young woman's mysterious disappearance. Arthur Conan *Doyle employs the character type in the person of Mycroft *Holmes, Sherlock *Holmes's older brother, who is even more brilliant at "observation and deduction" but is too addicted to the comforts of his club to be anything but an occasional consultant in investigations. In "The Greek Interpreter" (Strand, Sept. 1893), Sherlock Holmes says of his brother that, "if the art of the detective began and ended in reasoning from an armchair," Mycroft would be the greatest detective "that ever lived."

The most fully developed armchair detective is the creation of Baroness Emmuska *Orczy, in the series of stories about the *Old Man in the Corner, published between 1901 and 1925. The Old Man sits in the corner of a tea shop, tying intricate knots into a piece of string (as an "adjunct to thought") and recounts for the benefit of a young woman journalist his successes in solving famous crimes that have foiled the police. Although occasionally journeying to a crime scene or courtroom to verify a deduction, he arrives at his solution entirely on the basis of newspaper accounts of the crime. His interest lies in the intellectual challenge of the mystery and the chance

to show up official detectives, with whom he scorns to share his knowledge, even when it means a criminal gets away with a crime.

Later writers using an armchair sleuth include Agatha *Christie, who confines the inquisitive Miss Jane *Marple to dinner-table detecting in The Thirteen Problems (1932; The Tuesday Club Murders; Miss Marple and the Thirteen Problems), a series of stories in which a circle of village friends (lawyer, clergyman, former police inspector) take turns recounting some mysterious crime of which they have personal knowledge; invariably, Marple arrives at the solution before the teller reveals it. Isaac Asimov made use of a similar device in several volumes of short stories, beginning with Tales of the Black Widowers (1974), in which five professionals—writer, lawyer, chemist, artist, and cryptographer—meet monthly at dinner to match wits over a difficult *puzzle; the solution is regularly reached first by their waiter Henry.

As these examples suggest, inherent limitations in the armchair detection form make it more suitable to the short story than to the novel. Describing the crime indirectly, in a narration that becomes a virtual monologue of quotations within quotations, makes for a cumbersome structure, and emphasizing the *ingenuity of the detective, who is usually more attracted by the intellectual game than by the *pursuit of *justice, diminishes the human interest. Among the few writers who have used an armchair detective in a full-length work are Anthony *Boucher, whose Dr. John Ashwin, Professor of Sanskrit, solves a series of bizarre murders at a university in The Case of the Seven of Calvary (1937), and John *Rhode, whose Dr. Lancelot *Priestley, a prickly scientific genius in the vein of Jacques *Futrelle's Professor S. F. X. *Van Dugen, the Thinking Machine, appears in several novels, beginning with The Paddington Mystery (1925). Rhode achieved some variety by having Priestley leave his study occasionally to gather evidence or, more often, delegate the legwork to others—a device adopted by most later writers of armchair detection.

An example of this device is found in the work of Ernest Bramah, who introduced the first blind detective in a volume of stories, Max Corrados (1914). In the initial tale, "The Coin of Dionysius," coin collector Max Corrados realizes his wish to become a detective by teaming up with Louis Carlyle, an old school friend now turned private investigator. Carrados's acute senses of touch and hearing keep him from being an armchair sleuth in the strict sense, since they let him detect subtle physical clues invisible to others; but his partnership with Carlyle, carried on through two more volumes of stories, is the prototype of the relationship in which a reclusive or disabled detective takes on a younger, active partner. The best-known such pair is Rex *Stout's Nero *Wolfe, largely housebound by his girth and taste for comfort, and Archie *Goodwin, who functions as commentator and sidekick. Their partnership begins in Fer-de-Lance (1934; Meet Nero Wolfe) and continues in a series of books written over the next three decades. By making Archie Goodwin the narrator and developing the human side of his relationship with Wolfe, Stout overcomes the structural limitations of the armchair-detective form and suggests a way to extend its application, although not without compromising the central element of information obtained only by report; evidence and witnesses are brought to Wolfe for direct examination. Other writers have a sleuth temporarily become an armchair detective when he is immobilized by accident or illness, for example, Inspector Grant in Josephine *Tey's *The Daughter of Time* (1951) and Inspector *Morse in Colin *Dexter's *The Wench Is Dead* (1990).

The phrase "armchair detective" is sometimes used now in a more general sense to refer to the reader who, at the hands of a writer abiding by rules of fair play, has all the necessary clues for solving the crime before the writer reveals the solution. A similar meaning is implied in the title of the popular journal *Armchair Detective*, which since the 1960s has published articles and reviews on all types of mystery and detective fiction.

[*See also* Disability, Sleuth with; Great Detective, The; Reasoning, Types of; Sidekicks and Sleuthing Teams.]   —Mary Rose Sullivan

Armchair Detective, The. When *The Armchair Detective* magazine (popularly known as *TAD*) was founded by Allen J. Hubin in October 1967, the intent was to provide a central forum for mystery fans, allowing them to share knowledge, exchange books, and develop friendships. Hubin credited writer and critic Anthony *Boucher with spreading word about the magazine in his *New York Times Book Review* column. Boucher's work, like *The Armchair Detective* itself, is credited with legitimizing the genre in the eyes of critics and academics.

Largely sold by subscription, *The Armchair Detective's* readership includes fans of the genre, bibliophiles, and scholars. For two years it took on a more scholarly tone, after which it returned to its mission as a popular vehicle. It is now a slick magazine with color cover art.

In 1981, Hubin relinquished the editorial reins to Michael Seidman. Kathy Daniel assumed the editor's chair from 1989 to 1991, after which Kate Stine edited the magazine until 1997. Publishers of the magazine have included Hubin; Richard L. Roe and Publishers, Inc. of Delmar, California; Otto Penzler; and Judy Vause.

Particularly in the days before chat groups formed on the Internet, *The Armchair Detective* served as a reliable forum for its readers, with a sound reputation for its lively letters column, its tips on book collecting, its highly regarded reviewers, and its interviews of authors. Some of its most important feature articles included ground-breaking roundups of international crime writing and comprehensive listings of specialty bookstores. *The Armchair Detective* also served as a showplace for advertisers, particularly specialized bookstores, helping readers to find new and used books.

[*See also* Publishing, History of Magazine: American Magazines.]   —Robert Napier

ARMSTRONG, CHARLOTTE. (1905–1969), American author. After working as a fashion journalist, publishing some poems in magazines, and seeing two of her stage plays produced in New York, Armstrong turned to crime and mystery writing. Her first works in the genre narrated cases of a *sleuth whose name, MacDougal Duff, permitted the allusive titles *Lay on, Mac Duff!* (1942) and *The Case of the Weird Sisters* (1943). After carrying Duff into a third work, *The Innocent Flower* (1945; *Death Filled the Glass*), Armstrong abandoned the conventions of a serial detective, taking up as the focus of her next twenty-five novels the subjective experience of hazard in ordinary life. Sherry Reynard's father-in-law in *The Balloon Man* (1968) has a class-based but otherwise inexplicable dislike for her and employs an ambitious social climber to acquire evidence for use against Sherry in an impending child custody case. Once the situation is established, the novel's cadence of threat and escape intensifies until the familiar matter of domestic friction nearly reaches fatal conclusion. *Mischief* (1950), for which Armstrong wrote the screen adaptation (*Don't Bother to Knock*, 1952), capitalizes on the ordinary anxiety of parents leaving their children in someone else's care to introduce the peril of a baby-sitter whose apparent normality belies her deranged condition. *Lemon in the Basket* (1967) invades the territory of an eminently accomplished family to portray dangers consequent to the resentment of the one underachieving sibling and his resentful spouse. Armstrong constructs plots for her novels and the stories in her two collections of genre short works to create *suspense. Her characters represent the innate goodness of ordinary people in conflict with the self-serving excess that can arise in commonplace circumstances, all with the result of tapping her readers' fear that terror may invade everyday life.

[*See also* Allusion, Literary; Terror.]

• Myra Hunter Jones, "Charlotte Armstrong (1905–1969)," in *Great Women Mystery Writers: Classic to Contemporary*, ed. Kathleen Gregory Klein (1994): 18–21.

—John M. Reilly

ARSON, the willful act of setting fire to property for criminal purposes, is an insidious crime, as destructive as *murder and sometimes the means of it. The task of identifying arsonists is extremely difficult for the police, since there may be no apparent *motive and few *clues; the authorities must rely on the meticulous analysis of physical remains at the scene. Perhaps for this reason, arson figures less often than other crimes in fiction. Arson in a scheme of insurance fraud is common in real life but less so in fiction: Marge Piercy's *Fly Away Home* (1984) is thus unusual in its depiction of this crime. In fiction, arson is more often used to conceal a murder, thus challenging the investigator to identify and solve two crimes. Fire is set to destroy the corpse in a haystack, in R. Austin *Freeman's "The Funeral Pyre" (*Dr. Thorndyke's Casebook*, 1923; *The Blue Scarab*); in a barn, in Freeman Wills *Crofts's "The Case of the Burning Barn" (*Murderers Make Mistakes*, 1947); and in a residence, in H. C. *Bailey's "The Burnt Tout"

(*This is Mr. Fortune*, 1938). In *Burnt Offering* (1955), by Richard and Frances Lockridge, a burning firehall provides an opportunity for murder, and in Bailey's *Dead Man's Effects* (1944, *The Cat's Whisker*), a bonfire serves not only to destroy a corpse but also to guide enemy bombers to their target. Arson may be the murder method, as in the burning of the mansion in Leslie *Charteris's *Prelude for War* (1938; *The Saint Plays with Fire*). A fire is set in an attempt to kill the investigator Dr. John *Thorndyke and his colleagues, who narrowly escape death, in Freeman's *A Silent Witness* (1914). The *victim may even be soaked with a flammable substance and torched, as in Charteris's "The Sizzling Saboteur" (*The Saint on Guard*, 1945).

Some writers underscore the emotional devastation wrought by arson. In E. C. R. Lorac's *Fire in the Thatch* (1946), Nicholas Vaughan works hard and devotedly to restore a country cottage and enjoys deep happiness there; when the cottage is burned, it almost seems a greater crime than his murder. J. J. Marric's *Gideon's Fire* (1961), which treats this crime extensively, conveys the horror of a deadly fire for both the police and its victims. Fire brings an especially cruel death, and arsonists are rarely if ever presented with redeeming qualities.

Arson is not always committed for criminal purposes. Sherlock *Holmes employed the threat of fire to scare Irene *Adler into revealing the hiding place of a photograph in Arthur Conan *Doyle's "A Scandal in Bohemia" (*The Adventures of Sherlock Holmes*, 1892) and to flush out a criminal in "The Adventure of the Norwood Builder" (*The Return of Sherlock Holmes*, 1905). Fire accidentally started might even bring redemption for the criminal, as when the murderer rescues an elderly woman, his intended victim, from a burning museum in Margery *Allingham's *Hide My Eyes* (1958; *Tether's End*).

[*See also* Murder Weapons, Unusual; Violence.]

—William A. S. Sarjeant

ART AND ANTIQUES MILIEU. Many authors have found the art and antiques *milieu appealing because of the opportunity it can offer for the use of a historically rich *setting; thus, Timothy Holme draws upon a famed Italian locale in *The Assisi Murders* (1985) and Margaret Truman employs some of America's large art holdings in *Murder in the Smithsonian* (1983). Yet other authors people their fiction with characters from the art world, as does Michael *Innes in *A Private View* (1952; *One-Man Show*; *Murder Is an Art*), featuring art dealer Hildebert Braunkopf.

A growing number of writers, however, use the worlds of fine art, antiques, or antiquarian books as the milieu for virtually all of their crime novels, placing their series *sleuths in the ranks of expert professionals in those fields. Oliver Banks's art historian Amos Hatcher, Jonathan Gash's shady dealer Lovejoy, John Malcolm's art expert Tim Simpson, and Iain Pears's art historian Jonathan Argyll are all examples of this type. The detective work accidentally required of these figures comes naturally to them, for authenticating paintings or antiques and establishing their provenances involves the same combination of re-

search, speculation, and intuition as does solving a *murder. To say that the characters discovered in the world of art and antiques are shady is to understate matters; quite apart from out-and-out crooks, initially respectable individuals find that the lure of wealth or the satisfactions of acquisition and possession of rare items can lead them to operate on the far side of legality.

The crimes most commonly associated with art and antiques are *theft, *forgery, and *smuggling. For Gash's Lovejoy, fraud and its recognition are a way of life. As a result, the books are filled with tips on fakery, as in *Gold by Gemini* (1978), which includes explanation of the process for faking a nineteenth-century letter. Because Lovejoy is both hero and narrator of his tales, his own rampant dishonesty becomes something on the order of a personality quirk, especially as the *victims are often other crooked dealers.

The art milieu also allows writers to devise intricate plans for their culprit's frauds. In Banks's *The Rembrandt Panel* (1980; *The Rembrandt File*), the director of a museum needs a major acquisition to compensate for a dreadful mistake he has made; his "plan" is to paint over a newly discovered Rembrandt, enter it in a country auction, buy it, clean it, and "discover" the Rembrandt afresh. *The Sale of Lot 236* (1981) by Michael Delahaye places another intricate plan in the context of an auction, an event ripe for skulduggery. Here an art-restorer is blackmailed into helping two dealers uncover a thirteenth-century fresco, so it can be used to authenticate a crucifix they intend to purchase at auction. The restorer neatly turns the tables—first, by not revealing that there is no fresco, and second, by pushing the bidding artificially high at the auction.

A novel illustrating how much mileage can be obtained from dishonesty in the art and antiques milieu is *The Raphael Affair* (1990) by Iain Pears, which begins with reference to an eighteenth-century fraud: a painted-over Raphael that was to be smuggled into England. The agent arranging this was supposed to have perpetrated yet a further fraud, keeping the Raphael in Italy under its *disguise. Then it appears that the faker had not actually passed the disguised original over to its intended receivers. The *truth revealed by detection in the novel then compounds the *plot of fraud: the Raphael did reach England but was never cleaned and, therefore, never identified; by some amazing chance it came into the hands of a modern-day faker who unwittingly used it as a canvas on which to paint a fake—of the original Raphael.

Since the milieu of art and antiques offers writers access to familiar yet distinct settings, they are also encouraged to use the milieu in relating the more typical crimes of the detective mystery genre. Ngaio *Marsh—whose Inspector (later, Superintendent) Roderick *Alleyn marries an artist, Agatha Troy—set *Artists in Crime* (1938) and *Clutch of Constables* (1968) in the art world. In *Death Among the Artists* (1993) by J. D. Forbes, the former members of an artists' colony are killed by a supposed great artist who has been passing off as his own the works of a talented younger painter whom he murdered. In Robert Richardson's *The Book of the Dead* (1989), the owner of a privately printed Sherlock *Holmes story is murdered so that his wife can profit from inheriting and publishing the book.

As these latter cases indicate, the objects around which crimes revolve may have as much intrinsic interest as the milieu in which they appear. Add to this compelling attraction of the art and antiques milieu the expertise of some authors (Banks is an art consultant; Marsh was herself an artist), the skillful plotting of narrative by others, and the possibility for invention of ingenious characters by all writers who adopt the milieu, and the result is a formula to refresh the established conventions of detection fiction.
—Judith Rhodes

ASHDOWN, CLIFFORD. *See* Freeman, R(ichard) Austin.

ASSAULT is the unlawful attempt or threat to use force or *violence against another person. Although the term "battery" is reserved in legal usage for the completion of the threat by violence, in colloquial discussion assault tends to include the attack itself—bludgeoning, wife and *child abuse, *rape and other sex crimes and, of course, *murder. It may also refer to the harmful application of psychological and verbal force. Since the term "assault" is so elastic, its references are unavoidable in detective fiction. Murder in crime and mystery writing is assault taken to its extreme. The *underworld figures who populate *hard-boiled fiction commonly rely on the violence associated with assault, but assault also intrudes into the genteel world of the *cozy mystery; coshing and the use of a blunt instrument are obvious types of assault that occur in soft-boiled detective writing.

Assault weaves well into the fabric of the *detective novel in a technical sense, fulfilling its role as a *plot device. Assault is often used by the criminal as a means of intimidating the zealous detective; it is a violent act used as a warning to the detective to halt the investigation. For example, in Sara *Paretsky's *Indemnity Only* (1982), thugs grab private investigator V. I. *Warshawski at her apartment door in an attempt to pressure her to stay away from a certain case. As with many other detectives, however, this assault has the opposite effect, motivating the *sleuth to continue her investigation.

Assault can also be a preliminary step toward murder. If the *victim is incapacitated or put in a dangerous situation, his or her demise might be imminent. In Dick *Francis's *Smokescreen* (1972), Edward Lincoln is clobbered in a South African gold mine just before the mine is cleared for blasting in order to make his intended death appear to be an accident.

A history of assault can also be used to throw suspicion on a character. Diane Mott Davidson does this in *Catering to Nobody* (1992) when she lets the reader and her detective know that a character has been officially charged with assault in the past. The character's involvement in the novel's murder becomes more likely given this information. Finally, self-inflicted assault or a claim of assault can be a ruse to draw attention away from the murderer. Agatha *Christie employed this to good advantage in *Death on the Nile* (1937).

In detective fiction, however, violence cannot be passed off solely as a technical device. The social, legal, and moral implications of assault rendered in this genre portray the fragile state of society. Assault may also be used to comment on widespread gender- or race-based social attitudes. Many expressions of *prejudice are the violent release of the perpetrator's anger toward selected victims. Here the act of violence, apparently the solution to a problem with the victim, becomes itself a problem as it destroys the web of community. Contemporary authors' reliance on assault in detective fiction thus mirrors the cracking social order. The use of assault for symbolic purposes increasingly leads writers to show assault as quick and mindlessly violent. For example, harsh and explosive wife beating is central to Margaret Yorke's *suspense novel *Dangerous to Know* (1993). Seemingly mild-mannered Walter Brown hits his wife Hermione several times about the face because she finally refuses nonconsensual sex. This assault causes her at last to take action to protect herself from further attacks, including the rape she had been experiencing on a regular basis.

Using a medical examiner sleuth to describe the effects of assault on murdered victims, Patricia D. Cornwell uses the threat of further assault or serial killings to propel her characters to action and to keep her readers turning the pages. Along the way, she comments effectively upon random violence in American society. Mary Higgins *Clark similarly uses the threat of serial violence, including assault, to sustain *suspense in her novel *Loves Music, Loves to Dance* (1991).

The dramatic enactment of crime through representations of assault provides writers both the technical means of heightening suspense or increasing tension and the opportunity for social observation.

[*See also* Hard-Boiled Fiction; Serial Killers and Mass Murderers.]

• H. R. F. Keating, ed., *Whodunit? A Guide to Crime, Suspense, and Spy Fiction* (1982). Edward Margolis, *Which Way Did He Go? The Private Eye in Dashiell Hammett, Raymond Chandler, Chester Himes, and Ross Macdonald* (1982). David Geherin, *The American Private Eye: The Image in Fiction* (1985).
—Thomas Mavor

ATMOSPHERE. When the physical attributes of a place are selected by a writer to depict or mirror a psychological environment, atmosphere is created. In order to establish the atmosphere, or surrounding air of a place, the creative writer selects and describes physical details that possess metaphoric qualities, which tie in with the theme of the work. Atmosphere may then be used to arouse expectations and *suspense, along with feelings of pity, pleasure, or apprehension or moods ranging from the contemplative to the merry. In romantic literature, atmosphere was employed to mirror the emotions of the writer or his or her characters. In the *Gothic novel, it was used to establish an aura of fear or dread. In the crime and mystery genre, atmosphere is used not only to arouse emotions and underline themes, but it may also be employed for purposes of contrast, particularly to establish an ordered world that is disrupted by the intrusion of violent crime.

Atmosphere is linked to *setting and especially to *milieu, but it is richer than either; it exists when details of place are chosen to be more than trappings of a particular society, time period, or international setting. By this criterion, the trains that run reliably in the works of Freeman Wills *Crofts provide settings and setups for *alibis, unbreakable and otherwise, whereas the train hurtling through the night in Patricia *Highsmith's Strangers on a Train (1950) becomes a true psychological environment or atmospheric world with symbolic dimensions, since its isolation from the character's lives make it the ideal place to plot perfect crimes.

Orderly milieus, such as the English village and country house favored by writers of cozier fiction, are rarely atmospheric in the profound sense. Although the predictable routines and luxuries of life in such places contrast with the disruptive crime, the writer's purpose in employing these places is usually more concerned with establishing alibis and identifying wealth, privilege, and class than with exploring a rich psychological environment. When a guilty secret casts a dark shadow over the country house, as is the case in Daphne *du Maurier's Rebecca (1938), this setting becomes atmospheric in the true sense.

G. K. *Chesterton, whose sleuth enjoyed puzzling out paradoxes, used a quirky approach to creating atmosphere in stories where a comically bumbling character addresses *murder as the ultimate sin. Chesterton created what he considered to be the correct atmosphere for crime in a cityscape that nonetheless had the appeal of an enchanted country where "elfin coincidence" and paradox ruled. Here the *clerical sleuth Father *Brown wandered with his ever-handy umbrella, confounding the police and criminologists with his profound awareness of *evil. In his 1901 essay "A Defence of Detective Stories," Chesterton described the urban setting as appropriate for crime, and "more poetic than the countryside" because it is not only lonely but beautiful. It is the undertone of loneliness that takes Chesterton beyond setting and milieu into an urban environment that becomes atmospheric. Half a century later, in America, Frederic *Brown's The Fabulous Clipjoint (1947) makes a similar argument for the paradoxical atmospheric possibilities in the city of Chicago: It's beautiful, says one of the characters: "Beautiful as hell . . . but it's a clipjoint."

A certain amount of paradox endows the *mean streets milieu with atmosphere. In a cynical world overshadowed by the threat of *violence and undermined by deceit, it is the gritty detail that literally and figuratively leads the hero toward the truth, so that the narrative staggering through a deceptive world is finally steadied by realism.

Because a well-established atmosphere actively engages the reader's feelings, it is one of the chief qualities of literature that makes particular work memorable. The most readily remembered examples of atmosphere in detective fiction are found in Arthur Conan *Doyle's descriptions of Sherlock *Holmes's fog-enshrouded *London. Doyle was a master of establishing an air of mystery in a few lines, noting, for instance, the hoofbeats of a horse drawing a hansom cab over wet cobblestones. With details such as blooming jacaranda and heat simmering over hot pavement, Raymond *Chandler's Philip *Marlowe stories evoke a southern California where crime is waiting to flare up.

[See also Crime Novel.]

—Michael Cohen

AUDIENCE PARTICIPATION ACTIVITIES. For the mystery fan, the attractions of the genre extend far beyond the pleasure of curling up with a good book. All sorts of activities have been concocted to gratify a desire to "play detective": party games; audience participation plays in restaurants and theaters; hotel weekends, train trips, and ocean cruises; fan club reenactments of episodes from famous stories; pilgrimages and tours, and board games and computer games.

Elsa Maxwell, "the hostess with the mostest," claimed to have introduced the first murder game at a London dinner party. During the flowering of the country house murder mystery in the 1920s and 1930s, playing the murder game at house parties was enormously popular. After one of the guests was secretly given a token denoting him or her as the villain, the lights were suddenly extinguished and a game of hide-and-seek ensued. When the lights went on, the players emerged from hiding, the body was "discovered," and an investigation was conducted by a guest-cum-detective to determine "who done it."

The game inspired Ngaio *Marsh's first detective novel, A Man Lay Dead (1934), in which an actual murder occurs under cover of the make-believe crime. This device was also employed by Margery *Allingham in The Crime at Black Dudley (1929; The Black Dudley Murder), Mary Fitt in Three Sisters Flew Home (1936), Gladys *Mitchell in Watson's Choice (1955), and Agatha *Christie in Dead Man's Folly (1956). More recent examples include Marian Babson's Weekend for Murder (1985; Murder on a Mystery Tour), Joan Hess's Murder at the Murder at the Mimosa Inn (1986), and Max Allan Collins's Nice Weekend for Murder (1986).

The contemporary craze for murder games has produced a plethora of packaged kits, which supply guidelines for hosting a murder party at home. Such kits usually provide a cassette tape of a mystery story plus a cast list, *clues, physical evidence, invitations, costume suggestions, and even recipes. The tape is played or a fake murder is committed, and the guests then try to solve it by examining clues, interviewing each other, and even reconstructing the crime.

Many restauranteurs have been quick to see the advantage in offering their patrons a *whodunit play. Sometimes these dramas are staged in a separate part of the dining room, but usually professional actors mingle with the diners and create "scenes" in their midst throughout the evening. Patrons are often asked for their observations as witnesses. At the end of the evening the audience submits solutions and winners are given prizes.

This format has also been extended to longer time periods at various vacation venues: a weekend in a hotel, several days on a train journey, or a week's ocean cruise. The expanded time frame allows for more elaborate plots, with more than one murder occuring.

A train provides the perfect closed environment for enacting fictional murder, as Christie demonstrated in *The Mystery on the Blue Train* (1928) and *Murder on the Orient Express* (1934). Several railways in various parts of North America and Europe have provided venues for "let's pretend" violent death. Although it does not feature a murder puzzle involving patrons, the most popular of these trains remains the luxurious Venice Simplon Orient-Express, between London and Venice.

Audience participation whodunits have also been adapted for the commercial theater. Perhaps the best known of these productions was a dramatization of Charles *Dickens's *The Mystery of Edwin Drood* (1870), which was a huge success on Broadway in the 1980s. The drama followed the novel up to where Dickens left off, at which point the audience voted for the character they believed to be the *villain. The play then resumed, supplying an ending which explained the *means, motive, and opportunity for the crime. *Shear Madness*, produced in several cities around the world, was the longest-running interactive murder mystery, with 23,000 performances logged between 1980 and 1995 (*Time*, 20 Feb. 1995).

Such fan activities as theme tours and reenactments of favorite works vary widely in quality. Among the most authentic are those of the Sherlock Holmes Society of London and the other 413 *Sherlockian societies around the world. In May 1991, to celebrate the centenary of Sherlock *Holmes's decisive struggle with Professor *Moriarty at the Reichenbach Falls in 1891, one hundred members of the London society journeyed in period costume to Meiringen, Switzerland, where they followed in Holmes and Watson's footsteps to the falls and recreated the climax of "The Final Problem" (*The Memoirs of Sherlock Holmes*, 1894).

Both guided tours and individual walking tours are popular with mystery readers. Organized package tours usually focus on popular crime novelists and arrange visits to places in their books. Horace *Rumpole's legal London and Inspector's *Morse's Oxford, with talks by John *Mortimer and Colin *Dexter, might alternate with visits to the haunts of Holmes or *Jack the Ripper. In Britain, local tourist boards sometimes offer guided walking tours or create and distribute maps of recommended routes of sights to see associated with local authors and their books. The Christie Mile in Torquay, Devon, and the elaborately marked trails through Brother *Cadfael country in Shrewsbury, Shropshire, epitomize this kind of do-it-yourself tour.

For the more sedentary, there are board games and computer games. Using dice or cards, four to eight players compete to win the board games.

"Clue," or "Cleudo," a perennial favorite of board games, was invented in 1949 and quickly became ubiquitous on both sides of the Atlantic. The board for "13 Dead End Drive" is a two-dimensional cardboard model of a mansion with cutout characters located in various rooms. While awaiting the death of a wealthy relative, they seek to eliminate each other, thereby reducing the number of claims on the estate and increasing their personal legacies. Other board games include "221B Baker Street" and "Scotland Yard," both of which use schematic maps of key *London sites.

With computer games, an individual player pits his or her wits against those of the programmers who designed the software package. These games, exercises in virtual reality, usually contain a CD-ROM disk. The characters in the story present a *puzzle plot and offer the player the chance to solve the crime. The player can collect evidence, interview suspects, and form hypotheses. Each choice or answer determines the subsequent set of options. At almost any stage it may be possible to right an earlier wrong decision, but some wrong answers lead inevitably to defeat.

[*See also* Computer Detective Fiction.]

• Betty Lowry, "Class Trip," *Contra Costa Times* (25 June 1995): 11–21. Richard Corliss, "Murder Most Profitable," *Time* (20 February 1995): n.p.   —B. J. Rohn

AUSTRALIA, CRIME AND MYSTERY WRITING IN.

The authority for history of early Australian crime writing is Stephen Knight whose *Continent of Mystery: A Thematic History of Australian Crime Fiction* (1997) attributes to the earliest appearances of the genre a special character of absences. The *amateur detective and *police detective are rare. A high number of the stories leave investigation to the main characters rather than providing formal or specialized detectives. On the other hand, Knight relates that the Australian pioneer writers had their own subgenres deriving from historical conditions of settlement.

The preeminent instance of Australian uniqueness is the criminal saga. The first novel written and published in Australia—*Quintus Servinton* (1831)—introduced the type, and it continued throughout the nineteenth century under the hand of such writers as Marcus Clarke, author of *His Natural Life* (1872) and Eliza Winstanley, whose *For Her Natural Life* (1876), like Clarke's novel, details the harsh conditions experienced by convicts transported to Australia.

The continent's special history also stimulated the production of a subgenre termed "squatter thrillers" by Knight. These are represented by Henry Kingsley's *Recollections of Geoffry Hamlin* (1857) and *Irralie's Bushranger* (1896) by E. W. *Hornung. Squatter stories concern people in dangerous competition for rich land that they appropriate by a presumed right of settlement, but that remains an object of allure for others who can seize the land and squat on it also. The counterpart of these stories of the vast spaces is the urban thriller, which employs a similar *plot of threat of wealth and is usually set in Melbourne. Fergus Hume's *Mystery of a Hansom Cab* (1886) set the formal pattern for this subgenre.

The third Australian innovation is the goldfield story, works set in the mining areas of the continent and often relating police adventures, such as the short fiction published in the *Australian Journal* by Mary Fortune, the author most responsible for developing the narrative type with works such as "The Dead Witness" (1866) which served as a template for adaptations by her contemporaries.

More recent Australian crime writing bears closer relationship to the genre as it has been formed in other English-speaking countries. For example, the formal mystery is represented in the nearly two dozen books published by the writing team of Margot Goyder and Anne Neville Goyder Joske under the name of Margot Neville. Their series began with *Murder in Rockwater* (1945; *Lena Hates Men*, 1944) and usually featured the Sydney police officers Inspector Grogan and Sergeant Manning. An effective writer of the same period was A. E. Martin, whose leading character is a con artist named Pel Pelham who moves through a world filled with circus performers, giants, and armless wonders. One of his more memorable characters is the *private eye Rosie Bosansky in *The Misplaced Corpse* (1944). Arthur Gask, a prominent author of the 1920s, elaborated on the criminal saga with tales such as *The Red Paste Murders* (1923), which tells of Peter Wacks, a savage criminal under the influence of a mysterious Malayan drug and an evangelist in sane moments, and *The Secret of the Garden* (1924) which presents John Cups, a man whose appearance has been changed by dental and facial surgery.

The strong influence of British fashion in thrillers may be seen in writers such as Sidney Courtier, as well as Margot Neville. Neville's works are society *murder stories, Courtier's derivations from John *Buchan with the added attraction in such an example as *Ligny's Lake* (1971) of allusion to contemporary Cold War events—in this case the disappearance of Prime Minister Harold Holt.

British publishers have a natural interest in marketing their products in former colonies, which has the effect of inducing writers who seek a broad audience to write an international Anglo-style fiction which dispenses with particularized Australian detail. Geraldine Halls, who wrote as Charlotte Jay, won an American Edgar Allan Poe Award in 1953 for *Beat Not the Bones*, a novel set in New Guinea. Paul McGuire wrote many novels, including the well received *Burial Service* (1938; *Funeral in Eden*) but never set his works in his native Australia. A more subtle illustration of the international quality of crime fiction can be seen in the publications of Pat Flower, whose novels feature police—Inspector Swinton and Sergeant Primrose—but whose disposition is toward narratives of pathology akin to the fiction of Margaret *Millar, Patricia *Highsmith, and Ruth *Rendell. Patricia Carlon similarly illustrates the transnational appeal of psychological thrillers in her novel *The Whispering Wall* (1969).

A long view of Australian crime and mystery writing shows it to be held in tension between Australian particulars and formal generality. Two luminaries illustrate the point. Arthur W. *Upfield, exiled by his English father to Australia in 1910, developed a love of the Outback that led him to commemorate the Aboriginal/European origins of the nation in his character, the half-caste Inspector Napoleon "Bony" *Bonaparte who appeared in twenty-six of his thirty-eight books. Jon Cleary, author of more than forty books, sets his work in every part of the world, including Australia, but dedicates his craft to refining the *suspense story as an instrument for probing scenes of injustice wherever they may be. The great bulk of Australian crime writing arcs between these poles in a way that allows for the conclusion that ultimately it is hybridity that marks it as distinct.

[*See also* Great Outdoors, The; Rural Milieu]

—Ray B. Browne

AVIATION MILIEU. Powered heavier-than-air flight dates only from 1903, about the time Sherlock *Holmes retired from active practice. It did not take long for aviation to appear in the pages of crime fiction.

Early examples of the use of aircraft and aviation are found in the secret service *thrillers of William Le Queux, who produced examples like *The Zeppelin Destroyer* (1916), *Beryl of the Biplane* (1917), and *The Terror of the Air* (1920). Three of John *Buchan's Richard Hannay thrillers introduce airplanes: *The Thirty-Nine Steps* (1915), *Mr. Standfast* (1919), and *The Three Hostages* (1924).

As it boomed during the interwar period, air travel naturally became the background for mysteries by Golden Age authors. Freeman Wills *Crofts's inverted tale *The 12.30 from Croydon* (1934; *Wilful and Premeditated*) captures the thrill of flying then, as does Agatha *Christie's *Death in the Clouds* (1935; *Death in the Air*). Both feature an HP 42 airliner on the Le Bourget-Croydon route.

Prewar Croydon is described in Carter Dickson's (*see* John Dickson *Carr) *The Curse of the Bronze Lamp* (1945; *Lord of the Sorcerers*). Dorothy L. *Sayers's Peter Wimsey flies the Atlantic in *Clouds of Witness* (1926). Other prewar titles include William Sutherland's *Death Rides the Airline* (1934) and C. St. John Sprigg's *Death of an Airman* (1934). A. O. Pollard wrote several works centered around aviation including *The Phantom Plane* (1934) and later an anthology of short stories, *David Wilshaw Investigates* (1948), which contains "The Aerodome Explosion" and "The Murder Parachute" among other dramatically titled pieces.

Air raids figure in many 1940s detective stories, especially Christie's *Taken at the Flood* (1948; *There Is a Tide*), E. C. R. Lorac's *Murder by Matchlight* (1945), and John *Rhode's *The Fourth Bomb* (1942). The archetypal air hero, W. E. Johns's Biggles, became a detective sergeant in the *CID *"Air Branch"* after the war, appearing in *Biggles of the Special Air Police* (1953) and other works. Philip *Macdonald's Colonel Anthony *Gethryn investigates in *The List of Adrian Messenger* (1960) the death of Messenger, blown up, Lockerbie fashion, in an airliner days after giving *Scotland Yard a list of suspicious accidental deaths.

Hammond Innes (*Air Bridge*, 1951), Andrew Garve (*The Ascent of D-13*, 1969), and Roderic Jeffries (*Dead Clever*, 1989) have produced convincing aviation thrillers. Commercial aviation is the background of Douglas Rutherford's *The Perilous Sky* (1955), and air travel is the focus of Christie's *Passenger to Frankfurt* (1970).   —Philip Scowcroft

AWARDS. *This entry is divided into two parts, the first surveying numerous awards given in the United States and Canada, and the second describing the history of British awards given for works in the crime and mystery genre. Additional awards are presented by associations that bring together authors of other nationalities or language groups. The Association International des Escritores Policiacos of the International Crime Writers Association also presents awards celebrating the achievement of authors who write in this genre.*

North American Awards
British Awards

For further information, please refer to Crime Writers Association; Fans and Fan Organizations; Mystery Writers of America.

NORTH AMERICAN AWARDS

The first generally recognized mystery award was presented by the Mystery Writers of America, Inc. (MWA), in March 1946 for the best first novel published in 1945. Over the years, new categories have been added and some retired as the mystery genre evolved and gained higher visibility. There are now twelve categories: novel, first novel, paperback original, critical biographical work, fact crime, juvenile novel, young adult novel, short story, television feature or miniseries, television episode, movie, and play. Ceramic busts of Edgar Allan *Poe, called "Edgars," are presented to the winners in each category and nominees receive scrolls. The highest of all awards is the Grand Master Award, presented to an author who over a lifetime of achievement has proven himself or herself preeminent in the craft. The MWA also administers the Robert L. Fish Award, funded by the estate of Robert L. Fish, for the best first short story in the mystery genre. The Raven is presented to people who are not writers but are keenly supportive of the genre. The Ellery Queen Award is presented to writing teams or professionals in mystery publishing.

In 1979 the Wolfe Pack, a group of aficionados of the works of Rex *Stout awarded its first Nero Award. Only one award is given: for the book that best represents the spirit of the Nero *Wolfe novels. Since 1982, the Private Eye Writers of America (PWA) have honored the best in private-eye fiction, with their Shamus Awards. Their lifetime achievement award is the Eye. Categories are novel, paperback original, short story, and first novel. The Arthur Ellis Award, named after the *nom de travail* of Canada's hangman, is the mystery award sponsored by the Crime Writers of Canada (CWC). The award was established in 1984 and is limited to Canadian crime writers. Categories are novel, first novel, short story, true crime, juvenile, and play.

Although Bouchercon, the oldest and largest annual fan convention, was first held in 1971, its Anthony Award was not created until 1986. The works are voted by registrants for the convention. Categories are novel, first novel, critical work, true crime, short story, and anthology. Mystery Readers International sponsors the Macavity Award, established in 1987. Winning titles are voted by the subscribers. Categories are novel, first novel, critical/biographical, and short story. The Agatha Awards are presented annually at the Malice Domestic convention. The awards are voted by people attending "Malice" and were first presented in 1989. Categories are novel, first novel, short story, and nonfiction.

The International Association of Crime Writers (IACW) first presented the Hammett Award in 1992 to honor the best novel by an American or Canadian writer. The Dilys Winn Award was established in 1992 by the Independent Mystery Booksellers Association. Selection is based on the books that the membership most enjoyed selling during the year. The award is presented at the annual Left Coast Crime Convention held in February.   —Priscilla Ridgway

BRITISH AWARDS

The *Crime Writers Association (CWA), founded on November 1953 at the instigation of John *Creasey, is the only major presenter of awards for crime writing in the United Kingdom. Its first award, the Crossed Red Herrings, was presented in 1955 to Winston Graham for his novel *The Little Walls* (1955). Runners-up were Leigh Howard for *Blind Date* (1955), Ngaio *Marsh for *Scales of Justice*, (1955), and Margot Bennett for *The Man Who Didn't Fly* (1955). The Crossed Red Herrings was superseded in 1960 by the CWA Gold Dagger, which first went to Lionel Davidson for *Night of Wenceslas* (1960); the runners-up were Mary Stewart for *My Brother Michael* (1960) and Julian *Symons for *The Progress of a Crime* (1960).

The next decade saw various short-lived awards. The Best Foreign Crime Book of the Year was awarded to Patricia *Highsmith in 1964 for *The Two Faces of January* (1964), John *Ball in 1966 for *In the Heat of the Night* (1965), Sébastien Japrisot in 1968 for *The Lady in the Car with Glasses and a Gun* (1967), and Rex *Stout in 1969 for *The Father Hunt* (1968). Best British Crime Book of the Year was won by Gavin Lyall in 1965 for *Midnight Plus One* (1965) and Eric *Ambler in 1967 for *Dirty Story* (1967). The CWA Silver Dagger, runner-up to the Gold, was first presented in 1969, to Francis Clifford for *Another Way of Dying* (1968).

After Creasey's death in 1973, the CWA John Creasey Memorial Award was inaugurated to encourage new writers, the first winner being Kyril Bonfiglioli for *Don't Point That Thing at Me* (1972; *Mortdecai's Endgame*). Several winners have gone on to make their names in crime writing, among them Jonathan Gash (*The Judas Pair*, 1977), Paula Gosling (*A Running Duck*, 1978; *Fair Game*), Liza Cody (*Dupe*,

1980), Robert Richardson (*The Latimer Mercy*, 1985), Patricia Cornwell (*Postmortem*, 1990), and Walter *Mosley (*Devil in a Blue Dress*, 1990). The original citation for the Creasey Award, given for the best first crime novel, was made more specific after the award went to the first crime novel of a prolific author.

The CWA Non-Fiction Gold Dagger was presented for the first time in 1978. The first CWA/Cartier Diamond Dagger, for outstanding contribution to the genre, was awarded in 1986 to Eric Ambler, and the 1998 winner was Ed *McBain.

In 1993, as part of its fortieth anniversary celebrations, the CWA introduced the CWA/The Macallan Short Story Award, sponsored by The Macallan, for published stories by members of the association. Winners have included Reginald *Hill, Ian Rankin (twice), and Julian Rathbone.

From 1985 to 1987, the *Police Review* sponsored an award for the crime novel that best portrayed British police work and procedure. This was won in 1985 by Andrew Arncliffe for *Murder after the Holidays* (1985), in 1986 by Bill Knox for *The Crossfire Killings* (1986), and in 1987 by Roger Busby for *Snow Man* (1987).

In 1988 *Punch* magazine sponsored the Punch Prize for the funniest crime book of the year, won by Nancy Livingston for *Death in a Distant Land* (1988). This award was superseded the following year by the CWA Last Laugh Award, which ran from 1989–1996. The first winner was Mike Ripley, for *Angel Touch* (1989), and the last Janet Evanovich, for *Two for the Dough*.

In 1990 Hazel Wynn Jones, a member of CWA, sponsored the CWA '92 Award, to run for three years and mark Britain's entry into the European Community. It was for a novel set partly or wholly on the continent of Europe; sadly, its sponsor died before it could be presented. Also in 1990, the *New Law Journal* sponsored the CWA Rumpole Award, to be presented from time to time for the best crime novel of the year with a British legal setting. The first winner was Frances Fyfield for *Trial by Fire*.

Two awards for the author most popular with library borrowers, The Golden Handcuffs Award, superseded by Dagger in the Library, ran from 1992 to 1996.

The judges for the CWA fiction awards are reviewers of crime fiction on national or provincial newspapers and magazines. The nonvoting chairman of the panel is E. E. Pardoe of the *Birmingham Post*, who has served for over thirty years. Voting members serve for two consecutive years only. Judging for the CWA John Creasey Memorial Dagger has now been separated from the main fiction awards and is conducted by former Dagger winners, who serve a three-year term.

The nonfiction panel, chaired by a member of the CWA, is made up of a team of experts—doctors, lawyers, forensic scientists, police officers, and so forth.

Submissions in all categories are by publishers only.

There have been various sponsors over the years, including Securicor, Post Mortem Books, and Agatha Christie Ltd. The CWA John Creasey Memorial Award (now Dagger) has been sponsored for many years by Chivers Press. In 1995, sponsorship of the Gold and Silver Daggers was taken over by The Macallan, and their correct titles are now CWA/The Macallan Gold Dagger for Fiction, and so forth.

—Anthea Fraser

BAANTJER, ALBERT CORNELIS (b. 1923), Dutch crime author who writes under the single name Baantjer. With more than forty titles to his credit, Baantjer has sold more than four million copies in the Netherlands, a country of fewer than fifteen million inhabitants.

Baantjer's main character is a short, fat, irascible policeman named DeKok, who carefully spells his name to everyone he meets. Dekok's assistant is Vledder. Although Baantjer has been called "a Dutch Conan Doyle" by *Publishers Weekly*, and Dekok has been compared to Georges *Simenon's Jules *Maigret, both comparisons are off the mark. DeKok is a much more normal and less eccentric character than is Holmes, much warmer and more humanistic than Maigret.

Baantjer bases his writings on thirty-eight years' experience serving in the Amsterdam Municipal Police, with more than twenty-five of those years in the homicide division. He uses the upstairs office at 48 Warmoes Street (the real-life police station) as a setting where DeKok can look down a narrow street and see the notorious Amsterdam red-light district.

Several of Baantjer's works begin with a prostitute being fished out of one of the numerous canals in Amsterdam, the victim of a horrible *murder. The author displays great sympathy for such victims, viewing them as terribly abused by their customers. DeKok enjoys the prostitutes' trust and uses them in solving the crimes against them generally perpetrated by the wealthy and powerful, against whom Baantjer has unchanging animosity. Despite a deep-seated grumpiness, Baantjer has a warmhearted respect for all downtrodden people and for the human race in general.

[*See also* Police Detective; Police Procedural; Sleuth.]

• John Bakkenhoven, *Baantjer en de Cock*, 1990. Ray Browne, "Baantjer: New Major Voice in Crime Fiction in America." *Clues: A Journal of Detection* 16, No. 1 (spring/summer 1995): 155–67. —Ray B. Browne

BAGLEY, DESMOND (1923–1983), British author of adventure *thrillers with international *settings.

Born in Kendal, Westmorland (now Cumbria), England, the son of a miner, Bagley was brought up in a theatrical boardinghouse in Blackpool. He led a varied, interesting life, working as a broadcaster, editor, critic, wildlife photographer, and writer. After exploring Africa, he settled in South Africa and married Joan Margaret Brown, but following his successful

first novel, a sea adventure—*The Golden Keel* (1963) —he returned to England, living first in Devon and later, Guernsey. His novels, in the tradition of Hammond Innes, Gavin Lyle, Geoffrey *Household, and Alistair Maclean, reflect his love of nature and exotic places, his wide-ranging interests, his moral outrage at carelessness, waste, incompetence, and inhumanity, and his belief in the spirit and competence of the ordinary man. His style is straightforward, direct, and highly visual, with a fast-paced first-person narrative.

Bagley's quiet heroes, stubborn but coolheaded individualists forced to violent action by amoral villains, battle both hostile nature and human ignorance, corruption, and villainy. His exotic, vividly drawn settings test a man's mettle. Often this means using technological expertise effectively—a medieval warfare expert, for example, constructs crossbows to ward off modern villains—and involves discussion of such technical subjects as hurricane tracking, genesplicing, and complex computer programs.

[*See also* Great Outdoors, The; Heroism.]

• Deryck Harvey, "A Word with Desmond Bagley," *Armchair Detective* 7 (Aug. 1974): 258–60. —Gina Macdonald

BAILEY, H(ENRY) C(HRISTOPHER) (1878–1961), English fiction writer, who for over thirty years contributed richly to the form, producing twenty-one novels and perhaps a hundred stories, and creating two exceptional series detectives. Bailey deals in moral certainties: the protection of the innocent, the punishment of the guilty.

In the wake of the Great War he turned from the historical fiction with which he made his name to crime writing. In 1920 Reggie *Fortune appeared in *Call Mr. Fortune*, the first of the twelve collections that bear Fortune's name. Fortune is *Scotland Yard's foremost pathologist, a master of forensic evidence, whom nothing escapes. He features also in nine novels, occasionally appearing with Joshua Clunk, a wily solicitor, introduced in 1930, who also appears in novels on his own. Despite considerable differences, the two characters share a singleness of purpose: Once embarked on a course of action, neither fails to complete it.

Bailey makes demands on his readers, through his oblique and subtle approach and a style that is mannered, elegant, and elliptical. His narrative achieves a smooth and decorous surface that masks all manner of threats and tensions. The lines between victim and predator are continually smudged by ironies and ambiguities. While Bailey's writing might challenge the modern reader, once the reader is attuned to the idiom, the rest is pure pleasure. The short stories have always been admired, and their classic status is not in question. The novels have been undervalued and are now undergoing reassessment.

[See also Forensic Pathologist; Golden Age Forms; Gentleman Sleuth; Puzzle.]

• Erik Routley, The Puritan Pleasures of the Detective Story: A Personal Monograph (1972). Thomas D. Waugh. "The Parables of H. C. Bailey," Armchair Detective 6, no. 2 (Feb. 1973): 75–77. William A. S. Sarjeant, "In Defense of Mr. Fortune," Armchair Detective 14, no. 4 (fall 1981): 302–12; "The Devil Is with Power: Joshua Clunk and the Fight for Right," Armchair Detective 17, no 3 (summer 1984): 270–79.

—B. A. Pike

BALL, JOHN (1911–1988), American author, best known as the creator of the *African American sleuth Virgil *Tibbs. Born in Schenectady, New York, John Dudley Ball Jr. served in World War II with the U.S. Army Air Corps and was later a columnist, broadcaster, and director of public relations for the Institute of Aerospace Sciences in Los Angeles.

In the Heat of the Night (1965) introduced Tibbs, an astute black *police detective from Pasadena, California, who becomes inadvertently involved with murder in a racially and socially bigoted town in South Carolina. In this award-winning novel and the 1967 film adaptation, Ball's message was "don't judge minorities until you know what you're talking about." His social consciousness is also evident in Johnny Get Your Gun (1969; Death for a Playmate), in which he addressed the implications of gun ownership.

Ball prided himself on research into such fields as jade collecting and the import-export business (Five Pieces of Jade, 1972) and forensic detail, which was always crucial to the solutions he presented to his crimes. His impeccably researched *settings and police procedures are also evident in his books featuring Jack Tallon, beginning with Police Chief (1977), as well as in his nonseries works.

[See also Police Procedural; Prejudice; Racism.]

• Ray B. Browne, "John Ball's Humanism," in Heroes and Humanities (1986): 95–104. George N. Dove, "John Ball's Virgil Tibbs and Jack Tallon," in Cops and Constables, ed. Earl F. Bargainnier and George N. Dove, (1986): 43–54.

—Melvyn Barnes

BANKING AND FINANCIAL MILIEU. The *milieu of banking and finance offers fiction writers an obvious environment for crime stories, but, at the same time, it is one difficult to adapt for lively narrative. The world of fiscal dealings has intrinsic value for a genre such as detective fiction that arose in the historical conditions following the advent of capitalism, because it can typify the abstract power relationships determining the destiny of a modern society. Financial misdeeds, however, occur through paper manipulations and the shuffling of instruments of exchange in ways that may seem so arcane that readers fail to distinguish between illicit and normal modes of business. Moreover, paper crimes committed by financiers or their agents lack the immediate drama of physical action and character conflict.

As a result of these limitations on narrative use, banking and finance have more often been employed in the background of detective and mystery fiction than as the arena of central attention. Sigsbee Manderson, the victim in E. C. *Bentley's novel Trent's Last Case (1913; The Woman in Black) is a financier whose realm of business is briefly described in the book's opening, but the *plot of crime and detection occurs at a Golden Age country estate rather than in the City, *London's financial district. Financiers also figure in some of Agatha *Christie's stories of the detection exploits of Hercules *Poirot, but again their occupation and their work environment remain beyond the scope of narration, mentioned only to explain the characters' wealth and social position or the circumstances that produce motives for someone wishing them dead.

A partial exception to the practice of using banking and finance as a secondary narrative element is to be found in the novels of Emma *Lathen, whose sleuth, John Putnam *Thatcher, is senior vice president of Sloan Guaranty Trust. Thatcher's cases develop naturally out of inquiries undertaken to protect the interests of "the third largest bank in the world," with head offices on Wall Street in *New York City and branches in twenty-four countries. Actually, though, Thatcher's investigations go so far afield: Geographically they take him to Tokyo, Zurich, and London. In regard to business, he is less often engaged by crimes related to banking itself than by areas of business financed by the bank—areas as varied as fast food franchising, carpet imports, and ice hockey. Although Thatcher's success in detection is convincingly shown as arising out of his skill as a banker—his eye for the sort of anomaly or discrepancy that make the prudent lender suspicious—his creators evidently share the feelings of other authors that the banking milieu has decided limitations for narrative action and *suspense.

The closest rival to Lathen in the use of a banker as a series detective is the British writer David Williams. His hero, Mark Treasure, vice chairman of a firm of merchant bankers in the City of London, also becomes involved in cases as a result of his banking responsibilities. Williams describes the financial issues lucidly, but they seldom prove to be the cornerstone of a plot.

For illustration of the rare use of finance as sum and; substance of *thriller fiction, Paul E. Erdman provides the exhibits. In The Billion Dollar Sure Thing (1973, The Billion Dollar Killing) Erdman—who was educated at the Georgetown University School of Foreign Service, holds a Ph.D. in Economics, and has himself been a banker—leads his readers through a complex and clearly explained plot of international finance, in which the world created by banking becomes the direct subject of both narrative action and suspense. Erdman continued his saga of Swiss banking in The Silver Bears (1975).

Publishers' lists of nonfiction abound with books about finance, investment, and the stock and bonds market, but even in the present period of niche marketing, publishers and their authors do not see crimes in finance or banking giving serious competition to tales of *murder occurring in more accessible environments. Because it cannot be due to lack of interest on the part of the public, the scarcity of fictional crime in the world of finance seems to be a case of narrative need triumphing over contemporary importance.

[See also Briberg; Extortion.]

—Sarah Caudwell

BARNARD, ROBERT, (1936), British author of *detective novels and literary criticism. An Oxford-educated academic, Robert Barnard taught English at universities in Australia and Norway before returning to his home country in 1983. His first novel, *Death of an Old Goat* (1974) and his seventh, *Death in a Cold Climate* (1980), have Australian and Norwegian *settings, respectively, while many of his other books draw on his knowledge of politics, opera, and literary history. His *A Talent to Deceive: An Appreciation of Agatha Christie* (rev. ed. 1990) includes a perceptive analysis of *Christie's strategies of deception, and Barnard's depth of understanding of the genre and experience as a crossword compiler make it unsurprising that ingenious plotting is one of his hallmarks. The formal constraints of the short story suit his gifts; *Death of a Salesperson* (1989; *Death of a Salesperson and Other Untimely Exits*) is a strong collection. Barnard regards himself primarily as an entertainer, and his flair for comedy and distaste for pretension are evident in much of his work. He does not consistently employ a series detective, although Perry Trethowan and Charlie Peace are policemen who appear in several of his novels. His more darkly psychological novels, notably *Out of the Blackout* (1985), *A City of Strangers* (1990), and *A Scandal in Belgravia* (1991), are compelling and suggest that this versatile writer may yet extend his range even further. Barnard has also written historical novels under the pseudonym Bernard Bastable, including a series that features Wolfgang Amadeus Mozart as an amateur detective.

• Robert Barnard, "Growing up to Crime," in *Colloquium on Crime: Eleven Renowned Mystery Writers Discuss Their Work,* ed. Robin W. Winks (1986). John L. Breen, "Robert Barnard," in *St. James Guide to Crime and Mystery Writers,* 4th ed., ed. Jay P. Pederson (1996).

—Martin Edwards

BASEBALL MILIEU. *See* Sports Milieu.

BAXT, GEORGE (b. 1923), American author, creator of three popular detective series. In his first published novel, *A Queer Kind of Death* (1966), Baxt introduced Pharoah Love, an African American, irrepressibly gay New York homicide detective who follows his case through the byways of the homosexual world. This series continued with *Swing Low, Sweet Harriet* (1967) and *Topsy and Evil* (1968), which introduced still another *African American sleuth, Satan Stagg. Baxt set aside the well-received saga of Love for twenty-six years and then revived it with two additional works published in quick succes-

sion: *A Queer Kind of Love* (1994) and *A Queer Kind of Umbrella* (1995). In these later books, Love follows crime into a wider venue, but the earlier tone of irony and *satire continues.

The year after he started the Pharoah Love series, Baxt began his second sequence of novels with *A Parade of Cockeyed Creatures; or, Did Someone Murder Our Wandering Boy?* (1967), featuring Sylvia Plotkin, an author, and Max Van Larsen, another improbable New York *police detective. The relationship between Sylvia and Max is one of unconsummated and unstated love, but the cachet of their series lies in the carnival atmosphere of their section of Greenwich Village, peopled by zany characters with a penchant for zingers and a gift for falling into strange *plots, including the case of a thirty-six-year-old disappearance in *"I!" Said the Demon!* (1969). *Satan Is a Woman* (1987) marks another entry in this series.

In 1984 Baxt undertook his third distinctive series with *The Dorothy Parker Murder Case,* a rewrite of celebrity history. That formula continues in *The Alfred Hitchcock Murder Case* (1986) and *The Tallulah Bankhead Murder Case* (1987). Baxt has also authored nonseries novels, at least nine screenplays, and short stories usually published in *Ellery Queen's Mystery Magazine*.

[See also Couples: Sleuth Couples; Gay Characters and Perspectives.]

• Frankie Y. Bailey, *Out of the Woodpile: Black Characters in Crime and Detective Fiction* (1991).   —John M. Reilly

Beck, Martin. The main character of ten *police procedurals written between 1965 and 1975 by Sweden's Maj *Sjöwall and Per Wahlöö, Martin Beck is a Stockholm policeman who eventually rises to become head of the National Homicide Squad. Born in 1923, Beck is portrayed as the son of a lorry driver. He becomes a patrolman in 1944, then studies crime investigation at the police academy and joins the Stockholm CID. in 1951. The same year, he meets and marries Inga. They have two children, but the marriage goes downhill over the years and ends in divorce. Beck eventually meets a new woman (in every sense of the word), Rhea Nielson.

The stories about Beck and his colleagues, particularly the early ones, are fiercely realistic descriptions of crime and detection, yet Beck is also an idealized character, a model investigator, and a truly good cop. He keeps his grievances to himself and consequently suffers from a chronic bad stomach. Though loyal and strictly professional, he is increasingly aware of the deteriorating spirit inside his organization, and at a turning point of his career, almost loses his life in a Christ-like attempt to atone for his colleagues' sins.

Sjöwall and Wahlöö conceived their series as a whole, a ten-part "Novel of a Crime" of Balzacian scope, the crime in question being the betrayal of socialist ideals by the Social Democrat government. The criticism becomes more outspoken as the series progresses, but the authors' attitudes are expressed less by Beck than by his friend, the left-wing hedonist Lennart Kollberg, and by the fierce-tempered, well-dressed giant detective Gunvald Larsson.

[*See also* Europe, Crime and Mystery Writing in Continental: Nordic Countries; Police Detective.]

—Nils Nordberg

Beef, Sergeant. A series character created by Rupert Croft-Cooke writing as Leo *Bruce, the working-class Sergeant Beef is a stolid village policeman and an obvious contrast to the aristocratic sleuths and methodical inspectors of the day. Fond of darts, beer, and plain food, he is identifiable by his untidy ginger mustache and cockney speech. In his investigations Beef relies on doggedness and skepticism, interviewing relentlessly and recording all in a large notebook. When he is not promoted to *Scotland Yard after two successful cases, he resigns to become a *private detective. His cases are chronicled by the prim Lionel (sometimes Stuart) Townsend. Beef consistently reproaches Townsend for failing to make him famous, or at least as well known as other sleuths; Townsend in turn laments the poor material with which he has to work. The comic byplay between detective and chronicler that frames each case may reflect the author's disappointment with the course of his own literary career.

[*See also* Country Constable; Humor; Police Detective; Sidekicks and Sleuthing Teams.]

—Susan Oleksiw

BELLOC LOWNDES, MARIE ADELAIDE (1868–1947), British writer. Sister of the Roman Catholic historian and poet Hilaire Belloc, Marie Belloc was educated in convent school and, like her brother, lived for a time in France. She married F. S. Lowndes, a member of the staff of the London *Times*. Under the name Mrs. Belloc Lowndes, she earned a place in the literary history of the crime and mystery genre because of her imaginative analysis of the Jack the Ripper murder in her novel *The Lodger* (1912). That novel is both a skillful treatment of psychology and an early illustration of the *inverted detective story in which the killer is known from the start. *The Lodger* keeps readers attending closely to the story that gives away its solution by a dramatic rendering of the subjective experience of those in the house who wonder what their lodger is up to.

Belloc Lowndes published many other books, many of which feature female protagonists, predictive dreams, elements of the occult, and incidences of poisoning, placing them in the category of sensational crime writing. Her stories about Hercules Popeau are more direct contributions to detection fiction.

—John M. Reilly

BENSON, MILDRED WIRT. See Keene, Carolyn.

BENTLEY, E(DMUND) C(LERIHEW) (1875–1956), British journalist, biographer, and detective novelist who wrote during the heyday of the Golden Age of the *detective novel. He was educated at St. Paul's School, London, and at Merton College, *Oxford. Called to the bar in 1902, he later served as leader (i.e., editorial) writer (1912–34) and chief literary critic (1940–47) for the *Daily Telegraph*. Bentley is the author of two *detective novels, *Trent's Last Case* (1913, *The Woman in Black*) and, with H. Warner Allen, *Trent's Own Case* (1936); a collection of stories, *Trent Intervenes* (1938); and a mild *thriller, *Elephant's Work: An Enigma* (1950; *The Chill*). Among his other works are four volumes of light verse, starting with *Biography for Beginners* (1905), written in a verse form that he invented, the clerihew.

Bentley's reputation as a detective novelist rests on *Trent's Last Case*. This book, written in his spare time as an entry for a contest, is now considered to be one of the great examples of the *Golden Age form. The novel's chief innovation was the introduction of a fallible *sleuth. Bentley himself noted that he wrote the novel as a reaction against what he saw as artificial eccentricities and extreme seriousness in Arthur Conan *Doyle's Sherlock *Holmes. Bentley also was influenced by Émile *Gaboriau's *L' Affair Lerouge* (1866; The Widow Lerouge), a novel turning on the mistaken conclusions of a Great Detective in which Gaboriau concludes that "one's senses proved nothing."

Bentley also collaborated with other mystery writers on a roundtable book, *The Scoop and Behind the Screen* (1983). He edited works by Damon Runyon, and an anthology, *The Second Century of Detective Stories* (1938). Other works include *A Biography of Hester Dowden; Medium and Psychic Investigator* (1951) and *Those Days: An Autobiography* (1940).

[*See also* Conventions of the Genre; Pastiche.]

—LeRoy L. Panek

BERKELEY, ANTHONY, pseudonym of Anthony Berkeley Cox (1893–1971), British author of *detective novels and psychological crime fiction who also wrote as Francis Iles and A. Monmouth Platts. Cox began his literary career as a journalist known for his humor before introducing the inquisitive *amateur detective Roger Sheringham in his first detective novel, *The Layton Court Mystery* (1925), which offered a *locked room mystery. This book was at first published anonymously, as was *The Wychford Poisoning Case* (1926), a reworking of the Florence Maybrick case. Thereafter Cox made use of his forenames alone for the Sheringham novels, as well as for a number of nonseries books.

Berkeley had a flair for confounding the reader's expectations, although sometimes at the cost of anticlimax, as in *Top Storey Murder* (1931; *Top Story Murder*) and *The Silk Stocking Murders* (1928). In *Panic Party* (1934; *Mr. Pidgeon's Island*), the far from infallible Sheringham guessed correctly but did not attempt to bring the culprit to justice. "The Avenging Chance" (in *The World's Best 100 Detective Stories*, 2nd ed. Eugene Thwig, 1929) is a clever Sheringham short story which Berkeley turned, with characteristic *ingenuity, into *The Poisoned Chocolate Case* (1929), in which the Crimes Circle propounded a range of solutions to a *murder mystery. Sheringham's theory, correct in the short story, was this time debunked; the amateur sleuth who came up with the truth proved to be Ambrose Chitterwick, a mild little man who took a leading role in *The Piccadilly Murder* (1929). The Crimes Circle resembled in some respects the *Detection Club, which Berkeley helped to found; he contributed to several of the club's publications, notably the round-robin detective novel *The Floating Admiral* (1931).

In his preface to *The Wychford Poisoning Case*, Berkeley explained that he was trying to write a "psychological detective story." His dedication to *The Second Shot* (1930) reiterated the view that in detective stories of the future the element of *puzzle "will no doubt remain, but it will become a puzzle of character rather than a puzzle of time, place, motive, and opportunity."

Berkeley's experiments were not always successful, and some of them seem unsophisticated today, but he played a key part in the development of the genre. His first two novels as Francis Iles, *Malice Aforethought* (1931) and *Before the Fact* (1932), are notable examples of the *inverted detective story. Their main interest lies in the description of the murderer's behavior, rather than in his unmasking, yet they still offer *plot twists as ingenious as those of any conventional *whodunit. *Before the Fact* was filmed by Alfred Hitchcock as *Suspicion*, but with a very different ending. Both books had a long-term influence upon the development of crime fiction, but Iles published only one more novel, *As for the Woman* (1939). After starting to write and review as Iles, Cox soon lost interest in Sheringham, and the last three books he wrote as Berkeley were nonseries. Of these, critics agree that by far the best is *Trial and Error* (1937), again featuring Chitterwick, which in its description of Lawrence Todhunter's misadventures while trying to commit an altruistic murder displays to the full Berkeley's gifts of wit and originality.

[*See also* Golden Age Traditions: The British Golden Age Tradition.]

• William Bradley Strickland, "Anthony Berkeley Cox," in *Twelve Englishmen of Mystery*, ed. Earl F. Bargainnier (1984). Julian Symons, *Bloody Murder: From the Detective Story to the Crime Novel: A History*, 3d ed. (1992).

—Martin Edwards

BIGGERS, EARL DERR (1884–1933), American author and creator of Charlie *Chan. Born in Warren, Ohio, and educated at Harvard, Biggers began his writing career as a humor columnist for the Boston *Traveler*. Promoted to drama critic, he was fired for writing excessively scathing negative notices. Turning to the stage, he wrote an unsuccessful play, *If You're Only Human* (1912), before achieving major success with his first novel, *Seven Keys to Baldpate* (1913). A farcical mystery about a writer who holes up in an allegedly haunted inn to finish a story, *Baldpate* was adapted for the stage by George M. Cohan and subsequently filmed several times. Biggers, whose fictional impulses to pen humorously observed romance and gentle *satire seemed perfectly in tune with the tastes and requirements of his time, followed by other romantic mystery melodramas, *Love Insurance* (1914) and *The Agony Column* (1916), and several more plays.

Moving west to Pasadena, California, for health reasons, Biggers wrote for motion pictures. He made his major contribution to mystery fiction with the introduction of one of the great fictional detectives,

Charlie Chan of the Honolulu police, a character both lovable and formidable, whose image was intended to counter the sinister Chinese villains found in the works of writers like Sax *Rohmer, creator of *Fu Manchu. Ironically, Chan has himself come to be considered an ethnic stereotype, more because of the *film adaptations than Biggers's original novels. Chan's first case, *The House Without a Key* (1925), was followed by *The Chinese Parrot* (1926), *Behind That Curtain* (1928), *The Black Camel* (1929), *Charlie Chan Carries On* (1930), and *Keeper of the Keys* (1932). Though the early Chan books did not offer models of fair play, by the last book in the series Biggers had been influenced by such American Golden Age writers as S. S. *Van Dine and Ellery *Queen to place more emphasis on the generous planting of *clues. As a result of the immediate success of Chan, Biggers devoted most of his subsequent literary energies to the character, producing only one more nonChan book, the romantic novella *Fifty Candles* (1926), before his death from heart disease. The collection *Earl Derr Biggers Tells Ten Stories* (1933) was published posthumously.

[*See also* Ethnicity; Ethnic Sleuth.]

• Howard Haycraft, *Murder for Pleasure: The Life and Times of the Detective Story* (1941). Henry Kratz, "Earl Derr Biggers," in *Critical Survey of Mystery and Detective Fiction: Authors*, ed. Frank N. Magill (1988).

—Jon L. Breen

BLACKMAIL. *See* Extortion.

Black Mask. Though by no means the first magazine to publish exclusively detective stories, *Black Mask* was the finest and most influential of the many detective and mystery *pulp magazines. In its 31 years, the magazine had 340 issues and published approximately 2,500 stories by 640 authors, completely revitalizing a moribund literary genre and establishing certain literary formulas and genre conventions that remain in effect today.

The *Black Mask* was created by H. L. Mencken and George Jean Nathan as an attempt at saving the *Smart Set*, in financial trouble because its intended "cleverness" had failed to attract the readership or advertising necessary to make that magazine self-supporting. Approximately $500 was invested in the creation of the magazine, whose first issue is dated April 1920; Mencken and Nathan filled its pages with rejects from the *Smart Set* and, rumor has it, wrote some of the more dreadful pieces themselves. That the magazine proved reasonably popular from the beginning rather annoyed Mencken, who in April 1920 wrote to his friends that "our new louse, the Black Mask, seems to be a success. . . . The thing has burdened both me and Nathan with disagreeable work." In another letter he added that "The Black Mask is a lousy magazine—all detective stories. I hear that Woodrow [Wilson] reads it." Mencken and Nathan sold the magazine in November 1920 for $12,500 and had nothing further to do with it.

The first issues of *Black Mask* were edited by Miss F. M. Osborne and were subtitled "An Illustrated Magazine of Detective Mystery, Adventure, Romance, and Spiritualism." The stories she published were undistinguished, written in the style of the *Smart Set* by authors with no experience writing mystery fiction. In October 1922 George Sutton became editor, remaining until March 1924; the most notable events of his tenure were the appearance of series characters and the early appearances of writers who would later achieve fame. Dashiell *Hammett published his first story, under the name of Peter Collinson, in the issue of December 1922; in addition, the "Ku Klux Klan" issue of 1 June 1923, memorialized the Klan's activities and coincidentally marked the debut of Carroll John *Daly's enormously popular *hard-boiled detective Race *Williams; Erle Stanley *Gardner, Eustace Hale Ball, Ray Cummings, and J. Paul Suter also appeared in issues edited by Sutton. Philip C. Cody succeeded Sutton as editor in April 1924, lasting until October 1926; more series characters appeared, and the magazine's circulation grew, but Hammett, unable to get his pay raised to a penny a word, left and went into advertising.

Although he had no prior editorial experience, World War I veteran Joseph Thompson Shaw ("Captain Shaw") took charge of *Black Mask* in November 1926 and made immediate changes; the first issue under his aegis was subtitled "Western, DETECTIVE, and Adventure Stories," and in 1927 he shortened the magazine's name to *Black Mask*. He lured Hammett back and reawakened the interests of the writers whose careers had begun under previous editors. Shaw remained editor for ten years, during which time the magazine was completely redesigned, noted pulp artists providing the covers and illustrating the contents. He won a stable of writers by raising the payment rates to as high as six cents a word, arranged for book contracts, promoted the books in his editorials, and worked with Warner Brothers Studios to film the stories published in his magazine. In addition to Hammett, the roster of writers appearing under Shaw included Carroll John Daly, Lester Dent, Erle Stanley Gardner, Raymond *Chandler, Raoul Whitfield, Frederick Nebel, Horace McCoy, Dwight Babcock, and George Harmon *Coxe.

Shaw was fired in November 1936 over a salary dispute and replaced by Miss Fanny Ellsworth, who remained as editor until April 1940. Although she published early works by such writers as Cornell *Woolrich, Donald Wandrei, Wyatt Blassingame, Frank Gruber, and Steve Fisher, there was little innovation during her tenure. In early 1940, Popular Publications, Inc., bought the magazine, replacing Ellsworth with Kenneth S. White; he remained until November 1948, publishing works by Cleve F. Adams, D'Arcy L. Champion, Merle Constiner, William Campbell *Gault, and John D. *MacDonald, and an occasional atypical piece, such as Curt Siodmak's science fictional *Donovan's Brain* (1943). World War II hit the magazine hard. It became bimonthly, was printed on cheaper paper, and relied increasingly on reprints and materials published under such house names as "David Crewe"; circulation declined accordingly. No editor was listed on the issues published from January 1949 until its quiet death in July 1951, and the material published during those years is unmemorable. Sporadic attempts have been made to restart the magazine, and the name is currently used by an annual paperback series.

In *Black Mask* the best fiction was fast-moving and often violent, set in mean streets, dark alleys, and seedy dives and featured lower-class yet ethical detectives who were capable of hard-drinking and thinking, and were equally unafraid of using *violence in order to close a case or to achieve a measure of *justice. The altered focus on the characters and problems inherent in solving a crime marked the creation of a new and uniquely American form of fiction, the *hard-boiled detective story, and by popularizing it, *Black Mask* helped to establish the careers of virtually all of the hard-boiled fiction writers of the first half of the twentieth century.

[See also Conventions of the Genre: Hard-Boiled Conventions; Fiction Noir; Formula: Plot; Hard-Boiled Fiction; Hard-Boiled Sleuth; Mean Streets Milieu.]

• Joseph T. Shaw. *The Hard-Boiled Omnibus* (1946). E. R. Hagemann, *A Comprehensive Index to* Black Mask, *1920–1951, with Brief Annotations, Preface, and Editorial Apparatus* (1982). Michael L. Cook, ed., *Mystery, Detective, and Espionage Magazines* (1983). Michael L. Cook and Stephen T. Miller, *Mystery, Detective, and Espionage Fiction: A Checklist of Fiction in U.S. Pulp Magazines, 1915–1974* (1988).

—Richard Bleiler

BLACK MASK SCHOOL. The *Black Mask* school of detective fiction takes its name from *Black Mask* magazine and generally features a hard-boiled style of writing. Prior to Carroll John *Daly's story "Three-Gun Terry," which appeared in 1922, the *pulp magazine's detective fiction tended to feature *amateur detectives. Daly, and the wide popularity of his somewhat later but more influential professional detective Race *Williams, rang a new and harsher note in American crime fiction and set the course for what would become the *Black Mask* school of detective writing.

Daly's stories and those by writers following him generally take place in a grimly unromantic *urban milieu and emphasize fast action, *violence, interesting and interested ladies, mean streets, and meaner villains. Williams's fists and guns are for sale and are always aimed against clearly defined evildoers. The detective, streetwise and shifty, often operates outside the law to attain *justice as he defines it. Fittingly, the narrative style broke with genteel prose as it tended to be terse, wisecracking, gritty, and to make unapologetic use of current slang and underworld jargon.

Appearing in *Black Mask* only a few issues after Daly, Dashiell *Hammett's *Continental Op yarns brought a less exaggerated and more realistic toughness to counter the heightened violence and frenetic action of Williams. Unlike the virile and quick-fisted Williams, the Continental Op is short, almost forty, and overweight; in the *Black Mask* stories, he keeps his emotions under control in the interests of being an effective operative. As the employee of an established detective agency, he demonstrates the professionalism and tenacity that Hammett himself learned as a Pinkerton agent, and his adventures are told with the narrative directness and convincing detail of documented cases. The resultant realism gave readers a sense of understated immediacy that was thought of as American and modern rather than British or romantic.

But despite his differences from Williams, the Op is clearly of the *Black Mask* school. Violence is a tool he uses to get information and confessions, and he finds satisfaction in roughing up a criminal as well as excitement in the danger of being roughed up himself. Moreover, in the short stories, the narratives are essentially pursuits involving danger, escape, and surprise, rather than intricate *puzzles designed to challenge the reader.

When, in 1926, *Black Mask* came under the editorship of Joseph Thompson Shaw, the characteristics of the hard-boiled style were formalized into an editorial code. "Cap" Shaw viewed his magazine as a leader both in schooling American writers and in establishing a revolutionary direction for the detective story. Among the goals he urged on his contributors were simplicity in language and plausibility in *plot. He also insisted that action—violent or otherwise—must grow out of character. In these fiats, Shaw was expressing some of the truisms of American realism as it had developed under the leadership of William Dean Howells around the turn of the century and as those truisms were being interpreted and explored by such contemporary writers as Ernest Hemingway and Frank O'Hara.

Shaw's most famous contributor was Raymond *Chandler who began publishing in *Black Mask* in 1933, three years before the editor left the magazine. Although Chandler's wide influence on the mystery genre came after the demise of the *Black Mask* school, many of the fundamentals of Chandler's style can be attributed to Shaw's tutelage as well as to the influence of Hammett. In addition to strong and effective characterization and a crisp directness in language, Chandler developed the epigrammatic simile into a highly effective descriptive technique that combined a sardonic worldview with almost metaphysical wit: "[S]pring rustl[es] in the air, like a paper bag blowing along a concrete walk." Growing out of the terse *Black Mask* style, it was a technique that became an often overused hallmark of hard-boiled fiction.

Also making his debut toward the end of Shaw's editorship was George Harmon *Coxe, who began publishing in 1932. His action and prose style were fast moving and pared down, but the emphasis on violence was lessened as Coxe made use of more intricate plots.

Other notable mystery writers who made their early appearances in *Black Mask* include Erle Stanley *Gardner, Frank Gruber, and Cornell *Woolrich. In its forty years of publication, *Black Mask* developed into the leading vehicle for detective fiction in America during the *Great Depression, and the influence of its most talented writers, guided by Shaw, has been felt not only in the hard-boiled tradition of American detective fiction but in other literatures throughout the world.

[*See also* Characterization; Mean Streets Milieu; Realism, Conventions of; Voice: Hard-boiled Voice; Voice: Wisecracking Voice.]

• Geoffrey O'Brien, *Hard-Boiled America* (1981).

—Rex Burns

BLACK SHEEP. *See* Adventurer and Adventuress; Prodigal, Son/Daughter.

BLAKE, NICHOLAS, pseudonym under which the Irish-born poet Cecil Day-Lewis (1904–72; also known as C. Day Lewis) wrote a series of *detective novels. The son of a Church of Ireland clergyman, Day-Lewis was raised in England and educated at Sherborne and at Wadham College, Oxford, where he became part of the celebrated group of young poets (dubbed "MacSpaunday") whose other members were W. H. Auden, Louis MacNeice, and Stephen Spender. After graduating from Oxford, he found work as a schoolmaster, was active in left-wing politics, and published several poetry collections. Throughout the remainder of his life he pursued several careers simultaneously: poet, translator, critic, broadcaster, and crime writer. Notably, he was professor of poetry at Oxford (1951–56) and, from 1968 until his death, poet laureate.

When Day-Lewis found himself in need of £100 to repair his cottage roof, in the mid-1930s, he promptly wrote a detective novel and thereby marked out an alternative career for himself which continued right up until a year or two before his death. The opening novel of the series written under the pseudonym Nicholas Blake was *A Question of Proof* (1935), set in a boys' preparatory school, and brimful of the kind of insouciance and ingenuity associated with the first Golden Age of the detective novel. It introduces the cool-headed investigator Nigel *Strangeways, whose amiability is not as deeply ingrained as it might seem. Like all classic detectives, Strangeways's purpose is to establish the facts whatever the cost.

The early Blake novels are marked by a distinctly literary flavor and plot-making expertise, as well as being topically left-wing in approach (this is toned down later in response to changes in the world at large, and in the author's own circumstances; his membership in the Communist Party was short-lived). They are very high-spirited and agreeable in tone—apart from Blake's unaccountable tendency to go in for generalizations on the subject of women, as when he remarks that "in the last resort decisions should be made—where women are concerned at least—by the instinct." The author's mastery of the deft *plot is still evident as late as 1959. *The Widow's Cruise* of that year provides a good example of his craftsmanship; though after that, a slight touch of weariness sets in: *The Morning After Death* (1966), set in America, seems insufficiently resourceful; and in the last Blake novel of all, *The Private Wound* (1968; not a Strangeways title), an unresolved ambiguity in the author's attitude deforms the narrative. Interspersed with the Strangeways investigations are a number of out-and-out *thrillers, all enjoyable, indeed, but more conventional in spirit than the exercises in straightforward detection. Novels like *There's Trouble Brewing* (1937), *Minute for Murder* (1947), and *End of Chapter* (1957)—a classic example of a novel set in the *publishing milieu—are among the greatest pleasures of the genre.

[*See also* Allusion, Literary; Golden Age Forms: Golden Age Novel.]   —Patricia Craig

BLIND DETECTIVE. *See* Disability, Sleuth with a.

BLOCK, LAWRENCE (b. 1938), versatile American novelist, short-story writer, and writing teacher. Born in Buffalo, New York, Block initially wrote *paperbacks and magazine tales in the tough tradition, but most of his series characters established his reputation as a humorist. Examples of such characters include insomniac spy Evan Tanner beginning with the novel *The Spy Who Couldn't Sleep* (1966); Leo Haig, the would-be Nero *Wolfe of two parody-pastiches written under the pseudonym Chip Harrison, *Make Out with Murder* (1974; UK: *Five Little Rich Girls*, as Block, 1984) and *The Topless Tulip Caper* (1975); and professional burglar Bernie Rhodenbarr in *Burglars Can't Be Choosers* (1977) and sequels. The cases of unlicensed *New York *private eye Matt Scudder are in a much darker vein. The first three—*In the Midst of Death* (1976), *The Sins of the Fathers* (1976), and *Time to Murder and Create* (1977)—were overlooked paperback originals, but the hardcover cases, beginning with *A Stab in the Dark* (1981) and including the Edgar-winning *A Dance at the Slaughterhouse* (1991), are among the most honored products of the private-eye renaissance, combining classical plotting and a seemingly effortless style with a rare depth of character and emotional resonance. Block's own experiences with *alcohol and alcoholism inspired him to portray Scudder as a sleuth who also triumphs over the problem.

[*See also* Antihero; Characterization; Humor; Spy Fiction; Theft.]

• Lawrence Block, "Lawrence Block," in *Contemporary Authors Autobiography Series* 11 (1990). Lawrence Block and Ernie Bulow, *After Hours: Conversations with Lawrence Block* (1995).   —Jon L. Breen

BLOOD-AND-THUNDER FICTION. Closely related to the *Gothic novel of the late eighteenth century, blood-and-thunder fiction features malignantly motivated villains seeking to possess the hearts and souls of characters made vulnerable by their youth, gender, and penniless condition. The events of these stories, occurring in *settings distant from the workaday world, limn the obsessive behavior of these predatory characters whose deceptive exploitation of their victims' emotions work a psychological *violence never far from physical consummation. Making few concessions to verisimilitude, the blood-and-thunder narratives function as psychic dramas abstracted from the ordinary world of secondary contingencies, generating their *suspense by sketching the attenuated assault upon the ego of its prey by a relentless will to domination.

Critics explain the Gothic novel as it appeared in Great Britain in works like Ann Radcliffe's *The Mysteries of Udolpho* (1975) and Matthew Lewis's *The Monk* (1796) in terms of the haunting aftermath of medieval *religion and culture, mysteries unsubdued by the Protestant Reformation. For American works such as Charles Brockden Brown's *Wieland* (1778), the general explanation of origin refers to the artist's recognition of undercurrents of irrationality in the Age of Enlightenment. In either case, the critical analysis indicates that the unworldliness of Gothic fiction—the characters allegorically typed as good and *evil, the eerie and extraordinary settings—signifies that its actual locale is the deep recesses of the mind.

A similar explanation may be advanced for the blood-and-thunder kin of the Gothic novel. The recently recovered text of *A Modern Mephistopheles; or, The Fatal Love Chase;* (*ca.* 1866; published in 1995 as *A Long Fatal Love Chase*) by Louisa May Alcott serves to illustrate the traits of the school. The novel opens with young Rosamond's exclamation that she could gladly sell her soul to Satan in exchange for a year of freedom from the stultifying confines of life in the isolated home of her grandfather. Without missing a beat, the novel brings into the scene Philip Tempest, who is addressed by Rosamond's grandfather as Satan and whose appearance is identical to the portrait of Mephistopheles hanging in the hallway. Tempest then seizes Rosamond's affections, conceals a previous marriage, and pursues Rosamond through sites on the Mediterranean coast. Sexual desire on the part of both Rosamond and Tempest is an unstated theme in their relationship, but the true sensation of their story is to be found in Tempest's pornographic drive to subjugate Rosamond's being, to possess her completely.

That Tempest fails in his design is due to Rosamond's mental resilience. She is only eighteen years old, and her upbringing has limited her social experience, but she has a core of integrity and self-regard that Alcott presents as innate. This core makes her the match of "Satan," and shows, too, that the elemental structure of blood-and-thunder fiction presented the opportunity to make the case for an advanced guard of feminism.

Blood-and-thunder fiction often lacks a detective, and shows little concern to create the credibly empirical world that has become a convention of crime and mystery writing. Founded as it is, however, on representation of a landscape where criminal motive seeks vulnerable prey, the connection of blood-and-thunder fiction to the crime and mystery genre is firm and sure.

[*See also* Menacing Characters; Sex and Sexuality; Villains and Villainy.]

• Ralph Harper, *The World of the Thriller* (1969). Jerry Palmer, *Thrillers: Genesis and Structure of a Popular Genre* (1979).   —John M. Reilly

BLUESTOCKING SLEUTH. "Bluestocking," a term sometimes used derisively for women engaged in literary pursuits, was coined in the eighteenth century in reference to literary gatherings in *London at which the guests eschewed "full dress" and men wore blue worsted stockings instead of the customary black silk. The women who organized such soirées came to be known as Blue Stockingers or Blue Stocking Ladies. As a label designating a particular type of fictional female detective, the word "bluestocking" is used when the character in question is herself in some manner "bookish," often performing her amateur sleuthing in a *setting congenial to either literature or scholarship. "Bluestocking" can also imply "unworldly," and is sometimes used in tandem with "tomboy," another mildly derisive term signifying a noticeable lack of traditional femininity. A famous example of this convergence is the character Jo March in Louisa May Alcott's *Little Women* (1868–69). But, with regard to mystery fiction, the important attribute of bluestocking *sleuths is that it is, above all, their intellects that guide them. In addition like tomboys, they are stubbornly active and energetic when it comes to unraveling *clues and following a case to its conclusion.

Probably the genre's best-known example of the bluestocking type is Dorothy L. *Sayers's Harriet *Vane, who makes her first appearance in *Strong Poison* (1930)—the fifth novel featuring the debonair sleuth Lord Peter *Wimsey. A detective novelist by profession and herself a murder suspect in *Strong Poison* Vane is at center stage in a pair of books, *Have His Carcase* (1932) and *Gaudy Night* (1935). The latter novel is literally a convention of bluestockings, for it is set at Vane's old college, Shrewsbury—a lightly disguised version of Somerville College, Oxford—Sayers's own alma mater, where the annual convocation, or "gaudy," is taking place. Although Vane's investigations into a malicious letter-writing campaign and episodes of mischievous vandalism plaguing the close-knit Shrewsbury community are in the end undertaken with Wimsey acting as consultant, he is unavailable to her throughout much of the story's unfolding. No stranger herself to the volatile imbalance between emotions and intellect that lies at the heart of the college disturbances, Vane responds to the complex situation with the mix of empathy, intuition, and heartfelt concern. Vane's success proves that the bluestocking detective is very like her less erudite sleuthing sisters in all her most fundamental reactions and tactics, and that her tendency perhaps to overanalyze any given course of action can in fact be an added strength helping lead to an acceptable and humane resolution.

Another important bluestocking detective is Amanda *Cross's Professor Kate *Fansler, a member of the English faculty on a large New York City campus, whose debut case was *In the Last Analysis* (1964). The Fansler novels echo themes found in Sayers (who was, as Cross has testified, one of her major influences), for Kate Fansler, like Vane, is prideful and intellectually set apart from the average woman. Yet Fansler, too, is a woman who also readily allows herself to take risks in the name of intellectual curiosity and who often finds herself functioning as a source of steadiness in the midst of chaos when *murder intrudes into her *academic milieu.

Elizabeth Peters has created her own versions of the bluestocking detective three times over. Peters's characters Vicky Bliss (*Borrower of the Night*, 1973), Jacqueline Kirby (*The Seventh Sinner*, 1972), and especially Amelia Peabody (*Crocodile on the Sandbank*, 1975) all qualify as bluestockings because it is their confidence in their own learning that fuels their forthright independence; in turn, it is this quality which enables them to act as puzzle solvers and amateur agents of *justice.

Historically, the *spinster sleuth has always been far more common than the bluestocking detective (who may or may not be unmarried). Examples of bluestocking sleuths from the past are surprisingly rare. One could try to squeeze Mignon G. *Eberhart's Susan Dare (*The Cases of Susan Dare*, 1934) into the pigeonhole, since she, like Vane, makes her living as a author of mystery fiction. But in fact, Susan Dare is simply an example of a plucky "regular" girl whose adventures are marked by no "bookish" flavor. Lucy Pym, in Josephine *Tey's *Miss Pym Disposes* (1946), is also a writer, and her foray into detection takes place at a women's college, but there her resemblance with Vane ends, for the contagious joy Sayers takes in such things as the quote-capping duels between Vane and Wimsey, and in the scholarly sanctuary that Shrewsbury provides for its female fellows, is entirely missing.

[See also Academic Sleuth; Females and Feminists; Letters and Written Messages.]

• Michele Slung, ed., *Crime on Her Mind: Fifteen Stories of Female Sleuths from the Victorian Era to the Forties* (1975).

—Michele Slung

Bonaparte, Napoleon. Detective-Inspector Napoleon "Bony" Bonaparte, the creation of expatriate English author Arthur W. *Upfield, appears in twenty-nine of Upfield's thirty-four books and in numerous short stories. Bony is based on Tracker Leon Wood, a man whom Upfield met twice in his wanderings through Australia. Half British and half Aboriginal, Bony is in his early to middle forties. Like Herman Melville's Queequeg before him, Bony benefits from his mixture of races. He is described in *Sands of Windee* (1931) as "the citadel within which warred the native Australian and the pioneering, thrusting Britisher . . . a little superior to the general run of men in that in him were combined most of the virtues of both races and extraordinarily few of the vices." Five feet ten inches tall, he is slight of frame, and "was never handsome." Bony is married to "half-caste" Marie, who appears only as a reference point, and has three sons, all college graduates and headed toward success in life.

A man of multiple capabilities, Bony can train the wildest horses, endure great physical strain and pain, and be a savage antagonist or gentle advisor; but his greatest skill lies in tracking. Among a nation of aboriginals noted for their ability to read tracks, Bony is preeminent. Though a relentless pursuer of outlaws, Bony is gentle with people, especially young women of both races. Although he is well known throughout Australia, Bony is often the victim of discrimination, especially by young women, and is often called "Nigger." By his author he is properly called "The Spirit of

Australia," since he possesses great resilience and humanitarian spirit (such traits are frequently discussed in articles in the *Bony Bulletin*, edited by Philip T. Asdell and devoted exclusively to discussion of Upfield and Bony). To a world that knew little of the Australian Aborigine, Bony represents a fair and unprejudiced picture, though treated with what his author felt was the truth about his race. Bony was portrayed in a 1972 Australian television series. However, the character has been repudiated at Australia's aboriginal university, Monash University, for what is claimed to be an unsympathetic picture of the aboriginal people.

[*See also* Australia, Crime and Mystery Writing in; Pathfinder Fiction; Prejudice.]

• Ray B. Browne, "The Frontier Heroism of Arthur W. Upfield," *Clues* 7 (Spring/Summer 1985): 127–45.———, *The Spirit of Australia: The Crime Fiction of Arthur W. Upfield* (1988). Jessica Hawkes, *Follow My Dust: A Biography of Arthur Upfield* (1957). William A. S. Sarjeant, "The Great Australian Detective," *Armchair Detective* 12, no. 2 (1979): 99–105.   —Ray B. Browne

Bond, James, hero of a series of eleven novels, one novella, one short story collection, and several uncollected shorts written by Ian *Fleming. More crime fighter than espionage agent, as an agent in the British secret service and commander in the Royal Navy Volunteer Reserve (RNVR), Bond thwarts *murder, gem smuggling, the robbery of Fort Knox, nuclear extortion, and a plan to wage germ warfare, among other crimes. The *plots are varied, but the usual story line has Bond seducing the master criminal's exotically named woman companion and then killing the larger-than-life villain in a satisfyingly bizarre manner.

Fleming describes Bond as looking like the American popular composer Hoagy Carmichael, but a scar on his cheek adds a note of cruelty to his face. His "license to kill," a deft use of firearms, the frequent physical torture he endures, his encounters with beautiful women with broad-pleated skirts and unvarnished nails, and the number of brand-name products—soaps, perfumes, autos, and guns among them—proliferating through the novels gave critics a three-word recipe for the series' success: sex, sadism, and snobbery. After Fleming's death, Bond's adventures continued in books penned by John Gardner.

The Bond books form the basis of a popular film series that has flourished for more than three decades; most of the films, however, bear only superficial resemblance to Fleming's novels. Several actors have portrayed Bond on screen, but the first of these, Sean Connery, is by common consent regarded as the definitive 007.

[*See also* Adventurer and Adventuress; Femme Fatale; Sex and Sexuality; Spy Fiction.]

• Kingsley Amis, *The James Bond Dossier* (1965). Andrew Lycett, *Ian Fleming* (1996).   —Dana Bisbee

"Bony." *See* Bonaparte, Napoleon; Upfield, Arthur William.

BOOK CLUBS. Selling books through club memberships was introduced in the American market in the 1920s and in Britain in the 1930s. Mystery and detective fiction was distributed through clubs almost from their beginning. After the establishment in 1926 of the Book of the Month Club and the Literary Guild, both the Detective Story Club and the Crime Club made their appearance in 1928. The Detective Story Club's first selection, *The Cobra Candlestick* (1928) by Elsa Barker, was announced in the 3 November 1928 issue of *Publishers Weekly*. Members of the club received a publication, *Secret Orders*, with articles and information about the recommended books. The Detective Story Club was purchased by the Crime Club in 1930.

The Crime Club was never truly a book club in the traditional sense of selling books through the mail. Doubleday, Doran began the club to extend the sales of mystery and detective fiction by signing up subscribers through booksellers. The poet Ogden Nash served as the first editor, and four books were published each month. A committee of critics and writers chose one book each month as the club selection. This book was delivered to subscribing club members through bookstores. The first Crime Club selection, *The Desert Moon Mystery* by Kay Cleaver Strahan, was distributed in April 1928.

The Crime Club was involved in a variety of other activities that also promoted detective fiction. It produced a newsletter (*Crime Club News*), offered prizes, organized contests, and cosponsored a radio program from 1931 to 1936 to feature its books. The Crime Club evolved into a major publisher of mystery and detective fiction. In 1992, it was replaced with the imprint Perfect Crime, a joint venture of Doubleday and Bantam. In England, Collins operated a similar detective and mystery publishing line under the *Collins Crime Club name.

Book clubs had a slower start in Great Britain, due in part to the Net Book Agreement, originally negotiated between publishers and booksellers in the early 1900s. Under the agreement, publishers fixed the price of a book; discounting was prohibited, and booksellers were required to charge customers the cover price. Part of the advantage of book clubs is their discount pricing. In 1937, Foyle's bookstore in London sought to reach new and different buyers through book clubs and started six specialty clubs, a few years later adding the Thriller Book Club to sell mystery and detective fiction through the mail.

In 1942, another attempt to sell mysteries through the mail in the United States was initiated by the Detective Book Club. It offered members three-in-one volumes containing full reprints of previously published novels. The first volume, sent out in April, included *The Case of the Empty Tin* by Erle Stanley *Gardner; *Evil Under the Sun* by Agatha *Christie; and *A Pinch of Poison* by Frances and Richard Lockridge.

Unicorn Mystery Book Club entered the competition in 1945 by offering four novels in one volume. In 1948 Doubleday's Literary Guild decided to launch a new specialty club. Under the direction of Howard Haycraft, the Mystery Guild entered the market with extensive resources. It paid well for selections, advertised extensively, and offered famous authors. The introductory books for the club were *Ten Days Wonder* (1948), by Ellery *Queen, and *And Be a Villain* (1948), by Rex *Stout. For four years, until Unicorn folded in 1952, the market supported three mystery book clubs. The Mystery Guild and the Detective Book Club survived and continue to operate.

A variety of clubs and subscription services were started in the 1970s and 1980s, but most of them had short lives. Ellery Queen's Mystery Club began in the 1970s and published hardcover anthologies of short stories. This club was purchased by the Detective Book Club in 1978 and discontinued in 1983. Masterpieces of Mystery Library produced twenty short story anthologies sold by subscription between 1977 and 1979. In 1976, Mystery Library attempted to sell subscriptions to a series of classic mystery novels, with new introductions and supplementary material. They produced twelve volumes before their demise. Canada's Harlequin also tried to enter mystery publishing with Raven House Mystery Book Club in 1981, hoping to entice mystery fans into buying four numbered paperback books per month. Books were sold by subscription and on the newsstand. The line was discontinued within a year. The Mysterious Press Book Club, operated by Book of the Month Club, lasted from 1985 to 1992.

In England, a second mystery book club was established in 1972. Book Club Associates, which had been formed in the 1960s by W. H. Smith and Doubleday, inaugurated a British version of Mystery Guild. In the late 1980s the club became the Mystery and Thriller Guild, and the original Thriller Club operated by Foyle's bookshop disappeared. Book Club Associates is now partially owned by the German company Bertelsmann, which also owns Literary Guild and its family of book clubs.

Book clubs have played an important role in the distribution of mystery and detective fiction. Readers have benefitted from the advice of experts in selecting quality works in the genre. Books have been promoted in book club newsletters and readers who have not had easy access to bookstores have been able to order books through the mail. This role in distribution is currently being challenged by the growth in bookstore chains, superstores, and a growing number of mystery bookstores offering catalogs and mail order services.

• Michael L. Cook, *Murder by Mail: Inside the Mystery Book Clubs, With Complete Checklist*, rev. ed. (1983).

—Judy L. Solberg

BOOKSTORES, SPECIALIZED. The first bookstore devoted exclusively to selling mysteries was opened on June 1972, by Dilys Winn; Murder Ink was located on Manhattan's Upper West Side. It was followed shortly by Ruth Windfeldt's Scene of the Crime in Sherman Oaks, California (1975, now closed), Bruce Taylor's San Francisco Mystery Bookstore (1978, originally Murder Inc.), and Otto Penzler's Mysterious Bookshop in midtown Manhattan (1979). By 1983 there were approximately thirty mystery book-

stores across the United States, and in 1999 there were approximately 120 with more opening every month. Several retail stores—such as Tom and Enid Schantz's Rue Morgue in Boulder, Colorado (1980)—originally started life as mystery mail-order businesses in the early 1970s.

Although the United States has by far the most mystery bookstores, there are notable stores in other countries: Murder One and Crime Store in London; Gaslight Books of Woden, Australia; Sleuth of Baker Street in Toronto; Die Wendetreppe in Frankfurt; and Libreria Del Giallo of Milan.

The relationship of this hardy band of entrepreneurs to the swelling popularity of mysteries is complex. The huge popularity of certain mystery writers is not the leading indicator of the health of small independent bookstores. The large chain bookstores can and do regularly undercut their small competitors with substantial discounts on bestselling titles.

While reduced prices offered by the chain stores are an advantage to readers, specialty bookstores attract customers by holding titles on their shelves for longer periods and by stocking small press publications that chains may be unwilling to carry. Moreover, a typical mystery bookstore offers a trained and helpful staff that is intimately familiar with a wide-ranging genre. These stores attempt to emphasize customer service in a variety of ways. They may offer comfortable chairs, chatty newsletters and catalogs; provide special ordering, book searches and out-of-print and rare book want lists for collectors, and host special events such as mystery reading groups, author signings, readings, and teas. Many mystery bookstores offer ordering online, and there are some mystery bookstores that exist only online. In addition, many booksellers participate in the various mystery conventions, where they cultivate relationships with writers, editors, and readers.

The effect that an enthusiastic and well-read bookseller can have on a new writer's career cannot be overestimated. The word of mouth on Sue Grafton and Tony Hillerman, for example, started in the mystery bookstores, not in the media or the large chain stores. Savvy editors make use of this resource not only for talent scouting but for input on packaging, marketing, and sales potential.

Depth of stock is a major strength of these bookstores. There is also a particular emphasis on new writers and first novels that is partially—although certainly not entirely—due to the strong collector's market. Supplying collectors is a forte of many mystery bookstores as well as the numerous mystery mail-order businesses. This interest has been both encouraged and catered to by knowledgeable booksellers in the mystery genre. Most stores feature a mix of new titles and older used, out-of-print and collectable books in both hardcover and paperback.

The Independent Mystery Booksellers Association was formed in 1992. Guided first by Barbara Peters at The Poisoned Pen in Scottsdale, Arizona and then Jim Huang of Deadly Passions Bookshop in Kalamazoo, Michigan, the IMBA has successfully lobbied publishers for better service, set up bookselling forums for members, and generally begun to address the concerns faced by small specialized bookstores.

• Kathy Daniel et al., "The Armchair Detective Mystery Bookseller Survey," *Armchair Detective* 25, no. 4 (fall 1992): 475–89. A searchable list of mystery booksellers may be found at Mystery Net <www.mysterynet.com>.

—Kate Stine

BOUCHER, ANTHONY, pseudonym of William Anthony Parker White (1911–1968), American mystery writer and influential critic. Although his novels were considered "modest triumphs," Boucher was best known as a critic, editor, and anthologist. From 1951 to 1968, he wrote the popular "Criminals at Large" column for the *New York Times Book Review*. At the same time, he reviewed fantasy and *science fiction for the *New York Herald Tribune Book Review*.

The Case of the Seven of Calvary (1937), Boucher's first *detective novel, sets the stage for the six that follow. Like them, it has fair-play *puzzle plot in the tradition of the work of John Dickson *Carr and Ellery *Queen, favoring complex *clues and dry humor. The protagonist is Dr. John Ashwin, Professor of Sanskrit at the University of California. Although Ashwin never appears in any of the later novels, Boucher does use Irish private detective Fergus O'Breen in four of them: *The Case of the Crumpled Knave* (1939), *The Case of the Baker Street Irregulars* (1940; *Blood on Baker Street*), *The Case of the Solid Key* (1941), and *The Case of the Seven Sneezes* (1942). Under the pseudonym Theo Durrant, Boucher, with others, published *The Marble Forest* (1951, *The Big Fear*). Under the pseudonym H. H. Holmes he published *Nine Times Nine* (1940) and *Rocket to the Morgue* (1942), both featuring series character Sister Ursula. His mystery short stories, the best of which appear in *Exeunt Murderers* (1983), are highly regarded, especially those featuring Nick Noble, a former policeman and alcoholic. He also published two other short story collections: *Far and Away: Eleven Fantasy and Science-Fiction Stories* (1953) and *The Compleat Werewolf and Other Stories of Fantasy and Science Fiction* (1969).

Anthony Boucher was a true Renaissance man. In addition to novels, short stories, and radio plays, he edited eight anthologies of crime stories and two anthologies of *science fiction. The best of his numerous reviews were published in *Multiplying Villainies: Selected Mystery Criticism, 1942–1968* (1973). He also contributed frequently to *Opera News*, founded the Golden Voices program for Pacific Radio and hosted it for twenty years, served a term as president of *Mystery Writers of America, translated mysteries from French, Spanish, and Portuguese, and regularly indulged his passion for sports and poker.

Boucher was a three-time recipient of the Mystery Writers of America's Edgar Allan Poe Award for nonfiction. It is for his nonfiction that he is best remembered—those chatty, urbane, and unfailingly polite reviews in which he championed the literary merit of the mystery story. Quoting William *Shakespeare, he once referred to good detective stories as "the abstracts and brief chronicles of the time," pointing out

that they are invaluable records of the times they mirror. His pioneer efforts to gain recognition for the art of mystery writing are celebrated in an annual convention of authors and fans known as the Bouchercon, at which the awards known as Anthonys are presented.

[*See also* Awards: American Awards; Criticism, Literary.]

• "Anthony Boucher Dies on Coast; Mystery Story Writer and Critic," *New York Times*, 1 May 1968: 47. R. E. Briney, "Anthony Boucher," in *Twentieth Century Crime and Mystery writers*, 2nd ed., John M. Reilly (1985): 90–91. Isaac Asimov, "Anthony Boucher," in *I. Asimov: A Memoir* (1994).

—Thomas Whissen

BOW STREET RUNNERS. *See* Memoirs, Early Detective and Police; Police History: History of British Policing.

BOY DETECTIVE. *See* Juvenile Sleuths: Boy Sleuth.

BRADDON, MARY ELIZABETH (1835–1915), British author, a leading writer of the lurid *sensation novels that shocked Victorian moralists in the 1860s and later. Her own life caused her to question the hypocrisy of conventional morality. Her father, a solicitor, deserted the family when Braddon was four years old. In 1857, when she was twenty-two, Braddon went on the stage under an assumed name to support her mother and herself. In 1860, a wealthy admirer provided her with a means of support so that she could write, but she soon cohabited with John Maxwell, a London publisher of periodicals whose wife had been confined to a Dublin asylum. Braddon helped him to raise his five children and bore him five more, two of whom became novelists. Braddon married Maxwell in 1874, after the death of his wife.

Although Braddon also edited magazines, produced more than seventy novels, and wrote drama and poetry, her 1862 novel *Lady Audley's Secret* remains her best-known work. It concerns *arson, bigamy, child desertion, disguised identity, insanity, and *murder among the genteel classes. Such ingredients were the staples of a prolific output that earned her the sobriquet Queen of the Circulating Libraries.

Lady Audley's Secret was one of the earliest novels to feature an *amateur detective. Braddon's sleuth, Robert Audley, displays persistence, close observation, and inductive reasoning to unravel tangled *clues that point to his aunt's crimes. In this and other of her early novels, Braddon constructed mysteries around incident and focused on the techniques of detection. Later, she became more interested in characterization. In *The Fatal Three* (1888), regarded by her biographer Robert Lee Wolff as her best novel, the mystery is spun around the psychology of the characters.

Braddon also created a professional detective, John Faunce, who appears in *Rough Justice* (1898) and *His Darling Sin* (1899). Like other early creators of series sleuths, she endowed hers with a memorable habit—in Faunce's case, the reading of French novels. She was herself a Francophile and influenced by Balzac, Flaubert, and Zola.

[*See also* Suspense; Thriller: Psychological Thriller.]

• Robert Lee Wolff, *Sensational Victorian: The Life and Fiction of Mary Elizabeth Braddon* (1979).

—Michael Steed

Bradley, Mrs. Adela Beatrice Lestrange, a "little, thin, black-eyed, witch-like being" is the benign but alarming center of Gladys *Mitchell's *detective novels written over a span of more than fifty years. Medically qualified, she serves as a psychiatric adviser to the *Home Office. Her adherence to Freudian interpretations originally invoked police animosity, but her methods were justified by success. She also has an assistant who is married to a *CID detective; Bradley herself is related to most of England's chief constables.

Her "saurian smile" initially alarms, but her "beautiful, low, contralto voice" seduces all save the evil. She finds astonishing empathy with the young. Perhaps her open-minded approach wins their trust: She accepts the occult, ancient Greek mysticism, and revelatory dreams, and is prepared to believe in the Loch Ness Monster.

Her three marriages have left her tolerant of men but never easily deceived. Once involved in defending her son on a *murder charge, she is herself prepared to overlook murders or even commit one herself. Professionally, she encounters incest, gender-crossing, *impersonation, and *murders of—and by—children. None of it ever fazes her, although cruelty and malice provoke her anger. Her domestic staff, especially her chauffeur, serve her for decades, despite a daily round which might involve sheltering suspected criminals or fighting off Bradley's would-be attackers. Acknowledged by her young assistant as an Amazonian equal, she is capable herself in armed combat.

[*See also* Conventions of the Genre: Traditional Conventions.]

—K. D. Prince

BRAMAH, ERNEST (1868–1942), English author, the creator of Max *Carrados. Many details of his life are uncertain. Born Ernest Bramah Smith near Manchester, England, he spent time as a journalist on the magazine *Today* and as editor of the *Minister* and briefly was a farmer, a career he relates in *English Farming and Why I Turned It Up* (1894).

Bramah, who dropped the family name Smith from his author's byline, began a literary career with short stories concerning a Chinese storyteller published as *The Wallet of Kai Lung* (1900). The chinoiserie of these stories was evidently appealing enough to allow Bramah to continue the series through seven additional volumes, the last, *Kai Lung Beneath the Mulberry Tree*, appearing in 1940. Bramah's reputation in popular fiction rests, however, on the achievement of the three collections and one novel relating the cases of Carrados, who is both the genre's most compelling example of a blind sleuth and a successful example of the *Great Detective.

[*See also* Disability, Sleuth with a.]

—John M. Reilly

BRAND, CHRISTIANNA (1907–1988), British author, one of the last in the Golden Age tradition. She was born in the Far East, where her motherless first years were lonely and unhappy. This changed when she was sent to a convent school in England. After various short-lived and ill-paid jobs during the 1930s, she turned to writing and made a notably assured debut with *Death in High Heels* (1941), which included a fictional vengeance on one of her supervisors during her hungry years. Popular success came with *Green for Danger* (1945), which was filmed with Alistair Sim as the raffish, shabby, nicotine-stained Inspector Cockrill, her series detective based on her father-in-law.

Brand's high-spiritedness, often noted, should not be allowed to hide the craftsmanlike qualities of her books: They are meticulously planned, written with a sense of style rare in Golden Age writers, and the sympathetic characterization avoids stereotypes and caricatures. The exuberant and stylish *Tour de Force* (1955), with its corrupt and sinister island of San Juan, where the natives speak a bastard Italo-Spanish entirely of Brand's devising, represents her writing at its most sunny and energetic. *Cat and Mouse* (1950) is darker, fruitfully drawing on the traditions of the *Gothic novel. In *Green for Danger* the natural liveliness flourishes in a context of war and random devastation. Her last novel, *The Rose in Darkness* (1979), underappreciated and never published in the United States, displays a brilliant circularity in its plotting and a familiar interest in the self-absorption of the attractive young.

Brand was, like Ngaio *Marsh, a lover of intricate and involved *plots. Only in *Death of Jezebel* (1949) does this militate against the novel, becoming tiresome and unlikely, and destroying character interest. Elsewhere she always retains a light touch, so that her *ingenuity and her exuberance go hand in hand, carrying the reader along. In all her work there is a strong element of the comedy of manners: social gestures, public words and behavior, become indices of generosity or hardness of heart. Though she always emphasized that her aim was to entertain, writing a *whodunit was for her a rigorous intellectual discipline, and when other preoccupations prevented her giving her writing that kind of concentration she preferred to turn to less demanding forms. At the time of her death she was engaged on a crime novel featuring a duchess as detective and a barmaid called Topless among the cast list.

[*See also* Novel of Manners.]

• Robert Barnard, "The *Slightly* Mad, Mad World of Christianna Brand," *Armchair Detective* 19, no. 3 (summer 1986).

—Robert Barnard

Brandstetter, Dave, fictional insurance investigator and private detective in Joseph *Hansen's twelve-volume series, starting with *Fadeout* (1970) and ending with *A Country of Old Men: The Last Dave Brandstetter Mystery* (1991). Not only was Brandstetter the first gay protagonist in the genre to reach a large mainstream audience, but he is one of a very few characters in detective fiction to have aged at approximately the same pace as the novels appeared. Thus, when he suffers a fatal seizure in the final novel, he is in his mid-sixties. While Brandstetter's sex life is never a focus of the series, neither is it ignored. After the death of Rod Fleming, his lover of twenty-odd years (before the time of the first novel), Brandstetter meets Cecil Harris, a young African American news reporter, in *The Man Everybody Was Afraid Of* (1978); they establish a relationship in *Gravedigger* (1982) that, though rarely described in physical detail, provides a secondary storyline throughout the remainder of the series.

Hansen insisted that he hoped to destroy stereotypes of homosexual figures in mystery fiction by creating Brandstetter as a thoroughly masculine character who happens to be unabashedly gay. Although there is some *violence in nearly every book, Brandstetter is so sensitive and introspective—a lover of esoteric classical music, intellectually challenging literature, and gourmet cuisine—that he does not really fit into the hard-boiled mode. He is, therefore, a unique individual rather than a type, and has become a model for characters like Michael Nava's gay lawyer-detective, Henry Rios.

Most of Hansen's plots are structured in the pattern of the private-eye genre. In the middle and later novels, Brandstetter is involved in cases that center on socially and politically charged issues such as pornography, ultra-right-wing militias, environmental pollution, and AIDS. He is intensely aware of mortality and loss, a theme that becomes more dominant as the series draws to a close.

[*See also* Gay Characters and Perspectives; Males and the Male Image; Sex and Sexuality.]

—Landon Burns

BRIBERY, the offering or promise of money, property, or something else of value to induce someone to violate accepted standards of behavior, commit an illegal act, or to act against their better interests or will, is an especially versatile form of *corruption around which to plot crime fiction. Since bribery must be kept secret, if it is to have the full effect of deceiving or misleading onlookers about the cause of an action, it presents the possibility of stunning knowledge for a detective probing beneath surface appearances. Because bribery may plausibly follow upon a crime as an act meant to conceal wrongdoing or a criminal, it provides the attractive likelihood of a complex scheme for an author to expose in the final passages of a narrative. Moreover, because bribery introduces stress and the necessity for duplicity into a fictional *plot, it can also become the cause of further crimes.

In the hard-boiled rendition of crime, bribery becomes an element of the general corruption encountered by the *private eye, as in writings of Dashiell *Hammett such as *Red Harvest* (1929) and some of the stories about the *Continental Op, collected in two volumes published in 1945. While the practices of bribery are necessarily concealed until the detective reveals them, they have a public cast from the start, since bribery typically occurs in an institutional *setting—which is to say that the realms where bribery can be a way of doing business are typically political or legal. The journalist's adventure in Tony *Hillerman's *The Fly on the Wall* (1971) occurs in pursuit of information about scandalous and wholesale bribery in government contracts. *Police procedurals may exploit bribery among their crimes, and John Grisham's legal *thrillers work subtle variations on bribery extending from the "buying" of a young lawyer in *The Firm* (1991) to the use of bribery by indirection in *The Runaway Jury* (1996).

[*See also* Extortion.]

• Kelly R. Gordon, *Mystery Fiction and Modern Life* (1998).

—Helaine Razovsky

BROWN, CARTER, best-known of the pseudonyms used by the highly prolific novelist Alan Geoffrey Yates (1923–1985), who was English by birth and became a naturalized Australian citizen in 1948. He also used many pseudonyms, including Sinclair MacKellar, Dennis Sinclair, Paul Valdez, and various forms of his original name. Before he took up full-time writing in 1953, he served in the Royal Navy and worked as a sound recordist and a public relations agent. Yates's more than 270 novels followed models established by such American pulp writers as Robert Leslie Bellem, and his numerous *potboilers would have been perfectly suited for the spicy *pulp magazines. His fiction featured perpetually leering male series characters (Rick Holman, Larry Baker, Danny Boyd, Paul Donavan, Andy Kane, Randy Roberts, Al Wheeler) who during the course of their investigations invariably bedded gorgeous and improbably voluptuous young women. Yates's female series character is Mavis Seidlitz, whose body is as shapely as Mamie van Doren's and whose wit recalls that of Gracie Allen. In all novels, Yates's characters are subordinate to the plots, which in themselves require considerable suspension of disbelief on the part of the reader. In the early 1970s, Yates's work became known for explicit sexual descriptions. Yates was neither unintelligent nor uneducated, and his escapist fiction cannot completely hide the fact that he possessed a very capable mind.

[*See also* Australia: Crime and Mystery Writing in; Escapism.

—Richard Bleiler

Brown, Father, East Anglian Roman Catholic priest and *sleuth created by the British author G. K. *Chesterton and featured in fifty short stories collected in five volumes. The series began in 1911 with *The Innocence of Father Brown*; continued with *The Wisdom of Father Brown* (1914), *The Incredulity of Father Brown* (1926), *The Secret of Father Brown* (1927); and concluded in 1935 with the *Scandal of Father Brown*. The Father Brown stories tend to be conduits through which Chesterton, a Roman Catholic and a political and social traditionalist, communicated his theological and philosophical ideas. Although the plots generally emphasize symbolism rather than realism, they are made brilliant by clever characterization, lyrical writing, and constant wit.

Loosely based on a priest-friend of the author, Father John O'Connor, Father Brown is short, plump, myopic, and ostensibly absent-minded and unworldly. Yet this habitually umbrella-carrying cleric is unshocked by the most grotesque and morbid *murders and other crimes. The stories often involve Chesterton's favorite literary device, the paradox, and are concerned with the perception of the extraordinary within the seemingly most ordinary. This is perhaps best illustrated by the story of "The Invisible Man" (in *The Innocence of Father Brown*), where the criminal is revealed by Brown to be someone disguised as the mailman, a person so regularly seen and so disregarded that he is able to go about his illegal business unnoticed.

Father Brown relies on intuitive detection, psychological insight, and an extraordinary knowledge of theology and moral teaching. If he shares an asset with any other fictional detective, it would be Agatha *Christie's Miss Jane *Marple. Both are at first sight no apparent threat to wrongdoers and neither has any objection to being seen as innocent or naive, since such an image aids them in their work.

Ironically, Chesterton thought the Father Brown stories his least important works, believing them to be mere slingshots compared to the great artillery of his books of Christian philosophy, such as *The Everlasting Man* (1925), or his novels, such as *The Napoleon of Notting Hill* (1904). It is the Father Brown stories, however, that remain the most popular of Chesterton's massive output.

[*See also* Atmosphere; Clerical Milieu; Clerical Sleuth; Reasoning, Types of.]

• Maisie Ward, *Gilbert Keith Chesterton* (1943). Michael Coren, *Gilbert: The Man Who Was G. K. Chesterton* (1989).

—Michael Coren

BROWN, FREDRIC (WILLIAM) (1906–1972), American mystery and *science fiction writer. Brown began life as an office worker, but after one of his stories was accepted for publication when he was thirty, he became a proofreader and then a journalist. After a long apprenticeship writing some 300 stories for *pulp magazines, his *The Fabulous Clipjoint* (1947) won the *Mystery Writers of America Edgar award for best first novel. There followed twenty-two other mysteries, of which the most notable are *Night of the Jabberwock* (1951) and *Knock Three-One-Two* (1959). Brown's virtues at his best were his direct prose, his grip-of-iron storytelling, and his click-into-place *plots. His unique gift was to blend convincingly the highly romantic and the sturdily everyday, as illustrated by the fantastic and ominous title *The Screaming Mimi* (1949), where a doll of that name plays a central part, eventually revealed as a storekeeper's mnemonic for catalogue item SM1.

[*See also* Formula: Plot.]

• Newton Baird, *A Key to Fredric Brown's Wonderland* (1981).

—H. R. F. Keating

BRUCE, LEO, pseudonym of Rupert Croft-Cooke (1903–1979), English author. A prolific writer in his own name, he is now more celebrated for his pseudonymous works, all traditional detective novels written within and gleefully exploiting the *whodunit conventions. Eight books published between 1936 and 1952 feature William Beef, a plebeian provincial police sergeant who turns private investigator; a further twenty-three from 1955 to 1974 concern Carolus Deene, a wealthy history master at a minor public school. Both are outsiders: Beef because of his beery vulgarity, Deene because of a cynical detachment from life. The Beef books are less hidebound and range from a mischievous debut, in which Beef solves a mystery that has defeated Lord Simon Plimsoll, Amer Picon, and Monsignor Smith, to the somber episode that closes his career (apart from a few collected stories). The Deene series is more formulaic, with familiar rituals that lose their freshness only toward the flagging end of a long run. Bruce's level of dexterity is high: He is up to all the tricks and rings the changes on them with verve and daring. He is also consistently amusing, with a wit acknowledged by Noel Coward and a lively sense of his duty to entertain and satisfy the reader.

[*See also* Academic Sleuth; Beef, Sergeant; Ingenuity; Private Detective.]

• Earl F. Bargainnier, "The Self-Conscious Sergeant Beef Novels of Leo Bruce," *Armchair Detective* 18, no. 2 (spring 1985): 154–59.

—B. A. Pike

BUCHAN, JOHN (1875–1940), British author of *thrillers, the most famous of which remains *The Thirty-nine Steps* (1915). His father was a minister of the Free Kirk of Scotland, and both parents were fervent adherents of this severe and puritanical sect. Buchan, in reaction, gave his loyalties to England and the British Empire, serving as a lawyer and as a prominent figure in the worlds of education and politics.

A precocious writer, his first books were affected by the aesthetic movement (his work appeared in the *Yellow Book*), but in 1915, with the outbreak of World War I, he produced *The Thirty-nine Steps*. This blend of the patriotic spy novel and thriller was his first best-seller, and it led to a series of similar books.

The action of *The Thirty-nine Steps* begins in *London but soon shifts to Buchan's native Scotland. It is very much a novel of 1914, especially in dialogue, but the description of Scottish landscape, and of *pursuit and chase, derives from Robert Louis Stevenson's *Kidnapped* (1886). The espionage *plot may have been shaped by Buchan's reading of E. Phillips *Oppenheim; but his feeling for Secret Service work was probably more a response to the Rudyard Kipling of *Kim* (1901) and the stories about Strickland.

Implicitly, Buchan makes his conservative politics strongly felt in his thrillers. His heroes are often professional men, engineers (like Richard Hannay) or lawyers (like Edward Leithen), who take time out from their careers to save the nation. They are so depicted as to suggest to the reader that these are contemporary notables, thinly disguised. Buchan also introduces other social types, for instance the Glasgow grocer Dickson McCunn and the Gorbals slum boys, both of *Huntingtower* (1922), but he shows them following the lead of upper-class adventurers.

An idea often invoked in the thriller is that the crust of civilization, under which lies savagery, is fragile. Clearly this idea is useful to any thriller writer, but especially, as Buchan invokes it, to a conservative. It justifies his heroes in defending society against radicals and liberals, whom they see as a threat.

Although Buchan uses neither police nor *private detectives as his heroes, his influence was felt by his contemporaries writing during the Golden Age of the detective novel. For instance, Agatha *Christie toyed with espionage in her Tommy and Tuppence Beresford stories featuring overtones of the popular Buchan-style cloak and dagger plots.

Perhaps the most common device Buchan employs is to make his protagonist a hunted man, whether the hunters be sent out by a foreign power, as in The Thirty-nine Steps, or by a Napoleon of crime, as in The Three Hostages (1924). In this regard, his thrillers offer a certain parallel with the contemporary American private eye stories of Raymond *Chandler and his followers.

Buchan wrote fourteen thrillers between 1915 and 1941. By 1960 The Thirty-nine Steps had sold 355,000 copies, Greenmantle 368,000, Huntingtower 216,000, and so on. He also maintained a notable career in public office, climaxing when he became governor-general of Canada. He wrote other, more serious books, notably biographies, in which the same philosophy can be seen.

[See also Adventurer and Adventuress; Adventure Story; Conservative vs. Radical Worldview: Conservative Worldview; Heroism.]

• John Buchan, Memory Hold the Door (1940). Anna Buchan, Unforgettable, Unforgotten (1945). Janet Adam Smith, A Biography of John Buchan (1965). William Buchan, John Buchan (1982).
—Martin Green

BUSTED FLUSH, THE. See Addresses and Abodes, Famous.

"BUTLER DID IT, THE." The phrase "the butler did it" is a cliché widely used in jest by people who are not fans of detective fiction. In fact, there are surprisingly few *detective novels in which the butler is actually guilty of a crime. Far more common, however, are novels in which the butler is accused by household members or their friends, who refuse to believe one of themselves capable of *murder. Examples of this situation exist in Agatha *Christie's The Murder of Roger Ackroyd (1926), in which Dr. Sheppard casts suspicion on Ackyrod's butler, Parker, whose criminal past renders him vulnerable, and in Ngaio *Marsh's The Man Lay Dead (1934), in which Vassily's membership in a secret Russian brotherhood and subsequent disappearance lead almost everyone to accuse him. This pattern has prevailed long after the Golden Age. K. K. Beck employed the device in Murder in the Mummy Case (1986), set in 1928, which features a Chinese butler, Charles Chan, who leads a double life as a servant by day and owner of a *San Francisco speakeasy by night. Thus, whether the butler did it or

not, it is clear that it has become customary to accuse him. Because he usually is not guilty, the phrase has passed into lighthearted general parlance.

In speculating about the origin of the concept, one is led inevitably to examine the *country house milieu of the Golden Age, when butlers were in bountiful supply. One prominent example occurs in Arthur Conan *Doyle's "The Musgrave Ritual" (in The Memoirs of Sherlock Holmes, 1894) when Holmes deciphers the code of the Musgrave family's coming-of-age ceremony and discovers the body of the butler, Brunton, draped over a chest that had contained the family treasure. In this story the butler, guilty of betrayal and *theft, paid with his life for his perfidy.

Dorothy L. *Sayers used the device in "The Poisoned Dow '08" in Hangman's Holiday (1933) and in Gaudy Night (1935), in which a female servant at an Oxford college attempts murder for vengeance but does not succeed. Sayers's contemporary, Patricia *Wentworth, wrote two novels featuring criminal butlers: The Case Is Closed (1937) and The Ivory Dagger (1951), in which the butler, Marsham, stabs his master, who has caught him feathering his nest and is about to discharge him. Georgette *Heyer's Why Shoot a Butler? (1933) seems to convert the butler from *villain to *victim, but it emerges that he was killed because he was a blackmailer. This situation is similar to that in the Doyle story where the butler is a culprit who provokes his own death.

Philip *MacDonald's R.I.P. (1933; Menace) broadens the canvas beyond personal crime to embrace *revenge for military negligence during World War I when seven hundred men were killed by a mine blast despite a warning that the enemy had planted the charge. Rudolph Bastion, who was in the hospital when his company was destroyed, vowed to avenge their deaths on the four people he held responsible for the disaster. Five years later, having assumed a false identity, Bastion is hired as a butler by one of his intended victims and proceeds to seek vengeance. Victor L. Whitechurch's The Crime at Diana's Pool (1927) also deals with murder committed because of past political treachery.

Interest in villainous butlers survived in Britain beyond World War II and into the 1980s. In 1949 Freeman Wills *Crofts's Silence for the Murderer presents a butler who is both entrepreneur and inventor. Desirous of collecting a legacy promised him in his employer's *will, Boone creates a small bomb that simulates a pistol shot when exploded. Having shot his master, Sir Roland Chatterton, with a silenced gun, Boone then lights the fuse on his self-destroying bomb, leaves the crime scene, and provides himself with an *alibi by engaging in conversation when the bomb goes off. Some dozen years later Michael *Innes wrote A Connoisseur's Case (1962; The Crabtree Affair), in which the butler, Hollywood, cooperated with a distant cousin of the family in replacing valuable pieces of antique furniture at Scroop House with modern replicas and selling the originals for profit. At the end of the decade, Catherine Aird penned The Complete Steel (1969; The Stately Home Murder), in which a butler in a stately home engages in a scheme to steal paintings and replace them with forgeries. Michael Allen's *Spence at Marlby Manor* (1982) portrays a thoroughly modern butler, Tanner, who poisons his mistress's companion because she had threatened to reveal his compulsive gambling as well as kickbacks from suppliers.

Some American authors have also written books in which the butler did it. In Mary Roberts *Rinehart's *The Door* (1930), the butler works with an accomplice to commit murder. Links with the criminal underworld put an unmistakable American stamp on three other novels of the 1930s. In Jack R. Crawford's *The Philosopher's Murder Case* (1931), gangsters mistake a butler (who incidentally is a blackmailer) for another character and shoot him dead. *Organized crime makes its appearance in Clyde B. Clason's *The Purple Parrot* (1937) as a *red herring involving illicit transactions by a bootlegger. The murder itself is a straightforward affair committed by the butler Baines to cover his theft of a purple ceramic parrot whose eyes are rubies. In Gregory Dean's *Murder on Stilts* (1939), the butler, Peek, shoots his master after he has gone to bed in an elaborate effort to make the death appear as a locked room suicide.

Because the convention of the guilty butler is celebrated more in the breach than in the observance, readers rarely suspect the butler, the author derives maximum flexibility and surprise from employing him as the *least likely suspect. Because the butler can move about the house in the course of his duties with complete freedom and because he is so taken for granted by the other characters that no one pays attention to him, he makes an ideal culprit. Furthermore, because of the unbridgeable social gulf between master and man, the butler would seem to have no personal involvement with the closed circle of family members. Nonetheless, fictional butlers sometimes do act from the universal motives of revenge, self-protection, and *greed.

[*See also* Class; Closed-World Settings and Open-World Settings; Country House Milieu; Stock Characters.]

—B. J. Rahn

Cadfael, Brother, figure who is central to, and whose adventures are recounted in, novels and short stories written by Edith Mary Pargeter under her well-known pseudonym, Ellis *Peters. Set in twelfth-century Britain, the series—dubbed *The Chronicles of Brother Cadfael*—is set during the time of the war between King Stephen (who reigned from 1135 to 1154) and his cousin the Empress Maud for control of the English throne. The works especially concern the effects of that conflict on the West Midlands. A native Welshman, Cadfael ap Meilyr ap Dafydd serves as Peters's *amateur detective. At age fourteen he left his home in Trefriw, Gwynedd, to serve in the household of an English wool merchant living in Shrewsbury. Years later, after participating in the successful First Crusade (1095–1099) and other adventures abroad, Cadfael returned to England and joined the Benedictine monastery at the Abbey of St. Peter and St. Paul in Shrewsbury, serving as gardener, herbalist, and, occasionally, translator. The mysteries in which he appears develop from the multiple roles served by an abbey. As land and property owner, pilgrimage site, keeper of saints' relics, hospital, and guest hostel, the abbey garners a steady flow of people and information. Cadfael's wide experiences, his keen understanding of human behavior, his unceasing curiosity, his expertise as an herbalist familiar with medicines and poisons, and his dual nature—both of the world and separate from it—allow the monk to solve the mysteries presented to him.

[*See also* Clerical Milieu: The British Clerical Milieu; Clerical Sleuth; Poisons, Unusual; Poisons and Poisoning.]

• Rosemary Herbert, "Ellis Peters," *Publishers Weekly* (9 Aug. 1991). Anita Marissa Vickers, "Ellis Peters (1913–)," in *Great Women Mystery Writers*, ed. Kathleen Gregory Klein (1994).
—Kathryn Alexander

CAIN, JAMES M(ALLAHAN) (1892–1977), American author of *hard-boiled fiction, including short stories and, several *crime novels, notably the tough-guy novel *The Postman Always Rings Twice* (1934). Cain grew up in an *atmosphere of culture in two small towns in Maryland. His father was a teacher at St. John's College in Annapolis and president of Washington College in Chestertown. His mother's singing talent inspired Cain to consider a career as an opera singer; his *Serenade* (1937) and *Career in C Major and Other Stories* (1938) are about opera singers, and music is a major element in many of his novels.

Having taught mathematics and journalism at Washington College and St. John's, Cain pursued a long career in journalism. He benefitted from H. L. Mencken's guidance in Baltimore and, on returning from service in World War I, worked under Walter Lippman in New York. After a stint as assistant to Harold Ross at the *New Yorker*, he wrote filmscripts in Hollywood. Paradoxically, Cain's movie scripts failed, but most of his novels are inherently cinematic and have been made into movies—some more than once. Most of his works are set in California, but his favorite, and one of his finest, was *The Butterfly* (1947), a mystery of progeny, incest, and murder, set in the coalfields of West Virginia.

It was in *Los Angeles that he heard the hard-boiled, first-person voice that made him famous in *The Postman Always Rings Twice*. It is not until the end of this novel that the reader discovers, as in other Cain novels, that the compelling confessional voice that seems to speak aloud is spelled out in a written account. In most of his fiction, mastery of the aggressive American vernacular is the major characteristic of Cain's style. His narrators are average educated Americans who lust for a woman who can be won only by some extraordinary act—usually an act of *violence, in which the woman also plays a key role.

This pattern recurs in Cain's second-most-successful crime novel, *Double Indemnity* (1943; also published in *Three of a Kind*). Here an insurance agent helps his client's wife kill her husband so they can share the insurance and a life of passion. The theme of all Cain's novels is the wish that comes true, with catastrophic consequences. The man wishes to have the woman, the woman wishes to have the money, and the man has the means, a cunning intelligence, know-how, and violence. Forcing the wish to come true, the lovers suffer on what Cain called "the love rack." Usually, the woman betrays the man at the end, as in *Double Indemnity* and *The Magician's Wife* (1965).

The urban criminal *milieu is explored in *Love's Lovely Counterfeit* (1942; also published in *Three of Hearts*), and the inside-dopester details of the *white-collar crime of embezzlement is central to *The Embezzler* (1944; also published in *Three of a Kind*). The four novels of his later years, two of which were published posthumously, are interesting primarily in the different ways they employ familiar Cain elements, including *religion, the lure and power of information, and—a universal interest—food.

Crime, usually murder, plays a role even in novels

like *Serenade, The Moth* (1948), and *Galatea* (1953), all set in Cain's home state, Maryland, and in the two Civil War novels, *Past All Dishonor* (1946) and *Mignon* (1963). *Career in C Major,* a comedy that inspired three movie versions, and *Mildred Pierce* (1941), unusual in having a female protagonist and a third-person narration, lack the crime element. However, the first-person criminal confession is such a distinctive characteristic of Cain's novels that many readers mistakenly think of him as a detective novelist. His only detective narrators are the sheriff in *Sinful Woman* (1948) and the insurance investigator, modeled after Keyes in *Double Indemnity,* in *Jealous Woman* (1950); these were published together in a single volume (*Jealous Woman*) in Britain in 1955.

Compared with the voices and narration of private-eye novelists with whom he was often compared, Dashiell *Hammett and Raymond *Chandler, the diction of Cain's narrators has the pure simplicity of Horace McCoy and of the more literary Hemingway; his plots were more unified and tighter. Cain agreed with the observation that his best work was "pure"—conceived and executed to produce an experience for the reader, rather than to illustrate a moral or to lay out any other thematic trappings. That purity and the stacatto, metallic style of *The Postman Always Rings Twice* so affected Albert Camus that, in a revised version, he adapted it to the first-person narration of *The Stranger* (1942).

[*See also* Antihero; Femme Fatale; Sex and Sexuality; Voice: Hard-boiled Voice.]

• David Madden, *James M. Cain* (1970). Roy Hoopes, *Cain, The Biography of James M. Cain* (1982).

—David Madden

CAMBRIDGE is a market town and the county seat of Cambridgeshire in eastern England where a university was established in the thirteenth century, very shortly after its rival university was founded at Oxford. The university, at which women were not educated until late in the nineteenth century, consists of separate colleges, all but three exclusively for men until the late 1970s, when coeducation was introduced. Conflict between local residents and the university—"town and gown"—was prevalent, but has hardly been exploited as a theme of crime fiction. Indeed, unlike Oxford, Cambridge itself appears in remarkably few mystery novels.

This discrepancy may be due simply to the coincidence that most donnish detective novelists happen to have affiliations to Oxford. However, the crime writer Margaret Yorke, whose own books include several with an Oxford don as detective, postulated in *Murder Ink: The Mystery Reader's Companion* (1977) that Cambridge, being "strong in science," deals with criminological facts, while Oxford, whose *atmosphere induces introspection, inspires crime in fantasy.

The topographical nostalgia which both university towns evoke in their alumni is obvious. Some authors have written novels, as well as read them, at least partly in order to recreate beloved landscapes.

Professor Glyn Daniel, the first of whose two novels appeared in the name of Dilwyn Rees, was himself an undergraduate and later a don at St. John's College. Stationed in India during the Second World War, he dreamt of a precisely detailed Fisher College and the life its members led, in a Cambridge swept "by raw sharp winds which blew from off the dank fens and the grey-cold North Sea." *The Cambridge Murders* (1945) describes with a scholar's accuracy the life and *setting of a Cambridge college. The *amateur detective Sir Richard Cherrington is a typical Cambridge skeptic, unable to make up his mind whether scholarship was just another animal pleasure, like a squirrel's in collecting nuts, or whether in it could be found "something transcending brute nature, something of the spirit—the eternal, unsatisfied quest for truth."

Darkness at Pemberley (1932), one of the few other Cambridge-college detective novels, was the only really unsuccessful book T. H. White (the author of *The Sword in the Stone,* 1937) ever wrote, his fanciful talent being unsuited for the formulaic nature of a *locked room mystery. The university setting is clearly established in the novels of V. C. Clinton-Baddeley, whose series detective, Dr. Davie of the fictitious St. Nicholas College, first appeared in *Death's Bright Dart* (1967).

Of other mysteries set in the university, one may be Arthur Conan *Doyle's "The Adventure of the Three Students" (Strand, June 1904). Sherlock *Holmes has to identity which of three undergraduates has tampered with examination papers; it is one of the rare examples of Holmes not knowing what he was talking about. Whether the fictitious St. Luke's College is in Oxford or Cambridge has been inconclusively debated by Holmes scholars.

More recently, the antifeminism still surviving, hardly disguised, at Cambridge has provoked a polemic subtext in the American writer Nora Kelly's *In the Shadow of King's* (1984). The British feminist Joan Smith has used a Cambridge college, formerly for men only but now coeducational, in *Don't Leave Me This Way* (1990), one of a series featuring the English literature scholar Loretta Lawson. Smith uses the setting to make some trenchant points about the treatment of, and attitude toward, women in British university life. The American writer Elizabeth George makes similar use of Cambridge in *For the Sake of Elena* (1992); the endpapers of the American hardcover edition feature a map of the town, authentic in every detail save for the addition of the fictional St. Stephen's College.

The setting of P. D. *James's *An Unsuitable Job for a Woman* (1972), in which undergraduate life is described, is as much about Cambridge town and countryside as academia; the opportunity is taken to contrast the privileged life of students with that experienced in the outside world by the young woman detective Cordelia *Gray.

Cambridge city is the hiding place of a one-time undergraduate on the run in Jessica Mann's *Funeral Sites* (1981). It is the scene of an early novel by Margery *Allingham, *Police at the Funeral* (1931).

Allingham's intention was to use the setting to emphasize her belief that tradition can stifle natural human impulses and that intellect is less valuable than intelligence. The university does not feature strongly in the book and Allingham's use of the town as a setting is accurate but not evocative.

Unlike Oxford, Cambridge, the place, university, or even object of love, does not come to life, almost as a character in its own right, in crime fiction. Topographical accuracy rather than emotional atmosphere has been most often inspired by this setting.

[See also Academic Milieu; Academic Sleuth; Females and Feminists.]   —Jessica Mann

Campion, Albert. Originally envisioned as a secondary character, Albert Campion arrived somewhat inadvertently as the hero of Margery *Allingham's detective fiction. The intended hero of *The Crime at Black Dudley* (1929; *The Black Dudley Murder*), the first of twenty-one novels in which Campion is featured, was the cerebral and pompous consultant pathologist George Abbershaw. Campion himself was portrayed as possessing a police record as the petty criminal Mornington Dodd (Dodd's file was deleted from later editions.)

In his first appearance, Campion is an uninvited guest at Black Dudley, and his involvement in the house party there is never quite clear. He masks his intelligence with a vacancy of expression and a flippant air that is most pronounced in this and other early novels. Although he is emphatic that he never undertakes anything "sordid or vulgar," he has been hired by the *villains. This does not happen again. In Allingham's next novels, *Mystery Mile* (1930) and *Look to the Lady* (1931; *The Gyrth Chalice Mystery*), his employers are the great and the good. Later, in *Police at the Funeral* (1931), he is on comfortable terms with Inspector Stanislaus Oates and has donned a deerstalker in parody of Sherlock *Holmes. On the other end of the social scale, it is suggested that Campion's sidekick/valet Magersfontein *Lugg has underworld connections.

Although Agatha *Christie later commented that the early Campion seemed so like Dorothy L. *Sayers's Lord Peter *Wimsey that she wondered whether Allingham was a Sayers pen name, Allingham insisted that any resemblance between the two was coincidental. Both were products of the dedicated frivolity of the post–World War I period which also produced P. G. Wodehouse's Bertie Wooster. Allingham viewed Campion, Wimsey, Reggie *Fortune, Hercule *Poirot, and their peers as knights-errant "in fancy dress," displaced heroes in an age which had learned to distrust *heroism.

Campion is most like Wimsey—and least like himself—in Allingham's short stories (e.g., those collected in *Mr Campion and Others*, 1939), many of which were written for the *Strand. Allingham eventually considered these stories to be hackwork, and she became reluctant to use Campion for such purposes.

Campion's aristocratic connections are emphasized in the *Strand* stories and used to tantalize in the early novels. Allingham was interested in the concept of *class and was conscious that she was writing literature of escape in which an appeal to snobbery can provide a popular ingredient. She enjoyed teasing those of her admirers who enquired into the detail of Campion's genealogy and told the novelist Pamela Hansford-Johnson that he "came to the throne"—as King George VI.

The character of Campion changed as social attitudes developed. Although in *The Fashion in Shrouds* (1938) he becomes engaged to Lady Amanda Fitton (who proved to be very popular with readers), much of that novel is written in revulsion at the decadence and human vapidity of the 1930s rich. In Allingham's post–World War II novels much less is made of Campion's upper-class status. She experimented with alternative heroes such as the policeman Charlie Luke in *More Work for the Undertaker* (1948) and received many letters of complaint that she used Campion's Fitton connection so sparingly. In the two Campion novels—*Mr Campion's Farthing* (1969) and *Mr Campion's Falcon* (1971)—written by Allingham's husband, Youngman Carter, Campion is returned to club land.

Campion, "born with the century," aged and changed but resisted his author's efforts to displace him. There has been speculation about "real-life" models for the character, but Allingham claimed him as hers. "As the only life I had to give anybody was my own we grew very close as time went on." Close but not identical. Of creator and creation she added ironically, "As far as I am concerned one is just about as real as the other."

[See also Aristocratic Characters: Aristocratic Sleuth; Escapism; Silly-Ass Sleuth.]

• Margery Allingham, Preface to *The Mysterious Mr Campion* (1963). Margery Allingham, Preface to *Mr Campion's Lady* (1965). B. A. Pike, *Campion's Career: A Study of the Novels of Margery Allingham* (1987). Margery Allingham, "What to Do with an Ageing Detective," in *The Return of Mr Campion*, ed. J. E. Morpurgo (1989). Julia Thorogood, *Margery Allingham: A Biography* (1991).   —Julia Thorogood

CANADA, CRIME AND MYSTERY WRITING IN. Canada is a country for which an enduring national symbol is the policeman. In a country where the federal police force, the *Royal Canadian Mounted Police, has earned a reputation for benevolence and fairness in upholding the law—and an affectionate nickname, the "Mounties"—crime writing has leaned toward positive portrayals of authority. The earliest exemplars of Canadian crime writing depicted the adventures of Mounties, beginning with Gilbert Parker's *Pierre and His People* (1893), written just twenty years after the force was formed.

Those who study the question of law and order in Canadian crime fiction often cite the example of how Canadian authorities responded to the impending Gold Rush in the Yukon. It is significant to note that, in contrast to the neighboring United States, where sheriffs were brought in to tame lawlessness during the California Gold Rush, the Mounties anticipated their Gold Rush and arrived in the Yukon first, where they gained a reputation for helping settlers to survive, rather than exerting force over them. Whereas the American model for the fictional lawman is apt to be a maverick loner who makes decisions for himself, the Canadian Mountie tends to maintain the peace and to follow the letter of the law. In fact, in Canadian crime fiction, the elements of landscape and weather are often just as significant factors for the Mountie to face as are the challenges provided by criminals. This holds true in early twentieth century *adventure stories based on the exploits of real Mounties as well as in more recent fiction by a writer like Ted Wood, whose character solves cases in a mosquito-infested backwater in the company of a canine sidekick.

As was the case in other Western literatures, Canadian crime writing developed from the *sensation novel. Writing in English, novelists James De Mille, Agnes Fleming, and Anna Sadlier dominated the popular Canadian English-reading market for a time. French Canadian crime writing was also heavily influenced by the sensation novels of Georges Boucher de Boucherville's *La tour de Trafalgar* (1835) and Philippe-Ignace-François Aubert de Gaspé's *L'influence d'un livre* (1837). As the nineteenth century came to a close, novels and stories about the Mounties gained their audience. At the same time, Grant Allen anticipated E. W. *Hornung's creation of the *gentleman thief A. J. *Raffles by two years, when Allen created the eponymous rogue in *An African Millionaire: Episodes in the Life of the Illustrious Colonel Clay* (1897).

Early in the twentieth century, Robert Barr created a comic French detective in *The Triumphs of Eugene Valmont* (1906), set in France. Writing as Luke Sharp, he also wrote what may be the first parody of Sherlock *Holmes, "Detective Stories Gone Wrong: The Adventures of Sherlaw Kombs" (*Idler*, May 1892). In *The Adventures of Detective Barney* (1915), Harvey J. O'Higgins gave readers a believable juvenile detective in Barney Cook. O'Higgins also created John Duff who, in *Detective Duff Unravels It* (1929), represents the first serious attempt at psychoanalytical detection.

Some of the most popular crime writers of the 1920s and 1930s were Canadians: Arthur Stringer, Frank L. Packard, and Hulbert Footner. Despite the efforts in the 1940s of writers like Margaret *Millar and Francis Shelley Wees to set crime novels in Canada and feature Canadian detectives, the norm was for Canadians to set their novels outside of Canada. French Canadian writers were determined earlier than those writing in English to follow Continental models but to set their work at home. In the latter half of the twentieth century, French Canadian crime writing fell into three categories: the literary novel that has crime linked to theme, exemplified in Hubert Aquin's *Prochain Épisode* (1965); the *roman policier as represented by Chrystine Brouillet's *Le poison dans l'eau* (1987); and formulaic *paralittérature* including Bob Dutrisac's *Une photo vaut mille morts* (1989).

At the same time, English-language writers in Canada were turning out *police procedurals, *private eye novels, and stories about amateur detection. The Canadian taste for the public eye is satisfied in Eric Wright's Toronto police inspector Charlie Salter and Laurence Gough's Vancouver police officers Jack Willows and Claire Parker. The Canadian private eye is typified by Howard Engel's Benny Cooperman, who is, in his creator's words, "soft-boiled." Female private eyes include Lauren Wright Douglas's Caitlin Reece, an ex-Crown attorney who detects in Victoria, British Columbia, and Tanya Huff's Victory Nelson, an ex-police woman who works in Toronto. *Amateur detectives are most likely women with policeman lovers, like Alison Gordon's sportswriter Kate Henry or Medora Sale's photographer Harriet Jeffries.

Crime writing as a distinctive element within Canadian letters burgeoned sufficiently to warrant the founding of the Crime Writers of Canada in 1981, a time when Canadians were increasingly committed to telling their own stories, set in Canada, to themselves and to an increased international readership.

• Norah Story, ed., *The Oxford Companion to Canadian History and Literature* (1967). Edward McCourt, *The Canadian West in Fiction*, rev. ed. (1970). Margaret Atwood, *Survival. A Thematic Guide to Canadian Literature* (1972). James Hill, *The Northern Novel in Canadian Fiction* (1973). Carl Klinck, ed., *Literary History of Canada. Canadian Literature in English*, 2nd ed. (1976). Keith Walden, *Visions of Order. The Canadian Mounties in Symbol and Myth* (1982).

—David Skene-Melvin

CANON, THE. The sixty published cases of Sherlock *Holmes, written by Arthur Conan *Doyle, comprise a body of work known to fans and scholars as the Canon. Four of the works are novels and fifty-six are short stories.

The first work, *A Study in Scarlet*, was published in *Beeton's Christmas Annual* in 1887 and was first published separately in novel form by Ward, Lock in 1888. This edition was illustrated by the author's father, Charles Doyle, with six black and white drawings. The first American edition was published by the J. B. Lippincott Company in Philadelphia in 1890. *The Sign of the Four; or, the Problem of the Sholtos* was also first published in a magazine, *Lippincott's*, in February 1890, in both America and England. It was first published separately as a novel by Spencer Blackett in 1890 when it was given the title *The Sign of Four*.

Following the publication of these two novels, Doyle decided to write a series of short stories featuring Holmes, beginning with "A Scandal in Bohemia," which was published in the *Strand in July 1891. The first twelve stories were collected in *The Adventures of Sherlock Holmes* (1892). The next series of a dozen stories was collected in *The Memoirs of Sherlock Holmes* (1894).

From August 1901 to April 1902, Doyle's third Holmes novel, *The Hound of the Baskervilles*, was serialized in the *Strand* before it was published in book form in 1902. Following this, Doyle produced thirteen more short stories, collected in *The Return of Sherlock Holmes* (1905). Eight additional stories were collected in *His Last Bow* (1917), some of which were written before Doyle also published his last Holmes novel, *The Valley of Fear*, which was serialized in the *Strand* from September 1914 to May 1915 and was published in book form in 1915. The final collection of Holmes stories, *The Case-Book of Sherlock Holmes*, published in 1927, contains twelve stories.

[*See also* Short Story: The British Crime Short Story.]

• Arthur Conan Doyle, *The Annotated Sherlock Holmes: The Four Novels and the Fifty-six Short Stories Complete*, ed. William S. Baring-Gould (1960).   —Rosemary Herbert

CANONIZATION. Borrowing the ecclesiastical term for a body of law or the list of accepted sacred books, literary historians and critics often confirm that their choices of the most durable, influential, or important writings in a field or genre comprise a canon of standard works. In this respect, crime and mystery writing has a canon equivalent to those advanced by scholars for British drama, American literature, or the Great Books of Western civilization.

Canonization in crime and mystery writing may be said to have begun with the work of Ellery *Queen on detective short stories. Queen began the task with an essay in *101 Years' Entertainment: The Great Detective Stories, 1841–1941* (revised in 1946) and carried to greater length in *The Detective Story: A Bibliography* (1942). Considering strictly the original form of detective fiction as fathered by Edgar Allan *Poe— that is, the short story—and without reference to the detective novel, which Queen describes as "a short story inflated by characterization and description and romantic nonsense," Queen's introductory listing presents stories of "Pure Detection," stories of "Mixed Types," stories of "The Crooks, "Parodies and Pastiches of Holmes," "Pseudo-Real Life Stories," "Secret Service Stories," and "Anthologies." Topically the coverage is comprehensive, but the titles and authors Queen chooses to identify within the categories constitute a canon of works deemed to comprise the history of the form.

Despite claims that they distinguish the "best," canonical lists are not necessarily as brief as a culling of the wheat from the chaff suggests they might be. James Sandoe compiled "A Reader's Guide to Crime" (in *The Art of the Mystery Story*, 1946) that cites 194 titles. Popular success and durability in crime and mystery fiction depends upon a number of forces in the book market. The fact that series of novels with a recurrent sleuth sell well, the fact that there are definable niches that might assure sales and success for fiction stressing *suspense or that appeal to a male or female readership, and the chance that a book receives favorable reviews in major newspapers or is optioned for a film or television—all of these variables and more have their effect.

To complicate the matter, there are varying criteria for inclusion in a canon. Resemblance is one. If Agatha *Christie is indubitably the author of canonical works, a writer touted as a "new" Christie may enter the canon. For some makers of literary history, the works of importance are those that employ innovative *plots, portray distinctively different detectives, or examine an interesting *milieu. Still other critics prefer one of the familiar types—for instance, the *cozy mystery or *hard-boiled fiction—over others, and will naturally judge examples in that type as most worthy. Politics cannot be discounted either, not just the politics of canon making itself but the evident politics of writers, whether liberal, radical, or conservative in outlook.

This complexity makes the listing of the best, most important works as elusive in the crime and mystery genre as it is in other literary fields, reminding us that in its own fashion a canon, like the volumes it includes, is also a work of imagination.

[*See also* Criticism, Literary; History of Crime and Mystery Writing.]   —John M. Reilly

CAPER, a subtype of crime and mystery writing in which the *formula includes fast-moving action perpetrated by specialized thieves who precisely plan and execute often daring heists before making their escapes. Frequently their best-laid plans go awry, and much *suspense ensues as the protagonists are forced to improvise.

Even when narrated by a sidekick, as are some capers, the story is typically told from the criminal *antihero's point of view, extolling the thief's skill and inventiveness. The inverted plot sequence described by R. Austin *Freeman is sometimes employed.

Historically, the caper is an outgrowth of the *gentleman thief tradition, exemplified by E. W. *Hornung's A. J. *Raffles. The epitome of the English gentleman by day, Raffles is a brilliantly successful burglar by night, using his social connections to gain entry to wealthy homes, or confounding *Scotland Yard by robbing seemingly impregnable institutions like the British Museum. Other roguish gentlemen include the title character of Maurice *Leblanc's *Arsène Lupin, Gentleman Cabrioler* (1907; *Arsène Lupin, Gentleman Burglar*, 1910) and Leslie *Charteris's Simon Templar, also known as the Saint. Referred to as the "Robin Hood of Modern Crime," the Saint mostly steals from rich people who are portrayed as odious in short story collections including *Enter the Saint* (1930).

The caper novel takes a violent turn in James Hadley Chase's *No Orchids for Miss Blandish* (1939), where a gang of brutal criminals kidnaps an heiress. Chase combines the criminal point of view with the hard-boiled sensibility to produce something new in crime fiction. Gone is the gentlemanly sparring between master thief and *Scotland Yard detective: Chase depicts bloody shootouts and large body counts as crook and cops fight to the death.

Lionel White is one of the modern masters of the caper novel. *The Big Caper* (1955) features an intricate bank robbery, *The Snatchers* (1953) outlines a precise *kidnapping, and *Operation—Murder* (1956) details a well-executed train robbery. White excels at endowing his capers with realism. *Clean Break* (1955), the story of robbing a racetrack, was made into a classic movie, *The Killing* (1956), by Stanley Kubrick.

The acknowledged leader in contemporary caper novels is Donald Westlake. Early in his writing career he wrote a series of paperback originals as Richard Stark featuring a professional thief named Parker. In books like *The Hunter* (1962), *The Man With the Getaway Face* (1963), and *The Sour Lemon Score* (1969), he chronicles Parker's high-stakes capers: holding up an entire town, robbing an island's gambling casinos. The Stark books share the darkness and violence of Chase's caper novels but add the elements of exactness in the planning and execution of the capers. When Westlake found he could no longer write about the dark and bleak criminal world of Parker, he became one of the best-known writers of the comic caper. In *The Hot Rock* (1970), Westlake created John Dortmunder and his bumbling band of thieves. They steal the same diamond over and over and over again as their perfect plans somehow go awry. Even cleverer is another Dortmunder caper, *Jimmy the Kid* (1974), where the gang commits a kidnapping based on a caper novel by Richard Stark. Westlake continues the high-stakes caper even in these comic heists. In *Castle in the Air* (1980), the Dortmunder gang steals an entire castle.

Several well-known authors have worked in the caper subgenre. Eric Ambler's *The Light of Day* (1962; *Topkapi*) and Michael Crichton's *The Great Train Robbery* are examples by well-known authors who usually work outside the genre. Writing under the pseudonym Brian Coffey, best-selling writer Dean R. Koontz produced three caper novels featuring professional thief Mike Tucker. The middle book of the series, *Surrounded!* (1974), is a classic of *ingenuity and execution in the robbery of a shopping mall. Max Allan Collins, best known for his Dick Tracy, Mike Mist, and Eliot Ness works, wrote a series of seven caper novels with the main character Frank Nolan. The best of these, *Fly Paper* (1981), is about skyjacking. Bill Pronzini's thrilling *Snowbound* (1974) uses high-stakes capers as models when thieves rob an entire town that's cut off by the snowfall in the Sierra Nevada Mountains.

The latest innovation in the caper novel is the linking of the crime with terrorism. One of the first to do this successfully was Richard Jessup in his novel *Threat* (1981), in which terrorists threaten to blow up a skyscraper—twelve years before the World Trade Center bombing. Canadian writer Christopher Hyde develops this theme in his brilliant caper novel, *Maxwell's Train* (1984), about a terrorist plot to steal an Amtrak train carrying $35 million of Federal Reserve cash. Another example is Roderick Thorp's *Nothing Lasts Forever* (1979), which was made into the hit movie *Die Hard!* (1988) where criminals use terrorism as a front for their theft of hundreds of millions of dollars in bearer bonds from a recently completed corporate headquarters.

[See also Humor; Terrorism and the Terrorist Procedural; Theft.]

• John A. Dinan, "The Saint's Boston Caper" *Xenophile* 11 (Mar. 1975): 17–19. Theodore P. Dukeshire, "The Caper Novels of James Hadley Chase," *Armchair Detective* 10, no. 2 (Apr. 1977): 128–29. Lawrence Block, (1982), introduction to *The Mourner*, by Richard Stark. Walter Albert, *Detective and Mystery Fiction: An International Bibliography of Secondary Sources* (1985).
                                                    —George Kelley

Carrados, Max. The creation of Ernest *Bramah, Max Carrados is the genre's most famous blind detective. The author explains in an introduction to the second volume of short stories featuring Carrados the principle of compensation by which a blind person develops unusual sensitivity in his remaining senses. According to the background provided earlier in "The Coin of Dionysius" (*Max Carrados*, 1914) Carrados, who lost his sight in an accident, was born Max Wynn but changed his name as a condition of receiving an independent income from a wealthy American bearing that name. "The Coin of Dionysius" also joins the career of Carrados with that of the solicitor Louis Carlyle, who, approaching Carrados for help in this first exploit, becomes his sidekick for most of the remaining criminal cases.

The first volume of short stories, *Max Carrados*, was selected by Ellery *Queen as one of the ten best collections of mysteries. The basis of Queen's judgment, and the source of audience pleasure, lies with the characterization of Carrados as a witty, sometimes satiric man comfortably in command of circumstances, yet restrained by his author from excessive or self-pitying commentary on his disability.

After the debut volume, the blind detective appeared in two additional collections—*The Eyes of Max Carrados* (1923) and *Max Carrados Mysteries* (1927)—and a single novel, *The Bravo of London* (1934). One additional Carrados story appears in Bramah's *The Specimen Case* (1924).

[See also Disability, Sleuth with; Sidekicks and Sleuthing Teams.]
                                                    —John M. Reilly

CARR, JOHN DICKSON (1906–1977), American author of detective novels and historical crime fiction. He also wrote as Carter Dickson, Carr Dickson, and Roger Fairbairn.

Carr was born in Uniontown, Pennsylvania, the son of Julia and Wooda Nicholas Carr. His eclectic tastes in history and literature grew from happy boyhood hours spent in the vast library of his father, a lawyer and politician. Carr's first detective stories were written in his middle teens at the preparatory Hill School and at Haverford College.

Following the success of his first published *detective novel, *It Walks By Night* (1930), which introduced French Police Magistrate Henri Bencolin, Carr moved to England, where for the next fifteen years he wrote prolifically, averaging four novels a year. His most popular detectives were Dr. Gideon *Fell, a consultant to *Scotland Yard who first appeared in *Hag's Nook* (1933), Sir Henry *Merrivale, a barrister who debuted in *The Plague Court Murders* (1934), and Colonel March, chief of the Department of Queer Complaints, whose short stories were collected in 1940. The latter two detective series were written under the pen name Carter Dickson.

In his mastery of *impossible crimes—he is the undisputed master of the *locked room mystery—

and his love of bizarre characters and highly colored *atmospheres, Carr openly acknowledges the influence of his favorite writer, G. K. *Chesterton, whom he never met. Fell, like Chesterton's Father *Brown and Gabriel Gale, specialized in solving *murders that seem to have been committed through witchcraft and supernatural agencies, but whose solutions were entirely rational. Fell's best adventures, including the dazzling *Three Coffins* (1935); *The Hollow Man*) and *The Crooked Hinge* (1938)—and, indeed, almost all of Carr's work—were infused with a Chestertonian love of fair play, chivalry, and respect for the past. Indeed, Fell's appearance—his wheezing, vast bulk, bandit's mustache, shovel hat and cloak—resembled the rotund and revered Chesterton himself. The Fell series holds a high position among Carr's works, claims historian S. T. Joshi, in their "atmosphere of half-controlled lunacy": "It is as if everything Fell comes into contact with is bent slightly askew; and it is only he, with his self-parodically ponderous utterances, who can set it right again."

During World War II, Carr shuttled back and forth between America and England, writing propaganda programs and a weekly mystery radio series called *Appointment with Fear*. In later years he increasingly devoted his time to historical novels with crime and detection elements. Among these are *The Bride of Newgate* (1950), set in the Napoleonic era; *The Devil in Velvet* (1951)—one of his best selling works—set in 1675 London; *Fire, Burn!* (1957), a chronicle of the early days of Scotland Yard; (1957) and *The Hungry Goblin* (1972), in which author Wilkie *Collins solved a crime in 1869 London. Other projects included two collaborations with Adrian Conan Doyle, youngest son of Arthur Conan Doyle: the official biography of Sir Arthur (1949) and a volume of serious Sherlockian *pastiches, *The Exploits of Sherlock Holmes* (1954). In the early 1950s Doyle wrote a popular CBS radio series of exotic mysteries, *Cabin B-13* (the title story of which was filmed in 1953 under the title *Dangerous Crossing*).

Fantasy is relatively rare in Carr's oeuvre, confined mostly to some of the short stories appearing in *pulp magazines like *Horror Stories*, *Dime Mystery*, and *Detective Tales*, and in the collections *The Department of Queer Complaints*, *The Third Bullet and Other Stories* (1954), and *The Men Who Explained Miracles* (1963). Among the more than seventy novels, only *The Burning Court* (1937)—arguably Carr's greatest work—has a solution involving supernatural elements, although a rational solution is also offered. Significantly, the setting, contemporary Pennsylvania, is solid and detailed. It is only in this kind of realistic setting that fantasy is allowed to intrude; by contrast, the fantastic situations and bizarre settings of the other books—haunted tower rooms, sealed chambers of all descriptions, and a gallery of witches, hangmen, waxworks, and magicians—depend on entirely rational solutions. In that sense, he is the most distinguished successor to the Gothic legacy of Ann Radcliffe.

[*See also* Rules of the Game; Weapons, Unusual Murder; Whodunit.]

• John Dickson Carr, "The Grandest Game in the World," in *The Mystery Writer's Art*, ed. Francis M. Nevins Jr. (1970). Douglas G. Greene, "A Mastery of Miracles: G. K. Chesterton and John Dickson Carr," *Chesterton Review* 10, no. 3 (Aug. 1984): 307–15. S. T. Joshi, *John Dickson Carr: A Critical Study* (1990). Douglas G. Greene (1991), introductions to *Fell and Foul Play* and *Merrivale, March and Murder*. Douglas G. Greene, *John Dickson Carr: The Man Who Explained Miracles* (1995). —John C. Tibbetts

Carter, Nick, fictional *New York detective and master of *disguise, appeared in stories (1886–1936) published by Street & Smith that were written to appeal to boys and their fathers. He solved mysteries by a combination of observation, logic, and stamina with the assistance of Chick Carter (no relation), Patsy Murphy (later referred to as Patsy Garvan), and Ida Jones. His most persistent foe was Doctor Jack Quartz. Trained to be a detective by his father, Nick married Ethel Dalton, who was later murdered by one of his enemies. Nick Carter was created by John Russell Coryell; stories were written by *syndicate authors, most prolific of whom were Frederic Van Rensselaer Dey and Frederick William Davis. Over 700 novelettes and serials appeared in story papers, weekly periodicals, and *pulp magazines. Most of these were collected in paper-covered volumes signed by "Nicholas Carter." Updated versions of the characters appeared on a regular basis in a weekly radio show (1943–55) and a monthly series of paperbacks (1964–90).

[*See also* Juvenile Mystery: Boys' Juvenile Mystery; Radio: The Crime and Mystery Genre on American Radio.]

• J. Randolph Cox, "A Syndicate of Rascals: The Men Behind Nick Carter," *Dime Novel Round-Up* 63 (Feb. 1994): 2–12. —J. Randolph Cox

Castang, Henri. This member of France's Police Judiciaire (nonuniformed detectives) is a fictional detective first presented by Nicolas *Freeling as the rescuer of a kidnapped child in *Dressing of Diamond* (1974). Then living in a canalside flat in a "good, bourgeoise, frightened" district of an obscure town in northeastern France, Castang was class-conscious because of his hard-won route up from being the orphaned ward of a dipsomaniac aunt, and nationality-conscious through his marriage to a defecting Slovak gymnast. His problems were compounded by the *corruption of local politics, as seen in *Castang's City* (1980), domestic cruelty in *What Are the Bugles Blowing For?* (1975), terrorism in *Wolfnight* (1982), and, always, the temptations of his venal bourgeois surroundings.

Throughout, Castang is aware that he has neither the "temperament for excessive prudence nor discretion when in trouble." Even his promotions from his provincial northern town to Paris and to the Brussels headquarters of the European Community are merely expedient moves to get him away from where "he'd been a nuisance." Castang appreciates Humphrey Bogart's hard-boiled screen persona: He too operates in the *mean streets milieu. —K. D. Prince

CATHEDRAL CLOSE MILIEU. As the first Cathedral City to serve as setting for a fictional murder, Cloisterham, in *The Mystery of Edwin Drood* (1870), is the forerunner of many. Having recognized the power of the contrast between the vilest of crimes and the holiest of places, Charles *Dickens exploits it from the novel's opening words, in which John Jasper's "scattered consciousness" attempts to reconcile the spike on the Princess Puffer's bedpost with the tower at Cloisterham. At the end of the first chapter, as Jasper resumes his place in the cathedral, "the intoned words, 'WHEN THE WICKED MAN ———' rise among groins of arches and beams of roofs." The theme is made vividly explicit: In a sacred place, *evil is present.

Among the successors to *Drood*, this theme is more or less standard, implicit by virtue of the setting even where the cathedral is not an integral feature of the narrative. The more accomplished writers take pains to establish the edifice as well as those who serve it, so that, as in life, they may purposefully interact.

The humanity of the clergy is a further fertile theme. Despite their vocation, clergymen are subject to human frailty, vying for preferment, falling into dissension, and even committing *murder.

George A. Birmingham, himself a clergyman, sets *The Hymn Tune Mystery* (1930) in Carminster, where a dreadful discord arises in the cathedral when the organist falls dead across the keyboards. The significance of one of his compositions anticipates certain aspects of *The Nine Tailors* (1934) by Dorothy L. *Sayers.

In H. C. *Bailey's *The Bishop's Crime* (1940), the bishop of Badon wants to sell cathedral treasures and the archdeacon wants to stop him. The cathedral itself is a powerful presence, *fons et origo* of the action. It even brings Reggie *Fortune into the case, when dust from its fabric arouses his interest.

Edmund *Crispin's *Holy Disorders* (1945) takes Gervase *Fen to Tolnbridge, where a tradition of witchcraft appears to be reviving. Death and madness occur within the cathedral: The organist is demented, the precentor murdered. Besides Crispin's characteristic frivolous wit, the narrative achieves a potent sense of defilement.

In *Close Quarters* (1947), the earlier of Michael *Gilbert's Melchester mysteries, anonymous letters and practical joking bedevil the clerical community. When the head verger is murdered, the circumstances confine the crime to the close, pointing, correctly, to one of the clergy as the killer. In *The Black Serpahim* (1983), Melchester has moved on: The cathedral is seen as "an old-fashioned nuisance" and the dean's assertion of authority as obstructive to the police. The archdeacon dies in the cathedral; so does his murderer.

As an actual dean (of Durham), Cyril A. Alington trod gently in his clerical mysteries, with two archdeacons as his mildest of detectives. *Gold and Gaiters* (1950) is set in Garminster, noted for its massive Norman cathedral and left-wing bishop. The focus of interest is the cathedral library, from which gold Roman coins are stolen. John Trench's *What Rough Beast* (1957) includes a lyrical account of Cunningsbury cathedral, of which the "safety and immemorial certitudes" are threatened by organized *violence. A canon is accused of *theft and suspected of murdering his wife, found dead in the cathedral. Quotations from William Butler Yeats reinforce the theme of order under attack.

In Austin Lee's *Miss Hogg and the Dead Dean* (1958), the dean of Warchester dies by violence. Miss Hogg investigates with her customary sangfroid, undaunted by position and privilege. S. T. Haymon's *Ritual Murder* (1982) is a dark, disquieting novel, within the "literate" tradition but very far from cozy. A butchered choirboy appears to have been ritually sacrificed outside Angleby cathedral. The police envisage a psychopathic pedophile, but the truth is more shocking.

In David Williams's *Murder in Advent* (1985), a verger is murdered and fire destroys the library of Litchester cathedral, repository of a copy of the Magna Carta. Mark Treasure, urbane as ever, reconciles God and Mammon.

Deacon Theodora Braithwaite investigates the murder of the dean of Bow St. Aelfric in D. M. Greenwood's *Idol Bones* (1993). He lies in the close with his throat cut, an aggressive new broom no longer. In Kate Charles's *Appointed to Die* (1993) the dean of Malbury, likewise a turbulent priest, is arraigned for murder.

[See also Clerical Milieu; Clerical Sleuth; Closed-World Settings and Open-World Settings; Library Milieu.]

• Jon L. Breen and Martin H. Greenberg, *A Synod of Sleuths: Essays on Judeo-Christian Detective Fiction* (1990).

—B. A. Pike

CELEBRITY CRIME AND MYSTERY WRITERS. The 1980s and 1990s saw a flood of mystery novels bearing the bylines of celebrities from other fields, including entertainers, athletes, politicians (or their relatives), and journalists. The phenomenon first appeared in a major way in the forties with two novels signed by the striptease artist Gypsy Rose Lee, *The G-String Murders* (1941) and *Mother Finds a Body* (1942), both ghostwritten by Craig *Rice, who also wrote (with subghost Cleve Cartmill) the actor George Sanders's *Crime on My Hands* (1944). Leigh Brackett ghosted Sanders's *Stranger at Home* (1946).

While almost all celebrity mysteries are ghostwritten, there are exceptions—for example, no one suggests that Dick *Francis, a famous steeplechase jockey before the publication of his first novel, *Dead Cert* (1962), does not write his own books. And readers must assume the celebrity's actual authorship in the absence of evidence to the contrary. Among mystery and *thriller bylines have been presidential daughter Margaret Truman, journalist William F. Buckley Jr., entertainer Steve Allen, actress Dulcie Gray, vice presidential wife Marilyn Quayle (in collaboration with her sister, Nancy T. Northcott), former vice president Spiro T. Agnew, tennis star Ilie

Nastase, Kennedy administration press secretary Pierre Salinger, U.S. senators Gary Hart and William S. Cohen (who has also served as secretary of defense), former New Orleans district attorney Jim Garrison, and Watergate figures John Ehrlichman and G. Gordon Liddy.

Often, as with the two Gypsy Rose Lee novels and singer Helen Traubel's *The Metropolitan Opera Murders* (1951), ghosted by Harold Q. Masur, the true author's identity is not even hinted at on the book itself. Other times, the credit is subtle: The two Sanders novels are dedicated by name to their ghosts, and sometimes the ghost gets a note of acknowledgement from the putative author. Presidential son Elliott Roosevelt sometimes credits the advice and counsel of William Harrington, while actors George Kennedy and William Shatner thank Walter J. Sheldon and Ron Goulart, respectively. Sometimes a professional is credited, albeit usually in smaller letters, as a coauthor. Herbert Resnicow has written in ostensible collaboration with former New York mayor Edward Koch and sports stars Fran Tarkenton, Tom Seaver, and Pelé; Clifford Makins with British cricketer Ted Dexter; Arthur Lyons with Los Angeles coroner Thomas T. Noguchi; Thomas Chastain with actress Helen Hayes; and Paul Francis (Paul Engleman) with American disc jockey and television personality Dick Clark; Liz Nickles with tennis player Martina Navratilova; and Bill Crider with TV weathercaster Willard Scott.

Because most celebrity mystery novels are manufactured purely to make money, rather than written from any genuine creative impulse, they are rarely of lasting interest or value. But solving the mystery of *whodunit—and often, of who wrote it—has obvious appeal to mystery readers. —Jon L. Breen

CEREBRAL SLEUTH. *See* Great Detective, The.

CEREBRATION. *See* Reasoning, Types of.

Chambrun, Pierre, the best known of many series characters created by Hugh *Pentecost, is resident manager of *New York City's fictitious Hotel Beaumont, a luxury hotel patterned after the Waldorf-Astoria. Chambrun's early appearances are in novels and short stories involving traditional detection. In his first appearance, *The Cannibal Who Overate* (1962), he even solves a potential *murder *before* it takes place. In later cases, the culprits are often terrorists at his hotel, whose location near the United Nations headquarters makes it a convenient political target. Chambrun, a veteran of the French Resistance in World War II, must devise ways to free hostages without giving in to terrorist demands.

Pentecost increasingly showed his awareness of *violence and terrorism in the world, patterning his work after real events such as the Kitty Genovese slaying and, in *Remember to Kill Me* (1984), rioting in midtown Manhattan following a Central Park concert.

[*See also* Hotel Milieu; Terrorism and the Terrorist Procedural.]

• Hugh Pentecost, "Pierre Chambrun," in *The Great Detectives,* ed. Otto Penzler (1978): 47–55. Marvin Lachman, "Pentecost, Hugh," in *Twentieth Century Crime and Mystery Writers,* 3d ed., ed. Leslie Henderson (1991).

—Marvin Lachman

CHANCE. *See* Coincidence.

Chan, Charlie, fictional Honolulu police detective who appears in a series of six novels by the American writer Earl Derr *Biggers: *The House without a Key* (1925), *The Chinese Parrot* (1926), *Behind That Curtain* (1928), *The Black Camel* (1929), *Charlie Chan Carries On* (1930; *Charlie Chan Hangs On,* 1931), and *Keeper of the Keys* (1932). All of the novels were serialized in the *Saturday Evening Post* and were translated into several foreign languages.

Although Biggers's inspiration for Charlie Chan perhaps came partly from reading a newspaper account of the exploits of Chang Apana, a real Chinese policeman in Honolulu, Biggers had formed the idea for a *detective novel earlier, while visiting Hawaii: To this he added Chan as an unusual and amusing secondary character—a fat Chinese American policeman with numerous children, who speaks fractured English. It is to Biggers's credit that, within the limits of this character *formula, he managed to develop a complex and enduringly popular character, full of wisdom, warmth, and *humor.

In creating Chan, Biggers gave detective fiction a corrective to the sinister Asian stereotype personified in Sax *Rohmer's Dr. *Fu Manchu. And by making his *sleuth an Americanized Chinese, Biggers established two sources of conflict that helped him to develop Charlie's character: his Eastern-Western cultural duality, and his vulnerability to racial *prejudice. We see the former in Charlie's futile attempts to instill traditional Chinese values in his thoroughly Americanized children, and the latter in his encounters with racial discrimination, which he at first quietly endures but later counters with biting *humor.

Kindly, polite, protective, and sentimental, Charlie is a loyal friend, a devoted father, and an adroit matchmaker. But his most notable characteristic is his peculiar speech, in which he takes great pride. At first, Biggers has him say awkward things in tortured English for comic effect. But as the novels progress, Charlie's speech becomes increasingly flowery, aphoristic, and playful.

Charlie's detecting methods include gathering evidence from the crime scene, rummaging through old newspapers, and listing *suspects, whom he carefully observes for temperament and *motive. Then, out of this welter of *clues, he isolates the apparently insignificant detail with which he solves the case. While he can appear as impassive as a stone Buddha, Charlie acts swiftly and fearlessly when necessary. His success in solving crimes enables him to rise in rank from detective-sergeant to inspector of detectives. Nevertheless, he remains modest throughout the novels, and in contrast to some fictional sleuths, demonstrates a growing compassion toward the culprits he discovers.

Having created a fictional detective for whom the public clamored, Biggers did not tire of him (as Arthur Conan *Doyle did of Sherlock *Holmes and Agatha *Christie of Hercule *Poirot), but had further Chan adventures planned when he died in 1933. Biggers brought to the Chan novels the skill of an accomplished humorist and storyteller, firsthand impressions of exotic locales (including California, Nevada, and Hawaii), and characters drawn from his experiences in Boston, *New York, and Hollywood.

[*See also* Ethnicity; Ethnic Sleuth; Racism.]

• Jon L. Breen, "Murder Number One," *New Republic* 177, no. 5 (30 July 1977): 38–39. Neil Ellman, "Charlie Chan: The Making of an Immortal," *Indiana University Bookman* 8 (1967): 91–99.   —Jack Crowley

CHANDLER, RAYMOND (1888–1959), American author of *private eye novels, generally acknowledged as a primary influence on the development of the *hard-boiled fiction genre. Although educated in England, Chandler returned to the United States in 1912, engaging in a business career in California until he retired in 1933 to write full time.

Chandler's early work in the *pulp magazines *Black Mask, Dime Detective,* and *Detective Story* shows the influence of Dashiell *Hammett, as well as the pulp writers of his era. The pulp magazines provided a literary training ground for many mystery novelists, and Chandler was no exception. In his first and best-known novel, *The Big Sleep* (1939), published when he was fifty-one, he employed a technique that he would return to throughout his career: the blending and reworking of previously published short stories into a longer work, a technique he referred to as "cannibalization." *The Big Sleep* introduces private investigator Philip *Marlowe, whose genesis was in the narrators of these early stories. Marlowe is a complex character, full of contradictions. A tough man of the streets, he is also a romantic and an idealist with a self-evolved moral code. He is, at various times, compassionate and sentimental, brutal and indifferent. He is a master of the wisecrack, and his *humor often takes the form of wry self-mockery. Unlike many of his lesser imitations, Marlowe is no superhero; he freely acknowledges fallibility and fear.

Marlowe's *milieu is *Los Angeles and its environs, and his creator's language provides a rich, textured description of the locale and its inhabitants. Chandler's vivid use of metaphor engages the imagination, and his terse dialogue serves both to characterize and to advance the story. It has often been said that one needs only to read Chandler's works to understand what southern California was like in the 1930s and '40s. This assessment is accurate. Through his selective use of detail, Chandler brings this milieu to life with remarkable clarity.

The Big Sleep is a tale of corruption by money and power—both old and inherited and newly derived from racketeering. It is a theme that Chandler returns to in his second novel, *Farewell, My Lovely* (1940). Less convoluted in *plot than *The Big Sleep*,

this work represents a further refinement of the author's technique. Chandler relies on two apparently unrelated story lines that eventually dovetail, and—unlike his first novel—all loose ends are neatly tied up. Here, too, we find such Chandler hallmarks as Marlowe's uneasy, often antagonistic relationship with law enforcement personnel; the racketeer who is apparently above the law; the wayward and conniving woman; the wealthy individual threatened by blackmail and scandal. Many critics regard *Farewell, My Lovely* as its author's finest work; while this is open to debate, it definitely surpasses *The High Window* (1942), *The Little Sister* (1949; *Marlowe*), and *Playback* (1958).

In *The Lady in the Lake* (1943), Chandler again cannibalizes, using three pulp novelettes—"Bay City Blues" (*Dime Detective*, 1937), "The Lady in the Lake" (*Dime Detective*, 1938), and "No Crime in the Mountains" (*Detective Story Magazine*, 1941)—as his basis. He removes Marlowe from his customary urban setting and takes him to the mountains of San Bernardino County; his rich descriptions of this area and its people lend the novel an evocative, haunting quality.

Arguably, *The Long Goodbye* (1954) is Chandler's best work. Here Marlowe is at his most sentimental and compassionate, stepping forward time and again to rescue a dissolute and mostly undeserving friend from disaster. The plot is a natural outgrowth of the characters of Marlowe and his friend, Terry Lennox, and it is the interplay between the two men that makes the unfolding events and their shattering climax thoroughly believable. Again Chandler explores his theme of a person corrupted by money and power, and paints a memorable portrait of one man's slide into ruin. It is ironic that the character of Terry Lennox foreshadows the author's own deterioration as a result of alcoholism following the 1954 death of his wife, (Pearl) Cecily. He would never again write such a compelling and seamless novel.

Most critics would agree that without the works of Chandler, the American school of hard-boiled detective writing would have been very different. Following in the footsteps of Hammett, Chandler removed murder from the genteel confines of the country manor and placed it where it most frequently happens—in the streets and alleys of the city. He brought a gritty realism to the mystery novel by portraying, as he states in his essay "The Simple Art of Murder" (*The Simple Art of Murder*, 1950; *Trouble Is My Business*), "a world where no man can walk down a dark street in safety because law and order are things we talk about but refrain from practicing." With the publication of *The Big Sleep*, the private eye tale became one driven by events that could very possibly happen, rather than one driven by a set of improbable circumstances designed to formulate the classic *whodunit.

At the times of their publication, the response to Chandler's novels was overwhelmingly positive. With the passage of time, some critics have complained that Chandler was not adept at plotting; that he was a one-theme writer; that his characters are stock and dated. All of this may be true to some degree. However, when taken within the context of their times, the stories are remarkably fresh and powerful, the characters some of the most memorable in mystery fiction. Marlowe, in one way or another, is the prototype for every fictional private investigator—male or female—in print today.

Chandler collaborated with Billy Wilder on the screenplay of James M. Cain's *Double Indemnity*, and wrote an original screenplay, *The Blue Dahlia*. His novels were filmed numerous times, with varying degrees of success, the best of these efforts being *The Big Sleep*, starring Lauren Bacall and Humphrey Bogart. In addition to Bogart, Dick Powell, Alan Ladd, and Robert Mitchum have portrayed Marlowe on screen.

Chandler states in his introduction to the short story collection *The Simple Art of Murder* that "a classic is a piece of writing which exhausts the possibilities of its form and can hardly be surpassed. No story or novel of mystery has done that yet. . . . Which is one of the principal reasons why otherwise reasonable people continue to assault the citadel." In this statement Chandler's aim in writing private eye fiction is clear: He simply wanted to write the best detective story within his capability. In the hard-boiled category, his assaults come close to capturing the citadel.

[*See also* Hard-boiled Sleuth; Males and the Male Image; Realism, Conventions of; Voice: Hard-boiled Voice; Voice: Wisecracking Voice.]

• Dorothy Gardiner and Katherine Sorley Walker, eds., *Raymond Chandler Speaking*, rev. ed. (1973). Frank MacShane, *The Life of Raymond Chandler* (1976). Miriam Gross, ed., *The World of Raymond Chandler* (1977). Frank MacShane, ed., *Selected Letters of Raymond Chandler* (1981). T. R. Steiner, "Raymond Chandler," in *Twentieth Century Crime and Mystery Writers*, ed., Lesley Henderson (1991): 186–88. Tom Hiney, *Raymond Chandler: A Biography* (1997). William H. Pritchard, "Classic Chandler," *Hudson Review* 51, no. 1 (spring 1998).
— Marcia Muller

CHARACTERIZATION in fiction is an attempt by the author to convey, by the use of the written word alone, all that is usually able to be observed, heard, and sensed by someone when meeting a fellow human being in real life.

This is rather more of a requirement than when producing a simple pen-portrait, however skillfully delineated. Together with straightforward description, characterization has also to be conveyed to the reader the nuances normally portrayed in the living by the homogenous subtleties of body language, speech, and style, and experienced by those in contact one with another.

Similarly, the ordinary interlocutory exchanges of dialogue, when designed to be read on the printed page, must be enhanced by adverbs and adjectives that aim at conveying the accents, dialects, overtones, undertones, and emphases of normal speech. Verbal mannerisms, choice of words, and speech patterns have to be used for further definition. For example, slang and terseness are traditionally associated with *hard-boiled fiction, while learned and circumlocutory language is more common in those books set in the more leisurely academic world.

In crime writing there is the important additional factor that characterization always—and until relatively recently usually *only*—has to serve the action. An interest in the domestic life of the detective and the rounding out of his or her persona and background is a late development in a genre in which the sex life of the central character was once considered to be irrelevant at best and a hindrance at worst.

Apt but spare characterization has a particular significance in those detective novels that depend on keeping the identity of the murderer secret until the end of the story. The portrayal of characters in these works is thus commonly more basic than in other forms of fiction. Ideally, this characterization should be a little more than adequate but not too elaborate. While mere cypher is not enough, certain *stock characters do have their place in maintaining the pace of some styles of writing, especially when there are occupational connections clear to all.

Characters (and thus characterization) have naturally also become more complex as some authors, such as Patricia *Highsmith and Ruth *Rendell, have come to write crime novels rather than detective stories.

An additional factor in characterization has to be taken into consideration in crime writing as opposed to that in other fiction: the heightened awareness of action and tension within a scenario of deliberate confusion. The complexity of the writer's task is further compounded by having to demonstrate in varying degrees of detail how the characters in the story behave under significantly out-of-the ordinary stresses.

Police chases and arrests, viewing murdered bodies, blackmail, betrayal, becoming closely acquainted with weaponry and *violence, attending postmortems and inquests—these are experiences which, for the most part, the majority of readers can only imagine. Nonetheless, readers expect to share vicariously in the emotions generated by these activities through the responses to them of a character with whom they can identify and empathize.

Further than this, and more difficult, the crime writer has also to include at least one character whose behavior may be seen (in retrospect at least) to have been both completely rational and convincingly villainous. A convention here observed by most authors is that the murderer is not insane to the extent that the reader cannot be expected to work out the logic of his or her actions.

Some of this effect is achieved by a studied combination of description and action; sometimes it is achieved almost by dialogue alone. It is particularly effective where the author arranges for an image of a character to be slowly built up by being seen through the eyes of other characters. The opening of *Busman's Honeymoon* by Dorothy L. *Sayers (1937) is a good example of the presentation of different views of the same person other than by the authorial voice.

The exigencies of having a series character make

further demands in that the detective not only has to be clearly defined but also has to act consistently within those parameters at all times and within in every succeeding volume. That pivotal creation, who may be prim spinster, amiable and eccentric aristocrat, inquisitive *private eye, or hard-nosed *police detective, becomes in essence the author's stock-in-trade complete with the literary equivalent of his or her very own trademark. The name of Arthur Conan *Doyle, for instance, is less well known than that of his chief protagonist, Sherlock *Holmes, some of whose obiter dicta have passed into the language, while a catch-phrase written by Ian *Fleming—"The name's Bond. James *Bond"—is almost equally famous.

Some works stress the nature of the chief character more than the actual detection, notably Joyce *Porter's Chief Inspector Wilfred *Dover. It is, therefore, the sometimes arcane idiosyncrasies of the investigator which are then long remembered: the obesity of the triple-chinned Dr. Gideon *Fell, the hero of John Dickson *Carr; the blindness of Ernest *Bramah's Max *Carrados; and the enthusiasm for orchid-growing of Rex *Stout's Nero *Wolfe.

Routine police promotion and natural aging present further problems with the development of series characters. Margery *Allingham's Albert *Campion and Sayers's Lord Peter *Wimsey both begin their detective careers almost as caricatures but then mature within the oeuvres of their creators.

Certain types of series characters also exhibit particular distinguishing traits: self-pity, for example, appears to be an occupational disease of *private eyes, who are rarely happily married. Marital solitariness, however caused, is still a feature of many detectives. Agatha *Christie's husband-and-wife team Tommy and Tuppence Beresford are an exception to this. It is now uncommon to find a female detective—amateur, police or private investigator—though notably self-sufficient in almost all respects (including violence) to be without a male friend upon whom she can rely for judicious assistance in fields inaccessible to her.

Subsidiary characters, too, follow certain patterns. *Victims are commonly people who are not mourned overmuch—such as the tyrannical Mrs. Boynton in Christie's *Appointment with Death* (1938)—while the detective's sidekick is inevitably less clever than the detective. Of a whole host of such, it may be noted that the perspicacity of Doyle's Holmes invariably exceeds that of his assistant, Dr. John H. *Watson.

[*See also* Eccentrics; Formula: Character; Sex and Sexuality; Villains and Villainy; Voice.]

—Catherine Aird

Charles, Nick and Nora. Dashiell *Hammet created the sophisticated husband-and-wife sleuthing team of Nick and Nora Charles for only one novel, *The Thin Man* (1934), his last. However, they and their dog Asta have become immortalized largely as a result of six films and numerous radio adaptations. The comically offbeat pair is better known for their scintillating and teasing repartee—said to be based on Hammett's interaction with Lillian Hellman—

than for their detective skills. The well-heeled pair are most memorably portrayed in *film by William Powell and Myrna Loy. Nick Charles is a former operative for the Trans-American Detective Agency. His wife is a society type from California who persuades Nick to solve the crime that occurred among her social set. He serves as reluctant detective while she assists as a fond and witty sidekick.

[*See also* Alcohol and Alcoholism; Couples: Sleuth Couples; Humor; Marriage; Sidekicks and Sleuthing Teams; Voice: Wisecracking Voice.]

• "Charles, Nick and Nora," in *Encyclopedia Mysteriosa; A Comprehensive Guide to the Art of Detection in Print, Film, Radio, and Television*, ed. William L. DeAndrea (1994).

—Bernard Benstock

CHARTERIS, LESLIE (1907–1993), author who created Simon Templar, the figure known to millions of readers and viewers of film and television as The *Saint. Born Leslie Charles Bowyer Yin in the British colony of Singapore, he was educated at public schools in England, and spent two years at Kings College, Cambridge. In 1926, the year before publishing his first novel *X Esquire*, he changed his name legally to Leslie Charteris. While working at odd jobs and journalism in Malaya and Europe, he began contributing stories about Simon Templar, whose initials provided the opportunity for the nickname The Saint, to such magazines as the *Thriller*. The first Saint novel was *Meet the Tiger* (1928), followed by *The Last Hero* (1930) and a group of three novellas issued as *Enter the Saint* (1930). In 1935 Charteris relocated to the United States, where he continued steady production of at least a book a year about his latter-day knight-adventurer. In 1946 he relinquished his British citizenship to become a naturalized American.

In exacting retribution from those whom the law is powerless to touch, the gentleman outlaw Templar bears evident resemblance to such British clubland heroes as Bulldog *Drummond, but Charteris works his own variations on the *thriller of the 1920s and 1930s, most notably by redrafting his protagonist as a humane outsider rather than as an agent of a xenophobic establishment and by inscribing his narratives with humor and altruism.

With *The Saint in New York* (1935) and such later novels as *The Saint in Miami* (1940) and *The Saint Goes West* (1942), Charteris began to employ his new homeland for Templar's adventures. Charteris returned to the magazine world when he became editor of *Suspense* (1946–47), before founding his own publication, *The Saint Detective Magazine*, later known as *The Saint Mystery Magazine* (1953–67). Between 1945 and 1955 he also produced a syndicated comic strip portraying The Saint.

By the 1940s the fame of The Saint allowed Charteris to use the name, in the manner of Ellery *Queen, as the aegis for a series of mystery anthologies: *The Saint's Choice of Humorous Crime* (1945), *The Saint's Choice of Impossible Crime* (1945), and *The Saint's Choice of Hollywood Crime* (1946). It was the name and template of The Saint, not Charteris's own screenplays, that provided the subject for the many films and the television series about Simon

Templar. After 1967, additional books about The Saint were written by other authors under the supervision of Charteris.

[*See also* Adventurer and Adventuress; Club Milieu.]

• Bo Lundin, "Charteris, Leslie," in *Twentieth-Century Crime and Mystery Writers*, ed. Lesley Henderson (1991).

—Peter Ibbotson

CHASE, JAMES HADLEY, pseudonym of Rene Brabazon Raymond (1906–85). Chase entered the field of crime and mystery writing in 1939 with the stunningly successful novel *No Orchids for Miss Blandish*. Outside the circle of mystery readers the novel is best known for provoking a denunciation by George Orwell, who took it as representative of the worst trends in popular literature. Within the circle it is recognized as a hard-boiled detective version of William Faulkner's similarly lurid novel *Sanctuary* (1931). Both works exploit strains of *potboiler sadism, female vulnerability, *corruption, and perverse *villains and villainy. Chase adds to the mix the character of a *private eye, Dave Fenner. *Violence had been a staple of crime writing, on stage and off, but Chase turned the register up several notches in his debut novel and in subsequent works, of which there are more than eighty. Dave Fenner appeared once more in a book whose original title indicates its tone—*Twelve Chinks and a Woman* (1940). Chase introduced a California private eye named Vic Malloy in *You're Lonely When You're Dead* (1949); a Lothario named Mark Girland, who takes freelance assignments for the *CIA, in *This Is for Real* (1965); and an insurance investigator named Steve Harmas in *Tell It to the Birds* (1963). The character of Chase's protagonists leaves them unlikely candidates for audience heroes, but the pace of their actions firmly classes their exploits in the category of *thriller. Chase sets his fiction in the United States and makes his characters American presumably because that is a conventional expectation of the hard-boiled label, even though, as an Englishman whose books were all originally published in Great Britain, his knowledge of the *milieu is secondhand, making it difficult for him to achieve another convention of narrative, verisimilitude. The author also wrote as James L. Docherty, Ambrose Grant, and most extensively as Raymond Marshall, whose works feature Brick-Top Corrigan and Don Micklem.

[*See also* Heroism.]

—John M. Reilly

CHASE, THE. See Pursuit.

Chee, Jim, and **Joe Leaphorn,** members of the Navajo Tribal Police featured in the novels of Tony *Hillerman. Chee, the younger of the two, with the rank of sergeant (and later acting lieutenant) has retained a devout faith in the spiritual beliefs of the Navajo people, and returned to the reservation after college to join the police force and train to become a "singer," one who performs healing ceremonies. Leaphorn, a middle-aged married man in the earlier books and later widowed, is a lieutenant; he has been

a detective for more than two decades and is something of a legend among the members of the Navajo Tribal Police, from which he has retired in late-1990s installments of the series. Like Chee, he studied cultural anthropology; unlike Chee, and despite his fierce pride in the Navajo people, he favors rationality and logic over tribal ways. In spite of a deep respect for each other's abilities, the two detectives often clash: Leaphorn sees Chee's traditionalism as individualistic and romantic; Chee finds Leaphorn's skepticism about ancient Navajo beliefs disturbing.

[*See also* Native American Sleuth.]

• John M. Reilly, *Tony Hillerman: A Critical Companion* (1996).

—Lizabeth Paravisini-Gebert

CHESTERTON, G(ILBERT) K(EITH) (1874–1936), British author of over seventy books and collections of essays and creator of Father *Brown, the archetypal *clerical sleuth. Father Brown is a Roman Catholic priest who appears in five books containing a total of fifty short stories.

Chesterton was born in *London, prided himself on his "cockney" origins and placed most of his Father Brown stories in or near the city. Educated at St. Paul's School and at the Slade School of Art, he drifted into journalism and literature but immediately attracted a following of faithful readers. His literary style is characterized by the use of paradox and by a delight in the commonplace and things taken for granted. What could be more miraculous and wonderful, Chesterton argued, than an ordinary city street at night lit by gas flames and populated by shadows? His wit, too, was dependent on his playful approach to the ordinary and predictable. "If a thing is worth doing, it is worth doing badly," he wrote.

Chesterton championed Roman Catholicism after converting to that faith in 1922. He was also in favor of traditional values of family and nation. He possessed an uncluttered wisdom and an ability to cut to the heart of a problem, but he was also led—at least for a short period of time—into a mild form of *anti-Semitism by his younger brother Cecil Chesterton and by his close friend, the writer Hilaire Belloc.

Chesterton is best remembered for his Father Brown books, which began in 1911 with *The Innocence of Father Brown* and continued with *The Wisdom of Father Brown* (1914), *The Incredulity of Father Brown* (1926), and *The Secret of Father Brown* (1927) and concluded with *The Scandal of Father Brown* in 1935. Brown was based loosely on the author's friend Father John O'Connor. He stumbles his way through the books as a plump, short-sighted, untidy, and disorganized man carrying an umbrella and seemingly unaware of life around him. Of course, this is far from the truth. While discussing esoteric moral theology or worrying about where he left his prayer book, Brown can solve gruesome murders thanks to his keen sensitivity to *evil. Brown's own appearance of innocence is an advantage to his investigations because it causes criminals to dismiss him as innocuous.

Father Brown debuts in "The Blue Cross" (*Storyteller*, Sept. 1910), which fixes his character and introduces the style of the later stories. In this short story he is regarded by police and criminal alike as insignificant. As he travels along with an international thief, he manages to gain the man's trust and also to leave the police a clear trail by carrying out various absurd acts such as breaking windows or exchanging salt for pepper in a restaurant.

Chesterton's non–Father Brown stories brought him commercial and critical success. His biographies of Robert Browning (1903), Robert Louis Stevenson (1928), and various Roman Catholic saints; poetry and novels including *The Man Who Was Thursday: A Nightmare* (1908) and *The Napoleon of Notting Hill* (1904); and works of philosophy, history, and theology such as *Orthodoxy* (1908), *The Everlasting Man* (1925), and *Heretics* (1905), were also massively popular during his lifetime and are experiencing a renaissance today. He also founded and edited a small circulation magazine, known in its various stages as *Eye-Witness*, *The New Witness*, and *G. K.'s Weekly*. *The Chesterton Review* (the quarterly journal of the G. K. Chesterton Institute) is devoted to his life, work, and related subjects.

Chesterton wrote other stories featuring detective elements: *The Club of Queer Trades* (1905) is a collection of rather bizarre mystery tales, but they do not rival the undisputed genius of his Brown oeuvre.

• Maisie Ward, *Gilbert Keith Chesterton* (1943). Michael Ffinch, *G. K. Chesterton* (1986). Michael Coren, *Gilbert: The Man Who Was G. K. Chesterton* (1989).

—Michael Coren

CHILD ABUSE. As a genre, detective and mystery fiction traditionally has been interested in adult matters. Although writers of the genre have portrayed children as *victims of crime, they have only recently turned their attention to children as victims of systematic psychological, physical, and sexual abuse. For instance, while in H. C. *Bailey's story, "The Little House" (*Flynn's Detective Fiction*, 9 Oct. 1926) a child who is imprisoned, starved, and drugged is the victim of criminals intent on *revenge, more recent fictional criminals have made children the victims of their psychological disturbances and perversions. Discussion of child abuse in the news, the interest of feminist and other writers in *family relationships, and an emphasis on the criminal's psychological *characterization have stimulated the development of this topic in mystery fiction. Murders often are perpetrated in order to hide the fact of child abuse.

Many novels present child abuse as a symbol of the breakdown of the social and ethical norms that keep a community intact, especially when individuals responsible for children become their abusers instead. In P. M. Carlson's *Murder Misread* (1990), a professor of education has used his research to make children act out his sexual fantasies. Similarly, in Jonathan Kellerman's *When the Bough Breaks* (1985), a prominent child psychologist has helped sell the sexual favors of orphaned children to pedophiles. In Linda Grant's *Love Nor Money* (1991), a judge has sexually abused young boys in the charitable organizations where he volunteers his time. These novels focus on the sexual abuse of children and the psychological states of the abusers.

Other novels depict child abuse as symbolic of social breakdown reflected in the microcosm of the family. In Elizabeth George's *A Great Deliverance* (1988), a religious family man who secretly has abused his daughters is murdered. Sara *Paretsky's *Blood Shot* (1988) reveals a story of incest in an outwardly respectable family. Two British authors who write about child abuse within the family pay particular attention to the psychological state of the abuser and the pattern of repetition that turns abused children into adult murderers. P. D. *James creates two victims who turn into murderers, Mary Ducton in *Innocent Blood* (1980) and Dominic Swayne in *A Taste for Death* (1986); Frances Hegarty draws an extremely chilling portrait of a child abuser and potential murderer in *The Playroom* (1991).

[*See also* Deviance; Rape and Other Sex Crimes.]

—Marilyn Rye

CHILDERS, (ROBERT) ERSKINE (1870–1922), British writer, born in London. Childers served as a clerk in the House of Commons from 1895 to 1910, pursued careers in the military during the Boer War and World War I, and was a political pamphleteer; but he is best remembered for his only work of fiction, *The Riddle of the Sands: A Record of Secret Service* (1903). This tale of two contrasting protagonists cruising on the yacht *Dulcibella* in the Baltic and among the Frisian Islands was based on Childers's own sailing experiences in the region in 1897 and later. An exciting story of amateur espionage, with well-drawn background, absorbing nautical detail, and romantic subplot, the book was influential in calling attention to Germany as a potential enemy for England. It is also widely considered a precursor to the adventure *spy fiction of John *Buchan and to the work of such later writers in this genre as Graham *Greene, Geoffrey *Household, Andrew *Garve, Len *Deighton, and John *le Carré.

Childers settled in Dublin in 1919, joining the Irish Republican Army and working toward the goal of Irish Home Rule. In 1922 he was arrested, court-martialed, and executed by the government of the Irish Free State because of his armed opposition to the Treaty of 1922.

[*See also* Heroism; Nautical Milieu: Boating and Sailing Milieu; Spy Fiction; Thriller.]

• Tom Cox, *Damned Englishman: A Study of Erskine Childers* (1975). Andrew Boyle, *The Riddle of Erskine Childers* (1977). Maldwin Drummond, *The Riddle* (1985). Jim Ring, *Erskine Childers* (1996). —T. J. Binyon

CHILDREN'S DETECTIVE FICTION. *See* Juvenile Mystery.

CHINA, CRIME AND MYSTERY WRITING IN GREATER. China is an ancient and prolific source of crime and detective stories. Intriguing crimes, detection, and Socratic investigation figured in Chinese scriptural classics and histories from before the Common Era in the same ways as some Western critics see them in the Bible and *Oedipus Rex*. Master thieves and swindlers were stock fictional characters by the time of the Song dynasty (960–1127). Three extant vernacular stories, probably from the Yuan (1264–1368), if not the Song dynasty, have detection of culprits whose identity is concealed from the reader. Such plotting was a minor tradition in late imperial times.

More celebrated is the creation during the late Ming dynasty (late sixteenth century) of an "inverted" detective formula in short *gongan* (pronounced "goong an") or "court case" fiction. The culprit—sometimes a spirit—is revealed to the reader early on, but not to the *judge. The crimes are ingenious (e.g., imprisoning a person under a several-ton Buddhist temple bell until death by starvation) and not only solved but punished by a clever and incorruptible judge using stratagems, clever questioning, divine insight, and Solomonic shrewdness. The stories stand alone but were originally printed in pairs in novel-like books, sometimes with a single judge solving all the cases. Most famous was Judge Bao, a legendary series hero loosely based on the historical official Bao Zheng (Pao Cheng; 999–1062). Bao was deified in late imperial China; he could seek *clues from the underworld through spirit journeys and dreams, and he punished on his own authority, circumventing official obstruction of justice. Leon Comber's *The Strange Cases of Magistrate Pao* (1964) retells selected plots.

Judge Bao was already a hero in Yuan dynasty dramas (translated by George A. Hayden in *Crime and Punishment in Medieval Chinese Drama*, 1978) and fifteenth-century *chantefables* (narrated, with song). He lives on today in folk tales, Peking operas and drum songs, and temples dedicated to his worship. In some plots his most salient trait is probity rather than cleverness; he overturns the unjust verdicts of tyrants. To some Chinese, the "court cases" embody ancient folk culture and popular concepts of justice. And because the term *gongan* existed in the Song dynasty, in reference to certain puppet plays and oral narratives no longer extant, some claim for Chinese crime fiction a linear tradition not just one-and-a-half centuries but a millennium or more older than the Western one that began in the mid-nineteenth century. The Ming dynasty formula was indeed transnational, imitated in Japan by the seventeenth century. Yet neither the formula nor the term *gongan* survived continuously and consistently in later centuries. All fiction was déclassé to the literati, and most *gongan* were written in a hybrid language lacking the verve of the pure vernacular and the dignity of classical Chinese.

Biji, notational writings or "jottings" of the literati in classical Chinese, defined a genre with more staying power; some *biji* told of crimes and ingenious solutions of them. *Biji* were nonfiction, but only ostensibly so when crafted by classical-tale masters such as Pu Songling (1640–1715). The form flourished through the nineteenth century. A late-nineteenth-century novel celebrating the historical magistrate Di Renjie (630–700), *Wu Zetian si da qian* (Four Great Uncanny Cases from the Reign of Empress Wu Zetian)—made famous by the Dutch diplomat and sinologist Robert *van Gulik's translation of it as *Celebrated Cases of Judge Dee* (1949)—may reflect West-

ern influence, like van Gulik's own Judge Dee series mysteries, which he composed in English. The latter, and works by Chinese predecessors, do employ plot elements and *atmosphere from Chinese works from before the Western impact. Among the latter are casebooks of true crimes assembled by prideful magistrates such as Lan Dingyuan (1680–1733), author of *Luzhou gongan* (Cases Solved by Lan Luzhou), and a seminal text with many judges, some of whom perform chemical experiments, *Tangyin bishi* (1211; Parallel Cases Solved by Just and Benevolent Judges), which van Gulik published as *Parallel Cases from under the Pear Tree* (1956). The crime solutions in these books and in China's earliest classic of forensic science, the *Xiyuan jilu* (Manual for Redressing Injustice) of Song Ci (1186–1249), translated by Brian E. McKnight as *The Washing Away of Wrongs* (1981), are prized by China's crime aficionados. The great novelist Wu Woyao in 1906 revived *biji* to show that "Chinese detection" was superior to Sherlock *Holmes's, but by then Western imports were eclipsing every native genre; Wu adopted Western techniques in his own seminal detective story of 1906, *Jiuming qiyuan* (Nine Murders).

Most highly acclaimed internationally is China's tradition of great dramas and epic novels in the "vernacular" (partly based on Yuan and Ming dynasty speech), though literati prejudice prevented *canonization of such works in China until the twentieth century. *Shuihu zhuan*, a sixteenth-century novel variously translated as *All Men Are Brothers* (by Pearl Buck; 1933), *Water Margin* (1937), and *Outlaws of the Marsh* (1981), has swashbuckling episodes of outrageous crimes and injustices avenged by chivalric ruffians turned by fate into enemies of the state. Justice beyond the law has been celebrated since Sima Qian (145–87 B.C.E.?) included biographies of knights-errant and assassins in China's first great history, the *Shi ji* (Historical Records).

Legendary detective judges appeared again in long *gongan* novels during the last imperial dynasty (the Qing, 1644–1911), beginning with *Shi gongan* (1798; Judge Shi's Cases). *San xia wu yi* (1879; Three Heroes and Five Gallants) was the most influential work; it featured Judge Bao and was one of China's first lithographed novels, though literacy was not yet general. Judges in these novels functioned as symbols of justice served by a stable of chivalrous knights. Divided into dozens of episodic chapters each ending in *suspense, these epics resembled the great novels like *Water Margin* in structure, but their language was semiclassical without being truly literary. Adventure and weapons-play narratives gained new popularity in 1930s novels written in the modern vernacular. The formula became best-selling due to mass literacy in postwar Hong Kong, Taiwan, and, in the 1980s, mainland China, once communist proscriptions waned. Jin Yong (Louis Cha) of Hong Kong was the master, followed by Gu Long of Taiwan. Conceived as historical narratives focused less on detection and judicial acumen than on combat skills, stratagems, vengeance, and comradeship, such works are no longer called *gongan*, but *wuxia xiaoshuo* (martial-arts or chivalric novels). Attention to historical detail and the rhythms of classical Chinese, minus its difficult vocabulary, make this neotraditional genre a vehicle of Chinese ethnic pride.

After 1896, translations of Holmes stories and floods of sometimes anonymous imitations that constituted as much as a third of all fiction in print in the first decade of the twentieth century, triggered China's second boom in detective fiction since the sixteenth century. Arsène *Lupin mysteries by Maurice *Leblanc followed in the 1910s. Holmes and Lupin remain the favorite and paradigmatic Western detectives among Chinese today, including readers in Taiwan and its overseas orbit, for Taiwan banned mainland fiction while promoting Western writings after 1949. Holmes and Lupin originally attracted Chinese readers through classical-language translations, but in updated modern-language renditions made after the vernacular literary revolution of 1917, the Western detectives came to personify science and modernity. The Western-style *whodunit acquired an intellectual and progressive cachet other popular genres lacked.

The "Golden Age" of the Chinese detective story (1900–1949) thus belonged to Cheng Xiaoqing (1893–1976), creator of "the Sherlock Holmes of the Orient" (Huo Sang, with a "Watson," Bao Lang), and Sun Liaohong (1897–1958), whose series rogue-cynosure was Lu Ping, "the Arsène Lupin of the Orient." Both heroes were Shanghainese of very Westernized habits and dress. While bringing novelty to the Chinese literary world, Cheng and Sun no more created a new national subgenre or even a unique variation on the Holmes tradition than did Agatha *Christie— but their works are original and equal Christie's in plotting, suspense, attention to detail, and consistency of characterization and style. Also a translator, Cheng Xiaoqing created a readership in Chinese not just for the original Holmes, but for Philo *Vance, the *Saint, and Charlie *Chan.

Nearly all the above were banned after the communist revolution of 1949. Private detection and crime itself were deemed "bourgeois"; imperial judges, "feudal." Not only the mainland but Taiwan banned Cheng Xiaoqing's and Sun Liaohong's old works, since those authors remained in China. Some Soviet Eastern European, and Japanese "anti-spy" and "suspense" novels were translated in the People's Republic. Prior to the Sino-Soviet split, they influenced Chinese fiction and film having themes of police and militia tracking down spies and counterrevolutionaries (the same sort of menaces addressed in mainstream fiction of the time). Chinese bans on crime themes were far stricter than in the Soviet Union; suspense itself was politically heretical. The best imitations of Eastern Bloc works, by Li Wenda and other authors mostly forgotten today, generally date from the 1956–58 thaw. Fantastic, illicit hand-copied popular thrillers with detective interests circulated underground during the Cultural Revolution (1966–76).

In 1978–80, as Deng Xiaoping tolerated free expression to overthrow Maoism and open up China, two well-made crime genres emerged as if from thin air. China still lacked *private detectives, but fictional police heroes of dazzling deductive powers appeared in a genre more like the old whodunit than the *police procedural; Westernized young folk and people of "bad class background" made good *red herrings. Another genre made heroes of investigating judges, procurators (prosecutors), and dissident police, emphasizing their Judge Bao-like heroism in overturning unjust verdicts of the past. Wang Yaping's "Shensheng de shiming" (Sacred Duty; 1978) was a pioneer genre story bravely criticizing crimes of China's legal system. There were subgenres about juvenile offenders, inhumane prison camps (exposed by Cong Weixi), and muckraking reportage works by Liu Binyan about criminal communist bosses. Such works were suppressed again in 1980; reprints of Arthur Conan *Doyle's work and Christie's novels "about foreign crime" (sixteen million copies, 1980–81) stood in, until they, too, were squelched in 1983 campaigns against spiritual pollution and rising crime. Ye Yonglie, under contract with the police, was able to continue writing in a science fiction-detective subgenre. He created Jin Ming, a heroic Public Security detective and "scientific Sherlock Holmes"—a modernizer to equal his interservice rivals in the People's Liberation Army.

The heyday of Chinese crime fiction was 1984–89, when the mass campaigns stopped and the police (under dissident Public Security Ministry publisher Yu Haocheng) began to back crime fiction to profit from it, but were not fully able to control the genre. State subsidies were declining and fiction had to sell; crime fiction circulating in crime-genre periodicals dominated "serious" literature five-to-one, challenged in the end only by sudsy love stories newly imported from Taiwan and martial-arts novels from Hong Kong. All fiction magazine circulations declined through the 1980s and suffered from the 1989 Tiananmen massacre, but films and TV programs with crime themes took up the slack.

Representative novels, many of them written by current or former police, judges, and lawyers, include former prison guard Lü Haiyan's Bianyi jingcha (1985; Plainclothes Policeman), about a dissident young cop who opposes secret photographing of dissidents during the first (1976) Tiananmen demonstration; the novel speaks of "political prisoners" and gained new meaning after the second Tiananmen incident. Wang Xiaoying's Ni wei shui bianhu (1988; Whom Do You Defend) features myriad lawyers sleuthing and bravely arguing with the state in subplots as multifarious as those in China's grand old episodic novel tradition. Works by Wei Dongsheng, Xu Xiao, and Li Di mixed avant-garde and realistic narrative to probe the psychology of patrolmen and such unsympathetic characters as preliminary hearing interrogators (whose job it is to break the accused prior to his "arrest"). Zhang Xianliang's Xiguan siwang (1989), translated as Getting Used to Dying (1991), evokes a prison camp survivor's split personality in the style of Milan Kundera. Zhang Weihua with Zhang Ce, Jia Lusheng, Su Xiaokang, and a host of others probed official corruption in reportage. Li Jian and Wang Yonghong pioneered the feminist popular crime novel. Liu Heng wrote realistically of the travails of an ex-con in *Hei de xue* (1988), translated as *Black Snow* (1993). Liu Zongdai created a traditional-style popular crime *thriller of brave good cops overcoming evil cops and eerie mysteries in *Gongan hun* (1988; Public Security Spirits). Best-selling young author Wang Shuo, who reveled in the hip dialogue and cynicism of petty thieves and young social dropouts, before becoming China's favorite 1990s TV sitcom writer, explored the detective genre in *Wan de jiushi xin tiao* (1989), translated as *Playing for Thrills* (1997).

Crime and detective themes, Westernized and ripe for modernization but not yet "postcommunist," were ubiquitous in Chinese popular culture by the end of the twentieth century. This heralded the triumph of entertainment values and the Westernization of China's legal values—which was ironic, since Chinese officials, seeking to encourage writers to defend old-style socialist law and order, had christened writing about crime "Chinese legal system literature." Most readers continued to think of crime fiction as fun but immoral—like the West. Few authors admitted to being genre legal-system or crime writers. An exception was Chen Yuanbin, author of "Wan jia susong" (1991; Every Family's Lawsuit), whose tale of a peasant woman's fruitless quest for access to China's formal legal system was filmed by Zhang Yimou in the critically acclaimed *Qiuju da guansi*, or *The Story of Qiuju* (1992), starring Gong Li.

When Taiwan had its own cultural thaw in the 1980s, translated novels of *Matsumoto Seichō and other purveyors of the Japanese "social detective story" nearly swamped native efforts by Lin Foer (Lin Fo-erh), Ni Kuang (Ni K'uang), Ye Sang (Yeh Sang), and Ye Yandu (Yeh Yen-tu). But crime and detective themes and *plots were rife in modernist works like the introspective fiction of Ping Lu (P'ing Lu), and in crossover political crime satires by Zhang Dachun (Chang Ta-ch'un). Hong Kong published many thrillers, but the martial-arts novel and film were its main exports. China was fascinated with Western and Japanese crime writing; only Japanese aficionados returned the favor, but that reestablished an East Asian community of interest in crime.

• Yau-woon Ma, "The Textual Tradition of Ming *Kung-an* Fiction," *Harvard Journal of Asiatic Studies* 35 (1975): 190–220. Patrick Hanan, *The Chinese Vernacular Story* (1981). Huang Yanbo, *Zhongguo gongan xiaoshuo shi* (History of Chinese court case fiction; 1991). Meng Liye, *Zhongguo gongan xiaoshuo yishu fazhan shi* (History of the artistic development of Chinese court case fiction; 1996). Jeffrey C. Kinkley, *Chinese Justice, the Fiction: Law and Literature in Modern China* (2000). —Jeffrey C. Kinkley

CHIVALRY, CODE OF. The code of chivalry refers to the medieval system of knighthood, with its attendant duties and responsibilities. According to *Brewer's Dictionary of Phrase and Fable* (14th ed., 1989), "chivalry embodied the medieval conception of the ideal life, where valour, courtesy, generosity and dexterity in arms were the summit of any man's attainment." The true knight was brave, daring, honorable, and courteous, using his advantages to help the poor and weak. A contemporary definition of chivalry would include the concept of selflessly putting oneself at risk to protect another, above and beyond the call of duty.

The theme of chivalry occurs throughout mystery fiction. It is often the provenance of the *amateur detective and especially of the *private eye, since it is actually the job and duty of the police to put themselves at risk. The matter of motivation is important as well: The chivalrous detective becomes involved in solving crimes through concern for the *victim or because of a strong sense of *justice, rather than from sheer nosiness or intellectual curiosity. Thus Sherlock *Holmes, though he is often drawn into his investigations through the pleas of an attractive woman, cannot truly be considered a chivalrous detective, because his motivation is chiefly intellectual.

With his activities set in the twelfth century, which falls within the historical period of chivalry, Ellis *Peters's Brother *Cadfael behaves chivalrously. The fact that he is a cloistered monk rather than a knight does not make a great deal of difference. Throughout the series of detective novels in which he appears, Cadfael encounters beautiful young women in jeopardy and invariably brings about their rescue. For example, in *The Rose Rent* (1986), Cadfael is the self-appointed defender of an attractive young widow whose property makes her a target for unscrupulous suitors.

Raymond *Chandler's private eye Philip *Marlowe, often regarded as the quintessential tough guy, was in fact described by his creator in "The Simple Art of Murder" (*The Simple Art of Murder*, 1950, *Trouble is my Business*) as a modern knight "in search of a hidden truth." Marlowe, named to evoke the author of *Le Mort d'Arthur*, puts himself on the line to protect his often undeserving clients. In *The Long Goodbye* (1953) he allows himself to be jailed and savagely beaten rather than break faith with Terry Lennox, a man he regards as a friend. Similarly, private eye Travis *McGee was described by his creator John D. *MacDonald in a television interview as "a tattered knight on a spavined steed." McGee, like Marlowe, is motivated by loyalty and the desire to restore decency to the world. These and other private eyes trace their origins to Dashiell *Hammett's Sam *Spade, who in *The Maltese Falcon* (1929) begins his quest for justice by investigating his partner's death. All such detectives move through a world that looks sordid by contrast.

Altruistic impulses and a sense of honor often motivate the heroes of Dick *Francis to chivalrous behavior. Francis's heroes are decent and kind men who make a habit of protecting people who cannot look after themselves. In *Bonecrack* (1971) Neil Griffon faces blackmail and physical danger to shield his invalid father. Sid Halley undergoes similar ordeals in *Odds Against* (1965) on behalf of his father-in-law, and again in *Whip Hand* (1979) to save his calculating ex-wife. Incidentally, the root meaning of "chivalry" comes from the French word for horse, "cheval," which makes it a natural theme for Francis's books, largely set in the *horse racing milieu.

Dorothy L. *Sayers regarded her amateur detective Lord Peter *Wimsey as nothing less than a modern knight in shining armor, or at least in a top hat. Chivalry is part of his aristocratic baggage as well as a component of his personality, and he exhibits it throughout his adventures. But it is only when he meets Harriet *Vane in *Strong Poison* (1930) and falls in love that he mounts his charger in earnest, for Harriet is accused of poisoning her former lover and faces the gallows unless Wimsey can rescue her.

An unlikely knight-errant is Lindsey Davis's Marcus Didius Falco, a wisecracking private eye in ancient Rome. Much as he protests that he is motivated only by self-interest, he continually finds himself behaving in a chivalrous way. In the first chapter of *The Silver Pigs* (1989), he helps a beautiful girl escape from a bunch of pursuing thugs. He is unable to prevent the girl's eventual *murder, and his feelings of *guilt lead him to go undercover as a slave in the silver mines of Britain to find the murderer.

Romantic love is the motivation yet again in *The Franchise Affair* (1948) by Josephine *Tey. Robert Blair, a country solicitor, defends two women against a charge of kidnapping and assault. Gradually he falls in love with Marion Sharpe, one of the women, and finds himself entertaining the same grand fantasies he had as an adolescent. No one but Robert believes in the women's *innocence, but it is a matter of honor with him that they be exonerated. It is perhaps no coincidence that the house is called The Franchise: *The Shorter Oxford English Dictionary* gives as an alternate definition of franchise "nobility of mind; liberality; magnanimity." These are qualities of Robert Blair, as of the chivalrous knight in history—and in mystery fiction.

[*See also* Heroism.]

• Jacques Barzun and Wendell Hertig Taylor, *A Catalogue of Crime* (1971). Susan Oleksiw, *A Reader's Guide to the Classic British Mystery* (1988). Chris Steinbrunner and Otto Penzler, *Encyclopedia of Mystery and Detection* (1976). Julian Symons, *Bloody Murder: From the Detective Story to the Crime Novel: A History*, 3rd ed. (1992) Hillary Waugh, *Hillary Waugh's Guide to Mysteries and Mystery Writing* (1991).

—Kate Charles *and* Lucy Walker

CHRISTIE, AGATHA (Agatha Mary Clarissa Miller Christie Mallowan) (1890–1976), English author recognized around the world as one of the most important writers of detective fiction and arguably the most famous practitioner in the *British Golden Age tradition. Known for her prolificity and inventiveness, Christie turned out eighty-five books that can be categorized as detective novels or collections of mystery short stories. Her series characters include the Belgian private detective Hercule *Poirot, the *spinster sleuth Miss Jane *Marple, the detecting duo Tommy and Tuppence Beresford, and Superintendent Battle. Mr. Parker Pine, investigator, and Harley Quin appear in volumes of short stories. Christie also penned original plays and adaptations,

a series of psychological romances, autobiographical work, and a children's book.

Agatha Mary Clarissa Miller was born 15 September 1890 in Torquay, on the south coast of Devon, England, the third child of an American father and an English mother. A bashful and sensitive child, she was educated at home before attending finishing schools in Paris. Although she was an accomplished pianist, her extreme shyness and stage fright prevented her from pursuing a performing career. In 1914 she married Archibald Christie, an officer in the Royal Flying Corps. During World War I she served first as a volunteer nurse and then as a dispenser of drugs, gaining knowledge that would be invaluable to her career as a crime writer. She gave birth to her only child, Rosalind, in 1919.

In her posthumously published *An Autobiography* (1977), Christie revealed that she wrote her first *detective novel, *The Mysterious Affair at Styles* (copyright 1920; published in 1921) in response to a challenge from her sister Madge. She dashed off the manuscript during a scant two weeks in 1916. Published just over four years later, it was an instant success and is still regarded as among her masterpieces. The novel introduced Poirot, a prim and petite Belgian who characterizes his own immense cleverness as resulting from reliance on his "little gray cells," or brainwork. Poirot often works in tandem with Captain John Hastings, a less bright but ever eager sidekick figure. He is also assisted by his secretary, Miss Lemon, who is not averse to performing inquiries and other tasks beyond the typewriter.

Christie's great strength as a writer of classic mysteries centered around *puzzles was soon established: deliberate misdirection. A member of the elite *Detection Club, a group of authors who swore to play fair with their readers, Christie was a master at manipulating the *rules of the game or *conventions of the genre, generally laying *clues before her readers' eyes while guiding their scrutiny in the wrong direction. She was also notorious for breaking rules in her surprise ending to *The Murder of Roger Ackroyd* (1926), which proved that anyone can be a killer in a Christie novel. Many felt that the stunning solution departed from the fair-play convention of detective fiction, but they bought the book nonetheless, making this one of Christie's greatest best-sellers. *Murder on the Orient Express* (1934; *Murder in the Calais Coach*) was another rule-breaker proving that everyone can be guilty in a Christie work.

The same year that *The Murder of Roger Ackroyd* became a publishing sensation, Christie made news herself by vanishing for ten days, during which a nationwide search ensued. She was finally discovered registered at a resort hotel under the name of her husband's mistress. While Christie never explained the circumstances of the incident, many have speculated that she experienced an episode of stress-induced amnesia, inspired by the discovery of her husband's infidelity and by grief over the death of her mother that year.

Her divorce was finalized in 1928, just as the most prolific period of Christie's writing career was beginning. She introduced Miss Jane Marple in *Murder at* *the Vicarage* (1930). Marple succeeds as a personification of her creator's signature skill in *sleight of hand. This *elderly sleuth used her older appearance as an asset, allowing suspects to fail to take her seriously while she keenly investigated their activities. While Marple used the elderly stereotype to advantage, her sharp mind and physical courage also succeeded as strong and early arguments for the reversal of *stereotypes about the elderly. This was not so solidly the case, however, in some of the film versions of the Marple character.

In an effort to put her divorce behind her, Christie traveled to the Middle East in 1928, where she met Sir Max Mallowan, an accomplished archaeologist. She married Mallowan in 1930 and accompanied him on digs in Syria and Iraq, where she used her talents as a photographer to take official photographs recording his work. During these expeditions she also explored *settings that she would use in such works of detective fiction as *Murder in Mesopotamia* (1936) and *Death on the Nile* (1937). She later recounted some of her archeological adventures in *Come Tell Me How You Live* (1947), an autobiographical work.

Christie also launched her extraordinarily productive decade by publishing *Giant's Bend* in 1930. It was the first of six psychological romance novels that she penned under the pseudonym Mary Westmacott. During the 1930s she published four nonseries mystery novels, fourteen Poirot novels, two Marple novels, two Superintendent Battle books, a book of stories featuring Harley Quin and another featuring Mr. Parker Pyne, an additional Mary Westmacott book, and two original plays. She continued her prolific output, although not at the same pace, for the next three-and-a-half decades, causing readers to count on "A Christie for Christmas" until the year of her death. Her stage play *The Mousetrap* (1952) is another reliable production. Adapted from her short story "Three Blind Mice" (in *Three Blind Mice*, 1950; *The Mousetrap*), it has been playing continuously in London since its opening. The play is published in Christie's *The Mousetrap and Other Plays* (1978).

Christie is primarily associated in readers' minds with the Golden Age of crime and mystery writing, the period between the two World Wars when puzzle-centered detective fiction was built upon a conservative worldview. But during a writing career spanning the better part of six decades, Christie revealed herself as aware of changing realities of manners and mores, even if her works were often set in places where characters were comfortably situated, in terms of finances or leisure. In fact, even in the coziest of Christie's novels, where characters are enjoying relatively luxurious lifestyles, the solution to crime may reveal financial desperation as an underlying *motive for murder. Coziness, like so much else in Christie's work, is often a case of deceptive appearances.

Critics agree that Christie remains unsurpassed for her *ingenuity in plotting. While her contemporaries often relied upon pinning the crime on the *least likely suspect, Christie dared to allow the reader's attention to focus on the murderer as prime *suspect. Her forte was to then shift suspicion to an innocent character and thus cause the reader to dismiss the true murderer as a suspect.

Christie's work continues to be published in translation around the world and is said to outsell Shakespeare and the Bible. Her colleagues in crime writing voted to present her with the first Mystery Writers of America Grand Master Award in 1954. She became a Commander of the British Empire in 1956, and a Dame of the British Empire in 1971.

[*See also* Conservative vs. Radical Worldview: Conservative Worldview; Craft of Crime and Mystery Writing, The; Double Bluff; Plot; Whodunit.]

• Robert Barnard, *A Talent to Deceive: An Appreciation of Agatha Christie* (1980). Patricia D. Maida and Nicholas B. Spornick, *Murder She Wrote: A Study of Agatha Christie's Detective Fiction* (1982). Janet Morgan, *Agatha Christie; A Biography* (1985). Gillian Gill, *Agatha Christie: The Woman and Her Mysteries* (1990). Charles Osborne, *The Life and Crimes of Agatha Christie* (1990).

—Dana Bisbee *and* Rosemary Herbert

CHRISTMAS CRIME. The mystery story's association with Christmas dates back to the annual Christmas story tradition initiated by Charles *Dickens (*A Christmas Carol*, 1843) and carried on by the British Christmas annuals and Christmas numbers of popular monthlies of the nineteenth century. Arthur Conan *Doyle's only Christmas Sherlock *Holmes adventure. "The Adventure of the Blue Carbuncle," appeared in the *Strand* in January 1892. The tradition has continued in *Ellery Queen's Mystery Magazine* and the British annual *Winter's Crimes*. There are at least 130 novels and eight anthologies of short stories with seasonal associations.

In traditional or Golden Age crime and mystery writing, Christmas is seen as a season of innocent celebration, and goodwill is shattered by the intrusion of *violence and malice. The hard-boiled/procedural mystery accepts that there is a positive correlation between Christmas and crime, and stresses the contrast between the mundane reality and the romantic idealization of the season. The crowded stores and heedless shoppers are easy prey, and nowhere is there less cheer on Christmas Eve than among the cops at the precinct. Mysteries featuring the lonely cop at Christmas include Ed *McBain's *The Pusher* (1956), *Sadie When She Died* (1972), and *Ghosts* (1980); Joel Y. Dane's *The Christmas Tree Murders* (1938); Marian Babson's *The Twelve Deaths of Christmas* (1979); Thomas Chastain's *911* (1976, *The Christmas Bomber*); James McClure's *The Gooseberry Fool* (1974). Howard Engel's "The Three Wise Guys" (in *Mistletoe Mysteries*, ed. Charlotte MacLeod, 1989) includes the motif of the alienation of the Jewish cop at Christmas.

Urban mysteries often utilize the department store, as in M. P. Rea's *Death of an Angel* (1943), Jack Pearl's *Victims* (1973), Spencer Dean's *Credit for a Murder* (1961), and short stories such as Isaac Asimov's "Ho! Ho! Ho!" (in *Mistletoe Mysteries*), and Julian *Symons's "Twixt the Cup and the Lip" (*EQMM*, Jan. 1965).

Christmas mysteries often feature Santa Claus, or Father Christmas, as a figure conveniently in *disguise, appearing in every role from *victim to *villain to detective. Santa victims appear in George *Baxt's "I Saw Mommy Killing Santa Claus" (in *Mystery for Christmas*, ed. Cynthia Manson, 1990), Symons's "The Santa Claus Club" (*Suspense*, Dec. 1960), and Henry Slesar's "The Man Who Loved Christmas" (in *Mistletoe Mysteries*), in which a bigamist Santa gets his families mixed up and comes down the wrong chimney.

Santa is cast as villain in Jan Grape's "The Man in the Red-Flannel Suit" and Bill Crider's "The Night Before Christmas" (both published in *Santa Clues*, ed. Martin H. Greenberg and Carol-Lynn Rossell Waugh, 1993). In the same anthology, Santa is a *Robin Hood criminal, guilty, but true to the spirit of Christmas, in Christopher Fahy's "The Real Thing."

Detectives playing Santa occur in Stout's "Christmas Party" (*Collier's*, 4 Jan. 1957) and John Lutz's "Slay Belle" (in *Santa Clues*). The British tradition of Christmas pantomime provides other disguise opportunities, in G. K. *Chesterton's "The Flying Stars" (*Cassell's*, June 1911; included in *The Innocence of Father Brown*, 1911), and in Ngaio *Marsh's *Tied Up in Tinsel* (1972).

The British *cozy mystery and its American counterparts emphasize the more traditional *atmosphere of Christmas. Charlotte MacLeod's *Rest You Merry* (1978) evokes New England ambiance, while small-town settings are used by David William Meredith in *The Christmas Card Murders* (1951), whose chapter titles are taken from Clement Clarke Moore's poem "A Visit from St. Nicholas." Similarly, the carol "The Twelve Days of Christmas" is used as a structural device in Queen's *The Finishing Stroke* (1958). In Simon Brett's *The Christmas Crimes at Puzzel Manor* (1991), a series of clues have seasonal associations, including the hymn "Once in Royal David's City" and Mr. Weller's Christmas anecdote from *Pickwick Papers* (1836–37).

The quintessential Christmas mystery evokes the Dickensian archetype. Among those who have played the Dickens card is Agatha *Christie in "The Adventure of the Christmas Pudding" and, with more irony, in *Hercule Poirot's Christmas* (1938; *Murder for Christmas; A Holiday for Murder*), where Poirot and his host, Chief Constable Colonel Johnson, debate the colonel's contention of the unlikelihood of disturbance by violent crime at Christmas.

Other Christmas mysteries in an English country-house setting include Cyril Hare's *An English Murder* (1951), Georgette Heyer's *Envious Casca* (1941), C. H. B. Kitchin's *Crime at Christmas* (1934), and Michael *Innes's *There Came Both Mist and Snow* (1940; *A Comedy of Terrors*). An American variant is Edith Howie, *Murder for Christmas* (1941). In these works, the Christmas connection is often incidental, a matter of *atmosphere, but sometimes the Christmas spirit of reconciliation is operative, as in Chesterton's "The Flying Stars," H. R. F. *Keating's "Inspector Ghote and the Miracle" (*EQMM*, Jan. 1972), Georges *Simenon's "Maigret's Christmas"

(*EQMM*, Jan. 1954), and Alice Scanlon Reach's "Father Crumlish Celebrates Christmas" (*EQMM*, Jan. 1968).

[*See also* Holiday Mysteries; Religion.]

• Bill Vande Water, "Holidaying/The Christmas Mystery Lecture," in *Murder Ink/The Mystery Reader's Companion* (1977): 488–90. Jane Gottschalk, "Criminous Christmases," *Armchair Detective* 13, no. 4 (fall 1980): 281–85. Albert Menendez, *Mistletoe Malice: The Life and Times of the Christmas Murder Mystery* (1982).

—Peter V. Cenci *and* George L. Scheper

CIA. The Central Intelligence Agency, the first peacetime national intelligence service in the United States, was established by provision of the National Security Act of 1947. The need for such an agency had been impressed upon the government and public by the disastrous failure of the existing intelligence agencies to recognize and warn of the impending Japanese attack on Pearl Harbor in December 1941, and the realization that at the outbreak of World War II, the United States did not have an intelligence service on a footing with any of the warring powers.

The CIA is the direct descendant of the Office of Strategic Services (OSS), created by President Franklin D. Roosevelt in mid-1942. Under the command of Colonel (later Major General) William Donovan, the OSS was responsible for the collection and analysis of strategic information as required by the Joint Chiefs of Staff (JCS) and for "such special services as directed" by the JCS. In practice, these special services were espionage, sabotage, counterintelligence abroad, support to resistance activity, and a wide spectrum of covert action. The OSS organization, practices, and disciplines were strongly influenced by the British Secret Intelligence Service (SIS).

By the end of World War II, the OSS was fully operational in Europe and had a scattered presence in the Middle East, Africa, Southeast Asia, China, and elsewhere. When President Harry S. Truman abruptly abolished the OSS in October 1945, its research and analysis component was assigned to the Department of State. The remaining functions, operations, and personnel were transferred to the War Department's newly formed Strategic Services Unit. The intense competition among the State Department, the military services, and the *FBI for control of the future intelligence organization came to a head in 1947 when the National Security Act established the CIA as an independent agency.

Although many of the OSS responsibilities and a strong cadre of OSS veterans were incorporated into the CIA, emphasis was placed on the new agency's responsibility for gathering intelligence abroad and for evaluating and coordinating the national security intelligence reporting of all other agencies.

Post–World War II *spy fiction leans heavily to counterintelligence, particularly to the uncovering of traitors and penetration agents, with few authors giving much attention to intelligence collection or to the various forms of covert action. British authors like John *le Carré have frequently depicted stereotyped CIA operatives (called "the cousins" in British spy argot), cast in a generally unflattering light. However, the most revealing fictional glimpses of the CIA come from American authors, some of whom served in the agency. William F. Buckley Jr., for instance, published a series of spy novels featuring the CIA, in which he served briefly. These entertaining novels also serve as a platform for the author's political views. John Cassidy, another CIA veteran, used his knowledge of Vietnam to flesh out *A Station in the Delta* (1979), a strong novel about a CIA field officer and the tangle of events leading to the Tet Offensive of 1968.

Harris Greene, a retired CIA officer, has published several intelligence novels. *Inference of Guilt* (1982) explores the conflicts within the CIA when a senate investigation opens the case of a former Romanian Iron Guard officer. *Spy Wednesday*, by William Hood, an OSS/CIA veteran, involves a Soviet deception operation and the exfiltration of a *KGB defector from Hungary. This novel and *Cry Spy* (1990) give many details of spycraft. Another CIA veteran, John Horton, centers *The Hotel at Tarasco* (1987) around CIA activity in Mexico. *The Tears of Autumn* (1974), a novel by Charles McCarry, also a former CIA operative, gives another closely observed glimpse of secret intelligence activity.

Howard Hunt, a veteran of both the OSS and the CIA best known for his role in the Watergate affair, has published some fifteen espionage novels. Hunt's novels are heavy with spy terminology and conservative political and social comment.

Writers who do not possess CIA experience have also turned their skills to portraying the agency. Norman Mailer's *Harlot's Ghost* (1991) is an exhaustive account of the novelist's highly imagined CIA, while David Ignatius's *Agents of Innocence* (1987) is a revealing account of the CIA at work in the Middle East.

[See also Intelligence Organizations; KGB; MI5 and MI6.]

—William Hood

CID. At the heart of most English crime mysteries is the ubiquitous Criminal Investigation Department, or CID. Created in 1878 in succession to the Detective Department of the Metropolitan Police, the organization survives to the present day. Accommodated for years in an impressive turreted building designed by Norman North, and overlooking the River Thames next to the Palace of Westminster in *London, it retains the name New Scotland Yard after the site of its original headquarters at 4 Whitehall Place, overlooking Great Scotland Yard, even after its transfer in 1965 to the modern block it now occupies in Victoria Street.

For every independent investigator in popular fiction, there is a detective of the CID based at *Scotland Yard. Arthur Conan *Doyle's Inspector Lestrade, Agatha *Christie's Chief Inspector Japp, and Leslie *Charteris's Inspector Claude Eustace Teale are all essential figures in the crime genre. Often by convention the CID officer is portrayed as a bumbling bureaucrat, quite out of his depth in the complexity of a

mystery that can only be solved by an unorthodox *sleuth who has rejected the usual pedestrian methodology of the police for a more adventurous or a more cerebral approach. Thus the cocaine addict Sherlock *Holmes can make the most brilliantly intuitive deductions from the most obscure *clues without leaving his rooms in Baker Street, and Hercule *Poirot relies on his "little gray cells" to solve the most bizarre *puzzles, while Simon Templar prefers direct intervention to capture miscreants before the police can enter the scene. Ngaio *Marsh's Inspector Roderick *Alleyn is a CID man, as is P. D. *James's Adam *Dalgliesh, who is also perhaps the ideal representative of the CID detective in British fiction in the late twentieth century.

In reality, *Scotland Yard has established itself, over more than a century of operations, as a highly effective investigative organization, its reputation based on its comparatively very high clear-up rates for *murder (where the culprit is identified, if not actually convicted), the most popular topic for *thriller writers. This expertise, which is applied effectively in cases of domestic homicide, has enhanced the status of Scotland Yard's famed Murder Squad. Statistically, most murderers in Britain are members of the same family as their victims, thereby making the detective's task much simpler. The squad's activities have been especially attractive to writers because, as there has never been a national police force in England, it is the provincial forces that have been obliged to "call in Scotland Yard" to tackle a particularly challenging crime. This sets the scene for the kind of tensions—typically between bumbling local yokels and arrogant Londoners—that authors require to bring their characters to life.

Many of Scotland Yard's authentic detectives, such as Chief Inspector Greeno, Commander Burt, and "Fabian of the Yard" have achieved considerable fame in their own right as police officers whose exploits have caught the public's imagination, and who thereby become the models for successive generations of popular novelists. Even though the romantically titled Flying Squad has now been amalgamated with the more prosaic Robbery Squad, Scotland Yard is still the home of the CID of the Metropolitan Police, and will continue to offer promising *plots to aficionados of crime mysteries.

[See also Police Detective; Police History: History of British Policing.]

—Rupert Allason

CIPHERS AND CODE. Like so many other aspects of detective fiction, the cipher and code story traces its origins to Edgar Allan *Poe. His classic tale "The Gold-Bug" (*Dollar Newspaper*, 21 and 28 June 1843) remains today the most widely read of all cipher stories, still appearing in many anthologies. The story of a search for Captain Kidd's hidden treasure is not without its errors, both in the listing of the frequency with which various letters appear in written English and in the use of invisible ink, but the excellence of Poe's narrative overcomes them. As in subsequent stories of codes and ciphers, the secret message adds interest to the tale while presenting an additional challenge for the reader.

Novelists as different as William Makepeace Thackeray in *The History of Henry Esmond, Esquire* (1852) and Jules Verne in *Voyage au centre de la terre* (1864, *A Journey to the Center of the Earth*) made some slight use of cryptology during the second half of the nineteenth century, but the next important appearance of cryptology in detective fiction had to await the arrival of Sherlock *Holmes. In "The Adventure of the Dancing Men" (*Strand*, Dec. 1903), Arthur Conan *Doyle's master sleuth is confronted with five brief messages in which stick figures with their arms and legs in various positions stand for letters of the alphabet. Holmes solves the cryptograms, but not in time to prevent a *murder. He then devises a message of his own, using the same cipher symbols, to lure the killer into a trap. (Although the British editions of the story show the cipher message correctly, certain errors have crept into some American editions.) Secret messages figure to a lesser extent in other Holmes stories, and in the 1915 novel *The Valley of Fear* Holmes encounters a book code that makes use of a copy of *Whitaker's Almanac*.

Other early twentieth-century writers also attempted stories of codes and ciphers, with varying degrees of success. "Calloway's Code" (*Whirligigs*, 1910) by O. Henry is an amusing story of a foreign correspondent sneaking his scoop past the censor's eyes. Codes involving the names of flowers figure in Agatha *Christie's "The Four Suspects" (*Pictoral Review*, Jan. 1930) and in E. C. *Bentley's "The Ministering Angel" (*Ellery Queen's Mystery Magazine*, Sept. 1943). Lillian de la Torre's "The Stolen Christmas Box" (*EQMM*, Jan. 1946) finds a unique usage for one character's peg leg in solving a skytale cipher. Authors have devised all sorts of cryptograms, from Anthony *Boucher's use of the Library of Congress classification system for books to Elsa Barker's cipher based on a roulette wheel. More than one writer has made use of the fact that there are twenty-six letters in the alphabet and twice that many playing cards in a deck. Or that *JASON D* can simply refer to the initial letters of the last six months of the year.

One problem confronting authors is to use a code or cipher simple enough for the reader to grasp while still fulfilling its function as a secret communication. Lord Peter *Wimsey, the classic creation of Dorothy L. *Sayers, manages to solve a sophisticated Playfair cipher in the 1932 novel *Have His Carcase*, while Helen McCloy's *Panic* (1944) contains one of the most complex cryptograms ever to appear in a novel.

A fascinating view of code breakers at work is contained in an all-but-forgotten novel by Dennison Clift, *The Spy in the Room* (1944; *Espionage Agent*). A somewhat similiar milieu appears in the 1968 spy film *Sebastian*. Beginning in 1965 *Ellery Queen's Mystery Magazine* published more than seventy-five stories by Edward D. Hoch about British code breaker Jeffrey Rand, director of the mythical Department of Concealed Communications, though Rand finally retired from the code business and subsequently tackled more general types of espionage.

Among more recent novels built around codes and ciphers special mention should be made of Ken Follett's *The Key to Rebecca* (1980), which uses a copy of Daphne *du Maurier's famed novel for a book code during World War II, and Robert Harris's *Enigma* (1995), which builds a mystery around British attempts to crack the Nazis' Enigma code. Perhaps it is not surprising that modern novels of codes and ciphers are harking back to the Second World War. Today's computer-generated ciphers can be all but unbreakable, a boon for spies but hardly for fiction writers.

[*See also* Letters and Written Messages; Spy Fiction.]

• Raymond T. Bond, ed., *Famous Stories of Code and Cipher* (1947). David Kahn, *The Codebreakers*, rev. ed. (1996).
—Edward D. Hoch

CIRCUS AND CARNIVAL MILIEU. Traveling carnivals and circuses have proven entertaining grounds for *murder. From the debut of Clayton *Rawson's magician-sleuth, the *Great Merlini, in 1938, to Stuart M. Kaminsky's Russian circus in *A Fine Red Rain* (1987), the use of this *setting has brought an element of the grotesque and the flamboyant to the mystery genre. With casts of characters ranging from the eccentric to the freakish, and with physical environments offering singular opportunities for foul play, the *milieu allows for often bizarre creativity in the method and circumstances of death. Novels set in carnivals and circuses fully capitalize on the prevalence of *disguises, talent in deception, and extraordinary physical abilities of circus and carnival characters, as well as on the geographical mobility and nomadic ambience of the setting.

The setting was particularly popular in the 1930s and 40s. Rawson's *Death from a Top Hat* (1938) and *The Headless Lady* (1940) are two of the best-known carnival and circus mysteries. Rawson, an American magician whose stage name was the Great Merlini, was known as one of the most skilled illusionists of his time. His fictional hero, likewise the Great Merlini, was a professional magician and *amateur detective, born in a Barnum and Bailey circus car, who specialized in solving apparently impossible *locked room mysteries. The character's cases were known for magic feats and startling effects that sometimes stretched credibility but contributed nonetheless to their widespread popularity. Nigel Morland, a contemporary of Rawson's, set *The Corpse on the Flying Trapeze* (1941) in a traveling circus where his famous sleuth Mrs. Palmyra Pym investigates how and why an acrobat was beheaded while swinging from a trapeze in full view of an audience. Alan Melville (pseudonym of William Melville Caverhill) sets *Death of Anton* (1936) in a traveling circus where a tiger tamer has been murdered because of his knowledge of a dope-running scheme. The connection of the three-ring circus with drug trafficking or other smuggling operations is a frequent element introduced by Martin Joseph Freeman in *The Murder of a Midget* (1931). Stuart Palmer, in the first of two Howie Rook novels, *Unhappy Hooligan* (1956; *Death in Grease*

Paint), draws on his experience as a clown in the Ringling Brothers' circus in a novel that takes a light approach to murder. More recently, Kaminsky, in *A Fine Red Rain*, takes his Russian policeman Porfiry Rostnikov back to his childhood and the circus, where he defics the *KGB to protect a young female acrobat from murder. The plot follows the investigation of the murder of circus acrobats in connection with an immigration smuggling scheme. Kaminsky had used the setting earlier in *Catch a Falling Clown* (1982). Additional titles using the carnival and circus milieu as a setting include Ellery *Queen's *The American Gun Mystery* (1933; *Death at the Rodeo*), Leo *Bruce's *The Case with Four Clowns* (1939), Clifford Knight's *The Affair of the Circus Queen* (1940), Nigel Morland's *Corpse in the Circus* (1945), Jean Marsh's *Death Visits the Circus* (1953), and Mark McShane's *Night Evil* (1966).   —Lizabeth Paravisini-Gebert

CLARK, MARY HIGGINS (b. 1928), American author of best-selling mystery and *suspense novels. A *New York City native, Clark had a varied range of work and personal experience before she achieved fame and high standing as a writer. She has worked as an advertising assistant, airline flight attendant, radio scriptwriter, producer, and partner in a communications firm. In 1979 she completed a B.A. degree at Fordham University. It is not necessary to claim autobiographical content for her writing to see that lived experience has been a source of the feeling that readers find in her work.

In place of the process of detection that contours one prominent path taken by the crime and mystery genre, Clark explores the topography originally detailed by the *sensation novel. Her interest lies in the crime under way or yet to come if all goes wrong. Her narrative *point of view just as often illuminates the schemes and psychology of the culprit as it does the fears of the *victim. Her *plots examine familiar and, for that reason, unnerving circumstances and the material yielding the *suspense, which is the chief effect of her narratives, is generally associated with the experiences and interests of women. *Where Are the Children?* (1975), Clark's first novel and the start of her string of best-sellers, places two children in danger from a kidnapper exploiting a mystery in their mother's past. *A Cry in the Night* (1982) recounts a woman's discovery that the man she thought she knew well enough to marry is in fact a stranger. Yet, while culture associates the connection of destiny and *family as Clark presents it with the realm of life conventionally assigned to women, her narratives cannot be termed parochial, limited, or strictly feminine; Clark's insight is that the fears that may arise in the life of intimacy bespeak the needs at the foundation of social life for all.

With the publication of *Decked* (1992), Clark's daughter, Carol Higgins Clark, began a series that works its changes on the mystery formula by featuring a private detective named Regan Reilly who is the child of the famous crime writer Nora Regan Reilly.

[*See also* Kidnapping; Missing Persons; Pursuit; Stalking.]   —John M. Reilly

CLASS, or the organization of people into groups in a hierarchy according to birth, wealth, or occupation, has long played a role in crime fiction. Class may appear as a theme, as background information or description, or as the unconscious attitude of the author. Class consciousness in crime fiction parallels closely class consciousness in contemporary society, changing as the standards of society change.

Class occurs regularly, if rarely as a theme by itself. In *Trent's Last Case* (1913; *The Woman in Black*), E. C. *Bentley depicted his distaste for the new moneyed class being created by the fabulous wealth in America, and his longing for a return to what he saw as the stability, gentility, and familiarity of the traditional class system of England. Bentley's preference for the older class system, with its manor house and servants, was overt and thematic. Author Ann Bridge included a warm critique of the feudal system in *The Portuguese Escape* (1958), stressing its economic benefits for the poorer members of society.

In most instances, authors writing with an awareness of the class system oppose its many vices rather than uphold its virtues. Michael *Gilbert depicts the restrictions of class in the years before World War I in *Ring of Terror* (1995), reminding the reader of the power of class *prejudice to shape a life. Luke Pagan makes the mistake of capturing Sir George's son setting illegal snares and refuses to back down when challenged. Class rebellion cannot be tolerated, and Luke is forced to make his way in another world. In *Death and the Dancing Footman* (1942), Ngaio *Marsh depicts the brittle hollowness of the British class system before World War II; the upper classes seem to have forgotten the principles of generosity and fair play originally informing the laws of the land. Fifty years later, in *Blanche on the Lam* (1992), Barbara Neely's African American housekeeper, Blanche White, gives a working woman's perspective of the Southern aristocracy in a state of decline and a black woman's perspective of white people trying to maintain social superiority in an increasingly egalitarian world. This theme is taken up by Ruth *Rendell in *Simisola* (1994): Chief Inspector *Wexford investigates the death of a young black woman and uncovers the new class distinctions in England and their insidious effects. As Rendell illustrates, those with power and wealth, the result of education, birth, and occupation, can still do almost anything they wish within the structure of an orderly society, simply because they are removed from the world of police *suspicion.

More typical of mystery fiction has been the presence of cultural bias as an expression of the author's implicit worldview. Agatha *Christie deeply loved England and all things English, and offhandedly disparaged America and its goal of a classless society. The social *milieu in such stories as *A Murder Is Announced* (1950) is integral not only to the story but also to Christie's view that crime arises in part by people trying to be what they are not. Dorothy L. *Sayers, whose creation Lord Peter *Wimsey is the epitome of the illusions held about the upper classes, which she envied, revealed her biases more directly in *Gaudy Night* (1935) when she romanticized the world of the woman scholar and pinned the crime on someone of a class different from the other *suspects as well as the *victims. The explanations at the conclusion reveal Sayers's ambitions for herself as a scholar as well as her class of educated women. Gladys *Mitchell reveals her biases in favor of the upper class in the comments and behavior of her series character Mrs. Adela Beatrice Lestrange *Bradley, a psychologist; in *Death of a Delft Blue* (1964), class bias merges with *anti-Semitism. Almost any book from the *Golden Age tradition will supply an example of the author's class and cultural biases. Colin *Watson has analyzed these in *Snobbery with Violence* (1971), highlighting not only the class consciousness but also the racial, gender, and ethnic consciousness implicit in almost every line. One of the rare exceptions merits mention: Freeman Wills *Crofts's Inspector Joseph *French sticks strictly to detection, treating all with exactly the same respect.

Since World War II, numerous writers have become conscious of class and class biases in crime fiction, and have written about class with awareness and understanding. In part, this trend is related to the rise of the *police procedural (which is essentially a product of the postwar years and has a middle-class point of view) and, in part, to the lowering of class barriers. Occasionally an upper-class character makes an appearance as a police officer, such as the patrician Detective Chief Inspector Alistair Lingard in Jonathan Ross's series starring Inspector George Rogers or Detective Inspector Thomas Lynley in Elizabeth George's series, but such characters are now expected to move in a broader social milieu and must prove themselves to be of sound character. Suspects may still threaten to appeal to their good friend the chief constable, but this is much more likely to signal their *guilt than be taken as a failing in their social class, as it would have been during the Golden Age.

Some romanticization of the upper classes continues in Charlotte MacLeod's Sarah Kelling and Max Bittersohn mysteries, which feature the last remnants of Boston's codfish aristocracy, usually shown as wildly eccentric if not downright batty. Jane Langton's Homer Kelly books often include members of East Coast elites; and Julie Smith's Skip Langdon mysteries feature the New Orleans elite, defined by old money and old mores.

In contrast, several writers have chosen to focus on the other end of the social scale. Elmore *Leonard describes the world of a luckless but energetic criminal underclass in Detroit and Miami, "lowlifes" both black and white. George V. *Higgins, especially in his earlier novels, did the same for the Boston Irish operating on both sides of the law. The American term "lowlife" used by these and other writers signals an important perceptual shift, and obliquely reflects the biases of earlier authors. Probably the most sensitive social antennae of any American mystery writer were owned by John D. *MacDonald, who wrote a series of *thrillers in the 1950s and 1960s focusing on the postwar American middle class, newly enriched and full of fatal flaws.

In *spy fiction, upper-class origins can mark a vacant, nonprofessional, even amoral character. John *le Carré shows a touch of this class consciousness and Len *Deighton rather more. Gavin Lyall, in his Major Harry Maxim series, seems to fit somewhere between the two. The central theme of Brian Freemantle's Charlie Muffin spy thrillers is that Charlie, a professional but a prole, can expect to be betrayed by his well-bred masters. Only William F. Buckley Jr.'s Blackford Oakes thriller series suggests that class, defined by birth and education, can hold an advantage for the protagonist.

Class is never absent from crime fiction, but awareness of it as a vice or a *virtue varies with the corresponding view of contemporary society; few forms of literature record as accurately the changing perceptions of class and its effects on a community.

[See also Aristocratic Characters: The Aristocratic Sleuth; Aristocratic Characters: Secondary Aristocratic Characters; Bluestocking Sleuth; Conservative vs. Radical Worldview.]

• Colin Watson, *Snobbery with Violence: Crime Stories and Their Audience* (1971). —Dean A. Miller

CLERICAL MILIEU. *This entry is divided into two parts, the first surveying the use of the clerical milieu by British writers, and the second pointing out the manner in which the choice of the clerical milieu by American authors has a particular influence upon characterization and theme.*

The British Clerical Milieu
The American Clerical Milieu

For further information, please refer to Clerical Sleuth.

THE BRITISH CLERICAL MILIEU

A variety of *settings are employed within the British clerical milieu, including the vicarage, church or cathedral, convent, monastery, and retreat, wherever men and women religious gather to work, live, or pray. The detective pursuing the solution to a crime may be a man or woman religious, a police officer, an amateur, or a *private eye; there are no restrictions on who can serve as *sleuth in this *milieu. In a genre concerned with *justice, with bringing every culprit to a suitable punishment, the clerical setting allows the author to explore in greater detail issues of right and wrong, as well as the more specific moral issues of the time. In addition, the clerical milieu offers a closed community even more restricted than the usual village or small town while still including distinctive characters in some sort of hierarchy and social structure. The rules and codes by which clerical men and women live offer complications for the *plot.

The choice of a clerical setting does not always result in a discussion of *religion or ethics. In Agatha *Christie's *The Murder at the Vicarage* (1930), the vicarage of Saint Mary Mead is merely the site of the *murder of Colonel Protheroe and does not occasion grander speculations in the detective, Miss Jane

*Marple, or the police. Dorothy L. *Sayers expatiates on the little-known art of campanology, and on the restricted life of a rural vicar, in *The Nine Tailors* (1934). A different tack is taken by Ngaio *Marsh in *Death in Ecstasy* (1936), where she explores the deception and pettiness beneath the surface of pious behavior among members of a minor religious group. Edmund *Crispin's sleuth, *Oxford don Gervase *Fen, finds much of the same in the difficulties of a famous composer and organist invited to take over the services at a provincial cathedral in *Holy Disorders* (1945). The cathedral close has long been a popular setting, chosen by Colin *Dexter, Kate Charles, and others.

Catherine Aird's sleuth, Inspector C. D. Sloan, investigates the murder of a nun in a convent, exploring this closed community and the consequences of entering such a life for the woman and the *family left behind, in *The Religious Body* (1966). Robert *Barnard explores contemporary issues in *Blood Brotherhood* (1977), when a gathering of men and women religious to discuss the role of the church in the modern world leads to murder. The most comprehensive use of the clerical milieu is made perhaps by Ellis *Peters, whose Brother Cadfael series explores life in twelfth-century England. Her depiction of life in a monastery and its environs serves as a continuing commentary on contemporary life. In *The Leper of Saint Giles* (1981), Peters highlights the moral issues of compassion in ways not always possible in contemporary settings.

[*See also* Cathedral Close Milieu; Chivalry, Code of; Clerical Sleuth; Closed-World Settings and Open-World Settings.]

• Catherine Aird, "The Devout: Vicars, Curates and Relentlessly Inquisitive Clerics," in *Murder Ink: The Mystery Reader's Companion,* ed. Dilys Winn (1977; 1984). William David Spencer, *Mysterium and Mystery: The Clerical Crime Novel* (1989).
                                                   —Susan Oleksiw

THE AMERICAN CLERICAL MILIEU

The British clerical mystery had thrived for decades when American Anthony *Boucher, writing as H. H. Holmes, introduced Sister Ursula, the able investigator of locked room puzzles, in *Nine Times Nine* (1940) and *Rocket to the Morgue* (1942). Shortly after Sister Ursula's debut, the Protestant missionary Dr. Mary Finney, a worldly woman created by Matthew Head, appeared in *The Devil in the Bush* (1945). Margaret Ann Hubbard carried on the image of the practical nun in her fiction about Sister Simon, who, among other acts of boldness, capably holds a villain at gunpoint until the police arrive.

Some male clerics are fully as action-oriented as the practical women of the cloth. In Father Joseph Bredder, O. F. M., Leonard Holton created a *sleuth whose background as a former marine and boxer equips him to pursue adventures in East *Los Angeles. Yet Father Bredder, who first appeared in *The Saint Maker* (1959), is also a counselor of souls who can build evidence based upon "spiritual fingerprints" that are unseen by the police lieutenant who is his secular partner.

Beginning with *Friday the Rabbi Slept Late* (1964), Harry Kemelman built a series around Rabbi David *Small, who in another variation on the *clerical sleuth demonstrates that modes of reasoning derived from Jewish tradition are efficacious in solving crimes as varied as murder in a synagogue parking lot and an incident involving terrorism in Israel. Soon a television series introduced a new audience to Father Roger Dowling, created originally by Ralph McInerny in *Her Death of Cold* (1977). Like Rabbi Small and Father Bredder before him, and in the tradition set by G. K. *Chesterton in the stories of English priest Father *Brown, Father Dowling is as interested in the spiritual condition of the people he encounters as he is in their *guilt or *innocence in the eyes of the secular legal system. Under the pen name of Monica Quill, McInerny is also responsible for creation of another figure in the line of female clerics: Sister Mary Teresa (Dempsey), known as Attila the Nun among her familiars, a practitioner of armchair detection confident that her reasoning can outdo police procedure.

As the years have passed, the American clerical milieu has continued to take up themes in circulation among the news and entertainment media. In *Topless* (1991), for example, D. Keith Mano's Father Mike Wilson crusades against the "routine humiliation of women," and Father Andrew M. Greeley's fictional Monsignor John Blackwood "Blackie" Ryan displays as broad a set of concerns about the ills of the world and church as his prolific author does. Yet what will continue to fuel American authors who write about the clerical milieu may be that, in their view, to divorce the worlds of flesh and spirit is to betray an inability to see reality whole.

[*See also* Cathedral Close Milieu; Closed-World Settings and Open-World Settings; Religion.]
                                                   —William D. Spencer

CLERICAL SLEUTH. The significant position of the clergy in English literature is well documented. The age-old conflict between the church and crime has yielded much detective fiction and some clerical detectives, and has also been the subject of comment in theological and other publications.

Dorothy L. *Sayers, herself a daughter of the vicarage, postulated that the first clerical detective was the prophet Daniel. She argued that in the apocryphal stories of Susanna and the Elders and Bel and the Dragon, Daniel demonstrated his investigative skills in proving the innocence of Susanna and the perfidy involved in the worshipping of a false god.

G. K. *Chesterton's celibate Roman Catholic priest Father *Brown was an early clerical investigator in the genre, first appearing in the short stories that comprise *The Innocence of Father Brown* (1911). Although a notably compassionate man with an ability to put himself in other men's shoes with all their human weaknesses, nevertheless he takes a stern theological view of righteousness, as do his fictional peers. This trained capacity for making sound moral judgements is an important feature of clerical detectives, however lovable or idiosyncratic; so too is their uniform ability to make the sound, evidence-based judgments essential in the genre.

Clerical sleuths have advantages over other investigators in that they are usually able to go everywhere, talk to everyone—no one so spans the social spectrum as the clergy—and take as much time as they need. Nor, as a rule, are they answerable to any worldly body for their actions.

Some authors in this field have themselves been clerks in holy orders and thus observant in both senses. These include Canon Victor L. *Whitechurch, Dean Cyril A. Alington, Monsignor Ronald A. *Knox, and the Reverend Austin Lee who, although he wrote as both Julian Callendar and John Austwick, used his real name for *Miss Hogg and the Dead Dean* (1958). George A. Birmingham was in real life the Reverend James Owen Hannay. His *Hymn Tune Mystery* (1930) was church-based; but while an ecclesiastical *setting has become less usual over the years, a more ecumenical field of professionally unshockable clerical detectives has burgeoned.

These include Methodist minister Charles Merrill Smith's Reverend C. P. "Con" Randolph; Pauline King's Wesleyan Evan Morgan (in *Snares of the Enemy*, 1985); and Margaret Scherf's Episcopalian Minister, Reverend Martin Buell. Ellis *Peters's extensive series about Brother *Cadfael, a professed monk on the Welsh Marches in the turbulent twelfth century, began with *A Morbid Taste for Bones* (1977). In Umberto Eco's *Il Nome Della Rose* (1983; *The Name of the Rose*), set in a Franciscan Abbey in Italy in 1327, the sleuth is Brother William. A holy man is murdered in *La Puissance du Neart* (1982; *The Power of Nothingness*), by Alexandra David-Neel and Lama Youngden, in which the detection is done by a Tibetan Buddhist monk.

The cadre of heirs of Father Brown are in his tradition of the caring, endearing, shrewd but not wholly worldly; they include Andrew Greeley's fictional detective Monsignor John Blackwood Ryan, who made his debut in *Happy Are the Meek* (1985). Leonard Holton has created a series with Father Joseph Breddar as the investigator. Ralph McInery's considerable output of Father Roger Dowling stories began with *Her Death of Cold* and *The Seventh Station* (both 1977). William X. Kienzle's series hero, beginning with *The Rosary Murders* (1979), is Father Bob Koesler. Dorothy Salisbury *Davis's Father McMahon is more than usually tested in *Where the Dark Streets Go* (1969).

The higher Anglican hierarchy feature in the works of Thurman Warriner, whose hero is Archdeacon Toft, and in *Solemn High Murder* (1975) by Barbara Nirde Byfield and Frank L. Tedeschi, where the clerical sleuth is an aide to the Archbishop of Canterbury. The works of Freda Bream are set in New Zealand and cover the activities of the Reverend Jabal Jarrett, while those of John Armour are set in the outback of Australia.

In a different, older religious tradition are the works of Harry Kemelman, whose totally logical but endearing hero is Rabbi David *Small. Joseph Telushkin, an Orthodox rabbi, is the author of *The Unorthodox Murder of Rabbi Wahl* (1986; *The Un-orthodox Murder of Rabbi Moss*), in which the crime of the title is solved by his Rabbi Daniel Winter. And in *The Angel of Zin* (1984), by Clifford Irving, Rabbi Jacob Hurwicz investigates in a Nazi concentration camp.

Convents provide unlikely but effective bases for investigation, as in *Quiet as a Nun* (1977), by Antonia Fraser. Some sequestered religious sleuths, such as Anthony *Boucher's Sister Ursula, are hampered by grille and cloister, but the scholarly Sister Mary Dempsey, created by Monica Quill, is more mobile.

The Sister Fidelma novels of Peter Tremayne—for example, *Absolution by Murder* (1994)—have a seventh-century nun-lawyer of the Celtic church as their sleuth, while the works of Henry Catalan feature French nun Soeur Angele. More lighthearted is *A Nun in the Closet* (1975; *A Nun in the Cupboard*), wherein real-life Sister Carol Anne O'Marie has her detection performed by Sister Mary Helen.

A development reflecting recent ecclesiastical changes is the introduction of ordained women sleuths. The books of D. M. Greenwood feature Theodora Braithwaite, curate of London's St. Sylvester's, those of Isabelle Holland have as their sleuth the Reverend Claire Aldington, an American woman Episcopalian minister.

[See also Cathedral Close Milieu; Clerical Milieu; Religion.]

• Dorothy L. Sayers, introductions to *Great Short Stories of Detection, Mystery and Horror* (1928–34). F. E. Christmas, ed., *The Parson in English Literature* (1950). W. H. Auden, "The Guilty Vicarage," *Harper's Magazine* (May 1948). David G. Hawkins, "Whodunit Theology," *Anglican Theological Review* 71, no. 3 (summer 1989); revised version reprinted in *Christianity Today* 34, no. 16 (5 Nov. 1990).

—Catherine Aird

CLOSED-WORLD SETTINGS AND OPEN-WORLD SETTINGS. Those critics characterizing detective fiction as a movement from order through disorder to a final state of order—critics such as W. H. Auden, for one—doubtless also feel that the smaller the world under examination, the more effective will be the impression of restored order. A closed world also has the considerable practical advantage to writers of limiting the body of *suspects and, more or less, simplifying social differences. Edgar Allan *Poe declared "a narrow circumspection of space" the sine qua non of both the poem and short story, and it was he who first employed the limits of the most circumscribed of *murder scenes, the locked room. The crime of Wilkie *Collins's *The Moonstone* (1868) occurs in a country house; only the retribution is rendered in the metropolis. Charles *Dickens begins *The Mystery of Edwin Drood* (1870) in a seedy, anonymous *London but soon moves the narrative to a provincial cathedral town where the characters are all known to one another. Most of the cases that Arthur Conan *Doyle crafts for Sherlock *Holmes are centered in London, but the city is not so large that it cannot be encompassed by the Baker Street Irregulars.

Variants of nearly claustrophobic closed scenes deal with airplanes, trains, and ships. Agatha

*Christie found the narrow confines of transport useful in *Death in the Clouds* (1935; *Death in the Air*), *Murder on the Orient Express* (1934; *Murder on the Calais Coach*), and *Death on the Nile* (1937), while Ethel Lina White in *The Wheel Spins* (1936; *The Lady Vanishes*) presented the possibilities in a train-bound mystery that Alfred Hitchcock later exploited in his 1938 film adaptation, *The Lady Vanishes*.

Agatha Christie also offers the locus classicus for that most familiar closed world, the English country village. In the United States, Ellery *Queen may be the writer who most often rings the changes on closed circles for narrative action: from the island of *The King Is Dead* (1952) to upstate New York mansions in *The Finishing Stroke* (1958).

A recognizable hallmark of the closed-world is the linking of characters' lives. This is true of the ecclesiastical communities created by Ellis *Peters. It is even more recurrently true of the university, as in Dorothy L. *Sayers's *Gaudy Night* (1935), Helen Eustis's *The Horizontal Man* (1946), Thomas Kyd's *Blood Is a Beggar* (1946), Ross *Macdonald's *The Chill* (1964), Robert Bernard's *Deadly Meeting* (1970), and Antonia Fraser's *Oxford Blood* (1985), among others. Rivalling the ecclesiastical and academic worlds is the slightly larger, but still closed world of Hollywood, which entered detective fiction in a major way with Arthur B. *Reeve's *The Film Mystery* (1921). Since then the list has been long and has included such instances of hard-boiled writing as Raymond *Chandler's *The Little Sister* (1949) and Robert B. *Parker's *A Savage Place* (1981).

*Hard-boiled fiction, with its typical urban setting, seems to offer the fullest possibility for detective fiction in an open world—a world without carefully tended boundaries or efficiently enforced *class lines—but the mean streets may still represent a variety of closed world. That is what is to be found in Dashiell *Hammett's treatment of Poisonville in *Red Harvest* (1929). Hard-boiled fiction, just as often as Golden Age fiction, represents crime in the *setting of the *family, unquestionably one of the narrowest, and often closed, of worlds. And that vital subgenre of the hard-boiled, the *police procedural, although set in an anonymous and heterogeneous city, lodges its lead characters in the closed world of the station house, precinct, or central headquarters.

For an immeasurably open world, the reader turns to Arthur W. *Upfield, whose Inspector Napoleon *Bonaparte operates in the vast spaces of the Australian outback; or, among American writers, to Tony *Hillerman, whose characters Joe Leaphorn and Jim *Chee do their police business on the tracts of Native American reservations in the Southwest. Still, it is in Hillerman at least the geography that is vast and open. The world of society, the residence of *victims, bystanders, and killers has limits definite enough to support the argument that detective fiction, as Poe said, demands a limited world.

[*See also* Academic Milieu; Clerical Milieu; English Village Milieu; Locked Room Mystery; Railway Milieu; Travel Milieu; Urban Milieu.]

—Barrie Hayne

CLUB MILIEU. The gentleman's club as portrayed in detective fiction is typically a closed-world environment set at a *London or *New York City address, furnished with leather armchairs, populated with sleepy, stuffy, or eccentric characters, and exuding an *atmosphere of civility that makes a striking contrast with violent crime. The setting is also useful to the mystery writer in constituting an accidental meeting place and a jumping-off point for adventures, serving as an indicator of social status, and providing a nostalgic quality beloved of many readers of mysteries.

In some novels, the club itself has been the focus of the whole story. Dorothy L. *Sayers's *The Unpleasantness at the Bellona Club* (1928) is a classic specimen: The detective (Lord Peter *Wimsey), murderer, and *victim are indeed all members, and there is a supporting cast of other slightly Wodehousian clubmen. Similarly, in *The Lost Gallows* (1931), an early but powerfully atmospheric novel by John Dickson *Carr, the sinister Brimstone Club holds the key to the mystery.

These books were written, imaginatively, from the outside. In contrast, *My Foe Outstretch'd Beneath the Tree* (1968) by V. C. Clinton-Baddeley and *Conduct of a Member* (1967) by Val Gielgud are affectionate, knowledgeable, and amused portrayals of London club life. A more recent example, set almost entirely in one of New York's university clubs, is *This Club Frowns on Murder* (1990) by Albert Borowitz.

The Diogenes Club, a club for "the most unsocial and unclubbable men in London," gave Arthur Conan *Doyle an appropriate *setting in which to introduce Sherlock *Holmes's brother Mycroft *Holmes. And in Michael *Innes's *Silence Observed* (1961), the problem of a forged manuscript is first mentioned to Inspector John *Appleby at his club. Margery *Allingham's Albert *Campion was revealed to be a much grander person than he seemed to be when somebody spotted him entering one of the smartest clubs in *London.

For A. J. *Raffles-type stories, such as Frank L. Packard's Jimmie Dale series and much interwar pulp fiction, the protagonist's membership in an aristocratic club both fixed his own social position and facilitated piquant encounters with the district attorney or chief of police. Richard Usborne's *Clubland Heroes* (1953) entertainingly analyzes the novels of John *Buchan, Sapper, and Dornford *Yates, whose characters are denizens of clubland. And clubland constituted, for authors such as Ian *Fleming and William Haggard, a proper background to the daily lives of senior intelligence officers. In reality as in fiction, this milieu is visited by those in the intelligence game.

Because the very features—exclusivity and masculinity—which rendered clubland so useful to earlier crime writers were anathema to a new generation of leftish and feminist-influenced writers, clubs latterly have been presented as the habitat, even the symbol, of conspirators and *villains, rather than of heroes. Exceptionally, and a touch apologetically, Haughton Murphy has allowed his elderly protagonist Reuben Frost regular visits to a New York club referred to as his "play-house".

Club members and their guests, in volumes from

Sapper's *The Dinner Club* (1923) to Isaac Asimov's Black Widowers series, have told each other stories across the table. Carr's *He Who Whispers* (1946) begins with a frustrated meeting of a group not unlike London's *Detection Club, of which Carr was himself an enthusiastic member. *In the Fog* (1901) by Richard Harding Davis, although written by an American journalist, vividly depicts a London club almost certainly modelled on the Beefsteak.

Clubmen everywhere may frown on murder theoretically and deplore it on their own premises, but in fiction and in fact they love talking about it, which causes clubland to remain a hospitable ground for crime writing.

[*See also* Class; Males and the Male Image.]

—Anthony Lejeune

CLUES. In its archetypal form, the crime and detection story relates the crime and its aftermath of confusion requiring a detective to explain. It also recounts the work of detection, leading to the *sleuth's reconstruction of the hidden reality of the crime— the questions of who committed it, how, and why. In this literature, clues function as signposts on the road to the explanation of the mystery. Secondary characters will overlook the signs or misread them; readers may find them indecipherable or unremarkable until the detective translates them into language of exposition. But clues are in fact inert data given an instrumental place in the story where the detective explains all.

Writers vary the archetype, and in doing so have created distinctively different workings of the crime and mystery genre, but the economy of narration in any of its forms cannot afford loss of the generative power of clues. Stories employing the convention of the *Great Detective modeled on the character of the consulting wizard Sherlock *Holmes feature clues as the sleuth's raw material for dazzling solutions. However, illustration of the method for detection does not exhaust the function of clues. When the detective's sidekick, standing in as representative of the ordinary reader, draws inferences from clues and soon thereafter has those inferences corrected, clues serve to characterize the detective as fully worthy to preside over the story: The detective's readings of clues show an extraordinary ability to discover truth, sharply contrasting with the more ordinary capacities of the sidekick. Still, that is not all there can be to the function of clues in the Great Detective's story. The type of clue the detective works with helps to set philosophical and technical dimensions for the detective's world. When clues leading to the solution of a crime are physical or material ones, they imply that reality can be fully comprehended through the empirical techniques of natural science. Thus, they may lend an *atmosphere of optimism to the narrative. Additionally, the disciplines of investigation—chemistry, fingerprinting, forensic anatomy—besides certifying the efficacy of a detection method, give authors plausible means to introduce an intrinsically interesting *milieu into the story.

While many of the early Great Detective stories use clues to establish the eminence of sleuths who are in some way scientific, later authors have endowed their sleuths with cultural, rather than scientific, expertise used to guide them in interpreting clues. Arthur W. *Upfield's aboriginal Australian detective Napoleon *Bonaparte applies his native skills as a tracker to solution of crime. So do Joe Leaphorn and Jim *Chee, Tony *Hillerman's Navajo police officers. Each of these detectives, especially the Navajo protagonists, is meant by their authors to represent the rich life of non-European peoples. The clues discoverable in the natural settings of their fictions, therefore, educe cultural themes that serve to instruct readers.

As the illustrations from the annals of Great Detectives and ethnic detection show, clues function on two levels within crime and mystery narrative. Clues offer structure to description of detection, while on another level they are means for the author to entice the reader's interest. In *The Murder of Roger Ackroyd* (1926), Agatha *Christie conceals the identity of the murderer beneath the conventions of narration. The reader is led by past experience with detective fiction to believe that the first-person narrator is either the detective or an aide, but never the *villain. When the voice telling the story turns out to be the killer himself, the reader has to scramble to recall the subtle clues Christie has lodged in the manner of the narrator's accounting of the crime. In *Murder on the Orient Express* (1934; *Murder in the Calais Coach*) clues abound for the examination of Hercule *Poirot, but they seem to point to the *guilt of more than one person. Indeed, the crime has been a group project, defying once again a convention of criminous story telling. In each of these novels, Christie finds the opportunity to rework conventions by mining clues for their utility in founding narrative criminal plots.

Dorothy L. *Sayers, collaborating with Robert Eustace in *The Documents in the Case* (1930), produced what is perhaps the most extensive use of clues for plotting. While the story is a classical mystery, the narrative is almost entirely epistolary: A series of letters provides the clues that lead to the solution of the *puzzle. The remarkable twist here lies in the authors' replacing a report of clues with direct presentation of them, so that readers are invited to become actively engaged in the *plot of detection and to help produce the narrative of explanation. A similar exploitation of clues to pull readers into plotting the story occurs in the novels of Ellery *Queen. Queen's trademark "Challenge to the Reader" informs the audience that all the clues have been laid out, and the narrative takes a pause to allow readers to match wits with the detective.

The Ellery Queen stories belong to the category of crime and mystery writing in which clues are both material for demonstration of detection skill and opportunity for an intellectual game. These puzzle stories call upon authorial *ingenuity to arrange revelation of clues in a way that will baffle readers without treating them unfairly. Early examples can be found in the Uncle *Abner stories by Melville Davisson *Post. In "An Act of God" (*Uncle Abner, Master of*

Mysteries, 1918) Abner explains that a note purportedly written by a deaf man contains a phonetically inspired misspelling. The note is as available to the reader as it is to Abner himself; but Post, much like Christie, realized that his audience would read with merely normal care when special alertness is necessary. Post also wrote versions of the *locked room mystery, which demands a greater diversion of the audience. Masterful examples of clues concealed are rife in the locked room novels by John Dickson *Carr about Dr. Gideon *Fell. Carr diverts readers' attention by subordinating clues to distracting incidents, but is particularly notable in employing improbability. Readers will insistently relate occurrences to their real life experience when the novel is actually about a *puzzle, not reality.

The absence of certain clues can be as significant as their presence. This is the case in Dorothy B. Hughes's *The Expendable Man* (1963), where a young doctor is not revealed to be an African American until well along in the text when a bigoted police officer calls him a nigger. From that point on, the story is altered by the inclusion of America's racial obsession. Hughes's late insertion of a clue shifts the focus of the narrative and gives it a new cadence. Clues introduced early in a story can be equally functional in establishing atmosphere and setting the pace of narration. Patricia *Highsmith's *The Tremor of Forgery* (1969), for example, presents a character in its opening pages anxiously asking a hotel attendant if a letter has arrived. As H. R. F. *Keating points out in *Crime and Mystery: The 100 Best Books* (1987), this passage introduces a riddle that the reader cannot help wanting to solve and thus creates a mood of *suspense.

The examples from Hughes and Highsmith point to a significant change that clues undergo the further this genre moves from the classical forms. In *hard-boiled fiction, clues become increasingly nonmaterial even as the environment takes on a naturalistic form in which material conditions determine the destiny of life. For *hard-boiled sleuths, clues more often than not are circumstantial, insufficient to build a case for court but adequate to justify the detective's use of action and guile to pursue the presumptive villains. The wholesale marginalization of physical clues accords to those that remain a symbolic quality and function. Dashiell *Hammett's black bird, the object of the quest in *The Maltese Falcon* (1930) and the leading clue to the identity of the criminals, takes on the attributes of the cash nexus of capitalism, its exchange value providing the sole basis for human associations and purposes in the novel. The very titles of Raymond *Chandler's *The High Window* (1942) and Kenneth Fearing's *The Big Clock* (1946) signify things that have only the slightest value as physical clues aiding in solution of crime, but enormous importance as dominant symbols that set a tone for narration.

Predictably, the use of intangible clues has its greatest development in psychologically centered stories of crime and mystery. Georges *Simenon's Inspector Jules *Maigret infers clues from his imaginative entry into the behavior of criminals, and the novels of Ross *Macdonald present Lew *Archer his clues in the form of information about trauma and its dysfunctional results in the psyches of the characters. In Margaret *Millar's *A Stranger in My Grave* (1960) the initial clues setting the narrative in motion arrive in the form of a haunting dream, and Amanda *Cross's *Death in a Tenured Position* (1981; *A Death in the Faculty*) locates its conclusive clues in the tangle of character motivations. Even *police procedural stories, which by the nature of their attention to routine police methods might be expected to use only the most tangible clues, show that nonmaterial reality, in their cases reached through interrogation of suspects and knowledge of criminal profiles, can provide the clues for satisfactory solutions of crimes and satisfying reading.

The genre of crime and mystery writing might well be denominated by the literature of clues, for, apart from the representation of the detective characters themselves, nothing is more reflective of the inspiration at the core of the genre or more functionally productive for authors than clues.

[*See also* Ciphers and Code; Clues, Famous; Dying Message; Fingerprints and Footprints; Letters and Written Messages; Pathfinder Fiction; Red Herrings; Sleight of Hand.]
—John M. Reilly

CLUES, FAMOUS. From the earliest days of the genre, mystery writers have used elaborate clues as a means of seizing their readers' attention. Clues become especially memorable when they are obvious but at first indecipherable, or if they are ordinarily unnoticed items or events that may be put to bizarre use or interpreted in highly inventive ways.

*Ciphers and codes announce themselves as clues from the start. The first of many crime stories in which ciphers play a part was Edgar Allan *Poe's "The Gold-Bug" (*Tales*, 1845), in which the code provides directions for finding pirates' treasure. Arthur Conan *Doyle used a similar device for Abe Slaney's threatening hieroglyphs in "The Adventure of the Dancing Men" (*Strand*, Dec. 1903). The *dying message of a *murder *victim also offers scope for *ingenuity in providing a clue to the culprit's identity and a classic example is to be found in Ellery *Queen's "The Adventure Of The Bearded Lady" (*The Adventures of Ellery Queen*, 1934), in which a beard is painted on the chin of a woman in a Rembrandt copy. The crucial deduction is that Dr. Arlen was implying that his murderer was a person who seemed to be a woman but was really a man.

It takes a gifted fictional detective to interpret the seemingly inconsequential clue correctly. In Wilkie *Collins's *The Moonstone* (1868), Sergeant *Cuff rebukes a colleague who refers to a smear of paint on a door as a "trifle": The paint stain on Franklin Blake's nightgown appears to provide proof of his *guilt of theft of the diamond, but the solution is more complex than is at first apparent. The bell-pull in Doyle's "The Adventure of the Speckled Band" (*Strand*, Feb. 1892) is recognized by Sherlock *Holmes as a clue to an original method of murder, but perhaps the best-remembered illustration of Holmes's deductive skills occurs in "Silver Blaze" (*Strand*, Dec. 1892). He draws Inspector Gregory's attention to "the curious incident of the dog in the night-time." When Gregory points out that the dog did nothing in the nighttime, Holmes says that was the curious incident. The dog's silence indicated that the midnight visitor to the stables in which the dog was kept was someone whom it knew well. In much the same way, powder burns on the coat of the dead Miles Archer in Dashiell *Hammett's *The Maltese Falcon* (1930) lead Sam *Spade to the discovery of Archer's killer. Spade reasons that Archer would only have trusted Brigid O'Shaughnessy to stand so close to him in a dark alley.

Many of the most famous clues in the genre appear in the work of Agatha *Christie. *Death in the Clouds* (1935; *Death in the Air*) presents a significant clue hidden in a list of the belongings of passengers on an airplane in which a murder occurs. Christie made notable use of visual as well as verbal clues; by studying the bridge scores reproduced in *Cards on the Table* (1936) in the text, one may deduce who killed Mr. Shaitana. She also excelled at the art of designing clues that are not what they seem. The outstanding example occurs in *The ABC Murders* (1936; *The Alphabet Murders*), in which a multiple murderer's habit of leaving an ABC railway guide beside each body suggests homicidal mania. The truth, as Poirot eventually explains, is very different.

[See also Puzzle; Reasoning, Types of; Red Herrings; Rules of the Game.]

• Julian Symons "The Mistress of Complication," in *Agatha Christie: First Lady Of Crime*, ed. H. R. F. Keating (1977). Charles Osborne, *The Life and Crimes of Agatha Christie* (1982). Audrey Peterson, *Victorian Masters of Mystery* (1984). Julian Symons *Bloody Murder: From the Detective Story to the Crime Novel*, 3rd rev. ed. (1992).   —Martin Edwards

CODE. *See* Ciphers and Code.

COINCIDENCE. In every *plot, individuals and events must fit together—that is, coincide. The term "coincidence," taken as an artificial or noncausal conjunction of characters or events, appears in varying degree in the crime and mystery subgenres, being rejected by the classic *whodunit, tolerated in the *thriller, and embraced by the *hard-boiled novel. Crime and mystery readers who reject coincidence demand fully explicable causation in the solution to the story; those who accept this device appreciate the contribution of a frisson to a good story.

On one end of the continuum coincidence is never tolerated. In the classic detective story as defined by Edgar Allan *Poe and Arthur Conan *Doyle, the *sleuth follows a rigidly logical method, tracing a pattern of cause and consequence; mere coincidence has no place here. Detectives repeatedly stress their rigorously rational approach. Agatha *Christie's Hercule *Poirot is among the most cerebral, relying on "order and method." In *Murder on the Links* (1923) Poirot even goes so far as to disdain physical evidence in comparison with the power of his "little gray cells." When the *police procedural made its appearance in the 1940s and 1950s, technique, routine, and procedure replaced the *amateur detective's pursuit of logical connection and pattern, uncovered *clue by clue. Coincidence continued to be treated obliquely or with disdain; the emphasis was on the details of ordinary reality. At the opposite end of the continuum, the thriller and its variants, particularly the *Had-I-But-Known school, embrace coincidence, and could not succeed without it. In the work of Mary Roberts *Rinehart and her successors, the convolutions of the *puzzle have been shaken free of deductive logic and the detection of any sort of pattern.

The hard-boiled story remains the one subgenre where coincidence may be used as a plot device in association with detection of crime. Raymond *Chandler freely espoused coincidence as a plot device to extricate the writer from an impasse in the story, and his hero, Philip *Marlowe, regularly encounters by accident exactly the people he needs to help him along his way. Even when the coincidences are strained, the reader is for the most part accepting. In John D. *MacDonald's *Darker than Amber* (1966), Travis *McGee, while fishing under a Florida bridge at night, snags a woman thrown from the bridge and, following his line down into the water, releases her from the concrete block to which she had been wired. The statistical probabilities against such a rescue are, of course, astronomical, and MacDonald soon releases the reader from the strain of coincidence by having the girl killed a little later by the same villains who had thrown her off the bridge.

The suspension of disbelief and acceptance of coincidence may be reinforced by various techniques or by the introduction of other narrative devices. Ross *Macdonald's Lew *Archer novels introduce coincidence not only in space but also in time, tying up his perpetrators and their victims in long skeins of complicated events and consequences that sometimes require decades to work through. Macdonald's combination of the grim *private eye tradition with Freudian psychology, backed by his skill at delineating character, dominates, and usually excuses his nearly incredible structure of coincidence. In *Find a Victim* (1955), for example, accident begins the story and accident keeps it going. In *Yellowthread Street* (1975), William Marshall plays with the concept of coincidence by reversing the pattern: Events tumble randomly about the ears of the protagonists, with furious confrontations that make no sense at all—until, at last, coincidence is brought in as a solution: There is a reason for these events, a central rationale after all, and the events do somehow coincide. Marshall employs this tactic in subsequent novels in the Yellowthread Street series, but it is a risky and sometimes irritating and unsuccessful tactic. Tony *Hillerman's Joe Leaphorn and Jim *Chee mysteries, though much less frenetic than Marshall's stories, also demand that the reader follow his policemen as they trace disparate events, set in an immense physical space, until a rational pattern finally emerges.

Life is never entirely without coincidence, and the

best writers attempt to include it in their stories in a realistic manner. Indeed, the use or misuse of coincidence is one way to tell if an author is actually in control of his plot, even allowing for well-delineated characters and atmosphere that reduce the suspicion of improbability of any particular incident.

[See also Conventions of the Genre: Traditional Conventions; Craft of Crime and Mystery Writing, The; Realism, Conventions of; Rules of the Game.]

• Raymond Chandler, "The Simple Art of Murder" (1944), in *The Simple Art of Murder* (1950).   —Dean A. Miller

COLE, G(EORGE) D(OUGLAS) H(OWARD) (1889–1959) and **MARGARET (ISABEL) COLE** (née Postgate; 1893–1980), British economists and joint authors of detective novels and short stories. G. D. H. Cole, son of an estate agent (i.e., realtor), was educated at St. Paul's School and Oxford University. Margaret Postgate, daughter of a university don and sister of the author Raymond Postgate, was educated at Roedean School and Cambridge University. Married in 1918, they strongly influenced British socialism through their writing and lecturing, and Margaret (who in 1970 was awarded the D.B.E. and thereafter addressed Dame Margaret) long held office in the Fabian Society.

The Brooklyn Murders (1923), by G. D. H. Cole alone, introduced Superintendent Henry Wilson of *Scotland Yard. Subsequently, the Coles collaborated on some thirty novels. Critics agree that the Coles' crime writing is indistinguishable from other mediocre work of the interwar years. *The Murder at Crome House* (1927) is considered their best novel; Superintendent Wilson does not appear in this work, but is shown to advantage in the crisper short stories collected in *Superintendent Wilson's Holiday* (1928). In the rare instance in which the Coles' political and social views inform the novel—*The Murder at the Munition Works* (1940)—the characters, *plot, and commentary are fresh and absorbing.

[See also Conservative vs. Radical Worldview.]

• Margaret Cole, *The Life of G. D. H. Cole* (1971). Betty D. Vernon, *Margaret Cole, 1893–1980: A Political Biography* (1986).   —Melvyn Barnes

COLLEGE MYSTERIES. See Academic Milieu; Academic Sleuth; Cambridge; Oxford.

COLLINS CRIME CLUB. Despite its name, Collins Crime Club is not and never has been a *book club: It is the imprint, founded in 1930 by Sir William Collins, under which Collins (subsequently absorbed into HarperCollins) publishes crime fiction.

Collins already had a reputation for good crime fiction and had been publishing Agatha *Christie since 1926. The publisher had the idea of capitalizing on this reputation and on the popularity of the book clubs, then in their heyday. Newspaper advertisements invited the public to join The Crime Club free of charge and receive a newsletter detailing three titles per month—one "Choice" and two "Recommend-

eds"—specially selected for them by a panel headed by Dr. C. A. Alington, provost of Eton College and later dean of Durham Cathedral and himself a writer of detective novels. The books were produced in a uniform format and sold at a uniform price, a policy still maintained, although the editorial panel has long since disappeared, together with the invidious editorial distinction between Choice and Recommended.

The response to the advertisements was enthusiastic and sales of Collins crime fiction soared, even though the books could only be obtained via the circulating subscription libraries, then also in their heyday, or from bookshops at the full list price. Unlike the book clubs on which it was modelled, the Collins Crime Club never offered a discount.

The first title to appear under the new imprint, with its hooded gunman logo, was *The Noose* (1930) by Philip *MacDonald. The first Christie novel to be published in the Crime Club followed a few months later: *The Murder at the Vicarage* (1930), which introduced Miss Jane *Marple. Thereafter, with the exception of some of the early novels featuring the sleuth couple Tommy and Tuppence Beresford, which were loosely regarded as *thrillers, all Christie's crime titles first appeared in the Crime Club. Successive Crime Club editors have always striven to distinguish between these two genres, and the distinction grew increasingly necessary as the Collins general list became well known in the 1950s and '60s for such thriller writers as Alistair MacLean and Desmond *Bagley.

All Ngaio *Marsh's titles, beginning with *A Man Lay Dead* in 1934, appeared under the Crime Club imprint. Elizabeth *Ferrars, the author of some seventy crime novels, was first published by the Crime Club in 1946, and at the time of her death in 1995 was its longest-serving author. The list of Crime Club authors, past and present, is long and distinguished; it includes Catherine Aird, Marian Babson, Robert *Barnard, Gwendoline Butler, Liza Cody, Mignon G. *Eberhart, Jonathan Gash, Reginald *Hill, H. R. F. *Keating, Ross *Macdonald, Magdalen Nabb, Michael Pearce, Rex *Stout, Julian *Symons, and William G. Tapply.

In 1994 the contentious word "club" was dropped from the imprint's title and it became Collins Crime.

[See also Publishing, History of Book.]
          —Elizabeth M. Walter

COLLINS, (WILLIAM) WILKIE (1824–1889), English novelist, best known for *The Woman in White* and *The Moonstone*. Collins was a Victorian success. During the 1860s, when *The Woman in White* was a popular rage, his estimated annual income was over £10,000. Despite the appearance, so dear to the optimistic age, that this monetary attainment gave of energy and labor rewarded, Collins was otherwise not a conventional Victorian. The son of the landscape painter William Collins and godson of the painter Sir David Wilkie, whose name he bore, he led a bohemian existence of long sojourns abroad with his family, experienced extreme indecision about a career, and in maturity lived serially in two common-law families. He studied painting, undertook training with a firm of tea merchants, entered Lincoln's Inn to study law in 1846, and was called to the bar in 1851. All the while, though, he was also writing, so that his eventual career came upon him more by accident than by resolute pursuit. His first publication was a short story in 1843, and in 1848 he published a biography of his father in two volumes. Literary history, with hints from Algernon Swinburne and T. S. Eliot, has tended to regard Collins as a minor figure in the shadow of Charles *Dickens, whose close associate and friend he was. In the realm of popular fiction, however, Collins earned success by his own special talents.

Those talents included a gift for expert plotting of complex narratives that, at their best, become lucid after they have twisted their way to conclusion; precise and painterly descriptive powers; and an inventive approach to the use of narrative voice and point of view. He applied those talents to mystery first in short stories. "A Stolen Letter" (originally published as "The Fourth Poor Traveller" in *Household Words*, Christmas edition, 1854; reprinted as "The Lawyer's Story of a Stolen Letter" in *After Dark*, 1856) is, as its title suggests, reminiscent of Edgar Allan *Poe. "Anne Rodway [Taken from her Diary]" (*Household Words*, July 19 and 26, 1856; reprinted in *The Queen of Hearts*, 1859 as "Brother Owen's Story of Anne Rodway") claims interest because of its female detective and Collins's first use of a diary form, which would become one of his stocks in trade.

Through his friendship with Dickens, Collins became a regular contributor to Dickens's magazine *Household Words*. That journal's successor, *All the Year Round*, served as the outlet for the first publication of Collins's two stunning mystery novels, in serial form: *The Woman in White* was issued in installments starting in November 1859, and *The Moonstone* appeared from January 1868 on.

Apart from his work in the crime and mystery genre, Collins produced much doctrinaire fiction espousing the causes of illegitimate children and prostitutes, and attacking vivisection and the Jesuits. The bulk of this nondetective fiction belongs to the school of sensation, where the "secret" is indeed sprung upon the reader. His works that survive do so, however, because in them he exceeded the limits of both attenuated and sensational fiction.

The Moonstone, T. S. Eliot declared, is "the first, the longest, and the best of modern English detective novels." Even without the qualifications of "modern" and "English" the tribute would be just, for *The Moonstone* is incomparable. Told in a variety of voices, from the stolid but solid Gabriel Betteredge, steward in the noble household, to the religious crank Drusilla Clack, the poor relation hostile to the people Betteredge serves, the narrative is masterly in its balancing of sympathies as well as in its artful concealment and revelation of the truth. The secret—this being the essence of the difference between *sensation novel and *detective novel—is gradually revealed with the collaboration of the reader. The author plays fair. He does not spring the solution on

us, but instead provides a reconstruction of the crime and, in a foreshadowing of the wrap-up scenes that become de rigueur in classic crime stories, presents the answers with all *suspects assembled. There are several detectives in *The Moonstone*, but the principal two between them share qualities that have become characteristic of fictional *sleuths: Sergeant *Cuff, the policeman, rational, eccentric; and Ezra Jennings, the scientific artist, intuitive, also eccentric, and a social outcast. The Bi-Part Soul, both are needed to solve the crime.

The earlier novel, *The Woman in White*, more closely resembles sensation fiction. The secret is inaccessible to the reader until the end, and the story boasts two superb villains—Sir Percival Glyde, who is one dimensional, and Count Fosco, who is anything but. Indeed, one of the great villains of Victorian fiction, Fosco could have given Dashiell *Hammett suggestions for his portrayal of Casper Gutman.

Writing of the novelist in the Victorian age, Lord David Cecil says: "He had to be Mr. Galsworthy, Mr. Huxley, Mrs. Woolf, Mrs. Christie and Mr. Wodehouse in one." This was the kind of multifaceted novelist Collins was; but his forte was to have raised the mystery novel to a level higher than that of his contemporaries, and to have virtually invented the full-length detective novel.

[*See also* Eccentricity; History of Crime and Mystery Writing: Formation of the Genre; Truth, Quest for.]

• Kenneth Robinson, *Wilkie Collins: A Biography* (1951). Dorothy L. Sayers, *Wilkie Collins: A Critical and Biographical Study* (1977). Catherine Peters, *The King of Inventors* (1991).
—Barrie Hayne

COMPUTER DETECTIVE GAMES are role-playing investigations designed for play on a personal computer. Except for computer-generated party games, such as *Make Your Own Murder Party* (1986), computer games are graphic-textual or all-textual. In the 1980s, such games were marketed on floppy diskettes for computers with limited memory. Then, the more graphic a game, the less challenging it would be. Some pictorial games, such as the very popular Carmen Sandiego series, were designed to educate children. Others, such as *221B Baker Street* (1986), *Murder by the Dozen* (1983), and *Felony* (1984), packaged multiple cases or possible outcomes, reminiscent of board games (*Clue*) or chapters in the "Encyclopedia Brown," "Five-Minute Mysteries," or "Photo Crimes" series. Locations and suspects' statements were sorted out until the player was ready to propose a solution. Currently, *Foul Play* (1995) continues this board game approach, with thousands of possible solutions.

Of more interest to readers are the all-textual "interactive fictions." Each has extensive vocabularies to which characters respond. Against timed events—entrances, exits, interruptions, night, weather, crimes—and facing a maze of detailed locations, the player becomes an investigator, typing in dialogue and action. The best textuals, *Deadline* (1983), *The Witness* (1984), and *Suspect* (1985)—all available on a CD-ROM, *Classic Text Adventure Masterpieces of Infocom*

—feature a literate, sometimes parodic, hard-boiled style. Once accustomed to vocabulary limits, the player finds considerable challenges in analysis and mapping that may take up to twenty hours to complete. A "save" feature allows play to stop and restart. Saved positions allow repeat visits to earlier scenes or reinterrogations. As with violent adventure games, these positions also enable the player who has failed to restart at an advanced position. A "script" feature enables the player to print out important passages.

Textual games may disappoint readers who expect character individuality or want to force confessions from suspects. The culprit—as in many party games (the *Host a Murder* series) or second-rate novels—may be one of several logical suspects. But the ability to move about and engage in dialogue, even with stock characters, is a powerful inducement to play.

The advent of the Macintosh/Windows environment, supported by huge increases in computer memory, has allowed more complex narrative games. CD-ROM disks and Internet websites are capacious enough to support graphics and sufficient texts. *Deja Vu* (1985) foreshadowed many currently available features. With "graphic novel" detailing, it used mouse-menu options to examine parts of objects in a given scene, to open doors or drawers; it also supplied an inventory of keys, documents, weapons, food, and medicine for personal use. As with completely textual games, the player could interact with suspects, both conversationally and physically. Since 1990 CD-ROMs have featured videos of characters in such series as "Sherlock Holmes, Consulting Detective," "Who Killed . . . ," "D.A.: Pursuit of Justice," and "Santa Fe Mysteries." Actors play the roles, sometimes reenact key events, and respond to questions, though not as freely as in all-textual games. The effect is somewhat like watching the film *Clue* (1985), except that the player can open informational windows and more leisurely examine or print out evidence.

Online mysteries play somewhat like earlier graphic-textual games, since the player examines photos, videos, and documents without the pressure of a clock. Since 1995 *Crime Scene*, <www.crimescene.com>, has offered up to five cases at its web site. Updates, new developments, and E-mail interaction keep the player coming back. Some sites E-mail subscribers textual puzzlers, with aids or solutions available online. *The Mysterious Home Page*, <www2.db.dk/jbs/mysthome/>, has a large directory of links to detective game and author sites.

—W. M. Hagen

CONAN DOYLE, SIR ARTHUR. See Doyle, Arthur Conan.

CON ARTIST. The con artist is a specific type of fictional character who, having raised the techniques of deception, ingratiation, and tomfoolery to the level of an art form, cultivates the confidence of others to garner profit or the favors of the opposite sex or an avenue for escape. Superior wit; skill in the use of resources, including *disguise; adaptability; savoir faire; charm; and a continual desire to better his or her condition—these are some of the attributes of the con

artist at work to trick, beguile, maneuver, or manipulate others. Since the confidence game is generated by and predicated upon the human foibles of the *victim, the con artist's operations serve the turn of the satirist, the moralist, the critic of society who brings into view a world of dubious and doubting humanity, one that is populated by cheats, imposters, and fools.

The range of the con artist is immense. Among the British, Randolph Mason, a skilled, unscrupulous lawyer, cons his clients in Melville Davisson *Post's *The Strange Schemes of Randolph Mason* (1896). Arthur *Morrison's less-than-honest *private detective, Horace Dorrington, is both con man and thief in *The Dorrington Deed Box* (1897). Romney Pringle, a creation of R. Austin *Freeman and John James Pitcairn writing as Clifford Ashdown, poses as a literary agent who earns a living by swindling crooks out of their ill-gotten gains in *The Adventures of Romney Pringle* (1902). Dr. James Shepard, the narrator in Agatha *Christie's *The Murder of Roger Ackroyd* (1926), is a man of many masks: a moral monster, liar, blackmailer, and greedy gambler, who manipulates characters and readers alike with great guile and without any remorse. Constantine Dix is both lay preacher and thief in Barry Pain's *The Memoirs of Constantine Dix* (1905). Milward Kennedy created Sir George Bull in *Bull's Eye* (1933; *Corpse in Cold Storage*, 1934), a con man who assumes the role of a private detective to gain entrance to a wealthy social circle.

One version of the con artist is the *gentleman thief exemplified by E. W. *Hornung's A. J. *Raffles, cricketeer, gentleman, and thief in *The Amateur Cracksman* (1899; *Raffles, The Amateur Cracksman*). Writing as Barry Perowne, Philip Atkey imitates Hornung with his own gentleman-gone-astray, Raffles, in *Raffles After Dark* (1933; *The Return of Raffles*). The American master of parody, J. Kendrick Bangs, builds several stories around the adventures of Raffles's wife transplanted to American high society. She expands her name to Henriette Van Raffles and thrives in the heyday of Newport, Rhode Island, in *Mrs. Raffles: Being the Adventures of an Amateur Crackswoman* (1905). Another American, Christopher B. Booth, created that Chicagoan "confidence man de luxe," the title character of two volumes, *Mr. Clackworthy* (1926) and *Mr. Clackworthy, Con Man* (1927).

Particularly in America, the con artist emerged as a distinct literary convention in the 1830s out of an ancestry of seducers, pranksters, devils, or rogues. So suspicious are characters of each other in the American form of the genre that we can never be sure whether some apparently decent and good-hearted person may in fact be practicing pious fraud. Frederick Anderson introduces a master thief in *Adventures of the Infallible Godahl* (1914), and Frank L. Packard's Jimmie Dale (*The Adventures of Jimmie Dale*, 1917) poses as a New York club man, a crook dubbed the Gray Seal, an *underworld figure called Larry the Bat, and an unsuccessful artist known as Smarlinghue.

Gamblers, swindlers, hypocrites, and falsifiers also appear in the hard-boiled *private eye novels of Dashiell *Hammett, Raymond *Chandler, Mickey *Spillane, Ross *Macdonald, and John D. *MacDonald. In these authors' sometimes sordid and always cynical worlds, the rich make their fortunes through various scams, double crosses, and violent murders; the police, who should be able to see through these machinations, are instead incompetent and corrupt. If there is a sucker born every minute, there is also a con artist born to take advantage of human gullibility for his own selfish purposes.

[See also Antihero; Adventurer and Adventuress; Loyalty and Betrayal.]

• Frank Wadleigh Chandler, ed., The Literature of Roguery (1907). Robert C. S. Adey, "In Search of the 'Con Man'," Armchair Detective (July and Oct. 1967): 205; 259–61. Robert A. Baker and Michael T. Nietzel, Private Eyes: One Hundred and One Knights: A Survey of American Detective Fiction, 1922–1984 (1985). William E. Lenz, Fast Talk & Flush Times: The Confidence Man as a Literary Convention (1985). T. J. Binyon, "Murder Will Out": The Detective in Fiction (1989), 127–31.   —Dale Salwak

CONSERVATIVE VS. RADICAL WORLDVIEW

Introduction
Conservative Worldview
Radical Worldview

For further information, please refer to Political and Social Views, Authors'.

INTRODUCTION

The dominant precursors of crime and mystery writing were thief-catching memoirists and pioneering detectives such as Allan Pinkerton. Although they tell their readers that they often behaved as rogues, they always did so on behalf of the institutions that employed them. Often, too, their writings were authenticated by implied testimonials of the property owners or financiers they served, and consequently their actions in combating crime were sanctioned by established economic, political, or social elites. It was a small step from justification by the regimes that empowered the detectives, to advocacy that those regimes should be perpetuated, so the field of detective fiction was prepared for a conservative outlook—an outlook that linked the solution of crime and the resolution of disorder with the maintenance of social *class structures, the protection of property for those who possessed it, and the identification of criminal disorder with social destabilization. By the 1920s, the period that produced a stable set of rules for the literary genre, belief in social stability had also become an essential trait of the genre.

Just as social critics exposed the injustices and discrimination present in established social order, some writers of detective fiction redrafted the premises of their genre. While the writers of social fiction addressed the consequences of inequitable distribution of wealth, those writers of detective fiction who were as disaffected as the social critics were concerned to restore a beneficent order to the world in fiction. The critical view of these writers, implicitly claiming that they were dealing with the crime as it really occurred, radically transformed their treatment of crime, so that crime became a norm rather than a disruption as well as the practice and ethos of the detective, who in the hands of some authors became a champion of ordinary people instead of a defender of the status quo.

• John W. Cawelti, Adventure, Mystery, and Romance: Formula Stories as Art and Popular Culture (1976). Stephen Knight, Form and Ideology in Crime Fiction (1980). Dennis Porter, The Pursuit of Crime: Art and Ideology in Detective Fiction (1981).   —John M. Reilly

CONSERVATIVE WORLDVIEW

Crime in real life would appear to have existed as an integral part of the human condition since people began to live in societies. *Murder and *theft are proscribed in the Ten Commandments (Deut. 5: 6); throughout the ages, violation of these and later laws has attracted punishments of varying degrees of severity where and when the offender has been duly identified, apprehended, and judged guilty. Much crime and mystery fiction has followed this model.

The drafting and application of such laws, usually with the protection of either the state, property, or the person in mind, have led to their being defined, refined, and consolidated throughout history into (from the point of view of the writer and reader of detective fiction) a relatively and deceptively simple polarity of "right" and "wrong."

The possession of law in itself was seen by Rudyard Kipling as a benchmark of civilization when he referred, in his "Recessional," to "the lesser breeds without the Law." The importance of order in English society may be illustrated by the fact that until the Criminal Procedure Act of 1851, most criminal offences, including murder, were said to be committed "against the peace of our Lord the King" rather than against the individual *victim.

Notable and benign exceptions in legend to the implicit consensus disapproval of the breaking of the law include that of the early and persistent Robin Hood tradition of robbing the rich (of their ill-gotten gains) to pay the (deserving) poor. This notion may be found in the fiction of, among others, Leslie *Charteris and Ian *Fleming, where the means (bad) are intended to be seen to justify the end (good). Geoffrey *Household's Rogue Male (1939; Man Hunt) is concerned purely with bringing about the death of a bad man (implicitly, Adolf Hitler) set on world domination by a good man prepared to sacrifice himself in the process.

The greatly simplified stance of right and wrong is exemplified in the mystery plays found in all major European countries in early medieval times, and in the morality plays which succeeded them. It is possible that the conservative worldview in crime fiction descends from this presentation of enacted dramas in which there may be found a clear and moral position rather than any reflection of actual life. The approved view purveyed in these exemplary plays is that Good invariably succeeds over *Evil. The message is symbolically clarified still further by the convention in them that the Devil always enters from stage left—the sinister side.

Origins of another, similar aspect of crime fiction may be found in Dante Alighieri's Divina Commedia written in the early fourteenth century (and notably translated by Dorothy L. *Sayers and Barbara Reynolds, 1949–62), where well-known sinners from history are seen to receive their just deserts, although a genuine confidence in a conservative world perhaps is demonstrated by the willingness of many Golden Age writers to imply in their fiction the accepted impartiality of the judicial process and its award of condign punishment rather than to write about it more explicitly. In the works of Arthur Conan *Doyle, Agatha *Christie, Ngaio *Marsh, Margery *Allingham, and many others, the narrative often effectively ends with the arrest of the culprit, who is then immediately removed from the scene of the action by the police, although pages of explanatory detail may follow.

A parallel certainty is employed by these writers and their peers in the use of *stock characters, where the occupation of the character is closely related to status and therefore has reliable correlations with his or her presumed behavior in particular situations. Professions that carry firm overtones of integrity in a conservative English Golden Age setting include those of doctor, clergyman, lawyer, member of Parliament, and army officer. Hence the greater the element of surprise when the murderer is found to be a trusted figure, as in *Whose Body?* by Sayers (1923) and Christie's *The Murder of Roger Ackroyd* (1926).

In Sayers's *Gaudy Night* (1935), this faith is extended to both the scholar and the aristocracy. In her short story "The Professor's Manuscript" (in *In the Teeth of the Evidence*, 1939), the criminal, masquerading as a professor, is exposed by the fact that some of the actions he has taken are perceived to be unscholarly.

The same expectation of propriety (if not always of intelligence) is applied to members of the police force, even at the lowest levels: This is perhaps the most significant of all markers of the conservative view. However inept, unaware, or inefficient the fictional member of the constabulary is, in the years up until well after the Second World War, it is a sine qua non in English detective fiction that policemen are, if not exactly wonderful, at least both honest and courageous.

In her *Busman's Honeymoon* (1937), Sayers has her aristocratic hero, Lord Peter *Wimsey, clearly distressed at the possibility that the young police constable, Joe Sellon, might be lying to him and therefore perhaps guilty of murder. It is made equally clear, though, that if it becomes necessary to do so, Wimsey would, however reluctantly, denounce Sellon to his superiors. In Josephine *Tey's *Brat Farrar* (1949; *Come and Kill Me*), the clergyman destroys the incriminating evidence that would have led to the unnecessary identification of the murderer (who is by then dead): The Chief Constable is not able to do so, because he had his professional duty to consider, whereas the clergyman had only his conscience.

Importantly, notwithstanding any mitigating circumstances made available to the reader, the blame for any crime committed within the narrative is laid on the shoulders of its perpetrator and not on society at large. There is also the unwritten presumption

that in life as well as in law and theology, each individual is responsible for his or her actions. Furthermore, reader and fictional police alike seldom find it necessary to question the mechanics of how a confession is obtained, as a rule finding it a satisfactory method of confirming the rightness of the detective's deductions.

Into this area of law and order there also comes the principle of duty to one's country, very evident in the works of Sapper and John *Buchan, and in the detective novels of Dornford *Yates. Loyalty and obedience to public duty and proper administration may be read in the earlier novels of P. D. *James. The whole oeuvre of Emma *Lathen is dedicated to financial trustworthiness; that of Harry Kemelman assumes the total reliability of rabbinical probity and logic.

Another factor of considerable importance in a stance of orderly crime literature is the absence of anarchy, of necessity anathema to pure reasoning. If the reader is to be allowed—encouraged, even—to work out the detective *puzzle element in the story, then the actions of those characters within that story, together with the narrative element, must be sufficiently consistent, conventional, and logical.

Related to this is the fact that crime writing is seldom used in a proselytising way in order to further a change in the criminal law. Tey's *Kif: An Unvarnished History* (1929), first published under her other pseudonym, Gordon Daviot, is a polemic against capital punishment; but this sort of polemic is uncommon in the genre, suggesting perhaps that change is in itself considered undesirable rather than that the current situation is satisfactory in every possible respect.

The detective stories that most closely adhere to this worldview nearly always have as their detective hero or heroine an attractive, likable character with whom, however eccentric or remote, the reader is able to identify. These detectives—whether gifted amateur or thoroughgoing professional—are frequently mannered, but invariably mannerly. Similarly, it is customary for the personal lives of the characters within the story to remain unrevealed except where such information is absolutely necessary for the *plot.

Conservative detective fiction is usually set in ordered, secure, well-established societies in mainly rural surroundings. Few stories are centered in cities save ancient English cathedral ones—the provenance of *The Nebuly Coat* by J. Meade Falkner (1903), Michael *Gilbert's *Close Quarters* (1947), and Edmund *Crispin's *Holy Disorders* (1945), as well as the works of Cyril A. Alington and, earlier, of Charles *Dickens's unfinished *Mystery of Edwin Drood* (1870). Fewer still are set in towns, apart from the older university towns of *Oxford and *Cambridge, much written about by Michael *Innes, Crispin, J. C. Masterman, Lathen, Colin *Dexter, and Robert *Barnard.

The constant use of rural, cathedral or medieval university settings, which are presumed to be safe, reflects the public misconception that crime is a purely urban, industrial prerogative (or even phenomenon). Perhaps, too, these writers may be trying to perpetuate a rural idyll or possibly seeking to restore on paper an illusory status quo ante that may have existed only in wishful thinking. Alternatively, they may be attempting to rebut reality by collaborating with their readership in consciously retreating into a comfortable and undemanding haven in which there will be nothing worse than murder.

[See also Clerical Sleuth; Country Constable.]

• Richard Usborne, *Clubland Heroes* (1953). Colin Watson, *Snobbery with Violence* (1971). —Catherine Aird

RADICAL WORLDVIEW

When Marxist literary criticism flourished under state sponsorship in the Soviet Union and the German Democratic Republic, the arguments made by some of its adherents suggested that Western crime and mystery literature could never be fully radicalized, because the genre would wither away upon completion of political radicalism under socialism. The end of class conflict, Marxists maintained, and the replacement of the cash nexus that Karl Marx had declared to be the primary capitalist relationship, also would eliminate the struggle over scarce wealth and the living chaos of capitalist society. As history has shown, these critics were more utopian than realistic in the analyses that bolstered their claims for socialism. For its part, literary history demonstrates that criticism of the root and branch of existing societies—"root," after all, is the root meaning of "radical"—may occur under any regime and as an expression of worldviews in many times and in various places.

So it is that despite its appearance in Western capitalist and democratic societies, crime and mystery literature includes a radical worldview in opposition to the conservative worldview inherent in the early instances of detective writing and dominant in the genre's Golden Age. The radical worldview of crime and mystery literature avoids the utopianism of the Marxist critics as well as the social nihilism projected by the fierce vigilante-style writing that describes avengers in Mickey *Spillane's Mike *Hammer. Instead, the radical worldview appears through the social critique contained in the portrayal of character (especially among authors of *hard-boiled fiction), the description of social and physical setting of the mean streets, and in the open-ended story lines characteristic of fiction in which the efforts of a detective at best accomplish momentary resolution of a criminal problem.

Deriving an interest in exposure of the seamy environments of American life from literary *naturalism, the *pulp magazine writers of the 1920s and 1930s developed a plain but detailed manner of description, and made the gritty physical reality that was intended to represent the power of forces largely beyond human control a terrain for private investigators who spoke in the syntax of Ernest Hemingway and expressed the attitude of characters who had found emptiness in pursuing the American dream. The stylized utterances of detection-story naturalism conveyed the opinion that society was corrupt through and through, because money was the standard for success and its acquisition the motive for behavior. Neither the pulp writers nor the authors who carried the outlook of the pulps into longer, novel-length fiction made specific political or economic identification of the social reality they criticized. It was just the way things were.

Essentially, their writing worked to create narratives that undercut the legitimacy of *class structures by portraying the wealthy as debased, revealing the established institutions of law and order to be dysfunctional, indicating that the little fellow was the *victim of it all, and proving that everybody except the *private eye was out for the buck. The town of Personville that came to be known as Poisonville in Dashiell *Hammett's *Red Harvest* (1929), a novel that complements a series of short stories from the pulps about the *Continental Op, is representative of the world as it was radically viewed by hard-boiled writers; so too are many other works by writers in the hard-boiled tradition—writers such as Raymond *Chandler, of course, and W. R. Burnett, Paul Cain, Elmore *Leonard, Ross *Macdonald, Brett Halliday, Gil Brewer, Jim *Thompson, James *Ellroy, Robert B. *Parker, and Ed Gorman. The list makes it clear that the radical worldview is more than closely associated with the hard-boiled tradition.

The fact that many of the detective works embodying a radically critical worldview are set in *New York, *Los Angeles, or *San Francisco makes an important point. New York is the gateway to opportunity for immigrants from Europe; San Francisco, the access to the Golden Mountain for travelers from Asia; Los Angeles, the site where the West ends at the sea. When *corruption appears in these cities of hope, it is cause for anger. In America, anger resulting from the frustration of hope has commonly generated populist sentiment: Witness the revolt of farmers against land speculators and railroads in the Progressive Era. When the idealist program of populism—which amounts to more elections, more regulations, and more democracy—appears to result in more of the same old corruption, idealism turns to disillusion. This caricature of American disappointment lies at the heart of the radical worldview when it appears in crime and mystery writing.

The protagonists of radical hard-boiled writing usually are independent private investigators, not government agents or cops. This in itself offers relief for disappointment, because the private detective can become an exemplar of positive values in a debased society. Typically portrayed as a singular figure, the *private eye cannot be a hostage to corrupt institutions; because he or she is unaffiliated with social elites and, moreover, disaffiliated from their value systems, the detective independently creates the dominant values of the criminal narrative. These radical agents of forced individualism deal in *violence and often carry themselves with the same cynical arrogance as the criminals in their stories, but their purpose is good. The redemption of society lies beyond their power, but the ability to punish a few villains and to humanize life for their surviving victims does lie within the private eye's scope of business.

American authors do not have exclusive rights to the radical worldview in this genre, but writers in Great Britain, France, and elsewhere who employ a hard-boiled mode tend to accept the made-in-America brand of radicalism that has become an inherent part of tough narratives. This literary worldview has no underlying political or economic theory. It offers no program for reform beyond the example of a private eye's personal integrity. Yet the continued popularity of hard-boiled radicalism indicates that for many readers it is the honest way of looking at things.

[See also Loner, Sleuth as; Mean Streets Milieu; Resolution and Irresolution; Urban Milieu.]

• Stuart Hall and Paddy Whannel, The Popular Arts (1964). John M. Reilly, "The Politics of Tough Guy Mysteries," University of Dayton Review (1973). Leroy L. Panek, "The Naked Truth: The Origins of the Hard-Boiled School," Armchair Detective 21 (fall 1988): 363–75.   —John M. Reilly

Continental Op. Dashiell Hammett created the unnamed character known simply as the Continental Op while he served his apprenticeship as a hard-boiled detective fiction writer for *Black Mask* magazine from 1923 to 1927. Hammett wrote twenty-six short stories, a two-part novella—$106,000 Blood Money (1927)—and two novels—Red Harvest (1929) and The Dain Curse (1929)—featuring the Op. Hammett drew on his own experiences working for the Pinkerton Agency to give the stories authenticity.

When first introduced, the Op is thirty-five and has been an operative with the Continental Agency for fifteen years. Short and fat, he is ruthless in his work. The stories in which he appears are first-person narratives by the Op, told in a flat, matter-of-fact style enlivened by criminal slang. This straightforward style serves as a contrast to the graphic *violence and mayhem to come. In "The Gutting of Couffignal" (The Return of the Continental Op, 1945), a woman attempts to seduce the Op. He responds by saying, "You think I'm a man and you're a woman. That's wrong. I'm a manhunter and you're something that has been running in front of me. There's nothing human about it." Later in the story, when she doesn't believe his threat to shoot her and tries to leave, the Op shoots her in the leg. "I had never shot a woman before," he remarks to the reader, "I felt queer about it."

Although the Op felt queer about shooting a woman, he did it in order to do his job, for he lives by an ethical code ruled by loyalty to his agency and fellow detectives but excluding sentiment. The most important rule is that no operative can benefit monetarily from the solution of a case. This rule puts the Op above the *greed and *corruption of the *Prohibition society in which he works. Indeed, the Op shows no interest in money. He lives for his work.

The best-known example of his brutal work appears in Red Harvest, where he takes on an entire army of crooked cops and gangsters who run Personville, later Poisonville. The Op's method is to "stir things up," manipulating the crooked cops and the gangsters in ways that turn them against each other and destroy them.

• Lillian Hellman (1966), Introduction to The Big Knockover, by Dashiell Hammett. Steven Marcus (1974), Introduction to The Continental Op, by Dashiell Hammett.
                —George Kelley

CONVENTIONS OF THE GENRE

Overview
Traditional Conventions
Hard-Boiled Conventions

For further information, please refer to Craft of Crime and Mystery Writing, The.

OVERVIEW

The elements of narrative repeated in works by many authors become known as conventions. The word itself can suggest routine or uninspired usage; but more often, conventions serve to reveal the armature of a literary genre, the conception underlying form and the structure for writers' innovations. Conventions exist from the emergence of a genre, through its consolidation, and on into its newest appearances because they express the worldview or belief system inherent in the construction of the literary form.

That detective fiction will always offer a portrayal of an investigator seems to go without saying, just as the presence of a *puzzle about who is responsible for a crime appears to be inevitable in a work called a mystery. Yet, the self-evident requirements for a detective and a problem become endlessly repeatable, because the genre of detective and mystery fiction arose out of the modern historical conditions that made crime a problem contingent in everyday life; the circumstances of urbanization and social mobility made the creation of the new institution of official crime solvers—police—a necessity. With those historical conditions in place in the Western world as a result of industrialization, the rise of the economic system of capitalism, and the displacement of populations from the cultural and physical environments they had traditionally inhabited for centuries, it became inevitable that popular literature would develop types of writing to accommodate the new reality while formulating suggestive ways of psychological and social control. Humanity has always sought to know reality by the stories it tells. The case is no different when reality involves violation and *violence among people who are strangers to each other and living in social arrangements made opaque by their size and complexity.

Of course, what is different in the stories written about modern crime are the technical features employed to present crime and its control. These are the conventions of the body of popular literature known, because of its subject and its repeated elements of narration, as the genre of crime and mystery fiction.

According to most literary historians, the record of the genre begins with the prescient works of Edgar Allan *Poe, who first wrote stories about puzzling crimes, created an investigator to solve the puzzle, and devised from a secondary character the narrator standing in for the reader to express wonder at the means of solving the crime and satisfaction at its accomplishment. Poe's prescience lay in making the story of crime a subject of contemplation instead of an object of terror. He managed this by distancing the *plot of detection from the bloody facts of *true crime and turning the crude business of actual detective work into an elegant and cerebral exercise.

The distancing and intellectualizing evident in Poe's tales set a pattern for making the detective not only the central figure of the narrative but also a type of modern hero. Taking advantage of Poe's style of reformation of sensational writing, later writers, including the notable Arthur Conan *Doyle, burnished the image of the *sleuth into a figure of greatness. As treatments of the detective were repeated, it became evident that this protagonist had to be accorded special attributes in order to win the sympathy of readers and to create a level of confidence in the character's ability to master a crime in a believable way. This narrative necessity stimulated writers in the use of incidents secondary to the main plot that would illustrate the detective's possession of high intellectual skill or a peculiar quality of intuition. It also encouraged authors to assign biographical detail to the detective, making his or her specialness an evident consequence of innate character, learning, or faculties. Often the detail included eccentricities, but those too had utility in founding the basic convention of the detective and mystery genre—namely, the seemingly obvious need to have a sleuth central to the story. The sleuth was not only the star role but also one around which clustered additional conventions, such as unique habits, a penchant for delivering speeches on detection technique, or a distinctively described methodology. In turn, those conventions for personalizing the sleuth generated the further conventions needed to introduce exposition about the detective into the narrative. Notable among these conventional techniques are the continued use of a sidekick, a Dr. John H. *Watson figure who is companion to the detective and who provides references to cases other than the one in the immediate text, so that the credentials of the sleuth seem legitimate.

Most of the secondary conventions relating peculiarities and background surrounding the primary convention of the detective function to elevate the investigator to a position that idealizes a socially sanctioned type. The detective may be presented as an empirical scientist, as in the stories about Sherlock *Holmes; a master of intuitive psychology, as in the tales of Inspector Jules *Maigret; an accomplished gentleman, as in the Golden Age novels; or a rugged individualist, as in the hard-boiled variations of the genre. In each incarnation the detective's secondary attributes and abilities function on behalf of the primary convention that the sleuth be heroic in a way that is plausible because it is reinforced by audience values.

Inevitably, the crime addressed by the detective is also productive of fruitful convention. For Golden Age authors, a suitable crime—ordinarily murder—had to be presented in a rationally apprehensible manner, because their conception of the social world was premised on an assumption of fixed order, making rationalism the only appropriate basis for constructing a narrative of detection. As their detectives sought to repair the social order temporarily disrupted by the intrusion of a criminal act, they figured the power of order, which it was the goal of detection to restore, in the categorical logic of their preferred mode of detection. The rationalism extended as well to a general acceptance among Golden Age writers of certain *rules of the game for writing fiction that framed the stories as intellectual puzzles. The further consequence of emphasis upon rationally soluble puzzles was the tendency that became conventional to set the crime and solution in a tight community, the closed world of the village or country house.

If one considers the conventions of *setting and rational methodology of Golden Age writing alone, it seems a wonder that such writing could be thought to concern the modern world at all. Examination of the function of the conventions, however, diminishes the wonder as it becomes evident that, although the mean streets described by Raymond *Chandler as the truly appropriate site of detective fiction are absent from the stories of Agatha *Christie or Dorothy L. *Sayers, the artifice of those Golden Age conventions results from a desire to master the subject of crime and thus show it to be comprehensible to the human mind rather than a source of endless fear.

At first the conventions of hard-boiled writing may seem to dispense altogether with artifice, since they set crime among shady characters in settings quite distinct from the contented villages and houses of Golden Age sleuths. Still, though, the conventions developed by hard-boiled writers to make their protagonists distinctive and their cases typical of an urban society similarly advance an idealization, in this case the ideal of the practical American who can no longer be surprised by crime and who is able to fight it with grit and fire power. Here too are conventions working to convey, first, a worldview of corrupt social circumstances, and, second, the ideal of the self-reliant individual who can, with difficulty, master crime and what it represents.

All art depends upon a constant, dynamic tension between convention and invention. Each of the major schools of detective writing has innovated upon the initial genre form, and each writer within any of these schools hopes to work newer variations within the scope of established conventions. It is a challenge similar to writing a set verse form. Within its scheme much is possible. Outside of the scheme, the writing becomes something else entirely.

[See also Closed-World Settings and Open-World Settings; Formula.]

• George Grella, "Murder and Manners: The Formal Detective Novel," *Novel: A Forum on Fiction* (fall 1970): 30–49. George Grella, "Murder and the Mean Streets: The Hard-Boiled Detective Novel," *Contempora* (1970): 6–15. Colin Watson, *Snobbery With Violence: Crime Stories and Their Audience* (1971). Julian Symons, *Mortal Consequences: A History from the Detective Story to the Crime Novel* (1972, rev. 1985). Robin W. Winks, ed., *Detective Fiction: A Collection of Critical Essays* (1980). Dennis Porter, *The Pursuit of Crime: Art and Ideology in Detective Fiction* (1981).

—George Grella *and* John M. Reilly

TRADITIONAL CONVENTIONS

As writers of crime fiction, mostly in Britain, hammered out the form of the Golden Age detective story, various conventions of the genre were established. For the most part these were not necessities arising from the form itself but additions to it that readers enjoyed and came to expect.

One convention was that the *murder should not be, or appear to be, graphically violent. Early on the *detective story took on the quality of a game between writer and reader. In such fiction the actual murder was apt to be made sufficiently unreal to maintain an entertaining mood. It had to be sanitized. An excellent example is Agatha *Christie's *Curtain* (1975). Written at the end of the Golden Age in 1945 and stored away to be released later as the final appearance of Hercule *Poirot, it depicts a *victim with a neat hole in the middle of the forehead, a wound which, as every reader of the more realistic *whodunits of later years will know, would never be a tidy one.

Another convention arises from the structure of the detective story itself. This is the final confrontation in which, ideally, all the *suspects are gathered together in the library or similar enclosed and civilized setting; the detective demonstrates that each suspect in turn is capable of having committed the murder, and then clears each, one by one. Finally the sleuth reaches the last man or woman and produces a surprise solution. Sometimes, a writer will ingeniously revert to one of the already cleared suspects with a different version of how the murder was committed. "This time it was in the big drawing-room that Poirot assembled his audience," the final pages of Christie's *After the Funeral* (1953; *Funerals Are Fatal*) begin—a classic example.

In the choice of murderer to be unmasked in such a final confrontation, again certain conventions developed along with the genre. In keeping with the need for sanitization, the murderer had to be a person the reader would dislike. This presented authors of *puzzle stories with something of a dilemma: Make the hidden murderer someone thoroughly unpleasant, and with each stroke of character drawing you reveal more and more of the secret.

Two ways of dealing with this developed. The author could present the reader with an array of unpleasant people, finally, toward the end of the story showing one or more of them as less unpleasant than they had seemed. Christie does this in *The Murder of Roger Ackroyd* (1926). Alternatively, the author could portray a murderer as a sympathetic character and allow him or her to go free, as Gladys *Mitchell did in her debut novel, *Speedy Death* (1929). Another often used device was to grant an honorable *suicide, as Dorothy L. *Sayers does in *Murder Must Advertise* (1933).

Of course, on occasion the conventions could be used to deceive the reader. Christie was not only the originator of many of the most observed conventions but an adept manipulator of them.

Conventions also developed regarding the victim. To retain an entertaining *atmosphere in the classi-cal detective story, the victim had to be someone whose death would not upset the reader. Here, however, no dilemmas arose. Writers had simply to enjoy themselves painting the potential victim blacker and blacker before the victim's much deserved end. No better example of this perhaps can be found than Cyril *Hare's malicious portrait of the unjust judge in *Tragedy at Law* (1942). That book is itself an example of another of the conventions of the genre, the use of certain well-loved *settings. Hare's description of the world of the law is paralleled in books by Michael *Gilbert such as *Smallbone Deceased* (1950) and in almost all the novels of Michael Underwood, among which one might pick out *Menaces, Menaces* (1976), which begins with a man in the dock at the *Old Bailey whose predicament neatly establishes for him an *alibi for a later crime.

The alibi, indeed, is another convention employed in many of the books in the Golden Age tradition. The general principle employed here is to show a murder suspect as possessing an apparently unbreakable alibi and then to have the detective use *ingenuity, logic, or mere hard work to break it down. The hard-work variety is epitomized in Freeman Wills *Crofts and seen at its most pertinacious in *Inspector French's Greatest Case* (1924). A more modern example, solved by sudden detective understanding, is June Thomson's *Alibi in Time* (1980).

Two more conventions of the genre—the isolated setting and pinpointing of timing—are epitomized in the railway mysteries of Crofts. A murder in the course of a rail journey not only led to opportunities for alibi juggling but also put the suspects into a neat version of the necessary closed world. Undoubtedly the greatest example of such a book is Christie's *Murder on the Orient Express* (1934; *Murder in the Calais Coach*), where the suspects are not only confined to a single coach of the train but are also isolated by a heavy snowfall. Snow, indeed, was the classic method of ensuring the small closed circle of suspects. It is to be found cutting off the criminal in book after book, even in the title of Michael *Innes's *There Came Both Mist and Snow* (1940; *A Comedy of Terrors*), which is also a good example of an author taking full witty advantage of the *country house milieu.

Innes provides, too, a series of examples of another convention, one so strong indeed that it became a whole subgenre of the Golden Age novel. This is the donnish detective story, a murder mystery either set in a university or with a professor (a don) as detective. Much of the pleasure in such books derives from plentiful literary quotation and allusion woven into the telling. Fine examples besides Innes's own work are Amanda *Cross's *In the Last Analysis* (1964), set in the world of American academe, and the novels of Edmund *Crispin featuring Professor Gervase *Fen, who can be seen at work outside a university but in full literary flow in *Buried for Pleasure* (1948).

Crispin was, like Innes, a writer very conscious of the conventions from which his work could benefit. So he also incorporated, more than once, examples of the convention of the *locked room mystery or *impossible crime with the setting sometimes referred to as the hermetically sealed chamber, as in his first book *The Case of the Gilded Fly* (1944; *Obsequies at Oxford*). The master of this convention, however, was John Dickson *Carr, whose *The Three Coffins* (1935; *The Hollow Man*) has a whole chapter devoted to an exposition of the uses of this convention.

The detectives of Innes, Crispin, and Cross provide, as professionals in worlds other than that of the police, examples of a varied stream of such *sleuths who constitute perhaps the last of the conventions of the Golden Age worth examining. To a large extent the Golden Age preferred the *amateur detective. But this requirement again posed a problem for authors. How are their investigators to have sufficient leisure to investigate? A good many solved it by giving their sleuths wealth, such as Margery *Allingham's Albert *Campion with his hinted-at royal blood, seen at his wealthy idlest in *Look to the Lady* (1931; *The Gyrth Chalice Mystery*). But even police detectives were often endowed with upper-class manners, such as Ngaio *Marsh's Roderick *Alleyn or Innes's John *Appleby, who rises from inspector to detective inspector to commissioner.

A very different type of leisured detective, however, also came into being, the inquisitive spinster. In America we had Stuart Palmer's Miss Hildegarde *Withers (*Murder on the Blackboard*, 1932). In Britain there was Christie's Miss Jane *Marple, whose first appearance in a novel was in *Murder at the Vicarage* (1930), and Patricia *Wentworth's Miss Maud Silver, who appeared in a series of books from *Grey Mask* (1928) onward.

[*See also* Academic Milieu; Allusion, Literary; Closed-World Settings and Open-World Settings; Rules of the Game.]

• W. H. Auden, *The Guilty Vicarage* in *The Dyer's Hand* (1963). H. R. F. Keating, *Murder Must Appetize* (1975). Robert Barnard, *A Talent to Deceive: An Appreciation of Agatha Christie* (1980).   —H. R. F. Keating

HARD-BOILED CONVENTIONS

The map of the hard-boiled world shows no gridiron arrangement of passages from data to conclusions. Instead, it charts circular returns to a starting point, with interruptions, surprising byways, dead ends, and tunnels to the *underworld. The reader's companion on journeys in the hard-boiled regions is a *private detective with a street-level view, rather than a bird's-eye perspective of each avenue's proper place and direction. These properties of the hard-boiled world form the foundation for the secondary conventions of the genre type, while the attributes of the detective passing across the scene foster its primary conventions.

Hard-boiled narratives originate in the character of the detective, an independent self-employed man or woman, generally unattached to the routine of the work-a-day world and, typically lacking a spouse or close family, unencumbered by the fixed responsibilities of middle-class life. More often than not, the detective secures dominance in the fiction by serving as its narrator, thus making possible a revelation of character otherwise impossible with a figure so self-sufficient. From the early *pulp magazine stories that gave rise to the hard-boiled type—tales by Dashiell *Hammett about the *Continental Op, the episodes created by Paul Cain about the gambler Gerry Kells, or, among others, Raoul Whitfield's accounts of Jo Gar written under the name Ramon Decolta for *Black Mask*—to the recent modifications of hard-boiled adventure to be found in Marcia *Muller's series about Sharon McCone, Sue *Grafton's about Kinsey *Milhone, and Robert B. *Parker's concerning *Spenser, the authors of hard-boiled fiction have couched their stories in a readily identifiable vernacular language that stands as an identifying trait and convention of the form, even on the occasions when a third-person voice suits the writer's intent.

The narrative *plots of hard-boiled fictions are often dense, highly complicated, or nearly opaque, making it clear that the absence rather than the presence of linear order in the arrangement of scenes is the norm. Raymond *Chandler can baffle a reader who tries to compete with Philip *Marlowe, and Ross *Macdonald's sequences of events in his Lew *Archer stories work to destroy assumptions of conventional chronology by repeatedly looping backwards into the pasts of the clients.

As the crimes in hard-boiled fiction occur in the manner of a peculiar code that neither the rules of logic nor the principles of science are sufficient to explain, there can be no confidence that inferential reasoning will be sufficient to reach a solution; therefore, it has become conventional for the *sleuth to use an eclectic method of detection. It can include interpretation of material evidence but can also require dogged legwork and the use of informants. It demonstrates the power of intuition, and it may also demand that the detective actively intervene into relationships among the secondary characters in order to provoke useful reactions. Above all, the hard-boiled method of detection functions in terms of a convention of specialized knowledge. The detective knows the streets and is informed about the underworld, acquainted with people in all walks of life, and able to perform the shady tasks of breaking and entering, shadowing, and shooting as capably as most criminals. This knowledge reduces social distance, so that the hard-boiled detective is no more displaced when among thieves and *con artists than when mixing with presumably respectable people.

The possession of worldly knowledge informs what can be thought of as the philosophical conventions of hard-boiled fiction—namely, the detective's firm belief that things are not what they seem and the equally cherished assumption by detectives that a state of grace, which would be known by a condition of moral order and certainty, will never be reached. The first axiom results in the appearance of physicians who deal in dope, parents who abuse their children, hypocritical pillars of the community, and, in a reversal of sorts, cultured gangsters. The founding fathers of hard-boiled writing—Hammett, Chandler, Macdonald, and the other male authors who originally dominated the field of hard-boiled fiction—set the standard to represent this axiom. The founding mothers—Muller, Grafton, Sara *Paretsky, and others—have found it equally useful in their portrayals of hard-boiled society. The second basal principle—that the state of grace, which W. H. Auden wrote of as the condition a detective intends to restore, never existed and cannot be created at this late date—yields the hard-boiled convention of limiting the effects of solving a crime. A client may be saved from prison or have his or her personal or financial security protected for a time, or a killer might be caught; but crime will be with us always in the hard-boiled world, because the formula of character and social relations will always include a tainting dose of *corruption; it is in the nature of that world.

Collectively, the conventions of hard-boiled detective fiction present a Janus face. Literary historians have observed an association between hard-boiled stories and the school of *naturalism. Naturalists, blending the views of Darwinian science about the significance of environment with their own distaste for the poverty and social suppression consequent to monopoly capitalism and the industrial order, conceived of human character as the object of forces, sometimes physical, other times due to amoral decisions of the holders of wealth. Writers affected by literary naturalism—such as Émile Zola in France, Frank Norris and Theordore Dreiser in the United States—depicted a deterministic world with small room for free expression of individual will. The hard-boiled conventions of social description borrow from naturalism. The physical scene can contrast opulence with decay, mansions and rooming houses, while the continuous suggestion of debasement renders secondary characters as caricatures of mixed *motives. Moreover, the tone of pessimism and cynicism apparent in the speech of pulp magazine private detectives, as well as in the wisecracking speech of Nick and Nora *Charles, Spenser, Milhone, and V. I. *Warshawski, insinuates the notion that reality is ultimately beyond our grasp. The best that can hoped for is interpretation of the relative powerlessness of human beings in the face of reality.

Yet, at the same time as hard-boiled writers deploy conventions derivative from naturalistic determinism, they also elevate the *individualism of the detective. The characteristic emphasis on the personality of a *private eye conveyed through mannerisms of speech and attitude, the implicit indications through emphasis of the detective's uniquely personal code of behavior that the private eye is, as Chandler argued in his discussion of the mean streets, an ethical hero, and the construction of a fictional environment through which the private eye is the only safe guide—all of these conventions of a hard-boiled story work in tension with and partial contradiction of the equally requisite conventions governing the representation of a deterministic world.

The form, however, has never laid claim to rational logic. It was created by authors whose goal was to project into crime fiction a realism that they believed was lacking in the ratiocinative works of the Golden Age tradition. If their realism does not produce narratives that are neat and tidy, they can claim that result as the price of trying to make a fiction for the world that is, rather than a world that might be.

[See also Antihero; Characterization; Ethics of Detectives; Loner, Sleuth as; Voice: Hard-boiled Voice; Voice: Wisecracking Voice.]

• Gavin Lambert, The Dangerous Edge (1975). John M. Reilly, "Classic and Hard-Boiled Detective Fiction," Armchair Detective (1976). Dennis Porter, The Pursuit of Crime: Art and Ideology in Detective Fiction (1981). David Geherin, The American Private Eye: The Image in Fiction (1985).
—John M. Reilly

CORONER. Coroners, whose main duty is to ascertain the cause of any death that appears to be unnatural, regularly appear in mystery fiction, and the inquests they hold often play an important part in developing the story. In England and Wales coroners must have either legal or medical qualifications; in the United States they are often *forensic pathologists. In conventional mysteries, coroners are usually minor characters and the inquest is not the central event of the story, but Marc Connelly's much anthologized "Coroner's Inquest" (Colliers, 8, Feb. 1930) is an exception to the general rule, as is Percival Wilde's Inquest (1940). In an introduction to his novel, Wilde explained that, historically, in his own domain the coroner was czar, empowered not only to conduct the inquest as he wished but also able to pad out proceedings so as to increase his claim for expenses. Such abuses led to the abolition of the office in many parts of the United States and the appointment of state medical examiners, who are public servants paid regular salaries. Yet in Inquest itself, the Honorable Lee Slocum proves in the end to be much more astute than he initially seems.

In England and Wales, coroners' *juries are no longer entitled to bring in a verdict of willful *murder against a named individual, but in the past such accusations provided moments of drama in many novels, as is the case in Agatha *Christie's Death in the Clouds (1935; Death in the Air). The jury's verdict in Taken at the Flood (1948; There Is a Tide) seems equally to be a manifestation of local prejudice, yet with typical *sleight of hand Hercule *Poirot reveals in the end that, far from being ludicrous, the verdict was correct. In Michael *Gilbert's Roller Coaster (1993), Patrick Petrella reflects the professional policeman's distrust of a legal proceeding such as an inquest which is "without form and void."

In general, British writers have not attempted to exploit the potential of the coroner's office for mystery series to the same extent as their American counterparts. Lawrence G. Blochman's pathologist Dr. Daniel Webster Coffee investigates in many stories as well as one novel, while the medical examiner hero of the television series "Quincy M. E." appears in two novelizations (1977) written by Thom Racina. Of all the many coroners and medical examiners to have appeared in mystery fiction, however, perhaps the most notable is Dr. Kay Scarpetta, heroine of novels by Patricia Cornwell such as Postmortem (1990) and

All That Remains (1992). Scarpetta's work is an important part of her life, but the technical detail in the books does not slow down the action. On the contrary, the description of research techniques and use of DNA profiling effectively complement Cornwell's accounts of the painstaking hunt for serial killers.

[*See also* Clues; Poisons and Poisoning; Poisons, Unusual; Realism, Conventions of.]

• Paul Knapman, "The Crowner's Quest," *Journal of the Royal Society of Medicine* (Dec. 1993): 716–20.

—Martin Edwards

CORPSE. Golden Age writers made *murder a generic requirement. "There simply must be a corpse in a detective novel," wrote S. S. *Van Dine, "and the deader the corpse the better. . . . Three hundred pages is far too much bother for a crime other than murder." The amused tone of voice in which Van Dine issues his rule, and the nineteen others he declaimed as essential to the game, signifies the peculiar place for the corpse in mannered crime stories. Because the unnatural dispatch of the *victim produces the occasion for detection, the corpse has instrumental importance—the story cannot be imagined without it—but, as the narrative of Golden Age-style detective fiction unfolds, the corpse disappears from view, except as a datum, while a plot of consequential investigation plays at the center of narrative. The inevitable distancing of *violence when the corpse is quickly taken offstage accounts for the paradoxical effect by which some detective fiction transforms a frightful happening into the fine art that Thomas De Quincey said murder could be.

Some detective fiction does that, but not all. For hard-boiled writers, *police procedural authors, and other writers whose literary leanings go in the direction of realism and *naturalism rather than comedies of manners, the corpse offers an irresistible opportunity to signify inhuman conditions in a world of savagery.

Besides the telling importance obtained either because it is not seen or because its viewing is elaborated for effect, the corpse works as a prod to narrative composition. If there is to be a corpse in the story—for not all crime stories treat murder despite the demands of the Golden Age *rules of the game—then the author must determine a method of murder. John Dickson *Carr reveals some of the considerations in selecting a murder technique in the famous "locked room lecture" delivered by Dr. Gideon *Fell in *The Three Coffins* (1935; *The Hollow Man*), as does Dorothy L. *Sayers in her "brief selection of handy short cuts to the grave" appearing in the introduction to *Great Short Stories of Detection, Mystery and Horror* (1928–1934; *The Omnibus of Crime*).

In real-life murder disposal of corpses seems to occupy the minds of few killers, but in fiction there is a highly developed collection of expertise on the matter. Dr. John *Thorndyke in R. Austin *Freeman's *A Silent Witness* (1914) describes cremation. In P. D. *James's *Unnatural Causes* (1967) and Tony *Hillerman's *The Dark Wind* (1982), corpses are mutilated to prevent their identification. A corpse is given a false

identity in *The Conjure Man Dies* (1932) by Rudolph Fisher, and corpses are switched to confuse identity in Agatha *Christie's *The Body in the Library* (1942).

When an author does not choose to have a character dispose of the corpse, and when she or he elects to keep the corpse on view, it can become the object of forensic investigation as in the cases of Thorndyke and Patricia Cornwell's Dr. Kay Scarpetta. Lifeless the corpse may be in definition, but in the craft of crime and mystery writing it has a vital role in continuing to foster invention and variation of convention.

[*See also* Coroner; Forensic Pathologist; Realism, Conventions of.]

• Raymond Chandler, "The Simple Art of Murder" (*Atlantic Monthly*, 1944; rev. 1946). S. S. Van Dine, "Twenty Rules for Writing Detective Stories" (1928), in *The Art of the Mystery Story/A Collection of Critical Essays*, ed. Howard Haycraft (1946; 1974). John M. MacDonald, *The Murderer and His Victim*, 2nd ed. (1986).

—John M. Reilly

CORRUPTION. In crime and mystery fiction the perversion of integrity and debasement of standards or relationships signified by the term "corruption" is particularly associated with the writing of the hard-boiled school. While murderers of many sorts and conspiratorial plans for crimes such as robbery may be loosely designated "corrupt," it is the vision developed by hard-boiled authors of a world where crime is typical and tawdriness ubiquitous that makes corruption fundamental to narrative.

Dashiell *Hammett's *Continental Op in *Red Harvest* (1929) discovers a town made lawless by an alliance of gangsters, police, and politicians fostered by the wealthy Elihu Wilson. Raymond *Chandler's Philip *Marlowe contends with medical doctors violating professional ethics in nearly all of his adventures, and with shady police in *The Long Goodbye* (1953) and elsewhere. The third acknowledged master of the hard-boiled school, Ross *Macdonald, shows his sleuth, Lew *Archer, revealing the ties between people of wealth and the *underworld of Las Vegas in *Black Money* (1966) and a scheme for gangsters to fund film production in *The Barbarous Coast* (1956). In *The Moving Target* (1949; written as John Macdonald) and other works Macdonald also presents the corruption of *religion to be found in the cults that appeal to the lost souls he sees peopling California.

Earlier works had already made the corruption of society by the criminal underworld a staple in the American crime story. W. R. Burnett's *Little Caesar*, published in the same year in which *Red Harvest* established the gangster *antihero. Benjamin Appel filled in a picture of corruption in novels about the underworld of *New York City in *Brain Guy* (1934) and the corrupt practices on New York's waterfront in *The Raw Edge* (1958); Paul Cain's story of gangsters, *Fast One* (1933), set a level for representation of the brutal consequences of corruption that no other work has exceeded.

A signal effect of the body of writing relating the hard-boiled outlook has been to make an *atmosphere of pervasive corruption a convention of the crime genre. The convention functions to offer social commentary—as, for example, in the novels by Chester *Himes about Coffin Ed *Johnson and Grave Digger Jones that image the general corruption resulting from the taint of racism in all institutional life.

[See also Bribery; Conventions of the Genre: Hard-Boiled Conventions; Ethics of Detectives; Extortion.]
—John M. Reilly

COUNTRY CONSTABLE. The country constable, found predominantly in English crime fiction, is a popular *stock character in novels set in small towns or rural areas, but he is rarely presented as a main character or *sleuth. Like the New York patrolman's rank, constable is the lowest in the British police service; uniformed police constables and plainclothes detective constables are of equal rank, which is the lowest in their particular division. In fiction as in real life, the constable is answerable to a tier of supervisory officers, which severely restricts the freedom necessary for detective work. The constable is rarely able to make decisions of the kind required for a major investigation. The same applies to the patrolman, consequently these subordinate officers seldom feature as central characters in British or American crime fiction.

The stereotypical English country constable is male, middle-aged, red faced, very large, slow moving, and slow thinking; he lives in a village house, rides a bicycle, and speaks with a rustic accent. He is generally simpleminded, kindhearted, inoffensive, likeable, and malleable but often a man of deep wisdom about rural life and people. Happily married in many cases, he may or may not have children. The police station, sometimes within his house and sometimes in an annex, is usually small and contains the basics of his business: a desk, telephone, two chairs, a battered typewriter, and perhaps a notice board bearing posters of wanted criminals and warnings of animal diseases. Apprehended criminals are often confined to the cellar or a spare bedroom with a lock on the door.

Almost any British *crime novel of the first half of the twentieth century, particularly those featuring country house murders, will include a country constable. He will most often be depicted carrying out simple tasks such as guarding doors or conducting house-to-house inquiries under supervision rather than initiating his own tasks. Writers often use the stereotype of the inept and slightly stupid constable for comic relief. In Dorothy L. *Sayers's Clouds of Witness (1926), Lord Peter *Wimsey observes that, among several footprints in the ground, one belonged to an elephant, which had trampled across the borders; Wimsey's friend, Inspector Parker, observes that the marks in fact had been made by a very large and clumsy constable. By contrast, P. D. *James gives more credit to the constable in An Unsuitable Job for a Woman (1972). The first policeman to arrive on the scene is young and efficient; he conducts himself in a calm, professional manner by asking eminently sensible questions.

Frank Parrish makes good use of a constable as a secondary character in the Dan Mallett novels. Police Constable Jim Gundry, the village constable of Medwell Fratorum, is forever coming up against crimes committed by Mallett, a poacher who is also the main character and sleuth. The two men have a grudging professional respect for one another's skills and serve as foils to each other. Mallett, a former bank employee who now bears little respect for the institutions of this world and who uses his quick wits to successfully defy local powers, is the opposite of Gundry, who is quick to go for help but not quite quick enough to figure out Mallett's crimes (Fly in the Cobweb, 1986). The stolid tortoise loses out to the flamboyant hare.

Several writers have turned the constable stereotype on its head. Leo *Bruce introduced Sergeant *Beef (Case for Three Detectives, 1936) to spoof the eccentric and *aristocratic sleuths popular at the time. A man who loves darts and a large pint, Beef is the tortoise beating the well-dressed hares of detection. After two successful cases, he decides to go into business for himself as a *private detective if *Scotland Yard fails to recognize his remarkable abilities (Case Without a Corpse, 1937). Maurice Procter, a one-time Yorkshire policeman, also featured a constable as main character: Police Constable Daniel Burns is a patrolling officer in an urban environment in Each Man's Destiny (1947). With his No Proud Chivalry (1946), Procter was the first writer of *police procedural novels, predating both Hillary *Waugh's Last Seen Wearing —— (1952) and J. J. Marrie's (pseudonym of John *Creasey) Gideon's Day (1955; Gideon of Scotland Yard). In his semiautobiographical series of novels, Nicholas Rhea chronicles the work of a country constable in North Yorkshire during the 1960s, beginning with Constable on the Hill (1979). The stories are rich with *humor and nostalgia; crime investigation is not the dominant theme, though Rhea will investigate and detect crimes, both major and minor, that occur on his wild and romantic rural beat (Constable in Disguise, 1989). One of the constable's main protagonists is Claude Jeremiah Greengrass, the local poacher, petty thief, and general dealer. Rhea's relationship with the public (and even with Greengrass) shows a caring and sympathetic approach, at times defying his superiors, who do not understand his gentle method of policing.

Georgette *Heyer offers a different variation on the stolid constable in A Blunt Instrument (1938). The charming and generous Ernest Fletcher seems an unlikely candidate for murder, and the evidence argues that the crime was impossible anyway. The solution is not obvious: The constable did the deed, one minute before he "found" the body on his nightly rounds.

[See also Country House Milieu; English Village Milieu; Police Detective; Rural Milieu; Stereotypes, Reversals of.]
—Nicholas Rhea

COUNTRY HOUSE MILIEU. The attractions of the tightly contained world of the country house to the writer of *detective novels are particularly evident in those books written in the earlier years of the Golden

Age, when it was much more usual for these great houses to be in private ownership and still occupied by a family. Such edifices are historically situated on the outskirts of a village. In British fiction, they are often placed in an isolated *setting even deeper in the English countryside, though seldom in Wales, Scotland, or Northern Ireland. In American fiction, they are situated somewhere within reach of—but not too near—a major city, as is the case in Emma Lathen's *A Place for Murder* (1963).

In days gone by, the length of the carriage drive from entrance gate to house was an actual measure of the grandeur of a building—the longer the distance, the more prestigious the edifice was considered to be. At that time it was also quite usual for there to be no other dwelling visible from the windows of a stately home, although an ancient church was sometimes a permitted part of the landscape. Both these factors are of value to the crime writer in assisting to delineate and circumscribe the physical area within which the story takes place.

As well as providing the enclosed *milieu so useful to the crime writer, the ambience of the stately home is often much appreciated by readers whose actual knowledge of really grand houses is now likely to be confined to visits to those open to the public, first known as "Half-Crown Houses." Satirized by Noel Coward in his 1930s song "The Stately Homes of England," they were once a very important part of the social fabric of the countryside—a fact appreciated and much used by writers such as Michael *Innes, Agatha *Christie, E. X. *Ferrars, and Ngaio *Marsh.

While most of the houses about which they write are elegant, some are dour and forbidding, like the mansion Black Dudley, "standing in a thousand acres of its own land," "a great grey building, bare and ugly as a fortress," in *The Crime at Black Dudley* by Margery *Allingham (1929; *The Black Dudley Murder*). Some are beautiful, like The Grange, built on the site of an earlier monastic foundation, in *To Let, Furnished* by Josephine Bell (1952; *Stranger on a Cliff*), and Swanswater, an example of Georgian elegance, in *Suddenly at His Residence* by Christanna Brand (1947; *The Crooked Wreath*). Enderby Hall in Christie's *After the Funeral* (1953; *Funerals Are Fatal; Murder at the Gallop*), a vast Victorian pile built in the Gothic style, is feelingly described by the new cook as "a proper old mausoleum."

These large houses are peopled in crime fiction by their owners (usually old, ill, and wealthy), their heirs (often impoverished and sometimes undeserving), and assorted dependents and guests. Such is the great style of both the country houses and their owners that it occasions no surprise if visitors include the very distinguished, as in *The Rasp* by Philip MacDonald (1924). Similarly, where the detective is a well-connected amateur he or she is usually present first as a friend of the household and therefore numbered among the guests. The police may appear at chief constable level and the *coroner is likely to be an old friend of the owner, himself probably a justice of the peace for the county.

These disparate groups of *family and friends have often assembled for a weekend house party, ready for entertainment. This can include a masked ball, fancy dress parties (as in "The Queen's Square" by Dorothy L. *Sayers, in *Hangman's Holiday*, 1933), charades, and amateur theatricals as in *Hamlet, Revenge!* (1937) by Innes. All of these diversions offer opportunities for characters to be temporarily out of sight, disguised or otherwise unrecognizable, and licensed to behave oddly.

Christmas has proved a particularly popular festival in the literature of the country house murder with the added aid of footprints, or lack thereof, in the snow. *Tied up in Tinsel* by Marsh (1972) has a Santa Claus outfit used to advantage in Halberds Manor.

Confusion may be even further compounded by the existence in such historic old buildings of secret passages and hidden rooms. The owners live surrounded by visible reminders of their ancestors in the form of portraits and sporting trophies and quite possibly have a gun room. The buildings are the natural setting for famous paintings, valuable jewelry, and other similar artifacts, and the residents and staff keep to the time-honored routines that are a real aid to detection. The sounding of the dressing bell and the dinner gong, as well as church attendance on Sunday morning, are among the fixed points in the life of the household of that period, as is the butler's nightly security round.

The green baize door which traditionally divided the house from the servants' quarters existed in both fact and in metaphor. Old and omniscient butlers and other domestic staff have a part to play and are usually only suspect if fairly newly employed. Retainers of long standing are normally above *suspicion but often act as important purveyors of back-stairs information to the detective or to the sleuth's sidekick. Members of the squirearchy customarily would be expected to take responsibility for the welfare of their family, staff, and tenants in a manner linearly descended from the feudal tradition of livery and maintenance, and they have the authority and wealth to go with that responsibility.

The actual decline of the country house is seldom documented in detective fiction, although antiques and Hulliwell Hall (now open to the public) feature in Gladys Mitchell's *Noonday and Night* (1977). Developers, death duties, and decay pose a continual threat to the country house, and the imminent need for work to be done for its preservation may be an important part of a testamentary disposition or plausible motive.

If the murderer is of or related to the owner's family, he or she will be seen as someone not worthy of his or her inheritance—a gambler or a drinker or "not quite straight." Most of those who fall into the category of *suspect have a touch of this unworthiness about them.

The continual appeal of this milieu may have something to do with the gentle melancholy in G. K. Chesterton's poem "The Secret People" of "the last sad squires riding slowly down to the sea"; or, it may be a determined retreat into the apparently more ordered, secure world of yesterday.

[*See also* Class; Closed-World Settings and Open-

World Settings; Conventions of the Genre: Traditional Conventions; English Village Milieu.]

—Catherine Aird

COUPLES. *This entry is divided into two parts. The first surveys the roles of married and some unmarried but coupled pairs of *sleuths who are protagonists in the works in which they appear. The second section focuses on the challenges faced by the fictional sleuth, the author, and the reader when couples are used as secondary characters in a genre, that traditionally eschewed the use of elements of romance as complicating the detective's mission of discovering the truth.*

Sleuth Couples
Couples as Secondary Characters

For further information, please refer to Marriage; Sex and Sexuality.

SLEUTH COUPLES

Married couples who share in detecting emerged around the turn of the century but never came to dominate the genre, which prefers reason to romance. M. McDonnell Bodkin was among the first to portray married sleuths. The success of *Paul Beck, The Rule-of-Thumb Detective* (1898), followed by *Dora Myrl, The Lady Detective* (1900), encouraged him to bring his two detectives together in *The Capture of Paul Beck* (1909), in which Myrl and Beck compete, with the honors going to Myrl. At the end of the novel, the two sleuths decide to marry. Bodkin's series is notable for giving the woman equal importance. More typical is a series of pulp stories about the Honeymoon Detectives written by Arnold Fredericks that appeared between 1912 and 1917 and featured Richard Duvall, who relies on reason, and his wife Grace, who relies on intuition.

During the 1920s and 1930s, sleuth couples were often characterized by witty dialogue. The most famous detective couples were Tommy and Tuppence Beresford, created by Agatha *Christie, and Nick and Nora *Charles, by Dashiell *Hammett. The Beresfords first appeared as an unmarried pair in *The Secret Adversary* (1922) in which, despite having to be rescued, Tuppence is equal in importance to Tommy. In *Partners in Crime* (1928), the now-married couple opens a detective agency, and Tuppence is the brighter of the two. Nick and Nora Charles in *The Thin Man* (1934) are similar, although Nick had been a *private eye before marrying the socialite Nora.

It was their influence (more through the series of Thin Man movies than directly through the book) that led to a fad of married *sleuths during the late 1930s and 1940s. In 1936, Anne and Jeffrey McNeill first appeared in Theodora Dubois's *Armed with a New Terror*. They were followed by Craig *Rice's Jake and Helene Justus in *8 Faces at Three* (1939; *Death at Three*) and Kelley Roos's Jeff and Haila Troy in *If the Shroud Fits* (1941; *Dangerous Blondes*). The most popular of all were Pam and Jerry *North, created by Frances and Richard Lockridge in *The Norths Meet Murder* (1941; *Mr. and Mrs. North Meet Murder*). Unlike some of the sleuthing pairs, the Norths, who appear in twenty-six novels, have no professional experience as investigators. Much of the humor of the North books revolves around Pam's portrayal as a scatterbrain.

Sleuthing couples from the 1950s to the present reflect changes in traditional relationships and the emergence of nontraditional relationships including homosexual couples. Frequently, among traditional married couples, one partner is a police officer. Emmy Tibbett assists her husband, Chief Inspector Henry Tibbett, beginning in Patricia Moyes's *Dead Men Don't Ski* (1959). In many of Anne Perry's Victorian novels, Inspector Thomas Pitt's wife, Charlotte, takes advantage of her higher birth to investigate in situations where he cannot, as in *Paragon Walk* (1981).

Almost as frequently unmarried lovers work together as sleuths. Private investigator Catherine Sayler, in Linda Grant's *Random Access Murder* (1988), works with Peter Harmon, whom she describes as her "main squeeze." Beginning with Charlotte MacLeod's *The Family Vault* (1979), Sarah Kelling is first a friend, then the wife, of art investigator Max Bittersohn. Noteworthy are two other not-quite lovers, academics Penny Spring and Sir Toby Glendower, whose first case was *Exit Actors Dying* (1979) by Margot Arnold. In recent years, gay and lesbian partnerships have featured prominently in detective novels. In Sandra Scoppetone's series, *private eye Lauren Laurano is assisted by her lover Kip, as in *I'll Be Leaving You Always* (1992). As Scoppetone's books indicate, the competitiveness and repartee of earlier sleuth couples have gradually been replaced by the authentic soundings of deeper relationships.

[*See also* Gay Characters and Perspectives; Marriage; Sex and Sexuality.]

• Robert Sampson, *Yesterday's Faces: A Study of Series Characters in the Early Pulp Magazines*. Volume 4: The Solvers (1987). Julian Symons, *Bloody Murder: From the Detective Story to the Crime Novel: A History*, 3rd. ed. (1992).

—Douglas G. Greene

COUPLES AS SECONDARY CHARACTERS

Wilkie *Collins's *The Moonstone* (1868) establishes the essential problem of the couple in detective fiction. While the genre depends upon the revelation of secrets, the couple, by its very existence, suggests allegiances that threaten the detective's drive toward *truth. Suspecting her fiancé of the crime, Collins's heroine withholds evidence, delaying the resolution of the mystery; her loyal silence is read as evidence of *guilt. The detective *plot typically arrests romance: Rational exploration and private feeling cannot coexist. In Mary Roberts *Rinehart's famous example of the *Had-I-But-Known school, *The Circular Staircase* (1908), a young couple conspires to withhold crucial knowledge that might have saved lives. Yet early authors condone couples' secrecy, acknowledging alternative standards of privacy and loyalty that counter the detective's intrusive ethic.

Proscriptions of the 1920s and '30s on the detective novel's proper elements often stipulate "no love interest," marking the genre off from romance and signaling the ascendancy of rationality. The couple automatically becomes an object of *suspicion. Agatha *Christie manipulates this assumption. For example, *Hercule Poirot's Christmas* (1939; *Murder for Christmas; A Holiday for Murder*), the account of a family gathering at which the sadistic patriarch is murdered, opens with domestic scenes in which the *victim's children and their spouses reveal the interdependences that bind husband and wife. Establishing these networks, Christie puts into doubt all evidence offered by the coupled and diverts attention from her murderer. While Christie uses genre expectations to assemble a challenging intellectual *puzzle, for other Golden Age writers couples symbolize the disorder the detective must redress. In C. P. Snow's *Death Under Sail* (1932), *marriage is antithetical to purity. Each couple conceals discreditable secrets, innocent parties destroying evidence of spouses' murderousness. In the work of *Ngaio Marsh, *murder is often precipitated by sexual passion, whether fulfilled or frustrated. Both Marsh and Dorothy L. *Sayers portray couples as potential sites of sin. Antisocial forces are expressed as lust and adultery; in Sayers's *Clouds of Witness* (1926), these practices lead even Lord Peter Wimsey's *family to the brink of the gallows. The detective upholds a fragile civilization against the vast human depravity the couple often represents.

In the British novel *evil is natural and individual, the couple a means of its articulation. For the American hard-boiled school, focusing on corrupt social structures, the couple is less important. In the poisoned society of Dashiell *Hammett's *Red Harvest* (1929) or Raymond *Chandler's *The Big Sleep* (1939) transient individual alliances reflect a wider malaise. However, *hard-boiled fiction often validates the romantic couple as an idyllic alternative to the detective's damaged urban world. The couple at the center of *Spenser's investigation in Robert B. *Parker's *Mortal Stakes* (1975), though guilty of various crimes, is rescued from the text's real villain, *organized crime.

Couples as murderers are rare in detective fiction. But recent developments show couples sliding further into disrepute. Perhaps this reflects growing elasticity in how the term is defined: P. D. *James's *Shroud for a Nightingale* (1971) features a lesbian couple, one half of whom murders to shield the other, who responds by executing her would-be protector. While James evokes earlier authors' concern with the couple as breeding ground for individualistic passion, in recent feminist work by Sara Paretsky, *Barbara Wilson, and Katherine V. Forrest, the couple—specifically the married, heterosexual couple—embodies the evils of patriarchal society. The family becomes the place where wives collude in fathers' abuse of their female children. Forrest's *Murder at the Nightwood Bar* (1987), in which a timid housewife murders to protect her husband, only to immolate him when his incestuous past is revealed, is an extreme example of the feminist detective novel's attack on heterosexual couples and the abusive power relations they are seen to maintain.

[*See also* Loyalty and Betrayal; Sex and Sexuality.]

—Anna Wilson

COURTROOM MILIEU. An understanding of the narrative value of the courtroom *milieu is evident as early as Charles *Dickens's *Bleak House* (1852–53), but the setting does not find a firm place in the imagination of crime and mystery writers until the 1910s and 1920s. The emphasis in stories using this milieu moves among *lawyers, *judges, *witnesses, and jurors.

Arthur Train, a practicing lawyer and attorney general in Massachusetts, introduced his *lawyer sleuth Ephraim Tutt in short stories in the *Saturday Evening Post* and later in collections, beginning with *Tutt and Mr. Tutt* (1920). With his frock coat, stove pipe hat, and cigars, Tutt is a rich character who uses his privileged background and legal training to help the disadvantaged; Train's scrupulous regard for accuracy was appreciated by law schools and for many years was an exception in fiction with legal themes.

The figure of the brilliant lawyer showing his skill in a climactic courtroom scene continues in series featuring Erle Stanley *Gardner's Perry *Mason and Sara Woods's Antony Maitland. Cyril *Hare makes use of the British coroner's inquest as well as trial court. In *Tenant for Death* (1937) all the vital scenes occur at inquests. In *Tragedy at Law* (1942) Hare explores the adversarial relationship between prosecutor and defender, and depicts life for judges on the court circuit. With this novel, hare adapts the courtroom more closely to the country house mystery, with a limited group of characters and closed *setting.

In these early years the sympathy always lies with the defense lawyer rather than the prosecutor, on the assumption that the institution of law is being used to prosecute the innocent or the weak. An imaginative twist on this convention is C. W. Grafton's *Beyond a Reasonable Doubt* (1950) in which attorney Jess London is tried for the murder of his brother-in-law. He is guilty, but the murder is justified and London defends himself.

Gardner was one of the main proponents of the defense lawyer as hero, and his *sleuth, Perry Mason, was not above twisting the law to exculpate a client. Nevertheless, Gardner also developed a sympathetic prosecutor, district attorney Doug Selby, who first appears in *The D.A. Calls It Murder* (1937).

It wasn't long before writers advanced from using the courtroom as a stage for a lawyer to a setting to reveal character. In Frances Noyes Hart's *The Bellamy Trial* (1927) the entire action of the story takes place in the courtroom or in the judge's chambers. Two reporters record the testimony of witnesses, conveying all the *suspense of unexpected revelations and developments in personal relationships. Watching the truth of events unfold is equally riveting in Agatha *Christie's "The Witness for the Prosecution" (*The Witness for the Prosecution and other stories*, 1948), which plays in part on the reader's assumptions about *witnesses and lawyers. Margaret *Millar uses the same technique in *Beyond This Point Are Monsters* (1970), in which the mother of a man who has disappeared hopes desperately that he is still alive as she listens to testimony about his final hours. Although the witnesses are presented through one main observer, the technique enables the author to produce a story of multiple voices and perceptions, forcing the reader into the role of observer. This narrative device can evoke the immediacy of a real trial.

The courtroom does not have to be used to create *suspense, tell the entire story, or showcase lawyers and judges. Dorothy L. *Sayers uses the setting in *Strong Poison* (1930) to lay out the facts against Harriet *Vane, who is on trial for the murder of her lover, and give Lord Peter *Wimsey an opportunity to see and fall in love with her, as well as demonstrating the overlooked *virtues of women like Miss Katharine Climpson, the spinster whose vote postpones Vane's fate. The main purpose of the scene, to establish Vane as a sympathetic character, is achieved partly through the comments of the observers in the gallery, characters who are not normally given place in courtroom dramas.

In recent years, the lawyer sleuth who engages in pyrotechnics in the courtroom has gained in popularity, but two writers, both trained as lawyers, reach back to Arthur Train in the accuracy with which they depict the law and its workings. John *Mortimer's Horace *Rumpole chooses to defend the petty criminal and others who run afoul of the law, and does so with talent that depends as much on his wits as on the niceties of the legal system, which is an object of unrelenting satire. He appears in numerous short stories, beginning with *Rumpole of the Bailey* (1978). Lisa Scottoline, whose first book, *Everywhere That Mary Went* (1993), follows the work of lawyer Mary DeNunzio, also has avoided the trap of many lawyers-turned-writers of adjusting the law to suit the story, and is thus appreciated for the precision of her legal material as well as her *plots.

[*See also* Legal Procedural; Old Bailey.]

—Susan Docherty

COXE, GEORGE HARMON (1901–1984), American author of mystery novels, short stories, screenplays, and radio scripts. Coxe pioneered the use of a newspaper photographer as protagonist-sleuth with Flashgun Casey in short stories and novels, most of them for *Black Mask* magazine. He followed the burly, tough, somewhat disheveled Casey with a series about another photographer, the sophisticated, cynical sentimentalist Kent *Murdock, in novelettes for the *American Magazine*, many of which were later expanded into novels. Jack Fenner, the private investigator in the Murdock stories, appeared on his own in a later series, set in Boston—as were the Casey and Murdock stories. Coxe used other series characters, most notably Dr. Paul Standish, medical examiner, in short stories and novelettes for the slick magazines. Almost half of his sixty-two novels, however, do not have recurring characters, but are set in the Caribbean or South America, an area he visited frequently. Born in Olean, New York, Coxe attended Purdue and Cornell Universities, and worked for several West Coast newspapers and in advertising in New England before selling his first crime fiction to the *pulp magazines. His journalism background can be seen in the Casey and Murdock stories, all of which combine news reporting and crime. He was more interested in recognizable, interesting characters than clever *plot twists and often set two protagonists with differing backgrounds to solve the mystery. He never identified himself as a hard-boiled writer but wrote what the pulp market demanded.

[*See also* Journalist Sleuth.]

• J. Randolph Cox, "Mystery Master: A Survey and Appreciation of the Fiction of George Harmon Coxe," *Armchair Detective* 6, nos. 2 (Feb. 1973): 63–74, 3 (May 1973): 160–66, 4 (Aug. 1973): 232–41 and *Armchair Detective* 7, no. 1 (Nov. 1973): 11–24. Chris Steinbrunner and Otto Penzler, eds., *Encyclopedia of Mystery and Detection* (1976). George Harmon Coxe, "Flash Casey," in *The Great Detectives*, ed. Otto Penzler (1978). —J. Randolph Cox

COZY MYSTERY. A term first used in a review in the *Observer* 25 May 1958, "cozy" refers to a subgenre of the novel of detection defined by its light tone, element of fun, and closed world. A detective, amateur or professional, investigates the eruption of *violence in an apparently tranquil world; the cast of characters is limited, and suspects are known to each other. The *plot is often intricate, the story told with a sense of humor, the setting one of material comfort, and the emphasis on verbal jousting rather than physical violence. The quintessential cozy is a murder in a country house during a snowstorm as family and friends gather for a holiday, when no one can escape, or rescue the houseguests, from their opulent prison.

The cozy belongs to the twentieth century, but has nineteenth-century precursors. Wilkie *Collins defined the *setting, circle of *suspects, and central role of the detective in *The Moonstone* (1968). Robert Louis Stevenson in *The Wrong Box* (1889) and Mary Roberts *Rinehart in *The Circular Staircase* (1908) developed a lighthearted tone but lacked the necessary focus on detection to be classified as cozies.

E. C. *Bentley's *Trent's Last Case* (1913; *The Woman in Black*), with its well-sketched characters and literary *allusions, defined the new subgenre, which became one of the most popular forms during the Golden Age. Bentley introduced the fallible detective, which was followed by a diverse group of idiosyncratic sleuths often parodying Sherlock *Holmes, such as Agatha *Christie's Hercule *Poirot and S. S. *Van Dine's Philo *Vance. Although detectives become increasingly more interesting as characters, Ngaio *Marsh (*Artists in Crime*, 1938) was the first to recognize the necessity of making the detective a more realistic human being with a fully developed private life. Traditionally banned from detective fiction, romance was reintroduced, within limits, by Dorothy L. *Sayers in the Harriet *Vane books (*Strong Poison*, 1930); this writer also moved the form closer to the *novel of manners by exploring particular *milieus (*Murder Must Advertise*, 1933), as well as expanding the importance of setting (*The Nine Tailors*, 1934). The Golden Age writers developed another important quality introduced by Bentley: the treatment of the detective novel as a valid literary art form, replete with graceful writing and literary allusions.

The cozy respects unities of time and place, the story usually occurring in a single setting during a relatively short period of time, often a few days or a week. Typical settings are an estate (*The Affair of the Blood-Stained Egg Cosy*, 1975, by James Anderson), vicarage (*The Murder at the Vicarage*, 1930, by Agatha Christie), hotel (*The Mystery of the Cape Cod Tavern*, 1934, by Phoebe Atwood *Taylor), museum (*The Cat Who Talked to Ghosts*, 1990, by Lillian Jackson Braun), *convent (*The Religious Body*, 1966, by Catherine Aird), theater (*Panic in Box C*, 1966, by John Dickson *Carr), university (*Death in a Tenured Position*, 1981; *A Death in the Faculty*, by Amanda *Cross), or another site wherein the participants can be isolated. Bodies are found in the library (*A Night of Errors*, 1947, by Michael *Innes), on a church altar (*Death in Ecstasy*, 1936, by Ngaio *Marsh), or at a wedding reception (*Death of a Wedding Guest*, 1976, by Anne Morice), among other places. Murders occur at all times of the year, but holidays are an especially dangerous period, particularly Christmas (*Rest You Merry*, 1978, by Charlotte MacLeod).

The typical cozy relies on a wide range of *stock characters: the prominent family with a difficult or endearing patriarch and matriarch; prodigal son or daughter; ingenue; seductress; big-game hunter or adventurer; young man-about-town; student; doctor; vicar; ne'er-do-well; spinster; gauche foreigner; ambitious young writer; rake; professor; and so on. Any character may be in *disguise. In general, the solution to the crime lies within the given community or *class; therefore, no matter how suspicious he might be, the butler is seldom guilty (*Fair Warning*, 1936, by Mignon G. *Eberhart), though servants may supply *alibis (*Death and the Dancing Footman*, 1942, by Ngaio Marsh).

Novels may open with a list of characters, map of the village, or floor plan of the crime scene; the detective may later introduce timetables, facsimile letters, or other documents for the reader to study as *clues. Plots often include mechanical devices as murder weapons (*Murder Fantastical*, 1967, by Patricia Moyes), or alibis (*The Murder of Roger Ackroyd*, 1926, by Christie). As part of the reader-writer dialogue, the text may be studded with literary references (any novel by Innes), offer a commentary on a true crime (*Missing Susan*, 1991, by Sharyn McCrumb), contain quizzes about mystery fiction (*Death on Demand*, 1987, by Carolyn G. Hart), or instruct on a technical subject (archaeology in *Death at Hallows End*, 1965, by Leo *Bruce).

Plots are intricate, involving layers of secrets and a large number of clues; real-world events such as wars, depressions, or political upheavals are excluded or mentioned peripherally. In general, the murder is planned, the motive being one of four—gain, hatred, envy, or fear—listed by Christie in *Peril at End House* (1932)—and is a major cataclysm in the community; the murderer usually acts alone, rather than as part of a gang or conspiracy. The detective analyzes the evidence, building and revising cases against various *suspects as the novel proceeds. Several patterns are popular: Suspects are eliminated one by one as clues are discovered; a single suspect is guilty, then innocent, then guilty; the murderer is the *least likely suspect; or after much

investigation, the main suspect may be murdered, forcing the detective to start all over again.

An additional convention is the breaking of conventions. The most pointed of these is the concealment of the murderer in the guise of the detective, his assistant, or a policeman. Several writers have tried their hand at this, for example, Georgette *Heyer in *A Blunt Instrument* (1938). Christie wrote a series of novels devoted to breaking the rules.

Many writers of the cozy insist they are only writing light entertainment; this too is a convention, but it contains an important awareness that a failure in attitude can destroy the form. As a result, many writers concentrate on writing a *novel of manners; others strive to achieve a high standard in writing and storytelling while exploring issues of significance. Sayers poses questions on salvation and the nature of sin; Margaret Logan airs the problem of race and class in academia (*C.A.T. Caper*, 1990); and Barbara Neely describes the rich and class-conscious from the perspective of a housekeeper (*Blanche on the Lam*, 1992).

In the 1920s and 1930s, the cozy dominated the genre, supplying a welcome change from the *thriller novel and puzzle story of earlier decades. With the rise of the hard-boiled school of writing in the 1940s and 1950s and its emphasis on a gritty realism, however, such writer-critics as Raymond *Chandler and Julian *Symons declared the cozy less suited to conveying the complexity of modern life. Despite the charge that the cozy takes a frivolous view of crime and its aftermath, skillful writers still turned to the form to explore questions of community. Since the 1960s the cozy has enjoyed a resurgence in popularity and critical acceptance.

[*See also* Academic Milieu; Christmas Crime; Closed-World settings vs. Open-World Settings: Closed-World Settings; Conventions of the Genre: Traditional Conventions; Country House Milieu; Hotel Milieu; Library Milieu.]

• LeRoy Lad Panek, *Watteau's Shepherds: The Detective Novel in Britain, 1914–1940* (1979). Hanna Charney, *The Detective Novel of Manners: Hedonism, Morality, and the Life of Reason* (1981). LeRoy Lad Panek, *An Introduction to the Detective Story* (1987). Julian Symons, *Bloody Murder: From the Detective Story to the Crime Novel: A History*, 3rd. rev. ed. (1992).
—Susan Oleksiw

CRAFT OF CRIME AND MYSTERY WRITING, THE. Most authors approach the task of writing a crime or mystery narrative after having read hundreds of prototypes within the genre. From consuming stories of detection and crime, aspiring writers have learned along with every reader that stories in this genre share a basic structure. They also know that it is variation and invention in such apparently secondary matters as the character of the *sleuth, the peculiarity of the crime, or the *ingenuity displayed in resolution of the criminal problem—sometimes even the absence of a resolution and recognition that the problem is insurmountable—that makes the generic narrative successful. Still, much of the attraction of popular literature resides in its redundancy. Readers select texts from the popular literary genres because they can be dependably expected to give a familiar type of satisfaction. Interesting deviations and variations are the author's added gifts to readers.

Common possession of genre literacy among the audience and authors of crime and mystery literature indicates that the practice of writing in the genre can be readily understood as movement across a finite field of technical choices and their associated conventions. A writer may begin to draft a narrative in one of the distinct subtypes of the genre—*cozy mystery, *hard-boiled fiction, *police procedural, *caper story, and so on—due to personal taste for the type. Similarly, an author might set a story in one locale or another because it is actually or imaginatively familiar. Although the real *Los Angeles, for example, offers interesting terrain for fiction, the accretions of myth and popular imagery surrounding the "idea" of Los Angeles could be useful to a writer for other reasons. In any event, predisposition to favor a story type or to use a *setting amounts to making a choice and initiating a cascade of related, additional points of decision.

Comprising as they do a field of options, the contingencies of craft do not assume a linear order. One writer, hoping to inscribe his or her signature on the genre through *characterization, might begin by thinking about the character of the sleuth. Another writer, deciding that sleuths are generally portrayed as displaying implausible omnipotence, might found his or her conception of the eventual narrative on a decision to center attention upon the criminal and the crime. Regardless of where an author enters the field of choices, two things are clear about passage across the field. One is that the choices create a feedback system. Each technical decision introduces contingencies affecting each subsequent decision and modifying all prior decisions. The second clear thing about the field of options is that, precisely because the field has been created by the accumulation of all the previous instances of crime and mystery fictions, redundancy characterizes the range of choices, just as it typifies popular literature in the first place. In other words, the possibilities for technical choices are amenable to categorization.

The feedback system can be illustrated by imagining an author as having selected a geographical or physical setting. Immediately, *milieus begin to suggest themselves. The isolated country house raises thoughts of upper crust society, or possibly opportunity for scenes of horror that will be enhanced by the lonely surroundings. The selection of an urban setting like Miami offers options of using the milieu of tourism, the imagery of glitz, the complex overlay of Cuban American culture on the established routines of retirees from the northern United States, or maybe the hybrid cultural ways springing from legal and illegal international trade. An author's interest in a theme, his or her philosophical disposition, or a prior decision about a character type can guide the selection of milieu. A conservative social orientation that models society as a self-contained community could lead to selection of the isolated country house setting and upper-crust milieu. Conversely, a decision to place a story in such a setting inevitably forces the

writer to decide if a conservative image is, indeed, an aim of the story. Heirs to the Golden Age tradition and descendants of American hard-boiled writing can both use Miami as a geographical location, but the election of legal trade over illegal trade prods a story toward a milieu of legitimate finance, such as banking, rather than toward the grungy environs of the *underworld. Every decision in the process of crafting a narrative impinges on other decisions, narrowing the range for further options and amplifying the significance of decisions already made.

All decisions of craft are made within a framework of genre literacy. For intellectual convenience, readers and critics organize the details of their literacy taxonomically. Accumulated practices of characterization allow us to view protagonists and secondary figures according to type. The creative powers of past writers have been expended in imagining thousands of criminal actions, yet we can readily begin to classify crimes as violent and nonviolent; violent crimes can be further subdivided into kinds of *murder, *assault, and *rape and other sex crimes, some of which may be represented as spontaneous, others as premeditated, while nonviolent crimes lend themselves to arrangement as fraud, *extortion, *bribery, and so forth. Additionally, hundreds of precedents exist for the commission of nearly all the recorded types of crime. All of the categories making up the field of technical choices demand decisions from authors as they construct their narratives.

Some decisions about drafting the narrative are so bound up in previously existing dispositions or tastes—a personal philosophy, a background of experience, an interest in a milieu or knowledge of its intricacies—as to seem nearly spontaneous; others call for more deliberation. Either way, the story cannot become a story until the author decides on a *voice. Other choices are all of those associated with plotting the narrative, that is, arranging the events in a temporal frame, devising a basis for linking them, and determining how the events should be rendered or described. The plot, intimately related to the decision the author has made about voice, forms the armature of the narrative. Decisions about setting and milieu, character and crime, dress the armature with verisimilitude, or a sufficient resemblance to known reality to gain the credence of readers. But there is artifice in verisimilitude too, the artifice known as literary convention. When an author proceeds from technical decision to narrative development of the consequences of that decision, he or she can draw upon the level of accumulated narrative practice that, for example, surrounds one type of sleuth with an atmosphere of infallibility that makes him—and it is usually a him—the *Great Detective, while the contrasting attributes of the *hard-boiled sleuth have come through practice to include a degree of emotional vulnerability and a wisecracking manner of speech. As for plot, conventions generated by past practice apply there as well. When the *suspects in a crime are identified, according to one convention the *least likely suspect will prove to be the guilty party, whereas another convention operating in quite a different sort of story builds assurance throughout the narration that the suspiciously behaving character is correctly assumed to be the culprit.

The craft of crime and mystery fiction can be described usefully as a process of making selections within a field of interconnecting choices, but it is no more a mechanical activity than it is the sort of logical demonstration that old-time fictional detectives parade before the assembled suspects, and the reading audience, in a novel's final chapter. The form of the popular genre is redundant, but, then, so are all literary genres. The available technical choices are finite, but that is due to the nature of language and imagination, not to limitations peculiar to the crime and mystery genre. When critics acknowledge that originality is possible in the crime and mystery genre, they do it on the same basis as common readers do and in the full knowledge of how every skilled author has made craft original, namely, by taking different paths through the field of technical choices.

[See also Conventions of the Genre; Formula; Voice.]

• Tzvetan Todorov, The Poetics of Prose (1977). Gerard Genette, Fictions and Diction (1993).

—John M. Reilly

CREASEY, JOHN (1908–1973), English author who wrote more than five hundred books under some twenty names. Born in Southfields, Surrey, the seventh child of a coachmaker, Creasey was not academically inclined. While employed in various jobs, his passion for writing gained him more than five hundred rejection slips.

His first published novel was Seven Times Seven (1932), and he quickly became the doyen of *industry writers. In 1937 alone, twenty-nine of his books were published, while his later output so taxed his publishers that at least twenty new titles appeared posthumously. Some *pseudonyms were reserved for westerns, romantic novels, and children's books, but his fame rests on his crime fiction.

As Creasey, he created the gentleman-adventurer the Hon. Richard "The Toff" Rollison in Introducing the Toff (1938), *Scotland Yard's Roger "Handsome" West in Inspector West Takes Charge (1942), and the science fiction thrillers featuring Dr. Stanislaus Alexander Palfrey in Traitors' Doom (1942), but his earliest series featured Department Z in counterespionage stories beginning with The Death Miser (1933). He also contributed to the Sexton Blake Library. His other series included tales of Patrick Dawlish and "the Crime Haters" (as Gordon Ashe), Mark Kirby (as Robert Caine Frazer), "the Liberator" and Bruce Murdoch (as Norman Deane), Superintendent Folly (as Jeremy York), and psychiatrist Dr. Emmanuel Cellini (as Michael Halliday, but as Kyle Hunt in the United States). His novels as Anthony Morton, featuring reformed jewel thief John "the Baron" Mannering, began with Meet the Baron (1937; The Man in the Blue Mask), which was written in six days.

Creasey's Toff novels were straight *thrillers, although he sometimes grappled with social and political problems (The Toff and the Fallen Angels, 1970; Vote for the Toff, 1971). The West stories were often

excellent in structure (Look Three Ways at Murder, 1964), topicality (Strike for Death, 1958; The Killing Strike), and settings (Murder London-Miami, 1969). The Palfrey novels were allegorical and frighteningly prophetic (The Famine, 1967; The Smog, 1970).

He also achieved greatness in the *police procedural novel as J. J. Marric. Gideon's Day (1955) showed his Scotland Yard team pursuing six cases simultaneously, and later books developed the principal characters both personally and professionally.

• John Creasey, Good, God and Man: An Outline of the Philosophy of Self-ism (1967). William Vivian Butler, The Durable Desperadoes (1973). George N. Dove, The Police Procedural (1982).

—Melvyn Barnes

CRICKET MILIEU. See Sports Milieu.

CRIME INSPIRED BY FICTION. It is popularly believed that fictional crimes portrayed in crime and mystery writing sometimes inspire copycat crimes perpetrated in real life. Scrutiny of some criminal cases that at first appear to have been inspired by fictional crimes reveals that the connection is often far from convincing. In other cases, criminals have claimed that they have used ideas gleaned from fiction, although such claims need to be treated with skepticism.

In 1972 a young Hertfordshire man called Graham Young was convicted of murdering two work colleagues by thallium poisoning. Thallium, a metal similar to mercury and lead but more toxic than both, has rarely been used in homicides. However, its properties make it suitable for murderous designs: Its salts are colorless, almost tasteless, and can easily be dissolved, while the symptoms of ingestion resemble those of several common viral diseases, including influenza. The London Daily Mail published an article pointing out that Young's method was remarkably similar to that of the criminal in Agatha *Christie's The Pale Horse (1961).

Christie was distressed by the suggestion that her ingenious novel might have been used as a textbook by a would-be killer, but the suggestion that Young's crimes were inspired by her fiction does not stand up to close scrutiny. Young was an obsessive poisoner who yearned for publicity. At the age of fourteen he started administering doses of antimony tartrate to his family; following the death of his stepmother, he was sent to Broadmoor in 1962. He began another campaign of poisoning shortly after his release, but gave himself away for a second time by his eagerness to impress those investigating the sequence of deaths and sickness that had struck at his firm with his esoteric knowledge about the symptoms. Young's fascination with poison developed from a youthful passion for chemistry rather than overindulgence in the reading of mystery fiction. However, at his second trial he did claim that the secret diary notes confirming his guilt were no more than jottings for a novel.

Establishing that other novels have inspired real life crimes is equally difficult. It is most unlikely that reading a single mystery would turn an otherwise law-abiding citizen into a criminal, but those who are already intent upon committing crime may learn new methods—and perhaps better ways of escaping detection—from careful study of crime novels. A locked room plot in *Nena Sahib* (1858–59) by Herman O. F. Goedsche, writing as Sir John Retcliffe, is said to have given a carter named Conrad an idea for disguising his guilt of the murder of his wife and children. His crime, which took place in 1881, was nevertheless uncovered by the Berlin police and he was hanged. The risk of fiction serving as a how-to treatise for crime is increased by the fact that modern-day novels are apt to be carefully researched and accurate in matters of technical detail. Frederick Forsyth's thrillers read at times like documentaries; *The Day of the Jackal* (1971), which describes how a passport and a false identity might be obtained by using the birth certificate of a dead person (typically a child) who had never made a passport application, has been reported as the blueprint for several criminal schemes in real life. A blackmailer, Michael Norman, claimed at his trial in 1994 to have picked up ideas from *Banker* (1982) by Dick *Francis, and it has even been claimed that a murderer in Florida gleaned helpful information from Patricia Cornwell's *Post Mortem* (1990). In 1932 the Australian novelist Arthur W. *Upfield was called to give evidence at the trial for murder of John Thomas Smith, also known as Snowy Rowles, after it was suggested that Rowles's idea for disposing of human remains without trace came from conversations between Upfield and his friends about the *plot of the book eventually published as *The Sands of Windee* (1931). Rowles was convicted, but the similarity between his scheme and that discussed with Upfield may have been no more than coincidental. The danger is more acute in cases where an author has knowledge of an obscure means of committing murder that is particularly difficulty to identify. In a note at the end of *Thin Air* (1994), a book that propounds an ingenious murder method, Gerald Hammond explains that initially he had some doubt as to whether the book should be written; however, in deciding to proceed, he was influenced by the fact that his chosen scheme is already mentioned in diesel airgun literature available to the public.

The extent to which authors have a moral responsibility for their work has been much debated, not least by mystery writers themselves. Catherine Aird and others are careful never to provide a recipe for murder, making certain that their convincingly described poisons would not actually kill if used in real life. P. D. *James has long been concerned with the moral implications of detective fiction. Noting that contemporary society now lacks universally accepted philosophical or religious standards against which private morality may be judged, she has contended that all major novelists are concerned with the values by which people live and the dichotomy between one's desires and the rights and needs of others. In addition, authors are concerned about the way society attempts to reconcile private freedom with public order. Some raise the questions, How far does the author's own freedom extend to write about whatever he or she pleases? Should novelists bear in mind the possibility of their works being read by those who have weaker consciences than their own? The counterargument is that a writer's goal is to reflect something of the real world and to show people the truth about themselves, rather than disguising it. There is a risk, it may be claimed, that a crime writer's work may contribute to the state of moral confusion which encourages someone to believe that committing *violence is acceptable: Yet, as James has acknowledged, the days of moral absolutes in Western society have gone.

The debate continues as to whether the *taking of life can be inspired by fiction, but in a least one case, a detective novel helped to save a life. Agatha Christie's husband, Max Mallowan, reported a letter which his wife received from a woman whose knowledge of *The Pale Horse* led her to recognize and thwart a case of attempted murder. Moreover, shortly after Christie's death, a nurse who had read *The Pale Horse* helped to save a child's life by recognizing the symptoms of a hitherto undiagnosed ailment from the novel. Crime fiction may be as apt to save lives as to jeopardize them.

[*See also* Poisons and Poisoning; Poisons, Unusual; Weapons, Unusual Murder.]

• James Bland, *Crime Strange but True* (1911). Paul Plass, "Concerning *Nena Sahib*," *Armchair Detective* 6, no. 3 (May 1973). Charles Osborne, *The Life and Crimes of Agatha Christie* (1982). Diana Cooper-Clarke, "Interview with P. D. James," in *Designs of Darkness: Interviews with Detective Novelists* (1983). Colin Wilson and Donald Seaman, *The Serial Killers: A Study in the Psychology of Violence* (1990). Brian Lane, *The Encyclopedia of Forensic Science* (1992). Brian Lane and Wilfrid Gregg, *The Encyclopedia of Serial Killers* (1992). Douglas Wynn, *The Limits of Detection* (1992). Rosemary Herbert, "Patricia D. Cornwell," in *The Fatal Art of Entertainment: Interviews with Mystery Writers* (1994).
—Martin Edwards

CRIME NOVEL. The term "crime novel" has come into general use increasingly in the last two decades, but it is inevitably imprecise since the label can be applied to any tale involving detection or criminal *violence. Yet in practice the term marks out important areas of differentiation, particularly between a story concerned primarily with discovering the identity of a criminal and one dealing chiefly with criminal psychology and the reasons for the crime. The difference is between the *whodunit and the *whydunit. At the heart of the detective story is a *puzzle, while the core of the crime novel is a criminal's character.

The term is recent, and basically the form is too. Fyodor *Dostoyevsky's *Crime and Punishment* (1866) is literally a crime novel and so are Joseph Conrad's *The Secret Agent* (1907) and *Under Western Eyes* (1911), yet in these books punishment is the central preoccupation. The murder committed by Raskolnikov in *Crime and Punishment* and the terrorist act planned by Verloc in *The Secret Agent* are not much more than starting points for stories truly concerned with the redemption of the human spirit and the use and abuse of power. Of Wilkie *Collins's two most famous books, *The Moonstone* (1868) is certainly a *detective novel; and although *The Woman in White* (1860) contains a splendid villain in Count Fosco, Collins is not concerned with his psychology but his plotting.

Perhaps the first book to which the term can be properly applied is C. S. Forester's *Payment Deferred* (1926), which tells the story of a drably plausible murder in terms of the dully respectable killer. Five years later, *Malice Aforethought* (1931), written by Anthony *Berkeley under the pseudonym of Francis Iles, offered a full-blown investigation of a murderer's mind and procedures in the form of the genial but sinister Dr. Bickleigh. A second story, *Before the Fact* (1932), in which the heroine is complicit in her own *murder, was less successful, and Iles had few followers. The most notable of these were Richard Henry Sampson who wrote *The Murder of My Aunt* (1934) under the pseudonym Richard Hull and the historian C. E. Vulliamy who wrote *The Vicar's Experiments* (1932) as Anthony Rolls. The strict morality of the time, however, which demanded outright condemnation of any criminal, made both writers treat the plans of their chief characters with a facetiousness from which Berkeley himself was not entirely free.

In France, during this period and later, Georges *Simenon was writing crime novels scrupulous in their avoidance of similar moral judgement. These were not the Inspector Jules *Maigret stories, in which the detective's personality was always the center of interest, but what Simenon called his "hard" novels, several of which examine the cracks in personality that move very ordinary men (rarely women in Simenon) to criminal action. Often the characters play out two favorite Simenon themes, that of physical obsession with another person and the desire to break free of a life pattern the protagonist finds stifling. Sometimes the interest of these stories lies outside the limits of the crime novel, but just as often they are studies in personality elaborating the moment when apparently Harmless dreaming changes into dangerous action, and emphasizing that a stolid bourgeois face may hide a psychopath-ic mind.

It is significant that the decline of the detective story, a highly moral tale in which an evildoer was revealed and punished, marked also the rise of the crime novel in which *justice was only sometimes done. The change in manners and morals after World War II saw the emergence of writers more interested in the personality and social ambience of the criminal than in *clues, methods of detection, or the administration of justice. Among them were Margot Bennett, John Bingham, Nicolas *Freeling, and Ruth *Rendell in Britain, the Swedish collaboration of Maj Sjöwall and Per *Wahlöö, and, in the U.S., Helen Eustis, John Franklin Bardin, Patricia *Highsmith, and Ross *Macdonald.

On the whole, this approach to the crime story has found more adherents in Britain than elsewhere, and Highsmith, American by birth but for some years resident in Britain and later Europe, may be considered its exemplar. In her first novel, *Strangers on a Train* (1950), two previously unacquainted men agree to murder people unknown to them that the other would like to see dead, thus avoiding any obvious motive for murder. This is a highly unlikely arrangement, and Raymond *Chandler, who scripted the very successful film Alfred Hitchcock made from the

book, called it ludicrous. Highsmith's art, however, is to make this and similar apparently irrational motivations believable. Her characters, like those in Simenon's crime novels, have a surface normality which any small incident may tip over the edge into *violence. Tom Ripley, the attractive psychopath who appears in several books, has a moral code of his own which does not blink at murder when he feels it necessary to preserve his way of life, but at the same time he is made indignant by what seem to him wanton acts of cruelty.

Highsmith is by no means the head of a school of writers. The crime novel has great variety. Bennett used it for comedy with a sharp social edge, as in *Farewell Crown and Goodbye King* (1953) and the award-winning *The Man Who Didn't Fly* (1955); Freeling to comment on the way one human being can penetrate the thought processes of another, as in *Criminal Conversation* (1965). Bardin's *Devil Take the Blue Tail Fly* (1948) was original in showing a world seen wholly from a schizoid viewpoint. Ross Macdonald in his later books was concerned with the way inherited characteristics and past events could stain the personality, and like Freeling used a detective as a sort of psychiatrist. Wahlöö and Sjöwall drew Marxist implications from their sometimes semi-surrealist accounts of crime in Sweden. George V. *Higgins has exposed several kinds of social *corruption and the psychology of the corrupt through novels written almost entirely in dialogue.

So there is no school of crime novelists. It was once suggested by Edmund *Crispin, however, that detective story writers are almost always socially and politically conservative, crime novelists radical. This has a basis of truth, but there are exceptions. The most notable perhaps is Bingham, otherwise Lord Clanmorris, whose first book, *My Name Is Michael Sibley* (1952), was the first to give an accurate view of police interrogation methods and their effect on a weakly flexible personality. Bingham worked for years in MI6 and was suggested as the original of John *le Carré's George Smiley. He was firmly an establishment right-winger, but also a crime novelist primarily interested, as he said, in the psychological background to a crime and the mind of the criminal rather than in "who committed, say, the murder."

The interest in character and psychology that particularly marks the crime novelist is often accompanied by the desire to be treated as a writer treating criminal themes, rather than simply a "crime writer." Highsmith and Higgins have been particularly insistent that they should not be what they would regard as typecast, and Rendell has assumed a separate identity as Barbara Vine to produce books very different from the detective stories featuring Detective Chief Inspector *Wexford through which she first became known. It should be added that many crime writers have made gestures in the direction of the crime novel without fully committing themselves to it: Alain Robbe-Grillet, Leonardo Sciascia, Reginald *Hill, P. D. *James, William McIlvanney, Donald Westlake, Ed *McBain—and the list could be greatly lengthened to include work by writers whose intentions were only the practical ones of giving a specific public the kind of writing it wanted, like the psychological thrillers written by John *Creasey as Michael Halliday (the name Kyle Hunt was used for them in the U.S.) or the sadistic sex crimes given a thin covering of psychological speculation recently written by Americans. Another development has been the cautious gesture made in the direction of the crime novel by some highly regarded youngish novelists, including Ian McEwan and Martin Amis.

Every reader of crime stories will have a personal view as to whether a particular work is a crime novel. What seems certain is that this branch of crime fiction is often much nearer to the "straight" novel than is the detective story or that other modern development, the *police procedural. It is not likely to wither away, but its future is a matter of guesswork. The generation that follows such notable practitioners as Highsmith and Vine may move so far toward the straight novel that the crime element becomes subsidiary in their work. Bardin's remarkable study of abnormal psychology, written in the 1940s, did not find a publisher in his native America for twenty years, and a similarly original book might suffer the same fate. Yet it is also possible that a new generation may feel that the detective story as *puzzle is a worn-out form, and that the examination of the psychology of policemen and criminals is a better basis for *suspense fiction. Whatever the future holds, the crime novel has already produced work showing that the form of the crime story can be used to produce writing as various and talented as anything else in the modern novel.

[See also Antihero; Characterization; Deviance; Conservative vs. Radical Worldview.]

• Donald K. Adams, ed., The Mystery & Detection Annual 1972. Earl F. Bargainnier, ed., Twelve Englishmen of Mystery (1984). John C. Carr, The Craft of Crime: Conversations with Crime Writers (1983). Diana Cooper-Clark, Designs of Darkness (1983). John Raymond, Simenon in Court (1968). Ralph B. Sipper, ed., Ross Macdonald: Inward Journey (1984).

—Julian Symons

CRIMES, MINOR. In crime and mystery fiction, minor crimes are frequently portrayed. Minor crimes may be used to set up or foreshadow action, including major crimes. They may also be used to create a threatening *atmosphere or to provide background. Minor crimes are frequently used to complicate cases. In addition, such crimes either may propel the protagonist into action or may be committed by the hero in the course of solving crimes.

In Ed *McBain's Mischief (1993), a minor crime is used as prologue, setting an urban scene while setting up a *victim. A seventeen-year-old boy spray paints graffiti on a wall, only to be shot moments later by a killer who is stalking graffiti artists. In Edith Skom's The Mark Twain Murders (1989), set in the *academic milieu, *plagiarism and the theft of library books are minor crimes that precede a *murder that may involve both.

In Paul W. Valentine's Crime Scene at "O" Street (1989), minor crimes provide the opportunity for social commentary when a police officer discusses the various forms of legal and illegal hustling that take place in a poor community. Social commentary also accompanies the action of Lynda LaPlante's Cold Shoulder (1996), which details how alcoholism drives a woman to prostitution. A parallel storyline follows an investigation of the serial killing of prostitutes.

Minor crimes may be used effectively to convey a threatening atmosphere and to establish *suspense. Common examples of such crimes are the obscene phone call, the dead rat on the doorstep, racist grafitti, *poison pen letters, and blackmail messages. More unusual examples include a ten-foot alligator left in a judge's backyard in Elmore *Leonard's Maximum Bob (1991) and letters of condolence sent to people who have not been bereaved in Albert Borowitz's This Club Frowns on Murder (1990).

The use of a minor crime to complicate the case is exemplified in Anne Perry's Pentecost Alley (1996). Here an investigation into the death of a prostitute is compromised when a well-meaning character plants evidence in order to protect a character whom she believes is innocent.

Minor crimes often propel the protagonist into action. For example, in Barbara Neely's Blanche on the Lam (1992), Blanche White writes a bad check and, while fleeing from the consequences, finds herself involved in a murder investigation. Often detectives are called in to solve a minor crime only to find themselves investigating murder. In Val McDermid's Clean Break (1995) for instance, Kate Brannigan's case of industrial blackmail turns into a murder investigation.

*Sleuth protagonists sometimes commit minor offenses in the course of their investigations, often in order to save time during chases or in order to acquire information. Fictional sleuths rack up countless traffic and parking violations, but they are not above breaking and entering when they know that a clue is kept behind locked doors. For the most part, authors allow their sleuths to commit minor crimes in the interest of expediency. Occasionally a discussion of how the sleuth feels about breaking the law is used to develop his or her character.

[See also Murderless Mystery; Who-Gets-Away-with-It.]

—Frankie Y. Bailey

CRIME WRITERS ASSOCIATION. The Crime Writers Association was founded on November 5, 1953, when the prolific writer John *Creasey called a meeting at the National Liberal Club in London, attended by a dozen crime writing colleagues. Within twelve months there were sixty members, a crime book exhibition had been held, and arrangements had been made for a critics' panel to choose the best book of the year and for publication of a short story anthology. A journal was founded, first the occasional Crime Writer, then, from 1956 on, the regular monthly Red Herrings giving news of members' books and activities. Anybody who had published a crime story, short stories, or factual articles about crime, or who had film or TV credits, was—and is—eligible for membership.

In the first years the going was hard, and the energy and enthusiasm of Creasey played a large part in helping the association to survive. He was chairman for the first three years. Since then the post has changed yearly. Catherine Aird, Christianna *Brand, Simon Brett, E. X. *Ferrars, Dick *Francis, Gavin Lyall, H. R. F. *Keating, and Margaret Yorke are among those who have occupied the chair. The membership, which after the first years of hard work was still under a hundred, is now more than four times that number.

The association has no office, but monthly meetings are held at the Groucho Club in Soho. These gatherings are often addressed by experts on a branch of criminology, but are also valued for the chance of meeting old friends and making new ones. The Golden Dagger (originally Red Herrings) Award for the best book of the year has been maintained since 1955. The yearly short story collection began in 1956 with *Butcher's Dozen*, and is an annual event. It was called *John Creasey's Crime Collection* in memory of the founder, and was edited for more than a quarter of a century by Herbert Harris. With his retirement the anthology was renamed *Crime Waves*.

Two nonfiction works published for the CWA are *Crime in Good Company*: *Essays on Criminals and Crime-Writing* (1959), edited by Michael *Gilbert, and *Blood on My Mind* (1972), pieces about real crimes edited by Keating. There is a yearly weekend conference held in some attractive town or city (Edinburgh, Scarborough, and Brighton have been among the venues), and the Golden Dagger Award is presented at an annual dinner. Several chapters of the association have occasional meetings for members in their areas.

CWA is at the center of British crime writing. It has managed to avoid the two extremes of becoming either a trade Union battling with publishers, or a purely social organization concerned with dinners and cocktail parties. The association is influential, but does not try to lay down the law about any aspect of crime writing. The chairman is unpaid, the secretary and treasurer receive pittances for the amount of work they do. The association has never been able to afford an office or someone to run it, but for more than four decades it has managed without one. Altogether, the Crime Writers Association might be called a remarkable example of successful mutual aid.

—Julian Symons

CRIMINAL CASES, FAMOUS. *This entry is divided into two parts, each focusing on infamous criminal cases, many of which have inspired works of crime and mystery fiction, *true crime accounts, and films and stage dramas. The first surveys infamous American criminal cases, and the second surveys infamous crimes that occurred in Great Britain.*

Famous American Criminal Cases
Famous British Criminal Cases

For further information, please refer to Newgate Novel; Newspaper Reports, True Crime.

FAMOUS AMERICAN CRIMINAL CASES

Some criminal cases strike a chord in the American psyche. These cases symbolize something gone awry in American society. And they have the qualities that make any crime memorable—they embody the darker side of human emotions.

Perhaps the first famous American criminal cases were the 1692 witchcraft trials in Salem, Massachusetts. The Puritans perceived the trials as the appropriate response to the presence of "Satan disciples" in their midst. However, later historians have depicted the trials as the result of mass hysteria and class/political conflicts. The trials are retold as allegory in Arthur Miller's 1953 play, *The Crucible*.

By the nineteenth century, information about criminal cases was available to a broad cross-section of the American public. As the rate of literacy increased, improved technology brought down the cost of printed materials. Printed news became accessible to much of the population. Newspaper accounts of an unsolved crime served as the basis for Edgar Allan *Poe's second Dupin story, "The Mystery of Marie Roget" (*Snowden's Lady's Companion*, 2 Nov. 1842). The story was based on the 1841 murder of Mary Cecilia Rogers, a *New York City shopgirl whose body was found in the Hudson River. The *murder of Mary Rogers stirred the public imagination because of what it suggested about the dangers of the city.

Other nineteenth-century cases challenged assumptions about small towns and the sanctity of hearth and home. In 1892, Andrew Borden and Abby, his second wife, were murdered in their home in Fall River, Massachusetts. Lizzie, the Bordens' younger daughter, stood accused of the crime. The Borden case has inspired numerous fictional accounts— among them Lillian de la Torre's "Goodbye, Miss Lizzie Borden" (in *Murder Plain & Fanciful*, 1948), a one-act play. Among the nonfiction attempts to get to the heart of the Borden mystery is Victoria Lincoln's *A Private Disgrace* (1967).

In other criminal cases, the crime was committed in a manner as public as the lives of the principals. In 1906, an emotionally disturbed millionaire playboy, Harry Thaw, shot renowned architect Stanford White during a musical show in the magnificent rooftop club in New York's Madison Square Garden in front of hundreds of witnesses. The source of contention between the two men was the former showgirl Evelyn Nesbit, who had been White's mistress before she married Thaw. The case figures in the plot of E. L. Doctorow's *Ragtime* (1975).

If illicit affairs and murderous passions attracted public attention, the *kidnapping and murder of children riveted it. The first ransom kidnapping in the United States seems to have occurred Pennsylvania in July 1874, when Charles Ross and his older brother Walter were persuaded into a carriage by two men who promised to take them to a place selling fireworks. Walter was later abandoned in a candy store, but Little Charley was held for $20,000 ransom. Circulars were distributed nationwide. Two suspects, William Mosher and Joseph Douglass, were identified, but were killed while attempting a burglary in Brooklyn, New York. Mosher lived long enough to confess to the kidnapping, but not to provide information about the boy's whereabouts.

Christian Ross, Charley's father, continued his search for his son. In 1878, feeling the financial strain, Ross offered a book for sale by mail, *The Father's Story of Charley Ross*. The boy was never found.

Fifty years later, in May 1924, fourteen-year-old Robert "Bobbie" Franks, the son of a Chicago millionaire, was kidnapped by Nathan Leopold and Richard Loeb, brilliant scions of wealthy families. Influenced by the works of Friedrich Nietzsche, they sought to commit the perfect crime and chose Franks as their victim. When the pair made their ransom demand, they had already killed the boy. The police investigation focused on them, and Leopold and Loeb confessed to the kidnapping-murder. At their trial they were represented by Clarence Darrow, who opted to present their case before a judge rather than a jury; Darrow launched an attack against the death penalty. The judge sentenced Loeb and Leopold to life terms for murder and ninety-nine years for kidnapping. Loeb subsequently was killed in prison; Leopold was granted parole after serving thirty-three years of his sentence, and wrote an autobiographical account of his crime and punishment, *Life Plus 99 Years* (1958). Journalist Meyer Levin, who covered the case, wrote *Compulsion* (1956), a fictionalized account of the crime and the trial.

In March 1932, the twenty-month-old son of aviator Charles Lindbergh and writer Anne Morrow Lindbergh was kidnapped from the couple's New Jersey home. A ransom demand was made in a crudely written note; other ransom demands would be received as the Lindberghs attempted to cooperate with the police and, at the same time, to make use of other contacts. In May 1932, the child body's was found buried in a field near the Lindbergh home. Bruno Richard Hauptmann, a German-born carpenter living in the Bronx, was arrested, tried, and executed in 1936. There is still debate about whether Hauptmann committed the crime. The case resulted in federal legislation (the "Lindbergh Law") empowering the FBI to investigate kidnappings. *Stolen Away: A Novel of the Lindbergh Kidnapping* (1991) is an account of the case told in the form of fiction.

The Lindbergh kidnapping has a fictional parallel in Agatha *Christie's *Murder on the Orient Express* (1934; *Murder in the Calais Coach*), in which the murder of a wealthy "pseudophilanthropist" is motivated by his part in the kidnapping and murder of the three-year-old daughter of Colonel and Mrs. Armstrong.

On the other side of the continent, Hollywood was producing its own real-life crime dramas. Cases such as that of Roscoe "Fatty" Arbuckle and William Desmond Taylor were cited as evidence of Hollywood decadence. In 1921, beloved comedian Fatty Arbuckle held a Labor Day drinking party in his hotel suite. When starlet Virginia Rappe, who had taken ill at the party, died of a ruptured bladder, the hefty Arbuckle was charged with having caused her death by means of sexual assault. After three trials (two resulting in hung juries), Arbuckle was finally acquitted. But his career was over.

The same fate befell two actresses, comedian Mabel Normand and ingenue Mary Miles Minter, who was suspected in the 1922 murder of director William Desmond Taylor. The murder was never solved. But it was enough that their names had been linked to the scandal, especially when Mabel Normand's chauffeur was charged with the fatal shooting of an oil tycoon. These two cases provided fuel for the film censorship movement which culminated in the restrictive Hays Office Production Code.

By the 1950s, Americans were less easily shocked by crime. However, allegations of "malice domestic" such as the 1954 case of Dr. Sam Sheppard, an osteopath accused of murdering his wife, could still disturb. And the murder of the Cutters, a farm family in a small town in Kansas, stunned because it called into question the belief that there were still some safe places.

The intrusion of violent death into the peaceful existence of Holcomb, Kansas, is what Truman Capote explores in *In Cold Blood* (1965). In this work, Capote plots the converging paths of the four members of the Clutter family and that of the two men, Richard Hickok and Perry Smith, who were arrested, tried, and executed for the murders.

In the 1960s, amidst marches, sit-ins, and urban riots, a series of political assassinations changed the configuration of the government and of the civil rights movement. Three of these assassinations—those of John F. Kennedy, Martin Luther King, and Malcolm X—remain famous not only because of the victims but because of the continuing debates about whether or not the crimes involved conspiracies by politicians, law enforcement agencies, or secret rightwing groups. The theme of political assassination has figured in crime and mystery writing in works such as Hugh *Pentecost's *Hot Summer Killing* (1968) and Ellery *Queen's *The Black Hearts Murder* (1970).

During the late twentieth century, several cases have been added to the urban mythology of crime in the city. None is perhaps more infamous than the 1964 murder of Kitty Genovese, a young New York City woman who was attacked as she returned home from work late one night. Thirty-eight of her neighbors were awakened by her screams for help, but failed to respond. The case inspired research by social scientists who study "bystander intervention." It was the subject of a book, *Thirty-Eight Witnesses* (1964) by *New York Times* reporter A. M. Rosenthal.

[*See also* Missing Persons; Newspaper Reports; Rape and Other Sex Crimes; Taking of Life.]

• Hal Higdon, *The Crime of the Century: The Leopold and Loeb Case* (1975). Ernest Kahlar Alix, *Ransom Kidnapping in America, 1874–1974* (1978). David A. Yallop, *The Day the Laughter Stopped: The True Story of Fatty Arbuckle* (1976).
—Frankie Y. Bailey

FAMOUS BRITISH CRIMINAL CASES

Accounts of *murder cases, and transmutations of them, have a long history. The fourth chapter of the Book of Genesis presents a hearsay report on the case of Cain and Abel. And in Elizabethan times, the anonymous play *Arden of Feversham*—once attributed to Shakespeare—took its *plot from a murder recorded in Raphael Holinshed's *Chronicles of England, Scotland and Ireland* (1577), which was one of the story-sources of the murder plays that Shakespeare undoubtedly wrote.

The decade or so around the publication of Thomas De Quincey's innovative satire, "On Murder, Considered as One of the Fine Arts" (1827), was special in the sense that a number of things came together to give impetus to literary murder. With the foundation of the popular press—relatively cheap newspapers vying with catchpenny broadsheets devoted to particular events—the details of murders became common knowledge, public property; murders were no longer parochial affairs, with sensational details circulated chiefly by word of mouth. And, as it happened, the period had more than its fair share of picturesque cases.

Often, it was the embroidery on a story, asides from the criminal act, that intrigued contemporary writers such as Thomas Carlyle, Walter Scott, and Charles Lamb (who was not only suspected himself of being an accessory to a fatal mugging, but also had the perhaps unique distinction among English writers of living with a murderess—his sister Mary, who had stabbed their mother to death during one of Mary's bouts of madness). And one can link George Borrow and William Hazlitt, since they both encountered Jack Thurtell prior to 1823, when he was known simply as a low-life sportsman, not yet as the slayer of William Weare, a cardsharper and billiards player who had cheated Thurtell of several hundreds of pounds. Thurtell appears, scantily disguised as "Tom Turtle," in Hazlitt's essay "The Fight"; but a complete portrait, pockmarks and all, appears in Borrow's *Lavengro* (1851). Thurtell crops up again in Borrow's *The Romany Rye* (1857), though in this instance truth seems to have suffered in aid of an anecdote. A jockey in Thurtell's debt hastens to Hertford Jail for the latter's execution:

> Driving my Punch, which was all in a foam, into the midst of the crowd, which made way for me as if it knew what I came for, I stood up in my gig, took off my hat, and shouted, "God Almighty bless you, Jack." The dying man turned his pale grim face towards me—for his face was always somewhat grim, do you see—nodded and said, or I thought I heard him say, "All right, old chap."

The jockey's gig was not the famous one in the case. That belonged to Thurtell's victim. According to Carlyle, there was an exchange between a barrister and a witness at the trial. Question: "What do you mean by saying that Mr Weare was 'respectable'?" Answer: "He always kept a gig." The idea of associating a gig with respectability so enchanted Carlyle that he coined the term "gigmanity" for bourgeois social pretension.

The illustrious writers on the case were outshone by a penny-a-line broadsheet balladeer who cobbled together a verse that falsely spread the blame for the act of murder between Thurtell and two accomplices after the fact:

> His throat they cut from ear to ear,
> His brains they punch-ed in;

His name was Mr. William Weare,
Wot dwelt in Lyon's Inn.

That quatrain was a favorite of Robert Browning. He learnt it as a child, and still recited it with relish when he was old, by which time he himself had made several contributions to the literature of murder, most lengthily, inspired by an actual case, with *The Ring and the Book* (1868–69).

The murder of William Weare may be considered the gig that gave crime literary respectability. Throughout the Victorian age—thought by George Orwell to be "our great period in murder, our Elizabethan period, so to speak"—writers found inspiration in criminous reality. Wilkie *Collins's *The Moonstone* (1868) is the most noted example of a Victorian crime novel inspired by true events. Certainly, Collins borrowed incidents and characters from the Road House Mystery of 1860, the murder of four-year-old Savill Kent, probably by his half-sister Constance; and the episode in which Godfrey Ablewhite is lured to a house in Northumberland Street and there attacked is a retelling of the so-called Northumberland Street Sensation of 1861. The strangeness of that sensation—never explained—provoked a gasp from William Makepeace Thackeray: "The brave Dumas, the intrepid Harrison Ainsworth, the terrible Eugène Sue . . . never invented anything more tremendous. . . . After this, what is the use of being squeamish about the probabilities and possibilities in the writing of fiction?"

Twenty years before, Thackeray had been among the dense crowd of spectators at the execution of François Courvoisier, the Swiss valet who had practically decapitated his master, Lord William Russell. Charles *Dickens was there, too—drawn to the scene by what he termed "the attraction of repulsion." A report that Courvoisier had claimed in one of his many confessions that he was motivated to murder by reading Harrison Ainsworth's crime novel *Jack Sheppard* (1839) had caused quite a stir—augmented by a public argument between Dickens and Thackeray. The latter had condemned *Oliver Twist* (1838) as a primer for aspiring juvenile delinquents.

One cannot estimate the effects of what Dickens, primarily, and other Victorian authors wrote about crime and punishment—no more than one can do a head-counting exercise on how, in the twentieth century, the play of *A Pin to See the Peepshow*, F. Tennyson Jesse's 1934 novel about the Thompson-Bywaters murder case, persuaded proponents of capital punishment to change their minds. Dickens was an enthusiastic supporter of the New Police. He hero-worshipped detectives—in particular, Inspector Charles Field, who appeared undisguised or wearing the flimsy alias of "Wield" in articles in Dickens's periodical, *Household Words*, and as the fat-forefingered Inspector Bucket, probably the first police detective in English fiction, in *Bleak House* (1853). Another of the characters in that novel was drawn from life; or perhaps one should say death, for the original of Hortense, the murderous French maid, was Maria Manning, who, together with her husband Fred, was hanged in 1849, with Dickens looking on, for the murder of her erstwhile boyfriend Patrick O'Connor.

Among literally hundreds of twentieth-century crime novels based upon or with discrete borrowings from real cases, two by Josephine *Tey must be mentioned. *The Franchise Affair* (1948) represents an updating and combining of two eighteenth-century cases—the never-explained temporary disappearance of Elizabeth Canning and the torturing to death of servants by Elizabeth Brownrigg. In *The Daughter of Time* (1951), Tey's regular detective, Inspector Alan Grant, immobile in the hospital, conducts an investigation, à la Nero *Wolfe, of the Princes-in-the-Tower case of 1483.

Two cases especially have been useful to fiction writers. The Whitechapel Murders of 1888 were used in Marie Belloc Lowndes's *The Lodger* (1913), Thomas Burke's "The Hands of Mr Ottermole" in his *The Pleasantries of Old Quong* (1931), and Albert Borowitz's *The Jack the Ripper Walking Tour Murder* (1986). The killing of Julia Wallace in Liverpool in 1931 inspired Angus Hall's *Qualtrough* (1968; *Devilday*) Jonathan Goodman's *The Last Sentence* (1978), and John Hutton's *29 Herriott Street* (1979).

[*See also* Kidnapping; Missing Persons; Newspaper Reports; Rape and other Sex Crimes; Taking of Life.]

• Jacques Barzun and Wendell Hertig Taylor, *A Catalogue of Crime* rev. ed. (1989). James Sandoe, comp., "Criminal Clef" in *Murder Plain and Fanciful* (1948).

—Jonathan Goodman

CRIMINAL MASTERMIND. *See* Master Criminal.

CRIMINALS, TYPES OF. The authors and critics who first proclaimed the *rules of the game held that the only suitable crime for their favored fiction is *murder; nothing less is worth the bother. Very quickly, however, practitioners found that other types of crime could be worthy investments of their energy, but one self-evident rule remains inviolable: There must be at least one criminal in a story to gain its admittance to the genre of detective and mystery fiction. After satisfaction on that point, there appears to be a rich field for invention. How an author chooses to depict a criminal may depend on several factors. The nefarious character might be designed to reinforce the image of the detective, engage readers' attention, introduce social commentary, or convey a vision.

When a *sleuth has been conceived on the model of the *Great Detective, as was Sherlock *Holmes, accounts of his singular persona may require an extraordinary villain, a *master criminal who will make a dangerous and worthy adversary. Thus, Professor Moriarty comes on the scene to personify the forces of *evil that in mundane reality are dispersed among the hundred of *villains who commit just one crime or are embodied in the broadly general conditions of urbanism and industry. The formula of the master criminal character has similar value for such authors of patently fantastic tales of *heroism versus evil as Nick *Carter and Sexton Blake; Lester Dent, who wrote the Doc Savage stories for *pulp magazines under the

pseudonym Kenneth Robeson; and Ian *Fleming, whose James *Bond novels invest the force of evil in various Soviet KGB killers, Dr. No, and especially in the indefatigable Ernst Stavro Blofield, the chief executive of SPECTRE, Bond's foe in three novels.

The *gentleman thief is another criminal type from the fictional realms of fantasy. E. W. *Hornung, in a feat of economy converted the figure normally treated as the detective's nemesis into the protagonist of his series of stories about the gentleman A. J. *Raffles, who first appeared in *The Amateur Cracksman* (1899; *Raffles, the Amateur Cracksman*). Maurice *Leblanc did the same in the stories issued as *Arsène Lupin: Gentleman-Cambrioleur* (1907; *The Exploits of Arsène Lupin; The Seven of Hearts*), although in later appearances Lupin gradually came to work as a detective, in that respect perhaps an incarnation of the famous thief-taker *Vidocq whose *Mémoires de Vidocq* (1828–29; *Memoirs of Vidocq; Vidocq the Police Spy*) trace a similar adventure. Creation of gentleman thieves and other well-bred lawbreakers may be viewed as a process of imaginative rehabilitation that converts antisocial dreams into acceptable exploit.

The character of a writer's detective most obviously governs the selection of a criminal type when the detective is identified with a specific *milieu. John Putnam *Thatcher, the banker who figures as detective in the fiction of Emma *Lathen, typically confronts criminals from the world of business or finance. Jane Langton's Homer Kelly, a retired police officer turned scholar-teacher, meets his criminals in the worlds of education, art, or research. And most of the cases taken by Kate *Fansler, the creation of Amanda *Cross, occur in university literary circles.

The reverse of fantasy accounts for many writers' selection of criminals notable for their brutality. Minette Walters's *The Sculptress* (1993) places at the center of his journalist's investigation the story of a woman who murdered and dismembered her family. In *People of Darkness* (1980) Tony *Hillerman introduces Colton Wolf, whose total lack of feeling makes him a methodical killer for hire. Then there are the serial killers in Lawrence Sanders's *The Second Deadly Sin* (1977), Patricia D. Cornwell's *Postmortem* (1990) and *Body of Evidence* (1991), Julie Smith's *The Axeman's Jazz* (1991), and Lynn Hightower's *Flashpoint* (1995), where pathological criminal character is heightened by the fact that it must be inferred through the detective's examination of its shocking consequences.

The selection of criminal types for the purpose of introducing social commentary has particular importance to hard-boiled writing. Dashiell *Hammett's *Red Harvest* (1929) describes a town infested by criminal mobsters who are eventually explained as the hired hands brought in by a wealthy man who has lost his control of them. Valerie Wilson Wesley's series about Tamara Hayle, which began with the novel *When Death Comes Stealing* (1994), includes criminals and crimes that reflect life in the decaying city of Newark, New Jersey. Walter *Mosley's retrospective series about Ezekiel "Easy" *Rawlins in post–World War II California deploys criminals whose deeds take their peculiar form from the racial conditions of the time. In contrast to the authors who illustrate crime through the specifically individual psychology and behavior of their criminal figures, each of these hard-boiled writers and other practitioners in the school of writing that they represent, selects a type of criminal in whom social origins figure more prominently than personal psychology and whose behavior, therefore, can be read as representative.

James M. *Cain may be taken as indicative of the final category of criminal type: those selected to convey a vision of life. Frank Chambers, the condemned killer who serves as storyteller in Cain's *The Postman Always Rings Twice* (1934), describes an experience of sexual obsession and complicity in *violence expressive of utter amorality. He is Cain's pessimistic rendition of the alienated modern man.

When the modern problem of crime becomes the substance for a literary genre, as it has in detective and crime fiction, it invariably also distances the matter of crime from direct experience, making it the subject of technical choice. An author must think deliberately about portrayal of crime and the criminal. The decisions made about those issues of narrative composition in the end determine if the author bridges the distance back to reality.

[*See also* Antihero; Characterization; Formula: Character.]

• T. J. Binyon, *"Murder Will Out": The Detective in Fiction* (1989).
—John M. Reilly

CRIMINAL VIEWPOINT. If the crime story is, at least in part, an exploration of the dark side of the human psyche, then the crime story written from the point of view of the criminal can be the most intense and personal of such explorations. The criminal point of view is nothing new in crime literature; it is as old as writers' and readers' fascination with the intimate nature of *evil. Fyodor *Dostoyevsky used the criminal point of view in his 1866 novel *Crime and Punishment* as he explored the dual nature of the murderer Raskolnikov. Agatha *Christie used it to break new ground in her 1926 novel *The Murder of Roger Ackroyd*.

Writing from the criminal's viewpoint poses special problems and demands much of the writer. More must be revealed about psychological *motivation and the machinations of the crime itself than in stories told completely from the perspectives of others, even if the reader doesn't learn the identity of the culprit until the end of the story. Of course, in most fiction told from the criminal's point of view, the reader learns early on the identity of the criminal, and the work is more a psychological study or *suspense story than one of deduction relying mainly on curiosity for its effectiveness. Often these are procedural stories, focusing on the attempts of the criminal to outwit his or her pursuers. Such a story is British author Frederick Forsyth's 1971 novel of attempted political assassination, *The Day of the Jackal*.

While it is a challenge for the writer, the criminal viewpoint provides the richest possibilities for powerfully illustrating the complexities of morality,

honor, and self-image, and for the often painful examination of evil. Questions that confront the character sometimes are also questions that confront society as well as the reader personally. Sometimes the crime is not one listed in the statutes, but is a dark act of the soul that even the perpetrator doesn't regard as unethical or immoral, as in Stanley Ellin's short story, "The Question My Son Asked" (*Ellery Queen's Mystery Magazine*, Nov. 1962) in which a state executioner lectures his son, who he hopes will continue the family tradition and succeed him in what he considers to be a necessary and honorable occupation. The father rationalizes in an effort to lend higher status to his job, among other things referring to himself as an "electrocutioner" rather than an executioner. Only in the final sentence is the narrator and main character, along with the reader, forced to face the secret and horrifying engine that drives both the story and the protagonist.

In American short-story master Jack Ritchie's tale "For All the Rude People" (*Alfred Hitchcock's Mystery Magazine*, June 1961), the criminal's self-appointed mission is carried out in a more cavalier, guiltless fashion by a fellow almost casually gunning down those in society who are thoughtless, cruel, and impolite. Because of his criminality, the city in which the murders occur is stricken by an epidemic of consideration and flawless etiquette, and for a while society (at least that part of it other than the murdered individuals) is the better for the crimes. The protagonist is more a vehicle of expression than a deep psychological study, and Ritchie's characteristically succinct and powerful if amusing little story says a great deal about modern relationships.

When the reader finds himself or herself sympathizing with, even identifying with, the criminal, the reader becomes in a sense an accomplice in the crime. It can be a disturbing experience for some readers to discover they are pulling against the forces of law and order. Disturbing, but at the same time illuminating and leading to self-examination. When the criminal is finally forced to face himself or herself, the reader must ask and answer intensely personal questions and confront unsettling emotions. Dramatic structure has conditioned readers to the sense that the story will play itself out and the light of knowledge will illuminate all corners. It is this drama of inevitable, if eventual, confrontation with undeniable truth that attracts many writers and readers to the criminal viewpoint story.

Ruth *Rendell, especially in her work written as Barbara Vine, is adept at using the criminal viewpoint to create fictional criminals the reader finds especially repugnant. Yet at the same time, often because of her criminal's background or pathetic circumstances, as in her 1982 novel *Master of the Moor*, the reader's understanding and reluctant compassion are evoked as they might be only through the power of fiction.

The criminal point of view can provide illuminating glimpses of how some on the wrong side of the legal line cannot see themselves in an unfavorable light if their motives are guileless or well intended. In

Chekhov's 1885 short story "The Culprit," a magistrate tries without success to impress upon the defendant Denis Grigoryev that removing a nut from a bolt in a train track, thus endangering the passengers, was a serious crime even though Denis's intent was merely to acquire a sinker for his fishing line. The fact that many other peasants also sometimes used the nuts for sinkers reinforces Denis's notion that he is innocent of any criminality, thus undeserving of punishment. Despite the frustrated magistrate's efforts to convince him otherwise, as the guilty Denis is led from the courtroom he cries out words to the effect that he believes in punishing wrongdoers, but only if it is just punishment—as it certainly is not in his case, as he meant no harm. Every reader must at times have felt precisely that emotion. And whatever else the criminal viewpoint accomplishes in mystery fiction, perhaps its most valuable and fascinating function is, if only for brief and unexpected moments, to bring the reader face to face with . . . the reader.

[See also Antihero; Characterization; Formula: Character.]
—John Lutz

CRISPIN, EDMUND, pseudonym of the British novelist, composer, critic, and anthologist Robert Bruce Montgomery (1921–78). Born at Chesham Bois, Buckinghamshire, he attended Merchant Taylors' School, where his lameness caused him to direct his talents toward composing and writing. While studying modern languages at St. John's College, *Oxford, he spent two years as organ scholar and choirmaster, experience he put to excellent use in his first two novels.

"[S]omewhat of an intellectual snob" before he encountered John Dickson Carr's *The Crooked Hinge* (1938), Montgomery took up detective story writing in 1942 with the alacrity of his fictional hero, Gervase *Fen, an eccentric professor of English language and literature at St. Christopher's College, Oxford, and an irrepressible Renaissance man. Within the year he had chosen his pseudonym, taken from a character in Michael *Innes's *Hamlet, Revenge!* (1937), and was hard at work on his first novel.

Crispin's enduring reputation as a Golden Age detective novelist and *farceur rests on nine novels and two collections of short stories published between 1944 and 1979. *The Case of the Gilded Fly* (1944; *Obsequies at Oxford*, indulges Fen's passion for complex crime as he solves a triple *murder. *Holy Disorders* (1945) calls Fen to Tolnbridge cathedral in an adventure involving, drugs, ghosts, and Nazi spies. *The Moving Toyshop* (1946), perhaps his best novel, combines romance with rollicking chase scenes as Fen solves the "impossible" murder of an elderly heiress. In *Swan Song* (1947; *Dead and Dumb*), Fen solves the locked room murder of an opera company's principal bass singer. In *Love Lies Bleeding* (1948), Crispin draws on his teaching experience to craft a locked room mystery linking Shakespeare with chase scenes and heroism. *Buried for Pleasure* (1948) places Fen on the parliamentary hustings in a romp reminiscent of P. G. Wodehouse. In *Frequent Hearses* (1950; *Sudden Vengeance*) Crispin makes use of his knowledge of the British film industry to craft the story of a star-

let's suicide. *The Long Divorce* (1951; *A Noose for Her Neck*) sends Fen underground to do his sleuthing incognito.

After a twenty-five-year silence following his short-story collection *Beware of the Trains* (1953), Crispin produced his final novel, *The Glimpses of the Moon* (1977), which sets an older, more conservative Fen to solve a *puzzle in which dismembered *corpses compete for attention with car chases and a politicized constabulary. Another short-story collection, *Fen Country* (1979), was published posthumously.

Multitalented like his protagonist Fen, Crispin, under his real name, Montgomery, also composed choral and chamber works; wrote and conducted background scores for some forty films, including *Carry on Nurse* (1959); and edited six anthologies including *Best Detective Stories* (1959).

[See also Academic Milieu; Academic Sleuth; Eccentrics; Locked Room Mystery.]

• Robert Bruce Montgomery, "Edmund Crispin," *Armchair Detective* 12, no. 2 (spring 1979): 183–85.
—Jean A. Coakley

CRITICISM, LITERARY. Practitioners of the form gave crime and mystery writing its first body of literary criticism. Writers devoted to the crafting of cerebral *puzzle narratives offered axioms of construction (or *rules of the game) derived, it seemed, from acquaintance with a Platonic model. That the formulas presented by these *pontificators (R. Austin *Freeman, Ronald A. *Knox, S. S. *Van Dine, et al.) were actually intended to elevate the variety of the genre they wrote and preferred above the hastily written products of the mass market eventually mattered less than the fact that, despite its self-serving purpose, this early critical writing helped to define and, thus, to found, the *Golden Age tradition.

As the work of the rule makers illustrates, a primary function of literary criticism is definition, an inspection of texts to determine their relational features. Although he presented his findings in rhetoric alternately dismissive of the Golden Age style and romantically heightened in its treatment of his own preferred version of the genre, Raymond *Chandler performed such an exercise in definition when in "The Simple Art of Murder" (in *Atlantic Monthly*, Dec. 1944) he announced the appearance of a new mode of realism in detective fiction that would come to be labeled "hard-boiled." Yet again, Julian *Symons introduced a definition of great utility in *Bloody Murder: From the Detective Story to the Crime Novel: A History* (1972; *Mortal Consequences*) where he distinguished the *crime novel from both the Golden Age *detective story and the hard-boiled *detective novel. George N. Dove did the same with *The Police Procedural* (1982), a work that distills the essence of the subgenre while relating its history.

John Dickson *Carr included an excursion into type definition in *The Three Coffins* (1935; *The Hollow Man*), where Dr. Gideon Fell delivers a lecture on the locked room. The type later received full treatment, complete with bibliography, in Robert C. S. Adey's *Locked Rooms and Other Impossible Crimes* (1979).

Reference works such as *A Catalogue of Crime* by Jacques Barzun and Wendell Hertig Taylor (1971) do the work of subgenre definition in the course of establishing dependable listings and annotating bibliography. For pithy, illuminating descriptions and definitions of subtypes, however, one of the most useful efforts of literary criticism is a work conceived as a guide to writers. By indirection in *Writing Crime Fiction* (1986), H. R. F. *Keating distinguishes the detective novel from the detective story, characterizes the crime novel, *suspense fiction (plain and romantic), and *police procedurals, while also noting the essence of comic crime, farce crime, historical crime, and "real crime" writing.

Literary criticism bent upon the isolation of distinguishing traits of genre or type tends to produce definition synchronically: It conducts its study without regard to time periods. Since literature is, however, a historical product, it is equally important for criticism to take account of periods, to write about its subject across time periods. Diachronic criticism usually takes the form of literary history—that is, it embeds the theory, preferences, and taste of the critic-author in a linear narration that has as its primary purpose the recording of signal texts and developments in a temporal sequence.

H. Douglas Thompson initiated critical literary history of detective fiction in *Masters of Mystery: A Study of the Detective Story* (1931). In opening his history, Thomson alerts readers to his concern for the craft of writing and to his decision to stress the "best" stories. Thomson's first principle for selection of subjects leads him to introduce contrasting categories of intellectual and sensational detective stories, and his search for instances of the "best" examples permits discussion of some French works, a few American ones, and numerous British. Howard Haycraft opened his own full-length history of the genre in 1941 with the observation that "no adequate factual or analytic history" existed, by which he meant that Thomson's study had gone out of print and the two precedent works by François Fosca (*Histoire et Technique du Roman Policier*, 1937) and Regis Messac (*Le "Detective Novel" et l'Influence de la Pensee Scientifique*, 1929) were unavailable in English translation. In remedying the absence of an accessible history, Haycraft's *Murder for Pleasure: The Life and Times of the Detective Story* (1941) detailed the scheme of development that has remained authoritative to this day. Beginning with the genesis of detection fiction in the tales of Edgar Allan *Poe, proceeding through an English and an American romantic era (1890–1914), with a chapter on "The Continental Detective Story," into the Golden Age on either side of the Atlantic (1918–1930), and finally a chapter on "The Moderns," Haycraft named the books and authors that define distinct historical periods. That being done, he completed his examination with an essay attributing the vigor of the detective story to its origin in democratic societies, a presentation of a cornerstone library, and speculation on the future of the form.

Because Haycraft's history has been received as standard, subsequent historical criticism has been less expansive in scope, although more detailed in description and interpretation. Leroy Lad Panek's *Watteau's Shepherds: The Detective Novel in Britain, 1914–1940* (1979) critically scrutinizes the artifices of the Golden Age writers; his *Introduction to the Detective Story* (1987) distills patterns and their historical appearance; in *The Special Branch: The British Spy Novel, 1890–1980* (1981), Panek provides a detailed examination of connections between times and texts. Jerry Palmer has also taken advantage of the existence of a standard general history as opportunity to amplify a segment of that history in *Thrillers: Genesis and Structure of a Popular Genre* (1979), and Martin A. Kayman has revisited the period of genesis in *From Bow Street to Baker Street: Mystery, Detection and Narrative* (1992) for a probing study of detective fiction in relation to philosophical transformations engendered by modern urban conditions.

The specialization of criticism made evident by the appearance of period studies has a counterpart in specialized treatments of detective character, the preeminent example of which is T. J. Binyon's *"Murder Will Out": The Detective in Fiction* (1989). Unwilling to sacrifice accuracy in lineage to an image of the romantic genius, Binyon sets aside Poe as sole creator of the fictional detective to relate the origins of the type in works of Daniel Defoe, Voltaire, and William Godwin in the eighteenth century and to devote attention to the nineteenth-century instances of detective figures in Wilkie *Collins, Émile *Gaboriau, and Charles *Dickens. Having established a history of the character formation, Binyon concludes his study with a taxonomy of descendent types, including the "professional amateur," the "amateur amateur," "gentlemen burglars," "police," and "oddities."

For many devotees of crime and mystery fiction, their experience of literary criticism comes through the columns of newspaper or magazine book reviews, the utility of which varies greatly. Edmund Wilson had a problematic convention of review writing in mind when he said, in *Classics and Commercials* (1950), that "detective stories are able to profit by an unfair advantage in the code which forbids the reviewer to give away the secret to the public—a custom which results in the concealment of the pointlessness of a good deal of this fiction and affords a protection to the authors which no other department of writings enjoys." Of course, the code Wilson abjured is testimony to the success of the argument by early critics of the form that detective fiction is intellectual puzzle. To give away its ending would be to defeat its entertaining purpose. Justified or not in their code of concealment, reviews as a type of literary criticism function as a reader's guide. When the reviewer is widely read in the genre, well-informed about its practice, and sensitive to craft, the review columns provide a running commentary on the fortunes of the genre. The standard of excellence in this regard was set by William Anthony Parker White writing as Anthony *Boucher, whose work for the *San Francisco Chronicle* and the *New York Times* remains available in *Multiple Villainies: Selected Mystery Criticism, 1942–1968* (1973). Boucher did not hesitate to assert his judgment; thus, he declared

Cleve F. Adams a vulgar racist and evaluated Graham *Greene as deeper than the mainstream novelist John Steinbeck. He dissented from other authorities, taking issue with Ellery *Queen's selection of "most important" works and arguing with Jacques Barzun. Boucher's was an informed taste. He devoted annual columns to summing up trends; noted for his readers the appearance of scholarly works; and described the existence of library resources for research. And in the limited space of his columns he could trace the history of the *spy novel or explain effectively why Ross *Macdonald was a master.

Boucher evidently conceived of literary criticism in the manner of dialogue, a high level of discussion completely lacking in didacticism, a conversation aiming to invite responses and finally to illuminate. A similar spirit inspires such writing by Robin W. Winks as *Modus Operandi: An Excursion into Detective Fiction* (1982). Technically this book might be classed as reader-response criticism—that is, a weave of autobiography and revealing statements about the psychology of personal response to textual structures.

Evaluative writing such as Boucher's and Winks's, the specialized studies of subgenres and character types, historical narratives on genre development, and the essays in definition all have a utility secondary to their primary purpose: They help to form a body of dependable resource for future investigations. In recent years the compilation of resources has become an end in itself. When Allen J. Hubin founded the *Armchair Detective* in 1967, he formalized scholarship on crime and mystery writing. The pages of the journal became the venue of choice for publication of analysis and record, the appearance of which in turn stimulated further investigations along with a vigorous exchange of views in the letters column of the journal. As a regular reviewer of crime and detective fiction himself, Hubin also saw the need for definitive bibliography, so in addition to creating an organ for scholarly exchange, he produced the most accurate listing of works yet issued: *The Bibliography of Crime Fiction, 1749–1975* (1979), updated in 1984, supplemented in 1988 and reissued in a new edition (as *Crime Fiction II: A Comprehensive Bibliography, 1749–1990*) in 1994.

Fifty years ago Howard Haycraft lamented that scattered articles, a handful of prefaces, and some "how-to" books constituted the entire body of scholarship on crime and mystery writing. Today the secondary literature is so abundant that it has become possible to write not only more criticism of the primary works, but also criticism of the criticism, scholarship about scholarship.

[*See also* Craft of Crime and Mystery Writing, The; Reference Works.]

—John M. Reilly

CROFTS, FREEMAN WILLS (1879–1957), British detective novelist. Born in Dublin, Ireland, Crofts was educated in Belfast and spent his working life with the Belfast and Northern Counties Railway, joining as an apprentice engineer in 1896 and rising to chief engineer before retiring in 1929. Crofts's first detective novel, *The Cask* (1920), set the pattern for his later work. With its complex *plot in which an *alibi dependent on railway and cross-Channel timetables is gradually broken down, it was called by Anthony *Boucher "the definitive novel" of this type, and, as one of the first examples, is considered to be a significant landmark in the history of the genre. (A subsequent edition, published in 1940, contains a preface by the author describing the novel's genesis.) *The Cask* was followed by *The Ponson Case* (1921), *The Pit-Prop Syndicate* (1922), and *The Groote Park Murder* (1923), which has a South African background. Crofts's series detective, Inspector (later Chief Superintendent) Joseph *French, first appeared in *Inspector French's Greatest Case* (1925), is featured in twenty-eight other novels, including *The Sea Mystery* (1928), *The Box Office Murders* (1929; *The Purple Sickle Murders*), *Sir John Magill's Last Journey* (1930), *Crime at Guildford* (1935; *The Crime at Nornes*), and *Death of a Train* (1946). Crofts is one of the major writers in the *Golden Age tradition, and his plots—often with a railway or shipping background (as in *The Loss of the Jane Vosper*, 1936)—are put together with the care and precision of an engineer. Raymond *Chandler called him "the soundest builder of them all." His novels differ from those of most other writers of the time, however, in that French proceeds not by brilliant deduction but by the painstaking accumulation of minute detail; the reader is allowed to follow each step of the detective's ratiocination. Although French, with his bourgeois background, is more credible as a policeman than Ngaio *Marsh's aristocratic Roderick *Alleyn, Crofts knew little or nothing about the workings of the police force, and his work, unlike that of his contemporary Sir Basil Thomson (1861–1939), head of the *CID at *Scotland Yard, in no way adumbrates the later *police procedural novel. Crofts weaknesses are a pedestrian style, a certain dullness in narration, and the complete subordination of character to plot. His attempt to achieve more depth of characterization in the late *Silence for the Murderer* (1948) is a failure, though *The 12.30 from Croydon* (1934; *Wilful and Premeditated*), modeled on R. Austin *Freeman's *inverted detective story, in which the first half is narrated from the standpoint of the murderer, is not without merit. These qualities led Julian *Symons, in *Bloody Murder: From the Detective Story to the Crime Novel*, (rev. ed. 1992), to dub Crofts "a typical, but also the best, representative of what may be called the Humdrum school of detective novelists."

[*See also* Alibi, Unbreakable; Railway Milieu; "Time is of the Essence"; Transportation, Modes of.]

• Jacques Barzun and Wendell Hertig Taylor, *A Catalogue of Crime*, rev. ed. (1989).

—T. J. Binyon

CROSS, AMANDA, pseudonym of Carolyn Gold Heilbrun (b. 1926), American author and academic. Heilbrun taught English and Women's Studies at Columbia University, where she also received her doctorate, until 1992. Her academic writing—particularly *Toward a Recognition of Androgyny* (1973), *Reinventing Womanhood* (1979), and *Writing a Woman's Life* (1988)—explores the construction of women as individuals and as literary characters. Her criticism of detective fiction, notably as represented by the novels of Dorothy L. *Sayers and the comedy of manners, demonstrates the genre's literary connections. Her fiction, originally written under a pseudonym to protect her academic career, has received critical and popular acclaim: in addition to a scroll from the Mystery Writers of America, she received an Edgar nomination for best first novel for *In the Last Analysis* (1964) and the 1981 Nero Wolfe Award for *Death in a Tenured Position* (1981; *A Death in the Faculty*).

Cross's witty, literate detective novels are simultaneously academic mysteries, comedies of manners, and feminist fiction; their series detective, Professor Kate *Fansler, teaches English literature at a university much like Columbia. In the twenty-six years between the first novel and *The Puzzled Heart* (1998), Fansler ages little but grows both wiser and more feminist. Seeing the "ivory tower" from the inside, Fansler, Cross, and Heilbrun are increasingly discouraged by its politics, *sexism, *racism, and self-serving nature. Fansler detects like the literary scholar her creator is: She constructs narratives around the facts, *clues, *suspects, and inuendoes until one version emerges to accommodate most of what she has discovered. Beginning with the fourth novel, *The Theban Mysteries* (1971), whose setting and detection are based on Sophocles's *Antigone,* Cross addresses the feminist matters that dominate Heilbrun's academic work: The lives of women silenced, obscured, ended. Fansler detects more than murder as she reconstructs the narratives of women's experience.

[*See also* Academic Milieu; Academic Sleuth; Females and Feminists; Novel of Manners.]

• Steven R. Carter, "Amanda Cross," in Earl F. Bargainnier, ed., *10 Women of Mystery* (1981). Marty Knepper, "Who Killed Janet Mandelbaum and Indian Wonder? A Look at the Suicides of Token Women in Amanda Cross's *Death in a Tenured Position* and Dorothy Bryant's *Killing Wonder,*" *Clues: A Journal of Detection* 13, no. 1 (spring–summer 1992): 45–58.   —Kathleen Gregory Klein

Cuff, Sergeant. A *sleuth in *The Moonstone* (1868) by Wilkie *Collins, Sergeant Cuff is introduced to readers as the finest detective in England. Although he does not dominate events of the narrative, his approach to the criminal problem as a *puzzle to be solved piece by piece serves to anticipate the methodical demonstration of detection technique in the tales of the archetypal *Great Detective to be found in the works of Arthur Conan *Doyle and authors of the Golden Age. According to Howard Haycraft in *Murder for Pleasure* (1941), Cuff may be recognized as a fictional rendering of the real-life Inspector Whicher who figured in the sensational Constance Kent or "Road Murder" case of 1860. In any event, Cuff's professional position links his accomplishments to those of the official police whose exploits inspired the creation of the crime and mystery genre, as well as making him a prototype of numerous successors in fiction from every period in the history of the form.

[*See also* Eccentrics; Police Detective.]
                                        —John M. Reilly

CULINARY MYSTERY. *Murder and gastronomy are so compatible that the title *Murder on the Menu* has appeared at least thrice—on a cookbook and on two anthologies of short stories. Since Anthony *Berkeley's *The Poisoned Chocolates Case* (1929), culinary terms and references have graced numerous titles, including Rex *Stout's *Too Many Cooks* (1938), Lawrence G. Blochman's *Recipe for Homicide* (1952), Richard and Frances Lockridge's *Murder and Blueberry Pie* (1959), Gordon Ashe's *Murder with Mushrooms* (1950), Virginia Rich's *The Baked Bean Supper Murders* (1983), Diane Mott Davidson's *Dying for Chocolate* (1992), M. C. Beaton's *Agatha Raisin and the Quiche of Death* (1992) and *Death of a Glutton* (1993), and Nancy Pickard's *The 27-Ingredient Chili Con Carne Murders* (1993).

Several cookbooks have been published to appeal to readers who enjoy both crime writing and cooking. These include Jeanine Larmoth and Charlotte Turgeon's *Murder on the Menu* (1972), Stout's *Nero Wolfe Cookbook* (1973), Carolyn *Keene's *Nancy Drew Cookbook: Clues to Good Cooking* (1973) and Elizabeth Bond Ryan and William J. Eakins's *The Lord Peter Wimsey Cookbook* (1981). Lon Jane Temple, Davidson, Pickard, and Rich include recipes in their novels; Michael Bond, Nicolas *Freeling, Janet Laurence, and Robert B. *Parker evocatively describe cooking and meals.

The culinary arts provide creative possibilities for crime and mystery authors. Kitchens yield weapons in Rich's *The Cooking School Murders* (1982). Strongly flavored food disguises *poison: Lobster patties hide arsenic in E. X. *Ferrars's *Enough to Kill a Horse* (1955), pâté contains oleander in Laurence's *Recipe for Death* (1992). Culinary professionals have opportunities to add noxious substances to food, be framed for poisoning, and investigate a poisoner's activities. Restaurant crowds provide too many suspects. In Susan Dunlap's *A Dinner to Die For* (1987), chaos in a restaurant muddles a detective's attempts to solve a murder case.

Culinary *milieus serve distinct narrative functions by establishing *setting, delineating character, and creating mood. Tim Heald's *Just Desserts* (1977), Linda Barnes's *Cities of the Dead* (1986), Sherryl Woods's *Reckless* (1989), Dorothy Cannell's *Mum's the Word* (1990), Joan Hess's *Maggody in Manhattan* (1992), Sarah Shankman's *The King Is Dead* (1992), and Jacqueline Girdner's *Fat-Free and Fatal* (1993) are set in cooking classes or contests. Mealtimes figure in R. A. J. Walling's *Dinner-Party at Bardolph's* (1927; *That Dinner at Bardolph's*), Dorothy L. *Sayers's *Strong Poison* (1930), many Agatha *Christie novels, beginning with *Lord Edgeware Dies* (1933; *Thirteen at Dinner*), John Rhode's *Death at Breakfast* (1936), John Penn's *Deceitful Death* (1989; *Stag Dinner Death*), and in works by Christopher Bush, Jill Churchill, Jane Haddam, Carlton Keith, Davidson, Laurence, and Rich. Restaurants are scenes of skullduggery in Nan and Ivan Lyons's *The President Is Coming to Lunch* (1988), in novels by Leo *Bruce, Cynthia Laurence, Bond, Dunlap, and Rich.

Three types of gastronomes appear in detective fiction. Most numerous are those with an informed enjoyment of food and spirits: Charles *Dickens's In-spector Bucket, Sayers's Lord Peter *Wimsey, Stout's (and Robert Goldsborough's) Nero *Wolfe, H. C. *Bailey's Reggie *Fortune, Freeling's Inspector *van der Valk, and Bond's Monsieur Aristide Pample-mousse. Food writers investigate crime in the work of Bond, Laurence, and Page, as well as in Lilian Jackson Braun's *The Cat Who Saw Red* (1986). David-son, Lawrence, Pickard, Rich, and Gloria Dank write about sleuthing chefs. Frequently, a taste for food contributes to characteristics and *characterization: Simon Brett's Melita Pargeter in *Mrs. Pargeter's Pound of Flesh* (1992), Cannell's Ellie Simons Haskell in *The Thin Woman* (1984), and Wolfe are over-weight; Rich's Eugenia Potter dishes up baked beans while Davidson's Goldy Bear grills Sonoma baby lamb chops; Wimsey has an aristocratic taste in food and wine.

In novels of the 1980s and 1990s, food provides ambience: California trendiness in Lawrence's *Take-Out City* (1993), Thanksgiving on a Mayflower replica in Haddam's *Feast of Murder* (1992); southern France in Page's *The Body in the Vestibule* (1992), an English country inn in Patricia Moyes's *Twice in a Blue Moon* (1993). More generally, gastronomy creates a sense of place: Haddam's Armenian neighborhood, Bond's rural France, Rich's Maine coast, Pickard's Arizona ranch, and Braun's Moose County.

[*See also* Hotel Milieu; Nautical Milieu: Ocean Liner Milieu; Poisons and Poisoning; Poisons, Un-usual.]   —E. D. Huntley

Dalgliesh, Adam, detective protagonist in several novels by P. D. *James who rises from the rank of chief detective inspector to commander at *Scotland Yard. Dalgliesh is introduced in *Cover Her Face* (1962). A widower who lost his wife and son during childbirth when he was in his late twenties, he shows a melancholy, even saturnine, disposition. He had a lonely childhood, and he lives a solitary life as an adult. He feels some *guilt about his profession; more, he has a deeply rooted passion for *innocence, which he seeks to protect, in the elderly as well as the young, and a fear of emotional commitment which prevents his retaining the *love of a strong-minded woman met in *A Mind to Murder* (1963) and lost in *Unnatural Causes* (1967). Some readers hope he will become romantically attached to Cordelia *Gray, introduced by James in *An Unsuitable Job for a Woman* (1972), though the two seem ill matched. Dalgliesh is quietly competent, superb at interrogation, yet not infallible. While he can use calculated charm to good effect, his coworkers find him moody and at times aloof. Dalgliesh is a published poet—James provides one example of his writing, which is not without merit—and an acute observer of character. Though he can show compassion, he is committed to *justice for its own sake, and only once do we see his heart overrule his head.

Dalgliesh's presence is not as central or immediate in some of the later novels as it is in the earlier books, or so it seems—perhaps because his relatively high rank makes him less likely to be the on-the-scene investigator, more the supervisor of other detectives; or perhaps because James has been shifting her attention to other, secondary, characters.

Dalgliesh has been portrayed by Roy Marsden in a superior series of television films. James has said that Marsden is not at all as she imagined Dalgliesh, and one can see why, but each depiction is successful in its own right. It is appropriate that the reader view Dalgliesh in various lights—indeed, James spells his surname "Dalgleish" in her first book—for the novels in which he features change viewpoints, adding to their complexity and interest, so that at times the reader knows more than Dalgliesh does. In some of the television films, these shifts produce a choppy effect; in James's novels, the transitions are nearly seamless and almost always convincing. Thus readers do not grow tired of Dalgliesh as they might of an ever-present and hovering detective, and though they know he will produce order out of chaos in the end, they also expect that he will make human mistakes.

The result is one of the most convincing detectives in modern fiction, a man who is never endearing but always intellectually compelling.

[*See also* Loner, Sleuth as; Police Detective.]

• Norma Siebenheller, *P. D. James* (1981). Richard B. Gidez, *P. D. James* (1986). "P. D. James: Ordinary Lives, Extraordinary Deaths," in *13 Mistresses of Murder*, ed. Elaine Budd (1986): 65–74.　　　　　　　　　　　　—Robin W. Winks

DALY, CARROLL JOHN (1889–1958), American author credited with creating the prototype of the *private eye in his short story "The False Burton Combs" (*Black Mask*, Dec. 1922). The unnamed protagonist in this story is a hired impersonator who terms himself a "gentleman adventurer" and "soldier of fortune" who works on his own against crime but eschews any mission as a "knight errant." Daly's use of a tough, first-person vernacular, and of a character who is uninclined to take women seriously, anticipated the work of countless private eye writers to follow. These qualities were also shared by Daly's most famous series character, the hard-boiled private eye Race *Williams, and by two more gumshoes he created: Vee Brown, a private eye with a penchant for songwriting, and the New York cop Satan Hall. Another Daly creation, "Three-Gun" Terry Mack, appeared in the *pulp magazines.

Born in Yonkers, New York, Daly graduated from the American Academy of Dramatic Arts, began and then abandoned an acting career, and became a movie projectionist and an owner of a chain of movie theaters before he began a writing career that would win him recognition as the pioneer of the private eye story. At the height of his career, a *Black Mask* readers poll proved him to be more popular than Erle Stanley *Gardner and Dashiell *Hammett.

[*See also* Hard-Boiled Sleuth; Impersonation; Voice: Hard-Boiled Voice.]

• "Carroll John Daly," in *The Oxford Book of American Detective Stories*, ed. Tony Hillerman and Rosemary Herbert (1994, p. 162).　　　　　　　　　—Rosemary Herbert

DALY, ELIZABETH (1878–1967), American writer of sixteen well-plotted *murder mysteries featuring Henry Gamadge, a bibliophile *sleuth who solves his cases by means of logic and attention to detail. A New Yorker herself, Daly set her fictional crimes, written during the 1940s and 1950s, among a wealthy *New York social set. Influenced by the novelists of the Golden Age of the detective novel, she followed in their traditions, employing traditional *conventions of the genre: setting her work in a civilized *milieu, emphasizing the *puzzle element, and playing fair with the reader in the delivery of *clues. Her sleuth, initially a bachelor, eventually takes a wife, Clara, who shares his New York brownstone complete with laboratory.

Daly came from a privileged background. Born in New York City in 1878, she attended the exclusive Miss Baldwin's School, and earned a bachelor's degree from Bryn Mawr College in 1901 and a master's degree from Columbia University in 1902. She taught at Bryn Mawr from 1902 to 1906, and for many years enjoyed producing amateur theatricals. This Edgar Award-winning author began her mystery writing career at the age of sixty-one.

• Dorothy Salisbury Davis, "Some of the Truth," in *Colloquium on Crime*, ed. Robin W. Winks (1986).

—Rosemary Herbert

DAVIOT, GORDON. *See* Tey, Josephine.

DAVIS, DOROTHY SALISBURY (b. 1916), American author. Although Dorothy Salisbury Davis admits to a desire to create a series character like Georges *Simenon's Inspector *Maigret, her failure to develop a running character in her books looks like refusal of a convention: She has dedicated her work to a sympathetic investigation of characters undergoing stress which seems to demand a variety of milieus and portrayals rather than a formula.

Born in Chicago, Davis was raised as a Roman Catholic and educated at Holy Child High School in Waukegan, Illinois. She left the church when she married. Perhaps not surprisingly, crises of faith figure prominently in her fiction, most notably in *A Gentle Murderer* (1951) and *Where the Dark Streets Go* (1969), both of which feature priests as protagonists. The Midwest—Wisconsin and Illinois, rural and urban—often serves as the setting for Davis's books; but so too does *New York City in such novels as A Death in the Life* (1976), *Scarlet Night* (1980), *Lullaby of Murder* (1984), and *The Habit of Fear* (1987). The last of these is about Julie Hayes, a young fortune-teller in a seedy district of the city, who may become at last Davis's series character.

Psychology instead of detection provides the substance of Davis's short stories, even more so than in her novels. Her collection of fifteen short stories, *Tales for a Stormy Night: The Collected Crime Stories* (1984), displays a strong sense of suspense, a skillful ability to lure the reader into mistaken assumptions, and an especially strong way of sharing with readers the minds of female characters confronting hazards and crisis.

[*See also* Characterization; Religion; Rural Milieu; Urban Milieu.]

• Jean Swanson and Dean James, *By a Woman's Hand: A Guide to Detective Fiction by Women*, 2nd ed. (1996).

—John M. Reilly

DAY-LEWIS, CECIL. *See* Blake, Nicholas.

DEAF DETECTIVE. *See* Disability, Sleuth with a.

DEIGHTON, LEN (Leonard Cyril) (1929), English. Born in Marylebone, London on 18 February 1929, the son of a chauffeur and a cook, Leonard Cyril Deighton dropped out of school to help his father during the war, served in the Royal Air Force, Special Investigation Branch, and developed an interest in weapons, undersea diving, flying, and military history. He then studied commercial art at the Royal College of Art, graduating in 1953. He held diverse jobs from pastry cook to travel editor, news photographer, scriptwriter, and movie producer. His writing reflects his knowledge of gourmet cooking, his international travel, his artist's eye for detail and scene, and his expertise as a military historian.

Characterized by a sense of *humor, intriguing digressions, technical knowledge, and vivid rendering of place, Deighton's novels work against the spy novel tradition: They parody and mock the Ian *Fleming, W. Somerset Maugham, or Graham *Greene view, providing new perspectives on opposing ideologies, and debunking such sacred cows as Winston Churchill and public school aristocrats. *SS-GB: Nazi-Occupied Britain, 1941* (1979), for example, combines traditional detective novel and thriller conventions with a fascinating *science fiction scenario: what if Britain lost World War II and the German SS took control?

A typical Deighton novel celebrates the competence, professionalism, and humanity of the rank-and-file spy. Its typical protagonist, a street-tough loner caught up in internecine competition and double and triple crosses, is witty, irreverent, and deeply distrustful. He may be a young pawn put in play by scheming superiors (as is the anonymous spy in Deighton's first novel, *The Ipcress File*, 1962, and its sequels *Funeral in Berlin*, 1964, and *Billion-Dollar Brain*, 1966) or middle-aged and disillusioned, with limited loyalties (as is Bernard Samson in *Berlin Game*, 1983; *Mexico Set*, 1984; *London Match*, 1985). However, his working-class rudeness grates on his superiors, while his superior knowledge of everything from gourmet food to locale and language, his internal resources, his personal network of friends and enemies, and his marked professionalism help him survive deception and betrayal. The trilogies *Spy Hook* (1988), *Spy Line* (1989), and *Spy Sinker* (1990) and *Faith* (1995), *Hope* (1996), and *Charity* (1997) enmesh Sampson in trying post–cold-war games.

[*See also* Loner, Sleuth as; Loyalty and Betrayal; Spy Fiction; Thriller.]

• Fred Erisman, "Romantic Reality in the Spy Stories of Len Deighton," *Armchair Detective* 10 (Apr. 1977): 101–105. Edward Milward-Oliver, *The Len Deighton Companion* (1987). Lars Ole Sauerberg, *Secret Agents in Fiction: Ian Fleming, John le Carré and Len Deighton* (1984).

—Gina Macdonald

DETECTION CLUB, THE. At its founding, membership of the Detection Club was confined to writers of detective stories, the constitution and rules stating that "the term 'detective-novel' does not include *adventure-stories or *'thrillers' or stories in which the detection is not a main interest," and that writers of such works were excluded. The original twenty-six members included G. K. Chesterton, Dorothy L. *Sayers, Agatha *Christie, Anthony *Berkeley, E. C. *Bentley and Ronald A. *Knox.

The date, even the year, of the club's foundation remains uncertain, except that it was not 1932 as stated in *Verdict of Thirteen* (1979). An attempt to settle the exact date through a newspaper brought information suggesting that it was probably 1929, the founder Berkeley, perhaps in collaboration with Knox and Sayers. It was conceived and has continued as a dining club, meeting nowadays three times a year, with no purpose other than good fellowship.

The club's membership has gone through three phases. Before World War II, the rule insisting that members be pure detective story writers was strictly adhered to; after the war, it was relaxed with the election in successive years of Eric *Ambler, Andrew *Garve, and Julian *Symons; and in the 1960s and thereafter, the rule was abandoned altogether. The basic reason for the change was that few postwar writers produced pure detective stories.

The celebrated ritual for the induction of new members has also necessarily changed. It was almost certainly conceived originally by Sayers, perhaps in collaboration with Chesterton. The president entered wearing a black, scarlet-lined cloak, lighted by candles held by other members, and the ensuing ritual culminated in the new member placing a hand on Eric the Skull, whose eyes lighted up. The new member then swore by something held sacred to obey the club's unwritten laws. The trappings, cloak, candles, Eric, and the sacred oath have been retained, but the original ritual, now considered inappropriate and outdated, has changed out of recognition.

Election to the club remains by invitation. The presidents have been Chesterton (1932–36), Bentley (1936–49), Sayers (1949–57), Christie (1958–76, with Lord Gorell as co-president from 1958 to 1963), Symons (1976–85), succeeded by H. R. F. *Keating in 1985. The club has maintained itself financially by occasional publications contributed to by members. They include the early and fairly recently rediscovered *The Scoop & Behind the Screen*, written in 1930 and 1931; *The Floating Admiral* (1931); *Ask a Policeman* (1933); *Verdict of Thirteen: A Detection Club Anthology* (1979); and *The Man Who . . .* (1992). Berkeley's *The Poisoned Chocolates Case* (1929) is a wonderfully ingenious book containing a "Crime Circle" based on the Detection Club. Howard Haycraft's *The Art of the Mystery Story: A Collection of Critical Essays* (1946) includes an early version of the Detection Club oath.

[*See also* Crime Writers Association.]

• Julian Symons, introduction to *The Scoop & Behind the Screen* (1983).
                                                    —Julian Symons

DETECTIVE NOVEL. The detective novel is that form of long fiction centered upon investigation of a criminal problem. Typically the narrative presents the focal crime as seemingly insoluble by ordinary means and, therefore, requiring the techniques of inquiry honed by specialists in criminal matters. Those specialists may be professional police officers or other government agents, freelancing investigators, or amateurs who come upon a criminal case accidentally. Regardless of how they assume their commissions as *sleuths, though, the investigators of crime, rather than a crime's perpetrators, become the leading figures in a detective novel's narrative. Likewise the *plots of detective novels follow the pattern of the investigation, not the enactment of the crime itself. The sleuth's application of theory or reason to the details of the crime provides the dramatic action of the narrative. Following a trail of *clues and hypothesizing ways to relate them in a singular design, the detective tries out answers to the criminal problem that serve to exemplify detection methodology and to illustrate the sleuth's *ingenuity or genius. The tentative answers may be viewed not only as propositions to be tested by the sleuth's further inquiry, but also as drafts of the ultimate narrative to be composed by the detective when he or she has accounted for all the relevant data pertaining to the crime. When readers receive the final, true identity of the culprit and a satisfactory explanation of the *motive and means of the crime, the information arrives as a demonstration of the sleuth's ability to uncover knowledge that has been deliberately concealed in mystery by the mechanics of the text. The detective novel, thus, is constructed to represent a triumph of detective will and intellectual methodology.

A long period of gestation produced the detective novel. The interest in crime as a social problem arising from conditions of urbanization in the eighteenth and early nineteenth centuries fostered a large, popular literature about *violence and lawbreakers. The terror of the *Gothic novel shows a quality of uneasiness traceable to fears associated with the collapse of traditional consensus about the nature of good and *evil. The English genre of *Newgate novels, relating stories of real-life criminals, and the German variety of crime story labeled *Kriminalgeschichte*, helped create an audience for criminal sensation. In addition, a shift of attention from the crime to its solution appears in such works as the novels of Wilkie *Collins, but detection was still incidental. As Howard Haycraft puts it, in *Murder for Pleasure* (1941), what Collins essentially did in *The Woman in White* (1860) and *The Moonstone* (1868) "was to write a full-bodied novel in the fashion of his time, using detection . . . to catalyze the elaborate ingredients; much as another novelist of the same era might have employed a love or revenge motif." The process of hybridizing the detection motif and previously established forms remains baldly visible in the now famed debut of Sherlock *Holmes in *A Study in Scarlet Beeton's Christmas Annual*, (1887). There Dr. John H. *Watson introduces the incomparable Holmes and establishes his unique methods of detection, but Arthur Conan *Doyle also supplies his narrative with an account of events in the American West that undercut the formal coherence of the detection plot.

The stylized form of detection fiction was finally established not in the novel but in the short stories of Edgar Allan *Poe. The briefer form permitted Poe to strip his narrative of digression and secondary lines of action with the result that his "Murders in the Rue

Morgue"(*Graham's Lady's and Gentleman's Magazine,* Apr. 1841) and the successor stories crystallized the conventions that would prove continually useful to later writers. When almost a half century later the market demand from popular magazines encouraged writers with an interest in criminal detection to follow Poe's example and use the short story form for narration of criminal matters, the brief scope of the few pages publishers would allow for their stories discouraged both digression from the detection plot and any tendency toward extended development of theme or character. The effect of short-story discipline was to set the template of detection fiction and to produce a body of practice that settled the sleuth and detection squarely in the center of craft and custom.

A new preference among publishers for works of novel length following World War I forced the next generation of detective writers to complete the hybridization of the general novel and the newly emergent type of detective narrative. This they accomplished by incremental construction of *milieu, character, and event upon the armature of an intellectual process of detection—a concentration of effort that replaced the romance of outlaws and the sensation of violence with the type of heroic-comic narrative we know as the detective novel. Heroic because the sleuth, representative of either a natural or an inherent aristocracy, serves as a protector of the social commonweal, and comic, because the narrative plot of discovering knowledge leads to positive resolution promising a peaceful, if not graceful, future.

As a result of this literary labor, the novel was re-formed into a new genre. The writers active in the project had their specialties. Agatha *Christie excelled in plotting; Dorothy L. *Sayers elaborated the gentleman hero and gave him an emotional life; Margery *Allingham incorporated features of the *thriller; Ngaio *Marsh set an example in the use of an engaging milieu; Philip *MacDonald masterfully varied the pace of narration. Meanwhile in the United States S. S. *Van Dine and Ellery *Queen gave their talents to integration of the rules of the game into the novel, thereby completing the hybridization of criminal material and novel.

The collective designation of the period of the reforming project as the Golden Age testifies to the writers' success. The self-consciousness with which they undertook revision of the novel is evidenced by their creation of literary conventions distinctive to the detective novel. By repeated use, the writers of the Golden Age set *means, motive, and opportunity as the leading categories for a detective's analysis of crime. Through similarities in the tone of narrative voice and a regular practice of excluding actual commission of murder from the narration, they created the distance from violence that permits readers to enjoy criminal fiction as entertainment.

Once founded as a genre, the detective novel came to provide opportunity within its stylized framework for innovation. Francis Iles could rearrange the events of plot to make an "inverted" detective narration. And in the decades following the Golden Age, American authors dissatisfied with the too visible artifice of the established detective novel took the di-

rection soon labeled hard-boiled. Dashiell *Hammett's narrative about Sam *Spade, Raymond *Chandler's adventures of Philip *Marlowe, or Ross *Macdonald's accounts of the cases taken by Lew *Archer result from a reexamination of the detective novel, but unlike the earlier writers against whom the hard-boiled style was a reaction, Hammett, Chandler, Macdonald, and the dozens of later hard-boiled writers were not engaged in re-formation. Their negation of Golden Age conventions and manner was enabled by the already completed task of forming the genre that hard-boiled writers proceeded to appropriate to their own, different conceptions of crime and society.

[*See also* Amateur Detective; Conventions of the Genre; Craft of Crime and Mystery Writing, The; Crime Novel; Formula: Plot; Golden Age Forms; Golden Age Traditions; Hard-Boiled Sleuth; History of Crime and Mystery Writing; Police Detective; Private Eye.]

• Howard Haycraft, *Murder for Pleasure: The Life and Times of the Detective Story* (1941). Julian Symons, *Mortal Consequences: From the Detective Story to the Crime Novel: A History* (1972). Hillary Waugh, "The Mystery versus the Novel," in *The Mystery Story,* ed. John Ball (1976). LeRoy L. Panek, *Introduction to the Detective Story* (1987). Kate Stine, ed. *The Armchair Detective Book of Lists* (1995).

—John M. Reilly

DEVIANCE. Germinating in the emergent conditions of modern life, popular crime and mystery literature from the start was concerned with the disorder that resulted when the social contract was disregarded. To the extent that abiding by the law and assuming some degree of trust in economic exchange represented the desirable norm for behavior, violation of law, deceit, and unsanctioned *violence constituted deviance, and imaginary adventures in bringing concealed deviants to light through discovery of their motives and the methods of their crimes became the subject matter of the new popular writing about crime and its accompanying mysteries.

Early writers for the serial press and compilers of ostensible memoirs of police detectives were content to take an instructional attitude toward social deviance. Often they claimed for their revelations of inequity the higher purpose of instruction and warning. In time, writers interested in the power of literary technique to simulate a plausible world seized upon the formula of deviance and restoration of order to project social ideals as they entertained readers with tales of detection. Authors in the *Golden Age tradition, for instance, built narratives about the correction of social deviance upon their allegiance to the idea of an organic society. Under the aspect of detective fiction, writers such as Agatha *Christie, E. C. *Bentley, J. S. Fletcher, Freeman Wills *Crofts, Dorothy L. *Sayers, and Philip *Macdonald in England, and S. S. *Van Dine and Ellery *Queen in America, described fictional worlds that were ordinarily homogeneous in their populations. Both before the crime and after its solution, these worlds were comfortably arranged in a hierarchy of social station, and amenable to correction of their orbits by amateur sleuths whose full-time role when they were not detecting was to be the aristocrats whom the world's purpose had destined them to be. The literary logic of these closed societies, which classifies unassimilated outsiders, the disaffected, and critics as alien, often makes it economical for the dissonant interloper to be responsible as well for the criminal deviance, thereby confirming the rectitude of the worldview underlying the narrative. The evident gap between the actual modern world the Golden Age writers inhabited and the fictional world they imagined makes their work a variety of utopia.

By contrast, the social settings and physical sites of *hard-boiled fiction are mannered renditions of a reality where a fragile crust of civilization can barely contain the lawless behavior of professionalized criminals or the anarchic impulses of greed, envy, jealousy, and lust. The norm of order in narratives by Dashiell *Hammett, Raymond *Chandler, James M. *Cain, and the alumni of the *Black Mask school is at best circumscribed by the bounds of personal relationships, and even those relationships of *family and lovers may be jeopardized by *corruption. The hard-boiled detective has in mind an image of a social contract, but finds the ideal continually violated by deviant behavior. Correcting the deviance will never restore a condition of harmony in the general society, but it may provide relief, an enclave for goodness.

Both the Golden Age writers and the hard-boiled practitioners conceive of deviance in a fundamentally social way. Deviance also occurs, though, on subjective terrain, within the mind and consciousness. Margaret *Millar, Lawrence Sanders, Patricia D. Cornwell, Lynn S. Hightower, Mary Higgins *Clark—authors of *suspense fiction, and writers who chronicle the deeds of serial killers—all pursue deviance from psychological normality that results in antisocial behavior.

Once, in a time before detective fiction, violation of social expectations was defined as sin. With the rise of the popular literature about the problem of crime, that view was secularized. Deviance was portrayed by Golden Age authors as subversion of an organic society founded in a presumed natural order, and by hard-boiled writers as the manifestation of the essential condition of corruption in modern society. The reality of social change dispels the appeal of the Golden Age as an attainable ideal. Repetition of the hard-boiled view and real-world experience makes the idea of generalized corruption overly familiar. The remaining puzzle about deviance lies within the mind where contemporary writers increasingly turn their attention and narrative skills to plumb the internalized visions of a norm all people carry within them.

[See also Characterization; Closed-World and Open-World Settings; Formula: Character; Serial Killers and Mass Murderers.]

• Ernest Mandel, Delightful Murder: A Social History of the Crime Story (1984).
—John M. Reilly.

DEXTER, (NORMAN) COLIN (b. 1930), British author of detective fiction. Trained at Cambridge in the classics, which he taught in various schools, Dexter published his first *detective novel, Last Bus to Woodstock, in 1975 while employed by the Oxford Delegacy of Local Examinations. He is an avid fan of crossword puzzles, in which he has won national championships; his learning and love of puzzles inform his novels, which are formal *whodunits known for their elaborate *plots as well as their narrative verve and finely characterized series detective.

Through Death Is Now My Neighbor (1997), Dexter had published a dozen novels, all of them set in *Oxford and its environs, where he lives and which he lovingly details. In The Dead of Jericho (1981), for example, he explores the gentrification of an old working-class neighborhood. Many of his stories revolve around colleges, schools, or related institutions; The Silent World of Nicholas Quinn (1977) is set at an examinations board.

Chief Inspector Morse and Sergeant Lewis of the Thames Valley appear in every novel. Morse is a lover of Wagner, good beer, and crossword puzzles; Sergeant Lewis is the prosaic policeman, married with children. Through Morse, Dexter can display his love of words, theorizing, and general intellectual play. While Lewis slogs through the dull work of routine, Morse evolves theory after theory, sometimes wrongheaded, but always plausible and often brilliant. Dexter delights to show us the documents in the case, including epitaphs in The Wench Is Dead (1989) or handwritten letters in The Jewel That Was Ours (1991). Despite its linguistic precision and much exclamatory emphasis, Dexter's narrative is relaxed and informal, scattered with asides, jokes, and wry commentary.

[See also Academic Milieu; Allusion, Literary; Police Detective; Sidekicks and Sleuthing Teams.]
—Susan Oleksiw and Rosemary Herbert

DICKENS, CHARLES (1812–1870), British novelist, generally considered the greatest novelist of the Victorian age. Dickens's childhood was spent on the borderlines of poverty; central to his development was the emotionally crucial period when his father was imprisoned for debt and he, at the age of twelve, was sent to work for a pittance in a blacking warehouse. This period he kept a secret from his family and almost all his friends, but into many of the novels the words "Warren's Blacking" are inserted, as a sort of clue and reminder to himself.

It is not surprising that prisons should play such a large role in Dickens's novels. In each of the novels, crime is an important component—often the central motivator of the *plot. Some of his early novels are often classed with the *Newgate novels. Although Dickens does not fictionalize the lives of real criminals as do Edward Bulwer-Lytton and William Harrison Ainsworth, he takes fact as his springboard (the Gordon Riots in Barnaby Rudge, 1841; the fence Ikey Solomons as the model for Fagin in Oliver Twist, 1837–39), and these early works and sensationalize crime and present the criminal in a melodramatic or lurid light that almost transforms him into a hero. The treatment of Bill Sikes after the *murder of Nancy is a classic example of this.

In his great mature novels crime is still central. Most significant for the *whodunit is the murder of Mr. Tulkinghorn in *Bleak House* (1852–53). The treatment of Lady Dedlock's connection with the crime is one of the first uses of the *red herring technique; we have a surprise solution; and the use of Inspector Bucket, and Dickens's fascination with his methods of detection, bring us close to the twentieth-century crime novel. On the other hand, the atmospheric treatment of the semi-criminal waterside areas of *London in *Our Mutual Friend* (1864–65) made this novel a favorite with the Golden Age writers, who referred to it often when its reputation was not high. *The Mystery of Edwin Drood* (1870), though written at a much lower level of intensity, and perhaps in emulation of Dickens's friend Wilkie *Collins's successful fiction, bade fair to anticipate many more techniques of later crime novels, but it was only half finished at Dickens's death, and it has spawned more mysteries—and more proposed solutions—than any other of his novels.

*Prison scenes, a natural corollary of Dickens's preoccupation with crime, dot the books, from Pickwick in the Fleet to the projected scene of Jasper in the condemned cell that was to conclude *Edwin Drood*. They range in tone from the grand guignol of Fagin awaiting execution to the controlled *satire of Uriah Heep as a model prisoner—a critique of new penal thinking. More haunting still are the metaphorical prisons that pepper the novels, from the self-imprisonment of Miss Havisham and Mrs. Clennam, through imprisonment by political dogma in Mr. Gradgrind, to imprisonment by emotional repression in Mr. Dombey or Rosa Dartle.

Dickens's reputation dipped somewhat in his last years and in the decades immediately after his death, but in the twentieth century he has generally been regarded as Britain's greatest novelist. Central to that estimate is his handling of the themes of crime and punishment, *guilt and repentance.

[*See also* Characterization; Dostoyevsky, Fyodor Mikhaylovich.]

• Philip Collins, *Dickens and Crime* (1962). Peter Ackroyd, *Dickens* (1990).   —Robert Barnard

DIGEST-SIZED MYSTERY MAGAZINES. The era of the digest-sized mystery magazine began with the publication of *Ellery Queen's Mystery Magazine* (*EQMM*), its first issue dated fall 1941. Some pulp magazines had attempted a digest-size format earlier—notably Street and Smith's *Pocket Detective Magazine*, which lasted eleven months beginning in December 1936—but it was the immediate success of *EQMM* that brought about a lasting change.

Encouraged no doubt by wartime paper shortages, some pulps, such as the *Shadow*, soon went to digest size, but it was not until July 1945 that the first issue of *Mystery Book Magazine* presented a real challenge to *EQMM*. Like its predecessor it offered big-name mystery writers packaged within conservative, eye-catching covers that didn't need to be hidden from view like some of the older pulps. From the beginning, editor Leo Margulies made the magazine unique by specializing in the long form, publishing novelettes and novellas longer than anything *EQMM* ever used. Some were shortened versions of forthcoming novels by writers like Brett Halliday and Fredric *Brown; others were original novelettes by writers like Dorothy B. Hughes and Cornell *Woolrich.

Although it lasted for six years, *Mystery Book Magazine* never achieved the popularity of *EQMM*. Margulies decided he needed a mystery personality like Ellery *Queen on which to peg his next venture, and he traveled to England to meet with Leslie *Charteris, creator of the *Saint. He persuaded Charteris to become supervising editor of the *Saint Detective Magazine*, contributing a new Saint short story to each issue. Margulies even offered to have the stories ghostwritten by others, but Charteris was eager to do most of the writing himself. The magazine was a moderate success and continued long after Margulies left it in 1956 to start a similiar venture, *Mike Shayne Mystery Magazine*. In this case the monthly novelettes about the popular Miami *private eye were ghosted by others and Shayne creator Brett Halliday had no direct involvement with the magazine throughout its twenty-nine-year history.

Just a few months earlier than the *Saint*, with an issue dated January 1953, *Manhunt Detective Story Monthly* made its appearance. Bolstered by a four-part Mickey *Spillane serial, *Manhunt* was an immediate success. Its pages contained new stories by the best hard-boiled writers of the day, their names familiar to readers through paperback originals. Many were clients of the literary agent Scott Meredith, who with his brother Sidney played an active role in the magazine's early years. Some, like young author Evan Hunter, were even employees of Meredith.

The success of *Manhunt* inspired the founding of a host of short-lived imitators with names like *Guilty*, *Trapped*, and *Terror*. They paid less money and attracted lesser names, and they quickly failed along with *Manhunt*'s own spin-off, *Murder*. The publishers had much better luck in late 1956 with an entirely different sort of sister publication, *Alfred Hitchcock's Mystery Magazine* (*AHMM*). (Though *Manhunt* and *AHMM* were published by different corporations, they shared a Fifth Avenue address and, for a time, the same editor, William Manners.) An attempt to boost newsstand circulation led to the conversion of both magazines to a larger 8½" by 11" format early in 1957. They were back to digest size early the following year, but *Manhunt* was never quite the same. From the world's best-selling crime magazine it began a steady decline that lasted until its demise in 1967.

Most other mystery magazines, including *Rex Stout's Mystery Monthly* and *Ed McBain's Mystery Book*, had short lives in America. Some in England fared better. *John Creasey Mystery Magazine* was published from 1956 to 1965 and *Edgar Wallace Mystery Magazine* from 1964 to 1967. *London Mystery Magazine* lasted more than thirty years, though its authors were not household names and it relied heavily on fantasy.

During the 1980s in America the digest-sized *Espionage* had moderate success for a time, and a trade paperback, the *New Black Mask*, came close to resurrecting the excitement of its pulp predecessor, even publishing for the first time Dashiell *Hammett's screen treatment for *After the Thin Man*. After eight issues it ceased publication due to problems with rights to the *Black Mask* name.

The economics of the writing profession have worked against the short story in recent decades, and as markets dwindled fewer authors have been willing to devote their efforts to the form. Among digest-sized mystery magazines today only *EQMM* and *AHMM* have national distribution, though their circulation has held steady and even increased a bit in the 1990s.

• Michael L. Cook, *Monthly Murders: A Checklist and Chronological Listing of Fiction in the Digest-Size Mystery Magazines in the United States and England* (1982). Michael L. Cook, *Mystery, Detective and Espionage Magazines* (1983). Burl Barer, *The Saint: A Complete History in Print, Radio, Film and Television* (1993).   —Edward D. Hoch

DIME NOVEL, generic name for American paper-covered publications of the nineteenth and early twentieth centuries (1860–1915), issued at regular intervals, selling for a fixed amount (usually ten cents), and containing lurid adventures. The earliest example was *Malaeska, the Indian Wife of the White Hunter*, by Mrs. Ann S. Stephens, published in 1860 as the first number in the series called *Beadle's Dime Novels*. The dime novel exists in at least four publishing formats: small 100-page paperbacks measuring four by six inches; 250-to 300-page books measuring four by seven inches; and seven- by ten inch or eight-by eleven-inch pamphlets of sixteen to thirty-two pages. The cover illustrations (black and white until 1896; in color thereafter) were what attracted the purchaser's attention at the newsstand. Related to these were the story papers, newspaper-sized weekly publications that contained serialized novels and short fiction. The original dime novels were meant for an adult market, but by the 1890s the majority of readers were boys.

Frontier and western stories were the mainstay of the dime novel at first, but by the 1880s they were largely replaced by detective and mystery stories. The first dime novel detective story was *"The Ticket-of-Leave Man,"* (1865) a serial based on Tom Taylor's British play of the same name that appeared in the *Flag of Our Union*, a Boston story paper. It was followed by Harlan Page Halsey's *"Old Sleuth, the Detective"* in George Munro's *Fireside Companion* in 1872.

The dime novel detective story figures as part of the transition between such works as the *Mémoires de Vidocq* (1828–29; *Memoirs of Vidocq*, ca. 1828) by Eugène François *Vidocq and the appearance of the professional detective in the works of Arthur Conan *Doyle. Edgar Allan *Poe's Gothic tales as well as his stories of ratiocination inspired the writers of dime novels, while some of the earliest American translations of Émile *Gaboriau's *detective novels appeared as dime novels, and dime novel detective heroes were advertised as followers of Vidocq, the great French manhunter.

The influence of Poe's atmospheric writing may be seen in the publications of Frank Tousey, where the supernatural is prominent in titles, *plots, and the lurid woodcut cover illustrations. Haunted houses, bands of cloaked figures, skeletons, and suggestions of dark doings in the cemetery predominate. The opening installment of "Bats in the Wall; or, The Mystery of Trinity Church Yard," by P. T. Raymond (a house name) in the story paper *Boys of New York* dated 14 November 1885, is accompanied by an illustration of a mother pleading that her son not join an attempt to rob a bank. The background includes the Gothic church, dark tree branches, and a symbolic bat figure brooding over the scene.

An important feature of the dime novel mystery story, the detection and capture of the person responsible for a crime, derives from the model of Gaboriau's patient policemen and the revelation of *family secrets. Equally influential was Gaboriau's American counterpart, the private detective Allan Pinkerton, whose name was on the title pages of the Pinkerton accounts published from 1874 to 1884. It is the Pinkerton method—shadowing suspects, eavesdropping on conversations, and relying heavily on *disguise—that helped to establish in the dime novel the popular concept of detective work. The dime novel detective relied more on persistence than on reasoning, and the plots are filled with *coincidence and startling revelations. The motives of the criminal turn out to be simple *greed, and the final solution may include the real identity of the detective as well as the identity of the criminal.

Because the writers of dime novels were hidden behind pseudonyms, very little is known about the majority of them other than what they contributed to certain publications on a regular basis. The more successful writers were those who worked on a series with a famous fictional detective as protagonist, either as the creator or as one of the syndicate of writers assigned to keep the stories before the public.

Among the more prolific dime novel detective writers was Halsey, who wrote the stories of Old Sleuth, first under the pseudonym Tony Pastor (after the well-known showman) and then under the name "Old Sleuth." In this he originated the concept of the dual identity of protagonist and author and made the word "sleuth" synonymous with "detective."

The most significant detective stories Francis Worcester Doughty contributed to the Frank Tousey publications features Old King Brady. His stories written under the cognomen "A New York Detective" contained realistic details of the city where his stories took place. A characteristic of his style was the repetition of the story title in the final sentence of each story.

Walter Fenton Mott was primarily a writer of detective and adventure stories for Frank Tousey. His most significant contribution to the genre was the long series of stories about "Young Sleuth" in which the most interesting character was not the detective but his assistant. Jean Guillaume Jenkeau (referred to as Jenkins or the Count of No Account by his employer) served as welcome comic relief in the stories.

John Russell Coryell, Frederic Van Rensselaer Dey, and Frederick William Davis were the principal writers on Street & Smith's Nick *Carter series. Davis also wrote stories about other detectives (especially Felix Boyd) under his own pseudonym, Scott Campbell, and authored the Sheridan Keene series for Street & Smith's *Shield Weekly* as Alden F. Bradshaw.

W. I. James Jr., credited with writing the stories of Old Cap. Collier for Norman L. Munro, is as mysterious a figure as any he wrote about. Old Cap. Collier was created as a rival to the popular Old Sleuth stories published by Munro's brother George. A master of disguise, Old Cap. was called in when the local police were unable to solve the crime.

While Edward S. Ellis never wrote a series of stories about a single detective hero, a significant number of his story paper serials for Beadle & Adams belong to the genre.

The dime novel detective story belongs to that period of transition in the genre between the contributions of Vidocq and Doyle. It promoted many of the popular ideas about how detectives worked, packaged them in an appealing format, and priced them to be within reach of all American readers. The dime novel is as significant to the social historian as to the student of literature, if not more so.

[See also Industry Writers; Pathfinder Fiction; Syndicate Authors; Western, The.]

• Edmund Pearson, *Dime Novels; Or, Following an Old Trail in Popular Literature* (1929). Albert Johannsen, *The House of Beadle & Adams, Dime and Nickel Novels* (1950). E. F. Bleiler, *Eight Dime Novels* (1972). J. Randolph Cox, "The Heyday of the Dime Novel," *Wilson Library Bulletin* 55 (Dec. 1980): 262–66. J. Randolph Cox, "The Detective as Hero in the American Dime Novel," *Dime Novel Round-Up* 50 (Feb. 1981): 2–13.   —J. Randolph Cox

DISABILITY, SLEUTH WITH A. Relatively few writers have written crime fiction featuring a handicapped detective, probably because the limitation imposed by a disability adds another constraint to those already inherent in the form. Having deprived a detective of a sense or limb, it becomes necessary to demonstrate the lack and to bring it plausibly to bear on the development of a narrative. Ernest *Bramah's detective, Max *Carrados, was blinded by a branch while out riding. He has since refined his other senses in compensation and employs an invaluable manservant with eyes that miss nothing. Lest his powers seem excessive, his creator states clearly in a preface that his achievements, however remarkable, are founded on fact. In one story, Carrados confounds an old school friend by deducing—with expert knowledge and from handling a coin—the whole truth of a case he is investigating. In another, he turns the tables on his kidnappers by plunging them into darkness.

Thornley Colton is C. H. Stagg's detective, "totally blind since birth" but nonetheless a musician and man-about-town, with his secretary as guide. He, too, has trained his other senses and now has "won-derfully sharp ears" and "super-sensitive fingertips." In shaking hands, he rests his finger on the wrist, since a man cannot disguise his pulse rate, however impassive his face. Repeatedly, his fingers trace crucial details invisible to the eye: stitches in cushions, a tear in a lining, a scar in velvet.

Captain Duncan MacLain figures in Baynard Kendrick's novels, with two German shepherd dogs: Schnucke, his female Seeing Eye, and Dreist, his male protector. MacLain was blinded in World War I and has since worked ceaselessly "to perfect the senses of hearing, touch and smell." By counting footsteps he can estimate height and, after six years' practice, he can now "shoot at sound." Those who manipulate others by physical tricks are diminished by his presence.

Eric Ward has chronic glaucoma and suffers hideously in certain novels by Roy Lewis, with titles reflecting his condition but also commenting on the action: *A Certain Blindness* (1980); *A Limited Vision* (1983). Forced out of the police by his affliction, he becomes a solicitor, astute and observant, except when debilitated by an attack. An operation enables him, eventually, to lead a normal life. Stella Tower's *Dumb Vengeance* (1933) is a "semi-detective story" with Amelia Jenkins, a dumb woman, as its semi-detective. When her friend and host is murdered, she begins to "brood and watch and wonder," eyes and ears continually alert. Finally, aware of the truth and no longer passive, she intervenes drastically.

Drury Lane and Joe Binney are deaf, in works by Barnaby Ross and Jack Livingston, respectively. Lane has become deaf with age and lip-reading is a "latter-day accomplishment." It has "sharpened" his "powers of concentration": Once his eyes are closed, he enters a world of silence. Binney is a *private eye, whose hearing was destroyed in underwater demolition work with the navy. From lip-reading he has developed increased skill at "reading expressions" and it is "hard to hide a lie" from him.

Vicars Bell's detective, Dr. Douglas Baynes, lost a leg in World War I and still feels humiliated by his artificial limb, "wretched and somehow shameful." Despite his handicap, he drives a car and takes active part in Home Guard exercises.

Dan Fortune, in novels by Michael Collins, lacks his left arm and takes bleak comfort from the fact that he is right-handed. As a lawless seventeen-year-old he was looting a ship when he fell into a hold, smashing the arm so badly that amputation was necessary. Though always aware of his loss, he has developed "good legs and quick wits" in compensation and when matched against a single opponent can still fight and win.

Martin Cotterell is John Trench's detective, an archaeologist who lost his left hand in the desert during the Second World War. His "aluminium substitute" is attached by a harness and "covered by a glove." It allows him to drive and scale walls until it is "crushed and flattened" by a rock hurled by a murderer. Afterward, he needs help with his shoelaces. Later still, with a new "metal hook," he wards off a "swinging right" and disarms a youth with a razor.

In *Traitor's Purse* (1941) Albert *Campion suffers from amnesia and cannot recall his name, let alone the threat to national security he is working to avert. The story gains extraordinary tension from the cloud over Campion's brain: He has to rediscover not only the national secret but also himself.

—B. A. Pike

DISAPPEARANCES. *See* Kidnapping; Missing Persons.

DISGUISE. The use of disguise probably constitutes the oldest crime and mystery ploy, helping to complicate the *plot, establish the need for detection, and create *suspense regarding the identities of innocent and guilty. Often a climactic emotional moment occurs when the individual who has appeared to be the *least likely suspect is revealed as innocent, and the true *villain is exposed. In each instance the mode of disguise fits the crime; sometimes it is comical, sometimes deadly, but always it is an integral plot element in mysteries that involve spying, duplicity, equivocation, and betrayal.

The earliest English detective to assume false identities is Inspector Bucket in Charles *Dickens's *Bleak House* (1853), but the most famous is Arthur Conan *Doyle's Sherlock *Holmes, whose skill at disguise is one of his most prominent traits. On several occasions, his capacity for physical disguise is so convincing that he succeeds in fooling even Dr. John H. *Watson, as well as Inspector Lestrade of *Scotland Yard.

Others who employed disguise successfully include Albert *Campion in Margery *Allingham's *Sweet Danger* (1933; *Kingdom of Death*; *The Fear Sign*, 1961), who disguises himself as a maiden lady to break a case; and Dorothy L. *Sayers's series character Lord Peter *Wimsey. In *Murder Must Advertise* (1933), Wimsey plays several parts, including that of a harlequin, as he goes from group to group to test characters' reactions to him. John Dickson *Carr's series character Dr. Gideon *Fell dresses up as a cop in *The Mad Hatter Mystery* (1933) and as Professor von Hornswoggle in *The Eight of Swords* (1934). In *The Unicorn Murders* (1935), which Carr authored under the name Carter Dickson, the murderer, *victim, and detective all assume at least one disguise to manipulate people.

The ambiguous figure of the criminal who represents himself as a hero is an essential feature of detective novels, in which the disguised character wants to elude detection or deceive witnesses. This criminal-in-disguise motif appears in Agatha *Christie's *The Murder of Roger Ackroyd* (1926). In Christie's *The Secret Adversary* (1922), master of disguises Mr. Brown leads a plot to foment a general strike and even conceals his true identity to help Tommy and Tuppence Beresford with their detection. Other Christie disguisers include an international jewel thief (*The Secret of Chimneys*, 1925), four archcriminals intent on destroying the world order (*The Big Four*, 1927), and a burglar disguised as an archaeologist (*The Murder at the Vicarage*, 1930).

A most unusual disguise appears in Jane Langton's *Dark Nantucket Noon* (1975) when a man uses nature as his cover. Both Sophie Lang in Frederick Irving Anderson's *The Notorious Sophie Lang* (1925) and Four Square Jane in Edgar *Wallace's *Four Square Jane* (1929) are burglars who quickly change their appearance at the first sign of a policeman. The criminals in Sayers's *Unnatural Death* (1927; *The Dawson Pedigree*, 1929) and *Have His Carcase* (1932) also use disguises and establish double identities; in the latter, the criminal even has disguised accomplices.

Another variation occurs when a victim is disguised and must be unveiled before the crime can be solved; sometimes hidden beneath the disguise is a relationship between husbands and wives or between lovers. The potential victim may pose as a gentleman, but hide a dark secret, as does the evil Mr. Shaitana in Christie's *Cards on the Table* (1936), or pose as a philanthropist, as does the American kidnapper in *Murder on the Orient Express* (1934; *Murder in the Calais Coach*, 1934). The victim in Carr's *The Crooked Hinge* (1938) is a false claimant to a considerable country estate, and in *The Sleeping Sphinx* (1947) she is an adulteress masquerading as a respectable woman. In Nicholas *Blake's *The Widow's Cruise* (1959), the murderer impersonates the victim; the truth about Ianthe Ambrose reveals the killer's identity, motive, and modus operandi. In *Thou Shell of Death* (1936; *Shell of Death*) Fergus O'Brien actively collaborates in his own demise. Terminally ill and looking for a dramatic death, he poses as a victim of a staged knife fight, but not before he injects a walnut with poison, knowing that one of his targets will eat it.

In stories in which nothing is as it seems, the character in disguise misleads the more thoroughly persuasive he or she is, and is thus the ultimate reminder that this genre is always about the difficulty of identifying truth and the ease of deception.

[*See also* Adler, Irene; Circus and Carnival Milieu; Theatrical Milieu.]

• Page Heldenbrand, "Sherlock Holmes in Disguise," *Baker Street Journal: An Irregular Quarterly of Sherlockiana* (Jan. 1946): 318–22. Joy Rea, "Sherlock Holmes; Master Dramatist," *Baker Street Journal: An Irregular Quarterly of Sherlockiana* (Jan. 1954): 5–11. LeRoy Lad Panek, *Watteau's Shepherds: The Detective Novel in Britain, 1914–1940* (1979). Julian Symons, *Bloody Murder: From the Detective Story to the Crime Novel: A History*, rev. ed. (1985). T. J. Binyon, "*Murder Will Out*": *The Detective in Fiction* (1989).

—Dale Salwak

"DON'S DELIGHTS." *See* Academic Milieu; Academic Sleuth; Cambridge; Oxford.

DOPPELGANGERS. *See* Red Flags.

DOSTOYEVSKY, FYODOR MIKHAYLOVICH (1821–1881), Russian novelist and journalist. He entered the army as an engineer but resigned in 1844 to write. Sentenced to death in 1849 as one of a utopian socialist circle but reprieved immediately before execution, he was exiled to Siberia until 1859, spending 1850–54 in prison, of which *Notes from the House of the Dead* (1862; *Zapiski iz myortvogo doma*) gives a fictionalized account. Though his four great novels—*Crime and Punishment* (1866; *Prestupleniye i nakazaniye*), *The Idiot* (1868; *Idiot*), *The Possessed* (1872; *Besy*), and *The Brothers Karamazov* (1880; *Brat'ya Karamazovy*)—all deal with *murder, Dostoyevsky is not primarily interested in the detection of the crime or the psychology of the criminal. He sees murder as the result of the infection of society by Western ideas encouraging the selfish assertion of the individual will. In opposition to this he puts forward a Russian ideal of self-sacrifice and, in *The Brothers Karamazov*, the doctrine that all are guilty for the sins of all, in later journalism proclaiming Russia's messianic mission to save Europe. Dostoyevsky had a profound influence on subsequent Russian literature and thought. In the West he has been in the twentieth century the most widely read and influential of all Russian authors, as can be seen in the work, for example, of Albert Camus, André Malraux, and Jean-Paul Sartre. However, despite his remark, "I am called a psychologist; it is untrue, I am merely a realist in the highest sense of the word," he has been more generally viewed as a master of psychological narrative (Freud, "Dostoyevsky and Parricide," 1928). The crime novel, from R. L. Stevenson's *Dr. Jekyll and Mr. Hyde* (1886) onward, owes much to him: Most portrayals of lonely, obsessed murderers can be traced back to that of Raskolnikov in *Crime and Punishment*.

[*See also* Crime Novel; Europe, Crime and Mystery Writing in Continental: Russia.]

• René Wellek, ed., *Dostoevsky: A Collection of Critical Essays* (1962). Joseph Frank, *Dostoevsky*, 3 vols. (1979–88).

—T. J. Binyon

DOUBLE BLUFF is a technique of seducing the reader into making erroneous assumptions about the murderer or the *victim, or about the *villain's *motive, method, or *alibi, or about the detective's accuracy. Given that the author plays fair by following certain *conventions of the genre and presenting straightforward *clues, the reader ought to be able to deduce the correct solution to the case. But with the double bluff, the author manipulates accurate information so that the reader draws inaccurate inferences. The double bluff capitalizes on the reader's desire to try to outguess both *sleuth and writer; this is an example of the close engagement between writer and reader in the mystery genre. State the evidence, advises Raymond *Chandler, and the reader will mislead himself.

Wilkie *Collins, in *The Moonstone* (1868), was one of the earliest writers to demonstrate how to lure the reader into looking in the wrong direction by distributing suspicion among a number of candidates, one of whom turns out to be guilty. Robert Orr Chipperfield's *The Man in the Jury Box* (1921) offers a variation; here the guilty person turns out to be the *least likely suspect—a juror. Similar bluffs cause the reader to overlook the *guilt of unlikely suspects in Bernard Capes's *The Skeleton Key* (1919; *The Mystery of the Skeleton Key*) and Agatha *Christie's *The Murder of Roger Ackroyd* (1926). In a related twist, the reader presumes that an innocent man is guilty

(Christie's *The ABC Murders*, 1936; *The Alphabet Murders*) because he happens to be on the scene of all three murders.

Writers have devised numerous variations of the double bluff. The reader may believe the detective to be right when he is wrong, as in E. C. *Bentley's *Trent's Last Case* (1913; *The Woman in Black*). Or a suspect is initially cleared by an apparently unbreakable *alibi, but later turns out to be guilty after all, as in Freeman Wills *Crofts's *The Cask* (1920) and Ronald A. *Knox's *The Viaduct Murder* (1925). In Christie's *The Mysterious Affair at Styles* (1920), the obvious suspect hopes to be tried and acquitted so that he cannot be arrested for the same crime again. But Hercule *Poirot sees through the plan, prevents the arrest, and uncovers the flawed alibi. The reader is bluffed into dismissing the suspect because Poirot seems to be proving his innocence.

A popular variation is the false explanation. At the end of *The Burning Court* (1937), John Dickson *Carr indicates which of two explanations is correct, the false one having been put forward to conceal the true one. In *Drop to His Death* (1939; *Fatal Descent*), written by Carr as Carter Dickson, a theory advanced early in the book and subsequently discounted turns out to be the real solution after all. Peter Lovesey's *The False Inspector Dew* (1982) lulls the reader into accepting one solution to the crime, then reverses it, repeatedly instilling doubt in the reader's mind. The many parallel plots in Jane Langton's *The Transcendental Murder* (1964; *The Minuteman Murder*) are pure bluffs, intended to encourage the reader to leap to the wrong conclusion.

[*See also* Ingenuity: Rules of the Game.]

• Dorothy L. Sayers, introduction to *The Omnibus of Crime* (1929): 9–47. Dorothy L. Sayers, "Aristotle on Detective Fiction," *English* (January 1936): 23–35. Jacques Barzun, ed., *The Delights of Detection* (1961). John Dickson Carr, "The Grandest Game in the World," in *The Mystery Writer's Art*, ed. Francis M. Nevins (1970): 227–47. H. R. F. Keating, ed., *Agatha Christie: First Lady of Crime* (1977).

—Dale Salwak

DOUBLEDAY CRIME CLUB. One of the best-known publishing imprints in the crime and mystery genre, the Doubleday Crime Club was the brainchild of Daniel Longwell, Doubleday's advertising manager in the late 1920s. After a 1927 buying trip to England, Longwell decided to profit by the immense popularity of Edgar *Wallace's "thrillers" and the work of the authors who made up the newly formed *Detection Club by issuing a dedicated line of mystery novels with an identifiable logo. 1 April 1928, was the publication date of the first Crime Club book, *The Desert Moon Mystery* (1928) by Kay Cleaver Strahan. It wore what was to become the distinctive black cloth cover highlighted with crimson-inked titles and the Crime Club Gunman logo. The logo is made up of the letters that spell "crime," and it appeared on every book during the sixty-three-year history of the Crime Club. In the imprint's first three years, Doubleday published more than 150 books in the new series, prompting several other publishers to start their own mystery lines in the hope of duplicating the Crime

Club's popularity and profits. The Great Depression forced Doubleday for eleven months to reduce the price of the first editions to one dollar and for a period of several years to limit the number of titles.

Members of the Crime Club received their copies of the monthly main selection in advance of those readers who would either purchase one at a bookstore or borrow a copy through the then popular lending libraries. For many years the dust jackets for these member editions had a distinct motif, and the covers of these books were red cloth instead of the customary black. Dust jackets commissioned during the 1930s were cleverly designed, usually with vivid colors, and reflected the book's contents. Many covers were drawn by artists who later became well known in the commercial and fine art fields, often as illustrators of children's books. Notable artists who designed Crime Club dust jackets included Boris Artzybasheff, Paul Galdone, Vera Bock, and Andy Warhol.

In 1943 longtime editor Isabelle Taylor originated the Crime Club Bullseyes, a series of symbols classifying each book. The symbols were printed on the spine and on the bound-in blurb. They identified favorite categories popular with authors, readers, booksellers, and librarians. Among these symbols were a grinning skull that designated humor and homicide, an owl that promised suspense, and a shooting gun that suggested fast action. During this period, forty-eight books a year were usually published, even though World War II brought a major paper shortage that reduced print runs, trim size, and paper quality. Print runs increased after the war, but production values never matched their prewar levels.

During the sixty-three years that the Doubleday Crime Club was in existence, it published 2,492 titles and furthered the careers of such authors as Leslie *Charteris, Aaron Marc Stein, Margaret *Millar, Mignon G. *Eberhart, Charlotte MacLeod, Barbara Paul, Sax *Rohmer, and Jonathan Latimer.

—Ellen A. Nehr

Dover, Wilfred, comic *police detective created by Joyce *Porter. Detective Inspector Wilfred Dover is the *antihero of ten *police procedurals, beginning with *Dover One* (1964). Rude, overweight, lazy, hypochondriacal, slovenly, selfish, mean, occasionally violent, and always incompetent, Dover has achieved promotion only through being "kicked upstairs" by colleagues who could bear him no longer. He enjoys thwarting his priggish but competent assistant, Sergeant MacGregor, who longs to be transferred away from the man.

With his cynical view of humanity and inability to comprehend the importance of facts, Dover cares little if his chosen suspect is guilty or innocent. The isolated villages in which he works are parodies of the cozy milieus of Agatha *Christie's Miss Jane *Marple, populated by men and women equally mean-spirited and narrow who hinder Dover's search for creature comforts. In the end, circumstances and the *villain's own stupidity ensure that *justice, of a sort, is done.

[*See also* Country Constable; English Village Milieu.]

—Chris Gausden

DOYLE, ARTHUR CONAN (1859–1930), creator of the most famous detective in literature, Sherlock *Holmes, and his almost equally celebrated confidant, Dr. John H. *Watson. The second child and eldest son of Charles Doyle, who added to his small salary as a civil servant in the Scottish Office of Works by book illustration and painting, Doyle was born in Edinburgh, educated at the great Catholic school Stonyhurst, and decided on a medical career. In 1876 he enrolled at Edinburgh University, and five years later took his degree as bachelor of medicine. His father had declined into alcoholism and mental illness, and most of the decade before his death in 1893 was spent in nursing and mental homes. Doyle knew he must help to support his family. In 1882 he set up practice in Southsea, a small town on the south coast of England.

Doyle was by nature a man of action. He was an excellent cricketer and boxer, and before starting his own practice had made trips as ship's doctor to West Africa and the Arctic. But he was also ambitious to be a writer, and supplemented his modest income by writing short stories. In 1885 he married Louise Hawkins, the sister of a patient, and two years later published the first Holmes story, *A Study in Scarlet*, in *Beeton's Christmas Annual*. He sold the story outright for a mere £25.

The deductive powers of Holmes were based in part on those shown by Dr. Joseph Bell, one of Doyle's Edinburgh tutors. But the creation of Holmes owed something also to Edgar Allan *Poe's detective, the Chevalier C. Auguste *Dupin, to the French writer Émile *Gaboriau, and to the combination of mystical feeling with logical power and deductive skill in Doyle himself. This first Holmes novel was not particularly popular, nor was the second, *The Sign of the Four* (1890; *The Sign of Four*). In 1891, however, the appearance of six Holmes short stories in the newly founded *Strand magazine made their writer almost instantly famous.

To become famous as the creator of a fictional detective was almost an embarrassment for Doyle. He valued his historical novels much more highly, and both *Micah Clarke* (1889) and *The White Company* (1891) were popular and received critical praise. When two series of Holmes short stories had appeared, Doyle sent Holmes to his death in the embrace of the arch-villain Professor James *Moriarty. He told friends of his relief at being rid of the detective who, he said, kept him from better things. But popular demand and indignation were great, and Doyle felt it impossible to deny them.

After eight years' absence Holmes returned in *The Hound of the Baskervilles* (1902), and from then until Doyle's death Holmes stories alternated with other books and short stories, including the books and articles about the Spiritualist movement that increasingly absorbed Doyle in his last years. And at times the writing of fiction was subordinated to his activities as a public figure, something acknowledged when he was knighted in 1902. He was in command of a medical unit during the Boer War, and worked as what would now be called a war correspondent and propagandist in World War I. He was also a devoted family man. His first wife died in 1906, and in the following year he married Jean Leckie. There were two children of the first marriage, three of the second.

For his early readers the very character of Holmes revolutionized the crime story. To them he appeared a kind of intellectual Nietzschean superman in his ability to make amazing deductions and to dispense *justice when the law was erratic or impotent. For us it is the relationship between Holmes and Watson that comes through most clearly, and the world of gas lighting and Baker Street fogs that in the 1890s was very real now has a period charm.

The fifty-six short stories are more successful than the four novels. Their length is just right for the pyrotechnic display of Holmes's deductive skills, whereas the greater length places a strain on them. The difficulty Doyle found in maintaining the baffling phrases and ingenious deceptions called for by Holmes's presence is shown by the fact that three of the novels contain material relating to the past with which the detective had nothing to do. Even in the fourth, *The Hound of the Baskervilles*, there are several chapters in which Watson investigates and Holmes remains offstage.

There are factual flaws in the stories but they don't affect a reader's enjoyment, any more than do the inconsistencies in the depiction of Holmes that sprang in part from the need Doyle felt to make the detective less egotistic and more humanly agreeable. The stories survive triumphantly because Doyle was a greatly gifted story teller, and the best of the short stories are among his finest tales. It is not just the deductions that are gripping, nor even the relationship of Holmes and Watson, although this is one of the great partnerships in literature, along with that of Don Quixote and Sancho Panza.

The effect of these things is enhanced by that element of Celtic mysticism and sense of unease derived perhaps from Charles Doyle, whose drawings are full of fantastic figures sometimes merely whimsical but at other times frightening. There are elements in the Holmes stories that make one shiver on a second or tenth reading. They include the sound made by the snake as it comes down the bell rope in "The Adventure of The Speckled Band," the electric blue dress Miss Hunter is asked to wear in "The Adventure of the Copper Beeches," and the bloody, gory mess of Victor Hatherley's missing thumb in "The Adventure of the Engineer's Thumb," all of which are collected in *The Adventures of Sherlock Holmes* (1892). This element of something outside the stresses of everyday living pulses dangerously through many of the stories. They are a prime example of a writer working better, digging deeper, than he knew or intended. Quite casually, and without the wish to do so, Doyle created some of the finest short stories in crime or any other sort of literature.

• Hesketh Pearson, *Conan Doyle: His Life and Art* (1943). John Dickson Carr, *The Life of Sir Arthur Conan Doyle* (1949). Pierre Nordon, *Conan Doyle: A Biography*. Translated from the French by Frances Partridge (1966). Ronald Pearsall, *Conan Doyle: A Biographical Solution* (1977). H. R. F. Keating, *Sherlock Holmes: The Man and His World* (1979). Owen Dudley Edwards, *The Quest for Sherlock Holmes: A Biographical Study of the Early Life of Sir Arthur Conan Doyle* (1982).

—Julian Symons

Drew, Nancy. Nancy Drew is a girl sleuth created in 1929 by Edward Stratemeyer, who died in 1930, leaving the series in the charge of his daughter, Harriet Stratemeyer Adams. While Adams always claimed Nancy Drew as her "personal project," recent research credits Mildred Wirt Benson with writing most of the early stories, though Adams, of course, retained editorial control. The novels in which Drew appeared were written under the pseudonym Carolyn *Keene.

The series has been a staple for American girls aged eight to fourteen since the first book, *Secret of the Old Clock* (1930) appeared. The enduring attraction lies not in the *plots but in the Drew persona. She transcends the limitations of her young age (sixteen in the early books, eighteen later) and of her gender as few girls could in real life. The daughter of an attorney, she is independent, resourceful, unbeatably competent at absolutely everything, unfailingly successful at her sleuthing, respected and loved by all except "crooks" and the occasional jealous peer. She has two friends, George Fayne and Bess Marvin, and a boyfriend, Ned Nickerson, who is away at college.

The *formula keeps the spotlight on Drew. Never secondary to a male or an adult character, she is always the hero of the adventure, solving mysteries through intelligence, perseverance, and courage, accepting her well-deserved plaudits with becoming modesty. And all this she accomplishes without rejecting her femininity. Adams consistently denied feminist intentions, and nothing in the series she oversaw overtly contradicts her. Although the feminist messages in the Nancy Drew stories were powerful, they were veiled by a wholly conventional surface, allowing girls of every generation since 1930 to read them with both joy and comfort.

[See also Juvenile Sleuth: Girl Sleuth.]

• Bobbie Ann Mason, *The Girl Sleuth: A Feminist Guide* (1975). Deidre Ann Johnson, *Stratemeyer Pseudonyms and Series Books* (1982). Carol Billman, *Nancy Drew, the Hardy Boys, and the Million Dollar Fiction Factory* (1986). Anita Susan Grossman, "The Ghost of Nancy Drew," *Ohio Magazine* 10 (Dec. 1987): 41–43, 82–84.   —Anne Scott MacLeod

Drood, Edwin, a character in *The Mystery of Edwin Drood*, Charles *Dickens's last, uncompleted novel, serialized in 1870. Drood was by no means central to the story— as Dickens noted, "I call my book the Mystery, not the History of Edwin Drood." The spotlight instead was to be on John Jasper, an opium addict and the guardian of Rosa Budd, to whom Drood has been betrothed. Upon Drood's disappearance from the narrative, the presumption is that he has been murdered. The point is reinforced by the characterization, of Drood, who, being neither too sympathetic nor too contemptible, possesses qualities appropriate to a *victim. In conceiving *Edwin Drood* as a mystery, Dickens is thought to have been responding to the challenge presented by his friend Wilkie *Collins in *The Moonstone* (1868); for the reader, however, it is the book's unfinished state that gives it the air of a *whodunit.

- J. Cuming Walters, *The Complete Mystery of Edwin Drood* (1912). Felix Aylmer, *The Drood Case* (1964). Ray Dubberke, *Dickens, Drood, and the Detectives* (1992).

—Barrie Hayne

Drummond, Bulldog, hero of a series of fast-paced *thrillers written by H. C. *McNeile under the pseudonym "Sapper." Fighting *evil in a number of its forms—communism in the early novels, straightforward crime as well as assorted conspiracies that threaten Britain in the later ones—Hugh "Bulldog" Drummond is a representative of a wealthy upper-middle class equated with the British nation as such. Supported by his author-creator in his contempt for the law, which is viewed as a middle-class creation, Drummond takes things into his own hands in order to save the nation from criminals who are equally insensitive to the law's majesty and to the higher natural law that Drummond intuitively obeys. Well served by his enormous physical strength, his penetrating common sense, a "gang" of old war comrades (all officers, of course), and an extensive old-boy network upon which he can draw, Drummond unfailingly corners his criminal prey. He rounds off the hunt with a bout of combat—preferably unarmed but deadly nevertheless. One suspects that his taste for adventure was his reason for getting involved in the first place.

[*See also* Heroism.]

—Hans Bertens

DU MAURIER, DAPHNE (1907–1989), British author of historical romances and mystery novels. Du Maurier was born on 13 May in *London, daughter of Muriel (Beaumont) du Maurier and the actor Gerald du Maurier, and granddaughter of George du Maurier, author of *Trilby* (1894). She was educated privately and at a Parisian boarding school. In 1926, the du Mauriers bought Ferryside, a converted boathouse on the River Fowey in Cornwall. Here du Maurier began work on her first novel, a romance, *The Loving Spirit* (1931). In 1932 she married army major F. A. M. Browning; they had two daughters and a son and lived in Cornwall, in an ancient home, Menabilly, a few miles from Ferryside. Menabilly suggested the setting for her most popular work, *Rebecca* (1938), which is both a *Gothic novel and a murder mystery. Isolated at a remote seacoast estate, Manderley, with her brooding husband and a hostile housekeeper, the unnamed narrator of *Rebecca* feels caught in the spell of the first Mrs. de Winter, Rebecca, and the mystery surrounding her death. The book, reminiscent of Charlotte Brontë's *Jane Eyre* (1847) in its depiction of jealousy and madness, was extraordinarily successful, and du Maurier used similar elements—haunted landscapes, obsessional personalities, and sexual tensions—in other novels, notably *My Cousin Rachel* (1951), whose narrator struggles to determine his cousin's *guilt or innocence in her husband's poisoning. Du Maurier's short stories are marked by a sense of menace and bizarre psychological twists. Among the best known, both

published in *The Apple Tree: A Short Novel, and Some Stories* (1952; *Kiss Me Again, Stranger: A Collection of Eight Stories, Long and Short; The Birds and Other Stories*), are "The Birds," in which birds turn on humans, and "Kiss Me Again Stranger," in which a cemetery is the scene of a sinister sexual encounter. *Not After Midnight and Other Stories* (1971; *Don't Look Now*) includes "Don't Look Now," a story of *mistaken identities involving psychic twins and a dwarf. Like many of du Maurier's works, it was made into a popular film. Du Maurier, who became Lady Browning in 1946 and Dame Daphne in 1969, was in 1977 awarded the title of Grand Master by the Mystery Writers of America.

[*See also* Females and Feminists; Had-I-But-Known; Suspense.]

- Daphne du Maurier, *Growing Pains: The Shaping of a Writer* (1977; *Myself When Young: The Shaping of a Writer*). Margaret Forster, *Daphne du Maurier: The Secret of Life of the Renowned Storyteller* (1993).

—Mary Rose Sullivan

Dupin, The Chevalier C. Auguste, French *amateur detective created by Edgar Allan *Poe. Usually regarded as the first significant fictional detective, Dupin appeared in three stories: "The Murders in the Rue Morgue" (*Graham's Lady's and Gentleman's Magazine*, Apr. 1841), "The Mystery of Marie Roget" (*Snowden's Lady's Companion*, 2 Nov. 1842), based on the murder of Mary Rogers in New Jersey, and "The Purloined Letter" (*The Gift*, 1844). In these hugely influential stories Poe created the fictional detective so familiar thereafter. Dupin is an isolated figure, a *private detective who takes only those cases which stimulate his imagination. Well aware of his intellectual superiority, Dupin is particularly contemptuous of the painstakingly unimaginative methods of the police. He is accompanied on his cases by an unnamed friend, the narrator of the stories.

Dupin's friend provides few facts about the detective's personal life, undoubtedly because Poe wished to base Dupin's characterization exclusively upon his intellect. According to the narrator, apparently an American residing in Paris, Dupin, though from an "illustrious" family, has been reduced by a series of misfortunes to poverty and lives on a small inherited income. The two men meet in an obscure library where they are both in search of the same rare volume. Finding that they are kindred spirits, they move into a "time-eaten and grotesque mansion" in a "retired and desolate portion of the Fauberg St. Germain." A year later, after Dupin has solved the mystery in the rue Morgue, they are still together in the Fauberg St. Germain, though their residence is no longer described as a mansion, but as "chambers" at 33, rue Dunot.

The narrator never describes Dupin physically, confining himself to his friend's "mental character." Perhaps Dupin's most noteworthy idiosyncrasy, shared by his friend, is his fondness for darkness. At dawn he shutters all his windows, preferring the feeble rays of a couple of perfumed tapers for light. Indeed, when meditating, he prefers total darkness. Only at night does he venture out, "seeking . . . that infinity of mental excitement which quiet observation can afford."

Dupin's cases are built upon this contrast between physical darkness and intellectual illumination. In "The Purloined Letter," for example, Dupin is sitting in the dark when he is visited by Monsieur G, the "contemptible" prefect of the Parisian police, who scoffs at Dupin's "off idea" that physical darkness aids reflection. Monsieur G needs Dupin's help in finding a politically damaging letter, which has been stolen and hidden by the despicable Minister D. Characteristically, the prefect's method has been to tear up the Minister D's apartment in a vain attempt to bring to light what is hidden. Dupin, by contrast, takes no action at all until he deduces where the letter *must* be. Believing that the intellect creates its own light, Dupin places himself in the criminal's mind and concludes that the letter is not hidden at all.

In the first two Dupin stories, Poe seems to be groping toward a fiction to represent this idea. "The Murders in the Rue Morgue" seems at first to qualify. Dupin does correctly deduce that the murderer must be "of an agility astounding, a strength superhuman . . . and a voice foreign in tone to the ears of men of many nations." However, instead of following his train of thought to its logical conclusion (that the murderer must be an animal), he shows his friend a tuft of hair, apparently ignored by the Parisian police, which he found clutched in the murder victim's hand. His friend immediately comments that "this is no *human* hair," thus rendering Dupin's deductions utterly unnecessary. In the painstaking "Mystery of Marie Roget," Dupin's deductions are inconclusive at best. Only in "The Purloined Letter" does Poe provide his detective with a case truly worthy of his deductive powers. With this one brilliant solution, Dupin takes his place beside the greatest of fictional detectives.

[*See also* Eccentrics; Great Detective, The; Reasoning, Types of.]

• Robert L. Gale, *Plots and Characters in the Fiction and Poetry of Edgar Allan Poe* (1970) Umberto Eco and Thomas A. Sebeok, eds., *The Sign of Three: Dupin, Holmes, Peirce* (1983). John T. Irvin, *The Mystery to a Solution: Poe, Borges, and the Analytic Detective Story* (1994).   —Richard Steiger

DÜRRENMATT, FRIEDRICH (1921–1990), Swiss dramatist and fiction writer. Dürrenmatt received his secondary education in Bern, studied literature and philosophy in Zurich, and returned to his home city to attend the University of Bern. His first published narrative titled "Der Alte" ("The Old Man") appeared in 1945 in a Bern newspaper. After marrying Lotti Geissler, he pursued a career as playwright and novelist. His first dramatic success on the German-speaking stage was an account of community corruption, *Der Besuch der alten Dame* (1956; *The Visit*).

The first of his detective novels, *Der Richter und sein Henker* (1950; *The Judge and His Hangman*) introduces Kommissar Bärlach of Berne. A famous detective who faces death from inoperable cancer, Bärlach echoes the character of the loner detective established in American hard-boiled writing. The

Bärlach debut novel and its sequel, *Der Verdacht* (1951; *The Quarry*) originally appeared as serials in the Bernese *Beobachter* before being published as books. In *The Quarry*, Dürrenmatt gives his interest in philosophy broad scope through analysis of the character of the nihilistic villain Emmenberger, a sadistic physician who it seems was once, under another name, a doctor in a concentration camp who operated on patients without the use of anesthesia. *Das Versprechen* (1958; *The Pledge*), Dürrenmatt's third detective narrative, commits a parodic critique of the genre that the author evidently believed falsified reality by forcing it into literary formulas. Dürrenmatt's final work that critics assign to the mystery genre was *Die Panne* both a radio play and a short novel, translated as *Traps* (1956). In addition to the influence of hard-boiled detective fiction, critics also descry similarities in Dürrenmatt's work to the fiction of Franz Kafka and Fyodor Dostoyevsky.

[*See also* Police Detective; Sleuth as Loner.]

• Gordon N. Leah, "Dürrenmatt's Detective Stories," *Modern Languages* 48 (1967): 65–69. Murray B. Peppard, *Friedrich Dürrenmatt* (1969).   —John Michielsen

DYING MESSAGE. The *clue of the dying message, usually the written or spoken words of a murder victim just before death, has been a staple of mystery fiction for more than a century; it is one of the few elements of the genre that did not originate with Edgar Allan *Poe. The first use of a dying message probably came in Arthur Conan *Doyle's "The Boscombe Valley Mystery," in which Sherlock *Holmes determines that a dying man's reference to "a rat" really refers to someone from the Australian city of Ballarat. From that story in the *Strand* (Oct. 1891) to the present time, the dying message has been enlarged and refined to serve as a clue in scores of novels and hundreds of short stories.

One of the earliest uses of a dying message in a novel occurs in Agatha *Christie's first book, *The Mysterious Affairs at Styles* (1920), and by the time she wrote *The Seven Dials Mystery* (1929) she had added a neat double twist to the gimmick. In these books, as in Mignon G. *Eberhart's *Fair Warning* (1936), the *victim actually speaks the killer's name, but the listener does not realize the true import of the words. In John Dickson *Carr's *The Three Coffins* (1935; *The Hollow Man*) a victim names his killer, but evidence seems to show that the person must be innocent.

The title itself is the dying message in Christie's *Why Didn't They Ask Evans?* (1934), and it is an extremely clever one. The dying message is used, as a major or minor plot element, in novels as different from one another as Christie's *The Big Four* (1927), Dashiell *Hammett's *Red Harvest* (1929), Nicholas *Blake's *The Whisper in the Gloom* (1954), and John Dickson *Carr's *Patrick Butler for the Defense* (1956).

By its very nature, the dying message is seldom enough to carry an entire novel. For this reason, some of the best examples of the dying message are found in short stories. Doyle returned to the device in "The Adventure of the Speckled Band" (*Strand*, Feb.

1892) and "The Adventure of the Lion's Mane" (*The Casebook of Sherlock Holmes*, 1927), in both cases hinting at the creatures responsible for the deaths. There is even a dying message of sorts in Hammett's hard-boiled "Fly Paper" (*Black Mask*, Aug. 1929). Anthony *Boucher often used dying messages in his short stories. A deck of cards and a cribbage score figure in "Coffin Corner" (in *The Female of the Species*, ed. Ellery Queen, 1943.) and a Library of Congress book classification number in "QL696.C9" (*EQMM*, May 1943). Perhaps Boucher's crowning dying message appears in a short-short, "The Ultimate Clue" (*EQMM*, Oct. 1960). To identify which member of a football team has stabbed him, the dying man ripped the last page from a nearby book—a page that said "The End."

No writer during his career worked more variations on the dying message than did Ellery *Queen, in both novels and short stories. An early novel, *The Siamese Twin Mystery* (1933), devotes much attention to examining half of a playing card found clutched in the dead man's hand. Does the crumpled six of spades indicate the initials of Sarah Isere Xavier, the victim's wife? It is a false clue placed there by the real killer? What can Ellery deduce from the smudged fingerprint on the card? In a later novel, *The Scarlet Letters* (1953), a complex blackmail scheme runs through the letters of the alphabet until *murder finally occurs in the penultimate chapter and the dying man writes a bloody "XY" on the wall.

Two of Queen's novels about retired actor Drury Lane also feature dying messages. In *The Tragedy of X* (1932), the dying man crosses his fingers to form an X, a clue to the killer's occupation. In *The Tragedy of Z* (1933), the dying man's words are unimportant, but the fact that he was alive and able to speak them is vital.

It was in the short story that Queen excelled in variations on the dying message. An early story, "the Adventure of the Glass-Domed Clock" (*Mystery League Magazine*, Oct. 1933) and presents a false dying message, and another, "The Adventure of the Bearded Lady" (*Mystery*, Aug. 1934), has a visual message—a beard painted on a woman's portrait by the dying man. In other stories dying words are misunderstood. "Pair of dice" is heard as "paradise" in "Diamonds in Paradise" (*EQMM*, Sept. 1954), and "heroin" becomes "heroine" in "The Death of Don Juan" (*Argosy*, May 1962). In a late Queen story, "The Reindeer Clue" (*National Inquirer*, 23 Dec. 1975), the *victim indicates the names of Santa Claus's reindeer, one of which has a connection with a *suspect's name.

• R. W. Hays, "The Clue of the Dying Message," *Armchair Detective* 7, no. 1 (Nov. 1973).   —Edward D. Hoch

EBERHART, MIGNON G(OOD) (1899–1996), American mystery writer, originally associated with the *Had-I-But-Known school of writing. Born in Lincoln, Nebraska, she was educated at Nebraska Wesleyan University, and after marriage her worldwide travels provided background for many of her novels.

The Patient in Room 18 (1929) and other early novels had medical settings in which her series character nurse Sarah Keate was rescued from the perils of inquisitiveness by detective Lance O'Leary. Similarly, the short stories in *The Cases of Susan Dare* (1934) show the eponymous protagonist enmeshed in *murder in menacing circumstances.

Eberhart later began to fuse mystery, romance, and neo-Gothic *suspense, showing perceptive exploration of psychology and *motivation. In more than fifty novels, from early titles like *The White Cockatoo* (1933) to *R.S.V.P. Murder* (1965) and *Alpine Condo Cross Fire* (1984), she also conveyed the feel and color of her *settings and exploited their potential for *evil.

[*See also* Menacing Characters; Visitors Abroad.]

—Melvyn Barnes

ECCENTRICS. Eccentric characters fit into detective and mystery fiction much as the Gravedigger fits into *Hamlet* or the Porter into *Macbeth*, with this difference: that the comic form and structure of mystery fiction assimilates them more easily, and rather than being commentators on the action—still less, comic relief—they become kinsmen to the main characters. It is significant that in *hard-boiled fiction, which moves closer to tragedy than does the classic form, eccentric characters are much less in evidence.

In Wilkie *Collins's *The Woman in White* and *The Moonstone*, eccentrics abound. In the former novel, the villain, Count Fosco, is comically eccentric, though no less formidable for that, and the ineffectual but malign Mr. Fairlie, comic in his obsessive avoidance of stress, is one of fiction's most convincing hypochondriacs. In the latter novel, both detectives, Sergeant *Cuff and Ezra Jennings, are eccentric outsiders, much of whose effectiveness derives from their being so. Two others, Mr. Candy and Miss Drusilla Clack, one of the supreme creations of the genre, add to the comedy of the novel as well as providing *clues to the final solution. This is the double function of the eccentric character.

In the Sherlock *Holmes Canon, aside from the spectacular example of the *Great Detective himself, there are relatively few eccentrics. What eccentricity there is is suggested through characters' names, from Enoch J. Drebber in the first story to Josiah Amberley in the last. Both are villains, and it is in those who live on the other side of the law that Doyle gives freest rein to eccentricity, from Grimesby Roylott and Professor James *Moriarty to Baron Gruner and Charles Augustus Milverton. But the run of Holmes's clients are commonplace enough, as witness Jabez Wilson, who "bore every mark of being an average commonplace British tradesman, obese, pompous and slow. There was nothing remarkable about the man save his blazing red head"—which may be eccentricity enough.

While Dorothy L. *Sayers peoples her novels with eccentrics, as Edmund Wilson noted, some of these both advance the *plot and are interesting in themselves. Miss Alexandra Katherine Climpson's spinsterhood, turned to account in her auxiliary detection, is a more striking metaphor for the aftermath of the Great War than Lord Peter *Wimsey's shellshock. And in the same conventional between-the-wars world of Agatha *Christie, there is an overplus of eccentrics: The dotty old ladies who live in St. Mary Mead fall easily into the category. Sometimes the eccentric brings murder upon himself, like Mr. Shaitana in *Cards on the Table* (1936), or the detestable Mrs. Boynton in *Appointment with Death* (1938); sometimes the eccentric uses her eccentricity either to conceal her involvement in the crime, as Evelyn Howard does in *The Mysterious Affair at Styles* (1920), or simply to cover up another's crime, as Lady Angkatell, one of Christie's most convincing eccentrics, does in *The Hollow* (1946; *Murder After Hours*).

Christie often deals with a stage *milieu, rich in eccentrics. Sayers's world is wider, from club types to academics, as well as the ducal family itself, and her range of the dithering and the vaguely confused is correspondingly wider as well. And in the successors to Christie and Sayers—mostly English, like Ruth *Rendell and P. D. *James, and occasionally American, like Martha Grimes—eccentricity, if not the norm, at least comes as little surprise.

One place besides the English village where eccentrics are in their element is the little world of the school or university. The prototype may be Sayers's *Gaudy Night* (1935), followed closely by Michael *Innes's *Death at the President's Lodging* (1936; *Seven Suspects*), and pursued more recently by Colin *Dexter and Robert *Barnard (*Death of an Old Goat*, 1974) on one side of the Atlantic, and on the other by Thomas Kyd, Amanda *Cross, and, in his first novel, *The Godwulf Manuscript* (1973), Robert B. *Parker. Robert Bernard's two novels, *Death Takes a Sabbatical* (1967; *Death Takes the Last Train*) and *Deadly Meeting* (1970), among the best in this subgenre, introduce the reader to a variety of academic eccentrics. Though most of these novels deal with the murderous side of college politics and with the clash between earthly policemen and idiosyncratic dons, much of the emphasis is on the idiosyncracies. And other closed circles—libraries (as in Jane Langton's *The Transcendental Murder*, 1964), monasteries (as in Umberto Eco's *The Name of the Rose* 1983), and even the army (as in Richard Brooks's *The Brick Foxhole*, 1945)—provide characters who diverge from the behavioral norm.

A writer rich in eccentrics, in part because he is one of the most Dickensian of contemporary authors, is John *Mortimer. The judges before whom Horace *Rumpole appears, at the *Old Bailey and elsewhere; his colleagues in chambers, especially the most recent head, the relentlessly pious "Soapy Sam" Ballard, and the gaga Uncle Tom, blithely putting golf balls into the wastepaper basket; and not least his clients, beginning with the hereditary criminals the Timsons—all these are of the first order of eccentrics, though recognizably kin to the main character himself. And Jonathan Gash's Lovejoy, the antique dealer à la A. J. *Raffles, has gathered around himself, both as auxiliaries and adversaries, a remarkable array of originals: Tinker and Lady Jane, and the egregious Charley Gimble.

If eccentrics seem to predominate in British fiction, the reason lies in its *farceur quality and in its broad commitment to the classic form. In hard-boiled fiction, Dashiell *Hammett's Joel Cairo and Gutman in *The Maltese Falcon* (1930), even Raymond *Chandler's Moose Malloy in *Farewell, My Lovely* (1940) are arguable examples, but the incidental character whose sole raison d'être is his eccentricity barely exists; even such as the old man who claims to have seen something of the mass killing across the road twenty years before in Loren D. Estleman's *Sugartown* (1984) is essential to the plot, as are the numerous oddballs Philip *Marlowe meets in the prosecution of his cases, on which characters such as Estleman's are based.

[*See also* Academic Milieu; Humor; Library Milieu; Villains and Villainy.]

—Barrie Hayne

EIGHTY-SEVENTH PRECINCT, THE. *See* McBain, Ed; Police Detective; Police Procedural.

ELDERLY SLEUTH. Because popular literature reflects popular culture, detective fiction has produced a growing number of writers whose protagonists are energetic senior citizens. The earlier tendency to present elderly sleuths as figures of ridicule or amusement has diminished, and far fewer caricatures occur. Mild eccentricity or idiosyncrasy does survive, but on the whole mature adults are represented as more integrated into society and are depicted more realistically than they were previously in the twentieth century.

The inquisitive elderly spinster sleuth flourished during the Golden Age and prevailed through World War II. Free of conventional family duties, the spinster had time to observe human behavior and analyze its motives and consequences. The American Anna Katharine *Green contributed the prototype for the middle-aged spinster sleuth in the character of Miss Amelia Butterworth in *That Affair Next Door* (1897). She was succeeded by such figures as Mary Roberts *Rinehart's Rachel Innes and Nurse Hilda Adams (a. k. a. Miss Pinkerton), Stuart Palmer's Miss Hildegarde *Withers, Charlotte Murray Russell's Jane Amanda Edwards, D. B. Olsen's Rachel and Jennifer Murdock, and Phyllis Bentley's Miss Marian Phipps. Not the first in Great Britain but perhaps the best known, Agatha *Christie's Miss Jane *Marple belongs to this group of redoubtable spinster sleuths which also includes Dorothy L. *Sayers's Miss Alexandra Katherine Climpson, Patricia *Wentworth's Miss Maud *Silver, and Josephine *Tey's Miss Lucy Pym.

A small group of widow sleuths contains professional police detectives. Also socially marginal figures, these characters are eccentric to the point of being grotesque. The blatant caricature leads one to infer that only unattractive female misfits would elect to become detectives or that social mores of the time would not countenance married women engaged in criminal investigation. The first to appear, Edgar *Wallace's Mrs. Jane (also Emily) Ollorby, is ugly but cheerful, stout but quick, sentimental but indefatigable. Inspired by Mrs. Ollorby, Nigel Morland's Mrs. Palmyra Pym is also a *Scotland Yard professional. Equally eccentric but less physically tough, Gladys *Mitchell's Dame Beatrice Adela Lestrange *Bradley is probably best remembered among the Golden Age widows; she is a psychiatrist who acts as a consultant to the Home Office. G. D. H. and Margaret *Cole's Mrs. Elizabeth Warrender, the most conventional of the four, is an amateur who creates a cozy home in Hampstead for her son James, a professional investigator. Subsequently in the U.S., Erle Stanley *Gardner writing as A. A. Fair introduced Mrs. Bertha Cool, whose gray hair and sturdy figure, forceful speech, rough manners, and driving ambition owe a great deal to her doughty predecessors.

The spinster's counterpart, the eccentric but sagacious middle-aged or elderly man, is embodied in the armchair detective, Bill Owen, created by Baroness *Orczy in a series of short stories published in the *Royal Magazine* (1901–04). He would sit in the corner of a London tea shop knotting and unknotting a piece of string while discussing the details of intricate cases with Polly Burton, a young woman journalist. As a priest, G. K. *Chesterton's Father *Brown is socially separated yet enabled by his calling to expose unobtrusively the peccadillos of his fellow man. Christie's Hercule *Poirot was already retired from the Belgian police force when he first surfaced in England in 1920. In terms of physical image, larger-than-life personality, and unorthodox methods, John Dickson *Carr's rumbustious amateur detectives, Dr. Gideon *Fell and Sir Henry *Merrivale, are the counterparts of the Golden Age widows. In America the single male sleuth can be found in Melville Davisson *Post's short stories featuring Uncle *Abner. Like Carr, Phoebe Atwood *Taylor created two detectives "of a certain age": Asey *Mayo, called the "Codfish Sherlock"; and writing as Alice Tilton, retired Professor Leonidas Xenophon Witherall, a.k.a. "Bill Shakespeare."

In the last quarter of the twentieth century, almost fifty mature detectives emerged. Significant shifts in marital status are apparent. Spinsters and bachelors have been replaced by widows and widowers as the most common type of unmarried sleuth. Mixed sex partnerships occur much more frequently than before World War II.

At least one old-fashioned spinster sleuth survives in Hamilton Crane's new series (1991) extending the career of Heron Carvic's retired drawing mistress and yoga adept, Miss Emily Seeton, a. k. a. "the Battling Brolly." But on the whole, the conventional English maiden ladies of the past have given way to more contemporary characters. In two novels by J. S. Borthwick, Sarah Deane's Aunt Julia Clancy is owner and operator of a riding stable. Mary Bowen Hall's crusty Emma Chizzit, a California salvage company owner who does both the bidding for jobs as well as the physical work of salvaging, breaks conventional "feminine" stereotypes concerning woman as the weaker sex without being unattractively "masculine."

Two divorcées joined the lists of amateur detectives in the 1990s. Stefanie Matteson's Charlotte Graham, an actress of some repute, becomes involved in uncovering foul play against exotic settings such as the Buddhist treasure caves at Dunhuang, China. In England, M. C. Beaton's Agatha Raisin, a public relations executive who sold her prosperous London firm and took early retirement at fifty-three, discovers that a knack for investigation staves off boredom in her too quiet country village.

Modern widows, who are numerous, can be divided into types: homemakers and professional women. While all are independent and resourceful, and a few are zany, none exhibit the bizarre behavior of earlier gender models. Among the homemakers first in the field was Dorothy Gilman's madcap Mrs. Emily Pollifax, who becomes a CIA courier. In Virginia Rich's series, continued by Nancy J. Pickard, Mrs. Eugenia Potter shares her culinary lore with the reader while she stews over clues to mysterious deaths. Other examples are Serita Stevens and Rayanne Moore's Fanny Zindel, Eleanor Boylan's Mrs. Clara Gamadge, D. B. Borton's Catherine "Cat" Caliban, and Robert Nordan's Mavis Lashley.

Among the professional women, Kate Morgan's Dewey James, a retired librarian and widow of the former police chief in a small town, solves cases for her husband's incompetent successor. James McCahery's Lavina London is a former radio actress; more examples include Carolyn G. Hart's Henrietta O'Dwyer Collins ("Henrie O"), a retired reporter in her mid-sixties, and Simon Brett's Mrs. Melita Par-

geter, who lives on her husband's generous legacy.

Among the contemporary single men, only one bachelor works on his own. Joan Hadley's Theo Bloomer, retired from the florist business at sixty-one to devote himself to private horticultural pursuits, usually discovers foul play after being conscripted to chaperone or rescue his namesake niece in exotic environs such as Israel or Jamaica. A small group of widowers includes David Laing Dawson's Henry Thornton, a Canadian ex-car agency owner who uncovers murder in his nursing home. E. X. *Ferrars's Andrew Basnet, formerly a professor of botany at London University, applies scientific precepts to contemporary conundrums.

Married and unmarried couples also form a conspicuous group among elderly sleuths. Ann Cleeves's George Palmer-Jones, a former civil servant turned ornithologist in his mid-sixties, is often helped by his wife, Mollie, to explain illegal activities connected with birdwatching and wildlife conservation. In Suffolk, Anthony Oliver's retired police inspector John Webber is joined by the incorrigible Mrs. Lizzie Thomas in an informal partnership to expose skulduggery connected with the world of art and antiques. Another widower, Nancy Livingston's retired British tax inspector, G. D. H. Pringle, takes up detecting in order to support his passion for collecting paintings of the Manchester School. Pringle enjoys the company, cooking, and bed of a lady friend, Mavis Bignell, a red-haired barmaid of Rubenesque proportions and earthy common sense.

[See also Eccentrics.]

• "Senior Sleuths," Mystery Readers Journal 10, no. 3 (fall 1994).

—B. J. Rahn

Ellery Queen's Mystery Magazine (EQMM), best and most influential of the *digest-sized mystery magazines, first appeared in fall 1941. Originally envisioned as an anthology, it featured all reprints. Through the forties and fifties, more and more original material appeared, evolving toward the present policy of publishing almost all new stories with a smattering of distinguished reprints. The frequency changed from quarterly to bimonthly with the fourth issue, May 1942, became monthly in January 1946, adopted a schedule of thirteen issues per year in December 1979 and cut back to eleven per year in 1996.

The Ellery *Queen team (Frederic Dannay and Manfred B. Lee) had made their first foray into magazine publishing with the Mystery League Magazine, a high-quality *pulp magazine that numbered four issues in 1933 and 1934. Dannay was the guiding force behind EQMM until his death in 1982. Although the Queen byline was associated with the pure detective story of the Golden Age, all types of crime and mystery fiction appeared in EQMM. Alongside contributions of Agatha *Christie, Margery *Allingham, and John Dickson *Carr were rediscovered pulp stories by Dashiell *Hammett, Cornell *Woolrich, Frederick Nebel, and others. When the legendary *Black Mask finally folded in the early fifties, its name was acquired as a feature of EQMM.

Danny's three-pronged approach was to publish

the work of virtually every important mystery writer who wrote short stories (and to prod those who had not, to do so); to enhance the stature of crime fiction by presenting, usually in reprint, the work of famous mainstream literary figures; and, perhaps most significantly, to discover first stories from new writers. Among the hundreds of authors of *EQMM* first stories are James Yaffe, who was first published at age fifteen in 1943; Harry Kemelman; Stanley Ellin; Thomas Flanagan; Joyce Harrington; Robert L. Fish; David Morell; and Susan Dunlap.

All three editorial aims were furthered by the short-story contests held annually from 1945 to 1957. First prizes ranged from $1,500 to $3,000, still a handsome price for a short story and at the time more than an author could expect as an advance for a novel. William Faulkner was among the entrants in the first contest: His "An Error in Chemistry" was one of the second-prize winners behind Manly Wade Wellman's first-prize "A Star for a Warrior." Other entrants included T. S. *Stribling, Ngaio *Marsh, Michael *Innes, and Kenneth Millar (later known as Ross *Macdonald). Among subsequent first-prize winners were Georges *Simenon, Carr, Charlotte Armstrong, Flanagan, Roy Vickers, and Ellin.

Issues of the first decade were enlivened by Dannay's lengthy, learned, and enthusiastic story introductions, many of which were collected in *In the Queens' Parlor* (1957). The first book review columnist was Howard Haycraft, succeeded by Robert P. Mills (as editor of a feature quoting various reviewers), Anthony *Boucher, Carr, Allen J. Hubin, and Jon L. Breen. For a time in the seventies and eighties, the magazine included a section entitled "Ellery Queen's Mystery Newsletter" which included author interviews and news columns by Otto Penzler, Chris Steinbrunner, and finally "R. E. Porter" (Edward D. *Hoch). Under his own name, Hoch was the magazine's most prolific contributor through the 1990s, appearing in every issue since May 1973 with stories in a variety of series, mostly in the Ellery Queen tradition of fair play.

Eleanor Sullivan, long-time managing editor, took over the editorial reins on Dannay's death and was succeeded by Janet Hutchings in the year of her own passing, 1991. Both subsequent editors have continued Dannay's three-pronged approach successfully.

Originally published by Lawrence E. Spivak of American Mercury, Inc., the magazine appeared from 1957 under the banner of Davis Publications, Inc., headed first by Bernard G. Davis and subsequently by Joel Davis. In 1992, the magazine was sold, along with the other Davis fiction magazines, to Bantam Doubleday Dell. In 1996, the Dell magazines were sold to Penny Marketing.

[*See also* Short Story: The American Crime Short Story; Short Story: The British Crime Short Story.]

Michael L. Cook, comp., *Monthly Murders: A Checklist and Chronological Listing of Fiction in the Digest-Size Mystery Magazines in the United States and England* (1982). David H. Doerrer, "*Ellery Queen's Mystery Magazine,*" in *Mystery, Detective, and Espionage Magazines*, ed. Michael L. Cook (1983).
                                                          —Jon L. Breen

ELLIN, STANLEY (1916–1986), American master of the short story. The Brooklyn-born writer emerged in 1948 both as novelist, with *Dreadful Summit*, and as short story writer with the appearance in the May issue of *Ellery Queen's Mystery Magazine* of his best-known single work, the subtly chilling classic "The Specialty of the House." Ellin's short stories are marked by a variety of backgrounds, themes, and moods, as well as by unwavering craft, probing explorations of personal and ethical dilemmas, and a keen sense of irony. While the earliest tales, gathered in *Mystery Stories* (1956), may be the best, with "The House Party" and "The Moment of Decision" especially memorable, the Ellin touch rarely faltered. The quality of his equally varied novels, of which *The Eighth Circle* (1958) and *Mirror, Mirror on the Wall* (1972) are most frequently cited, has not eclipsed his primary niche as one of the two or three finest short story writers of this century in the crime field.

[*See also* Short Story: The American Crime Short Story.]

• Edward D. Hoch, "Stanley Ellin," in *Twentieth-Century Crime and Mystery Writers*, ed. Lesley Henderson, 3d ed. (1991).   —Jon L. Breen

ELLROY, JAMES (b. 1948), American author, practitioner of *hard-boiled fiction, or *fiction noir, and a self-educated ex-convict, employed at various jobs, including caddying. An active novelist since 1981, Ellroy centers all of his works on a quasi-historical vision of midcentury *Los Angeles governed by institutional and individual *corruption and brutality. His dense, dark crime novels feature police who are only marginally better than his stomach-churning *villains. His first novel is the semiautobiographical *Brown's Requiem* (1984). Investigation into the *true-crime mutilation murder of Elizabeth Short in 1947 provides the basis for the plot of *The Black Dahlia* (1987) and becomes a recurring motif through most of his novels. In his works, including the *Los Angeles Quarter* (*The Black Dahlia* 1987; *The Big Nowhere*, 1988; *L.A. Confidential*, 1990; and *White Jazz*, 1992), Ellroy chronicles the often futile attempts of damaged individuals to navigate in a world ruled by *violence and duplicity.

[*See also* Deviance.]   —LeRoy L. Panek

ENGLAND, STATE OF. To generalize about the state or condition of England is to invite swift and crushing contradiction. The country is small, but the character of its society is complex. Yet mystery writers have, albeit often unconsciously, provided many clues for those wishing to understand England and the English. Julian *Symons identified William Godwin's *Caleb Williams* (1794) as the novel that first struck "the characteristic note of crime literature." Godwin was an anarchist who became the intellectual leader of the English radical movement, and he intended his novel to show the corruption inherent in any legal system through which one man has power over another. His *villain, Falkland, is driven to *murder as a result of being betrayed by the society in which he invested his faith.

The French Revolution had taken place the year before *Caleb Williams* was published, and in the decades that followed, lawlessness was rife in many parts of England. Calm only began to be restored after the establishment of the first professional paid police force in 1829. Thereafter, the detective came to be seen as the protector of English society. The conditions were thus set for the development of the *detective novel, in which fictional *sleuths fulfilled a similar role, providing a rational explanation for baffling mysteries and restoring order after an outbreak of crime. The two major writers who were early exponents of the form, Charles *Dickens and Wilkie *Collins, based Inspector *Bucket in *Bleak House* (1853) and Sergeant *Cuff in *The Moonstone* (1868) respectively on the real-life policemen Field and Whicher. Bucket and Cuff were men whose work caused them to move among members of all classes; but, as guardians of the social fabric, they were careful to pay due regard to distinctions of birth and background. By the time Arthur Conan *Doyle created Sherlock *Holmes, the British Empire stretched across the globe and patriotic fervor was at its height. Although at first blush, the depressive drug addict of *The Sign of Four* (1890; *The Sign of the Four*) seems an unlikely hero for the supposedly sober Victorian age, the loyalty of this Nietzschean superman to Queen and country was absolute. In a similar vein, E. W. *Hornung's A. J. *Raffles, the amateur cracksman, died heroically serving England during the Boer War. Colin Watson has pointed out that "sport" is a key word in the Raffles stories—and has argued that the ascribing of "unsportsmanlike" motives to enemies is a propensity of the English. After the First World War, Ronald A. *Knox sought to lay down in his Detective Decalogue "rules" for writing detective stories. These rules reflected notions of sportsmanship: The criminal must be mentioned early in the story, for example, and the detective must not be aided by accident or intuition. Agatha *Christie, whose first book was published in 1920, took particular pains to play fair with her readers, even in the famously tricky *Murder of Roger Ackroyd* (1926). Christie was in many ways a typical Englishwoman of the upper-middle class, deeply conservative in her outlook. But she was never afraid to exploit conventional assumptions about character and society. In *One, Two Buckle My Shoe* (1940; *The Patriotic Murders*; *An Overdose of Death*), an unpleasant young radical proves to be harmless, the culprit being a pillar of the English establishment. Nor does Christie, even in a book published soon after the start of the Second World War, shrink from the implications of her plot; she, like Hercule *Poirot, is content for the potential savior of the society she loved to pay the penalty for his crimes against private individuals, however unworthy they were, despite the potential cost to England.

Symons pointed out that English crime novels of the Golden Age were written at a time of high unemployment and economic hardship, yet the reality of poverty was seldom addressed by writers of the period—even those who held strong socialist views, such as the prolific husband and wife team of G. D. H and Margaret *Cole, and Ellen Wilkinson, the member of Parliament known as "Red Ellen," who wrote *The Division Bell Mystery* (1932). Apart from eccentrics such as Poirot, the principal detectives were usually either professional policemen such as Freeman Wills *Crofts's Inspector Joseph French or members of the upper class or aristocracy, notably Margery *Allingham's Albert *Campion and Dorothy L. *Sayers's Lord Peter *Wimsey. *Thrillers and *spy fiction provided insights into the condition of England which were sometimes appealing but often unattractive. John *Buchan's Richard Hannay expounds his love for England lyrically in *Mr. Standfast* (1919), but lesser writers, such as Dornford *Yates, E. Phillips *Oppenheim, and H. C. *McNeile writing as "Sapper" reflected the snobbery and xenophobia of many of their readers.

After 1945, the world changed and so did England. Although Christie and others continued to write stories set in mythical villages and market towns of the type characterized by Watson as *Mayhem Parva, the unreality of the society they described became ever more obvious. Symons was one of the first English writers of the postwar era to move away from lighthearted confections and toward more realistic studies of crime, and his willingness to explore the secrets which lie behind bland, conventional appearances made him one of the most skilled analysts of the state of England. Yet the duality of approach between writers of radical outlook and those with conservative instincts has persisted. In the field of espionage, Ian *Fleming's novels about James *Bond echoed those of Yates and Sapper in their distaste for foreigners and appeal to snobbish values. John *le Carré and Len *Deighton struck a more sceptical note and le Carré's books about George Smiley provide a penetrating assessment of English social mores. The strength of such questioning writers as Symons and le Carré has been their realization that the story must come first; some of their successors, in seeking to cast light upon the society in which they live, have fallen into the trap of didacticism or self-indulgence. The long period of Conservative political domination from 1979 to 1997 gave rise to many dismal books from those who disliked the establishment: An example is Derek Raymond's *Dead Man Upright* (1993). Subtler writers have made their points more obliquely, but more entertainingly. Michael Dibdin's *Dirty Tricks* (1991) wittily indicts the superficial materialism of the economic boom years of the late 1980s. Reginald Hill's *Pictures of Perfection* (1994) in one sense is a pastoral idyll with fairy tale elements, yet in another portrays the destruction of traditional ways of life and the sense of community long associated with the villages of England in a manner that is subtly subversive. In *Simisola* (1994), Ruth *Rendell's depiction of *racism, both conscious and unconscious, in Kingsmarkham is integrated with a plot in which a wealthy family enslaves a black girl. Today, even English writers of conservative instinct, such as P. D. *James, seldom portray the moral landscape of their country in the uncritical manner of so many of their predecessors. James's vision in powerfully imagined books such as *Devices and Desires* (1990) is bleak, but gentler books in the fair play tradition continue to appeal. The Americans Elizabeth George and Martha Grimes have each created successful series that draw heavily on a perception of English society reminiscent of that of the Golden Age. The distinctions between writers sympathetic toward the status quo and those hostile to it have become blurred in recent years, but still remain. As a result, mystery fiction presents a complex picture of the state of England that is entirely appropriate to the subject.

[See also Conservative vs. Radical Worldview; Realism, Conventions of; Rules of the Game.]

• Ronald Knox, "The Detective Decalogue," in Best Detective Stories of 1928. Richard Usborne, Clubland Heroes (1953, rev. ed. 1974). Colin Watson, Snobbery with Violence (1971, rev. ed. 1979). Erik Routley, The Puritan Pleasures of the Detective Story (1972). Julian Symons, Bloody Murder: From the Detective Story to the Crime Novel, 3rd ed. (1992). William Vivian Butler, The Durable Desperadoes (1973).

—Martin Edwards

ENGLISH VILLAGE MILIEU, quintessential *setting during the Golden Age, defining the boundaries within which the detective must solve the crime and the group among whom he must search for *suspects. Because this deceptively reassuring community appears to be untainted and peaceful, *murder (usually of someone everyone knows) is unheard of, and the subsequent investigation by an outsider precipitates a crisis. Relationships that once were strong are pushed to the extreme, family members and neighbors grow suspicious of one another, and tensions mount as gossip grows, providing an abundant opportunity for *humor, *suspense, and social criticism. With the arrest (or *suicide) of the criminal, order is restored, and life goes on much as before.

In his essay "The Guilty Vicarage" (Harper's Magazine, May 1948), W. H. Auden defined the village setting as the "Great Good Place," and added, "the more Eden-like it is, the greater the contradiction of murder." In the early novels of Agatha *Christie, the village stands for permanence in a changing world, a simpler, stratified way of living that contrasts with the fragmenting complexity of city life. Christie fills her novels with the expected social types or apparent *stock characters from the country—local gentry, doctors, vicars, coroners, postmen, lawyers, mothers, teachers, village "characters," and occasional visitors—and most of them keep secrets about themselves in order to preserve the stability of the community. This Edenic imagery reflects Christie's desire to recapture in her novels a time and a place already dissolved by the time she is writing.

Against this background of order and harmony, behind this mask of kindness and respectability, crime is the exception, motivated by emotions that seemingly have no place here, like *greed or jealousy or hate. Once the murder has occurred, a transformation gradually takes place: The investigation leads to the discovery of all kinds of disorder in the world. "Those we trust will deceive us" is a lesson that Christie's Miss Jane *Marple learns all too well from a lifetime spent watching the inhabitants of St. Mary Mead, the small village in which she lives (The Murder at the Vicarage, 1930).

Newcomers disrupt the tenuous balance; they are seldom welcome without *suspicion in the country villages, and many authors explore how the closed community reacts against an outsider and the balance tips, often toward crime. In Philip *MacDonald's The Link (1930), a young veterinarian becomes a likely *suspect when the husband of the lady he loves is shot to death. When a young shopgirl is found dead in June Thomson's Not One of Us (1971), the villagers quickly turn on a stranger in their midst, and the town's peace is forever shattered. In M. C. Beaton's Death of a Perfect Wife (1988), newcomer Trixie Thomas interferes with the rhythms and customs of the village life and is poisoned.

With the violence of two world wars, with depression and increasing crime in the cities, with the dehumanization of modern society through technology and science, the fictional portrayal of English village life loses its idyllic feeling of wholeness and unity. Behind Dorothy L. *Sayers's Unnatural Death (1927; The Dawson Pedigree, 1928) and Christie's The Pale Horse (1961) is the suggestion of a complex and unpredictable world with a potential for *evil arising anywhere, at anytime, from anyone.

Gone is the assumption inherited from the eighteenth and nineteenth centuries that the world amenable to human reason and control, that those who disturb the established order are always found and punished. Darkness and chaos encroach upon the apparent order of family and class in Margery *Allingham's The Crime at Black Dudley (1929; The Black Dudley Murder), Mystery Mile (1930), and Sweet Danger (1933) with the invasion of the idyllic English village by foreigners, gangsters, or millionaires.

In No Medals for the Major (1974) by Margaret Yorke, random *violence alters everything in a small quiet village, and a visitor who intended to retire there must face the anger and suspicion of his new neighbors. In The Small Hours of the Morning (1975), concealed beneath the civilized life of a village are many passions: The wife of the deputy librarian meets her lover; a young man plans a series of robberies; and a silent watcher sees them all and more.

In The Watersplash (1951) by Patricia *Wentworth, it is easy for Miss Maud *Silver (and the reader) to become acquainted with all the members of this closed community, although occasionally everyone in the village will fall under suspicion. Blackmail often leads to murder; it is most vicious in a village where neighbor suspects neighbor, as in Wicked Uncle (1947).

Victimization, small cruelties, hopelessness, a struggle for survival all characterize the village milieu created by Sheila Radley. From the squalor and deprivation in Death and the Maiden (1978; Death in the Morning, 1979) to the dislikeable people in Chief Inspector's Daughter (1980), from the empty marriage in A Talent for Destruction (1982) to the mindless victimization in Fate Worse than Death (1985), her novels typify the more realistic portrayal of village life in recent years.

• Geraldine Penderson-King, "Detective Stories and the Primal Scene," in *Dimensions of Detective Fiction*, ed. Larry N. Landrum et al. (1976): 58–63. Elaine Bander, "The English Detective Novel Between the Wars: 1919–1939," *Armchair Detective* 11, no. 3 (July 1978): 262–73. Deborah Bonetti, "Murder Can Happen Anywhere," *Armchair Detective* 14, no. 3 (summer 1981): 257–64. Dennis Porter, *The Pursuit of Crime: Art and Ideology in Detective Fiction* (1981). Earl F. Bargainnier, ed., *Comic Crime* (1987). Robert Barnard, "Ordinary People," *Armchair Detective* 25, no. 1 (winter 1992): 14–19.   —Dale Salwak

ESCAPISM may be defined as a tendency to escape from reality and everyday routines by means of imaginative activities, and the term has long been applied to popular genres such as crime writing. Although the idea of entertainment (the *divertissement* of the **roman policier*, a form of *littérature d'évasion*) rarely arouses marked disapproval, the patronizing reference to **suspense fiction (Literatur vor dem Einschlafen, littérature de chevet)* reduces it to a soporific. If the German term *Trivialliteratur* suggests insignificance, "escapist" and "escapism," particularly as applied to the British cozy tradition that began in the 1920s, connote artistically, psychologically, or socially irresponsible flight from reality into delusion. Although early criticism tends to focus on moral concerns, such as crime fiction's potential for arousing antisocial behavior, later appraisals, specifically of detective novels, often involve substantial literary and ideological issues.

The long arm of criticism has placed both writers and readers in the dock on a general charge of stiffening inspired models of fictional detection (from Edgar Allan **Poe and others) into a formulaic repetitiveness. A **red herring diverting readers from the artistically richer crime fiction heralded by Thomas De Quincey's "On Murder Considered as a Fine Art" (1827), the puzzle-centered mystery was accused of being reprehensibly escapist from the start. Preoccupied with the sleuthing process, detective fiction is sometimes seen as trivializing through emotional neglect. For instance, professional devotee Harrison R. Steeves calls the genre "culpably unserious" for its "artistic failure" to generate emotional intensity in "A Sober Word on the Detective Story" (*Harper's Magazine*, 1941). Another complainant, Colin Watson, charges British puzzle mystery writers with ignoring the realities of criminal violence the better to divert, soothe, and reassure readers in *Snobbery with Violence* (1971). In *The Puritan Pleasures of the Detective Story, a Personal Monograph* (1972), like "false religion," Erik Routley warns, the guaranteed solution of a crime novel fosters "trivial-mindedness." With true postmodernist epistemological skepticism, in *The Doomed Detective: The Contribution of the Detective Novel to Postmodern American and Italian Fiction* (1984), Stefano Tani considers the British puzzle-solution mystery no longer viable, its rationalism useful only for the purpose of being subverted.

Satisfying readers' needs can turn a writer into an escape artist. Offering his chronically guilt-ridden reader an "illusion of innocence," the cozy is merely subartistic "escape literature," W. H. Auden says in "The Guilty Vicarage" (*Harper's Magazine*, May 1948). Likened by Nicholas **Blake to a "drug addict" spreading the "habit," the writer is turning the reader into a suspense-addicted "opium smoker," according to Edmund Wilson's "Who Cares Who Killed Roger Ackroyd?" (*New Yorker*, 20 Jan. 1945). Routley charges that this "addiction" encourages a socially "reactionary" moral narrowness, and Ernest Mandel characterizes the genre as middle-class "opium" against urban stress in *Delightful Murder* (1984). George Orwell's wartime distress at the "totalitarian" nature of popular American-style realism expressed in "Raffles and Miss Blandish" (*Horizon*, Oct. 1944; *Collected Essays*, 1961), eventually becomes exposure of the British cozy's quietism, its settings ahistorically insulated from the social conditions actually producing crime in the view of Dennis Porter in *The Pursuit of Crime: Art and Ideology in Detective Fiction* (1981). Again, the **police procedural assuages public uneasiness with bureaucratic surveillance in the service of corporate capitalism, say Robert P. Winston and Nancy C. Mellerski in *The Public Eye, Ideology and the Police Procedural* (1992).

Marjorie Nicolson vindicates detective fiction as a self-justifying game that gives the reader intellectual rather than emotional satisfaction in "The Professor and the Detective" (*Atlantic Monthly*, Apr. 1929). The mystery novel is, in her view, an escape from psychological literature and a return to the novel of plot and incident. Another defense spotlights the excellence of individual works and writers, such as Raymond **Chandler's insistence in "The Simple Art of Murder" (*Atlantic Monthly*, Dec. 1944) on the literary eminence of Dashiell **Hammett's *The Glass Key*. George Grella traces British detective fiction conventions to mainstream literary types, the comedy of manners, and the pastoral novel in "The Formal Detective Novel" (*Detective Fiction: A Collection of Critical Essays*, ed. Robin W. Winks, 1988).

Although the genre is the subject of postmodernist obituaries, it refuses to die. In part because of television serialization, traditional British detective fiction is undergoing a renaissance. Increasingly popular are American police procedurals and private eye fiction with ethnic or feminist slants. The college setting that Auden preferred for fictional murder is now the site of numerous courses on crime and detective fiction, some of which are described in B. J. Rahn's collection of thirty-five syllabi in *Murder Is Academic* (1993).

The crime novel has achieved respectability among both writers and critics, leading to studies of individual writers, such as the collection of articles in *Ngaio Marsh*, edited by B. J. Rahn (1995) and to critical studies of aspects of the genre, such as *Mysterium and Mystery: The Clerical Crime Novel* by William Daniel Spencer (1989).

• Marie J. Rodell, *Mystery Fiction: Theory and Technique* (1943; rev. ed. 1954). Stanley Cohen and Laurie Taylor, *Escape Attempts: The Theory and Practice of Resistance to Everyday Life* (1976). Peter Nusser, *Der Kriminalroman*, (rev. ed. 1992). Richard Raskin, "The Pleasure and Politics of

Detective Fiction," *Clues: A Journal of Detection* 13, no. 2 (fall/winter 1992): 71–114.   —Richard Smyer

ESPIONAGE FICTION. *See* Spy Fiction.

ETHICS OF DETECTIVES. While the main purpose of the writer of detective fiction may be to raise questions of *means, motive, and opportunity, most writers in this genre also grapple with ethical concerns that naturally arise in literature dealing with crime, *justice, and the discovery of *truth. Like a great deal of popular literature, detective fiction appears to confirm the generally held values of a readership. It is not surprising, therefore, that detectives in books frequently work in the interests of the acknowledged legal system: They want to solve crimes, which are acts against society, and bring criminals to justice, which means they represent accepted notions of law and order and work for the common good. But a close examination of the genre also reveals numerous cases where *sleuths subvert accepted legal standards. The ethics of detection does not always conform to a simple, universally accepted code—do the right thing, catch the criminals, and clear the innocent. In English detective fiction those simple rules are complicated by a social order in which *class and privilege dominate. In the American counterpart the rules are interpreted and manipulated by the romantic personality of the protagonist. Therefore, in both British and American detective fiction motivation and conduct often turn out to differ widely from the accepted norms and even the expectations of the readers.

In its earliest manifestations, detective fiction sometimes evades any sort of ethical standard. Edgar Allan *Poe's Chevalier C. Auguste *Dupin, who holds the police in contempt, appears to work for the most part to amuse himself and to settle some personal scores. He wants to clear the *suspect in "The Murders in the Rue Morgue" (*Graham's Lady's and Gentleman's Magazine*, Apr. 1841) because he owes the man an unspecified favor, and he relishes the implication of Minister D—— in "The Purloined Letter" (in *The Gift*, 1845) for exactly the opposite reason—he desires revenge. Arthur Conan *Doyle's Sherlock *Holmes, who mostly finds the police laughable, conducts a personal vendetta against both Professor *Moriarty, "the Napoleon of crime," and Colonel Sebastian Moran in several stories, in which the official forces of law and order seem impotent; in many stories, he is content to see a sort of natural justice working out. G. K. *Chesterton's Father *Brown, of course, is always far more interested in the *criminal's immortal soul than in the normal business of the law; even for some of the earlier and more distinguished fictional detectives, then, personal codes of belief and conduct far outweigh the official, so that the detective extends his function beyond analysis to judgment.

Perhaps following the example of the great originals, a surprising number of writers have their detectives consciously violate the accepted code of ethics, generally by intentionally avoiding the usual methods of justice. The detective may find the murderer but refuse to have him or her arrested, may seek some alternative source of justice or may even facilitate the murderer's escape. Most of the major practitioners of the form have allowed their sleuths to break both the law and the unwritten code that lies behind the fictional business of criminal investigation.

If the *victims of crime are themselves especially bad people—in the English novel, most victims somehow deserve their fate—then their murderers can escape retribution. In Agatha *Christie's *Murder on the Orient Express* (1934; *Murder in the Calais Coach*), Hercule *Poirot decides that because the victim was a vicious kidnapper, his murderers should go free. Questions of *class cause John Dickson *Carr to allow the murderer in *The Crooked Hinge* (1938) to go free, since his victim was a lower-class impostor falsely claiming to be the heir to a fortune. Most of the classic writers also permit the more socially acceptable killers to foil justice by committing *suicide, presumably to escape the obloquy of publicity, trials, prisons, executions—for example, Christie in *The Murder of Roger Ackroyd* (1926), Dorothy L. *Sayers in *Whose Body?* (1923) and *The Unpleasantness at the Bellona Club* (1928), and Carr in *Hag's Nook* (1933) and *The Sleeping Sphinx* (1947).

On the other hand, in *The Maltese Falcon* (1930) by Dashiell *Hammett, Sam *Spade provides a long list of reasons for turning his client (and lover) over to the police, most of them professional. To let her go, he says, would be "bad business . . . bad for every detective everywhere," and unnatural, "like asking a dog to catch a rabbit and let it go." Spade's argument essentially establishes the ethical code for all the American *private eyes who follow him. They may bend the law, hide things from the police, drink too much, sleep with their clients, and make wisecracks, but they will always do their job.

Spade's colleagues and his successors generally follow a personal rather than an objective code of conduct. Raymond *Chandler's Philip *Marlowe, for example, almost invariably prefers mercy to punishment, even in some extreme cases; in *The Big Sleep* (1939) he protects a psychopathic murderer from the law, mostly out of regard for her aged father. In books as different as *Farewell, My Lovely* (1940) and *The Little Sister* (1949), he involves himself in complicated cases simply because he cares about the people who ask his help. Marlowe's direct descendant, Ross *Macdonald's Lew *Archer, extends the subjective interpretation of his job beyond any of the other private eyes. In the nineteen novels in which he appears, Archer grows more and more saintly and compassionate, so that his investigations increasingly resemble ongoing journeys into the depths of the human spirit. He practices his profession to help others and to understand himself; he cares far less about crime and punishment than about protecting the innocent and even finding some redemption for the guilty.

Although the *detective novel may appear to endorse the ethical status quo, a great many writers suggest in their explicit or implicit ethical code a discernible conflict with those values. In England, the *amateur detective tends to subordinate the law to his own judgment of the social acceptability of the culprit and the moral subtleties surrounding the crime. In America, the private eye—assisted by the common national distrust of authority—trusts himself far more than he trusts the law, so he must reach his own conclusions and sometimes even choose the means of punishment. In a significant number of works by a variety of writers on either side of the Atlantic, the detective's personal code of ethics conflicts with accepted standards of conduct. When this happens, the detective novel often turns out to be an astonishingly subversive form.

[See also Chivalry, Code of; Heroism.]

• George Grella, "Murder and Manners: The Formal Detective Novel," *Novel: A Forum on Fiction* 4 (fall 1970): 30–48. George Grella, "Murder and the Mean Streets: The Hard-Boiled Detective Novel," *Contempora* 1, no. 1 (1970): 6–15. Colin Watson, *Snobbery with Violence: Crime Stories and Their Audience* (1971). Julian Symons, *Bloody Murder: From the Detective Story to the Crime Novel*, 3rd rev. ed. (1992). George Grella, "Evil Plots: Ross Macdonald," *New Republic* (26 July 1975): 24–26. Robin W. Winks, ed., *Detective Fiction: A Collection of Critical Essays* (1980). Dennis Porter, *The Pursuit of Crime: Art and Ideology in Detective Fiction* (1981).
—George Grella

ETHNICITY. In literature, as in life, ethnic identity may be assigned or deliberately assumed. In the familiar occurrence of ethnic assignment, people who are distinguishable from a majority culture because of their complexion, language, or heritage are perceived as distinctly "other" than the dominant crowd and, consequently, become known by rubrics intended to enforce upon consciousness their peculiar differences. Lexicons of popular usage more often than not record the labels as pejorative, because they bespeak subordination in a social and economic power relationship that legitimates itself through insult. Even when the hurtful terminology is neutralized, as, for instance, it ordinarily must be in census and ethnographic reports, the assignment of an ethnic label can indicate that the objects of labeling do not share possession of the traits of universality presumed to rest with the group that has the power to study and name the other.

On the other hand, members of groups who feel themselves culturally distinct from those who seem to dominate a society may elect to reify their appearance, belief systems, language, or heritage in order to enhance their singularity. They celebrate their color as a cultural marker, employ their beliefs as means of apprehending reality in a manner alternative to the methods endorsed by the social majority, practice linguistic innovation in hybridizing their native language with the standard usage of society, and relate themselves to a history parallel to that history taught by mainstream schools and publications.

When ethnic identity is assigned it invariably yields stereotypes that are either partial truths at best or, more likely, defamation. Early detective novels seized upon assigned ethnicity to signal culpability and sinister intentions. Wilkie *Collins's The Moonstone* (1868) serves to illustrate the use of ethnicity as a threatening element in narrative. The house steward for the wealthy Verinder family, Gabriel Betteridge, writes with automatic *suspicion about the Indians who have come to recover the stolen jewel. Their dark skin immediately suggest to him that they must be crude and unmannerly; when they turn out not to be so, they become all the more suspicious. Collins does not restrict distrust of "others" to Betteridge, for the unfolding *plot of the novel increases suspense by capitalizing on English readers' stereotypes of dark-skinned people and by stressing the desperateness of the Indians' spiritual devotion. Collins's Indians are, however, more noble than the religious hypocrite who is the real *villain and whose appearance fits the stereotypical British hero.

For years assigned ethnicity proved handy for furnishing sinister *atmosphere. Suggestively Jewish characters appear as outsiders in Golden Age fiction, African Americans in hard-boiled stories, all in decidedly subordinate roles suggestive of both the stereotypes incident to assigned ethnicity and the debasement of other that is acceptable to contemporary readers. Among major characters, however, Charlie *Chan was a production in prose fiction as momentous in the history of ethnic exploitation as the radio shows about Amos and Andy. Earl Derr *Biggers, the creator of Chan, equips his *sleuth with impenetrable detection methods that play off of the stereotypical inscrutability of Asians. The prolific father of eleven children, a speaker of broken English, and parodic in his dispensing of Eastern wisdom, Chan was evidently intended to be a comic figure. In that regard, he is the polar opposite of Sax *Rohmer's Eastern villain, *Fu Manchu—opposite but just as much a product of the Western practice of crude portrayal of people of color.

Considerably distanced from these treatments of Asian "others" by Western writers is the series of detective novels about Judge Dee. Robert H. van Gulik found inspiration for the character of a real life magistrate of ancient China by translating *Dee Goong An* in 1949, an anonymous eighteenth-century novel about an historical figure who was immortalized in Chinese popular stories and plays. Following the success of his translation, van Gulik produced a series of original stories described by E. F. Bleiler as "the finest ethnographic detective novels in English" (*Twentieth Century Crime and Mystery Writers*, 1991).

Completing the transition from novels that use characters with assigned ethnicity to those who present characters who adopt ethnicity as an identity of choice are the novels by Chester *Himes about Grave Digger Jones and Coffin Ed *Johnson, Harlem police officers who appear in a cycle of absurdist crime works published between 1957 and 1969. These books are marked by a complex relationship between other and the established institutions of majority culture. Since the dominant social order mistrusts and mistreats ethnic others, the upholders of that order such as police, teachers, and detectives earn suspicion from the oppressed. Himes's officers understand and share this suspicion, but nevertheless they recognize social disruption as a threat to their community and proceed to employ their knowledge of African American reality as the foundation for a hard-boiled code of *justice.

The novels of Donald Goines are even more un-compromising than Himes's in their depiction of a ghetto code. Passion and degradation mark Goines's stories of pimps, *con men, addicts, and bad guys, while his series about Kenyatta (under the name Al C. Clark) carry self-chosen ethnicity to the extent of describing a black revolutionary campaign led by the hero Kenyatta against the exploitation infesting inner city life. The heroic Kenyatta remains linked to stereotypes fostered by the majority culture. In contrast, the recent works of Walter *Mosley represent a profound interpretation of the social psychology of American ethnicity in their portrayal of Ezekiel "Easy" *Rawlins, a character living in racially segregated Los Angeles in the 1940s. A reluctant detective, Rawlins becomes involved in cases illustrating the indeterminate borders between races and the ambivalent mentality of a man living, as W. E. B. Du Bois put it, with double consciousness.

Rawlins's attachment to his identity is matched by Barbara Neely's Blanche White, a domestic worker who is another *accidental sleuth. Blanche taps into the black domestic worker neighborhood gossip line to solve her first mystery, Blanche on the Lam (1992) and, in a feat of reversal, manipulates white stereotypes about blacks. There is, in fact, a growing body of writing about African American detectives, all of it illustrative of the deliberate selection of ethnicity as identity and subject. Valerie Wilson Wesley's novels about Tamara Hayle, a *private eye in Newark, New Jersey, provide another example.

Just as ethnic community and culture are keys to understanding the trespasses in recent African American detective novels, Edna Buchanan's novels about the Miami crime reporter Britt Montero, who debuted in Contents Under Pressure (1992), show Montero repairing the disruption of the Cuban American community through her natural ethnic connections. Buchanan's Cuban American Montero relishes her otherness as a rich alternative to the boring white community that her mother represents, and finds that her special cultural knowledge empowers her detecting ability as well.

Gloria White's Veronica (Ronnie) Ventana, who first appeared in Murder on the Run (1991) is another part-Hispanic, part-Anglo character described as the child of cat burglars in *San Francisco. The tension between Ronnie's ethnic status and the authorities becomes part of the plots of White's novels, indicating that the hard-boiled practice of setting sleuth against cop has new utility for authors of ethnic narratives.

Tony *Hillerman introduces a significant variation on the tensions between legal authority and sleuths by making his detectives, Joe Leaphorn and Jim *Chee, members of the Navajo tribal police. His novels generally hinge upon knowledge of the myths, rituals, and customs of Native Americans, but an equally important contribution to their success as narratives lies with Hillerman's skill in creating multidimensional characters who grapple with their roots and their relationship to the Anglo world.

Fiction about ethnic sleuths inevitably makes an appeal to readers because of its presentation of a unique *milieu. The challenge to the author is to control the presentation of information about ethnic culture and practices so that it will be received as knowledge of human society rather than exotic data about curious folk. It must depart from the manner of popular ethnography and employ the narrative techniques of literature, so that readers cross over the borders of difference and complete an identification with characters and situations. Ethnic crime fiction may be a literature of observation, but it must also be a literature of participation. Among the successful practitioners of participatory ethnic literature are such authors as Linda Barnes, whose sleuth Carlotta Carlyle is Irish Jewish American; Sara *Paretsky, whose V. I. Warshawski is Italian Jewish Polish American; and Dana Stabenow, whose character Kate Shugak is native Alaskan. For these characters, ethnic roots are integral sources of self; and for their readers, ethnicity is integral to satisfying narrative.

[See also Prejudice; Racism; Stereotypes, Reversals of.]

• Greg Goode, "The Oriental in Mystery Fiction: The Orient, Part II" Detective 15 (1982): 306–13. Thomas S. Gladsky, "Consent, Descent, and Transethnicity in Sara Paretsky's Fiction." Clues: A Journal of Detection 16, no. 2 (fall–winter 1995): 1–15. John M. (John Marsden) Reilly, Tony Hillerman: A Critical Companion (1996). Stephen F. Soitos, The Blues Detective: A Study of African American Detective Fiction (1996).
—Catherine E. Hoyser

ETHNIC SLEUTH. The ethnic sleuth entered crime and mystery fiction at the very outset. The Chevalier C. Auguste *Dupin, the "ratiocinative" Paris metaphysician in Edgar Allan *Poe's "The Murders in the Rue Morgue" (Godey's Lady's and Gentleman's Magazine, Apr. 1841), "The Mystery of Marie Roget" (Snowden's Lady's Companion, Nov. 1842), and "The Purloined Letter" (The Gift, 1845), serves as a founding ethnic sleuth—along with, in England, the figure of Count Fosco in The Woman in White (1860) by Wilkie *Collins.

For modern purposes, however, the key figure is Charlie *Chan, Earl Derr *Bigger's mandarin Hawaiian detective who makes his entrance in The House Without a Key (1925). Chan's amiable good manners, sing-song pidgin, and "Confucian" unraveling of each foible, *theft, and *murder immediately charmed audiences. Here lay the perfect rebuke to the "Yellow Menace" villainy of *Fu Manchu, first introduced by Sax *Rohmer in "The Zaya Kiss" (The Story-Teller, 1912) and typically sinister in President Fu Manchu (1936).

Chan and other stereotypes of inscrutability have not fared well in a latter-day multicultural age any more than has Fu Manchu or any other fantasy "oriental" villain possessed of a will to global domination and a dark, hardly concealed sexuality, like Shiwan Khan (one of Lamont Cranston's prime antagonists in the Shadow series) or Emperor Ming of the Flash Gordon stories and films. For as in film, cartoons, and every other kind of literature, ethnicity in mystery writing has never been less than an ambiguous element. If Chan, or another notably accented puzzle solver like Agatha *Christie's Hercule *Poirot, can bring an outsider's vantage-point to the "plots" of mainstream society, classic detectives like Dashiell *Hammett's eponymous sleuth in *The Continental Op* (1945) can use "ethnicity" (whether Asian or not) to suggest an especially alien or sinister criminality.

The writer who chooses to use an ethnic sleuth has some advantages in particularizing the hero's identity. Further, the ethnic cop, gumshoe, or *private eye can not only investigate "mainstream" society but also enter and decode a Chinatown, ghetto, *barrio*, tribal homeland, or particular religious community. For the most part, these communities remain closed to most nonethnic investigators. Ethnicity, used well, thus calls up not just the difference of a name or appearance or setting but of a whole psychology, an interior and understanding derived from "other" roots and mores.

In this respect American fiction offers a panorama—Japanese sleuths in the mold of John P. Marquand's Mr. *Moto introduced in *Ming Yellow* (1935) and of Howard Fast/E. V. Cunningham's Masao Masuto in *The Case of the One-Penny Orange* (1977); Elizabeth *Linington/Dell Shannon's Mexican Luis Mendoza of the San Diego force in *Case Pending* (1968) and its successors; Marcia *Muller's Santa Barbara chicana heroine, Elena Oliverez, in *The Tree of Death* (1983) and *Legend of the Slain Soldiers* (1985); John *Ball's Virgil *Tibbs, the black Pasadena cop whom Sidney Poitier portrayed in the film version of *In the Heat of the Night* (1965); Harry Kemelman's Rabbi David *Small of bestsellers like *Friday the Rabbi Slept Late* (1964); the mestizo Denver cop, Gabe Wager, whom Rex Burns first introduced in *The Alvarez Journal* (1975); and Barbara Neely's Blanche White in *Blanche on the Lam* (1992).

Inevitably, the issue of authenticity has arisen. For better or worse, there is debate over whose mysteries offer the more legitimate ethnicity: those written from an outside or an inside perspective? Some would argue that in the case of Afro-America, and of Harlem especially, Ernest Tidyman's John Shaft thrillers simply by dint of being white-written fall short of Chester *Himes's work featuring Coffin Ed *Johnson and Grave Digger Jones. In the case of a chicano milieu, some ask if Margaret *Millar's San Diego mystery *Beyond This Point Are Monsters* (1970) ranks below Rolando Hinojosa's Tex-Mex "Belken County" mystery *Partners in Crime* (1985). Has the acclaimed Navajo-Pueblo series of Tony *Hillerman featuring Sergeant Jim *Chee and Lieutenant Joe Leaphorn—especially a "historical" novel like *A Thief of Time* (1988), which involves the "detection" of the lost Anasazi tribe—eclipsed all others? Or should not Hillerman's cycle coexist with Indian-written mysteries like those of the Oklahoma and Choctaw-born Todd Downing? Certainly the question is accentuated in the multicultural portrait in Ed *McBain's Eighty-seventh Precinct series, where the local police squad includes the Italian Steve Carella, the Jewish Meyer Meyer, the African American Arthur Brown, the Puerto Rican Frankie Hernandez, and the Irish Peter Byrnes.

In the European tradition, similar controversies arise. The ingenious Judge Dee stories by the Dutch-born Robert H. *van Gulik, especially the two he chose to write in English, *The Chinese Bell Murders* (1958) and *The Chinese Maze Murders* (1962), may be open to the charge of ethnic-historical fantasia, but they nevertheless offer a shrewd lens through which to measure contemporary society. If Inspector *Van der Valk, first introduced by Nicolas *Freeling in *Love in Amsterdam* (1962), gives an English-eye view of Amsterdam, there is still a larger story in play— that of the modern city as maze and bureaucracy (a nice comparison could be drawn with the Rio de Janeiro patrolled by Robert L. Fish's Captain Jose da Silva of Brazil's federal police). H. R. F. *Keating's Inspector Ganesh Ninayak *Ghote of the Bombay CID can be read as an assiduous, genuinely nuanced attempt to decipher Indian culture as, notably, in *The Perfect Murder* (1964).

The major shift in ethnic mysteries has been the rise in the number of ethnic authors. In this Chester Himes holds a special place for the labyrinthine, gallows-humor, and often surreally violent Harlem of the *romans policiers* he began with *For Love of Imabelle* (1957). In his wake have come Ishmael Reed with his Vodoun, "Neo-Hoodoo," and postmodern Papa LaBas in *Mumbo-Jumbo* (1972); Walter *Mosley with his Ezekiel "Easy" *Rawlins series set in postwar black and white *Los Angeles and inaugurated with *Devil in a Blue Dress* (1990); and the black Guyanese British Mike Phillips, whose *Blood Rights* (1989) and *The Late Candidate* (1990), with journalist gumshoe Sam Dean, unravel not only murder but a fast-emerging multicultural England. In *Point of Darkness* (1994) Phillips transfers Dean to a multicultural Bronx and Queens in a plot that extends to California and Arizona. In like manner, the Cuban American Alex Abella writes a chicano East L.A. mystery (*The Killing of the Saints*, 1991) and Martin Cruz Smith explores Hopi culture in *Nightwing* (1977). Smith, in addition, can lay claim to Roman Grey, the Romany investigator of *Gypsy in Amber* (1971) and *Canto for a Gypsy* (1972).

The development of the ethnic sleuth and continuing popularity reflect the broadening of themes and audience of crime fiction, and its maturity as literature.

[*See also* African American Sleuth; Characterization; Native American Sleuth; Racism.]

• Edward Margolies, *Which Way Did He Go? The Private Eye in Dashiell Hammett, Raymond Chandler, Chester Himes and Ross Macdonald* (1982). Bill Pronzini and Martin H. Greenberg, eds., *The Ethnic Detectives: Masterpieces of Mystery Fiction* (1985). Werner Sollors, *Beyond Ethnicity: Consent and Descent in American Culture* (1986).   —A. Robert Lee

EUROPE, CRIME AND MYSTERY WRITING IN CONTINENTAL. *The tradition of crime and mystery writing in the following regions and countries is outlined below.*

The Netherlands and Flanders
Nordic Countries
Russia
Spain

INTRODUCTION

European crime writing in general shows a broadly similar pattern of growth and development to that experienced in both the United States and the United Kingdom. This is in spite of some of its practitioners variously having to contend with difficulties engendered by civil war, censorship, political propaganda, repressive regimes and bilingual states, and memories of former hostility and oppression which may sometimes surface.

The tradition begins with an early moving away from the established straight novel toward the novel of detection. A marked trend emerges in almost all European writing in the first half of the nineteenth century and is soon consolidated, as in the English-speaking world, when it becomes a discernible entity as crime fiction.

The genre burgeoned on the Continent up to and between the two world wars, slowly changing direction afterward from cozy to hard-boiled—fallible detectives seem to have come earlier on the Continent—and then moving from the roman noir toward a modified psychological approach.

Writers in most of the countries have been subject to cross-fertilization from translations, usually from English, but also from French and German. Crime writing in almost all of Europe shows the influence of writers such as Edgar Allan *Poe, Arthur Conan *Doyle, Peter Cheyney, Raymond *Chandler, Dashiell *Hammett, Agatha *Christie, and Patricia *Highsmith.

Even so, each country has also established its own individual tradition, at the same time giving the works of writers such as the French Maurice *Leblanc, the Belgian Georges *Simenon, and the Italian Umberto Eco to the rest of the world in translation. Among the strongest of these national traditions are the French and the Scandinavian, with the occasional writer such as the Swiss Friedrich *Dürrenmatt remaining international.

As elsewhere, the style and content of the European mystery story continue to reflect national and international political and sociological changes, the former being most evident in twentieth-century German writing. The rise in feminist writing is perhaps best instanced by the work done by a women authors' cooperative with origins in Catalan writing collectively under the name Ofèlia Dracs. In the work of one of its members, Maria-Antónia Oliver's Estudi en Lila (1985; Study in Lilac, 1987), the role of the female detective is as mediator and problem solver.

[See also Roman Policies.]

• Kathleen McNerney, preface to Estudi en Lila (1985).

—Catherine Aird

EASTERN EUROPE

The detective genre first began to take root in Eastern Europe during the period between the two world wars. Early productions, written in almost every subgenre including the *puzzle story, the *police procedural, and the novel of *suspense, tended to be highly derivative of Western models, and few of them received any attention internationally. Then, with the coming to power of Communist regimes in the aftermath of World War II, virtually anything that could be construed as being even indirectly critical of the status quo—and this included much crime fiction—was suppressed. Only ideologically acceptable work could be published, such as the espionage novels of the Romanian Theodor Constantin and the Pole Zbigniew Safjan, and police procedurals that celebrated the triumphs of "socialist *justice," for example those of the Bulgarians Bogomil Rainov and Andrei Guliashki (the latter also wrote a parody of the James *Bond *thriller), the Czech Eduard Fiker, the Pole Jerzy Edigey, and the Croatian Pavao Pavličič.

Having to work in the face of constant censorship and political pressure would spur other, better writers to approach their subjects ironically, by playing with conventions of the genre. In Czech literature this mode of writing originated with the great Karel Čapek, coiner of the word "robot." Čapek's detective stories, offering a blend of parody and *pastiche, attracted a number of emulators. Arguably, the most accomplished is Jiři Marek, whose collection of mystery short stories set in Prague are notable for their inventiveness and gentle comedy. The major, and much translated, Czech émigré writer Josef Škvorecky made several humorous forays into the field, creating the idiosyncratic detective Sergeant Boruvka. The Hungarian Jenö Rejtö, a contemporary of Čapek's, was a prolific author whose tongue-in-cheek mysteries, disguised as adventure novels, won renewed popularity with the decline of Communist rule. In Poland, the foremost practitioner of the pastiche *whodunit is Joe Alex (pseudonym of the noted literary critic Maciej Slomczynski), whose novels, invariably set in the West, are narrated—and their mysteries unraveled—by a character named Alex. Elegant *plots and an impeccable style are hallmarks of the "ironic mysteries" of another Pole, Joanna Chmielewska. Although he is best known internationally for his *science fiction, Stainslaw Lem addresses in his later work mysterious crimes that give rise to apparently unrelated solutions or are left essentially unsolved. Throughout Eastern Europe, meanwhile, a new wave of writers has begun to explore such topics as ethnic conflict, political terrorism in societies still in the throes of the transition from communism, and the rise of mafias.

[See also Spy Fiction.]

—Vassily Rudich

FRANCE AND BELGIUM

The creation of specialized detective fiction series in the 1930s in France stimulated an explosion of French and Belgian writers of crime and mystery literature. In France, Jacques Decrest's elegant police inspector Monsieur Gilles, Noël Vindry's examining magistrate Monsieur Allou, Pierre Véry's magic realism, and Juliette Pary's L'homme aux romans *policiers* (1933) created a French version of the classic British *detective novel.

In Belgium Jean Ray, inspired by turn-of-the-century French classics Fantômas and Arsène *Lupin, developed his Harry Dickson series, known as an American Sherlock *Holmes. With his French police commissioner Jules *Maigret, Georges *Simenon, although Belgian, created the archetype of the French detective hero. Simenon focused on *atmosphere and psychological character study.

The works of Stanislas-André Steeman are emblematic of the evolution of Belgian mystery and crime fiction from the 1930s to the late 1960s. His early works, notably *Six hommes morts* (1931; Six Dead Men), which introduced his suave and charming detective hero Monsieur Wenceslas Vorobeitchik, resemble those of Agatha *Christie. An interest in psychology also marked Steeman's work, as in *La maison des veilles* (1935).

As editor of *Le Jury* (1940–44), Steeman contributed to the emergence of a "golden age" of detective fiction in war-isolated Belgium. Louis-Thomas Jurdant with his predilection for English decor and detective heroes à la Edgar *Wallace, Louis Dubrau (pseudonym for Louise Scheidt), A. P. Duchateau, Paul Kinnet, and Thomas Owen, whose mix of supernatural in the detective *plot mirrored the work of John Dickson *Carr, participated in establishing an identifiable Belgian school of writing.

The postwar years witnessed a dual evolution of both French and Belgian detective novels. Steeman accelerated the shift of Belgian detective fiction toward a psychologically driven drama, continuing the trend exhibited in Carine's *Champs-Dormant* (1942); other examples include Anne Sylvius in *Guignol* (1944) and Jules Stéphane, whose inspector Savignon resembles Maigret in his humanistic and psychological approach to crime. In *Haute tension* (1953) and *Une veuve dort seule* (1960), Steeman reasserted his tendency toward the examination of criminal character and *motive. In France, Pierre Boileau and Thomas Narcejac in *Celle qui n'était plus* (1952; The Woman Who Was No More) developed the psychological suspense novel, followed by Sébastien Japrisot in *La dame dans l'auto avec des lunettes et un fusil* (1966; The Lady in the Car with Glasses and a Gun) and Laurence Oriol in *Le tueur est parmi nous* (1983).

Influenced by the American-style *hard-boiled detective novel, (*roman noir* in French), Belgian Max Servais's *La mort de Cléopâtre* (1941), featuring an action-driven *plot, realistic *milieus, everyday language, and *private detective Nicky Noël, was a precursor to Léo Malet's Nestor Burma series, beginning with 120, rue de la Gare (1943), and to the French *roman noir* of the 1950s. Coinciding with the creation of Frédéric Dard's detective hero San Antonio, Steeman introduced a Lemmy Caution/Mike Hammer-inspired detective, Désiré Marco, in *Madame la mort* (1951). Yvan Dailly's *J'ai bien l'honneur* (1950–51), André Duquesne's *Retour de femme* (1958), and Georges Tiffany's (pseudonym of Jacqueline de Boulle) *Etes-vous Emilie?* (1967) continued this trend. Whereas Belgian writers emigrated to French

publishing houses after the war, thus diluting the specificity of their work as a group, Jean Amila, Auguste Le Breton, Albert Simonin, and Jean-Patrick Manchette developed a distinctively French-style *roman noir* in the 1970s and 1980s.

[*See also* Roman Policier.]

• Danny de Laet, *Les anarchistes de l'ordre,* (1908–1980. Luc Dellisse, *Le policier fantôme: Mise en situation du roman policier belge de type classique, suivi d'un répertoire des auteurs et des collections* (1984). Michel Lebrun and Jean-Paul Schweighaeuser, *Le guide du "polar:"* (1987). Norbert Spehner and Yvon Allar, *Ecrits sur le roman policier: Bibliographie analytique et critique des études et essais sur le roman et le film policiers.* (1990). —Deborah E. Hamilton

GERMANY

Contrary to a widely held view, Germany possesses a rich tradition of popular crime and detective fiction, the memory of which, however, was lost after World War II. Only a few works by established writers are usually cited today as rare examples of German crime and detective fiction, notably Johann Christoph Friedrich Schiller's *Der Verbrecher aus verlorener Ehre* (1786; A Criminal, in Consequence of Lost Reputation), E. T. A. Hoffman's *Das Fräulein von Scuderi* (1819; Mademoiselle de Scudéry), Annette von Droste-Hülshoff's *Die Judenbuche* (1842; The Jew's Beech), Theodor Fontane's *Unterm Birnbaum* (1885; Under the Pear Tree), and Wilhelm Raabe's *Stopfkuchen: Eine See- und Mordgeschichte* (1891; Tubby Schaumann: A Tale of Murder and the High Seas).

Toward the end of the eighteenth century, in the wake of François Guyot de Pitaval's *Causes célèbres et intéressantes* (1734ff.; Famous and Interesting Cases), case histories and crime stories, often based on real cases, became an important medium for examining the causes of criminality. Anselm Feuerbach's *Merkwürdige Criminal-Rechtsfälle* (1808–11; Noteworthy Law Cases), his *Aktenmäßige Darstellung merkwürdiger Verbrechen* (1828–29; Documentary Accounts of Remarkable Crimes), and Julius Edward Hitzig's and Wilhelm Häring's *Der neue Pitaval* (1842–90; The New Pitaval), as well as crime stories by other writers satisfied the interest in crime.

Detective fiction emerged in the first half of the nineteenth century with Adolph Müllner's *Der Kaliber: Aus den Papieren eines Criminalbeamten* (1829; The Calibre: From the Papers of a Magistrate), considered to be the first of its kind in Germany. The abolition of torture earlier in the century and changes in the criminal code after 1848 stimulated public interest in crime detection and led to the publication of an increasing number of detective stories in the popular journals. Some of Hubertus Temme's stories and Adolph Streckfuß's *Der Sternkrug* (1870; The Crossroads Tavern) are early examples of detective fiction.

Toward the end of the nineteenth century, under the influence of Arthur Conan *Doyle's Sherlock *Holmes, the *detective novel became dominant. In the following years important contributions were made by Augusta Groner (*The Man with the Black Cord*, 1911), Balduin Groller (*Detektiv Degoberts*

Taten und Abenteuer, 1910–12; Detective Dagobert's Exploits and Adventures), and Paul Rosenhayn (*Joe Jenkins' Case Book*, 1930). Other noteworthy writers of the period were Hans Hyan, Ferdinand Runkel, and Fred Andreas (*Der Mann, der zweimal leben wollte*, 1932; *Death at Heel*, 1933; *Alias*, 1933).

During the Nazi era, crime and detective fiction served the Nazi ideology and the war effort. After 1945, most detective novels failed to address the postwar situation, and could not compete with the growing number of translations from English-speaking countries. During the fifties, however, Fred Arnau introduced the realistic *police procedural, set mostly in the United States. In his wake, a new generation of crime writers began to employ American and other European models in order to comment on the political unrest that gripped West Germany during the 1960s. Among the pioneers of the revival of German crime fiction were Hansjörg Martin (*Kein Schnaps für Tamara*, 1966; *Sleeping Girls Don't Lie*, 1976); Michael Molsner, who acknowledged the influence of Raymond Chandler; Irene Rodrian, whose novels are reminiscent of Patricia Highsmith; Friedhelm Werremeier, whose police procedurals feature Kommissar Trimmel; and Horst Bosetzky, who pioneered the *Sozio-Krimi*, a crime novel with a pronounced sociocritical tendency as influenced by Maj *Sjöwall and Per *Wahlöö. The sociocritical trend continued to be popular with writers in the 1970s.

During the eighties many talented writers made their debuts. Women made significant contributions, which included introducing feminist issues into the genre. Doris Gercke tackled the responsibility of every citizen for the corrupt and oppressive institutions of Germany in *Weinschröter, du mußt hängen* (1990; *How Many Miles to Babylon*, 1991).

East German crime fiction developed independently. Although originally frowned upon by the authorities, by the mid-1970s the crime novel was accepted as a useful vehicle for the transmission of socialist values. Important writers were Fritz Erpenbeck, Gerhard Neumann, and Tom Wittgen.

After the fall of the Berlin Wall, writers like Tom Wittgen (*Eine dreckige Geschichte*, 1991; An Ugly Story), Leo P. Ard and Michael Illner (*Gemischtes Doppel*, 1992; Mixed Doubles), and Jürgen Kehrer (*Killer nach Leipzig*, 1993; Killer to Leipzig), focused their attention on the political situation in the new Germany.

• Hans Otto Hügel, *Untersuchungsrichter, Diebsfänger, Detektive: Theorie und Geschichte der deutschen Detektiverzählung im 19. Jahrhundert* (1978). Karl Ermet and Wolfgang Gast, eds., *Der neue deutsche Kriminalroman: Beiträge zu Darstellung, Interpretation und Kritik eines populären Genres* (1985). Knut Hickethier, "Der alte deutsche Kriminalroman," *Die Horen*, 31, no. 4 (1986): 15–23. H. P. Karr, *Lexikon der deutschen Krimi-Autoren* (1992).   —Dieter Riegel

ITALY

Emilio de Marchi's Dostoyevskian novel *Il cappello del prete* (1887; The Priest's Hat) is considered to be the progenitor of the modern detective novel in Italy. It contained many of the ingredients that were to typify the best Italian novels in the genre: the concentration on a confined milieu, an element of irony, and an almost fatalistic belief in the role of fortune. Detection as such plays little part; the criminal is known from the start, and it is the priest's hat of the title that serves to trap him.

The novel had no immediate successors, and it was not until the 1930s that an Italian school of detective fiction can be said to have arisen. Although popular with readers, the classic detective novel seemed less congenial to Italian writers; the novels of the period relied heavily upon conventions of the genre and the use of the dandified *sleuth. A notable exception was Augusto De Angelis, who indulged in conscious parody.

After the war, some new writers emerged who were less dependent on foreign models. The distinguishing feature of their writing is its intensely local flavor. Giorgio Scerbanenco's novels of the sixties such as *Tradition di tutti* (1966; *Duca and the Milan Murders*, 1970) draw a bleak picture of Milan, Loriano Macchiavelli's Inspector Sarti novels a less jaded one of Bologna; Attilio Veraldi concentrates on the violent underworld of Naples as in *La mazzetta* (1976; *The Pay off*). With copious use of local dialect, Andrea Camilleri depicts contemporary and nineteenth-century life in a fictional Sicilian town, Vigáta. The tendency to emphasize *setting is perhaps seen at its best in Renato Olivieri's novels about Commissario Ambrosio including *Maledetto Ferragosto* (1988; Hellish August), which describe the world of bourgeois Milan with painstaking topical exactitude.

Carlo Fruttero and Franco Lucentini wrote two long and witty detective novels set in Turin, *La donna della domenica* (1972; *The Sunday Woman 1973*) and *A che punto è la notte?* (1979; At What Point Is the Night?). In 1991 they returned to the genre with *Enigma in luogo di mare* (*An Enigma by the Sea*), set in a holiday community in Tuscany. The detective is an ex-depressive who undertakes the investigation for therapeutic purposes.

The *amateur detective is comparatively rare in Italian fiction, as is the *private eye. Most writers choose policemen or examining magistrates as their protagonists, and this is generally true of Leonardo Sciascia, the most important Italian writer to have used the genre. His novels, *Il giorno della civetta* (1961; *Mafia Vendetta; The Day of the Owl*) and *Una storia semplice* (1989; A Simple Story) show minor-ranking officials doing their honest best to untangle a web of corruption. This reflects his belief in the value of the law in a Mafia-ridden society, but justice rarely prevails in Sciascia's pessimistic view of Sicily and Italy.

Two other major writers who have adopted the genre are Carlo Emilio Gadda and Umberto Eco. Gadda's novel *Quer pasticciaccio brutto de via Merulana* (1957; *That Awful Mess on Via Merulana*), although constructed around a murder investigation, is more interested in the multiplication of viewpoints than the discovery of the murderer. Eco, however, undoubtedly produced a detective novel with *Il nome della rosa* (1980; *The Name of the Rose*). His fascination with conspiracy theories is explored in *Il pendolo di Foucault* (1988; *Foucault's Pendulum*).

The 1990s saw the emergence of Carlo Lucarelli, who began with a trilogy of atmospheric novels set in the Fascist and post-Fascist period and has also written novels about contemporary Italy in a vigorous colloquial style.

• Loris Rambelli, *Storia del "giallo" italiano* (1979). Carlo Fruttero and Franco Lucentini, "Yellow Books: Why the Italians Prefer Reading Thrillers to Writing Them," *Times Literary Supplement* 4574 (30 Nov.–6 Dec. 1990): 1289.

—Gregory Dowling

THE NETHERLANDS AND FLANDERS

The first exemplars of crime and mystery writing in the Netherlands and Flanders were modeled on foreign works, particularly those in the English language. In response to perceived readers' taste, these works mainly featured non-Dutch and non-Flemish characters and *settings. In fact, Maarten Maarten's *The Black Box Murder* (1889), considered to be the first detective novel written by a Netherlands author, was originally written in English and published in England. Jacob van Schevichaven, a contemporary of Arthur Conan *Doyle, wrote highly successful formula stories under the name Ivans, modeling his work after the Sherlock *Holmes stories. During the first half of the twentieth century, H. van der Kallen used the pen name Havank when he wrote twenty-nine humorous novels about his popular and eloquent character, the Shadow, an inspector with the Parisian police. However, in the 1930s, Willy Corsari, Mr. A. Roothaert, and Jan de Hartog, using the pseudonym F. R. Eckmar, wrote thoroughly Dutch detective novels.

Until the 1960s, traditional puzzle-centered *plots and *police detectives dominated Dutch detective fiction, while topical themes were less important. Police detectives investigated crimes in a dozen novels by the Flemish Dr. Louis van den Bergh writing as Aster Berkhoff, in thirty-two novels by the Dutch sisters M. A. Wierdels-Monsma and H. S. Paauwe-Monsma using the joint pseudonym Martin Mons, and in twelve books by W. H. Haasse writing as W. H. Van Eemlandt. More realistic police routine is described in four well-written novels by Joop van den Broek writing as Jan van Gent. During the 1960s, more novels featuring police investigators were written by Pim Hofdrop, A. C. *Baantjer, and Ton Vervoort. Robert H. *van Gulik is in a category of his own, with *historical mysteries featuring Judge Dee, set in seventh-century China.

Grim realism entered Netherlands crime literature with *Parels voor Nadra* (1953; Pearls for Nadra) by Joop van den Broek, the first hard-boiled *thriller by a Dutch author, set in postcolonial Indonesia: It was followed by a series of adventures published over four decades. Theo Eerdmans and John Hoogland also turned out hard-boiled thrillers. The more traditional work of Rico Bulthuis and Bert Japin and the psychological thrillers of Ab Visser all have remarkable literary quality. Around the same time Ted Viking and H. J. Oolbekkink were producing *spy fiction.

During the 1960s, Gerben Hellinga, writing as Hellinger, and Anton Kuyten, writing as Anton Quintana, continued the hard-boiled form while the brothers Faber and Heere Heeresma produced burlesques and crime critic Rinus Ferdinandusse turned out satirical novels. A great stimulus to the genre remains the successful series of *police procedurals by Janwillem *van de Wetering, featuring eccentric Amsterdam plainclothes duo Grijpstra and De Gier.

Due to this success accompanied by the rise of a new generation of authors during the 1980s, led by Willem Hogendoorn writing as Tomas Ross, crime fiction in the Netherlands began to achieve status and recognition, while demonstrating a shift to realism and issue-oriented fiction. Ross's writing can be termed "faction," since it fixes its plots around commonly known historical and political facts. Ross's work, reflecting conflicts of modern history in ingenious plots, finds equals in the novels of Flemish authors Jef Geeraerts and Bob Mendes. Big-city settings are to be found in the thrillers of Theo Capel and Gerben Hellinga, who set their work in urban Amsterdam; Jacques Post's Rotterdam novels; and in intriguing novels by Peter de Zwaan. During the same time period, Koos van Zomeren analyzed internal politics and Martin Koomen turned out a fine series of espionage novels set in the 1930s. Traumas engendered by the German occupation play a part in *Geweten* (1996; Conscience), one of the oppressive psychological thrillers by René Appel, Rippen, and in an expressive novel, *Sporen* (1988; Traces), by Chris Rippen. Bert Hiddema, Charles den Tex, and Niels and Lydia Rood, who write as Rood and Rood, also deal with environmental issues. *Organized crime is everywhere, exemplified in the thrillers by Jacob Vis and Jac Toes.

The Association of Netherlands Crime Writers, or Het Genootschap van Nederlandstalige Misdaadauteurs, was founded in 1986 to promote the position of crime literature by authors who write in Dutch or the closely related Flemish language. The organization annually confers the BRUNA Golden Noose (Gouden Strop) award and Shadow (De Schaduw) debut prize. In 1995, the group assumed membership in the International Association of Crime Writers.

• Jan C. Roosendaal, "Misdaad in Holland," in *Moord in doodslag*, ed. Julian Symons (1976).   —Chris Rippen

NORDIC COUNTRIES

Scandinavian writers were producing crime and mystery fiction before Edgar Allan *Poe's "The Murders in the Rue Morgue" (*Graham's Lady's and Gentleman's Magazine*, Apr. 1841). In 1825 the Norwegian Maurits Christopher Hansen published "Kaeden eller Klosterruinen" (The Chain of the Cloister Ruin), a crime story with subsidiary *plots, and followed it up with "Mordet paa Maskinbygger Roolfsen" (The Murder of Engine Builder Roolfsen). The Dane Steen Steensen Blicher's "Praesten i Vejlbye: En criminalhistorie of herresfoged Erik Sorensens Dagbog" (The Vicar of Vejlbye), published in 1829, is considered the first fictitious crime story of literary value written in Scandinavia. As early as 1822 the Swede Carl Jonas Love Almqvist had published the novel

Amorina: Eller historien om de fyra (Amorina), part mystery and part fantasy. His *Drottningens juvelsmycke* (1834; The Queen's Necklace) is the story of the *murder of King Gustavus III, and his "Skällnora kvarn" (1838; The Mill of Skällnora) is a short story of crime and detection.

It was not until century's end that Scandinavian writers returned to the genre. For decades the market was dominated by pale imitations of English, German, and American mysteries. Beginning in the 1930s, however, writers succeeded in shaking off foreign influence and typical national mysteries emerged.

The first modern Swedish mystery novel appeared in 1893 with the publication of *Stockholmsdetektiven* (The Stockholm Detective) by Fredrik Lindholm writing as Prins Pierre. The only writer of note during the early decades of the twentieth century was Frank Heller, whose books have been translated into many languages. Stieg Trenter updated the genre, and Vic Suneson introduced the Swedish *police procedural. In the 1960s Jan Ekström emerged as the master of *locked room mysteries, Maj *Sjöwall and Per Wahlöö began their partnership with the first of their ten books featuring Martin *Beck and his colleagues, Staffan Westerlund developed the ecological thriller, and Ulf Durling created masterpieces of psychological mystery. Three of the most important mystery writers currently at work are Kerstin Ekman, with *Händelser vid vatten* (1993; *Blackwater*, 1997); Henning Mankell, who has breathed new life into the police procedural; and Jan Guillou, whose spy novels have broken best-seller records. The *hard-boiled mystery has never taken root in Sweden.

Palle Rosenkrantz became Denmark's first modern mystery writer with his first novel, *Hvad Skovsøen gemte: Detectivroman* (1903; What Is Hidden in the Lake). The 1960s and 1970s were the high point of the genre in Denmark. Anders Bodelsen gained international fame for his psychological novels; Poul Ørum combined the police procedural and the psychological crime novel; Torben Nielsen's police procedurals analyzed the contemporary scene; and Frits Remnar tried his hand at various categories of crime novel writing, most successfully about the average man in conflict with his conscience. In the 1980s Dan Turèll introduced his nameless Copenhagen-based *private eye, and in the 1990s Fleming Jarlskov wrote hard-boiled works also set in Copenhagen, yet without slavishly copying American models. Turèll and Jarlskov each put a Danish spin on an American tradition.

Among the earliest Norwegian mystery writers was the poet Olaf Bull, who published *Mit Navn er Knoph* (My Name Is Knoph) in 1913. As was true elsewhere in Scandinavia, most early Norwegian mysteries were set in the capital, the books often bearing titles alluding to the "big city" and its horrors. The most popular and prolific of the early writers were Stein Riverton (pseudonym of Sven Elvestad) and Øvre Richter Frich—the former a skillful writer and stylist, the latter somewhat primitive in his handling of plot and character. Jonas Lie, Vidkun

Quisling's police minister during the German occupation of World War II, wrote a handful of mysteries as Max Mauser; Bernhard Borge (pseudonym of the poet André Bjerke) also wrote psychological crime novels in the 1940s. Police procedurals and spy novels began to appear in the 1960s and 1970s. In Denmark and Sweden the success of Sjöwall and Wahlöö inspired many imitators, but Norway produced only one novelist of the police procedural, Tor Edvin Dahl writing as David Torjussen. In 1977 Jon Michelet published *Orions Belte: En roman fra Svalbard* (Orion's Belt), a thriller that evoked the novels of Hammond Innes. In four books over ten years, Kim Smage combined the feminist novel with hard-boiled conventions. Gunnar Staalesen writes in the hard-boiled private eye tradition, setting his stories in the town of Bergen.

The leading pioneer of the genre in Finland was Uuno Hirvonen, whose *Gyldenbrookien kunnia* (The Honor of the Golden Brooks) was published in 1918. Mika Waltari achieved fame as a mystery writer in his own country but was better known elsewhere for his works about ancient Egypt. The policeman Matti Joensuu's police procedurals present a realistic picture of the society in which they are set.

Iceland is almost a blank spot on the map of mystery fiction, even though interest in the genre is enormous. Most of its crime fiction has been based on true cases. In 1999 only two crime writers were active in Iceland: Gunnar Gunnarsson and Thor Vilhjálmsson.

• Jörgen Elgström and Åke Runnquist, *Svensk mordbok: Den Svenska Detectivromanens Historia*, 1900–1950 (1957). Bjørn Carling, *Norsk kriminallitteratur gjennom 150 år* (1976). Harald Mogensen, *Mord og mysterier* (1983). Keijo Kettunen and Risto Raitio, "The History of Finnish Crime Fiction" in *Rapport, Proceedings: Nordkrim '92* (1992). Kristinn Kristjánsson, "Den islandske krimi" in *Rapport, Proceedings: Nordkrim '92* (1992). Willy Dahl, *Dødens fortellere* (1993). Bo Lundin, *Århundradets svenska deckare* (1993).

—K. Arne Blom

RUSSIA

As a distinct subgenre of popular literature, the Russian crime novel dates from the second half of the nineteenth century. The first practitioner to achieve any renown was Alexandr Shkliarevskii (1837–1883), the author of tales drawn largely from the world of police practice and unfolding against a squalid background of petty officialdom and the demimonde. The setting is similar to that portrayed by Fyodor Mikhaylovich *Dostoyevsky, at least three of whose major novels *Prestuplenie I nakazanie* (1866; *Crime and Punishment*), *Besy* (1872; *The Possessed*), and *Brat'ia Karamazovy* (1879; *The Brothers Karamazov*) revolve around crime and its exposure. During the rest of the prerevolutionary period, little else of intrinsic literary merit was produced within the genre.

In the early years of the Soviet regime the entire genre was denounced as an offshoot of bourgeois society, but it was tolerated when it was dressed up as anticapitalist *satire, as in Marietta Shaginian's *Mess-mend* (1924), or purported to expose the nefarious schemes of class enemies both within and without the "socialist fatherland," as in the crudely didactic works of the prominent judiciary official Lev Sheinin, and the spy novelists Nikolai Shpanov and Lev Ovalov. It was not until the 1970s that the detective novel, despite and in defiance of the stifling political climate in the so-called "period of stagnation," began to achieve quality and stature. Since Soviet reality left no room for the existence of the *private eye, the majority of these works are more akin to *police procedurals, dealing as they do with criminal investigations conducted by officers of the national militia, the Ministry of the Interior, or the Office of the Public Prosecutor. Two competent professionals are Arkadii Adamov and Mikhail Chenyonok, who are capable of constructing intricate and suspenseful works; more remarkable, however, are the novels of Eremei Parnov which contain elements of both the historical novel and *science fiction; and, particularly, those of the brothers Arkadii and Georgii Vainer, who display a keen interest in social and psychological analysis. Their sequence of novels *Petlia I kamen' v zelenoi trave* (A Loop and a Stone in the Green Grass) and *Evangelie ot palacha* (published 1991 and 1992, written in the mid-1970s; The Gospel According to an Executioner) authentically communicate the terror Experienced by the Soviet intelligentsia in the wake of Stalin's anti-Semitic campaigns of the late 1940s and early 1950s.

Of espionage fiction, still by far the most popular—owing in part to the TV series based upon it—is Yulian Semyonov's multivolume saga featuring the Soviet intelligence agent Isaev-Stierlitz, whose adventures are largely set during and in the aftermath of World War II. A mainstream writer Vladimir Bogomolov achieved fame with his excellent novel *Moment istiny* (1980; The Moment of Truth), which describes in detail a Soviet counter-intelligence operation against the Nazis. Finally, two emigré authors, Friedrich Neznansky and Edward Topol, writing as collaborators and separately, have produced political thrillers, some of them first-rate, unmasking military adventurism and power struggles within the Kremlin.

The arrival of perestroika and the subsequent collapse of the Soviet Union triggered a veritable avalanche of crime fiction. Much of it, written often by former KGB officers, has little or no literary value and exhibits anti-liberal and chauvinist sentiments. Other authors, such as Daniil Koretskii, Georgii Mironov, and, notably, Nikolai Leonov, expose the corruption within the new economic system and the rise of mafia-style organized crime. The work of Aleksandra Marinina, distinguished by subtle characterization and extravagant plots, seems to exercise a particular appeal to the public.

[*See also* Spy Fiction.]

—Vassily Rudich

SPAIN

In 1853, just thirteen years after the publication of Poe's "Murders in the Rue Morgue," Spaniard Pedro de Alarcón published the short story "El clavo" (The Nail), generally considered the first formal detective story in Spanish, about a woman who dispatches her husband by driving a nail through his head while he sleeps. Novelist Emilia Pardo Bazán contributed to the new genre with "La gota de sangre" (The Drop of Blood) in *Belcebú: (Novelas cortas)* (1912), and in the late nineteenth century many crime-centered penny novels appeared, often written by authors who used English-sounding *pseudonyms. Translations from English and French were avidly read, and by 1909 Joaquin Belda produced a spoof of Sherlock *Holmes and other detectives in ¿Quién dispaó? (Who Fired?). A farcical play that premiered in 1916, *Sebastián el Bufanda, o el robo de la calle Fortuny* (Sebastián the "Scarf," or Robbery on Fortuny Street), by José Ignacio de Alberti and Enrique López Alarcón, introduced several key characteristics of detective fiction in Spain. The first is an absolute refusal to create an omniscient, omnipotent detective who never fails. The variety of Spanish sleuths is great, but one will not find the virtual mind-reader like Poe's Chevalier C. Auguste *Dupin or an infallible righter of wrongs like Sherlock *Holmes. The Spanish detective is above all things human and fallible. The play also makes great use of criminal slang, continuing in the tradition of Miguel de Cervantes and Francisco de Quevedo. Last, and probably the most outstanding characteristic of Spanish detective fiction, is a basic distrust of the police.

The confusion of the prewar years and the destruction that occurred during the Spanish Civil War (1936–39), followed by World War II, severely curtailed literary production of all kinds. In Spanish detective fiction only one name emerged during the war itself: E. C. Delmar published three novels, set in Barcelona and Holmesian in format. During the dictatorship of Generalísimo Francisco Franco (1939–75), harsh censorship discouraged the development of a Chandlerian novel and exploration of police *corruption. Translations from English and French detective fiction were popular.

In 1953, Mario Lacruz published *El inocente* (The Suspect, 1956), a Kafkaesque tale of a man on the lam from corrupt policemen, but it was only in 1965, Francisco García Pavón published the first of a string of novels and stories featuring Plinio, that a well-known detective series was launched in the small town of Tomelloso, Ciudad Real, investigated small, everyday crimes and local problems, and thus the books were not considered threatening by Francoist censors.

While García Pavón was developing a rural *cozy mystery tradition in the central plains, writers to the north in Catalunya were struggling in the face of censorship to produce a Catalan-language *novella negra (roman noir)* after Dashiell *Hammett, Raymond *Chandler, James M. *Cain, and Chester *Himes. Manuel de Pedrolo published *L'inspector fa tard* (The Inspector Arrives Late) in 1953, followed by a series of experiments in various genres, including the *roman noir*, the most famous of which is *Joc brut* (1965; Dirty Pool) a tale strongly flavored by Cain. Pedrolo's most notable follower of the 1970s was Jaume Fuster, whose *De mica en mica s'omple la pica* (1972; Little by Little the Basin Fills) is the first of a number of detective works that run a gamut from cozy to avant-grade to hard-boiled.

In the late seventies and early eighties a number of writers already famous for more "serious" fiction contributed detective novels. Eduardo Mendoza contributed two outrageously funny books starring an unnamed paranoid schizophrenic released by the Barcelona police to serve as an informant, and Fernando Savater and Lourdes Ortiz also wrote a detective work each, Ortiz's with the only female Spanish sleuth to that date—Barbara Arenas. The most significant detective work to appear in the seventies, was Manuel Vázquez Montalbán's *Tatuaje* (1974; Tatoo) featuring Pepe Carvalho, a former Marxist turned CIA agent turned private investigator. Other important contributors since the 1980s have been journalist Juan Madrid and Andreu Martín, who is prolific in both Spanish and Catalan and whose works include dual-language juvenile detective novel.

A strong tradition developed in the Catalan language following Pedrolo. Under the pseudonym Ofèlia Dracs, a collective published *Negra i consentida* (1983; Hardboiled and Spoiled), a potpourri of detective fiction in different styles by a dozen authors. Both the Majorcan Maria-Antonia Oliver and the Valencian Isabel-Clara Simó have created strong female heroines whose exploits have been translated into English. Mercè Rodoreda, Maria-Aurelia Capmany Margarida Aritzeta, Assumpta Margenat, and Assumpcio Maresma are other women who have written detective fiction in Catalan.

American and British criticism of detective fiction in Spain tends to focus on one or two "literary" novels with some characteristics of the mystery, such as Juan Benet's *El Aire de un Crimen* (1980; The Air of a Murder), while ignoring more Authentic examples of the genre.

Various novels of crime and detection began to appear in Euskera the Basque language and Galician in the late 1980s and early 1990s.   —Patricia Hart

EVIL. In the era of the radio serial a popular program of crime and detection asked, "Who knows what evil lurks in the hearts of men?" The narrator assured the audience, "The Shadow knows." The popularity of the mystery tale suggests that readers are interested in some literary resolution of the issues of crime, guilt, and suffering, which wrestle with the question of evil.

Evil is experienced, in the external world and within the human heart, in the divide between human experience and the expectation of goodness. It is not only the fact that the good does not always happen, also the reality that something seems actively to resist goodness, which leads to the exploration of evil.

Crime and mystery fiction can explore evil at several levels. It may, by illustration, give expression to the existence and limits of evil. It may speculate about the source or cause of evil. It may examine the adequacy of explanations of evil, and it may suggest the degree to which it is possible to resist, constrain, or defeat evil.

That there is crime, even *murder, does not in itself explain much about the nature of evil. But what crime suggests about the sources of evil, and about how wide it is spread, begins to help to describe the human condition. For instance, classical writers of detection such as Agatha *Christie and Arthur *Conan Doyle tend to present evil as a containable disruption occasionally introduced into an otherwise good society. By defeating or constraining the *villain, as Sherlock *Holmes constrains his nemesis Professor *Moriarty, the protagonist both preserves *innocence and restores order to society. In contrast, the hard-boiled detectives of writers like Dashiell *Hammett, Raymond *Chandler, and Ross *Macdonald typically inhabit a world in which evil in endemic. The detective's investigation reveals that evil is to be found not in a single identifiable villain but with in a circle that grows ever wider as the investigation goes on. This is sometimes portrayed, as in Hammett's *The Maltese Falcon* (1930) or Fredric Brown's *The Screaming Mimi* (1949), in the guilt of the detective's beloved. In such stories *innocence is much harder to maintain. Between these extremes, the genre is capable of illustrating a wide range of arguments about the existence and extent of evil.

However wide or narrow the circle of guilt, the next question is the source of the evil portrayed. Crime and mystery fiction asks: Is evil caused by some malevolent force, or by a few wicked people? Or is it a part of the fabric of social life? Is evil potentially harbored in every human heart? The work of three American writers of the hard-boiled school Provides three different perspectives. Mickey *Spillane's *private eye, Mike *Hammer, and those close to him are good. Others, such as the villainous Lilly Carver in *Kiss Me Deadly* (1952), are evil and must be defeated before further harm befalls the innocent. For Macdonald, evil is explained psychologically. As in his *The Underground Man* (1971), the sufferings of the present generation can only be explained by the wounds passed down from previous generations; solutions to present mysteries are worked out in light of the history of tragedy in the family. Author Sara *Paretsky tends to think in sociological and economic terms. Her *Burn Marks* (1990) opens with a family problem, and the hero has a measure of personal guilt. But, for Paretsky, evil's true locus is the large institutions of business, politics, and *religion.

The problem of evil emerges in theological reflection from the assumption of an omnipotent creator willing the good. A source of "ought" makes evil a philosophical problem. In her novel *Clouds of Witness* (1926), Dorothy L. *Sayers brought a theological consciousness to crime fiction while seldom seeming to write about matters of religion. Starting about 1910 with G. K. *Chesterton's Father *Brown stories, the genre has made room for numerous clerical detectives whose experience of evil leads them to reflect theologically on the great mysteries of the human condition. The genre is also capable of representing other religious perspectives. In *The Blessing Way* (1970) and subsequent tribal *police procedurals, Tony *Hillerman attempts to represent a Navajo worldview. Whether evil is introduced by Navajo skin walkers (witches) or by the disruptive incursions of the white world, the solution requires not only the identification of the guilty but also the ritual return to a balanced "way of beauty" in keeping with the actions of the first people.

At least as far back as the biblical Book of Job, literature has evaluated the cultural justifications offered for evil. Is the guilt of the sufferer always the explanation of suffering? The mystery story seems to reject such an assertion out of hand. It is the apparent innocence of the client that typically requires the detective's action. In the *whodunit tale, such as Doyle's "The Red Headed League," (*Strand*, Aug. 1891) the explanation of the cause is less important than the identification of the perpetrator.

In the hard-boiled tradition a far darker vision of the world is explored. The famous "Flitcraft parable," in Hammett's *The Maltese Falcon*, is an assertion of moral ambiguity. In a world where tragedy and evil strike randomly one must adapt to present realities. A more romantic Chandler shares Hammett's worldview but offers in Philip *Marlowe a hero of less ambiguous virtue. Chandler's *The Big Sleep* (1939) opens with an only mildly ironic analogy between Marlowe and Saint George slaying the dragon. This idealization of the hero points to a limitation in the genre's ability to fully plumb the limits of evil. The serial nature of so much of the genre, even in a series which expresses a quite dark view of the world, points to the genre's romantic hope. In order to preserve the possibility of the reader's innocence, the detective must rise above the evil that corrupts others. Evil may be real, the world fallen, but the hero models some possibility of *virtue. Only the writer who is at least willing to entertain the possibility of the hero's corruptibility can examine the full range of the problem of evil.

If evil exists, then there remains the question of human response. Is it possible to resist evil? And if so, is it likely that people will? One solution, popular with those who think of themselves as good, is the sort of predestinarian divide between good and evil portrayed in the works of Spillane cited above. Far more complicated and ambiguous schema are explored by others. Chandler's famous essay "The Simple Art of Murder" (*Atlantic Monthly*, Dec. 1944) lays out the traditional hard-boiled vision of a world in which *corruption is easy, and evil an ever present and often banal temptation. His is a world in which society itself corrupts, and in which evil can be resisted by moral individuals only at considerable social cost.

The mystery story is capable of exploring the questions of evil. Its focus on crime and guilt makes it a form that illustrates the existence and variation of evil. Practitioners have used it to express and question suggestions about the source and locus of evil, to examine human nature, and to consider how evil might be constrained. However, it must be acknowledged that the romantic presentation of the protagonist limits the ability of the genre to explore fully the corruptibility of the human heart.

[*See also* Characterization; Femme Fatale; Master Criminal.]

• Radoslav A. Tasnoff, "Problem of Evil," in *Dictionary of the History of Ideas*, ed. Philip P. Wiener (1973). W. H. Auden, "The Guilty Vicarage," in *Detective Fiction Criticism: A Collection of Critical Essays*, ed. Timothy W. Johnson and Julia Johnson (1981). Paul Ricoeur, "Evil," in *The Encyclopedia of Religion*, ed. Mircea Eliade (1987). William David Spencer, *Mysterium and Mystery* (1989). Jeffrey H. Mahan, *A Long Way from Solving That One* (1990).
—Jeffrey H. Mahan

EXPEDITIONS. The expedition mystery can have it both ways: The principals are removed to a wide-open, foreign, even threatening *milieu where anything seems possible—yet the expedition itself can function as a closed-world setting, virtually a transplanted village. The wide-open element aligns it with the *thriller, the closed-society aspect with the traditional mystery. Constant features include the exploitation of local color and the use of expedition artifacts as unusual murder *weapons. In these stories, the advancement of knowledge must compete with the monetary value of the sought-after artifacts, and frequent parallels are made between detection and such activities as tracking and excavating: observing minute detail and sifting, sorting, and reconstructing on-site evidence.

Expedition mysteries set in the Old World favor colonial and former colonial settings, particularly East Africa, Egypt, and the Near East, where hunting or archaeological interests mix with international politics which run the gamut of colonialist, anticolonialist, and postcolonialist attitudes. One subgenre is the safari novel, including works by Elspeth Huxley, Dorothy Gilman, and Karin McQuillan. A British imperial atmosphere pervades Huxley's *Murder on Safari* (1938), which traffics in a Conradesque exoticizing of Africa and a Hemingwayesque romanticizing of big-game hunting. Gilman's *Mrs. Pollifax on Safari* (1977) has a grandmotherly secret agent outwitting international enemies in an "emerging" Africa whose representations alternate between Rhodesian freedom fighters and depictions reminiscent of Tarzan movies. In contrast, McQuillan, a former Peace Corps volunteer in Africa, incorporates bona fide African natural history and indigenous cultural history into her three Jazz Jasper mysteries, in which the native bearers of colonial-era novels are replaced by Kenyan professional police who can provide authentic cultural readings.

Another popular setting is the scientific expedition. In Aaron Elkins's *Icy Clutches* (1990), the murder that occurs during a botanical expedition to Alaska's Glacier Bay National Park is related to another that took place on a prior expedition. Physical anthropologist Gideon Oliver is able to read the evidence of the thirty-year-old bones. Other Elkins mysteries featuring the "skeleton detective" are set in *archaeological milieu, from Mayan ruins to British barrows.

Another favorite venue for archaeological expeditions is the Near East. Peter Levi's *The Head in the Soup* (1979) concerns the apparent discovery of the great menorah and other liturgical objects looted by the Romans from the Second Temple of Jerusalem in

A.D. 70. As Oxford archaeologist Ben Jonson's research takes him from archive to archive, he points up parallels between archaeology and detection, even to the "stratification" of papers on a desk. The legendary treasures of the First Temple, the Temple of Solomon, underlie *Zadok's Treasure* (1980), by Margot Arnold. Arnold introduces not only a fictional Dead Sea fragment giving specific directions to the location of the treasure but another, more sensational fragment referring to Jesus as a member of the Essene community, thus proving the historicity of Jesus and sparking a worldwide religious revival. Discovery of a "Jesus document" is the ultimate "what if?" scenario of such archaeological thrillers as James Hall Roberts's *The Q Document* (1964), Peter Van Greenaway's *Judas!* (1972; *The Judas Gospel*), and Barbara Woods's *The Magdalene Scrolls* (1978).

Elizabeth Peters's *The Mummy Case* (1985) combines the popular interest in new "Jesus scrolls" and in Egyptian mummies. Peters, who has a Ph.D. in archaeology, writes campy narratives that play on upper-class British perceptions of Egypt as a contradictory place of romance and squalor; patronizing Anglo-Saxon prejudices extend to everything foreign, from Arabs to Catholics, but the reader is meant to be amused.

The most popular setting for expedition mysteries is Egypt, although often the archaeology is just a matter of background, as in *The Curse of the Bronze Lamp* (1945), by John Dickson *Carr writing as Carter Dickson. Agatha *Christie has used Egypt in a straight travel context, but "The Adventure of the Egyptian Tomb" in *Poirot Investigates* (1924) is an expedition story. Christie's *Murder in Mesopotamia* (1936) and *They Came to Baghdad* (1951) are set in an Iraq whose squalid locales undercut any Arabian Nights romanticism.

Many recent archaeological mysteries have focused on the American Southwest. In *Clay Dancers* (1994) Cecil Dawkins uses an excavation at a pueblo site to present a feminist revision of Native American cultural history. Tony *Hillerman's southwestern series twice focuses on archaeological excavations. In *A Thief of Time* (1988), two projects become intertwined: that of a pottery specialist who believes she can trace the movements of a thirteenth-century potter, and that of a physical anthropologist conducting unauthorized excavations of Anasazi skeletons. In *Dance Hall of the Dead* (1973), an embittered archaeologist support his controversial theory that Folsom Man adapted rather than dying out.

[*See also* Closed-World Settings and Open-World Settings, Pathfinder Fiction.]

• C. W. Ceram, *Gods, Graves and Scholars* (1951). Jacquetta Hawkes, ed., *The World of the Past*. 2 vols. (1963). Riane Eisler, *The Chalice and the Blade: Our History, Our Future* (1987). Douglas Ubelaker and Henry Scammel, *Bones: A Forensic Detective's Casebook* (1992).

—Peter V. Cenci *and* George L. Scheper

EXTORTION. The attempted extraction of payments (usually in money but sometimes in "favors") by means of threat is used in both Golden Age and hard-boiled fiction. In either case, extortion can be viewed as the reverse of bribery, in that it originates with the receiver of the funds or favors rather than with the giver. Extortion, or blackmail as it is synonymously termed, generally has a tightly personal focus, since the threat to the *victim is that he or she will be revealed as living a lie. For the threat to be effective, however, there must be a public, or at least a *family set, to whom it will make a difference if the victim's image is tarnished. In Golden Age detective fiction the victim of extortion very likely fears the blackmailer's ability to destroy social reputation, and considering the propriety of the conservative world inhabited by the classical detectives and their clients, it is not surprising that the threat to reveal past amours or indiscretions begins with the history of the genre, namely, in Edgar Allan *Poe's "The Purloined Letter" (*The Gift*, 1844), where readers are invited to imagine the contents of the letter in question could be lurid. The idea of social blackmail is fully developed and exemplified, then, in Arthur Conan *Doyle's "A Scandal in Bohemia" (*Strand*, Sept. 1891).

Hard-boiled writers introduce blackmail as part of their general representation of social *corruption, implying also that the suppressed truths are themselves instances of corruption. Raymond *Chandler's *The High Window* (1942) stands as an example. Among the successor authors who have modified the *private eye story, Dick *Francis's *Reflex* (1980) suggests that blackmail can be a viable source of criminal *plot in a broad range of milieus. Apart from the opportunity that the crime of blackmail affords for complicating plots and allowing an author of detective fiction to capitalize an investment in the deception of appearances, blackmail or extortion have an inherent significance for the genre of detective fiction. For the detective character as a seeker of knowledge, extortion is a fruitful crime because it is entangled with the suppression and revelation of truth.

—John M. Reilly

FAIRY TALE. Part of the universal and lasting appeal of the crime novel is its resonance from childhood. At first glance, this echo may seem to come from *nursery rhymes, since so many mystery stories have kidnapped titles from that source: Clifford Witting's "There Was a Crooked Man" (1960), Donald Henderson's "Who Killed Cock Robin?," Ed *McBain's *Snow White and Rose Red* (1985) and *Rumpelstiltskin* (1981), and Agatha *Christie's *Ten Little Niggers* (1939; *And Then There Were None*), among innumerable others. Because the fairy tale represents one's earliest immersion in narrative about adult experience, a much more profound link connects the mystery and fairy tale.

The detective story, like the fairy tale, is linked to the collective imagination and makes an ideal vehicle for expression of the moral ambiguities and fears of the times in which it is written. The crime novel accomplishes for the adult what the fairy tales does for the child: It expresses and thereby banishes universal, libidinous, and perennial fears and guilts. Gertrude Stein, a devotée of crime fiction, claimed that *murder is the desire most deeply hidden, and that melodrama, including the crime novel, covers up our bottom nature. The *detective novel and fairy tale are modern forms of allegory whose function it is to pull rabbits out of hats, to exert moral magic (although the fairy tale has more license—it can use the supernatural, the fantastical, the outright magical). Both fictions gratify the reader's love of riddling, itself one of the oldest literary types. This is evident in the abundance of secrets, mysteries, proscriptions, which baffle both reader and characters.

The heroes of fairy tale and detective novel undertake central quests. The hero of the mystery novel undertakes a quest for *the* truth that explains an event, an outrage; the fairy tale hero is on a quest which will test his or her mettle, or worthiness, to perform some deed—to overcome obstacles or vanquish *evil. These two quests share obvious similarities. The heroes and, more recently, the heroines of both narratives use cunning and courage, and operate on the assumption that truth will out. Both presume a rigid dichotomization between good and evil, or right and wrong. Both employ confrontation and recognition. The villainy of the wicked stepsisters in *Cinderella* is revealed; the accursed prince transformed into a frog is restored to manhood by true love. The detective story also traditionally assumes that its deceitful or evil characters will be exposed and their identities disclosed. The mystery novel

and the fairy tale share a longing for order; having reestablished order, they also share happy endings. A consequence of the allegorical underpinning of these fictions is that both villain and hero are *archetypal characters. Necessarily therefore, for both, *plot rather than character development is of the highest significance.

Insofar as it affords poetic justice, the mystery novel is a kind of fairy tale. Both forms of narrative are concerned with the depiction and conservation of the status quo; both are rooted in bourgeois values. As W. H. Auden pointed out in "The Guilty Vicarage" (*Harper's Magazine*, May 1948), this is why the more innocent the *setting—the vicarage for example—the more heinous the crime appears, and the greater will be the reader's satisfaction when innocence is restored to the violated community.

Both narratives follow a trajectory from danger to security, and the reader finds a hero who is more successful, more powerful, resembling the protagonists of allegory. In *K Is for Killer* (1994) Sue *Grafton's investigator Kinsey *Milhone boasts that she has never had a case without a resolution. This power means that the *sleuth has nine lives—he or she doesn't die. Whatever physical assault or perilous condition is inflicted, the investigator emerges miraculously. What is real is what we are circumventing, or escaping, or countering. Finally, both fairy tale and mystery fiction embed messages for the superego. If the fairy tale told in the nursery had the purpose of making children obedient, as Plato alleges, the crime novel instructs its followers that "crime doesn't pay."

This is the background of their common stock. But both have diverged significantly from their traditional models, though in different ways. The fairy tale form has within itself the potential for utopian critique. Examples are George Macdonald's "The Princess and Curdie" (1887) and Oscar Wilde's "The Selfish Giant" (in *The Happy Prince, and the Selfish Giant: Two Stories of Loving Service*, 1894), which inveigh against the materialism and hypocrisy of upper-class Victorian England.

At the same time that the truth of fairy tales is being revised, the detective novel has departed radically from its assumption that truth will out. Some modern crime fiction goes further and parodies the detective's role, its sense of mission and code of values. A number of contemporary works depict an America lacking that code, a country more akin to T. S. Eliot's "The Waste Land" (1922) than to Christie's St. Mary Mead. James Crumley's *The Last Good Kiss* (1978), for example, reflects the fragmentation of the American dream, and the decay of traditional values.

There may be, however, a salutary consequence of the detective novel's rejection of an innocent/guilty polarity and the certainty of moral judgment that implies. In their stead may come relativism—the acknowledgment that codes reflect a particular time, a particular culture. When writers employ a postreligious sense of right and wrong instead of an absolute good and evil, the relation of law to justice, of law to moral judgment, can be explored.

As fairy tale and mystery novel move away from the earlier allegorical patterns they held in common, they move further apart. What they share now is the breakdown of formulaic pattern and the reformulation of new and contemporary sensibilities within their worlds.

• Bruno Bettelheim, *The Uses of Enchantment: The Meaning and Importance of Fiction* (1989). Ruth Bottigheimer, *Grimm's Bad Girls and Bold Boys* (1989).

—Nadya Aisenberg

FAMILY. A new focus on the family is a noteworthy development of contemporary crime fiction. Although past mysteries featured husband and wife sleuthing teams, the family was not otherwise considered relevant to the mystery. Even the unions of married professional policemen such as Ngaio *Marsh's Inspector Roderick *Alleyn, wedded to sculptor Troy Alleyn, and Inspector Henry Tibbett, married to housewife Emmy Tibbett, occupy little of the psychological or narrative interest of the novels. Rather, the model pair remained Sherlock *Holmes and Dr. John H. *Watson: a hero and his sidekick. This male collegiality does not pretend to be family. In late-twentieth-century writing, however, a new trend can be spotted. In all sorts of guises, social issues centering on the family claim a place within the expanding boundaries of the mystery novel.

For example, in Jane Smiley's *Duplicate Keys* (1984), *murder is the central event, and the quest for the identity of the murderer impels the narrative. Yet this is equally a novel about *friendship and social relations. *Duplicate Keys*, rooted in social realism as were the novels of Dashiell *Hammett and Raymond *Chandler, updates their scene. Drug-taking among post-hippie generation musicians of the middle class—Smiley's characters are neither down-and-outers nor the decadent idle rich—is the background to murder. But the reader has another *puzzle, in addition to murder, to solve. Why has this tightly knit group of protagonists, who began their move to New York with "duplicate keys" to each others' apartments, frayed and come apart? The author seriously considers the cost of being socially mobile and asks if a group of friends can become a viable surrogate family subject to the same strains and stresses as a biological family.

The importance of family may also be conveyed by the sense of loss that its absence precipitates. The mystery novels of P. D. *James, for instance, are marked by such loss. Her fiction depicts characters who are burdened with anxieties and self-doubts; it is suggestive that these characters are, at the same time, children of dead or departed mothers, foolish and irresponsible fathers, broken marriages, and failed love affairs. For the most part, the personal world in James's novels is not a support. The family is yearned for, but not present—especially the good mothers. James's female detective, Cordelia *Gray, deserves to be deemed a success as much for overcoming her own losses as for her competent performance on the job. The quest for relation rings a note of sadness through all James's work; no longer is the detective loner a character to admire and emulate.

Home can no longer be assumed to be a base of security; rather, it is often a place of treachery, hostility, and abandonment. Instability and insecurity, a lack of "natural" familial feeling pervading all classes, is overwhelmingly evident in the fiction of Ross *Macdonald, Raymond *Chandler, and James Crumley, to cite but a few. Children don't find their feet, are lost, go on drugs. Lew *Archer himself is divorced and has no familial attachments; his home is where he sleeps. Agatha *Christie, despite the highly formulaic novels she produced, portrayed the family early on not as a cohesive and benign social unit, but as a place of falsity to which her own experience attested.

What is true for these writers holds especially true in the work of Ruth *Rendell. Particularly in those novels written under the pseudonym of Barbara Vine in which, critics agree, Rendell allows herself greater freedom to explore character and its dark underside, most often the family is broken down. We find mothers who are pathologically possessive, sexually jealous of their daughters and fathers who are deserters.

Counterbalancing this, many contemporary female sleuths created by women mystery writers declare their emotional need for relation, and find ways to gratify it. Sue *Grafton's Kinsey *Milhone, Sara *Paretsky's V. I. *Warshawski, Linda Barnes's Carlotta Carlyle, Jane Logue's Laura Malloy—all voice their desire for connection, though they are all unmarried and function within the sleuth as *loner tradition of the *private eye. This tradition makes Milhone in *"K" Is for Killer* (1994) feel ambivalent about the claims of newly discovered family.

The social realism of these novels featuring women sleuths and written by women does more than provide background; it raises contemporary issues and conflicts faced by women. For instance, a lesbian couple with children is the center of Diana Macrae's *All the Muscle You Need* (1988); one of the two women is the detective. In *Glory Days* by Rosie Scott (1989), a single mother, the amateur who becomes inadvertently involved in the pursuit of the criminal, sings in a night club to support her child. In the highly competitive, masculinist world of police investigation, however, Linda LaPlante's *Prime Suspect* (1991) Inspector Jane Tennison, her high rank challenged by her male cohorts, must be satisfied with a makeshift personal life in order to remain in control professionally. She is not married, gets pregnant by mischance, and decides to have an abortion. For her, the job comes first—or, she knows, she goes.

Women authors have not only changed the emphasis on family, but its definition. For contemporary women investigators, the definition of "family" is expansive—if, in *"K" Is for Killer* Milhone is digesting the news that she has family she hasn't discovered until now, neither has she gone without emotional (and practical) support. Throughout the series, she turns to her elderly landlord Henry and to a neighborhood restaurant owner, Rosie; Carlyle and Warshawski both adopt "kid sisters"; Warshawski also reaches for counsel and encouragement to an older Austrian woman doctor; Malloy has deep affection for her widowed father, and forms strong friendships with other women. The family has become a web of extended kinship, evidencing the profound human need for that emotional support conspicuously lacking in both the cozies, where, if present at all, it is relegated to the background, and in the tough-guy thrillers, where it is outside the picture.

—Nadya Aisenberg

FANS AND FAN ORGANIZATIONS. Crime and mystery fiction is a reader-driven genre, and it is not surprising, therefore, that fans have created a world of newsletters, conventions, and awards celebrating their favorite reading material. The Baker Street Irregulars, founded in 1934 by Christopher Morley, was the first official organization of mystery fans. It was then and is still limited to male devotees of Arthur Conan *Doyle's Sherlock *Holmes, and membership is by invitation. This group holds an annual meeting in New York City on 12 January, the date they have discerned from their studies of the *Canon to be Holmes's birthday. Local groups, called scion societies, all named after titles of or incidents in the stories, meet in cities all over the world, publish newsletters, and encourage the further proliferation of Sherlockian knowledge. Another group, The Adventuresses of Sherlock Holmes, is made up of women with similar interests.

Some groups devoted to specific authors focus on the authors' works. Most publish newsletters for members as a part-time activity on an irregular basis. These usually contain articles about the author's characters and their backgrounds, and sometimes offer suggestions to the authors about future plots. Meetings of group members are unlikely due to geographical spread, but the newsletter is usually quite sufficient to maintain a sense of camaraderie. The most active groups are those focusing on Dorothy L. *Sayers, Margery *Allingham, R. Austin *Freeman, Lillian Jackson Braun, Charlotte MacLeod, Elizabeth Peters/Barbara Michaels, and Lawrence *Block.

Fans of the orchid-fancier *sleuth Nero *Wolfe formed the Wolfe Pack in 1978. They hold their Black Orchid Banquet annually on the first Saturday in December and bestow the Nero Wolfe Award on an author whose work reflects the best qualities of the Rex *Stout legacy. In addition, they publish the *Gazette: The Journal of the Wolfe Pack*.

Mystery Readers International is an umbrella organization for a number of groups that meet on a regular basis, many at mystery bookstores in the United States, Canada, and England. The *Mystery Readers Journal* was first published by Janet Rudolph in 1984; each of the quarterly issues is dedicated to a specific mystery subject such as history, sports, art, music, or legal issues. Members of MRI annually vote for the Macavity Award.

Fans can gather at a growing number of conventions devoted to the genre. Bouchercon, the World Mystery Convention, first held in 1969, moves to a different location every year. Here groups and individuals meet, discuss favorite authors and subgenres within the mystery world, listen to authors discuss their work, and have books signed. Members of the convention also vote on the Anthony Awards (named after Anthony *Boucher). Copies of new and used books as well as magazines are available for sale in the dealers' room. Held each spring in Washington, D.C., Malice Domestic is a convention specifically devoted to that aspect of the mystery. The membership bestows the Agatha Award to the best novel, best first novel, best short story, and best nonfiction book that reflects the area of interest of the members. The convention also provides the platform for original short-story collections of the "cozy" style, and has published a cookbook compiled by prominent authors and fans. EyeCon, a convention specifically honoring the *private eye, was first held during the summer of 1995 in Milwaukee, Wisconsin. Shots on the Page is held in Nottingham, England, where it is paired with Shots in the Dark, a convention focusing on film.

Each of these conventions honors a living author as guest of honor and, in many instances, recognizes a fan who has contributed substantially to the mystery field. Regional conventions also have proliferated, with several taking place in Philadelphia, Pennsylvania, and Austin, Texas, in recent years.

—Ellen A. Nehr

Fansler, Kate. A feminist professor of English literature with a sleuthing sideline, Kate Fansler is the creation of the former Columbia University professor Carolyn Gold Heilbrun, whose nom de plume is Amanda *Cross. Introduced in 1964 in *In the Last Analysis*, Fansler uses the methods of academic research to solve mysteries, not all of which are murders. Described by her creator as a fantasy self, Fansler is middle-aged, independently wealthy, elegantly slim, and sophisticated. Her most striking characteristics are quick intelligence, acerbic wit, and a gift for brilliant conversation, replete with literary *allusions and quotations. In the early novels Fansler expresses love for the academy, but beginning with *Death in a Tenured Position* (1981; *A Death in the Faculty*) her view of academe becomes more critical. Fansler's most important relationships are with her niece and nephew and with her husband, attorney Reed Amhearst. She investigates the abduction of the latter in *The Puzzled Heart* (1998).

[*See also* Academic Milieu; Academic Sleuth; Females and Feminists.]

• Carolyn Heilbrun, *Writing a Woman's Life* (1988). Maureen T. Reddy, *Sisters in Crime: Feminism and the Crime Novel* (1988).

—Maureen T. Reddy

FARCEURS. The farceurs were identified by Julian *Symons in *Bloody Murder: From the Detective Story* *to the Crime Novel: A History* (1972; *Mortal Consequences*) as "those writers for whom the business of fictional murder was endlessly amusing." Symons said that the early farceurs functioned in interwar Britain, a place he felt was more conducive to lightheartedness about crime than the streets of cities like Chicago or Paris. But more recently writers of other nationalities have enjoyed playing with the *conventions of the genre in a high-spirited manner, too.

The authors specifically identified as farceurs by Symons are Philip *MacDonald, Ronald A. *Knox, A. A. Milne, Michael *Innes, and Edmund *Crispin. Although there is a vast difference between the sophisticated and skilful writing of Innes and Crispin and what Symons calls the "desperate facetiousness" of Knox, these five writers have much in common in their approach to the *rules of the game and the spirit in which they play with them. The subgenre of farceur writing grew out of the conventions of detective writing generally followed in England during the 1920s and 1930s, when the construction of mysteries was perceived by authors as a civilized game played according to rules, ten of which were outlined by Knox himself in his famous Decalogue (reproduced in his introduction to *The Best Detective Stories of the Year 1928*).

In their introductions to their books, the farceurs themselves made frequent references to the importance of the joke or *puzzle elements in their writings. In his introduction to *The Maze* (1932), MacDonald refers to his work as "an exercise in detection." Milne, introducing his only mystery novel, *The Red House Mystery* (1922), sets out his intentions in a typically facetious fashion, making it clear that he is not taking matters seriously, nor does he expect the reader to do so. Years later, Innes—writing under his real name, J. I. M. Stewart, in his autobiography *Myself and Michael Innes: A Memoir* (1987)—revealed that his *Appleby on Ararat* (1941) and *The Daffodil Affair* (1942) were "two extravagances" intended to "bring a little fantasy and fun into the detective story. But the impulse has always been present with me, and has justly earned for me Mr. Julian Symons's label as a *farceur* in the kind. Detective stories are purely recreational reading, after all, and needn't scorn the ambition to amuse as well as to puzzle."

Crispin believed that detective stories should be "essentially imaginative and artificial in order to make their best effect." On occasion the reader is actually admitted into the farce: In *The Moving Toyshop* (1946), the character Gervase *Fen refers to Crispin as well as to the book's publisher. (Innes had already made a similar joke: In *The Daffodil Affair*, Inspector Appleby facetiously refers to Innes by name.)

Farceurs commonly use the upper-class society and the *country house milieu characteristic of Golden Age detective fiction. Crispin and Innes continued to feature such settings right into the 1970s and 1980s. Elements that immediately mark out these novels as farces include the use of puns in the naming of characters. For example, the family name of Lord Mullion in Innes's *Lord Mullion's Secret*

(1981) is Wyndowe. Exaggerated or ludicrous naming occurs when the insurance company employing Ronald Knox's series detective, Miles Bredon, is called the Indescribable Insurance Company.

The detectives created by farceurs are usually amateurs, and are nearly always urbane, sophisticated, and intellectual. Even Innes's John *Appleby, although a professional policeman, bears these hallmarks of the gifted amateur. Other characters are frequently caricatured, often marked out as such by comic nomenclature: A rather backward jobbing gardener is called Solo Hoobin in Innes's *An Awkward Lie* (1971), while a college butler is endowed with the name Slotwiner in Innes's *Death at the President's Lodgings* (1936; *Seven Suspects*).

More recent authors who engage in the spirit of fun echoing that of the farceurs include Charlotte Macleod, Donald Westlake, Alfred Alcorn, and Lawrence *Block with his Bernie Rhodenbarr series. The works of present-day farceurs rely on lively pace, puzzling situations, and often witty dialogue to keep the reader relentlessly entertained.

Melvyn Barnes's categorizing in his *Murder in Print: A Guide to Two Centuries of Crime Fiction* (1986) is typical of the critical response to this farceur fiction: He refers to it as "the 'Here's a murder, what fun!' school."

[*See also* Allusion, Literary; Humor; Pastiche; Pontificators, The.]

—Judith Rhodes

FAR EAST. *See* China, Crime and Mystery Writing in Greater; Japan, Crime and Mystery Writing in.

FASHION AND DESIGN MILIEU. Beginning with Rex *Stout's *The Red Box* (1937; *Case of the Red Box*), in which Nero *Wolfe solves a *murder in couturier Boyden McNair's elegant Fifty-second Street, *New York, fashion house, some two dozen notable crime and mystery novels have been set in the fashion and design *milieu. *Settings range from classic salons to catalogue shippers and trendy hairdressers in cities from New York to Shanghai. Focused on a swiftly changing industry, these novels tend to provide striking pictures of the social and business worlds in which they are set. Visual imagery is often vivid and essential to the placement of *clues. And flamboyant personalities are portrayed with verve and often wit. The colorful milieu is used to display attitudes from snobbery to political points of view. And with its emphasis on the up-to-date, the milieu is particularly attractive to writers who are concerned to use crime and mystery writing to examine issues contemporary to their times.

The prototypical example of detection in the fashion world is Margery *Allingham's *The Fashion in Shrouds* (1938), which portrays the "special snobbism and . . . conscious striving for effect" that are "the very parents of fashion." In this novel, Allingham sketched a world of innovation where entrepreneurship is a metaphor for modernity and murder a remedy for inconvenience.

Dorothy B. Hughes continues this focus on snobbishness in *The So Blue Marble* (1940), which pits a

Hollywood designer against international criminals. Christianna *Brand's *Death in High Heels* (1941) and Patricia McGerr's *Fatal in My Fashion* (1954) zoom in on the world of haute couture models.

The Cold War shifted the focus to espionage in Patricia Moyes's *Murder* à la *Mode* (1963) and Jocelyn Davey's *A Killing in Hats* (1965). Ellery *Queen cracks a designer's code in *The Fourth Side of the Triangle* (1965), exposing a killer, while Emma *Lathen's *The Longer the Thread* (1971) is a case of thwarted sabotage in an offshore pants factory.

Michael Collins's *The Slasher* (1980), which traces a model's quest for the mother who has abandoned her, spotlights the late-twentieth-century fascination with dysfunctional *families. Alisa Craig added a dash of intrigue in *The Terrible Tide* (1983), in which a disfigured model turned detective foils a murderer. Caroline Crane's *Man in the Shadows* (1987) shows a mother's move to protect her children from a stalker, while James Melville's *Kimono for a Corpse* (1987) examines Japanese family relationships while unmasking a murderer. Charles Cohen's *Silver Linings* (1988) spoofs suburban recreations from sex to playgroups while a murder is solved in an upscale boutique. Robert L. Duncan's *China Dawn* (1988) moved the action in flashbacks to prewar Shanghai, where a Japanese fashion designer and her half-Western daughter discover the motives of modern saboteurs threatening their garment line.

Thomas H. Cook's *Flesh and Blood* (1989) introduces a lively new line—the police procedural set in the cutthroat world of fashion. Gwendoline Butler's *Coffin in Fashion* (1987) shifts the action from New York's Seventh Avenue to *London, where her plot unfolds in a trendy clothing factory. Mary Higgins *Clark's *While My Pretty One Sleeps* (1989) introduces a new wrinkle, a *police procedural with a double murder solved by a retired commissioner's boutique-owner daughter.

Christopher Newman's *Knock-Off* (1989) looks at the seamier side of Seventh Avenue fashion, exposing a crooked Treasury agent and scams ranging from design theft and Treasury bond *forgery to premeditated murder.

Liza Cody's *Backhand* (1991), which traces a design thief from London to a fashionable tennis club in the Florida Keys, and Leslie Meier's *Mail-Order Murder* (1991), where an upscale Maine clothier is killed during the Christmas rush, demonstrate the growing popularity of female *amateur detectives. Erica Quest's *Model Murder* (1991), featuring a female detective chief inspector investigating rape and murder, reveals the often problematic life of the professional policewoman.

Sandra Brown's *French Silk* (1991) and Sophie Dunbar's *Behind Eclaire's Doors* (1993) illustrate contemporary trends in fashion and design venues. In the first, a lingerie designer is charged with murdering a televangelist who accused her of publishing pornographic photographs; in the second, an haute coiffure designer must clear her ex-husband of murdering her manicurist.

[*See also* Banking and Financial Milieu.]

—Jean A. Coakley

FAULKNER, WILLIAM. *See* Incidental Crime Writers.

FBI. The Federal Bureau of Investigation (FBI), a branch of the United States Department of Justice, was created in 1908 to address violations of federal criminal laws, issues of national security, and civil matters involving the U.S. Government. In its earlier years, the FBI was a little-known agency, but when J. Edgar Hoover was appointed director in 1924, he focused both the organization's and the public's attention on a well-publicized battle against gangsters who built their illicit empires on the profits to be made by violating the laws of *Prohibition and the criminals emboldened by a popular tolerance of illegality. After such notable adventures as the tracking of John Dillinger and the adoption of the practice of advertising the Ten Most Wanted criminals, the FBI became the most visible, and seemingly most professional, law enforcement organization in the nation.

Because of the support it receives from the U.S. Congress, the Treasury, and public opinion, the FBI has been able to build criminal and forensic laboratories, databases, and a training academy serving police everywhere. In a country that jealously protects the sovereignty of states and localities, the FBI has attained the standing that would elsewhere be the purview of a national police force.

During the 1930s Hoover began to appropriate political radicalism as an object of FBI surveillance, and throughout the Cold War he worked assiduously to portray his agency as a frontline force in the struggle against domestic communist subversion. More recently, federal legislation (the RICO laws) directed against organized crime has recast the agency, under Hoover's successors, in a contest against crime that crosses political boundaries and exceeds the power of localities to control.

Popular literature has joined efforts of the agency to burnish its image. For example, the Judy Bolton series of children's mysteries by Margaret Sutton finds Judy and her fiancé starry-eyed at his decision to become an agent in *The Secret of the Barred Window* (1943). Gordon Gordon, a former FBI agent, collaborated with his wife on *The FBI Story*, featuring Special Agent John Ripley. The dustjacket breathlessly describes the book as a look at "a fabulous organization at work."

Even negative presentations of the FBI, among them Rex *Stout's condemnation of Hoover himself in the Nero *Wolfe mystery *The Doorbell Rang* (1965) play a part in sustaining the FBI's image as a stock example of law enforcement. FBI "profilers" are featured in Thomas Harris's *The Silence of the Lambs* (1988), along with a special agent who becomes the protagonist. Of course, Margaret Truman's series of Washington novels includes one about the bureau, *Murder at the FBI* (1985). Finally, the conventional appearances of the FBI in fiction receive a self-reflexive criticism from Jane Haddam's Gregor Demarkian in *A Great Day for the Deadly* (1992).

[*See also* CIA; Forensic Pathologist.]

• Athan G. Theoharis, ed., *From the Secret Files of J. Edgar Hoover* (1991). Ronald Kessler, *The FBI: Inside the World's*

Most Powerful Law Enforcement Agency (1993). John Douglas, *Mindhunter: Inside the FBI's Elite Serial Crime Unit* (1995). Diarmuid Jeffreys, *The Bureau: Inside the FBI* (1995).

—Sue Feder

Fell, Dr. Gideon. John Dickson *Carr based his character Dr. Gideon Fell on G. K. *Chesterton, a writer he greatly admired. Fell resembles Chesterton physically, with his great weight and enormous mustache, and in dress, using two walking sticks and wearing a shovel hat and tent-like cape. Fell also wears pince-nez and smokes a pipe. Meeting him, his creator says, is like meeting Old King Cole or Father Christmas.

Introduced in *Hag's Nook* (1933), Fell appears in twenty-three novels. He has a B.A. and Ph.D. from Harvard, as well as an M.A. from *Oxford and a law degree from Edinburgh, but he never practiced. He is a lexicographer and historian who writes books on such pseudo-learned subjects as the mistresses of the British kings and English drinking customs, the latter topic quite appropriate for the eccentric, beer-loving Fell.

It is to Fell that *Scotland Yard turns when faced with seemingly *impossible crimes. He is at his best in the *locked room mystery, a subgenre of which Carr was the recognized master. In *The Three Coffins* (1935; *The Hollow Man*) Fell delivers the now-famous lecture on locked rooms. Fell deals with apparent criminal impossibility also in novels such as *The Problem of the Wire Cage* (1939), in which the *victim is murdered on a muddy clay tennis court by a killer who leaves no footprints.

Many Fell novels and short stories involve bizarre *settings and unusual murder *weapons, such as the crossbow. Because of his love of the *outré*, Fell is especially happy when dealing with witchcraft, ghosts, magic, and satanism. Although his creator was known for his use of logic and fair play, typical features of the *Golden Age form, Fell is less orderly in his thinking and often reaches the solution by pursuing the bizarre questions that come to his mind but no one else's.

Fell reflects the British and U.S. influences in the life of Carr; Fell's assistants or American-born Watsons are often thinly disguised versions of Carr. When the detective expresses disgust with Britain's postwar socialist government, he is speaking for Carr; after 1948, when Carr first returned to the United States, Fell solved most of his cases there.

[*See also* Clues, Famous; Eccentrics; Fingerprints and Footprints; Ingenuity.]

• Marvin Lachman, "The Life and Times of Gideon Fell," *Mystery Fancier* (May 1978): 3–18. S. T. Joshi, *John Dickson Carr: A Critical Study* (1990). Douglas G. Greene, *John Dickson Carr: The Man Who Explained Miracles* (1995).

—Marvin Lachman

FEMALES AND FEMINISTS. Women writers have been a mainstay of crime and mystery writing. Nineteenth-century British sensationalist writers like Mrs. Henry *Wood and Mary Elizabeth *Braddon contributed to the "mystery" even as Americans Seeley *Regester and Anna Katharine *Green (known as

the mother of the detective novel) created early detectives and crime solving methodology. Although Green's first detective was a policeman, Ebenezer Gryce, she later created both the *spinster sleuth Amelia Butterworth and an early paid woman detective, Violet Strange. In the *Golden Age of detective fiction from 1921 to 1930, five women took top honors: British writers Agatha *Christie, Dorothy L. *Sayers, and Margery *Allingham were joined by Josephine *Tey (pseudonym of Elizabeth Mackintosh) from Scotland and New Zealander Ngaio *Marsh. They developed and polished the classic detective formula with its heroic protagonist, intrusive criminal, and eventual restoration of order. In similar fashion, American women writers of the 1980s and 1990s have redefined the hard-boiled private eye novel, with Marcia *Muller, Sue *Grafton, and Sara *Paretsky, among others, capturing the mean streets for women *private eyes.

Between these two notable events, talented women writers extended and reconfigured the conventions of the genre. Suspenseful psychological *thrillers from Patricia *Highsmith, Margaret *Millar, and Ruth *Rendell (also writing under the pseudonym Barbara Vine) unnerved readers with their careful dissection of the *evil done by ordinary women and men. While Elizabeth *Linington (also writing as Dell Shannon) and the husband and wife team of Per Wahlöö and Maj *Sjöwall gave new dimensions to conventional *police procedurals, Dorothy Uhnak and Lillian O'Donnell went further by introducing the first credible women police officers in procedurally organized novels. In the "Great Detective" model of the Golden Age—but always with a twist—P. D. *James and Elizabeth George continued the tradition of the erudite police inspector—a "gentleman" of at least comfortable means, highly placed in his professional world, and eccentric. James's Adam *Dalgliesh is a published poet, and George's Thomas Lynley is a titled aristocrat. But George and James broke the mold with their introduction of two working-class women police officers—Sergeant Barbara Havers and Detective Inspector Kate Miskin—whose lives and ideas contrast sharply with those of their superiors. The feminist reevaluation of the male detective model is found consistently from the 1970s on in the works of Antonia Fraser, Amanda *Cross, Anne Perry, Barbara Wilson, Barbara Neely, and numerous others.

Despite their important presence, women writers have consistently received less space in review columns and fewer nominations or awards for their work. In 1986 *Sisters in Crime was founded in the U.S. as an advocacy group for women writers, in particular, but also readers, editors, and booksellers.

Female characters play many roles in mystery and detective fiction. They have been *victims, *suspects, murderers, accomplices, narrators, *detectives, and onlookers—everything except the orangutan. Although *sensation novels focused on the restrictiveness of women's domestic lives, Braddon's Lady Lucy Audley provides an early example of misdirection as an innocent-looking woman who plots and executes crime; her better known "sister in crime" in the nineteenth century is Irene *Adler, Sherlock *Holmes's nemesis, who not only blackmails his client but successfully evades the *Great Detective.

With the rise of hard-boiled detectives in *Black Mask* magazine and subsequent novels by Dashiell *Hammett and Raymond *Chandler, the tempting *femme fatale moved to center stage to charm and deceive the wary detective. In *The Maltese Falcon* (1930), Sam *Spade successfully unmasks the guilty woman before the reader has begun to suspect her; despite their intimacy, he has no reservations about turning her over to the police. Mickey *Spillane's Mike *Hammer takes an even harder line with Charlotte Manning in *I, the Jury* (1947) when he eliminates this threatening woman by killing her. In the hard-boiled novels, female sexuality becomes a metaphor for wickedness which the detective had to root out; like Eve in the Garden of Eden, these women are temptations to be resisted even by a tarnished hero.

As detectives, women first came to the genre as police officers in the 1860s novels by Andrew Forrester, Jr. and William Stephens Hayward as well as in the American *dime novels published by Beadle and Adams. Amateur sleuths spanned the continuum from Green's astute Butterworth or Christie's indomitable Miss Jane *Marple to Mary Roberts *Rinehart's more naive heroines, captured in their repeated excuse, "had-I-but-known."

The greatest impact on women as writers, characters, and readers has been the feminist movement from the 1960s to the present in both Britain and the U.S. Independent characters, often as first-person narrators of their lives, their investigations, and their novels have displaced passive stereotypes. *Forensic pathologists, private eyes, college professors, bookstore owners, lawyers, business owners, caterers, and reporters have solved crimes; from teenagers to senior citizens, women as detectives have taken the heroic role in *cozy mysteries, *novels of manners, police procedurals, and hard-boiled fiction, matching women's changing roles in society.

[See also Adventurer and Adventuress; Characterization; Gender; Had-I-But-Known; Heroism; Males and the Male Image; Sex and Sexuality.]

• Kathleen Gregory Klein, *The Woman Detective: Gender & Genre* (1988; rev. ed., 1995). Maureen T. Reddy, *Sisters in Crime: Feminism and the Crime Novel* (1988). Jean Swanson and Dean James, *By a Woman's Hand: A Guide to Mystery Fiction by Women* (1994).
—Kathleen Gregory Klein

FEMME FATALE. The femme fatale is any woman whose presence reveals the vulnerability of a man to sexual charm and thereby threatens the stability of his world. The beguiling sirens of ancient myth luring male mariners to their doom founded the perdurable image of the fatal female, leaving it to generation after generation of males to inscribe her a place in all the genres of art and literature, not excepting popular crime and mystery writing.

Writing that is reflective of a normally populated social environment where the sexes are equal in number makes scant use of the femme fatale; thus,

the *Golden Age tradition, despite its artifice, has no significant place for characters who are ominous because they are female. On the other hand, the memoirs of early detectives written in the manner of fiction, works such as Edward Crapsey's *The Nether Side of New York; or, The Vice, Crime and Poverty of the Great Metropolis* (1872) and John H. Warren, Jr.'s *Thirty Years' Battle with Crime; or, The Crying Shame of New York* (1874) relate accounts of urban enclaves of prostitution where women's sexuality accords them the power to be active agents of crime. Critical analysis of the memoirs and the successive forms of pulp writing, *hard-boiled fiction, and the paperback original novels of the 1950s that bear them close relationship, indicates that the trope of the femme fatale becomes more likely to occur when the social *milieu of fiction segregates rich from poor, men from women, established ethnic groups from "others."

The critically acknowledged parents of hard-boiled writing, Dashiell *Hammett and Raymond *Chandler, also both make extensive use of the femme fatale. In *The Maltese Falcon* (1930), Brigid O'Shaughnessy deploys her wiles to lure Sam *Spade's partner to his death. Her amoral use of sexual power justifies for Spade his own duplicitous treatment of her, but despite his efforts to overcome her force, at novel's end he remains emotionally in thrall, as he says, perhaps in love with her. Nearly all of Chandler's novels include a female character who toys with Philip *Marlowe, enticing him with promises of sex that would compromise his work on a case, and, if not that, then destablize his ethical system.

Other hard-boiled writers share an intuitive sense of the utility of female sexuality as a snare for men. James M. *Cain's best-known novels, *The Postman Always Rings Twice* (1934) and *Double Indemnity* (in *Three of a Kind*, 1944), concern the passionate entanglements of men who lose control of reason and masculine detachment in the arms of women.

The femme fatale was more than a literary convenience for hard-boiled writers: She was a staple of their worldview, literally giving body to anxieties resulting from the sharp demarcation of male and female realms. When the provenance of adventure and real business is dominantly men's, and there is neither language nor protocol available to naturalize sexually generated feeling and to manage it in the interests of the heterosexual companionship that would be possible if the genders were deemed equal, then the unsettling intrusion of women requires a reductive description that can serve both to limit the role of women in the plot of adventure and to justify the habitual segregation of men and women into separate spheres. The trope of the siren or the femme fatale originated for such utility and remains current through all sorts of social change.

The worldview insinuated into hard-boiled fiction at its inception continues to set contested boundaries between male and female. The phenomenon of paperback original publishing in the 1950s kept the image of the femme fatale before audiences by a typical use of cover art picturing near-nude female sex objects and by commonly presenting women in language suggesting ultimately inexplicable character traits. Novels by Jim *Thompson such as *The Getaway* (1959) and *The Grifters* (1963) capture some resonances of the femme fatale, showing that the image has become a staple, while in the fiction of Mickey *Spillane's Mike *Hammer, introduced in *I, the Jury* (1947), the woman, in body and mind, is the vengeful negative force whose sexual difference from men usurps the place usually played in the hard-boiled *plot by inequities of wealth. Taking the femme fatale to an historic apex, Spillane practically redrafts the story of crime fighting as a battle of the sexes.

More recent authors of detective fiction, however, are working a reversal of the fatal female trope. Walter *Mosley's *White Butterfly* (1992), for example, opens with echoes of the image but dispels expectations of it as the plot continues. Robert B. *Parker's multivolume project of revision of the hard-boiled *private eye novel includes a redefinition of female character along humanly realistic lines. Most important of all in this respect, the women private eyes in the fiction of Marcia *Muller, Sara *Paretsky, Sue *Grafton, Linda Barnes, Julie Smith, and others their jobs as the full equals of their male counterparts, reconfiguring the world of adventure, making it sexually integregated, more natural, and no longer hospitable to femmes fatale.

[*See also* Archetypal Characters; Gender; Paperbacks; Sex and Sexuality.]

• Rachel M. Brownstein, *Becoming a Heroine: Reading about Women in Novels* (1984). Michelle Barrett, "Ideology and the Cultural Production of Gender," in *Feminist Criticism and Social Change*, ed. Judith Newton and Deborah Rosenfelt (1985). —John M. Reilly

Fen, Gervase, series detective created by the British composer and anthologist Robert Bruce Montgomery writing as Edmund *Crispin. Fen appeared in five novels and several short stories. A late example of a Golden Age detective, and an *academic sleuth, Fen is an eccentric *Oxford don who is both erudite and comic. Although there was a lapse of twenty-six years between the last two novels in which he appeared, *The Long Divorce* (1951; *A Noose for Her Neck*) and *The Glimpses of the Moon* (1977), Fen's portrayal is remarkably consistent. His obliviousness to much that occurs around him contrasts comically with his intuitive and logical methods of solving crimes. Arrogant, learned, paradoxically both cynical and naive, he is an effective central character of novels that are broadly farcical in tone and sharply satiric in social commentary. His spiky hair and his use of literary allusions such as the exclamation, "Oh, my paws and whiskers," borrowed from the White Rabbit in *Alice's Adventures in Wonderland* (1865), make Fen a memorable character.

[*See also* Academic Milieu; Farceurs; Humor.]

• Mary Jean DeMarr, "Edmund Crispin," in *Twelve Englishmen of Mystery*, ed. Earl F. Bargainnier (1984).
—Mary Jean DeMarr

FERRARS, E. X., pseudonym of Morna Doris MacTaggart Brown (1907–1995), British writer of *detective novels in the malice domestic or *cozy tradition who also wrote as Elizabeth Ferrars. Born in Burma, she was educated at the Bedales School in Petersfield, Hampshire, and at University College, London, receiving a diploma in journalism in 1928.

A founding member of the *Crime Writers Association, she authored more than seventy books in five and a half decades, working within the Golden Age conventions of the 1920s and 1930s long after that era had passed. Witty and highly literate, her novels are peopled with educated upper-middle-class characters. Her books do not have a constant series detective, although a few characters appear in more than one novel. Toby Dyke, a Bertie Wooster/Lord Peter *Wimsey type who follows in the tradition of the *gentleman sleuth, is featured in novels written in a genteel voice in the early 1940s. Retired professor of botany Andrew Basnett, an *elderly sleuth with endearing habits and methodical detection techniques, appeared in the 1980s, and the unusual detective team of an estranged wife and husband, Virginia and Felix Freer, are central to Ferrars's last novels. She also wrote short stories about a crusty old *amateur detective called Jonas P. Jonas. Publishing more than a book a year throughout her writing career, Ferrars explored many *milieus, including the *theatrical milieu, the *country house milieu, and other *settings on both British and foreign shores. Her flair for titles is evident in *Frog in the Throat* (1980), *Skeleton in Search of a Cupboard* (1982; *Skeleton in Search of a Closet*), and *Skeleton Staff* (1969).

[*See also* Titles and Titling; Voice: Genteel Voice.]

• David Gordon, "E. X. Ferrars, Morna Doris Brown," in *Critical Survey of Mystery and Detective Fiction*, ed. Frank N. Magill (1988): 599–604. Mary Helen Becker, "Elizabeth Ferrars," in *Twentieth Century Crime and Mystery Writers*, ed. Lesley Henderson, 3rd ed. (1991): 358–60. Jean Swanson and Dean James, "E. X. Ferrars," in *By a Woman's Hand* (1994).
—Barbara Sloan-Hendershott

FICTION NOIR depicts the controlled depravity and existential absurdities faced by men and women caught in a web of random *violence, amorality, and lust for sex and money. This bleak view of life is a result of the *Great Depression, when personal ethics and ability were coopted by forces totally beyond the control of the individual.

Dashiell *Hammett's *Red Harvest* (1929) is not usually categorized as fiction noir, but the novel contains all the characteristics of the *hard-boiled detective novel as well as those of fiction noir, save one: The hero really is a hero. The world is corrupt, deaths are violent, drug use and casual sex are rampant, but the *Continental Op is a relative saint compared to his corrupt adversaries. He survives by falling to their level, getting them to kill each other, and killing those who will not fall for his chicanery. The town is cleansed, but the moral question remains just as it does in all fiction noir: What is the value of life and what is the true nature of man?

James M. *Cain is perhaps the best known early writer of fiction noir. He plays with the concept of Pandora's box; once it is opened, it cannot be closed and all the efforts of the unfortunate *victim mean nothing. In *The Postman Always Rings Twice* (1934), drifter Frank Chambers succumbs to the brutal demons of lust and money, helping Cora Papadakis kill her husband, Nick, as they seek their corner of the American dream. In *Double Indemnity* (1943), insurance agent Walter Huff cannot resist the promise of quick money and sex with Phyllis Nirdlinger, who seduces him into planning her husband's *murder. Huff soon realizes he has made a major blunder but cannot escape; he is trapped by his own ego and by the dogged claims agent Keyes.

Paul Cain's *Fast One* (1933) is nonstop action with an amoral hero, Gerry Kells, whose name is a play on the word "kills." In the story that's what he does, but without any redeeming motive. He breezes into *Los Angeles, tries to make a big score, enrages the mob, and dies violently and desperately alone after a car wreck in which his girlfriend dies. Horace McCoy's *They Shoot Horses, Don't They?* (1935) is a marathon dance of death in which Robert Syverten performs a mercy killing on his dance partner Gloria Beatty so that she may know in death the happiness she has never known in life.

McCoy's stream-of-consciousness gangster novel *Kiss Tomorrow Goodbye* (1948), with its hauntingly realistic psychotic narrator, led to the nightmare world of Jim *Thompson. Thompson's best remembered novel, *The Killer Inside Me* (1952), shows the darkest side of fiction noir; the deputy sheriff investigating a series of murders in a small town is actually the psycho killer responsible for them. Thompson's dark world is best presented in *Savage Night* (1953), *A Hell of a Woman* (1954), and *Pop, 1280* (1964).

Cornell *Woolrich, who wrote some acknowledged classics in this genre, seems to offer a slightly more positive version of the doomed universe but upon reflection the reader finds this world permeated by unrelieved despair. In his "black" series of novels, random chance is the true enemy in an uncaring universe. These novels add unbearable *suspense to the tension. His best include; *The Bride Wore Black* (1940; *Beware the Lady*), *The Black Curtain* (1941), and *The Black Angel* (1943).

Richard Stark brought noir to its logical conclusion with his Parker series, beginning with *The Hunter* (1962; *Point Blank*). Parker is a *master criminal, the brains behind innumerable heists, at odds with the world and true only to his own amoral code. He is presented as the hero but in this world things often go terribly wrong. Parker may get the money, but he's usually not overly happy about it. Stark's novels are more enjoyable and not nearly so sordid or hopeless as those from the 1950s.

The best-known contemporary practitioner of noir fiction is James *Ellroy, whose *Brown's Requiem* (1981) begins a series of stories about Los Angeles and its inhabitants whose humanity is lost beneath a surfeit of perverted passions and impulses.

Although noir is strictly an American creation, several British writers have contributed to the genre. In Graham *Greene's *A Gun for Sale* (1936; *This Gun for Hire*) a hit man's boss turns on him after he's killed his victim. In James Hadley Chase's *No Orchids for Miss Blandish* (1939; *The Villain and the Virgin*),

psycho Slim Grisson refuses to release his heiress hostage. Peter Cheyney imitates the idiomatic American style in his Lemmy Caution stories, such as *This Man Is Dangerous* (1936).

[*See also* Antihero; Corruption; Deviance; Sex and Sexuality.]

• Geoffrey O'Brien, *Hardboiled America: The Lurid Years of Paperbacks* (1981). Julian Symons, *Bloody Murder: From the Detective Story to the Crime Novel*, 3rd rev. ed. (1992).

—James L. Traylor *and* Max Allan Collins

FILM. As compounds of light, shadow, and illusion, the movies have always been apt vehicles for crime and mystery stories. Soon after the introduction of the first brief story films and actualities in France, England, and America in 1895–96, filmmakers like Georges Méliès, Cecil Hepworth, and Edwin S. Porter began scavenging the police blotter, newspaper headlines, stage melodramas, and the dime detective novels for material. A few examples from that first decade confirm that the standard movie formulas of crime and detection were quickly established. *Sherlock Holmes Baffled* (1903), from the Biograph studio, was the first of many portraits to come of Arthur Conan *Doyle's famous detective hero; *A Search for Evidence* (1903), also from Biograph, was an early example of the *police procedural story; *The Ex-Convict* (1904), an Edwin S. Porter film from the Edison studio, was a sympathetic character study of a criminal; *The Bold Bank Robbery* (1904), from the Lubin studio, was a typical cops-and-robbers chase; and *The Great Jewel Robbery* (1905), another Biograph, was drawn from newspaper accounts of an actual bank robbery of the day.

The brevity of these early silent films—*Sherlock Holmes Baffled* is only thirty seconds long—and their dependence upon explanatory titles limited *plot and character development. But story formats grew longer by 1912, and Holmes and other well-established detectives and talented cracksmen of literary and stage fame had more space to work in, so to speak. The first series of Holmes adventures were two-reelers from Nordisk Films of Denmark (1908–11). The first features in America were William Gillette's *Sherlock Holmes* (1916), based on his popular stage play, John Barrymore's *Sherlock Holmes* (1922), and Buster Keaton's visually imaginative fantasy *Sherlock Jr.* (1924). In England Eille Norwood made nearly fifty British films in the 1920s. On the other side of the aisle, among the famous cracksmen to first make it to the screen were E. W. *Hornung's A. J. *Raffles, who first appeared in print in 1899 and came to the American screen just six years later. In 1917 John Barrymore played him in *Raffles, the Amateur Cracksman*. Arsène *Lupin, Raffles's rival in France, who first appeared in book form in 1907, reached the screen in 1917 in a film titled *Arsène Lupin* and in 1919 in *The Teeth of the Tiger*.

By far the most popular and influential movie crime melodramas of the period were the French chapter-plays, or serials, drawn from newspapers and pulp fiction. Louis Feuillade's five Fantômas serials (1913–14) chronicled the adventures of the mysterious criminal Fantômas and his dedicated pursuer, detective Juve. Packed with bizarre crimes, embattled heroines, resourceful heroes, chases, and hairbreadth escapes, they quickly were imitated in America by three Elaine serials, based on Arthur B. *Reeve's Craig Kennedy detective stories, which pitted the *scientific sleuth against the masked "Clutching Hand."

Less bizarre than the serials—at least in a surreal sense—but sensational in their depiction of vice and *corruption, were a number of police-procedural films that were drawn from contemporary reform movements like the investigations of the Rockefeller grand juries. The granddaddy of these was George Loane Tucker's feature-length *Traffic in Souls* (1913), an "exposé" of white slavery by police investigators in American cities. Graphic screen *violence and controversial subject matter inevitably aroused public protests. "They are intended to stimulate and exploit the morbid interest in the harrowing details of a sickening and revolting aberration of the human soul," reported the *Moving Picture World* in 1914.

The modern gangster film had its genesis in the slum melodramas of D. W. Griffith in 1910–12, like *A Child of the Ghetto* (1910) and *The Musketeers of Pig Alley* (1912). Indeed, the word "gangster" can be found in many titles of the day, as registered in the Catalogue of Copyright Entries of the Library of Congress. *Musketeers*, in particular, reflected the gang wars and Tammany Hall corruption of New York's Lower East Side. It created the first modern movie gangster, the "Snapper Kid," a tough, aggressive, yet sympathetic character with an omnipresent cigarette dangling from his lip. The location shooting, sophisticated editing and camera work, and sympathetic examination of the environmental, social, and psychological issues behind urban crime made it a landmark in cinema. Other noteworthy and relatively sophisticated portrayals of criminals in the 1920s included some of Lon Chaney's films, like *Outside the Law* (1921), and Josef von Sternberg's late-silent classic, *Underworld* (1927).

In the late 1920s the gangster genre got a fresh boost with Prohibition-related gangland activities, a popular wave of gangster melodramas on Broadway, and the development of synchronized-sound technology at Warner Brothers studio. After a tentative experiment with Bryan Foy's *The Lights of New York*, Warner Brothers' first all-talking feature in 1928, other, more successful gangster talkies included play adaptations like Paul Fejos's *Broadway* (1929), Roland West's *Alibi* (1929), and Howard Hawks's *The Criminal Code* (1930). Attracted to the novelty of sound, audiences reveled in the squeal of tires, the wail of sirens, the rattle of machine guns, the tapping of policemen's nightsticks, and the verbal pepper of underworld slang.

A second wave of films, from 1931 to 1935, celebrated gangsters as heroes, all of them descendants of the Snapper Kid—Edward G. Robinson as Rico Bandello in *Little Caesar* (1931), James Cagney as Tom Powers in *The Public Enemy* (1931), Spencer Tracy as Bugs Raymond in *Quick Millions* (1931), and Paul Muni as Tony Camonte in *Scarface* (1932).

When the Volstead Act was repealed in 1933, racketeering turned from bootlegging to labor and transportation. The new gangsters personified those models of successful Americans, the robber barons Jim Fisk, Jay Gould, and Cornelius Vanderbilt (not to mention the notorious criminals of the day like Al Capone) as charismatic, clever, and ruthless men whose rapid rise to wealth and power had made them laws unto themselves.

The violence and content of these pictures were tempered in the mid-1930s by the newly toughened Motion Picture Production Code. Gun-toting James Cagney now wore a badge in *G-Men* (1935), for example, which initiated a new cycle of police procedurals based on the activities of J. Edgar Hoover's *FBI. Still implicit, however, was the message that in Depression America it was, indeed, crime that paid, and crime that brought in the big box-office dollars.

Not to be forgotten were the "gentlemen crooks" and fiendish masterminds of yore who successfully bridged the gap between silent and sound films. O. Henry's reformed crook, Jimmy Valentine, who had first appeared in *Alias Jimmy Valentine* (1915), portrayed by Robert Warwick, now reappeared in *The Return of Jimmy Valentine* (1936), with Roger Pryor. Based on a character created by Norbert Jacques, the villainous mastermind Dr. Mabuse became the subject of four Fritz Lang films beginning with *Dr. Mabuse, der Spieler* (1922), and made his first talkie appearance in *Das Testament des Dr. Mabuse* (1933), a thinly disguised allegory of the rise to power of Adolf Hitler. Maurice *Leblanc's Arsène *Lupin, "Prince of Thieves," who first appeared in print in 1907, benefited from the inimitable voice and delivery of John Barrymore (*Arsène Lupin*, 1932), and Melvyn Douglas (*Arsène Lupin Returns*, 1938). And Sax *Rohmer's *Fu Manchu, the insidious Chinese criminal, first appeared on screen in 1923 in a series of short British films with Harry Agar Lyons as the doctor.

The master detectives, too, quickly made their way into the talkies. Holmes's first talkie was *The Return of Sherlock Holmes* (1929), with the debonair but stiff Clive Brook. H. C. *McNeile's Bulldog *Drummond (Captain Hugh Drummond), who had first appeared on screen in *Bulldog Drummond* (1922), played by Carlyle Blackwell, was a great success in his first talkie, *Bulldog Drummond* (1929) with Ronald Colman. Colman played the role again in *Bulldog Drummond Strikes Back* (1934). S. S. *Van Dine's Philo *Vance, the most popular detective in literature during the late 1920s, was played four times by William Powell, most notably in *The Canary Murder Case* (1929), an early example of the sophisticated use of sound technology, and *The Kennel Murder Case* (1933), one of the screen's finest detective movies. Rex *Stout's corpulent Nero *Wolfe, who first appeared in *Fer-de-Lance* (1934), made it to the screen two years later, as played by Edward Arnold in *Meet Nero Wolfe*. Dashiell *Hammett's Nick and Nora *Charles were impersonated with witty sophistication by William Powell and Myrna Loy in the six-film Thin Man series (1934–47). Among the female detectives was Stuart Palmer's Hildegarde *Withers, a thin spinster teacher turned detective who first appeared in 1931 in *The Penguin Pool Murder* and was portrayed by Edna May Oliver in three RKO pictures, beginning with *The Penguin Pool Murder* (1932). Other actresses included Helen Broderick (*Murder on the Bridle Path*, 1936) and Zasu Pitts (*The Plot Thickens*, 1936).

With the establishment of double-bills in American movie theaters in the 1930s and 1940s, there was a greater need for formula pictures, programmers in all genres, to complement the A pictures. All the major studios had B units, and a number of smaller studios, like Monogram and PRC, were expressly formed to crank out low-budget cheapies. Not for nothing were these latter studios dubbed "Poverty Row." The number and variety of detective and crime thrillers increased radically; however, as their budgets decreased and the shooting schedules shortened, the quality of the productions declined.

The Rathbone/Holmes series, for example, after two top-drawer entries for Fox studios, *The Hound of the Baskervilles* (1939) and *The Adventures of Sherlock Holmes* (1939), was transferred to the humbler domain of Universal Studios, where production values sagged and the stories were updated (to the consternation of purists). Other popular detectives and reformed crooks now relegated to the B-movie ghetto included series programmers the Falcon (RKO), the Lone Wolf (Columbia), the *Saint (RKO), Fu Manchu (Paramount, Metro-Goldwyn-Mayer, Seven Arts, etc.), Nick *Carter (Metro-Goldwyn-Mayer), Ellery *Queen (Republic and Columbia), the Crime Doctor (Columbia), Bulldog Drummond (Paramount), the Shadow (Columbia and Monogram), Michael *Shayne (Twentieth Century-Fox), Dick Tracy (Republic), the Green Hornet (Universal), and Boston Blackie (Columbia). Several series programmers included movies adapted from juveniles. Nancy *Drew, whose first book appearance was in *Secret of the Old Clock* (1930), reached the screen in the late 1930s in a Warner Brothers series of four films with Bonita Granville.

Among the Asian detectives in the low-budget programmers of the 1930s and 1940s were John Marquand's Mr. *Moto, whose portrayals by Peter Lorre for Twentieth Century-Fox ceased with the anti-Japanese sentiments of World War II; Mr. Wong, who was incarnated by Boris Karloff in five films for Monogram Pictures; and Charlie *Chan, who was portrayed in forty-six films by a number of actors, including Warner Oland, Sidney Toler, and Roland Winters. (Chan has never been portrayed by a Chinese actor.)

During World War II many of the aforementioned characters found themselves embroiled in the *war effort. Even the gangsters got into the act, as when Humphrey Bogart's mob took on the Nazis in *All Through the Night* (1942). But the most important impact of the war on crime and detective films was the emergence of the genre dubbed "film noir" by the French critics. Neat *puzzle problems and debonair *sleuths no longer belonged in a world that had gone mad. More in keeping with the times were convoluted, mazelike plots, brutal violence, hard-boiled detectives, and the fatalistic vision of the *Black Mask*

school of fiction, led by authors Dashiell Hammett and Raymond *Chandler. Other important influences were the cynical "poetic realism" of the French director Marcel Carné (*Le jour se lève*, 1939) and the German Expressionist visual style—baroque chiaroscuro, skewed camera angles, distorted set design—imported from Europe by filmmakers Fritz Lang and Alfred Hitchcock.

Leading the way among the noir detective movies was John Huston's *The Maltese Falcon* (1941), based on the 1929 Hammett novel, with Bogart as a much tougher Sam *Spade than had been portrayed by Ricardo Cortez and Warren William in, respectively, 1931 and 1935. Lightweight leading man Dick Powell underwent a startling and persuasive transformation into a tarnished knight in *Murder, My Sweet* (1944), based on Chandler's *Farewell, My Lovely*. Two years later Humphrey Bogart played him in another noir classic, Howard Hawks's *The Big Sleep*.

Foremost among the practitioners of murder and mayhem on screen is Alfred Hitchcock. Indeed, his name has become synonymous with movies of intrigue (*The Thirty-Nine Steps*, 1935; *Foreign Correspondent*, 1940; *Torn Curtain*, 1966), paranoia (*The Lady Vanishes*, 1938; *The Wrong Man*, 1956), gothic guignol (*Psycho*, 1960), the chase (*North by Northwest*, 1959), and the psychological thriller (*Rebecca*, 1940; *Vertigo*, 1957; *Marnie*, 1964). Hitchcock further popularized the genres on his television series, *Alfred Hitchcock Presents* in the 1950s and 60s, for which he himself occasionally directed, and in which he introduced TV viewers to the works of such masters of the form as Robert Bloch, John Collier, and Ray Bradbury.

Although the classical black-and-white noir exhausted itself in America in the mid-fifties, culminating with Orson Welles's baroque *Touch of Evil* (1958) and Robert Aldrich's nihilistic Mike *Hammer thriller *Kiss Me Deadly* (1955)—the most notable in a series of pictures drawn from Mickey *Spillane's hard-boiled investigator—its influence has been felt in recent decades in the work of some of the screen's premier international directors, including the documentary-like police procedurals of Japan's Akira Kurosawa (*Stray Dog*, 1949; *High and Low*, 1963), the psychoneurotic ambiguities of Italy's Bernardo Bertolucci (*The Spider's Stratagem*, 1970; *The Conformist*, 1970), and the work of French stylists like Henri-Georges Clouzot (the horrific *Les diaboliques*, 1954) and the New Wave and Second Wave directors, like Jean-Luc Godard (the anarchic *Breathless*, 1959, with its many references to noir icons like Bogart) and Jean-Pierre Melville (the stylishly ritualized portraits of cops and robbers, *Le doulos*, 1962; *Le deuxième souffle*, 1966; *Le samouraï*, 1967). Modern American disciples of the noir tradition include John Frankenheimer (*The Manchurian Candidate*, 1962), Sidney Lumet (*Prince of the City*, 1981), Martin Scorsese (*Mean Streets*, 1973; *Taxi Driver*, 1976; *GoodFellas*, 1990), and Francis Ford Coppola (the acclaimed *Godfather* trilogy—1972, 1974, 1990—which brought the activities of the Mafia to the screen in the multigenerational saga of the Corleone family, based on stories by Mario Puzo).

Movies like these shocked public sensibilities with a hitherto undreamed-of degree of graphic violence and sex. Since the 1950s the more genteel detectives, crooks, and policemen had gone over to the new medium of television. In Hollywood in the mid-1960s the censorious Motion Picture Production Code and the studio system that had supported it—both in place since the late 1920s—were collapsing. As a result, filmmakers were ready—and able—to reflect in their crime and detective films the developing social, racial, and cultural upheavals of the 1960s. As Robert Warshow had predicted in his classic essay "The Gangster as Tragic Hero" (1954), the crime thriller was becoming "the 'no' to that great American 'yes' which is stamped so big over our official culture and yet has so little to do with the way we really feel about our lives."

Pessimism, corruption, and defeat marked the "revenge" and "vigilante" cycles, like the Charles Bronson *Death Wish* pictures; the so-called "blaxploitation" pictures of the 1970s, Gordon Parks's *Shaft* (1971) and Gordon Parks Jr.'s *Superfly* (1972), which were metaphors of black power and racial conflict; the "rap" and "hood" pictures about ethnic youth gangs, notably Dennis Hopper's *Colors* (1988), Mario Van Peebles's *New Jack City* (1991), Edward James Olmos's *American Me* (1992), and John Singleton's *Boyz N the Hood* (1991); and the conspiracy dramas, which had had a brief cachet in the right-wing anti-communist thrillers of the early 1950s (*Big Jim McLain*, 1952), and which now reemerged in post-Watergate films such as Alan J. Pakula's *The Parallax View* (1974) and *All the President's Men* (1976), Oliver Stone's *JFK* (1991), and John MacKenzie's *Ruby* (1992).

Films like these cast wide their nets of guilt and recrimination. Their mazelike constructions were, in historian Carlos Clarens's words, "concentric circles of involvement that become more and more diffuse; the paranoid syndrome of universal malevolence encroaching on the individual." If Clarens is correct, these new films not only reflect an ongoing crisis in our social structure but also the breakdown of the detective and crime film genre itself: "It is the systematic dissolution of binary values like good/evil, right/wrong, true/false, inside society/outside society." Thus it has always been that, quite apart from their entertainment value, these films have become seismic readings of our times, even if they risk self-destruction in the process.

[*See also* Formula: Character; Formula: Plot.]

• Robert Warshow, *The Immediate Experience: Movies, Comics, Theatre and other Aspects of Popular Culture* (1962). William K. Everson, *The Bad Guys: A Pictorial History of the Movie Villain* (1964). William K. Everson, *The Detective in Film* (1972). James Robert Parish and Michael R. Pitts, *The Great Gangster Pictures* (1976). Alan G. Barbour, *Cliffhanger: A Pictorial History of the Motion Picture Serial* (1977). Eugene Rosow, *Born to Lose: The Gangster Film in America* (1978). Carlos Clarens, *Crime Films* (1997). Oscar Rimoldi, "The Detective Movies of the 30s & 40s." Parts 1 and 2. *Films in Review* 44, no. 5/6 (1993): 165–73; no. 7/8 (1993): 225–33.

—John C. Tibbetts

FINGERPRINTS AND FOOTPRINTS, which may be used to identify the perpetrators of crimes as well as to exonerate the innocent, have long been among the most important *clues in the arsenal of the detective writer. Fingerprints, which serve as absolutely individual identity markers, are among the most reliable clues in real life and fiction. Footprints, especially those made by footwear, are significantly less reliable identifiers of particular individuals, since the footwear can be donned by a person other than the owner of the footwear. Nonetheless, footprints remain a popular clue type, perhaps because they can be manipulated by the author, who can use them to advance the detection process without necessarily solving the case based on footmarks alone.

Although schemes for the organization of fingerprints into systems that are useful to law enforcement are popularly believed to have appeared only during the twentieth century, fingerprints have long been used as identification markers in many societies around the world. In ancient Assyria and Babylonia, digital impressions upon clay tablets seem to have been used as identity marks. The British Museum holds an artifact recording that a Babylonian officer was ordered to make property confiscations and arrests and to secure defendants' fingerprints.

In Europe, it was not until the seventeenth century that fingerprints were considered to be important identity markers. In 1684, Dr. Nehemiah Grew, a fellow of the College of Physicians and Surgeons of the Royal Society, London, published his observations on fingerprints. In Italy, Marcello Malpighi, a professor of anatomy at the University of Bologna, published his research on fingerprints beginning in 1686. His work on the subject was so highly regarded that one of the layers of the human skin is named for him.

Before fingerprints could be used for the purposes of law enforcement, they had to be classified. A major step in this direction was taken in 1823 when Johannes Evangelist Purkinje published his doctoral thesis at the University of Breslau. In it he classified fingerprint types into nine groups and described their features. Twenty-five years later, Sir William Herschel, who was working for the British government in Bengal, India, fingerprinted the Indians with whom he did business. Believing one business associate to be particularly unreliable, he required him to provide an imprint of his hand rather than a signature in handwriting. Herschel later decided that an imprint of the last finger joint would serve as well as a whole handprint.

Around the same time, Dr. Henry Faulds, a Scotsman working in Japan, became fascinated by the finger marks he found on some ancient pottery. Faulds began an in-depth study involving the collecting of fingerprints from people of Japanese and other origins, looking for ethnological markers. He also studied the prints of monkeys. In 1880, he stated in a letter his observation that "the scientific conviction of the perpetrator [of a crime] may be effected" through the identification of fingerprints. In that letter, he described two classic cases of finger marks at the scenes of crimes and stated, "If the fingerprints that have been taken are known, they certainly offer stronger proof than the customary 'birthmark' of the dime novel." Faulds eventually wrote a textbook on fingerprint procedure in which he recommended printing all ten fingers.

In Argentina, another fingerprint researcher, Juan Vucetich, compiled the largest file of fingerprints in the world before 1900. Working at the same time, the Englishman Sir Francis Galton published a book on the topic in 1892. It included his analysis of his predecessors' work and practical advice for recording fingerprints. He also identified three groups of fingerprint patterns, which he called arches, loops, and whorls. His A-L-W method, named for the first initials of those pattern types, formed the basis for his system of fingerprint registration. These are still used by modern fingerprint experts. Sir Edward Richard Henry, head of the metropolitan police in London, published his *Classification of the Uses of Finger Prints* in 1900. His system and that of Vucetich are cornerstones of most fingerprint systems that are used today.

An early exemplar of the use of the science of fingerprinting in detective fiction appears in a classic scientific detective novel, *The Red Thumb Mark* (1910), by R. Austin *Freeman. This *inverted detective story shows Dr. John *Thorndyke applying the scientific method, and some knowledge about fingerprinting, to a case in which the identity of the killer is known from the start.

In recent years, laser technology has made possible the reading of fingerprints left on skin and other surfaces from which fingerprints could not be lifted previous to the advent of this technology. Patricia D. Cornwell describes this process in her novel *Post Mortem* (1990).

The prints of bare feet may also be used to establish personal identification, particularly of babies, whose footprints have been recorded at birth, but such footprints are used more rarely than footwear impressions in crime fiction. One of the more memorable works in which footprints of shoes figure is *Clouds of Witness* (1926) in which Dorothy L. *Sayers describes a host of puzzling footprints discovered outside of the conservatory at Riddlesdale Lodge. There is a squelchy-looking print from a bedroom slipper, the print of a woman's strong shoe, the marks of galoshes, and a policeman's boot mark, all of which lead Lord Peter *Wimsey to ponder upon the footwear worn that night by his brother, who is the chief *murder *suspect.

[See also Forensic Pathologist; Scientific Sleuth.]

• Berthold Laufer, "History of the Finger-Print System," in *Annual Report of the Board of Regents of The Smithsonian Institution . . . for the Year Ending June 30, 1912* (1913). B. C. Bridges, *Practical Fingerprinting* (1942). Frederick R. Cherrill, *The Finger Print System at Scotland Yard: A Practical Treatise on Finger Print Identification for the Use of Students and Experts and a Guide for Investigators when Dealing with Imprints Left at the Scenes of Crime* (1954). Michael Kurland, *How to Solve a Murder: The Forensic Handbook* (1995).

—Nicholas Rhea

FLEMING, IAN (1908–1964), English journalist and novelist, creator of the British *secret agent James *Bond. The second son of a prominent Scottish family, Ian Lancaster Fleming was expelled from both Eton and Sandhurst before attending Tennerhof, the experimental school in Kitzbühel, Switzerland. Before World War II he worked as a foreign correspondent for Reuters. His breeding and charm subsequently landed him a wartime post as personal assistant to the director of Britain's Naval Intelligence.

In 1952 Fleming married Ann Charteris, who suggested that he write fiction. Close contact with espionage operations during the war, his experience as a journalist, and the novels of Dornford *Yates, H. C. *McNeile ("Sapper"), and John *Buchan, which he had read as a youngster, all inspired Fleming. When he introduced Bond in *Casino Royale* (1953; *You Asked for It*), Fleming created one of the most popular fiction series ever. Although his deliberately formulaic novels (which intersperse brief bursts of fantastic action with extended passages of detailed description) met with critical disdain, they also brought him the financial success he sought. Moreover, his work found admirers in Raymond *Chandler and Kingsley Amis, among others; John F. Kennedy acknowledged that *From Russia, With Love* (1957) was one of his favorite books.

The Bond books usually pit the gentleman superspy against a master villain, often a puppet of the Soviet Union. Serving an unimpeachably trustworthy and virtuous British secret service, Bond always triumphs over his adversaries while enjoying the favors of several superficially depicted females. Spending about two months each year writing at his home, Goldeneye, in Jamaica, Fleming wrote twelve Bond novels; all have been filmed, although the screen versions bear little or no resemblance to the books on which they are purportedly based. He also wrote three nonespionage books: *The Diamond Smugglers* (1957), a nonfiction work; *Thrilling Cities* (1963), a travel narrative; and *Chitty-Chitty-Bang-Bang* (1964), a children's story, which was also filmed. *Octopussy* (1966), a collection of previously published short stories, was published after Fleming's death from a heart attack.

[See also Adventurer and Adventuress; Gentleman Adventurer; Heroism; Sex and Sexuality; Spy Fiction.]

• Andrew Lycett, *Ian Fleming: The Man Behind James Bond* (1995).

—Matthew Cohen

FOOTBALL MILIEU. *See* Sports Milieu.

FORENSIC PATHOLOGIST. In the real world of homicide, it is not uncommon that the identity of the assailant quickly becomes known, the assailant having informed the police of the occurrence and details of the killing. The role of the forensic pathologist in such cases may be mere confirmation of the alleged cause of death, although it is not impossible that the pathological findings may complicate what otherwise appears to be a straightforward case. Where a body is found in apparent suspicious circumstances and the details of the events leading to death are unknown, then, again, the role of the forensic pathologist is to determine the cause of death. Moreover, the forensic pathologist will endeavor to gather from the postmortem examination information that may be of assistance in testing the truth of any account of events leading to the death given by an alleged assailant, when—and if—an assailant is found. The forensic pathologist is only one among the representatives of many disciplines and professions that make up the investigating team: As the first person to examine the body in detail, another important function is to recognize and preserve appropriately any evidence upon or within the body which may be analyzed by other members of the team.

It should not be surprising, therefore, that the forensic pathologist as protagonist looms small in detective novels and detective stories. Given the geographical and historical differences between the medical examiner in America and the *coroner in England and Wales, it is equally unsurprising that a single medical examiner figures frequently in a "supporting role" to an American "series detective"—Dr. Emanuel Doremus to Philo *Vance, or Dr. Multooler to Thatcher Colt, for example. In Great Britain, where a coroner still retains the legal right to direct a deceased's general practitioner to perform a postmortem examination—even though that practitioner may have no experience of pathology—and where pathology as a separate discipline is relatively young, it is again unsurprising that postmortem examinations in the detective novels and stories of the Golden Age were carried out largely by frequently anonymous police surgeons. The conclusions given by these characters furnish the basis for the investigation by the protagonists whom they support; but, as befits their supporting role, details of the examinations that yield those conclusions are generally absent.

A similar absence of detail exists in the exploits of the earliest protagonist with a specific forensic bent, Surgeon-Colonel John Hedford, whose exploits were chronicled with sardonic melodrama by Robert Cromie, in collaboration with T. S. Wilson. Appearing first in the periodical Black and White, these twelve exploits were collected in The Romance of Poisons (1903). Despite the title—and his soubriquet, "The Specialist in Poisons"—about half of these crimes involve microbiology—typhoid, cholera, an "obscure fungus"—rather than toxicology.

For many, the preeminent practitioners in the field—although for different reasons—are Dr. John *Thorndyke, introduced by R. Austin *Freeman in The Red Thumb Mark (1907), although the biography prepared by the author for Sleuths, 1931, cites his work for the defense in Regina versus Gummer, 1897, as his first case; and Reggie *Fortune, introduced by H. C. *Bailey in Call Mr. Fortune (1920). In the Thorndyke novels and stories, everything is subordinate to the detail of the pathological and scientific evidence by which Thorndyke brings home the crime to its perpetrator or, as in real life, demonstrates the absence of a crime. That Thorndyke can be both forensic pathologist and forensic scientist reflects the

field of knowledge available in the early years of the twentieth century. Where knowledge has advanced to make a comment by Thorndyke unacceptable to the modern reader, as in his remarks concerning the lack of a method allowing identification of an individual from blood in "The Pathologist to the Rescue" in The Magic Casket (1927), this serves only to enhance the period flavor. This is particularly so where the advance does not detract from the method used within that story which, although not giving individual identity, yields sufficient information to allow comparison between three disputed blood samples and deductions as to the characteristics of the person who has shed the blood from which one sample is derived. This effect of the "evolution of knowledge" is by no means confined to the early years of the century: The author of The Expert (1976), the eminent forensic pathologist Bernard Knight, writing under the pseudonym Bernard Picton, would place far less reliance, less than twenty years later, on the "signs of asphyxia" than does his forensic pathologist, Dr. John Hardy—otherwise the forensic pathologist's fictional forensic pathologist.

What is less acceptable to today's forensic pathologist is the overinterpretation by Thorndyke—however necessary for the *plot—of his findings at a postmortem examination in Mr. Polton Explains (1940). In this novel a body that has "been exposed to such intense heat that not only was most of its flesh reduced to mere animal charcoal, but the very bones, in places, were incinerated to chalky whiteness" is found in the cellars of a house which has been "burned out from the ground upwards" without "even part of a floor left." The deceased had a room on the first floor. "Looking at that odontoid process" (a part of the second bone of the neck which articulates with the first), Thorndyke is of the opinion that "it was broken before death; that, in fact, the dislocation of the neck was the immediate cause of death." This opinion cannot be supported from the evidence, given those circumstances: If the dislocation of the neck were the cause of death then that dislocation must have occurred during life, evidence for which would be the presence of bleeding, visible to the naked eye, or inflammation, visible under the microscope. Given the description of the remains, it appears difficult to accept that such evidence may still be visible; even if it were, how can Thorndyke exclude the dislocation having occurred as a result of the movement of the body from the first floor to the cellar during the collapse of the house?

The outstanding characteristics of Fortune are his emphasis upon the importance of evidence and his outrage at the failure of the police to appreciate that importance or, worse still, to ignore or resist its thrust where it does not accord with the preconceptions of "the official mind." In these days of "miscarriages of justice," it is remarkable that critics of the genre fail to appreciate this crusading quality in Bailey's writing—save for Erik Routley in his masterly exegesis in The Puritan Pleasures of the Detective Story (1972). The paradox of Fortune, given the scarcity in real life of objective pathological evidence that indicates the guilt of a named individual, is his manipulation of events to bring about what he regards as justice, a particularly chilling example being the means he uses to "finish off the case" in "The Dead Leaves" in *Clue for Mr. Fortune* (1936; *A Clue for Mr. Fortune*). Such behavior requires that the conclusions Mr. Fortune draws from the pathological evidence must be unobjectionable but, sadly, this is not always the case. In a cameo appearance in *Clunk's Claimant* (1937; *The Twittering Bird Mystery*), he examines two skeletons found in a garden grave and gives the opinion at the graveside: "time of burial, say twenty years ago. . . . Don't expect to revise that or add." There is even today no method that would allow the dating of skeletal remains within a period of more than five years and less than one hundred years.

Thorndyke and Fortune have sufficient veracity to make credible their extended careers: Given the statements of other fictional forensic pathologists, their sporadic appearances are wholly comprehensible. In *Fatality in Fleet Street* (1933) C. St. John Sprigg's Sir Colin Vansteen, consultant pathologist to His Majesty's Home Office, merely from his examination of a brain can say that the victim was stabbed while asleep!

Equally comprehensible is the subsidiary role of the police surgeon Dr. Jaynes, the narrator of two series of stories by Douglas Newton for *Pearson's Magazine* in 1932 and 1935, whose hero is Paul Toft, a detective with a clairvoyant faculty. In "The Mystery of the Firework Man" (July 1932), his examination of a dead body at the scene of its discovery is so perfunctory that he does not remove the boots, only doing so at Toft's suggestion to discover that a red hot iron had been applied to the soles of the feet. Such a lack of attention to detail might explain the ability of the general practitioner in "Murder on the Fen" in *Physicians' Fare* (1939) by C. G. Learoyd to perform a postmortem on a body, recovered from a river after having been missing for four months so that the condition of the body is "that jellified you could have sucked her through a straw," in three minutes and forty seconds.

In America, the earliest appearance of the medical examiner as protagonist of a series of stories appears to be in 1926 in the pages of *Detective Story Magazine*: Dr. Aloysius Moran, the creation of Ernest M. Poate, appears to Robert Sampson, "afflicted in the head" (*Yesterday's Faces, Volume 4: The Solvers*).

Although not himself a medical examiner, a knowledge of forensic medicine assists Dr. Colin Starr in the cases chronicled by Rufus King in *Redbook*, seven of which were collected in *Diagnosis: Murder* (1941). George Harmon *Coxe's uncollected stories about Dr. Paul Standish, medical examiner of Union City, Connecticut, published in *Liberty* and *Cosmopolitan* from the middle to late 1940s, are quietly absorbing, although there is little overt pathology. The same may be said of the Standish novel *The Ring of Truth* (1966).

Pathology returns to the fore in *Diagnosis: Homicide* (1950), the first collection of stories featuring Dr. Daniel Webster Coffee, pathologist at Pasteur Hospital, Northbank, the creation of Lawrence G. Blochman. This volume and its successor, *Clues for*

Dr. Coffee (1964), have introductions by distinguished medical examiners—Thomas Gonzalves in the former and Milton Helpern in the latter. Despite the competence of the pathology, Dr. Coffee lacks the personality of Thorndyke or Fortune.

Not lacking personality—only credibility—is the glamorous Dr. Tina May, heroine of three novels written in the 1980s by Sarah Kemp (pseudonym of the late Michael Butterworth). In *No Escape* (1985), a dismembered torso is found in an advanced state of decomposition; May gives evidence that this victim had taken an amount of whisky before death, in apparent ignorance of the possibility of production of alcohol in the process of decomposition of the body and, even could such postmortem artifact be excluded, the impossibility of determining from what liquor the alcohol found in the body was derived. Such ignorance—together with her deductions as to the state of mind of an assailant from the wounds to the body of a victim (the wise pathologist refrains from forays into forensic psychiatry)—makes one doubt the claim in her newspaper biography that she "wrote, at 23, a book on Forensic Medicine which has become a standard textbook. . . . "

The suspension of disbelief necessary to the detective story becomes strained when the performance of the protagonist is not in accord with the recorded reputation. In *Old Bones* (1987), Aaron Elkins's "Skeleton Detective," Professor of Anthropology Gideon P. Oliver, fails to realize for some sixty hours the significance of "beadlike nodules on the ends of the ribs" of a skeletal torso found in a French manoir. When one learns that the motive for a murder committed during that period of forgetfulness was to prevent recognition of the significance of the nodules by the victim—who had been a medical student for one or two years several decades previously—suspension of disbelief is difficult to maintain.

There is no difficulty in believing the paranoia engendered by a political background to a system of medicolegal investigation of death, a state of mind readily apparent in the fictional chief medical examiner for the Commonwealth of Virginia, Dr. Kay Scarpetta, protagonist of Patricia Cornwell's *Postmortem* (1990) and later novels. Surrounded by the latest technology of forensic science—from physical evidence recovery kit (PERK) to laser—and supported by experts in criminalistics and forensic psychiatry, forensic pathology, as in real life, does not by itself crack the problems in the Cornwall books. It is curious that this renaissance of the forensic pathologist in crime fiction boasts only female protagonists, May and Scarpetta being followed by Clare Rayner's Dr. George Barnabas and Nigel McCrery's Dr. Samantha Ryan while Gideon Oliver's distaff is Kathy Reich's Dr. Temperance Brennan. John Knox might have had some comment upon this phenomenon.

This historical perspective of fictional forensic pathologists reveals an apparent lack of accuracy on the part of their creators, raising the questions, What part does forensic pathology play in the mechanics of the genre, and, Is inaccuracy inevitable?

The evidence of the fictional forensic pathologist may define critical parameters of the *puzzle, most obviously those necessary to the apparently unbreakable *alibi. Where none of the methods of determination of time of death—body temperature, development of rigor mortis, the concentration of potassium in the vitreous humor (a fluid in the eyeball), the rate of digestion or emptying of the stomach—in real life can give a margin of error of less than several (if not many) hours, it appears desirable that, in fiction, these temporal niceties be ignored. Christopher Bush was particularly dependent upon the state of the stomach contents of the deceased—in The Case of the Running Man (1958), for example—despite Perry *Mason's destruction of the autopsy surgeon's evidence on this point in The Case of the Rolling Bones (1939).

An alternative but equally invalid approach to determining time of death is an opinion as to how long the victim would have lived after having sustained an injury. L. T. Meade and Robert Eustace in "The Luck of Pitsey Hall" (The Brotherhood of the Seven Kings, 1899) have it that death must be instantaneous when a man is stabbed through the heart. The interval before death and the victim's capability of movement during that interval are unpredictable and may be astonishing, as is acknowledged by S. S. *Van Dine in The Kennel Murder Case (1933). It is a sad irony that the victim of a method of murder which probably would cause almost instantaneous collapse, if not death, walks, hails a taxi and dies five hours later in the Savoy Hotel in One, Two, Buckle My Shoe (1940; The Patriotic Murders) by Agatha *Christie.

It may be that a knowledge of forensic pathology affords a novel method of murder, but that method impresses more if the knowledge is applied correctly. That is not the case in Dorothy L. *Sayers's Unnatural Death (1927; The Dawson Pedigree), where air is introduced into an artery rather than a vein to cause death by air embolism. Sayers redeems herself by the novel change rung on the theme of identification from dental evidence in her story "In the Teeth of the Evidence" (Help Yourself Annual, 1934). This theme was introduced into fiction by Joseph Sheridan le Fanu in "The Room in the Dragon Volant" (In a Glass Darkly, 1872) and elaborated by Rodrigues Ottolengui in "The Phoenix of Crime" in Final Proof (1898). It is of interest to be the birth of forensic dentistry is considered to be the identification of the victims of the fire at the Bazar de la Charité in Paris in May 1897.

The reasons for these forensic fallacies in fiction may be lack of research by the authors or, as already hinted, the evolution of factual forensic knowledge; the references consulted by the authors of the Golden Age might now be considered themselves erroneous. Consider the "real" cause of death of Chloe Pye in Margery *Allingham's Dancers in Mourning (1937; Who Killed Chloe?). An acknowledged, if poorly defined, entity in pathology until two or three decades ago, status lymphaticus is now regarded as nonexistent, a form of words used by the pathologist where the postmortem examination failed to reveal the cause of death. It has been replaced by the accurate, if less abstruse, term "unascertained." An author is well advised to consult the textbooks contemporary with the period of his fiction; contemporary accuracy cannot guarantee freedom from criticism by the forensic pathologist of the future.

Detective fiction is not devoid of instances of curious prescience. Roy Vickers's "The Three-Foot Grave" (Pearson's Magazine, Nov. 1934; "The Impromptu Murder") foreshadows by almost fifty years events that followed the discovery of human remains in a peat bog at Lindow Moss in Cheshire (Regina v. Reyn-Bardt, 1983). The means of reconstruction of facial features from the skull, pioneered in real life by the Russian palaeontologist Gerasimov and employed by the crime-sculptor Imro Acheson Fitch in Anthony Abbot's About the Murder of a Startled Lady (1935; Murder of a Startled Lady), caught the public imagination when used by Richard Neave, a medical illustrator at Manchester University, in the case of a skeleton found buried in a carpet in Cardiff in 1989. The method used to murder Sir Raymond Ramillies in Allingham's The Fashion in Shrouds (1938) was not brought home to a perpetrator in real life until Regina v. Barlow, 1957.

The concern of the factual forensic pathologist with the accuracy of the opinions expressed by fictional counterparts is natural. Potential jurors may be expected to have read more detective fiction than textbooks of forensic pathology; their expectations of the limitations of forensic evidence are more likely to be guided by the former.

[See also Reasoning, Types of.]

—Stephen Leadbeatter

FORGERY is the act, usually illegal, of imitating or counterfeiting documents, letters, signatures, or works of art, in order to deceive. The forger's motives are the usual ones: *greed, fear, hatred, or envy, or to conceal a *murder. Although successful forgery is becoming more difficult with advances in technology, forgery remains a popular focus for mystery writers.

As a physical object, a forged paper might have no intrinsic value, as is the case with the popular forged will used by numerous detective writers, or the forged confession exemplified in Anna Katharine *Green's The Leavenworth Case (1878). A more unusual example of a forged paper item is the railway ticket with faked conductor's punch which establishes a false *alibi in Dorothy L. *Sayers's Suspicious Characters (1931; The Five Red Herrings).

However, certain forged paper can have an actual value, as with the checks or share certificates that are the focus of innumerable mysteries. Paper can have an aesthetic as well as a monetary value. In August Derleth's The Adventure of the Unique Dickensians (1968), Solar Pons proves a purported Charles *Dickens manuscript to be forged by showing that the watermark was created at a later date. Elizabeth *Daly's The Book of the Lion (1948) concerns a lost Chaucerian poem sold to a millionaire who dies with it in an airplane crash. In Margery *Allingham's Flowers for the Judge (1936; Legacy in Blood), a publishing company boasts of its private ownership of an unknown, scabrous play by William Congreve. The manuscript, titled The Gallivant, proves to be a nineteenth-century fake, the original having been sold by a vanished director.

Forgery of works of art follows logically. In Allingham's *Death of a Ghost* (1934), the annual showing of a painting purportedly by a deceased artist is used to boost the studio's profits. In Michael *Gilbert's *The Family Tomb* (1969; *The Etruscan Net*), an Italian professor sells forged "finds" of Etruscan treasures. In Arthur Lyons's *Other People's Money* (1989), an art expert is fooled by apparently priceless pre-Hittite artifacts; this is an admitted tribute to *The Maltese Falcon* (1930) by Dashiell *Hammett, the self-confessed *detective novel parody, in which ruthless competing persons seek the legendary Templar's tribute, found to be stripped of its jewels.

Forgery as a confidence trick involves substituting a fake for the real object already examined. In Charlotte MacLeod's *The Family Vault* (1979) a forger with a supply of fake jewels sells them as the originals. Morris Hershman's *A Matter of Pride* (1966) offers a satisfying variation on this theme: One dealer is selling fakes to another, who is paying in counterfeit money. Jaime Sandival used fake paintings in *Art for Money's Sake* (1970). In *Set a Thief* (1984; *The Man Who Stole the Mona Lisa*), Martin Page suggests that the Mona Lisa was copied when the real life thief Adam Worth stole it in 1911.

Forged forgery is the key to Michael *Innes's *Silence Observed* (1961), in which a collector of forgeries discovers that he has purchased the forgery of the work of an established forger. Discovery of the forgery leads to murder. In Jonathan Gash's *The Gondola Scam* (1984), a collector substitutes fakes for the originals at risk during the Venetian floodings.

[*See also* Art and Antiques Milieu.]

• Henry Taylor Fowkes Rhodes, *The Craft of Forgery* (1934). Sepp Schuller, *Forgers, Dealers, Experts: Strange Chapters in the History of Art* (1960). Frank Arnau, *Three Thousand Years of Deception in Art and Antiques* (1961). Henry F. Pulitzer, *Where is the Mona Lisa?* (1967). Tom Keating, *Geraldine Norman, and Frank Norman, The Fake's Progress: Being the Cautionary History of the Master Painter & Simulator Tom Keating as recounted with the utmost candour & without fear or favour to Frank Norman* (1977). Colin Wilson, *Written in Blood: a History of Forensic Detection* (1989).

—John Kennedy Melling

FORMULA. *This entry is divided into two parts, the first surveying formulas for the characterization of hero protagonists in crime and mystery fiction, and the second examining formulaic plots in this genre and their attraction for the crime and mystery writer.*

Character
Plot

For further information, please refer to Craft of Crime and Mystery Writing, The; Theory, Prescriptive Theory.

CHARACTER

A description of the formulas of the *detective novel and the *mystery story is also the history of the genre, but a history that has received nourishment from many other literary genres. In the corpus of detective and mystery fiction can be found formulaic and thematic elements from literary genres as diverse as the traditional *Gothic novel, the *sensation novel, the penny dreadful, the *dime novel, the pulp *thriller, the bildungsroman, the clerical novel, the *western, the historical novel, the classical *ghost story, the hard *science fiction story, and the social *novel of manners.

Nevertheless, what distinguishes crime and mystery fiction from the above genres is the presence of the person who works (often systematically and logically) to uncover or resolve a crime or mystery, often to right a wrong and to clear a client who has been unjustly accused. The existence of a detective as an independent operative who investigates because he or she has been requested to do so rather than because he or she is mandated to do so distinguishes detective and mystery fiction from the formulaically related but distinct types of the *police procedural, *spy fiction, the thriller, and the *crime novel. These boundaries are, however, frequently nebulous and always debatable.

Fictional *private eyes and *amateur detectives had appeared prior to the April 1841 advent of Edgar Allan *Poe's Chevalier C. Auguste *Dupin. Dupin's character contained virtually all the thematic ingredients for what rapidly became established as the prescriptive formula for the character of a *private detective who was independent and often eccentric but always a supremely ratiocinative individual, brilliantly capable of surmising a tapestry of crimes from the most threadbare *clues. In Poe's usage, and in the majority of the subsequent uses of this formula, the detective is openly contemptuous of established police procedures and policemen, and has an admiring sidekick narrating his adventures but missing the significance of the clues.

As this formula was used by successive generations of writers, their stories became close and circular, with a clear resolution, a genteel *setting, and, as subject matter, crimes motivated by passion or material greed. The detectives were often independently wealthy and from the upper classes, casually solving complicated crimes that baffled the obtuse investigators of *Scotland Yard or the police. Small variations exist in the treatments of this formula, but detectives cleaving to its basic patterns can be found in the works of writers as superficially diverse and distinct as Arthur Conan *Doyle (Sherlock *Holmes), Arthur *Morrison (Martin Hewitt), H. C. *Bailey (Reggie *Fortune), A. A. Milne (Antony Gillingham), Vincent *Starrett (Jimmie Lavender), Dorothy L. *Sayers (Lord Peter *Wimsey), John Dickson *Carr (Dr. Gideon *Fell), and Agatha *Christie (Hercule *Poirot and Miss Jane *Marple). Nor was this formula unrecognized by its early contemporaries: T. S. *Stribling's first Professor Henry Poggioli stories parodied it by pitting independent detective Poggioli against *villains who were better prepared and more intelligent; Poggioli's ingenious solutions came invariably too late.

In a conscious inversion of the established formula, *armchair detectives never visited the scene of the crime or looked for *clues, remaining in relative or absolute isolation, and depending upon media or friends to convey information to them. The first arm-chair detective—the *Old Man in the Corner—was created by the Baroness Emmuska *Orczy. Succes-sive notable armchair detectives were Jacques *Futrelle's Professor Augustus S. F. X. *Van Dusen, also known as the Thinking Machine, and M. P. Shiel's Prince Zaleski. The last significant armchair detective was Rex *Stout's largely sedentary and ago-raphobic Nero *Wolfe.

At the end of the nineteenth and beginning of the twentieth centuries, the established formula began to develop elaborate variations. The *psychic sleuth and the scientific detective flourished briefly and died slowly. The former either possessed psychic powers or was thoroughly cognizant of all psychic rituals; notable examples were William Hope Hodgson's Car-nacki, Algernon Blackwood's John Silence, J. U. Giesy's Semi-Dual, and Seabury Quinn's Jules de Grandin. The scientific detective story was more for-mulaic, invariably being structured around a de-nouement featuring the trappings of the latest inves-tigative technology; Arthur B. *Reeve's Craig Kennedy was the most important and influential sci-entific detective.

Substantially more durable were the *medical sleuths, the legal detectives, and sleuths who sur-mount disabilities. The former applied technical as-pects of their medical or psychological training to solving crimes, with notable medical detectives like R. Austin *Freeman's Dr. John *Thorndyke, Max Rit-tenberg's Dr. Xavier Wycherley, and Ernest M. Poate's Dr. Thaddeus Bentiron, and medical detectives en-dure in the works of such contemporary writers as Jonathan Kellerman's Dr. Alex Delaware. Lawyers were introduced to serve as detectives, as in Arthur Train's stories featuring the ingenious Ephraim Tutt; they continue to do so, as in the novels of John Gr-isham and Scott Turow. Ernest Bramah created the first notable sleuth with a disability, the blind Max *Carrados, whose senses were nevertheless so acute he could read a newspaper's headlines with his fin-gertips, and additional writers created detectives who were blind, amnesiac, crippled, and even hemo-philiac. The handicapped detective continues to be used in stories by writers as varied as Edward D. *Hoch and Dick *Francis.

In addition, and at roughly the same time as the above, rogues and "bent heroes" were introduced as detectives, solving crimes to atone for their past mis-deeds and to win the love of faithful women; and vir-tually every profession, including nurse, journalist, and stock speculator, had its practitioners function-ing as detectives and solving crimes. Detective stories written for juvenile audiences were the staple of nu-merous *dime novels (featuring Nick *Carter, Old Cap Collier, and others) and, slightly later, in juvenile series books (e.g., the series featuring Nancy *Drew and the Hardy Boys).

The most significant modification to the hitherto established formulas occurred during the second and third decades of the twentieth century, when Ameri-can detective and mystery writers combined melo-dramatic fantasy with the tropes of American literary *realism. They created stories in which detectives op-erated in an ethically ambiguous but morally rigid world; in these stories, lower-class detectives walked dilapidated neighborhoods and absorbed physical abuse while investigating crimes born of social pathology and *greed, yet remained generally free from *corruption even while consorting with the rich; often they delivered death to miscreants. These hard-boiled detectives originated in the *pulp maga-zines. The first hard-boiled series character, Gordon Young's "Don Everhard," appeared as a series charac-ter in the enormously influential *Adventure*, and the first hard-boiled series detective—Carroll John *Daly's "Three-Gun Terry Mack"—appeared in *Black Mask*. Daly soon created the enormously popular and influential Race *Williams, a private investigator whose shooting was invariably accurate and lethal. Superior hard-boiled detective stories by Dashiell *Hammett rapidly appeared. Hammett brought to his fiction literacy and a seeming realism (based par-tially on his experiences as a Pinkerton detective); when Joseph T. Shaw became editor of *Black Mask*, Hammett's formulas were consciously adopted as the standard to be used in writing detective and mystery stories, and other magazines followed suit. Addi-tional notable writers of hard-boiled detective and mystery fiction include Lester Dent, Erle Stanley *Gardner, Raymond *Chandler, Raoul Whitfield, Frederick Nebel, Horace McCoy, Dwight V. Babcock, and George Harmon *Coxe, among many.

At the close of the twentieth century, Hammett's basic formula for the hard-boiled detective endures and dominates, for it offers substantially greater nar-rative possibilities than earlier formulas. Neverthe-less, although traditional hard-boiled detective fic-tion is still being written, significant variations have been introduced. The characters of the detectives have been humanized and modernized, and many of the finest contemporary writers are women, their sto-ries featuring women as detectives: Sara *Paretsky, Sue *Grafton, and Marcia *Muller offer consistent innovations to the hard-boiled formula, even while remaining cognizant of their origins, and numerous other writers have expanded the hard-boiled formula to accommodate gays and lesbians, racial and ethnic minorities, and even the mentally ill as detectives.

[*See also* Characterization; Conventions of the Genre.]

• Howard Haycraft, ed. *Art of the Mystery Story* (1946). John Ball, ed. *The Mystery Story* (1976). Robin W. Winks, *Modus Operandi: An Excursion into Detective Fiction* (1982). Robert Sampson, *Yesterday's Faces: A Study of Series Characters in the Early Pulp Magazines*; 6 vols. (1983–1993).
—Richard Bleiler

PLOT

In a highly regarded essay entitled "The Concept of Formula in the Study of Popular Literature" (*Journal of Popular Culture*, 1969), John G. Cawelti describes formula as "a conventional system for structuring cul-tural products," which is to say that formula "repre-sents the way in which a culture has embodied both mythical archetypes and its own preoccupations in narrative form." Employing Cawelti's concept of for-mula as an instrument for analysis, the student of crime and mystery writing will quickly conclude that the popular genre is inherently formulaic, because the visible foundation in all of its subtypes and variations is the attempt to remedy the specific instance of social disorder known as crime. Whatever form it appears in, the story of criminal detection seems to be the product of anxiety about the danger of violation of the social contract by an unlawful appropriation of wealth or the destruction of life. Moreover, the genre invariably addresses the problem of crime by posing in opposition to it a character representing civilized values. The values may be ethical or moral; they may express a collective faith in reason or in scientific method, as well as the aptitude of a singular individual, or, in the case of the *police procedural, the force of an official agency such as the police.

The *Golden Age traditions provide one way of using the elemental formula, and the hard-boiled manner of writing detective fiction another, but the stylistic differences among schools of crime and mystery writing are secondary to the root formula, ways of translating it into affecting means of conveying the central formula to different readers.

Since the romantic period, literary taste has valorized authorial originality to the point where writing that displays evident signs of formulaic inspiration is regularly demoted by critical judgment to subliterary rank. Originality, however, has many forms of expression. Before the invention of technology making possible rapid, inexpensive reproduction of books through a far-flung network of distribution, literature not uncommonly had an allusive weave. It referred to earlier writings, invoked classical models, displayed its learning ostentatiously, and commented liberally on texts outside itself. With the rise of publishing houses that could economically give whole libraries of works to consumers of printed matter, authors responded to the change in conditions for their employment by altering aesthetic theory so it could argue for the uniqueness of each new book.

Writers of earlier ages knew, however, that there was originality in the execution of familiar motifs, and authors who devote themselves to popular genres today know it too. Use of formula has great attraction for a writer precisely because it entails, a review of a familiar pattern. For one thing, because the groundwork for formula narrative has already been prepared, writers and their readers shift their attention to execution—how this or that writer manages the pursuit of suspects, how he or she will embody the promise of order restored in traits of the detective character, and, on a less conscious level, how the writer will use *voice and *plot to delay the narrative so the reader's *suspense will rise, or how the writer will hide *clues and develop the detective's reconstruction of the crime. For another thing, the frequency of formula repetition certifies the attraction it holds for people who share with the author the anxieties and hopes contained in the formula. This produces an invisible literary community that produces a third advantage to the use of formula: the possibilities it offers for philosophical themes.

Despite the dismissive treatment given to popular literature by some critics, as a product of a historical culture it is freighted with commonly held ideas about life. It seems to be a mirror reflecting culture back upon an audience; but if it is a mirror, it is a two-way one. The formula plot of crime detection constitutes a quest for understanding and, ultimately, meaning; thus, its latent content is investigation of how to know reality. In short stories about the ratiocinative Sherlock *Holmes and novels about R. Austin *Freeman's Dr. John *Thorndyke, reality is revealed by application of empirical science. In Ross *Macdonald's narratives, Lew *Archer follows paths to reality blazed by Sigmund Freud. In the police fiction of Elizabeth *Linington and Ed *McBain, reality becomes the object of a collective enterprise of investigation aided by forensics, methodical interviewing, and legwork. Rex *Stout's Nero *Wolfe can remain settled in his armchair while detecting because he projects a trained imagination onto the nonmaterial data presented to him. Resolutely hard-boiled detectives may find that the contours of reality are not in the end amenable to being mapped. Reality's essence is elusive. Hercule *Poirot and Inspector (later Superintendent) John *Appleby proceed with confidence that brain work will restore normative order, but Robert B. *Parker's *Spenser and Sue *Grafton's Kinsey *Milhone figure that the site where order is possible has a narrow and not always comfortable circumference. In the cases taken by these detectives, and in the cases followed by every other detective in every other story or novel about crime and mystery, variations on the epistemological theme seem limitless—just as limitless as variations on the basic conventions of sleuth characterization and the plotting of fictional crimes. Finally, though, the variations on formula conceived by writers of mysteries and detective stories keep readers turning the pages because these works play on a formula deeply structured into popular consciousness. The search for a renewed social order and for ways to comprehend reality speaks to universal modern interests. The formula for the search is a boon to writers, a never completed adventure for readers.

[See also Conventions of the Genre; Rules of the Game.]

—John M. Reilly

Fortune, Reggie. Highly popular in his day, Reggie Fortune, medical consultant and gadfly to *Scotland Yard, appears in ninety-five detective stories and novels written by H. C. *Bailey between 1920 and 1948. These works are notable for the terse wit of the main character and a recurring urgency to protect future victims. The well-fed Reggie moves from his couch to the *corpse on the dissecting table, never surprised by villainy, never restrained in his comment on human folly, and seldom hesitating to act as the agent of Providence. He characteristically appears in long stories published six to those volume; they are variously humorous *puzzles, slices of career crime, tales of elaborate *revenge, or accounts of twisted love. Fortune concentrates on facts: "You never know what you're looking for, so you have to look for everything," he remarks in "The Greek Play" (in Delineator, Mar. 1930).

—Nancy Ellen Talburt

FRANCIS, DICK (b. 1920), British author of mysteries set in the *horse racing milieu. The son of a horse trainer, Francis grew up in Wales, aspiring to be a jockey. After serving as an airframe fitter and pilot in the Royal Air Force during World War II, he pursued his racing dreams despite being a little old for a novice and too large to be a flat-racing jockey. As a steeplechase rider, he won his first competitive race in 1947. By 1954, he was champion jockey of Britain. After near victories at the Grand National (the pinnacle of steeplechasing competition), in 1956 Francis was out in front just fifty yards from the finish line when his horse, Devon Loch (owned by Queen Elizabeth the Queen Mother), suddenly and inexplicably stopped. The event was such a sensation that a publisher contracted for Francis's autobiography, *The Sport of Queens: The Autobiography of Dick Francis* (1957). Though he had no previous writing background, Francis's book became a best-seller in Britain. Encouraged by this success, and by his wife's suggestion that he write a *thriller, he then produced *Dead Cert* (1962). Each year until 1998 he published at least one new novel, all of them proving so popular that since 1980 his American publisher has promoted him as a "mainstream" best-seller.

There are many affinities between the usual Francis hero and the kind of hard-boiled protagonist described in Raymond *Chandler's "The Simple Art of Murder" (1944). The typical Francis hero is a vulnerable yet stoical loner struggling to do the best he can against *corruption but with few illusions about changing the world. Although he always connects his hero (frequently a jockey or former jockey) to the world of racing, Francis rarely repeats a main character. The individual's struggle to retain his honor, professionally and morally, against the forces of *evil is Francis's primary interest. His ability to describe pain is one of his most powerful skills as an author, but he never glamorizes brutality.

[*See also* Gambling, Illegal; Loner, Sleuth as.]

• Melvyn P. Barnes, *Dick Francis* (1986). J. Madison Davis, *Dick Francis* (1989).   —J. Madison Davis

FREELING, NICOLAS (b. 1927), author of crime fiction. Born in London, reared in France, and residing near Strasbourg, France, Nicolas Freeling, by his life and writing, belongs to that still unusual population better termed European than known by allegiance to a singular culture. In his youth Freeling followed an apprenticeship in French hotel restaurants, which he eventually memorialized in *Kitchen Book* (1970); *The Kitchen: A Delicious Account of the Author's Years as a Grand Hotel Cook*. With the family he started with his Dutch wife in 1955, he lived and worked for hotels in England, Holland, and France—a pattern of relocation that Freeling has described as a continuation of the vagabond existence of his youth.

That life, however, yielded the material Freeling used for release from itinerant employment. When he published his first novel, *Love in Amsterdam* (1962; *Death in Amsterdam*), featuring the cosmopolitan couple, Amsterdam police officer Inspector Piet *van der Valk and his French wife, the talented cook Arlette, Freeling launched a successful career as a crime writer. As the detective protagonist of twelve *police procedural novels, van der Valk is often likened to George *Simenon's Inspector Jules *Maigret because of his disregard for the conventions of bureaucracy and his subjective entry into the lives of the criminals and *victims he meets; van der Valk is also considerably more political than his purported model.

Despite the popular following Freeling developed for van der Valk, he concluded the series with the assassination of the inspector in *A Long Silence* (1972; *Aupres de ma Blonde*). Because Arlette has been Piet's partner in detection throughout the series, Freeling can comfortably shift to her narrative perspective in the final section of the novel. He also has given Arlette encore volumes of her own: *The Widow* (1979), *One Damn Thing After Another* (1981; *Arlette*).

Freeling's third detective series bears similarity to the van der Valk books. Henri *Castang is also a police officer, this time in France, and his wife Vera, a Czech, serves as a partner whose cultural distance from her husband's home equips her with lenses that improve the vision of crime.

[*See also* Police Detective.]

• Carol Schloss, "The van der Valk Novels of Nicholas Freeling," in *Art in Crime Writing: Essays in Detective Fiction*, ed. Bernard Benstock (1983).   —John M. Reilly

FREEMAN, R(ICHARD) AUSTIN (1862–1943), creator of Dr. John *Thorndyke, detective fiction's foremost medico-legal expert. Born and raised in *London, Freeman, with exactitude and respect, used London as the setting for thirty of his sixty-five tales.

In 1887 Freeman qualified for membership in the Royal College of Surgeons, then went on to serve with the British colonial administration in Africa. Upon his return to England, four years hence, his health gone, he looked to his pen for income. While making shift as interim medical officer at Holloway Prison, he wrote (as Clifford Ashdown), with J. J. Pitcairn, *Adventures of Romney Pringle* (1902), tales about an engaging miscreant not unlike E. W. *Hornung's A. J. *Raffles. In 1904 the pair wrought tales about a fledgling surgeon-sleuth. Dr. Wilkinson. Striking out on his own, Freeman introduced Thorndyke in a move, he said later, that "determined not only the general character of my future work but of the hero." When Freeman was forty-five Thorndyke made his first full-fledged appearance in *The Red Thumb Mark* (1907), the book extolled by Howard Haycraft as "one of the undisputed milestones of the genre." Over the next thirty-seven years, Thorndyke presided in twenty-two novels and forty short stories. Though he knew the man only through his epoch-making text *The Principles and Practice of Medical Jurisprudence* (1865), Freeman identified Thorndyke's prototype as Alfred Swaine Taylor, the father of medical jurisprudence.

Not only was Freeman the first writer to introduce genuine science into detective fiction, at Gravesend in Kent, his home from 1903 onward, he maintained a laboratory in which he conducted experiments essential to Thorndyke's investigations, contriving there solutions sound enough to stand up in a court of law. Years ahead of the official police in applied criminology, for example, analyzing blood, hair, or fiber, utilizing X-rays, Thorndyke set standards later emulated by law enforcement agencies. His omnipresent tote kit, for example, became regulation issue for the French *Sûreté. In law schools Thorndyke became required reading.

Though he created more than 600 characters, Freeman's best were Thorndyke himself and Thorndyke's humble factotum, Nathaniel Polton, lauded by P. M. Stone as "one of the most fascinating, finely portrayed, convincing characters in the entire gallery of detective fiction." Thorndyke's digs, at 5A Kings Bench Walk, in London's Inner Temple, of themselves a presence in the stories, have a mood of snugness and replenishment rivaling Sherlock *Holmes's 221B Baker Street habitat. In *The Singing Bone* (1912) Freeman achieved another major breakthrough for the genre with the creation of the *inverted detective story. The final Thorndyke tale, *The Jacob Street Mystery* (1942), was written (while German bombers soared overhead) in a bomb shelter that the unthwartable Thorndykean octogenarian built in his garden. In September 1979, with the mayoress of Gravesend and fellow novelists H. R. F. *Keating and Catherine Aird looking on, American admirers set a tombstone in place on Freeman's hitherto unmarked grave. The R. Austin Freeman Society and its journal, the *Thorndyke File*, founded in 1976, continue to provide a forum for a readership unwavering in its loyalty to the man whose two sons, with quiet awe, identified as "the Emperor."

[*See also* Addresses and Abodes, Famous; Medical Sleuth.]

• P. M. Stone, ed., introduction and "5A King's Bench Walk," in *Dr. Thorndyke's Crime File* by R. Austin Freeman (1941). Norman Donaldson, *In Search of Dr. Thorndyke* (1971). John McAleer, ed., *Thorndyke File*, 22 issues (1976–88). Oliver Mayo, *R. Austin Freeman: The Anthropologist at Large* (1980).
—John McAleer

French, Inspector Joseph, *Scotland Yard detective created by Freeman Wills *Crofts, appeared in some thirty *detective novels and many short stories from 1924 to 1957, latterly as chief inspector and superintendent. Sometimes ploddingly pedantic, sometimes ruthlessly insistent and brilliantly intuitive, his success rate is impeccable.

French is happily married and ordinary, from his clean-shaven look to his almost medium height and roughly medium build. His geniality is evidenced by twinkling dark blue eyes, and his nationality proclaimed by tweeds and bowler hat. He takes regular meal breaks, irrespective of his location or the pressing nature of his enquiries. Yet he is no home bird, for he enjoys his holidays and relishes every opportunity to pursue his investigations well away from *London.

From his first appearance in *Inspector French's Greatest Case* (1924), involving robbery and *murder in London's Hatton Garden diamond district, French quickly established a reputation for demolishing the supposedly unbreakable *alibi. While he is consistently meticulous, with his cases as neatly dovetailed as the railway timetables which were his creator's stock-in-trade, this does not mean that his exploits are less readable than those of the more extrovert or omniscient detectives (usually amateurs) created by other writers of the Golden Age. There is an excitement in accompanying French every step of the way, sharing his thoughts, his disappointing leads and lucky breaks, and being presented with every *clue at the same moment as the detective.

Although most of the French novels are straightforward narratives with the criminal's identity ultimately exposed, *The 12.30 from Croydon* (1934; *Wilful and Premeditated*) shows the murderer executing his plan and then gives French's explanation of how he closed the case. This inverted technique is used also in many of the short stories included in *Murderers Make Mistakes* (1947) and *Many a Slip* (1955).

[*See also* Inverted Detective Story; Railway Milieu; Time Is of the Essence.]
—Melvyn Barnes

FRIENDSHIP. In crime and mystery fiction, as in life, much depends on friendship. Although the device and notion of friendship appears to be at odds with a genre conventionally featuring fictional protagonists largely isolated from other people, writers have consistently relied on friendship both as a structural device (e.g., the traditional *sleuth/sidekick relationship) and as a thematic concern allowing reflection and comment on social mores.

By virtue of eccentricity, personal peculiarity, intellectual prowess, or ego, the fictional detective has not on the whole been an easy person to befriend or live with. A figure full of contradiction and often righteous to the point of obsession, the prototypical detective frequently exasperates those who are close to him or her. The sleuth's faithful friend, then, is both an expression of the isolated investigator's uneasy stance vis-à-vis society and a representative of the normality to which the detective is restoring things. An important paradox in the genre is the extent to which the mythically self-reliant and self-sufficient investigator is rarely without the support of a friend of some description. For the historically male, unmarried, and reclusive detective, the friend often functions as something of a spouse substitute, tying the detective into a semblance of a "normal" domesticity.

The origins of the device of sleuth and companion can be traced back to Edgar Allan *Poe's Chevalier C. Auguste *Dupin stories, published in the 1840s. The relationship of the intellectually superior Dupin and the anonymous narrator is the blueprint for an enduring convention of crime and mystery fiction: the renowned sleuth assisted by a trusted but less able friend who does the legwork, keeps order (domestic and otherwise), and tells the story from a perspective of admiration and utter loyalty.

Also in the Dupin stories is the prototype of another enduring thematic treatment of friendship—the claim of friendship as a rationale for the detective's initial involvement in an investigation. It is, for instance, Dupin's "old acquaintance, Monsieur G—, the Prefect of the Parisian police," who prevails upon Dupin to solve the problem of "The Purloined Letter" (in *The Gift*, 1845).

By the 1890s, Arthur Conan *Doyle was successfully incorporating these narrative devices in his popular stories of the *Great Detective Sherlock *Holmes and the awestruck auxiliary Dr. John H. *Watson. Thus was a pattern set: from the late nineteenth century onward, fictional detectives had their Watsons in one form or another, as well as an endless succession of fictional friends, relations, and friends of friends asking for help in the name of acquaintanceship.

For many decades, however, the fictional sleuth/sidekick relationship, ostensibly based on friendship, continued in fact to rely not so much on principles of mutual benevolence and reciprocity as on a condition of superiority/inferiority. The detective's social, educational, and economic circumstances are usually more privileged than those of the sidekick. This dichotomy ensured that the powerful bonds of friendship rarely developed to a point where they might compromise the detective's *heroism or even eclipse the sleuth's legendary power. Close personal relationships bear the price tag of accountability. Early writers in the genre stuck to the convention that the generic detective's style of placing him/herself in potential danger in order to further the investigation should not be jeopardized by the problem of close personal ties.

Famous fictional friends of eccentric, egotistical, and acutely intelligent sleuths include Hercule *Poirot's Captain John Hastings in Agatha *Christie's novels, Nero *Wolfe's Archie *Goodwin in Rex *Stout's work and Dr. John Evelyn *Thorndyke's Dr. Jervis in the fiction of R. Austin *Freeman. As friends and assistants, they display folkloric qualities of loyalty, courage, patience, resourcefulness, and, particularly in Captain Hastings's case, a boundless capacity for stubborn obtuseness. They ask for little in return beyond the privilege of keeping the great one company.

Friendship was treated differently in hard-boiled private investigator fiction of the 1920s and 1930s. The traditional sidekick was dispensed with for more transitory and uneasy liaisons with an assortment of pals claiming friendship on the basis of for instance, shared wartime experiences or favors owed. Interestingly, both Dashiell *Hammett and Raymond *Chandler, creators of archetypal American lone *private investigators with neither friends nor a permanent social context to speak of, produced novels dealing with the question of friendship. Hammett's *The Glass Key* (1931) is, according to James Sandoe, a detective story offering "an exceptionally delicate scrutiny of friendship." Chandler's *The Long Goodbye* (1954) has the private investigator Philip *Marlowe embarking on an intense, though short-lived, friendship with war veteran Terry Lennox. The protagonists in both

novels are dragged into their investigations through the personal connection of friendship but are betrayed by friends who prove unworthy. The relationships are severed, the sleuths thus reinstated as heroes who rarely answer to the demands of love or friendship, immune from the vulnerabilities that beset the rest of the human race.

Refreshing new slants on friendship have been offered by crime and mystery writers of the last thirty years. The genre currently abounds in fictional sleuths engaged in complex and challenging relationships both at work and at home. Many of these friendship networks reflect changing attitudes toward class, race, *gender, sexuality, and age. The work-based partner/friendship of Reginald Hill's British policemen Superintendent Andrew Dalziel and Peter Pascoe transcends *class boundaries and the attendant chasm of educational background. In a similar vein, the American writer Faye Kellerman explores the nonsexual but loyal and affectionate partnership between her police sergeant Peter Decker and police detective Marge Dunn as they bolster each other's egos and spirits across traditional gender and religious boundaries. Robert B. *Parker's Boston-based detective *Spenser's initial relationship with his employee, Hawk, is that of professional colleague, but before long the two forge a profound trust based on literal reliance on each other in life-and-death situations.

In the work of many contemporary women crime and mystery writers, both British and American, independent, unmarried female sleuths form networks of friends who support them both emotionally and practically. Sara *Paretsky's Chicago-based V. I. *Warshawski has a friendship with Dr. Lotty Herschel, an older woman of personal and professional stature. V. I.'s other friendships draw attention to her past and to her firmly antiracist and antisexist approach to life, and are used in contrast to her courage and independence to show her vulnerability as a human being. Most of her investigations are undertaken at the behest of female family members or acquaintances from the past. Sue *Grafton, too, provides her character Kinsey *Milhone with a network of neighbors and friends. American author Linda J. Barnes's detective Carlotta Carlyle not only maintains a network of friends, but also acts as big sister to the young Paolina, growing up in a family constrained by grinding poverty. Befriending Paolina involves Carlotta in a relationship that frequently tests her, while it demonstrates that strong bonds can bridge divisions of age, race, income, and experience. Amanda *Cross's feminist protagonist Kate *Fansler, the New York-based university lecturer and *amateur detective, often concerns herself with questions of female friendship. In *Death in a Tenured Position* (1981; *A Death in the Faculty*), one erudite character reiterates Virginia Woolf's assertion, earlier in the twentieth century, of the importance of women's friendships in the struggle to change their lot.

[See also Loner, Sleuth as; Loyalty and Betrayal; Sidekicks and Sleuthing Teams.]

• John G. Cawelti, *Adventure, Mystery and Romance: Formula Stories as Art and as Popular Culture* (1976). Howard Haycraft, *The Art of the Mystery Story: A Collection of Critical Essays* (1983). Patricia Craig and Mary Cadogan, *The Lady Investigates: Women Detectives and Spies in Fiction* (1986). Kathleen Gregory Klein, *The Woman Detective: Gender and Genre* (1988). Maureen T. Reddy, *Sisters in Crime: Feminism and the Crime Novel* (1988). T. J. Binyon, *Murder Will Out: The Detective in Fiction* (1989).

—Margaret H. Kinsman

Fu Manchu. The repeated appearance in book after book over nearly fifty years of the Chinese criminal genius Fu Manchu illustrates the capacity of popular literature to create and reinforce stereotypes. Reportedly the journalist Sax *Rohmer found the model for his character in London, but the inspiration for the portrayal of a "sinister Oriental" who embodies the alleged mysteries of Asia in combination with mastery of Western learning arose from the bigotry and xenophobia that trumpeted the fearful threat to Western civilization from what was sensationally termed the "Yellow Peril." Rohmer introduced his character in a single short story, "The Zayat Kiss," published in 1912. Within a year the crafty figure began to appear in novel-length works: *The Mystery of Dr. Fu Manchu* (1913; *The Insidious Dr. Fu Manchu*), *The Devil Doctor* (1916; *The Return of Fu Manchu*), and *The Si-Fan Mysteries* (1917; *The Hand of Fu Manchu*). After a hiatus while Rohmer wrote of other criminal doings, the wily doctor reappeared in *Daughter of Fu Manchu* (1931), beginning a series of eight more novels running to 1949. Following another break in publication, Rohmer brought him back in *Re-enter Dr. Fu Manchu* (1957) and *Emperor Fu Manchu* (1959), by which time he had taken the role of an anti-Communist seeking to cleanse his homeland. In his heyday, however, Dr. Fu Manchu moved through vividly atmospheric settings suggesting the ominous purposes he pursued, while eluding his nemeses, the putative heroes of the West—Sir Denis Nayland Smith and his sidekick Dr. Petrie. Racial prejudice has its own appeal, but Rohmer's undoubted narrative skill enhanced its ugly face with the features of a cultural archetype.

[*See also* Archetypal Characters; Ethnic Sleuth; Ethnicity; Oriental Sleuth; Prejudice; Racism; Stock Characters.]

—John M. Reilly

FUTRELLE, JACQUES (1875–1912), American author, known for his "Thinking Machine" detective who solves *impossible crimes. Born in Pike County, Georgia, Futrelle worked as a newspaperman in Richmond, Virginia, and in Boston, Massachusetts, while publishing short stories featuring a variety of detectives. In 1905 the *Boston American* serialized as part of a contest for readers Futrelle's "The Problem of Cell 13," in which Professor Augustus S. F. X. *Van Dusen, known as the Thinking Machine, proves he can escape from an impregnable prison. The character caught the public's imagination and Futrelle used him in *The Chase of the Golden Plate* (1906), in two collections of stories, *The Thinking Machine* (1907; *The Problem of Cell Thirteen*) and *The Thinking Machine on the Case* (1908; *The Professor on the Case*), and in a novelette, *The Haunted Bell* (1909). Other

novels, without the Van Dusen character, combine elements of mystery with romance, such as *The Diamond Master* (1909) and *My Lady's Garter* (1912). Futrelle was aboard the *Titanic* on its fateful maiden voyage, and died when the ship sank. His wife, L. May Futrelle, also a mystery writer, later expanded his *The Simple Case of Susan* (1908) into *Lieutenant What's-His-Name* (1915). Some uncollected stories published in the *Ellery Queen Mystery Magazine* in 1949–50 brought the total of Thinking Machine stories to almost fifty.

The Thinking Machine is in the tradition of the eccentric genius of Edgar Allan *Poe; the Chevalier C. Auguste *Dupin's name may be detected in Augustus Van Dusen's. A caricature of the cerebral scientist, he has many titles (from Ph.D. to M.D.) and an "almost grotesque" appearance: He is thin and colorless, with eyes "squinting" behind thick spectacles, and a huge head. Arrogant and cantankerous, he emerges from his laboratory only to take on an intellectual challenge, such as the claim, in "The Problem of Cell 13," that "no man can *think* himself out of a cell." He escapes in a week's time, with some help from a reporter friend, but mainly by applying his engineering skills and keen eye for the habits of rodents and jailers.

The solving of an impossible crime by a surprising but rational explanation is the hallmark of the Thinking Machine: He discovers jewels cunningly concealed, in "The Missing Necklace" (*Cassell's*, 1908), and a car vanished from a closely guarded road, in "The Phantom Motor" (*Cassells*, 1908). The device, a variation of the *locked room mystery, was used not only by Poe and Arthur Conan *Doyle but by such contemporaries of Futrelle as Israel *Zangwill, in *The Big Bow Mystery* (1892), and Gaston Leroux, in *The Mystery of the Yellow Room* (1908; *Murder in the Bedroom*). It was particularly popular in the 1930s among such writers of the *puzzle plot as Agatha *Christie and Ellery *Queen, and John Dickson *Carr devoted a chapter of *The Three Coffins* (1935; *The Hollow Man*) to various locked room scenarios. Futrelle's contribution to the impossible-crime tradition lay in leavening his *sleuth's implausible analytical skills with *humor and irony while playing fair with the reader by providing clear clues. "The Problem of Cell 13" remains one of the most frequently anthologized mystery stories and, along with other original and ingenious tales of Futrelle's, assures the author—despite the brevity of his career—an important place in the history of the genre.

• "Jacques Futrelle," in *The Oxford Book of American Detective Stories*, ed. Tony Hillerman and Rosemary Herbert (1996). Julian Symons, *Bloody Murder: From the Detective Story to the Crime Novel*, 3rd rev. ed. (1992).

—Mary Rose Sullivan

FUTURE, USE OF THE. The future has been an anomaly in crime and mystery writing, perhaps because, to paraphrase Isaac Asimov's preface to *The Caves of Steel* (1954), it isn't fair to the clue-seeking reader if the author can "at will drag in futuristic devices." Nonetheless, both this book, set in a future *New York, and its sequel, *The Naked Sun* (1957), manage to be fair to the reader because the crime's solution depends on laws of robotics that have been explained fully. The robot detective R. Daneel Olivaw carries the Sherlock *Holmes tradition of logical deduction to its logical extreme, but it is his human partner Elijah "Lije" Bailey who solves the crime, because R. Daneel cannot match Bailey's understanding of primitive human emotion and intuitive reasoning.

Asimov is nonetheless correct: Today's future fiction is the province of *science fiction, a publishing category quite distinct from crime and mystery. When crime and mystery writers use a future *setting it is generally incidental. Thus in Reginald *Hill's One Small Step (1990), the scene of the crime is a colonized moon of the future, but series characters Andrew Dalziel and Peter Pascoe solve the mystery of the murdered Italian astronaut entirely by interrogating the astronaut's banal colleagues in a fashion that would have worked out the same in a country home of the 1930s. To be sure, among the shapers of crime and mystery writing were Edgar Allan *Poe and Arthur Conan *Doyle, who also helped to shape future fiction; indeed, the "science fiction" of both has been collected. Poe's cosmological fantasy Eureka (1848) provides a dimension to his work that is analogous to what the future provides in later writers, and which illuminates such mystery stories as "The Fall of the House of Usher" (Burton's Gentle-

man's Magazine, Sept. 1839) and "The Masque of the Red Death" (Graham's Lady's and Gentleman's Magazine, May 1842) as stemming primarily from cosmic forces. Doyle's best-known futuristic stories are in the Professor Challenger series, which are essentially mystery stories with scientific solutions.

Asimov's contention notwithstanding, one could argue that today's future fictions are mystery (and at times crime) stories, the solution to which is either a scientific discovery or the sociological result of one. Thus, the time-traveler narrator of H. G. Wells's The Time Machine (1895) solves the crime and mystery of the split of future humanity into two species, the Eloi and the Morlocks. Similar solutions obtain in Robert A. Heinlein's classic Orphans of the Sky (1963); Asimov's greatest story, "Nightfall" (Astounding Science Fiction, Sept. 1941) Ray Bradbury's "The Third Expedition" (Planet Stories, 1948); Walter M. Miller's A Canticle for Leibowitz (1960); and Arthur C. Clarke's 2001: A Space Odyssey (1968). Jorge Luis Borges in "The Garden of Forking Paths" (EQMM, Aug. 1948) gives us the form of a spy story with the reality of alternate cosmology, as in Poe's Eureka. The effect of the future is to broaden the implications of the mystery.

• George Edgar Slusser, Asimov: The Foundation of His Science Fiction (1980).
—Curtis C. Smith

GABORIAU, ÉMILE (1832–1873), French author of sensational novels of crime. Born in the small town of Saujon, Charente-Maritime, he was apprenticed to a notary but enlisted in the army. Leaving as a sergeant major after four years' service, he settled in Paris in 1856, and worked as a writer and journalist, becoming secretary to Paul Féval, a newspaper editor, dramatist, and popular novelist.

After composing much ephemeral fiction, Gaboriau became famous after the 1865 serialization of his novel *L'affaire Lerouge* (1866; The Widow Lerouge; The Lerouge Case) in the newspaper *Le Pays*. This was followed by *Le crime d'Orcival* (1867; The Mystery of Orcival), which appeared simultaneously in two newspapers; *Le dossier no. 113* (1867; File No. 113; Dossier No. 113); and *Monsieur Lecoq* (1868; Monsieur Lecoq; Lecoq the Detective). Although Gaboriau believed that all his novels belonged to one type, which he termed *le roman judiciaire*, only these four have a substantial detective element; others, such as *La clique dorée* (1871; The Clique of Gold, The Gilded Clique) and *La dégringolade* (1872; The Downward Path, The Catastrophe), deal with crime but do not present a mystery. The four that involve detection feature a police detective, Lecoq (who plays only a minor role in *L'affaire Lerouge*). However, Gaboriau is careless in his use of names and the four Lecoqs, though sharing a name and a profession, otherwise have little in common. An *amateur detective, Père Tabaret (or Tirauclair), formerly a pawnbroker's clerk, has the main role in *L'affaire Lerouge*, and is consulted by Lecoq in *Monsieur Lecoq*. Gaboriau took from Edgar Allan *Poe the detective's ratiocinative method. He was also influenced by earlier French sensational literature, and by his study of past criminal cases: His facts are accurate, and his description of the French legal system exact. His *plots, which usually turn on some sexual scandal, are, however, repetitious; the novels lapse into melodrama and are overly dependent on *coincidence. Nevertheless, Gaboriau's influence on later authors is considerable. The admirable opening scenes of *Monsieur Lecoq* (in which the detective deduces, from a detailed examination of the scene of the crime, what has occurred and arrives at a description of the participants) were imitated by Arthur Conan *Doyle in the first chapters of *A Study in Scarlet* (*Beeton's Christmas Annual*, 1887). Gaboriau's method of describing the crime in the first part of a novel and the events that engendered it in the second (in *Monsieur Lecoq* the two parts are so tenuously connected that the second is usually omitted in translations) was also imitated by Doyle, who writes in *Memories and Adventures* (1924), "Gaboriau had rather attracted me by the neat dovetailing of his plots." With Lecoq, Gaboriau gave detective fiction its first *police detective, and with Père Tabaret he carried on the tradition of Poe's Chevalier C. Auguste *Dupin. Though now most of Gaboriau's work can only interest the literary historian, the first volume of *Monsieur Lecoq* is still eminently readable.

[*See also* Europe, Crime and Mystery Writing in Continental: France and Belgium; Reasoning, Types of; Sensation Novel.]

• Nancy E. L. Curry, *The Life and Works of Émile Gaboriau* (1971). Roger Bonniot, *Émile Gaboriau, ou, la naissance du roman policier* (1985).   —T. J. Binyon

GAMBLING, ILLEGAL. Crime and mystery novels based on games of chance for illicit gain lend themselves to all the elements that make for engaging *thrillers: danger, tension, the unexpected, deception, and *violence. Crime novelists traditionally set their stories in the *milieu of authorized gambling—casinos and racetracks—in order to highlight the criminals who hope to either guarantee their odds, exploit novice gamblers, or launder money.

Dick *Francis's books set in the world of British horse racing reveal the ruthless tactics of horse owners, trainers, and jockeys who often are under the influence of blackmailers or the mob. In *Nerve* (1964) horses are drugged in order to fix races and ruin uncooperative jockeys. In *Bolt* (1986) horses are killed as part of an elaborate racing scam. Following Francis's lead, writers from both sides of the Atlantic, such as Virginia Anderson in *King of the Roses* (1983) and *Blood Lies* (1989), John Birkett in *The Last Private Eye*, (1988) and *The Queen's Mare* (1990), William Murray in *Tip on a Dead Crab* (1984) and *The Getaway Blues* (1990), and James Sherburne in *Death's Pale Horse* (1980) and *Death's Bright Arrow* (1989), have emphasized the *horse racing milieu in their mysteries.

Las Vegas casino settings have inspired scores of novels, spawning a subgenre of gambling fiction. Mysteries set in Nevada frequently stress the shadowy connections between casinos and mob syndicates. Local Las Vegas gangsters are the villains in an early casino-based mystery, *The Honest Dealer* by Frank Gruber (1947). Nearby Death Valley and Hoover Dam often serve as dramatic backdrops to climactic chases. The entrepreneurs and entertainers typically drawn to Las Vegas often inspire the *plot: in *To Cache a Millionaire* (1972) Margaret Scherf constructs a tale around the business dealings of a Howard Hughes–type millionaire recluse. Prostitution and pandering, traditionally associated with the gambling milieu, often are the impetus behind the crimes committed. In *Shakedown* (1988) Gerald Petievich tells of a tenacious *FBI agent in Las Vegas who, on the tail of a shakedown artist, uncovers multiple scams connected with vice crimes.

Other crime and mystery novels based on illegal gambling have focused on the high stakes associated with professional sports. The world of golf has served as a backdrop for Charlotte and Aaron Elkins, the world of boxing for Dashiell *Hammett and William Campbell *Gault. More often, however, football and baseball have been the sports of choice for American writers. Bookies and managers/coaches are frequently either *victims or *suspects. Michael Geller's *Major League Murder* (1988) tells of a scandal over doctored baseballs, and Robert B. *Parker's *Mortal Stakes* (1975) involves a star pitcher accused of shading a game. Fran Tarkenton and Herb Resnicow (*Murder at the Super Bowl*, 1986) and William X. Kienzle (*Sudden Death*, 1985) have employed National Football League settings.

[See also Extortion; Sports Milieu; Underworld; Underworld Figure.]

—Margaret Broom Harp

GANGSTERS. *See* Film; Menacing Characters; Underworld Figure.

GARDENING. The uses to which mystery writers put the innocent fruits of Mother Earth are infinitely diverse and generally devious. Catherine Aird turns three underfed and not quite ripe tomatoes into a thoroughly satisfying book called *Passing Strange* (1980). Reginald Hill gets splendid results in *Deadheads* (1983) from the gardener's simple chore of slicing bygone blossoms off rose bushes.

General Sir Richard Hannay has been feasting his war-weary eyes on the flowering blackthorn and the primrose blooming among the hedgerows when the call to duty comes yet again. Hannay might have known that his creator, John *Buchan, would wrest him away from his primroses and drag him through the multiple agonies of *The Three Hostages* (1924), his only clue a scrap of doggerel with a strong horticultural slant, his only weapons his wits and an over-developed sense of noblesse oblige.

Far less obliging is Nero *Wolfe, for whom being a famous detective is only a way of financing his two great loves—his meals and his orchids. The four hours a day he devotes to his phalaenopsids and cattleyas are sacrosanct. In Rex *Stout's *Murder by the Book* (1951), Wolfe's aide-de-camp Archie *Goodwin has just seen the woman he had been on his way to interview sprawled dead on the sidewalk seventeen stories down. Shaken, he goes back to Wolfe, finds him in the rooftop potting shed surrounded by *Dendrobium chrysotoxum*, and is snapped at for interrupting Wolfe's potting. Archie concedes that his

report can wait, since the *victim is now dead and the orchids are still alive.

When a wicked nurse in Agatha *Christie's *Sad Cypress* (1940) injects herself with a fast-working emetic after drinking poisoned tea, she thinks she can pass off the needle's mark as a scratch from a thorn on the rose tree that grows by the kitchen door. Hercule *Poirot already knows, however, that not every rose has its thorns.

The laurels for most varied usage of horticultural materials should probably go to Margery *Allingham. In *The Fear Sign* (1933; *Sweet Danger*), Dr. Edmund Galley plants his back garden with flowers under the influence of the Moon, Venus, and Mercury; those under the Sun, Mars, and Jupiter grow at the front of the house. In *Flowers for the Judge* (1936), an anguished young widow has to sit through her lover's trial looking at the dour old judge's colorful nosegay, a relic of the time when the flowers were intended to ward off the plague and defend His Honor's august nose from the stench of the courtroom. In *More Work for the Undertaker* (1949), Miss Jessica Palinode gives detective Albert *Campion a lesson in how to live on nothing a week by picking weeds in Hyde Park and cooking them in treacle tins. *The Beckoning Lady* (1955) shows Campion's friend Charlie Luke falling in love with a beautiful anachronism and reminiscing about his botany teacher, who first gave him a reason to learn the language of flowers. *Black Plumes* (1940) brings flowers galore and the macabre dignity of a hearse drawn by six black-brown horses with silver sconces on their heads holding black plumes.

—Charlotte MacLeod

GARDNER, ERLE STANLEY (1889–1970), American author who started by writing for *pulp magazines and went on to achieve great success with his books. Despite a busy law practice, between 1921 and 1932, in his spare time, he wrote about 300 stories and created twenty-five series featuring such colorful characters as Speed Dash "The Human Fly," Fishmouth McGinnis, the Patent Leather Kid, and Lester Leith, confidence man. After he wrote *The Case of the Velvet Claws* (1933), introducing lawyer-detective Perry *Mason, Gardner was able to become a full-time writer. Although there had been *legal procedurals before Gardner, his books quickly achieved enormous popularity as the first series to combine the inherent drama of the courtroom with action and complex detective *puzzles.

As a California lawyer, Gardner had defended the downtrodden—for example, illegal Chinese immigrants. He made Mason the advocate of defendants whose rights were put in jeopardy by questionable police tactics. Mason was especially adroit at juggling physical evidence, usually guns or bullets, but sometimes items as exotic as birds. In having Mason discredit police procedure, Gardner employed tactics he had successfully used in his own law career.

In 1948, Gardner co-founded with the magazine *Argosy*, an unofficial board of investigators, the Court of Last Resort, lending his time and money to investigate cases of people he considered falsely convicted of *murder and other serious crimes. He wrote many articles about this organization and a book (*The Court of Last Resort*, 1952) which won him a *Mystery Writers of America Edgar for real crime writing in 1952.

After 1932, Gardner remained prolific, publishing almost 500 more stories and articles, as well as about 150 books, including two or three a year featuring Mason. He wrote a series of nine books about Doug Selby, a small-town California district attorney who, in an interesting twist, has to contend with a wily defense attorney, A. B. Carr. In 1939, Gardner adopted a pseudonym, A. A. Fair, so that he could write more books for his publisher, William Morrow. The result was another successful series—twenty-nine books about Bertha Cool and Donald Lam. Gardner's method of writing became well publicized. He dictated his work to a battery of secretaries in one of his many isolated rural retreats, where he could also pursue his love of nature, including his hobbies of archery and horseback riding.

As one who learned his trade in the pulps, Gardner was primarily a storyteller, relying on almost nonstop action and lively courtroom climaxes. His characters were essentially one dimensional, yet they proved popular with the public, especially Mason and his supporting cast: Della Street, Mason's loyal secretary; Paul Drake, the private detective he employs; and District Attorney Hamilton Burger, his hapless opponent. Mason's clients usually appear to be guilty, and many make his job more difficult by lying to him. However, despite the concerns of Street and Drake, Mason risks disbarment for these clients, sometimes using illegal means to get evidence, which he then produces as a surprise in court.

The *setting for most Gardner books is *Los Angeles, but the city seldom comes alive, since there is little regional description. Occasional books, like *The Case of the Drowsy Mosquito* (1943) are set in such rural areas as the California desert, and their settings are better realized, reflecting Gardner's interests.

The Gardner Canon is generally consistent, though the Mason books of the 1930s are considered best due to their vigorous writing, intricate *plots, and *Great Depression *atmosphere. By the 1940s, Gardner's books had begun to appear in the *slicks (slick magazines) before publication, and though his plotting and courtroom scenes continued to be strong, he made Mason a bit smoother than the pulp-based Mason, who often functions like a tough *private eye. In two of his first three cases, Mason never even enters a courtroom. The books produced during the last decade of Gardner's career are not as well plotted or imaginative, and some even suggest that Gardner was a victim of the success of the Perry Mason television show, which ran for nine seasons (1957–66). A frequent television device, due to time constraints, was a scene in which the killer, illogically, suddenly confesses in court. That never occurred in the earlier Mason books, but did beginning with *The Case of the Long-Legged Models* (1958).

After the Miranda ruling and other U.S. Supreme Court decisions in the 1960s, Mason's unconven-

tional, zealous advocacy of defendants' rights seemed dated and unnecessary. Although the television Mason remains in syndication, there has been a general falling off of interest in Gardner's books. Despite his once being the most popular American mystery writer, with paperback reprints of his work in the millions, Gardner has seldom been reprinted in the 1990s.

[*See also* Courtroom Milieu; Judge; Jury; Justice; Sidekicks and Sleuthing Teams.]

• Alva Johnston, *The Case of Erle Stanley Gardner* (1947). Charles W. Morton, "The World of Erle Stanley Gardner," *Atlantic* 219 (Jan. 1967): 79–86, 91. E. H. Mundell, *Erle Stanley Gardner: A Checklist* (1968). Dorothy B. Hughes, *The Case of the Real Perry Mason: A Biography* (1978). Francis L. Fugate and Roberta B. Fugate, *Secrets of the World's Best-Selling Writer: The Storytelling Techniques of Erle Stanley Gardner* (1980).   —Marvin Lachman

GARVE, ANDREW, pseudonym of Paul Winterton (b. 1908), British author who also wrote as Roger Bax and Paul Somers. In the course of his career, he worked as a journalist for the *Economist* (1929–33) and the *News Chronicle* (1933–46), being the newspaper's for foreign correspondent in Moscow from 1942 to 1945. Beginning with *Death Beneath Jerusalem*, (1938, published under the Bax pseudonym), Garve has written forty novels exhibiting great diversity in *plot and *setting. Though most deal with crime, they are usually not *detective novels, but adventure novels or *thrillers, sometimes with a romantic element, in which a lone hero—who may be a criminal, as in *The Megstone Plot* (1956)—narrates his efforts, often involving extreme physical endeavor, to clear his name, foil a plot, or make his fortune. Garve uses his knowledge of Russia to good effect in *Murder in Moscow* (1951; *Murder Through the Looking Glass*) and *The Ascent of D-13* (1969), but most often small boats and the sea form the background as in *Came the Dawn* (1949, as Bax; *Two If by Sea*) and *A Hero for Leanda* (1959). The novels are short, tense and exciting narratives which, though individual, perhaps owe something to John *Buchan. Additional important titles are *No Tears for Hilda* (1950) and *The Ashes of Loda* (1965).

[*See also* Adventure Story; Adventurer and Adventuress; Heroism; Nautical Milieu.]

• Jacques Barzun and Wendell Hertig Taylor, *A Catalogue of Crime*, rev. ed. (1989).   —T. J. Binyon

GAULT, WILLIAM CAMPBELL (1910–1995), American author of mystery and *private eye novels and sports fiction for the juvenile audience. Gault, who also wrote as Bill Gault, Will Duke, and Roney Scott, emerged from the *pulp magazine field to win an Edgar for his first novel. *Don't Cry for Me* (1952). He went on to write a number of excellent nonseries mysteries, but he is perhaps best known to mystery readers for his two series featuring private eyes Joe Puma and Brock (the Rock) Callahan. While both men are solidly in the hard-boiled tradition of tough heroes, Gault's treatment makes each man unique.

Their ethics are their own, but they are men of principle in a world that does not necessarily share their values. Such solidly plotted books as *The Convertible Hearse* (1957) and *Sweet Wild Wench* (1959) demonstrate Gault's feel for character and the telling detail. Gault's short story "See No Evil," published in *New Detective* in 1950, is both an early example of pulp fiction treating the social issue of young Mexican American males attracted to violent recreation and of Gault's skill in endowing male characters with both strength and sensitivity.

[*See also* Hard-Boiled Sleuth; Heroism.]

• "PQ Interview with William Campbell Gault," *Paperback Quarterly* 2, no. 2 (summer 1979): 9–13. Art Scott, "William Campbell Gault," in *Twentieth-Century Crime and Mystery Writers*, 2d ed., ed. John M. Reilly (1985).

—Bill Crider

GAY CHARACTERS AND PERSPECTIVES. For decades, gay and lesbian characters in detective fiction were not overtly identified as such, and the way in which they were depicted tended to reinforce negative stereotypes about homosexuals. For example, in Dashiell *Hammett's The Maltese Falcon* (1930) and Ross *Macdonald's The Barbarous Coast* (1956), the gay characters are thieves, murderers, and gangsters. In Raymond *Chandler's Farewell, My Lovely* (1940), Lindsay Marriott is a weak, effeminate man who is involved in *theft and blackmail. The killer in one of Agatha *Christie's Miss Jane *Marple mysteries is a lesbian whose attraction to a young heterosexual girl leads to *murder when the girl becomes involved with a man.

Perhaps the works of Mickey *Spillane offer the most offensive portrayal of gay characters. In *I, the Jury* (1947), Spillane includes a group of loud, flamboyant homosexuals at a tennis weekend on a country estate apparently for no other reason than to allow Mike *Hammer to make derogatory comments about them. Spillane's *Vengeance Is Mine!* (1950) chronicles Hammer's attraction to Juno Reeves (the head of a modeling agency), ending with the outrageous revelation that Juno, like her namesake, is in fact a "real queen"—a man in drag.

The first crime novel featuring a gay detective is George *Baxt's A Queer Kind of Death* (1966), which introduces Pharoah Love, a black New York City homicide detective. However, this book and the two subsequent novels in the series provide little insight into the realities of the gay subculture (or of black society, for that matter). Instead, the novels are more reminiscent of the Philo *Vance mysteries by S. S. *Van Dine that portray wealthy New York society, use a limited number of *suspects, and employ witty dialogue.

Joseph *Hansen's *Fadeout* (1970) marks the true development of the gay detective novel. From *Fadeout* through *A Country of Old Men: The Last Dave Brandstetter Mystery* (1991), the twelfth and final novel in the series, the reader follows the life of Dave *Brandstetter, an insurance investigator. His intelligence, courage, honesty, and concern for others make him a touchstone for later gay detectives.

Since 1980 a fairly large number of novels featuring gay detectives have appeared, and the image of gay males has become increasingly positive in them. Several common characteristics are found in these gay detectives. The modern gay detective is open about his sexual orientation. Donald Strachey, an Albany *private eye in a series by Richard Stevenson, and Henry Rios, a California lawyer in a series by Michael Nava, are good examples of men who do not "shout out" the fact that they are gay—but neither do they attempt to conceal the fact.

Second, the modern gay detective contrasts with the effeminate or weak stereotypes of the past in several ways. Today, he is traditionally masculine in speech and appearance. Both Brandstetter and Strachey, for example, have to turn down amorous advances from women who are attracted to them and who are surprised to discover that the men are gay. Moreover, the contemporary gay detective is connected to traditionally masculine occupations and interests. For example, Dave Brandstetter and Donald Strachey both served in the army; Tom Mason and Scott Carpenter (the two amateur detectives in a series by Mark Richard Zubro) are respectively a Vietnam veteran and a professional baseball player; Doug Orlando, in a series by Steve Johnson, is a New York City homicide detective. Finally, the present-day gay detective is able to handle himself physically when the need arises and is not cowardly or fearful.

Third, in contrast to the stereotype of the promiscuous homosexual, the modern gay detective is usually in a monogamous relationship. At the start of the Brandstetter series, Brandstetter is mourning the loss of his lover of twenty-five years to cancer. In the course of the series, Brandstetter develops another long-term relationship (with Cecil Harris, a young black television reporter). As almost half of the Brandstetter series was written in the 1970s, Dave's monogamous relationships are clearly a matter of choice, not a reaction to fear of contracting AIDS.

With the advent of the AIDS crisis in the 1980s, however, monogamy becomes less a choice than a requirement for survival. This change is mirrored in novels from this period. For example, in the first two Donald Strachey mysteries, from the early 1980s, both Strachey and his lover Timothy Callahan have sex with other people. In the later novels, however, both have accepted the need for sexual fidelity. Donald, while still at times attracted to other men, tries to envision a skull and crossbones on their foreheads.

After years of stereotypical presentations, gays in detective fiction are now likely to be depicted as competent professionals, caring individuals, concerned citizens, and productive members of society. The novels show men who are people first, with their sexual orientation being only a part of their lives.

• Michael Nava, ed., *Finale* (1989). James Levin, *The Gay Novel in America* (1991). Ed. Gorman et al., eds., *The Fine Art of Murder: The Mystery Reader's Indispensable Companion* (1993). Anthony Slide, *Gay and Lesbian Characters and Themes in Mystery Novels: A Critical Guide to Over 500 Works in English* (1993).

—David C. Wallace

GENDER. A significant contribution of the women's movement has been to separate the terms "sex" (biology) and "gender" (social roles). The latter is now seen as a cultural construct, differing according to time and locale, as societies place values on specific behavior for women and men. Whereas men are required to be active, brave, and virile, women must be passive, timid, and virginal; whereas boys are forbidden tears or dolls, girls are forbidden footballs and boxing gloves.

With its roots in nineteenth-century Britain and the United States detective fiction, like all forms of popular or mass culture, has reflected the pattern of its times. Important early examples of the genre like Edgar Allan *Poe's and Arthur Conan *Doyle's short stories celebrate ratiocination, the brain power their societies reserved for men. The shock for readers in "A Scandal in Bohemia" (*Strand*, July 1891) was that a woman, Irene *Adler, could think as well as or better than a man, Sherlock *Holmes; but readers' cultural sensibilities are reassured upon learning that she is "*the* woman," a unique specimen unlikely to be replicated in their own homes.

Two important gender battles have highlighted the twentieth-century history of the genre. The first pitted Golden Age writers against hard-boiled novelists. During the 1920s, Agatha *Christie, Ngaio *Marsh, Dorothy L. *Sayers, Margery *Allingham, S. S. Van *Dine, Ellery *Queen, and Josephine *Tey dominated the mystery field with *gentlemen sleuths, country house murders, bodies in the library, and mannerly novels. Enter Dashiell *Hammett and Raymond *Chandler, out to rescue *murder for real men. When Chandler wrote in "The Simple Art of Murder" (*The Simple Art of Murder*, 1950) that murder belongs to "a man fit for adventure," he had only one definition of "a man" in mind: tough, physical, unsentimental. The tension between these two forms of mystery fiction—golden age and hard-boiled—is based on gender imperatives.

The second battle began in the 1970s when women writers in particular seized *police procedurals and hard-boiled *crime novels for women protagonists. Dorothy Uhnak and Lillian O'Donnell's female cops joined forces with Marcia *Muller, Sara *Paretsky, and Sue *Grafton's female *private eyes to demand equal access to the action. These writers created women who jogged for fitness, took firearms practice, tackled criminals, and walked down mean streets into worlds—professional and social—previously reserved for men. The success of their followers—at least one hundred characters have been introduced in the past twenty-five years—belies the original skepticism of critics, editors, and publishers.

The generic split into oppositional camps has been presumed to reflect reader preferences as well. Unlike romances, *westerns, or *science fiction, which tend to have gender-specific audiences, crime fiction as a whole is the single genre read equally by women and men. Conventional wisdom holds that women prefer classic mysteries and men choose hard-boiled fiction. Although anecdotal evidence to the contrary exists, no extensive survey of mystery readers has yet been done. Noting that women writers receive far less than their share of reviews, prizes, and bookstore shelf space, an advocacy group called *Sisters in Crime was established in the U.S. in 1986 to promote women writers, reviewers, booksellers, editors, and readers.

The genre has always relied heavily on stereotypes, whether upholding or undermining them. Christie's Miss Jane *Marple, Patricia *Wentworth's Miss Maud *Silver, and Sayers's "Cattery" challenge the expected view of elderly spinsters by demonstrating their extraordinary sleuthing skills. Robert B. *Parker's macho hard-boiled *sleuth *Spenser, who cooks complex dishes, shatters a similarly limited view of masculine behavior. In Travis *McGee, the conventional stereotyping is reinforced: John D. *MacDonald's hero is a dirty fighter and a tender, healing lover—a knight errant, an improbably romantic figure. And P. D. *James calls her first Cordelia *Gray novel *An Unsuitable Job for a Woman* (1972), simultaneously confirming and denying the title. Both approaches work with readers who enjoy having their *prejudices upheld as much as they like being surprised.

Lesbian and gay writers are the most likely to use the genre to investigate gender imperatives as their detectives unravel crimes. Much lesbian detective fiction (especially the many novels published by Naiad) mesh a coming-out novel with the crime novel; a character, usually the detective, explores her own sexuality against the expectations of her culture, often finding that she too is perceived as a criminal. Slowly moving out of small presses and into mainstream houses, gay and lesbian detective fiction like Joseph *Hansen's Dave *Brandstetter series or Sandra Scoppettone's three novels about Lauren Laureto challenge culturally mandated heterosexuality as a social norm. Cross-dressed characters play a similar role in challenging the readers' and detectives' unspoken assumptions. Tey's famous portrait of Leslie/Lee Searle in *To Love and Be Wise* (1950) and Queen's misleading transvestite in *The Last Woman in His Life* (1969) show the darker side of gender crossing, whereas Barbara Wilson's *Gaudi Afternoon* (1990) is a seriocomic challenge to socially restrictive expectations. Perhaps the most clever manipulation of gender expectations is found in Sarah Caudwell's refusal to specify whether her scholar-sleuth Hilary Tamar is male or female. By employing ambiguous descriptions and carefully avoiding personal pronouns, Caudwell either delights or infuriates fans. But the trick may have overshadowed the novels; and, finally, gender is not her concern.

[*See also* Females and Feminists; Femme Fatale; Gay Characters and Perspectives; Lesbian Characters and Perspectives; Males and the Male Image; Sex and Sexuality.]

• Derek Longhurst, ed., *Gender, Genre and Narrative Pleasure* (1989).   —Kathleen Gregory Klein

GENIUS. *See* Great Detective, The; Superman Sleuth.

GENTEEL WOMAN SLEUTH. The *sleuth as a woman of genteel background and breeding is as old as the mystery genre itself. Valeria Woodville in Wilkie *Collins's *The Law and the Lady* (1875) is a twenty-three-year-old woman determined to invalidate the Scotch verdict against her husband; well bred, sensible, and intrepid, she sets a standard of investigation for years to come.

Anna Katharine *Green turned Collins's heroine into two character types. In *That Affair Next Door* (1897), Miss Amelia Butterworth is an amiable spinster in her fifties who enjoys solving crimes while worrying about the proprieties. In *The Golden Slipper and Other Problems for Violet Strange* (1915), Violet Strange is a debutante who becomes a detective to make money on the sly; she moves gracefully through the upper layers of society, never doubting her place among the highest social *classes. The former led to the elderly, unmarried woman sleuth whose grandmotherly looks conceal her sharp mind, epitomized by Agatha *Christie's Miss Jane *Marple in *The Murder at the Vicarage* (1930). The latter led to the professional woman detective, such as Patricia *Wentworth's Miss Maud *Silver, introduced in *Grey Mask* (1928).

In the 1920s and 1930s, the sleuth is a professional woman, which facilitates her involvement in criminal investigations. Mignon G. *Eberhart's Nurse Sarah Keate and Mary Roberts *Rinehart's Nurse Hilda Adams take on medical cases connected to police matters; both are respectable spinsters who brook no nonsense. In the 1960s and later, the genteel woman sleuth sought her place in almost every corner of the professional world; she was also younger, smarter, livelier. Amanda *Cross's Kate *Fansler is a university professor engaged in the issues of her time; Anne Morice's Tessa Crichton is an actress; Antonia Fraser's Jemima Shore is a TV journalist.

The earliest sleuths rely on standard techniques of investigation: reason, deduction, physical pursuit of evidence, and interrogation. By the 1920s, however, praise for the sleuth's intellectual abilities is offered in place of demonstration. Always ready to follow a *suspect late at night, Eberhart's Keate has a look "like an X ray" and the knack of "being around when things are happening"; Rinehart's Adams looks like a "baby-faced owl" and has a gun. Wentworth's Silver listens closely to gossip and Christie's Marple studies character. Much is made of *clues and detecting, but in fact the genteel woman sleuth comes to rely more on intuition, social observation, and *coincidence than on evidence and logic.

There are comparable changes in her relations with the authorities. Whereas Woodville persuades others by uncovering evidence, and Butterworth gradually wins the intellectual admiration of a skeptical *police detective, Keate receives amused respect from the police and Adams receives a marriage proposal. In turn, Silver and Marple may treat the police detective as a bright young nephew. In every instance, the genteel woman sleuth is deemed to be different from other women because of her crime-solving abilities.

The question of her involvement in a police matter is solved in a variety of ways. Keate and Adams are introduced as necessary employees, Marple is a harmless old lady nosing about, and Elizabeth Peters's Dr. Victoria Bliss is a sprightly young woman following her curiosity. Beginning in the 1960s, though the genteel woman sleuth continues to investigate crimes involving people related or known to her, she may gain legitimacy by marrying a policeman, as did Crichton, Shore, and Anne Perry's Charlotte Pitt, or an assistant district attorney, as did Fansler.

The type is easy to parody. In Rinehart's *The Circular Staircase* (1908), Miss Rachel Innes is forever rushing from one suspicious noise to another; in Gladys Mitchell's *Speedy Death* (1929), Mrs. Beatrice Adela Lestrange Bradley treats superstitions as seriously as psychoanalysis, and gives both more credence than reason.

Throughout her history, the genteel woman sleuth challenged the definition and role of women in society. Butterworth is a superb reasoner at a time when men assume women lack intellectual capacity, Keate exudes competence and fearlessness in facing physical danger, and Adams demonstrates imaginative resourcefulness. Fansler legitimates an intellectual life for women, even after marriage, and Pitt is not hampered by raising children. As an elderly woman this sleuth undermines assumptions about physical and mental decline; age is never a bar to her investigative activities. Butterworth may have eye trouble, Keate may have neuralgia, and Adams a weak heart, but Marple's mind typically remains as sharp as any police officer's.

[See also Bluestocking Sleuth; Females and Feminists; Gentleman Sleuth; Voice: Genteel Voice.]

• Earl F. Bargainnier, ed., *Ten Women of Mystery* (1981). Patricia Craig and Mary Cadogan, *The Lady Investigates: Women Detectives and Spies in Fiction* (1981). Kathleen Gregory Klein, *The Woman Detective: Gender and Genre* (1988).

—Susan Oleksiw

GENTLEMAN ADVENTURER. The protagonist of good birth and social standing, who is courteous, gracious, and considerate, can be a soldier of fortune, a rogue, or a secret service agent. His adventures are often not of his own choosing—he tends to react to rather than initiate situations—but he still strives to set right that which he perceives to be wrong from a sense of duty or to uphold ideals or merely to rescue someone in need of rescuing. His wealth and position often allow him the freedom to pursue adventure, while his profession, if he has one—journalism, for instance—makes his presence on the scene plausible. He conveys the "idea" of being a gentleman by putting others at ease; he is self-sufficient and sporting at all times. He dresses well and belongs to the right club, but may also be skilled with *weapons and have a wide range of knowledge that will be useful in his adventures. He is a larger-than-life figure able to defeat a band of conspirators almost single-handedly.

The seeds of this character type were planted in 1894 with Rudolf Rassendyll's adventures in Ruritania in Anthony Hope's *The Prisoner of Zenda*. Rassendyll is a thorough gentleman and does not choose adventure; it chooses him.

The type was developed further by Baroness Emmuska *Orczy, who chronicled the adventures of Sir Percy Blakeney in a series of novels and short stories beginning with *The Scarlet Pimpernel* (1905). With Blakeney came the concept of the dual identity by which the hero gives the illusion of being ineffective in order to work undercover. Blakeney, the hero, is able to learn secrets that he can use in his other guise—that of the Scarlet Pimpernel. Johnston McCulley borrowed the concept in 1919 for the first of his stories about Zorro, the masked avenger whose other self was the fop Don Diego de la Vega. In both examples the public persona was that of the gentleman. Orczy also introduced a coterie of followers who could be called upon to aid the hero. In another variation on the role of the gentleman adventurer, John Buchan introduced the *plot device of the hunter who becomes the hunted in *The Thirty-nine Steps* (1915), in which Richard Hannay crosses the wilds of Scotland to thwart a conspiracy. This became a popular device and was repeated by numerous writers, including Geoffrey *Household in *A Rough Shoot* (1951) and *A Time to Kill* (1951).

During the period between the two world wars the gentleman adventurer took on additional features, including a service record from World War I, and gained the assistance of a gentleman's gentleman, usually someone who had served as the adventurer's batman in the war. His other followers were often drawn from those with whom he had attended school.

Dornford *Yates returned to Anthony Hope's Ruritanian setting in his Chandos novels such as *Blind Corner* (1927) and *Perishable Goods* (1928), setting up a contrast between the *virtues of the hero and the rugged challenges he faces, symbolized by the landscape. Richard Chandos receives a pet dog from a dying man and later discovers that the dog is holding directions to a treasure. He sets off with two other friends and three servants to find the treasure; in the second book the villains strike back.

Under Leslie *Charteris's hand, the gentleman adventurer became more urbane and cosmopolitan and less tightly connected to the British upper classes. Charteris's Simon Templar, though clearly a rogue in many ways, fits the definition of the gentleman adventurer and frequently displays a sense of altruism. In such early books as *The Last Hero* (1930; *The Saint Closes the Case*) he has his own coterie of followers, but he goes it alone in the later years.

The gentleman adventurer has proved to be an enduring figure, and the basic character traits continue to appear generation after generation, even in a cool professional like Ian *Fleming's James *Bond and his successors.

[See also Adventure Story; Adventurer and Adventuress; Club Milieu; Disguise; Heroism.]

• Colin Watson, *Snobbery with Violence: Crime Stories and Their Audience* (1971). William Vivian Butler, *The Durable Desperadoes* (1973). Patrick Howarth, *Play Up and Play the Game: The Heroes of Popular Fiction* (1973). Richard Usborne, *Clubland Heroes: A Nostalgic Study of Some Recurrent Characters in the Romantic Fiction of Dornford Yates, John Buchan and Sapper*, rev. ed. (1975). Philip Mason, *The English Gentleman: The Rise and Fall of an Ideal* (1982). A. J. Smithers, *Dornford Yates: A Biography* (1982).
—J. Randolph Cox

GENTLEMAN SLEUTH. The term "gentleman," when used to modify "sleuth," may denote the character's position in the upper class or connote that the detective is a true amateur. The two attributes—being of the monied *class and investigating crimes for no payment other than the satisfaction of seeing *justice done—work well together, since they allow the character leisure to pursue investigations unhindered by the demands of an ordinary work life.

The most memorable exemplars of gentlemen sleuths are Dorothy L. *Sayers's Lord Peter *Wimsey and Margery *Allingham's Albert *Campion. The second son of the fifteenth duke of Denver, Wimsey attended Eton and is a graduate of Oxford University. He sports such upper-class mannerisms as dropping his final *gs* in conversation and is a connoisseur of wine, a collector of incunabula, and an accomplished pianist. His sidekick, Bunter, who is also his valet, looks after him at their *London address at 110 Piccadilly.

Campion's pedigree is more mysterious and exalted. His exact position in the British aristocracy is never pinpointed, but Allingham is said to have told a colleague that her *sleuth was in line to inherit the throne. Created six years after Wimsey was introduced, Campion was conceived as a *silly ass sleuth, who cultivated an appearance of foolishness to mask his intense scrutiny of suspects. His sidekick is a manservant, Magersfonteyn *Lugg, whose resume includes burglary and imprisonment.

Philip *MacDonald's Colonel Anthony Ruthven *Gethryn is introduced as the son of an English squire and a Spanish actress in *The Rasp* (1924). Gethryn is the publisher of an investigative journal, *The Owl*, whose mission is to anticipate crimes before they occur. Another character possessing an independent income is Alan Grant. Originally created by Josephine *Tey under the pseudonym Gordon Daviot, Grant was introduced in *The Man in the Queue* (1929) and makes his most famous appearances in *The Franchise Affair* (1948) and *The Daughter of Time* (1951). In the latter, the bedridden sleuth engages in bibliographic detective work in an effort to prove that England's King Richard III did not kill his nephews.

A British policeman who possesses a pedigree is Ngaio *Marsh's Roderick *Alleyn. Named by the author after the actor Edward Alleyn, this sleuth's social position as the second son of a baronet provides him with entrée into the homes and confidence of the upper crust. His diplomatic experience also helps when it comes to their discovery that he is there to invade their privacy. Alleyn's sidekick is Inspector Fox, whose first name is never revealed, although he is sometimes referred to as "Br'er Fox" by his superior.

Another English policeman, Inspector (later Superintendent) John *Appleby, proves the point that gentlemanliness in detectives need not be strictly confined to those who sport pedigrees. This creation of Michael *Innes, himself an *Oxford don, Appleby uses erudition to insinuate himself into the company of the educated classes and the landed gentry. His appreciation of art and his eye for literary *allusion help him to discover many abstruse *clues in a series of novels sometimes cited as prime examples of the *farceur school of writing.

Another character whose intellectual erudition enhances his gentlemanly qualities is Nicholas *Blake's Nigel *Strangeways. This character, who seems not to need to earn a living, is identified as an Oxford graduate who always seems ready to help out *Scotland Yard's Inspector Blount or any number of well-heeled friends in a pinch.

Although the gentleman sleuth is most likely to be a British creation, this character type appeared on the other side of the Atlantic as well. The best remembered example is S. S. *Van Dine's Philo *Vance, whose snobbishness outdoes his gentlemanliness. He lives in luxury in his *New York penthouse where his narrator S. S. Van Dine is kept at his beck and call. He speaks with an affected British upper-crust accent, dropping his g's as does Wimsey. He uses a cigarette holder for his Regie cigarettes and possesses an encyclopedic knowledge of obscure facts, some of which are expounded upon in footnotes in the novels.

[See also Addresses and Abodes, Famous; Allusion, Literary; Sidekicks and Sleuthing Teams.]

• E. C. Bentley, Those Days: An Autobiography (1940). Barbara Reynolds, "The Origin of Lord Peter Wimsey," Times Literary Supplement (Apr. 22 1977). Philip L Scowcroft "Some Thoughts on Josephine Tey's The Daughter of Time," Deadly Pleasures Issue 21 (1998) 58–59. Philip L. Scrowcroft "Trent's Last Case," CADS 9 (1988), 1477.

—Rosemary Herbert

GENTLEMAN THIEF. The gentleman thief is a man of good breeding who makes his living by dishonest means. A literary descendant of the gallant highwayman found in such early fiction as "The Squire's Story" by Elizabeth Gaskell (1853; reprinted in Lizzie Leigh and Other Tales, 1855), the gentleman thief was a popular contrast to the *Great Detective epitomized by Arthur Conan *Doyle's Sherlock *Holmes. Most notable among such characters and the prototype of the gentleman thief is E. W. *Hornung's A. J. *Raffles: cricketer, burglar, and gentleman (The Amateur Cracksman, 1899; Raffles, the Amateur Cracksman). A criminal who is willing to contemplate *murder (though he does not commit it) to avoid arrest, Raffles has at the same time, as George Orwell points out ("Raffles and Miss Blandish," Horizon, Oct. 1944), a strict code of honor: He will not steal from his host, though a fellow guest is fair game; he is intensely patriotic, returning a stolen antique gold cup to Queen Victoria, and enlisting in the army during the Boer War to die a hero's death in South Africa. Raffles is not only the first, but perhaps also the only pure example of the type: The criminal element is not underplayed, as it is elsewhere, but is the raison d'etre of his character; the stories in which he appears are, from a literary point of view, undoubtedly the best in this genre. A French equivalent is Maurice *Leblanc's Arsène *Lupin (Arsène Lupin: Gentleman-Cambrioleur,

1907; The Exploits of Arsène Lupin); here, however, comic exaggeration leads to parody.

Few followed the Raffles model in every detail. Frank L. Packard's New York club man, Jimmie Dale, the "most puzzling, bewildering, delightful crook in the annals of crime," remains close to the model of Raffles (The Adventures of Jimmie Dale, 1917), as does Bruce Graeme's mystery writer and thief Richard Verrell (Blackshirt, 1925) in a series continued by the author's son Roderic Graeme.

Contemporary with the development of the Raffles character were two variations; the first of these, the crooked *lawyer or investigator, was perhaps more typical of early crime fiction, in which the protagonist was almost as often a criminal as a detective. Examples include Melville Davisson *Post's short stories featuring lawyer Randolph Mason (The Strange Schemes of Randolph Mason, 1896), Arthur *Morrison's detective Horace Dorrington (The Dorrington Deed-Box, 1897), and Clifford Ashdown's (pseudonym of R. Austin *Freeman and J. J. Pitcairn) literary agent Romney Pringle (The Adventures of Romney Pringle, 1902). Pringle, a professional who uses his standing to act the role of Robin Hood, links the two variations. In the second, the protagonist is an honest professional who engages in illegal activity only to right a wrong. Arnold Bennett's Cecil Thorold (The Loot of Cities, 1904) and William Le Queux's Italian aristocrat, Bindo di Ferraris (The Count's Chauffeur, 1907) follow this pattern.

The gentleman thief evolved into the *gentleman adventurer, epitomized by Leslie *Charteris's Simon Templar, known as The *Saint, whose career spans almost sixty years from his introduction in Meet the Tiger (1928). Though living beyond the law, Templar has little or nothing of the criminal about him. A modern Robin Hood, pursued by the police in Britain and America, he rights wrongs, succours the poor, and brings criminals to justice through unlawful means. Despite his long career, Templar belongs to the interwar years, just as Raffles belongs to the Victorian era. An updated version is offered by John *Creasey's the Honourable Richard Rollison, known as the Toff (Introducing the Toff, 1938).

Later attempts to make the criminal (whether active or reformed), a central character focus on the criminal element rather than on the breeding and code of honor, a sign that this character is perhaps bound more by time and culture than others in crime fiction.

[See also Club Milieu; Robin Hood Criminal.]

—T. J. Binyon

Gethryn, Colonel Anthony Ruthven, an *amateur detective created by the British author Philip *MacDonald, was a product of the genre's Golden Age. Born around 1885, the son of an English country gentleman and a Spanish actress who also danced and painted, Gethryn was educated at *Oxford, saw army service in World War I, was subsequently in the Secret Service, and ultimately solved crimes in the *country house milieu and the *English village milieu.

The first of Gethryn's dozen appearances, in *The Rasp* (1924), finds the sleuth in rural retirement with his wife Lucia disturbed by the murder of a cabinet minister. Later, in *The Noose* (1930), Gethryn has just five days to clear a condemned man. His exploits are characterized by sound detection, conducted in an *atmosphere reminiscent of that created by Alfred Hitchcock, and featuring wraith-like criminals. *Plots in the Gethryn stories hinge upon small *clues, and are presented with whimsical *humor combined with touches of the bizarre. *The Nursemaid Who Disappeared* (1938; *Warrant for X*) and *The List of Adrian Messenger* (1959) exemplify Gethryn at his best.

[*See also* Gentleman Sleuth.]   —Melvyn Barnes

GHOST STORY. Ghosts have an ancient cultural lineage, but literary ghost stories—deliberate fictional constructions designed to make readers feel pleasurably afraid—are of relatively recent origin. Their main characteristics evolved during the nineteenth century and have remained remarkably constant, emphasizing both their conservative nature and the resilience of their appeal.

As a genre within the wider category of supernatural fiction, ghost stories are defined by their basic *plot dynamic: The dead intrude upon the living. In general, they differ from horror stories designed to inspire feelings of physical shock by the relative decorum of their effects and by their intention to induce subtler states of unease. Such distinctions, however, are far from absolute, and there are many stories that can be classified in either genre. Again, though the returning human dead predominate in the mainstream ghost story tradition, other forms of supernatural visitant are common and strict typology is impossible.

The ghost story's immediate literary antecedent is Gothic romance, particularly the short stories and fragments common in English periodical literature in the last three decades of the eighteenth century. The short story has remained the dominant form for ghost stories—appropriately for a genre with its roots in oral storytelling—with magazines and anthologies consequently playing an important role in establishing and maintaining their popularity. The crucial innovation for the form was the domestication of setting and incident. Where Gothic fiction had been remote in its settings and flamboyantly atemporal, ghost stories (like Victorian sensation fiction) became anchored firmly in the contemporary, or near-contemporary, here and now. The German short-story writer E. T. A. Hoffmann (1776–1822) was among the first to infuse supernatural incident with a strong sense of the everyday, and his work inspired the stories of Edgar Allan *Poe, although Poe's idiosyncratic fantasies had less influence on the mainstream ghost story tradition than on the broader class of supernatural horror writing. It was in Britain that ghost stories developed as a distinct genre, and they have remained largely a British phenomenon. In Sir Walter Scott's "The Tapestried Chamber; or, The Lady in the Sacque," (*Blackwood's Edinburgh Magazine*, 1818), many of the genre's essentially anti-Gothic qualities are foreshadowed. These are more fully developed in J. S. Le Fanu (1814–73), the first great ghost story specialist, whose first collection, *Ghost Stories and Tales of Mystery*, a landmark in the genre, was published in 1851.

The influence of Charles *Dickens (1812–70) on the mid-Victorian ghost story derived as much from his editorship of the monthly magazine *Household Words* and its successor *All the Year Round* (launched April 1859), in which many classic Victorian ghost stories (including "The Phantom Coach," 1864 by Amelia B. Edwards and Dickens's own "The Signalman," 1866) appeared, than from his own contributions to the genre. Thereafter ghost stories became staple items in middle-class magazines of the 1860s and 1870s such as *Temple Bar*, *Belgravia*, and *London Society*, notably in the special Christmas numbers, and later in the illustrated monthlies of the 1890s typified by the *Strand* and *Pearson's Magazine*. Throughout the nineteenth century, women writers—M. E. *Braddon, Rhoda Broughton, Mrs. J. H. Riddell, and others—were prominent providers of ghost fiction for the magazine market.

From roughly 1880 to 1930 both the quantity and quality of ghost stories made this period the genre's golden age, the muster of writers including Violet Paget writing as Vernon Lee, Arthur Quiller-Couch, E. Nesbit, Henry James, Algernon Blackwood, H. Russell Wakefield, A. M. Burrage, W. F. Harvey, Edith Wharton, Oliver Onions, E. F. Benson, and Walter de la Mare, to name but a few. Among the most influential of the early twentieth-century specialists was M. R. James (1862–1936), an admirer of Le Fanu who skillfully deployed scholarly expertise to lend authenticity to his fictional world. James's first collection, *Ghost Stories of an Antiquary* (1904), stands at the head of a tradition of antiquarian ghost stories stretching from those in the immediate line of his influence like E. G. Swain (*The Stoneground Ghost Tales*, 1912) and R. H. Malden (*Nine Ghosts*, 1943) to a host of minor imitators, and his presence can still be felt in contemporary writers such as Russell Kirk and Ramsey Campbell.

In the twentieth century, many ghost stories have successfully utilized the landscapes and technology of modern urban life; but on the whole the genre is deeply imbued with its own past and innovation has come more through reinterpreting conventions than radical departure from them. A representative sampling of modern authors who have contributed significantly to the genre would include L. P. Hartley, Elizabeth Bowen, Robert Aickman, Rosemary Timperley, James Turner, Jessica Amanda Salmonson, Fred Urquhart, Mary Williams, and Alison Lurie—a list that emphasizes the continuing importance of women writers. Despite the popularity of more graphic forms of supernatural fiction, traditional literary ghost stories continue to enjoy a devoted readership, though it is now served mainly by anthologies and small press publications.

Ghost stories and tales of detection have long shared readers, and several authors whose reputations are primarily in the mystery field—Wilkie

*Collins, Arthur Conan *Doyle, John Dickson *Carr, and Edmund *Crispin among others—have also written ghost stories. A few ghost stories—such as Collins's "Mrs. Zant and the Ghost" (1885; *Little Novels*, 1887) or M. R. James's "The Treasure of Abbot Thomas" (*Ghost Stories of an Antiquary*, 1904), which involves the unraveling of a cipher—contain elements of the mystery or detective story. Conversely, and more commonly, "ghosts" have been used as plot devices in crime and mystery writing—for example, in Robert Barr's "The Ghost with the Club Foot" (1906), Ernest Bramah's "The Ghost at Massingham Mansions" (*The Eyes of Max Carrados*, 1923), and G. K. *Chesterton's "The Ghost of Gideon Wise" (*The Incredulity of Father Brown*, 1926).

A more obvious fusion is the subgenre of psychic detective stories. Anticipated by Le Fanu in the character of Dr. Martin Hesselius ("Green Tea," in *All the Year Round*, 23 Oct. 1869) and directly inspired by the success of Sherlock Holmes, the *psychic sleuth first appeared in the Flaxman Low stories of "E. and H. Heron" (the mother and son writing team of Kate and Hesketh Prichard), serialized in *Pearson's Magazine* beginning in 1898 and collected as *Ghosts* (1899). Other examples include Algernon Blackwood's John Silence (*John Silence, Physician Extraordinary*, 1908), William Hope Hodgson's Carnacki (*Carnacki, the Ghost-Finder*, 1913), Dion Fortune's Dr. Taverner (*The Secrets of Dr. Taverner*, 1926), Margery Lawrence's Miles Pennoyer (*Number Seven, Queer Street*, 1945), and Joseph Payne Brennan's Lucius Leffing (*The Casebook of Lucius Leffing*, 1973).

[See also Gothic Novel; Horror Fiction; Occult and Supernatural Literature; Sensation Novel; Terror.]

• Glen Cavaliero, *The Supernatural and English Fiction* (1995). Stewart M. Ellis, in *Mainly Victorian* (1925). H. P. Lovecraft, *Supernatural Horror in Literature* (1945). Jack Sullivan, *Elegant Nightmares: The English Ghost Story from le Fanu to Blackwood* (1978).   —Michael Cox

GHOSTWRITERS. Ghost writing, sometimes referred to as "ghosting," is the use of someone other than the attributed author to do the actual work of writing. Ghosting is common and often expected when celebrity authors are involved. But when a professional writer's byline appears, the reader assumes truth in labelling. However, some books signed by "real" writers have been entrusted to ghostwriters, whether because the original writer died, retired, overcommitted, or wanted to increase the cash flow on a saleable name. In the genre of crime and mystery, ghostwriters often have been employed to extend the lives of highly popular series characters.

Brett Halliday turned the writing of Michael *Shayne novels over to ghostwriters Robert Terrall and W. Ryerson Johnson in the 1950s and 1960s, while the lead stories in *Mike Shayne Mystery Magazine* were the work of such writers as Dennis Lynds, Michael Avallone, James M. Reasoner, and the team of Hal Blythe and Charlie Sweet. Leslie *Charteris employed Harry Harrison to ghost *Vendetta for the Saint* (1964), but in later books Charteris credited his collaborators. A couple of paperback originals about

Ernest Tidyman's John Shaft were the work of Robert Turner, while posthumous books credited to William Ard were written by John Jakes or Lawrence *Block. Paperbacks of the 1960s and early 1970s attributed to Ellery *Queen (joint pseudonym of Frederic Dannay and Manfred B. Lee) but not concerning the character Ellery *Queen were written by Stephen Marlowe, John Holbrook Vance, Talmage Powell, Richard Deming, Fletcher Flora, Walter J. Shelden, and Edward D. *Hoch.

A practice related to ghost writing is the use of silent partners. Third collaborators, including Avram Davidson, Theodore Sturgeon, and Paul W. Fairman, were recruited to write Queen novels based on Dannay's outlines in the 1960s. In the 1940s, Anthony *Boucher relieved Dannay's heavy workload by becoming Lee's collaborator on Ellery Queen radio scripts. Some of Margery *Allingham's novels were written in collaboration with her husband, P. Youngman Carter, while C. L. Moore assisted on mysteries credited to her husband, Henry Kuttner. A Cleve F. Adams novelette was posthumously expanded into a novel by Robert Leslie Bellem. Warren B. Murphy, who created the paperback Destroyer series with Richard B. Sapir, used uncredited collaborators, including Richard S. Meyers, Robert J. Randisi, and Molly Cochran. At present, the series is ghosted by Will Murray. The later books in Don Pendleton's Executioner series have been ghosted, with the true authors credited on the verso of the title page.

"House names"—bylines owned by a publisher or packager—were common in the heyday of the *pulp magazines, as was the case with *The Shadow's* Maxwell Grant (usually written by Walter B. Gibson) and *Doc Savage's* Kenneth Robeson (usually written by Lester Dent). In *dime novels, pulps, and paperback originals, any number of writers have ghosted works with byline Nick (or Nicholas) *Carter.

[See also Celebrity Crime and Mystery Writers.]

• Allen J. Hubin, *Crime Fiction, 1749–1980: A Comprehensive Bibliography* (1984); *1981–1985 Supplement* (1988).

—Jon L. Breen

Ghote, Inspector Ganesh Vinayak. Created by H. R. F. *Keating, Inspector Ghote of the Bombay Criminal Investigation Department (CID) appears in some twenty novels and numerous short stories. Beginning with *The Perfect Murder* (1964), Ghote, with his bony shoulders weighed down by life, seems easily intimidated by the rich and mighty. Dominated by his superiors, nagged by his wife Protima and cajoled by his beloved son Ved Ghote appears diffident, overwhelmed, and error-prone. Yet in pursuit of a criminal, he is shrewd and intelligent. Beneath the humorous figure of a downtrodden policeman lies a formidable adversary.

A man of honor, Ghote struggles to do what is right. In *Under a Monsoon Cloud* (1986), he protects a longtime hero from prosecution and faces an inquiry; in *The Iciest Sin* (1990) he witnesses a venerated scientist commit a *murder. In *Inspector Ghote Trusts the Heart* (1972), he draws on his deep compassion when the son of a poor man is kidnapped. An admirer of Hans Gross, early criminologist and author of *Criminal Investigations*, Ghote combines basic principles of detection with intuition and common sense.

[*See also* Ethnic Sleuth; Ethnicity; Humor; Visitors Abroad.]

• Otto Penzler, ed., *The Great Detectives* (1978). H. R. F. Keating, *Inspector Ghote, His Life and Crimes* (1989).

—Melvyn Barnes

GILBERT, MICHAEL, (b. 1912), English author, a Grand master of the MWA, recipient of the 1994 Diamond Dagger Award. Gilbert was a fledgling lawyer when he began his first novel, but World War II intervened and he did not become either solicitor or novelist until his return to civilian life in 1946. He joined a leading law firm in Lincoln's Inn and set about completing and revising the unfinished novel, published in 1947 as *Close Quarters*. Until his retirement from the law, he sustained two careers, writing his novels and stories in the trains that carried him to and from his legal work. From the start he showed his versatility, determined never to write the same book twice. *Close Quarters* is a classical closed-circle mystery set in the *cathedral close milieu. *They Never Looked Inside, (1948; He Didn't Mind Danger)*, which followed, is a taut and lively *thriller exploiting the tensions of postwar London. Since then, diversity has been a hallmark of Michael Gilbert's work; as Eric Forbes-Boyd remarked, he has shown himself equally adept "with wig and gown or cloak and dagger."

This means that it is not possible to characterize the typical Gilbert novel. *Smallbone Deceased* (1950) is a legal *whodunit long assured of classic status; *Death Has Deep Roots* (1951) takes us into an *Old Bailey trial; *Death in Captivity* (1952; *The Danger Within*, 1952) draws on the author's experience as a prisoner of war, combining detection with a war story; and *Blood and Judgement* (1959) is a rare full-length case for Patrick Petrella, the protagonist of numerous police stories. *The Etruscan Net* (1969; *The Family Tomb*, 1970) investigates art frauds in postdiluvian Florence; *The Body of a Girl* (1972) and *Death of Favourite Girl* (1980; *The Killing of Katie Steelstock*) are complex *police procedurals with less predictable policemen than the decent Petrella; *The Night of the Twelfth* (1976) gives a chilling account of sadism and *murder at a prep school; and *Trouble* (1987) is an ambitious thriller dealing in terrorism and racial tensions.

The story collections are equally varied. Two featuring Petrella present a traditional, reassuring image of the police force; two involve Messrs. Calder and Behrens, senior spies who play a grim game without rules; while another, with Jonas Pickett, a semiretired solicitor, shows a world still secure despite the weakening of its "bastions"—"religion, family life, the rule of the law."

Gilbert's respect for established authority is everywhere apparent, and his attitudes do not waver. Criminals are outlaws demanding society's vengeance. Brutes should expect brutality in return, and a righteous end may justify equivocal means.

Throughout, Gilbert writes with confidence, ease, and *humor. As a narrator he is masterly, able to assemble from diverse encounters and events a tense, absorbing pattern that gains in coherence until the denouement completes the design.

[*See also* Legal Procedural; Spy Fiction; Terrorism and the Terrorist Procedural.]

• B. A. Pike, *The Short Stories of Michael Gilbert: An Annotated Checklist* (1998).

—B. A. Pike

GIRL DETECTIVE. *See* Juvenile Sleuths: Girl Sleuth.

GODWIN, WILLIAM (1756–1836). Author of *Things as They Are; or, The Adventures of Caleb Williams* (1794), a novel considered to be a precursor of the novel of mystery and detection, William Godwin became a student of philosophy at the Hoxton Presbyterian Academy. From 1778 to 1783 he served several dissenting congregations as minister. Following his doubts about organized *religion, he become an atheist and left the Church for work as writer and political activist. He was connected with the extreme Whigs, worked as a writer for *New Annual Register*, and started a publishing firm, which failed despite its issue of the famous *Tales from Shakespeare* (1807) by Charles Lamb.

Godwin was an associate of the English Romantic writers—it was Samuel Taylor Coleridge who drew him back from atheism to theism—and became their de facto social theorist. His notable work of political theory was *Enquiry Concerning Political Justice* (1793), published during a decade of great activity by Godwin. In 1794 he published the narrative of Caleb Williams, in 1797 he married Mary Wollstonecraft, and in 1803–1804 he issued a two-volume study of Chaucer.

Caleb Williams focuses at its opening on Falkland, a wealthy squire whom critics regard as a forerunner of Dr. Jekyll and Mr. Hyde because he is both affable and a murderer. The eponymous hero of the story is Falkland's secretary, who finds evidence of his employer's *guilt and flees when Falkland threatens to lay the guilt on Williams. Eventually Falkland confesses his crime and Caleb Williams suffers remorse for having contributed to Falkland's disgrace. Politically the work concerns the *corruptions of power. In terms of its place in the literary history of crime and mystery it represents a union of the tale of *pursuit with an investigation of *motive and evidence.

• R. Glynn Grylls, *William Godwin and His World* (1975). William St. Clair, *The Godwins and the Shelleys: The Biography of a Family* (1989).

—John M. Reilly

GOLDEN AGE FORMS. *This entry is divided into two parts. The first surveys exemplars of tales of detection written during the Golden Age of the Short Story, which can be dated from the creation of Sherlock Holmes in 1887 to the close of the Second World War. The second discusses the Golden Age Novel of detection, which began to develop previous to World War I,* *had its fullest flowering between the two world wars, and remains a nostalgic form used to this day.*

The Golden Age Short Story
The Golden Age Novel

For further information, please refer to Golden Age Traditions.

THE GOLDEN AGE SHORT STORY

According to Julian Symons, the Golden Age of the detective short story begins with Sherlock *Holmes and ends with the Second World War—a period of about half a century. During that time, society was significantly altered, reading habits changed, and the popularity of the short form waxed and waned. Holmes made his short story debut in the July 1891 issue of the *Strand* magazine, which first appeared in January of that year. The enormous public enthusiasm for Holmes soon caused the *Strand* and its competitors to encourage other writers to develop series detectives in the hope of emulating Doyle's success. The rivals of Sherlock Holmes included Arthur *Morrison's Martin Hewitt, a "plain man" who represented a reaction against Holmesian eccentricities, and G. K. *Chesterton's Father *Brown, a more effective and memorable figure. Brown was equally unflamboyant in appearance, but more subtly conceived as an agent of social *justice whose moral theology helped him to explain how miraculous *murders could have been committed by men who were merely mortal.

The personality of the detective was crucial to the tone and, often, the quality of short stories until near the end of the Golden Age. As much ingenuity was devoted to the creation of distinctive heroes as to the construction of complicated *puzzles; there were few heroines and those who did emerge were, like Baroness Emmuska *Orczy's Lady Molly de Mazareen of Scotland Yard, distinctly second rate. Among the more memorable heroes were the vegetarian hypochondriac Thorpe Hazell, a specialist in railway detection created by Canon Victor L. Whitechurch, and Ernest *Bramah's Max *Carrados, whose acute intelligence and other senses compensated for his blindness. Orczy's most interesting sleuth, the *Old Man in the Corner, was the ultimate *armchair detective; sitting in the corner of a tea shop consuming milk and cheesecake and tying and untying knots in string, he was able to solve cases that baffled the police. Across the Atlantic, Jacques *Futrelle's stories about Professor Augustus S. F. X. *Van Dusen, "The Thinking Machine," have long been acknowledged as ingenious classics, although they do not have the atmospheric depth or moral force of the stories that Melville Davisson *Post wrote about Uncle *Abner, a Virginian squire of the Jeffersonian era. Later, C. Daly King's Trevis Tarrant appeared in a number of "episodes," which Ellery *Queen considered "the most imaginative detective short stories of our time." In comparison to Queen himself, one of the few Golden Age detectives who appeared to equal advantage in both the short and long form, Tarrant nowadays seems a minor figure.

The British author R. Austin *Freeman was an innovator of the first rank. The *inverted detective stories in *The Singing Bone* (1912) showed that a reader could from the outset be furnished with all the facts of the crime and yet still be fascinated to learn how the detective would solve the mystery. More generally, in his stories about Dr. John *Thorndyke, an expert in medical jurisprudence, Freeman used his technical knowledge to show how science could assist in the detection of crime. More ambitious were H. C. *Bailey's stories about Reggie *Fortune; the strength of Fortune's passion for justice gave the best of Bailey's stories a depth that Freeman could never match. Other writers found that a successful fictional sleuth need not always be on the side of law and order. Morrison's crooked investigator Horace Dorrington, although less celebrated than Martin Hewitt, is a more interesting character, and in A. J. *Raffles, the amateur cracksman, E. W. *Hornung created a likeable *antihero who has stood the test of time.

The best Golden Age stories, such as Anthony *Berkeley's "The Avenging Chance" (*The Best Detective Stories of the Year 1929*, 1930; *The Best English Detective Stories of the Year*) and "The Tea Leaf" (*Great Short Stories of Detection, Mystery, and Horror*, Vol. 1, 1928) by Edgar Jepson and Robert Eustace, dazzled readers with their twists and turns. Yet harsh economic realities began to threaten the form. Magazine markets slowly dried up when authors such as Agatha *Christie and Dorothy L. *Sayers found it made commercial sense to develop their better ideas at novel length and readers started to obtain their fiction more regularly from lending libraries than from railway bookstalls. Many notable stories that appeared in the 1930s were independent stories with not a *Great Detective in sight, written by writers who are now largely forgotten. Yet as the Golden Age drew to its close, in stories like Thomas Burke's chilling "The Hands of Mr. Ottermole" (*Pleasantries of Old Quong*, 1931; *A Tea-Shop in Limehouse*), Hylton Cleaver's ironic "By Kind Permission of the Murdered Man" (*Strand*, Mar. 1934), and Loel Yeo's witty "Inquest" (*Strand*, Apr. 1932), the seeds were sown for the development of the short form in the postwar era.

[*See also* Eccentrics; Ingenuity; Plainman Sleuth.]

• Jack Adrian, ed., *Detective Stories from the Strand Magazine* (1991). Patricia Craig, ed., *The Oxford Book of English Detective Stories* (1990). Dorothy L. Sayers, ed., introduction to *Great Short Stories of Detection, Mystery and Horror*, 2nd Series (1931). Julian Symons, *Bloody Murder: From the Detective Story to the Crime Novel*, 3rd rev. ed. (1992).

—Martin Edwards

THE GOLDEN AGE NOVEL

To identify the Golden Age novel as a form that belongs wholly to the years between the two world wars is to constrain a period that was in reality more elastic. This is especially so since the initial development of the genre from its nascent state in the years immediately before World War I was slow. The strong retrospective factor was emphasized by stories set in wartime (for example, Agatha *Christie's *The Mysterious Affair at Styles*, 1920) or in the aftermath of *war (such as Dorothy L. *Sayers's *The Unpleasantness at the Bellona Club*, 1928, in which a character suffers from shell shock).

Such authors as H. C. *McNeile, Leslie *Charteris, and John *Buchan, in whose books positive action is a feature, continued for rather longer to echo undertones of war. For these writers, patriotism is the highest virtue and treason the most venal sin.

The popularity of writers already famous from even earlier eras, particularly Edgar Allan *Poe, Wilkie *Collins, G. K. *Chesterton, and Arthur Conan *Doyle, was in no way diminished by the increasing number of their successors. Detective fiction after World War I also showed some evidence of regression in its persistent harking back to the confidence of the Edwardian heyday, whose comforts and opulence were conspicuous by their absence in the economically straitened and deflationary 1920s and 1930s.

More importantly, readers continued to share perceptions of right and wrong with the author. During the Golden Age all crime—but especially *murder— was seen as an offense against the established order. In its implicit endorsement of the rule of law, the Golden Age novel mirrored the support usually given by the British public to the police.

Little sympathy was customarily extended to the criminal in fiction—Gordon Daviot's *Kif* (1929) was a notable exception to this rule—and only rarely was much made by authors in the way of attempts at understanding the actions of the murderer or mitigation of the crime.

The comfortable, predictable, and ordered world of this period in detective fiction manifested itself in, among other features, a deliberate under-characterization of those depicted in the action and a noted, if unreal, felicity of phrase and quotation. The nature of the *settings in which the detective action took place is also significant. These were usually rural and often at first sight pastorally idyllic; indeed, some works are almost novels of place. *The Sittaford Mystery* (1931; *Murder at Hazelmoor*) by Christie, whose writing career spanned the entire period, and Sayers's *The Nine Tailors* (1934) both portray familiar parts of the English countryside with insight and affection.

Furthermore, the houses in which the crimes often took place tended to be large, stately even, and usually well-staffed by live-in servants. The legend that it was the butler who committed the murder was later labeled "The Body in the Library School." That books of this type were read mostly by those without either butlers or libraries gave them an element of wish fulfillment which only served to heighten their burgeoning popularity throughout the period.

Even when the action did not take place in a stately home, it was taken for granted that the smooth running of a household was a laudable end in itself. The powerful constraints of that which is "not done" in polite society affected the content of the genre, as did the importance of the minor social events that punctuated life in this stratum of society. This is exemplified in Francis Iles's *Malice Aforethought* (1931), in which the tennis party is prominent.

Similarly, mealtimes were significant markers of the day, although the exact nature of the menu was dealt with only superficially unless poisoning was suspected. As was then usual in real life, clothes were seldom commented on in great detail—they were merely noted in passing as good, fashionable, or perhaps well-worn but clean. Sex was never explicit, and love, however ardent, never went beyond the bedroom door.

If the mise-en-scène was urban, the setting was usually either a quaint cathedral city or one of England's two traditional university cities, *Oxford or *Cambridge. Mean streets featured less commonly, even when the action took place in *London, and work in the industrial sense was rarely written about. Financial malpractice and *white-collar crime in the fiction of Henry *Wade, Christopher Bush, and Freeman Wills *Crofts, among others, reflected several spectacularly successful frauds perpetrated on the public in these years.

In the earlier part of this period there was much emphasis on the concept of the genre as a game that ought to be played according to agreed rules. This was felt especially by writers such as Ronald A. *Knox and S. S. *Van Dine. The concept underlined the categorization of Golden Age fiction by some as merely escapist reading. This negative opinion, however, was not endorsed by those who saw it more as a worthy academic exercise in intelligent puzzle-solving.

The genre's *puzzle aspect was itself later to expand into the specialized *locked room mystery, also known as the *impossible crime. The doyen of this increasingly ingenious field was the prolific author John Dickson *Carr, who brought the genre to its apogee in *The Three Coffins* (1935; *The Hollow Man*). Its chronicler was Robert C. S. Adey in *Locked Rooms and Other Impossible Crimes* (1979).

Some of the important developments that succeeded the backward-looking, nostalgic school were made by writers whose hard-boiled style followed that which had been previously designated "tough" writing. Dashiell *Hammett's books, including *Red Harvest* (1929), *The Glass Key* (1931), and *The Maltese Falcon* (1930), feature detectives owing allegiance only to their own conception of justice. Peter Cheyney's Lemmy Caution, who first appeared in *This Man Is Dangerous* (1936) is in a similar mode. In some senses the two creations of H. C. *Bailey, the mannered Reggie *Fortune and Joshua Clunk, also made their own rules of behavior.

A very slow and still incomplete move away from the gifted amateur with ample means as crime investigator began in the interwar years. This mirrored the public's perception of improvements in actual police procedure and in the expansion of forensic science.

R. Austin *Freeman's Dr. John *Thorndyke and his microscope were the forerunners of a whole school of fictional *forensic pathologists with increasingly sophisticated instruments and techniques. Crofts's Inspector Joseph *French first appeared in *Inspector French's Greatest Case* (1924). His famously methodical approach and meticulous attention to detail put him among those who paved the way for future police procedurals, such as Henry *Wade's *Constable, Guard Thyself* (1934).

Two books firmly in the old tradition of patriotism and stylized amateurism presaged the European war to come. They were Geoffrey *Household's *Rogue Male* (1939; *Man Hunt*) and Ethel Lina White's *The Wheel Spins* (1936; *The Lady Vanishes*). The writing of these prewar days continued after the 1939–45 war in the same way as it had done in the 1920s.

Robert Graves and Alan Hodge in their social history of the years 1919 to 1939, *The Long Weekend* (1940), were of the opinion that lowbrow literature was then dominated by detective fiction. It is even more noteworthy that the writers in this genre who were famous at the time have not only retained their readership but, in comparison with most authors of straight fiction of the same period, are more likely to have remained household names.

[*See also* "Butler Did It, The"; Cathedral Close Milieu; Country House Milieu; English Village Milieu; Escapism; Rules of the Game.]

• A. E. Murch, *The Development of the Detective Novel* (1958). Julian Symons, *Bloody Murder: From the Detective Story to the Crime Novel*, 3rd rev. ed. (1992).   —Catherine Aird

GOLDEN AGE TRADITIONS. *As the novel supplanted the short story as the commercially favored form for criminous narrative, writers faced with such possibilities in the longer form as room to complicate *plot, elaborate *setting, and expound the cast of characters also sought to legitimate their entertainments as intellectually challenging literature. Prescriptive statements of rules for playing fair with the reader, introduction of well-educated and socially elevated detectives, and extended development of detectives' talk about their methods all enforced the idea that the heart and aim of the detective narrative is to provide readers with worthy *puzzles to test their wits but not to pander to emotion or display atmospherics. Of course, the emerging practice of detective writing carried a unified set of values—conservative, upper-class, and set off from the contingencies of history—but more important for the writers, their combined practice in forging new, longer narratives resulted in a collection of distinct conventions readily adaptable for repeated use and quite popular besides. The result has come to be called the Golden Age, meaning the period when the conventions initially flourished (roughly 1920–39) and, then, also signifying the conventions themselves as they prove endlessly attractive to authors and readers alike.*

This article consists of two parts:

The British Golden Age Tradition
The American Golden Age Tradition

THE BRITISH GOLDEN AGE TRADITION

The years following World War I and leading to the start of World War II are conveniently labeled the Golden Age of Detective Fiction. The oddity and particularity of the traditions adhered to during this Golden Age have become masked by the extraordinary popularity books of this sort acquired as well as by the influence they came to have. But look at the tradition objectively and it can be seen as curious indeed. It stipulated in principle that crime novels be written to a strict and consistent formula bearing only the haziest true relation to life as it was known at that time in Britain.

This tradition, though springing originally from the enormous success of the Sherlock *Holmes stories, was very different from storytelling based on the probabilities of real life. Although the novels of this new era paid obeisance to the normalities, these were almost exclusively the normalities of its expected readership, the floating mass of the British middle class, especially its women. The desire for simple and uncomplicated mental comfort equally played its part in the creation of the genre. The time, although free of the actual dangers of war, was still far from pleasant, with widespread unemployment, financial difficulties, and the nervous casualties of the huge conflict still all too evident (note the effects of trench warfare on Dorothy L. *Sayers's Lord Peter *Wimsey).

The formula for the books thus brought into being has been described most clearly perhaps by a later writer, who yet owes more than a little to its conventions, P. D. *James. She has often stated that the detective story must have a mysterious death as its core and that there must be a closed circle of people or *suspects, who could have brought that death about. Each of these suspects must have a credible *motive, opportunity to commit the crime, and reasonable access to whatever means was used to commit the deed. There must, too, be a person who unravels the mystery by logical inference from facts put directly before the reader (though not necessarily in their true form) and this person, the *detective, whether an amateur such as Sherlock *Holmes or a police officer, must be central to the story.

These traditions, which came to be regarded as rules, were codified in the heyday of the Golden Age by Monsignor Ronald A. *Knox, who combined his religious duties with the occasional writing of light-hearted stories in the genre. In the preface to *Best Detective Stories of the Year 1928* (1929; *The Best English Detective Stories of 1928*), he laid down Ten Commandments for the writing of detective fiction, which can be summarized as: The criminal must be mentioned early in the narrative; no supernatural element is permitted; only one secret passageway is allowed; no undiscovered poisons are acceptable; no "Chinamen" (that is by implication exotic, rules-free villains) can be featured; the detective may never succeed through a mere accident or by an unaccountable intuition; the detective must not be the murderer; all *clues must be shown at once; the Watson figure must betray his every thought; unprepared-for twin brothers are not to appear.

But, as with any set of seemingly rigid commandments, there proved to be always room for infinite scrupulous adjustment. Perhaps the most notorious manipulation of the rules occurs in Agatha *Christie's *The Murder of Roger Ackroyd* (1926), whose conclusion continues to be controversial to this day.

But rule-breaking, or bending, in sport justly creates more fury than the weavings and dodgings of life. And the traditional British detective story was very much a sporting contest, much like the game of cricket. Knox, indeed, said elsewhere it should be a kind of game between writer and reader. The object is to see whether reader or author unravels the mystery first. Moreover—and here is a bonus for the author—the reader who solves the *puzzle first is delighted, but equally the reader who fails to solve it is delighted with the cleverness of the writer.

Among those who, with the champion Christie, most often achieved the latter happy result (because an insufficiently adroit writer earns the reader's contempt) there should be mentioned Sayers with her first book *Whose Body?* (1923), Margery *Allingham with *Police at the Funeral* (1931), Ngaio *Marsh with *Enter a Murderer* (1935), Anthony *Berkeley with *The Poisoned Chocolates Case* (1929), and Gladys *Mitchell with *When Last I Died* (1941).

But there were many other practitioners who, while lacking the panache in plotting of a Christie, produced books that solidly satisfied their audience in the years between 1920 and 1940. And there are still readers who, demanding no more than the pleasures of the chase, derive enjoyment from these books, hard though they are to find. Total oblivion, however, ought not to be the fate of the best constructed work of John *Rhode, E. R. Punshon, the brother and sister team of G. D. H. and Margaret *Cole (though the fact of their interchangeable dual authorship indicates how the standard detective story could be produced in such quantities), or of J. J. Connington, Christopher Bush, or R. A. J. Walling.

Nor should it be thought that with the advent of World War II the genre disappeared. Britons under aerial onslaught found immense comfort in the simplicities of detective stories which continued to be written under wartime difficulties. Although the major effect of the disruption and disenchantment brought about by the war was to produce what might be called crime novels of unease, the *cozy story continued to be written in some quantity, and fresh examples can still be found.

Peter Dickinson's earlier books featuring Superintendent James Pibble were squarely in the tradition, despite the extraordinariness of the setting of, for instance, *Skin Deep* (1968; *The Glass-Sided Ants' Nest*). Robert *Barnard, a writer a good deal more waspish than the standard detective story authors of the 1920s and 1930s, works largely and very effectively in the same mold. *Death in a Cold Climate* (1980), though set in a Norwegian university rather than an English manor house, is a characteristic example. Catherine Aird has produced some excellent specimens of the genre, lightened with quiet wit and with a police detective rather than the amateur whose existence in the postwar years was more difficult to account for. An exemplary Aird novel is *The Religious Body* (1966).

It should not be forgotten, either, that the classical detective story as written in the Golden Age provided a blueprint for crime stories of, often, very different sorts. Its fundamental outline can be seen, for instance, in all the early novels of a writer as seemingly different as John *le Carré. Its influence on a writer with aims much more profound than providing a simple pastime, James, has already been noted. The glow from the Golden Age reaches far down the years.

—H. R. F. Keating

THE AMERICAN GOLDEN AGE TRADITION

At least in its early years, the British dominated the Golden Age of Detection. Prominent names in American mystery fiction of the early twenties—Arthur B. *Reeve, Carolyn Wells, Lee Thayer, Octavus Roy Cohen—didn't threaten the British. Some Americans, Melville Davisson *Post, for example, shunned the novel form in favor of short stories. Perhaps Jacques *Futrelle, had he survived the sinking of the *Titanic* in 1912, would have become an American classicist comparable to Agatha *Christie, Dorothy L. *Sayers, and their British colleagues.

One of the most important conventions of the time was the depiction of the memorable series character. It is not surprising, then, that the first major American writer to emerge in the period was Earl Derr *Biggers, whose 1925 novel, *The House Without a Key*, introduced Sergeant Charlie *Chan of the Honolulu police, still one of the best-known fictional detectives. But the early Chan novels were closer to slick-magazine romantic mystery fiction than to the rigorous, generously clued puzzle making favored by British writers. Biggers would fully achieve this kind of fair-play plotting, which was a hallmark of classic detective fiction, only with his last novel, *The Keeper of the Keys* (1932).

America's first truly important Golden Age writer was S. S. *Van Dine, who introduced mannered and erudite *gentleman sleuth Philo *Vance in *The Benson Murder Case* (1926) and followed him through eleven subsequent cases, ending with the posthumous *The Winter Murder Case* (1939). Van Dine owes his place not only to the high quality of his early novels but to his "Twenty Rules for Writing Detective Stories" (1927), which were often broken even in his own books. The proclivity for rule making was a Golden Age pastime Van Dine shared with Father Ronald A. *Knox, Sayers, and the members of Great Britain's *Detection Club. Van Dine's tendency to play up the bizarre elements and hype every case as the most baffling mystery ever confronted was carried on, if more subtly, by his successors. In fact, the determination to go for the big effects every time represents the main contrast between American Golden Age detective fiction and its more matter-of-fact low-key British equivalent.

Van Dine and Vance set the stage for a whole series of American puzzle spinners and *sleuths, many of whom are forgotten—Will Levinrew's (William Levine's) Professor Herman Brierly, Cortland Fitzsimmons's Arthur Martinson—but some of whom would surpass their progenitors. The greatest of all American Golden Age figures, Ellery *Queen, appeared first as author and detective in *The Roman Hat Mystery* (1929), a narrative awash with the accoutrements of classical detection: a list of characters, a map of the *murder scene, and Queen's own innovation, stopping the action when all *clues have been revealed to present a formal Challenge-to-the-Reader. Though Queen would develop and change with the times, always retaining an adherence to the demands of the formal fair-play puzzle, the early Queen was very much influenced by Van Dine, as were Anthony Abbot in the series about *New York police commissioner Thatcher Colt, beginning with *About the Murder of Geraldine Foster* (1930), and Clyde B. Clason in *The Fifth Tumbler* (1936) and subsequent cases about elderly *academic sleuth Theocritus Lucius Westborough. Though Clason did not share Van Dine's love of footnotes, he carried the display of erudition one step further by including a three-page bibliography at the beginning of *The Man from Tibet* (1938).

Two American writers, C. Daly King and Clifford Knight, experimented with another piece of Golden Age window dressing, albeit one that didn't quite catch on: the Clue Finder, or Index of Clues (King's *Obelists at Sea*, 1933; Knight's *The Affair of the Scarlet Crab*, 1937), in which the author appends a list of all the ostensible clues to the solution, keyed to the page on which they appear. Anthony *Boucher, a writer in the Queen tradition who later became dominant among American mystery critics, took the gimmick one step further, listing the clues and their page references *before* revealing the solution in his first novel, *The Case of the Seven of Calvary* (1937).

John Dickson *Carr, master of the *locked room mystery, made his debut in book form in 1930 with *It Walks by Night*. Because he rarely used an American background until late in his career and lived for a good part of his life in Britain, Carr has often been bracketed with the British writers. Though several contemporaries (Queen, King, and Clason among them) sometimes included *impossible crimes in their stories, Carr's most prominent acolyte in always providing such a situation was Clayton Rawson, author of the Great Merlini series beginning with *Death from a Top Hat* (1938).

Among the other prominent classical-style writers of the thirties were Stuart Palmer, who introduced schoolteacher-detective Miss Hildegarde *Withers in *The Penguin Pool Murder* (1931); George Bagby (Aaron Marc Stein), whose Inspector Schmidt solved *Murder at the Piano* (1935), the first of more than a hundred novels signed Bagby, Stein, or Hampton Stone; Vincent *Starrett, the Sherlock *Holmes scholar who wrote short story mysteries about Jimmie Lavender and book-length ones about Walter Ghost, notably *Dead Man Inside* (1931), and Riley Gatewood; and Helen McCloy, whose first novel, *Dance of Death* (1938; *Design for Dying*), came near the end of the Golden Age period. Mignon G. *Eberhart, though most often classed as a writer of romantic *suspense (or, less complimentary, the *Had-I-But-Known school), belongs at least marginally with the Golden Age writers, as does Leslie Ford (Zenith Brown), who also wrote novels set in Britain as David Frome.

Also making their debuts in the thirties were a number of writers who drew almost equally on the hard-boiled tradition of the *pulp magazines and the puzzle-spinning expertise of the classicists: Erle Stanley *Gardner, who introduced lawyer-detective Perry *Mason in *The Case of the Velvet Claws* (1933); Brett Halliday, who wrote two puzzle novels as Asa Baker before creating Miami private detective Michael *Shayne in *Dividend on Death* (1939);

George Harmon *Coxe, whose photographer-sleuth Kent *Murdock first appeared in *Murder with Pictures* (1935); and, perhaps most notably of all, Rex *Stout, who combined a breezy humorous narrator, Archie *Goodwin, with an eccentric *Great Detective, Nero *Wolfe, to create a unique (if often imitated) variation on the Holmes-Watson relationship in *Fer-de-Lance* (1934) and subsequent novels.

Though styles and trends in crime fiction changed, many later American writers continued in the Golden Age tradition. Hake Talbot produced two novels in the Carr mode, *The Hangman's Handyman* (1942) and *Rim of the Pit* (1944), as would John Sladek thirty years later in *Black Aura* (1974) and *Invisible Green* (1977). Sladek also followed Carr's lead in his use of a British background. James Yaffe began writing as a teenager for *Ellery Queen's Mystery Magazine* with some fine stories of impossible crime, drawing on both Carr and Queen for inspiration, but pursued a primarily mainstream career as novelist and playwright in the decades to follow, returning to detective fiction with *A Nice Murder for Mom* (1988) and other novels about a character introduced in *EQMM* short stories of the fifties. Herbert Brean showed a strong Carr influence in *Wilders Walk Away* (1948) and subsequent books. Isaac Asimov brought the purest kind of Golden Age puzzle-spinning to a science fiction setting in *The Caves of Steel* (1954) and *The Naked Sun* (1957). Emma *Lathen introduced her Wall Street banker-detective John Putnam *Thatcher in *Banking on Death* (1961). Among the other contemporary American practitioners with obvious Golden Age roots are William L. DeAndrea, Jane Haddam (Orania Popazoglou), Francis M. Nevins Jr., Herbert Resnicow, Barbara D'Amato, Richard Forrest, Jean Hager, Susan Dunlap, Parnell Hall, and Michael Bowen.

Queen and Carr were as adept in the short-story form as they were at novel length. Much of the American Golden Age tradition has been maintained in short stories, both in *Ellery Queen's Mystery Magazine* (through the works of such puzzle spinners as Edward D. *Hoch, William Brittain, and James Holding) and other periodicals (e.g., the stories of the Carr-inspired Joseph Commings).

[*See also* Conservative vs. Radical Worldview; Conventions of the Genre; Rules of the Game.]

• Howard Haycraft, *Murder for Pleasure* (1941). Marvin Lachman, *A Reader's Guide to the American Novel of Detection* (1993).   —Jon L. Breen

GOLF MILIEU. *See* Sports Milieu.

Goodwin, Archie, the first-person narrator of Rex *Stout's Nero *Wolfe series. Through thirty-three novels and thirty-eight novelettes, Goodwin serves not only as Wolfe's active investigator, but also as his amanuensis and conversational foil. Because Wolfe is almost neurotically opposed to leaving his brownstone on New York's West Thirty-fifth Street, Goodwin does the legwork in the cases they accept.

Goodwin is a sharp-tongued wit and cynic, realistic enough to know that he cannot keep up with Wolfe's superior powers of ratiocination, but confident enough to maintain his self-esteem in their tense, but mutually respectful, relationship. Stout gives Goodwin a private life, including his frequently mentioned but seldom-seen romance with Lily Rowan and his weekly poker games with Saul Panzer. Wolfe's gruff acknowledgment of Goodwin's indispensable place in his life is particularly spelled out in the short story "Christmas Party" (*And Four to Go*, 1958), in which Wolfe leaves his brownstone and disguises himself as a bartending Santa Claus in order to assure himself of Goodwin's well-being.

[*See also* Friendship; Sidekicks and Sleuthing Teams.]

• William S. Baring-Gould, *Nero Wolfe of West Thirty-fifth Street: The Life and Times of America's Largest Private Detective* (1969).   —Landon Burns

GOTHIC NOVEL. The Gothic novel arouses terror and dread, typically involving enclosed settings such as old castles or mansions, and emphasizing themes of imprisonment, persecution, and decay. The first important example of the genre was Horace Walpole's *The Castle of Otranto* (1764), but the full flourishing of the Gothic novel occurred in Britain and Ireland in the three decades after 1790, closing with the appearance of Charles Robert Maturin's *Melmoth the Wanderer* (1820). During this period, the leading practitioner was Ann Radcliffe, whose novels *The Mysteries of Udolpho* (1794) and *The Italian: or, The Confessional of the Black Penitents* (1797) set the pattern for numerous imitators; of these, the most striking is Matthew Lewis, whose novel *The Monk* (1796; *Ambrosio*) reached new levels of sensational *violence. The term "Gothic" in this context means "medieval," and by implication "barbaric." Radcliffe, Lewis, and Maturin set their novels in the Catholic countries of southern Europe in the sixteenth and seventeenth centuries, alarming their largely Protestant audience with tales of the Spanish Inquisition and of villainous, hypocritical monks and nuns. Some of their contemporaries and immediate successors, however, managed to achieve comparable effects of apprehension and claustrophobia in novels with more modern settings: William *Godwin in *Things as They Are; or, The Adventures of Caleb Williams* (1794; *Caleb Williams*), his daughter Mary Shelley in *Frankenstein; or The Modern Prometheus* (1818), and the Scottish writer James Hogg in *The Private Memoirs and Confessions of a Justified Sinner* (1824). All evoked powerful unease without medieval trappings. Although each of these three novels includes prominent *prison scenes, the principal strength is the evocation of psychological torment, *guilt, self-division, and paranoid delusion. There are some grounds for excluding these works from the strictest definitions of Gothic fiction, but they are nonetheless commonly grouped with the work of Radcliffe and Lewis.

After the 1820s, the effects associated with the Gothic novel were adopted in various forms by nineteenth-century writers. The novels of the Brontë sisters, for example, are strongly Gothic in flavor, whereas Charles *Dickens concentrates his Gothic touches upon particular characters such as Miss Havisham in *Great Expectations* (serialized in *All the Year Round*, 1860; published in book form in 1861). Three special bodies of writing in the nineteenth century inherit and adapt the achievements of the early Gothic novel: the American short story, from Edgar Allan *Poe to Charlotte Perkins Gilman; the so-called *sensation novels of the 1860s in England; and a group of sinister fin de siècle novels including R. L. Stevenson's *The Strange Case of Dr. Jekyll and Mr. Hyde* (1886), Oscar Wilde's *The Picture of Dorian Gray* (*Lippincott's*, 1890), and Bram Stoker's *Dracula* (1897). In the twentieth century, the novels and stories of William Faulkner and other writers of the American South gave a powerful new impetus to Gothic literary devices. Daphne *du Maurier's *Rebecca* (1938) memorably revived the central Gothic motif of the defenseless heroine virtually imprisoned in the house of a secretive-master figure, and inspired countless formulaic imitations in the popular market.

The Gothic novel has some importance as a forerunner of modern mystery and crime fiction, chiefly because it habituated the nineteenth-century reading public to the heightened manipulation of *suspense (notably by Radcliffe) and to the sensational treatment of violent crimes and of the secret conspiracies involved with them. The missing element is usually that of detective investigation, for which there is often little scope in true Gothic fiction: Typically, the heroine finds herself imprisoned in a castle or mansion by a powerful man who tries to force her into marriage in order to obtain her fortune, as in Radcliffe's *The Mysteries of Udolpho*. The criminal's identity and *motives are usually known, and the novel focuses on the heroine's apprehensions rather than on any mystery surrounding the identity of a malefactor. Some rudimentary investigation—in the form of domestic spying—is common in Gothic novels, but is usually restricted by the enclosed space in which the investigator is permitted to move, and characterized by mistaken inferences, as in *The Mysteries of Udolpho*. In general, a concentration on *atmosphere rather than on logical deduction distinguishes Gothic fiction from modern crime and detective fiction. It is also worth observing that Gothic novels are typically set in zones outside the reach of the law, such as remote castles or mansions, and are therefore alien to the world of the police novel.

The two traditions are connected, however, by a common inheritance. The eponymous hero of Godwin's semi-Gothic *Caleb Williams* is sometimes cited as the first important detective in the English novel (for example, by Ian Ousby in *Bloodhounds of Heaven: The Detective in English Fiction from Godwin to Doyle*, 1976), although he might be better defined as a spy who becomes a fugitive. It is hard to believe that it is merely coincidence that the author who perfected the Gothic short story—Edgar Allan Poe in "The Fall of the House of Usher" (*Burton's Gentleman's Magazine*, Sept. 1839)—was also a principal founder of the detective tradition in English: The relentless logic whereby hidden secrets are exposed seems to be similar in Poe's detective and Gothic fictions. The sensation novels of the mid-Victorian period, such as Wilkie *Collins's *The Woman in White* (1860) and J. Sheridan Le Fanu's *Uncle Silas* (1864), are poised midway between the crime/mystery and Gothic traditions.

A more direct connection between the two traditions may be found in Arthur Conan *Doyle's "The Adventure of the Speckled Band" (*Strand*, Feb. 1892) and "The Adventure of the Copper Beeches" (*Strand*, June 1892), as well as in his novel *The Hound of the Baskervilles* (1902). All show strikingly Gothic features such as the incarcerated heiress, the gloomily deserted wing of an old and isolated building, and the superstition of the *family curse. While such Gothic elements hark back to archaic forms of despotism or cruelty, the intervention of the detective as illuminator of dark places leads in another direction, toward the security of modern rationality. The hybrid Gothic-detective genre is, then, internally contradictory: *The Hound of the Baskervilles*, the most celebrated example of such a mixture, is more successful in establishing Gothic setting and atmosphere than in maintaining the suspense of a crime mystery.

A faint shadow of Gothic fiction may seen to lie across the mystery set in the English *country house milieu, inasmuch as each takes advantage of the spatial restrictions of the rural building. In the Gothic novel, however, the convention serves to create a sense of claustrophobic apprehension. In the murder mystery, it is used principally to limit the number of *suspects—again, the interests of atmosphere compete with those of forensic logic. In modern crime and mystery fiction as well, distant echoes of Gothic traditions may be discernible in stories that are set in remote times (medieval monasteries, for example) or in which sinister family secrets such as incest and hereditary madness are uncovered.

[*See also* Closed-World Settings and Open-World Settings; Ghost Story: Horror Fiction; Occult and Supernatural Literature; Terror.]

• David Punter, *The Literature of Terror: A History of Gothic Fictions from 1765 to the Present Day*, 2 vols., 2nd ed. (1996). Linda Bayer-Berenbaum, *The Gothic Imagination: Expansion in Gothic Literature and Art* (1982).

—Chris Baldick

GRAFTON, SUE (b. 1940), American creator of the sassy California *private eye Kinsey *Milhone, who appears in books entitled after letters in the alphabet. The daughter of lawyer and sometime detective novelist C. W. Grafton and chemistry teacher Vivian Harnsberger, Grafton grew up in a household that revered the written word. She has termed her home "classically dysfunctional," since both of her parents were alcoholics. Making an advantage from a liability, Grafton has said that her parents' alcoholism built in her a sensitivity to subtle cues in behavior, and her relatively unsupervised childhood in Louisville, Kentucky, allowed her generous time for outdoor play centered upon the construction of imaginary *adventure stories. Often playing the role of the heroine, Grafton said she never depended upon others for rescue but was determined to save herself. These qualities are carried over into the creation of her *sleuth, Milhone.

Grafton married at eighteen and earned a degree in English from Western Kentucky State Teachers College. She became the mother of three, hoping to create an ideal family life that had eluded her when she was a child, but was married three times before she found real happiness. Grafton tried homemaking and work as a consciousness-raising group leader before turning her hand to writing two mainstream novels and numerous screenplays and teleplays. Then, inspired by a sense of helplessness during a custody battle over her children, Grafton created the independent, capable Milhone, a champion of the helpless, and also found her true calling as a detective novelist. Milhone is introduced in *"A" is for Alibi* (1982). Alcoholism is a theme in *"D" is for Deadbeat* (1987).

[*See also* Females and Feminists; Hard-Boiled Sleuth; Heroism.]

• Rosemary Herbert, "Sue Grafton," in *The Fatal Art of Entertainment: Interviews with Mystery Writers* (1994): 29–54. Natalie Hevener Kaufman and Carol McGinnis Kay, *G. Is for Grafton: The World of Kinsey Milhone* (1997).

—Rosemary Herbert

Gray, Cordelia, resourceful fictional *private investigator created by P. D. *James and introduced in the 1972 novel *An Unsuitable Job for a Woman*. Upon the *suicide death of her mentor and business partner, Bernard "Bernie" G. Pryde of Pryde's Detective Agency, Gray, who "had brought no qualifications or relevant past experience to the partnership and indeed no capital except her slight but tough twenty-two-year-old body, [and] a considerable intelligence," picks up the pieces and limited resources of the detective agency and proves that detective work is a perfectly fitting career for a woman possessed of intelligence, determination, and courage when she pursues the case of Mark Callender, whose father, a famous scientist, hires Gray to discover why Mark committed suicide.

Gray is remarkably self-possessed for her age, a result of her unusual and unsupportive upbringing. Her mother died when Gray was just one hour old, leaving Gray's father, an "itinerant Marxist poet and amateur revolutionary" either to drag their child around with his "comrades" from lodging to lodging or to farm her out to a succession of foster mothers. Gray's irregular education included convent schooling that offered her incompetent instruction in the sciences but an excellent acquaintance with literature. She puts the latter to good use in interpreting clues in *An Unsuitable Job for a Woman*. Gray is also the protagonist in *The Skull Beneath the Skin* (1982), and she is mentioned in *The Black Tower* (1975) when she sends a hand-picked bouquet of flowers to Commander Adam *Dalgliesh, who is recuperating from atypical mononucleosis at the novel's start.

James has said that she identifies with Cordelia and enjoyed working with "a youngish woman: vulnerable, but I think courageous in setting out regardless." James added, "I suppose I *approve* of Cordelia very much."

• Rosemary Herbert, "P. D. James," in *The Fatal Art of Entertainment: Interviews with Mystery Writers* (1994).

—Rosemary Herbert

GREAT DEPRESSION, THE. The Great Depression of the 1930s is depicted directly in much literature, but it features more obliquely in the mystery genre. It is possible to read mysteries from either side of the Atlantic and be unaware of the social conditions that resulted from the crash of the *New York stock market in 1929. Mystery fiction of the 1930s continued to reflect personal tragedies of World War I and treated even *anti-Semitism and *racism more fully than they did the economic disaster, as is the case in Rex *Stout's *Too Many Cooks* (1938).

Popular writers made occasional references to strikes and the National Recovery Act as did Ellery *Queen in "The Lamp of God" (*Detective Story Magazine*, Nov. 1935) and Stout in *Royal Flush* (1934). Robbery and forgery, which may have increased during the era, were also mentioned as in Edgar *Wallace's "The Treasure Hunt" (*Grand Magazine*, Dec. 1924). Generally, however, authors who had begun writing earlier in the Golden Age, during the 1920s, continued to cover the worlds of manor houses, resorts, and clubs. Such props as expensive cars, and *stock characters like butlers or stereotyped characters like sweet young things, provided a fantasy quality that caused some to declare that the reading of mysteries had become pure *escapism. Only occasionally did writers portray a sense of frenzy among stockbrokers, the despair of stockholders, or a glimpse of a stark room in a boarding house.

In *Cause for Alarm* (1938), Eric *Ambler gives a candid, but brief, account of suffering at the tail end of the depression. Professionals such as Ambler's character Nicholas Marlow lose positions due to the "trade recession" and either remain unemployed or take jobs at a fraction of their former salary. During Marlow's extended unemployment, he becomes psychologically depressed, yet he recognizes that the unskilled are the real casualties, for they have little hope of gainful employment. Agatha *Christie's cozy mysteries include little about the depression, and Dorothy L. *Sayers makes only passing reference to the tight job market (*Murder Must Advertise*, 1933).

James M. *Cain and Cornell *Woolrich (also writing as William Irish) best capture the *atmosphere of despair, grubbiness, sleaziness, and uncertainty of America in the 1930s. Much of the action in Cain's *The Postman Always Rings Twice* (1934) occurs in a greasy roadside lunchroom and filling station in California. Frank, a drifter, bums lunch, stays on to pump gas, takes up with the Greek proprietor's wife, falls in love with her, and helps to *murder her husband for his insurance. Frank wants her to drift with him; but, having worked for two years in a hash house in Los Angeles, she sees no allure in this way of life. She knows intuitively that the mountains she dreams about are impossible to attain. Although Cain does not refer to the depression directly, he creates its atmosphere, and his charactes are its *victims.

Woolrich captures the lives of unskilled workers in New York City during the 1930s. Writing as William Irish, he treated the personal tragedies of World War I veterans while vividly depicting the squalid life of a taxi dancer in "The Dancing Detective" (*Black Mask*, Feb. 1938). Ginger, who posesses both moral scruples and sensitivity, works hard at a dance hall, carefully garnering dance stubs for which she receives two cents each. Condemned to a drab, lonely existence in a boarding house, she also suffers the indignities of an autocratic boss and the propositions and pawings of her male customers. In "Murder at the Automat" (*Dime Detective*, Aug. 1937) the author creates a drab, gray atmosphere of *greed and desperation. The poisoned baloney sandwich in the automat is as unappetizing as the victim's derelict walkup. The military lineup of taxi dancers as they walk to the dance floor in the one story and the machine-like atmosphere of the sterile automat in the other become metaphors for the stark entrapment of the depression.

[*See also* Urban Milieu.]

• C. R. Hearn, *The American Dream in the Great Depression* (1977). LeRoy Panek, *Watteau's Shepherds: The Detective Novel in Britain, 1914–1940* (1979). Peter Clarke, *Hope and Glory: Britain 1900–1990* (1996).   —Wilson J. Hoffman

GREAT DETECTIVE, THE. As the literature of ancient Greece and Rome employed the figure of apotheosis, or elevation of a heroic personage to the rank of a god, so the popular genre of crime and mystery writing uses a secularized version of the device to raise the character of the detective to a position of extraordinary distinction. In both cases, the technique expresses cultural values. The ascription of divinity to a champion of war or statecraft becomes possible when it is believed that the realm of gods interrelates with the world of human beings in such an intimate way as to make moral power personal, the sacred and the mundane interchangeable. The creation of a detective possessing singular powers of discernment and the dauntless ability to restore civil order signifies the modern belief that moral ends, at least so far as they pertain to social order, may be achieved through the resources of individual genius and the techniques of disciplined reasoning.

Given the historical circumstances that form the source of crime and mystery writing, it was inevitable that the detective would take a central narrative role, for the complexity and confusion of modern urban society raise a popular desire for an agency that will explain and control events when the older systems of religious and social order seem no longer to do so. For problems of property the agency of explanation became the system of law, and for the problem of crime there had to be an independent force, perhaps a government bureau in the real world, but in the world of imagination, where the profound needs and wishes of a culture take dramatically tangible appearance, disorder was countered by the aggressive mind and engaging personality of the lone detective.

From their beginnings in early detective and police *memoirs, narratives of thief catching and crime solving placed an aura of superiority around the detective. The varied adventures of Eugène François *Vidocq gain what unity and coherence they have from portrayal of Vidocq himself. The tales related by Allan Pinkerton from the archives of his detective agency are distinguished by the consistently superior guile and nerve of his agents and by the background presence of Pinkerton presiding over his agency's exploits like King Arthur at the Round Table.

When detection narratives became deliberately and frankly fictitious, as they did in the inventive short stories of Edgar Allan *Poe, their authors crafted nearly all of their technique for the purpose of enhancing the figure of the detective. For example, readers hear of the cases of the Chevalier C. Auguste *Dupin from the distance of a secondary character's memories. The effect is to engender awe, wonder, and no little mystery about Dupin, since the narrative distance prevents him from becoming commonplace. Moreover, Dupin has no family, no evident occupation, no involvement in pedestrian daytime reality. He is free from any responsibility, except that which he chooses to assume, he is independent in his opinions, stellar in his reasoning. The stories are designed to progress intellectually, complete with brief lectures on reasoning from Dupin, so that there is little to detract from the presentation of his mental superiority—no actions occurring within the story, no competing characters, no background material beyond what is required to set the scene and the circumstances of the crime. Dupin is the only figure of consequence in the world Poe makes, and he is inevitably its greatest inhabitant.

The techniques Poe pioneered for stories of detection became the template and convention for his successors. Arthur Conan *Doyle's Sherlock *Holmes is also a man without domestic connection or responsibility, and his cases, too, are the tales told by a sidekick. What Doyle adds to the formula of the Great Detective is detailed eccentricity: pensiveness, the habit of escaping into music, a possible drug habit, and a disarming way of dominating conversations with axioms about observation and reasoning. Some of these assigned behaviors are not particularly functional to the progress of the narratives, but they are decidedly important to the job of distancing Holmes from the ordinary person and making him, thereby, extraordinary.

Once the literary success of the convention of the Great Detective became evident, it spawned great *ingenuity. There was the blind detective Max *Carrados created by Ernest *Bramah whose extraordinary abilities include super elevation of his remaining senses, the *Thinking Machine whose feats related by Jacques *Futrelle outdid Dupin's. There were the *gentlemen sleuths of the Golden Age, characters such as Lord Peter *Wimsey and Hercule *Poirot whose mannered eccentricities were designed to reinforce the grand accomplishments of their detection and to assure their inclusion in the list of great, because unusual, detectives. Even as the original models receded into the past, the convention retained vitality. Rex *Stout's Nero *Wolfe, assisted by Archie *Goodwin, a character somewhat hardboiled, displayed the unusual ability to solve crimes throughout the city from the comfort of his armchair where he settled his hugely obese body, all the while conducting the opinionated conversation that by now has become requisite for any Great Detective.

The advent of hard-boiled detectives such as Dashiell *Hammett's Sam *Spade and Continental *Op or Raymond *Chandler's Philip *Marlowe altered but did not erase the Great Detective. Kinship with predecessors from the Golden Age and earlier can be seen in the isolated status of hard-boiled sleuths. They, too, are sleuths as *loners; consequently, their narratives can center entirely on their practice of detection. They are not thinking machines or even especially men of reason, needing instead to use more active means of solving crimes. Still, their authors assign them traits suggesting singularity—sometimes a mood of disappointment, at other times unusual knowledge of seamy life, and always a peculiarly personal tone in their worldly wise voices. The world the hard-boiled detective inhabits seems to show little possibility for any sort of greatness, but, as Chandler argued in his famous essay "The Simple Art of Murder" (*Atlantic Monthly*, Dec. 1944), the detective in a city of mean streets "is not himself mean. . . . He is the hero, he is everything." In other words, the detective embodies an improvisational morality uncharacteristic of most other people. He is great. Although the hard-boiled mannerisms seem to be spent, and authors increasingly normalize their protagonists as women and men beset by fear and loneliness that earlier writers never would have assigned their characters, the archetype of the Great Detective continues to resonate. The detectives in the fiction of Tony *Hillerman, Sue *Grafton, or Robert B. *Parker are drawn with traits more common than extraordinary, except for the mystique that inspires their careers. They are detectives, after all, trying to put the world right.

[See also Conventions of the Genre; Eccentrics; Formula: Character; Gentleman Sleuth; Reasoning, Types of; Superman Sleuth.]

• Howard Haycraft, *Murder for Pleasure: The Life and Times of the Detective Story* (1941). Otto Penzler, ed. *The Great Detectives* (1978). William Roehlmann, *Saint with a Gun: The Unlawful American Private Eye* (1974).

—John M. Reilly

GREAT OUTDOORS. When Captain Arthur Barlowe first gazed upon the coastline of Virginia in 1584, he found a "delicate garden abounding with all kinds of odoriferous flowers." He watched the natives catch fish and thought them "most gentle, loving and faithfull, voide of all guile and treason." In 1620 William Bradford viewed the Cape Cod landscape from the anchored *Mayflower* and saw a "hideous and desolate wilderness, full of wild beasts and wild men."

These two contradictory visions of the great outdoors and its native inhabitants have informed crime and mystery fiction from the beginning. The natural world offers rich opportunities to establish mood. Not surprisingly, images of nature's malevolence dominate early works. Thus the "dark and stormy night" soon became a cliche. Edgar Allan *Poe's landscapes are typically dreary and hostile. Arthur Conan *Doyle expresses a similar attitude in *The Hound of the Baskervilles* (1902), wherein the "huge expanse of the moor . . . mottled with gnarled and craggy cairns and tors . . . that desolate plain" portends evil and danger.

Nature's forces—weather, climate, topography—participate actively in mystery *plots. The ebb and flow of the tide on a barren beach, for example, is a key factor in Dorothy L. *Sayers's *Have His Carcase* (1932). The migration of a rare gyrfalcon to the Montana mountains motivates the storyline in Judith Van Gieson's *Raptor* (1990), while Ted Wood's Reid Bennett investigates a suspected bear mauling in the Canadian barrens in *Fool's Gold* (1986).

The men and women who live harmoniously in the great outdoors bring their understanding of the natural world to their mystery solving. Tony *Hillerman's Lieutenant Joe Leaphorn (*The Blessing Way*, 1970) uses his Navajo wisdom to solve crimes that baffle urban sleuths. Dana Stabenow's Aleut heroine Kate Shugak (*A Cold Day for Murder*, 1992) treks through the frozen Arctic by sleddog in search of a missing park ranger.

Among British writers in the genre, John *Buchan is arguably the premier exponent of the great outdoors. Buchan contrasts the elemental danger of the natural world with the deceit and suspicion that breeds in the civilized indoors. Utterly at home in the wild, his heroes rely on their uncanny ability to blend into—and to live off—the land while eluding a pursuer or stalking a quarry, as do Richard Hannay in the Scottish highlands in *The Thirty-nine Steps* (1915) and *The Three Hostages* (1924) and David Crawfurd on the South African veld in *Prester John* (1910; *The Great Diamond Pipe*).

Many mystery protagonists move easily between civilization and the great outdoors. Cyril *Hare's Inspector John Mallett investigates a *murder at a pastoral English trout-fishing club in *Death Is No Sportsman* (1938), and Philip Craig's Jeff Jackson in *A Beautiful Place to Die* (1989) finds *clues while surfcasting for bluefish off the beach at Martha's Vineyard. John D. *MacDonald was among the first American writers to move hard-boiled crime fiction off the city's mean streets. His Travis *McGee tracks *villains from *The Busted Flush*, his houseboat moored in Fort Lauderdale, into the inland swamps and uninhabited coastal islands of Florida. Rick Boyer's Boston-based oral surgeon Charlie (Doc) Adams is drawn into a showdown in the trackless mountains of western North Carolina in *The Daisy Ducks* (1986).

Crimes against the natural world provide contemporary mystery writers with new forms of evil to investigate. The draining of the Everglades and the potential destruction of its ecosystem motivates Carl Hiaasen's oddball character Skink in *Tourist Season* (1986), while Jane Langton's *God in Concord* (1992) examines the ramifications of commercial development in the pristine woodlands surrounding Thoreau's Walden Pond.

These mystery writers, and many others, understand that amoral nature holds up a mirror to humanity. Her ruthless but lawful eat-and-be-eaten code is "hideous" only to those villains who would violate it.

[*See also* Rural Milieu; Settings, Geographical.]

• William Bradford, *Of Plymouth Plantation* (1857). Leo Marx, *The Machine in the Garden* (1964).

—William G. Tapply

GREED, or an excessive desire for wealth, appears early in the mystery genre and continues as a powerful motive for crime. Greed is implicit in Edgar Allan *Poe's "The Gold Bug" (*Philadelphia Dollar Newspaper*, 21 June, 1843), where it appears in the pure form of desiring money and wealth for its own sake. Greed leads to *murder in Wilkie *Collins's *The Woman in White* (1860) and to the theft of jewelry in *The Moonstone* (1868). Arthur Conan *Doyle often used greed as a theme in his Sherlock *Holmes stories. In *The Hound of the Baskervilles* (1902), a distant member of the family uses a local legend to try to unseat the rightful heir to the estate. G. K. *Chesterton explores the same theme in "The Purple Wig" (*The Complete Father Brown*, 1982).

Greed was a prominent theme in the *cozy mysteries of the 1920s and 1930s. Agatha *Christie believed that her stories were the modern equivalent of medieval morality tales, and explored the effect of greed on characters in several stories. In *Hercule Poirot's Christmas* (1939; *Murder for Christmas*; *A Holiday for Murder*), greed triggers the murder of a family head who made his fortune in South African diamonds. In Cornell Woolrich's "Murder at the Automat" (*Dime Detective*, Aug. 1937) a psychopathic wife enlists the aid of her greedy paramour to murder her miserly husband with a cyanide-laced baloney sandwich planted an automat machine. Her partner shows no remorse.

In the cozy novels, greed was individualized and localized. It frequently motivated a family member to commit a crime, usually within the confines of the family estate, and the morally defective perpetrator was almost always caught and punished. This pattern changed in the 1930s with the appearance of the hard-boiled novel. Sex, immorality, and *violence became intertwined with greed; the individual's desire for power and fame came to be seen as manifestations of greed. Writers explored these forms of greed in stories about corporations and their corruption, depicting men and women corrupted by the desire for wealth.

James M. *Cain, an early hard-boiled writer, portrayed men and women desperate to escape their lives in his classic novels *The Postman Always Rings Twice* (1934) and *Double Indemnity* (1943). In Cain's hands, greed now came to symbolize deeper character flaws. The broadening understanding of greed is especially evident in mystery novels written since World War II and reflects the changing role of the individual in society as well as the rise of a corporate and consumer society. In *Passenger to Frankfurt* (1970), Christie speculates about the threat posed to society by charismatic, irresponsible demagogues lusting for power. Her story is a fantasy, but not an impossible one. Robert *Barnard in *A Hovering of Vultures* (1993) wrestles with fanaticism and manias leading to greed, and John D. *MacDonald in *Free*

Fall in Crimson (1981) views the "artistic imperative" of Kesner, an inept moviemaker, as greed. Fame is his aim, and he will do anything, including videotaping rape scenes, to achieve it.

In *One More Sunday* (1984), MacDonald wrote a scathing novel about "psychic epidemics"—television evangelists and religious right-wingers whose greed for power, money, and sex corrupts them and leads to murder. The novel's hero is a simple country preacher who rejects the lures of corporate *religion. Simon Brett, in *Mrs. Pargeter's Pound of Flesh* (1992) explores greed in the cosmetic industry. Sue Fisher, goddess of consumerism, boasts that she uses no animals in testing her products, hiding the fact that, instead, humans are used and that they are often disfigured and sometimes even killed by these products. The power behind her is a third-rate chemist who is striving to develop a formula to turn fat people into thin ones—a formula which, if it works, will make him famous and rich. In the meantime, at least one person has died for his so-called scientific research.

In Jonathan Gash's novels, his characters, though lovable, are unabashedly greedy, and the antique business, which is riddled with scams, is a metaphor for human behavior that operates on "ruthless greed." In *Jade Woman* (1989), his amoral sleuth Lovejoy argues that we are all greedy and fakes but recognize such qualities only in other people. "Greed," Lovejoy says, "is the only appetite that never fails—all others weaken with satiation."

Greed has been used extensively as a motif in mystery novels since their inception. Persons who commit socially unacceptable acts motivated by greed are discovered and punished by society, sometimes ingeniously by writers such as Brett and Cain. Redemption is rarely possible. Yet, in the tradition of morality tales, there is always hope. In M. C. Beaton's *Death of an Outsider* (1988), Ross curbs his undue ambition and greed and is redeemed.

[*See also* Advertising Milieu; Art and Antiques Milieu; Banking and Financial Milieu.]

• LeRoy Panek, *Watteau's Shepherds: The Detective Novel in Britain, 1914–1940* (1979). Audrey Peterson, *Victorian Masters of Mystery from Wilkie Collins to Conan Doyle* (1984).

—Wilson J. Hoffman

GREEN, ANNA KATHARINE (1846–1935), American author, frequently denominated as the "mother of the detective novel." Green was born in Brooklyn Heights, *New York, to a family that traced colonial New England forebears on both sides. She lived in Brooklyn and Manhattan in her early years, married Charles Rohlfs in 1884, and moved to Buffalo, New York, in 1887. Having lost her mother at age two, Green was highly influenced by her father, James Wilson Green, a lawyer prominent in Republican party politics in New York City. She was the only one of his four children sent to college, gaining a B. A. at Ripley Female Seminary in Vermont in 1866 or 1867. Hoping for recognition as a poet, she submitted work to Ralph Waldo Emerson for his criticism; in a carefully worded response dated 30 June 1868, he advised her to write if she felt the desire, but not to try to make a profession of poetry. She put poetry aside and worked for five years on a "criminal romance," producing her landmark novel, *The Leavenworth Case: A Lawyer's Story* (1878), which remained a bestseller for decades and established the type.

Green's novel emphasized rational detection, and developed the early series detective New York City police officer Ebenezer Gryce, nine years before Sherlock *Holmes's appearance in fiction. Such now familiar conventions as the body in the library, the wealthy man about to change his will, the locked room, the use of ballistics evidence, a coroner's inquest, a sketch of the scene of the crime, and a partially burned letter all appeared in this novel. A. E. Murch, in her ground-breaking study *The Development of the Detective Novel* (1958), describes Green as virtually the creator of the *detective novel. Green was influenced by Émile *Gaboriau's *roman policier*, with its typically French social and legal procedures, but her novels are distinctively American, many of them set in New York City in the elegant mansions of lower Fifth Avenue. *The Leavenworth Case* attracted the attention of Wilkie *Collins, who wrote commenting on her fertility of invention and depiction of strong women.

Nineteen years and eighteen books later, Green created a *spinster sleuth, a forerunner of Agatha *Christie's Miss Jane *Marple, in Miss Amelia Butterworth (*That Affair Next Door*, 1897). (Christie credits her influence, mentioning Green specifically in her *Autobiography*.) Green also created a young debutante sleuth, Violet Strange. Although Green wrote fiction in order to gain recognition for her poetry, she was spurred by the success of her first novel to go on writing detective fiction: Widely anthologized, her works ran in serial form in newspapers and magazines such as *The Century*, *Lippincott's*, *Frank Leslie's Illustrated Newspaper*, *The New York Ledger*, and later, *The Ladies' Home Journal*. Her last book, *The Step on the Stair* (1924), completed a lifework of thirty-six detective novels, four collections of short stories, one volume of poetry (*The Defense of the Bride*, 1882), and one verse drama (*Risifi's Daughter*, 1887). None of her later works equalled the success of her first book, which continued to sell in many different versions for forty years; still she reigned as a grande dame of detective fiction. Contemporary reviewers praised her ingenious and intricate plotting as surprising from a female writer; some suggested the author might be a male using a pseudonym. Green's melodramatic style won some scornful reviews, but British prime minister Stanley Baldwin, speaking in London in 1928, praised *The Leavenworth Case* as "one of the best detective stories ever written," and the book was used at Yale Law School to demonstrate the weaknesses of circumstantial evidence.

[*See also* Females and Feminists; History of Crime and Mystery Writing: Formation of the Genre (1841–1888); Poets as Crime Writers.]

• Barbara Welter, "Murder Most Genteel: The Mystery Novels of Anna Katharine Green," in *Dimity Convictions: The American Woman in the Nineteenth Century* (1976). Michele Slung, introduction to *The Leavenworth Case* (1981). Joan Warthling Roberts, "Before 'Sherlock Holmes' There Was Anna Katharine Green," *MS* 13, no. 10 (Apr. 1985). Patricia

D. Maida, *Mother of Detective Fiction: The Life and Works of Anna Katharine Green* (1989). Joan Warthling Roberts, "Amelia Butterworth: The Spinster Detective," in *Feminism in Women's Detective Fiction*, ed. Glenwood Irons (1995).

—Joan Warthling Roberts

GREENE, GRAHAM (1904–91), British author, a major figure of twentieth-century letters of biography, plays and screenplays, essays, and criticism, as well as *thrillers. Greene was often named as a Nobel Prize candidate, though he never won the award. As for his forays into crime writing and *spy fiction, he himself dismissed these most popular of his works as "entertainments." These thrillers include *Stamboul Train* (1932; *Orient Express*) *Brighton Rock* (1938), *The Confidential Agent* (1939), and *The Ministry of Fear* (1943), among others. He also wrote or co-wrote the film adaptations of these books.

The author of twenty-four novels over a sixty-year career, Greene created memorable male characters possessed of wavering morals, trying to make a stand in an equally unsteady world. This is true of the teen killer in *Brighton Rock* (1938). In addition, the unnamed Mexican priest in *The Power and the Glory* (1940; *The Labyrinthine Ways*) is an alcoholic, or "whiskey priest," and has fathered a child. He is on the run from the dogged *pursuit of an army lieutenant because, in a society where the church is persecuted by a military government, priests are being executed. This priest is no righteous Jean Valjean, though: He is an immoral man who must live by his wits, placing others in mortal danger by his actions. If he makes a moral stand, it will be at the expense of his own life. In *The Third Man* (1950), Rollo Martins name Holly in the 1949 film must tiptoe through the political and moral debris of post–World War II Vienna as well as its physical rubble. At each step, Martins's beliefs about his closest boyhood friend, Harry Lime, increasingly crack like one of the city's war-ravaged buildings.

The Catholic Church condemned *The Power and the Glory* for its portrayal of the unorthodox priest. Other Greene novels received official condemnation from national governments. In the United States, *The Quiet American* (1955) and *The Comedians* (1966) were read as attacks on America's foreign policy in Vietnam and Haiti, respectively. Yet, while Greene may have had strong liberal opinions about church and government, his topic was really the human soul.

Greene was born in Berkhamsted, Hertfordshire, England. His father was headmaster of Berkhamsted School, which Greene attended preparatory to Balliol College, *Oxford. His childhood was unhappy: He suffered a nervous breakdown at Berkhamsted and was treated by a psychiatrist. At Oxford, Greene joined the Communist Party. In 1927, at age twenty-two and just out of Oxford, he converted to Catholicism in order to marry the Catholic Vivien Dayrell-Browning. Years later, he would resist the term "Catholic writer," but religion was central to many of his books, as well as those of his contemporaries. Following Oxford, he worked at the *Times* of London as a copy editor, eventually leaving to become a film critic for several newspapers and journals, including

the *Spectator*. He supported his family in that role while writing his earlier novels.

During World War II, he was an intelligence officer with the Foreign Office. He was sent to West Africa in 1942. He traveled widely during and after the war, his globetrotting lasting as long as he was physically able. Many of his destinations became locales for his stories.

Greene wrote two autobiographies: *A Sort of Life* (1971) and *Ways of Escape*. (1980). Divorced, he died in Vevey, Switzerland, at the age of eighty-six.

[*See also* Antihero; Heroism; Males and the Male Image; Religion.]

• Norman Sherry, *The Life of Graham Greene*, 2 vols. (1989, 1995). Michael Shelden, *Graham Greene: The Enemy Within* (1994). —Dana Bisbee

"GREY SEAL, THE." *See* Adventurer and Adventuress.

GUILT. The establishment of, or culpability for, an offense or crime is a major concern of writers and readers of crime and mystery fiction. W. H. Auden argued that the interest in detective fiction lies in "the dialectic of innocence and guilt." Julian *Symons said that readers use crime fiction to exorcise guilt through ritual and symbolic sacrifice of the murderer, who is a "permanent scapegoat."

In a traditional detective story, the guilt of the culprit is finally unequivocal and often limited to a determination of the fact of who is guilty of a crime. But sometimes guilt or remorse drives the perpetrator of a crime to perform an act of conscience. This is the case in Edgar Allan *Poe's "Thou Art The Man" (*Godey's Lady's Book*, Nov. 1844), the prototype for the *"least likely suspect" murder mystery. Mr. Pennifeather is convicted of the *murder of his uncle and sentenced to death, but the narrator discovers that the real killer is Charley Goodfellow. Shocked by an accusation—apparently from his dead *victim— Goodfellow provides an immediate, detailed confession, and the "guilty wretch" is then obliging enough to drop dead. The narrator is vindicated in his reliance upon the killer's conscience to reveal the truth, and Pennifeather, having inherited a fortune, turns over a new leaf.

It was inevitable that as soon as conventions were established in the genre, writers would tinker with them. Arthur Conan *Doyle made it clear that Sherlock *Holmes was prepared, on occasion, to commute a felony in order to save a soul, as in "The Blue Carbuncle" first published in the *Strand in 1892. Agatha *Christie sometimes challenged comfortable assumptions regarding guilt. In *Murder on the Orient Express* (1934; *Murder in the Calais Coach*), Hercule *Poirot establishes that *all* the *suspects are guilty. In *Ten Little Niggers* (1939; *And Then There Were None*), a judge gathers together a group of people who, although responsible for the deaths of others, have escaped the law, and arranges for them to receive *justice. This theme is also used in Saho Sasazawa's "An Invitation from the Sea" (*Ellery Queen's Japanese Golden Dozen*, 1978). In other books Christie recognizes the limitations of the law in more ortho-dox fashion, as in *Five Little Pigs* (1943; *Murder in Retrospect*) and *Mrs. McGinty's Dead* (1952; *Blood Will Tell*), where innocent people have been convicted of murder.

Among Christie's American contemporaries, Dashiell *Hammett and Raymond *Chandler demon-strated that when police are corrupt, the distinction between guilt and innocence becomes blurred and sometimes impossible to establish. Later, Patricia *Highsmith explored issues of moral responsibility for crime. Her books about the appealing but amoral Tom Ripley portray the extremes of action open to a person who does not suffer from a sense of guilt.

Today, on both sides of the Atlantic, major practi-tioners of both the traditional and modern schools of crime writing reveal in their work an acute awareness of the ambiguities of guilt. The title of Scott Turow's *Presumed Innocent* (1987), for example, is ironic. The novel opens with prosecutor Rusty Sabich making an accusation of guilt and closes with his being asked to "give a guilty conscience a chance."

Few mystery novelists have addressed questions of personal guilt as consciously as P. D. *James, who has argued that it is the writer's attitude toward guilt that "distinguishes the true crime novel from mere entertainment." James is a very different writer from Highsmith, but is similarly interested in free will and its limits. In *Original Sin* (1994), her central theme is reinforced by the history of the building in which much of the action takes place; it emerges that Fran-cis Peverell, who built Innocent House in the nine-teenth century, became obsessed with the place, and killed his wife because of it. The principal culprit claims to seek justice, but is in reality trying to purge his own sense of guilt. In a final bitter irony he learns that all he has achieved is to murder the innocent.

[*See also* Corruption.]

• W. H. Auden, "The Guilty Vicarage," *Harpers Magazine* (May 1948). David Lehman, *The Perfect Murder: A Study in Detection* (1989). Tony Hilfer, *The Crime Novel: A Deviant Genre* (1990). Julian Symons, *Bloody Murder: From the Detec-tive Story to the Crime Novel*, 3rd rev. ed. (1992). Rosemary Herbert, "P. D. James," in *The Fatal Art of Entertainment: In-terviews with Mystery Writers* (1994).

—Martin Edwards

GUMSHOE. *See* Hard-Boiled Sleuth; Private Eye.

HAD-I-BUT-KNOWN, a term generally applied to a first-person detective story narrated (usually) by a woman who learns from experience that things are not always what they seem. Hence, the notion—whether spelled out or not—of "had I but known" figures in the narrative in many places, letting the reader know that the obvious solution, or the solution that the narrator has been favoring, is not the correct one. The Had-I-But-Known, or HIBK, often has Gothic elements, including a high level of *suspense, a cast of *menacing characters, and a romantic interest. In some of these novels the narrator is not only narrating a mystery, she is telling us a story of how she came to wisdom through the experience of discovering a *murder and its solution.

Typically, the HIBK is narrated by a young, naive woman who in the course of the story finds not only the solution to the mystery but also true love. Although the *plot centers on her amateur efforts at puzzling out mysterious circumstances and facing threatening situations, this narrator is not the official *sleuth. It could be said that the first HIBK is Charlotte Brontë's *Jane Eyre* (1847), in which Jane comes to the Rochester home innocent but sees any number of odd incidents that cannot be explained until her proposed wedding day, when the mystery of Bertha Rochester is explained. In many ways, *Jane Eyre* is an excellent prototype for this kind of novel, for although the heroine is young and inexperienced, she is also observant and rational and has a strong sense of herself and her moral values. Another HIBK is Wilkie *Collins's *The Woman in White* (1860). In both of these novels *coincidence plays a large role in helping the characters to peel away layers of deception until the central secret is revealed.

Twentieth-century HIBK heroines tend to be less staunch and self-confident than Eyre. They may be young and unmarried, although their youth is relative. While these women are not cowardly in the physical sense, naiveté and a willingness to be carried along by circumstance makes them easy prey to the *villain. Invariably they are rescued by a hero-detective figure, as in Mignon G. *Eberhart's Nurse Sarah Keate series or in Leslie Ford's Grace Latham series. Often, the detective-hero is only introduced to the heroine at the beginning of the book, and the romance that sometimes develops between these two characters is usually postponed by their *suspicion that the other has committed the crime.

The social *milieu of these novels is important. The powerful characters tend to be of high socioeconomic class; the *setting is often a large country house, such as Manderley in Daphne *du Maurier's *Rebecca* (1938). Usually, money is a factor in the crime committed; often the family has fallen upon hard times, like that in Mary Roberts *Rinehart's *Episode of the Wandering Knife* (1950; *Wandering Knife*). Much of the misunderstanding between the two major characters is caused by assumed differences in social status. Any character who is a stranger to the environment—often the narrator—is immediately assumed to be of lower socioeconomic class than the rest of the major characters. The objectivity that results from this assumed difference in social standing frequently enables the heroine narrator to solve the mystery, but this same objectivity is also perceived as a major obstacle to any romance.

Family conflict with roots in secrets from the past is a mainstay of the HIBK. Sometimes present-day conflict occurs within a *marriage, which is disrupted by an old secret unknown to one of the partners. Usually the wife assumes that she is unworthy of her husband's love, as the second Mrs. de Winter assumes in *Rebecca*. These conflicts are caused by failure of communication between spouses or by local society's views of a supposedly unequal marriage. Lack of self-confidence often causes the heroine to resist asking direct questions, especially of the male love interest.

Ghosts may seem to appear in the HIBK, but they are usually laid to rest by the end of the novel. However, for a significant part of some of these novels, the supernatural is seriously considered as an explanation for the apparently unexplainable. Many times, the country houses in which these novels are set have developed a reputation for being haunted, but the solution reveals that the inhabitants are being haunted only by their own painful memories and poor choices.

[See also Females and Feminists; Gothic Novel.]

• Ann B. Tracy, "Gothic, Had-I-But-Known, Damsel-in-Distress: Stalking the Elusive Distinction," in *Murderess Ink: The Better Half of the Mystery*, ed. Dilys Winn (1979): 14–17. Patricia Craig and Mary Cadogan, *The Lady Investigates: Women Detectives and Spies in Fiction* (1981).

—Mary P. Freier

HALLOWEEN. *See* Holiday Mysteries.

Hammer, Mike. The hard-boiled detective Mike Hammer appears in twelve of the twenty-one works Mickey *Spillane produced between 1947 and 1988, but his first appearance is his most notorious. At the climax of I, the Jury (1947), he shoots his naked fiancée in the abdomen when he discovers that she has brutally murdered his old army buddy and five others. This first novel established the fevered sexuality and Manichaean perspective of Hammer's world, one that both captured and created the emotional tenor of Cold War America.

Although his *pursuit of vigilante *justice never again scales such luridly sexual heights, Hammer continues to mete out extreme punishment to the guilty. Showing a preference for smashing faces, fingers, and kneecaps over reasoned contemplation, he solves cases by a literal process of elimination: The last to remain alive is the culprit. An untrammelled id who repeatedly explodes in messianic rage—against effete intellectuals and homosexuals, against legal niceties and social conventions that impede his quest for vengeance, against oppression of the "little guy" by such organizations as the Mafia and the Communist Party—he has been little changed by his forty years of violent activity. When Hammer reappears in The Girl Hunters (1962) after a decade's absence, he is a drunken wreck consumed with *guilt for sending his secretary Velda to what he mistakenly believes to have been her death, but by the novel's end he has mended.

Spillane intended his sketchy physical descriptions of Hammer—as a large and emphatically unattractive man—to allow readers to imagine themselves in the hero's shoes. Indeed, Hammer is a fantasy of irresistible masculine potency. Women often rip their clothes open in his presence, proffering an invitation he accepts with gleeful sadism that, readers are assured, they find exciting. Despite the sexual banter between Hammer and the voluptuous Velda, however, she is meant to preserve her virginity until the day he consents to marry her. The pair finally consummate their love in The Snake (1964), but Velda does not get her wedding ring.

[See also Hard-boiled Sleuth; Sex and Sexuality; Violence.]

• Christopher La Farge, "Mickey Spillane and His Bloody Hammer," Saturday Review (6 Nov. 1954): 11–12, 54–59. J. Kenneth van Dover, Murder in the Millions: Erle Stanley Gardner, Mickey Spillane, Ian Fleming (1984).

—Jesse Berrett

HAMMETT, DASHIELL (1894–1961), American author whose writing career lasted no more than a decade, but who in that short span of time created a specifically American kind of crime story, loosely called the tough-guy or hard-boiled tale, and made it respectable. Hammett had the hard and varied youth endured by many American writers, working on the railroad, then as a Pinkerton operative whose duties included occasional strike-breaking, then enlisting in the Army during World War I. He was discharged as tubercular and given a small pension, married his hospital nurse, had two children, and suffered poverty before making some money by writing short stories for the *pulp magazines that became immensely popular in the U.S. during the 1920s.

As a writer, Hammett began by using and romanticizing his Pinkerton experience. The stories were told in the first person by a short, fat detective called the *Continental Op. The Op had few opinions about anything except his work, which he carried out with ruthless efficiency. Many of the stories were extremely violent, and they were written in a style deliberately bare, stripped of adjectival color. The action is colorful, the writing plain. The style resembles that of early Ernest Hemingway, although any direct influence of either writer on the other is very unlikely.

Hammett wrote mostly for *Black Mask, the best of the pulps, and quickly became their most popular writer. He also learned his craft. His first novel, Red Harvest (1929), is sophisticated and stylized in a way that would have been beyond Hammett's capacities a year or two earlier. There are two dozen deaths in the book, yet among the gunplay and gang warfare are characters vividly realized, including Hammett's first convincing woman. This is Dinah Brand, called a deluxe hustler and a soiled dove, who has "the face of a girl of twenty-five already showing signs of wear," is a tremendous drinker—and one of the most sexually attractive women in crime literature.

Hammett called The Dain Curse, published in the same year, a silly book, and it is easy to agree with him. In it he moved away from things he knew about—gunmen, shysters, and local politicos—to deal with family curses and religious cults. But The Maltese Falcon (1930) made Hammett famous, and The Glass Key (1931) consolidated the fame. In them the Continental Op has been replaced by the dubiously honest but physically attractive Sam *Spade and Ned Beaumont, respectively. *Violence is greatly reduced, and almost all of it takes place offstage. The distinctive Hammett style has now been perfected. Characterization is achieved in part through a scrupulous, often detailed account of physical appearance (as of Gutman in the Falcon), in part through the revelations of dialogue. The Maltese Falcon is a *thriller, The Glass Key offers the *puzzle of who killed Taylor Henry, but both transcend their *plot origins. The first poses particular questions about a detective's ethics and, by extension, about morality in general, the second is about the power and limits of loyalty. Both were recognized as remarkable novels, especially by American critics. Hammett was a prophet honored in his own country.

His last novel, The Thin Man (1934), gave a sanitized view of his relationship with Lillian Hellman, and may also be seen as an account of a decadent society viewed from the inside. Hammett had been taken up by Hollywood, and was living in the way which his friend Nunnally Johnson said made sense only if "he had no expectation of being alive much beyond Thursday."

He had also become actively involved with left-wing political causes. In World War II he enlisted in the army (with difficulty because of his health); spent three years mostly in Alaska, where he founded and edited a camp newspaper; and was known to the youngsters as "Pop." In 1951, called to give evidence in a case involving Communists who had jumped bail, he refused to answer questions by pleading the

Fifth Amendment, and was sentenced to six months in prison. When he came out it was to find the three radio shows based on his characters taken off the air, his books proscribed and removed from libraries, and all his sources of income removed. He survived for another ten years, but wrote only a Hemingwayesque fragment of a novel called *Tulip*.

The life may be seen as tragic, although Hammett would have deprecated such sentiment. Nor did he think highly of his writing, conceding only in an interview that *The Glass Key* was "not so bad." His standards were high, and often he did not live up to them: but he set his stamp permanently on American crime fiction, and his two finest books provide a benchmark few have reached.

[*See also* Hard-boiled Fiction; Hard-boiled Sleuth; Loyalty and Betrayal; Private Eye.]

• Diane Johnson, *Dashiell Hammett: A Life* (1983). Richard Layman, *Shadow Man: The Life of Dashiell Hammett* (1981). William F. Nolan, *Hammett: A Life at the Edge* (1983). Julian Symons, *Dashiell Hammett* (1985). Christopher Metress, ed., *The Critical Response to Dashiell Hammett* (1994).

—Julian Symons

Hanaud, Inspector. A. E. W. *Mason's Inspector Hanaud of the Paris *Sûreté appeared in five novels and three short stories between 1910 and 1946, without showing much development. Writing twenty years after introducing his creation, Mason stated the four specifications he had laid down for his detective: He should be a professional; he should be as physically unlike Sherlock *Holmes as possible; he should be a friendly soul; and he should be willing to act on his intuition. Accordingly, Hanaud is the first important professional policeman after Charles *Dickens's Inspector Bucket, Wilkie *Collins's Sergeant *Cuff, and Émile Gaboriau's *Monsieur Lecoq. He is a big bear of a man, rumpled and jowly, looking like a prosperous comedian. His geniality is disarming, and he uses it to entrap his adversaries. Moreover, his insistence that the facts be viewed with "imagination on a leash" puts him solidly in the line of descent from the Chevalier C. Auguste *Dupin's Bi-Part Soul. Mason's own values are distinctly British and Edwardian, and Hanaud is clearly the projection of these; his main Gallic attribute is his demotic English, more witticism than malapropism, as when he calls Paris one's "spirituous home," or refers to the ^ACID as the QED. With his finicky, wine-fancying widower friend Julius Ricardo, he is one-half of one of the more pleasing Holmes-Watson combinations in the genre.

[*See also* Police Detective; Visitors Abroad.]

—Barrie Hayne

HANDICAPPED SLEUTH. *See* Disability, Sleuth with a.

HANSEN, JOSEPH (b. 1923), American crime writer, self-consciously concerned with "gay" issues. Born in Aberdeen, South Dakota, and educated there and in Minneapolis, Minnesota, and Pasadena, California, Hansen settled in California. Like the feminist novelists Barbara Wilson, Eve Zaremba, and Mary

Wings, Hansen belongs to that group of contemporary writers eager to exploit the *crime novel to investigate pressing social issues, reappraising questions of *gender and sexuality arising from more traditional detective fiction. Just as the female writers challenge the belittling representations of women in hard-boiled crime writing, so Hansen takes issue with what he sees as the implicit homophobia of Raymond *Chandler. His recurrent central figure is the middle-aged *private eye and insurance investigator Dave *Brandstetter, unapologetically homosexual. From the excellent first novel, *Fadeout* (1970), onward, the interaction of the investigator's troubled private life and the mysteries in which he becomes embroiled is compellingly and sensitively handled. In that novel, Brandstetter's lover dies; as the central character mourns his loss, he becomes involved in a *murder case. *Fadeout* was well-received, and started Hansen on his extensive series of Brandsetter adventures, principally set in southern California.

In the tradition of Ross *Macdonald and Armistead Maupin, Hansen is a witty and shrewd chronicler of the fads and eccentricities of that life. Indeed at times his eagerness to indulge in social commentary distracts from the momentum of the *plot, and the narratives of some later books, such as *Gravedigger* (1982) and *Nightwork* (1984), seem implausible. However, when Hansen is fully engaged with challenging issues, he is a vivid and distinctive writer within the Chandler tradition. *Death Claims* (1973) and *Early Graves* (1987) are adjudged to be the best novels in the Brandsetter series. The latter proves that crime writing can deal effectively with the issue of AIDS. Hansen also writes fiction outside the private eye genre, under his own name and as James Colton and as Rose Brock, but this work has not yet attracted the attention accorded his Brandstetter mysteries.

[*See also* Gay Characters and Perspectives; Males and the Male Image; Sex and Sexuality.]

—Ian Bell

HARD-BOILED DICK. *See* Hard-Boiled Sleuth; Private Eye; Williams, Race.

HARD-BOILED FICTION. Now popular worldwide, the hard-boiled school of crime writing originated in America during the 1920s, though it has ancestry in James Fenimore Cooper's *pathfinder fiction and in the straight-shooting cowboy of nineteenth-century *dime novels. Accustomed to *violence—indeed, often relishing it—the *hard-boiled sleuth began as a loner, unaffiliated with the police or government and lacking a woman friend, pitting himself against villains of gigantic stature in a corrupt and nihilistic world. A gun for hire, he worked on the edge of the law and beyond it, relying on his fists and wits and adopting a personal code of ethics to justify his actions.

Until the last quarter of the twentieth century, hard-boiled fiction was almost exclusively the domain of male authors and their male *private eyes. The milieu was the underside of the city. Its mean streets reflected the cynicism of *Prohibition, the disillusionment following World War I, and, later, the grimness of America during the *Great Depression. His world was pervaded by *greed, *corruption, and alienation in the face of ill-defined but massive economic and social threats. Nonetheless, the *private eye often maintained a personal, albeit bruised, faith in values he felt ought be upheld in a fallen world: loyalty to his code and the few who shared it, self-honesty, unsentimental charity toward the weak and defenseless, pride in doing a hard job well, and a sardonic belief that human nature will ultimately reveal itself in the worst light. In many ways, these values paralleled the disillusioned romanticism of F. Scott Fitzgerald's *The Great Gatsby* (1925).

Appearing in the *Black Mask*, Carroll John *Daly introduced an unnamed tough guy in 1922, but the first hard-boiled private eye was his "Three-Gun" Terry (May 1923). Terry was quickly superceded by Daly's far more popular Race *Williams (June 1923) who was a prototype for Sam *Spade, Michael *Shayne, Mike *Hammer, and many others. Violent, even brutal, Williams brought down criminal kingpins. Minimal *plots focused on *pursuit and vengeance rather than on *puzzle or multiple storylines. Characters were uncomplex, *villains driven by greed and lust for power, Williams by clear evidence of their wrongdoing. Williams's moral codes were unpolished and pragmatic: "I ain't afraid of nothing providing there's enough jack in it." Although the prose style of the first-person narratives is forced and Daly's us of *setting lacks complexity, the Williams yarns were widely popular for their action and anti-idealism.

A few months after Williams's debut. Dashiell *Hammett's *Continental Op appeared in *Black Mask*. Fat, nameless, and middle-aged, the Op was intended as a realistic contrast to the British puzzle mysteries then prevalent. But he, along with Hammett's later Sam Spade, also contrasted with the exaggerations of Race Williams to establish a polarity that persists in the hard-boiled genre: the romance of violence versus the reality of crime. The first, emphasizing strident action and bizarre characters, moves toward unreality, while the second, not eschewing violence, stresses real figures, identifiable settings, and the crime found in police reports. Hammett's best style is terse, quick moving, and factual, making use of understatement to hint at the complexities of the Op or Spade, and of sharp wisecracks to deflate falseness and pretension.

When Joseph T. "Cap" Shaw became editor of *Black Mask* in 1926, he honed the hard-boiled style, advocating compression, telling detail, fast storyline, and more believable characters. The writer he chose as a model was Hammett. Among the many contributors Shaw advised were Raymond *Chandler, Frederick Nebel, Lester Dent, Raoul Whitfield, Erle Stanley *Gardner, and George Harmon *Coxe.

With "Return Engagement" (*Black Mask*, spring 1934), Coxe introduced the first newspaper reporter to feature in a hard-boiled yarn. A combat veteran, hard drinking, quick fisted, and thoroughly professional, "Flashgun" Casey led his own crusade against evil. Notable for its pared-down quality, Coxe's writing did not portray violence for its own sake. Rather he offered more complex plots and workmanlike detection; his Kent Murdock character was a predecessor to the protagonists created much later by Ross *Macdonald and Robert B. *Parker, since Murdock adhered to a more gentlemanly code than did other tough heroes of the time.

Nebel, a drinking buddy of Hammett, also used a reporter, Kennedy, as the sidekick of Captain Steve MacBride. Both were unsentimental about human weakness, but Nebel's main contribution was the often frenetic and witty comedy of Kennedy which challenged authority and convention and provided a human contrast to the soulless world of Richmond City.

Like Nebel, Chandler was influenced by Hammett and Shaw. Chandler's indelible mark on the genre was made with such novels as *The Big Sleep* (1939). Like Hammett, he wanted to represent "real" crime. Among other major contributions in style, setting, tone, and theme, the Chandler protagonist was less pathologically violent, though certainly able to defend himself. His virtues tattered by a harsh world, Philip Marlowe is a lone knight often fighting dragons from the past, trying existentially to establish a moral point in an aimless and destructive cosmos.

James M. *Cain, who disliked being compared with Hammett and Ernest Hemingway, nonetheless shared the traits of the genre in works such as *The Postman Always Rings Twice* (1934) and *Double Indemnity* (1943). To the swift pace and grim worldview, Cain added the psychological study of the effects of greed or illicit passion, while Cornell *Woolrich portrayed a bleak world verging on the deranged.

Combining conventions of the puzzle mystery with those of the hard-boiled school, Jonathan Latimer in 1935 introduced Bill Crane who enjoyed a wide, if brief readership.

In pre–World War II England, Gerald Hersh's novels ran counter to the popular British cozies and puzzles. Considered weak in plot, the stories had graphic scenes of *London's low-life. But Reginald Southouse (Peter) Cheyney was the first British writer to admit the influence of the hard-boiled school. His London-based private eyes, Lemmy Caution in *This Man is Dangerous* (1936) and Slim Callaghan in *Urgent Hangman* (1938), influenced by Williams, appeared in action-filled and intricate plots. Like his American cousins, Callaghan was cynical, tough, and marginally mannered. After midcentury, P. D. *James introduced the modern female hard-boiled detective Cordelia *Gray in *Unsuitable Job for a Woman* (1972). Adam Hall combined espionage and the hard-boiled story in the Quiller tales, and Liza Cody began her Anna Lee series. Though not as prominent in Britain, the traditional hard-boiled detective yarn was continued by Dick *Francis with two Sid Halley tales and by Dan Cavanaugh's Duffy series. William McIlvanney combined the *police procedural with hard-boiled conventions. Gillian Slovo used the form to present feminist and socialist issues, Mike Ripley offered a comedic version of the genre, and Mike Phillips, originally from Guyana, used the conventions to delve into the harsh world of Afro-Caribbean immigrants.

America after World War II saw the wide popularity of Mickey *Spillane's Mike Hammer. Aptly named both physically and intellectually, Hammer outtoughed a world filled with gratuitous and even grotesque savagery. Like the writing, the direct and uncomplex plotting leaned toward the romance of violence. Jim *Thompson in the 1950s also emphasized violence; but by telling his stories through the eyes of the criminal, he blended psychological realism with hard-boiled characteristics, pointing to the novels of Lawrence Sanders.

Originally writing as a *noir* novelist for Marcel Duhamel, the African American author Chester *Himes broadened the genre to include a new region and protagonists who were cops. Coffin Ed *Johnson and Grave Digger Jones patrolled a hard and often manic Harlem. Himes provided a precursor for later African American writers such as Gar Anthony Haywood and Walter *Mosley, as well as the absurdist tales of Carl Hiaasen.

Continuing the Knight-errant figure, Ross *Macdonald's Lew *Archer made his first appearance in *The Moving Target* (1949), and John D. *MacDonald's Travis *McGee began his career in 1964. Robert B. *Parker developed that tradition further, adding a sophistication and sensitivity to his *Spenser that merited the term "soft-boiled." The traditional figure stayed alive with Bill Pronzini, George V. *Higgins, and others, while Elmore *Leonard's often blackly comic views of East Coast criminal life were told in a telegraphic street vernacular born of cinematic imagery.

New and popular, the modern female hardboiled private eye appeared in America in large numbers during the latter third of the century. Following P. D. James's lead, Marcia *Muller introduced Sharon McCone of San Francisco. Sue *Grafton's Kinsey *Milhone respresented the Los Angeles area. Sara *Paretsky's V. I. *Warshawksi, harder than Milhone and more concerned with social issues, was based in Chicago.

Just as the form expanded its boundaries in character and theme, so, by the end of the century, it did in setting. Robert J. Randisi's Nick Delveccio series took place in a Brooklyn undergoing seismic cultural changes. Detroit was the home of Loren D. Estleman's Amos Walker. In Denver, Michael Allegretto's Jacob "Jake" Lomax represented the traditional private eye, while Warwick Downing's Joe Reddman made a brief appearance as a *Native American sleuth. Dan Roman, created by Edward Mathis, fought his way across Texas; Raymond H. Ring set his stories in rural Arizona; James Crumley, in Montana and the West. Jonathan Valin, in Cincinnati. In Cedar Rapids, Iowa, Ed Gorman's "Jack Walsh" showed that the mean street could be Main Street.

Vibrant and innovative, hard-boiled writers maintained a core of traditional private eyes who ranged from realistic to caricature, as well as blending traits from other types of fiction. The genre also reflected the general movement in literature during the late twentieth century to regionalism and multiculturalism.

[*See also* Conventions of the Genre: Hard-Boiled Conventions; Heroic Romance; Loner, Sleuth as; Loyalty and Betrayal; Mean Streets Milieu; Voice: Hard-Boiled Voice; Voice: Wisecracking Voice.]

• David Geherin, *The American Private Eye: The Image in Fiction* (1985). Larry N. Landrum, Pat Browne, and Ray B. Browne, eds., *Dimensions of Detective Fiction* (1976). Frank N. Magill, ed., *Critical Survey of Mystery and Detective Fiction*, 4 vols. (1988). Martin Priestman, *Detective Fiction and Literature: The Figure on the Carpet* (1991). John M. Reilly, ed., *Twentieth-Century Crime and Mystery Writers*, 2nd ed. (1985). Chris Steinbruner and Otto Penzler, eds., *Encyclopedia of Mystery and Detection* (1976). Ralph Willett, *Hard Boiled Detective Fiction*, BAAS Pamphlets in American Studies 23 (1992).   —Rex Burns

HARD-BOILED SLEUTH. Narrative elements surrounding the detective are normally brought forward to characterize hard-boiled writing: a tinsel-town *milieu, scenes of repeated *violence, a tone of cynicism about wealth and authority, and a general sense of disorder. Detective fiction, however, above all concerns detectives doing their jobs. In that, hard-boiled fiction differs not at all from the classic tales of the Golden Age. A case can be made that the hard-boiled detective inhabits a world vastly different from that of that of the sleuth who is at home in the *cozy mystery. Still, when the matter of a detective's work is considered as an issue of narrative construction, rather than a means to document the reality existing outside the text of a fiction, the detectives of literature have an inevitable uniformity in their narrative function.

In both cases, the reader encounters crimes that present a mystery. The criminals are unknown; or perhaps they are known, but retribution for the crime seems impossible. A client seeks the assistance of the detective, forming at least a tacit contract requiring the detective to solve the mystery. To fulfill the contract, the detective by whatever means must construct a cogent explanation of the criminal events. In other words, the detective is employed to produce a hypothesis that will withstand scrutiny. Another way of putting it is to say the detective must discover the true story behind the mystery, but even that is not the whole of it. The detective of fiction also must craft the findings about cause and *motive, crime and its intended consequences, into a statement of explanation. That statement becomes a second narrative, a narrative within the framework of the inclusive story which the client sets in motion by seeking the detective's assistance.

This way of looking at detective fiction yields the idea of a double structure. First is the overall story that relates the crime and the detective's method of seeking its explanation. This first story comes to readers in the voice of the story or novel. Second, there is the discourse of explanation created by the detective. This second discourse originates in the detective's mind and may be expressed in a fragmentary way, as the detective's thoughts are shared with readers, or it may be related in a burst of final exposition, as in the characteristic wrap-up scenes where Charlie *Chan, Lord Peter *Wimsey, Hercule *Poirot, or a similar figure—the detective—assembles all the suspects to audit his explanation of whodunit.

Using the idea of the dual narrative, the sleuths of hard-boiled writing can be distinguished by their rare use of the wrap-up scene. They cannot summon the confidence in their intellectual powers to prepare such a performance. For example, while Dashiell *Hammett's Sam *Spade finds himself among all of the suspects at the ending of *The Maltese Falcon* (1930), they have not congregated to hear him but to keep a watch on him. When Spade undertakes his explanation, it is at best fragmentary, and, in any case, his mind becomes concerned with emotional control of himself, as he tells Brigid O'Shaughnessey why he will turn her over to the police. Having lost intellectual command of events, Spade is relieved when the timely arrival of the police brings his case to its conclusion.

This drama in *The Maltese Falcon* of the detective's mind struggling for control of the novel's second narrative illustrates the circumstances of the hard-boiled sleuth. Preceding detective fiction had valorized the power of reason to explain reality. As a result, detectives such as Sherlock *Holmes and the revised versions of the *Great Detective who populate Golden Age stories treated crimes as intellectual problems, so that they could render their solutions in the form of well-structured demonstrations of mental acuity. For the hard-boiled sleuth, mysteries become existential. Chester *Himes's detective partners, the very tough Coffin Ed *Johnson and Grave Digger Jones, confront the most absurd sorts of crimes, and they are never in doubt, nor are readers, about the inadequacy of reason alone to manage their causes or consequences. The nine books about their adventures form a saga that explores the conditions created by systemic racial prejudice and exploitation that are so corrupt no single mind can fully explain them, let alone institute reasonable order in the world made by *racism.

Of course, the speech of hard-boiled sleuths also illustrates their view of the mysteries they meet. Terse, rarely abstract but instead direct and vascular, the sleuths are Huckleberry Finn's cousins in the American vernacular. Perhaps more often than any other type of detective fiction, hard-boiled narratives are written from the first-person detective's point of view. That technical choice, then, simplifies narration, because it eliminates the separation between the voice of the novel and the voice of the sleuth; all of the story's discourse originates in the consciousness of the detective. Ross *Macdonald has described the process of centering the story in the detective's mind as making "the mind of the novel . . . a consciousness in which the meanings of other lives emerge." The economy of narration does not establish a control of mystery. On the contrary, in Raymond *Chandler's stories told by Philip *Marlowe, for instance, the dominance of a weary, disillusioned detective voice affirms the limitations of the mind, while Paul Cain's fictional voice in *Fast One* (1933) and in a short story such as "Trouble-Chaser" (*Black Mask*, Apt. 1934) can seem to be entirely devoted to a record of action.

Under more technical analysis, too, the use of American vernacular in the dialogue and narration of hard-boiled writing illustrates the character of the sleuth and the nature of his world. Complex sentence structures that employ syntactical subordination for purposes of intellectual analysis are considerably rarer in the sleuth's hard-boiled speech than are compound or simple sentences that simply juxtapose thoughts. The stories by Carroll John *Daly, who is considered to have begun the whole mode of hard-boiled writing with "The False Burton Combs" (*Black Mask*, Dec. 1922) and to have set its early patterns in the stories for *Black Mask* about Race *Williams, serve to illustrate the point, as do Hammett's stories about the *Continental Op, who was introduced in *Black Mask* in 1923, or the language used by Raoul Whitfield when he wrote under his own name or as Ramon Decolta.

The weaknesses or afflictions of hard-boiled sleuths sometimes contribute the limitation on their ability to dominate reality through reason. Frederick Nebel's Kennedy, who appeared in *Black Mask* stories in the 1930s, is a drunk. So is Jonathan Latimer's screwball detective Bill Crane, featured in a series of novels beginning with *Murder in the Madhouse* (1935), and Lawrence *Block's Matt Scudder, who debuted in *The Sins of the Father* (1977). In other instances, the sleuths are world weary loners. Yet others, we are told by their stories, have just seen too much sleaze.

Still and all, the hard-boiled sleuth who gradually developed in the pages of *Black Mask*, *Dime Detective*, *Detective Story*, and other *pulp magazines, and then in paperback and hardcover novels, does not express nihilism. A hard-boiled detective can place no faith in conventional verities, but he (and, more recently, female characters too, such as Marcia *Muller's Sharon McCone and Sara *Paretsky's V. I. *Warshawski) does have a code of behavior. Like the philosophical existentialists they resemble, the hard-boiled private eyes practice situational ethics. Relentlessly honest and consistently devoted to the victims in society, the hard-boiled sleuth resists blandishment and bribery and sets his or her own high standards without regard for the conventions of a fictional world in which their style of morality seems unique, although Robert B. *Parker's *Spenser, for one, indicates that the code of tough guy behavior derives from the philosophy to be found, of all places, in the pulp magazine stories of hard-boiled detection.

The argument has been made that the hard-boiled private eye is an American hero descended from James Fenimore Cooper's archetypal Leatherstocking; thus, George Grella has stated that the private detective chooses an instinctive code of *justice over "the often tarnished justice of civilization" and "replaces the subtleties of the deductive method with a sure knowledge of his world and a keen moral sense." For Grella, therefore, the hard-boiled story must be classed with the American romance, which the critic Richard Chase suggested was preoccupied by an "interest in alienation and disorder." Regardless of that argument, though, the hard-boiled sleuth also works as a putative philosopher, just as every detective undertaking the fictional genre's requirement to construct the story's second narrative of explanation must be. The traditional detective was a philosopher of order and reason. The hard-boiled sleuth thinks those neoclassical values are inauthentic for the world he or she knows, and that is what makes all the difference.

[*See also* Characterization; Chivalry; Conventions of the Genre: Hard-Boiled Conventions; Formula: Character; Loner, Sleuth as; Voice: Hard-Boiled Voice; Voice: Wisecracking Voice.]

• George Grella, "The Gangster Novel: The Urban Pastoral," in *Tough Guy Writers of the Thirties*, ed. David Madden (1968). George Grella, "Murder and the Mean Streets: The Hard-Boiled Detective Novel," *Contempora* 1 (1970): 6–18. E. R. Hagemann, ed., *A Comprehensive Index to Black Mask, 1920–51* (1982). Edward Margolies, *Which Way Did He Go?: The Private Eye in Dashiell Hammett, Raymond Chandler, Chester Himes, and Ross MacDonald* (1982).

—John M. Reilly

HARDY BOYS, THE. *See* Juvenile Sleuths: Boy Sleuth.

HARE, CYRIL, pseudonym of Alfred Alexander Gordon Clark (1900–1958), British author of cozy detective novels. He derived his pseudonym from his London residence, Cyril Mansions, in Battersea, and his Temple chambers, Hare Court. A barrister who became a county court judge, Hare made excellent use of his legal knowledge in his fiction. His early books featured Inspector John Mallett of *Scotland Yard. *Tragedy at Law* (1942), considered his finest book, introduced Francis Pettigrew, an aging and unsuccessful barrister. Pettigrew reappeared in *With a Bare Bodkin* (1946) and other books, but he remained a reluctant detective; in *That Yew Tree's Shade* (1954; *Death Walks the Woods*), he remarks how much he loathes "this business of detection." *An English Murder* (1951; *The Christmas Murder*) is a spoof of the *cozy mystery set in a snowbound castle. The crime is solved by a Czech refugee, Dr. Wenceslaus Bottwink, a character employed by the author to comment on English eccentricities. *He Should Have Died Hereafter* (1958; *Untimely Death*) reunited Pettigrew and Mallett. The posthumously published *Best Detective Stories of Cyril Hare* (1959; *Death Among Friends and Other Detective Stories*), edited by his friend Michael *Gilbert, shows Hare's mastery of the short as well as the long form. Gilbert remembered Hare as having a striking physical resemblance to Sherlock *Holmes and as possessing superb skills as a public speaker.

[*See also* Conventions of the Genre: Traditional Conventions; Country House Milieu; Farceurs; Humor.]

• Charles Shibuk, "Cyril Hare," in *St. James Guide to Crime and Mystery Writers*, 4th ed., ed. Jay P. Pederson (1996). Julian Symons, *Bloody Murder: From the Detective Story to the Crime Novel: A History*, 3rd rev. ed. (1992).

—Martin Edwards

HAUTE COUTURE. *See* Fashion and Design Milieu.

HEARING-IMPAIRED DETECTIVE. *See* Disability, Sleuth with a.

HEROIC ROMANCE. That crime and mystery writing is a decidedly modern genre has been well established. Despite the attempts of Golden Age apologists to claim an ancient lineage for their ventures, the conception of crime as a social problem at the heart of mystery fiction, the characterization of the protagonist as a specialized empirical investigator, and the use of narrative techniques to represent a known reality, all of these qualities, and others besides, demonstrate that crime and mystery fiction arose as a literary marker for urban, middle-class industrialized society. Historically it is even younger than the novel.

When we turn our attention from the question of origins and ancestry, however, to chart literary genres according to their functions, a strong case can be made for associating crime and mystery fiction with such venerable forms as the heroic romance. Sagas of mighty deeds and the exploits of armed champions evolved in many cultures. In Europe they hybridized into a cycle of tales relating an evidently endless quest for the relics of Christianity carried on by a loosely joined posse of warriors. While the tales in various languages indicate that the group bears loyalty to a great king presiding over the court where they each have won a place, the adventures of the tales concern extraordinary individuals undergoing the trials of combat with foes they encounter on a continuous journey devoted to finding the opportunity for noble accomplishments. Viewed as products of culture, the heroic romances may be understood as enactments of cherished *virtues. The heroes are brave and selfless. They apply their military skills to socially positive ends, such as protection of the weak and poor, redemption of the vulnerable. Their bearing is athletic, their mien handsome. They are heroes of collective good acting individually, and sometimes individualistically, on its behalf.

The original heroes of romance appeared in manuscripts purporting to record oral accounts of the dateless period of King Arthur's Round Table and Charlemagne's days, but their avatars endured in the printed literature of the nineteenth century. Sir Walter Scott reconstructed the past history of Scotland in *Ivanhoe* (1819), *Kenilworth* (1821), *The Fortunes of Nigel* (1822), and *Quentin Durward* (1823). Heeding the acclaim earned by Scott, other writers undertook their own historical reclamations. In the United States James Fenimore Cooper wrote his famous Leatherstocking tales, a series of six novels about the northern frontier from the days of the forest wilderness to the time when settlement reached the western prairies, the last of them published in 1841. The southern frontier of the United States found its chronicler in William Gilmore Simms, who fashioned a set of "Border Romances" set in South Carolina and published between 1834 and 1859. Scott, Cooper, and Simms thus were near contemporaries responding in a time of great social and economic change to a popular interest in the seemingly more stable past. Providing their readers a myth of national origins, each expressed also his culture's conception of enduring values of behavior, a template for *heroism.

The functional similarity of these heroic romances to detective fiction is not hard to see. Where the hero was once a knight or a frontiersman, the *sleuth is a man or woman of urban society; but the techniques of the prose novel, like the techniques of the romance, show the protagonists to be the extraordinary figures in their stories, doing deeds as their precursors did to protect society from instability. Robert B. *Parker underlines the relationship in naming his detective *Spenser, after the British author of the heroic romance of The Faerie Queene (1590–96) and by showing Spenser to be self-consciously devoted to a code of altruistic performance. Because detective fiction typically presents itself in the dress of the immediate present rather than garbed in a romantic past, its relationship to the tales of old is opaque; but writers like Arthur Conan *Doyle and Agatha *Christie have known that, for all of their eccentric ways, fictional detectives serve as exemplars of social virtue, just as heroes always must, and writers like Raymond *Chandler and Joseph Wambaugh have even risked explicit reference to heroism by seriously terming the *private eye and police officer of their fiction knights. What the writers have known, readers sense: that a detective story may be an essay in triumphing over the dragons.

[See also Chivalry; Urban Milieu.]

—John M. Reilly

HEROISM. It is a peculiar quality of crime and mystery writing that in bookish conversation examples of the genre are often identified by the name of their lead detective more often than by the name of the author. Book buyers and library users search for stories about Sherlock *Holmes, Miss Jane *Marple, Adam *Dalgliesh, or any other figure whose narrative has given past pleasure. Early appearances of crime writing, however, featured the sensation of the crime above any character. Thieves' confessions regaled readers with lurid details of wrongdoing. The three-volume, anonymously written work known as Richmond; or, Scenes in the Life of a Bow Street Runner, Drawn Up from His Private Memoranda (1827) offered episodic treatments of crimes categorized by type: gambling or fraud, among others. Similarly, the memoirs of the American detective Allan Pinkerton that appeared in the 1870s and after offered accounts of the battle of his agency against commercial crimes. The more purely literary form of crime story known as the *sensation novel, and illustrated, for example, by Lady Audley's Secret, published by M. E. *Braddon in 1862, engaged readers with its tale of madness more than it did with amateur detective Robert Audley.

The balance among narrative elements in the typical crime story shifted, though, in the years following the appearance of Arthur Conan *Doyle's A Study in Scarlet (1887) featuring the redoubtable Holmes, whose character and its accentuated displays of a detection method based upon inferential reasoning became the center of narration. What was true for Holmes held constant for his nineteenth-century rivals in detection and set the pattern for practically all subsequent fictional treatments of crime. Strictly speaking, the shift in narrative focus from episodes of crime to the work of the detective is not attribut-

able to Doyle and Holmes because they were first; priority goes to Edgar Allan *Poe and the hero of his detection stories, the Chevalier C. Auguste *Dupin, who first appeared in "The Murders in the Rue Morgue" (Graham's Lady's and Gentleman's Magazine, Apr. 1841). But Holmes, almost fifty years after, was the protagonist who achieved the popularity to create both an extensive audience for illustrious deeds of detection and the model for other writers sensitive to popular interest.

As popular fiction addresses a general love of story among readers, so popular detective writing feeds the desire to read and hear about outsized characters or heroes. For detective fiction written since the redirection of attention from crime to *sleuth, the term "protagonist" nearly always means the same as "hero." The detective's accomplishments are extraordinary. He or she removes a threat of *violence or disorder from the community by explaining a baffling set of circumstances that no one else is equipped to interpret. Yet, for all of that, the detective also expresses consensual values of the audience. In the case of Holmes, the values include a high regard for empirical investigation, a point especially well made for readers at the dawn of a scientific age. Other detectives reflect contemporary interest in finding means to institute order in the impersonal surroundings of modern cities. Some embody idealizations of manly, or competent womanly, behavior, while yet others perform their deeds in towns and cities similar to the environs of their readers. It is a likely truism that we know reality by the stories we tell of it, in which case the story of the heroic detective expresses a popular wish about reality.

Critics and writers have promoted the idea of a kinship between the fictional detective and traditional heroes. Most notably Raymond *Chandler in The Simple Art of Murder (Atlantic Monthly, Dec. 1944) equated the *private detective with the knight of medieval romance. Dorothy L. *Sayers, in The Omnibus of Crime (1929), identified the detective with the mythic character of James Fenimore Cooper's Leather-stocking romances. The validity of such comparisons can be extended to such familiar traits of fictional detectives as the independence from social ties and freedom from routine employment that they share with romantic heroes; the serial trials they endure like epic heroes; and, in the case of male detectives, the attraction they hold for women because they are so aloof.

Yet detective protagonists are definitely modern heroes. Their turf is usually the city, in both its rudest quarters and its exotic ways. They are citizens of a mass society, even when they bear residual titles of the aristocracy. Their detection methods are informed by knowledge of psychology or of forensic science or the practical experiences of contemporary life. They may have an ancient ancestry, but their creators craft their adventures to make them the object of our current aspirations.

[See also Characterization; Chivalry; Formula: Character; Reasoning, Types of.]

—John M. Reilly

HEYER, GEORGETTE (1902–1974), British author of mysteries and historical novels, best known for her Regency romances. In *The Talisman Ring* (1936) and *The Corinthian* (1940) she successfully combined history and mystery. A lifelong best-selling author, Heyer (who also wrote as Stella Martin) remained an intensely private person. She received little critical acclaim for the wit and craftsmanship of her comedies of manners, written, according to Heyer, as a mix of Dr. Johnson and Jane Austen.

Born in Wimbledon, England, Heyer was privately educated. Her first book, *The Black Moth* (1921), was published when she was nineteen. She was a thorough researcher: *An Infamous Army* (1937) retells the Battle of Waterloo. Altogether Heyer published fifty-six novels and a book of short stories.

Beginning in 1932, Heyer wrote twelve *thrillers. Howard Haycraft in *Murder for Pleasure* (1941) said that Heyer's lively style showed a new and harder veneer, while in *Bloody Murder: From the Detective Story to the Crime Novel: A History* (1972) Julian *Symons called her one of the last *farceurs of the Golden Age, whose ethical standards were implicit in their social values.

Footsteps in the Dark (1932) appeared the year her son was born, but she regarded the third, *Death in the Stocks* (1935; *Merely Murder*) as her first "real" crime story, featuring the *CID's Sergeant Stanley Hemmingway and Superintendent Hannasyde. Her barrister husband, George Ronald Rougier, worked out the *plots, while Heyer brought the characters to life; but biographer Hodge suggests that working with her husband inhibited Heyer's genius. Rouget's legal background informs *Duplicate Death* (1951), but most of the mysteries, like *They Found Him Dead* (1937), are set in the *English village milieu. Many critics consider *The Blunt Instrument* (1938) and *Envious Casca* (1941) her best books, but Heyer remains best known to readers for her depictions of stately homes and what Dilys Winn, in *Murderess Ink: The Better Half of the Mystery* (1979), termed "that ultra-dry British humor."

[*See also* Country House Milieu.]

• Jane Aiken Hodge, *The Private World of Georgette Heyer* (1984).
—Alzina Stone Dale

HIGGINS, GEORGE V(INCENT) (b. 1939), popular American crime novelist. Educated at Boston College and Stanford University, Higgins was admitted to the Massachusetts bar in 1967. He has been both a federal prosecutor in the Massachusetts office of the U.S. attorney general and a defense attorney, as well as a reporter, columnist, and critic. The main elements of his style were evident in his first novel, *The Friends of Eddie Coyle* (1972): characters drawn from sleazy individuals from both sides of the law, a *plot depicting, often with considerable sympathy, the everyday struggles of these characters, and, above all, extraordinarily realistic dialogue that makes few concessions to the conventions of grammar and punctuation that undermine the verisimilitude of most fictional dialogue. Later works of note include *The Digger's Game* (1973), *Cogan's Trade* (1974), *Kennedy for the Defense*, which introduced recurring character Jerry Kennedy (1980), and *A Choice of Enemies* (1983).

[*See also* Urban Milieu; Underworld, The.]
—Richard Steiger

HIGHSMITH, PATRICIA (1921–1995), American author who for many years made her home in Europe. Born in Fort Worth, Texas, as Mary Patricia Plaughman, she later took the name of her stepfather. In Europe, particularly in Britain, France, Germany, and Spain, Highsmith is regarded as one of the greatest modern crime novelists. In her native country her reputation is less high but has been growing.

Her first novel, *Strangers on a Train* (1950), later a very successful film directed by Alfred Hitchcock, set the wholly individual pattern of her writing. As Graham *Greene said when introducing a collection of her short stories, her *The Snail-Watcher and Other Stories* (1970; *Eleven*), her world is claustrophobic, irrational, and dangerous. Her protagonists are not ruled by the standards and limits of behavior regarded as normal. In that first novel and in several later ones, strangers are emotionally bound to each other through acts of *violence in relationships that waver between love and hatred. Characters are obsessed by fantasies that turn into disconcerting reality. In *This Sweet Sickness* (1960), a young chemist buys and furnishes a house for a woman who has never seen it and has no interest in him. *The Story-Teller* (1965; *A Suspension of Mercy*) finds a young writer pretending he has killed his wife and making a mock burial of her body; he subsequently gets in deep trouble when she actually disappears. Highsmith's books contain no *puzzles, and *justice is rarely done in them. Emotional problems turn into violent actions, and our concern is to see how they will come out.

This is especially true of her most popular books, the novels about the pleasant, totally amoral young American Tom Ripley, who gets away with crimes including forgery and murder. *The Talented Mr. Ripley* (1955) is the first and perhaps the best of them, although *Ripley Under Ground* (1970), in which he impersonates a dead artist and is drawn into murder when the deception is about to be discovered, is also chillingly memorable. The later Ripley stories, including *Ripley Under Water* (1991) are less successful.

Highsmith always resisted being typecast as a crime novelist, and as well as crime fiction also wrote "straight" novels, including the powerful *People Who Knock on the Door* (1983), in which fundamentalist *religion wrecks an apparently ordinary and secure family in midwest America. An early novel about a lesbian relationship, originally published under the pseudonym Claire Morgan in 1952 as *The Price of Salt*, was reissued in 1990 as *Carol* under Highsmith's own name.

It may be the variety of her work, and the fact that it cannot be categorized—if she is basically a crime novelist she is emphatically not a writer of detective stories—that has delayed American appreciation of her extraordinary talent. Almost every one of the dozen books she wrote between her first novel and *Ripley Under Ground* is unique in the different ways they make irrational behavior seem inevitable. She has also been, without intending it, a prophet: The terrors and delusions driving her psychopaths to violent action are the ones we see enacted now in the apparently motiveless crimes recorded in our daily newspapers.

[See also Antihero; Characterization.]

• Franz Cavigelli and Fritz Senn, eds., Über Patricia Highsmith (1990). Julian Symons, Bloody Murder: From the Detective Story to the Crime Novel: A History, 3rd rev. ed. (1992).

—Julian Symons

HILL, REGINALD (b. 1936), the British author best known as the creator of the Yorkshire policemen Andrew Dalziel and Peter Pascoe. More recently, he has introduced the black private investigator, Joe Sixsmith, a character Hill bases in Luton, near London. Hill has also produced work under pseudonyms. Under the name Patrick Ruell, derived from his wife's maiden name, Patricia Ruell, he has penned several *thrillers that combine international intrigue with mystery elements. As Dick Morland and Charles Underhill, he has examined futuristic problems in works that might be classified as *science fiction. He also took Dalziel and Pascoe into the *future in *One Small Step* (1990), a slim novel, set in the year 2010, when the pair investigate a *murder on the moon.

The son of a professional football (i.e., soccer) player and a factory worker, Hill won a scholarship to Oxford University. Upon graduation, he became a schoolmaster and the a lecturer in a teacher's college before he took up writing full time. He resides in a Victorian vicarage in England's Lake District.

A subtle writer, he has won many awards, including Gold and Diamond Daggers from the *Crime Writers Association. His *plots are complex, his characterization sharp, and his dialogue liberally laced with humor. The Dalziel and Pascoe series began conventionally enough with *A Clubbable Woman* (1970) and *An Advancement of Learning* (1971), the latter drawing upon Hill's experience as a college lecturer. *Deadheads* (1983) centers on whether an apparently amiable rose grower is a killer, while in *Exit Lines* (1984) the focus is upon older poeple and the inevitability of death. The grim theme is complemented with much dark *humor, including famous last words that head each chapter. Dalziel, fat and course, and Pascoe, intelligent and sensitive, contrast superbly; they respect each other but have irreconcilably different outlooks. Increasingly, Hill has sought to explore aspects of British life including a mining community ravaged by the aftereffects of a disastrous industrial dispute in *Underworld* (1988) and the *country house milieu in *Recalled to Life* (1992).

[See also Police Detective; Sidekicks and Sleuthing Teams.]

• Jon L. Breen, Novel Verdicts (1986). Rosemary Herbert, The Fatal Art of Entertainment; Interviews with Mystery Writers (1994).

—Martin Edwards

HILLERMAN TONY, (b. 1925), American author, best known as the creator of the *Native American sleuths Joe *Leaphorn and Jim *Chee, tribal police officers whose territory is the Four Corners area of the American southwest where New Mexico, Arizona, Utah, and Colorado meet. On a philosophical level, these police detectives pursue their work in another intersection, the area where Anglo- and Native American cultures meet.

Hillerman's acquaintance with Native American peoples dates from his boyhood. He was born in the dust-bowl village of Sacred Heart, Oklahoma, where he found it easier to identify with his Potawatomie and Seminole Indian friends than with the town boys. The son of a farmer and jack-of-all-trades and a homemaker who had worked as a registered nurse, Hillerman was raised until the age of twelve in a household without a telephone, running water, or electricity, where storytellers were valued and books were luxuries. Nonetheless, Hillerman discovered the work of Arthur *Upfield, whose stories set in the Australian outback featured *sleuths of mixed racial heritage.

Hillerman began work his way through Oklahoma State University, but his academic career was cut short by World War II. Serving in the U.S. Army, he was wounded in action in France while home on convalescent leave, Hillerman experienced two serendipitous occurrences. He met a reporter who had read his letters sent home from the front, who encouraged him to try his hand at writing. Then, while driving a truck on the Navajo reservation, he witnessed a curing ceremony that was to become the inspiration for his first novel *The Blessing Way* (1970).

Hillerman's long experience as a journalist is reflected in his second novel, *The Fly on the Wall* (1971), and in his 1996 novel, *Finding Moon*. Despite his clean style, Hillerman is remembered by readers for his vivid visual depictions of the southwest scene, which he establishes through the use of telling details that also illustrate the uneasy meeting of Native American traditions and contemporary American culture.

In addition to authoring novels for adults, Hillerman wrote one children's book, several nonfiction works about the southwest, including an account of *The Great Taos Bank Robbery and Other Indian Country Affairs* (1973). He edited *The Mysterious West* (1994), an anthology of crime and mystery stories, and coedited *The Oxford Book of American Detective Stories* (1996). The Navajo people found Hillerman's writing so convincing that they declared him a Special Friend of the Dineh, or tribe.

• Martin Greenberg, ed., ed. The Tony Hillerman Companion: A Comprehensive Guide to his Life and Work. Rosemary Herbert, The Fatal Art of Entertainment: Interviews with Mystery Writers (1994).

—Rosemary Herbert

HIMES, CHESTER (BOMAR) (1909–1984), African American novelist best known for his darkly comic tales of criminal life in Harlem, and for the creation of *African American sleuths Coffin Ed *Johnson and Grave Digger Jones. Himes came to the writing of crime fiction with firsthand knowledge of the life of the petty criminal, convict, and street hustler living on the edge. Although born into a middle-class family, by 1929 he was in prison for armed robbery. He began writing in prison, first publishing in small-circulation African American magazines. In 1932, his work came to the attention of Arnold Gingrich and began to appear in *Esquire*.

His early novels, beginning with *If He Hollers Let Him Go* (1945), reflected his preoccupations with the destructive power of *racism and interracial sexuality. Although marginally successful critically, his failure to gain financial security, combined with the breakup of his marriage, provided the impetus for his emigration to France in 1953.

After several very lean years in Europe, Himes was offered the chance to write for Editions Gallimard's *Série noire*, an acclaimed series of translated American crime fiction. The resulting novel, published in French in 1958 as *La reine des pommes* (*For Love of Imabelle*, 1957; *A Rage in Harlem*), was an instant hit, winning for Himes the prestigious *Grand prix de la littérature policière*, the first such award to a non-French writer. *The Real Cool Killers* (1959), *The Crazy Kill* (1959), *The Big Gold Dream* (1960), and *All Shot Up* (1960) quickly followed. In each, he juxtaposed absurdly comic characters with dark, sinister situations and set them against the grimly realistic backdrop of a teeming, degraded ghetto.

In many of his works, a good-hearted black male, often just trying to get along, finds himself caught up in a desperate struggle for life itself. A morally ambiguous, light-skinned woman is often at the heart of his trouble. Flamboyant religious charlatans, hard-edged gamblers, and drug-crazed killers are also regular members of Himes's "domestic" cast.

As the series grew, Johnson and Jones developed from minor characters into spokesman through which Himes articulated his rage at the cruelty and injustice of American racism. As the series drew to a close with *Cotton Comes to Harlem* (1965), it began to mirror his hopelessness at the race problem. In *Blind Man with a Pistol* (1969) Himes saw such *corruption and chaos that even his indomitable heroes could not prevail against it. In *Plan B* (unfinished but published in the United States in 1993), he envisioned a racial apocalypse that would kill his detectives and eventually destroy America.

Himes is best remembered for his remarkable fusion of the sociological protest novel with the hard-boiled detective tale. Like Raymond *Chandler, Himes used the detective story to mirror his times and to articulate his social concerns. Johnson and Jones were the models for Shaft and other black heroes of the sixties and seventies, and Himes's influence can be seen in the work of such diverse writers as Donald Goines, Walter *Mosley, and James Sallis.

[*See also* New York; Prejudice; Realism, Conventions of; Sex and Sexuality.]

• Edward, Margolies, *Which Way Did He Go?: The Private Eye in Dashiell Hammett, Raymond Chandler, Chester Himes, and Ross Macdonald* (1982). Robert E. Skinner, *Two Guns from Harlem: The Detective Fiction of Chester Himes* (1989). James Sallis, *Difficult Lives: Jim Thompson, David Goodis, Chester Himes* (1993).   —Robert E. Skinner

HISTORICAL FIGURES IN CRIME AND MYSTERY WRITING. *This entry points out figures from history who are used as characters in crime and mystery writing. The piece is divided into two parts, the first focusing upon royalty, politicians, and statesmen used as figures of fiction, and the second looking at celebrities who become characters in this genre.*

Royals, Politicians, and Statesmen
Celebrities

For further information, please refer to Historical Mystery.

ROYALS, POLITICIANS, AND STATESMEN

Because *period mystery novels, like their ancestors and cousins historical novels, reach into the past for their *plots and characters, it is not surprising that actual people from the past appear in such books. And, as in historical novels, the roles of these historical figures vary greatly.

One of the first to use historical figures in his *detective novels, John Dickson *Carr, employed them in a variety of ways. Joseph Fouché, Napoleon's director of the secret police, was the antagonist in *Captain Cut-Throat* (1955); the first two commissioners of the London Metropolitan Police, Charles Rowan and Edward Mayne, were authority figures in *Fire, Burn!* (1957), as was Sir John Fielding, founder of the Bow Street Runners, in *The Demoniacs* (1962); and Wilkie *Collins served as the investigator in *The Hungry Goblin* (1972).

Our earliest example (in real time), however, may be the fourth-century B.C. philosopher Aristotle, in Margaret Doody's *Aristotle Detective* (1978); he appears not as the protagonist but rather as a proto–Mycroft *Holmes, to whom the actual hero, Stephanos, brings his *clues and questions. The first-century A.D. Roman emperor Vespasian serves, in the novels of Lindsey Davis, both as an initiator and rewarder (as in *Silver Pigs*, 1989). Many of the players in the fall of the Roman republic in the last century B.C., men and women like Cicero, Sulla, Caesar, Clodius, Clodia, and Milo, appear at the edges, and seduce or attempt to murder, or befriend Decius Caecilius Metellus, the hero of John Maddox Roberts's novels (e.g., *SPQR*, 1990). This subsidiary role for historical figures is true as well in the novels of Steven Saylor (*Roman Blood*, 1991; *Arms of Nemesis*, 1992), in which Gordianus the Finder, like Roberts's Decius, moves among the great of late-republican Rome.

Beyond the classical period, other prominent figures provide a general background against which the story is set. In Ellis *Peters's chronicles of Brother *Cadfael, beginning with *A Morbid Taste for Bones* (1977), the monk-detective must work out the tangles of his mysteries while, beyond his home in Shrewsbury—and even within the town in *One Corpse Too Many* (1979)—King Stephen and the Empress Matilda (also called Maud) fight out their bloody and seemingly endless civil war. In Leonard Tourney's series featuring Matthew Stock, the constable of Chelmsford, Elizabeth I and her chief minister, Sir Robert Cecil, occasionally appear. Cecil himself may set Stock on the course of an investigation in *Old Saxon Blood* (1988), and Elizabeth's minor roles range from provider of rewards to the target of an attempted assassination in *The Bartholomew Fair Murders* (1986).

In more modern settings, Lillian de la Torre, inspired by the relationship between Sherlock *Holmes and Dr. John H. *Watson, produced a series of books in which Samuel Johnson and his biographer, James Boswell, fill the roles of the two Victorians (e.g., *Dr. Sam: Johnson, Detector: being a light-hearted collection of recently reveal'd episodes in the career of the great lexicographer narrated as from the pen of James Boswell* . . . , (1946). Here, we can observe historical figures playing the role of the protagonist. Cast as protagonists elsewhere are such figures as Albert Edward, the Prince of Wales, in works by Peter Lovesey (e.g., *Bertie and the Tinman*, 1987); Teddy Roosevelt, as the commissioner of the New York City police in, Lawrence Alexander's *The Big Stick* (1986); and Eleanor Roosevelt, who features in a series by Elliot Roosevelt, of which (*Murder in the West Wing*, 1993) is a typical title. (According to Allen J. Hubin some or all of Roosevelt's works were "apparently ghost-written" by William Harrington.) Somewhat different is Josephine *Tey's *The Daughter of Time* (1951), in which the bedridden Inspector Alan Grant investigates (through the printed word) the allegation that King Richard III was responsible for the deaths of the two princes in the Tower in the 1480s.

The advantages of employing an actual historical figure as a detective are several. First, as in the case of Lovesey's "Bertie," the historical character can provide his readers with an entree into a world difficult for the ordinary investigator to penetrate. One has only to observe the constant snubs and sometimes complete rejections that Anne Perry's imaginary Inspector (later Superintendent) Thomas Pitt and Inspector Monk receive in middle-class Victorian homes to understand what Bertie—and Lovesey—have given us. Second, there is the sheer fun for the writer of recreating a famous (or infamous) person and employing that person in a way more natural to our age than earlier periods. Third, there is the delight for the reader in seeing such a figure come to life in an unexpected way, creating new biographical material, as it were, to add to our actual historical knowledge. This pleasure can even be combined with in-jokes about the figure or period—"Bertie" is an absolute blunderer as an investigator—to turn the form inside out, allowing for a sort of subliminal commentary in which the historical person can be employed to solve the mystery even while being laughed at as an improbable figure for the job.

[*See also* Milieu.]

—Carolyn Higbie *and* Timothy W. Boyd

CELEBRITIES

A number of crime and mystery writers have woven stories around real-life celebrities. An early example is S. S. *Van Dine's *The Gracie Allen Murder Case*, (1938; *The Smell of Murder*), in which the author captures the essence of the title comedienne—her zany wit, non sequiturs, impulsiveness, and use of a running gag about her missing brother. Three years later, the versatile Craig *Rice, in her capacity as ghost-writer for Gypsy Rose Lee, created *The G-String Murders (The Strip-Tease Murders*, 1941) a novel featuring the stripper. Ghostwriting for George Sanders a few years later, Rice introduced the actor as a character in *Crime on My Hands* (1944).

During the 1930s and 1940s, Clayton Rawson, a magician known professionally as "the Great Merlini," published a series of detective novels and short stories under his stage name. The author himself appears as the magician *sleuth in these works, which draw heavily on his professional experience and which established him as one who could perform *sleights of hand on the page as well as on stage.

Celebrityhood is put to another use in Peter Lovesey's *Keystone* (1983), a work of fiction built around such historical figures as Mack Sennett, Mabel Normand, Fatty Arbuckle, and the Keystone Kops. This well-researched novel incorporates numerous factual details including references to the Kops as former tumblers and acrobats, the assignment of the most dangerous stunts to the newest member of the group, and the portrayal of the tumultuous love affair between Sennett Mark and Normand.

Celebrity-based fiction may be closely allied with the *true crime narrative in which speculations upon unsolved actual cases serve as *plot vehicles. James *Ellroy's *The Black Dahlia* (1987) was inspired by the *murder of his own mother as well as the torso killing in 1947 of Elizabeth Short, a bit player in the movies. The 1976 murder of Sal Mineo, which baffled Los Angeles police until 1979, was the basis for Susan Braudy's *Who Killed Sal Mineo?* (1982). The author takes liberties with certain facts but tells an engaging tale of a young *New York female reporter turned *amateur detective in the hard-boiled tradition.

Stuart Kaminsky, Andrew Bergman, and George *Baxt have written celebrity-based mysteries laced with elements of parody and *satire. Kaminsky and Bergman create plots in which unknown *private eyes handle awkward situations for famous clients. Kaminsky's Toby Peters conducts quiet, secret investigations to avoid scandal for Judy Garland in *Murder on the Yellow Brick Road* (1978), to stop the blackmailing of Errol Flynn in *Bullet for a Star* (1977), and to locate Bette Davis's missing husband in *The Devil Met a Lady* (1993). Bergman enjoys pairing entertainers and politicians in his work—for example, Humphery Bogart and Richard Nixon work together convincingly in *Hollywood and LeVine* (1975). Baxt vividly blends the worlds of politics and entertainment in *The Tallulah Bankhead Murder Case* (1987). He brings other celebrities to life in *The Dorothy Parker Murder Case* (1984) and *The Alfred Hitchcock Murder Case* (1986).

A celebrity himself, Steve Allen drew on his many years in show business and his cerebral *humor to write *The Talk Show Murders* (1982), *Murder on the Glitter Box* (1989), *Murder in Vegas* (1991), *The Murder Game* (1993), and *Wake Up to Murder* (1997). Allen and his wife, Jayne Meadows, play variously heroes, *suspects, and patsies.

[*See also* pastiches.]

• Marvin J. Wolf, and Katherine Mader, *Fallen Angels: Chronicles of L.A. Crime and Mystery* (1986). Michael Munn, *The Hollywood Murder Casebook* (1987).

—Katherine M. Restaino

HISTORICAL MYSTERY. Despite whatever universal explanatory power they have, schemes for interpretation of reality bear traces of their origin in specific times and places. Sigmund Freud's theory of *family pathology has evident roots in the late nineteenth-century bourgeois culture of central Europe, but it nevertheless has utility in anachronistic application to examination of, say, the conflicts of medieval churchmen with papal authority. A similar anachronism informs the entertaining practice of relating adventures set in the past through the modern genre of crime and detective fiction. Although the genre sprang from the conditions of modern life that define crime as a major social problem and created the necessity for professional detectives, writers face little difficulty in using the narrative genre conditioned by present social experience to "read" events of the past.

Ellis *Peters wrote twenty novels featuring as detective Brother *Cadfael, a twelfth-century Benedictine monk. Lindsey Davis produces a series about Marcus Didius Falco, whose career in ancient Rome follows the occupational pattern of a *private eye, and Margaret Doody places *Aristotle Detective* (1978) in Athens in the year 332 B.C.

Most writers who historicize the mystery genre, however, prefer *settings in the more recent past. One of the most highly regarded of these is Peter Lovesey, who introduced the Victorian detectives Sergeant Cribb and Constable Thackeray in *Wobble to Death* (1970), followed the next year by the memorably titled *The Detective Wore Silk Drawers*. While Cribb and Thackeray are fictional characters, Lovesey's novels *Bertie and the Timman* (1987), *Bertie and the Seven Bodies* (1990), and *Bertie and the Crime of Passion* (1993) use "Bertie"—Albert Edward, Prince of Wales (later King Edward VII)—as detective. Others using the Victorian *milieu include the novels by Elizabeth Peters about the archaeologist Amelia Peabody, and Anne Perry, who writes two series about the period: novels featuring Police Inspector Thomas Pitt and his wife Charlotte, who assists him with investigations, and the works about Inspector William Monk, a detective whose career in fiction begins when he awakens in a hospital in 1850 with no recall of his identity.

Works of historical mystery-making set in nineteenth-century America naturally employ cultural scenery different from that of Victorian England, and include distinctly American events. Miriam G. Monfredo writes about Glynis Tryon, a librarian and women's rights exponent whose home is Seneca Falls, New York, the site of the 1848 meeting on suffrage, where the fictional Glynis meets the historic Elizabeth Cady Stanton in *Seneca Falls Inheritance* (1992). Wendi Lee writes a series about Jefferson Birch, a detective in the Old West. With *The Strange Files of Fremont Jones* (1995), Diane Day begins a series set in turn-of-the-century *San Francisco about a young woman who runs a typing service. Teona Tone introduced a wealthy lady detective residing in Washington, D.C. in 1899 with *Lady on the Line* (1983).

Like "straight" historical fiction, historical mysteries require their authors to research customs and institutions of the past to achieve verisimilitude, or appearance of actuality, necessary in a genre that provides readers a guarantee of realism. But there is also a body of historical mystery that willingly accepts the constraints of the historical record in order to explore actual *puzzles from the past. Edgar Allan *Poe based "The Mystery of Marie Roget" (*Snowden's Lady's Companion*, Nov. 1842) on a real *murder of a young woman. Robert H. *van Gulik initiated his series about Judge Dee with a translation of an anonymous account of actual cases. Colin *Dexter's *The Wench Is Dead* (1989) treats an unsolved case of a woman found dead in an *Oxford canal. F. Tennyson Jesse's *A Pin to See the Peepshow* (1934) imaginatively recreates the circumstances surrounding a marital crime Jesse covered as a court journalist. Margaret Atwood has contributed to the genre with her novel *Alias Grace* (1996). Reminiscent of Jesse's work, it speculates about the circumstances surrounding Grace Marks's imprisonment for murder in Toronto in 1843. The greatest number of fictionalized treatments of actual past crimes, however, can be generally categorized as clustering around five historical puzzles: the death of the princes in the Tower (Richard III); the identity of Jack the Ripper; the T. J. Wise forgeries; the conspiracy theories about John F. Kennedy's assassination; and the death of Christopher Marlowe.

Possibly the most famous historical mystery is *The Daughter of Time* (1951), by Josephine *Tey—not because it is set in the past, but because it deploys Inspector Alan Grant of *Scotland Yard to work retrospectively on the disappearance of King Edward V and his brother Richard, the duke of York. In a simulation of the writer's own task, Tey presents Grant researching the case and reasoning his way to the conviction that Richard III was innocent of the *murder of the princes. Actually, then, *The Daughter of Time* is not a historical re-creation but a novel about a historical mystery. The same must be said about other attempts to address the Ricardian puzzle, such as Elizabeth Peters's *The Murders of Richard III* (1974) and Guy M. Townsend's *To Prove a Villain* (1985). The circumstances in Peters's novel concern a meeting of Ricardians in an English manor house for an announcement of absolute proof of Richard's *innocence. Townsend uses the historical crime as a classroom history exercise, debunking Tey's theory by citing academic essays and historical documents that suggest Richard's *guilt.

For Elizabethan enthusiasts, the ambiguities surrounding Christopher Marlowe's death are examined in Martha Grimes's *The Dirty Duck* (1984), Judith Cook's *The Slicing Edge of Death* (1993), and Charles Nicholl's *The Reckoning* (1992). In Grimes's book the historical matter is again presented as the object of modern investigation. Grimes interweaves information about Marlowe's death with the murders of American women tourists, so that the *family jealousy that motivates the modern mystery echoes the political jealousies of the Marlowe murder. By contrast with Grimes, Cook recreates the *atmosphere of the Elizabethan theater world, develops Marlowe as a character, and restores the political intrigues of the Renaissance. Two "literary" novels about the Marlowe mystery are George Garrett's *Entered from the Sun* (1990) and Anthony Burgess's *A Dead Man in Deptford* (1993).

The oldest of the fictions about Jack the Ripper is *The Lodger* (1913) by Marie *Belloc Lowndes, who mingles the Ripper murders with the crimes of Dr. Neill Cream, noted in his day as a copycat Ripper. Hilary Bailey in *The Cry from Street to Street* (1992) uses the Ripper murders as a means of rendering Victorian *London from the point of view of the women being hunted by the Ripper. Other writers have taken the Ripper's crimes as material to weave into fictional *pastiche, most notably the works linking the crimes of the Ripper with Sherlock *Holmes: *The West End Horror* (1976), by Nicholas Meyer; *The Last Sherlock Holmes Story* (1978), by Michael Dibdin; *The Mycroft Memoranda* (1984), by Ray Walsh; and *The Whitechapel Horrors: A Sherlock Holmes Novel* (1992), by Edward B. Hanna.

The T. J. Wise forgeries, discovered in 1934, serve as inspiration for at least three novels about manuscript forgeries. In Julian *Symons's *Bland Beginning* (1949) the illegitimacy of the second son's claim to a family fortune is a secret buried in forged documents. Lee Thayer in *Murder Stalks the Circle* (1947) employs *forgery as a basis for murder and adds an historical fillip with a recreation of the Mark Twain house in Hartford, Connecticut. William H. Hallahan trumps the Wise case in *The Ross Forgery* (1973), which relates a labyrinthine tale of scholars forging the forgeries.

The neverending fascination with John F. Kennedy has yielded several fictional treatments of the historical circumstances alleged to surround the assassination. Charles McCarry's *Tears of Autumn* (1975) sets the investigator Paul Christopher to a search for details of a conspiracy including Vietnamese, Soviet, and Cuban connections. Don DeLillo's *Libra* (1988) uses the historical assassination as an opportunity to profile Lee Harvey Oswald, as does Norman Mailer in *Oswald's Tale: An American Mystery* (1995). And there is even a pastiche by Edmund Aubrey entitled *Sherlock Holmes in Dallas* (1980) that compounds anachronism by setting the *Great Detective to the case of the murder of JFK.

Finally, there are historical mysteries that employ historical personages in fictional circumstances. Elliott Roosevelt's series featuring his mother Eleanor Roosevelt playing detective serves as an example of this subtype, as does the Toby Peters series by Stuart Kaminsky in which the detective addresses criminal problems having to do with famous celebrities of the past.

[*See also* Historical Figures in Crime and Mystery Writing; Memoirs, Early Detective and Police; Newgate Novel; Newspaper Reports; Realism, Conventions of.]

• Alison Weir, *The Princes in the Tower* 1992. *Mystery Readers Journal* 9, 2 & 3 (1993). Jennifer S. Palmer, "Mysteries of the Ages. Four Millennia of Murder and Mayhem in Historical Mysteries." *Armchair Detective* 30 (spring 1997): 156–64. Kathryn Kennison, "Past Mysteries, Present Masters," *Armchair Detective* 30 (spring 1997): 176–84.

—Catherine E. Hoyser

HISTORY OF CRIME AND MYSTERY WRITING.

*Common sense suggests that literature in some way or another always expresses the time and place of its creation. The familiar way of making this point is to say literature reflects society. If that were true, though, imaginative literature would read like ethnography laced with precise references to established customs and usual behavior, or would resemble travel articles that include the names and addresses of places the reader is invited to visit. Surely that is not how literature works, for fiction is licensed to invent places, even when they bear known names, and to describe ways of behaving that have never before occurred. Still and all, literature carries within itself evidence of its origin in an actual time and place of origin. This is simply to say that literature always is historical. It was produced through circumstances peculiar to a period of time and a specific venue, and, while writers do not transcribe those periods and venues, their work mediates the originary reality. Despite the best efforts of the Baker Street Irregulars in advancing the pretense that Sherlock *Holmes actually lived and breathed, readers discover that the "truth" of Arthur Conan *Doyle's tales emerges not in the accuracy of the railroad schedules Holmes has committed to memory or in the catalogue of cigar ashes he has compiled. Instead, the tenor of Victorian Britain is embodied in an invented image of a Great Detective who manifests the optimism about reason and science characteristic of middle-class English society in the nineteenth century.*

All literature is a mediation of history. So, too, does literature possess a record of production, which forms another sort of history. The essays to follow constitute a review of that record for the crime and mystery genres. They form a history of this popular literature's mediated rendering of the time and place of its origins.

This entry is divided into six parts providing a chronological survey of the development of the crime and mystery genre:

Precursors of the Genre (to 1840)
Formation of the Genre (1841–88)
The Genre in the Late Nineteenth and Early Twentieth Centuries (1889–1917)
American and British Developments in the Genre (1918–45)
Diversification of the Genre (1900s–60s)
Establishment of the Genre (1970s–90s)

For further information, please refer to Craft of Crime and Mystery Writing, The.

PRECURSORS OF THE GENRE (TO 1840)

A loose interpretation of the attributes of crime and mystery writing can locate the origins of the genre whenever human communities first turned their gaze upon the issues of *evil and morality. For some historians, therefore, *Oedipus Rex* qualifies as a mystery story, as does the Hebrew narrative of Susanna and the Elders. In her introduction to the *Omnibus of Crime* Dorothy L. *Sayers nominates the unknown authors of the Apocrypha, as well as Herodotus and Virgil, as forerunners of the modern form. Other critics assign a share of paternity to the stories with *puzzles, such as the narrative about the princes of Serendip (1719) by Chevalier de Mailly, a story adapted by Voltaire in *Zadig Memnon* (1747); or stories of lowly life, such as Daniel Defoe's *Moll Flanders* (1722). Especially notable too is William *Godwin's political thriller *Things As They Are; or, The Adventures of Caleb Williams* (1794), whose *plot involves concealed *guilt and eventual exposure.

Critics making these genealogical claims seem determined to establish an antique origin for crime and mystery writing that will distinguish it from the ephemeral and sensational works so commonly denigrated as merely popular, or even mass, literature. Still there is no escaping the fact that, while themes of evil and guilt in literature certainly are ancient and universal, the narrative form centering upon a criminal problem appears only in recent times. Dorothy L. Sayers maintains that the form could not develop beyond the instances she cites as forerunners of detection stories, because time had to pass before public opinion was on the side of the law, rather than of its violators, and before there was widespread interest in the use of material proof. To put the point more exactly than Sayers does, the narrative form occupied with criminal acts and their solution arose when societies discerned crime as a distinct problem. It was not always so, for although it might issue from evil, crime is different from sin. Crime as a social problem accompanies the growth of urban centers housing large populations in conditions that create anonymity and aggravate the differences between property and poverty. Where sin might be sufficient explanation for violations of order in stable, traditional communities where the dominance of a lord or squire capped a system of control, the broader term and idea of crime was required to explain disruptions of order in the incipiently capitalist cities with their complex property arrangements, landless inhabitants, and fluid social relationships. As crime became a recognizable problem, its control eluded the grasp of the established order of church or state. By the process of division of labor characteristic of complex communities, a new agency for order emerged—in time, to become the familiar bureau of police, but at first working in an improvisational fashion.

Against this background of the historical sources for the problem of crime, the literary lineage of crime and mystery writing can well begin with such a work as *The Newgate Calendar, or, Malefactors Bloody Register . . . from . . . 1700 to the Present Time* (1773), a compilation employing a traditional code of honor as it tracked the deeds of a new criminal class. The appeal of the *Calendar's* accounts of crime lay in the sensation surrounding the details. Similarly, a spate of cheaply printed pamphlets alleging to contain the true confessions of culprits facing execution offered their readers proof that crime was abroad in the land.

As such news of crime spread, the subsequent appearance of popularly written recollections of "thief catchers" presented the challenge to disorder and crime. Priority in these narratives belongs to Eugène François *Vidocq, whose *Mémoires* first appeared in 1828–29. It has been suggested that the vivid portrayal of the *underworld in his memoirs owes a lot to Vidocq's personal experience outside the law before he turned on the brotherhood of thieves. In any case, his writings are a marked departure from moralizing treatments of wrong doing into the new area of a secular contest between the lawless and the agents of social order.

As early as 1748, Henry and John Fielding, magistrates of the Bow Street Court in London, established an organization of constables dubbed the Bow Street Runners. Anticipating the eventual techniques of police procedure, the Runners developed skills in gathering information about criminals and crime and in investigation at the scenes of crimes. The adventures of the Runners were memorialized in *Richmond; or, Scenes in the Life of a Bow Street Runner, drawn up from his private memoranda* (1827). Clearly a work of fiction rather than a documentary record, the story of Richmond, written by an anonymous author, introduces its lead character as an aimless youth familiar with criminals and proceeds to follow him as he joins the Runners and works on five detailed cases involving abduction, swindling, and other confidence games (but not murder).

Two years after the publication of Richmond's two-volume novel, the period of improvisational policing ended in England with the passage of Sir Robert Peel's Metropolitan Police Act, which introduced a uniformed corporate force charged as much with the prevention of crime through patrols and vigilance as with the pursuit of thieves. In the United States, local governments established metropolitan police forces later in the century. Meanwhile, Charles *Dickens introduced the official police of *London into popular literature with a set of articles about the Detective Police, whose office was established in 1842. Published in the magazine *Household Words* between 1850 and 1859, and later in *All the Year Round* between 1859 and 1870, Dickens's articles portrayed the detectives as dauntless and ingenious, engaging in person and skillful in their profession. In short, the articles by Dickens countered a lingering public dislike of spying and sneakiness with characterizations of new heroes fit to use the law in a never-ending struggle with crime.

[*See also* Memoirs, Early Detective and Police; Newgate Novel; Newspaper Reports; Penny Dreadful; Police History: History of British Policing.]

• Frank Wadleigh Chandler, *The Literature of Roguery*, 2 vols. (1907). A. E. Murch, *The Development of the Detective Novel* (1958). John M. Reilly, "Beneficent Roguery: The Detective in the Capitalist City," *Praxis* 3 (1976): 154–63.

FORMATION OF THE GENRE (1841–88)

The historical developments that forced the problem of crime before the public simultaneously created in that public an avid interest in reading about crime. Some of the works created to meet that interest exploited dangers to detectives and offered vicarious thrills to readers. In England that was the motif in the collections of stories by William Russell, writing between 1852 and 1870, and publishing usually under the pseudonym "Waters." Seeking to feed the apparent public hunger for documentary details about crime, Russell presented his narratives as accounts of real-life experience as a detective. Other writers also claimed the memoir as their genre, among them the American George S. McWatters, whose *Knots Untied; or, Ways and By-Ways in the Hidden Life of American Detectives* (1871) describes the detective as "dishonest, crafty, and unscrupulous when it is necessary to be so," because "he is the outgrowth of a diseased and corrupted state of things, and is, consequently, morally diseased himself." The famed Allan Pinkerton, presenting a whole series of alleged memoirs in the 1870s and after, showed his agents to be sly as those in McWatters, but rather than *antiheroes, Pinkerton's detectives are complete champions of commercial order and social progress. The apotheosis of the detective in memoir became complete in America when Julian Hawthorne published a series of romances ostensibly derived from the diaries of Thomas Byrnes, head of the New York City Detectives. Published in the 1880s, the Hawthorne romances relate bizarre stories of international criminal rings, declassed nobles, and attenuated love; but presiding over all in brief episodes and scenes is Thomas Byrnes, a genius in inferential reasoning, possessed of incomparable knowledge of the criminal world, and the inevitable executive for a worldwide network of amateurs who follow his direction in pursuit of *clues to solve the cases he undertakes.

To say the least, it was farfetched to imagine that Hawthorne's stories provided genuine documentation of crime. On the other hand, in colonizing the romance genre with criminal circumstances his writing represents the detective edging into the realm of archetypal hero. *Dime novels present a similar process. Originating as adventurous narratives of the Western frontier and before that of patriotic wars, the American dime novel began in the 1870s to set its action-filled *plots in the *underworld, with amateur and *private detectives (as well as police) racing through episodes whose chief effect was that of elevated *suspense. The most durable name in the dime novel format was Nick *Carter, cast in a legendary mold by many house writers who willingly concealed their own identities. John Russell Coryell began the serial with a trilogy in the *New York Weekly* in 1886, and Frederick Merrill Van Rensselaer Dey took over in 1891, writing more than four hundred additional adventures. Other American writers carried on the name and the saga even until recent years. In Great Britain, the counterpart to Nick Carter is Sexton Blake, a house name originated in 1893 for publication in boys' papers. Reportedly he has lived through more than four thousand adventures written by over two hundred authors—a clear record.

When documentation of criminality was the motive for writing in the nineteenth century, narrative often suffered, even if it was highly fictionalized. Plots were loosely constructed and characterization slight, for the stories were meant to create shock and surprise at the strange happenings reported. When writers took their models from the genres of romance and adventure, the narratives loosed their moorings from the circumstances of actual crime. In either case, these narratives packaged crime as a commodity in familiar wrappings. By contrast, the period was also marked by literary experimentation that resulted in the production of the new and distinct genre of detective fiction.

No history of crime and mystery writing challenges the premiere place accorded Edgar Allan *Poe. In three short stories written for popular audiences he fashioned conventions and patterns that made a new type of literature. "The Murders in the Rue Morgue," published in *Graham's Magazine* in April 1841, linked the element of the *impossible crime in a sealed room with the character of an eccentric and brilliant investigator. "The Mystery of Marie Rogét," published in *Snowden's Lady's Companion* in November 1842, gave Poe's *sleuth the Chevalier C. Auguste *Dupin a historical murder to solve from his armchair. And "The Purloined Letter," appearing in *The Gift* (1845), provides a display of ratiocination by which Dupin's unusual talents triumph over the earthbound techniques of police procedure. In addition, Poe's stories establish the use of a secondary narrative voice in the detective genre, someone to represent the audience in the presence of the *Great Detective, and they give prominence to the idea that a detective's mind can explicate the most puzzling events with a chain of cause and effect beyond the ken of other people. For all of their achievements, and all of the promise for later writing that we see in them, Poe's stories did not at once find imitators. It was as if the stories were archived while other influences stimulated the development toward the new genre.

One of these influences was the form of narrative classified in *Blackwood's Magazine* in 1862 as *sensation novels. The extraordinarily popular *Lady Audley's Secret* (1862) by the English author M. E. *Braddon, a tale of insanity and amateur detection, may stand for the type, along with Mrs. Henry *Wood's *East Lynne* (1861), with its subplot of *murder. Related as well to the sensation novel, and displaying the growing interest among writers in using the materials of crime, are the works of the Irish writer Joseph Sheridan Le Fanu, famed for his *ghost stories but also highly regarded for his use of the new science of forensics in such works as *Wylder's Hand* (1864) and *Checkmate* (1871). Wilkie *Collins's *The Woman in White* (1860) is said to have influenced Braddon, and shares traits with the work of other sensation writers. Collins's *The Moonstone* (1868), however, is more completely a detection fiction than the others' writing.

All of these works are distinguished by complex plotting and detail of the sort characteristic of Victorian fiction in all genres. None shows indications of following Poe. One possible explanation for the archiving of Poe's detective fiction lies in the differences in the nineteenth century between writing for magazines and writing for the established book-buying public. The modes differed according to the vehicle of distribution. Books allowed readers to luxuriate in lengthy description and convolutions of *plot. The serial publication of magazines, and of dime novels too, demanded economy and a single effect. As a consequence, crime and mystery writing followed several streams of development. There was the flow of memoir-styled fictions, a stream of adventures and romances that adapted the problem of crime to existing conventions, and the surging current of long fictions. All were quite apart from the short story form in which Poe excelled. Each stream has its differential history.

As for the novel, in the United States historians cite either Seeley *Regester or Anna Katharine *Green as the parent of book-length detective fiction. Regester was the pseudonym of Metta Victoria Fuller Victor who produced, among other works, a book entitled *The Dead Letter* (1866) which chronicles a detection process aided by the detective's clairvoyance. Green, however, completed a series of detective works, beginning with *The Leavenworth Case: A Lawyer's Story* (1878) and continuing until she published her last book, *The Step on the Stair*, in 1923. Green's best-known detective, Ebenezer Gryce—a lawyer, police officer, and narrator of the cases—appears in eleven of Green's books, working on cases in Manhattan society. In her time, Green won a large readership with Gryce, and sustained it while introducing two additional detectives: the elder Miss Amelia Butterworth and the youthful Violet Strange, each in her way an anticipation of later female detectives in fiction.

In France, full-length detective fiction debuted in *L'Affaire Lerouge* (1866), a work known in English as *The Widow Lerouge*, written by Émile *Gaboriau. The book, which appeared first in serial publication, introduced the consulting detective Pere Tabaret. A reprint of the Lerouge story in 1873 made Gaboriau famous at home and abroad, preparing him an audience for subsequent detection narratives relating the cases of M. Lecoq of the *Sûreté. Gaboriau, unlike the nineteenth-century crime novelists of England and America was decidedly willing to acknowledge the influence of Poe on his narrative form, but he also diligently studied the literature of factual crime and the workings of the police court. Gaboriau thus merged two of the streams of crime writing, so that as he remains important for the quality of his writing in itself, he assumes the historical importance of completing the formative period of the genre.

[*See also* Memoirs, Early Detective and Police; Police History.]

• H. Douglas Thomson, *Masters of Mystery: A Study of the Detective Story* (1931). T. J. Binyon, *Murder Will Out: The Detective in Fiction* (1989). Martin A. Kayman, *From Bow Street to Baker Street: Mystery, Detection, and Narrative* (1992).

THE GENRE IN THE LATE NINETEENTH AND EARLY TWENTIETH CENTURIES (1889–1917)

No view of late nineteenth-century popular literature can overlook the phenomenon of Fergus Hume's *The Mystery of a Hansom Cab* (1886), which was the blockbuster best-seller of its time. The accepted account of its origin holds that the Australian Hume extracted the narrative formula for his *potboiler from the mysteries of Émile *Gaboriau intending to cash in on the public taste for crime stories. The historical importance of this derivative mystery lies not in any literary quality. Despite years of trying, Hume could not repeat his initial success. Instead, the remarkable sales of inexpensive editions of *The Mystery of a Hansom Cab* testify to the emergence of the large audience whose eagerness for diverting tales provided the opportunity for the fuller literary development of crime and mystery fiction.

The course of that development was charted by both narrative and commercial invention. The chief narrative innovation was the *Great Detective, who entered literature in the character of Sherlock *Holmes presiding in the investigations of "A Study in Scarlet," published in *Beeton's Christmas Annual* for 1887. In literary terms, that debut was as important as the birth of the detective story itself forty-six years earlier when *Graham's Magazine* published Edgar Allan *Poe's "The Murders in the Rue Morgue." While Poe sketched the pattern and conventions of the genre, Arthur Conan *Doyle gave the genre its human interest. But as effective a character as Holmes was, he still needed a vehicle to secure a large, regular audience. The periodical press, employing technology that allowed for rapid and inexpensive printing and a mass distribution network that could serve readers their weekly or monthly helpings of entertainment, provided that audience. The American publisher of *Lippincott's* issued the second long Holmes story, "The Sign of Four," in 1890. Doyle's Holmes series subsequently began a long run in the *Strand, a popular monthly magazine published in London. The first twelve stories appeared from July 1891 to June 1892, followed by another twelve that concluded with "The Final Problem" in December 1893. Eventually Doyle published fifty-six Holmes stories and four novellas. In another brilliant commercial practice, the stories were regularly collected for publication as books, beginning with *The Adventures of Sherlock Holmes* (1892).

Besides the human interest to be found in a character with compulsive habits and eccentricities, a biography that suggests past influences continuing into his present life, a degree of justified arrogance, and a stylized way of speaking, the Holmes stories also contribute to the genre of detective fiction the grounds for modern *heroism. Poe's Chevalier C. Auguste *Dupin was an abstract "ratiocinative" thinker, but Doyle's Holmes, as an empirical detective with laboratory training, could be readily linked to the general readers' nineteenth-century optimism about the accomplishments of the scientific method. Moreover, as a consulting detective rather than as a government official, Holmes suited the middle-class belief in *individualism that made business entrepreneurs heroes of their time. In short, Doyle gave his character, too, the traits of a culture hero.

Finally, Doyle popularized for other writers notable features of narration. The use of series characters is one of these features. Designing the series character's sidekick as the narrator of the stories was another, as was the formation of an economical sequence for the *plot. The series character encouraged reader identification with the series figure and provided a simple means for rounding out character in the limited space of a short story. The sidekick storyteller keeps the subjective life of the detective concealed yet present nonetheless, while introducing into the narrative someone to ask questions that are on the reader's mind and to signal the appropriate attitudes of puzzlement or awe at the detective's procedure. The *plot sequence—a client presents a problem, the detective and sidekick investige, and the solution is explained in—maintains the narrative focus on intellectual challenge and marginalizes issues of legality, punishment, and morality.

The potent influence of Doyle's modeling of the detective story is readily apparent upon his contemporaries writing in 1890–1910. Arthur *Morrison, also writing initially for the *Strand*, followed the Holmes formula of *characterization and plot arrangement through eighteen stories about Martin Hewitt, a law clerk whose journalist friend chronicles the adventures. Those adventures also were reissued in three volumes of the collected stories appearing between 1894 and 1896. Baroness Emmuska *Orczy, most famous for the costume *thriller *The Scarlet Pimpernel* (1905), had earlier success with a series of stories about Bill Owen, the *Old Man in the Corner of a restaurant who explains to the journalist Polly Burton the solutions to crimes reported in the newspapers. There are thirty-eight of these stories, a clutch of them collected in *The Old Man in the Corner* (1909). As the circumstances of the stories indicate, Orczy inscribes her own touches on the Holmes model by making her figure an *armchair detective and by centering most of the narrative attention on relating the solution of the crime; yet the inspiration for her Old Man is the image of the *Great Detective.

The dominance of that image challenged writers to devise engaging variations on Holmes. One such variation exaggerated the mental powers of the detective while minimizing the significance of crime. Beginning with "The Problem of Cell 13" (*The Thinking Machine*, 1907), the American writer Jacques *Futrelle prepared forty-three stories about Professor S. F. X. *Van Dusen, whose brainy and often flamboyant solutions of problems earned him approbation as the Thinking Machine. Where Futrelle's detective narratives were meant to impress readers with the workings of genius, R. Austin *Freeman took as his emphasis the scientific method of the Great Detective. *The Red Thumb Mark* (1907) introduced the forensic scientist Dr. John *Thorndyke in a case of falsified fingerprints related by his assistant Dr. Christopher Jervis. Throughout a long series of stories and novels, Thorndyke's laboratory and his encyclopedic knowledge of experimental findings convinced readers of the potency of science for criminal investigation. Freeman's methodological emphasis and interest in the laboratory milieu led him also to a major innovation in detection story plot: the *inverted detective story. In this variety of problem story, the narrative reveals everything to the reader in

its opening—who committed the crime and how—leaving for the body of narration an account of the detective figuring it all out. Still another emphatic treatment of the intellectual element of detection originating in the image of Holmes as *the* Great Detective can be found in *The Mystery of the Yellow Room* (1908) by the French author Gaston *Leroux, who also wrote *The Phantom of the Opera* (1911). This mystery, which includes lengthy passages about the processes of thinking, complicates the examination of criminal suspects by revealing the culprit to be, indeed, the *least likely suspect—namely, the professional detective. As a consequence, the unofficial detective Joseph Rouletabille assumes the position of the wonderful reasoner whose accomplishment is recorded by his friend Sainclair.

Among the original Great Detective's skills was *disguise. In the Holmes stories this is a decidedly secondary interest of narration. Thomas W. Hanshew, however, elevated the aptitude in his stories about Hamilton Cleek, the protagonist of *The Man of the Forty Faces* (1910), to the level of detection method. A much more substantial variation on the detective formula, but one destined to wait decades before fulfillment, was changing the *gender of the detective to female. C. L. Pirkis's *The Experiences of Loveday Brooke: Lady Detective* (1894; *Loveday Brooke*) and Orczy's tales in *Lady Molly of Scotland Yard* (1910) represent the early innovation in the short story of equipping the lead character of a genre fostered by male authors and framed in masculinist values with the insight and experiences of a woman. In the full-length novel of the period, however, there were very strong and influential efforts by Anna Katharine *Green and her younger contemporary Mary Roberts *Rinehart. *The Leavenworth Case* (1878) presents Green's lawyer detective Ebenezer Gryce. *That Affair Next Door* (1897) assigns Amelia Butterworth to the case as Gryce's associate, and *The Golden Slipper and Other Problems for Violet Strange* (1915) introduces a female detective as central character. As its length suggests it might, Green's writing retains the ponderous detail and leisured pace of late Victorian novels at a time when the more economical, faster moving short story dominated the genre. Still, Green had her influence, not least upon Rinehart, who stripped down the novel of detection to create the mystery centered upon the fears and feelings of the innocent central character. Rinehart is often charged with inventing the *Had-I-But-Known school of writing in which a narrator, usually female, foreshadows her telling of events by expressions of rueful regret. Rinehart's output, which began with *The Circular Staircase* in 1908, appears by contrast with other genre fiction of the period to be a form entirely different. Criminal investigation is minor, the detection process more intuitive than methodical, and the detective scarcely figures. What Rinehart retains, though, is the situational feeling of the crime and detective story. When the Great Detective is on the scene, peril is distanced but still it is there. Rinehart eliminates that distance and lures the reader into participation with her protagonist in emotional adventure.

English-speaking readers have a continuing fascination with French detectives. There were Dupin, the detectives created by Gaboriau, Leroux's Rouletabille, and, beginning in 1910 with the novel *At the Villa Rose*, Inspector Gabriel *Hanaud of the *Sûreté, the leading character of the English author A. E. W. *Mason. In contrast to his scientific colleagues in detection, Hanaud thinks that detectives are "servants of chance" not confident investigators. Robert Barr also determined that French nationality was appropriate for the detection business, and created the society detective Eugene Valmont, whose humorous manner and style of speech anticipate Agatha *Christie's Belgian sleuth, Hercule *Poirot. The stories about Valmont appeared in magazines in the United States as well as Great Britain before their collection in *The Triumphs of Eugene Valmont* (1906).

Departure from the enthusiasm for empirical detection methods can be seen as well in G. K. *Chesterton's stories of Father *Brown, whose career begins in the stories collected in *The Innocence of Father Brown* (1911). In portraying the priest, Chesterton drastically altered important features of the Great Detective. Brown is physically unimpressive, a bit bumbling. He employs no science and has little adventurous action in his career. Instead, he serves as an exponent of Chesterton's religious beliefs, seeking solutions to crime by means of his clerical knowledge about human *evil, exploring and explaining the crimes in his stories in aid of Chesterton's interest in points of doctrine. The sharp differences between Brown and Holmes or Thorndyke effectively illustrate the broadening of the terrain for detective fiction at the turn of the century. With the audience established and the thirst for detective fiction increasing, authors had increasing opportunity, as well as the increasing necessity, for variation and development within the genre.

If the exploits of a detective thrill an audience, so might the adventures of a *master criminal. Such reasoning accounts for the appearance of A. J. *Raffles created by E. W. *Hornung, Doyle's brother-in-law. In his own way Raffles was as exemplary as Holmes, for he was a model gentleman, although a thief; a man motivated by a desire to employ his remarkable skills, as well as by a need for money; and a figure accompanied by a loyal friend, Bunny, who writes up the exploits in an admiring style, as in *The Amateur Cracksman* (1899; *Raffles, the Amateur Cracksman*, 1906). Among other authors who turned their hand to writing about thieves was R. Austin *Freeman who, with John James Pitcairn, coauthored a series of stories about Romney Pringle under the pseudonym Clifford Ashdown. The character of the engaging thief also found French incarnation in the work of Maurice *Leblanc, whose series about Arsène *Lupin began in 1907.

These stories of characters on the other side of the law owe something to traditions of rogue literature along with a debt to detective fiction, for like the narratives of lawless highwaymen they celebrate the brigands. By way of contrast, this period in the history of the genre also introduced fiction of the master criminal. Exploiting both the *prejudice against

Asians that encouraged fear of the "Yellow Peril" and attributes of the gentleman hero of adventure fiction, Sax *Rohmer produced a series about the nefarious doings of *Fu Manchu, beginning with "The Zayat Kiss" (1912). The gentleman of the stories was Sir Denis Nayland Smith, sworn enemy of Fu Manchu and champion of Anglo-Saxon civilization.

A survey of detective writing before World War I must properly end with E. C. *Bentley's *Trent's Last Case* (1913). It fits within the arbitrary time period and presents the action of an elite detective fashioning the solution to the criminal problem—several solutions, in fact. Bentley seemed to have wanted his novel to be received as "an exposure of the detective story." For that reason, he revealed the fallibility of Philip Trent and his susceptibility to the allure of a chief suspect. For all of that, however, the narrative actually renewed the detective story by giving it a new kind of character, the useful *milieu of an upper-class estate, and a pleasingly witty and erudite style. Concluding a period chronologically, it announced the coming of another that would be known as the Golden Age.

[*See also* Eccentrics; Formula;Character; Formula; Plot; Gentleman Thief; Reasoning, Types of; Sidekicks and Sleuthing Teams; Superman/Superwoman Sleuth.]

• Howard Haycraft, *Murder for Pleasure: The Life and Times of the Detective Story* (1941). Sutherland Scott, *Blood in Their Ink: The March of the Modern Mystery Novel* (1953). Ian Ousby, *Guilty Parties: A Mystery Lover's Companion* (1997).

AMERICAN AND BRITISH DEVELOPMENTS IN THE GENRE (1918–45)

The second and third decades of the twentieth century have been dubbed the Golden Age of crime and mystery writing. Appropriately enough, writers of detective fiction were themselves responsible for the demarcation of their work during the time as special. Through an emphasis upon *puzzles at the heart of their detective stories and the jocular compilation of *rules of the game, writers such as Ronald A. *Knox with his ten commandments for detective writing characterized their works as intellectual exercises and, thus, maintained that they were significantly different from both the sensational action stories about crime in *pulp magazines and *dime novels and from the avant garde experimental writing that was emerging in mainstream literature. Setting off this niche for themselves, writers of detective fiction acting as critics also encouraged a protocol for reviewing detective stories: They assumed that good fiction was a chaste narration of the solution to a puzzle without digressions into improbability, sentiment, or unnecessary descriptions of character or scene.

There was a larger field of historical influences to promote such self-consciousness. One of the influences was the rise of commercial lending libraries specializing in the kind of contemporary and popular writing that public libraries could not supply. Publishing houses also promoted detective novels as commodities and entered competition with the periodical press in supplying the market. Slimming down the length of books from the size to which they had grown in the Victorian period, employing technology to yield economies in large scale production, and capitalizing on the attraction for readers in following a series detective, publishers succeeded in making the novel a preferred mode for telling detective stories. To encourage "brand loyalty" in another way, shrewd publishers and distributors invented the crime *book clubs to make detective fiction available by subscription and to encourage awareness of the continuing supply of criminous entertainment.

Crime and mystery writing had been a predominantly male enterprise, but the new conditions of the market soon attracted female authors who quickly became the stalwarts of the so-called Golden Age. Agatha *Christie introduced Hercule *Poirot in 1920 in The Mysterious Affair at Styles. Her forte was her skill in challenging the rules of the game, along with ingenious plotting. Assured of success with Poirot, she invented yet other series characters: Tuppence and Tommy Beresford, whom she introduced in The Secret Adversary (1922); Miss Jane *Marple, who started her long career in The Murder at the Vicarage (1930); and Superintendent Battle, who took his first case in The Secret of Chimneys (1925).

Margery *Allingham introduced the *sleuth Albert *Campion in The Crime at Black Dudley (1929; The Black Dudley Murder). An element of romance for Campion's life and a sharply observant style of relating his adventures were the hallmarks of Allingham's work during the Golden Age. Dorothy L. *Sayers also allowed romance a role in her stories of Lord Peter *Wimsey, introduced in Whose Body (1923)—so much so, in fact, that adherents to the original values of the rules of the game still feel they must take her to task for pursuing the love affair of Wimsey and the crime novelist Harriet *Vane through several books, including Gaudy Night (1935), in which they agree to marry, and Busman's Honeymoon (1937), in which they solve a crime while on their wedding journey.

Josephine *Tey also allowed men and women an equal place. Writing as Gordon Daviot, she introduced her series figure Inspector Alan Grant in The Man in the Queue (1929; Killer in the Crowd), provided an amateur female sleuth in Miss Pym Disposes (1946), and featured a male lawyer turned detective in The Franchise Affair (1948). Critical tradition adds yet another woman to the list of top Golden Age authors—Ngaio *Marsh. Marsh's series detective, Inspector (later Superintendent) Roderick *Alleyn, first appears in A Man Lay Dead (1934). Alleyn, like Wimsey, also marries in the course of his adventures.

The United States has its own Golden Age practitioners. One of the founding fathers in America was the art critic Willard Huntington Wright, who deliberately analyzed the formula of detective fiction while he lay ill; he emerged with ideas he embodied in twelve novels that he wrote as S. S. Van *Dine featuring the wealthy *amateur detective Philo *Vance. The series began with The Benson Murder Case (1926). Complicated in their plots and highly mannered in their style, Van Dine's novels represented a transplant of aristocratic character and values to the American scene. The transatlantic amalgam was completed by

Van Dine's "Twenty Rules for Writing Detective Stories" American Magazine, Sept. 1928) that defined the genre as "a kind of intellectual game."

The other American parents of the Golden Age were the cousins Frederic Dannay and Manfred B. Lee, who wrote together as Ellery *Queen and as Barnaby Ross. The Ross novels related the cases of the actor Drury Lane, beginning in The Tragedy of X (1932). The long series of Queen novels, which concern the fictitious writer Ellery *Queen and his father Inspector Richard Queen, began in 1929 with The Roman Hat Mystery. In their conception, these stories owe a deep debt to Van Dine that can be seen in the intellectualized speech of Ellery the son and in the milieu of tony society. The execution of the narratives, however, displayed a personal signature that became increasingly distinctive as the authors developed their characters and cases. That signature can be found in the vigor Queen the author gives to the fundamental process of detection. Complicated plots, a range of *suspects, tours de force in reasoning, and a trademark of introducing a pause in the narrative to invite readers to match wits with Queen, the detective when they have all the clues illustrate how attractive a *puzzle story can be. Besides their exemplary novels, the Queen writers also contributed to the art of detective fiction a flood of secondary materials, including anthologies and bibliographies. In addition, these writers lent support to the continuing production of detective fiction in short story form through Ellery Queen's Mystery Magazine, beginning in 1941 and principally edited by Dannay, and they adapted the genre for radio with the series Adventures of Ellery Queen (1938–41).

A third American writer deserving notice as a founder of the Golden Age traditions was John Dickson *Carr, who developed several series detectives: Henri Bencolin who debuted in It Walks by Night (1930); Dr. Gideon *Fell, a specialist in *locked room mysteries, who started his career in Hag's Nook (1933); and Sir Henry Merrivale, chronicled by Carr (writing as Carr Dickson and then Carter Dickson) beginning with The Bowstring Murders (1933).

A second tier of writers includes Philip *MacDonald, who created a hero without a taste for *violence in Colonel Anthony Ruthven *Gethryn in The Rasp (1924). The educated taste of the Golden Age writers can be found in high relief in the works of Nicholas *Blake, whose Oxonian sleuth Nigel *Strangeways appeared in more than sixteen novels starting with A Question of Proof (1935), and in the novels by Michael *Innes featuring John *Appleby, beginning with Death at the President's Lodging (1936; Seven Suspects).

The period was a veritable big tent under which many innovations were possible. Anthony *Berkeley Cox introduced the offensive man-about-town Roger Sheringham in The Layton Court Mystery (1925). Writing as Francis *Iles in Malice Aforethought (1931), Cox focused on a man's plan to kill his wife. The husband and wife team of G. D. H. *Cole and Margaret Cole wrote a series of novels about Superintendent Henry Wilson that took on the form of highly intellectual procedural stories. G. D. H. Cole wrote the first of these, *The Brooklyn Murders* (1923), on his own, but afterward the books bore both Cole names. A. A. Milne, the children's author, produced a book, *The Red House Mystery* (1922), that has been praised as among the best of Golden Age novels. Devout attention to detail and logical detective work was the hallmark of Freeman Wills *Crofts, who created Inspector Joseph *French for *The Cask* (1920). Carolyn Wells, who actually began her writing career before the turn of the century, contributed the stylized plots of Fleming Stone's detection in upper-class circles to what would become the Golden Age, beginning with *The Clue* (1909), and continued this series and others through eighty novels. Wells also added to the secondary literature a practical guide for writers, *The Technique of the Mystery Story* (1913). Melville Davisson *Post, who began a series about the unscrupulous lawyer Randolph Mason with *The Strange Schemes of Randolph Mason* (1896), anticipated the Golden Age interest in character in his historically based tales of *Uncle Abner, Master of Mysteries* (1918).

The vitality infused into the detective fiction genre during the period when the Golden Age was invented was matched by the creation, first in American pulp short story magazines and then in novels, of hardboiled *fiction. Unlike the self-promoting Golden Age writers, the pulp authors had few literary pretensions. They were originally allied in their techniques with the action writers of *adventure stories. The narratives were clear-cut combats between good and evil, without much concern for the gradations of morality or the philosophy of crime solving. The criminals were either masterminds or stupid, but always brutal. The skillful editorial guidance of Joseph T. Shaw of *Black Mask* magazine made considerable difference, though. In Shaw's words, the magazine wanted "simplicity for the sake of clarity, plausibility, and belief." Shaw also noted that "action is meaningless unless it involves recognizable human characters in three-dimensional form."

The field of influence responsible for creating the hard-boiled manner of writing extended far beyond the agency of one person, however. Shaw needed a stable of authors who would contribute regularly to the magazine and make money for it, since it had been started by the owners of *Smart Set* as a way of funding their more serious and sophisticated project. The writers, of course, needed usable subject matter. This they found in conditions of postwar America as *Prohibition encouraged tolerance for illegal activity, crime became organized, gangsters celebrated, disparities between rich and poor exaggerated, and scandal seemed commonplace in government and circles of high and low society.

The cadre of writers responding to the opportunity to publish in the newer pulp detective magazines included Carroll John *Daly, who is said to have been somewhat like Edgar Allan *Poe in that he laid down the outline for the new way of writing with a series of stories written in the 1920s about Race *Williams; Frederick Nebel, who portrayed the alcoholic reporter Kennedy, and the tough guys Cardigan and

Danny Donahue; George Harmon *Coxe, who created a series about Flashgun Casey, a newspaper photographer with a skill for being on the scene of crimes; Robert Leslie Bellem, who set the womanizing Hollywood detective Dan Turner loose in wisecracking stories; Raoul Whitfield, who wrote under the name of Ramon Decolta about the ex-cop from Manila, Jo Gar; Dashiell *Hammett, whose adventures of the *Continental Op were published first as pulp stories; and Raymond *Chandler, who started writing about *Los Angeles for the *pulp magazines when he was already forty-five years old.

The strenuous job of writing for the poor-paying pulps left little time for reflection, so the common features that allow historians to cluster the hardboiled writers as a school emerged through intuitive responses to the models the writers set for each other and through the commercial success their motifs found. Like populists in politics, the hard-boiled writers were enthralled by the American belief in *individualism but angered by conditions that prevented the little guy from fulfilling his dream. Unequal distribution of wealth was the fundamental object of their enmity; as a result, hard-boiled stories are filled with examples of corrupt rich people. Since most institutions could be thought of as tainted by the inequities induced by wealth, the police, the professions, the political system, and much of the business world was represented as shady and untrustworthy. Given a social world imaged in this fashion, an honest person was naturally alienated, alone, and aloof. Such a person might very well become a freelance detective, since that job allows one to be of some service when the cards are stacked against the folks who are salvageable because they have little stake in the corrupt society. But the detective must be without illusions that success in solving a crime amounts to more than temporary relief, and obviously the detective cannot be an instrument in support of the social order contrived by wealth and bureaucracy. This intuitively devised worldview has an American lineage traceable to the frontier, populist politics, and popular interpretation of American civil values. The worldview is linked as well to cultural traditions that have elevated the independentminded hero in literature and general consciousness. Those sources also lent their influence to the characterization of the hard-boiled *private eye as a figure with a personal code of conduct.

Although hard-boiled writing took its form without much conscious deliberation, it does have some notable statements of its rationale—notably, Chandler's essay "The Simple Art of Murder" (*Atlantic Monthly*, Dec. 1944), which sets up the fiction written by Hammett and himself in clear opposition to classical Golden Age writing. Where Golden Age fiction is artificial, the new style of the *Black Mask* school is realistic. Where the detectives of the well-plotted stories are cardboard, the private eyes are like medieval knights in their devotion to service.

Chandler's declaration in behalf of the hard-boiled school has about as much validity as the Golden Age claims that detective fiction is primarily an intellectual operation; but nevertheless the school did flourish, and it did take its techniques from the pulp magazines into the form of the novel. Hammett worked some of his Continental Op stories into longer narratives, such as *Red Harvest* (1929), and when he wrote about Sam *Spade and Nick and Nora *Charles he chose to use the novel as his medium. Chandler also gained his largest audience through novels. With their success, the way was opened for publishers to issue the work of other hard-boiled specialists. Jonathan Latimer created a series about Bill Crane (introduced in *Murder in the Madhouse*, 1935), who uses logic and deduction, whiskey too. Cleve F. Adams used the milieu of the insurance business to relate the cases of excessively male chauvinist, bigoted, and protofascistic Rex McBride, who joined the hard-boiled school in 1940 in *And Sudden Death*. Brett Halliday, who wrote sixty-nine books and sponsored a magazine, introduced the action hero Michael *Shayne in *Dividend on Death* (1939). And Robert Wade and Bill Miller teamed up as Wade Miller to develop the house detective Max Thursday in six cases, starting with *Guilty Bystander* (1947).

[*See also* Conventions of the Genre; Impossible Crime; Ingenuity; Publishing, History of Book; Publishing, History of Magazine; Realism, Conventions of; Whodunit.]

• Dorothy L. Sayers, introduction to *The Omnibus of Crime* (1929). Victor E. Neuberg, *Popular Literature: A History and Guide* (1977). David I. Grossvogel, *Mystery and Its Fiction: From Oedipus to Agatha Christie* (1979). David Geherin, *The American Private Eye: The Image in Fiction* (1985).

DIVERSIFICATION OF THE GENRE (1900s–60s)

Branches of the crime and mystery genre may wither when new growth begins to flourish, but life continues to flow in the older forms, sometimes taking on surprising new shapes. For example, between the two world wars a type of *thriller concerning gentlemen outlaws grew from the adventurous tales about Sexton Blake and Nick *Carter. Blake and Carter had been *pulp magazine heroes acting out their struggles against *evil for an audience of young men, but in 1919 H. C. McNeile, writing under the name Sapper, assigned the traits of the white, male freebooter to Captain Hugh "Bull Dog" *Drummond and gave him life in stories with the scope of an entire book instead of the single series short story of his predecessors. Although the work entitled *Mufti* (1919) set the formula, the full title of Sapper's second book expresses the protagonist's motives: *Bull-Dog Drummond: The Adventures of a Demobilized Officer Who Found Peace Dull* (1920). The particulars of this new figure were conceived out of a nationalist enthusiasm, bigotry, and complacency. He despises foreigners, mistrusts the Bolshevik radicals threatening civil order, classifies women as either bad or requiring the protection of an able man, always prefers action as it is codified by such sports as boxing to intellectual effort, and produces dialogue that sounds like a parody of British upper-class speech.

Within a few years the popular literary market produced counterparts to Drummond who shared in the new thriller's astonishing sales. Writing as Bruce Graeme, Graham Montague Jeffries created a mystery writer who becomes a *sleuth at night. The costume he dons for his night-work gains him the name Blackshirt, and he figures as the lead character in thirteen volumes of adventures, beginning with *Blackshirt* (1925) and *The Return of Blackshirt* (1927). John *Creasey's ceaseless industry created another member of the club in *Introducing the Toff* (1938). Writing as Anthony Morton, Creasey also developed a series about John Mannering, a gentleman known as The Baron, who came on the scene in *Meet the Baron* (1937; *The Man in the Blue Mask*). Yet another of these thriller heroes, who as a group the critic William Vivian Butler has labeled "The Durable Desperadoes" in a book of that name (1973), was Simon Templar, The *Saint, created by Leslie *Charteris. The Saint, whose long career began in *Meet the Tiger* (1928), is cut closer to the pattern of a modern Robin Hood than his fellows Drummond, Blackshirt, The Toff, and The Baron, but the evidence of their continuing presence among the best-selling works of popular literature indicates that they all were responses to an audience taste for unmodified derring-do.

The mass of stories about such characters who are shown to operate mostly outside the law but are crafted to seem the embodiment of normative attitudes eventually makes them sources of influence upon audience preference as well as responses to it. This effect indicates why tales of adventurous champions of simple values continue to appear throughout the later history of crime and mystery writing, even as they assume new forms. The nationalist hero bored by peacetime regularity has a rebirth in such figures as Ian *Fleming's James *Bond. An agent of a clandestine intelligence agency, Bond has official sanction to use any means necessary to gain his ends, but since his debut in *Casino Royale* (1953; *You Asked for It*), his relationship to the old club of gentleman outlaws has been clear, although the rough edges of blatant bias have been softened. In contrast to these very upper-class English sorts of fantasy heroes, the genre also shows another variation with the exaggeration of hard-boiled mannerisms to be found in the populist avenger introduced in Mickey *Spillane's *I, The Jury* (1947). At first glance, Spillane's Mike *Hammer seems to come from an entirely different world than Drummond or Bond. Recognition, however, of the action-centered plots where all the good is on one side, all the bad on the other; the investment in a masculinist code of behavior; the impatience with legal due process and humanistic tolerance; and the arrogant appropriation of *violence by the protagonists, leads inexorably to the conclusion that they are all cousins in a similarly conceived family.

While these rogue-heroes provide examples of the way that an early form of detective adventure story has gained new life by adapting its form, changes in the hard-boiled version of detective fiction, apart from those made by Spillane, represent a grafting of new sensitivity onto the story of the lonely *private eye. In *The Moving Target* (1949; *Harper*) Ross *Macdonald introduced the sleuth who works as the compassionate explorer of troubled souls. Lew *Archer shares the melancholy but not the cynicism of the older American private detective. At first modeled on Raymond *Chandler's Philip *Marlowe, by the late 1950s Archer showed the guiding influence of Sigmund Freud as Macdonald made him the catalyst prodding his clients to plumb their familial pasts. The toughness of the hard-boiled private eye was softened in another way by Thomas B. Dewey, whose character Mac; originating in *Draw the Curtain Close* (1947; *Dame in Danger*), displays a deep devotion to clients that grants them an integrity rarely seen before in hard-boiled writing. Dennis Lynds, who introduced Dan Fortune in *Act of Fear* (1967; under the pseudonym Michael Collins), Kane Jackson in *A Dark Power* (1968; under the pseudonym William Arden), and Paul Shaw in *The Falling Man* (1970; under the pseudonym Mark Sadler), turns the hard-boiled mode toward what Lynds calls socio-drama. A criminal plot is useful, because it generates stress and tension, but the aim of the Lynds private eye stories is to explore character and environment, not to engender the security to be found in tales of detection.

As the private eye story gains shading and tone through writers' combining it with sensitivity previously found more often in mainstream fiction, the vintage *Great Detective story also undergoes transformation, most notably in the work of Rex *Stout. Beginning with *Fer-de-Lance* (1934; *Meet Nero Wolfe*), Stout rivaled Arthur Conan *Doyle in portrayal of the quarters and manners of a detective marked by eccentricity and a stunning method of solving crimes. Unlike Doyle's Sherlock *Holmes, Stout's Nero *Wolfe is the consummate *armchair detective. Working from his house on West Thirty-fifth Street in Manhattan, Wolfe has a sidekick who brings to his narratives another important variation on the model: Archie *Goodwin, who resembles a hard-boiled private eye rather than a plodding companion. Goodwin does the legwork, speaks the American vernacular in contrast to Wolfe's transatlantic English, and confounds his employer with a yen for women.

At the same time, Zenith Brown (writing as Leslie Ford) capitalized on the tradition's social *milieu and its exhibition of *settings while writing about Lieutenant Joseph Kelly in novels beginning with *Murder in Maryland* (1932). Ford also created Colonel John Primrose, whose series began with *The Strangled Witness* (1934), and Grace Latham, who accompanied Primrose in adventures in *Ill Met by Moonlight* (1937). As David Frome Brown created a series about Evan Pinkerton that opened with *The Hammersmith Murders* (1930). Nearly all of her detective fiction, series and nonseries alike, appeared first in well-paying slick magazines such as *The Saturday Evening Post*, directed toward a very different audience from the poor-paying pulp magazines.

Phoebe Atwood *Taylor, Mignon G. *Eberhart, Frances and Richard Lockridge, and the Gordons were legatees of the Golden Age and *suspense traditions. Taylor injected humor and the virtues of a simple life into stories of the Yankee sleuth Asey Mayo, who first took up detection in *The Cape Cod Mystery* (1931). Eberhart followed the example of Mary Roberts *Rinehart's earlier conversion of the detection story into the *Had-I-But-Known suspense tale starting with a novel about Nurse Sarah Keate and Lance O'Leary called *The Patient in Room 18* (1929). The Lockridges incorporated a sleuth *couple (the memorable Mr. and Mrs. *North), the charm of intimate banter, and a comic tone into the classic detection story when they started their durable series in *The Norths Meet Murder* (1940). Mildred Gordon and Gordon Gordon generally preferred nonseries fiction, as did Rinehart before them. Much like Rinehart, and Eberhart, they turned the refinements of Golden Age writing—its social milieu, the amateur status of the sleuth, and the controlled element of romance—into matter for psychological suspense fiction.

Two other occurrences in the history of the form are innovative. The first of these is *police procedural fiction, which drastically alters a premise of the established detective story, as well as the underlying formal structure of the novel itself. Where the protagonist of the *detective novel had been a remarkable individual, the *police procedural gives the role of protagonist to an entire unit of police officers. The collective focus of the narrative, then, allows an opportunity to feature the routine techniques of police work, especially the necessarily cooperative requirements of it. Lawrence *Treat introduced the new form in *V As in Victim* (1945). Shortly thereafter, Maurice Procter set the police procedural in England with *The Chief Inspector's Statement* (1951; *The Pennycross Murders*), and Hillary *Waugh continued the form in America starting with *Last Seen Wearing* (1952). Within the decade the vitality of the new type of narrative burgeoned in work by Ed *McBain, starting with *Cop Hater* (1956), John *Creasey's series about Commander George Gideon of *Scotland Yard written under the name J. J. Marric and opening with *Gideon's Day* (1955; *Gideon of Scotland Yard*), and three series by Elizabeth Linington: Those attributed to Dell Shannon and introducing Lieutenant/Detective Luis Mendoza in *Case Pending* (1960), the novels begun as Lesley Egan with *A Case for Appeal* (1961) concerning Jesse Falkenstein, and the stories about Sergeant Ivor Maddox that started with *Nightmare* (1961), published under the names Elizabeth *Linington and Anne Blaisdell.

The second departure to be recorded in the genealogy of the crime and mystery genre in the years following World War II is the appearance of the type of narrative that the critic Julian *Symons terms the *crime novel. Often these novels will have no detective at all, nor any *clues in the terms that conventions provide for them. Characterization becomes central, and plot finds form as it follows motive through commission of a crime. The list of notable examples of such narratives begins with Patricia *Highsmith is *Strangers on a Train* (1950), in which suspense is attached to the psychopathic designing of companion crimes. In the set of novels about Tom Ripley initiated in *The Talented Mr. Ripley* (1955) she takes a charming man, shows him to be unstable and lacking *guilt, and sets him off on a career in which crime is the normal expression of his personality. Shelley Smith has indicated the move from detection of crime to dramatization of the criminal in a statement where she explains that she began writing *whodunits only to find that her deepest interests lay in the psychology of the criminal, which is as neat a statement about the emergence of the crime novel as can be found. Her first published novel, *Background for Murder* (1942), illustrates Smith's original use of a detection story, while *The Ballad of the Running Man* (1961) can stand for the direction she chose when the criminal character became her focus.

The originality of the authors in the crime and mystery genre serves to explain much of the diversity to be found between 1946 and the 1970s, but other factors in the literary marketplace had a role too. One of these factors was the end of slick magazine fiction. Stalwart publishers of diverting fiction lost business to news and pictorial magazines. As a result, authors directed their energies away from the novellette and toward longer narratives that could be published as novels. In the 1950s, growth in the established market for paperbound books at the same time as most of the pulp magazines folded led to the introduction of paperback original volumes that became an outlet of choice for authors of rapidly written stories of crime. In addition, television and newspaper coverage of sensational murders and criminal trials bred an interest in real accounts of crime that set conditions for the creation of *true crime books. These changes, coupled with creative variations in the patterns of Golden Age and hard-boiled writing, the emergence of the police procedural story and the crime novel, gained crime and mystery writing a nearly universal audience. The huge audience set favorable conditions for the greatest diversity crime and mystery writing had ever had, and the insatiable taste that had been cultivated for crime and detection fiction through nearly a century of popular literary production assured that the genre would never want for readers.

[*See also* Conventions of the Genre; Club Milieu; Gentleman Adventurer; Males and Male Image; Paperbacks; Robin Hood Criminal; Slicks; Whydunit.]

• David Geherin, *Sons of Sam Spade: The Private-Eye Novel in the '70s* (1980). Julian Symons, *Bloody Murder: From the Detective Story to the Crime Novel*, 3rd rev. ed. (1992). Ralph Willett, *Naked City: Urban Crime Fiction in the USA* (1996).

ESTABLISHMENT OF THE GENRE (1970s–90s)

In the last third of the twentieth century the detection and mystery genre continues to provide readers a wealth of opportunities to experience the aesthetics of crime. Each of several types of genre story remains vibrant and dynamic, settled into a niche of reader preference yet capable of development. The recent literary history of the genre, thus, becomes a record of variety between far horizons.

Examples of hard-boiled writing still flow steadily into the marketplace, and at least four important innovations serve to indicate its inherent vitality. The first notable innovation has carried the *private eye away from home bases in *Los Angeles, *San Francisco, and *New York. Indianapolis has Michael Z. Lewin's Albert Samson and police Lieutenant Leroy Powder at work on the scene, Samson debuting in

Ask the Right Question (1971) and Powder in *Hard Line* (1982). Jonathan Valin introduced Cincinnati's private eye Harry Stoner in *The Lime Pit* (1980). New Orleans has provided the setting for at least two detectives in the private eye tradition: James Lee Burke's Dave Robichaux, an ex-police officer who tangles with the mob, crime, and ghosts in such novels as *The Neon Rain* (1987); and Julie Smith's Skip Langdon, a product of high society who has become a police officer. Smith introduced Langdon in *New Orleans Mourning* (1990). Before that, she had set up Rebecca Schwartz, an attorney, as a *sleuth in the familiar terrain of *San Francisco. The Schwartz series opens with *Death Turns a Trick* (1982). One of Boston's private eyes is John Francis Cuddy, created by Jeremiah Healy for a series begun with *Blunt Darts* (1984). Together, these writers, and others who are setting their stories in new locales, are generalizing the private eye tradition by carrying it well beyond the cities with reputations for crime, and localizing it at the same time by investing their books with details of place names and atmosphere. The result has been familiarization of the hard-boiled type.

A second important trend in the hard-boiled literature continues the sympathetic mode of detection begun by Ross *Macdonald's Lew *Archer. Robert B. *Parker's Boston private eye, *Spenser, exemplifies the development of a sensitive sleuth who has dispensed with the machismo and taciturnity of his elders and found that a normal life of intimacy and companionship with a woman enables him to show the adaptability of the tough guy code of detective behavior.

Chronologically, the third major alteration of the hard-boiled tradition has been its reconstruction as a vehicle for feminism. The American private eye originated as the protagonist of a form bearing the freight of socially constructed views of *gender. The hero was male and unattached. As an updated counterpart of the romantic hero of the forest and the adventurous voyager on the sea, the private eye inhabited a world controlled, and corrupted, by men—a world in which women were distractions. Arguably, the form was so deeply invested with masculinist values that it could not accommodate women in major roles; yet, a string of successes by Marcia *Muller, Sue *Grafton, Sara *Paretsky, and others shows that revision was only a matter of time.

Besides being steeped in masculinist values in its original days, the hard-boiled private eye story was also emblematic of racial chauvinism. Black characters appeared occasionally but always in stereotypical ways, and although the mannered *naturalism of hard-boiled writing laid claim to revelations about American social *corruption, it scarcely noticed racial segregation or institutional racism. That has changed. African Americans are no longer the "other people" in detective fiction. Even more important than that are the numbers of *African American sleuths on the scene. Walter *Mosley has become well known since he began a series about Ezekiel "Easy" *Rawlins, an *accidental sleuth, in *Devil in a Blue Dress* (1990). Mosley gives striking pertinence to the point about the past invisibility of black characters by setting up his series to explore life in immediate postwar *Los Angeles when the end of wartime prosperity exacerbated race relations. Barbara Neely has also adopted the device of the accidental detective in her series about the African American domestic Blanche White, who came to life first in *Blanche on the Lam* (1992). Valerie Wilson Wesley has chosen to make her protagonist, Tamara Hayle, a professional private eye and, like many of her counterparts, an ex-cop. Hayle, whose career began with *When Death Comes Stealing* (1994), also contributes to the localizing of hard-boiled writing by carrying on her business in Newark, New Jersey.

What has been begun by African American writers who have informed their detective fiction with the soul of the distinctively ethnic blues has begun to be matched in the works of other writers who have selected detectives from America's minority groups. The best-known example to date is Tony *Hillerman, who began a series of stories about Navajo police lieutenant Joe Leaphorn in *The Blessing Way* (1970) and about Navajo sergeant Jim *Chee in *People of Darkness* (1980). Chicano culture enters the detective genre in the fiction of Rudolfo Anaya about Sonny Baca, an Albuquerque private eye who had his first outing in *Zia Summer* (1995). The importance of these African American, Native American, and Hispanic characters lies not in the fact that they are "firsts," for indeed they are following in the footsteps of earlier characters. (Chester Himes had created black tough guys in a series of books that started in 1957, and he was not even the first. That honor goes to Rudolph Fisher who published *The Conjure Man Dies*, a mystery set in Harlem and peopled by a broad variety of characters of African descent, in 1932.) The new *ethnic sleuths are not any longer lone travelers in the land of detective mystery. They are settling the territory, just as women detectives are doing.

The diversification of detective characterization evident in the appearance of women and African American sleuths extends as well to matters of sexual preference and orientation, which was as hidebound in earlier hard-boiled writing as the assumptions about gender and *ethnicity. Homosexual characters were invariably villainous, creatures from another world than the detective's world. Joseph *Hansen's gay detective Dave *Brandstetter, who first appeared in *Fadeout* (1970), is both straightforward about his sexual preferences and as skilled in his professional craft as any other tough-guy sleuth. Still, the subculture of gay life does figure significantly in his stories. That culture becomes more prominent in the numerous novels now written by women authors about lesbian private eyes and sleuths. An example is Ellen Hart's series of novels about Jane Lawless, a Minneapolis restaurant owner, which began with *Hallowed Murder* (1989).

The vigorous life exhibited in the newer hard-boiled writing finds a match in the continuing work of authors inspired by Golden Age traditions. The prevalence of works that frankly acknowledge their debt to Agatha *Christie and others who set the parameters for classic detection writing has made it necessary to coin a new term, the *cozy mystery. To some, the term may suggest a sneer, but the successful practice in the form really converts the tone to affection. The British origins of the cozy are clear in the work of Martha Grimes and Elizabeth George, two American writers who use traditional British settings and portray detectives from *Scotland Yard.

In the fiction of both, the parallels to be found with earlier British detective writing go beyond derivation. George especially creates a large cast of additional characters linked by work, love, *marriage and participation in the mutually satisfying job of crime solving.

Although the cozy type of detective fiction has a special English flavor, it does transport well. The novels of Amanda *Cross about Professor Kate *Fansler, introduced in *In the Last Analysis* (1964), constitute a transatlantic variety of sleuth story. The same might be said about the fiction of Jane Langton, who sets her tales of the affable retired policeman turned Henry David Thoreau scholar Homer Kelly in the center and environs of Cambridge, Massachusetts. If Cambridge's Harvard is America's equivalent of the ancient university in *Oxford, Kelly, who came to notice in *The Transcendental Murder* (1964; *The Minuteman Murder*), a novel about a mystery of scholarship concerning Thoreau and Emily Dickinson, is the Americanized version of the Oxonian don.

Three additional types of crime and mystery writing deserve mention in illustration of the vigor in the established genre. The first of these is the historical detective story, that is, the tale given a setting in the past. Lillian de la Torre calls herself a histo-detector, a writer who sets about solving mysteries of the long-ago. De la Torre's eighteenth-century puzzles featuring the "real" man of letters Dr. Samuel Johnson four are published in volumes of collected stories, starting with *Dr. Sam: Johnson, Detector* (1946). John Dickson *Carr also set some of his mysteries in the past—for example, *The Bride of Newgate* (1950). Easily the most popular of the writers of retro detection has been Peter Lovesey, who introduced Victorian detectives and Victorian crimes in *Wobble to Death* (1970). Another variety of *historical mystery that has a longer lineage than Lovesey or Carr's work is found in the neverending production of Sherlock *Holmes sequels. Nicholas Meyer reanimated the *Great Detective *pastiche in *The Seven-Per-Cent Solution* (1974) and *The West End Horror* (1976). The charm of these ingenious novels includes the introduction of Holmes to the other great detective of the nineteenth century, Sigmund Freud. Laurie R. King has converted pastiche into sequel with a series about Mary Russell, who goes from being Holmes's student to being his lover in *The Beekeepers Apprentice* (1994), and and who becomes his wife and collaborator in detection in the subsequent volumes.

The sheer mass of publication at present defies any effort to comprehensive coverage. The subtype of crime fiction set in courtrooms has gotten a hearty boost from the blockbuster success of Scott Turow, author of *Presumed Innocent* (1987) and John

Grisham, whose train of best-sellers starting with *A Time to Kill* (1989) promises to make him as dominant a figure in *legal procedurals as Erle Stanley *Gardner. Dick *Francis has elevated the *thriller to classic form, and Charles McCarry, with such works as *Shelley's Heart* (1995), has shown the durability of the thriller for investigation of politics. The stories Joan Hess sets in Arkansas—for example, the Arly Hanks series begun with *Malice in Maggody* (1987)—bring raucous *humor to detection. Nevada Barr in *Track of the Cat* (1993) and its sequels shows that national parks can be viable scenes of crime and detection, and park rangers successful sleuths. Aaron J. Elkins has made forensic anthropology the skill for detection in novels such as *Old Bones* (1987), while Patricia D. Cornwell has renewed the character of the scientific detective by writing about Dr. Kay Scarpetta, chief medical examiner of Richmond, Virginia, in a series initiated by *Postmortem* (1990). Margaret Maron has invented a way for a judge to be also the detective on her cases in the stories of Deborah Knott, beginning with *Bootlegger's Daughter* (1992), but Knott is her newest sleuth. Maron's first sleuth, New York policewoman Sigrid Harald, has been on the force since *One Coffee With* (1981).

This overview confirms the verdict of literary history. The end of the twentieth century found the genre of crime and detective fiction fully established, highly diverse, and evidently a continuing source of aesthetic satisfaction for the readers whose fictional literacy prepared them to reward inventive authors with continued attention.

[*See also* Females and Feminists; Gay Characters and Perspectives; Native American Sleuth; Regionalism.]

• Bonnie Zimmerman, *The Safe Sea of Women: Lesbian Fiction, 1969–1989* (1990). Kathleen Gregory Klein, *The Woman Detective: Gender and Genre*, 2nd ed. (1995). Stephen F. Soitos, *The Blues Detective: A Study of African American Detective Fiction* (1996).   —John M. Reilly

HOCH, EDWARD D(ENTINGER) (b. 1930), American author who exemplifies the working writer practicing his craft in a dedicated, reliable fashion. Hoch has written five novels and is the respected editor of anthologies, but his great achievement lies in writing more than 800 short stories and earning his living for more than three decades largely through the writing of short fiction. For more than two and a half decades, beginning in May 1973, he contributed at least one short story per issue to *Ellery Queen's Mystery Magazine*. A native of Rochester, New York, Hoch began to write detective stories when he was in his teens. He continued to write while he was a student at the University of Rochester, during two years in the U.S. Army, while he was employed by Rochester Public Library, during a short stint with Pocket Books in New York City, and while working in advertising and public relations in Rochester. His first story, "Village of the Dead," was published in *Famous Detective Stories* in December 1955 when he was twenty-five. Hoch turned to writing full time in 1968, after he won the Edgar Allan Poe Award for the Best

Short Story of 1967 with "The Oblong Room" (in *The Saint*, July 1967). Writing under his own name and seven pseudonyms, he created twenty-six series characters and was one of several writers who wrote as Ellery *Queen, turning out one novel and one short story under that pseudonym. He edited individual theme anthologies and two long-running annual series: *Best Detective Stories of the Year* (from 1976 to 1981) and *The Year's Best Mystery and Suspense Stories* (from 1982 to 1995). He served as president of the *Mystery Writers of America in 1982–83.

[*See also* Short Story: The American Crime Short Story.]

• Tony Hillerman and Rosemary Herbert, eds., "Edward D. Hoch," in *The Oxford Book of American Detective Stories* (1996). June M. Moffatt and Francis M. Nevins Jr., *Edward D. Hoch Bibliography* (1991; updated annually).
                    —Clark Howard

HOLIDAY MYSTERIES. Holidays, or occasions when religious or secular events are commemorated and celebrated, have often been used in crime and mystery writing to provide reasons for disparate characters to gather together. Moreover, the holiday *setting provides contrast between the happy or solemn occasion and the violent intrusion of the crime. The meanings associated with holidays may also be used as thematic elements. In addition, individual holidays have also been used by editors as unifying aspects for anthologies and by publishers as a marketing tool, especially for major occasions like Christmas, that may spur readers to purchase holiday-themed books as gifts.

Christmas is the most often featured holiday in crime and mystery fiction, but other holidays have been used to advantage as well. Major events associated with these occasions are often portrayed in mystery novels and short stories. Such is the case in Lee Harris's *The Saint Patrick's Day Murder* (1994), which uses the fact that the *New York City Police Department is well represented in that city's annual Saint Patrick's Day Parade. The *murder of a police officer contrasts with the celebratory mood; it is all the more shocking that he is killed while surrounded by officers of the law. Similarly, the festivities associated with Patriot's Day in New England provide the occasion for murder when Jane Langton has a citizen killed during the annual reenactment of the American Revolutionary Battle of Lexington and Concord in *The Transcendental Murder* (1964; *The Minuteman Murder*). Another Patriot's Day tradition is the Boston Marathon, a famous annual race that provides a setting for Linda Barnes's *Dead Heat* (1984). Valentine's Day, associated with romantic love, is the opening date in Ruth *Rendell's *A Judgement in Stone* (1977) and in Carolyn G. Hart's *Deadly Valentine* (1990). In these books, thwarted characters ultimately loose control on a holiday whose loving associations are in stark contrast to the realities of the murderers' lives. Harry Kemelman, too, has his series sleuth, Rabbi David *Small, investigate a murder that occurs on Valentine's Day in *That Day the Rabbi Left Town* (1996).

Passover, a holy day for those of the Jewish faith,

is celebrated with the seder, a dinner during which it is traditional to open a door and pour a glass of wine to welcome the prophet Elijah. In Lee Harris's *The Passover Murder* (1996), a young woman gets up to open the door and is never seen alive again. Harris also uses a Christian holy day as central to her *The Good Friday Murder* (1992), while Mary Daheim portrays the trappings of Easter celebrations in *Holy Terrors* (1992).

The Jewish New Year, which culminates in Yom Kippur, is traditionally a day of prayer and meditation when Jews ask forgiveness of God and of one another. Faye Kellerman uses this theme to effect in *Day of Atonement* (1991) when a detective's birth mother seeks forgiveness in a *plot complicated by the disappearance of a child. Kemelman weaves the intricacies of Jewish law into his Yom Kippur murder in *Saturday the Rabbi Went Hungry* (1966).

Halloween, with its connection to witchcraft and hauntings and its open use of *disguise for celebratory purposes, provides a backdrop to murder in Leo *Bruce's *Death on Allhallowe'en* (1970). The trickery associated with April Fool's Day, when elaborate hoaxes are the order of the day, is the occasion for *The Last Laugh* (1984), by John R. Riggs.

Secular New Year's Eve celebrations are often raucous congregations for friends and strangers, where the consumption of liquor and use of disguises, noisemakers, and music can be the perfect cover for murder. H. Paul Jeffers sets his *Rubout at the Onyx* (1981) during a New Years's Eve in *New York City just after the repeal of Prohibition. Colin *Dexter's Chief Inspector *Morse investigates the murder of a man known only by the costume that won him a New Years party prize in *The Secret of Annex 3* (1986).

[*See also* Christmas Crime.]

—Sue Feder

Holmes, Mycroft. The elder brother of Sherlock *Holmes, Mycroft Holmes takes part in the action of two stories and is mentioned in just two more tales among the sixty works centered around the *Great Detective. Nevertheless, Mycroft Holmes remains memorable for his superior reasoning powers, which he exercises from the comfort of his armchair in the Diogenes Club or his Pall Mall, *London, lodgings. Corpulent and lacking in energy and ambition, he makes his way to Baker Street only twice, in "The Greek Interpreter" (*Strand*, Sept. 1893), in which Sherlock Holmes says, "When I say, therefore, that Mycroft has better powers of observation than I, you may take it that I am speaking the exact and literal truth," and in "The Bruce-Partington Plans" (*Strand*, Dec. 1908), in which Holmes, citing his brother's importance to the government in Whitehall, remarks, "Again and again his word has decided the national policy."

[*See also* Armchair Detective; Canon, The.]

• Joseph A. Kestner, *Sherlock's Men: Masculinity, Conan Doyle, and Cultural History* (1997). Arthur Conan Doyle, *The Annotated Sherlock Holmes: The Four Novels and the Fifty-six Short Stories Complete*, ed. William S. Baring-Gould (1960).

—Rosemary Herbert

Holmes, Sherlock. Created early in 1886 by the young English doctor Arthur Conan *Doyle, Sherlock Holmes was destined, with Edgar Allan *Poe's Chevalier C. Auguste *Dupin, to become one of the two most important characters in the history of detective fiction. Known for his talent for observation, powers of reasoning, eccentric personality, habits of living, and memorable turns of phrase, this *Great Detective so captured the imaginations of readers that he has often been regarded as a living person rather than as a fictional character. The adventures of the consulting detective are narrated by his friend Dr. John H. *Watson in the form of four novels and fifty-six short stories, known to Sherlockians and literary historians as the *Canon.

Holmes came to life when Doyle sketched out notes for a piece of fiction in order to while away idle hours in a rather unsuccessful medical practice in Southsea, Hampshire. Headed "A Study in Scarlet," these notes marked a solid basis for the Holmes series, revealing that the author was initially more concerned with character than *plot and that Doyle prized dialogue in the creation of character. The importance of the narrator, too, is obvious from the fact that he is mentioned first: "Ormond Sacker—from Afghanistan. . . . Lived at 221B Upper Baker Street with Sherrinford Holmes." Doyle changed the characters' names to Watson and Holmes before he penned the work, which was first published in *Beeton's Christmas Annual* in 1887.

Undoubtedly best known for his powers of reasoning, Holmes possessed a flair for drawing conclusions from keenly observed details that was modeled in part on the talents of Doyle's own medical mentor, Dr. Joseph Bell, whom Doyle met at Edinburgh University and to whom he dedicated the first collection of his short stories, *The Adventures of Sherlock Holmes* (1892). A lecturer and surgeon, Bell amazed students with his ability not only to diagnose illnesses but to infer life circumstances based on observations of complexion and other physical characteristics along with wardrobe and behavior. While the popular view holds that Holmes used deductive reasoning, in fact, Holmes generally reasoned abductively, as did Bell, working from the observation of out of the ordinary particulars to form a hypothesis, on the basis of which the observations would be expected. One of the most memorable aspects of the Holmes character is his ability to deliver surprising conclusions based on his recognition of the significance of details that others see as trifles. Holmes's talents in this regard are underlined for the reader by exclamations of astonishment and awe from the narrator, Watson.

Watson is not unmindful, however, of Holmes's dark side, which is detailed in the opening pages of *The Sign of the Four* (1890; *The Sign of Four*). Here Holmes is shown as having been taking three injections of cocaine per day for a period of months. Depressed when he is not engaged in work, Holmes can lie on his sofa "for days on end" in a lethargy hardly broken by his "scraping away" on his violin. Later, his cocaine habit is explained away as "a protest against the monotony of existence."

Otherwise, Holmes is portrayed as a man immune

to human weaknesses. With the exception of Irene *Adler, the diva who dupes him in "A Scandal in Bohemia" (*Strand*, July 1891), no woman arouses Holmes's ardor—and although Holmes refers to Adler as "the woman" and requests her photograph in payment for his services, it may be argued that his admiration is more inspired by her cleverness, boldness, and singing ability than by her sexual appeal.

If Holmes "never spoke of the gentler passions, save with a gibe and a sneer," he also found it difficult to express himself as a friend. He is an inconsiderate roommate, smoking up the place with dangerous chemical experiments; shooting bullet holes in the wall on a whim; storing things—like tobacco in a Persian slipper—in bizarre locations; and rousing his sidekick at all hours to accompany him on cases. A master of *disguise, Holmes also enjoys startling Watson by appearing in their digs or elsewhere in convincing costume. In "The Adventure of the Speckled Band" (*Strand*, Feb. 1892), a story that demonstrates Holmes's physical courage and emotional nerve, he fails to inform Watson of the mortal danger in which he puts him when the two await the arrival of a poisonous snake in confined quarters. His profound attachment to Watson is, however, revealed in "The Adventure of the Devil's Foot" (*Strand*, Dec. 1910) when, after Holmes and Watson are nearly killed while exposing themselves to a deadly poison, Holmes directly apologizes for putting his friend at risk, causing Watson to reflect, "I had never seen so much of Holmes's heart before." In "The Adventure of the Three Garridebs" (*Colliers*, 25 Oct. 1924), Holmes is even more demonstrative regarding his concern for Watson. When Watson receives a gunshot wound, Holmes exclaims, "You're not hurt, Watson? For God's sake, say that you are not hurt!" Watson observes, "It was worth a wound—it was worth many wounds—to know the depth of loyalty and love which lay behind that cold mask." Otherwise, Holmes is a more devoted adversary than friend, as is demonstrated by his perseverance in eliminating "the Napoleon of crime," Professor James *Moriarty.

Not only does Holmes generally hold himself above the niceties of *friendship, but he often places himself above the law, describing himself in *The Sign of the Four* as "the last and highest court of appeal in detection." Holmes allows culprits to escape in "The Adventure of the Blue Carbuncle" (*Strand*, Jan. 1892), "The Adventure of the Abbey Grange" (*Strand*, Sept. 1904), "The Adventure of the Devil's Foot" (*Strand*, Dec. 1910), and other stories. Holmes also occasionally lets accomplices to go unpunished, as in "Silver Blaze" (*Strand*, Dec. 1892).

"Silver Blaze" also contains one of the most memorable exchanges of dialogue in the Canon:

> "Is there any other point to which you would wish to draw my attention?"
> "To the curious incident of the dog in the night-time."
> "The dog did nothing in the night-time."
> "That was the curious incident."

This passage at once illustrates Doyle's gift for writing original and fluid prose and Holmes's application of imagination to aid in his reasoning process.

Because Holmes can imagine the scene in the nighttime so fully as to picture and hear it, he recognizes the silence of the dog as a vital *clue to the solution of the case.

Doyle was concerned to relate stories or adventures centered around his *sleuth rather than to detail the particulars of Holmes's antecedents or education. Because Holmes took on a life of his own in readers' imaginations, much "biographical" information has been drawn by others from the Canon itself and from other research. The name Sherlock may have come to Doyle's mind since the Sherlocks were landowners in County Wicklow, Ireland, where the Doyle family once held estates. This Irish name is a Gaelic version of the Anglo-Saxon word for short locks or one with short hair: *scortlog*. Doyle borrowed his sleuth's last name from the American jurist Oliver Wendell Holmes, whom Doyle admired.

The only family member who is portrayed in the Holmes stories is the sleuth's elder brother, Mycroft *Holmes, a "corpulent" man who may possess greater talents for observation than his brother but who is too sedentary to pursue a career in crime solving. Evidence in the Canon suggests that one of Holmes's grandmothers was a sister to the French artist Vernet. Otherwise, family background for Holmes is speculative, as is the place of his schooling.

There is no question, however, about Holmes's enduring influence upon the crime and mystery genre and his place in the popular imagination. From Doyle's day to the present, imitators and those who would spoof Holmes have been legion, while Doyle and Holmes have been the subject of numerous biographical and countless academic studies. Television, film, and stage and radio dramas have also featured Holmes and Watson. Virtually all writers of crime and mystery fiction, especially stories of true detection, acknowledge the influence of Holmes on their own work. Holmes carved out the niche of consulting detective and made it his own. In applying the scientific method to the understanding of human affairs, Holmes is an original hero who rights wrongs through the application of the intellect.

[*See also* Clues, Famous; Eccentrics; Ingenuity; Pastiche; Short Story: The British Crime Short Story; Sidekicks and Sleuthing Teams; Spoof Scholarship; Superman Sleuth.]

• Arthur Conan Doyle, *The Annotated Sherlock Holmes; The Four Novels and the Fifty-six Short Stories Complete*, ed. William S. Baring-Gould (1960). William S. Baring-Gould, *Sherlock Holmes of Baker Street: The Life of the First Consulting Detective* (1965). Thomas Sebeok and D. Jean Umiker-Sebeok, *You Know My Methods: A Juxtaposition of Charles S. Peirce and Sherlock Holmes* (1980).

—Rosemary Herbert

HOME OFFICE, the government department primarily concerned with matters of administration affecting the internal well-being of England and Wales so far as those matters are not especially vested in other departments. It is presided over by the home secretary, a senior cabinet member who exercises extensive powers of administration, supervision, and control. They include powers connected with *coroners, civil defense, licensing and inspection under the law relating to controlled drugs, and, most significantly, public order. The home secretary has wide authority with regard to immigration and extradition and is responsible for the organization of the magistrates' courts, as well as the general supervision of the police and prisons. Inevitably, home secretaries and the Home Office have played a crucial role in the administration of justice over the years. Recent years have seen increasing criticism of that role in cases involving apparent miscarriages of *justice. The campaigning journalist Bob Woffinden, for example, has argued that Home Office staff have been too willing to defer to the courts even where they have felt disquiet about particular verdicts.

Traditionally, mystery novelists in whose work the innocent have been found guilty have paid little attention to the Home Office's possible involvement in miscarriage cases, although in Peter Lovesey's *Waxwork* (1978) a photograph sent to a Victorian Home Secretary casts doubt on Miriam Cromer's confession to *murder. Although home secretaries often feature in mystery fiction, they are apt to be peripheral characters. Examples may be found in Golden Age *whodunits, such as Anthony *Berkeley's *Death in the House* (1939) and espionage novels, like Stanley Hyland's *Top Bloody Secret* (1969), both of which have parliamentary settings. The often uneasy relationship between police officers and their ultimate political masters has been reflected in an increasing number of books in modern times, including Reg Gadney's *Just When We Are Safest* (1995). In *Floating Voter* (1992) Julian Critchley, a Conservative Member of Parliament when the book was published, mixes a number of real-life political figures with his fictional creations and Kenneth Baker—a home secretary in Margaret Thatcher's government—discovers the drowned body of a female delegate to a Conservative Party conference. Douglas Hurd, also a home secretary during the Thatcher era, earned a reputation as an author of accomplished *thrillers before achieving political eminence. P. D. *James was employed by the Home Office for many years, and her *Death of an Expert Witness* (1977) benefits from its authoritative description of a Home Office forensic laboratory in East Anglia and the people who work within it.

[See also Spy Fiction.]

• Paul Begg, Martin Fido, and Keith Skinner, *The Jack the Ripper A to Z* (1991). Lord Hailsham of St. Marylebone, Ed. in Chief, *Halsbury's Laws of England*, Vol. 8 (4th ed.) (1974). Donald McCormick and Katy Fletcher, *Spy Fiction: A Connoisseur's Guide* (1990). Bob Woffinden, *Miscarriages of Justice* (1988).   —Martin Edwards

HOMICIDE. *See* Murder; Taking of Life.

HORNUNG, E(RNEST) W(ILLIAM) (1866–1921), British author of fifteen crime novels and ten volumes of short crime stories. There can be little doubt that the fame of Hornung rests upon his twenty-five stories and one novel about A. J. *Raffles, cricketer and gentleman thief, appearing in three volumes including *the Amateur Cracksman* (1899; *Raffles, the Amateur Cracksman*), *The Black Mask* (1901), and *A Thief in the Night* (1905), and later collected editions. The Raffles stories were, in the words of Hornung's brother-in-law, Arthur Conan *Doyle, "a kind of inversion of Sherlock Holmes." Hornung also wrote a novel and two plays in which Raffles appears, but much of his other fiction dealt with crime and convicts in nineteenth-century Australia, where the author lived for three years because of the poor health that plagued him all his life. Hornung was a fine craftsman, creating in Raffles one of the great characters of crime fiction whose name has entered our language.

[See also Adventurer and Adventuress; Gentleman Adventurer.]

• Jeremy Lewis, introduction to *The Collected Raffles* (1985).   —Edward D. Hoch

HORROR FICTION encompasses all literature in which the forces of the unknown or demonic threaten the realm of the ordinary or everyday. Horror fiction is therefore not necessarily concerned with the supernatural but rather with forces, psychological, material, spiritual, or scientific, that can be "supernaturalized" and made into a force that threatens the living with annihilation.

Early horror fiction such as Ann Radcliffe's *The Mysteries of Udolpho* (1794) and Charles Robert Maturin's *The Fatal Revenge* (1807) may be distinguished from its folk precedents by its bourgeois concerns, its obsession with the boundaries of material and rational existence, its literary nature and its fear of, and fascination with, a mythologized medieval or folk past. Female middle-class *innocence is pitted against an aristocratic and erotic past returned to haunt the living in concerns over legacies and legitimacy.

From these early roots, two types of horror tale emerge; one is determined by a threat from "real" outer forces, either supernatural or scientific but always monstrous. This category includes the tales of Sweeney Todd and Varney the Vampire, and works by Guy de Maupassant, Wilkie *Collins, M. R. James, and H. P. Lovecraft. It has recently been manifest in the very material horrors of bodily functions and displaced organs depicted in William Peter Blatty's *The Exorcist* (1971), Stephen King's *Carrie* (1974), and James Herbert's *The Rats* (1974). The second type of horror fiction, which is connected to both the materialistic forms of horror and detective fiction, is that based on the increasing fascination since the last century with psychological and criminal depravity. This social darwinist horror links Robert Louis Stevenson's *The Strange Case of Doctor Jekyll and Mr Hyde* (1886) to the real world of Jack the Ripper, Henry James's *The Turn of the Screw* (1898), Elizabeth Bowen's *The Cat Jumps and other Stories* (1934), and Ruth *Rendell's *A Demon in My View* (1976).

The first great tales of detection were written by a master of horror fiction, Edgar Allan *Poe, who understood that both genres share one prerequisite: The moment of origin and the recovery of that moment is demonized in *guilt and *corruption.

*Murder governs both genres. The defining quality of detective fiction, that obsessional "need-to-know," is exemplified both in Poe's supernatural pieces and in his tales of ratiocination. "The Man of the Crowd" (*Burton's Gentleman's Magazine*, Dec. 1840), for example, is preoccupied with rational explanation and the descent into its inversion paranoia and monomania, a horror whose monster is democratic man and whose demons are psychological and political.

These affinities between horror and detective fiction have not been lost upon crime writers; after all, criminality, blood, murder, *violence, secrecy, and psychopathology all play their part in stories of detection. Authors of detective fiction have borrowed freely from the formal properties of horror fiction and the generalized gothic. Arthur Conan *Doyle, for example, was at pains to provide scientific explanations to tales of horror, as, for instance, in "The Adventure of the Sussex Vampire" in *The Case-Book of Sherlock Holmes* (1927), but he is also willing to allow the properties of horror fiction to add color to his detective tales and to add a dimension of ambivalence to tales in which a rational explanation is offered. *The Hound of the Baskervilles* (1902) is an exercise in supernatural debunking that nevertheless does not explain the original legend of the Baskerville demon. The story is dominated by the scientific and yet bizarre concept of hereditary degeneracy into depraved *evil.

In America both James M. *Cain and Cornell *Woolrich used the gothic and horror to heighten effect. In *Night Has a Thousand Eyes* (1945), Woolrich, writing as George Hopley, conceives of a detective who is a romantic dreamer and of a tale that is gothic in its features and its props. In *The Bride Wore Black* (1940), the central figure is both demonic muse and terrible harpy, a seductress and vampire. Cain's *Double Indemnity* (1943) with its twistings, its inexorable and unavoidable fate, and its gothic trappings conjures up both the tragedy of William *Shakespeare's *Macbeth* (1623) and the traditional vampire woman in order to refine the horror of the everyday and the mundane.

Finally, Thomas Harris's *The Silence of the Lambs* (1988), purportedly based on the psychopathology of known serial killers and real cases, owes much to its gothic horror origins; Clarice Starling takes the role of an Anne Radcliffe heroine in an adventure in a dungeon-basement filled with deathshead moths and a charnel house of bodily parts and terrified *victims secreted in an obliette. Harris's Hannibal Lector, with his deformities, gross appetite, and ludicrous knowledge, is at once Dr. *Fu Manchu, Dr. No, and Count Dracula. Here the real ordinariness of the psychopath is supernaturalized for popular consumption.

[See also Gothic Novel; Menacing Characters; Sensation Novel; Terror.]

• Clive Bloom, ed. *Gothic Horror* (1998).

—Clive Bloom

HORSE RACING MILIEU. Few crime writers have exploited the racetrack's compelling possibilities as background. Of those who have, even fewer remain in print. (Among the missing are the popular turn-of-the-century British author Nat Gould, after whom the Archers named a steeplechaser, and the American author Michael Crichton, who in the 1960s under the pseudonym John Lange wrote several racing thrillers.) However this small number includes some of the genre's most brilliant work.

Financial *motives spur the racing industry: huge purses multiplied by legal and illegal *gambling, breeding fees and million dollar foals from winning stallions and broodmares, insurance settlements for valuable bloodstock. Distractions and *red herrings materialize everywhere. Characters can be glamorous, dangerous people at all social levels: greedy owners, desperate trainers, corruptible jockeys and grooms, dishonest vets, crooked gamblers. *Clues can hide, and danger lurk, in atmospheric backgrounds like the idyllic horsefarm, the lonely heath where training strings come and go in the dawn mist, the teeming track grandstand, or the backstretch world of grooms, hotwalkers, trainers, and hangers-on.

Arthur Conan *Doyle, despite his own athleticism and aristocratic Irish ancestry, was not a racing man (and he said himself the story was full of howlers), but the gripping "Silver Blaze" (*Strand*, Dec. 1892) makes textbook use of its racing *milieu, culminating with the ingenious *disguise of the *murder weapon. Holmes understands the racehorse and the stable dog; thus, he understands the crime. Here, as in most subsequent racing mysteries, the horse is a noble innocent beyond the strictures of law and society, an instinctive judge of human good and *evil.

Beginning at the turn of the century, the prolific and wildly popular Edgar *Wallace published more than a hundred *thrillers. An elaborate bookmaking scheme in the horseracing novel *The Green Ribbon*, (1929) reflects Wallace's passion for betting. Though Trigger the bookmaker is believably, even lovingly drawn—and at some length—the filly Field of Glory gets barely a hundred words in which to win the great Cambridgeshire Handicap. Wallace's accurate psychology, his gift for intimate domestic detail, dark-of-night excursions upon the heath, secret caverns, an international cast of characters, and easy command of racing routines all look forward to the great Dick *Francis (who read Wallace as a child), if the omniscient Inspector Luke does not.

Among Golden Age writers, Josephine *Tey devotes an entire book to the world of horses. Technically, psychologically, and descriptively stunning, *Brat Farrar* (1949; *Come and Kill Me*) is as close as the racing milieu mystery gets to a pastoral form. The stud farm Latchetts is an English Eden, threatened by the snake who turns horses into murder weapons. The hero-sleuth is a superior rider as well as a morally superior person. Ultimately he unmasks the villain and establishes a new Adam and Eve in Eden, ensuring that the garden of beautifully bred horses will flourish.

Somewhat later, Henry *Wade's *A Dying Fall* (1955) makes classic use of the horseracing milieu. In a steeplechase, the Shankesbury Royal Cup, the filly Silver Eagle carries all her owner's fortune on her back. A worthy literary descendant of Silver Blaze, she captures the reader's attention. At the end of this well-crafted book, the opening chapter is revealed to be a paradigm of the larger story. Of course, the main character has been allowed to change the ending. Wade teases the reader, asking if horsemanship equals good morality, and if Eden has been lost.

From the early 1960s on, the racing milieu is the undisputed domain of its greatest practitioner, the retired champion jockey Dick *Francis. Francis's heroes only begin with a racing background. Later they branch out into other professional worlds, tied into racing secondarily if at all. Again, characters' attitudes toward horses are a barometer of moral worth. Perhaps because race riding is such a rootless life, the concept of home is terribly important to Francis and his heroes. This genius for domesticity makes the varied habitats, or *series milieu (Francis seldom uses the same character in more than one book) as comforting and intimate as Holmes's familiar Baker Street rooms.

Francis worked with coeditor John Welcome on story anthologies using the horse racing milieu. Welcome, who served as a senior steward of the Irish National Steeplechase Committee, also wrote several nonfiction books about racing. His own thrillers, featuring secret agents Richard Graham and Simon Harald, touch on the racing milieu.

The 1980s produced several fine hard-boiled American series with racetrack backgrounds. Michael Geller, a racehorse owner in real life, gives Francis-like authenticity to *Dead Fix* (1989) and the other Ken Eagle mysteries. In the tradition of Raymond *Chandler and Ross *Macdonald, William Murray's *Tip on a Dead Crab* (1984) revels in a southern California locale. Detective Shifty Anderson, a Las Vegas magician, lives with an unlikely professional horseplayer who lolls on the beach during morning workouts, bets several races on a card, and wheels multiple sucker bets.

Professor-turned-detective Thomas Theron goes racing in Robert Reeves's debut, *Doubting Thomas* (1985). In addition to the track, Theron charges through most of New England's seamy underside; academia is not the least of it.

California racing pervades Jon L. Breen's *Listen for the Click* (1983; *Vicar's Roses*), a believable track mystery that manages to parody many conventions of the genre. Yet when Jerry Brogan narrates the Surfside Handicap, the excitement is real because the race is a vital plot turn. Breen makes his racing totally authentic to support suspense, while secondary characters and some off-track scenes function as pure *satire.

It's always August racing season in Stephen Dobyns's *Saratoga Swimmer* (1981). Track security man Charlie Bradshaw is a plainspeaking, flawed hero à la Francis. Outcast from his stodgy family, Charlie belongs at the training barns, among the animals and people he trusts. Dobyns's psychology is keen, his dialogue spare and accurate. Once again, the moral man is the one who knows and cares for horses.

[*See also* Sports Milieu.]

• Melvyn P. Barnes, *Dick Francis* (1986).

—Margaret Byer

HOSTAGES. See Kidnapping; Terrorism and the Terrorist Procedural.

HOTEL MILIEU. The hotel in crime fiction ranges from the elegant luxury hotel in an exclusive area to the seediest dive in the worst possible neighborhood; the hotel serves as refuge, resort, hideout, and home. In a story in which every character is concealing something, the hotel milieu provides an additional layer of deception: the false face of people on their best behavior in public. When hotels, like homes, play host to *evil and *murder, there is a deep sense of betrayal, for a refuge has been violated. The reader is left with the impression that no place is truly safe.

Hotels provide a microcosm of society in a confined *setting—essential for any good, tightly drawn mystery—but the very nature of the setting, a place for transients, tends to press the writer to conform more closely to the unities of time, place, and action. In Agatha *Christie's *Evil Under the Sun* (1941), a flamboyant actress is murdered at a seaside resort, and the crime's setting ensures that the guests are the only *suspects. *Sleuth Hercule *Poirot asserts that he can never truly relax, for he, at least, must always be vigilant against evil. In Christie's *At Bertram's Hotel* (1965), Miss Jane *Marple stays in the hotel of the title and observes the parade of American and British guests and staff. With characteristic shrewdness, she pierces the perfect Edwardian facade of the hotel, for she knows full well the impossibility of recapturing the past.

The bed-and-breakfast setting brings *violence closer to home, for the murder takes place in a home-like setting where the owners of the B&B live, but the supporting features of a hotel—staff and strangers in close proximity with a strict schedule—are maintained. In this version of the hotel setting, the conflict between the false world of the holiday and the more down-to-earth *virtues of ordinary life is underscored. In Mary Daheim's *Just Desserts* (1991), for example, B&B hostess Judith McMonigle deals with a snowstorm, a squabbling family of guests, a murder, the serving of multiple meals, and an obnoxious cat.

The traditional view of the hotel as refuge from the wearying world is used to good effect in Dorothy L. *Sayers's *Have His Carcase* (1932). For Harriet *Vane, the Hotel Resplendent is the perfect escape after her unsettling discovery of a body on the beach. In the safe haven of the hotel, Vane can wear a claret-colored frock and dance and detect with Lord Peter *Wimsey.

Hotel staff make excellent sleuths, for they can use their privileged position to get to the bottom of mysteries involving their guests that might tarnish the hotel's reputation for efficiency and respectability. In Hugh *Pentecost's series featuring the Hotel Beaumont, the luxury hotel run by dapper general manager Pierre *Chambrun is itself an international city within the city of *New York; the hotel is run with

"Swiss watch" precision. Pentecost uses this luxurious setting to throw into relief the violence of the modern world—particularly terrorism—and its costs. In *Remember to Kill Me* (1984), Central American terrorists take hostages in the hotel, demanding the release of eight political prisoners. In Alan Russell's *The Hotel Detective* (1994), Hotel California assistant general manager Am Caulfield juggles a double murder, an apparent *suicide, and the mysterious disappearance of $3,000 worth of desserts.

Far removed from the rarefied *atmosphere of the luxury hotels are the sordid venues of deception and betrayal along Raymond *Chandler's mean streets. In his stories "The King in Yellow" (*Dime Detective*, March 1938) and "Pickup on Noon Street" (*Pick-Up on Noon Street*, 1953), cheap, dimly lit hotels are the settings for murder and frameups of the hard-drinking *private detective. In Cornell *Woolrich's chilling "Walls That Hear You" (1934), the narrator takes revenge against an unbalanced doctor who performs back-room abortions and amputates a man's tongue and fingers in the Hotel Lyons. E. Phillips *Oppenheim brings the seedy into the well-heeled Milan Hotel in *The Adventures of Mr. Joseph P. Cray* (1925). Industrialist and ex-YMCA volunteer Cray recuperates at the hotel from World War I by drinking like a fish and trapping slick con artists and war profiteers; he is a one-man system of *justice with the perfect place to exercise his moral judgment.

[*See also* Closed-World Settings and Open-World Settings.]

• Raymond Chandler, *The Simple Art of Murder* (1950).
—Elizabeth Foxwell

HOUSEHOLD, GEOFFREY (1900–1988), British author of *thrillers. Educated at *Magdalen College*, Oxford, he embarked on international career that would provide backgrounds for his fiction. He worked as a banker in Romania, a marketing manager in Spain, an encyclopedia writer and composer of children's radio plays in the United States, and as a salesman in Europe, the Middle East, and South America. During the Second World War, he served as a member of the British Intelligence Corps in the Middle East.

The author of some thirty-seven books including novels, short story collections, juvenile fiction, and an autobiography, Household was, in his thrillers, a master of the first-person narrative and the confessional journal that reveals the psychology of the self-reliant yet suspicious protagonist. His novels can be said to link the outdoor adventures of John *Buchan to the flight-and-chase novels of Lionel Davidson. Household's work was inconsistent, but at its best—in *Rogue Male* (1939; *Man Hunt*), *Watcher in the Shadows* (1960), and *Dance of the Dwarfs* (1968)—it exemplified description of manly action in the outdoors with the evocation of *terror inspired by politically motivated threatening situations. Household was unsurpassed in showing how the hunter can become the hunted.

[*See also* Great Outdoors, The; Heroism; Pursuit.]

• Michael J. Hayes, "The Story of an Encounter: Geoffrey Household's *Rogue Male*," in *Spy thrillers: From Buchan to le*

Carré, ed. Clive Bloom (1990): 72–85. Household, Geoffrey, *Against the Wind: An Autobiography* (1958).
—Robin W. Winks

HOWDUNIT, a type of story in which a rational explanation is found for a seemingly impossible event, most commonly a *murder committed in a locked or sealed room. Often only one person, who the reader is certain must be innocent, appears capable of having committed the crime. In other cases, the crime may appear to be *suicide or an accident, or a supernatural agency may seem to be at work, only to be ruled out in the end.

Though Edgar Allan *Poe's "The Murders in the Rue Morgue" in (*Graham's Lady's and Gentleman's Magazine*, Apr. 1841), generally regarded as the first real detective story, is also sometimes credited as the first *locked room mystery, Robert C. S. Adey cites Joseph Sheridan Le Fanu's "A Passage in the Secret History of an Irish Countess" (1838) for the honor. Le Fanu reused the same problem and solution in "The Murdered Cousin" (1851) and his celebrated novel *Uncle Silas* (1864). Best-known early classics of the howdunit are Israel *Zangwill's *The Big Bow Mystery* (1892) and Gaston Leroux's *The Mystery of the Yellow Room* (1908). Writers of the early twentieth century who were particularly attracted to impossible situations included G. K. *Chesterton, Jacques *Futrelle, Thomas W. Hanshew, and Carolyn Wells. Edgar *Wallace's *The Four Just Men* (1905) includes a locked room problem, and he would return to howdunit situations occasionally in the years to follow.

Arthur Conan *Doyle involved Sherlock *Holmes in *impossible crimes in "The Adventure of the Speckled Band" (*Strand*, Feb. 1892) and "The Problem of the Thor Bridge" in the *Strand*, Feb. 1922). In the quasi-Sherlockian tale "The Lost Special" (*Strand*, Aug. 1898; "The Story of the Lost Special"), Doyle first posed one of the great howdunit situations, the disappearance of a train, a problem later tackled by August Derleth in "The Adventure of the Lost Locomotive" (*The Memoirs of Solar Pons*, 1951) and by Ellery *Queen in "Snowball in July" (*This Week*, 31 Aug. 1952; "The Phantom Train"). In later variations, a jumbo jet vanishes in Tony Kenrick's *A Tough One to Lose* (1972), a houseboat in Richard Forrest's *Death on the Mississippi* (1989).

The writer most associated with locked rooms, and the supreme master of the type, was John Dickson *Carr, who from his debut in *It Walks by Night* (1930) included such a situation in nearly every novel and story he wrote, whether under his own name or as Carter Dickson. In "The Locked Room Lecture," a chapter of Carr's *The Hollow Man* (1935; *The Three Coffins*), the sleuth Dr. Gideon *Fell discusses and classifies all the possible variant solutions.

In another type of impossible crime, no footprints, save perhaps the *victim's, are evident in the snow, on the wet sand, on a clay tennis court, or on some comparable surface. Prominent examples are Carr's *The Problem of the Wire Cage* (1939) and William L. De Andrea's *Killed on the Rocks* (1990). The impossible disappearance is typified by the Sherlock Holmes adventure—a story referred to but never told by

Doyle and a favorite of *pastiche writers—wherein Mr. James Phillimore returns into his house for his umbrella and is never seen again. Herbert Brean's *Wilders Walk Away* (1948) concerns a family of multi-generational vanishers.

Most of the best-known Golden Age writers turned to the howdunit at least occasionally; examples include Eden Phillpotts's *The Grey Room* (1921), Anthony Berkeley Cox's *The Layton Court Mystery* (published anonymously in 1925), Agatha *Christie's *Why Didn't They Ask Evans?* (1934; *The Boomerang Clue*), Margery *Allingham's *Flowers for the Judge* (1936), Ngaio *Marsh's *Death and the Dancing Footman* (1941), R. Austin *Freeman's *The Jacob Street Mystery* (1942; *The Unconscious Witness*) S. S. *Van Dine's *The "Canary" Murder Case* (1927), and Ellery Queen's *The Chinese Orange Mystery* (1934) and *The King Is Dead* (1952). The period's most significant American impossible crime specialists after Carr were Clayton Rawson, whose sleuth, the Great Merlini, first appeared in *Death from a Top Hat* (1938); C. Daly King, whose 1935 collection *The Curious Mr. Tarrant* is rich in impossible situations; and Clyde B. Clason, whose Theocritus Lucius Westborough confronts many such situations in the series of novels beginning with *The Fifth Tumbler* (1936). Britain's Golden Age produced fewer specialists, though Anthony Wynne's Dr. Eustace Hailey solves many such problems in a long series of novels and Walter S. Masterman frequently practiced the howdunit.

Though Howard Haycraft prematurely buried the locked room in his classic history *Murder for Pleasure* (1941), numerous writers who have developed since then have made good use of it, including Edmund *Crispin, most notably in *The Moving Toyshop* (1946); Hake Talbot, in *The Hangman's Handyman* (1942) and *Rim of the Pit* (1944); John Sladek, in *Black Aura* (1974) and *Invisible Green* (1977); Francis Selwyn, in the Sergeant William Verity series; *science fiction writers Isaac Asimov (in *The Caves of Steel*, 1954, and *The Naked Sun*, 1957) and Randall Garrett (in *Too Many Magicians*, 1967, and numerous short stories about Lord Darcy), and such contemporaries as Bill Pronzini, Michael Bowen, Richard Forrest, and Herbert Resnicow. Latter-day short-story writers with a special interest in impossible crimes include Joseph Commings, whose Senator Brooks U. Banner is reminiscent of Carr's Dr. Fell and (writing as Dickson) Sir Henry Merrivale; and Edward D. *Hoch, whose characters Simon Ark, Captain Leopold, Nick Velvet, and especially small-town physician Sam Hawthorne frequently encounter howdunit situations. Barbara D'Amato's *Hard Tack* (1991) is an outstanding recent example, proving the type is not dead.

The howdunit has sometimes been taken as being synonymous with the inverted crime story or *inverted detective story, in which the process of committing a crime is described, with the criminal known, in the first portion of the book before the detective solves it in the second. The term has also been applied to any work that focuses on describing how the crime is committed. However, the howdunit is more commonly seen as having parallels with the *whodunit, implying an unknown factor to be revealed at the end. The two definitions converge in the sort of story that could be called a how-will-it-be-done, in which an apparently impossible event is contemplated, then the means of accomplishing it described. Examples include the jailbreak bet in Jacques Futrelle's anthology staple "The Problem of Cell 13" (in *The Thinking Machine*, 1907) and big *caper novels like Michael Crichton's *The Great Train Robbery* (1975).

[*See also* Ingenuity; Who-Gets-Away-With-It.]

• Robert C. S. Adey, *Locked Room Murders and Other Impossible Crimes: A Comprehensive Bibliography*, rev. ed. (1991).

—Jon L. Breen

HUMOR arises out of the funny, incongruous, or ludicrous in people or events. In general it may make a serious situation less onerous, or balance a tragic event with the relief of gentle laughter. In mystery fiction, the author may use humor to hide *clues, reveal the innocent, distract the reader or a character, or comment on society and contemporary issues. In addition to offering pure entertainment, humor is also used to comment on this genre through parody.

Not all writers and critics approve of the use of humor in crime and mystery fiction. At the 1992 Shots in the Dark Conference in Nottingham, England, for example, Robert Cook argued that crime is too serious to be treated lightly, that misery and death are inappropriate subjects for mere *puzzles and entertainments. One who would disagree is Michael *Innes, who considered detective stories purely recreational reading and quite openly strived to amuse as well as puzzle the reader. Innes developed his sense of farce to a fine pitch, in one case having Sir John *Appleby dress as Robin Hood to investigate at a village fete and later make his escape by hot-air balloon in (*Sheiks and Adders* (1982).

Most writers use humor to achieve specific goals. In Barbara Paul's *But He Was Already Dead When I Got There* (1986), six characters rearrange the evidence at a murder scene, leaving the reader frantic to keep the clues straight while obscuring the question of the identity of the murderer. In Agatha *Christie's *The Murder of Roger Ackroyd* (1926), the narrator's comic descriptions of Caroline Sheppard underscore her innocence; only *suspects appear without humorous qualities. The pathetic state of Rowan Rover, the tour guide in Sharyn McCrumb's *Missing Susan* (1991), leads to one ludicrous situation after another but also tells the astute reader something of what to expect in the climax.

The vehicle of humor in many instances is the principal character, often a *sleuth with a comic or eccentric appearance or personality. The comic detective is depicted as the opposite of the super-human sleuth in either one or several qualities. As depicted in *Dover One* (1964), Joyce *Porter's Detective Wilfred *Dover is everything Sherlock *Holmes is not: fat, greedy, slovenly, prejudiced, and incompetent. John *Mortimer's Horace *Rumpole is a slovenly crusading barrister henpecked by his wife and tolerated by his colleagues, but in the end a superb barrister. S. S. *Van Dine's Philo *Vance turns his investigations somewhat fey with his applications of psychology and discourses on art in *The Benson Murder Case* (1926). Phoebe Atwood *Taylor's Asey *Mayo is also both brilliant and hilarious in *Octagon House*, (1937). Margery *Allingham's eye for the absurd is given full expression in the person of the lugubrious Magersfontein *Lugg, as in *The Case of the Late Pig* (1937). Slightly different are series featuring hapless heroes. Lawrence *Block's books featuring Bernie Rhodenbarr follow the burglar cum bookseller through a series of compromising situations, usually murder, (as in *Burglars Can't Be Choosers*, 1977), for example. In Donald E. Westlake's comic novels, young men stagger from one disaster to another, as they do in *Enough!* (1977).

Concentrating the humor in secondary characters may allow the writer to comment on contemporary behavior. Catherine Aird pokes gentle fun at the stewards of old homes struggling to survive in the modern world in *The Complete Steel* (1969; *The Stately Home Murder*); Georgette *Heyer paints droll portraits of foolish women and girls in *No Wind of Blame* (1939); Emma *Lathen wittily sketches banking colleagues of her detective, John Putman *Thatcher, in *Murder Without Icing* (1972). Edward Mackin shows just how bizarre the modern college has become in *The Nominative Case* (1991), and Henry Cecil depicts the absurdities commonly emerging from witnesses to an accident or a crime in *Independent Witness* (1963). Margeret Scherf (*The Owl in the Cellar*, 1945) and Charlotte MacLeod (*Something the Cat Dragged In*, 1983) describe the ludicrous in people, manners, and mores in small communities.

The wise-cracking humor of the hard-boiled school took two directions. Dashiell *Hammett's tough-guy humor of sarcasm and self-mockery turned into screwball comedy in *The Thin Man* (1934), his later work featuring Nick and Nora *Charles. And Craig *Rice parodied the genre through Chicago lawyer John J. Malone in *Trial by Fury*, (1941). Hammett's hard-boiled style also led to the wry self-mockery in a character like Sue *Grafton's Kinsey *Milhone, who longs for the peanut butter sandwich waiting for her at home, instead of a whisky, in *"H" is for Homicide* (1991).

[*See also* Eccentrics; Farceurs; Pastiche; Silly-Ass Sleuth; Spoof Scholarship.]

—Rosemary Herbert *and* Susan Oleksiw

HUNTER, EVAN. *See* McBain, Ed.

ILES, FRANCIS. *See* Berkeley, Anthony.

IMPERSONATION. Mystery writers have long recognized the *plot possibilities that open up when one character impersonates another. There is a tradition of detectives adopting false identities: Sherlock *Holmes, for instance, bamboozled Dr. John H. Watson in "The Adventure of the Empty House" (*Strand*, Oct. 1903) when he played the part of an elderly, deformed book dealer. Although *disguise was beyond a man of such precise appearance as Hercule *Poirot, even he assumed another name and pretended to be a representative of a refugees' charity in *After the Funeral* (1953; *Funerals Are Fatal*; *Murder at the Gallop*). Members of the official police force have much less freedom to impersonate at will than do *amateur and *private detectives, but Eileen Dewhurst's *A Nice Little Business* (1987) offers a remarkable example of a *Scotland Yard man, Inspector Neil Carter, dressing up as a woman for most of the book as he pursue an unofficial investigation. The exploits of Thomas W. Hanshew's rascal Hamilton Cleek, a master of disguise who appeared in books such as *The Man Of The Forty Faces* (1910; *Cleek, the Master Detective*), require total suspension of disbelief, but Irwin M. Fletcher, who made his debut in Gregory Mcdonald's *Fletch* (1974), is a rather more plausible character. Fletch is an investigative reporter who assumes a wide range of characters in his quest for a story as well as in finding the answer to questions such as why a rich man should hire a beach bum to commit his own *murder.

Impersonation is a recurrent element in books about returning prodigals, such as Josephine *Tey's *Brat Farrar* (1949; *Come and Kill Me*) and Martha Grimes's *The Old Fox Deceiv'd* (1982), but the variety of ways in which it can be employed by those with criminal intentions is infinite. Impersonation may be incidental to the commission of the crime, typically as a means of creating confusion about the precise time of a *victim's death and thus helping the culprit to establish an apparently watertight *alibi; Jill McGown's *The Other Woman* (1993) is an example of this time-honored device. Often, the impersonation is central to the criminal design, as in books where one character fakes his or her identity with a view to laying claim to an inheritance. Emma *Lathen has pointed out that in three of her most successful postwar novels, Agatha *Christie played games with the readers' expectations when death stalks the wealthy; the imposter is not one of the obvious suspects, but

the monied person who was prepared to kill to protect his or her illicitly gained wealth.

Experienced mystery readers are alert for the *clues to a story which depends upon impersonation. A character with theatrical experience is often a promising *suspect, while the discovery of a *corpse whose features are rendered unrecognizable usually paves the way for a final revelation that the identity of the deceased was not as everyone originally believed. The diversity of books in which impersonation is an element is remarkable: Consider two contemporaneous works that are otherwise very different from one another, Raymond *Chandler's *The Long Goodbye* (1953) and Margot Bennett's *Farewell Crown and Good-Bye King* (1952). *The Norwich Victims* by Francis Beeding (1935) is unusual in that it includes photographs of the chief characters; the gimmick has a serious purpose, since few readers will realize that two of the pictures are of one and the same man. The superficial physical dissimilarity in the illustrations reinforce the cunningly contrived text, in which a multiple murderer leads two distinct lives as a means of covering his tracks. Equally noteworthy was Robert Player's first novel, *The Ingenious Mr. Stone* (1945), although Julian *Symons, an admirer of the book, described Player's use of more than one disguise as "outrageous."

Impersonation raises questions about identity that writers of talent can be expected to explore further in the years to come. The theme of sexual identity has been explored for some time, but even books as good as Tey's *To Love and Be Wise* (1950) and Ruth *Rendell's *A Sleeping Life* (1978) are far from offering the last word on the subject. Walter *Mosley's *Devil in a Blue Dress* (1990), points the way ahead: When Ezekiel "Easy" *Rawlins discovers that a black girl called Ruby Hanks has been passing herself off as a white torch singer, Daphne Monet, he not only solves a mystery but also learns something about what it is to be black in a society dominated by whites.

[*See also* Mistaken Identity; Prodigal Son/Daughter; Sex and Sexuality.]

• Emma Lathen, "Cornwallis's Revenge," in *Agatha Christie: First Lady of Crime* (1977), ed. H. R. F. Keating. Julian Symons, *Bloody Murder: From the Detective Story to the Crime Novel*, 3rd rev. ed. (1992).   —Martin Edwards

IMPOSSIBLE CRIME. The first mystery story was an impossible crime; in Edgar Allan *Poe's "The Murders in the Rue Morgue" (*Graham's Lady's and

Gentleman's Magazine, Apr. 1841) two women are murdered in a locked room. The *locked room mystery became a special category in crime fiction, but did not remain the only impossible crime detailed by writers. Beginning in the 1890s writers exhibited ingenuity in the creation and solution of impossible crimes, including an unseen *murder in full view of witnesses or the disappearance of buildings, trains, people. In every story the reader is brought face to face with the deceptiveness of appearances.

In "The Case of Roger Carboyne" (*Strand*, Sept. 1892) by H. Greenhough Smith, one of the earliest examples of an impossible crime, a man vanishes without a trace from a mountain track and appears later, dead, on a higher plateau. The device of the disappearing person or *corpse proved a popular one, and Anna Katharine *Green's *Miss Hurd: An Enigma* (1894), wherein a woman vanishes inexplicably, was among the earliest impossible disappearance novels. The most famous was undoubtedly Ethel Lina White's *The Wheel Spins* (1936; *The Lady Vanishes*), which was filmed by Alfred Hitchcock, but the most satisfying remains *Into Thin Air* (1928) by Horatio Winslow and Leslie Quirk. Other books have featured people jumping from cliffs or buildings without landing, as in Norman Berrow's *Don't Jump, Mr. Boland* (1954), or disappearing from a swimming pool, as in S. S. *Van Dine's *The Dragon Murder Case* (1933).

Some writers focused on vanishing objects large or small. Will Scott provided *The Vanishing House* (1934) for his tramp-detective, Giglamps, and Edmund *Crispin's *The Moving Toyshop* (1946) did just that. Norman Berrow removed a complete street in *The Three Tiers of Fantasy* (1947). A railway train was made to vanish as early as 1898 in Arthur Conan *Doyle's "The Lost Special" (*The Black Doctor and Other Tales of Terror and Mystery*, 1925) and was followed by Melville Davisson *Post's *The Bradmoor Murder* (1929; *The Garden in Asia*). A truck vanished in H. S. Keeler's *The Vanishing Gold Truck* (1941), an airliner in Karen Campbell's *Suddenly, in the Air* (1969; *The Brocken Spectre*), and a houseboat in Richard Forrest's *Death on the Mississippi* (1989). One of the simplest yet most convincing disappearances was Jacques *Futrelle's "Phantom Motor Car" (*Cassell's Family Magazine*, Mar. 1908).

Several writers focused on *clues, such as footprints. In "The Flying Death" (*Strand*, Apr. 1903), Samuel Hopkins Adams recounts murder on a beach unmarked except for the prints of a gigantic prehistoric bird. Harriet *Vane pondered the absence of footprints on a beach leading to a corpse in Dorothy L. *Sayers's *Have His Carcase* (1932).

Another popular impossible crime was death by invisible agency, wherein the victim was apparently on his own when struck down. The form began with Melvin L. Severy's *The Darrow Enigma* (1904) and an impossible case of poisoning. It was John Dickson *Carr who explored virtually every variation in the form in such books as *The Three Coffins* (1935; *The Hollow Man*), and *The Reader Is Warned* (1939), written under the pseudonym Carter Dickson.

Some problems defy categorization. Israel *Zang-will's *A Nineteenth Century Miracle* (1897) concerns a man swept from a channel packet boat and deposited moments later through a London studio skylight. Corpses were made to drive cars in Nevil Monroe Hopkins's "The Moyett Case" (in *The Strange Cases of Mason Brant*, 1916). Untraceable fingerprints began with Hugh Austin's *The Upside Down Murders* (1937). Devil's hoofmarks appear on occasion, the most ingenious use appearing in the medieval setting in Arthur Porges's "The Devil Will Surely Come."

Porges was one of a band of American authors who produced innumerable twists using the short story format. He demonstrated how a blood sample can be taken from an unwilling suspect, a strong man can be strangled by a child, an immovable block can be used as a blunt instrument. Joseph Commings, with his sleuth Senator Banner, faced a vampire killer confined to a mausoleum for 150 years, and a scarecrow able to use a shotgun, and, in "The X Street Murders" (*Mystery Digest*, Mar./Apr. 1962), a killer using a pistol and then having it produced seconds later from a sealed envelope in an adjoining room. Edward D. *Hoch makes a complete circus disappear, presents a fatal bullet wound with no entry, strangles a skydiver during a parachute jump, and, in "The Problem of the Invisible Acrobat" (*EQMM*, mid-Dec. 1986) makes an acrobat vanish while on the high wire.

The emphasis on working out what appears to be an impossible turn of events often shifts the attention away from character development and *atmosphere or *setting, but few other categories of crime and mystery fiction challenge the reader so relentlessly to question his or her basic perceptions and assumptions.

[*See also* Fingerprints and Footprints; Impersonation; Ingenuity; Railway Milieu; "Time Is of the Essence."]

• Robert C. S. Adey, *Locked Room Murders, and Other Impossible Crimes. A Comprehensive Bibliography* (1979; rev. and expanded 1991). Roland Lacourbe, *99 Chambres Closes. Guide de Lecture du Crime Impossible* (1991). Steve Lewis, "Locked Rooms and Other Impossible Crimes," *Crime and Detective Stories* 20 (Mar. 1993), 21 (Aug. 1993), 22 (Jan. 1994), 23 (May 1994). Michel Sonpart et al. *Chambres Closes, Crimes Impossibles* (1997).   —Robert C. S. Adey

IMPOSTORS. *See* Impersonation; Mistaken Identity.

INCIDENTAL CRIME WRITERS. Throughout the history of the mystery genre, writers best known for work in other areas have occasionally added mystery fiction to their list of works.

In its earliest years, crime fiction was regarded as one genre among several available to the writer. Wilkie *Collins, Elizabeth Cleghorn Gaskell, and Robert Louis Stevenson moved freely from one form of the novel to another. By the time Arthur Conan *Doyle began writing his historical novels, the lines between genres were becoming stricter, at least in the eyes of the reading public. Nevertheless, many writers have continued to move among the genres, choosing the form most appropriate to the story.

Their crime novels sometimes become more well known than the rest of their work; mainstream novelist C. H. B. Kitchin, for example, is chiefly remembered for *Death of My Aunt* (1929), the first of four sober, understated *whodunits narrated by a prim stockbroker, Malcom Warren. But it was equally likely that the crime fiction was subsumed by the writer's larger body of work. A. A. Milne, celebrated author of *Winnie the Pooh* (1927), turned his hand to many forms of writing, including essays and drama. His talents in mystery writing are well exhibited in *The Red House Mystery* (1922); his crime stories appear in two mixed collections, *Birthday Party and Other Stories* (1948) and *A Table Near the Band* (1950). William Faulkner, the quintessential novelist of the American South, used the techniques of detective fiction in some of his major works: *Absalom, Absalom!* (1936) and *Intruder in the Dust* (1948). His story collection *Knight's Gambit* (1949), featuring an astute rural attorney, is authentic detective fiction. Mainstream novelist C. P. Snow's first and last novels are detective stories: *Death Under Sail* (1932), a meticulous formal exercise, and *A Coat of Varnish* (1979), more somber and serious of purpose.

The appeal of the genre may be its formal structure or its ability to accommodate variation through a series of books. Winifred Ashton (writing as Clemence Dane) and Helen Simpson together wrote three graceful detective novels featuring the actor-manager Sir John Saumarez, a walk-on in *Printer's Devil* (1930; *Author Unknown*), but otherwise the lead. Several of the novelist, dramatist, and critic J. B. Priestley's works qualify as criminous: two apocalyptic thrillers, *The Doomsday Men* (1938) and *Saturn over the Water* (1961); two diverse spy novels, *Black-Out in Gretley* (1942) and *The Shapes of Sleep* (1962); and a lively whodunit, *Salt Is Leaving* (1966), with a dogged provincial doctor as detective. F. Tennyson Jesse introduced Solange Fontaine, who employs a "delicate extra sense" that warns her of *evil in *The Solange Stories* (1931), and offers a harrowing version of the infamous Thompson-Bywaters murder case in *A Pin to See the Peep-Show* (1934).

The genre has appealed also to writers in nonfiction. The Shakespearean scholar Alfred Harbage wrote four detective novels under the pseudonym Thomas Kyd; a determined policeman, Sam Phelan, figures in these, notably *Blood of Vintage* (1947). Ralph Arnold, a social historian, published a small body of detective novels beginning in the 1930s. Robert Bernard, the literary biographer, follows an eccentric scholar, Millicent Hetherege, in *Deadly Meeting* (1970) and *Illegal Entry* (1972). The critic and historian Audrey Williamson published two stylish whodunits late in her life, both with Superintendant Richard York as the detective. *Funeral March for Siegfried* (1979) draws effectively on her Wagnerian expertise. The critic and commentator William F. Buckley Jr. has written more than half a dozen spy novels about Blackford Oakes, an American secret agent. The first, *Saving the Queen* (1976), is typical in its political astuteness.

Among contemporary novelists also working in detective fiction, perhaps the best known is Jorge Luis Borges, whose best work includes "The Garden of Forking Paths" in *Ficciones* (1962) and "Death and The Compass" in *Labyrinths* (1962). Paco Ignacio Taibo II has also turned to detective fiction; his *Life Itself* (1994) comments on political life in Mexico.

—Susan Oleksiw

INDEPENDENT SLEUTH. Largely associated with American hard-boiled *private eye fiction, the depiction of the *sleuth as an independent character without personal entanglements is an important tradition in the literary history of the broader genre. Early in the development of the genre, writers realized that it was advantageous to keep the hero's personal attachments limited so that the character could believably pursue *clues and *suspects at all hours and in dangerous circumstances. A detective without a family might be inclined to take greater personal risks than would one with a spouse or family. A sleuth who is not romantically attached is also useful to the writer who is interested in creating new relationships in the course of a narrative.

Intellectual prowess turned some sleuths into loners. The first private detective, Edgar Allan *Poe's Chevalier C. Auguste *Dupin, had powers of observation and analysis far superior to those of the people around him. Arthur Conan *Doyle's Sherlock *Holmes, too, remained an essentially solitary figure who was more befriended by than connected to his devoted sidekick and narrator, Dr. John H. *Watson. In fact, most of fiction's *Great Detectives essentially stood apart from others—including the professional police—who held them in awe and were not their intellectual equals.

The sleuth as *loner came of age in distinctly American fiction published in the 1920s in *Black Mask magazine. It may be no coincidence that this magazine, initially created by H. L. Mencken to showcase *westerns and *horror fiction along with crime stories, welcomed stories featuring individualist heroes drawn from the loner hero traditions of America's Old West. Significantly, these heroes did not rely on sidekicks to narrate their work, but instead poured them out in their own vernacular.

The prototypical private eye was Carroll John *Daly's Race *Williams, who first appeared in *Black Mask* in 1923. He set out the hard-boiled hero's philosophy when he said: "Right and wrong are not written on the statutes for me, nor do I find my code of morals in the essays of long-winded professors. My ethics are my own. I'm not saying they're good and I'm not admitting they're bad, and what's more I'm not interested in the opinions of others on that subject." This attitude is a direct descendent of the mythic codes of honor spelled out in westerns: When the agents of law and order have been bought and corrupted, honorable individuals are bound to take the law into their own hands to preserve fundamental, immutable *justice. Of course, some westerns portray official lawmen as honorable, but they are often seen to stand alone against a corrupt crowd. Earlier stories emphasized sparring, both physical and verbal, while more recent stories are stronger on internal monologues, resulting in more profound character development.

Raymond *Chandler's Philip *Marlowe further defined private investigation as the preserve of the lone male hero when he wrote, in his essay "The Simple Art of Murder" (in *Atlantic Monthly*, Dec. 1944): "Down these mean streets a man must go who is not himself mean, who is neither tarnished nor afraid." Chandler identified his private eye prototype as "a lonely man" with a chivalric approach to his work. Many writers after Chandler relied upon his conventions, creating characters who champion the underdog or the poor, are good in a fight, and are introspective to the point of brooding. Ross *Macdonald perfected the brooding sleuth in Lew *Archer, who first appeared in *The Moving Target* in 1949. Late twentieth-century women feminists have proven that the mean streets are not the exclusive preserve of male private eyes, and that the lonely search for the *truth can be achieved by a woman.

[*See also* Chivalry; Conventions of the Genre; Formula: Character; Individualism.]

• Robert A. Baker and Michael T. Nietzel. *Private Eyes: 101 Knights* (1985). John G. Cawelti, *Adventure, Mystery, and Romance: Formula Stories as Art and Popular Culture* (1976). Kathleen Gregory Klein, *The Woman Detective: Gender and Genre* (1988). Maureen T. Reddy, *Sisters in Crime: Feminism and the Crime Novel* (1988).　—Sara Paretsky

INDIVIDUALISM. Among the ideological values transmitted by crime and mystery fiction, none is more significant than individualism. Created in an historical period characterized by diminishment of community ties, the decline of surety about one's place in any divine plan, and the erosion of collective belief systems that had rooted a person in a traditional caste or *class, the genre of fiction about criminal detection made the singularity of character its sole fixed point. The extraordinary appeal of detective fiction, thus, came to rest in the reassuring implication of narrative designs showing that an individual's personality can be sufficient resource to comprehend and, possibly, even control a world of alienating and opaque forces.

The prototypical detective was crafted as a figure whose mental acuity surpasses that of any other character in the fiction, an acuity compounded of exceptional reasoning powers and an ability to intuit patterns and connections others miss. The detective's mental powers, therefore, expressed the fact of independence from the conventions that constrain the minds and behavior of ordinary citizens and the possession of a personal code that allows the *sleuth to serve as ethical *judge as well as investigator of crime. This prototype of the individualist detective appears almost completely formed in the stories by Edgar Allan *Poe about the Chevalier C. Auguste *Dupin. Indifferent to the perquisites of social class, Dupin places himself apart from the law and decorum. He enters apartments in search of *clues, climbs over roofs, and in and out of windows.

The later incarnation of the great (individualist) detective as Sherlock *Holmes displays even greater willingness to follow his own course of judgment. In "The Adventure of the Blue Carbuncle" (*Strand*, Jan. 1892), Holmes condones a felony in the hope of saving a soul. In "The Adventure of Abbey Grange" (*Strand*, Sept. 1904), Holmes and Dr. John H. *Watson decide to withhold the identity of the killer from the police. And, in "The Adventure of Charles Augustus Milverton" (*Strand*, Apr. 1904), they turn blind eyes to a woman's shooting of a blackmailer.

Writers often choose to emphasize the individualism of their detectives by attributing eccentricity to them. Wilkie *Collins's Sergeant *Cuff has a predilection for rose growing. Rex *Stout's Nero *Wolfe consumes great quantities of beer, is an expert orchid grower, vents fierce opinions about descriptive linguistics in dictionaries and women in general, and can scarcely be budged from his armchair. H. C. *Bailey's Joshua Clunk likes singing hymns and sucking sweets. James H. "Jim" Hanvey, the creation of Octavus Roy Cohen, affects a gold toothpick and relishes strong cigars.

The development of American hard-boiled writing served only to reinforce the individualism of detectives. Although Dashiell *Hammett's *Continental Op sets out to reform the town of Personville in *Red Harvest* (1929), he determines that he must be as lawless as the gangsters and crooked politicians to accomplish his end, not because he is personally corrupt but because, on the contrary, he has an exacting code of *justice that directs his behavior in a fallen world. Raymond *Chandler's Philip *Marlowe, Mickey *Spillane's Mike *Hammer, Ross *Macdonald's Lew *Archer, John D. *MacDonald's Travis *McGee, and Robert B. *Parker's *Spenser are all individualistic kin in their relentless *pursuit of a justice and *truth they interpret in terms of their own sense of integrity. They react swiftly against the immoral rich, venal politicians, corrupt police, and petty hoodlums, placing little faith in conventions intending to constrain ordinary citizens; like all detective heroes, they are confirmed in the rectitude of the values they create for themselves.

At times the individualistic sleuth may also be a loner, but that is a secondary trait reflective of the particularized experiences allotted by authors to their detectives for reasons apart from expression of fundamental individualism. The confident individualism of detectives who make their own rules may also sanction brutality inexcusable to anyone else, but even such excess illustrates the fundamental truth that the detective character is a product of a world that often seems to writers, and to readers, lacking in any basis for morality other than individualism.

[*See also* Chivalry; Eccentrics; Formula: Character; Heroism; Independent Sleuth; Loner, Sleuth as.]

• Christopher Metress, "Dashiell Hammett and the Challenge of New Individualism: Rereading *Red Harvest* and *The Maltese Falcon*," *Essays in Literature* (fall 1990): 242–60. Michael F. Logan, "Detective Fiction as Urban Critique," *Journal of American Culture* (fall 1992); 89–94.

　—Dale Salwak

INDUSTRY WRITERS. All genres of *formula fiction naturally lend themselves to mass production. The formulas exist because they appeal to a reliable market, and they also provide the writer with a replicable product. The special nature of the detective story formula invites replication to a unique degree. The defining character of the genre—the detective—is, like the catalyst of chemical processes, unaltered by the actions and reactions of any given case. Unlike the usual fictional hero, the detective concludes each case possessing essentially the same status as at the beginning, ready and intact for the next case.

Ever since Edgar Allan *Poe created the Chevalier C. Auguste *Dupin and used him in three mysteries, the possibility of future adventures has probably been a factor in the conception of nearly all fictional detectives. The author knows that if the audience buys the prototype, it will buy a succession of reproductions. Few writers compose models intended to be unique to their first tale; sometimes, when they do, as E. C. *Bentley did in *Trent's Last Case* (1913), they are later tempted to repetition anyway. In this sense a large proportion of detective fiction can claim an industrial premise. But the term "industry writer" is reserved for those whose prolificity has led to their names (and often the names of their *sleuths) becoming household words.

In some cases the fame of the character and presumed author has been the work of a changing cast of industrial workers; thus, the house names Nick *Carter (in the United States; first novel 1886) and Sexton Blake (in England; first novel 1893) have been the bylines for literally thousands of similar products (an estimated 4,000 for Blake) created by an interchangeable battery of writers.

A step up from the laborers who assembled episodes for Carter and Blake are the one-man fiction factories whose output can claim the integrity of a single engineer. The phenomenal exemplars are Erle Stanley *Gardner and John *Creasey. In the fifty years of his writing career (1921–1970) Gardner published more than a thousand titles. Creasey's production was even greater: Between 1932 and 1979 he published more than 500 novels. After his death in 1973 the backlog resulted in the appearance of some twenty posthumous titles. In a single year, 1939, Gardner published at least four novels, eighteen novelettes, two short stories, and five articles. In the same year Creasey published at least thirty-eight novels.

Though they share an almost superhuman capacity for production, Gardner and Creasey pursued different industrial strategies. Gardner invented a character who has become an icon. Although he made efforts to develop subsidiary series, he eventually subsided into producing ever more mechanical copies of the archetypal Perry *Mason scheme: a narrow class of characters with a limited menu of *motives working at cross-purposes until lawyer Mason extracts the *truth. Despite their popularity, none of Creasey's prominent detectives—Richard Rollison "The Toff"; Roger West; Dr. Palfrey; or Commander George Gideon—approached Mason's eminence. On the other hand, Creasey took his writing seriously

enough to revise his work with care and to create a three-dimensional fictional world. The Gideon books, for example, written under the J. J. Marric pseudonym, have received special critical praise for their realism.

A number of writers not as prolific as Gardner or Creasey may also be placed in the industrial class. Edgar *Wallace, who between 1906 and 1932 published more than 170 books, more than half of them mysteries or thrillers, belongs in the category; so does Phillips *Oppenheim, with more than 150 novels and short story collections issued between 1887 and 1944.

Georges *Simenon represents the acme of industrial writing: an extremely prolific author who produced 220 novels, eighty-four of them Inspector Jules *Maigret mysteries. In the eleven months between May 1932 and April 1933, he wrote ten novels; at the height of his career he averaged more than five novels a year. Although Simenon accepted the essential structural formula of the genre—murder, investigation, discovery—and relied upon recurring figures, the formulas are subordinated to exploration of character and environment, an exploration which seems to be new in each case, an effect demonstrating that an industry writer can create a quality product.

[See also Series and Serial Publication.]

• Quentin J. Reynolds, *The Fiction Factory; or, From Pulp Row to Quality Street: The Story of 100 Years of Publishing at Street and Smith* (1955). John G. Cawelti, *Adventure Mystery and Romance* (1976). Francis L. Fugate and Roberta B. Fugate, *Secrets of the World's Best-Selling Writer* (1980).
—J. K. Van Dover

INGENUITY, or the quality of being clever, original, or inventive, has almost universal appeal. So it was to be expected that mystery writers should seize on opportunities to demonstrate it in their fiction. Ingenuity is used in two ways, first by an author in devising a *plot or in telling a story, and second by the *sleuth in finding the solution (which is, of course, primarily the author as well).

The second approach dates from the beginning of classical crime fiction itself. The ingenuity of the solutions found by Edgar Allen *Poe's Chevalier C. Auguste *Dupin in the story collection *Tales* (1845) is still breathtaking. Some of the stories in the first of Arthur Conan *Doyle's collections, *The Adventures of Sherlock Holmes* (1892), are every bit Dupin's equal.

There have, however, been later writers with sleuths of almost equal ingenuity. Among them, working from the depths of a huge armchair, is Rex *Stout's Nero *Wolfe, typically in *A Family Affair* (1975). Equally smart with solutions, propounded in the courtroom, was Erle Stanley *Gardner's Perry *Mason. Among his many cases, *The Case of the Sleepwalker's Niece* (1936) is a good example.

For ingenuity of plot one of the earliest writers in the genre, Jacques *Futrelle, still perhaps bears the palm. "The Problem of Cell 13," in *Best Thinking Machine Detective Stories* (1973), his story of prison escape featuring Professor S. F. X. *Van Dusen, the Thinking Machine, is purely dazzling. It is rivaled perhaps by two examples of ingenuity in the method of *murder. The first, incorporating a locked room complication, was written by John Dickson *Carr under his pseudonym Carter Dickson, *The Judas Window* (1938; *The Crossbow Murder*). The second, which has been hailed as the cleverest method of murder ever devised, comes in Christianna *Brand's *Green for Danger* (1944).

Ingenuity can also be displayed in the way a murderer is concealed from the reader. In this subdivision a neat example is provided in Ngaio *Marsh's *Overture to Death* (1939), in which the *victim is maneuvered into bringing about his own death. A killer is equally well concealed, but in an entirely different way, in Raymond *Chandler's *The Big Sleep* (1939). Here the method of concealment is the extraordinary complicatedness of the whole affair until all the pieces finally fall into place.

Complication of plot is an essential device in another form of the ingenious mystery story, the comic crime novel. Here, as in many comic novels without any crime backbone, complication and convolution are the writer's best weapons, as in Donald Westlake's *God Save the Mark* (1967).

The writers may concentrate their ingenuity in the actual telling, that is, in the very problem writers set themselves in spinning some particular tale, as in Agatha *Christie's dilemma of having a series of murders in English towns each beginning with a successive letter of the alphabet. The pleasure of *The ABC Murders* (1936; *The Alphabet Murders*) lies as much in watching how Christie does it as in the actual mystery.

A different dilemma was set for herself by Helen Eustis in *The Horizontal Man* (1946). Whereas Christie located a large part of her story in the outside world of events and discussions, Eustis sets her story largely in the minds of her characters. But her surprise solution is as ingenious as that of Christie. Again, Stanley *Ellin's *Mirror, Mirror on the Wall* (1972) takes place all within one mind, and a pretty mixed-up mind at that. Only in the last pages does one realize just how ingenious Ellin has been.

While Christie was at the height of her ingenuity, Francis Iles was advancing the art into new waters. In *Before the Fact* (1932) the reader can see from the start who the murderer will be and who will be his victim. But half the pleasure of the book lies in watching the ingenuity with which Iles edges his story ever nearer the expected climax.

Ingenuity is sometimes the whole of a book, as in Barbara Paul's *But He Was Already Dead When I Got There* (1986). More often it is, as it were, a second locomotive driving the train along at a yet more cracking pace. This is the case with Julian *Symons's *The End of Solomon Grundy* (1964). Symons intended the book to be a mystery exposing middle-class hypocrisy, and so devastatingly it is. But at the same time he provided twist on twist of ingenuity, and it is that which holds the reader's nose firmly down in the pages. Far from being a mere trick, ingenuity challenges the reader to look beyond the superficial.

[*See also* Clues, Famous; Impossible Crime; Locked Room Mystery; Weapons, Unusual Murder.]
• Robert Barnard, *A Talent to Deceive* (1980).

—H. R. F. Keating

INNES, MICHAEL, pseudonym of J(ohn) I(nnes) M(ackintosh) Stewart (1906–1994), British author, literary critic, and *Oxford don. He produced detective novels under his pseudonym, and mainstream novels, including the *Staircase in Sturry* quintet, and literary criticism under his own name. He also used the Stewart name for his works of literary biography, including a study of English novelist and poet Thomas Hardy, and for his contribution to the *Oxford History of English Literature* series.

He took to writing crime fiction in 1936 to pass the time during a sea voyage from Liverpool, England to Adelaide, Australia, where he was a professor of English at the University of Adelaide for ten years, and he continued to write clever, cultivated mysteries for a further fifty years. He is a master of the high, polite tradition of detective fiction and one of the best known of the *farceurs, variously characterized as donnish, civilized, and literate. His detective novels are distinguished by mischievous wit, exuberant fancy and adroit contrivance, with literary *allusion a sine qua non. At times his work achieves a bizarre, almost manic brilliance, pushing the form well beyond conventional limits. *Appleby on Ararat* (1941) maroons a picturesque company on a Pacific island; *The Daffodil Affair* (1942) concerns a vanished horse with extrasensory perception; *A Night of Errors* (1947) features identical triplets; and *Operation Pax* (1951) combines the novel of threat and tension with a full-scale intellectual *puzzle.

Many of Innes's books have country-house *settings, with priceless assets as the focus for criminal complications. Precious paintings and manuscripts recur as objects of devious desire; equivocal butlers hover and dubious scholars take their chances. The style throughout is immaculate mandarin, irresistible in its poised precision and self-mocking pedantry. Educated jokes abound and abstruse vocabulary enhances the effect of intellectual bravura. Thus, a resounding boom is "latrant, mugent, reboatory"; and a company plays a parlor game requiring them to quote in turn from William *Shakespeare on the theme of bells. The sequence from *Death at the President's Lodging* (1936) to *Christmas at Candleshoe* (1953) is especially memorable and includes some perfect masterpieces: *Lament for a Maker* (1938), a tortuous, protean narrative shared among five narrators, set in a snowbound Scottish mansion, remote, and rat-infested; *Stop Press* (1939; *The Spider Strikes*), an ambitious tour-de-force, dense and elaborate, yet light and subtle, with a fictional master criminal who rises from the page to haunt his creator; *Appleby's End* (1945), an intricate farce, antic and exhilarating, involving a resourceful family in a hectic sequence of fantastic events, in which life appears to imitate art; and *Christmas at Candleshoe* (1953), an entrancing tale with its own magic, lyrical, formal, oblique, and unpredictable.

The later works are less substantial, less closely wrought and teasing to the wits; but even the least of them is deft, intriguing and amusing. Several feature Charles Honeybath, a distinguished painter, much in demand for portraits.

For most of the time John *Appleby is in charge, the least procedural of policemen, worldly and self-possessed, with a natural authority. A man of infinite resource and acute practical intelligence, he is at ease in any company and wholly unfazed by eccentric persons or odd events. He is also supremely well-informed, with a formidable range of cultural reference and an infallible gift for apt quotation. His recorded career covers fifty years, from the murder of Dr. Umpleby in 1936 to that of Lord Osprey in 1986. Few fictional detectives have served so long and few crime writers have given such intense pleasure over so many years.

[See also Academic Milieu; Country House Milieu; Gentleman Sleuth; Humor.]

• George L. Scheper, *Michael Innes* (1985). J. I. M. Stewart, *Myself and Michael Innes* (1987). —B. A. Pike

INNOCENCE. Every story in the crime and mystery genre raises the question of innocence: What is it? And how is it to be recognized or determined? Writers work with a variety of definitions of innocence, such as freedom from legal *guilt; freedom from moral guilt, or sin; or freedom from duplicity.

In the simplest form of detective fiction, a crime is committed and a detective tracks down the guilty party and vindicates everyone else. Once the guilty party is removed from the community, the original, innocent world is restored. In Margery *Allingham's *Look to the Lady* (1931; *The Gyrth Chalice Mystery*), for example, Albert *Campion not only prevents the loss of a valuable family chalice to a syndicate of avaricious collectors but also restores a scion to his family. This pattern of affirming traditional society is common among authors working in the *Golden Age traditions.

The pattern is consistently inverted in American *hard-boiled fiction, where there are only *corruption and cynicism. In this American Puritan version of romance, the *private eye alone represents honor and innocence. In Dashiell *Hammett's *The Maltese Falcon* (1930), Sam *Spade swims through a sordid world to avenge the death of his partner. The *formula persists until the post Mickey *Spillane version of the tough-guy protagonist forsakes any claim to innocence whatsoever.

These two types, combined with the *conventions of the genre that aid in deceiving the reader, have given rise to conventions about who is innocent. In novels with private detectives, whether professional or amateur, the official police *suspect is almost certainly innocent. Clients of lawyer detectives are usually innocent, but not so the clients of private eyes. Amnesiacs who stand accused are almost always innocent, as are those first observed at the scene of a crime. Policemen, spinsters, and vicars (if genuine) are usually innocent, as are servants (unless bogus), gypsies, vagrants, and foreigners (except in thrillers).

The love interest or the confidant of the detective is probably innocent, except in hard-boiled stories. *Sidekicks and narrators are presumed innocent. And every one of these conventions has been turned upside down by writers.

These conventions do not mean, however, that nothing adverse happens to the innocent. Indeed, one strand of this genre is the exploration of how the innocent cope with the relentless pressure put on those presumed to be guilty or cope with blackmail, planted evidence, or the miscarriage of *justice. False accusation is the theme of Josephine *Tey's *The Franchise Affair* (1948); an innocent party is used as a pawn in Agatha *Christie's *The ABC Murders* (1936; *The Alphabet Murders*); and characters are framed in Arthur Conan *Doyle's "The Adventure of the Norwood Builder" (*The Return of Sherlock Holmes*, 1905).

The effort to exonerate the innocent inevitably rouses the villain. In Christie's *Ordeal by Innocence* (1958), a whole *family resists reopening the case of a man convicted of murdering his mother because that would refocus *suspicion on the rest of them. In P. D. *James's *Innocent Blood* (1980) and *An Unsuitable Job for a Woman* (1972), the protagonists conceal incriminating evidence to protect the innocent. In Edward Gorman's *Murder on the Aisle* (1987), Tobin, a movie critic, must find the murderer while staying one step ahead of the police, who are growing tired of his influential friends.

Other writers raise the most complicated question: What constitutes innocence? In many stories the murderer is deemed to be innocent of any crime, and the detective allows him or her to go on with life; in these cases, the murderer is someone who follows an acceptable mode of life and is implicitly considered more valuable than the victim. In Doyle's "The Adventure of Charles Augustus Milverton" (*Strand*, Apr. 1904), blackmail is considered justification for murder. The protagonist of Anthony *Berkeley's *Trial and Error* (1937) commits a "morally justifiable" homicide, but then must strive to exonerate someone else who is convicted of the murder; the protagonist's innocence is derived in part from his commitment to protecting another. Again, the murderers are deemed justified in Christie's *Murder on the Orient Express* (1934; *Murder in the Calais Coach*); in Gwen Moffat's *Pit Bull* (1991) a neighbor arranges the death of a young man who has been harassing a young girl of whom he is fond.

In the preceding examples, the innocence of those who are driven to homicide is not compromised, and the violent act seems to be the only adequate response to *evil. But other writers challenge this perception. In the ultimate subversion of the formula there is no innocence or catharsis; justice may not be done; characters may be successfully framed; a guilty protagonist may be punished for the wrong crime; and victims may incite their own murder, as in Francis *Iles's *Before the Fact* (1932), or bystanders may be complicit by unwittingly inciting or consciously concealing knowledge of the crime, as in Marie *Belloc Lowndes's *The Lodger* (1913).

G. K. *Chesterton's Father *Brown would probably not dispute this bleak view of the world, but his creator insists on focusing on the possibility of redemption. Father Brown's capacity to identify with the heart and mind of the criminal enables him to solve such mysteries as "The Hammer of God" (*Storyteller*, Dec. 1910) and to exact repentance rather than impose punishment. Indeed, he condemns the preaching of a false theology of innocence in "The Eye of Apollo" (*The Innocence of Father Brown*, 1911).

[*See also* "Butler Did It, The"; Characterization; Whodunit.]

• Hanna Kurz Charney, *The Detective Novel of Manners: Hedonism, Morality, and the Life of Reason* (1981). George Grella, "Murder and the Mean Streets: The Hard-Boiled Detective Novel," *Contempora* 1, no. 1 (March 1970): 6–15. Tony Hilfer, *The Crime Novel: A Deviant Genre* (1990). Robert S. Paul, *Whatever Happened to Sherlock Holmes: Detective Fiction, Popular Theology, and Society* (1991). Colin Watson, *Snobbery with Violence: Crime Stories and Their Audience* (1971). Robert Zaslavsky, "The Divine Detective in the Guilty Vicarage," *Armchair Detective* 19, no. 1 (Winter 1986): 58–68.
—George L. Scheper *and* Peter V. Cenci

INTERPOL. During the early twentieth century, the need for cooperation between nation states in policing serious crime became urgent. Although police contacts had been made between European countries before 1914, it was in that year that the first International Police Conference was held in Monaco, mainly with European representatives but with a few from South America and Asia.

World War I immediately sabotaged the success of this conference, and it was not until 1923 that a second conference was convened in Vienna. The outcome was the establishment of the International Criminal Police Commission (ICPC), which functioned most effectively in Central Europe until the Nazis seized control in 1938 and moved the headquarters to Berlin. This terminated the ICPC until after World War II, when it was revived at a Brussels conference in 1946 and its headquarters France, still with a predominantly European membership.

To mark the adoption of new statutes in 1956, the ICPC changed its name to the present International Criminal Police Organization—Interpol. Since then, Interpol has grown enormously with most countries represented at the United Nations now holding membership. When coined, the term "Interpol" excited a great deal of media attention so that an organization little known previously to the general public suddenly became famous, stimulating popular TV and radio series like *The Man from Interpol* (a.k.a. *Interpol Calling*) and *Dossiers de l'Interpol*. Even so, Interpol has featured in fiction much less than have national or regional police forces, perhaps because of the complexity of its structure and operations and the consequent difficulty in writing about it convincingly.

Since the 1950s, Interpol has been particularly active in countering drug trafficking, terrorism, and financial crimes such as money laundering. Interpol remains the most important organization of multilateral police cooperation in the world, but it works closely with other international bodies, especially United Nations agencies.

• Malcolm Anderson, *Policing the World: Interpol and the Politics of International Police Co-operation* (1989).
—Peter Lewis

INVERTED DETECTIVE STORY. The weight of convention and practice shows that crime and mystery writers have found that dramatic effect lies most predictably in narrative *plots building toward conclusive revelation. The crime is detailed, *clues are sorted, *suspects interrogated, and, in a demonstration of the efficacy of investigative method, the story reaches its finish when the *detective ties the facts together to expose the criminal. Despite its continued repetition, the design of fiction that deliberately withholds full portrayal of the criminal action until a *sleuth is prepared to recount it secondhand seems never to lose its appeal. Yet, as though to prove there are other ways to achieve *suspense, a small body of authors has reversed the established way of constructing the criminal story to achieve different effects.

Critical opinion attributes the invention of the inverted detective story to R. Austin *Freeman. In stories featuring Dr. John *Thorndyke originally written for *Pearson's Magazine* and collected under the title *The Singing Bone* (1912; *The Adventures of Dr. Thorndyke*), the reader is informed fully about the crime at the beginning through scenes identifying the killer and showing him at work. The body of each narrative is then devoted to Thorndyke's process of discovery. Freeman's evident interest in detective fiction lay in the opportunity it affords for delineation of scientific techniques of detection. His debut detective novel, *The Red Thumb Mark* (1907), for example, presents exhaustive detail of Thorndyke's investigation of a case of forged fingerprints. His innovative creation of the inverted detective story thus became Freeman's means for replacing the human-interest *plot of a detective hunting a criminal with an abstract intellectual drama of problem-solving.

In the same year that Freeman published *The Singing Bone*, Marie *Belloc Lowndes independently produced another type of the inverted detective story. *The Chink in the Armour* (1912; *The House of Peril*) practically dismisses detection, allowing the reader to receive the information about the crime filtered through the consciousness of the *victim of *murder. Howard Haycraft, in *Murder for Pleasure* (1941), labeled Belloc Lowndes's narrative an inside-out crime story, a type that creates its effect through displacement of narrative point of view from the detective to a participant in the crime—the killer, as in the story of Jack the Ripper, or the victim.

Anthony *Berkeley, writing as Francis Iles, replicated the experiment in a series of novels beginning with *Malice Aforethought* (1931), which follows a husband's planning for the murder of his wife. Haycraft contrasts Iles's experiment with inverted narrative to Belloc Lowndes's by pointing out that while the latter deals with crime as abnormality, Iles achieves the effect of terror in such books as his masterpiece, *Before the Fact* (1932), by setting the tale of murder in cozy circumstances. Both authors, though, reconstruct the conventional order of detective story narration in order to explore character.

Acknowledging the influence of Francis Iles, Richard Henry Sampson, writing as Richard Hull, undertook a continuation of the inverted story with *The Murder of My Aunt* (1934), a first-person narration by a nephew trying three times to complete the perfect crime. *Murder Isn't Easy* (1936) elaborates upon the use of a killer's point of view to allow several participants to narrate the death of their victim.

Because the inverted form of crime story may use the criminal as protagonist, some authors have found it as useful for recreating historical crimes. Writing under the pseudonym Joseph Shearing, Gabrielle Margaret Vere Campbell enacts a feat of imagination in *For Her to See* (1947; *So Evil My Love*) to portray the people involved in an unsolved poisoning case from 1876. In *A Pin to See the Peepshow* (1934), F. Tennyson Jesse traces the life, crime, trial, and execution of a character based on the leading figure in a murder case of 1922. These works appeal to readers' interest in *motive as well as to their presumed fascination with celebrated criminal cases. Pursuing either interest allows for a look at the way an individual's story intersects with social reality. That intersection impels interest in Raymond Postgate's *Verdict of Twelve* (1940), an inverted type of story that abandons actual history but, through an account of a fictional criminal trial, turns attention to the interplay of social environment and character.

The inverted detective story has become a familiar construction to viewers of the *Columbo* television series, but nevertheless it serves the crime and mystery genre primarily as an experimental form. It offers no substantive competition to the long-preferred structure of detective structure that saves its criminal revelations for the end, but it remains a demonstrably effective means for writers seeking innovation.

[See also Point of View, Narrative; Resolution and Irresolution.]
                                                    —John. M. Reilly

IRISH, WILLIAM. *See* Woolrich, Cornell.

ISLAND MILIEU. Islands represent isolation, but also power exercised without social inhibition. The island may be W. H. Auden's Great Good Place, an untouched Eden, but it may also be a self-contained Hell, ruled over by a malign manipulator. In crime and detective fiction, it is often a combination of both. An archetypal story is Richard Connell's "The Most Dangerous Game" (in *Collier's*, Jan. 19, 1924), in which the hero is washed overboard and on to Ship-Trap Island, presided over by General Zaroff, a sportsman who is hunting the ultimate quarry—man.

The classic and most familiar use of the island in crime fiction is Agatha *Christie's, in *Ten Little Niggers* (1939; *And Then There Were None; Ten Little Indians*). Ten people who have committed crimes which society cannot punish are brought to the island and killed one by one, according to the prescription of the *nursery rhyme(s) of the title(s). Christie's novel also

well illustrates the allure of the island for the writer of mystery fiction: It gives her a tiny *milieu for the crime, limits the number of *suspects, and suspends over the whole an air of claustrophobic paranoia. Similar fears are evoked by placing a small group of people in peril from a threatening criminal or criminals: John D. *MacDonald effects this well on an island in *The Executioners* (1958; *Cape Fear*), and Andrew Garve achieves similar results in a lighthouse in *The Sea Monks* (1963).

There are a number of writers, MacDonald included, whose locales, for the sake of novelty, range over much of the world. Inevitably, their detectives fetch up sooner or later on islands, and MacDonald's Travis *McGee is on Granada, for instance, in *A Tan and Sandy Silence* (1971). Where actual geographical islands are used, they are usually represented as places of *corruption, or ingrown chauvinism. They may be paradisiac, though they pall beside the city's seductions: Inspector Charlie Salter in Eric Wright's *A Body Surrounded by Water* (1987) finds Prince Edward Island very much a bucolic backwater after his own city of Toronto. On the other hand, just north of Toronto, Ted Wood's Reid Bennett, the one-man police force of Murphy's Harbour, the center of a network of islands, finds just as much crime and corruption there as the city has to offer.

A detective on an island is often a detective on holiday, and several novels take their detectives to exotic good places where crime, predictably, invades. Hercule *Poirot is on Smuggler's Island, off the coast of Devon, in *Evil Under the Sun* (1941), a reworking of an earlier Poirot story, "A Triangle at Rhodes" (in *Dead Man's Mirror*, 1936). Christianna *Brand's Inspector Cockrill is caught up in *murder while vacationing in the fictional Mediterranean isle of San Juan el Pirata in *Tour de Force* (1955). Ruth *Rendell's Chief Inspector *Wexford is holidaying in "Achilles Heel" off the Dalmatian coast when a murder claims his attention.

Real islands, as well as providing exotic color, may carry certain mythologies with them. Charlotte Jay sets several of her mysteries on one of the world's largest islands, New Guinea, where the mixture of voodoo and savagery, especially in *Beat Not the Bones* (1952) enlivens an otherwise conventional *suspense novel. Two other actual island locales which have been widely used are the Hawaiian Islands and the Western Isles of Scotland. The former provides a multiracial civilization, most notably in the six Charlie *Chan novels written by Earl Derr *Biggers between 1925 and 1932. The Scottish islands import another element, in their immemorial age and their accretion of legend. Inspector Alan Grant, in Josephine *Tey's last novel, *The Singing Sands* (1952) is there partly to recuperate, partly in pursuit of a criminal. Mary Stewart expertly explores the magical superstitions of the Isle of Skye in *Wildfire at Midnight* (1956), and Antonia *Fraser works the same vein, with some Stuart pretending thrown in, in her second novel, *The Wild Island* (1978).

In an age of nationalism reduced to absurdity, the island may itself be a nation, ruled, according to the *formula, by a despot. Ellery *Queen, who very nearly exhausted the possibilities of the closed circle, did not forgo the island republic, and in *The King is Dead* (1952) Ellery and his father go to Bendigo Island, "somewhere in the Atlantic," to guard the totalitarian King Bendigo against threats to his life. Still more in the realm of moral allegory (and comedy) is Brand's *The Three-Cornered Halo* (1957), in which San Juan el Pirata, with Cockrill replaced by his sister, is caught up, from its grand duke on down, in the campaign to canonize a long-dead member of the ruling family.

Perhaps the work that most successfully brings together all the elements of islandness is P. D. *James's *The Skull Beneath the Skin* (1982). A play is being performed on a privately owned island (whose history is as symbolically freighted as is the Maltese Falcon's), and the obnoxious leading lady is murdered. There are suspects aplenty in this closed world, but the final issue is one of autocratic control of this world and the preservation of the Great Good Place, which is here seen in its most complex ambiguity. Can it be the Great Good Place if it is not accessible to all? This may be, at last, the central question posed by the detective genre.

[*See also* Closed-World Settings and Open-World Settings.]
—Barrie Hayne

JAMES, P(HYLLIS) D(OROTHY) (b. 1920), British writer, considered one of the finest authors of crime fiction and the first author in the genre in modern times to have triumphantly passed over the barriers into mainstream fiction. P. D. James, the Baroness James of Holland Park, has been compared to Jane Austen who, it is said, would be as interested today in murder and death as she was in her time in pride and prejudice. James cites Austen, as well as Evelyn Waugh, Graham *Greene, and Anthony Trollope, as deep influences on her work.

Born in Oxford and educated at Cambridge Girls' High School, James worked as a Red Cross nurse during World War II. She married Connor Bantry White in 1941; he returned from the war mentally ill and she helped nurse him until his death in 1964. From 1949 to 1968 she administrated several psychiatric units for the National Health Service, from which she took background for portions of her novels. Most of her books deal with the failure of one of the institutions by which society hopes to hold back death: concern for unwed mothers in *Cover Her Face* (1962); a psychiatric outpatient clinic in *A Mind to Murder* (1963); a nurses' training school in *Shroud for a Nightingale* (1971); a home for the disabled and dying in *The Black Tower* (1975); a forensic laboratory in *Death of an Expert Witness* (1977); the Anglican Church in *A Taste for Death* (1986); a nuclear power station in *Devices and Desires* (1989); the world of publishing in *Original Sin* (1994); and the courts and barristers' chambers in *A Certain Justice* (1997). Each book reveals a bit more about James's series figure Adam *Dalgliesh, who rises at *Scotland Yard from inspector to commander. Each demonstrates a growing command over *plot and character: James insists that plot must never twist character out of authenticity. After 1968 James worked as an administrator for the Home Office, in the police department, and in the criminal policy department. From 1979 to 1984 she also was a magistrate, and in recent years she has been much involved with service for the Church of England, especially on the Liturgical Commission—all capacities in which she has occasion to think deeply about death, *guilt, and punishment. Indeed, her elevation to the House of Lords in 1991 was as much for her public service, which has included acting as a governor of the BBC. She is a member of the Society of Authors, Fellow of the Royal Society of Literature, and Fellow of the Royal Society of Authors.

James has had the courage to grow, not allowing her increasing and very substantial sales to prevent experimentation. She does not consider the genre limiting, as some commentators do, but liberating. Perhaps twice she has written conscious parodies of the genre, though not all critics recognized them as such; arguably in *Unnatural Causes* (1967), and clearly in *The Skull Beneath the Skin* (1982). In the latter, she dared to use the oldest chestnut there is—a small group of individuals trapped for a weekend on an island off the Dorset coast, surely an obeisance to Agatha Christie's *Ten Little Indians* (1939)—and drew affectionately upon many other plot devices while nonetheless writing a novel enjoyable at more than one level. *Innocent Blood* (1980) moved away from formal mystery to moral fiction, demonstrating how the *truth could work to evil purposes. Each subsequent book was a major financial success, and those featuring Dalgliesh spawned an admirable television series with Roy Marsden in the role of the pensive detective. In *The Children of Men* (1992), a morality tale set in 2021, James shows a derelict English society incapable of procreation or community though not, in the end, of love.

James created a second series figure, Cordelia *Gray, in *An Unsuitable Job for a Woman* (1972). Only twenty-two, Gray takes over a ramshackle detective agency from her partner after he commits *suicide. James uses Gray as Dorothy L. *Sayers used Harriet *Vane, particularly in *Gaudy Night* (1935), to explore aspects of feminism, though the novel remains a well-crafted mystery, and, to some critics, James's finest book. James's own favorites are *The Black Tower*, *A Taste for Death*, and *Original Sin*. Gray returns in *The Skull Beneath the Skin*.

James's work is notable for the strength of its plots, for the precision of its *settings, and for the way in which the narrative grows out of revealed character. She is an elegant stylist, a stern moralist, and a person of alert and orderly mind: Her descriptions show a concern for architectural exactitude, for the rich particularity of place, and for a most subtle laying down of clues.

• Norma Siebenheller, *P. D. James* (1981). Richard B. Gidez, *P. D. James* (1986). Rosemary Herbert, "P. D. James," in *The Fatal Art of Entertainment: Interviews with Mystery Writers* (1994). Dennis Porter, "P. D. James," in *Mystery and Suspense Writers: The Literature of Crime, Detection, and Espionage* (1998).
—Robin W. Winks

JAPAN, CRIME AND MYSTERY WRITING IN. Although isolated examples of crimes and outlaws occur in early and medical Japanese literature, it was with seventeenth-century trial narratives such as Ihara Saikaku's *Honchō ōin hiji* (1689; Tales of Japanese Justice, 1980) that Japanese crime writings first showed signs of coalescing as a genre in their own right. Following the Chinese stories that inspired his collection, Saikaku places at the center of the action not a criminal or detective per se, but rather a wise *judge, the aptness of whose decisions invariably silences all protest. The similar stories in the anonymous *Ōoka seidan* (Tales of Ōoka's Rulings) are partly inspired by verdicts of the renowned Ōoka Tadasuke, a city commissioner under the Edo government from 1717 to 1736. The collection, versions of which first circulated in the late eighteenth century, also includes stories from the same Chinese tradition Saikaku knew, stories based upon rulings by commissioners other than Ōoka, and pure fabrications.

In the nineteenth century, dramatists such as Kawatake Mokuami enjoyed popular success with plays about thieves and outlaws. The rise of newspapers in the 1870s and 1880s prompted a boom in serialized and freely embroidered biographies of criminals—particularly those of women who put their charms to nefarious purpose. Most notorious among these *dokufu*, or "poison women," was Takahashi Oden, a murderer and *con artist beheaded for her crimes in 1879. Following Oden's execution, her life was retold in newspapers, cheap pamphlets, ballads, and plays. *Takahashi Oden yasha monogatari* (1879; The Story of Takahashi Oden the She-Devil), a multipart pamphlet by Kanagaki Robun, is the best-known version; although populated by characters who are conventional types, it contains occasional descriptions whose realism anticipates twentieth-century crime writing.

It was, however, only with the influx of Western literature in the 1880s and 1890s that the classic detective story began to take hold in Japan. In 1887 Edgar Allan *Poe's "Murders in the Rue Morgue" appeared in a condensed Japanese translation. Anna Katharine *Green's *XYZ* was published in translation that same year, and Arthur Conan *Doyle's *Adventures of Sherlock Holmes* had been translated by 1899. Kuroiwa Ruikō's tabloid newspaper *Yorozu chōhō* (Morning Variety), which was the most widely circulating daily in Tokyo by 1902, greatly increased the Japanese audience for detective stories. In it Ruikō ran, in serial format, translations and adaptations of over sixty works by nineteenth-century Western authors such as Green, Wilkie *Collins, and Émile *Gaboriau, as well as others less well remembered, such as Fortune du Boisgobey. Ruikō's own short detective story "Muzan" (1899; In Cold Blood) is the earliest example, and a deft one, of a story written in Japanese using the structure of the classic *whodunit.

Between 1917 and 1936, the Kabuki playwright Okamoto Kidō wrote sixty-eight period detective stories about the exploits of Hanshichi, an expert *okappiki* (thief catcher) informally connected with the Edo police force. The stories, most of which are told as reminiscences of the retired Hanshichi, tend to the formulaic, and as a rule the reader is not privy to all the information needed to solve the cases. But Kidō's nostalgic evocation of the bygone world of Edo—in which the clues always added up and justice was always served—was enthusiastically welcomed by a readership eager for relief from the complexities of life in a modernizing Japan. With his stories, which have been collected in several editions under the title *Hanshichi torimono-chō* (Hanshichi's Arrest Records), Kidō inaugurated the Japanese subcategory of crime writing known as *torimono-chō*, or stories of detection set in the Edo period (1600–1868), often in the city of Edo itself (now Tokyo). Later examples of this enormously popular genre include Nomura Kodō's series *Zenigata Heiji torimono hikae* (1931–57; Memoirs of Zenigata Heiji's Arrests), Yokomizo Seishi's *Ningyō Sashichi torimono-chō* (1938–68; Ningyō Sashichi's Arrest Records), and Ikenami Shōtarō's *Onihei hanka-chō* (1967–90; Case Records of Onihei). Yet another variation on the period crime story is Ikenami's series about Fujieda Baian, a *master criminal of Edo who is equally adept at acupuncture and assassination. Of this series, *Koroshi no vonin* (1972) has been translated as *Master Assassin: Tales of Murder from the Shogian's City* (1991), and *Baian ari jigoku* (1980) has been translated as *The Bridge of Darkness: The Return of the Master Assassin* (1993).

By the early 1920s, writers of literary repute, such as Tanizaki Jun'ichirō, Satō Haruo, and Akutagawa Ryūnosuke had begun experimenting with crime and detective stories. Tanizaki's 1920 *Tojō* (Along the Way) is a tongue-in-cheek story about a man's scheme to kill his wife. Satō Haruo's "Shimon" (1918; "The Fingerprint," 1996) vividly mixes opium dreams and *murder, and Akutagawa's "*Yabu no naka*" (1922; "In a Grove," 1952) presents the reader with irreconcilably conflicting first-person testimony concerning a rape and a stabbing death.

But it was only with the arrival of Edogawa Rampo (sometimes transliterated as Ranpo), whose pen name is homonymous with the Japanese pronunciation of "Edgar Allan Poe," that Japan could claim its first full-time professional crime writer. Rampo's large oeuvre is uneven and recycles a relatively limited number of favorite themes (voyeurism, false or multiple identity, dismemberment, sadomasochism, doll-like people, and human-seeming dolls). But at his best Rampo was startlingly original, and he is widely considered the father of Japanese detective fiction. His debut piece, the 1923 story "Nisen dōka" (The Two-Sen Copper Coin), cleverly incorporates cryptographical tricks along the way to its surprise ending. Subsequent works such as the 1925 "Ningen isu" ("The Human Chair," 1956), *Yaneura no sanposha* (1925; The Attic Walker), and his masterpiece *Injū* (1928; Dark Beasts) established him as a mainstay of the magazine *Shinseinen* (New Youth), which continued from the 1920s until World War II as the most important forum in Japan both for native and translated crime stories. Translations into English of ten stories by Rampo, some in slightly abbreviated form, are included in *Japanese Tales of Mystery and Imagination* (1956).

By the mid-1920s, crime writing in Japan had divided into two schools; the so-called orthodox (*honkaku-ha*) and the unorthodox, or innovative (*henkaku-ha*). Writers of the orthodox school, which prided itself on fastidiously fair presentation of *puzzles to the reader, included the early Rampo, Kōga Saburō, Hirabayashi Hatsunosuke, and, in some of his works, Yokomizo Seishi. The unorthodox school abandoned pure detection to focus on the fantastic, the macabre, the psychotic, and the erotic, often for their own sake. This school comprised such writers as the later Rampo, Ōshita Udaru, Yumeno Kayūsaku, and Unno Jūza. Rampo's *Mōjū* (1931; Blind Beast), for example, is about a blind sculptor turned serial killer. He locks one of his victims in a pitch-dark room, the more easily to take sexual advantage of her. She gradually loses her sight and comes to enjoy his assaults. Their quest for ever greater stimulation leads to sadomasochistic play with knives, and ultimately the sculptor dismembers the woman.

During World War II, crime and detective stories were banned in Japan, and many writers of both schools turned to spy and *science fiction stories. The Japanese appetite for detective stories was, if anything, increased by this wartime hiatus, and the sheer abundance and variety of mystery writing in postwar Japan has matched that seen in any other country. Immediately following the war, Yokomizo Seishi's now classic *Honjin satsujin jiken* (1946; The Old Inn Murder), which introduced his *private eye Kindaichi Kōsuke, rekindled interest in the orthodox style. The novel effectively combines the British Golden Age device of the locked room—the author acknowledges the inspiration of John Dickson *Carr in the first chapter—with the Japanese color of its traditional village setting. The writings of Yokomizo Seishi, along with contributions by Takagi Akimitsu, Ayukawa Tetsuya, Sasazawa Saho, and others, made the magazine *Hōseki* (Gem) the undisputed postwar successor to *Shinseinen*. Takagi Akimitsu's *Mikkokusha* (1965) has been translated as *The Informer* (1971). Sasazawa Saho's short story "Umi kara no shōtaijō" appears as "Invitation from the Sea" in *Ellery Queen's Japanese Golden Dozen* (1978). The story, which is reminiscent of the work of Agatha *Christie, throws together a group of strangers who have accepted mysterious invitations to visit a Japanese seaside resort. Once there, they discover that all of them are connected to a long-past apparent suicide.

If such writers tended to confirm their membership in the orthodox school by taking inspiration from Western predecessors, beginning in the late 1950s the mysteries of *Matsumoto Seichō made a new departure by using crime fiction as a medium for social criticism. Seichō's mysteries, which inspired what came to be known as the social school (*shakai-ha*) of writers, typically concern average citizens who became caught up in crimes engineered by members of a corrupt elite, few of whom are ever brought to justice. Kuroiwa Jūgo, Minakami Tsutomu, Kajiyama Toshiyuki, and a host of others have since followed Seichō's practice of setting crime stories against realistic, contemporary backgrounds in order to give them a critical barb.

In the 1980s and 1990s, perhaps predictably, there has been a reaction against the social school and a renewal of interest in the demanding craft of pure and original puzzle-making Ayalsuji Yukito, in particular, has been accused of setting the clock backward by his insistence that extraneous social commentary not be allowed to overpower the essential ingredients of crime fiction: master detectives, seemingly locked rooms, parades of *suspects, and stunningly ingenious solutions. His *Jukkaku-kan no satsujin* (1987; The Ten-Sided-Building Murder) was a manifesto for the movement to revitalize the classic mystery novel in Japan. Ayatsuji followed it with five other novels, all of which are set in buildings with some architectural peculiarity. Writers who have joined Ayatsuji in the so-called third wave of orthodox writing include Norizuki Rintarō, Kitamura Kaoru, Kyōgoku Natsuhiko, and Kasai Kisai Kiyoshi.

Another important postwar trend in Japanese crime fiction has been the use of *humor and parody. Akagawa Jirō has demonstrated his light touch in over seventy popular *detective novels, most famously in his series devoted to the bumbling inspector Ōnuki (published between 1982 and 1993), who gets his man in spite of his less than flawless chains of reasoning. In Hoshi Shin'ichi's short sendup "Ashiato no nazo" (translated as "The Mysterious Footprints," *The Spiteful Planet and Other Stories*, 1978), a Japanese gumshoe is called to a snowbound burglary scene. When he finds that the trail of footprints left in the snow by the escaping culprit comes to a sudden end, much comical theory-spinning ensues. Higashino Keigo's collection *Meitanteinookite* (1996; The Rules of Master Detection) likewise is a reminder that not all crime writing need take itself seriously.

Notable female Japanese crime writers of the postwar period include Natsuki Shizuko, Togawa Masako, Takamura Kaoru, and Miyabe Miyuki. Natsuki Shizuko, who is most closely associated with the social school of writers, is admired for her psychologically convincing portrayals of the maternal instinct, upon which her plots often hinge. Among her works available in translation are the 1982 *W no higeki* (*Murder at Mount Fuji* 1984) and the 1978 *Daisan no onna* (*The Third Lady*, 1990). Togawa Masako (who has had a career as a professional singer) is also known for her memorable female characters. Her translated works include *Ōi naru gen'ei* (1962; The Master Key) and *Ryōjin nikki* (1963; The Lady Killer). (Miyabe Miyuki is associated with the "third wave" of orthodox crime writing; her novel *Kasha* (1992) has been translated as *All She Was Worth* (1996).

Japanese crime and mystery writing can now look back upon a rich native tradition; its longstanding cosmopolitanism also remains undiminished. The variety of crime fiction in stock in virtually every bookstore in the country, in the continuing enthusiasm of its readers, and the array of prizes that have been established to encourage new talent all suggest the genre will not go stale anytime soon.

[*See also* Locked Room Mystery; China, Crime and Mystery Writing in Greater.]

—Mark Silver *and* Rosemary Herbert

Johnson, Coffin Ed, and **Grave Digger Jones,** two Harlem police detectives created by Chester

*Himes. Carrying identical .38-caliber revolvers, clad in dark suits, and driving a battered Plymouth sedan, Coffin Ed Johnson and Grave Digger Jones inspire fear, respect, and awe as do the "bad men" of African American folklore. Like Chandler's "lonely knight," they are the best men in their world.

Grotesquely scarred by acid flung by a *con man in *For Love of Imabelle* (1957; *A Rage in Harlem*), Johnson is subject to lethal rages. Although more contemplative, Jones also finds it difficult to maintain his balance amid death, betrayal, and the ever present *racism that distorts black lives.

In *Blind Man with a Pistol* (1969), the two detectives lose their struggle against chaos and *corruption. But before Himes makes this last bitter statement, readers journey in eight previous novels with his heroes through a world both terrible and comic, sharing jazz, soul food, and their comradeship.

[*See also* African American Sleuth; Police Detective; Police Procedural, The American Police Procedural; Prejudice; Sidekicks and Sleuthing Teams.]

• Robert E. Skinner, *Two Guns From Harlem: The Detective Fiction of Chester Himes* (1989). —Frankie Y. Bailey

JOKESTERS. *See* Farceurs.

JOURNALIST SLEUTHS. Journalists rank high among those who legitimately go about asking questions and, so, are plausibly involved in criminal investigation. The modern investigative journalist deliberately seeks out crime, as the source of the next story. The press are usually early on a *murder scene and sometimes get there first. Fictional crime reporters have friends at court or, at least, a sparring partner within the official ranks.

An early journalist sleuth is Joseph Rouletabille, a reporter for the Parisian newspaper *L'Epoque*. He is featured in novels by Gaston Leroux, preeminently *The Mystery of the Yellow Room* (1908; *Murder in the Bedroom*), which he brings to a successful and startling conclusion while still in his teens. Philip Trent works as "special investigator" for the *Record*, most notably in *Trent's Last Case* (1913; *The Woman in Black*). On occasion his dispatch, which travels by train, forms part of the narrative, and in "The Old-Fashioned Apache" (1938; *Trent Intervenes*) it serves as exposition. Roger Sheringham is a popular novelist, employed as "unofficial special correspondent" by the *Daily Courier*, to which he contributes "chattily written articles on murder." His journalism is essentially a sideline and hardly affects his hit-or-miss detective activities. Nigel Bathgate alternates as Boswell and Watson for Superintendent Roderick *Alleyn before the war. A gossip columnist for an unnamed "perverted rag," he is unaccountably absent from the high-society murder of *Death in a White Tie* (1938). In 1939, in *Overture to Death*, he represents the *Evening Mirror* as crime reporter.

Among the various detectives of George Harmon *Coxe are two newspaper photographers, both based in Boston: Flash (sometimes "Flashgun") Casey on the *Globe* and, later, the *Express*, and Kent *Murdock on the *Courier-Herald*. Casey is rougher and tougher than Murdock but both are highly paid and expert at their jobs. Both tend also to be at odds with the official investigators. Barney Gantt appears in novels by John Stephen Strange as a staff photographer on the *New York Globe*, where his shots of murders invariably make the first edition and his future wife writes the "problem page." He wins a Pulitzer Prize and produces special postwar features for *Blue Book*. Reynold Frame, who after eight years with the *New York Herald-Tribune* becomes a freelance writer and photographer, figures in four of Herbert Brean's novels, with a notably odd assignment in *Wilders Walk Away* (1948) and an immensely dangerous one in *The Clock Strikes Thirteen* (1952).

Quinn, contributor of a daily crime column to the *Morning Post*, appears in novels by Harry Carmichael, solo on occasion but more usually with John Piper, an insurance assessor. An abrasive *antihero, unkempt and insecure, Quinn employs direct, aggressive methods that perfectly complement those of his subtler collaborator. In four novels by Kenneth Hopkins, Gerry Lee acts as feature writer for the *Post*, running into murder whatever his assignment, the paper's crime reporter coming a poor second. In 1963 he lectures on English journalism in Texas and encounters a *Campus Corpse*. Kate Theobold, the journalist wife of a barrister, is featured in six novels by Lionel Black. She works for the *Daily Post*, initially on the cookery column, later as roving reporter, resourceful but headstrong. Her subjects of investigation include a health farm and, in "the silly season," a seaside hoaxer.

Lillian Jackson Braun's Jim Qwilleran is a veteran newsman with a distinguished past and two Siamese cats who participate in his investigations. After a stint in the Midwest as art editor of the *Daily Fluxion*, he comes into money and moves north to Pickax, where he writes a column for the local paper. Barbara Ninde Byfield's novels feature Helen Bullock, a photojournalist with an international reputation who made her name on the *Globe* and, like Barney Gantt, has a Pulitzer Prize among her credits. Known as "Holocaust Helen," she has a reputation for fearlessness and raw candor: Both her writing and photographs have an "unedited 'here-it is' quality." In Lucille Kallen's novels C. B. Greenfield edits and owns the *Sloan's Ford Reporter*, a small-town weekly out to "vanquish corruption, greed, injustice, disease and inferior English teachers in the school system." His cases are narrated by Maggie Rome, his quizzical chief reporter and long-suffering legman.

Rain Morgan is a gossip columnist, sufficiently eminent to have her picture appear in her *Morning Post* column and to be recognized in pubs. She figures in several novels by Lesley Grant-Adamson, of which one, *Wild Justice* (1987), draws heavily on the *Post* for its setting and personnel. The victim is the paper's proprietor.

Amanda Roberts and Samantha Adams are investigative journalists in Atlanta in novels by, respectively, Sherryl Woods and Alice Storey (who also write together as Sarah Shankman). The former joins *Inside Atlanta* as a feature writer after a murder investigation releases her from humdrum assignments; the latter, on the staff of the *Atlanta Constitution*, chooses her own stories and thereby runs repeatedly into danger. In novels by Barbara d'Amato, Cat Marsala works freelance in Chicago, seeking whomever she may righteously and profitably devour.

[*See also* Mean Streets Milieu; Urban Milieu.]

—B. A. Pike

JUDGE. While judges rarely, if ever, function as protagonists in crime novels, they must nevertheless preside over climactic scenes of courtroom trials in which the issues are settled and the culprit identified. In his or her courtroom, the judge controls the flow of permissible testimony and constrains opposing counsel from exceeding the bounds of legitimate advocacy.

An established *convention of the genre requires the judge to mediate between a zealous defense attorney and a relentless prosecutor avid for career advancement or political office. With both sides mobilizing their legal stratagems and cunning subtleties, frequent objections are inevitable. The judge must sustain or reject, and his rulings provide an author with the opportunity to engage the reader's emotions. Thus, if a reader identifies with the accused whose fate hangs in the balance, an unfavorable ruling will evoke in the reader a sense of misgiving, anxiety, or apprehension.

The stereotype that commonly appears in crime and mystery writing is the judge as generally a political animal, an irritable man who threatens contempt proceedings and is concerned about being reversed in a higher court. Judges lacking in moral compass are less stereotypical and may produce far more engrossing complications. And judges lacking in intelligence but rich with eccentricities can provide both tension and *humor as exemplified in stories by John *Mortimer.

In formulaic novels the judge's role is usually marginal. Fans of Erle Stanley *Gardner, anticipating a courtroom confrontation, are often rewarded with a last-minute confession extracted by Perry *Mason's adroit cross-examination. The judge in these cases exists largely to sustain or dismiss objections and to bang the gavel when Mason has satisfactorily wrapped up the case.

In more recent novels, authors have been mining a richer vein for the man with the gavel. In *Death Penalty* (1993), William J. Coughlin (himself a senior United States administrative law judge) introduces several jurists, two of whom—the chief justice of an appellate court and his former colleague on the bench—are egregiously corruptible. The second acts as bagman for the first, who offers to sell his critical vote upholding a lower court's multimillion dollar award in exchange for half the winning lawyer's fee. The parts played by these venal characters—and by a third judge, a man of unimpeachable rectitude and decency, who helps to bring them down—are integral to the main story line, which indeed could not exist without them.

A judge's flagrantly prejudicial conduct is on display in Barry Reed's *The Verdict* (1980). Because of

his relationship to a high-ranking prelate, the judge favors a church-affiliated hospital while presiding over a malpractice suit involving the death of a patient. His blatantly biased rulings and cavalier treatment of the plaintiff's lawyer infuriate the reader.

Scott Turow's *Presumed Innocent* (1987) is arguably a pivotal performance in this particular category. Here the judge is a presence of considerable import, both at pretrial conferences and in the courtroom, a take-charge figure, testy, assertive, and quick to censure any deviation from accepted protocol. These traits contribute color and urgency to a novel that demonstrates how solid *characterization and *atmosphere can enhance a genre that is viewed primarily as escape literature.

[*See also* Courtroom Milieu; Eccentrics; Legal Procedural.]

• Joseph C. Goulden, *The Benchwarmers: The Private World of the Powerful Federal Judges* (1974). Donald Dale Jackson, *Judges* (1974).

—Harold Q. Masur

JURY. Though most big-trial novels and courtroom mysteries include a jury, relatively few have focused on the jurors themselves, and those few rarely put the system in a favorable light. Fictional jurors ignore admonitions not to discuss the case or absorb media accounts, stubbornly apply their own *prejudices to considerations of the evidence, and even bring to the jury room extraneous evidence from their own independent investigations. In Dorothy L. *Sayers's *Strong Poison* (1930), Miss Climpson's account to Lord Peter *Wimsey of jury deliberations in the trial of Harriet *Vane shows the arbitrariness with which a juror's charge is sometimes carried out.

Eden Phillpotts's satirical *The Jury* (1927), the first novel to concentrate its action in the jury room, presents a typically jaundiced view. The jurors in George Goodchild and C. E. Bechhofer Roberts's similarly structured *The Jury Disagree* (1934) at least concentrate on the evidence. The best-known and most successful attempt to dramatize jury deliberations, Reginald Rose's 1955 television play *Twelve Angry Men*, includes the quirks and prejudices, but ultimately presents a somewhat more optimistic view of the process's validity. Showing how the one juror voting for acquittal of a Puerto Rican youth gradually brings the other eleven around, Rose's play was subsequently adapted for film and stage versions.

Two of the best British novels focusing on jurors and their deliberations, though not confining their action to the jury room, are Raymond W. Postgate's *Verdict of Twelve* (1940) and Gerald Bullett's *The Jury* (1935). More recent examples include Michael Underwood's *Hand of Fate* (1981), B. M. Gill's *The Twelfth Juror* (1984), and John Wainwright's *The Jury People* (1978). Michael *Gilbert's *The Queen Against Karl Mullen* (1991) provides a rare description of British jury selection, while Donald MacKenzie's *The Juryman* (1957) centers on efforts to fix a juror.

Many American trial novels, including such classics as Robert Traver's *Anatomy of a Murder* (1958) and Al Dewlen's *Twilight of Honor* (1961), devote considerable space to the jury selection process. William

Harrington's undervalued debut *Which the Justice, Which the Thief* (1963) may be the most extensive fictional treatment ever of how jurors are chosen. Steve Martini's *Compelling Evidence* (1992) has another of the best sequences on jury selection, while Vincent S. Green's *The Price of Victory* (1992) is unusual in offering details of military jury selection. Warwick Downing's *The Water Cure* (1992) has an unusual angle on the process, with the prosecution's and defense's usual priorities reversed by the nature of the case. Ellery *Queen's *The Glass Village* (1954) shows a small-town court intentionally selecting a bad jury to avoid lynch law and guarantee any conviction will be reversed on appeal. John Grisham's first novel, *A Time to Kill* (1989), provides details of a Mississippi lawyer's jury research prior to trial, the actual process of selecting a jury, and finally their deliberations, including one juror's inventive and brave measure to bring the deadlocked group to a verdict. Two American novels, Harvey Jacobs's somewhat absurdist *The Juror* (1980) and Parnell Hall's *Juror* (1990), emphasize the jury-duty experience more than specific cases.

[*See also* Courtroom Milieu; Justice; Legal Procedural.]

• Jon L. Breen, *Novel Verdicts: A Guide to Courtroom Fiction* (1984).
—Jon L. Breen

JUSTICE. The quest for justice is a central theme of mystery fiction which has preoccupied succeeding generations of writers and sparked much of the finest work in the genre. Those working within the tradition of the classic *whodunit often regard *detective novels as the modern equivalent of the medieval mystery play which describes the triumph of good over *evil. The counterargument is that justice is not only an abstract but also an ambiguous notion which is frequently at odds with strict application of the letter of the law. The latter may seem a modern view, yet it is implicit in stories written by one of the genre's founding fathers, Arthur Conan *Doyle. In "The Adventure of the Abbey Grange" (*Strand*, Sept. 1904), Sherlock *Holmes says that once or twice in his career he felt that he had done more real harm by his discovery of the criminal than had been done by the crime and that this had led him to prefer to play tricks with the law of England rather than with his own conscience. Thus in "The Adventure of the Blue Carbuncle" (*Strand* Jan. 1892) he is prepared to commute a felony in the hope of saving a soul, while in "The Adventure of Charles Augustus Milverton" (*Strand*, April 1904) he does nothing to expose the killer of the eponymous blackmailer. Later supermen of detection such as Philo *Vance in S. S. *Van Dine's *The Bishop Murder Case* (1929) and Hercule *Poirot in Agatha *Christie's *Curtain* (1975) are even willing to kill in order to achieve a "higher justice." In the postwar age, detectives like Inspector Morse in Colin *Dexter's *The Way Through The Woods* (1992) see the quest for justice as an "eternal problem." In *Corporate Bodies* (1991) by Simon Brett, Charles Paris concludes that abstract justice is fairly meaningless, while V. C. Clinton-Baddeley's Doctor Davie is dis-

armingly frank in *To Study a Long Silence* (1972) when he acknowledges to himself that he is spurred to detection not from a desire to see justice done but rather from a simple wish to exercise his mind.

A similar dichotomy appears in novels focusing directly upon the legal system. Erle Stanley *Gardner's Perry *Mason articulates the conventional outlook in *The Case of the Drowning Duck* (1942) with romantic passion when he declares his commitment to the blind woman for whom he works: "They call her Justice." Contemporary writers of the *legal procedural are apt to be more cynical. At the start of Scott Turow's *Presumed Innocent* (1987), Rusty Sabich demands of the jury: "What is the hope of justice if the truth cannot be found?" Yet at the end of the book he has to ask himself what is harder, knowing the truth or finding it, telling it or being believed?—and the murder of Carolyn Polhemus remains officially unsolved. Turow's success has prompted a host of other trial lawyers to draw upon their own knowledge of the justice system in constructing novels dealing with important social issues. A notable example is Richard North Patterson's *Degree of Guilt* (1993), in which a woman charged with murder claims self-defense on the grounds that her *victim had attempted to rape her. British lawyer-authors such as Michael *Gilbert and Frances Fyfield have been equally prepared to address the gulf between law and justice in their fictions, although their work fits less easily into the pigeonhole of the courtroom *thriller. Although writers in Britain have generally portrayed the forces of law and order with less angry contempt than Americans of the hard-boiled school—Raymond *Chandler, for instance, toyed with giving the title of *The Law Is Where You Buy It* to the book which eventually became *Farewell, My Lovely* (1940)—they have nevertheless long been prepared to cast an ironic eye over the mysterious way in which justice works. C. S. Forester's *Payment Deferred* (1926) broke fresh ground with the eventual punishment of the guilty William Marble not for the murder of his wife but for another death of which he was innocent. Francis *Iles's *Malice Aforethought* (1931) was similarly conceived and, as Anthony Berkeley, the same writer explored questions about justice in mysteries such as *Roger Sheringham and the Vane Mystery* (1927; *The Mystery at Lovers' Cave*) in which the culprit escapes scot-free. A similar theme lies at the heart of Josephine *Tey's *Miss Pym Disposes* (1946): A woman who has written a best-seller about psychology runs into trouble when she seeks to apply her expertise in the real world, and when she tries to act as a superwoman above the law in the manner of a Holmes or a Poirot, the results are disastrous. Even more powerful is *Reputation for a Song* (1952), in which Edward Grierson depicts the thwarting of justice by a murderer who succeeds in blackening the name of his victim. A kind of rough justice is achieved in Richard Hull's *The Murder of My Aunt* (1934) where the victim outmaneuvers her would-be killer.

Patricia *Highsmith famously expressed a minority opinion in finding the public passion for justice "quite boring and artificial, for neither life nor nature cares if justice is ever done or not," and novels such as *The Talented Mr. Ripley* (1955) reflect that view of the world. The narrator of Michael Dibdin's *Dirty Tricks* (1991) is wittily contemptuous: "There is no such thing as justice, only winners and losers." But many mystery writers would agree with the murderer in Margot Bennett's *The Widow of Bath* (1952), who says, "I believe in justice, not in the law." Moreover, justice can, as Greg Hocking argues in Robert *Barnard's *Posthumous Papers* (1979; *Death of a Literary Widow*), take many forms. Greg opts for a kind of justice which involves not the murderer's arrest and conviction but rather his fear of a long-deferred but inevitable humiliation, which he had sought to avoid by committing the crime. Such an outcome may not accord with legal orthodoxy, but is in a wider and more meaningful sense wholly just.

[*See also* Courtroom Milieu.]

• Raymond Chandler, "The Simple Art of Murder," *Atlantic monthly* (Dec. 1944). Tony Hilfer, *The Crime Novel* (1990). Julian Symons, *Bloody Murder: From the Detective Story to the Crime Novel: A History*, 3rd ed. (1992).

—Martin Edwards

JUVENILE MYSTERY. *This entry is divided into two parts, the first surveying mysteries targeting boy readers and the second surveying mysteries written for girls.*

Boys' Juvenile Mysteries
Girls' Juvenile Mysteries

For further information, please refer to Juvenile Sleuth.

BOYS' JUVENILE MYSTERIES

Popular boys' fiction of the past century and a half stressed action, adventure and, very commonly, mystery. In the early hardcover books for juveniles, however, the mystery was only one of many problems that confronted the youthful hero.

Such popular English writers for boys of the late nineteenth century as G. A. Henty, Harry Collingwood, William Henry Giles Kingston, and R. M. Ballantyne stressed action and adventure, with some use of mystery to heighten *plot interest. However, the juvenile heroes only solved incidental problems and were not presented as sleuths as such. This is also true in the writings of such popular American writers of the late 1800s as Horatio Alger Jr., Harry Castlemon, Oliver Optic, and Edward Ellis. Mystery may well be present as a part of the plot but is subordinate to the action and adventure. The most common mystery faced by many a young hero (as exemplified, for example, in various novels by Alger) is the *puzzle of his past. The search for lost fortunes and for noble or at least respectable parentage were common themes.

In the twentieth century, writers began to place more emphasis on the mystery itself. Significantly, the word "mystery" became common in the titles of boys' books, both in England and the United States. In England, Percy Westerman wrote *A Mystery of the Broads* (1930), *The Mystery of the Key* (1948), and *The Mystery of Nix Hull* (1930). Random examples in the United States include *Dave Fearless and the Cave of*

Mystery (1918), by Roy Rockwood; *The Putnam Hall Mystery* (1911), by Arthur M. Winfield; *Bob Dexter and the Radio Mystery* (1933), by Willard F. Baker (1933), *The Mystery of the Brass Bound Box* (1937), by Howard R. Garis; *The Mystery of the Galloping Horse* (1954), by Bruce Campbell; *The Blue Ghost Mystery* (1960), by John Blaine; and *The Happy Hollisters and the Whistle-Pig Mystery* (1964), by Jerry West. It might be mentioned that these are all titles in various boys' series and the listed authors, except for Garis, are all pen names. The mystery theme was so popular with the boys that several multivolume series were built around it. Among these were the Mystery Hunters series, by Capwell Wyckoff; the Mystery Boys, comprising one series by Howard Garis and another by Van Powell; and Mystery Stories for Boys, a series by Roy J. Snell.

The boys' detective story, in which boy characters consciously act as *amateur detectives, also evolved during the twentieth century and was closely related to the boys' mystery story. In 1922 A. Hyatt Verrill wrote a four-volume Radio Detective series whose contents were described as adventure and mystery stories. *Detectives, Inc.* (1935), by William Heyliger, was advertised as "A Mystery Story for Boys." In England, Captain W. E. Johns's Biggles continued his adventures by becoming a successful air detective.

Several later popular series that emphasize juvenile detectives and detecting are the Ellery Queen Jr. Mystery Stories (published between 1941 and 1954); the Brains Benton Mysteries (1959–61), by Verral and Wyatt; the Encyclopedia Brown detective stories (1963–83), by Donald J. Sobol; and the Alfred Hitchcock Mystery Series written by various authors between 1964 and 1979.

By far the most popular boys' detective series is that featuring the Hardy Boys, which originated in 1927 and has continued since. Both the Hardy Boys and Nancy *Drew Mystery Stories series were produced (though not written) by Edward Stratemeyer and the Stratemeyer Syndicate. Stratemeyer was unquestionably the most important figure in the juvenile mystery field in his day. He had written about twenty-six of the Nick *Carter detective stories in the 1890s as well as numerous boys' *adventure stories. The detective story *dime novels, while tremendously popular and undoubtedly read by boys, were actually written for an adult audience. When Stratemeyer formed his syndicate, in about 1904, he hired competent writers to do the actual writing of his boys' series following his own outlines and plots.

In the twentieth century, boys' juvenile mysteries evolved as part of the subgenre of popular series books. Few of the boys' mystery series, except for the Hardy Boys and the few similar juvenile detective series, bear much resemblance to adult detective fiction. At the end of the century, action and adventure remained the major focuses of boys' series books.

[*See also* Heroism; Pursuit.]

• Ralph D. Gardner, *Horatio Alger, or The American Hero Era.* (1964). Roger Garis, *My Father Was Uncle Wiggily* (1966). Leslie McFarlane, *Ghost of the Hardy Boys* (1976). John T. Dizer, *Tom Swift & Company: "Boys' books" by Stratemeyer and Others* (1982). Deidre Johnson, *Edward Stratemeyer and the Stratemeyer Syndicate* (1993).

—John T. Dizer

GIRLS' JUVENILE MYSTERIES

Like their adult counterparts, girls' juvenile mysteries take various forms: They encompass virtually every subgenre except the police procedural. There are juvenile *detective novels, espionage tales, *cozy mysteries, *thrillers, historical crimes, *locked room mysteries, parodies, psychological explorations, and *whodunits tailored to a specific readership. Stories for very young children feature such "mysteries" as missing pets, and those for older teens use mystery to explore questions rich with moral ambiguity.

Girls' mysteries evolved into a distinct genre during the 1920s. Previously, mysteries in girls' fiction were primarily subplots that provided necessary conflict: missing examination papers in a school story or a heroine's unknown parentage in a "Cinderella" novel. But as adult mysteries gained popularity in the 1920s, children's novels followed suit. In *You're a Brick, Angela:* (1976), Mary Cadogan and Patricia Craig note that girl detective Sylvia Silence, created by John W. Bobin writing as Adelie Ascott, was featured in British story papers as early as 1922. By 1928, the juvenile mystery genre was so well established that at least one publisher was marketing titles under the rubric "Mystery and Adventure Series for Girls."

In quality, these early works were uneven. Many continued, often clumsily, to mix mystery with such genres as school stories, romances, domestic tales, and adventure novels. The more formulaic titles frequently violated the emerging "rules" of adult mysteries: Questions remained unanswered, solutions depended on coincidence and luck rather than strictly logical detection, and crucial information was withheld from the reader. But, perhaps because of children's preference for the safely predictable, the formulaic novels eventually became the best-selling girls' mysteries.

In 1930, the advent of Nancy *Drew established the continuing-character series as the most durable of girls' mystery formats. Drew was quickly followed by other heroines whose main purpose was to solve cases: Judy Bolton (in mysteries published from 1932 to 1967), the Dana Girls (1934–1979), nurse Cherry Ames (1944–1968), and more. In England, the Valerie Drew series began its long run in the *Schoolgirls' Weekly* in 1933. Enid Blyton's many continuing characters (the Famous Five, the Adventurers, and the Secret Seven, among others) made her one of the most popular children's authors in Britain.

The literary quality of such series varied. In the Nancy Drew stories, for instance, detection was all; family, friends, social issues, and personal development were secondary to the mystery, if they appeared at all. Eventually, in the weakest series, the plots became so streamlined that almost nothing remained except the *puzzle, the *clues, and the chase. Non-series mysteries frequently offered more thematic scope. The puzzle was often combined with a parallel story of the heroine's or other character's developing

identity or maturity. In the first Edgar-winning juvenile, Phyllis *Whitney's *The Mystery of the Haunted Pool* (1960), the heroine learns to deal with family illness and a friend's physical disability while discovering the secret of a long-lost treasure.

Until the middle to late 1960s, most girls' mysteries presented little threat to the status quo; though many characters experienced personal growth, the basic security of their world was rarely disrupted, its rightness rarely questioned. In the late 1960s, however, juvenile fiction in general began to exhibit what has been called the "new realism"—a more explicit, challenging, and less reassuring presentation of adolescent problems. Illegal drugs, sex, peer pressure, and violence are all treated in this fiction, and racial and ethnic minorities began to take slightly larger roles. In mysteries, danger became more acute, moral issues became less clear-cut. Even books for young girls, such as Willo Davis Roberts's *Megan's Island* (1988), forced heroines to come to terms with a world less ordered and fair than the one they inhabited when the story began.

In the decades following the 1960s, girls' mysteries included such growing juvenile dangers as the threat of being kidnapped or stalked. *Murder, a crime previously taboo even in most young-adult mysteries, became much more common as an element of plot in juvenile mysteries forming the basis of Joan Aiken's *Night Fall* (1971), among others. More sophisticated narrative strategies also appeared. In *The Stalker* (1985), Joan Lowery Nixon included the thoughts and plans of a murderer. Often, characters' entire world and sense of self underwent significant changes. In Lois Duncan's *Killing Mr. Griffin* (1978), a studious "good" girl must face the consequences of a prank that leaves her teacher dead.

Though much about girls' mysteries has changed over the years, much has stayed the same. The "new realism" resulted in many works that challenged the secure world of more traditional incarnations of the genre, but few juvenile mysteries were completely cynical or despairing. Optimistic endings continued to be the norm, however tempered that optimism might be. Formulaic series, safe cozies, and comedies never disappeared. With some exceptions, scholarly neglect or disparagement of girls' mysteries remained constant as well. Nevertheless, the popularity of the form has not faltered.

[*See also* Adventure Stories; Heroism; Realism, Conventions of.]

• Mary Cadogan and Patricia Craig, *You're a Brick, Angela!: A New Look at Girls' Fiction from 1939 to 1975* (1976). Bobbie Ann Mason, *The Girl Sleuth: A Feminist Guide* (1975; reprinted with new introduction, 1995). Zena Sutherland and May Hill Arbuthnot, *Children and Books,* 8th ed. (1991).

—Kathleen Chamberlain

JUVENILE SLEUTHS. *This entry is divided into two parts both of which survey outstanding examples of youthful characters who play the role of sleuth in fiction written for young people. The first part examines the appeal of the young detective hero as portrayed in books marketed to boys. The second notes the impor-*

tance of the female sleuth as a capable role model for girl readers.

Boy Sleuth
Girl Sleuth

For further information, please refer to Juvenile Mystery.

BOY SLEUTH

The inquisitiveness of young people makes them natural detectives. It follows, then, that fictional juvenile detectives offer young readers, as Carol Billman has pointed out in her study of the *Stratemeyer Syndicate, "mythic figures who answer to the dreams of American youth culture and to the perennial psychological needs of the young as they set out to discover life's secrets."

The early years of the century were boom times for detective enthusiasts, especially young readers. "[Boys] had discovered with joy and gratitude that wherever there is a criminal in a play, there must, of course, be a detective, sometimes many detectives," wrote novelist Booth Tarkington. Detectives figured in books, *dime novels, comics, newspapers, magazines, plays onstage and on the radio, and in films.

Prototypes of the boy sleuths were the Baker Street Irregulars, the "unofficial force" of street urchins who first appeared in Arthur Conan *Doyle's *The Sign of the Four* (1890; *The Sign of Four*). Led by the redoubtable Wiggins, their tasks consisted primarily in assisting Holmes in matters of surveillance.

Six years later Tom Sawyer turned to sleuthing in Mark Twain's *Tom Sawyer, Detective* (1896), in which Tom employs some genuine deduction in a mystery surrounding a diamond theft, double-crossing thieves, and identical twins.

Tarkington's *Penrod Jashber* appeared in 1929. Readers of the earlier stories of twelve-year-old Penrod Schofield were already familiar with Penrod's fascination with crime and detective stories. Indeed, Penrod's own literary efforts, surreptitiously written in the sawdust box in the woodshed, were a pastiche of the Holmes-Moriarty stories, pitting the bloodthirsty road agent Ramorez against the wily detective George Jashber. Deciding that detectives were more admirable than road agents, Penrod assumed the persona of Jashber and undertook, through a series of deductions and shadowings, to solve the mystery of some stolen horses.

The Hardy Boys series remains the most enduring creation of the prolific Edward L. Stratemeyer. The Franklin W. Dixon *pseudonym was but one of many employed for a wide variety of juvenile series. Between 1889, when he sold his first story to *Golden Days*, a boys' magazine, and his death in 1930, Stratemeyer either wrote, outlined, or edited more than eight hundred books under sixty-five pseudonyms, selling an estimated total of two hundred million copies. Founded in 1906, his Stratemeyer Syndicate became a kind of literary assembly line, creating books in a month's time and mass marketing them for fifty cents. Other boys' series created by Strate-

meyer centered around Tom Swift, Don Sturdy, and The Rover Boys. Writing in *Tom Swift and Company*, John T. Dizer calls Stratemeyer's literary syndicate "the most important single influence in American juvenile literature," in his volume *Edward Stratemeyer and the Stratemeyer Syndicate* (1986).

Crime solving, which had always been an element in and other series The Rover Boys, came to the fore in the Hardy Boys books. *The Tower Treasure* appeared in 1927 and introduced Frank and Joe Hardy, sixteen and fifteen, respectively, who lived with their detective father, Fenton, and eccentric Aunt Gertrude in the snug little New England coastal town of Bayport. The *formula consisted of fast-paced investigative action, the paraphernalia of gadgets and *disguises, and healthy doses of fortuitous coincidence and moral uplift. Each case is handed down to the boys by their father, who is always setting out on a case of his own. The boys' adversaries sport colorful monikers, like Mortimer Prince, Vordo Blecker, and The Chameleon.

As of 1984 the series had run to eighty volumes, and more than seventy million novels had been sold. There had been changes along the way, of course. All titles written before 1959 have been substantially revised so the boys could enjoy rock music, display new hairstyles, and extend their investigations into international espionage. However, as the dust jackets boast, the essential tone of the stories remains the same: "Believing that right will triumph—that lawbreakers can be brought to *justice—the Hardys work day and night to accomplish their ends." Indeed, as Carol Billman notes in her study of the Hardys, "The Hardys remain locked in that period between childhood and adult life . . . the quiet and deep sleep of fairy tale characters that precedes awakening into maturity."

Meanwhile, the boys' fame spread into comic books and television. In America, the Hardy Boys adventures were part of Walt Disney's *The Mickey Mouse Club* show, starring Tommy Kirk and Tim Considine as Joe and Frank. This debuted in the 1950s. A Saturday morning cartoon series appeared on ABC in 1969, and an hour-long series began on ABC in 1977 with Shaun Cassidy and Parker Stevenson.

Contemporaries of the Hardys included Emil Tischbein, a German boy who was featured in two highly regarded juvenile mysteries by Erich Kästner, *Emil and the Detectives* (1929) and *Emil and the Three Twins* (1934), and a series of boys' mysteries written under the name Ellery Queen, Jr. (a pseudonym for mystery novelist James Holding) that began in 1941 with *The Black Dog Mystery*. Ten more titles were published before the series' demise in 1965 with *The Purple Bird Mystery*.

Adolescent readers growing up in the late 1940s savored the adventures of Rick Brant, a cross between Tom Swift and Craig Kennedy (but with a more realistic science background) and Ken Holt, a young man who displayed solid deductive powers. The Ken Holt Mystery Stories were the product of Samuel Epstein, writing under the pseudonym Bruce Campbell. Epstein brought a strong science background and solidly crafted plots to these adventures. Ken Holt was the son of Richard Holt, of the Global News Service. Beginning with *The Secret of Skeleton Island* in 1949, his series ran to eighteen titles, concluding in 1963 with *The Mystery of the Sultan's Scimitar.*

Rick Brant's Science Adventure series were written by John Blaine, a pseudonym for Harold Leland Goodwin, a scientist with a background in atomic physics and oceanic research. Rick was the son of scientist Hartson Brant, who conducted scientific studies from his laboratories on Spindrift Island. His twenty-two adventures, spanning twenty years and locations ranging from Egypt, Nigeria, and China to the Western Pacific, began with *The Rocket's Shadow* (1947) and continued through such evocative titles as *The Whispering Box Mystery, Caves of Fear, The Electronic Mind Reader,* and *The Rocket Jumper.*

For those young readers still in elementary grades, there have been numerous adventures and crimes to solve. The Stratemeyer Syndicate had frequently injected crimes and *puzzles into the Bobbsey Twins series (*The Bobbsey Twins Solve a Mystery,* 1934), and in 1935 it began a new series of mysteries, the Mary and Jerry Mystery Stories. The five-volume series about the young twins of the Denton family included such low-key problems as a missing clown and a stolen piggy bank. In 1953 the syndicate established another mystery series, The Happy Hollisters. Written by syndicate partner Andrew Svenson under the pen name Jerry West, it numbered thirty-three titles in seventeen years.

More recent popular boy detectives among younger readers between ages five and eight are the Encyclopedia Brown, Nate the Great, and The Three Investigators series. Donald J. Sobol's Leroy "Encyclopedia" Brown, of Idaville, first appeared in 1963. "He was like a complete library walking around in sneakers," notes the author. To date there have been nineteen volumes of stories. Readers are presented all the clues and have the opportunity to solve the mysteries themselves. Sobol has won a Special Edgar from the Mystery Writers of America. Marjorie Weinman Sharmat's first Nate the Great book appeared in 1972. Nate is a precocious child who never eats on the job—except for the inevitable plate of pancakes. The Three Investigators were the creation of Robert Arthur. Working from their headquarters in the Jones Salvage Yard in Rocky Beach, California, Jupiter Jones, Pete Crenshaw, and Bob Andrews have as their motto "We investigate anything!" *The Secret of Terror Castle* began the series in 1964; later, Alfred Hitchcock's name was added to the books, and brief introductions to each story bore his name. Since Arthur's death, other writers have continued the series, including William Arden. Another series are the Piet Potter stories, by Robert Quackenbush, about a boy who lives with his family in *New York City.

[See also Juvenile Mystery; Juvenile Sleuth: Girl Sleuth.]

• John T. Dizer, *Tom Swift and Company: "Boys' Books" by Stratemeyer and Others* (1982). Carol Billman, *The Secret of the Stratemeyer Syndicate* (1986). Deborah Felder, "Nancy Drew: Then and Now," *Publishers Weekly* 229, no. 22 (30 May 1986): 30–34. Bruce Watson, "Tom Swift, Nancy Drew and Pals All Had the Same Dad," *Smithsonian* 22, no. 7 (Oct. 1991): 50–61. Carole Kismarie and Marnin Heiferman, *The Mysterious Case of Nancy Drew and the Hardy Boys* (1998).

—John C. Tibbetts

GIRL SLEUTH

Since they first appeared in *dime novels, girl sleuths and their sidekicks have empowered readers to see themselves positively, think clearly, face danger squarely, and strive vigorously to see justice done. The genre's first efforts were transitional novels by popular motivational authors, such as Oliver Optic's (William T. Adams) *Poor and Proud; or, The Fortunes of Katy Redburn* (1858), Horatio Alger's *Helen Ford* (1866), *Tattered Tom; or, the Story of a Street Arab* (1871), and Carrie L. May's Sweet Clover series beginning with *Sweet Clover; or, Nellie Milton's Housekeeping* (1865). By 1877, when Edward Wheeler, creator of Deadwood Dick and Calamity Jane, brought out *Hurricane Nell, the Girl Dead Shot* and *Edna, the Girl Bandit,* following in 1880 with *New York Nell, the Boy-Girl Detective; or, Old Blakesly's Money,* the female dime novel detective was a sure seller. Over the next three decades Irish and professional operatives prevailed, such as F. Lusk Broughton's *Belle Kingston, the Detective Queen; or, the Stolen Bonds* (1883), Detective Edenhope's *Nellie Kelly's Nerve; or, Japanese Joe's Chinese Chase* (1893) and *Foiled by a Female Detective* (1910), until the genre's feisty "new women" traded their shock value for more socially potent guises.

It was L. Frank Baum, prolific author of *The Wizard of Oz,* not Edward Stratemeyer, who created the classic girl sleuth. Beginning with *Annabel* (1906) written as Suzanne Metcalf, his well-crafted mysteries include *The Daring Twins: A Story for Young Folk* (1911) and *Phoebe Daring* (1912), issued under his own name, and the Mary Louise series (1916–19), written as Edith Van Dyne, the pseudonym he used for his popular Aunt Jane's Nieces series. Here, fully formed, is the familiar socially adept, autonomous, orphaned, educated, white, upper-middle-class, thoroughly modern girl detective. Aided by loyal family, friends, and servants, she uses observation coupled with insight and technical skills to solve mysteries, calling on authority figures as needed.

When Street and Smith hired Edward Stratemeyer as a ghostwriter in 1892, it laid the groundwork for the most productive fiction factory of all. By 1904, he had launched the Rover Boys and Bobbsey Twins series and formed the Stratemeyer Syndicate which would produce some 59 series before he died in 1930. Among these was Honey Bunch (1923–55; updated as Honey Bunch and Norman, 1957–63), a spin-off of his tot series starring a fetching five-year-old, for which Mildred Augustine Wirt Benson wrote five titles between 1937 and 1941. In 1930 at the height of mystery writing's Golden Age, Carolyn *Keene rolled out blond Nancy *Drew and her roadster, creating a publishing blockbuster. When Benson submitted her draft of *The Secret of the Old Clock* (1930), the first of her twenty-five Drew titles ending with *The Ghost of Blackwood Hall* (1948), Stratemeyer angrily voiced his displeasure. Nancy was much too fresh for his taste, not at all what he wanted. Readers would not accept a character who behaved so outrageously. He was wrong.

In 1934 Clair Blank launched The Beverly Gray College Mystery series (twenty-six titles, 1934–55) with *Beverly Gray Freshman*, which follows her heroine to Vernon, her mother's elite alma mater. That same year new CEO Harriet Stratemeyer Adams published the syndicate's first Dana Girls mystery, *By the Light of the Study Lamp*, as by Carolyn Keene, which sent assertive orphans Louise and Jean Dana to Starhurst, a posh boarding school. The series survived till 1979, with Benson ghosting twelve early titles.

Probably the most prolific British author of children's mysteries is Enid Blyton, whose series continues although her comfortably well-bred child sleuths, the five find outers, who are introduced in *The Mystery of the Burnt Cottage* (1943), and *The Secret Seven* (1949; *The Secret Seven and the Mystery of the Empty House*) have fallen out of favor since the 1960s. While fellow Briton Edith Pargeter is better known as Ellis *Peters for her popular Brother *Cadfael series, her *Piper on the Mountain* (1966) and *Black Is the Colour of My True Love's Heart* (1967) introduce Dominic Felse's fiancée, Tossa Terrell, a well-drawn modern girl sleuth.

No discussion of girl sleuths would be complete without mentioning the popular syndicated series that now constitute a substantial part of children's library collections and circulate at a phenomenal rate. The oldest, Gertrude Chandler Warner's Boxcar Children (1924–present), developed to motivate her students, tells of four practical-minded orphans who set up housekeeping in an abandoned boxcar before being reunited with their wealthy grandfather. Ann M. Martin's twenty-seven Babysitters' Club Mysteries (1986–present), are a subset of the popular series dealing with upscale Stoneybrook's seven-member teenage Babysitters' Club and its clients. Recent series for younger readers featuring girl sleuths and their sidekicks worth noting are David A. Adler's Cam Jansen series (1980–present) and The Fourth Floor Twins (1985–present), and Patricia Giff's Polka Dot Private Eye (1987–present), which move the venue to the city and employ logic to solve contemporary *puzzles, and Irene Schultz's Woodland Gang (1984–present), whose five orphaned sleuths live in a group home and include a minority child and a child in a wheelchair.

• Albert Johannsen, *The House of Beadle and Adams and Its Dime and Nickle Novels: The Story of a Vanished Literature*, 3 vols. (1950–62). Carol Billman, *The Secret of the Stratemeyer Syndicate: Nancy Drew, The Hardy Boys, and the Million Dollar Fiction Factory* (1986). Faye Riter Kensinger, *Children of the Series and How They Grew; or, A Century of Heroines and Heroes, Romantic, Comic, Moral* (1987). Kimberley Reynolds, *Girls Only? Gender and Popular Children's Fiction in Britain 1880–1910* (1990). Robert Druce, *This Day Our Daily Fictions: An Enquiry into the Multi-Million Bestseller Status of Enid Blyton and Ian Flemming* (1992). Deidre Johnson, *Edward Stratemeyer and the Stratemeyer Syndicate* (1993). Mildred Wirt Benson, "Fulfilling a Quest for Adventure," in *Rediscovering Nancy Drew*, ed. Carolyn S. Dyer and Nancy Tillman Romalov (1995), 59–65.

—Jean A. Coakley

**KEATING, H(ENRY) R(EYMOND) F(ITZWAL-
TER)** (b. 1926), novelist and critic, has been a central
figure in British crime writing for at least four
decades. He was for fifteen years crime critic of the
Times, and since 1985 has been president of the famous *Detection Club. He has edited several books
about crime fiction, including *Whodunit? A Guide to
Crime, Suspense, and Crime Fiction* (1982) and a collection of essays about Agatha *Christie, written a biography of Sherlock *Holmes, and played the game
of choosing his hundred best crime stories in *Crime
and Mystery: The One Hundred Best Books* (1987). All
his critical writing is marked by a conspicuous generosity of mind, scholarship lightly borne, and perceptions both sharp and subtle.

But creation is more important than criticism, and
the tone and manner of Keating's crime stories are
wholly original in modern crime fiction. They spring
from a mind attracted to philosophical and metaphysical speculation, with a liking for fantasy held in
check by the crime story's requirements of *plot.
Early books like *Zen There Was Murder* (1960) and *A
Rush on the Ultimate* (1961) gave readers the pleasure of seeing a writer kick up his heels in defiance of
any critical perception of what a crime story *ought* to
be like. It is typical of Keating's intense imaginative
powers that when Inspector Ganesh *Ghote of the
Bombay Police first appeared in *The Perfect Murder*
(1964), his creator had not visited India, and did not
do so for another decade. That first Ghote novel won
the *Crime Writers Association's Golden Dagger
Award and launched its author on the series of books
in which Ghote is the central character.

The ambience of the little Indian detective allowed
full play to Keating's offbeat humor, and Indian
habits and attitudes held an evident attraction to a
mind unsatisfied by Western rationalism. Preferences among the Ghote books vary from reader to
reader. *Inspector Ghote Hunts the Peacock* (1968),
which finds the detective astonished by English
ways, and *Under a Monsoon Cloud* (1986), where he
is confronted by a moral problem, suggest the range
of comedy and seriousness the series can comprehend. *The Murder of the Maharajah* (1980) is a brilliant variation on the classical crime formula, perhaps underrated by its creator.

Keating likes to experiment. Using the name Evelyn Harvey, he wrote in the 1980s three crime stories
with a period *setting in which the central character
was the governess Harriet Unwin. After 1986, however, he abandoned the Harvey pseudonym and Vic-

torian crime and returned to Ghote.

Yet the Ghote stories have not stretched Keating's
talent to its limits. That he recognizes this himself is
suggested by two of his four excursions into the
"straight" novel, *The Underside* (1974) and *A Long
Walk to Wimbledon* (1978). The first offered a view of
the Victorian sexual underside that was realistic yet
infused with fantasy, the second an after-the-bomb
vision, a journey through chaos the more powerful
because confined to a single viewpoint. If Keating
can fuse such themes into a crime story's framework,
the result might be his masterpiece.

[*See also* Ethnic Sleuth; Humor; Period Mystery.]

• Meera T. Clark, "H. R. F. Keating," in *Twelve Englishmen of
Mystery*, ed. Earl F. Bargainnier (1984).

—Julian Symons

KEENE, CAROLYN, pseudonym used by the Stratemeyer Syndicate for the author of two teen detective
series for girls centered around characters Nancy
*Drew and the Dana Girls. With the pseudonym, the
syndicate could employ different writers to continue
the multivolume series. The first three (possibly four)
Nancy Drew stories, beginning with *The Secret of the
Old Clock* (1930), were outlined by Edward Stratemeyer. After his death, his daughter Harriet S. Adams
created the outlines, often based upon considerable
research, which other writers then expanded into
books. She also undertook substantial rewriting of
manuscripts before publication. Volumes 1–7, 11–25,
and 30 of the Nancy Drew series were written by Mildred Wirt Benson, a journalist and author of other
children's books.

The Dana Girls mysteries, introduced with *By the
Light of the Study Lamp* (1934), featured two sisters
at boarding school. Although they never attained the
household-word status of Nancy Drew, the Dana
Girls nonetheless were built upon a similar premise:
Unusually talented heroines solved cases by means of
luck and pluck. Leslie McFarlane, who wrote many
Hardy Boys books, wrote the first four Dana Girls
mysteries. Benson also produced several volumes in
this series.

The Stratemeyer Syndicate, along with the name
"Carolyn Keene," was sold to publisher Simon &
Schuster in 1984. By the late 1990s, "Carolyn Keene"
was credited with more than 140 Nancy Drew mysteries, 34 Dana Girls titles, and many titles in spin-off
series such as "Nancy Drew Files," "Nancy Drew
Notebooks," and "Nancy Drew on Campus."

[*See also* Juvenile Mystery: Girls' Juvenile Mysteries; Juvenile Sleuth: Girl Sleuth; Syndicate Authors.]

• "Benson, Mildred (Augustine Wirt)," *Something about the Author* 65 (1992): 7–11. Deidre Johnson, *Edward Stratemeyer and the Stratemeyer Syndicate* (1993). Carolyn Dyer and Nancy Romalov, *Rediscovering Nancy Drew* (1995).

—Kathleen Chamberlain

KGB. The Komitet Gosudarstvennoy Bezopatnosti, or Committee of State Security, the Soviet foreign intelligence and security service was founded as the Cheka in December 1917. It was envisaged as a temporary expedient for the "revolutionary settlement of accounts with counter-revolutionaries," but swiftly became an all-pervasive element in Soviet life.

Its greatest strength lay in the ideological appeal of Communism, which was responsible for the major intelligence coups of the interwar years when highly motivated spies such as "the London Five"—Guy Burgess, Donald Maclean, Kim Philby, Anthony Blunt, and John Cairncross—were recruited, In *Familiar Strangers* (1979; *Strangers*), Bryan Forbes traces the history of a man who knew Burgess. The British situation was mirrored in the United States by the recruitment of Harry Dexter White, the Silverman Ring, and Alger Hiss. In *Show Me A Hero* (1992), Ted Allbeury describes a spy network that operated in the United States for forty years. Again, some of those engaged on working on the development of the A-bomb were persuaded to betray its secrets to the Soviets—notably Klaus Fuchs, Allan Nunn May, and Bruno Pontecorvo.

The ideology had profound drawbacks, notably by inspiring conspiracy theories that persuaded both the institution and the Soviet leadership to see themselves surrounded by capitalist and counterrevolutionary plots. This frame of mind was largely responsible for Stalin's murder of millions of Soviet citizens, the murders being carried out by the institution. It was also responsible for the erroneous evaluation of much good raw intelligence collected by the service, since the heads of service and the leadership could only view it through a distorted perspective. Warnings of the approaching Nazi invasion were catastrophically ignored, while every effort was made to find and destroy purely imaginary plots. Eric *Ambler explores some of this thinking in *Judgment on Deltchev* (1951).

Emigré opponents of the regime could be assassinated or kidnapped by the service—so-called wet affairs—as in the cases of the White Russian leaders Generals Kutepov (1930) and Miller (1937), and the former People's Commissar for Foreign Affairs, Leon Trotsky (1940). As world opinion turned against this sort of operation, the KGB relied increasingly on disinformation making extensive use of forged documents, too many of which were such poor products that they had little impact in the West.

Efforts were made from the 1970s to close the economic gap between the West and the Soviet Union by stealing scientific and technological material, but this could not tip the balance. With the break up of the Soviet bloc and the impending collapse of the Soviet Union, senior officers of the KGB played a lead-ing role in the attempted coup of 1991. They were arrested after its failure and the organization was disbanded at the end of the year. Martin Cruz Smith's *Gorky Park* (1981) pits a Moscow homicide investigation against the KGB in what has turned out to be one of its final stages.

[*See also* Intelligence Organizations; Loyalty and Betrayal; Spy Fiction.]

• Christopher Maurice Andrew and Oleg Gordievsky, *KGB: The Inside Story of its Foreign Operations from Lenin to Gorbachev* (1990).   —Michael Occleshaw

KIDNAPPING. As early as the seventeenth century, the act of stealing or carrying off a person, especially a child, was referred to as kidnapping. During ensuing centuries, the term has been applied to the capture against their will of people of all ages, often involving informal imprisonment in some concealed place. The crime of kidnapping is often accompanied by other offenses, including *extortion, terrorism, rape, and *murder.

The earliest recognized examples of mystery writing include suggestions or clear depictions of kidnapping. Edgar Allan *Poe's evil Montressor abducts and entombs his prey in "The Cask of Amontillado" (*Godey's Lady's Book*, Nov. 1846). Wilkie *Collins's eponymous character in *The Woman in White* (1860) makes her first appearance as a person in flight from being held against her will. Abduction is also important to Arthur Conan *Doyle's "The Greek Interpreter" (*Strand*, Sept. 1893) and "The Adventure of the Priory School" (*Strand*, Feb. 1904).

Since then, writers of detective fiction, psychological *thrillers, and *true crime have continued to explore kidnapping as a crime around which to center their work. Notable examples of short stories from the Golden Age of puzzle-centered mysteries include Agatha *Christie's "The Kidnapped Prime Minister" (*Hercule Parrot Investigates*, 1924) and Ellery *Queen's "Child Missing!" (*This Week*, 8 July 1951).

Real-life kidnapping cases have on occasion inspired mystery novels. The action in Christie's *Murder on the Orient Express* (1934; *Murder in the Calais Coach*) bears a striking resemblance to the kidnapping of Charles Lindbergh's son and takes advantage of the widespread revulsion inspired by that crime. Josephine *Tey's *The Franchise Affair* (1948) is a modern reworking of the eighteenth-century case of Elizabeth Canning. Mary Willis Walker's *Under the Beetle's Cellar* (1995), which concerns hostage taking by a fundamentalist religious cult, was influenced by the seige of the Branch Davidian compound at Waco, Texas. A British Foreign Office minister is captured in Geoffrey Archer's thriller *Java Spider* (1996), which has parallels with the 1996 kidnapping in Irian Jaya (West Papua) of a group of Cambridge postgraduates by tribesmen protesting the appropriation of their lands for a new mine.

Mystery novelists have found invented kidnapping useful in constructing their fiction. *The Only Game* (1991), by Patrick Ruell, begins with the disappearance of a young boy. The initial *puzzle as to whether he has run away, been killed, or been kidnapped is developed into a complex *plot. Conversely, after the philanderer Ken Crossland goes missing in Stephen Murray's *Death and Transfiguration* (1994), the police start to suspect a serial killer, only to find that Crossland had been held captive by a deranged woman.

Private eye novelists are fond of sending their *sleuths out on *missing persons cases. Robert B. *Parker's *Spenser seeks to rescue an abducted author in *Looking for Rachel Wallace* (1980), and in Liza Cody's *Bad Company* (1982), private investigator Anna Lee is herself kidnapped, along with a teenaged girl. *The Baby-Snatcher* (1997), by Ann Cleeves, is a British regional police story in which Inspector Ramsay investigates a series of short-term child abductions. Ray Harrison's *Facets of Murder* (1997) is a *historical mystery in which Constable Morton's fiancee is abducted by a gunman raiding a jewelery shop in Victorian *London.

Increasingly, crime and mystery writers look at the effects of the crime on the people concerned, including the perpetrator, the investigator and especially the *victim and the victim's loved ones. Barbara Vine's *Gallowglass* (1990) emphasizes psychological *suspense and delineation of character. The same author, writing as Ruth *Rendell, provides new insights on her series character, Inspector Reginald *Wexford, when he investigates a hostage taking that involves his own wife in *Road Rage* (1997).

The horrific subject of child abduction, abuse, and murder is handled with sensitivity in Andrew Taylor's *The Four Last Things* (1997), in which Lucy Appleyard, the four-year-old daughter of a policeman and a woman cleric, is snatched from a child minder. Children are also abducted in two American books published in 1995, both centered around a strikingly similar premise. In the aforementioned *Under the Beetle's Cellar*, Samuel Mordecai and his followers abduct from a school bus eleven children and their driver, a veteran of the Vietnam War. Jeffrey Deaver's *A Maiden's Grave* begins with a group of hardened criminals kidnapping eight deaf children and their teachers, again from a school bus. Both books derive much of their strength from the description of the authorities' race against time to free the captives before they are killed. Authors who center their stories around kidnapping have an advantage, in that readers may find it easy to identify with the victims or their loved ones, whose lives are suddenly changed by this violent and sometimes random crime that could happen to anyone.

[*See also* Blackmail; Rape and Other Sex Crimes; Terror; Terrorism and the Terrorist Procedural.]

—Martin Edwards

KITCHIN, C. H. B. *See* Incidental Crime Writers.

KNOX, RONALD A(RBUTHNOTT) (1888–1957), British priest, scholar, satirist, author, and one of the foremost *pontificators on the subject of detective fiction, regarded the *detective novel as an intellectual test. In his six classic novels he demonstrated his skill at using distinctive British *settings, such as the River Thames near *Oxford in *The Footsteps at the Lock* (1928) or the Scottish highlands (*Still Dead* (1934); however, he has been criticized for constructing implausible *plots. Believing that the mystery writer should always play fair with the reader, he provided page numbers for his clues, in case the reader had missed them. He is perhaps best remembered for constructing a set of ten rules for crime writers, known as the Decalogue. These were published as part of his introduction to *Best Detective Stories of the Year 1928* (1929). Knox was one of the first to publish scholarship on Sherlock *Holmes. His "Studies in the Literature of Sherlock Holmes," on which Conan Doyle congratulated him in some amazement, appeared in *The Blue Book 1912*.

[*See also* Conventions of the Genre; Craft of Crime and Mystery Writing, The; Criticism, Literary; Formula; Golden Age Forms; Golden Age Traditions; Rules of the Game.]

• Evelyn Waugh, *The Life of the Right Reverend Ronald Knox* (1959). Penelope Fitzgerald, *The Knox Brothers* (1977).

—Penelope Fitzgerald

Kramer, Lieutenant, and **Sergeant Zondi,** creations of James *McClure, a native South African now resident in England. The pair are introduced in *The Steam Pig* (1971), the first in McClure's series of police procedurals. Trekkersburg, modeled on McClure's hometown of Pietermaritzburg, is a solid Afrikaner laager in which blacks are "kaffirs" and Englishmen are reviled. Lieutenant Tromp Kramer, a member of the city's murder and robbery squad, is a hard-boiled Boer detective whose belief in Afrikaner supremacy is only slightly mollified by his friendship with his Zulu sergeant, Mickey Zondi, who provides a counterweight to the dominant, white view of society. Both men are committed police officers who daily confront the injustices of apartheid as well as crime.

[*See also* Ethnic Sleuth; Prejudice; Racism; Sidekicks and Sleuthing Teams.]

—Chris Gausden

LAST WORDS. *See* Dying Message.

LATHEN, EMMA, joint pseudonym of the late economist Mary Jane Latsis (1927–1997) and Martha B. Henissart (b. 1929), a lawyer. The American writing pair, who collaborated on novels of amateur detection set against the backgrounds of *New York's Wall Street and the Washington, D.C., political *milieu, put together the Lathen name by combining the first three letters of each of their last names. Initially they used the pseudonym to hide from their colleagues their identities as mystery writers; later they cultivated a mystique about their identities and an elusiveness that meant they were rarely seen in public together.

The pair introduced their most famous character, John Putnam *Thatcher, executive vice president of Sloan Guaranty Trust, in *Banking on Death* (1961). During a thirty-six-year collaboration, they portrayed Thatcher as using business savvy and urbane wit to investigate mysteries in a variety of business *settings. In *Murder Sunny Side Up* (1968), under the joint pseudonym R. B. Dominic, they introduced another popular series character, Congressman Ben Safford. Safford solves crimes mostly set in Washington, D.C. The success of both series had much to do with the authors' ability to make readers feel like insiders in the worlds they depicted. This is achieved in part by Lathen's insertion of sager pronouncements about the states of affairs in these two realms, expressed in the characteristically debonair and witty dialogue that became the Lathen hallmark.

The characters themselves are powerful and intelligent. Thatcher is rich, handsome, unattached, and endowed with keen intelligence and a huge store of common sense. Safford is a government insider. Both men, in the *Golden Age tradition, solve crimes by noticing and remembering details that are more or less furnished to the reader but whose significance is lost to everyone else.

[*See also* Banking and Financial Milieu; Bribery; Extortion; White-Collar Crime.]

• John C. Carr, *The Craft of Crime* (1983), 176–201. Shakuntala Jayaswal, "Emma Lathen," in *Critical Survey of Mystery and Detective Fiction*, ed. Frank Magill (1988), vol. 3, 1021–26.
—Rosemary Herbert

LATIN AMERICA, CRIME AND MYSTERY WRITING IN. Crime and mystery writing in Latin America has been inhibited by a marketplace saturated with translated works from abroad and by a sense that the *conventions of the genre are incongruous in the new context. The task of appropriating a genre so profoundly associated with British and North American cultures has been viewed as unprofitable and unwieldy, and relatively few Latin American authors have cultivated the form. Those who have done so tend to produce works of great variety and often of a sophisticated nature.

The centers of crime and mystery writing in Latin America are Argentina, Brazil, Cuba, and Mexico. The earliest and the most examples come from Argentina. In the late nineteenth century, Paul Groussac and Eduardo Ladislao Holmberg were among the first to experiment with the detective story. The use of *satire and parody in Holmberg's "La bolsa de huesos" (1896; The Sack of Bones) is typical of Latin American crime and mystery writing. The genre is also frequently employed to construct the kind of metaphysical narrative for which Argentina's most distinguished author, Jorge Luis Borges, is well known. Borges's masterpiece, "La muerte y la brújula" (1942; Death and the Compass), undermines the symmetry of the tidy crime-to-solution *formula to reveal an unpredictable universe ruled by paradox and uncertainty. Borges's cultivation of the detective story gave it prestige and created a sense of national identification with a form Latin Americans generally considered alien to their cultural and literary traditions. Borges also wrote in a satirical vein in his collection of detective stories *Seis problemas para don Isidro Parodi* (1942; Six Problems for Don Isidro Parodi). Whether playful or erudite, parodic or metaphysical, crime and mystery writing from Latin America tends to develop from a sense of transgression. Authors violate the codes inscribed in the imported genre as a means of expressing difference.

Social protest is also characteristic of Latin American crime and mystery writing. In Argentina, authors such as Ricardo Piglia, Juan Carlos Martini, José Pablo Feinmann, and Osvaldo Soriano began using the North American hard-boiled model to comment on institutionalized violence and repression. These authors produced works that are memorable for their tense, searching, often elliptical indictments of society, and for the casting off of real world logic in the tradition of Borges and the metaphysical. Piglia's "La loca y el relato del crimen" (1975; The Crazy Woman and the Story of the Crime) pays homage both to Borges and to the North American hard-boiled authors by challenging the linear structure of the conventional crime narrative and by using the detective story to denounce social injustice. From Holmberg in the nineteenth century, to Leonardo Castellani's Padre Metri stories from the 1930s through the 1950s, to Rodolfo Walsh's *Operación masacre* (1957; Operation Massacre) which integrates crime fiction techniques and documentary narrative to investigate a case of human rights violations, Argentine authors have applied the genre to explore social issues.

Social criticism is an important element of Brazilian crime literature as well, starting with the first work published there, *O Mystério* (1920; The Mystery), collectively authored by a group of intellectuals including Coelho Neto and Afrânio Peixoto. Maria Alice Barroso's acclaimed mystery novel *Quem matou Pacífico?* (1969; Who Killed Pacífico?) uses the form to examine violence practiced with impunity by powerful landowning families. Crime fiction by Ignácio de Loyola Brandão and Rubem Fonseca explores dehumanization and violence in modern Brazilian society. José Louzeiro is the best known of those Brazilian authors who cultivate nonfiction narratives documenting and analyzing actual crime cases. Parody, satire, and farce are also common in Brazilian crime fiction.

Until the 1970s, there was virtually no crime and mystery writing in Cuba. Since then, with the encouragement of government-sponsored competitions, the genre has flourished. While the didactic aims of revolutionary crime fiction tend to limit the genre's possibilities, authors such as Ignacio Cárdenas Acuña, Juan Angel Cardi, and Arnaldo Correa have found ways to exploit conventional devices and strategies while still projecting a socialist point of view.

Arguably the most important detective fiction from Mexico is Vicente Leñero's novel *Los albañiles* (1964; The Bricklayers). The author's metaphysical mystery integrates a portrait of class conflict with a mythical vision of cultural disintegration. Leñero's confrontation with the "other" is a motif that surfaces throughout Mexican crime and mystery fiction. The theme is developed in works by the first Mexican to cultivate the genre, Antonio Helú, in the 1920s, and is taken up by authors such as Rodolfo Usigli, José Emilio Pacheco, and Paco Ignacio Taibo, who cultivate unconventional configurations of the genre.

• Donald A. Yates, ed., *Latin Blood: The Best Crime and Detective Stories of South America* (1972). Jorge Lafforgue and Jorge B. Rivera, eds., *Asesinos de papel* (1977). Paulo de Medeiros e Albuquerque, *O mundo emocionante do romance policial* (1979). Luis Rogelio Nogueras, *Por la novela policial* (1982). Vicente Francisco Torres, ed., *El cuento policial mexicano* (1982). Amelia Simpson, *Detective Fiction from Latin America* (1990). Amelia Simpson, trans. and ed., *New Tales of Mystery and Crime from Latin America* (1992).

—Amelia Simpson

LAWYER. *Lawyers are important characters in crime and mystery writing, sometimes playing the role of sleuth as well as legal advisor or advocate, and in other cases appearing simply as secondary characters whose legal expertise or access to privileged information is essential to the development of the plot. This entry is divided into three parts, the first two surveying outstand-* ing examples of fictional American and British lawyers who become lead characters performing detective work and the third examining the role of the lawyer as a secondary character. It is important to note that some lawyers who are seen as hero-sleuths actually engage in very little hands-on detective work themselves. Despite the fact that they use private detectives to do their footwork, they are seen as sleuths, since their cases are solved by the application of their intellectual powers and legal expertise. Erle Stanley Gardner's Perry Mason is an example of such a lawyer sleuth.

American Lawyer-Sleuth
British Lawyer-Sleuth
Lawyers as Secondary Characters

For further information, please refer to Courtroom Milieu.

THE AMERICAN LAWYER-SLEUTH

The fictional American lawyer-sleuth has had a long and varied history. Melville Davisson *Post's Randolph Mason, more rogue than detective in *The Strange Schemes of Randolph Mason* (1896; *Randolph Mason: The Strange Schemes*) and *The Man of Last Resort or, The Clients of Randolph Mason* (1897), finds loopholes to help his clients cheat the law. In the later adventures, collected in *The Corrector of Destinies* (1908; *Randolph Mason, Corrector of Destinies*), he reforms somewhat and performs more like a traditional detective. Post's other continuing lawyer-sleuth, Colonel Braxton, whose cases were gathered in *The Silent Witness* (1930), operates in rural Virginia like the more famous Uncle *Abner. Arthur Train's *Saturday Evening Post* character Ephraim Tutt, who appeared in a long series of collections beginning with *Tutt and Mr. Tutt* (1920) and one short novel, *The Hermit of Turkey Hollow* (1921), only occasionally functions as a detective.

By far the most famous lawyer-detective, Erle Stanley *Gardner's Perry *Mason, first appeared in *The Case of the Velvet Claws* (1933), a novel that did not employ courtroom drama. Most of the more than eighty subsequent Mason books, through the posthumous *The Case of the Postponed Murder* (1973), included the patented courtroom climax that later writers have tried, usually not as successfully, to emulate. C. W. Grafton's Gil Henry, a promising lawyer-sleuth in the Mason tradition, appeared in only two books, *The Rat Began to Gnaw the Rope* (1943) and *The Rope Began to Hang the Butcher* (1944). Another successful novel in the Mason tradition was *A Handy Death* (1973), by Robert L. Fish with attorney Henry Rothblatt, but advocate Hank Ross never appeared again. Television lawyer Sam Benedict, based on J. W. Ehrlich, appeared in several somewhat Masonesque novels, most successfully a pair by Brad Williams and Ehrlich, *A Conflict of Interest* (1971) and *A Matter of Confidence* (1973). Jack Donahue's Harlan Cole and D. R. Meredith's John Lloyd Branson are other less successful attempts to create a new Perry Mason. Most competent in capturing the writing and plotting style of Gardner's series has been Parnell Hall writing as J. P. Hailey in the series about

Steve Winslow, beginning with *The Baxter Trust* (1988). Thomas Chastain has continued the Mason series proper with a couple of *pastiches, beginning with *The Case of Too Many Murders* (1989).

Some of the best-known American lawyer detectives eschew the courtroom and operate more in the tradition of *private eyes: Craig *Rice's John J. Malone, Harold Q. Masur's Scott Jordan, William G. Tapply's Brady Coyne, and Ed *McBain's Matthew Hope, who finally argues a case in *Mary, Mary* (1993).

Since the accused person is usually innocent in detective stories, defense lawyers have predominated among fictional sleuths. Gardner gave the prosecution not-quite-equal time with small-city district attorney Doug Selby, hero of *The D.A. Calls It Murder* (1937) and subsequent novels. *The Corpse in the Corner Saloon* (1948) launched a series by Hampton Stone (pseudonym of Aaron Marc Stein) whose protagonist, Jeremiah X. "Gibby" Gibson, is an assistant district attorney in *New York but never gets near the courtroom. Changing social attitudes have made prosecutor heroes more frequent in recent years. Robert K. Tanenbaum's Roger "Butch" Karp, who first appeared in *No Lesser Plea* (1987), is a New York assistant district attorney in a more realistic mode.

Lawyer-sleuths, like fictional sleuths generally, were predominately male for many years. Barbara Frost's defense attorney Marka de Lancey, who appeared in three novels beginning with *The Corpse Said No* (1949), was ahead of her time as an independent female professional. A pioneer on the prosecutorial side was Barbara Driscoll, who appeared in only one novel, *Criminal Court* (1966), by William Woolfolk writing as Winston Lyon. The 1990s saw a plethora of female lawyer-sleuths, including Margaret Maron's Judge Deborah Knott, who first appeared in the Edgar-winning *Bootlegger's Daughter* (1992), Julie Smith's Rebecca Schwartz, Lia Matera's Willa Jansson and Laura di Palma, and Carolyn Wheat's Cass Jameson.

Many lawyer-sleuths have been the creation of lawyer-writers. Among the characters introduced in the seventies by real-life lawyers were Francis M. Nevins Jr.'s law professor Loren Mensing and Joe L. Hensley's small-town defender Donald Robak. With the best-selling success of Scott Turow's *Presumed Innocent* (1987), law-trained novelists became a hot commodity. Warwick Downing made an organization rather than a single lawyer the hero in his National Association of Special Prosecutors series, beginning with *A Clear Case of Murder* (1990). Other distinguished attorney-created sleuths are William Bernhardt's Ben Kincaid, who first appeared in *Primary Justice* (1992), and Steve Martini's Paul Madriani, who appears in *Compelling Evidence* (1992) and *Prime Witness* (1993). The novels of John Grisham, beginning with *A Time to Kill* (1989), feature lawyer-sleuths but, to date, no continuing characters.

Though American legal fiction tends to contain less humor than the works of British writers like Henry Cecil and John *Mortimer, an exception exists in the comic trial scenes of Paul Levine's Jake Lassiter novels, beginning with *To Speak for the Dead* (1990). Challenging the rule that lawyer fiction is

usually contemporary are Raymond Paul's Lon Quinncannon series, beginning with *The Thomas Street Horror* (1982), which is set in the nineteenth century, and Richard Parrish's novels featuring Joshua Rabb, who first appeared in *The Dividing Line* (1993), and who operates in the period just following World War II.

[*See also* Courtroom Milieu; Justice; Legal Procedural.]

• Jon L. Breen, *Novel Verdicts: A Guide to Courtroom Fiction* (1984).   —Jon L. Breen

THE BRITISH LAWYER-SLEUTH

The enduring popularity of legal mysteries in Britain is due largely to the skill with which succeeding generations of writers have developed the lawyer-sleuth. That so many lawyers should turn detective is plausible: The work of many solicitors and barristers brings them into contact with crime and criminals, police officers and *suspects. The lawyer-sleuth is usually a maverick, prepared to bend or even flout the law in the hope of avoiding ordeals for the innocent and the risk that the guilty will walk free. The danger is that for a professional man or woman regularly to behave in such a way may destroy credibility—a weakness, for example, of Anthony Gilbert's novels about the rumbustious solicitor Arthur Crook and those by H. C. *Bailey about the hymn-singing hypocrite Joshua Clunk.

A sea change in the portrayal of the lawyer-sleuth occurred with the publication of Cyril *Hare's *Tragedy at Law* (1942). In real life, Hare was a barrister and he captured the insular nature of circuit life as well as creating in Francis Pettigrew a barrister-detective all the more credible because he did not win every case and was apt to lapse into melancholy. Later writers built on the foundations laid by Hare; many, like him, have been lawyers and have taken pains to combine a believable picture of the legal world with strong *plots which frequently turn on a quirk of law. Hare's most notable disciple has been Michael *Gilbert, a *London solicitor whose clients included Raymond *Chandler. In *Smallbone Deceased* (1950), a *corpse of a trustee is found in a deed box; the legal knowledge of a young solicitor, Henry Bohun, helps Inspector Hazlerigg to solve the mystery. Nap Rumbold, another London solicitor, appeared in a number of books and short stories; in *Death Has Deep Roots* (1951), Gilbert intersperses courtroom scenes with Nap's exploits in France, as he tries to establish the *innocence of his client. Gilbert's preferred method is to confront a likable young solicitor with a legal mystery which can only be resolved by heroic actions, as in *The Crack in the Teacup* (1966). In *Flash Point* (1974), narrated in part by an employee of the solicitors' professional body, the Law Society, Gilbert combines a lively tale about secret service dirty tricks with a series of skilfully contrasted court scenes. *The Case Against Karl Mullen* (1991), a late and undervalued work, introduces Roger Sherman, who makes good use of his army training after taking on as a client a member of the South African security forces with powerful enemies. In contrast, the *elderly sleuth Jonas Pickett has an ex-circus strongman to help with the rough stuff in the ironically titled story collection *Anything for a Quiet Life* (1990).

The legal profession in England and Wales is divided between barristers and solicitors; lawyers who turn, in fictional terms, to crime, almost invariably write about the branch of the profession to which they personally belong. John *Mortimer, a Queen's Counsel, is the creator of Horace *Rumpole, scourge of the Establishment and firmly within the tradition of idiosyncratic amateur *detectives. Less radical, but equally entertaining, are Sarah Caudwell's books about the tax barrister Julia Larwood and her colleagues; they show that even tax law and high finance can supply the raw material for mysteries in the classic tradition. Historically, solicitors have been regarded as leading less glamorous lives than barristers, who perform more regularly in the theatrical atmosphere of the courts. Yet solicitors' work brings them more directly into contact with the outside world—and in particular with clients who are suspects, culprits, and, occasionally, *victims. M. R. D. Meek's Lennox Kemp has had a checkered career; having at one time been struck off the roll of solicitors, he spent several years working as a *private eye before being allowed to reenter the profession. Roy Lewis seeks to get the best of two worlds: His solicitor-detective, Eric Ward, combines criminal and corporate work and often finds that the two spheres of his practice overlap. Legal series have kept up-to-date with the changing face of the profession in Britain, and lawyers are no longer stereotyped as middle-aged, middle-class, and male. Michael Underwood's Rosa Epton, who first appeared in *The Unprofessional Spy* (1964) is notable as the first British female lawyer-sleuth. Martin Edwards's Harry Devlin, based in Liverpool, is one of the few provincial solicitor-detectives, while Helen West works, like her creator Frances Fyfield, in the Crown Prosecution Service.

Today, the lawyer-sleuth is as likely to have a working-class background and to have a clientele composed of the underprivileged (as well as the all too often guilty) as to be a member of a social elite based in elegant chambers in Lincoln's Inn. The books in which such characters appear range from the grimly realistic to the avowedly cerebral and demonstrate that no profession offers so many possibilities for the amateur detective as the law.

[*See also* Courtroom Milieu; Justice; Legal Procedural.]

• Breen, Jon L. *Novel Verdicts: A Guide to Courtroom Fiction* (1984).

—Martin Edwards

LAWYERS AS SECONDARY CHARACTERS

Lawyers have appeared as supporting characters in any number of crime fiction works, whether serving as the Watson figure, adversary, *victim, *suspect, *murderer, reader of the will to the assembled heirs of the murder victim, or handy legal consultant for the detective. Lawyers play every kind of role, from family adviser to ambulance-chasing shyster to flamboyant courtroom performer. Even in today's lawyer-baiting climate, their roles range from the heroic to the venal.

S. S. *Van Dine's gentleman *amateur detective Philo *Vance is brought into his cases by his friend John F.-X. Markham, district attorney of *New York County, who acts as Greek chorus and slightly smarter equivalent of dumb cop sergeant Heath. Arthur Train's long-running attorney Ephraim Tutt, whose partner is a younger lawyer also named Tutt but unrelated (thus the title of the 1920 collection *Tutt and Mr. Tutt*), has recurring villainous adversaries in small-town lawyer Squire Hezekiah Mason and New York assistant district attorney William Francis O'Brion. Similarly, Erle Stanley *Gardner's Perry *Mason invariably opposes a district attorney, in early books Claude Drumm and later the better-known Hamilton Burger, whose primary function is to put the wrong suspect on trial. To liven up the series about prosecutor hero Doug Selby, Gardner introduced a character he seemed to have greater fondness for, sneaky defender A. B. Carr, in *The D.A. Draws a Circle* (1939)—while Carr is invariably vanquished, he proves a much more interesting character than Drumm, Burger, or (most ironically) Selby.

Some British legal series characters have whole casts of continuing associates. John *Mortimer's Horace Rumpole of the Bailey shares chambers with a variety of fellow advocates—Claude Erskine-Brown, Phillida Trant ("the Portia of our chambers"), Uncle Tom, the outspokenly evangelical Soapy Sam Bullard, the left-leaning Fiona Allways, and most notably the trouble-prone Guthrie Featherstone, QC, M. P., who somehow rises from head of chambers to the High Court bench. Rumpole also appears repeatedly before the dreaded Judge Bullingham. Sara Woods's Antony Maitland is supported by his uncle and housemate, Sir Nicholas Harding, QC, and frequently has the same junior counsel (Derek Stringer), prosecution opponent (Bruce Halloran), and presiding judge (Carruthers).

Several secondary lawyer characters recur in Henry Cecil's comic fiction, most notably Mr. Tewkesbury, the drunken solicitor who first appears in *The Painswick Line* (1951). The brilliant advocate Sir Impey Biggs recurs in Dorothy L. *Sayers's Lord Peter *Wimsey novels, most memorably in *Clouds of Witness* (1926). Michael Underwood's solicitor Rosa Epton has a partner, Robin Snaith, and a romantic interest, Peter Chen, who reappear from book to book. Oliver Rathbone, QC, became a more and more important secondary figure in Anne Perry's series about amnesiac Victorian detective William Monk and Crimean War nurse Hester Latterly.

Most of the better big-trial novels have vivid and interesting lawyer characters in supporting roles. The secondary characters in Robert Traver's *Anatomy of a Murder* (1958), prosecutor Claude Dancer and Judge Harlan Weaver, are especially effectively drawn. The old lawyer, sometimes a drunk, who is drawn in to help the younger hero has become something of a *stock character in such books. A recent example is disbarred alcoholic Lucien Wilbanks, who helps out Jake Brigance in John Grisham's *A Time to Kill* (1989). Among the most interesting secondary characters in the 1990s flood of legal *procedurals are those in Steve Martini's novels *Compelling Evidence* (1992) and *Prime Witness* (1993): Quite a few of them are (if only to the naive nonlawyer, perhaps) incompetent beyond belief, particularly the laggardly assistant district attorney Roland Overroy. Both books also feature money-hungry defenders with more interest in book and film contracts than justice.

[*See also* Sidekicks and Sleuthing Teams.]

• Jon L. Breen, *Novel Verdicts: A Guide to Courtroom Fiction* (1984).   —Jon L. Breen

LEAST LIKELY SUSPECT, a narrative convention or device that entails, in its simplest form, ultimately pinning the crime on the character who appears to be most innocent, most helpful to the investigation, least suspicious in conduct, least obvious in *motive, or least physically capable of having committed it. Readers enjoy finding *guilt in unexpected places— witness some of the "celebrity" solutions offered for real-life crimes like the Jack the Ripper murders and the John F. Kennedy assassination.

As a fictional device, the least likely suspect dates back at least to Edgar Allan *Poe's "Thou Art the Man" (*Godey's Lady's Book*, Nov. 1844), in which the pleasant and well-liked Charlie Goodfellow proves to be the culprit, an unsubtle revelation that paradoxically neither surprises the reader nor appears to be intended to do so. While some commentators on *whodunit technique have counseled writers to appear to consider but clear the real murderer early in the going, John Dickson *Carr believed the culprit in a well-crafted detective story must be someone on whom serious *suspicion has not fallen.

Listing examples breaks the normal rule of mystery criticism that insists on maintaining the secrecy of solutions, so readers disturbed by such revelations should now skip to the final paragraph of this article.

Early least likely *suspects were often of the servant *class, such as the secretary in Anna Katharine *Green's *The Leavenworth Case* (1878), thus exonerating the upper-crust main characters from blame. Few books have actually embodied the cliché that the *butler did it, however, and those that employ this solution, such as Catherine Aird's *The Complete Steel* (1969; *The Stately Home Murder*), generally do so conscious of its irony. At least in old films, pinning the crime on a character apparently confined to a wheelchair was a frequent and soon shopworn device. A type of surprise that developed surprisingly early was to point the finger at the official policeman investigating the case or even the *Great Detective himself: Early examples include Israel *Zangwill's *The Big Bow Mystery* (1892), Marie Connor Leighton and Robert Leighton's *Michael Dred, Detective* (1899), and Gaston Leroux's *Le mystère de la chambre jaune* (1908; *The Mystery of the Yellow Room; Murder in the Bedroom*). Later variations appear in Barnaby Ross's *Drury Lane's Last Case* (1933; reprinted as by Ellery *Queen) and Agatha *Christie's final Hercule *Poirot novel, *Curtain* (1975).

Christie has been more renowned than any other writer for producing surprising murderers. In her very first novel, *The Mysterious Affair at Styles* (1920), she achieves a double reverse, as the person on trial for the murder, and thus by detective fiction logic automatically innocent, turns out to be guilty after all. In her 1926 classic, *The Murder of Roger Ackroyd*, the Watson narrator proves to be the murderer, bringing forth cries of reader outrage and charges of unfairness. While Ronald A. *Knox created a retroactive rule to prohibit the practice—the killer "must not be anyone whose thoughts the reader has been permitted to follow"—Christie's defenders insisted that the reader was charged with suspecting *everyone*. The ethics of the *Ackroyd* solution remain controversial to this day. Though seemingly unrepeatable, the *Ackroyd* surprise has been resprung by a surprising number of later writers, including Anthony *Berkeley in *The Second Shot* (1930), Mickey *Spillane in the novella "Everybody's Watching Me" (*Manhunt*, Jan.–Apr. 1953), and Christie herself in *Endless Night* (1967). Others, such as Scott Turow in *Presumed Innocent* (1987), have had fun tantalizing their readers with the possibility of an Ackroydal murderer. In another famous example of Christie's whodunit surprises, *Murder on the Orient Express* (1934; *Murder in the Calais Coach*), all the suspects committed the murder as a team, while in *Ten Little Niggers* (1939; *And Then There Were None; Ten Little Indians*), the murderer is a character believed to be dead. In *Crooked House* (1949), a child is the killer. In this last device, Christie was untypically anticipated by another writer: Barnaby Ross, in *The Tragedy of Y* (1932; reprinted as by Ellery Queen). Margery *Allingham used a similar gimmick even earlier in *The White Cottage Mystery* (1928).

Other writers have made a continuing series character the criminal, a variant seen in Clayton Rawson's *The Footprints on the Ceiling* (1939) and in Rex *Stout's *A Family Affair* (1975). The ploy of making the protagonist's ostensible love interest the culprit occurs most memorably in Dashiell *Hammett's *The Maltese Falcon* (1930) but has been repeated countless times since, including occurrences in any number of romantic *suspense novels, always with an alternative love interest available. Too frequent to require an example are stories in which the culprit is seemingly attacked and wounded by the killer. Most unlikely, and perhaps most disappointing of all to the reader, is the solution in which it is revealed that there was no killer at all; the apparent murder turns out to have been a suicide or an accident, as in Ronald A. *Knox's *The Three Taps* (1927).

Every type of character in a mystery has been cast as murderer at one time or another. The necessity of having a surprising murderer sometimes leads writers to falsify character and introduce physical and psychological impossibilities in the interest of fooling the reader. The lesser Golden Age writers constantly threw consistency and plausibility to the winds in the cause of bamboozlement. Achieving both believability and astonishment is difficult but not impossible: A recent example is Julie Smith's *The Axeman's Jazz* (1991).

[*See also* Conventions of the Genre: Traditional Conventions; Formula: Character; Rules of the Game.]

• Howard Haycraft, *Murder for Pleasure* (1941). Dorothy L. Sayers, introduction to *The Omnibus of Crime* (1929).

—Jon L. Breen

LEBLANC, MAURICE (MARIE ÉMILE) 1869–1941), French writer who created the gentleman burglar Arsène *Lupin. Leblanc is, with Gaston Leroux, the leading figure in early French detective fiction.

Leblanc was born in Rouen. Early novels (*Une femme*, 1893; *L'oeuvre de mort*, 1896) and short stories (*Des couples*, 1890) reveal the influence of Flaubert and Maupassant.

In 1905 he was solicited to contribute a short story, to be written in the manner of the Sherlock *Holmes tales, to a new French magazine that was modeled on the *Strand*. "L'arrestation d'Arsène Lupin" was published in July of that year. (It was translated as "The Arrest of Arsène Lupin" in *The Exploits of Arsène Lupin*, 1909.) Leblanc subsequently detailed the adventures of the exceptional thief, treasure hunter, Don Juan, and shrewd detective in a series of novels including *L'Aiguille creuse* (1909; *The Hollow Needle*, 1910) *813* (1910), and *La demeure mystérieuse* (1929; *The Melamare Mystery*) and collections of short stories such as *Arsène Lupin contre Herlock Sholmes* (1908; *Arsjene Lupin versus Holmlock Shears*, 1909). Novels in addition to the Lupin series include *Dorothée, danseuse de corde* (1923; *Dorothy the Rope Dancer*) and the *science fiction work *Les trois yeux* (1920; *The Three Eyes*, 1921).

[*See also* Gentleman Thief.]

• Jacques Derouard, *Maurice Leblanc, Arsène Lupin malgré lui* (1989).

—Jacques Baudou

LE CARRÉ, JOHN, pseudonym of David John Moore Cornwell (b. 1931). British author of *spy fiction, considered the most outstanding political novelist of the Cold War period. Le Carré began to write while working for British intelligence, so he knew the secret world from the inside. At the time, Ian *Fleming's James *Bond novels were immensely popular, but in published interviews le Carré made it clear that he did not share the current enthusiasm. An important stimulus for his writing was his desire to create an alternative form of *thriller, replacing glamorizing fantasy and facile heroics with a more authentic portrait of the intelligence world and of Cold War realities.

George Smiley, the series character le Carré launched in his first two novels, *Call for the Dead* (1961) and *A Murder of Quality* (1962), is Bond's antitype, a short, fat, middle-aged, bespectacled, and inconspicuous cuckold. With his much more original third novel, *The Spy Who Came in from the Cold* (1963), le Carré achieved a huge international success and transformed the spy novel. This terse, chilling, and powerful story of multiple deception and be-

trayal explores the rhetoric and ethics of the Cold War in order to subvert standard pieties, especially those of the supposedly morally superior West concerning freedom, *justice, and democracy. For the Circus, le Carré's fictional equivalent of *MI5, the end justifies the means, as it does for its Marxist counterparts, and the lovers central to the novel are exploited and sacrificed in the name of expediency. The vulnerability and fragility of human love in a world of power politics is an important theme in le Carré's novels. In *The Looking Glass War* (1965), le Carré's bleak, pessimistic narrative of a British intelligence operation that goes terribly wrong focuses on the department responsible, which lives nostalgically in its glory days. Out of touch with reality, this organization is a microcosm of British society, like the public school in *A Murder of Quality*, so that both books are "condition of England" as well as genre novels.

By the mid-1960s le Carré was a full-time writer and his style subsequently became more expansive and detailed than it was in his spare, compact early novels. In *A Small Town in Germany* (1968), an intelligence probe into the disappearance of a supposed defector is a way of dealing with the shadow cast on contemporary German politics by the Nazi past. Le Carré then abandoned mystery and spy conventions for the first and only time, but his most self-consciously literary novel, *The Naive and Sentimental Lover* (1971), was not well received. Le Carré immediately returned to Smiley, the Circus, and Cold War espionage with the widely praised *Quest for Karla* trilogy he wrote during the 1970s: *Tinker, Tailor, Soldier, Spy* (1974), *The Honourable Schoolboy* (1977), and *Smiley's People* (1980). These books established his reputation as one of the most important of postwar English novelists. The scope of this realistic yet mythic trilogy is vast, geographically, politically, and humanly. It encompasses such themes as *loyalty and betrayal, memory, time, *innocence, love, and the conflict between public and private values, and contains brilliant analyses of postimperial Britain, bureaucratic institutions, and the corporate mind. The trilogy was not exactly le Carré's farewell to Smiley, who is the unifying figure in *The Secret Pilgrim* (1991), something of a literary throwback, but all his other novels since 1980 have broken new ground. *The Little Drummer Girl* (1983) explores the Israeli-Palestinian conflict in considerable depth. *A Perfect Spy* (1986), his most autobiographical novel as well as one of his best, relates the extraordinary English childhood of a spy to his later success as a "perfect" double agent. *The Russia House* (1989) was le Carré's response to the Gorbachev phase of glasnost and perestroika, when the Cold War was ending but the organizations that fought it were still intact, and *The Night Manager* (1993), about the vast business of drug smuggling, was his first reply to the question, Where does the spy novel go after the Cold War? Succeeding novels have provided a variety of answers. In *Our Game* (1995) the complex relationship between two Englishmen formerly engaged in Cold War intelligence leads both of them, hunter and hunted, into the dangerous world of Caucasian religion and politics in the 1990s. Very different is his much-lauded

Central American novel, *The Tailor of Panama* (1996), in which machinations and intrigue arise from concern about the future of the Panama Canal. A British Customs intelligence investigation into financial corruption on a vast international scale is central to the fast-moving and action-packed *Single & Single* (1999), which resembles *A Perfect Spy* in being an English father-and-son story while also featuring a prominent Russian mafia family.

[*See also* Pursuit.]

• Tony Barley, *Taking Sides: The Fiction of John le Carré* (1986). Peter Lewis, *John le Carré* (1985).

—Peter Lewis

LEGAL PROCEDURAL, a type of novel that shows lawyers engaged in the business of law. It is likely to have a lawyer as detective and at some stage may take the reader into a courtroom. At its best, it will turn on a specific point of law.

Legal procedure figures in the earliest detective novels: Charles *Dickens's *Bleak House* (1852–53), where the law is a major preoccupation and the abuse of his power by Mr. Tulkinghorn, the Dedlock family lawyer, is crucial to the narrative; Wilkie Collins's *The Moonstone* (1868), where Matthew Bruff tells part of the story; and Dickens's *The Mystery of Edwin Drood* (1870), where Hiram Grewgious is most scrupulous in the discharge of his duty to his ward. Bruff and Grewgious are prototypes of the army of devoted family solicitors in later detective fiction, including Mr. Murbles, who represents the Wimsey family in Dorothy L. *Sayers's work; Mr. Rattisbon, in Ngaio *Marsh's novels; and Mr. Rumbold, in novels and stories by Michael *Gilbert.

In formal American detective fiction, sleek or portly attorneys protect the rich from unwelcome police attention and are instantly on hand when the trouble starts—Mr. Archer in Leslie Ford's *The Clue of the Judas Tree* (1933), Eldridge Fleel in S. S. *Van Dine's *The Kidnap Murder Case* (1936), Chester Bigelow in Barnaby Ross's *The Tragedy of Y* (1932), and Mortimer Peabody in Rufus King's *The Lesser Antilles Case* (1934). In Sac Prairie, Wisconsin, they send for Ephraim Peck, the wily old *judge in August Derleth's novels.

When Ludovic Travers is seconded to a law firm in Christopher Bush's *The Death of Cosmo Revere* (1930; *Murder at Fenwold*), his employer speaks for all who fear the consequences of *murder in the family: "Everything that *can* be hushed up has got to be." The client's interests are paramount: In Charlotte Murray Russell's *The Case of the Topaz Flower* (1939), Denby Rogers defies Captain Bain, insisting that the letter addressed to his daughter shall go to her and not to him. Some solicitors go well beyond the routine calls of duty: Anthony Gilbert's Arthur Crook, a crusader who sometimes overrides the law; Joshua Clunk, H. C. *Bailey's second-string, ferreting for justice within the law by sometimes questionable means; and Robert Blair, who defies a whole community in the course of *The Franchise Affair* (1948), by Josephine *Tey. Others follow Mr. Tulkinghorn and abuse their trust: Andrew

Pennington in Agatha *Christie's *Death on the Nile* (1937), a notable exponent of the "sign here" school of law, and Abel Horniman, who uses his privileged position to feather his nest in Gilbert's *Smallbone Deceased* (1950).

The inquest is a staple of detective fiction, though often a mere formality, quickly adjourned. Coroners range from the disconcerting veteran Albert Amblesby in Colin *Watson's Flaxborough novels, conducting inquests with a "certain sardonic sharpness" unnerving to witnesses, to the officious Mr. Salley, who instructs the jury in the inquest on Paul Brande, in Margery *Allingham's *Flowers for the Judge* (1936), that they may legitimately make a specific charge of murder. In R. A. J. Walling's *The Coroner Doubts* (1938; *The Corpse with the Blue Cravat*), Daniel Rose questions a verdict of *suicide pronounced in his own court and enlists Philip Tolefree to investigate further.

Juries in the high court also reach the wrong verdict. Walter Eustiss is condemned by a wayward *jury in *Death in Perpetuity* (1950) by Douglas G. Browne, but is acquitted on appeal and later vindicated by Harvey Tuke, the deputy director of public prosecutions. In Dorothy Le Sayers's *Strong Poison* (1930), only Miss Katharine Climpson saves Harriet *Vane from hanging, resisting the verdict of her co-jurors to force a retrial and give Lord Peter *Wimsey time to establish the truth. In *Clouds of Witness* (1926), Wimsey's brother is tried by his peers in the House of Lords. *The Twelfth Juror* of B. M. Gill's novel (1984) has inside knowledge of the case he is judging. Unable to judge dispassionately, he makes dangerous, destructive decisions. *Verdict of Twelve* (1940), by Raymond Postgate, also brings its jurors to life while demonstrating how they contribute to a trial. Gilbert applauds the "account of the machinery of the law in action" in this novel. Gilbert's own *Death Has Deep Roots* (1951) takes us to the *Old Bailey for the trial of *Rex* v. *Lamartine*.

Cyril *Hare's novels draw expertly upon legal niceties. In *Tragedy at Law* (1942), a circuit judge is the *victim and the rituals of provincial assizes buttress and nourish the narrative. Sarah Caudwell's novels involve five barristers and a law professor. Trust funds and tax planning occupy their attention.

[*See also* Courtroom Milieu; Truth, Quest for.]

• Jon L. Breen, *Novel Verdicts: A Critical Guide to Courtroom Fiction* (1984). —B. A. Pike

LEGAL SYSTEMS. *General perceptions of the workings of U.S., English, and Scottish legal systems arise from the reading of crime and mystery fiction. Divided into three parts, this entry outlines some of the basic legal concepts and precepts from the United States, England, and Scotland that often underly aspects of plot in crime and mystery writing. Subgenres in which appreciation of legal points are especially useful include the legal procedural, true crime, and detective fiction that turns on a point of law.*

The English Legal System
The U.S. Legal System

The Scottish Legal System and the "Not-Proven Verdict"

THE ENGLISH LEGAL SYSTEM

The English legal system is known as a common law system from the system of justice instituted by medieval English kings to provide a body of laws common to the entire land as opposed to local customs and practices. Derived from medieval guilds, the four Inns of Court are responsible for regulating admissions to the bar; those who have been called to the bar (admitted to practice) may join one of the societies of the Inner Temple, Middle Temple, Lincoln's Inn, and Gray's Inn. In addition to barristers, who present cases in court, solicitors have a similar history, beginning as general business agents and eventually joining exclusively the Inns of Chancery. This system played a crucial part in mystery novels from the Victorian age to the present day. Although the system, like the genre, continues to evolve, the fundamental principle of criminal law has always been that a defendant is regarded as innocent unless *guilt is proved beyond reasonable doubt. A criminal trial is concerned with proof, rather than with truth, and complex rules govern the admissibility of evidence. Until 1898 an accused person was generally not allowed to give evidence on his or her own behalf; the Police and Criminal Evidence Act of 1984 sets out procedural requirements that investigating police officers must observe. Prior to 1987, the police also often acted as prosecutors, a role that has now passed to the Crown Prosecution Service. Magistrates deal with most minor offenses, but more serious cases are referred to a judge and jury in the Crown Court, which replaced the assize courts, court sessions held periodically in English counties by traveling judges (the circuit) to try civil and criminal cases and abolished in 1971. Until 1948 a member of the House of Lords could elect for trial by his peers, as the Duke of Denver did in Dorothy L. *Sayers's *Clouds of Witness* (1926). *Juries have been allowed to reach majority verdicts since 1967, but *judges retain the power to sentence. The punishment of hanging for *murder was for all practical purposes abolished in 1965; the crime now attracts a mandatory life sentence. The Scottish verdict of "not proven" is not permitted, and the legal system of Scotland also differs from that of England and Wales in many other respects.

The English system aims to treat the accused fairly, but numerous authors, both radical and conservative, have shown how apparently desirable technical rules may assist the guilty. For example, the principle of *autrefois acquit* (i.e., that the law does not permit a man to be twice in peril of being convicted of the same offense) is the cornerstone of the *plot of Agatha *Christie's *The Mysterious Affair at Styles* (1920). The unpredictability of the human beings who make up a jury has been powerfully conveyed by Raymond Postgate in *Verdict of Twelve* (1940), whereas in Edward Grierson's *Reputation for a Song* (1952) the presumption of *innocence enables a guilty man to walk free. Conversely, strict application of the law may result in unjust convictions; in Richard Hull's *Excellent Intentions* (1938; *Beyond Reasonable Doubt*), a judge exploits his own powers in an unusual way so as to prevent a grievous wrong. Many novels depict courtroom action, but F. Tennyson Jesse's *A Pin to See the Peepshow* (1934), Edgar Lustgarten's *A Case to Answer* (1947; *One More Unfortunate*), and Bruce Hamilton's *Let Him Have Judgement* (1948; *Hanging Judge*) are notable for the strength of their antihanging sentiments. Cyril *Hare's *Tragedy of Law* (1942) is notable for its depiction of the life of judges in the circuit of assizes, and John *Mortimer depicts the world of the criminal lawyer in *Rumpole of the Bailey* (1978). Of trial scenes written by nonlawyers, Anthony *Berkeley's account of a private prosecution for murder at the *Old Bailey in *Trial and Error* (1937) is ingenious and imaginative, whereas Julian *Symons's *The Progress of a Crime* (1960) provides a grimly realistic description of the legal process. Symons's fictionalized account of the nineteenth-century case of Adelaide Bartlett, *Sweet Adelaide* (1980), is equally compelling and well researched.

The 1990s saw widely publicized miscarriage of justice cases that have called the quality of English justice into question. In fiction, miscarriage of justice stories often have a retrospective element. Reginald *Hill's *Recalled to Life* (1992), with its echoes of the 1960s, is a contemporary example, but even Christie was prepared to acknowledge that the innocent might be convicted of murder, as in *Mrs. McGinty's Dead* (1952; *Blood Will Tell*) and *Five Little Pigs* (1943; *Murder in Retrospect*).

[See also Courtroom Milieu; Legal Procedural; Witness.]

• Jon L. Breen, *Novel Verdicts: A Guide to Courtroom Fiction* (1984).

—Martin Edwards

THE U.S. LEGAL SYSTEM

The U.S. legal system reflects the substantial influence of the English institutions from which most American law and legal procedures were originally drawn. Basic concepts familiar to English criminal process—trial by *jury, the presumption of *innocence, the right to cross-examine witnesses, and the right to be represented by counsel—have from the beginning characterized American trials.

The U.S. Constitution also provides specific guarantees against what Americans regarded as abusive measures employed in English political trials. These include prohibition of double jeopardy, the privilege against forced confessions, the rights to speedy and public trial and to subpoena defense witnesses, detailed prescription of the place of trial, and prohibition of "excessive bail . . . and cruel and unusual punishments." The Fourteenth Amendment's due process clause was eventually held to make these guarantees applicable in state as well as federal courts.

Responsibility for criminal justice in the United States is divided between state and federal governments. Federal criminal jurisdiction is limited to areas of specific federal interest, such as crimes that cross state lines. The vast majority of *murder prosecutions take place in state courts, and American courtroom fiction has focused primarily on those courts.

Unlike federal judges, who receive lifetime appointments, most state judges are popularly elected, usually at the county level and often in contested races. So are the district attorneys who, under various titles, are responsible for state-level prosecutions. Serious crimes, including all felonies, are triable in state courts of general jurisdiction, variously called "circuit courts," "district courts," and "county courts." Lesser offenses are triable in municipal or "police" courts, which function at the city and village level rather than the county level.

Grand jury indictment is constitutionally required for federal felony prosecutions (unless waived by the defendant), but most states allow district attorneys to press charges on their own authority. At neither the state nor the federal level do police officers decide whether criminal charges will be brought. Police officers file complaints against accused criminals, but prosecutions do not proceed unless district attorneys decide that they will.

In most states and in the federal system, criminal charges must withstand scrutiny by either a grand jury, or a magistrate at a preliminary hearing that the defendant may contest. If the grand jury indicts or the magistrate determines that the charge is supported by "probable cause," the defendant must proceed to trial. The defendant has the right to jury trial, where the prosecution must prove every element of the offense charged beyond a reasonable doubt. In the vast majority of states a unanimous vote of the jurors is required for conviction, although unanimity is not constitutionally required and some states permit conviction by a qualified majority.

The Perry *Mason series by Erle Stanley *Gardner (e.g., The Case of the Sulky Girl, 1933, and The Case of the Crimson Kiss, 1970), which dominated the American courtroom fiction genre through much of the twentieth century, exemplifies its state court orientation and its general focus on factual rather than legal issues. In dozens of novels and hundreds of television episodes, almost all of Mason's adventures took place in state court and turned on sharply disputed issues of fact, contested through the cut and thrust of direct and cross-examination. The same thing is true of numerous fictional American lawyers less well known than Mason, such as Joe L. Hensley's Donald Robak (e.g., Song of Corpus Juris, 1974).

Substantive criminal law, though broadly similar among the states, can differ from state to state in important ways. To take one of the most striking examples, a majority of the states provide the death penalty for murder under varying circumstances, while a substantial minority do not allow that penalty at all. The 1958 classic Anatomy of a Murder by Robert Traver exemplified fictional use of state law variation by exploiting a version of the insanity defense that was recognized in Michigan but not in most other states.

Constitutionally prescribed procedural limitations, combined with the exclusionary rule which bars illegally obtained evidence, has caused many criminal prosecutions since 1960 to turn on pretrial motions to suppress evidence rather than on juries' determinations of transactional fact. The U.S.

Supreme Court's decision in Mapp v. Ohio made the legality of police searches and arrests a centerpiece of many courtroom dramas, and the Court's decisions in Escobedo v. Illinois and Miranda v. Arizona turned the stereotype "Miranda warning" ("You have the right to remain silent ... ") into a household phrase. Scott Turow's Presumed Innocent (1987) is one of many pieces of courtroom fiction that give a realistic place to such procedural sparring both before and during trial.

American law typically allows one appeal as a matter of right from a criminal conviction, with further appeals only by permission from the court appealed to. (Where a death sentence is imposed, however, many states require automatic review by the state supreme court.) Appellate courts freely review issues of law (e.g., whether evidence was improperly admitted) but only allow very limited challenges to the factual accuracy of the jury's verdict.

A state court defendant who has been unsuccessful in the highest state court may ask the U.S. Supreme Court to review federal constitutional issues (e.g., a claim that the state deprived the defendant of his or her right to counsel), but not issues arising under state law. The Supreme Court grants review in only a small percentage of cases.

[See also Courtroom Milieu; Guilt; Judge; Witness.]

• Sanford Kadish and Monrad Paulsen, Criminal Law and Its Processes, 2nd ed. (1969). Phillip Johnson, Criminal Law, 2nd ed. (1980). Jon L. Breen, Novel Verdicts: A Guide to Courtroom Fiction (1984). Lawrence M. Friedman, A History of American Law (1985).

—Michael Bowen

THE SCOTTISH LEGAL SYSTEM AND THE "NOT-PROVEN" VERDICT

Scottish law, which is based on Roman law, differs in some significant respects from that which applies in the rest of the United Kingdom. A number of these differences are reflected in some, but not all, detective fiction set in and about Scotland.

The one most apparent in crime novels is the procedure following a death other than from natural causes. In England, a *coroner, who has independent and autonomous powers, makes the inquiries and then conducts an inquest. In Scotland, the procurator fiscal, who is essentially a prosecutor, decides whether to hold a "fatal accident inquiry" after a sudden and unexplained death. The procurator fiscal is answerable to the Crown Office whose principal is the Crown agent. One such procurator fiscal, a notably engaging man, appears in Five Red Herrings (1931; Suspicious Characters) by Dorothy L. *Sayers, in which he remarks "that he had been much struck by the superiority of the Scots law to the English in these matters."

The highest criminal court in Scotland is the High Court of Justiciary in Edinburgh (the Scottish equivalent of the *Old Bailey), presided over by the lord justice general. The highest civil court in Scotland is the Court of Session, founded in 1532. It is presided over by the same judge but under a different title, namely the lord president of the Court of Session. An appeal lies from the Court of Session to the House of Lords, but not from the High Court of Justiciary. The Sheriff (not Sheriff's) Court deals with lesser civil and criminal business. Minor criminal matters are dealt with in the District Court. The Scottish equivalent of the English barrister is the advocate; solicitors appear in the lower courts. The solicitor-advocate is a recent innovation.

A number of Scottish solicitors, mainly in Edinburgh, enjoy the status of being "writers to the signet." The signet is a seal which has to be affixed to a writ before it can be served in the Court of Session. Writers to the signet have descended historically from the days when important writs had to be written by lawyers sufficiently educated to do so. Michael *Innes features one such prestigious solicitor in his *Lament for a Maker* (1938), while John Dickson *Carr includes both a procurator fiscal and a writer to the signet in his *The Case of the Constant Suicides* (1941).

Importantly, there exists in Scotland a verdict not applicable under English law. This is that of "not proven" and is applied where the Crown has been deemed not to have proved its case beyond reasonable doubt even if the *judge or *jury are not satisfied of the *innocence of the accused. The most famous instance of this occurred in the classic real-life trial of Madeline Smith, accused of poisoning.

Christianna *Brand includes her and the outcome of this case in her short story "Cloud Nine" in the Detection Club Anthology *Verdict of Thirteen* (1978). In this, there is postulated a heavenly tea-party in which the murderess Mrs. Florence Maybrick sums up the verdict of "not proven," saying to Madeline Smith, "They know you did it, honey, but they think you didn't. Peculiar to Scotland and typical of the British."

Sayers was clearly fascinated by the possibilities of the not proven verdict and refers to it in three of her other works, although these are all set in England. They are *Clouds of Witness* (1926), *The Unpleasantness at the Bellona Club* (1928), and *Strong Poison* (1930).

The police establishment in Scotland is not dissimilar to that obtaining in other parts of the United Kingdom. Bill Knox and Peter Tumbull are the authors of many police procedurals set in Glasgow. Other writers of Scottish police procedurals include Ian Rankin, who is noted for books centered on his detective inspector John Rebus.

Some funeral customs apply only in Scotland. One of these features in *The Fifth Cord* by D. M. Devine (1967), which is set round the strict protocol applied to the custom of inviting family and friends of the deceased to take the cords which lower a coffin into the grave.
—Michael Macmillan

LEGAL THRILLER. *See* Legal Procedural.

LEONARD, ELMORE, (b. 1925) leading contemporary American author of realistic crime fiction. He was born on 11 October in New Orleans and raised in Detroit. After service in the navy during World War II, he enrolled at the University of Detroit. Following graduation in 1950, he worked for the next decade as an advertising copywriter. His earliest publications

(written in the early mornings before he left for work) were short stories aimed at the *western *pulp magazines which were still flourishing in the early 1950s. His first five novels were also westerns (as were several original screenplays he wrote). But when the western market began to disappear in the early 1960s, he shifted his attention to contemporary crime fiction, beginning with *The Big Bounce* (1969).

In 1972, after reading George V. *Higgins's *The Friends of Eddie Coyle*, a comic novel about small-time Boston hoodlums narrated largely through dialogue, Leonard began experimenting with new ways of telling his stories. He began relying more heavily on realistic dialogue while limiting the narrative perspective to his increasingly colorful characters. The result of this experiment was *Fifty-Two Pickup* (1974), his first major success as a crime novelist.

In 1978, Leonard was commissioned by the *Detroit News* to write a nonfiction article about the local police. Originally planned as a brief assignment, Leonard's visit with the police eventually lasted for over two months as he found himself fascinated by the colorful parade of characters, criminals and police alike, who passed through the squad room. This experience led to *City Primeval* (1980), his first novel to feature a policeman as protagonist. Four novels quickly followed over the next three years—*Split Images* (1981), *Cat Chaser* (1982), *Stick*, and *LaBrava* (both 1983)—earning him a reputation as a fresh new voice in contemporary crime fiction.

To further enhance the realism of his work, Leonard also began drawing upon the efforts of a part-time researcher. Whether the subject is Atlantic City gambling casinos or the federal witness security program, Leonard's novels provide an authentic behind-the-scenes view along with a richness of detail that heightens their believability.

With the publication of *Glitz* (1985), Leonard's popularity finally caught up with his growing critical reception. Since then, his novels have routinely shot to the best-seller lists while his critical reputation continues to soar.

Rather than employing a single recurring hero, Leonard's novels instead feature a changing cast of memorable characters set against a variety of vividly portrayed urban backgrounds (Detroit, Atlantic City, New Orleans, Miami Beach). His characters range from cops and *judges to thieves, drug dealers, bookies, loan sharks, and assorted killers. However, by intentionally blurring the distinction between the "good guys" and "bad guys," Leonard creates the kind of unpredictable interaction between his characters that produces fast-moving *plots filled with unexpected twists. Despite their importance, *setting and plot never overshadow character development, which is the hallmark of a Leonard novel. Leonard is particularly skilled at humanizing his villains. He possesses an uncanny ability to mimic the distinctive *voices and to get inside the heads of his characters, allowing their quirky thoughts and pungent language to carry the story. The result is an impressive body of fiction (over twenty crime novels to date) that is notable for its richness of detail, comic dialogue, and fascinating variety.

[*See also* Police Detective; Police Procedural; Realism, Conventions of; Urban Milieu.]

• Greg Sutter, "Researching Elmore Leonard's Novels," parts 1 and 2, *Armchair Detective* (Winter 1986): 4–19; (spring 1986): 160–72. Barbara A. Rader and Howard G. Zettler, eds., *The Sleuth and the Scholar: Origins, Evolution, and Current Trends in Detective Fiction*. (1988), 101–10. David Geherin, *Elmore Leonard* (1989).   —David Geherin

LESBIAN CHARACTERS AND PERSPECTIVES.

With a history of being considered a marginal genre and with its emphasis on secrets, detective fiction is particularly suited as a forum for the concerns of lesbian writers. Women writers of traditional detective fiction have presented lesbian characters as part of their densely peopled lists of *victims and *suspects. In *Unnatural Death* (1927; *The Dawson Pedigree*), Dorothy L. *Sayers presented Vera Findlater, a nasty villain who hates men and has decided to live with another woman, despite Miss Climpson's hope that eventually a nice man will come along for each of them. Harriet *Vane in *Strong Poison* (1930) has a lesbian friend. Agatha *Christie's Miss Jane *Marple offers Miss Murgatroyd and her companion, Miss Hinchliffe, in *A Murder Is Announced* (1950).

The 1980s saw an explosion of lesbian detectives, as members of the police, private investigators, or inquisitive women in the right place when crime occurred. Often these detectives are involved with crime directed toward the lesbian and gay communities. In Katherine V. Forrest's *Murder by Tradition* (1991), Kate Delafield recognizes a *murder as part of a pattern of gay bashing, and in investigating the murder she is threatened with being revealed as gay, or "outed," in her department.

Claire McNab's Carol Ashton books, set in Sydney, also feature a police inspector whose colleagues support her when she is threatened with being outed. While readers of detective fiction are never surprised when the detective becomes romantically involved with a suspect, Ashton's lack of restraint in *Lessons in Murder* (1988) is shocking. Among the most interesting aspects of the Ashton stories are the dilemmas she sometimes faces, whether in pursuing a straight woman or, in *Dead Certain* (1992), telling her son about her lesbianism.

Penny Sumner's Victoria Cross, introduced in *The End of April* (1992), is a document analyst and *private eye who won't carry a gun or do divorces; this rich, well-written debut includes coming out, pornography, drugs, and gay-bashing issues as well as homophobic college administrators. A strong political message is conveyed in Lauren Wright Douglas's *The Daughters of Artemis* (1991), featuring Caitlin Reece as a lesbian private eye addressing vigilantism and rape. *Keeping Secrets*, Penny Mickelbury's 1994 debut, presents a conflict between police lieutenant Gianna Maglione, head of the Hate Crimes unit in Washington, D.C., and Mimi Patterson, a reporter, over issues of public information involving multiple murders of gays. In the insightful *Long Goodbyes* (1993), Nikki Baker's Virginia Kelly, a lesbian financial analyst in Chicago, confronts the problem of coming out in her middle-class African American *family.

In *Murder in the Collective* (1984), Barbara Wilson, cofounder of Seal Press, introduced Pam Nilsen as an amateur sleuth recognizing herself as a lesbian. *The Dog Collar Murders* (1989) is intriguing for its discussion of the pornography debate in the feminist community, especially as it affects lesbians; the rescue of an elderly woman accused of murder is the backdrop for discussions of language theory, European history, and goddess worship in *Trouble in Transylvania* (1993), part of the Cassandra Reilly series.

Probably the most popular lesbian detective in mainstream detective fiction, Lauren Laurano from Sandra Scoppetone's *Everything You Have Is Mine* (1991), enjoys wordplay and wit and is embroiled in familiar detective concerns: helping out a friend with her professional services and looking for *missing persons. Her identity as a lesbian rarely is a strong factor in her work, but her marriage, her partner's gay brother, AIDS, and the gay and lesbian community they live in are important plot elements. Ellen Hart's series featuring Jane Lawless, a Minneapolis restaurateur, is also winning a mainstream audience, although it doesn't dodge issues and even depicts homophobic characters confronting Jane about her lifestyle in *Stage Fright* (1992) and in *Hallowed Murder* (1989). These novels' lightness of tone often makes the mayhem seem less threatening.

With Lindsay Gordon in *Report for Murder* (1987), Val McDermid explores the life of a lesbian journalist from Scotland; in *Union Jack* (1993) she writes about homophobia in the media while showing how the passage of ten years has changed it. Laurie R. King's *A Grave Talent* (1993) features Kate Martinelli, an inspector for the *San Francisco Police Department who is investigating a series of child murders while facing the problem of a closeted lesbian whose partner wants her to come out.

Other lesbian detectives have various reasons for becoming involved in crime: *Final Session* (1993) by Mary Morell features Lucia Ramos, a lesbian police officer who addresses issues of sexual abuse; Joanna Michaels's *Nun in the Closet* (1994) presents Callie Sinclair, an alcoholic, and the effects of abuse on adult survivors as well as the issue of lesbian nuns; Maria-Antonia Oliver's Lonia Guiu in *Antipodes* (1987), Claudia McKay's Lynn Evans in *The Kali Connection* (1994), and Diana McRae's Eliza Pirex in *All the Muscle You Need* (1988) investigate missing persons while pursuing love interests; Carole Spearin McCauley's bisexual Pauli Golden talks of being a "litmus test" for her lovers as she investigates the murder of one of them in *Cold Steal* (1991). Other writers presenting lesbian heroes or strong lesbian characters, some in international settings, include Elizabeth Bowers, Stella Duffy, Lisa Haddock, Randye London, Mary Logue, Elizabeth Peterzen, Rosie Scott, Carol Schmidt, Jean Taylor, and Pat Welch.

Several mainstream straight women detectives recognize lesbians in their communities, notably in Sara *Paretsky's *Killing Orders* (1985), Martina Navratilova and Liz Nickles's *The Total Zone* (1994), McDermid's Kate Brannigan series, and Patricia D.

Cornwell's *All That Remains* (1992) and *The Body Farm* (1994). In *Final Option* (1994), Gini Hartzmark depicts a character's lesbianism negatively, as evidence of her instability.

Lesbian detective fiction enables writers to engage in open and sympathetic political discussion of lesbian concerns and to depict lesbian romance as much as detection plots. Moreover, in this fiction, readers explore the implicit boundaries of mainstream life and the deceptions that keep them in place. In *The Case of the Not-So-Nice Nurse* (1991), for example, Mabel Maney reminds us just how compulsory the heterosexuality of the 1950s was, offering a vivid contrast to the sensitive exploration of self and sexuality possible today.

[*See also* Females and Feminists; Gay Characters and Perspectives; Rape and Other Sex Crimes; Sex and Sexuality.]

• Maureen T. Reddy, *Sisters in Crime: Feminism and the Crime Novel* (1988). Barbara Wilson, "My Work" in *Inversions: Writing by Dykes, Queers and Lesbians*, ed. Betsy Warland (1991). Kathleen Gregory Klein, *Great Women Mystery Writers Classic to Contemporary* (1994). Sally R. Munt, *Murder by the Book?: Feminism and the Crime Novel* (1994). Jean Swanson and Dean James, *By a Woman's Hand: A Guide to Mystery Fiction by Women* (1994).   —Georgia Rhoades

LETTERS AND WRITTEN MESSAGES. Ever since Edgar Allan *Poe wrote "The Purloined Letter" (*The Gift*, 1845), letters and written messages have played an important part in mystery stories and novels. Documentary *clues and *plot devices come in many forms, including wills, *ciphers, and codes, but crime writers have made especially ingenious and varied use of letters in developing their story lines. The letter form may even be integral to the structure of a mystery. An early example is Wilkie *Collins's "Brother Griffith's Story of the Biter Bit" (*The Queen of Hearts*, 1859), with its extracts from the correspondence of the *London police. "The Letters in Evidence" by C. S. Forester is skillfully composed, and Morris Hershman's "Letter to the Editor" (*Detective Story*, Sept. 1953) has a startling and effective climax. When Robert *Barnard turned to historical fiction and published *To Die like a Gentleman* (1993) under the name of Bernard Bastable, he made abundant use of confessional letters as well as secret diaries and third-person narrative, but the most remarkable novel to adopt the epistolary form is *The Documents in the Case* (1930) by Dorothy L. *Sayers writing in collaboration with Robert Eustace. Sayers admired the first-person narrative technique which Collins employed in *The Moonstone* (1868) and sought to adapt it to a mystery with a complex scientific theme. The design of the novel precluded the participation of Lord Peter *Wimsey, but the skillful way in which Sayers portrays the character of the letter writers through both their own eyes and those of others compensates for the absence of her series detective. *A Stranger in My Grave* (1960) by Margaret *Millar is notable in that each chapter of the book begins with a short first-person extract from a letter which is distinct from the main third-person narrative about Daisy Fielding Harker's "times of terror." It becomes

apparent that the letter was written by another character, but the revelation of the author's true identity at the end of the book still comes as a surprise.

In many short stories as well as full-length mystery novels, an urgent message initiates the action. Arthur Conan *Doyle's "The Adventure of Missing Three-Quarter" (*The Return of Sherlock Holmes*, 1905) opens with a brief and enigmatic telegram which puzzles even Sherlock *Holmes and leads him to investigate the disappearance of a famous rugby player. A summons from the millionaire Renauld at the start of *The Murder on the Links* (1923) by Agatha *Christie catches Hercule *Poirot's interest when he sees through the subterfuge implicit in a scrawled postscript. At the beginning of *The Tragedy of X* (1932), by Ellery *Queen writing as Barnaby Ross, an extract from Drury Lane's letter to the *New York district attorney claims that Lane has solved the problem of who killed John Cramer; a telegram in reply makes it clear that the culprit's confession substantiates Lane's deduction and asks for help with the Longstreet murder. Philip MacDonald's *R.I.P* (1933; *Menace*) is more conventional, opening with a series of menacing anonymous letters to Lady Destrier, while death threats to the actress Clarissa Lisle cause Cordelia *Gray to investigate in P. D. *James's *The Skull Beneath the Skin* (1982). Two novels published in 1990 in which suicide notes create an aura of mystery are noteworthy. The last message which Clara Stern leaves for her lawyer-husband Sandy in Scott Turow's *Burden of Proof* (1990) says simply: "Can you forgive me?" In *Bones and Silence* (1990) by Reginald *Hill, one of the *puzzles is to identify the woman who writes to superintendent Andrew Dalziel disclosing an intention to kill herself.

Practitioners of the classic form of detective novel, such as Christie, Sarah Caudwell, and Colin *Dexter, have made frequent use in their work of letters and written messages, but the devices can be found in the work of writers whose concerns extend beyond the creation of the baffling puzzles. Julian *Symons has highlighted the way in which two distinguished novelists from widely divergent backgrounds, Joseph Sheridan Le Fanu and Dashiell *Hammett, employed letters in a similar way in *Wylder's Hand* (1864) and *The Thin Man* (1934). In each case the letters are a means of creating uncertainty as to whether or not a character who has vanished but apparently remained in contact by correspondence is dead or alive. When a facsimile of a handwritten letter is printed in the text of a mystery novel, the author has the opportunity to play visual tricks or plant clues of an unusual kind, as in Christie's *Lord Edgware Dies* (1933; *Thirteen at Dinner*) and Dexter's *The Jewel That Was Ours* (1991).

Anonymous messages are a common ingredient of mystery fiction: In a typical *plot, a spate of *poison pen letters received within a closed community results in tensions which lead to murder. Christie's *The Moving Finger* (1942) shows how the application of simple psychology can reveal the culprit: The murderer was prepared to write an unpleasant letter to himself, but balked at the prospect of sending one to the girl he loved. *Avenging Angel* (1990) by Anthony Appiah offers a twist appropriate to a novel set in academia: The anonymous notes are in Latin. Cryptic messages from multiple murderers are found in novels as different as Cornell *Woolrich's *Rendezvous in Black* (1948) and Robert B. *Parker's *Crimson Joy* (1988) and contribute to the building of *suspense by indicating the disturbed mental state of the killers.

Mystery novels occasionally end with letters, typically from murderers confessing to their crimes. Such a device needs to be handled with care lest the truth be revealed in too heavy-handed a manner, but in Christie's *Why Didn't They Ask Evans?* (1934; *The Boomerang Clue*), for instance, the criminal's letter to Bobby Jones skillfully completes a lighthearted but ingenious story. Philip MacDonald's *Rynox* (1930; *The Rynox Mystery*; *The Rynox Murder Mystery*) is unusual in that the final letter reveals than an apparent murder was, in fact, a suicide contrived so as to facilitate an insurance fraud.

[*See also* Clues; Clues, Famous.]

• James Brabazon, *Dorothy L. Sayers* (1981). Tony Hilfer, *The Crime Novel: A Deviant Genre* (1990). Julian Symons, *Bloody Murder: From the Detective Story to the Crime Novel*, 3rd rev. ed. (1992). H. R. F. Keating, "Dorothy L's Mickey Finn," *Dorothy L. Sayers: The Centenary Celebration*, ed. Alzina Stone Dale (1993), p. 129–30. Barbara Reynolds, *Dorothy L. Sayers. Her Life and Soul* (1993).   —Martin Edwards

LIBRARY MILIEU. In his classic prescription for successful crime fiction, "The Guilty Vicarage" (*Harper's*, May 1948), W. H. Auden describes the desired *milieu as a closed society characterized by such *innocence that *murder will be a shocking violation of the usual state of grace. One milieu suiting Auden's prescription is the library. The quintessential harmlessness of the library underlines the horror of the murder and makes the ultimate return to a state of order all the more satisfying to readers.

Many authors who use the library milieu emphasize the calm, the quiet, and the sense of reverence for what Charles J. Dutton describes in *Murder in a Library* (1931) as the "glorious heritage of the world's life . . . all the beauty and intelligence which the mind of man has discovered during the entire history of civilization." Such of view of libraries leads Police Chief Rogan to complain early in the book, "Did you ever hear of a fool crime like this, in a library, a place filled with books . . . ? What under heavens is there in a library to bring a crime?" As though to underline the point, Agatha *Christie writes in the preface to *The Body in the Library* (1942): "The library in question must be a highly orthodox and conventional library. The body, on the other hand, must be a wildly improbable and highly sensational body." Christie places just such a body, clothed in tawdry satin, in Colonel Bantry's sedate library to create a *puzzle only Miss Jane *Marple can solve. Before the murderer is confronted in an eerie storage vault in *The Widening Stain* by W. Bolingbroke Johnson, (1942), the librarian remarks, "I like it here. It makes a nice solitary retreat for me, when I want to get away from all the to-do in the catalogue room. I even like the smell, so cool and musty. The smell of dead books." In *Murder in the Stacks* (1934), Marion M. Boyd demonstrates how such a setting becomes eerie

when she describes the light in a library as "a faint twilight singularly appropriate to these bound thoughts of writers many of whom were long since dead." Given the conditioned feelings about libraries, their architecture—the crypts, the domed reading rooms, the balconies and lonely stack areas, even the glass floors found between stack levels where a body can be seen from below—may become sinister.

A library also provides opportunity to employ exotic murder *weapons unique to the *setting. In *Death Walks in Marble Halls* (1951), by Lawrence Blochman, the *victim is stabbed with a brass catalogue drawer spindle. Jo Dereske repeats the use of the same weapon in *Miss Zukas and the Library Murders* (1994). The police are baffled by the use in murder of the blade of a large paper cutter in *Dewey Decimated* by Charles A. Goodrum (1977). Even the books in libraries can be deadly. Umberto Eco in *Il Nome Della Rosa* (1983; The Name of the Rose) kills off victims with an application to the pages of a rare book that unsuspecting readers ingest when they lick their fingers to help turn the pages. In *The Cruelest Month* by Hazel Holt (1991), a cataloguer at *Oxford's Bodleian Library is murdered by being brained with a heavy calf-bound volume of Horsley's *Britannia Romana*.

As Auden implies they should, the rituals and routines practiced in libraries represent order and harmony. One such convention is the classification scheme used to organize books. *Dewey Death* (1956) by Charity Blackstock features the interlibrary lending of microfilm as a means of illicit drug delivery. The title of each chapter uses the peculiar style of Melvil Dewey and is accompanied by a call number ("deth," for example, is 236.1). "Librarians," writes Blackstock, "worked in a world enmeshed in the decimal code. To them, enforced devotees of Mr. Dewey, . . . hell was not a fiery furnace; it was simply 237.5." The classification scheme is also the focus of a short story by Anthony Boucher, "QL 696. C9" (in *Ellery Queen's Mystery Magazine*, May 1943), which makes the murder victim a cataloguer who discovers a spy using library books to convey code. Her dying phrase, "L. C.," at first thought to mean "Elsie," instead explains her typed Library of Congress classification number that gives the story its title. The call number identifies books about birds in the swift family and also identifies Stella Swift, junior librarian, as the spy and murderer. Library rules figure as well in *Murder within Murder* (1946) by Frances and Richard Lockridge (1946). When Amelia Gipson is poisoned in the library where everyone knows you are forbidden from eating or drinking, what baffles the authorities is how the murderer could have administered poison.

Many library *plots revolve around the holdings in a collection. In those cases the crime may be *theft of valuable manuscripts or books. In *The Gutenberg Murders* (1931) by Gwen Bristow and Bruce Manning, the library collection includes a hundred-year-old French text of philosophy that has value to the murderer because of its inclusion of a recipe for burning victims to death by painting phosphorus on their clothing.

The unprepossessing library milieu also provides a

home for a rich assortment of characters useful to writers, ranging from the psychotic library patron who mutilates books and young women in Jonathan Valin's *Final Notice* (1980) to all the stereotypical "cranky old maids" and unsuitably sexy librarians, such as those in *Murder in a Library*, helpmates like Helen Marsh in Charlotte MacLeod's Peter Shandy series, and the almost magically skilled reference librarians like Miss Pierre, described as "a treasure" in J. S. Borthwick's *The Student Body* (1986).

Libraries may also be used by writers to help characterize their sleuths. Notable examples are Dorothy L. *Sayers's Lord Peter *Wimsey and Rex *Stout's Nero *Wolfe. Even Edgar Allan *Poe's Chevalier C. Auguste *Dupin is said to get by without superfluities, since books are his sole luxury.

• Jane Merrill Filstrup, "The Shattered Calm: Libraries in Detective Fiction," *Wilson Library Bulletin* (December 1978): 320–27; (January 1979): 392–98.
                                                          —Janet L. Potter

LININGTON, ELIZABETH (1921–1988), American author of some eighty novels, most written in the *police procedural, multi-storyline tradition. Born in Aurora, Illinois, she settled in California where, in addition to achieving her prolific output as a novelist under her own name and the pseudonyms Anne Blaisdell, Lesley Egan, Egan O'Neill, and Dell Shannon, she was a right-wing political activist, principally for the John Birch Society.

She is the author of three series. Her first, written as Dell Shannon, is her most long-running and successful, incorporating thirty-eight books published over twenty-seven years. It features Luis Mendoza of the *Los Angeles Police Department. When he was first introduced in *Case Pending* (1960), Mendoza was a relatively rare example of a Mexican American protagonist in this genre. His relationships with his fellow police officers and his personal life are developed throughout the series.

Under her own name, Linington created Sergeant Ivor Maddox and other members of the Hollywood Police Department in a thirteen-book series that also features the capable policewoman Sue Carstairs (later Maddox). Beginning with *Greenmask!* (1964) this series uses domestic detail and the details of the characters' romantic lives as a counterpoint to crime-solving. As Lesley Egan she created two occasionally overlapping series focusing on Jesse Falkenstein, a lawyer, and Vic Verallo, a policeman, and the crimes that each encounters.

Overall the moral imperative in this author's work is strong. There is a clear opposition of good and *evil and a marked sensitivity to the suffering endured by the *victims of crime. While she makes a deliberate effort to deglamorize police work and to deal with the realities of urban life, Linington's style is not a bluesy vernacular. In fact, even when dealing with the grimmest details, she exercises a kind of constraint (not to be confused with prudishness) that makes hers a memorable delivery of the details of police procedure.

[*See also* Police Detective; Urban Milieu.]

• Mary Jean DeMarr, "Elizabeth Linington," in *Great Woman Mystery Writers*, ed. Kathleen Gregory Klein (1994). Dove, George N., *The Police Procedural* (1982).
                                                          —Frankie Y. Bailey

LITERARY ALLUSION. *See* Allusion, Literary.

LITERARY CRITICISM. *See* Criticism, Literary.

LOCKED ROOM MYSTERY stories began with Edgar Allan *Poe's "The Murders in the Rue Morgue" (*Graham's Lady's and Gentleman's Magazine*, April 1841), in which the murderer had managed to leave a victim in a locked room, with the key still inside. This conundrum challenged the Chevalier C. Auguste *Dupin's considerable analytical powers and fired the imaginations of later writers. (Poe's solution bore similarities to a device used by Joseph Sheridan Le Fanu in an earlier story, albeit that Le Fanu's featured neither detective nor ratiocination). In April 1852, *Household Words* published Wilkie *Collins's "A Terribly Strange Bed", wherein the narrator locked himself into a gambling salon bedroom but still found his life threatened in a most diabolical fashion. It was a tale so appealing that it was often imitated. American Fitz-James O'Brien devised a different means of sealing a murder room in *The Diamond Lens and Other Stories* (1858), but it was Israel *Zangwill who applied new *ingenuity to the problem in *The Big Bow Mystery* (1892). His explanation was daring and original, with a simplicity that marked the best treatments. In "The Adventures of the Speckled Band" The (*Strand*, Feb. 1892), Arthur Conan *Doyle tackled his one genuine locked room puzzle.

Later writers vied to inject originality into the form. In "The Problem of Cell 13" (*Boston American*, Oct. 30 1905), Jacques *Futrelle set his detective, "the Thinking Machine," the task of escaping from a locked cell under police guard. The solution was a minor miracle of ordered complexity. In *The Mystery of the Yellow Room* (1908; *Murder in the Bedroom*) the Frenchman Gaston Leroux not only described a new and startlingly simple method for murder behind locked doors but also told the story in a sharply dramatic style that proved influential. Thomas W. Hanshew's Hamilton Cleek, "the Man of the Forty Faces," appeared in a long series of adventures, many of which featured locked room murders. The exclamatory writing was no better than most of the solutions, but Cleek displayed an attractive dynamism. In 1911 G. K. *Chesterton's Father *Brown met his first locked room problem in "The Wrong Shape" (*Storyteller*, Jan. 1911). The later "The Absence of Mr. Glass" (*London Pall Mall Magazine*, Mar. 1913), however, was more typical of Chesterton's style. Carolyn Wells wrote more than twenty sealed room novels, most of them involving Fleming Stone, with solutions as banal as the writing, starting with *A Chain of Evidence* (1912).

The short stories of Melville Davisson *Post and the novels of S. S. *Van Dine, both American, also were meritorious contributions to the tradition.

Post's Uncle Abner in *Uncle Abner: Master of Mysteries* (1918) solves two locked room tales, of which "The Doomdorf Mystery" (*Saturday Evening Post* 18, July 1914) has been much anthologized. Van Dine's detective, Philo *Vance, drawled his way through a dozen books; *The Canary Murder Case* (1927) was a most effective handling of the sealed room. Another American, John Dickson *Carr, made his debut with *It Walks by Night* (1930), which featured the Parisian *juge d'instruction* Henri Bencolin and concerned a decapitation in a room under constant observation. Neither the solution nor the detective was quite top flight, but the writing, conveying *atmosphere and a sense of the dramatic, was. Bencolin appeared in several more works, including one locked room mystery and as Carr, later Carter, Dickson, the author introduced and retired John Gaunt in *The Bowstring Murders* (1933). With Dr. Gideon *Fell in *Hags Nook* (1933) and Sir Henry *Merrivale in *The Plague Court Murders* (1934), Carr, writing as Carter Dickson, found detective characters suited to his flamboyant style of writing. Fell (who supposedly was based on Chesterton), and Merrivale (who contained a dash of Winston Churchill) were larger-than-life figures, eccentric, with distinctive speech and exceptional detective abilities. The thirties were a very fertile period for both of them. Fell moved on to snowbound *London for *The Three Coffins* (1935; *The Hollow Man*), his most illustrious case, during which he delivered his famous lecture on the art and science of locked room crimes. Merrivale, after two further successes, tackled *The Judas Window* (1938), in which he revealed in a gripping court room scene the secret of death by bowshot in a closed study. Carr's boundless ingenuity is exemplified in *He Wouldn't Kill Patience* (1944) as Carter Dickson; here the problem was complicated by the fact that the murder room was hermetically sealed. Carr continued to publish until 1972, when *The Hungry Goblin* appeared.

The Golden Age produced other locked room writers of quality. Ellery *Queen wrote three noteworthy tales of which *The Chinese Orange Mystery* (1934) contained a particularly fascinating gimmick, and Anthony *Boucher, as H. H. Holmes, was at his most inventive in *Nine Times Nine* (1940). Jonathan Latimer pitted private eye Bill Crane against three sealed room murderers, and fellow American Theodore Roscoe wrote two quite extraordinary books. Australian Max Afford's *The Dead Are Blind* (1937) was the cleverest of several clever books. The Great Merlini, Clayton Rawson's magician detective, made his bow in *Death from a Top Hat* (1938). Just as Rawson specialized in *solving impossible crimes, so did Hake Talbot in two books, the second of which, *Rim of the Pit* (1944), was one of the most ingenious and original. As time went by, tastes changed and the classic *puzzle lost ground to the *crime novel. Nevertheless, famous writers continued to create sealed room problems. John Russell Fearn, a Carr aficionado writing under several pseudonyms, constructed locked room mysteries for each of his detectives, including Adam Quirke, a scientist of the *future (in novels written as Volsted Gridban). The

Woman in the Wardrobe (1951), by Peter Antony, featured an eccentric cast of characters, none more so than detective Mr. Verity, and a new solution to the old problem. Science fantasist Randall Garrett devised an alternate universe for his detective, Lord Darcy, and in a series of novels and short stories beginning with *Too Many Magicians* (1967) provided rational explanations for apparently irrational problems. *Science fiction author John Sladek wrote two exceptional mysteries, *Black Aura* (1974) and *Invisible Green* (1977), in the classic tradition, and Bill Pronzini, in successfully combining locked room puzzles and *private eyes, as in *Hoodwink* (1981), almost performed the impossible himself. Joseph Commings, Arthur Porges, and the prolifically inventive Edward D. *Hoch continue to employ the locked room situation in the short story form.

• Robert C. S. Adey, *Locked Room Murders and Other Impossible Crimes: A Comprehensive Bibliography*, rev. ed. (1991). Roland Lacourbe. *99 chambers closes: Guide de lecture du crime impossible* (1991). Steve Lewis, "Locked Rooms and Other Improbable Crimes," *Detective Stories* (CADS), nos. 20–22 (Mar. 1993–Jan. 1994). Michel Soupart et al., *Chambres Closes, Crimes Impossibles* (1997).

—Robert C. S. Adey

LONDON. Celebrated in song and story since it was established as Londinium by the Romans in A.D. 43, London has long been a setting for a variety of fiction. Greater London today sprawls over eight hundred square miles; Gothic, classic, and Victorian buildings vie for space with contemporary steel and glass. Since Charles *Dickens created the first fictional police detective, Inspector Bucket, in *Bleak House* (1853), London's crowded streets as well as grand homes and lucrative businesses have served as a *setting for uncounted tales of *greed, vengeance, and despair in crime and mystery writing. In *The Woman in White* (1860) Wilkie *Collins recalls a familiar path in his description of Walter Hartright's moonlit walk from his mother's cottage in then suburban Hampstead and his encounter with the desperate woman in white. The personality of the city creates an *atmosphere that impregnates and shapes Dickens's final novel, the unfinished *The Mystery of Edwin Drood* (1870).

Victorian London is so much a part of the stories and novels of Arthur Conan *Doyle that it is almost impossible to think of Sherlock *Holmes without picturing gaslit streets and hearing the rattle of hansom cab wheels over cobblestones. The close association between London and crime and mystery writing in readers' imaginations is in part the result of Doyle's depiction of the minor details of daily life in the city throughout his fiction. A hansom cab is always at hand for the frenetic Holmes, urchins are eager to do his errands, and alleys and mews as well as mansions and boardinghouses vainly shelter criminals from the *Great Detective. Indeed, Dr. John H. *Watson's very first meeting with Holmes defines the detective as a thoroughly urban man; they meet in a laboratory in a wing of an urban hospital in *A Study in Scarlet* (*Beeton's Christmas Annual*, 1887). G. K. Chesterton plays on the anonymity of modern urban life in "The Blue Cross" (*Storyteller*, Sept. 1918) Aristide Valentin's chase through London after master criminal Flambeau and the little priest with him. E. W. *Hornung's *Raffles moves in upper-class society in *The Amateur Cracksman* (1899), a world that is still isolated and disdainful in Ngaio *Marsh's *Death in a White Tie* (1938), a story of *blackmail within London's most glamorous circles.

As the world changed, London changed, and fiction reflected this. Writers such as Agatha *Christie, Josephine Bell, Josephine *Tey, and Margery *Allingham explored other aspects of London in their work, describing a changing metropolis teeming with life and pulsating with hidden secrets. Dorothy L. *Sayers's Lord Peter *Wimsey, after suffering the horrors of the First World War, takes up residence and the remnants of his life at 110A Piccadilly, and investigates the charge of murder against Harriet *Vane, a resident of Bloomsbury, in *Strong Poison* (1930). His investigation leads him into the bohemian corner of urban life.

At times London is more than a rich *setting, becoming a character that leaves its imprint upon action and outcome alike. This is the case in Allingham's *The Tiger in the Smoke* (1952), set in the period immediately following World War II. The remains of the war are everywhere, creating a theme of confusion and temporality in life. The city is hidden, shrouded, and forbidding. The "smoke" of the title has a double meaning, referring both to the thick fog for which London has long been famous and to the city itself, a slang term for which is "the Smoke." In Christianna *Brand's *Fog of Doubt* (1943; *London Particular*) a thick London fog is the setting for murder.

The changing populations, neighborhoods, and social life of London have been documented by more recent writers as well. In Marian Babson's *Queue Here for Murder* (1980; *Line Up for Murder*), sweet, middle-aged Dorothy Witson records the changes in the metropolis from her vantage point on the sidewalk, where she is camped out in the hope of being among the first for the great New Year's sale at Bonnard's. The population around her is a reminder of Britain's colonial history and how far away that past is. *Christie explored precisely this theme earlier in *At Bertram's Hotel* (1965), when Miss Jane *Marple enjoys a visit to a *hotel that manages to cling to its Edwardian past while all around it foreign tourists and young Brits underscore how different the world is from then. Nor is London as a setting restricted to one period or one area. Anne Perry in such books as *The Cater Street Hangman* (1979), *Callander Square* (1980), and *Farriers' Lane* (1992) re-creates the terraces and squares of fashionable Victorian London as she reveals the evil that infects each level of society.

Writers rarely make an effort to disguise the city of London, so that readers of crime and mystery writing readily recognize references to and descriptions of Piccadilly Circus, the Inner and Middle Temples, Inns of Court, Somerset House, Trafalgar Square, Fleet Street, and many other locales. Holmes's Baker Street Irregulars are replaced by families of squatters; Hornung's glittering social world preyed on by Raffles gives way to the world of the theater where Simon Brett's Charles Paris struggles to hold onto his career. Through it all, the city remains, an eternal presence that alters the character and lives of its inhabitants.

[*See also* Addresses and Abodes, Famous; Urban Milieu.]

• Alzina Stone Dale and Barbara Sloan-Hendershott, *Mystery Reader's Walking Guide: London* (1987).

—Barbara Sloan-Hendershott

LONER, SLEUTH AS. There are several explanations for the established image of the fictional detective as loner. First and most obviously, the crime and detective fiction genre derives from the previously formed genre of the novel. A product of the post-Renaissance Western world, the novel gave importance to the texture of ordinary life and especially to the career of a singular protagonist as armature for the narrative in an approach resulting from modern conceptions of personality and modern interest in social mobility. When authors enclosed their criminal stories in the framework of the novel, they adopted not only the form but its cultural freight as well.

The convention of the detective as solitary figure is based as well in the special ethos and *virtues of the detective as they relate to the historical origin of modern crime control. Precursors of modern crime writers, the detective memoirists and thief takers, wrote up their cases as exploits of individual daring and skill because, of course, they had themselves as primary subject. Even after the foundation of official police forces, written accounts of detective work, like the periodical articles by Charles *Dickens, dramatized individual officers' defense of order against crime.

A wish to present the detective as heir to earlier social heroes was at work in this writing. The culture of the West conditioned its participants to interpret the *plot of experience as the encounter of individuals with resistance to their aims, and the plot of history as an account of the deeds performed by extraordinary persons. Faced with the complexity of an urbanizing society and rampant capitalism, an environment in which crime became an immense "problem," writers of the new detective fiction gave their readers revised stories of *heroism that crafted the developing techniques of criminal investigation and detection into the means for comforting resolution of crime.

As the emerging genre of detective fiction constructed the character of its heroic protagonist, a set of conventions resulted with a stress on the powers of the *Great Detective and a mode of description that set the detective off from the common run of humanity. These conventions, appearing first in Edgar Allan *Poe's portrait of the Chevalier C. Auguste *Dupin, mark all major detectives from the time of Sherlock *Holmes through the Golden Age. *Sleuths have been comic, foppish, garrulous, and gruff, but always they are presented as separate and special. The use of narrative point of view underscores uniqueness of character, whether in first-person narration by sidekicks such as Dr. John H. *Watson and Hercules *Poirot's chronicler John Hastings, or in third-person controlled narration that keeps readers at bay while the detective thinks his thoughts and drafts his theories for our wonder, as is most commonly the style of narration in the Golden Age; in each case, the narrative eye rarely leaves the detective.

Whereas in classic detective fiction the sleuth was set apart in a process of heroizing, hard-boiled writers used the device as a commentary on modern society, which they saw as endemically alienating. Because satisfying and close personal relationships were next to impossible, hard-boiled detectives were unmarried, never parents, and suspicious about sexuality. What is more, the world could not be repaired where there had been no order to begin with, so Dashiell *Hammett's Sam *Spade, Raymond *Chandler's Philip *Marlowe, and their countless descendants such as James Lee Burke's Dave Robicheaux necessarily existed in isolation.

A recent trend has been to reintegrate the detective into society. Fewer are neurotically disaffected; some like Julie Smith's Skip Langdon, Jane Langton's Homer Kelly, and Robert B. *Parker's *Spenser, have emotional relationships with companions. The techniques of narration, however—point of view, focus, characterization, and the disposition of detective plots to dramatize exploits as a contest of sleuth against criminals—continue to set the sleuths apart and to render their journeys to criminal solutions as lonely quests. The condition of loner is nothing less than a necessity of the literary form.

[See also: Characterization; Hard-Boiled Sleuth; Independent Sleuth; Milieu.]   —John M. Reilly

LOS ANGELES, with its glitz and glamor contrasting with gritty reality, has long been been a favored *setting for detective fiction. By the 1930s, some of the genre's best writers were at work describing the city *Black Mask magazine had labeled "the New Wild West."

Despite its attractions—or perhaps because of them—Los Angeles was not a safe place. *Violence came from nature in the form of earthquakes, fires, droughts, and harsh winds, and from humankind in acts of *theft, battery, and homicide. Hard-boiled writers, particularly, found it an ideal cityscape for their fiction.

James M. *Cain (The Postman Always Rings Twice, 1934) and the British novelist Eric M. Knight writing as Richard Hallas (You Play the Black and the Red Comes Up, 1938) were among those challenging the Hollywood-based fantasy that the area was a land of opportunity and renewal; their protagonists' dreams of sex and wealth turn into nightmares of tabloid violence. Raoul Whitfield's Death in a Bowl (1930) features a *private eye made cynical by a city that casually mixes tranquility with brutality. In Paul Cain's Fast One (1933), the locale is so lacking in *justice that the protagonist feels compelled to create his own destiny, however amoral.

Raymond *Chandler had been observing southern California for twenty years before writing about it. Narrated by private eye Philip *Marlowe, his novels take the reader on an informed tour of the territory in the depressed 1930s and the pre- and postwar 1940s, matching precise locales—a seedy bookstore on Hollywood Boulevard here, a Pasadena mansion there—to the action and the cast of characters. His descriptions are so detailed that even renamed locations are identifiable. In the early novels the author seems to have found a measure of solace in his surroundings—poetically recalling the scent of honeysuckle or the splendor of sunsets—but The Little Sister (1949) shows Marlowe bitterly denouncing the city as beyond hope. Most of Chandler's last completed novel, Playback (1958), occurs away from Los Angeles in the neighboring towns of San Diego and La Jolla (called Esmeralda in the novel), to which the writer himself had relocated.

By then, a number of other investigators had taken up residence in Angel City, chief among them Lew *Archer, the creation of Kenneth Millar writing as Ross *Macdonald, an author whose attention to place nearly matched Chandler's. His California was not a paradise where losers began afresh and lived happily ever after but rather a purgatory where the sins of generations past made future happiness doubtful. In early novels like The Moving Target (written as John Macdonald; 1949) and The Way Some People Die (written as John Ross Macdonald; 1951), Archer leads readers through the area's booming post–World War II years. In The Zebra-Striped Hearse (1962) and, especially, The Instant Enemy (1968), he sagely observes the generation gap and the drug-fueled aimlessness of Sunset Stripped youths. Later novels are concerned with misuse of the environment as typified by a devastating fire in The Underground Man (1971) and an offshore oil spill in Sleeping Beauty (1973).

The last several decades have seen changes in Los Angeles–based crime fiction. Joseph Wambaugh, a veteran of the Los Angeles Police Department, almost single-handedly reinvented the *police procedural with novels like The New Centurions (1971). The subgenre flourished in the 1980s, but waned in the 1990s, possibly because of well-publicized incidents (the Rodney King beating, the O. J. Simpson trial) that cast local lawmen in a less than heroic light. Meanwhile, Joseph *Hansen's homosexual insurance investigator Dave *Brandstetter was expanding the bounderies of detective fiction by exploring aspects of the city's gay life that could not have been hinted at in Chandler's day. Social injustices that occurred in the city's past come under examination in the novels of Walter *Mosley, creator of the *African American sleuth Ezekiel "Easy" *Rawlins. A Red Death (1991) recalls the communist witch hunts that destroyed many a Hollywood career in the 1950s; White Butterfly (1992), set in the city's Watts section in the year 1958, paints a vivid picture of the kind of racial persecution that would within a decade trigger rioting and open warfare against the police.

The unsolved 1947 "Black Dahlia" murder case has inspired at least two novels of note—John Gregory Dunne's True Confessions (1977), which also explores the city's Roman Catholic community, and James *Ellroy's The Black Dahlia (1987). The latter was the first of the four ultraviolent, elliptically written novels that make up Ellroy's "Los Angeles

Quarter," in which real people and incidents are grist for the author's anarchic imagination.

Today, many writers are ignoring major metropolitan areas in favor of smaller, less familiar locales. But the aforementioned and other novelists like Michael Connelly, Robert Crais, Jonathan Kellerman, Faye Kellerman and Gerald Petievich continue to keep southern California in the crime fiction mainstream.

[See also Historical Figures in Crime and Mystery Writing: Celebrities; Mean Streets Milieu; Urban Milieu.]

• Philip Durham, *Down These Mean Streets a Man Must Go: Raymond Chandler's Knight* (1963). David Madden, ed., *Tough Guy Writers of the Thirties* (1968). Peter Wolfe, *Dreamers Who Live Their Dreams: The World of Ross Macdonald's Novels* (1976). Ron Goulart, *The Dime Detectives* (1988). Mike Davis, *City of Quartz: Excavating the Future in Los Angeles* (1990).   —Dick Lochte

LOYALTY AND BETRAYAL. The commission of crime carries an implicit sense of betrayal. Whether as a violation of the trust of an individual or of the conventions of a society, acts of *murder, *theft, and *blackmail shatter normal patterns. The world becomes more uncertain, more untrustworthy. The ramifications of betrayal and the corresponding nuances of loyalty are popular themes for mystery writers.

Within the genre, writers have explored not only crime as betrayal, but also betrayal as a *motive for crime, the destructive power of loyalties, the psychological costs of divided loyalties, and justifications of allegiance. The works of Daphne *du Maurier, Graham *Greene, Julian *Symons, and P. D. *James, in particular, offer powerful reflections of these ideas. Du Maurier's *Rebecca* (1938) is a study of the destructive power of betrayal and misguided loyalty. Rebecca's treachery lies in her ability to create false appearances and in her inability to love others. Incapable of loyalty, she is the embodiment of deceit; her crimes are compounded by the loyalty she evokes in Mrs. Danvers. This misguided loyalty twists Danvers into an instrument of hate and destruction. Their legacy of betrayal taints all other characters forcing them all to become silent accomplices to crime.

For Symons, betrayal leads directly to crime. This theme is most evident in *Something Like a Love Affair* (1992). Judith Lassiter, an ordinary homemaker, is finally broken by a complex series of betrayals. As she is seduced by a cousin, abandoned by her family, married to a closet homosexual, her identity and connections to society are relentlessly unraveled by lies and the selfish pragmatism of those who claim to love her. Lassiter's public crime stands in ironic contrast to the private betrayal and duplicity she has endured. While only her crime is officially punishable, the others share culpability in their acts of betrayal.

The search for personal identity and the legacies of betrayal are central to James's novels. In *Innocent Blood* (1980) a young woman's search for her biological mother uncovers a pattern of abuse and isolation. She must finally form an identity based on the truth of her heritage. James's detectives, Cordelia *Gray and Commander *Dalgliesh, share a sense of isolation. Gray's is the most intense, a self-imposed exile based on her loyalty to her mentor, Bernie Pryde. Believing him to have been betrayed by *Scotland Yard, she pursues a private definition of *justice. Dalgliesh's isolation is defined in part by his status as a widower and in part by his introspective nature. His *pursuit of justice demands that he confront the disjunction between personal sympathies and ultimate loyalties.

Similar themes permeate the work of Greene. The fragility of faith and the ease of betrayal underscore the *plots of *A Gun for Sale* (1936; *This Gun for Hire*) and *The Ministry of Fear* (1943). In Greene's novels ordinary people may be caught up in international conspiracies; their only defense becomes their belief in goodness, in protecting the innocent from *evil. By maintaining small loyalties, they can stand against greater betrayals.

While not quite an ordinary character, Georgia Strangeways struggles with questions of loyalties and betrayals in Nicholas *Blake's *The Smiler with the Knife* (1939). To expose a political plot, she must lose her husband and friends and enter a world where all relationships are dangerous. She must rely on her wits and instincts for reading people to uncover a series of conspiracies. Blake is most critical of those who are more concerned about reputations than honesty, especially upper-class characters who hide behind secret societies rather than openly declare their loyalties.

John *le Carré presents a more cynical account of the struggle between small loyalties and political betrayals in his spy novels. The distinction between good and evil is less clear. In le Carré's world, *innocence has been sacrificed to political expediency. George Smiley is constantly aware of how little divides him from his enemies.

Abuse of power and impersonal regulations also raise questions of loyalty to police departments and political bureaucracies. In the novels of Margaret Truman and Patricia D. Cornwell, corrupt politicians create complications and even commit crimes to protect themselves. Robert B. *Parker's *Spenser is an ex-cop who operates best outside the system. John D. *MacDonald's Travis *McGee not only operates outside the law, he prefers to live outside the conventions of a society corrupted by commercialism and corporate *greed.

Arthur W. *Upfield's mixed race Australian, Napoleon *Bonaparte, is caught between societies. This tension is shared by Tony *Hillerman's Navajo police officers Jim *Chee and Joe Leaphorn, Chee recognizes the conflict between Navajo and Anglo justice systems and in *The Sacred Clowns* (1993) is forced to choose between them. He risks his career to retain his sense of identity and location in the world.

Other writers have used the personal loyalties of their detectives to comment on social values and mores. As noted in Jessica Mann's *Deadlier than the Male: An Investigation into Feminine Crime Writers* (1981), Dorothy L. *Sayers used the plot of *Gaudy Night* (1935) to present intellectual integrity as a virtue. Throughout the novel characters argue for the right of women to the intellectual life and support the suitability of that life. Harriet *Vane's actions as a detective are circumscribed by her loyalty to her college and women's rights. This theme is echoed in the works of Amanda *Cross and more humorously by Elizabeth Peters.

In the diverse arena of *clerical sleuths, questions of loyalty arise in relation to specific institutions and broader theologies. G. K. *Chesterton's Father *Brown pursued a justice defined by his faith, seeking more to restore souls than to mete out punishments. Following in his wake are Harry Kemelman's Rabbi David *Small, Kate Gallison's Mother Lannia Gray, and William X. Kienzle's Father Bob Koesler. These detectives may rely upon their faith in solving crimes but also find themselves at odds with church hierarchies and traditions. These conflicts provide the authors with opportunities to comment on faith, *gender roles, and abuse of power in a broader context.

[See also Friendship; Guilt.]

• Aaron Marc Stein, "The Mystery Story in Cultural Perspective," in The Mystery Story, ed. John Ball (1976). Ernest Mandell, Delightful Murder: A Social History of the Crime Story (1984). William David Spencer, Mysterium and Mystery: The Clerical Crime Novel (1989).   —Jan Blodgett

Lugg, Magersfontein. Created by Margery *Allingham, Magersfontein Lugg is Albert *Campion's unorthodox manservant and assistant in detection. Lugg's first name commemorates a British victory in the Boer War; his surname defines his work and hints at his lugubrious nature. Though a former cat burglar once sentenced to Borstal (a reform institution for youth), he now moves like a circus elephant and has a large white face. A Cockney with a rich, eccentric utterance, he is by turns a valet, heavy, underworld expert, and nanny. He has served as a bohemian butler and pig-keeping air-raid warden, faced near-death at the hands of the Kepesake murderer, and survived a pretentious spate of self-improvement when a peerage loomed for his employer. He is Campion's sense of humor.

[See also Sidekicks and Sleuthing Teams.]

—Susan Oleksiw

LULLABIES. See Music and Song; Titles and Titling.

Lupin, Arsène. A *gentleman thief created by French writer Maurice *Leblanc in the short story L'Arrestation d'Arsène Lupin (in the magazine Je sais tout, 1905), Arsène Lupin is the hero of fourteen novels and five collections of short stories as well as several plays and radio dramas by Maurice Leblanc (some of them in collaboration with other writers).

Born in 1874, Arsène Lupin is the son of Mademoiselle d'Andrésy and of Théophraste Lupin, a boxing teacher and crook who was jailed and who died in the United States. His vocation as a burglar begins early: At the age of six, he steals the famous Queen Marie-Antoinette necklace in order to avenge his mother for the humiliations inflicted by her family. In him the thief is always partly a dispenser of *justice.

Grown up, he practices burglary as an art, with gallantry. He attacks the rich, stealing their purses, their jewelry, their works of art, and sometimes their secrets, too, with inventive and virtuoso plans; he is also very keen to amuse the public, and never wastes an opportunity to have his feats celebrated in the press, or to duel with his adversaries: Herlock Sholmès, Isidore Beautrelet, l'Inspecteur Ganimard.

Lupin is also a consummate actor, able to juggle his many identifies: Horace Velmont, Don Luis Perenna, Prince Paul Sernine, Jim Barnett, or, more paradoxically, Victor Hautin, Inspecteur de la Brigade Mondaine, or Monsieur Lenormand, Chef de la Sûreté. Last, but not least, he is a great seducer and a great lover, terribly sentimental. Many of his adventures deal with historic secrets, such as the secret of the kings of France exposed in L'Aiguille creuse (1909; The Hollow Needle).

In the 1970s, Pierre Boileau and Thomas Narcejac imagined a continuation of Arsène Lupin's adventures in Le secret d'Eunerville and other works.

• Europe 604–605 (Aug.–Sept. 1979). Special issue on Arsène Lupin.   —Jacques Baudou

LUST. See Fiction Noir; Sex and Sexuality.

MACDONALD, JOHN D(ANN) (1916–1986), American writer, born in Sharon, Pennsylvania. His seventy-plus novels and over five hundred short stories range from "straight" novels, *science fiction, and fantasy to his preferred subject, crime.

MacDonald's career tracks one of the major developments in mid-twentieth-century American crime and mystery fiction. Beginning in the 1920s, when publications such as *Black Mask* began to present the innovative treatments of crime written by the hard-boiled school, *pulp magazines served as a venue of choice for authors of the naturalistic tales of private investigators in a tough world. Although the most successful among these writers often drew upon their pulp stories to craft full-length novels, the pages of the pulp magazines continued through the 1930s and 1940s to provide writers the space for experimentation and the opportunity for speedy publication. The growing popularity of paperback books changed that. In the 1950s, Fawcett Gold Medal and other imprints entered the market, peddling books written for original paperback publication, priced at a cost only slightly higher than the older pulps.

MacDonald became an established writer at that historic moment. Educated at Syracuse University, where he completed a B.S. in 1938, and Harvard University (M.B.A., 1939), he served with the Office of Strategic Services during World War II. Following the war, he wrote pseudonymously and under his own name for pulp magazines, but ended his apprenticeship with the publication of his first paperback original novel for Fawcett, *The Brass Cupcake* (1950).

His work culminated in the enormously popular Travis *McGee series, in which earlier themes, attitudes, concerns, and ideals find memorable expression. MacDonald excels at characterization, and much of the series's popularity stems from McGee's complexity: an unofficial *private eye, an honest *con man who swindles the swindlers. Leading a sybaritic existence aboard his houseboat *The Busted Flush* in Fort Lauderdale, Florida, he serves as a court of last resort for those who have been cheated by the wealthy and powerful, who seem beyond the reach of legality. Calling himself a "Salvage Consultant," McGee takes fifty percent of what he recovers.

MacDonald showed McGee's relationship to the rough hard-boiled detective tradition by depicting him as a man of great size, quickness, and strength who is a formidable opponent in a fight. His active sex life is viewed by author and character as therapeutic for McGee's female partners. It also involves considerable soul-searching, expressions of affection, and honest self-doubt. With his introspection and his preference for using his wits rather than his brawn whenever possible, McGee displays qualities similar to Ross *Macdonald's sleuth Lew *Archer and Robert B. *Parker's *Spenser.

McGee's economist friend Meyer, who lives on a nearby houseboat, occasionally becomes co-protagonist of the novels. Meyer's engaging personality, expertise in business and finance (reflecting McDonald's M.B.A.), professional contacts, and perceptive insights make him an ideal sidekick.

The McGee novels are serious, penetrating exposes and analyses (with sermonic asides by McGee) of important social issues. The abuses that lust for money and power may engender underlie all the plots, which explore subjects such as corruption in business and government, environmental depredation, the dissolution of purpose and meaning in modern life, and the vagaries of personal relationships.

Thematically and technically MacDonald did not discover new ground for detective fiction, but he did explore the established territory with a skill that helped to bring some matters to the forefront of popular consciousness. Starting with Junior Allen in the first McGee book, *The Deep Blue Goodbye* (1964), MacDonald portrayed the now chillingly familiar type, the sadistic psychopath. An even greater service is MacDonald's early and repeated commentary on environmental destruction. The nonseries book *A Flash of Green* (1962) describes efforts to save a bay from developers, while the McGee series extends environmental concern in passages such as the two-page, scientifically accurate lecture on the ways we have ravaged the Everglades (*Bright Orange for the Shroud*, 1965) and the account of harbor pollution in Pago Pago (*The Turquoise Lament*, 1973).

After two decades of producing paperback originals which, despite their great popularity, seldom were promoted or reviewed like mysteries in hardcover, MacDonald became a crossover author. The phenomenon of paperback originals had passed, but this stalwart author survived the loss and began to publish steadily with firms who issued his books as part of their preferred list of A-line mysteries, thus completing a career that epitomizes the fortunes of hard-boiled writing both in terms of the art of fiction and the currents of publishing history.

[*See also* Addresses and Abodes, Famous; Serial Killers and Mass Murderers; Sidekicks and Sleuthing Teams.]

• David Giherin, *John D. MacDonald* (1982). Edgar W. Hirshberg, *John D. MacDonald* (1985). —Donald C. Wall

MACDONALD PHILIP (1899–1981), British author of *detective novels, who also wrote as Martin Porlock, Oliver Fleming, and Anthony Lawless. After collaborating on two books with his father Ronald,

Philip MacDonald created Colonel Anthony Ruthven *Gethryn in *The Rasp* (1924). Gethryn was a conventional upper-class Englishman, but several novels in which he appeared, such as *The Choice* (1931; *The Polferry Riddle*, *The Polferry Mystery*), had *plots which were ingenious and extraordinary even by Golden Age standards. *Murder Gone Mad* (1931) and *X v. Rex* (1933; *Mystery of the Dead Police*, *The Mystery of Mr. X*, published under the name Martin Porlock in the United Kingdom) were fascinating nonseries novels. MacDonald moved to Hollywood in 1931 and he collaborated on the screenplay of *Rebecca* (1940). He also wrote short stories, three of which featured the seer-detective Dr. Alcazar. After a long absence, Gethryn returned in MacDonald's last novel, *The List of Adrian Messenger* (1959), an unorthodox mystery which became a gimmicky but entertaining film.

[*See also* Ingenuity.]

• Melvyn Barnes, "Philip MacDonald," in *St. James Guide to Crime and Mystery Writers*, 4th ed., ed. Jay P. Pederson (1996).   —Martin Edwards

MACDONALD, ROSS, is the pseudonym of Kenneth Millar (1915–1983), who is the Canadian-American author widely credited, along with Dashiell *Hammett and Raymond *Chandler, with elevating *hardboiled fiction to the status of literature.

"We never forgive our childhood. What makes a novelist is the inability to forget his childhood," Macdonald said in 1974. Poised uneasily between these imperatives, Macdonald's considerable body of work ponders at length the possibility and necessity of escaping an often terrifying past. So thoroughly do his fiction and life intertwine that consideration of Macdonald's writing properly begins with his origin.

Born in Los Gatos, California, Kenneth Millar spent his childhood scuttling across Canada, living on the charity of relatives with his impoverished mother. His father had abandoned them when the boy was three, in quest of a series of wild fantasies that he pursued until his death in 1932. Millar later recalled that he had lived in fifty different rooms by the age of sixteen. At six he was nearly placed in an orphanage, a narrow escape he would remember all his life. Yet the pain of these years fired his imagination: *Oliver Twist* was an early favorite of his, and Charles *Dickens's own difficult childhood furnished constant inspiration. He also took Dickens as his model of the democratic artist whom the critics respected but the masses could read. As an adult Millar reread F. Scott Fitzgerald's *The Great Gatsby* annually and repeatedly introduced Gatsbyesque figures into his novels, usually depicting them with a pained understanding that honors the quality of their dreaming but attends to the devastation they wreak.

He attended college on the proceeds from his father's dying bequest, then married and began graduate school at the University of Michigan, where he studied European literature under W. H. Auden. Encouraged by Auden's love of mysteries and by the quick success of his wife, Margaret *Millar, in the field, he turned out his first novel in only one month. Discharged from the navy in 1946, he settled in Santa Barbara, California, with his wife and began to write in earnest. His next three novels did not so much develop a voice as pay homage to Hammett and Graham *Greene, but flashes of incisive *characterization and sociological acuity hinted at what was to come.

With *The Moving Target* (1949) he began to explore his major themes. Published under the name "John Macdonald"—in memory of his father, John Macdonald Millar—it was the first novel to feature the private eye Lew *Archer. (After protest from John D. Macdonald, Millar wrote as John Ross Macdonald and, after 1956, Ross Macdonald, though his identity was revealed on the cover of *Find a Victim* (1954). For Macdonald nothing was clear-cut. As Archer explains in his first appearance, "Evil isn't so simple. Everybody has it in him, and whether it comes out in his actions depends on a number of things. Environment, opportunity, economic pressure, a piece of bad luck, a wrong friend."

Family tragedy stimulated Macdonald's art; further pain forced its maturity. Shattered by his daughter Linda's arrest for vehicular homicide as well as "seismic disturbances" rising from his past, in 1956 Macdonald suffered a breakdown and spent a year in psychoanalysis. Both of his succeeding novels, *The Doomsters* (1958) and *The Galton Case* (1959), probe tormented *families to discover roots of present trauma in the betrayal of children by parents and suggest that the worst *violence is that which individuals inflict on themselves. Archer becomes less interested in meting out justice than in simply listening to and understanding others.

In *The Galton Case* Macdonald rewrote his own youth along Oedipal lines: A young man who is stolen from his parents' estate and raised in poverty eventually regains his true birthright. Over the next decade he turned out a succession of classic novels that worked repeated variations on the theme of troubled children fleeing and coming to terms with damaging pasts. His *plots, generally of Byzantine complexity, drive down the mean streets of every subdivision in suburban southern California, sympathizing with both puzzled adults and angry children poisoned by "a kind of moral DDT" bequeathed by parents whose dreams have gone irrevocably sour. Concurrently, ecology and the ruin of the environment, which he had touched on as early as *The Drowning Pool* (1950), became a major theme in *The Underground Man* (1971) and *Sleeping Beauty* (1973).

From the first, Macdonald won the admiration of critics in the mystery field, particularly his longtime friend and supporter Anthony *Boucher. In the early sixties he began to attract academic attention. Paul Newman's *Harper* (1967), the film version of *The Moving Target* (which was released in England under the book title), made him wealthy, but the real break came in 1969, when the front page of the *New York Times Book Review*, carrying a review by Eudora Welty, proclaimed his work "the finest series of detective novels ever written by an American."

• Bernard Schopen, *Ross Macdonald* (1990). Matthew Bruccoli, *Ross Macdonald* (1984). Ralph B. Sipper, ed., *Ross Macdonald: Inward Journey* (1984).   —Jesse Berrett

Maigret, Inspector Jules, the creation of Georges *Simenon, quiet, plodding "mender of destinies" and *commissaire* of the Paris police. He appeared in more than seventy novels and over two dozen short stories. Maigret does not solve crimes by making logical deductions based on shrewd observation, but rather by his patience and ability to understand human nature. He is described as tall and bulky, but otherwise no details of his facial features are given.

Jules-Amédée-François Maigret was born in central France, near Moulins, his grandfather a tenant farmer. His mother died when he was eight years old. A few years later Maigret became a medical student at the Collège de Nantes but quit school on the death of his father. He joined the police force and rose in the ranks from bicycle patrolman to homicide detective. Such details are found in *La première enquête de Maigret* (1949; Maigret's First Case) and *Les mémoires de Maigret* (1951; Maigret's Memoirs).

Throughout the original French series Maigret is promoted in his profession, but the books were translated out of sequence and a reading in English in the original published sequence can be confusing. Different 1963 English translations of three 1931 titles render his title as inspector, chief inspector, and superintendent. In *Une confidence de Maigret* (1959; Maigret Has Doubts) he is a *commissaire*, or superintendent, while in *Maigret aux Assises* (1961; Maigret in Court) he has been promoted to *commissaire divisionnaire*, translated as divisional chief inspector.

His wife, Madame Louise Maigret, is introduced in the final chapter of the first book written, *Pietr-le-Letton* (1931; The Strange Case of Peter the Lett; Maigret and the Enigmatic Lett), and shares an apartment with him in the Boulevard Richard-Lenoir. It is to Madame Maigret that her husband imparts his thoughts on difficult cases; in later years their social group includes Dr. and Mrs. Pardon. That apartment and the office in the Quai des Orfèvres, with the office stove valiantly keeping off the chill, have become as familiar to readers as Baker Street. Maigret is seldom without his pipe and on his desk in his office he keeps a selection of several pipes. The pipe, his bowler hat, and his overcoat are recognizable to every follower of the series. Maigret's colleagues Coméliau, the examining magistrate, and his assistants Lucas, Janvier, and Lapointe comprise his official family. Another one of these assistants, Torrence, was killed in *Pietr-le-Letton* in 1931, but later resurrected because Simenon forgot the details of the earlier story.

The Maigret stories fall into two distinct groups: those published between 1931 and 1934, when he retires, and the remainder, in which he returns without reference to retirement, published between 1942 and 1972. For many readers, the earlier books filled with *atmosphere and character are superior to the rambling later ones. Others prefer the dark complex vision of the world in the later novels to the relatively simple, uncomplicated early period. By the final novel, *Maigret et Monsieur Charles* (1972; *Maigret and Monsieur Charles*) the *commissaire* is offered the position of head of the Police Judiciaire, but he is more interested in contemplating his real retirement.

[*See also* Addresses and Abodes, Famous; Europe, Crime and Mystery Writing in Continental: France and Belgium.]

• Thomas Narcejac, *Le cas "Simenon"* (1950; The Art of Simenon). John Raymond, *Simenon in Court* (1968). Julian Symons, "About Maigret and the Stolen Papers," in *Great Detectives: Seven Original Investigations* (1981). Fentons Bresler, *The Mystery of Georges Simenon: A Biography* (1983). Patrick Marnham, *The Man Who Wasn't Maigret: A Portrait of Georges Simenon* (1992).   —J. Randolph Cox

MALES AND THE MALE IMAGE. Despite the fact that the first full-length detective novel was the work of a woman—with Seeley *Regester and Anna Katharine *Green contending for the honor—the crime and mystery genre entered popular literature as an indisputably masculine type of writing. The *dime novels and penny dreadfuls that nurtured an audience for crime fiction were dedicated to action-adventure, and the numerous published memoirs of real-life detectives such as Allan Pinkerton recollected cases in which both culprits and *sleuths were typically male. Not only were they male in *gender, but the aggressive manner of the detectives and their assumption of the role of defender of the powerless expressed values associated with life in a man's world.

The literary refinement of the genre in the hands of Arthur Conan *Doyle, Arthur *Morrison, Arthur B. *Reeve, R. Austin *Freeman, and others who developed the image of the detective figure as practitioner of contemporary scientific detection did not diminish his masculine traits. In his confident mastery of technique and dauntless *pursuit of truth the detective remained in conformity with popular views of what it meant to be a male in society. To the extent that such authors elevated the detective figure to a place alongside frontiersmen, sea captains, soldiers, statesmen, industrialists, and other social heroes, the creation of the *Great Detective amounted to erection of another pedestaled statue in a male pantheon.

Since males are capable of variation and subtlety, after all, the male image lent itself to additional development during the Golden Age of the genre. E. C. *Bentley's Philip Trent, Agatha *Christie's Hercules *Poirot, Margery *Allingham's Albert *Campion, Ngaio *Marsh's Roderick *Alleyn, and S. S. *Van Dine's Philo *Vance are all men of superior intellect who have been conditioned by a superb education and a society in which complex rituals and manners control the tendencies it may harbor for offense and disturbance. In fact, that it is the point of the fictions in which they figure. The detectives are gentlemen protective of a gentle world. Regardless of their smoothness and facility, however, they are still male figures; whether the creations of female or male authors, they occupy positions available almost exclusively to males and exercise privileges of free movement that are denied to women of their time. Moreover, the fact remains that a strong figure dominates events, controls information by insistently providing its true interpretation, and returns a *family or other small social group to its normative condition of order. Thus *plots of detective fiction, even when they bear the impress of Golden Age manners, reveal their kinship to the fantasy life of males.

Dorothy L. *Sayers conducted a significant interrogation of the male image and plots of detective fiction when she introduced Harriet *Vane as a moral heroine who gains the heart of Lord Peter *Wimsey in *Strong Poison* (1930). As she developed their relationship in subsequent novels Sayers removed the male figure from his pedestal, and in doing so created a model for a type of detective fiction that could feature a loving couple as near equals who might be thought to make up an androgynous whole. Dashiell *Hammett's Nick and Nora *Charles (*The Thin Man*, 1934) and Frances and Richard Lockridge's Mr. and Mrs. *North (who first appeared in *The Norths Meet Murder*, 1940) have been the best known of these sleuth *couples, but the modification and balance the heterosexual couple introduces in place of an exclusively male, or for that matter exclusively female, center for detection has continuing vitality.

Genders are socially defined by their contrast to one another. In the realm of fiction, this has meant that male figures are represented by their difference from females, whereas oftentimes the purpose of female figures is simply to be "other" than male. This is generally the case in nineteenth-century and in Golden Age detective fiction. With the advent of hard-boiled writing, the latent meaning of the device becomes increasingly overt. Most hard-boiled characters operate in a world where women are either absent or secondary. Raymond *Chandler's Philip *Marlowe, however, is vulnerable to females whose sexuality and wiles pose a predatory threat. The male becomes an object of prey just because he is a male, and consequently the male image gains definition as a sexually embattled figure. Mickey *Spillane takes hold of implications in the characterization of Marlowe and turns his Mike *Hammer into a violent avenger who destroys females. The famous scene in Spillane's debut novel (*I, the Jury*, 1947) in which Hammer shoots the alluring female *villain in the stomach marks the eruption of a maleness that is not just different from femaleness but is actively malevolent toward it, the justification being self-defense.

The male image as presented by Spillane reappears in the work of other writers, but, then, so do variations on the male Great Detective and on the crime-solving couples of Sayers and those who followed in her footsteps. Important further developments include the treatment of male figures in *police procedural writing as ordinary cops who work as a team rather than acting as sole saviors and the introduction of intimacy and affection into the life of the male detective in such fiction as Robert B. *Parker's stories of *Spenser and Susan Silverman. This last development, along with a general softening of the hard-boiled image evident earlier in the fiction of Ross *Macdonald, and later in the work of Bill Pronzini and Lawrence *Block, can be seen as the natural accompaniment to the broadening audience and authorship of crime and mystery writing. Great numbers of women are writing stories about women and about men detectives, and the audience for this popular literature appears to have expanded to include thousands of female readers who seek the same entertainment from it as male readers—all of this signifies that the genre of crime and mystery writing is no longer a male preserve. The male image, like male detectives and male writers, has accommodated the healthy change.

[*See also* Adventurer and Adventuress; Chivalry, Code of; Gay Characters and Perspectives; Gentleman Adventurer; Gentleman Sleuth; Gentleman Thief; Heroism; Sex and Sexuality; Truth, Quest for.]
—John M. Reilly

MANDERLEY. *See* Addresses and Abodes Famous; Du Maurier, Daphne.

MANNERS, NOVEL OF. *See* Novel of Manners.

Marlowe, Philip. Raymond *Chandler's Philip Marlowe is one of the most persistently interesting detectives in the history of mystery literature. Arguably the most famous hard-boiled *private eye, Marlowe is thirty-three years old in *The Big Sleep* (1939), the first of his seven appearances, and forty-two nineteen years later in his last (*Playback*, 1958); in between he appears in *Farewell, My Lovely* (1940), *The High Window* (1942), *The Lady in the Lake* (1943), *The Little Sister* (1949), and *The Long Goodbye* (1954).

He is ruggedly attractive at just under 6'1" and 190 pounds, with brown hair and eyes; he has no siblings, his parents are dead, and he has no close living relatives. Born in 1906 in Santa Clara, California, he attended a state university in Oregon before drifting to southern California where he became an investigator, first for an insurance agency and then for the district attorney of *Los Angeles County, a position he lost for being insubordinate. At this point he went into business on his own.

In the hard-boiled private eye tradition that he helped to shape, Marlowe is single, talks tough, and delivers memorable wisecracks. He is celebrated for his deftness with figurative language, especially similes, as when he says in *The Big Sleep* (1939) of an enfeebled old man that "a few locks of dry hair clung to his scalp, like wild flowers fighting for life on a bare rock." If Marlowe too often overindulges his appetite for metaphor, this is consistent with his character: He smokes and drinks excessively too. His cigarette of choice is a Camel, which he fires up with kitchen matches snicked to life with his thumbnail, and he also smokes pipes in his more contemplative moods. Although he dislikes sweet drinks, he will eagerly and frequently—imbibe almost any other alcoholic beverage. He has the private eye's obligatory bottle in the office drawer and drinks from it alone or with clients; at home he is often a solitary drinker.

Marlowe's primary points of reference—his office and apartment—are predictably anonymous. His place of business occupies a room and a half on the sixth floor of an office building, and is furnished institutionally: a few chairs, a commercial calendar on the wall, a squeaky swivel chair behind a glass-top desk, and five green metal filing cabinets, "three of them full of California climate." He has no partner, secretary, or referral service, underscoring his independence, his professional marginality, and his rejection of middle-class values.

If Marlowe's office provides him with a link to the workaday world, such is seldom the case with his apartment. A sixth-floor efficiency, Marlowe's apartment complements his office and reflects the spareness of his existence; he has a radio, a few books and pictures, a chess set, and some old letters containing his memories. It may not be much, but it is a refuge from the tawdry, threatening world outside.

Although he has a network of professional associates, Marlowe has no friends; nor, until the end of his career, does he have a love interest. He entertains himself by listening to classical music, going to movies, and pondering chess problems. He is, in the tradition of American heroes, a loner.

Marlowe's modus operandi is pragmatic—he follows his nose, often bruising it and other parts of his anatomy in the process. He doesn't use snitches or hobnob with *underworld figures. He would never be mistaken for a ratiocinator like Sherlock *Holmes or Hercule *Poirot: although he moves about energetically, he observes, questions, listens, and waits for the truth to find him.

Marlowe's name is an amalgam of literary reference to Sir Philip Sidney, Christopher Marlowe, and the Marlow who occupies the moral center of several of Joseph Conrad's tales. Chandler originally intended to name his detective Mallory, alluding to Sir Thomas Malory whose chivalric romance, Le morte d'Arthur (1485), simultaneously dramatizes the heroic deeds of the Arthurian knights and portrays the less glamorous side of knighthood. Indeed, Marlowe is often a knightly hero. He places himself in the service of others; he is honest, brave, self-effacing, stoic, and witty in the face of danger; he resists temptations (except alcohol use) and constantly risks his life in pursuit of *justice and truth. His code is his character.

Marlowe is not perfect, to be sure. He harbors many of the *prejudices of his age, notably *racism and homophobia. Because he decries homosexuality yet is reluctant to sleep with women, it has been suggested that Marlowe is himself a homosexual. Perhaps in response, Chandler involved Marlowe in two casual sexual encounters in Playback and planned to marry him off in Poodle Springs, an unfinished novel.

It could be argued that Marlowe's character changed over time. Surely he developed a greater tolerance for *evil by the end of the series and became wearier and more disillusioned. Still, he is the best man in Chandler's world—"and a good enough man for any world," as Chandler puts it in "The Simple Art of Murder" (Atlantic Monthly, Dec. 1944).

[See also Chivalry, Code of; Hard-Boiled Sleuth; Independent Sleuth; Individualism; Loner, Sleuth as; Private Eye; Truth, Quest for; Voice: Hard-Boiled Voice; Voice: Wisecracking Voice.]

• Philip Durham, Down These Mean Streets a Man Must Go: Raymond Chandler's Knight (1963). Frank MacShane, The Life of Raymond Chandler (1976). Miriam Gross, ed., The World of Raymond Chandler (1977). Raymond Chandler, Selected Letters, ed. Frank MacShane (1981). Jerry Speir, Raymond Chandler (1981). William Marling, Raymond Chandler (1986).   —David Rife

Marple, Miss Jane, an *amateur detective and *genteel woman sleuth created by Agatha *Christie,

first appeared in short stories in the late 1920s. Christie did not perceive her as a rival to Hercule *Poirot, but in the end Miss Marple was featured in twelve novels and twenty stories. She became the quintessential detective of the *cozy mystery.

Introduced at sixty-five to seventy years old, Miss Marple could only live to a great age. In At Bertram's Hotel (1965) she looks a hundred and throughout the Canon her great age is stressed. Her hair is white, her face sweet, placid, pink, and crinkled; her china blue eyes appear innocent. She flutters and twitters, and her hands are often occupied with knitting. In her old-fashioned clothes she is every inch a lady. Indeed her childhood, apart from some education in Italy, was spent in a cathedral close. She has high-ranking and aristocratic relatives, and her circle of acquaintances is large. *Gardening is among her chief interests. She helps with Girl Guides and serves on an orphanage committee. Cultural pursuits are not important to her: In *London she prefers shopping to visiting galleries or museums, although she likes the outdated artists Charles-Blair Leighton and Sir Lawrence Alma-Tadema. Other than a preference for devotional books for late-night reading in bed and film magazines for research, she exhibits little interest in literature; she has a good literary background, however—she understands the significance of the John Webster quotation in Sleeping Murder (1976).

All in all, Miss Marple seems a very unlikely investigator of crime, but her background, appearance, and age are no handicap; instead, they camouflage her detective abilities and agile mind. Police officers who encounter her are amazed at her shrewd mind, adjectives used by Inspector Curry in They Do It with Mirrors (1952; Murder with Mirrors) and Inspector Neele in A Pocketful of Rye (1953), among others. Mr. Rafiel describes her as conscientious and as having a logical mind in A Caribbean Mystery (1964). Her friend Sir Henry Clithering, formerly of *Scotland Yard, marvels that her mind can plumb the depths of human iniquity, and do it merely as part of a day's work, in The Body in the Library (1942).

The secret of her success lies in her English village background, with its network of gossiping ladies and servants. St. Mary Mead seems to be a tranquil, conservative place—Marple's nephew Raymond West calls it a stagnant pool. His aunt, however, observes that nothing is so full of life under a microscope as a drop of water from a stagnant pool. Her years of observing village life, sometimes with binoculars, have thus given her an understanding of human nature and behavior on which to base deductions in her crime cases. She always believes the worst because she has seen so much *evil in villages. Her own hobbies, usually gardening, sometimes provide clues.

St. Mary Mead itself is the setting for crimes in three novels and many of the stories, but thanks to her network of friends and her nephew's generosity, Marple is able to travel and thus use her skills elsewhere. Strange locations do not intimidate her; she merely draws comparisons with people and situations she has previously encountered. In two cases she is forced to rely on information fed to her by associates, in 4:50 from Paddington (1957; What Mrs. McGillicuddy Saw!) and The Mirror Crack'd from Side *to Side* (1962; *The Mirror Crack'd*). In the latter book she is confined to her house because of old age and illness, and bitterly regrets her inability to tend her garden. When the book was published Christie herself was seventy-two and beginning to chafe against the constraints imposed by age. Yet despite her frailness, Marple went on to solve three more cases, even facing physical danger in *Nemesis* (1971).

[*See also* Addresses and Abodes, Famous; Conservative vs. Radical World View; Elderly Sleuth; English Village Milieu; Hotel Milieu; Spinster Sleuth; Whodunit.]

• Anne L. Hart, *The Life and Times of Miss Jane Marple* (1985).
—Christine R. Simpson

MARRIAGE, while portrayed in mystery and crime writing with great regularity, is more often than not peripheral to *plot. However, some writers give center stage to marriage and its attendant difficulties, complications, or benefits.

In Arthur Conan *Doyle's short story "The Adventure of the Dancing Men" (*Strand*, Dec. 1903), for instance, the plot focuses on a troubled husband who has promised never to inquire into his wife's past but who is driven to seek Sherlock *Holmes's help in the matter of puzzling messages left in his home. For this desperate husband, marriage culminates in tragedy. Doyle's intent is not to probe the nature of marriage, however, but rather to investigate the mystery associated with the wife's unusual request.

In contrast, F. Tennyson Jesse in *A Pin to See the Peepshow* (1934) uses marriage to comment directly on the position of women, on the *class system, and on the social mores of England. The novel is a biting indictment of marriage, suggesting that it drains energies, cripples spirits, and creates a virtual imprisonment for middle-class women in the early decades of the twentieth century. For women seeking escape from such restraint, rebellion can even prove fatal.

Dorothy L. *Sayer's *Gaudy Night* (1935) explores similar, questions regarding marriage and women's role in society. But whereas both *Gaudy Night* and *A Pin to See the Peep Show* examine in detail the complexities of the human heart and mind and the potentially devastating effects of marriage, Sayers's novel is much more positive about the possibility for happiness within marriage for both men and women.

Andrew *Garve's *No Tears for Hilda* (1950) depicts the worst of wives as a portrait of a monstrous woman emerges through the dogged persistence of her husband's friend, who sets out to find the wife's murderer and to exonerate the husband. The eponymous character turns out to have been an indifferent homemaker, a lousy mother, and a manipulative and vicious woman. A telling aspect of this novel is the implied commentary on the way in which a wife's insidious effects on everyone around her can somehow escape the attention of her husband.

An example of the way in which marriage is treated in a *private eye novel is William Campbell *Gault's *Come Die with Me* (1959). This novel begins when the wife of a jockey asks *private detective Brock "the Rock" Callahan to investigate her husband's connection with a notorious hoodlum. When Brock sets out to find the person who murders the

jockey, he has ample opportunity to comment on relationships, marital or otherwise, including his own love affair with a woman who will not marry him because of his profession.

An ingenious treatment of the theme of marriage occurs in Sheila Radley's *A Talent for Destruction* (1982). In this novel, the villain, a stunningly beautiful young woman who derives pleasure from destroying stable marriages, operates on the premise that marriage is a process of mutual destruction. While the young woman's deadly manipulation of a dangerously possessive rector and his naive wife leads to disaster, the couple remain steadfastly supportive of one another and emerge with their marriage intact.

As society in general has become more knowledgeable about and sensitive to the nature and extent of domestic *violence, some writers have begun to explore the problem in their fiction. A good example is Nancy Pickard's *Marriage Is Murder* (1987), which highlights the horrors of domestic violence by centering on a series of murders of husbands who have been physically and emotionally abusive. An interesting twist is that the protagonist herself is about to be married to a policeman investigating the murders.

Unhappiness in marriage provides the basis of many plots, as in Julian *Symons's *Something Like a Love Affair* (1992), which finds a childless couple entering their fifteenth year of marriage with serious problems lying beneath an apparently calm surface. While the husband engages in secretive homosexual encounters, the wife has an affair with a man fifteen years her junior, hires a hit man to kill her husband, and ends up committing murder herself.

The treatment of marriage has necessarily altered over time as attitudes toward women, men, and their roles in society have changed. But the theme itself remains a constant, recurring with regularity in a variety of ways that comment on crime and on society.

[*See also* Couples; Family; Femme Fatale; Friendship; Loyalty and Betrayal.]

—Katherine Anne Ackley

MARRIC, J. J. *See* Creasey, John.

MARSH, (EDITH) NGAIO (1895–1982), New Zealand author and theater director; one of the "Queens of Crime" in the British Golden Age. She established herself firmly in the classical tradition of the English *detective novel with her first book, *A Man Lay Dead* (1934), written during her first visit to England. Trained as a painter at Canterbury College School of Art in Christchurch, where she was born, she continued to paint and sketch all her life, but by the 1930s she had begun to realize that her greatest talent lay with words, not in paint.

Her background was not wealthy (her English-born father was a bank clerk), but her parents valued education and the arts and as an only child her talents were cherished. From her mother came a great love of the theater, and the whole family were enthusiastic amateur actors. Marsh went on to become a formative influence on the development of theater in New Zealand, and it is for this work, not for her writing, that she is best remembered in New Zealand today.

Marsh claimed that her first novel was swiftly

written in imitation of existing popular styles, but she soon began to develop an individual approach which was very much character-led: "I invariably start with people. . . . I must involve one of them in a crime of violence. . . . I have to ask myself which of these persons is capable to such a crime, what form it would take and under what circumstances would he or she commit it." By carefully building and defining her characters, she attained high praise in the United States in the 1940s for the psychological depth of her fiction. As with all crime writers who focus on *characterization rather than relying on intricate turns of the *plot to hold the reader, Marsh was sometimes in danger of conflicting with the accepted restrictions of the genre, and of reluctantly introducing tidy solutions which jar with the complexity of her created world.

She increasingly found her life divided between two very different spheres of operation. At home in New Zealand she would lock herself away to write her novels, then work with huge energy to produce plays by William *Shakespeare with young actors from Canterbury University College. On her regular visits to England, always traveling by ocean liner, she would stay with her aristocratic English friends who lived in country houses in the Home Counties or in fashionable flats in London. Somewhat to her surprise Marsh found herself feted in the United States (she made one visit in 1962) and in England as a detective novelist. She had been awarded the OBE in 1948, and in 1966 was created Dame Commander of the British Empire (in her words, "her damery").

The services of Inspector Roderick *Alleyn, Marsh's series detective, are retained throughout all thirty-two novels—"I've never got tired of the old boy," she said—and the author passes on to him her love of theater and an ability to quote Shakespeare. Whether there is wish fulfillment in creating his wife Agatha Troy as a painter is hard to say, but Marsh herself retained her independence and never married, remaining a private person all her life who seldom revealed her feelings to any but her very close friends.

The novels of Marsh fall naturally into four thematic categories, but even these overlap slightly. Many are set in comfortable country houses in small English villages not far from London: *Death and the Dancing Footman* (1941), one of her most popular books, is an example. Some deal with the world of the theater; Marsh had a particularly acute ear for the repartee of actors, revealing both their pretensions and their insecurities, as in *Killer Dolphin* (1966; *Death at the Dolphin*). The role of Troy dictates the plot in several novels, where commissions to paint famous people such as the African politician in *Black as He's Painted* (1974) can unexpectedly lead to the involvement of Alleyn in solving a violent crime. Finally, Marsh's love for the landscape of New Zealand emerges strongly in the four novels set in her native country, but undoubtedly the most ingenious is *Colour Scheme*, written in 1943, which uses a boiling mud pool as a murder weapon.

The achievement of Marsh will always be associated with the elegance of her writing, her wit, and her painterly ability to evoke a scene. Admired during her lifetime for her skill at extending the confines of the classical form without losing its definition, she is appreciated by a new generation who respond to her sharp observation of social structures and the freshness of her invention.

[*See also* Allusion, Literary; English Village Milieu; New Zealand: Crime and Mystery Writing in; Theatrical Milieu: Legitimate Theatre, Amateur Theatre, and Touring Companies; Violence; Weapons, Unusual Murder; Whodunit.]

• Ngaio Marsh, *Black Beech and Honeydew: An Autobiography* (1965). Margaret Lewis, *Ngaio Marsh: A Life* (1991).

—Margaret Lewis

MASON, A(LFRED) E(DWARD) W(OODLEY) (1865–1948), British author of detective, historical, and adventure novels, short mystery and espionage fiction, crime and courtroom drama. London-born, Oxford-educated, Mason began his career as an actor and playwright. His experiences as a Liberal Party member of Parliament for Coventry (1906–10) and an operative in British naval intelligence during World War I resulted in a political novel, *The Turnstile* (1912), and short stories of espionage. His best-selling work was a nonmystery, *The Four Feathers* (1902), and he also wrote a biography of Francis Drake and a stage history. His best-known character, *Sûreté Inspector *Hanaud, debuted in *At the Villa Rose* (1910). In the tradition of Wilkie *Collins, Mason employs varying points of view, especially those of the innocent and threatened, to inspire fear. He deromanticizes the detective, draws characters from his experience, and never repeats his ingenious *plots.

[*See also* Adventure Story; Police Detective; Police Procedural; Spy Fiction.]

• Roger Lancelyn Green, *A. E. W. Mason* (1952). Barrie Hayne, "A. E. W. Mason," in *Twelve Englishmen of Mystery*, ed. Earl F. Bargainnier (1984).   —Michael Cohen

Mason, Perry, lawyer-detective hero in extremely popular novels by Erle Stanley *Gardner. He first appeared in *The Case of the Velvet Claws* (1933), which was followed by eighty-five other novels (five of them published posthumously), a number of short stories, and two authorized novels by Thomas Chastain published in 1989 and 1990. The continued popularity of his exploits was doubtless enhanced by eight films in the 1930s, a radio program in the 1940s, and especially the popular television series, starring Raymond Burr, which played for nine seasons (1957–66) and lives on in reruns. The series was reprised in twenty-six television movies that appeared at irregular intervals from 1985 until Burr's death in 1993.

The novels are simply written (most of them dictated) and contain a good deal of dialogue. While they all adhere to the same *formula, they are fast-moving, often with extremely complicated *plots and a number of surprises along the way. Mason practices law in *Los Angeles, where he is assisted by his able and attractive secretary, Della Street, and Paul Drake, the head of a detective agency. Perry typically uses a number of quasi-legal tricks to protect his clients or establish their *innocence, often moving them around from one address to another to escape the police, to the constant annoyance of Lieutenant Tragg of the Los Angeles Police Department. Drake and Street are constantly warning Perry Mason that he is "skating on thin ice," but he is not deterred. He maintains that his tactics are within the letter if not the spirit of the law, and they change as the law of the land changes. It is in the courtroom, however, when his client stands trial, that Perry proves his or her innocence after a display of legal pyrotechnics that exasperates the district attorney, Hamilton Burger, and trips up the killer on the witness stand.

[See also Courtroom Milieu; Judge; Jury; Justice; Legal Procedural; Sidekicks and Sleuthing Teams.]

—Henry Kratz

MASTER CRIMINAL. The threatening figure of the master criminal, or the criminal mastermind, has been prominent in crime writing since the late nineteenth century, often embodying the motiveless principle of *evil which the virtuous protagonist has to combat and to overcome. In more simple allegoric forms, the master criminal is evil incarnate, and his confrontation with the hero represents a stylized form of the constant fight between the forces of good and evil in the world—witness the conflict between Superman and Lex Luthor, or between Batman and the Joker, the Penguin, and Catwoman, or between James *Bond and Ernst Stavro Blofeld. These quasi-allegoric forms retain a residual presence in a great deal of crime and spy writing—the evil in the Erskine *Childers's The Riddle of the Sands (1903) or in John *Buchan's stories may be conspiratorial rather than individualized, but there is always the sense of some unidentified and invisible hand orchestrating the mayhem. However, in the more strictly generic forms of crime writing, the master criminal may share similarities with the hero, whatever his differences with the readership, as he so clearly does in Fantômas (1911) by Pierre Souvestre and Marcel Allain.

In the Sherlock *Holmes stories, the *Great Detective faces a number of powerful adversaries, including Irene *Adler and Charles Augustus Milverton, but his archenemy is the evil Professor James *Moriarty, "the Napoleon of crime." Author of a brilliant treatise on the binomial theorem at the age of twenty-one, and renowned throughout Europe as a mathematician, the ex-Professor Moriarty has devilish cunning and an insatiable appetite for evil, but it is suggested that he is at least a worthy opponent for the equally gifted detective, and at the moment of Holmes's death at the Reichenbach Falls, described in "The Final Problem" (Strand, Dec. 1893), he is symbolically entangled with his greatest adversary. No less brilliant than Moriarty, Holmes's intelligence is at the service of *justice where his opposite number's does tremendous harm by stealth, and the conflict between the two extravagantly gifted figures greatly intensifies the drama of the tales.

Holmes and Moriarty may be equals in their gifts, but later versions of the master criminal do not put him alongside a commensurate adversary. In the highly melodramatic *Fu Manchu tales by Sax Rohmer (pseudonym of Arthur Sarsfield Ward), written between 1913 and 1959, the evil mastermind has diabolical plans to rule the world, and his opponents are at first no more (and no less) than fairly ordinary citizens, personified by the dogged Nayland Smith, the Burmese commissioner. In his earliest appearances, Fu Manchu represents the "yellow peril," the xenophobically constructed Oriental plot to conquer the West. In later appearances, he changes sides, if not colors, and takes on the fight against the "red menace" of Communist China, proving himself even wilier than before, as well as versatile in his capacity to create or allay anxieties. The Fu Manchu stories are extremely lurid and sadistic, as well as shoddily written, and it is hard to take them seriously now.

Two other variants on the theme of the master criminal need to be mentioned. In Ed *McBain's Eighty-seventh Precinct series of *police procedurals, the carefully crafted urban realism is suspended in some stories by the appearance of an arch-villain called "the Deaf Man." This character haunts the life of Steve Carella and his fellow cops by committing the most awful crimes and disappearing without a trace. He makes his first appearance in The Heckler (1960), and reappears in Fuzz (1968) and in Let's Hear it for the Deaf Man (1973). His longevity and continuing vitality are on display in Mischief (1993), in which he orchestrates a particularly violent *caper. The use of this master criminal seems incongruous in McBain's otherwise scrupulously realistic technique, but the enigmatic nature of the central character makes it surprisingly successful.

The final version of the master criminal comes from the notion of organized crime. In many stories about the Mafia, or Cosa Nostra, individual figures are brought to the fore as the principal custodians of evil in contemporary society. The best example of this is the patriarchal Don Corleone in Mario Puzo's The Godfather (1969), who presides over his own criminal empire. Puzo's novel is profoundly ironic, in that it paints Corleone as both the master criminal and the most responsible of citizens, representing a belief in family and in loyalty which lie at the heart of American ideology. Corleone does not exhibit the diabolical ingenuity of Moriarty, the grotesqueness of Fu Manchu, or the motiveless malignity of the Deaf Man, but in his stealthy organization of society around his criminal aims, he stands for the most modern and plausible version of the master criminal.

[See also Deviance; Spy Fiction; Underworld Figure; Villains and Villainy.]

—Ian Bell

MATSUMOTO SEICHŌ, pseudonym of Matsumoto Kiyoharu (1909–1992), Japanese novelist. Born to working-class parents in Kokura city on the island of Kyūshū, Seichō worked odd jobs after finishing middle school; during and after World War II, he designed advertisements for the Asahi newspaper. His literary career blossomed only in 1952, when his "Aru Kokura nikki den" (1952; A Story of the Kokura Diary) won the prestigious Akutagawa Prize. By the mid-1950s he had turned to crime literature, rejecting what he called the "haunted-house" contrivances of prewar Japanese mysteries in favor of the painstaking study of *motive and, above all, the critical portrayal of contemporary society. In his typical 1957 best-seller *Ten to sen* (*Points and Lines*, 1970), detectives break the alibis of a businessman and a powerful bureaucrat whose scheme to conceal a bribery scandal involves killing an ordinary waitress. Seichō's injection of anti-establishment consciousness into the *crime novel won it unprecedented popularity with the general reader in Japan. Besides his dozens of mysteries, he wrote historical fiction, *science fiction, history, and criticism. *Suna no utsuwa* (1960-61) has been translated as *Inspector Imanishi Investigates* (1989). *The Voice and Other Stories* (1989) contains some of his shorter fiction.

[*See also* Japan, Crime and Mystery Writing in; Political and Social Views, Authors'.]

• Gorda Manji, "Crime Fiction with a Social Conscience," *Japan Quarterly* (Apr.–June 1993). —Mark Silver

MAYHEM PARVA is a term coined by Colin *Watson in *Snobbery with Violence* (1971) for a subgenre of the mystery characterized by semi-isolated *settings epitomized by the English country village. In such a setting the predictable is the norm, at least until *murder occurs in the midst of a limited cast of characters who generally take a back seat to the *puzzle being presented. The denizens of Mayhem Parva generally hold ordered and conservative world views, and share a pervasive sense of law, *justice, and morality, which may or may not correspond to the morality of the world at large, but which, in the context of the story, allows for a tidy ending. Mysteries that belong to the Mayhem Parva subgenre play fair with the reader and represent the beginning of the *cozy or malice domestic mystery. For much of the Golden Age of mystery fiction they occupied center stage.

Some critics have maligned the Mayhem Parva subgenre as unrealistic and characterless. Such critics view the characters as little more than cardboard cutouts placed in a story to see the puzzle through to its end, a view taken by Julian *Symons in *Bloody Murder: From the Detective Story to the Crime Novel* (1972; *Mortal Consequences: A History from the Detective Story to the Crime Novel*). Watson, however, points out that stories of the Mayhem Parva subgenre must be considered on their own. "To characterize the fiction of the Mayhem Parva school as 'two dimensional' is not to question its adequacy as entertainment. It could not have offered what it did . . . if it had possessed that third dimension which gives a story power to affect the reader in much the same way as actual experience." Robert *Barnard, in *A Talent to Deceive* (1980), adds, "It is in many ways an unrealistic, stylized world. . . . But *cozy*, safe, ordered? Only on the surface."

Perhaps the most important practitioner of this subgenre was Agatha *Christie. Particularly in Christie's mysteries with Miss Jane *Marple investigating crimes in the English village, the subgenre receives its fullest treatment. These mysteries are populated by characters who are types: the retired colonel of the Indian army, the vicar, the baronet, the slightly easy and uncultured secretary or serving girl. In a parody called "Holocaust at Mayhem Parva" (*A

Classic English Mystery, ed. Tim Heald, 1990), Symons names his characters after those found in the popular board games Clue and Cluedo.

Regardless of how some critics might view the subgenre, some mysteries of the Mayhem Parva school have become classics in the field of mystery fiction, for example A. A. Milne's *The Red House Mystery* (1922), many of the works of Christie, the Sir Henry *Merrivale mysteries of John Dickson *Carr, and Ngaio *Marsh's *The Crime at Black Dudley* (1929; *The Black Dudley Murder*).

Many of today's cozier mysteries published on both sides of the Atlantic are direct descendants of the Mayhem Parva school. Writers such as Charlotte MacLeod, Carolyn G. Hart, Katherine Hall Page, Deborah Adams, and Dorothy Cannell owe a good deal of the *atmosphere and structure of their novels to the work of the early Mayhem Parva school. Other writers have composed individual works that reflect a Mayhem Parva heritage. For instance, there is more than a bit of the Mayhem Parva spirit displayed in Barnard's *Disposal of the Living* (1985; *Fete Fatale*) and *Sheer Torture* (1981; *Death by Sheer Torture*).

[*See also* Conservative vs. Radical Worldview: Conservative Worldview; English Village Milieu; Whodunit.] —Steven Riddle

Mayo, Asey, protagonist in a series of twenty-four books published between 1931 and 1951, and an archetypal American *amateur detective. A scion of Mayflower stock, Mayo lives on Cape Cod in Wellfleet, Massachusetts, where his creator Phoebe Atwood *Taylor maintained a summer cottage. A jack of all trades—mechanic, carpenter, and seafaring man of the world—he relies on common sense and Yankee *ingenuity to solve cases that are masterpieces of comic mystery. His personal history is ambiguous, since he seems to have engaged in secret work during World War I but once claimed to have spent the war years peeling potatoes. It is known, however, that he went to sea at age eight; sailed on the last of the clipper ships; drove a Porter automobile coast to coast in 1899; and tested racing cars at Daytona Beach in 1904. During a brief stint as police constable in Wellfleet he solved two *murders, but decided to quit while he was ahead—a typical Taylor irony, given his subsequent career as a famous *sleuth, frequently pictured in rotogravures and labeled the "Codfish Sherlock." Of indeterminate age, he is described as tall, thin, tough, tanned, and rugged, with twinkling blue eyes. Dressed in corduroys, a flannel shirt, and either a Stetson or a yachting cap, he is comfortable in any company.

—Mary Helen Becker

MCBAIN, ED (b. 1926), pseudonym of Evan Hunter, American author of *police procedurals and other crime fiction. Although he maintains "The city in these pages is imaginary," he has used *New York City, where he was born, raised, and educated, as a model *setting for the forty-plus novels in his Eighty-seventh Precinct series. Another series featuring lawyer Matthew Hope is set in Florida. After writing for *pulp magazines he achieved success with *The

Blackboard Jungle (1954), based in part upon his experiences teaching in a Bronx high school. Under his legal name of Evan Hunter he has written sixteen more novels and screenplays. He has been named a Grand Master by the *Mystery Writers of America.

Cop Hater (1956) was his first police procedural. Although he was determined to have as his hero the entire detective squad, Steve Carella quickly emerged as the chief player in McBain's ensemble approach to character and action. Other mainstays include Lieutenant Peter Byrnes, Meyer Meyer, Cotton Hawes, Bert Kling, Arthur Brown, Andy Parker, Hal Willis, and Eileen Burke.

Carella confronts many villains but has one nemesis as sinister and as indestructible as Sherlock *Holmes's Professor James *Moriarty: the Deaf Man, who appears in several books.

McBain says he conceives of each Eighty-seventh Precinct novel as a chapter in one long book. He plans for these chapters to appear even after his own death.

Despite detours into political satire in *Hail to the Chief* (1973) and the supernatural in *Ghosts* (1980), McBain concentrates on the day-to-day operation of the justice system. A stickler about the details of police work, he often lightens descriptions of routine with touches of *humor. He learned the routine by visiting station houses, jails, and labs and continues to keep current on procedures and forensic science. For example, his detectives no longer attend lineups. Sam Grossman, head of the police lab, usually explains scientific advances during telephone conversations with Carella.

About half the novels have a single dominant *plot, but others are built on multiple story lines, which may or may not be related. Only the *coincidence in timing ties them together. In *'Til Death* (1959) the apparent single plot bifurcates at the end. In *Hail, Hail, the Gang's All Here!* (1971) each detective pursues his own case.

Lean prose and crackling dialogue propel the Precinct and Hope books, although in the Hunter novels the style varies with the subject. One of McBain's trademarks is the insertion into the text of visuals, such as police forms or handwritten notes.

[*See also* Police Detective; Police History: History of American Policing.]

• George N. Dove, *The Boys from Grover Avenue: Ed McBain's 87th Precinct Novels* (1985).
—John D. Stevens

MCCLURE, JAMES (b. 1939), British writer born in Johannesburg, South Africa, and educated in Pietermaritzburg. McClure worked as a photographer, teacher, and reporter before emigrating with his family to England. He has worked for newspapers in Scotland and England. Inspired by Ed *McBain and Chester *Himes, McClure turned to the *police procedural to explore the world of and relationship between Afrikaner lieutenant Tromp Kramer and his Zulu sergeant Mickey Zondi. With his first book, *Steam Pig* (1971), McClure began a painful but honest depiction of life in South Africa. Kramer and Zondi trust and respect each other, but under the crippling rule of apartheid they must hide their friendship and

alter their public behavior. The crimes they investigate arise out of the distortions of South African society: A white family is reclassified as Cape Coloured in *The Steam Pig*; the racist activities of a young boy lead to his *murder in *The Caterpillar Cop* (1972); and a government spy is murdered in *The Gooseberry Fool* (1974). The ugly experience of life under apartheid is tempered with *humor and compassion. McClure has also written a *thriller and two nonfictional studies of police in Liverpool and San Diego.

[*See also* Ethnic Sleuth; Ethnicity; Police Detective; Prejudice; Racism; Sidekicks and Sleuthing Teams.]
—Susan Oleksiw

McGEE, Travis, hero in a series of twenty-one mystery novels written by John D. *MacDonald. A self-described beach bum. McGee lives aboard *The Busted Flush*, a fifty-two-foot houseboat moored at Slip F-18, Bahia Mar, Fort Lauderdale, Florida. McGee is not a professional detective but what he terms a "salvage expert": He retrieves valuable lost items for friends and keeps half of what he recovers.

What ordinarily prompts McGee to abandon his pleasurable retirement aboard his boat is not the promise of reward but a quixotic sense of knight-errantry. McGee rushes to the defense of the defenseless (especially if they are beautiful women) and risks his life for his clients, all while struggling to adhere to a personal code of moral behavior.

McGee is also a knowledgeable man who (along with economist buddy Meyer) imparts fascinating tidbits of information on a wide array of subjects. MacDonald routinely employs McGee as a vehicle for expounding his views on social issues, especially those related to the destruction of the environment of his beloved Florida.

McGee's comfortable lifestyle excites escapist fantasies while his courage and bravery earn admiration. Add to this his insistence upon proper moral behavior, and he exemplifies the virtues of both living well and doing right.

[*See also* Addresses and Abodes, Famous; Chivalry.]
—David Geherin

MCNEILE, H(ERMAN) C(YRIL) (1888–1937), short story writer and novelist; he used the pseudonym Sapper in his native Britain. He served in the Royal Engineers during the First World War and was awarded the Military Cross. His pseudonym was suggested by Lord Northcliffe, proprietor of the *Daily Mail*, in which the author's war stories appeared. Described by a reviewer as "far more terrible than anything Kipling or Stephen Crane or Tolstoy or Zola ever imagined," these stories were collected as *The Lieutenant and Others* (1915) and *Sergeant Michael Cassidy, R. E.* (1915; *Michael Cassidy, Sergeant*). Each collection sold over 200,000 copies in a year. Equally successful were Sapper's postwar works: the series of novels, for which he is best known, in which the hero is Captain Hugh "Bulldog" *Drummond (the first of which is *Bull-Dog Drummond: The Adventures of a Demobilized Officer Who Found Peace Dull*, 1920); and the novels and short stories with Ronald Standish—sometimes a detective, sometimes a secret service agent—or the adventurer Jim Maitland as hero. Gerard Fairlie (1899–1983), an officer in the Scots Guards and noted amateur boxer, on whom Drummond was modeled, and who continued the series after McNeile's death, quotes (in *With Prejudice: Almost an Autobiography*, 1952) the latter, a fanatical golfer, as likening the perfect short story to "the perfect iron shot." Certainly the best short stories ("The Man in Ratcatcher," for example, in *The Man in Ratcatcher and Other Stories*, 1921) are technically excellent—McNeile's favorite authors were Guy de Maupassant, Ambrose Bierce, and O. Henry (whose stories he edited)—and superior to the novels, which suffer from repetitious *plot elements. Though, as a popular writer, Sapper has few equals for exciting narration, his work, with its reactionary political views, *anti-Semitism, and curious blend of *chivalry and brutality, belongs to the interwar years and is scarcely acceptable to the modern reader.

[*See also* Heroism; Prejudice; Racism; Spy Fiction; Suspicious Characters.]

• Richard Usborne, *Clubland Heroes*, rev. ed. (1983). Sapper, *The Best Short Stories*, selected and introduced by Jack Adrian (1984).   —T. J. Binyon

MEANS, MOTIVE AND OPPORTUNITY. The categorical trinity—means, *motive, opportunity—provides a structure for detection method that has become either an expressed or subliminal convention in narratives that present the *sleuth at work in a world amenable to reason. Working through the list of *suspects, the detective in a version of Boolean inquiry seeks to establish linkages: Which suspect has knowledge of the means of committing the crime or the ability to apply the means? Which suspect possessing knowledge and ability also had adequate opportunity to commit the crime? And what needs or desires (fear, jealousy, *greed, resentment, etc.) would motivate a suspect to seize upon an opportunity to execute the crime? The works of author Ellery *Queen are especially notable for their overt use of the trinity. Ellery *Queen, the character, and his father, the police commissioner, typically assemble the evidence in a case so that readers may be assured, in a formal challenge that interrupts the story, that by that point they know all that the sleuth Ellery knows. The challenge effectively invites readers to sort the information they have acquired about means, motive, and opportunity and to check their conclusions against Queen's retelling of the commission of the crime in the novel's finale.

Critics in the Golden Age who represented crime and mystery fiction as a high-level intellectual enterprise spoke implicitly of means, motive, and opportunity when they promulgated *rules of the game forbidding improbability and unnatural interventions in the *plot. Reviewers readily acceded to the idea that solutions to fictional crimes should be based in logic and often judged a book's worth in terms of consistency of motives and plausible techniques of *murder. Hard-boiled writing, which stresses character and *setting above detection method, naturally makes less use of means, motive, and opportunity,

but many *police procedurals, however hard-boiled they may be in tone, reveal an underpinning of the classic categories when officers are dispatched in search of forensic information that will tie the means of committing the crime to suspects with relevant motives and definite opportunities to carry it off.

The convention of the triple avenues of investigation owes its durability in no small measure to the way it underlines the appeal of stories about the mind's making sense of reality. Amid all the changes in style and setting that detective fiction has undergone, there seems always to be reason for a character to declare, as Lieutenant Genesko does in *Something to Kill for* (1994) by Susan Holtzer, "the classic approach is to identify means, motive, and opportunity." True to that instruction, and true also to her profession as a computer programmer, Holtzer's amateur detective Anneke Haagen proceeds to draw up lists detailing exactly that for every suspect. And, of course, it works, because that is the way of conventions.

[*See also* Conventions of the Genre; Formula: Plot; Whodunit.]   —John M. Reilly

MEAN STREETS MILIEU. The term "mean streets" may first have been applied to the stories of British writer Arthur *Morrison. In 1894, a collection of Morrison's stories dealing with life and death in the *London slums appeared with the title *Tales of Mean Streets*. But it was left to the American writers of the 1920s and after to perfect the concept of the mean streets as the symbolic representation of the crime and *violence of urban America. The most notable use of the literary term appeared in Raymond *Chandler's 1944 *Atlantic Monthly* essay "The Simple Art of Murder." "But down these mean streets a man must go who is not himself mean, who is neither tarnished nor afraid" is Chandler's description of the urban *sleuth and the detective found in American detective fiction. The city itself might be *San Francisco or *Los Angeles or *New York, but whatever the particular location, the description was the same: a dangerous place, frequently viewed at night, filled with strangers capable of violence, motivated by *greed, lust, and hatred; even the people one knows in the mean streets may not be what they seem. The city's size and variety of lifestyles afforded the writer a wide range of possible *suspects and *victims and threats to the detective and his or her clients.

The pulp writers of the 1920s first used this *urban milieu in their detective stories, and Dashiell *Hammett went on to perfect its use in his stories and novels set in San Francisco. In Hammett's *The Maltese Falcon* (1930), murders occur at night and characters hide in the shadows of doorways or slip in through alleys. These city streets are frightening, filled with unknown dangers. Raymond *Chandler's detective, Philip *Marlowe, operates in Los Angeles. In *The Big Sleep* (1939), Marlowe uses his car on the busy streets to tail suspects; he can disguise himself and be lost among the other city inhabitants; murders occur at night on rain-slicked streets, behind the closed doors of mysterious dwellings. Forty years later, Ross *Macdonald used the same lonely, threatening urban setting for his Lew *Archer tales.

Later detective fiction writers have used the mean streets concept in their work with some interesting variations. John D. *MacDonald expanded the streets of Fort Lauderdale, Florida, to include the marinas as well; MacDonald's *private eye Travis *McGee lives on and works from a houseboat, *The Busted Flush*. Sara *Paretsky sends her female private eye, V. I. *Warshawski, down the menacing streets of Chicago, while Walter *Moseley has Ezekiel "Easy" *Rawlins solving crimes and confronting *racism in the Los Angeles of the 1950s.

The mean streets setting used in *hard-boiled fiction acts as a concrete representation of societal conditions. Violence occurs quickly and frequently in the darkened city streets. The detectives working in this *milieu often appear to be of questionable character, if not to the reader, at least to other characters. To succeed in the mean streets setting, detectives must understand the violence there and sometimes be changed by it. Few innocents inhabit the mean streets, but the *hard-boiled sleuths working in this milieu see their jobs providing some *justice within this merciless, dangerous setting.

[*See also* Chivalry, Code of; Heroism; Truth, Quest for.]

• George Grella, "The Hard-Boiled Detective Novel" in *Detective Fiction: A Collection of Critical Essays* (1980). Ernest Mandel, *Delightful Murder: A Social History of the Crime Story* (1984). LeRoy Lad Panek, *An Introduction to the Detective Story* (1987).

—Bonnie C. Plummer

MEDICAL MILIEU. The medical *milieu encompasses hospitals, medical offices and research facilities, and the professional world of the medical practitioner, including doctors whose primary objective is to cure or prevent disease and *coroners or medical examiners whose concern is to establish cause of death. This milieu offers the crime and mystery writer a host of unusual murder *weapons and a distinctive and hierarchical closed community. It also provides the writer the opportunity to look at *clues from a scientific perspective.

R. Austin *Freeman is credited with developing the possibilities of the medical environment in his novels and stories featuring the *scientific sleuth Dr. John *Thorndyke. In *The Red Thumb Mark* (1907), Thorndyke says of his career, "my sphere of influence has extended until it now includes all cases in which a special knowledge of medicine or physical science can be brought to bear upon law." The detailed, accurate descriptions of medical and scientific researches in Freeman's day retain a dateless quality, probably due to the paucity of reference to historic events.

Thorndyke is often found in places where forensic medicine is practiced or testified to—the *murder scene, autopsy room, laboratory, and witness box. A number of Freeman's novels begin with a narrative of a young general practitioner encountering crime, Thorndyke appearing subsequently as a senior colleague and medico-legal consultant. An exception, *Mr. Polton Explains* (1940), presents Thorndyke at the beginning of his career, discharging the routine duties of house physician in the wards of a London hospital.

Physicians and hospitals figure prominently in the output of Dr. Doris Bell Collier Ball, who wrote under the pseudonym Josephine Bell. Her early novels, beginning with *Murder in Hospital* (1937), feature young, idealistic Dr. David Wintringham, who frequently works in connection with Inspector Mitchell of *Scotland Yard. Bell's fiction marks a distinct transition from British *Golden Age traditions. The omniscient *Great Detective is absent, replaced by dedicated professionals including police detectives, lawyers, and medical doctors all working conscientiously to uncover the truth against a well-drawn background of a society facing prewar industrial depression, wartime restrictions, and postwar austerity.

The nursing home, or long-term care facility, is a medical milieu that is useful for displaying the skills of both doctors and nurses in a closed community where the stresses of confinement may enhance character development. Ngaio *Marsh, writing in collaboration with Dr. Henry Jellett, used this setting in *The Nursing Home Murder* (1935), in which Inspector Roderick *Alleyn investigates the suspicious death of the British home secretary following an operation. The carefully constructed solution to the crime involves the then-fashionable pseudoscience of eugenics.

A nursing home for the disabled and the terminally ill is the *setting of P. D. *James's (*The Black Tower* (1975), in which a claustrophobic, morbid *atmosphere is established through the isolation of the setting. James is fond of medical settings. She uses a psychiatric clinic in *A Mind to Murder* (1963) and a training college for nurses in *Shroud for a Nightingale* (1971). James has commented on the usefulness to the writer of the hierarchical medical community in which a patient may feel vulnerable and anxious and where the medical staff operates according to definite rules, conventions, and timetables.

In the United States, Robin Cook builds the vulnerability that James mentions into a state approaching paranoia. Typically, a Cook novel features a courageous individual who uncovers conspiracy and grotesque murders hidden behind the facade of medical professionalism, elitism, and bureaucracy. In *Blindsight* (1992), for example, pathologist Dr. Laurie Montgomery risks her career and her life to find the links among a wealthy ophthalmologist, a Mafioso, and a number of deaths resulting from cocaine overdoses.

An earlier American example that conveys a sense of criminal conspiracy in the medical milieu is Emma *Lathen's *A Stitch in Time* (1968), in which investment banker John Putnam *Thatcher uncovers *corruption among physicians prescribing and dispensing overpriced drugs under their own labels. Writing as R. B. Dominic, the same pair of collaborators revisits the subject of medical conspiracy in *The Attending Physician* (1980), in which congressman Ben Safford investigates elaborate Medicaid fraud and murder among a group of wealthy doctors in his Ohio congressional district.

Patricia D. Cornwell uses the technology and skills of the *forensic pathologist to examine death in more ways than one. Her medical examiner sleuth Dr. Kay

Scarpetta not only establishes the factual cause of death; she uses forensic evidence gathered in the morgue and at the scene of the crime to pursue murderers and bring them to justice.

[See also Medical Sleuth; Poisons and Poisoning.]

• Norman Donaldson, In Search of Dr. Thorndyke: The Story of R. Austin Freeman's Great Scientific Investigator and His Creator (1971). Bernard Benstock, "The Clinical World of P. D. James," in Twentieth-Century Women Novelists, ed. Thomas F. Staley (1982).   —Christopher Bently

MEDICAL SLEUTH. The popularity of the medical *sleuth dates from the opening of the twentieth century, a time, not incidentally, of growing fascination with science and the scientific view of life. In many ways the medical detective seems an ideal choice for a sleuth, given his or her precise knowledge of the physical world. The medical sleuth has grown and changed since then, but writers have returned to this template time and again.

R. Austin *Freeman created the definitive medical sleuth in Dr. John Evelyn *Thorndyke, who first appears in The Red Thumb Mark (1907). Thorndyke, qualified in both medicine and law, lectures on medical jurisprudence at a *London teaching hospital. He is an expert in the examination of cadavers and fragmentary human remains, demonstrating in The Eye of Osiris (1911; The Vanishing Man) that a supposed Egyptian mummy is the *corpse of a recent *murder *victim, and identifying the traces of cumulative arsenic poisoning in a lock of hair from a dead girl in As a Thief in the Night (1928). Unlike many contemporary sleuths, Thorndyke is on good terms with the police and respects the work of his assistants. He is entirely professional, even distant, with clients. Although this can make for dry characterization, the best stories are absorbing cases of material *clues.

Among later writers who continued the pattern established by Freeman is Lawrence G. Blochman. His detective, Dr. Daniel Webster Coffee, a pathologist at a hospital in a fictional midwestern city, uses recondite knowledge and skilled laboratory work to solve crimes in numerous short stories and one novel, Recipe for Homicide (1952). Another rigorous approach to criminal pathology is found in Patricia D. Cornwell's Dr. Kay Scarpetta, chief medical examiner for the Commonwealth of Virginia. In her first appearance (Postmortem, 1990), Scarpetta battles institutional sexism while assembling the forensic evidence necessary to find a serial killer.

Not all scientific detectives demonstrate or rely on true scientific reasoning. H. C. *Bailey's Reggie *Fortune, a London physician and surgeon and a special adviser to the *CID, demonstrates little medical knowledge. In The Shadow on the Wall (1934), Fortune attends a Buckingham Palace garden party and then proceeds to Lady Rosnay's ball, where he encounters attempted murder. Throughout these mannered writings Fortune is more of a socialite and talented *amateur detective than a doctor. Margaret Scherf's Dr. Grace Severance is a retired pathologist who relies more on intuition than on expert knowledge; in To Cache a Millionaire (1972), she investi-

gates the disappearance in Las Vegas of a fictional counterpart of Howard Hughes. Jonathan Stagge's Dr. Hugh Westlake is a general practitioner in a small Pennsylvania town who correctly suspects murder behind inexplicable or apparently supernatural occurrences. Turn of the Table (1940; Funeral for Five) includes a seance in which a murder is accurately predicted as well as a killer who may be a vampire.

Many writers turned to the psychologist as sleuth and found here greater scope for character development within the range of scientific worlds. Gladys *Mitchell's Mrs. Beatrice Adela Lestrange *Bradley is a psychiatric consultant to the British Home Office in a long series beginning with Speedy Death (1929) and reaching a peak in the author's favorite, The Rising of the Moon (1945), a vivid, atmospheric work in which the narrator is a thirteen-year-old boy with knowledge of a serial killer. The psyche of the child becomes central in the unflinching, sometimes harrowing novels of Jonathan Kellerman. His series investigator is Dr. Alex Delaware, a child psychologist in *Los Angeles, who usually works with police detective Milo Sturgis. In Private Eyes (1991), Delaware is drawn back into the traumatic life of a teenage girl who had been his patient nine years before. In some cases the professional title can be little more than costuming. Professor Henry Poggioli appears in stories by T. S. Stribling, some of which are collected as Clues of the Caribees (1929). Although he has a degree in medicine and teaches psychology at Ohio State University, the whimsical Poggioli generally solves crimes by applying skepticism to the deceptively exotic.

A major advantage of the medical sleuth is that the doctor remains a respected figure whose dispassionate view commands the trust of the reader. The doctor can go anywhere and ask almost anything without raising *suspicion; he or she has almost as much freedom as a police officer. J. B. Priestley used this figure to advantage in Salt Is Leaving (1966). Dr. Salt, an unconventional, restless widower who has been working in general practice in a grim English Midlands town, delays his departure in order to investigate the disappearance of a young woman patient. Ignoring obscure threats and the indifference of the local police, he uncovers a domineering industrialist's *family secrets, including a bizarre murder, and finds a new wife for himself. C. F. Roe's Dr. Jean Montrose seems fully occupied by her general practice in Perth, Scotland, and by the demands of her family, but is sometimes consulted on questionable and suspicious deaths by Detective Inspector Douglas Niven. Death by Fire (1990) finds her investigating an apparently authentic case of spontaneous human combustion complicated by the possibility of supernatural intervention. Roe's novels, with their regional flavor and realistic portrayal of a physician integrated into the daily life of a small community, suggest the continuing viability of the medical sleuth.

[See also Coroner: Poisons and Poisonings; Reasoning, Types of.]

• Norman Donaldson, In Search of Dr. Thorndyke: The Story of R. Austin Freeman's Great Scientific Investigator and His Creator (1971). Chris Steinbrunner and Otto Penzler, Encyclopedia of Mystery and Detection (1976). P. D. James, "A Fictional Prognosis," in *Murder Ink: The Mystery Reader's Companion*, ed. Dilys Winn (1977). Oliver Mayo, *R. Austin Freeman: The Anthropologist at Large* (1980).

—Christopher Bentley

MEMOIRS, EARLY DETECTIVE AND POLICE. The nineteenth-century popular press and reform literature of the United States reveal deep anxiety about an impending *class conflict that was thought likely to follow from the massive immigration of impoverished peasants from Europe, the congregation of the poor in major cities, and unrest among the new industrial working class. Charles Loring Brace did not mince words in titling his personal account of twenty years' work as a reformer, calling it *The Dangerous Classes of New York* (1872); in it he declares that the wretchedness to be found in *New York is more dangerous than that in *London, and that Americans should not expect that the terrible communist outbreaks in Paris will be confined to the French.

Writing about the foundations of literary *naturalism, the critic June Howard demonstrates further cultural connections to the fear of class conflict, among them the widespread stereotyping of immigrants and workers in popular discourse as brutes and the theories of Cesare Lombroso and others that linked the heredity of the "other people" (i.e., immigrants, the poor, and industrial workers) to social problems. Howard's historical analysis might very well extend to the early writings of detective memoirs, for they, too, can be seen to represent fears of the underclass among the literate and well-off.

New York's legendary chief of detectives Thomas Byrnes contributed to the public awareness of a criminal class a volume entitled *Professional Criminals of America* (1886), in which he categorizes criminal modes of operation from those of sneak thieves to confidence men and offers his readers photographs, descriptions, and the records of 204 actual criminals. Expression of a more explicit debt to the studies of Lombroso can be found in *Our Rival, The Rascal, A Faithful Portrayal of the Conflict Between the Criminals of This Age and the Defenders of Society—The Police* (1896), written by Benjamin P. Eldridge, superintendent of police in Boston, and Chief Inspector William B. Watts. In their preface Eldridge and Watt maintain that "the rascal" is an eternal type, while in their survey of the causes of crime they say that "the logical induction seems to be that environment is the ultimate controlling factor in determining careers, placing heredity itself as an organized result of environment." Although the arguments in their book hesitate between an essentialist idea about innate criminal tendencies and the effect of circumstances in conditioning for criminal behavior, the statistics of Eldridge and Watt adhere to the presentation of a dangerous class: more than eleven percent of male prisoners and thirteen percent of female prisoners are under the age of twenty, making up a cohort that is annually renewable and likely to be perpetual.

Possibly the most prominent and most frequently reproduced memoirs of detection are those issued under the name of Allan Pinkerton. Interestingly, the many volumes taken from the case records of the Pinkerton agency rarely relate the crime of murder. Instead the focus remains steadily upon crimes of fraud, commercial deceit, labor agitation, abduction, and *theft—all of them crimes directed against wealth and economic order and all of them, therefore, illustrative of popular anxieties about the safety of property in an expansive capitalist age.

Some early detective memoirs evidence the outlines of later fictional genres. Notable in this regard is *Recollections of a New York Chief of Police* (1887) by George W. Walling, whose anecdotal record of crimes he has observed frequently digresses into description of police procedures and the personnel requirements for an effective police force.

Frank Wadleigh Chandler, the scholar whose two-volume study *The Literature of Roguery* (1907) remains valuable as a standard work of literary history, observes that both the picaresque narrative and the old rogue's literature are supplanted in the nineteenth century by a literature of crime detection. It begins, Chandler indicates, as a type of realism, as in the memoirs of Eugène François Vidocq (1828–29) and the perfection of early French crime writing in the fiction of Émile *Gaboriau. A later development noted by Chandler occurs when the author of fiction collaborates with the detective. Julian Hawthorne's novels purporting to be from the diaries of Inspector Byrnes are his leading exhibits, but considering the probability that a professional author ghosted the works of Pinkerton, it may be argued that the conversion of documentary records into legend reached an acme in the many, many volumes about the Pinkerton agency.

Although early detective memoirs display features in common with fictional narratives, their immediate progeny are not the famous inventions of Arthur Conan *Doyle and his contemporaries but rather *dime novels and pulp fiction. The rise of the publishing houses of Beadle and Adams and their competitors Street and Smith coincided with the processes of industrialization and growth of big business. The timing made these firms' mass market publications the natural outlets for treatment of the problem of crime, and their style of filling narratives with action heroes and elemental morality lent strength to what seems in historical retrospect to have been an all-out cultural campaign in defense of establishment values.

[See also Conservative vs. Radical World View; Ethnicity; Realism, Conventions of.]

• June Howard, *Form and History in American Literary Naturalism* (1985).

—John M. Reilly

MENACING CHARACTERS. The long-standing practice whereby detective fiction *puzzles distance the crime from its solution leaves little room for representing characters with an *evil mien, since one of the intended effects of closed circle stories is to present crime as an unusual intrusion into stable or commonplace life. When writers take a contrary view of society, however, seeing it as disorderly and unfortunately hospitable to crime, characters with an aura of menace about them become highly functional.

The memorable radio drama of the 1940s "Sorry, Wrong Number" features the harassment of a bedridden woman by the repeated ringing of her telephone by an anonymous caller preying on her condition of solitude. Although the caller is faceless, genderless, and voiceless, his or her messageless signals are sufficient to suggest that beyond the *victim's bedroom lies not a mundane world but one that poses threatening *violence. In this case the villain is nothing more than menace adumbrated. By contrast, menace takes on the particulars and traits of the antagonist who challenges the detective protagonist in such stories of serial killers as Lawrence Sanders's *The Second Deadly Sin* (1977), with the result that the two figures assume roles as champions of the light and darkness of the world.

The works of Robert Bloch and Jim *Thompson extend the use of menacing characters to the point that they create the diametrically opposite world to that of classic puzzle stories. Bloch's *The Scarf* (1947), *The Kidnapper* (1954), and the renowned *Psycho* (1959) all produce fictional realms where peril and danger are the norm, because the narrative leads are taken by psychopaths. Thompson elevates the sense of menace even further by using disturbed, deeply sick narrators to relate the stories in *The Killer Inside Me* (1952), *Savage Night* (1953), *After Dark, My Sweet* (1955), and *Pop. 1280* (1964). The deceptively ordinary but actually dysfunctional narrators of Thompson's books include such characters as a police officer and a hit man whose occupations have something to do directly with crime, but who are also megalomaniacs, alcoholics, and certifiably distressed souls. Collectively they populate an environment beyond reason and predictability.

While the entrance of a menacing character into crime fiction generally signals that an uncommon side to pedestrian reality is to be revealed, the character does not necessarily remake the fictional world of the short story or novel in his or her image. Sherlock *Holmes's nemesis Professor James *Moriarty and Dr. Grimesby Roylott, the *villain in "The Adventure of the Speckled Band" (*Strand* Feb. 1892), challenge the Great Detective without destroying the optimistic expectation that the narratives will show order restored by application of the eccentric detective's brilliant method. Menace is contained in another fashion in such thrillers as Eric *Ambler's *The Mask of Dimitrios* (1939; *A Coffin for Dimitrios*) where the eponymous character is found by the detective writer Charles Latimer to typify the sordid reality of Europe on the eve of *war without the revelation's obliterating the humanistic values that form the source of Latimer's, and the reader's, shock.

Even writers of *hard-boiled fiction will make use of characters who serve to signify the presence of base motives yet whose menacing aspects are softened by a mannered veneer. Caspar Gutman, his armed bodyguard Joel Cairo, and Brigid O'Shaughnessy in Dashiell *Hammett's *The Maltese Falcon* (1930) typify this sort of balanced use of menacing characters.

[*See also* Atmosphere; Master Criminal; Suspicious Characters; Underworld, The; Underworld Figure.]
—John M. Reilly

Merrivale, Sir Henry, series character created John Dickson *Carr Writing as Carter Dickson. Better known as "H. M." or "the Old Man," from 1934 to 1955 he appeared in twenty-two *detective novels and one novelette, all of them requiring him to solve *locked room mysteries or other *impossible crimes. He is in his sixties, and his features—big belly, bald head, wrinkled face, small eyes behind tortoise-shell glasses—are those of a bespectacled Buddha. He expresses his opposition to affectation and artificiality in many ways, including favoring a rather shabby mode of dress, displaying a predilection for risqué books and movies, and communicating in phrases of his own coinage. A composite of several people, including Winston Churchill and Carr himself, H. M. is variously described as barrister and physician, as Britain's chief of intelligence and the former head of espionage, even as a lifelong, energetic socialist, a connection that Carr drops in the late 1930s. Through this character, Carr attacks pretense, provides *humor, and connects H. M.'s love for games with his abilities as a detective who solves the case by determining the murderer's *motive.

[*See also* Eccentrics; Ingenuity.]

• LeRoy Panek, *Watteau's Shepherds: The Detective Novel in Britain, 1914–1940* (1979). S. T. Joshi, *John Dickson Carr: A Critical Study* (1990).
—Dale Salwak

MI5 AND MI6. In 1909 the British government established a Secret Service Bureau with two aims: to uncover hostile agents in Britain and to gather intelligence abroad. Almost immediately the Bureau became two separate organizations, which have often been rivals. The first of these, devoted to counterintelligence at home, became Military Intelligence 5 (MI5) or the Security Service, while the second, involved in running agents overseas, became MI6, or the Secret Intelligence Service (SIS).

With the outbreak of World War I in 1914, both grew considerably and MI5 in particular was highly successful. The author W. Somerset Maugham was an MI6 agent in Russia in 1917 and later wrote convincingly about the secret world in his collection of stories *Ashenden* (1928). Peace in 1918 led to huge cuts in the funding of both MI5 and MI6.

When World War II began in 1939, MI5 and MI6 expanded enormously and changed radically, with a large influx of young academics and intellectuals. Both achieved great successes, such as MI5's brilliant Operation Double-Cross and MI6's Ultra (the successful decoding of German military radio communications using the Enigma machine). The downside of World War II recruitment did not become clear until years later with the gradual exposure of the Cambridge graduates who had been recruited as moles by Soviet intelligence in the 1930s and subsequently betrayed many of their country's secrets, the four best known being Anthony Blunt, Guy Burgess, Donald Maclean, and, above all, Kim Philby.

For more than forty years after World War II, British intelligence was preoccupied with the Cold War, including the betrayal of atomic secrets to the Soviets and the sometimes paranoid quest for more moles and traitors within MI5 and MI6 themselves, including the supposedly top-level "fifth man." *Spycatcher* (1987), the "candid autobiography" of a senior MI5 officer, Peter Wright, illustrates the latter tendency. Philby and his fellow moles also inspired some outstanding novels of the Cold War, including John *le Carré's *Tinker, Tailor, Soldier, Spy* (1974) and Graham *Greene's *The Human Factor* (1978). The Cold War spawned a huge amount of fiction as well as nonfiction by British authors about the secret world and its "wilderness of mirrors," to use *CIA agent James Angleton's famous phrase. One of the best fictional evocations of Cold War espionage is le Carré's influential *The Spy Who Came in from the Cold* (1963). Like le Carré and Greene, several of the best-known spy novelists had firsthand experience of intelligence work during or after World War II, including Ted Albeury and Ian *Fleming. If Fleming's heroic *adventure stories about James *Bond represent one end of the fictional spectrum, le Carré's grimmer and more realistic novels involving George Smiley exemplify the other.

Since the late 1960s with a return of "the Troubles" to Northern Ireland, MI5 and MI6 have been very active in the province. Both have also played a major part in the struggle against international terrorism and drug trafficking, and with the end of the Cold War *spy fiction has reflected these changes.

[*See also* Heroism; Terrorism and the Terrorist Procedural; War.]

• R. G. Grant, *MI5 MI6: Britain's Security and Secret Intelligence Services* (1989).
—Peter Lewis

Milhone, Kinsey. Introduced in the 1982 novel *"A" Is for Alibi* by American author Sue *Grafton, Kinsey Milhone is one of the earliest female private investigators in the hard-boiled tradition. In Milhone's first nine appearances in the alphabetically titled series, Grafton's *private eye operates in the tradition of the *sleuth as loner. Orphaned at age five, Milhone is twice divorced and lives simply and on her own. Milhone is slow to establish intimate connections despite genuine affection for her elderly landlord, Henry Pitts, and the owner of her favorite bar. However, in *"J" Is for Judgment* (1993), Grafton introduces Milhone's previously unknown relatives, inevitably changing both the future course of the novels and the construction of her detective.

Grafton sets up her character plausibly. A former police officer, Milhone has experienced sex discrimination firsthand. An independent private investigator, she often questions her *motives, methods, and successes. She typically wisecracks her way through confrontations, usually winning the verbal battles. She is also physically tough: she runs, engages in target practice, and continually tests herself; but she also gets attacked, shot at, and beaten. Still, she describes her job as methodical and routine, comparing it to women's typical work. In *"B" Is for Burglar* (1985), she notes that "there's no place in a p.i.'s life for impatience, faintheartedness, or sloppiness. I understand the same qualifications apply for housewives" (even though Milhone eschews housework).

The cases which Grafton details through Milhone's first-person narration, like those of Ross *Macdonald's Lew *Archer, tend to focus upon the past. In *"A" Is for Alibi*, Milhone reopens a *murder case when a convicted killer, newly released from prison, hires her. A seventeen-year-old murder draws her into *"F" Is for Fugitive* (1989); in *"I" Is for Innocent* (1992), she takes over a murdered colleague's reinvestigation of the Isabelle Barney case. In *"G" Is for Gumshoe*, Milhone finds herself threatened by a killer she had fingered. Despite significant evidence of the shortcomings of the traditional legal/police system, Milhone persists in believing in its efficacy. Although many of her cases arise from errors perpetrated by the legal system, she typically hands over the criminals she has uncovered to the legal establishment.

The novels in which Milhone appears are told in a straightforward manner. Grafton uses an opening prologue in which her *sleuth reintroduces herself to the reader as though in a report to a client. As of *"F" Is for Fugitive*, Grafton occasionally drops the epilogue that she had used in the earlier novels, with its formal closing, "Respectfully submitted, Kinsey Milhone."

[*See also* Females and Feminists; Hard-Boiled Sleuth; Titles and Titling; Voice: Wisecracking Voice.]

• Peter J. Rabinowitz, "'Reader, I Blew Him Away': Convention and Transgression in Sue Grafton," in *Famous Last Words: Women Against Novelistic Endings*, ed. Alison Booth (1993). Priscilla Walton, "'E' Is for En/Gendering Readings: Sue Grafton's Kinsey Milhone," in *Women Times Three: Writers, Detectives, Readers*, ed. Kathleen Gregory Klein (1995).
—Kathleen Gregory Klein

MILIEU is a story element that includes intangible features that may direct the affairs of characters. (It differs from *setting, which may be little more than a backdrop against which a story takes place.) Tony *Hillerman's *The Fly on the Wall* (1971), for example, as a journalistic procedural story, includes the processes of investigating stories, following up on tips, drafting, and rewriting that are the typical activities of a newspaper office like the capital city bureau featured in the novel. Similarly, the police procedural stories written by J. J. Marric, Ed *McBain, Dell Shannon, and Joseph Wambaugh are filled with details of the way police officers use informants, conduct interrogations, collaborate with their peers, and deal with citizens. Whether at the news bureau or on the police force, occupational routines influence the actions of the characters in a way that distinguishes them as participants in a distinctive milieu.

As the example of the police narrative indicates, milieu may serve to generate *atmosphere as well. In the police story, it is an atmosphere of a prevalent crime. The mean streets and corrupt burgs visited by the hard-boiled *private eye likewise serve for more than setting, more even than the milieu of back alley lawlessness. Dashiell *Hammett's *Continental Op, Raoul Whitfield's Jo Gar, and Robert Leslie Bellem's Dan Turner move through milieus indicative of their creators' views of social *corruption.

Dorothy L. *Sayers draws upon her own work experience in situating Lord Peter *Wimsey undercover in an advertising firm in *Murder Must Advertise* (1933), just as Dick *Francis uses the *horse racing milieu for Sid Halley's investigations. Wimsey, however, merely adopts the persona of an adman for the purposes of his case, thus presenting a sharp contrast to Halley and Francis's other jockeys and horsemen, products of their milieu whose values, ethics, and self-esteem flow from their involvement in a unique sport. In that regard, it can be said that the detectives of the hard-boiled world are also products of milieus, for their distrust of authority and their enforced loneliness are the results of living a reality wherein power disappoints and personal relationships cannot last long.

The intangible social relationships within a milieu can signify larger social and economic relations too, as when the homogeneous *family or community of the country house mystery expresses the elite status of a privileged upper *class. Within the closed world of an aristocracy reared upon a system of fixed order, the intrusion into the milieu of outsiders or of *violence gives the writer a wealth of opportunity to lay symbolic stress on characters and clues that represent a threat to order. In the same way, the supposition that rational thought and civil discourse are the norm in milieus such as academic societies and libraries allows writers to heighten shock when they introduce *murder into the study or the stacks.

Depending on their experience or the energy they have for research, writers can conjure up numberless milieus that grow out of distinctive occupations and styles of action. Each encompasses a community of more or less like-minded individuals who have invested belief in their shared codes and rules. Sports offer useful milieus where conformity to rules determines success. The arts, the world of antiques, the theater, and the academy provide communities guided by agreed standards of quality. Medical and religious milieus present the conditions for communities dependent for their existence upon specialized knowledge and a shared morality. Under these circumstances a crime may represent subversion of values held in common, and in every case the existence of a collective code of conduct and known rules of procedure permit the author of a mystery story to present a crime as a violation of the social contract. The more loosely definable milieus of the corrupt city of politics will imply general standards rather than display them explicitly, standards such as the right of people to live free of deceit or abuse, but even those milieus can enforce the inherent theme of crime as subversion of community.

The use of a physical setting may be determined by the convention of verisimilitude or the requirement that a narrative simulate reality. It may be as basic for the writer as the decision about who will tell the story: detective, sidekick, or authorial voice. Once a writer makes a decision about setting or voice, however, the opportunity presents itself for a greatly enriched narrative. Setting can become a milieu conveying a theme, creating turns of *plot, shaping character, and supporting the commentary of the narrative voice. Milieu thus is a matter of conscious craft.

[*See also* Academic Milieu; Advertising Milieu; Archaeological Milieu; Art and Antiques Milieu; Banking and Financial Milieu; Cathedral Close Milieu; Circus and Carnival Milieu; Clerical Milieu; Club Milieu; Country House Milieu; Courtroom Milieu; English Village Milieu; Expeditions; Fashion and Design Milieu; Medical Milieu; Musical Milieu; Nautical Milieu; Publishing Milieu; Railway Milieu; Rural Milieu; Theatrical Milieu; Travel Milieu; Urban Milieu.]
—John M. Reilly

MILITARY MILIEU. Since a great tradition in crime and mystery writing is to have the disruptive *violence of crime occur in an otherwise secure and predictable world, the military milieu, particularly as depicted in wartime, is not a common place for fictional crime to be set. When it is used, the military *setting in crime and mystery fiction is incidental, as opposed to integral, to the mystery itself. A corollary to this is the fact that many of the novels contain inaccuracies about things military. Mysteries set in this milieu have little homogeneity regarding locale, type of crime, or period in which they are set.

An exemplary British novel is Clifford Witting's *Subject-Murder* (1945), which deals with a *murder committed on an air-defense base during World War II. In *Night Exercise* (1942; *Dead of the Night*) by John Rhode, the disappearance of a home guard colonel during an anti-invasion exercise early in World War II becomes the mystery. *Death in Captivity* (1952; *The Danger Within*) by Michael *Gilbert concerns the death of a Greek soldier in an Italian prisoner of war camp housing mostly British military personnel. Patricia Moyes's *Johnny Underground* (1965) has *Scotland Yard looking back into an ace pilot's death at an air base during World War II. Two peacetime mysteries set in Britain are *Corporal Smithers, Deceased* (1983) by Jack S. Scott and *The Medbury Fort Murders* (1929) by George Limnelius.

The Night of the Generals (1963) by Hans Hellmut Kirst is principally the story of a brutal serial killer on the German General Staff during World War II, but carries a strong anti-war message in its understory. The wife of the commandant of a German concentration camp in World War II is killed in *The Murder of Frau Schutz* (1988) by J. Madison Davis.

Mason Wright's *The Army Post Murders* (1931) is exceptional in that the murders and *motive are both related to the U.S. Army milieu. In Virginia Hanson's *Death Walks the Post* (1938) and *Casual Slaughters* (1939), however, the army post is simply the backdrop for each story. The same is true for the slaying of a Russian officer killed while observing a U.S. Army exercise in *Murder at Maneuvers* (1938) by Royce Howes. Two American novels set in World War II—*Watchful at Night* (1945) by Julius Fast and *The Corpse in Company K* (1942) by Robert Avery—are only loosely connected to the U.S. Army and the motives for murder are not related to the military. *The Brass Chills* (1943) by Hugh *Pentecost and *The Sulu Sea Murders* (1933) by Van Wyck Mason are *potboilers that are considered inauthentic military-wise. *Murder in the Navy* (1955) by Richard Marsten, later reissued as *Death of a Nurse* (1964), by Ed *McBain, is exactly as its two titles suggest. Margaret Truman's

Death at the Pentagon (1992) deals primarily with political intrigue, and its military connection is tenuous. *Dress Gray* (1978) by Lucian K. Truscott IV, while concerned with the murder of a West Point cadet, is also the author's castigation of the army. Two army CID agents investigate the murder of a nightclub dancer in Seoul, Korea, in *Jade Lady Burning* (1992) by Martin Limon. *The General's Daughter* (1992) by Nelson DeMille is set in a southern fort where the post commander's daughter (who is also an army captain) is found raped and murdered.

—Don Sandstrom

MILLAR, MARGARET (ELLIS STURM) (1915–1994) was born in Ontario, Canada, and educated in Canada before she met and married Kenneth Millar, who later gained fame writing as Ross Macdonald. She wrote her first mystery novel while convalescing from a heart ailment and soon became known for her psychological development of characters and talent for evoking uneasiness, exemplified in her novel *A Stranger in My Grave* (1960).

Millar's first three novels—*The Invisible Worm* (1941), *The Weak-Eyed Bat* (1942), and *The Devil Loves Me* (1942)—were *novels of manners. They featured a *sleuth, lightly patterned after such Golden Age characters as Philo *Vance, to whom Millar assigned the profession of psychiatrist and amusingly named Dr. Paul Prye. She continued the practice of using a dominant sleuth to preside over the narrative in two subsequent novels presenting Inspector Sands of the Toronto Police Department—*Wall of Eyes* (1943) and *The Iron Gates* (1945). The more significant change represented by the Inspector Sands stories, however, was Millar's modernization of conventions of the *Gothic novel for the serious purpose of investigating human psychology. Description of the workings of the mind—illusions and deceptions, latent influences on behavior, and apparent *deviance—became such a compelling interest to Millar that she replaced the sleuth at the center of her narratives with strongly plotted accounts of eruptions from the depths of the unconscious: a stunning example of dual personality in *Beast in View* (1955); the story of a woman who first dreams about, and then sees her own grave in *A Stranger in My Grave* (1960); the distortions of personality created by the stress of past associations in a present setting of a religious cult in *How Like an Angel* (1962); and the indeterminancy of mental illness in *The Fiend* (1964).

In her later work Millar revived the use of a dominant sleuth for a series of novels about Tom Aragon, who searches for a missing husband in *Ask for Me Tomorrow* (1976), a young retarded woman in *Mermaid* (1982), and the solution to the mystery surrounding a wealthy widow in *The Murder of Miranda* (1979).

The observation that Margaret Millar was married to Kenneth Millar (i.e., Ross Macdonald) is included in most critical comment on her work, as is the remark that both writers probed the complexity of family relationships in a Freudian manner. More to the point, however, is the fact that Margaret Millar placed her own personal signature upon the mystery genre with a skillful handling of narrative *atmos-

phere that conveys a profound sense that the ultimate mysteries are mental.   —John M. Reilly

MILNE, A. A. *See* Incidental Crime Writers.

MISSING PERSONS. A missing person is one who has disappeared for a specified period of time, and is not presumed to have died by *murder or accident. The causes for the disappearance are various, and the incident may shade into a number of crimes: *murder, *kidnapping, espionage, blackmail, and so on. The theme of the missing person is prominent in detective fiction, perhaps because the fear of being lost, never to see family or home again, is one of childhood's worst. Reports of missing persons, ships, or aircraft are extensively covered in newspapers, and often serve as the basis for crime fiction.

The missing person theme appears in one of the earliest detective stories, Edgar Allan *Poe's "The Mystery of Marie Roget" (*Snowden's Lady's Companion*, Nov. 2, 1842), which is based on the real-life disappearance of the beautiful cigar-store clerk Mary Rogers. In Poe's story, the young Marie Roget disappears for a week, returns amid much speculation about what might have happened to her, then disappears a second time, about five months later; she is finally found drowned in the Seine. The suspense created by the disappearance and reappearance makes the theme attractive to all subgenres of crime fiction. In William Irish's haunting work *Phantom Lady* (1942), a man searches for a mysterious woman in an orange hat, whose testimony alone can save his friend from the electric chair; she is a woman whom witnesses say does not exist. In the *police procedural *So Long as You Both Shall Live* (1976) by Ed *McBain, a policeman's bride becomes a missing person on her wedding night. There is a military police background in *The Third Man, and The Fallen Idol* (1950; *The Third Man*) by Graham *Greene; Rollo Martins, a second-rate writer, goes to visit his friend Harry Lime in post–World War II Vienna, but Lime dies in a car accident before Martins arrives. Soon Martins begins to question what he knows about his dead friend, and to search for the third man at the accident scene, who disappeared immediately afterward. In Robert Bloch's thriller *Psycho* (1959), a woman looks for a girl last seen heading out of town with someone else's money. Lawrence *Block's private eye Matt Scudder hunts for a missing *New York actress in *Out on the Cutting Edge* (1989). F. R. Buckley uses the theme in a historical adventure, "Of a Vanishment" (*Adventure*, Mar. 1930), in which a Renaissance duke disappears from the midst of his troops at the moment of victory.

The missing person *plot may encourage a greater emphasis on surprise endings. The killer in Jonathan Latimer's rowdy novel *The Lady in the Morgue* (1936), for example, steals a *corpse to prevent its identification and the inevitable revelation of the killer. Writers also often use the theme to explore contemporary social problems: lonely hearts columns and the people they attract in *Loves Music, Loves to Dance* (1991) by Mary Higgins *Clark; child sex rings in

Bump in the Night (1988) by Isabelle Holland; drug rings in *The Bohemian Connection* (1985) by Susan Dunlap; antiques rackets in *Pearlhanger* (1985) by Jonathan Gash.

The missing person device may be one element in a bizarre or fantastic crime. In Herbert Brean's *Wilders Walk Away* (1948) an entire *family disappears, and in Edmund *Crispin's *The Moving Toyshop* (1946) a poet steps into an open toyshop, discovers the body of an elderly woman, gets hit on the head, and awakes in a closet; he escapes and returns with the police, but the toyshop is gone.

The missing person plot has produced a subgenre of its own: stories based on real people and ships, for example, that disappear without a trace. Arthur Conan *Doyle's short story "J. Habakuk Jephson's Statement" (in the *Cornhill Magazine*, Jan. 1884) offered a solution to the mystery of the brig *Mary Celeste*, which was found drifting off the Azores in 1872 with no trace of captain or crew. Mary Roberts *Rinehart's novella "The Buckled Bag," in *Mary Roberts Rinehart's Crime Book* (1933). was based on two cases, the disappearance of Elizabeth Canning in London in 1753 and that of heiress Dorothy Arnold on a wintry day in *New York in 1910. Josephine *Tey's *The Franchise Affair* (1948) is a modern retelling of the Canning case. Karen Campbell, a former stewardess, based her novel *Suddenly in the Air* (1969; *The Brocken Spectre*) on the real losses of two Tudor IV airliners, in 1948 and 1949. In the novel, a plane loaded with gold is flying the South Atlantic route over which another gold-carrying plane had disappeared only a year earlier.

[*See also* Kidnapping.]

• Allen Churchill, *They Never Came Back* (1960). Robert J. Nash, *Among the Missing* (1978).

—Frank D. McSherry, Jr.

MISTAKEN IDENTITY is a *plot device creating mystery through misidentification. Emerging in the *sensation novel and the *roman policier, it later became a stock device of the *penny dreadfuls, *dime novels, juvenile, and Golden Age forms of detective fiction. Mistaken identity can be established and manipulated by the author by the use of physical *disguise or it can be a function of secrets (especially *family secrets or skeletons in the closet) that are typically uncovered in the course of investigation of a crime. Over the years since the Golden Age, the dependence upon physical disguise has declined, except in *spy fiction and the *thriller, to be replaced with an emphasis on essential secrets of identity and the use of more subtle psychological and social masks to conceal real character.

As early as 1794, William *Godwin's novel *Things as they are; or, The Adventures of Caleb Williams*, sometimes considered the first *detective novel, depends upon the escape of the *suspect in disguise. Disguised detectives regularly appear in Eugène François *Vidocq's *Mémoires de Vidocq* (1828–29; Memoirs of Vidocq; Vidocq the Police Spy) and in Eugene Sue's *Les Mystères de Paris* (1843–44; *The Mysteries of Paris*, 1843–46), among others.

The Victorian sensation novel relied heavily upon both physical disguises and questions of family relationships. Wilkie *Collins's *The Woman in White* (1860) is not only the progenitor of the form but one of the best examples of it. Mrs. Henry *Wood's *East Lynne* (1861), Mary Elizabeth *Braddon's *Lady Audley's Secret* (1862), and Charles *Dickens's *Our Mutual Friend* (1864–65) are also driven by similar questions of identity and family secrets. Anna Katharine *Green, who is acknowledged as one of the first writers deliberately to shape her fiction as detective stories, depends heavily upon mistaken identity, for example in *A Matter of Millions* (1890). Arthur Conan *Doyle's Sherlock *Holmes fiction memorably employs the devices, from the disguised heir to the Baskerville estate in *The Hound of the Baskervilles* (1902) to the disguised reappearance of Holmes himself in "The Adventure of the Empty House" (in *The Strand*, October 1903). Holmes also gains entry to the home of the clever Irene *Adler by means of disguise in "A Scandal in Bohemia" (in *The Strand*, July 1891), and Doyle even disguises a horse in "Silver Blaze" (in *The Strand*, December 1892).

During the Golden Age of crime and mystery writing and the period leading to it, mistaken identity and, less frequently, disguises reinforce characteristic *conventions of the genre in a literature where the *puzzle is more important than psychological depth in characterization. G. K. *Chesterton relies extensively on disguises and mistaken identity in his metaphysical detective novel *The Man Who Was Thursday* (1908) and in many Father *Brown stories such as "The Sins of Prince Saradine" (in *Cassell's*, May 1911); so does Maurice *Leblanc's Arsène *Lupin in *The Exploits of Arsène Lupin* (1907). Questions of identity underlie many works by Agatha *Christie, from the suspense stories "Accident" and "The Girl in the Train," both published in *The Listerdale Mystery* (1934) and *Murder in the Calais Coach* (1934; *Murder on the Orient Express*) to her record-breaking play, *The Mousetrap* (1954), in which the devices are so prominent as to provoke Tom Stoppard's parody in *The Real Inspector Hound* (1968).

By 1928, however, the use of physical disguise and doppelgängers was considered by some to be shopworn. In his "Twenty Rules for Writing Detective Stories" (1928), S. S. *Van Dine proscribes the pinning of crime on a twin or relative who resembles the culprit, while Ronald A. *Knox, in the introduction to *The Best Detective Stories of the Year 1928* (1929), also rules out the use of twins or doubles in his "detective story decalogue." Howard Haycraft, in *Murder for Pleasure; The Life and Times of the Detective Story* (1941), remarks that disguise is as obsolete as women's bustles; in "The Simple Art of Murder" (1944), Raymond *Chandler seriously attacks A. A. Milne's *The Red House Mystery* (1922) for its assumption that forensic techniques would not penetrate a superficial disguise. Mistaken identity is still used, however, especially in *spy fiction and the *thriller, as is the case in John *le Carré's *Tinker, Tailer, Soldier, Spy* (1974). Colin *Dexter makes use of mistaken identity in *The Riddle of the Third Mile* (1983) and *Service of All the Dead* (1979).

Increasingly, however, emphasis on character development has caused the disappearance or transformation of the device. As early as the 1930s, Mary Roberts *Rinehart reserved mistaken identity for personalities needing to remake themselves, as in *The Album* (1933) and *The Wall* (1938); the device does not exist for its own sake but as part of complex psychological characterization. Similarly, human minds devise new versions of themselves in Margaret *Millar's *Vanish in an Instant* (1952) and *Beast in View* (1955). L. P. Davies, in *The Artificial Man* (1965) and other novels, depicts mental disorientation as a result of injury in accidents or from drugs in works that are considered to blend mystery and *science fiction. Gladys *Mitchell, beginning with *The Saltmarsh Murders* (1932), turned mistaken identity into psychological personae behind which seemingly innocent persons mask sins and crimes; this is an increasingly innocent persons mask sins and crimes; this is an increasingly common twist on the device in *cozy mysteries such as Charlotte Macleod's *The Withdrawing Room* (1980) and Jane Haddam's detective novels *Precious Blood* (1991) and *Quoth the Raven* (1991). More sophisticated are P. D. *James's *A Taste for Death* (1986), in which Commander Adam *Dalgleish must cut through the many psychological masks worn by victim Sir Paul Berowne in order to understand the murder, and Elizabeth George's *For the Sake of Elena* (1992), in which artificial attitudes toward the physically impaired must be stripped away to reveal the real causes of the death of a Cambridge University student.

Physical disguise and costume are apt in fiction that focuses upon discerning the truth of events and the simple reality of whodunit. But as writers refine the potential of these conventions, they query the nature of identity itself. When detective fiction tackles such fundamental reality, the *whodunit becomes the who-is-it.

[*See also* Kidnapping; Prodigal Son/Daughter.]

• Howard Haycraft, ed., *The Art of the Mystery Story: A Collection of Critical Essays* (1946). Howard Haycraft, *Murder for Pleasure: The Life and Times of the Detective Story*, rev. ed. (1951). Colin Watson, *Snobbery with Violence*, rev. ed. (1979). Julian Symons, *Bloody Murder, From the Detective Story to the Crime Novel: A History*, rev. ed. (1985). Frank N. Magill, ed., *Critical Survey of Mystery and Detective Fiction: Authors*, 4 vols. (1988). Martin A. Kayman, *From Bow Street to Baker Street: Mystery, Detection and Narrative* (1991).

—Betty Richardson

MITCHELL, GLADYS (MAUDE WINIFRED) (1901–1983) was a British author in the classical school. Born in Oxfordshire, Mitchell attended the University of London and University College, *London, receiving a degree in history in 1926; she enjoyed a long career as a secondary school teacher. Mitchell's novels are more striking and idiosyncratic than the term "classical" would suggest; they often contain an element of spoof or *satire as well as accommodating the untoward, ambiguous, or unaccountable, giving them a unique flavor. Indeed, some are constructed on the thicket principle in detective writing with complications abounding, leading the odd commentator to take the playful author to task.

In her first novel, *Speedy Death* (1929), Mitchell introduces her sleuth, Mrs. (later Dame) Beatrice Adela Lestrange *Bradley, an elderly psychologist who consults for the *Home Office. Unlike the typical sleuth, Bradley is not physically attractive, often holds questionable moral positions, and is not above committing *murder. Fascinated by myth, folklore, and the occult, Mitchell often packs her stories with supernatural monsters as in *Winking at the Brim* (1974) or witchcraft as *Tom Brown's Body* (1949). Several novels including *The Saltmarsh Murders* (1932), feature vivid descriptions of place. Others describe corners of working life, such as pig farming in *Spotted Hemlock* (1958).

[*See also* Elderly Sleuth; Females and Feminists.]

—Patricia Craig

Moriarty, Professor James. Created by Sir Arthur Conan *Doyle to serve as an arch-enemy and intellectual equal to Sherlock *Holmes, Professor James Moriarty is portrayed as possessing the greatest criminal mind in England. As "The Napoleon of crime," Moriarty is said to be responsible for half of the *evil and most of the undetected crime in *London.

Moriarty's genius is chronicled in seven stories also featuring Holmes, who respects the professor's brilliant organizational powers, which permit the Moriarty to do little himself other than plan. By delegating authority to his subordinates, he is able to "sit motionless like a spider in the center of his web" while his agents carry out their sinister tasks.

Moriarty is also revealed to be a man of great academic scholarship. His treatise on the binomial expansion earned him a university chair in mathematics prior to his taking control of London's *underworld. His book, *The Dynamics of an Asteroid*, was found by Holmes to have "ascended to such rarefied heights" that no one was capable of criticizing it.

Doyle captured the public's imagination by depicting Moriarty as a figure of mythical proportions. The professor's protruding forehead and peering eyes staring out of an oscillating head suggest the appearance of a terrifying human reptile.

The dramatic confrontation between the two contrasting masterminds, Moriarty and Holmes, in the latter's lodgings, ranks as a great moment in English storytelling. The dynamics of their dialogue set the stage for their later inevitable duel to the death at Reichenbach Falls, where the two personify nothing less than the struggle between evil and good.

The exploits of Moriarty may not be true crime. Nonetheless, in literature, his acts are truly criminal.

[*See also* Master Criminal; Villains and Villainy.]

—Joe Fink

MORRISON, ARTHUR (1863–1945), British writer of realistic accounts of life in *London's East End slums, short detective fiction, lighthearted short stories, and a significant study of Japanese painting. Born to working-class parents, he was employed as a clerk for a charity institution before doing editorial work for the London *Globe*. His realistic fiction (*Tales of Mean Streets*, 1894; *A Child of the Jago*, 1896; and *The Hole in the Wall*, 1902) are minor classics, while his chief contributions to detective fiction remain his creation of the solicitor's clerk-cum-sleuth, Martin Hewitt, a "cheerful" average man who used ordinary talents to solve crimes, in the Sherlock *Holmes tradition, and his stories about the unscrupulous Horace Dorrington. The Hewitt stories were collected into three volumes, *Martin Hewitt, Investigator* (1894), *Chronicles of Martin Hewitt* (1895), and *Adventures of Martin Hewitt* (1896), with a fourth volume of connected episodes, *The Red Triangle: Being Some Further Chronicles of Martin Hewitt* (1903). Dorrington appears in only one collection, *The Dorrington Deed-Box* (1897). Morrison conformed to the status quo, working smoothly within established tradition without breaking new ground. Hewitt does not claim to employ a special system in his detective work, merely common sense and good eyesight. His ability as a detective is equal to that of Holmes, but he lacks the ego of his contemporary.

[*See also* Plainman Sleuth.]

• E. F. Bleiler, Introduction to *Best Martin Hewitt Detective Stories* (1976). Richard Benvenuto, "Arthur Morrison," in *Dictionary of Literary Biography: British Writers, 1860–1919*, vol. 70 (1988).
—J. Randolph Cox

Morse, Inspector, is a fictional police detective featured in the works of British author Colin *Dexter. A middle-aged bachelor, Morse (whose Christian name is not divulged until his appearance in *Death is Now My Neighbor*, 1997), is a chief inspector in the Thames Valley Police *CID whose cases frequently bring him into contact with *Oxford's academic community. Unorthodox, restless, and headstrong, he works largely by a process of free association, trial and error, and sheer inspiration rather than by following strict police procedure. While his reasoning is often flawed and his conclusions premature, Morse is tenacious. A loner by nature, he is both tender and tetchy. His sympathy for the *victims of crime and his wistful longing for unattainable women match his disgust with criminal behavior, his disdain for abusive authority figures, and his impatience with the pretentious and superficial; he understands that life is far more complex than sociology or the law would have us believe. Morse brings a passion for real ale, the operas of Mozart and Wagner, crossword puzzles, and poetry to bear in his investigations. He is assisted by the ordinary but able Sergeant Lewis, who regards Morse with both awe and annoyance. Actor John Thaw portrayed Morse vividly in a British television series in the 1980s and 1990s.

[*See also* Academic Milieu; Allusion, Literary; Police Detective; Sidekicks and Sleuthing Teams.]
—John Drexel

MORTIMER, JOHN (CLIFFORD) (b.1923), British novelist, playwright, screenwriter, journalist, critic, and translator, is best-known to readers of crime and mystery fiction as the creator of the rumpled, eccentric, poetry-spouting barrister Horace *Rumpole. Known to many as "Rumpole of the Bailey," after the title of one of the several volumes of short stories and the television series that Mortimer also penned, Rumpole was modeled on Mortimer's father, a distinguished barrister who specialized in divorce cases. Other regular characters and some incidents depicted in the series were inspired by people and events that Mortimer encountered or witnessed during his own career in the law.

Mortimer is the only child of a highly literate and eccentric barrister and his wife. He was raised in his parent's flat in *London's Inner Temple and later in a house and garden designed by his father, situated in England's Chiltern Hills. He spent a rather solitary childhood during which he enjoyed acting out scenes by William *Shakespeare on his own and taking long walks in the company of his father, who recited Sherlock *Holmes stories to him from memory. His father, who was blinded in an accident in his garden, was a great influence on Mortimer, convincing him to practice law and serving as a model not only for Rumpole but for the father figure in Mortimer's autobiographical play, *A Voyage Round My Father* (1971).

Mortimer attended the Dragon School in Oxford, then Harrow, and Brasenose College at Oxford University. During World War II, Mortimer served as an assistant director and scriptwriter in the Crown Film Unit, making documentary films. He then studied law and was called to the bar in 1948. He worked as a divorce barrister before practicing criminal law as a Queen's Counsel. During the latter part of his law career, he defended in celebrated cases concerned with questions of freedom of expression and censorship.

Mortimer's first courtroom drama was *The Dock Brief*, penned for radio in 1958. In it an old barrister and an unsuccessful criminal converse in a jail cell. In the 1970s Mortimer decided to create another barrister character, and penned the first of many Rumpole stories and screenplays, sometimes writing the latter first for television. Two of Mortimer's novels that do not feature Rumpole have strong crime elements. *Summer's Lease* (1988) is plotted around mysterious circumstances investigated by an English housewife holidaying with her family in Italy. *Felix in the Underworld* (1997) examines a paternity suit that turns out to be a murder case. Another novel, *Dunster* (1992), features a key courtroom scene. Mortimer is also editor of *The Oxford Book of Villains* (1992), a nonfiction work.

• John Mortimer, *Clinging to the Wreckage; A Part of Life* (1982). John Mortimer, *Murderers and Other Friends; Another Part of Life* (1994). Rosemary Herbert, *The Fatal Art of Entertainment: Interviews with Mystery Writers* (1994).
—Rosemary Herbert

MOSLEY, WALTER (b. 1952), son of a schoolteacher mother and a reputedly footloose father who worked as a school custodian, born in South Central Los Angeles, an African American neighborhood famous for its dramatically resistant attitude to the city's predominantly white police force. Educated in the public schools of Los Angeles and at Johnson State College, Vermont, Mosley worked in a variety of occupations, including potter and computer programmer, before beginning a serious study of writing at the City University of New York. His first novel, *Gone Fishin'*, was completed in the 1980s but did not see print until 1996. By that time he had built an enviable reputation with a series of novels that chronicle the adventures of Ezekiel "Easy" *Rawlins, an unlicensed investigator, and his sociopathic sidekick Raymond "Mouse" Alexander.

Taking the American hard-boiled first-person style of narration and combining it with African American oral and protest traditions, Mosley has crafted a series that has been critically hailed for its affinity to the foundational works of hard-boiled writing. This affinity is found in the serious use to which Mosley puts the popular genre—examination of *racism's constraints of liberty—and in his use of a Southern California setting of the 1940s and 1950s that was contemporary for Dashiell *Hammett and Raymond *Chandler but reconstructed history for Mosley.

Although African American crime writing has included the notable series about Harlem cops written by Chester *Himes in the 1960s, and instances of criminal *plots and detection in popular writing appearing in African American magazines throughout the century, Mosley's novels about Rawlins are the first major works in the crime genre to induce a large biracial audience to cross over the line that typically separates the black and white mainstreams of popular literature.

The stories in which Rawlins is the reluctant detective and *Gone Fishin'*, in which he is the narrator, are but one way Mosley explores the reality of American multicultural life. In *R. L.'s Dream* (1995) he recaptures the career of Robert Johnson in a genre he terms the blues novel, and in 1997 he introduced a new protagonist, Socrates Fortlow, a philosophically minded ex-convict, in *Always Outnumbered, Always Outgunned*.

[*See also* African American Sleuth; Prejudice.]

—Robert E. Skinner *and* John M. Reilly

MOTIVATION, PSYCHOLOGICAL. From its beginnings in the short stories of Edgar Allan *Poe, modern crime and detective fiction has displayed the keen interest of its authors in processes of the mind. "The Murders in the Rue Morgue" (*Graham's Lady's and Gentleman's Magazine*, Apr. 1841) begins with a discourse on intellectual methods of analysis. In "The Mystery of Marie Roget" (*Snowden's Lady's Companion*, 2 Nov. 1842) Poe's detective, the Chevalier C. Auguste *Dupin, applies a "calculus of probabilities" in an effort to solve a case bungled by the police, and the *plot of "The Purloined Letter" (in *The Gift*, 1845) develops a contrast between the empiricism of the police and the imaginative ratiocination of Dupin. Poe's exercises in detective investigation present a version of nineteenth century faculty psychology that permitted Samuel Taylor Coleridge to draw his distinctions between fancy and imagination, offered a theory to sanction Romanticism, and encouraged Poe's successors in detective fiction to portray their *Great Detectives in possession of acute analytic powers that they employed at the expense of their emotions.

Apart from its usefulness in the creation of detective protagonists, however, psychology, as thought of at the end of the twentieth century, played a small part during the early years of the genre in the depiction of crime and criminals. The culprits in Arthur Conan *Doyle's stories of Sherlock *Holmes are generally motivated by material ends, as are culprits in other writings from the last quarter of the nineteenth century, such as the series of novels by Anna Katharine *Green beginning with *The Leavenworth Case* (1878) and the Martin Hewitt stories by Arthur *Morrison, published mostly in the 1890s. On the other hand, the *armchair detective formula used by Baroness Emmuska *Orczy in her tales of the *Old Man in the Corner, G. K. Chesterton's intuitive detection stories of Father *Brown, and the Thinking Machine stories by Jacques *Futrelle about Professor S. F. X. *Van Dusen reinforce the point that for the first period of its existence writers working in the detective genre gave their interest in psychology over to portrayal of *sleuth protagonists.

As experiments in detective character accreted into a tradition of conventions about investigative method, modes of popular literature other than detective fiction delved deeper into psychology. The so-called *sensation novel represented by M. E. *Braddon's *Lady Audley's Secret* (1862) includes a rendition of insanity within a plot covering attempted murder. Mrs. Henry *Wood's stories, including her famous *East Lynne* (1861), evoke the psychological currents running beneath Victorian middle-class life. In the new century Marie *Belloc Lowndes's retelling of the Jack the Ripper murders in *The Lodger* (1913) kept the interest in abnormal psychology flowing until it freshened detective fiction.

That did not occur immediately, however, for the Golden Age tradition of detective fiction generally kept the plot so tightly focused on the doings of the *sleuth in a mannered society that little acknowledgment of subjective reality was possible. Dorothy L. *Sayers was an important exception, for by creating Harriet *Vane in all her complexity she allowed the entry of such patterns of psychology as displacement of emotion, in *Gaudy Night* (1935), and a fear of intimacy in the extended courtship of Vane and Lord Peter *Wimsey. For the most part, however, Golden Age fiction used for its motivation of crime a psychology nearly medieval in its dependence upon *greed, envy, and other death-producing sins.

Detective fiction began to be more sophisticated in its use of the psychology of motivation at the same time as other types of literature, that is, after the popularization of Freud's theories. Prominent writers like Margaret *Millar and her husband Ross *Macdonald draw heavily on Freud's insights, especially in their handling of familial relations and the dead hand the past can lay upon the present, but generally speaking the entry into popular consciousness of Freud and other members of the European psychoanalytic school produced a sensitizing experience rather than a conversion for detective writers.

The masterful works of Patricia *Highsmith are illuminating examples of the inventive possibilities following on the application of a writer's imagination to the conception of human nature conveyed by modern psychology. *Strangers on a Train* (1950) brilliantly strips away the normality of two characters to reveal their underlying corruptibility, and

Highsmith's novels about Tom Ripley, starting with *The Talented Mr. Ripley* (1955), are a cavalcade of protean experience showing the protagonist freeing himself from *guilt, changing identity, reviving his previous character, and improvising a new self that engages in crime for whim as well as purpose. All of Ripley's engaging antics are constructed from suppositions about the complex byways of personality discoverable through psychological investigation.

Equally profound in her use of psychology is Highsmith's younger contemporary, Ruth *Rendell, whose devotion to character portrayal has resulted in revision of the classic detective series figure and the production of a striking number of independent novels. Her series character, Chief Inspector Reginald *Wexford, is gifted with perceptual powers that he uses to probe criminal *motive in the manner of Georges *Simenon's Inspector Jules *Maigret. In addition, Rendell associates him with *family, friends, and fellow officers who give rise to complex subplots about their own subjective experiences. Among her non-series novels, *A Judgement in Stone* (1977) uses the *inverted detective story structure to study the effects on a woman of social isolation; *A Demon in My View* (1976) pairs the stories of a psychopath and a criminal psychologist to display the similarities of their struggles to remain functional; *The Face of Trespass* (1974) turns the novelist's attention to the psychology of an author experiencing writer's block; and penned under the Barbara Vine *A Dark-Adapted Eye* (1986) portrays the condition known as codependence. These latter works, occurring in the Canon of an author who also writes detective stories using a series sleuth, demonstrate the fuller development and merger of two popular channels of literature that under the rubrics of detective fiction and the sensation novel were once distinctly separate.

Margaret Yorke is another author who has worked in the once separate types. In 1970 she began a series of novels about the donnish detective Patrick Grant, but with *No Medals for the Major* (1974) she gave the English village story a psychological spin by plumbing the lives of ordinary residents as they are affected by crime. Her characters are not psychopathic but rather kindred to many of Yorke's readers. As H. R. F. *Keating has written of Yorke's *The Hand of Death* (1981), her technique, buttressed by psychological insight, plausibly shows "how a nice man like you, or your brother, can become a hooded rapist" (*Twentieth Century Crime and Mystery Writers*, 2nd ed. 1985).

At the end of the twentieth century detective fiction abounded in skillful handling of motive in terms of complex psychology. Detective psychology remained prominent, but faculty psychology in the sleuth had been replaced by holistic conceptions of mentality, such as found in P. D. *James's Commander Adam *Dalgliesh or Batya Gur's Israeli Chief Inspector Michael Ohayon. And, as the works about *Scotland Yard police cases written by Elizabeth George, the *Los Angeles cop stories by Joseph Wambaugh, and the hard-boiled adventures of John Marshall Tanner written by Stephen Greenleaf demonstrate, modern psychology had become as indispensable to characterization of the motive and

personality of *suspects and *villains as it had to description of detective protagonists.

[*See also* Characterization; Formula: Character; Reasoning, Types of.]

• Julian Symons, *The Modern Crime Story* (1980). George Dove, "The Criticism of Detective Fiction," in *Detective Fiction: A Collection of Critical Essays*, ed. Robin W. Winks (1980).
—John M. Reilly

MOTIVES. Crime fiction is known for its realistic treatment of crime, and insofar as art imitates life, motives for *murder in the genre follow common patterns of human behavior in the real world. Except for commercially inspired murders depicted in *thrillers, *police procedurals, and some *private eye novels, which investigate deaths resulting from organized crime such as racketeering and drug dealing, most detective novels tell of private or personal murders. Although several authors have commented on motive in crime fiction over the years, few systematic studies have been written. In her landmark study of true crime, *Murder and Its Motives* (1924), F. Tennyson Jesse stipulates six motives: gain, revenge, elimination, jealousy, conviction, and blood lust. In a more recent analysis, *The Reason Why* (1995), Ruth *Rendell also differentiates six separate types of motive: gain, revenge, escape, altruism or duty, insanity, and impulse or curiosity. Using different terminology both writers recognize gain, revenge, and self-protection, as well as jealousy, conviction, and criminal mania. Rendell includes envy and ambition, while Jesse omits them. Rendell alone contemplates what might be termed mercy killing and deals with murders of impulse, chance, and experimentation. Thus, a composite list yields about a dozen motives. Rendell believes that crime fiction readers are attracted to the genre by a desire to know what has gone on in a murderer's mind and heart, what has led the murderer to violate the old commandment, "Thou shalt not kill." Certainly, the growing emphasis on *characterization in the genre in the latter half of the twentieth century and the increasing prominence of the *whydunit would seem to justify her claim.

Although, neither Jesse nor Rendell creates a comprehensive or mutually exclusive system of classification for motive, when crimes are classified teleologically, that is, by the desired end result, four logically separate groups emerge, which contain subdivisions with related but independent motives. Under the heading practical motives are *greed (murder for gain) and self-protection (elimination of a threat). Under emotional satisfaction appear revenge, envy, and jealousy, plus love—the desire to possess or protect someone. Ambition can be fueled by both practical and emotional needs. A third category includes crimes designed to achieve intellectual, ideological, or spiritual goals such as political, social, religious, and aesthetic ideals, that is, murders stemming from conviction. The final general heading would designate crimes committed by the criminally insane, whose motives may or may not be understandable.

Probably the most common cause of *murder in real life and in fiction is greed—desire for the good things life offers. A quick trawl through the major writers of the genre reveals that "the lust for gain in the heart of Cain" motivates the majority of fictional murders. For example, in the cases of Sherlock *Holmes, cupidity consistently takes precedence over concupiscence. Examples of fictional crimes committed for gain occur in Dashiell *Hammett's *The Maltese Falcon* (1930), Philip *MacDonald's *The List of Adrian Messenger* (1959), and P. D. *James's *The Skull Beneath the Skin* (1982).

Murder for self-protection aims at eliminating an individual who threatens the killer's well-being. A combination of hatred and fear of the tormentor motivates these crimes. The villain acts in self-defense to remove the danger, whether it be blackmail or exposure of some sort of malfeasance followed by private and/or social disgrace. From Arthur Conan *Doyle's "The Adventure of Charles Augustus Milverton" (in *The Strand*, April 1904) to James's *Death of an Expert Witness* (1977), malefactors seek to preserve the equilibrium of their lives when it is jeopardized.

The revenge killer is impelled by a feeling of self-righteousness, a sense of the fitness of things, or a desire to put things right in his or her personal universe. This killer is determined to redress an injury whether it be physical, emotional, social, or material. Retaliation for injured pride produced by sexual and/or emotional rejection falls into this group, as do slights to personal or family honor. The perpetrator's feelings may be detached or passionately engaged. Elaborate plans may be made, with the killer waiting for the victim to fall into a carefully laid trap, or the murderer may strike out impulsively in blind rage. The more interesting revenge murders are those with subtly contrived schemes designed to achieve the satisfaction of retribution for the culprit and yet enable him or her to elude the law. Edgar Allan *Poe's short story "The Cask of Amontillado" (in *Godey's Lady's Book*, Nov. 1846) is a classic study in revenge of this type. Ngaio Marsh's *Photo-Finish* (1980) exemplifies the remorseless vendetta that is pursued tortuously but relentlessly from generation to generation as a matter of clan honor, often by people who have not been personally injured, while in C. F. Roe's *A Classy Touch of Murder* (1991), an individual acts more directly to protect the family name. Murderers in Edmund *Crispin's *Frequent Hearses* (1950), Agatha *Christie's *The Mirror Crack'd from Side to Side* (1962; *The Mirror Crack'd*), June Thomson's *The Long Revenge* (1974; *Sudden Vengeance*), Martha Grimes's *Help the Poor Struggler* (1985), and P. M. Carlson's *Audition for Murder* (1985) all seek to even the score by claiming a life for a life. James's *Unnatural Causes* (1967) illustrates the hell-like fury of a scorned woman, while in Frances Fyfield's disturbing story of Oedipal jealousy, *Trial by Fire* (1990; *Not That Kind of Place*), a would-be lover murders a rival and arranges for the desired partner to be arrested for the crime. Barbara Paul's *The Fourth Wall* (1979) is a most exquisite study in revenge, as the avenger contrives to make the punishment suit the crime. Elizabeth George's *For the Sake of Elena* (1992) contains one of the most subtle revenge motives in the genre.

Envy and jealousy are often confused, but they are not the same thing, even though a killer may be motivated by both, as in Thomson's *Death Cap* (1973). Envy is based on resentment of another's possessions, achievements, or status so that he or she becomes an object of hostility. Envy occurs presumably because its object seems manifestly less worthy or deserving than the self, and/or because the envied one makes the envious one feel inadequate. Hatred of the object of envy can grow so intense that it can be satisfied only by the removal of its cause, as in Hammett's *The Dain Curse* (1929) and Maureen O'Brien's *Close-up on Death* (1989).

Jealousy involves resentment of another individual who attracts the attention, affection, and/or sexual desire of a loved one. Jealous rage is composed of a sense of devastating loss plus outrage at being betrayed, feelings that give rise to the desire to injure those responsible for the pain. Children may become jealous of a favored sibling who seems to attract an inordinate share of parental concern or parents may harbor feelings of possessive love toward children, as in Josephine *Tey's *Brat Farrar* (1949), Christie's *Nemesis* (1971), Thomson's *Deadly Relations* (1979; *The Habit of Loving*), and Liz Rigby's *Total Eclipse* (1995). In adult life, jealousy usually occurs when one of the partners in an established relationship is attracted to a third party, who is then resented by the second partner for alienating the affections of his or her beloved. Sometimes all hatred is directed against the interloper and the injured partner seeks to redress the situation by eliminating the detested rival, hoping that by doing so he or she will reclaim the love of the partner and restore the status quo. This hot-blooded *crime passionnel* is regarded more leniently by society, as is the case in Rendell's *A Guilty Thing Surprised* (1970), than premeditated schemes to remove a loathed competitor, as in Rex *Stout's Novella, *Immune to Murder* (in *Three for the Chair*, 1957). Sometimes the anger of the jealous individual is directed only against the partner who betrays as in Thomson's *No Flowers, by Request* (1987). At times the jealous avenger cannot be satisfied till both are dead as in Raymond Chandler's *The Long Goodbye* (1953). Occasionally, the third party murders his or her married lover for refusing to leave the marriage, as in Christie's *Five Little Pigs* (1942; *Murder in Retrospect*).

These cases must be distinguished from those where no jealousy is involved but in which the murder of a spouse is committed as a matter of convenience so the lovers can be united. These crimes are prompted by erotic love whose motivation is selfish and possessive. This situation occurs in Christie's *Murder at the Vicarage* (1930) and James M. *Cain's *The Postman Always Rings Twice* (1934) and *Double Indemnity* (1943).

Sexual attraction sublimated as possessive love can also lead unmarried people to murder rivals in the hope of securing or maintaining a desired relationship, as portrayed in the passionate and disturbing story of sexual rivalry in Elizabeth George's *Playing for the Ashes* (1994).

The human need to love can assume almost atavistic intensity in the desire to possess and nurture a child. Rendell portrays this primitive drive in *Murder*

Being Once Done (1972) and again writing as Barbara Vine in *A Dark-Adapted Eye* (1986) and *Asta's Book* (1993; *Anna's Book*, 1994). In Robert Barnard's *Fete Fatale* (1985; *The Disposal of the Living*), a woman transfers this love to her pet dog and kills to avoid being separated from him.

Not all crimes committed in the name of love are selfish. The most sympathetic murderer is the unselfish or altruistic killer who strikes out to protect the innocent. Frequently, the crime is committed for purely personal reasons, to prevent suffering or shield a loved one, as in Marsh's *Hand in Glove* (1962), James's *Shroud for a Nightingale* (1971), Thomson's *Alibi in Time* (1980), Dorothy Simpson's *Six Feet Under* (1982), and P. M. Carlson's *Bad Blood* (1991). Occasionally, however, the crime is sparked by a desire to avert danger from an intended victim, as in George's *A Great Deliverance* (1988). Other ethically inspired murderers may seek to fulfill an obligation, pay a debt, or perform a duty, as in James's *Devices and Desires* (1989).

Crimes motivated by ambition are stimulated by desire for power and/or an obsession to achieve professional goals, political office, or social prominence. Dorothy L. *Sayers's *The Unpleasantness at the Bellona Club* (1928), Leo Bruce's *Die All, Die Merrily* (1961), Robert Robinson's *Landscape with Dead Dons* (1963), and Lillian O'Donnell's *A Private Crime* (1991) all depict characters driven to kill by ambition. The desire for personal power over another is also a facet of ambition, and murder represents total dominion, as stated by the villain in Barnard's *Death in Purple Prose* (1987; *The Cherry Blossom Corpse*).

Sometimes the motive is broader in scope, deriving from a sense of social responsibility that leads to crime fueled by conviction. An individual thus motivated is often concerned to avoid anti-social acts by removing their probable instigator, as in Amanda *Cross's *Poetic Justice* (1970). The perpetrator can also be prompted by zeal for a social or political cause or devotion to a religious ideal that results in extreme hostility toward alternative creeds and belief systems. Murders prompted by social issues such as homophobia, abortion rights, or animal protection belong in this group. Political beliefs underlie murder in A. J. Orde's *A Little Neighborhood Murder* (1989). Murders committed in the name of religion may involve a ritual demanding blood sacrifice, punishment for breaking rules, or merely intolerance of another's beliefs. Marsh's *Spinsters in Jeopardy* (1953; *The Bride of Death*) and *Last Ditch* (1977) deal with cult ritual and religious mania. Religious bigotry leads to murder in Bruce's *Furious Old Women* (1960). Gladys *Mitchell's *Death at the Opera* (1934; *Death in the Wet*) provides a rare example of murder committed on purely aesthetic grounds.

Mental illness in its various manifestations—delusion, obsession, compulsion—often results in murder. Paranoid delusion leads to violent death in Rendell's *A Judgement in Stone* (1977), and the compulsion to kill is clearly illustrated in her *A Demon in My View* (1976). A small group of murderers, surely also insane, kill just for the experience of knowing what it is like to take a human life and/or to outwit the authorities. Curiosity, experimentation, or vanity seems the best way to describe this kind of motive, which appears in Israel *Zangwill's *The Big Bow Mystery* (1892) and Bruce's *Crack of Doom* (1963, *Such Is Death*).

The most upsetting and alienating kind of murder is that of blood lust. These killers are driven by psychopathology to seek victim after victim. Early examples occur in Marsh's *Singing in the Shrouds* (1959) and John Fowles's *The Collector* (1963). Since the 1980s, when the psychological profile of the serial killer became public knowledge, a spate of novels has appeared featuring psychopathic villains. Among the most well known are Thomas Harris's *The Silence of the Lambs* (1988), Patricia D. Cornwell's *Postmortem* (1990), and Caleb Carr's *The Alienist* (1994). These works, which reveal the well springs of the dark side of human nature, may provide insight and lead to understanding of human behavior, but they do not condone antisocial acts. In helping to interpret the shadows on the cave wall, their insight brings comfort.

• Jesse, F. Tennyson, *Murder and Its Motives* (1924). Philmore, R. and Yudkin, John. "Inquest on Detective Stories," *Discovery* (April 1938). Rptd. in Howard Haycraft, *The Art of the Mystery Story* (1946): 423–35. Obstfeld, Raymond, "Opus in G Minor on a Blunt Instrument: The Development of Motive in Detective Fiction," *The Armchair Detective*, 14, no. 1 (1981): 9–13. Pearson, Col. Fred. "A Motive for Murder," *Police Times* (12 August 1988): 6, 17. Rendell, Ruth, ed. *The Reason Why*, (1995).
                                                      —B. J. Rahn

Moto, Mr. A fictional character created by the American author John P. Marquand, Mr. Moto is portrayed as Japan's top *secret agent. Moto appears in six novels, beginning with *No Hero* (1935; *Mr. Moto Takes A Hand*). All are set in exotic locales including Hawaii, Singapore, and Peking and are worked around a formula featuring young European or American couples who become involved either professionally or inadvertently in international espionage.

The stories are told from the perspectives of these Western protagonists who encounter Moto as they struggle to deal with the threatening situations they are facing. In fact, Moto sometimes seems peripheral to the action, but when he is on stage, the delicately made, self-effacing secret agent steals the scene.

Educated at two American universities, Moto is a skilled linguist who speaks perfect English. He is a dapper dresser, sometimes tending toward flamboyant European outfits. Moto is a master of *disguise who at various times masquerades as manservant, bartender, or tourist. His talents include a proficiency in judo.

The American agent in *Stopover: Tokyo* (1957; *The Last of Mr. Moto, Right You Are, Mr. Moto*) suspects that Moto is a member of the Japanese aristocracy. Whatever his background, Moto has enough influence with an "august personage" to be able to circumvent the military's actions. Although this is a touchy diplomatic matter, as always Moto is cool in a tight spot, and efficient in dealing with his foes. In this last book in the series, however, Moto reveals his fallibility by making two serious errors of judgment.

Moto, like his contemporary Charlie *Chan, is the

antithesis of the "yellow peril" characters symbolized by Sax *Rohmer's Dr. *Fu Manchu, generally emerging as an ally of the Western hero. And yet, much about Mr. Moto remains a mystery.

[See also Couples as Secondary Characters; Ethnic Sleuth; Ethnicity.]

• John G. Gross, *Marquand* (1963).　　　—Frankie Y. Bailey

MUGGING. *See* Assault.

MULLER, MARCIA (b. 1944), American author of *private eye novels, anthologist, and critic of crime fiction. Muller was born in Detroit, Michigan, and earned a bachelor's degree in English and a master's degree in journalism from the University of Michigan in Ann Arbor. After holding several jobs, she became a full-time writer in 1983. Credited with creating the first contemporary American female private eye, Sharon McCone, in *Edwin of the Iron Shoes* (1977), Muller has written three series centered on women detectives. These heroines are McCone, a professional detective who eventually opens her own agency; Joanna Stark, co-owner of an art security firm, introduced in *The Cavalier in White* (1986); and Elena Oliverez, art museum director and *amateur detective, introduced in *The Tree of Death* (1983). In collaboration with her husband, Bill Pronzini, Muller wrote *Beyond the Grave* (1986); with Oliverez investigating a century-old mystery. All three series are set in California, where Muller has lived for more than two decades.

Personal and professional relationships between the sexes form a significant theme in the McCone books, as the detective struggles to balance work and love, often learning that men find her job troubling. In the McCone and Oliverez series, race and *ethnicity are also recurring themes, as both detectives are minority group members—McCone is part Native American and Oliverez is Latina—who sometimes confront *prejudice.

• Marcia Muller and Bill Pronzini, *1001 Midnights: The Aficionado's Guide to Mystery and Detective Fiction* (1986).
　　　—Maureen T. Reddy

MURDER. From the time of its origin as an Old English word until today, the term "murder" has meant the most heinous kind of ᴬtaking of life, the killing of one or more than one human being by another, also known as homicide. According to *The Oxford English Dictionary*, the Old English word "morðor" or was applied to "any homicide that was strongly reprobated." The term often denoted secret homicide, and it carried the senses of great wickedness, deadly injury, and great torment. In the laws of England, Scotland, and the United States, murder is defined as the criminal killing of a human being with malice aforethought, or willful murder. In the law courts of these nations, conviction on a charge of willful murder rests upon establishing that the perpetrator was of sound mind when the act occurred.

Throughout the history of crime and mystery writing, murder has been the crime of choice around which writers have centered *detective novels, *police procedurals, and *private eye novels, all forms of fiction that depend upon a central *sleuth discovering the truth on behalf of a *victim—who is no longer alive to right the wrong done to him or her—and so acting as the protector of society. Murder is viewed as a sufficiently heinous crime to sustain the attention of the reader through the long form of a novel in which the writer may develop puzzling *plot twists, mysterious *clues, and revelation of character, especially in regard to *motive, while the reader tries to determine which character had the *means, motive, and opportunity to perpetrate the crime. In inverted crime novels, in which the murderer is identified from the start, the crime writer often examines psychological *motivation along with any material motive that may drive the actions of the perpetrator. Fyodor *Dostoyevsky's *Prestuplenie I nakazanie* (1866; *Crime and Punishment*) and Francis Iles's *Malice Aforethought* (1931) and *Before the Fact* (1932) exemplify the inverted form. Books about psychopaths driven to kill and about those who have accidentally perpetrated murders are also likely to take a psychological approach to the subject, as are narratives about murder perpetrated under mitigating circumstances. An exemplar of the latter is Susan Glaspell's "A Jury of Her Peers" (*Everyweek*, 5 Mar. 1917), in which a farmer's wife kills the husband who murdered the joy of her life, a beloved canary bird. In this story, the author ruminates not only on questions of crime and punishment but on the issue of *guilt experienced by the friends of the murderess, who realize how they have failed their neighbor even as they recognize that their friend has committed a crime.

Crime writers have almost always stayed very close to the oldest definition of murder when centering stories around it, regarding it as a malicious and serious crime for which society can only gain restitution through the earnest action of the hero-sleuth. The seriousness of the quest to discover who perpetrated a mysterious crime was, however, sometimes treated rather lightheartedly in puzzle-centered *whodunits in which the sleuth or the suspects in the case were portrayed in an intentionally farcical manner. In such detective fiction, however, the act of killing and the result of the murder—the *corpse—are generally kept offstage, undercutting the awful reality of murder in order to allow readers to look at the *puzzle as an entertainment. Even in books of this lighthearted nature, the fact of murder is usually taken seriously to the point that the reader believes the sleuth will stop at nothing until the murderer is identified. Some inverted detective novels may also use *humor, which may be easily sustained when a would-be murderer keeps bungling the job, as is the case in Richard Hull's *Murder of My Aunt* (1934) and Nigel Williamson's *The Wimbledon Poisoner* (1990). More unusual is the novel in which murder has been done and the writer dares to make the corpse itself a figure of fun while also deflating the pretensions of sleuth and suspects alike, as in Alfred Alcorn's *Murder in the Museum of Man* (1997).

[See also Inverted Detective Story.]
　　　—Rosemary Herbert

MURDERLESS MYSTERY. Murderless mysteries are more common in earlier crime and mystery writing than in later; they are more frequent in the British than in the American tradition; and they are far more likely to be short stories than novels. Among murderless mysteries, certain types of crimes are predominant, foremost among them *theft. Within this general category, two types are especially frequent: jewel theft and theft of government documents or secrets. Jewel theft tends to locate the story in an aristocratic *milieu governed by gentlemen's codes and club rules, where honor is more at issue than legality; it provides the high-toned setting for the exploits of *gentleman thieves, such as E. W. *Hornung's A. J. *Raffles or Clifford Ashdown's Romney Pringle. A subset of the jewel-theft genre is the eye-of-the-idol story. The prototype is Wilkie *Collins's The Moonstone (1868)—although it does include a murder—with its attendant Orientalist themes.

Other common, symbolically resonant theft motifs in murderless mysteries are thefts of artworks, rare books or coins, and the related crimes of art *forgeries, swindling, and *plagiarism, all of which represent appropriations of objects not only valuable in themselves but symbolic of civilization or cultural values. Another common category is fraud, including embezzlement, swindles, and con games—these being the most common motifs in American murderless mysteries—often in connection with *impersonation or blackmail. A recurring motif in the British tradition concerns missing false claimants, missing inheritances, and wills that have been tampered with. Other murderless mysteries may involve violent crimes that do not eventuate in *murder, notably abduction, and there is a whole category that involves the motif of attempted, unsuccessful murder (stories that otherwise are no different from murder mysteries).

In the vast corpus of Victorian and Golden Age work jewel theft is prominent, notably in collections devoted to the theme, such as Max Pemberton's Jewel Mysteries I Have Known (1894; Jewel Mysteries from a Dealer's Notebook), and I. D. B.; or, the Adventures of Solomon Davis on the Diamond Fields and Elsewhere (1887) by W. T. E. (pseudonym of W. T. Eady). Sherlock *Holmes recovers precious gems twisted from the royal crown in "The Adventure of the Beryl Coronet" (Strand, May 1892) and recovers a jewel pilfered from a *London hotel room in "The Adventure of the Blue Carbuncle" (Strand, Jan. 1892). Holmes's contemporary, Arthur *Morrison's Martin Hewitt, cracks a code encapsulated in a musical score to discover the hiding place of jewels in "The Case of the 'Flitterbat Lancers'" (Windsor Magazine 3, Jan.–June 1896). Similarly, the Thinking Machine shows how pearls have been transferred from a boat to shore by homing pigeons, in Jacques *Futrelle's "The Missing Necklace" (Cassell's Magazine, 1908). Among other early mysteries, the series called "The Count's Chauffeur" by William le Queux (Cassell's Magazine, 1906), includes four jewel theft stories. G. K. *Chesterton stories featuring jewel theft include Flambeau's designs on African jewels in "The Flying Stars" (Cassell's Magazine, June 1911) and on a jeweled church relic in "The Blue Cross" (Storyteller, Sept. 1910).

Other murderless jewel or precious object thefts include Baroness Emmuska *Orczy's "The Affair at the Novelty Theatre," and *Old Man in the Corner story (Royal Magazine, 1904), "The Case of Major Gibson," a "skin o' my tooth" Patrick Mulligan story (Windsor Magazine, Aug. 1903); Guy Boothby's "The Duchess of Wiltshire's Diamonds" (Pearson's Magazine, Feb. 1897); C. L. Pirkis's "Drawn Daggers" (Ludgate Magazine, June 1893); Ernest *Bramah's "The Mystery of the Vanished Petition Crown," featuring the blind detective Max *Carrados (Max Carrados Mysteries, 1927); and Rodrigues Ottolengui's "The Aztec Opal" (Idler, Apr. 1895). The latter belongs to the eye-of-the-idol subgenre, as does Agatha *Christie's "The Adventure of 'The Western Star'" (Poirot Investigates, 1924). Dorothy L. *Sayers's most famous tale of jewel theft is "The Necklace of Pearls" (Hangman's Holiday, 1933).

Art theft is central to Hornung's Raffles story "Nine Points of the Law" (Cassell's Magazine, Sept. 1898), in which a Velazquez painting goes missing; the theft of a recently discovered Rubens occurs in Christie's "The Girdle of Hippolita," and of a Cellini goblet in "The Apples of the Hesperides" (both in The Labours of Hercules, 1947; almost all the stories in Labours are murderless). Art-related murderless mystery novels by Michael *Innes include From London Far (1946; The Unsuspected Chasm); Christmas at Candleshoe (1953; Candleshoe); A Family Affair (1969; Picture of Guilt); Money from Holme (1964); and Honeybath's Haven (1977). Valuable antiquities are stolen in R. Austin *Freeman's "The Antropologist at Large" (Pearson's Magazine, 1919), and in other cases featuring Dr. John Evelyn *Thorndyke.

Another prominent crime in murderless mysteries, theft of government documents, is the subject of Arthur Conan *Doyle's "The Naval Treaty" (The Memoirs of Sherlock Holmes, 1894) and "His Last Bow" (Strand, Sept. 1917); Morrison's "The Case of the Dixon Torpedo" (Strand, June 1894); and Victor L. Whitechurch's "The Affair of the German Dispatch-Box" (Thrilling Stories of the Railway, 1912).

Several stories involve the favorite British theme of eccentric wills, exemplified in Robert Barr's "Lord Chizelrigg's Missing Fortune" (Triumphs of Eugene Valmont, 1906); Fergus Hume's "The Florentine Dante" (Hagar of the Pawn-Shop, 1898); and Christie's "Strange Jest," in which Miss Jane *Marple locates a fortune in a priceless postage stamp (Three Blind Mice, 1950; The Mousetrap), and "The Case of the Missing Will" (Partners in Crime, 1929).

The use of impersonation to commit fraud is a common feature of claimant novels, such as Josephine *Tey's Brat Farrar (1949; Come and Kill Me), which is murderless in the narrative present, or Julian *Symons's The Belting Inheritance (1965).

Abduction is sometimes the method used to engineer an impersonation, as in Morrison's "The Case of Laker, Absconded" (in Chronicles of Martin Hewitt, 1895), or George A. Bests's "The Counterfeit Cashier" (Cassell's Magazine, May 1902). More commonly, abduction is aimed at obtaining a ransom, as in Christie's "The Adventure of Johnny Waverly" (The Mousetrap and Other Stories 1949; Three Blind Mice and Other Stories), or to achieve a political end, as in "The Kidnapped Prime Minister" (*Poirot Investigates*, 1924). Nonlethal assault and abduction occur in Chesterton's "The Resurrection of Father Brown," (1924; *The Incredulity of Father Brown*, 1926) and abduction of a favorite to influence the outcome of a race occurs in "The Loss of Sammy Crockett" (*Martin Hewitt, Investigator*, 1894). Abduction to enlist domestic services is the charge laid against the two female protagonists of Tey's *The Franchise Affair* (1948), by a young schoolgirl, as a way of explaining her lengthy disappearance from home.

Many Victorian and Golden Age stories deal with varieties of frauds and swindles. Swindling and conspiracy feature in L. T. Meade and Robert Eustace's "The Arrest of Captain Vandaleur" (*Harmsworth Magazine*, July 1894); Allingham uses counterfeiting in "The Psychologist," insurance fraud in "Little Miss Know-All," and the receipt of stolen goods in "The Lie-About" (all in *The Allingham Case-Book*, 1969).

Chesterton said that a mystery must have a death to have life in it, yet he himself generated a good number of murderless mysteries, all those involving Flambeau before his reformation, for instance. There is no crime at all in "The Scandal of Father Brown," "The Blast of the Book" (both in *The Scandal of Father Brown*, 1927), "The Absence of Mr. Glass" (*Wisdom of Father Brown*, 1914), or "The Secret of Father Brown" and its companion, "The Story of Flambeau" (both in *The Secret of Father Brown*, 1927). Two of the principal motifs of the murderless mystery come together in "The Insoluble Problem" (*The Scandal of Father Brown*, 1927), in which a "murder" is staged to distract Flambeau from investigating a theft.

It is common in the tradition for murder to be disguised as suicide, but Christie's "Murder in the Mews" (*Murder in the Mews*, 1937; *Dead Man's Mirror*) and the parallel "The Market Basing Mystery" (*The Under Dog and other Stories*, 1951) have a more unusual, suicide-disguised-as-murder plot, and still another variant of this latter puzzle is Christie's "Wasp's Nest" (*Double Sin and Other Stories*, 1961), which involves both attempted suicide and attempted murder by framing for murder. Other variants of this suicide-disguised-as-murder plot include Philip MacDonald's *Rynox* (1930; *The Rynox Murder Mystery*), which includes the concoction of a fictional murderer, and E. C. Bentley's *Trent's Last Case* (1913; *The Woman in Black*), in which a tycoon intends to commit suicide as a way of framing his secretary for murder, but whose plan results in suspicion of murder based on what proves to be accidental death.

A major contribution to the murderless mystery that does not fit into the above categories is Sayers's *Gaudy Night* (1935), an account of a series of vindictive vandalisms perpetrated against an Oxford women's college. Many of Innes's whimsical, donnish mysteries are murderless; in addition to the examples already noted, his early mystery novel of manners, *Stop Press* (1939; *The Spider Strikes*), deals with a variety of interwoven bizarre plots, some innocent and some criminal, but focused mainly on stopping a mystery writer from continuing to publish his series.

• Erik Routley, *The Puritan Pleasures of the Detective Story* (1972). LeRoy Panek, *Watteau's Shepherds: The Detective Novel in Britain 1914–1940* (1979). Audrey Peterson, *Victorian Masters of Mystery* (1984). Julian Symons, *Bloody Murder: From the Detective Story to the Crime Novel*, 3rd rev. ed. (1992).
—Peter V. Cenci *and* George L. Scheper

MURDER WEAPONS, UNUSUAL. *See* Weapons, Unusual Murder.

Murdock, Kent. Kent Murdock, newspaper photographer, is a series *sleuth whose adventures owe much to the journalism experience of his creator, George Harmon *Coxe. An *amateur detective, whose profession regularly puts him at the scenes of crimes, Murdock may depend upon physical and photographic evidence to solve his cases.

Coxe often required Murdock to rescue himself from awkward situations. His first appearance, *Murder with Pictures* (1935), has a murder in Murdock's apartment building and a female suspect hiding in his shower—while he is using it. In both *Four Frightened Women* (1939) and *The Fifth Key* (1947), knockout drops are placed in Murdock's scotch, and he awakens in the same room as a female *corpse.

He is honeymooning in *The Barotique Mystery* (1936), and his wife is later featured in *Mrs. Murdock Takes the Case* (1941), but then disappears from the series. Coxe explained that he realized he had created so strong a character in the wife that she was in danger of upstaging Murdock.

[*See also* Journalist Sleuth.]

• J. Randolph Cox, "Mystery Master: A Survey and Appreciation of the Fiction of George Harmon Coxe; Chapter Three: The Sophisticated Young Photographer and Other Series Characters," *The Armchair Detective* (Aug. 1973): 232–41. Unsigned article, "Kent Murdock," in *Encyclopedia of Mystery and Detection*, ed. Chris Steinnbrunner and Otto Penzler (1976), p. 293.
—Marvin Lachman

MUSICAL MILIEU. The musical milieu has long been used by crime and mystery writers as a background to their fiction. Over the years, detective fiction set in this *milieu has made use of stereotyped characters and attitudes popularly believed to be typical of the music worlds ranging from opera companies to jazzy dance halls.

Some writers endow their characters with musical accomplishments to make them seem more dramatic or appealing, as is the case in "A Scandal in Bohemia" (*Strand*, July 1881) when Arthur Conan *Doyle gives Irene *Adler status as an operatic prima donna, which raises her in the estimation of Sherlock *Holmes. This story is typical of many that are cited as having musical elements; however, it is not set specifically in the musical milieu, although Adler's musical accomplishments along with her cunning intelligence make her memorable.

Another frequently cited "musical" work of detective fiction is Dorothy L. *Sayers's *The Nine Tailors* (1934). Here the bell tower where much action takes place serves as a musical milieu, as does the hotel dance hall described in *Have His Carcase* (1932), which works as an atmospheric environment for the action, rather than a mere location or background for a story. Cornell *Woolrich's seedy dance halls epitomize the desperation people experienced during the *Great Depression.

Musical productions are especially rich territory for crime writers, who may use to advantage dramatic or stereotyped characters, timing and stage cues, and the atmospheric qualities engendered by types of music. Jane Langton has written two novels in which crime occurs in the midst of musical productions. Her *The Memorial Hall Murder* (1978) is set in the titular hall at Harvard University, during a performance of Handel's *Messiah*. Langton's *Murder at the Revels* (1997) is set in the same building during rehearsals and performances of the annually produced *Christmas Revels*. A leading music festival is the backdrop for Lucille Kallen's C. B. Greenfield's *The Tanglewood Murder* (1980), which follows the struggle for possession of a priceless eighteenth-century Guarnerius violin.

Operatic productions are used as background to professional jealousies in Helen Traubel's *The Metropolitan Opera Murders* (1951), which depicts a deadly feud between fictional sopranos. James Yaffee imagines real sopranos, Maria Callas and Renata Tebaldi, feuding in "Mom Sings an Aria" (*EQMM*, Oct. 1966), but violence is done by their fans. Someone is killing the world's leading tenors in *Gala* (1987) by Metropolitan Opera tenor William Lewis; professional jealousy is assumed to be the *motive. In *Death on the High C's* (1977), opera lover Robert *Barnard has a police detective who is knowledgeable about opera solve a case centered around a hateful mezzo-soprano working with a small English opera troupe. Barbara Paul fictionalized Enrico Caruso and Geraldine Farrar into series detectives beginning with *A Cadenza for Caruso* (1984).

Gilbert and Sullivan's operatic comedies are highlighted in Isaac Asimov's "The Gilbert and Sullivan Mystery" (*EQMM*, Jan. 1981), which serves as a paean to Gilbert's witty lyrics, and in Gladys *Mitchell's *Death at the Opera* (1934), set during a school production of *The Mikado*. American musical comedy is the milieu for Herbert Resnicow's *The Gold Gamble* (1988) in which the author depicts a revival of *Guys and Dolls*. A musical produced in a West End, *London theater is the scene of Simon Brett's *Star Trap* (1977).

The jazz world is shown in Bart Spicer's *Blues for the Prince* (1950), set in Philadelphia. Malcolm Braly's *Shake Him Till He Rattles* (1963) concerns a sadistic policeman who assumes all jazzmen use drugs. More recent mysteries with jazz backgrounds are set in New Orleans. Exemplars are Clark Howard's "Horn Man" (*EQMM*, June 1980), John Lutz's *The Right to Sing the Blues* (1986), and Julie Smith's *The Axeman's Jazz* (1991), which portrays a serial killer who loves jazz so much that he promises to spare those who will listen to it. Dishonesty within the commercial aspects of the contemporary popular music industry comes under the scrutiny of Evan Horne, Bill Moody's *private eye, in *Solo

Hand (1994). While most writers use one kind of musical background, William Bankier's tastes and skills are catholic, as demonstrated in stories set in the worlds of jazz, dance hall music, and symphonic music. Bankier's "Concerto for Violence and Orchestra" (*EQMM*, June 1981) uses disco music, which he dislikes, as a metaphor for civilization's deterioration.

The rock-and-roll world is used as background to fiction featuring Elvis Presley impersonators, including Art Bourgeau's *The Elvis Murders* (1985) and Lynne Barrett's Edgar Award–winning "Elvis Lives" (*EQMM*, Sept. 1990). Jesse Sublett, a musician who words in rock bands, created the guitar-playing *sleuth Martin Fender in *Rock Critic Murders* (1989), and rock guitarist and singer Douglas Allyn explores Detroit's popular music in "The Sultans of Soul" (*EQMM*, March 1993) and other stories that are informative about the Motown sound.

[*See also* Music and Song; Theatrical Milieu.]

• Marvin Lachman, "Murder at the Opera," *Opera News* (July 1980): 22–30. Philip L. Scowcroft, "Music in English Detective Fiction," *(CADS)* (Apr. 1986): 13–23.

—Marvin Lachman *and* David Whittle

MUSIC AND SONG. While the *musical milieu, with its colorful personalities, professional jealousies, and dramatic *settings, is a popular place to set crime and mystery fiction, elements of music and song are used in crime and mystery writing that may be set in *milieus that may or may not be strictly musical. These elements range from the use of lines from lullabies, popular ditties, and songs to create catchy titles to the use of musicological expertise to perpetrate crimes or to interpret vitally important clues.

The use of lullabies in titling is exemplified in Mary Higgins *Clark's *The Cradle Will Fall* (1980) in which a rhyme usually sung to children as they are being safely tucked into bed contrasts with the horror a mother experiences when her children are missing. Most crime writers use titles taken from recognizeable tunes similarly, contrasting their associations with childhood, safety, and happy holidays with the disruptive crime depicted in the fiction. Examples of titles taken from sung rhymes are Agatha *Christie's "Sing a Song of Sixpence" (*A Century of Detective Stories*, 1935) and her *A Pocket Full of Rye* (1953). Julian *Symons's "The Flowers That Bloom in the Spring" (*EQMM*, July 1979) and Hal Dresner's "By the Sea, By the Sea" (*AHMM*, Oct. 1962) take their titles from lighthearted songs. Lyrics to songs aimed at children have also been used in mystery titling, as is the case in Richard Levinson's and William Link's collaboratively written short story, "Whistle While You Work" (*EQMM*, Nov. 1954). Lines and titles from Christmas carols also appear in crime fiction titles, as is the case in Baynard Kendrick's "Silent Night" (*Sleuth Mystery Magazine*, Dec. 1958) and Frank Sisk's "O Tannenbaum" (*AHMM*, Oct. 1975).

The use of musicological know-how to perpetrate a crime is seen in "The B-Flat Trombone" (*Average Jones*, 1911), by Samuel Hopkins Adams, in which the instrument of the title emits a note with a resonance perfectly suited to triggering an explosion.

Perhaps the most famous use of musical noise to perpetrate a crime is seen in Dorothy L. *Sayers's *The Nine Tailors* (1934), a work in which campanology, or the art of bell ringing, is essential to the *plot.

Clueing and the interpretation of *clues based on musical knowledge is seen in Edmund *Crispin's *The Case of the Gilded Fly* (1944; *Obsequies at Oxford*). The absence of clarinets in a performance of Mozart's *Prague Symphony* points to the killer in Cyril *Hare's *When the Wind Blows* (1949). The English folksong "Bushes and Briars," heard played at a distance on a native pipe in the unlikely setting of the Czech mountains, proves vital to the discovery of a missing person in Ellis *Peters's *The Piper on the Mountain* (1966).

[*See also* Clues, Famous; Nursery Rhymes; Titles and Titling.] —David Whittle

MYSTERY STORY. No term in the literary lexicon is more ambiguous than "mystery." In a past known to comparative religionists and within circumstances familiar only to initiates of secret lodges in the present, mystery refers to concealed rites. For students of the European Middle Ages, "mystery story" refers to the popular dramatic presentations of the birth, death, and resurrection of Jesus Christ once associated with religious holidays. Even today in theological circles the word retains religious significance when used in reference to the Eucharist or to matters unknown except by divine revelation. It would seem, then, that "mystery" once meant the subject and source of humanity's most meaningful stories of destiny.

The impact of the changes associated with the emergence of a modern world can be observed in the narrowing of "mystery" to signify uncertainty surrounding a crime, for in secular society anxiety issues less from existence itself than from the fact that it can be extinguished by a violent act. "Mystery" thus comes to denominate stories about identification of criminals. Not without imprecision, though, because "mystery" commonly comes paired with the term "detective story," which, of course, is also a type of narrative about *pursuit of villains and the rendering of explanatory solutions for criminal events. In the binary coupling of "mystery" and "detective story" the two become near-synonyms employable separately or in combination. As if that were not vexing enough, "mystery" can come paired alternately with "crime," as in "crime and mystery writing," where the one term, "mystery," seems to modify "writing" as if there were stories to be considered that are not criminal in their mystery.

When the genre of crime and mystery writing was young, prescriptive criticism like that written in earnest behalf of the *rules of the game might have insisted with some effect on clear distinctions, with the *detective novel seen to focus on the *sleuth hero and the process of detection, the crime novel centered upon psychology, and the mystery novel serving as a narrative that gets to the heart of perplexing matters through the peeling away of layers of confounding wrapping until the central truth is revealed. At this late date, however, stipulation of that sort is no more possible than archaeological recovery of a forgotten meaning that mystery once held in writing about the problem of crime. The best that can be accomplished by way of definition is a process of teasing out of the complex practices of narrative writing the undeclared sense of how the element of mystery gives peculiar shape to story.

Wilkie *Collins's *The Woman in White* (1860), an undisputed foundation work in the genre of crime and mystery, presented a *plot of changed identities, fortune-hunting connivance, and pursuit of a villain by a courageous woman and a surprisingly intrepid drawing master. Mary Elizabeth *Braddon's *Lady Audley's Secret* (1862), a work associated with the *sensation novel as well as crime and mystery writing, exploited a plot of insanity. Marie Adelaide *Belloc Lowndes contributed to the formation of the genre a psychologizing study of an analogue to Jack the Ripper in *The Lodger* (1913). Predating the purification of narrative into a tale of cerebral detection in the Golden Age and differing decidedly from the sleuthing stories of Sherlock *Holmes and his contemporaries in their inclusion of character and incident not contributing directly to detection, the works of Collins, Braddon, and Belloc Lowndes remind us that in their origin the novels about crime employed more melodrama and subjective sentiment than they did detection. Although the way the history of crime and mystery writing is conventionally told portrays the rise of the new genre as a process through which detection shook itself free of the vestigial elements of the novel that are extraneous to an account of cerebral *puzzle solving, the history could just as well, and more accurately, be understood as the record of varying narrative methods. One method led in the direction of the *Great Detective and development of attendant conventions effecting a transformation of the novel into tales of detection, but an equally vital and long-lived type of narrative retained a display of heightened action and emphatic *atmosphere in its treatment of crime. If the history were to be so revised, then the mystery story could be seen as the parallel to the detective story.

For parallel it is, in the sense that the mystery story is generated from an instance of violation, just as the detective story is. Where it differs is in its displacement of detection in favor of attenuating the experiences consequent to violation. The works of Mary Roberts *Rinehart, for example, usually locate violation in the realm of intimacy. A romantically involved woman fears that the man she believes she knows is capable of unspeakable deeds. A *family member is haunted in some way by the actions or experiences of a relative. An anxiety as frightening as fear of violent death comes close to home.

Unsympathetic critics, nothing the technique of foreshadowing in such works of intimacy by the protagonist's rueful statement that, had she but known what was to occur, she would not have proceeded so blithely, have contrived the dismissive label of the *Had-I-But-Known school to express their ridicule. Labored as the convention may be, it is, after all, simply a shorthand introduction of atmosphere, the same in its own way as the description of mean streets in hard-boiled writing or the introduction of the country house setting as an emblem of the closed society of Golden Age fiction.

If the point about foreshadowing is accepted, it readily follows that a collection of repeated elements or conventions can serve to define the mystery story. Among these conventions are emphasis upon emotion as well as intellect in a protagonist; a plot that introduces peril to the protagonist accidentally rather than as a result of a professional or avocational role as a detective; a tendency to present the crime of the story more as violation of personal security than as felonious assault, which means that *murder is not required; a striking preference for centering stories upon female characters and upon *settings common rather than exotic. All mysteries do not contain all conventions, nor do they exist in anything like a "pure" form. Among practicing writers today, Phillis A. *Whitney stands as exemplar of mystery tradition, her works a template of the basic mystery. For examples of highly inventive turns on the mystery pattern, Margaret *Millar earns top billing with her adaptation of Gothic motifs and the psychological thriller to the purposes of uncovering the mystery in ordinary life.

As Millar's books illustrate, the mystery story readily hybridizes. Millar herself incorporated detection into accounts of emotional distress. P. D. *James's fiction about Cordelia *Gray, detective, resonates with elements of the mystery story. The studies of psychopathic behavior in the fiction of Patricia *Highsmith emphasize mystery over crime, the labyrinths of psychology instead of the assembly of evidence. Finally, the stories of Kate *Fansler written by Amanda *Cross demonstrate a happy blend of series detection with mystery element. To satisfy the aficionados of detection stories there are plots of murder and solution, but Cross also presents the satisfactions of mystery convention by placing crime in the presumably unlikely settings of academic and literary life, equipping her protagonist with an emotional life complete with a complement of vulnerability, and portraying the subjective consequences of threat and violation to be as bitter as actual violence.

Without doubt booksellers, publicists, reviewers, and writers themselves will continue to use the term "mystery" interchangeably with "detective story" and in tandem with the descriptor "crime." The lesson in that may well be that the genre the terms describe is a vital mix, always revising its appearance.

• David Grossvogel, *Mystery and Its Fictions: From Oedipus to Agatha Christie* (1979). Julian Symons, *Bloody Murder: From the Detective Story to the Crime Novel: A History* (1985).
—John M. Reilly

MYSTERY WRITERS OF AMERICA. Founded in New York City in 1945 by a group of prominent American mystery and crime writers, Mystery Writers of America, Inc. (MWA) was inspired by The *Detection Club of *London. Although MWA had some of the same goals as that organization, it differed in opening its membership to all published writers in the field and in making annual awards for achievement in the genre. Headquartered in *New York City, the organization boasts a membership numbering in the thousands and including many of today's most prolific and well-known writers.

Membership is available in four categories: Active, for published, professional writers of fiction or nonfiction in the crime/mystery/suspense field; Associate, for professionals in allied fields, such as editors, critics, agents, and booksellers; Affiliate, available by petition only to writers not yet professionally published; and Corresponding, for writers qualified for active membership who live outside the United States. Only active members may vote or hold office.

The stated goals of MWA are as follows:

1) To promote and protect the interests and welfare of mystery writers; 2) To advance the esteem and literary recognition of the genre; 3) To monitor tax and other legislation affecting writers; 4) To receive inquiries through the national office and direct them to the applicable committee or chapter; and 5) To circulate important information and provide the opportunity for stimulating association with other professionals in the field.

Its motto, "Crime doesn't pay—enough," reflects both the early and ongoing concern of the organization, to ensure equitable treatment for new and established writers and to monitor developments in legislation and tax laws to protect the economic interests of mystery and crime writers.

The organization holds monthly meetings; offers mystery writing courses, workshops, and seminars; publishes an annual anthology of short stories by members; publishes a newsletter, *The Third Degree*; maintains a reference library of works in and related to the genre at its headquarters; and periodically convenes an international congress to assemble crime writers from all over the world. Its most well-known activity is the annual Edgar Allan Poe Awards banquet. The highly coveted "Edgars" have been awarded since 1947 to authors of distinguished work in such areas as the short story, the novel, fact crime, juvenile and young adult fiction, and television and motion picture screenplays. The most prestigious and coveted award is the Grand Master, which recognizes not only important contributions to the genre over time but also consistently high-quality work.

• Barry T. and Angela Zeman, "Mystery Writers of America, Inc: An Abbreviated History," *Armchair Detective* (spring 1993): 36–41, 100–106. Brochure, Mystery Writers of America, National Headquarters, New York City.
—Katherine Anne Ackley

NAMES, AMBIGUOUS. *See* Red Flags.

NAMES AND NAMING OF CHARACTERS. Crime and mystery fiction has long been the preserve of the memorably named character. Distinctive names for primary and secondary characters may reflect the wit, whimsy, personal history, or artfulness of their creators. Perhaps the best-documented case of a sleuth's name is Arthur Conan *Doyle's Sherlock *Holmes. Doyle borrowed "Holmes" from Oliver Wendell Holmes, another physician-writer, whom Doyle admired. For Holmes's first name, Doyle originally considered Sherringford, or Sherrinford, until Sherlock finally came to him, from a family of landed gentry in the part of Ireland where the Doyles came from. Agatha *Christie's Hercule *Poirot reflects in his first name his great strength in solving crimes, though he has a small, pear-shaped body, suggested by his last name.

The names of detectives reflect the history of the genre as well. During the Golden Age, detectives' commitment to an ordered, aristocratic world reassured their audience. Their names buttressed that reassurance, with a dash of *humor: Dorothy L. *Sayers's Lord Peter *Wimsey, going where his whimsy takes him; Ngaio *Marsh's Roderick *Alleyn, not pronounced as it is spelled, a well-established appeal to snobbery; and Margery *Allingham's Albert *Campion, suggesting royalty as well as that other Golden Age, the Elizabethan. Even the detectives of the hard-boiled school may carry names invoking a world of chivalry, though they belong to a time without aristocracy and often without order. Raymond *Chandler's Philip *Marlowe, based on the medieval Sir Thomas Malory, is the prime example, but Ross *Macdonald's Lew *Archer (the chaste hunter) is almost as obvious.

Even when names seem nondescript, there may be an artfulness in the author's choices. G. K. *Chesterton's cleric, Father *Brown, is a down-to-earth man with spirituality. Nothing could be plainer than Christie's Miss Jane *Marple, but the surname suggests her adamantine qualities, and her associates never address her without the "Miss." A detective with only one name seems dignified, mysterious, or independent: Jonathan Gash's Lovejoy and Robert B. *Parker's *Spenser are examples. The single first name has a similar effect; in the names of Adso of Malk or Brother *Cadfael, there is no familiarity. Or the detective may have no name, such as Bill Pronzini's nameless sleuth and Len *Deighton's nameless spy; such anonymity preserves their superiority. A detective may be named after a place (Joyce *Porter's Inspector Wilfred *Dover, Karen Kijewski's Kat Colorado), after a historical figure (Arthur W. *Upfield's Inspector Napoleon *Bonaparte, Michael Connelly's Inspector Hieronymous Bosch), after animals (June Thomson's Inspector Finch, William Campbell *Gault's Joe Puma).

The name of the detective's auxiliary establishes his ordinariness. Doyle wisely changed Ormond Sacker to Dr. John H. *Watson. The name Archie *Goodwin balances the imperious and gormandizing qualities of Rex *Stout's Nero *Wolfe. Christie's partner for Poirot, Captain Arthur Hastings, is quintessentially English with a name referring to the crucial battle of 1066. His name also suggests his haste to draw (often erroneous) conclusions, and a winning eagerness. Allingham achieved the same with Campion's partner, Magersfontein *Lugg, the first name commemorating a British triumph in the Boer War and the second emphasizing his role as carrier and listener.

The name of the villain can be as important as that of the *sleuth. Godfrey Ablewhite in Wilkie *Collins's *The Moonstone* (1868) is a whitened sepulchre of hypocrisy. Holmes's most formidable opponents have a family resemblance: Professor James *Moriarty, Colonel Sebastian Moran, Charles Augustus Milverton. Dashiell *Hammett's Casper Gutman, exotic and obese, is one of the most suggestively named villains in *hard-boiled fiction.

Even secondary characters speak for their creators. John *Mortimer's penchant for Dickensian names, in a sometimes Dickensian legal system, produces a black teenager named Oswald Gladstone and an aging manufacturer named Percival Ollard. In hard-boiled fiction, the names may be more realistic and pedestrian. The stability evoked by the name of the Sternwood family in Chandler's *The Big Sleep* (1939) is endangered by the younger daughter, Carmen.

At one time foreign names flagged the villain in both hard-boiled and *detective fiction, testifying to the systemic conservatism of the genre. Count Fosco in Collins's *The Woman in White* (1860) is diabolical, as are Sax *Rohmer's *Fu Manchu and Hammett's Paul Madvig in *The Glass Key* (1931). The attitude toward detectives with ethnic names has also changed; whereas Earl Derr *Biggers's Charlie *Chan was always mildly patronized, Sara *Paretsky's V. I. *Warshawski is never so treated.

—Barrie Hayne

NARRATIVE THEORY. Every literary genre subscribes to a particular narrative theory (sometimes to more than one) and adheres to a specific set of narrative conventions. Formula fiction, as its name suggests, is especially reliant on its emblematic constructions, and detective fiction, as an exemplar of formula fiction, comprises one of the most rigidly defined genres in the history of literature. Indeed, one crime writer, S. S. *Van Dine, formulated a list of rules to which "proper" murder mysteries would adhere. The list included such prescriptions as: "The novel must have at most one detective and one criminal, and at least one *victim (a *corpse)"; "love has no place in detection fiction"; and "everything must be explained rationally." Ronald A. *Knox, the founders of London's *Detection Club, and others laid down rules of a literature that is considered to be an interactive game played against the readership.

The narrative theory that governs classic detective fiction is straightforward. There is the discovery of the crime, the *pursuit of information by the detective, the climactic revelation of the solution, and the resolution or explanation of the solution. As Tzvetan Todorov points out in his *The Poetics of Prose* (1977), *whodunits contain two stories: the story of the crime and the story of the investigation. The chief emphasis in the second story—the story of the investigation—is upon learning rather than action.

The two narrative movements Todorov sees in detective fiction support the novel's thematic message that "the truth will out." This message is delivered overtly through the exposure of the criminal and also, more covertly, through the story of the investigation. The genre subscribes to a specific set of narrative conventions and formulaic patterns, and it also conforms to a belief that that which is seen can be known and that which is known can and must be explained. *Great detectives like Arthur Conan *Doyle's Sherlock *Holmes and Dorothy L. Sayers's Lord Peter *Wimsey are able to explain the mysteries they encounter through the use of superior reasoning abilities.

Clearly, the strictures of the detective genre place constraints upon the crime writer, who seeks to produce a novel that adheres to the narrative conventions already established. At the same time, however, working within these narrow confines allows authors to play with the conventions and to produce works that both conform to and subvert the traditional detective paradigm.

The American tradition of *hard-boiled fiction constitutes a move to break down the *class structure preserved in traditional detective fiction. In contrast with classic detective fiction, which is often set in country houses or small villages, hard-boiled novels take place in the mean streets of major urban centers and focus on the blight and *corruption pervading the social order. In this mode, the detective is lower-class, and often he differs from the criminal only insofar as he is upholding the law, which is itself frequently shown to be problematic. Hard-boiled detective fiction usually employs a first-person narrative technique, which serves to generate a sense of immediacy, and works to implicate the reader in the scope of the social critique.

More recently, such writers as Sara *Paretsky, Sue *Grafton, and Marcia *Muller subvert the formerly sexually specific basis of the hard-boiled genre by portraying female detectives who are as tough and streetwise as their male counterparts. Other writers, like Joseph *Hansen (whose detective is gay) and Walter Mosley (whose detective is African American), have used the genre in a similar fashion. Such strategic generic modifications highlight the exclusive nature of traditional detective fiction when they undercut its rigid codes of *gender, race, and sexual preference. In so doing, these writings also draw attention to some of the reasons for the popularity of a genre that provides its readers with an opportunity to explore, fictively, the cultural tensions and anxieties posed by a world in transition. As a result, crime writing not only offers a pleasurable reading experience, it also serves as a useful tool for mediating and assimilating social change.

• Catherine Belsey, *Critical Practice* (1980). John Cawelti, "The Study of Literary Formulas," in *Detective Fiction: A Collection of Critical Essays*, ed. Robin W. Winks (1980). Glen W. Most, and William W. Stowe, *The Poetics of Murder: Detective Fiction and Literary Theory* (1983).

—Priscilla L. Walton

NARRATIVE VOICE. *See* Point of View, Narrative; Voice.

NARRATOR AS CRIMINAL. While the vast majority of crime and mystery fiction is narrated by sleuth, sidekick, or reliable third-person narrator, the use of a criminal or murderer as story teller has produced some of the most memorable and controversial work in the genre. Even before Edgar Allan *Poe's "The Telltale Heart" (*Pioneer*, Jan. 1843), which succeeds as a deranged speaker's confession of murder, Charles *Dickens's "A Confession Found in a Prison in the Time of Charles the Second" (*Master Humphrey's Clock*, 1840) used the device of a murderer describing his crime and the compulsion to confess. Although Dickens's unfinished *The Mystery of Edwin Drood* (1870) was evidently intended to conclude with the murderer describing his crime, the first noteworthy example of a novel narrated by a murderer is Oliver Onion's *In Accordance with the Evidence* (1912), a killer's cool description of how he got away with hanging his rival.

In *The Murder of Roger Ackroyd* (1926), Agatha *Christie introduced the narrator-murderer into the *puzzle mystery and created a critical uproar. Objecting to her concealing the narrator's *guilt, Ronald A. *Knox in his "Ten Commandments of Detection" or "detective fiction decalogue" in his introduction to the *Best Detective Stories of the Year 1928* (1929) forbade any future use of a villain "whose thoughts the reader has been permitted to follow," but Dorothy L. *Sayers defended Christie as having vouched only for the narrator's function and not for his honesty. The debate provoked Edmund Wilson's essay "Who Cares Who Killed Roger Ackroyd?" (*New Yorker*, 20 Jan. 1945), but the consensus now is that Christie "played fair" by allowing the reader to detect a crucial gap in the duplicitous Dr. Sheppard's chronology of events.

Technically difficult, the "Ackroydal device" is rarely used. Most writers disclose a speaker's criminality immediately and rely on other devices for surprise. *The Murder of My Aunt* (1934), for example, by Richard Henry Sampson writing as Richard Hull is the diary of a bungling would-be killer who is finally killed, as a postscript reveals, by his intended *victim. A complex variation is *The Face on the Cutting-Room Floor* (1937) by Ernest Borneman writing as Cameron McCabe, in which the narrator's revelation that although acquitted of *murder, he is guilty, is followed by a newspaperman's speculations about who else may be guilty and the disclosure that he is himself a murderer. Eric Mowbray Knight writing as Richard Hallas gives the theme of misdirected *justice an American *setting in *You Play the Black and the Red Comes Up* (1938) with a narrator who, intending to murder one woman so he can marry another, kills the wrong one and is freed by a *suicide's false confession.

Narrator-killers in American crime novels are often agents in *pursuit of private justice, such as Dashiell *Hammett's *Continental Op, who goes on a bloody vendetta in *Red Harvest* (1929), and Nick Corey, Jim *Thompson's small-town sheriff in *Pop. 1280* (1964), who engineers with impunity his enemies' deaths for personal *motives. Irish writers, by contrast, tend to subordinate *violence to epistemological concerns, as in John Banville's *The Book of Evidence* (1989) and *Ghosts* (1993), narrated respectively by a murderer on the loose and one who has served his sentence, and in *The Third Policeman* (1940, published 1967) by Brian O'Nolan writing as Flann O'Brien in which a killer is blown up attempting to claim his victim's money and recounts the rest of his bizarre story from his afterlife in hell.

Black humor can also be achieved by utilizing the criminal as narrator. Such is the case in Nigel Williams's *The Wimbledon Poisoner* (1990), concerning a suburban husband who would like to do in his wife and in Ellis Parker Butler's "Our First Burglar" (in *Everybody's Magazine*, 1909; later published as "The Silver Protector") in which a paranoid homeowner constructs a Rube Goldbergesque burglar trap that kills the intruder. It was Christie who found one more variation for the narrator as murderer in the puzzle story *Curtain: Hercule Poirot's Last Case* (1975). Her *Endless Night* (1967) is narrated by a murderer but without the *Whodunit element. Written in the 1940s but published only shortly before Christie's death, *Curtain* served both to close the career of master detective Hercule *Poirot and, by reworking the Ackroydal device, to answer her critics. The narrator, Captain Arthur Hastings, utterly trustworthy as reporter, comes perilously close to committing a murder like Dr. Sheppard's in *Ackroyd*, after which Poirot takes over as narrator, in a confession written before his death, disclosing that he has himself committed a murder.

[*See also* Who-Gets-Away-with-It.]

• Julian Symons, *Bloody Murder. From the Detective Story to the Crime Novel*, 3rd rev. ed. (1992). Tony Hilfer, *The Crime Novel: A Deviant Genre* (1990).   —Mary Rose Sullivan

NATIVE AMERICAN SLEUTH. The introduction of the Native American sleuth into detective fiction has added new dimensions to the genre. These include cultural materials that, when organically connected to the *plot, expand the methods of detection to incorporate different value systems and processes of thought; the invocation of spaces, such as the harsh and inhospitable landscapes of the southwestern reservations, previously unexplored in detective fiction; and the opening of the genre into political processes such as the rights of indigenous peoples and the ecological impact of the commercial exploitation of resources on cultures closely tied to the land. Native American detectives first appeared in the popular *dime novels of the 1880s. Judson R. Taylor's *Phil Scott, the Indian Detective: A Tale of Startling Mysteries* (*Phil Scott, the Detective*), published in 1882, marks one of their earliest appearances in book form. Popular interest in the conquest of the American West and in Native American cultures then perceived as exotic led to numerous reprints of titles like T. C. Harbaugh's *Velvet Foot, the Indian Detective, or, The Taos Tiger* (1884). Even Buffalo Bill, best known for his Wild West Show, penned a mystery with a Native American detective, *Red Renard, the Indian Detective, or, The Gold Buzzards of Colorado: a romance of the mines and dead trails*, published in 1886. *Pawnee Tom, or, Adrift in New York: A Story of an Indian Boy Detective* by Old Sleuth appeared in 1896. The "Indian detective" of these titles had skills in tracking, an intimate knowledge of the landscape, spoke several languages, and could negotiate several cultures with ease. In "A Star for a Warrior" (*EQMM*, Apr. 1946), Manly Wade Wellman introduced tribal policeman David Return, a member of the Tsichah, an imaginary tribe for the creation of which Wellman borrowed Cheyenne and Pawnee elements. Return's methods of deduction arise out of deep knowledge of traditional mythology and ceremonials.

In the 1970s, Brian Garfield published *Relentless* (1972) and *The Threepersons Hunt* (1974) featuring a Navajo protagonist, Arizona state trooper Sam Watchman, who investigates crimes closely linked to the landscape, such as battles over water rights and the complex relations between state and federal agencies and the reservations. In 1971 Richard Martin Stern published the first in his series about Johnny Ortiz, a part-Apache, part-Spanish officer in the Santa Cristo Police. In *Murder in the Walls* (1971), *Death in the Snow* (1973), and *Missing Man* (1990), Ortiz and his African American cultural anthropologist friend, Cassie Enright, investigate crimes stemming from clashes between traditional Pueblo cultures and progressive urbanization.

The best-known series of Native American mysteries are Tony *Hillerman's novels featuring Sergeant Jim *Chee and Lieutenant Joe Leaphorn. Alongside his convincing *puzzles, Hillerman offers in-depth studies of Navajo and Zuni culture and folklore and considerable insight into the idiosyncrasies of the Native American character. Their popularity inspired three more recent series. Jean Hager has developed two interconnected series featuring Oklahoma Cherokee detectives Mitchell Busyhead, a police chief introduced in *The Grandfather Medicine* (1989), and Molly Bearpaw, a young female officer who is featured in *Seven Black Stones* (1995) and *The Spirit Caller* (1997). Jake Page introduced his blind Santa Fe sculptor detective Mo Bowdre and his Anglo-Hopi girlfriend Connie Barnes in *The Knotted Strings* (1995). Here, and in its 1996 sequel, *The Lethal Partner*, Page writes with authority and feeling about Hopi tribal life, offering glimpses into kachina ritual dances and writing movingly of a tribal elder's grief over the loss of his gods. More recently, Aimee Thurlo has introduced a series centered on Pueblo Indians featuring half-Navajo botanist Belara Fuller, beginning with *Second Shadow* (1993).

In the wake of multiculturalism, the Native American detective has emerged as a popular figure in juvenile literature, where the mystery genre is put to the task of educating children about Native American cultures, religions, and oral traditions. Examples are Anna Hale's *Mystery on Mackinac Island* (1989), Kate Abbott's *Mystery at Echo Cliffs* (1994), Rob MacGregor's *Prophecy Rock* (1995), and Nat Reed's *Thunderbird Gold* (1997).

[*See also* Ethnic Sleuth; Ethnicity; Heroism.]

—Lizabeth Paravisini-Gebert

NATURALISM. American literary naturalism grew out of philosophic, scientific, and literary developments in eighteenth-and nineteenth-century Europe. The development of Newtonian science in the seventeenth century, which posited nature as equal in importance to spirit, gave rise to the eighteenth-century philosophy of deism, which saw nature as God's revelation. In the nineteenth century, August Comte in his *Course of Positive Philosophy* (1830–42), developed the theory of positivism, which rejected the notion of first causes and absolute truths, sought effective causes from which all laws could be deduced, and viewed all phenomena as subject to physical laws. Naturalism, which stated that the essence of God, nature, and the human individual could all be found in the principle of reason, developed from these philosophic traditions.

In the nineteenth century, the social sciences also contributed ideas that became part of the tradition of naturalism. Charles Darwin in *On the Origin of Species* (1859) asserted that new biological species were the result of a random process of natural selection operating without the assistance of divine purpose. Herbert Spencer in *The Synthetic Philosophy* (1860–96) attempted to synthesize all the social sciences into a system whose unifying principle was evolution, and Karl Marx asserted in *Capital*, published beginning 1887, that the basic principle of social evolution was class struggle. Key ideas that the naturalists extracted from these works were a vision of the world as an essentially violent and godless *milieu, the randomness of cause and effect as this principle relates to individuals, and the idea of *class struggle, which translated for many of them into a criticism of the wealthy and corrupt strata of society.

In *The Experimental Novel* in 1880, Émile Zola applied the new methodologies to literature. He sug-

gested that the novelist observe certain patterns of human behavior and acts, place a character endowed with them in a controlled environment, and interfere in the manner of an experimenter by modifying the circumstances and surroundings without deviating from the laws of nature. Zola's twenty-volume Rougon-Macquart series, about the evolution of hereditary powers and maladies in members of a family who represent almost every social class and profession of the French Second Empire, became an inspiration for writers on both sides of the Atlantic.

Will versus fate is a controlling theme in the work of the naturalist writer. An interest in depicting the taboo as a corrective for the nineteenth-century dictum that only the pleasant and morally correct were suitable subjects for literature became one of the hallmarks of the movement. Focus on the lives of the rural and urban poor often led to social criticism as writers sought to analyze the causes of unequal distribution of wealth. An objective presentation of material is one of the most often noted characteristics of naturalistic style, but critics have also cited the documentary, the impressionistic, the satiric, and even the sensational as variants within the naturalistic mode. Stephen Crane, Frank Norris, Jack London, Theodore Dreiser, and Ernest Hemingway rank among the most important practitioners of American literary naturalism.

Naturalism exercised its most important influence on crime and mystery writing in the hard-boiled detective fiction of the 1930s and 1940s. But several thematic concerns link naturalism to the writings of earlier mystery writers as well.

The naturalistic insistence on the primacy of reason is an important element in mystery and crime writing. It may be seen in the classical detective story as far back as Edgar Allan *Poe and Arthur Conan *Doyle. The element of ratiocination was essential to these stories, and led to the development of the detective who examined *clues and questioned *suspects solely with the aim of solving a mystery. Poe's Chevalier C. Auguste *Dupin, Doyle's Sherlock *Holmes, Agatha *Christie's Hercule *Poirot, and Dorothy L. *Sayers's Lord Peter *Wimsey all function in this manner. The *police procedural tale, in which the reader's interest is directed toward the actions taken to solve the crime, also depends on reason by involving the reader in the attempt to solve the mystery. John *Creasey, Ed *McBain and Georges *Simenon are all practitioners of this genre.

The importance of crime in the mystery and detective story is a natural outgrowth of the naturalistic fascination with crime as a symptom of social *corruption. In the classical detective story, the establishment of the criminal's identity and of a *motive for the crime are important parts of the *formula. The location of the detective in a *setting isolated from the chaos and corruption of the world that bred the crime underscores this notion. Poe's Dupin and Doyle's Holmes both operate within such settings as the reader becomes aware that the supremely rational and, for the most part, law-abiding classical detective stands in sharp contrast to the rest of society.

The hard-boiled school of detective fiction, which most critics predicate began with the fiction of Dashiell *Hammett in the 1920s and was developed in the work of Raymond *Chandler, Erle Stanley *Gardner, and others in the 1930s and 1940s, exhibits many thematic and stylistic links to naturalism. As in the classical detective story, the setting is an important element. In *hard-boiled fiction, the setting is most often the modern city, and it is depicted as a moral wasteland, the breeding ground of *violence and crime. The rich and powerful, with whom the detective almost always has contact during his work, are often depicted as either morally corrupt or enervated and boring; the implied criticism of the wealthy and powerful is similar to that of many of the literary naturalists.

The hard-boiled detective exists somewhat apart from the world of wealth and corruption, but he inevitably becomes involved with it when he is sought out to solve a crime. Though he is not of this world, he understands it and can move through it and emerge from it relatively unscathed. Often he is forced, because of a threat to his safety or because of his emotional involvement with one or more of the criminals, to take a moral stance toward the criminal or the crime. Hammett's Sam *Spade falls in love with Brigid O'Shaughnessy but turns her in at the end in The Maltese Falcon (1930), for example, and Chandler's Philip *Marlowe views his solution of crimes as part of a personal crusade for *justice. This moral direction also underscores the social criticism theme.

The naturalistic insistence on the random operation of the universe is most notable in the works of Hammett. Sam Spade's rendition of the Flitcraft incident in The Maltese Falcon is the most often cited example of Hammett's statement of this theme. But throughout his novels and most of those of other practioners of the genre, hard-boiled detectives do not control their fates. Fate is subject to chance.

The detailed descriptions of criminal activity, violence, and *sex and sexuality portrayed in hard-boiled detective fiction are all outgrowths of the naturalistic tendency to focus on the unpleasant side of reality. The depiction of women as sexual temptresses rather than romantic heroines, as in Hammett's O'Shaughnessy and Chandler's Carmen Sternwood (The Big Sleep), also spring from this tradition.

The style of the hard-boiled detective writer is based on simple, stripped-down sentences; the objectification of people by the use of equal amounts of description of humans, actions, and objects; the use of understatement; the portrayal of actions as series of component movements; and an emphasis on brutality. This style follows closely the stylistic lead of such naturalists as Crane, London, and Hemingway, whom many of the hard-boiled detective fiction writers read and admired.

[See also Chivalry, Code of Femme Fatale; Realism, Conventions of; Reasoning, Types of; Voice: Hard-Boiled Voice.]

• Lars Ahnebrink, The Beginnings of Naturalism in (1950). Charles Child Walcutt, American Literary Naturalism: A Divided Stream (1956). Donald Pizer, Realism and Naturalism in Nineteenth Century American Literature, rev. ed. (1984). June Howard, Form and History in American Literary Naturalism (1985). Lee Clark Mitchell, Determined Fictions: American Literary Naturalism (1989).   —Susan Ward

NATURAL WORLD, THE. See Great Outdoors, The; Settings, Geographical.

NAUTICAL MILIEU. This entry is divided into two parts. The first section surveys fiction that is set on board ocean liners and ferries. The second part provides selected examples of crime and mystery writing set in the worlds of boating and sailing in smaller vessels, including motorboats, yachts, fishing boats, canal boats, and a canoe. While writers who use the ocean liner milieu have the most obvious opportunity to isolate their suspects in a setting that is a world in itself, all writers who place their characters in the boating scene can keep them confined to an atmospheric setting.

Ocean Liner and Ferry Milieu
Boating and Sailing Milieu

For further information, please refer to Setting.

OCEAN LINER AND FERRY MILIEU

Transatlantic liners, and ocean liners generally, reached a peak in popularity and prestige in the years between 1920 and 1940, detective fiction's Golden Age. This was also the period when *murder in detective fiction was an upper-class activity. Not surprisingly, many detective authors of the period combined the two, staging murders on oceangoing vessels. A liner offers the detective novelist a closed community, albeit a potentially large one, in an exotic or unusual *setting. The *atmosphere of luxury piquantly contrasts with the sordid business of murder and the often light-hearted wit suggests the holiday spirit.

Writers have used both real and fictional liners: The Titanic figures in John Dickson *Carr's classic The Crooked Hinge (1938), and the Lusitania in Agatha *Christie's The Secret Adversary (1922) and in M. McDonnell Bodkin's "The Ship's Run" (The Quest's of Paul Beck, 1908). Fictional ships are more common, however. Carr twice sailed the North Atlantic on liners: As Carr he wrote The Blind Barber (1934), a murder case featuring *clues as jokes, and as Carter Dickson he wrote Nine—and Death Makes Ten (1940; Murder in the Submarine Zone), which takes place just after war has broken out. South African liners figure in Christie's The Man in the Brown Suit (1924), inspired by the author's own voyage to the cape as part of a working world cruise with her first husband, and later in Ngaio *Marsh's Singing in the Shrouds (1958). Other liner examples are Bruce Hamilton's Too Much of Water (1958), set on a Barbados-bound passenger vessel, and C. Daly King's Obelists at Sea (1933).

Freeman Wills *Crofts's Found Floating (1937) is one of the few novels in which the author describes the working of the ship. The murder is committed on board, and there is a characteristic Croftsian *alibi.

In Crofts's *Fatal Venture* (1939; *Tragedy in the Hollow*) the cruise ship sails round the British Isles as a floating gambling casino while outside territorial waters; the murder takes place ashore, and the vessel is again well depicted. From the same period come Q. Patrick's *S. S. Murder* (1933), written in the form of letters, and Earl Derr *Biggers's *Charlie Chan Carries On* (1930), describing cruises to Rio and in the Pacific, respectively.

Though transatlantic passengers increasingly traveled by air, not liner, cruises remained popular both in reality and in detective fiction. Nicholas *Blake's *The Widow's Cruise* (1959), Miles Burton's *Murder in Absence* (1954), Andrew Garve's *The Late Bill Smith* (1971), and, though the cruise is but a prologue, Elizabeth Lemarchand's *Cyanide with Compliments* (1972) are all set in the Mediterranean, a popular destination for cruises.

The Caribbean is the scene of Edward Gorman's witty *Several Deaths Later* (1988), Robert James's *Board Stiff* (1951), Leo *Bruce's *Death in the Middle Watch* (1974), Josephine Bell's *The Fennister Affair* (1969), and Frances and Richard Lockridge's *Voyage into Violence* (1956). Africa is the destination in Marian Babson's *The Cruise of a Deathtime* (1984).

Short sea ferries also figure in detective fiction: Crofts's *Man Overboard* (1936), set in the Irish Sea, and *Mystery in the Channel* (1931; *Mystery in the English Channel*); Patricia Moyes's *Night Ferry to Death* (1985), set on the Harwich-Hook North Sea crossing; and Chris Rippen's "Ferry Noir," in *Murder on Deck! Shipboard and Shoreline Mysteries* (1998). The *Murder on Deck!* anthology and *Ellery Queen's Crime Cruise Round the World* (1981) prove that the shipboard milieu works well in the crime short story.

• Philip L. Scowcroft, "Ships, Boats and Harbours in Sayers' Detective Fiction," in *Sidelights on Sayers*, vol. 4 (1984): 3–8; "Murder on the Water," *CADS* 5 (Feb. 1987): 30–32; "Crossing the English Channel: Wimsey's Preferred Route," in *ibid.*, vol. 42 (1994): 49–50; and "Transportation Themes in the Detective Fiction of Freeman Wills Crofts, *CADS* 25 (Mar. 1995): 19–22.
—Philip L. Scowcroft

BOATING AND SAILING MILIEU

When Sherlock Holmes takes to a Thames river police launch to hunt down his quarry in *The Sign of the Four* (1890), he is only one of many to take to the water. Many of the early works set in the boating and sailing milieu are *adventure stories, that launched a crime and detection theme into an established story type. Erskine *Childers's *The Riddle of the Sands* (1903) is replete with yachting detail and charts of the north German coast, making the spy element seem almost a bonus, with a minimum of *violence, heard about only in retrospect. Small boats appear marginally in John *Buchan's *The Thirty-nine Steps* (1915) and *The Island of Sheep* (1936). In A. G. Macdonell's Buchan-influenced *The Crew of the Anaconda* (1940), a German spy ring is rounded up at the start of World War II by an unusual group of characters based on a sleek motor cruiser. A. E. W. *Mason, a secret agent in 1914–18, was a keen yachtsman, a fact reflected in *The Dean's Elbow* (1930).

In addition to heightening the sense of danger in chase scenes, the milieu offers writers other opportunities. In R. Austin *Freeman's *The Shadow of the Wolf* (1925), an *inverted detective story, a murderer is identified by means of a marine growth on his yacht peculiar to Land's End (the "Wolf" is Wolf Rock lighthouse). Freeman Wills *Crofts used small boats primarily to construct characteristically impregnable *alibis. A small boat in *The Sea Mystery* (1928) carries two fishermen who find a body. Motor boats play a crucial role in carrying out murderous intents in *Sir John Magill's Last Journey* (1930), *Mystery on Southampton Water* (1934), and *Mystery in the Channel* (1931; *Mystery in the English Channel*). Dorothy *Sayers's *The Five Red Herrings* (1931; *Suspicious Characters*), set in Galloway, Scotland, includes a suspect boat, which is a *red herring. Each body of water poses its own problems and dangers, from treacherous storms in the English Channel, as in Mason's *The House in Lordship Lane* (1946), to navigating usually calm rivers. The several novels set on rivers or canals offer vivid *settings and *plots adapted to the movements of rivers through marshes, fields, and locks. In Peter Lovesey's *Swing, Swing Together* (1976), the pursuit of a suspected murderer follows the leisurely pace of a river tour in 1888. In Ronald A. *Knox's *The Footsteps in the Lock* (1928), a Miles Bredon tale, two brothers who hate each other take a canoeing expedition on the River Thames above *Oxford; C. P. Snow's first novel, *Death Under Sail* (1932), is set in the Norfolk Broads. An American yachting example is Mignon G. *Eberhart's *The Patient in Cabin C* (1983).

Writers have taken the opportunity to explore various locales. Andrew *Garve explores the East Anglian coast in *The Far Sands* (1961) and *The Cuckoo Line Affair* (1953), the Scillies in *The Riddle of Samson* (1954), English canals in *The Narrow Search* (1957), the northeast coast in *The Megstone Plot* (1956), and the Indian Ocean in *A Hero for Leanda* (1959). J. R. L. Anderson writes about Devon in *Redundancy Pay* (1976; *A Death in the Channel*), Cornwall in *Festival* (1979), the Bristol Channel in *The Nine-Spoked Wheel* (1975), the east coast of Britain in *Death in the North Sea* (1975), and *London's river in *Death in the Thames* (1974). A sailing accident off the coast of Scotland begins P. M. Hubbard's *The Causeway* (1976). The East Anglian coast features in P. D. James's *Devices and Desires* (1989), the northeast coast in Douglas Clark's *Plain Sailing* (1987). Colin Dexter's *The Wench Is Dead* (1989) is the finest of all canal-set crime novels.

[*See also* Travel Milieu.]

• Roger Lancelyn Green, *A. E. W. Mason* (1952). Andrew Boyle, *The Riddle of Erskine Childers* (1977), esp. ch. 4. Philip L. Scowcroft, "Murder on the Water," *CADS* 5 (Feb. 1987): 30–32; and "Transportation Themes in the Detective Fiction of Freeman Wills Crofts," *CADS* 25 (Mar. 1995): 19–22.
—Philip L. Scowcroft

NEWGATE CALENDAR. *See* Newgate Novel.

NEWGATE CALLENDAR. *See* Criticism, Literary.

NEWGATE NOVEL. Newgate novels, which were in vogue in the 1830s in England, have as their subject matter *London crime and criminals. They are named for London's Newgate Prison, which dated from the twelfth century. The prison was so named for its original location during the Middle Ages in the gatehouse of the principal west gate of the city of London. The prison was enlarged during the fifteenth century and burned down in the Gordon Riots of 1780. It was rebuilt after the riots and operated until 1902, when it was demolished so that the Central Criminal Court, known as the *Old Bailey, could be constructed on the site.

Newgate Prison earned an unsavory reputation, due to both the conditions and the inmates within it. Novels named for the place have long been associated in the popular mind with sensationalism, probably due in large part to the fact that executions performed just outside the prison attracted large crowds until as late as 1868.

Newgate fiction also derived its name from written sources upon which writers of the genre relied. *The Newgate Calendar,* begun about 1773 and published in five volumes, was a record of notorious actual criminal cases. Later compilations of crimes included *The Malefactor's Register* (1779) and *Criminal Chronology* (1809), compiled by Andrew Knapp and William Baldwin. Another *Newgate Calender* was issued from 1824 to 1826, and *The New Newgate Calendar* sated the public appetite for *true crime in 1826.

During the heyday of the Newgate novel in the 1830s, some writers received criticism for attempting to understand and explain criminal motivation in their work. Edward Bulwer Lytton's *Paul Clifford* (1830) and *Eugene Aram* (1832) and William Harrison Ainsworth's *Rookwood* (1834) and *Jack Sheppard* (1839) are exemplars of this approach to the criminal character. Charles *Dickens, whose *Oliver Twist* (1837–38) also examined criminal life, disassociated himself from Newgate novelists in his preface to the third edition of that novel. While Dickens does portray sympathetic characters such as Oliver Twist and Nancy as involved in a criminal coterie, his view of these characters as the *victims of criminals and of social ills distinguishes his work from the writings of true Newgate novelists. Another contemporary of the Newgate novelists, William Makepeace Thackeray, penned his novel *Catherine* (1839–40) in indignant reaction to the notion of romanticizing the criminal life. He mined *The Newgate Calendar* for information about the deeds of the murderess Catherine Hayes and then set out to make her circumstances and actions appear sordid, but some critics say that Thackeray depicted a sympathetic heroine, in spite of himself, in the lively *Catherine.*

Earlier and notable works said to be derived from accounts in *The Newgate Calendar* include Henry Fielding's *The Life of Jonathan Wild the Great* (1743), which traces the life of the eponymous thief and thief-taker from cradle to gallows, and William *Godwin's *Things as They Are; or, The Adventures of Caleb Williams* (1794), one of the most important progenitors of the *crime novel.

• Richard Altick, *Victorian Studies in Scarlet* (1970). Bernard O'Donnell, *The Old Bailey and Its Trials* (1950). Rayner Heppenstall, *Reflections on the Newgate Calendar* (1975).
—Rosemary Herbert

NEWSPAPER REPORTS. Raymond Williams, in *The Long Revolution* (1961), divides the history of printed news into seven periods, the first four of which are: 1665–1760, early middle-class press; 1760–1836, the struggle for press freedom and the new popular press; 1836–55, the popular press expanding; and 1855–96, the second phase of that expansion. What is noteworthy in these dates is that it is not until the entry of a press accessible to the populace at large that recognizable mystery stories appear, and it is not until the nineteenth-century climax of that journalistic evolution that the literature of crime takes on a real identity. Williams points out that the *Times* of London did not achieve a circulation of ten thousand until the 1820s, about the same time that papers were beginning to give significant space "to detailed accounts of murders, rapes, seductions, and similar material." He notes that this phenomenon in the press grew rapidly through the introduction of the Sunday papers (which were comparable to the supermarket tabloids of today) and the illustrated weeklies of the 1840s, culminating with the 1856 introduction of the first penny daily, the *Telegraph,* an event that Matthew Arnold depicted as the arrival of a "new journalism."

Richard D. Altick's *Victorian Studies in Scarlet* (1970) more explicitly addresses crime reporting. From about 1600, Altick states, homicides were recounted in broadsheets hawked on streetcorners and, most particularly, to the crowds that attended public hangings. From Daniel Defoe in the early eighteenth century onward, Grub Street authors produced catchpenny biographies of eminent criminals. By 1773, *The Newgate Calendar,* a popular book-length collection—supportive of conventional morality, as was most contemporary journalism—of these profiles in villainy began to appear and continued to do so into the next century. The interest of editors and, by inference, of the general populace in criminal matters was intensified, Altick believes, because of the decline in war news after the battle of Waterloo (1815). This was symbolized by the enthusiasm with which the press leaped in 1823–24 at the trial and execution of John Thurtell, a rogue with aristocratic connections who arranged for the robbery and murder of one of his gambling associates. Indeed, by that time an enterprising fellow named James Catnach had begun to print up trial transcripts for sale, and his account of the Thurtell trial—which had already been milked dry by all classes of newspaper—managed to sell five hundred thousand copies. Sales of Catnach's "execution papers" burgeoned for two decades after this—as did sensational crimes—culminating in the distribution of no fewer than 2.5 million broadsides on the trial and execution of Maria Manning and her husband for murdering her Irish lover and burying him in their basement.

Aided by urban population growth and technological developments such as the telegraph and the railroad, print communications mushroomed. When the government abandoned taxation of paper and stamp duties in the early 1850s, the steady increase became a flood and papers became cheaper, longer, more graphically detailed, and significantly—since many of these details concerned a criminal lowlife at odds with the so-called official consciousness of a self-congratulatorily pious and affluent society—a tendency to subversive editorial commentary. (A similar pattern emerged in America, though at a later date, due to the Civil War and the slower pace of urbanization.)

It is therefore no surprise that the emergence of a coherent body of mystery and *thriller fiction that is at once literate, realistic, and laced with explicit and implicit social commentary, is contemporaneous with these breakthroughs in crime reporting. Many of the great fictional successes of the age drew elements of style, character, *plot, and message from police reports. These included Charles *Dickens's *Bleak House* (1853)—with a murderess modeled on Maria Manning—and his last dark criminal explorations of the 1860s; Wilkie *Collins's *Woman in White* (1860)—whose experimentation in multiple points of view the author likened to witnesses in a trial—and *The Moonstone* (1868); and the other so-called *sensation novels of the period by M. E. *Braddon, J. S. Le Fanu, Charles Reade, and many others. The Dean of St. Paul's was compelled to attack these "newspaper novels" as beneath contempt. Henry James, on the other hand, praised their ability to echo "today's newspaper" while he capsulized in a line the evolution of crime fiction from the long-ago-and-far-away Gothic fantasy, not to mention the Newgate morality tale, of the more primitive days of the news media: "Mrs. Radcliffe's mysteries were Romances sure and simple; while those of Mr. Wilkie Collins were stern reality." Certainly the innovations in media technology at the end of the twentieth century—video and computers in the courtroom, the cyberspace revolution—will have comparable long-term effects on crime and mystery writing.

• Richard D. Altick, *The English Common Reader: A Social History of the Mass Reading Public, 1800–1900* (1957). Thomas Boyle, *Black Swine in the Sewers of Hampstead: Beneath the Surface of Victorian Sensationalism* (1989). H. J. Dyos, *Exploring the Urban Past: Essays in Urban History* (1982).   —Thomas Boyle

NEW YEAR'S DAY. *See* Holiday Mysteries.

NEW YORK CITY has been identified with the mystery since the American inventor of the genre, Edgar Allan *Poe, used a New York crime as the basis of "The Mystery of Marie Roget" (*Snowden's Ladies' Companion*, Nov. 1842). A generation later New Yorker Anna Katharine Green published *The Leavenworth Case: A Lawyer's Story* (1878), one of the first detective novels written by a woman and one of the all-time best-sellers.

Manhattan symbolizes the urban New World, both mecca and menace. Leslie *Charteris wrote in *The Saint in New York* (1935) that it was the wonder island of the West, a modern Baghdad where civiliza-

tion and savagery climbed on each other's shoulders. Manhattan is the scene of the crime not only for society mysteries set in brownstones or penthouses, but for cops-and-robbers *violence in ethnic neighborhoods. Its authors range from native-born writers such as S. S. *Van Dine and Ellery *Queen, whose urbane sleuths Philo *Vance and Ellery *Queen deal with the rich and powerful, to the broader canvas of clients helped by Rex *Stout's "immigrants," Montenegrin Nero *Wolfe and midwesterner Archie *Goodwin, to Chester *Himes's portraits of the Harlem underclass.

In many mysteries Manhattan itself is a major character because, to make their settings realistic, New York writers use actual neighborhoods, such as Greenwich Village, and street names, such as Broadway or Fifth Avenue. This gives their mysteries a sharp outline, for as Margaret Maron noted in *Past Imperfect* (1991), because New York was really just a collection of villages whose inhabitants rarely ventured outside their areas of work and home, it was possible for eight million New Yorkers to walk down a Manhattan street and see familiar faces.

The glaring exception to this rule is the prolific Ed *McBain, who insists that his *police procedurals about the fictional Eighty-seventh Precinct, starring NYPD detective Steve Carella, are not about New York. Most readers, however, agree with British author and critic H. R. F. Keating, who replies, "As a matter of fact, the city can be seen to be New York turned on to its side."

As the Big Apple is a center of the arts, publishing, merchandising, and high finance, these occupations are also used as mystery *milieus. In *Banking on Death* (1961) Emma *Lathen pointed out that Wall Street is the world's banker, and their Sloan Guaranty Trust banker John Putnam *Thatcher is the epitome of the observant, worldly-wise but tolerant New Yorker. In *The Big Killing* (1989) Annette Meyers's women headhunters Xenia Smith and Leslie Wetzon work the Street, while Haughton Murphy's retired lawyer Reuben Frost, in mysteries such as *Murder for Lunch* (1986), acts as a cynical commentator on the business community in general.

The Times Square theater world has been another popular setting since Van Dine's *The Canary Murder Case* (1927) and Queen's *The Roman Hat Mystery* (1929). Stage stories include Patrick Quentin's *Puzzle for Players* (1938), Edgar Box's *Death in the Fifth Position* (1952), and Dorothy Salisbury *Davis's *Lullaby of Murder* (1984). Newer series include Jane Dentinger's, featuring actress Jocelyn O'Roarke, and Stefanie Matteson's with retired actress Charlotte Graham as a sleuth who is also a Katharine Hepburn look-alike.

Fifth Avenue appears in Dashiell *Hammett's hard-boiled social commentary *The Thin Man* (1934), where Nick *Charles waits in a bar for his wife Nora and their dog Asta to finish shopping. In Frances and Richard Lockridge's cozy *The Norths Meet Murder* (1940; *Mr. and Mrs. North Meet Murder*), Pam North shops the street for a whole new outfit to put off her pursuer. Famous New York hotels from the Algonquin to the Waldorf-Astoria to the Plaza appear in mysteries such as Jerome Charyn's *Paradise Man* (1987), in Hugh *Pentecost's series about hotel manager Pierre *Chambrun, and in Steve Allen's zany *Murder in Manhattan* (1990), while Grand Central Station is the hub of Mary Higgins *Clark's thriller *A Stranger Is Watching* (1978).

Central Park appears in mysteries as varied as George Chesbro's *Bone* (1989), P. M. Carlson's *Murder Unrenovated* (1988), and Amanda *Cross's *In the Last Analysis* (1964), where intrepid professor Kate *Fansler hikes back and forth, ignoring the park's dangers. New York landmarks, such as the Empire State Building, appear in Rex Stout's *Too Many Clients* (1960), as does Rockefeller Center in Donald E. Westlake's John Dortmunder mystery, *Good Behavior* (1985).

Amateur sleuths' occupations also determine their Manhattan settings, from the Establishment Episcopal churches of Isabelle Holland's series about the Reverend Claire Aldington to Jerome Charyn's policeman Isaac Sidel who inhabits a Balzacian urban Jewish jungle with echoes of long ago. Female NYPD detectives include Margaret Maron's Lieutenant Sigrid Harald, Dorothy Uhnak's detective Christie Opara, and Lillian O'Donnell's Sergeant Norah Mulcahaney, who later became a lieutenant.

Historical mysteries about New York combine real characters with fictional ones to give the reader a sense of the past. Maan Meyer's *The Dutchman* (1992) stars coroner John Tonneman of pre–Revolutionary War Manhattan, William Marshall's *New York Detective* (1989) tells about building the Brooklyn Bridge, and William DeAndrea's *The Lunatic Fringe* (1980) is about Police Commissioner Teddy Roosevelt.

From its founding as a Dutch colony in 1621, New York has been a scene of the crime, which will continue to be true in the twenty-first century because, as William L. DeAndrea says in "Mysteries of New York," "There are eight million stories in the Naked City. And a lot of them are mysteries."

[*See also* Mean Streets Milieu; Urban Milieu.]

• Alzina Stone Dale, *Mystery Readers Walking Guide: New York* (1993).
—Alzina Stone Dale

NEW ZEALAND, CRIME AND MYSTERY WRITING IN.

One of the most successful crime novels ever published was written by New Zealand barrister Fergus Hume. *The Mystery of a Hansom Cab*, inspired by the novels of Émile *Gaboriau and set in Melbourne, Australia, was published by Hume himself in 1886 after he had been told that "no Colonial could write anything worth reading." The book sold 375,000 copies in Britain alone and even more through American editions.

Despite this promising beginning, New Zealand remained lukewarm to the crime genre; though it was considered entertaining and widely read, crime fiction, particularly the classic English detective story, often dealt, with a social world alien to the developing nation. This ambivalence haunted Ngaio *Marsh throughout her long career. Her first novel, *A Man Lay Dead* (1934), introduced Inspector Roderick *Alleyn, a series character drawn from the English

aristocracy. Only four of her thirty-two novels are set in her native country but her penultimate novel, *Photo Finish* (1980), brings Alleyn and his wife Troy to the breath-taking landscapes of the South Island.

For some time New Zealand crime and mystery writers continued to publish abroad and to set their work in overseas locales. Colin D. Peel has published numerous international *thrillers; typical is *Covenant of the Poppies* (1992), in which an arms buyer overstays his visit in a village in Afghanistan and witnesses mass murder. Joan Druett successfully published *Murder at the Brian Boru* (1992) in the United Kingdom as did Patricia Donnelly with *Feel the Force* (1993). Rose Beecham published her series of Amanda Valentine mysteries with Naiad Press in the United States.

A taste for mystery writing set in New Zealand developed during the 1990s with small presses providing opportunities for new writers. Carol Dawber's *Backtrack* (1992), published by River Press in Picton, deals with the death of a backpacker on one of New Zealand's famous long-distance tracks. Gaelyn Gordon has published several mysteries in New Zealand, including *Above Suspicion* (1990) and *Strained Relations* (1991). In the late 1990s Hazard Press in Christchurch brought out a historical mystery, *The Dancing Man* (1997), by Edmund Bohan; *Click* (1997), a psychological thriller by Ray Prebble; and *Mates* (1998), a *police procedural by veteran crime writer Laurie Mantell, whose previous novels were all published in the United Kingdom.

The world of international terrorism and political activism has come closer to home during the past decade. Paul Thomas's *Old School Tie* (1994), *Inside Dope* (1995), and *Guerilla Season* (1996) bring wit, pace, and political sharpness to New Zealand thrillers, helped by the sardonic voice of his chief investigator, a bad-tempered and worldly wise Maori, Detective Sergeant Tito Ihaka. *Friendly Fire* (1998), by ex-government adviser Michael Wall, shows that political conspiracy and violence can function as stylishly in New Zealand as anywhere else on the world stage.
—Margaret Lewis

NOIR FICTION. *See* Fiction Noir; Roman Policier.

North, Mr. and Mrs. Though they were not the first, much of the popularity of husband-wife detective teams derives from the success of Pamela and Jerry North, creations of Frances and Richard Lockridge. They appeared in twenty-six novels and one short story.

They are suspects in their first case, The Norths Meet Murder (1940; *Mr. and Mrs. North Meet Murder*), when Pamela rents a Greenwich Village apartment for a party but discovers a *corpse in its bathtub. Lieutenant Bill Weigand, who investigates, becomes their friend. Though exasperated by the frequency with which Pamela discovers corpses, he is usually glad for the Norths' assistance. In *Death of a Tall Man* (1946), Pamela sees Weigand driving to a murder scene and follows him. She barges in, but he lets her stay.

Jerry, busy earning a living in publishing, plays a smaller role, though he occasionally provides important *clues. The detective work is done by Weigand and, unofficially, by Pamela, who frequently is stalked by the killer. Often, Bill and Pamela arrive at the solution simultaneously, albeit by different methods. Though she has a reputation for dizziness (perhaps because played in the movies by Gracie Allen), Pamela is bright; she just speaks in a way that seems strange to those who don't understand her mental shorthand.

The background of many North books reflects the Lockridges' experience. Richard was a drama critic, and Frances held important positions with charities. They were known for their love of Siamese cats, and those owned by Pamela and Jerry were based on the cats who shared the Lockridge household.

Frances Lockridge died in 1963. Though Richard wrote mysteries for another twenty years, he abandoned the Norths, saying Pamela had been based too closely on his wife.

• R. Jeff Banks, "Mr. and Mrs. North," *Armchair Detective* 9 (1976): 182–83. Richard Lockridge, "Mr. and Mrs. North," in *The Great Detectives*, ed. in Otto Penzler (1978): 155–63.

—Marvin Lachman

Norton, Irene. *See* Adler, Irene

NOSY PARKER SLEUTH. Nosy parker *sleuths, or amateur detectives who invite themselves to explore the private lives of people who are strangers to them or with whom they have only slight acquaintance, are frequently found within the pages of mysteries. Self-appointed and driven by their own curiosity or a perceived sense of *justice, these often zany sleuths confuse the issues, discard obvious *clues, jump to unwarranted conclusions, and interfere with the official investigators. They frequently promote a romance between two characters who are most affected by a crime, one of whom is apt to be a *suspect. Authors use these characters as farcical figures who provide contrast to dogged but nonetheless unsuccessful official sleuths. Given their muddled approach to crime solving, it is entertaining and surprising to find that, in the end, nosy parkers manage to identify the culprit and explain the *motive.

Unlike *amateur sleuths, who are invited by police or neighbors to get to the truth of a situation, or *surrogate sleuths, such as journalists and medical personnel, who use professional credentials in fields other than detection to gain entrée to crime scenes and who employ specialized skills to interpret clues found there, nosy parker sleuths have no legitimate reason for involving themselves in a case. They may be *accidental sleuths, who happen to be on the scene when a crime occurs. More likely, they have barged their way into such scenes, inspired by irresistible curiosity.

A prime example of the self-appointed snooper is Jane Amanda Edwards, identified as "Pauline Pry" by her author, Charlotte Murray Russell. This nosy neighbor prides herself on knowing all there is to know about the private lives, incomes, and social standing of the denizens of Rockport, Illinois, where she intrudes and interferes with great aplomb in adventures written during the 1930s and 1940s, including the aptly titled novel *The Bad Neighbor Murder* (1946).

—Ellen Nehr

NOVEL OF MANNERS. Novels of manners are longer works of fiction that aim to serve as mirrors reflecting sharp likenesses of society. Deriving from Restoration comedies of manners, the novel of manners was polished to perfection by eighteenth- and nineteenth-century novelists including Henry Fielding, Jane Austen, and Anthony Trollope, writers who possessed astute powers of observation and lively senses of *humor. These authors and others who have produced novels of manners, including crime and mystery writers, often present witty observations laced with satire or irony, with the goal of pointing out society's verities and bursting pretensions and social codes.

In order for a mystery novel to succeed as a novel of manners, the writer must be concerned with presenting a penetrating view of society along with creating a puzzling *plot. In the early days of the genre's development, this approach was often taken in shorter fiction, in which detectives like John Kendrick Bangs's Mrs. Raffles were seen to operate in high society, solving cases through acquaintance with and participation in societal pretensions that are deflated by the author.

But the full-length detective novel as a novel of manners was developed most dramatically between the world wars, when the *country house milieu, the *cathedral close milieu, and the *academic milieu were in vogue for authors of mysteries. These closed-world settings served as microcosms of society in which the social order could be examined. Some writers, like Michael *Innes and Edmund *Crispin, used such broad humor in their works that they have been termed *farceurs. Richard Hull, in *Murder of My Aunt* (1934), also uses elements of farce in that novel, whose plot to kill a relative is echoed much later in Nigel Williams's *The Wimbledon Poisoner* (1990). Others, like Dorothy L. *Sayers, Margery *Allingham, and Ngaio *Marsh, were less effervescent in their approach to commenting on society.

Despite her initially playful approach to her lead series character, Lord Peter *Wimsey, Sayers focused increasingly on issues such as the manipulation of the populace by means of advertising, and serious social problems such as wife battering, making her novels of manners weightier than some. Sayers's fiction proves that she was at home in a fictional women's college in *Oxford, in the country house, and in an advertising office. Allingham, too, could set a puzzler in a country house in *The Crime at Black Dudley* (1929; *The Black Dudley Murder*), but she had her confidential investigator Albert *Campion step out of the country house and into the business world to expose communities where trade wears the cloak of gentility. Marsh chronicles the more problematic transition of aristocrat Roderick *Alleyn from the Foreign Office to gentleman policeman in *A Man Lay Dead* (1934). Alleyn's posh background endows him with entrée and equal status when he investigates upper-crust crimes, but he is less at ease with his subordinates.

While the interwar period saw the development of the mystery as novel of manners, writers continue to explore and develop the form. Other writers whose mysteries may be classified in this category include Cyril Hare, whose spoof *An English Murder* (1951; *A Christmas Murder*) reveals the point of view of a foreign visitor to the country house milieu; Anne Morice, who focused on the *theatrical milieu; Sarah Caudwell, who examines the legal establishment; Robert *Barnard, who turns a sharp eye on worlds ranging from British boys' schools to a committee trying to rescue a literary landmark; Catherine Aird, who uses her wit and wits to portray English village life; Jane Langton, whose academic sleuth detects in Concord, Massachusetts, and in international settings, including Oxford, England; Joan Hess, who proves that the novel of manners can illuminate the anything-but-posh social scene in a redneck Arkansas community; and Alfred Alcorn, who deflates academic pretensions in a natural history museum.

• Colin Watson, *Snobbery with Violence: Crime Stories and Their Audience*, 1971.   —Jean A. Coakley

NURSERY RHYMES. The term "nursery rhyme" vidently did not appear until toward the end of the nineteenth century, but the rhymes themselves are a much older form of folk literature. Some scholars have dated the oral transmission of many rhymes, such as "Humpty Dumpty" and "London Bridge," to well before 1599. Few rhymes were recorded, however, until the 1700s. The earliest extant nursery rhyme book is *Tommy Thumb's Pretty Song Book*, published in London in 1744 and containing thirty-eight rhymes, all of which were probably well known by the time they were recorded. Many are familiar today, such as "Sing a song of sixpence," "Hickory dickory dock," and the famously mournful "Who killed Cock Robin?" *Mother Goose's Melody* appeared around 1760 and influenced all subsequent collections, especially in the United States.

The increase in the recording of nursery rhymes during the mid-eighteenth century corresponds approximately with the distribution of the pamphlets that were later collected as the *Newgate Callendar* (1773), which some historians believe to be a chief forerunner of today's crime fiction. According to Stephen Knight in *Form and Ideology in Crime Fiction* (1980), the stories of crime and punishment that made up the Newgate pamphlets and later the *Calendar* presented criminals as ordinary people, the family as representative of the social order, and crime as revealed and punished without any special detection: "The stories imply that just as society can sometimes suffer from disorderly elements, so it can deal with them by its own integral means."

Similarly, ordinary people and disorderly behavior are the hallmarks of the nursery rhymes, and punishment is generally administered internally, if at all. Unlike *fairy tales, whose characters and settings are often fantastic, the rhymes are set in the village, ale-

house, or barnyard and generally describe Jack, Elsie, Mary, and Mrs. Bond going about their daily lives. These lives are often marked by anger, deceit, thievery, *revenge, and *murder, for monetary or sexual reasons or simply from frustration or meanness. In a rhyme probably intended to teach the days of the week, Tom "married a wife on Sunday" and "beat her well on Monday"; she dies by Saturday and Tom is glad to bury her on Sunday. Billy, in one of the oldest known rhymes (which may be based on the old ballad "Lord Randal") has been poisoned by a beautiful woman and comes home to die. "Taffy the Welshman's" constant thieving drives the narrator of that rhyme to all sorts of insulting injuries. The old man in "Goosey Goosey Gander" is discovered in a lady's chamber and thrown downstairs. Gratuitous *violence appears even in a riddle: "When I went up Sandy-Hill, I met a sandy-boy; I cut his throat, I sucked his blood, and left his skin a-hanging-o." (The answer is an orange.)

In 1952, in a plea for reformation of the rhymes, Geoffrey Handley-Taylor catalogued the violence in them: deaths by hanging, drowning, squeezing, boiling, starvation, decapitation, and devouring, as well as instances of *kidnapping, maiming, drunkenness, house burning, and whipping, among many allusions to graves, misery, poverty, and quarrelling (cited in William S. and Ceil Baring-Gould, *The Annotated Mother Goose*, 1962). But except for obviously didactic ones like counting rhymes and alphabets, the rhymes were never intended solely for children; products of a time when neither adults nor children expected to be shielded from unsavory realities, they acknowledge societal disorder as part of the human experience. Jacques Barzun and Wendell Taylor in the revised edition of *Catalogue of Crime Fiction* (1989) believe this same attitude characterizes crime fiction, which "accepts character and society ready-made and offers no searching or reformist criticism."

Crime and mystery writers since Agatha *Christie have found nursery rhymes a rich source of titles as well as themes. The ironic contrast between their lilting rhymes and jolly rhythms and the mayhem they describe suggests not only a similar irony in a crime novel but the elemental pleasure to be had in reading it. "Sing a song of sixpence, a pocket full of rye," for example, has provided many titles: *Sing a Song of Cyanide* by Nigel Morland (1953), *Sing a Song of Homicide* (1940; *Sing a Song of Murder*) and *A Pocket Full of Clues* (1941; *A Pocketful of Clues*) both by James R. Langham, John Wyllie's *A Pocket Full of Dead* (1978), and of course Agatha Christie's *A Pocket Full of Rye* (1953). At least four authors have used the title *Sing a Song of Murder*: Langham, George Worthing Yates (1936), Robert Portner Koehler (1941), and Andrew Spiller (1959). "Who killed Cock Robin?" has inspired crime and mystery titles such as Roy Fuller's *With My Little Eye* (1948), and given its name to a crime fiction publishing imprint issued by Macmillan: Both Emma Lathen and Amanda Cross published "Cock Robin Mysteries." Crime and mystery fiction for young people has also borrowed from the rhymes; naturalist and children's writer Jean Craighead George has posed an "ecological mystery" in *Who Really Killed Cock Robin?* (1971), and Robert Cormier's *We All Fall Down* (1991), written for a young adult audience, details the results of a crime perpetrated by a group of teenage boys.

The most controversial title taken from a nursery rhyme is Christie's *Ten Little Niggers* (1939). This rhyme began as an American rhyme composed before 1869, "Ten Little Injuns"; around 1869 Frank Green rewrote it for the British musical stage as "Ten Little Niggers," the term "nigger" being in common use in England to refer to any dark-skinned person. Even before the 1960s, when racial protests increased, U.S. publishers began to substitute "Indians" for Christie's original "niggers," or to use the last line of the rhyme for the book's title: *And Then There Were None* (1940). This novel is also an exemplar of the nursery rhyme being used throughout the book to create a sense of tension essential to the atmosphere of *suspense.

[*See also* Titles and Titling.]

• Iona and Peter Opie, *The Oxford Dictionary of Nursery Rhymes* (1951). Ernest Mandel, *Delightful Murder: A Social History of the Crime Story* (1984). Dick Riley and Pam McAllister, eds., *The New Bedside, Bathtub, and Armchair Companion to Agatha Christie* (1986). Lucy Rollin, *Cradle and All: A Cultural and Psychoanalytic Study of Nursery Rhymes* (1992).

—Lucy Rollin

OBTUSE SLEUTH. *See* Plainman Sleuth.

OCCULT AND SUPERNATURAL LITERATURE.
Supernatural fiction deals with occult forces or
forces from a spiritual realm that break through into
common reality. Such forces take shape as ghosts,
spirits, demons, and fairies, and challenge rationalist
and scientific assumptions. Inherent in these stories
is the belief that the world of ordinary reality is surrounded by an often hostile, inexplicable, and powerful spiritual world. Supernatural and occult literature may have as its intent *horror, as in M. R.
James's "The Rats" (*Collected Ghost Stories*, 1931), or
whimsy, as in E. G. Swain's "Bone to His Bone" (*The
Stone Ground Ghost Tales: Compiled from the Recollections of the Reverend Roland Betchel, Vicar of the
Parish*, 1912), or merely conveying the fantastic, as in
the work of Lord Dunsany or James Branch Cabell.

The supernatural tale has a long history, but the
literary supernatural tale dates from the latter half of
the eighteenth century and accompanies the rise of
the *novel of manners. Matthew Lewis's *The Monk*
(1795), an early example, is set in Madrid during the
Inquisition and is the story of a monk who succumbs
to sexual desire, a ghost known as the Bleeding Nun,
and lovers separated by imprisonment. It is a story of
terrifying encounters with the otherworldly, confinement in tombs, and violent hypocrisy. This and other
tales are products of a general cultural and ambivalence over the rise of materialistic, scientific, and rational culture and a general move into city life and
industrial mass society. The 1840s saw the appearance of the two faces of materialistic culture: the invention of the term "scientist" and the first table-
turning spiritualist activities, which dominated the
drawing rooms of late Victorian life. Fueled by a popular taste for spiritualist works and organized within
the new mass publishing, writers, whether journalists such as Charles *Dickens, whose most famous
*ghost story is *A Christmas Carol* (1843), or clergymen such as S. Baring-Gould, who also wrote "Onward Christian Soldiers" (*Church Times*, 1865), could
earn a good living providing tales of the supernatural
to magazines. Bram Stoker's *Dracula* (1897) was only
one of many vampire tales to capture readers' imaginations. By contrast, Henry James's *The Turn of the
Screw* (1898) veers away from indisputable ghosts
and supernatural forces and offers a tale of ambiguous possibilities where the *evil might be a projection of a disturbed mind, a separate entity, or both.

Despite the emphasis on ghosts and inexplicable
events driven by forces of the spirit realm, much of
the fiction classed as occult or supernatural relied on
down-to-earth depictions of events that could be investigated and contrasted with events from the spirit
realm. In his first novel, *The Cock and Anchor* (1845),
Joseph Sheridan Le Fanu established a pattern of horrifying atmosphere, inexplicable events, and material
*clues. In this story he presented a detailed under-
standing of the working of the system of *justice, and
in later books he relies on material clues to advance
parts of the *plot. In *Wylder's Hand* (1864) the climax
depends on identifying a particular kind of soil.

The supernatural tale continued to develop alongside the *detective novel, but instead of giving up the
advances it had made in using physical evidence to
affix *guilt or determine *innocence, the supernatural tale adapted the role of the detective to investigating crimes or problems from the spirit realm. In
Le Fanu's *In a Glass Darkly* (1872), Dr. Hesselius investigates supernatural problems. Algernon Blackwood's Dr. John Silence, a physician who specializes
in nervous disorders, investigates supernatural
crimes in *Dr. John Silence, Physician Extraordinary*
(1908). For example, when a writer seeks his help to
fend off the psychic attacks of a dead woman, Silence
meets her on her own terms and defeats her. William
Hope Hodgson's detective also defeats assaults from
the hostile spiritual world in *Carnacki, the Ghost
Finder and a Poem* (1910).

For the most part, the supernatural no longer enters the world of the detective novel except in very restricted circumstances. In Arthur Conan *Doyle's *The
Hound of the Baskervilles* (1902), Sherlock *Holmes
sets out to disprove the legend of a mad hound that
attacks people on the moors at night. Many of John
Dickson *Carr's stories revolve around debunking
seemingly supernatural events, giving readers the opportunity to indulge in terrifying tales before withdrawing to a rational explanation that is also comforting, ensuring a world safely within the bounds of
human understanding. In *The Burning Court* (1937),
for example, a woman claims to be the reincarnation
of a seventeenth-century she-devil.

In the last few years the supernatural has taken
another turn. In Tony *Hillerman's stories about the
Navajo, many of the characters have extraordinary
qualities, such as in *Listening Woman* (1978), or refer
to mythical figures whose reality is left open, as in
Skinwalkers (1987). The matter-of-fact way the dimension of the spirit world is presented and accepted contrasts with Doyle's and Carr's debunking

and makes a legitimate place again for the supernatural in detective fiction.

[*See also* Menacing Characters; Sensation Novel.]

—Clive Bloom

OLD BAILEY. The Old Bailey was part of the defensive wall, originally Roman, protecting the city of *London between the gates of Newgate and Ludgate. It is referred to from the twelfth century onward as terra de Bali (*ca.* 1166), La Baillye (1431), and Old Balee (1556). The prefix was probably added to differentiate it from a side street called Little Bayly, which did not disappear until circa 1760. The Old Bailey is a street, not a building, but has always been understood to mean the Sessions House, originally constructed in 1539 adjacent to Newgate prison, and since 1907 to mean the Central Criminal Court built on the site of the demolished eighteenth-century prison and Sessions House.

From 1783 to 1868 the Old Bailey, outside Newgate prison, was where most of London's public executions took place. The last woman to be burned for counterfeiting was executed there in 1789. Both Charles *Dickens and William Makepeace Thackeray witnessed the execution of François Courvoisier there for the murder of Lord William Russell in 1840.

By tradition, the judges carry at certain times nosegays as a reminder of the era when there was a constant risk of infection from the malodors and jail fever of the prisoners from Newgate jail. More than seventy people died in the Black Assize of 1750.

The present Old Bailey building has nineteen courtrooms. Its normal jurisdiction is that of Greater London, although it will often hear cases, requiring greater impartiality or security, from other parts of the country or when it is required to help reduce the backlog of cases from other courts. In 1981 this led to the court's youngest defendant this century, a twelve-year old girl, standing in the dock accused of stealing a doughnut and iced bun.

Famous trials held at the Sessions House included those of Quakers William Penn and William Mead (1670) for unlawful assembly and preaching, who plotted to assassinate the entire British Cabinet including the prime minister, the Cato Street conspirators (1820), and Oscar Wilde (1895). Since 1907 the present building's Number One courtroom has been where most of the great criminal and *murder trials of this century have taken place. Among those tried for murder have been Dr. Hawley Harley Crippen (1910), J. R. Christie (1953), the Kray twins (1968), and serial killer Peter Sutcliffe, "the Yorkshire Ripper" (1981).

It is this background of real-life drama that mystery writers such as Agatha *Christie have capitalized on and that, more recently, John *Mortimer, in his Rumpole of the Bailey chronicles, has made the setting for his wonderfully bilious Old Bailey hack, Horace *Rumpole.

Contrary to popular myth, the figure of Justice, holding sword and scales, on the dome, is not blindfolded. She can see which way the scales dip and where to strike if necessary. Above the main entrance is a massive stone figure of the Recording Angel flanked on either side by Truth and Fortitude. Cut into the stone is the prayer book version of a verse from Psalm 72: "Defend the Children of the Poor: Punish the Wrong-Doer."

—Donald Rumbelow

Old Man in the Corner. The creation of Baroness Emmuska *Orczy, the Old Man in the Corner is the prototype of the *armchair detective, an *amateur detective for whom crime solving is an intellectual exercise conducted at a distance from the scene of the crime. Snuggled up in a *London tearoom, he works out his solutions to puzzling crimes recounted to him by journalist Polly Burton. Stories featuring him were first published between 1901 and 1904 in the *Royal Magazine*. A total of thirty-eight tales are collected in *The Case of Miss Elliott* (1905), *The Old Man in the Corner* (1909; *The Man in the Corner*), and *Unravelled Knots* (1925).

While drinking glasses of milk and untying knots in a piece of string, the Old Man works the case backward, noting details that the police overlook and making deductions based on ratiocination and intuition. Although he bases most of his solutions upon *newspaper reports, he does attend inquests and trials and makes visits to crime scenes after the fact in some cases. Therefore, he is not wholly sedentary.

Orczy never names the Old Man, but in "The Mysterious Death in Percy Street" (*The Old Man in the Corner*), she suggests that he is Bill Owen, who likely murdered his aunt. In his narrative, however, the Old Man tells Burton only that the uncaptured killer was "one of the most ingenious men of the age" and his crime "one of the cleverest bits of work accomplished outside Russian diplomacy."

[*See also* Great Detective; The Reasoning, Types of.]

• Howard Haycraft, ed., *The Art of the Mystery Story* (1946). Fred Dueren, "Was the Old Man in the Corner an Armchair Detective?," *Armchair Detective* (summer 1981): 232–33.

—Gerald H. Strauss

OMNISCIENT SLEUTH. *See* Great Detective, The; Superman Sleuth.

110A PICCADILLY. *See* Addresses and Abodes, Famous; London; Wimsey, Lord Peter.

OPPENHEIM, E(DWARD) PHILLIPS (1866–1946), British *thriller writer of the Golden Age who also wrote as Anthony Partridge. Oppenheim left England for France and Guernsey in 1922 and served in the Ministry of Information during World War I. His prolific output of 115 novels and 44 collections of short stories made him enormously wealthy, and he lived like many of his heroes.

In his thrillers, a fabulously rich man uses his wealth to gain power over business or government and bring an end to *evil; pacifism, the virtues of wealth and the aristocracy, and redemption through philanthropy are recurring themes. For example, in *Up the Ladder of Gold* (1931), the hero seeks to end war for forty years. Oppenheim's detectives are usually amateurs with a modest public persona, such as Louis, the crippled maître d' of the Milan Hotel, or the wealthy layabout who redeems himself through meeting unexpected challenges in *The Great Impersonation* (1920).

[*See also* Amateur Detective.]

• Robert Standish, *The Prince of Story-Tellers* (1957).

—Chris Gausden

"Op, The." *See* Continental Op, The.

ORCZY, BARONESS EMMUSKA (Emma Magdalena Rosalia Maria Josefa Barbara), (1865–1947), British author, known for creating the *armchair detective and for her early portrayals of the capable female sleuth. Hungarian-born daughter of musician Baron Felix Orczy, she was educated abroad and in *London, where she studied art and married illustrator Montagu Barstow in 1894. She is best known for *The Scarlet Pimpernel* (1905), and her main contribution to detective fiction is the development of detection based entirely on reported information, foreshadowed in Edgar Allan Poe's "The Mystery of Marie Roget" (*Snowden's Lady's Companion*, Nov. 1845). In a series of stories collected in *The Case of Miss Elliott* (1905), *The Old Man in the Corner* (1909; *The Man in the Corner*), and *Unravelled Knots* (1925), the Old Man sits in a café, playing with string and working out, in conversation with a newspaperwoman, solutions to baffling crimes. Armchair detection, as this came to be known, was adapted by Ernest *Bramah, for his blind Max *Carrados, and by Agatha *Christie, for her amateur crime solvers in *The Tuesday Club Murders*. Orczy also created a woman detective in *Lady Molly of Scotland Yard* (1910), in which the aristocratic heroine, heading the "Female Department of the Yard" while working to clear her husband's name, is assisted by her maid, who also narrates their adventures. Lady Molly de-Mazareen is a forerunner to the contemporary feminist detective who breaks cases by wit and daring rather than intuition.

[*See also* Aristocratic Characters: The Aristocratic Sleuth; Females and Feminists.]

• Emmuska Orczy, *Links in the Chain of Life* (1947).

—Mary Rose Sullivan

ORGANIZED CRIME is a phrase which, over the years, has expanded in significance. The planning of criminal operations by the leader of a gang constitutes organized crime. The coordination of activities by a group of criminals acting in concert or alliance is also organized crime on a greater scale of iniquity. Such organizations are shapeless yet frightening— evil octopuses with tentacles reaching out unseen to grasp and manipulate business leaders, politicians, even the police. Through their power and reach, they operate with virtual impunity.

At the heart of organized crime there is always the gang. Gangs have a long history. Some became legendary because they were beneficent to the poor. The deeds of Robin Hood, that shadowy figure of medieval England, were commemorated in contemporary ballads and have been recounted in many novels, among them Nicholas Chase's *Locksley* (1983).

The smugglers of the English Channel are featured in Russell Thorndyke's stories of *Doctor Syn* (1915, and later works); the bushrangers of Australia, in Rolfe Bolderwood's *Robbery under Arms* (1888) and obliquely in Arthur W. Upfield's *Bony and the Kelly Gang* (1960; *Valley of Smugglers*). Other gangs began as patriotic movements against alien oppressors but grew into exploitative monsters with well-merited reputations for evildoing: The Camorra of Naples and the Mafia of Sicily are examples.

These gangs operated essentially in the countryside, at least at the outset. Not all were benign; the Chauffeurs, who plundered isolated farms in eighteenth-century France, were altogether *evil. Yet it was in the industrial cities that organized crime really took shape. In British industrial towns, gangs were numerous enough. In the 1920s Sheffield was dominated by the Mooney and Garvin gangs, Derby had its race gangs, and Glasgow the South Side Stickers, the San Toy Gang, and James "Razzle-Dazzle" Dalziel's Parlour Boys. Most were eliminated before the Second World War. Unfortunately, the postwar years saw the rise of new gangs. *London's gangland environment has been portrayed with sympathy by Charles Raven (*Underworld Nights*, 1956), humorously by Frank Norman (*Too Many Crooks Spoil the Caper*, 1979), and seriously by Michael *Gilbert (*Fear to Tread*, 1953). Bill Knox portrayed the postwar resurgence of organized crime in Glasgow in *The Tallyman* (1969) and *Draw Batons!* (1973).

However, it was in the United States that the gangs reached their apogee—becoming, as Edgar Lustgarten noted in *The Illustrated Story of Crime* (1967), groups who were more likely to wage war among themselves than against the public. As Lustgarten pointed out, their ultimate genesis was in "the Great Migration westwards" from Europe to the major U.S. cities. Herbert Asbury sets the genesis of *The Gangs of New York* (1927) at the beginning of the nineteenth century, in the streets around the Five Points. By the century's end, they were numerous and powerful; notable were the Gas House Gang, the Gophers, and the Hudson Dusters. Unexpectedly, P. G. Wodehouse gave a good portrait of them in *The Prince and Betty* (1912; rewritten as *Psmith, Journalist*, 1915). In Chicago, there were the gangleaders styled by Lloyd Wendt in *The Lords of the Levee* (1943), notably Michael "Hinky Dink" Kenna and "Bathhouse John" Coughlin. The Gold Rush brought gangs and the wars of the Chinese tongs to California, as described in Herbert Asbury's *Barbary Coast* (1933).

Paradoxically, it was the passing of the Eighteenth Amendment to the United States Constitution in 1920 that gave greatest impetus to the gangs. The prohibition of alcohol, initially applauded, swiftly became unpopular. Suddenly, criminals became friends of most ordinary Americans, with bootleggers acquiring a respectability almost comparable to that of doctors. (Wodehouse treats this humorously in *Hot Water*, 1932.) The long-term consequence was serious; when *Prohibition was repealed in 1933, the gangs were too strong to contemplate dissolution and instead concentrated upon activities hitherto marginal—prostitution, selling narcotics, and illegal *gambling.

The most infamous gangleaders were all products of Prohibition. *New York spawned such criminals as Arnold Rothstein, Jack "Legs" Diamond, Owen "Owney" Madden, and Dutch Schultz (featured, thinly disguised, in Leslie *Charteris's *The Saint in New York*, 1935). Detroit had its Purple Gang, Kansas City its Pendergast machine, and Cincinnati its George Remus, "the gentle grafter." However, it was the gangs of Chicago that attained greatest notoriety. Dominant was the gang led successively by "Big Jim" Colosimo, Johnny Torrio, and Al Capone; this eliminated its rivals led by the Genna brothers and Dion O'Banion. These events have inspired many novels, the best being W. R. Burnett's *Little Caesar* (1929).

By the time of Prohibition's repeal, some gangs had been broken by oblique means, such as Capone's conviction for tax evasion. Organized crime's most formidable hit group, notorious as Murder, Incorporated, had been exposed; one of its leaders, Louis "Lepke" Buchalter, was executed, while another, Charley "Lucky" Luciano, fled to Sicily. However, the gangs swiftly recouped these losses and emerged as powerful as ever. To this day they remain strong. Their wars continue and their leaders—though often identified—are rarely convicted. Mario Puzo's *The Godfather* (1969) reveals their philosophy; Harry Grey's *The Hoods* (1952) recounts the rise and moral degeneration of a gangster; and Richard Condon's *Prizzi's Honor* (1982) humorously portrays a Mafia hit man. Organized crime's stretching forth into law is depicted in John Grisham's *The Firm* (1991).

The struggle against the power of organized crime is so difficult that it tends to be a minor theme in fiction. Though mentioned often in *police procedurals, only peripheral successes are scored. The encounters of Rex *Stout's Nero *Wolfe with Arnold Zeck cost him much personal suffering before the third (*In the Best Families*, 1950; *Even in the Best Families*, 1951) brings triumph. When Charteris's Simon Templar ventures against the Mafia in Sicily (*Vendetta for the Saint*, 1965), his success is limited, and when the Honorable Richard Rollison fights organized crime, his victory costs him prolonged hospitalization (John *Creasey, *The Toff in New York*, 1956). Ross *Macdonald's Lew *Archer combats organized crime in *Los Angeles (*The Way Some People Die*, 1951), and Jonathan Valin's Harry Stoner wages a bitter war in Cincinnati (*The Lime Pit*, 1980), but even in the hard-boiled genre, organized crime is not a common theme.

[*See also* Underworld; Underworld Figure.]

• Patrick Pringle, *Honest Thieves: The Story of the Smugglers* (1938). Craig Thompson and Allen Raymond, *Gang Rule in New York: The Story of a Lawless Era* (1940). Herbert Asbury, *The Great Illusion: An Informal History of Prohibition* (1950).
—William A. S. Sarjeant

ORIENTAL CRIME WRITING. *See* China, Crime and Mystery Writing in Greater; Japan, Crime and Mystery in.

OUR SOCIETY. Having inherited a love of the theater from his father, the great Sir Henry Irving, Henry Brodribb (H. B.) Irving became an actor manager. His father had wished him to train for a more reputable career, so he studied at Oxford and was called to the bar in 1894. He retained an interest in criminology and wrote several books, which included a biography of Judge Jeffreys (1898) and several collections of essays on causes célèbres.

On 5 December 1903, H. B. Irving invited five friends to dinner at his London home. That evening the six decided to establish a regular dining club with the object of discussing legal and criminological topics. To avoid any legal repercussions, papers were not to be read or discussed until servants had departed. Membership soon increased, and it became known as Our Society, or, unofficially, The Crimes Club.

Many officers of the society have served for long periods. The first president and honorary secretary, Arthur Lambton, a founding member, remained in office for thirty-two years. His successors, Sir Percy Everett and Eveleigh Nash, held the post for shorter periods until 1952. Then the much respected lawyer, Judge Henry Elam, took over as honorary secretary, holding the position for forty-one years until his death at age eighty-nine in 1993.

Over the years many distinguished doctors, lawyers, and authors have become members or have addressed the society. Arthur Conan *Doyle joined in 1904 and gave several papers, including "The Psychic in Crime." Other author members included A. E. W. *Mason, Gilbert Frankau, Ian Hay, P. G. Wodehouse, and E. W. *Hornung. Sir Edward Marshall Hall, Viscount Jowitt, and Sir Bernard Spilsbury were among those distinguished in the forensic field.

Famous cases, like those of the Brides in the Bath, Dr. Hawley Harley Crippen, James Hanratty, the Great Train Robbery, and the Moors murders have been discussed, as well as subjects more generally related to crime. Among the latter have been "Sexual Abnormality" (1931) and "Hysterical Women" (1938), presented by Harold Dearden, M.D.

George R. Sims, a stalwart member, fought successfully for the release of Adolph Beck, who he believed was wrongly convicted of fraud. Doyle also campaigned effectively on behalf of those he saw as victims of injustice, especially Oscar Slater and George Edalji.

The society's pattern of meetings is little changed today. Three or four times a year, following dinner at the Imperial Hotel in London, members are generally presented with a paper on a current or classic crime, followed by questions and discussion.

HRH Prince Philip is the society's patron and occasionally attends meetings. He is not the first royal member. HRH the Duke of Kent was a member for ten years until his tragic death in 1942.

Membership of the society is limited to six life members and seventy-five ordinary members. Only those who have dined as guests, and have thus been "vetted," are eligible to join. There is a waiting list.

Jonathan Goodman became honorary secretary in 1993.
—Christine R. Simpson

OUTCASTS AND OUTSIDERS. The universe of crime and mystery fiction abounds in closed worlds that serve as microcosms for demonstrating the consequences and possible remedies for social violations. Whether the closed worlds comprise an enclave of wealthy residents, academics, hardened criminals, professionals, or residents of a set locality, they have indigenous manners, tastes, and, of course, a common background and value system.

The task for the writer plotting a tale of attack upon a particular social order is to enact the eruption of crime. An excellent means of doing so is through interlopers who may be, or appear to be, catalysts for criminal disorder. Associated with outbreaks of crime, the conventional character type of the alien outsider or its allied type, the deviant, appears to deserve to be cast out of the community.

In fiction that shows closed worlds as positive ideals for human society, such as Golden Age writing, the outsider may be described in terms resonant of comedies of manners; thus, the villain eventually revealed in Dorothy L. *Sayers's *Gaudy Night* (1935) is a woman who sides with the cause of men in what she presumes is the battle against them initiated by the female academics of the Oxford college. Besides despising the inherently feminist outlook of the women in the community, her background, education, and social *class differ entirely. In essence, therefore, she is totally alien, the complete outsider. A similar rendition of the outsider figure appears in the stories by Agatha *Christie about Miss Jane *Marple, doyenne of a timeless village, whose adventures are littered with hints that the newcomer is a person who must be watched carefully.

A curious modification in the use of the outsider as the likely criminal in upper-class society can be discovered in stories of *gentleman thieves like the adventures of A. J. *Raffles related by E. W. *Hornung. Raffles possesses sufficient accomplishments of learning and style to be the consummate insider, yet his actions put him in the role of the invasive outsider, violating the expectations of mannered behavior. The witty effect of this play with stereotypes is further heightened by observable similarities between Raffles, the violator, and Sherlock *Holmes, the idealized defender of the social order.

Away from the environs of social privilege, in the gritty cities where hard-boiled writers place their stories, social *milieus take other forms, but they can be just as closed as the habitats of the wealthy and just as protective against outsiders. The police officers in Joseph Wambaugh's *The Onion Field* (1973) become tragic outcasts when they give up their guns to criminals, thereby violating the decorum of police behavior. In a variation on this formula, E. Richard Johnson's *Case Load—Maximum* (1971) tells of a parole officer who faces ostracism from his occupation because he has lowered the defensive shield of wariness and trusted a parolee when he should not have.

Law enforcement, as a matter of fact, provides especially rich opportunities for authors to develop themes about closed environments through the use of outsider characters. Dorothy Uhnak's *Law and Order* (1973), in telling of generations of Irish American police officers, plays on the insider-outsider theme by demonstrating that insiders within a corrupt department are a better hope for reform, because of their knowledge, than high-minded outsiders. Uhnak's other significant treatment of an outsider is her story of Christie Opara, a woman officer in the male-oriented police force. Characters who are inevitably outsiders, although they are official cops, also appear in Chester *Himes's series about the Harlem detectives Grave Digger Jones and Coffin Ed *Johnson. Effective enforcers of law, but also sympathetic protectors of the little people of Harlem, Jones and Johnson can never be anything but outsiders, because in a society and city run by a predominantly white power structure, blacks are always the "other."

In confirmation of the utility of outsiders or outcast characters the authors of underworld stories use them to convey the sense of Mafia exclusivity, as in the Godfather film and stories of Mario Puzo. The adopted Irish boy grows up to be the organization's lawyer, but without the all-important blood ties he can never be a fully fledged member of the crime family.

Other examples of outsiders who can never integrate into the tight crime family are to be found in the classic *puzzle stories deriving from the patterns of the Golden Age, which show that most often this character type is used to best advantage in secondary roles. This only stands to reason, for despite the intrinsic interest an author may have in such characters, their greatest usefulness lies in the way they mark the boundaries of the many closed worlds in crime and mystery literature.

[See also Closed-World Settings and Open-World Settings; Deviance; Prodigal Son/Daughter.]

• Glenn W. Most and William W. Stowe, eds., *The Poetics of Murder: Detective Fiction and Literary Theory* (1983). Colin Watson, *Snobbery with Violence: Crime Stories and Their Audience* (1971).
—John M. Reilly

OUTDOORS, THE. *See* Great Outdoors.

OXFORD, the country seat of Oxfordshire. England, is a city on the River Thames that has been the site of university studies since 1167. Throughout the twentieth century it has been frequently used as a *setting for detective and mystery stories, and is, indeed, the most popular of all *academic milieus. As a university city, Oxford is a natural habitat for the *academic sleuth; while the small enclosed community of the Oxford college provides for the classical tale of detection an environment akin to that of the traditional *country house milieu. And, since a large number of detective novelists—Ronald A. *Knox, G. D. H. and Margaret *Cole, E. C. *Bentley, Dorothy L. *Sayers, Michael *Innes, H. C.*Bailey, Edmund *Crispin, J. C. Masterman, Antonia Fraser, and Nicholas *Blake, among others—were educated at the university, it is not surprising that they should return to it in their work.

One of the first Oxford detective novels is *The Oxford Murders* (1929) by Adam Broome, interesting for its portrayal of the town, but negligible in other respects; the same might be said of David Frome's *The Body in the Turl* (1935) and of *Off With Her Head!*

(1938) by the Coles. However. *An Oxford Tragedy* (1933), set in the imaginary St. Thomas's College, by Masterman, later provost of Worcester College, makes superb use of the enclosed environment and of academic rivalry. Equally successful is Sayers's *Gaudy Night* (1935) which uses a fictional women's college as the setting for her exploration of the issue of women's education and of the problem as to whether the scholarly pursuit of truth should override all other considerations. The setting of Innes's first novel. *Death at the President's Lodging* (1936: *Seven Suspects*), and of Victor L. Whitechurch's *Murder at the College* (1932; *Murder at Exbridge*) is obviously Oxford, though both purport to take place in fictional towns. Innes also uses Oxford in a *thriller. *Operation Pax* (1951: *The Paper Thunderbolt*), whose climax is a chase through the underground stacks of the Bodleian library. Crispin makes much use of real Oxford localities: In his *The Case of the Gilded Fly* (1944: *Obsequies at Oxford*) characters drink at the pub frequented by the group known as the Inklings, whose members included J. R. R. Tolkien and C. S. Lewis. *The Missing Link* (1952) and *Gownsman's Gallows* (1957) by Katherine Farrer and *Untimely Slain* (1947) by Jonathan Gray have admirable openings set in Oxford, though the action is later transferred elsewhere. More of a tourist's view of the city is given by Amanda *Cross, whose American academic Kate *Fansler spends a sabbatical at Oxford in *The Question of Max* (1976). Two excellent humorous detective novels set in the university are *Landscape with Dead Dons* (1956) by Robert Robinson and Timothy Robinson's *When Scholars Fall* (1961)—a parody of the *academic sleuth novel. Colin *Dexter's long series of novels, beginning with *Last Bus to Woodstock* (1975), in which the detective is Inspector *Morse, make admirable use of the topography of Oxford and its surroundings: some have a college, some an urban background. Finally, in Fraser's *Oxford Blood* (1985) her detective, Jemima Shore, pursues an inquiry at the imaginary Rochester College, designed by Nicholas Hawksmoor, who was in fact the architect of the library of The Queen's and the north quadrangle of All Soul's College.

The Oxford detective novel is generally light in tone, indulgent to academic eccentricity, and inquisitive as to the rites and customs of the senior common room: Undergraduates are, with some exceptions, usually ignored. Only, perhaps, in Dexter's novels is the university seen as but part of a large city, and Oxford itself placed in the context of the country as a whole.

[*See also* Closed-World Settings and Open-World Settings; Eccentrics.]

—T. J. Binyon

PAPERBACKS. The advent of paperback publishing profoundly extended the range of the crime and mystery genre by increasing the list of available titles and winning a larger readership. A signal American contribution to extending readership was the provision of Armed Services Editions—pocket-size paperbacks—to military personnel in World War II: 1,324 titles were published, a significant percentage of them mysteries.

In addition, inexpensive production encourages the marketing of books as commodities. Low-cost and frequent reprinting attracted casual first-time readers, many of whom became regular fans. Publishers quickly learned to target audiences, such as devotees of the *cozy mystery, through cover design, and to create new audiences, such as, readers whose fondness for action stories would lead them to try hard-boiled crime fiction. This was achieved at first by instinct and eventually by means of market research.

Bantam Books and Pocket Books were early industry leaders, but after World War II, Avon, Dell, and Popular Library were healthy competitors. In Britain, Penguin led the field. American rights to Penguin and Pelican titles were acquired by Victor Weybright and Kurt Enoch of England, who left Penguin to found their own company, New American Library (NAL). On both sides of the Atlantic, the early model for the industry was to reprint titles already successful in hardcover.

In 1950, Fawcett Publications changed paperback publishing forever by embarking on an ambitious publishing program featuring entirely original work. Fawcett also compensated its writers more generously: The author received an immediate $3,000 advance against royalties. At the time, most hardcover publishers would not pay writers until after publication.

The impact was immediate. Fawcett Publications attracted superior writers of crime fiction in the fifties: John D. *MacDonald, Charles Williams, Bruno Fischer, David Goodis, and Harry Whittington. Other paperback publishers hurried to follow Fawcett's example. By 1955, a third of all genre paperbacks were original works.

The fifties also saw the publication of one of the most ambitious crime and mystery series in paperback history: the Dell mapbacks. Dell sought to differentiate itself from the competition by featuring four-color covers with a map or diagram on the back illustrating the scene of the volume's crime. Although not all five hundred mapbacks were mysteries, the series concentrated on crime and mystery titles. Mapbacks were also known for their distinctive "eye in the peephole" logo and brilliant stylized abstract covers. Featured authors were Dashiell *Hammett, Agatha *Christie, Brett Halliday, Mary Roberts *Rinehart, Rex *Stout, George Harmon *Coxe, Ellery *Queen, and Mignon G. *Eberhart. From hard-boiled detective novels to cozies, the Dell mapback collection included a wide selection of all types of mystery fiction.

In the early 1980s Dell issued the Scene of the Crime/Murder Ink series featuring seventy mysteries by mostly British writers, including Robert *Barnard, Colin *Watson, Simon Brett, and Martha Grimes. Early covers featured a jigsaw puzzle motif.

Another unique design was the ACE Double. A. A. Wyn's ACE Books with editor Donald A. Wollheim featured two complete novels bound back to back, with each half having its own cover illustration and title page. The first ACE Double (D-1) was Samuel W. Taylor's *The Grinning Gismo* and Keith Vining's *Too Hot to Handle* (1951)—both mysteries. Most of the ACE Doubles were hack writing, but the most famous number, D-15, contained *Junkie* (1953) by William Burroughs writing as "William Lee."

In the 1960s many smaller, now defunct, paperback publishers started significant mystery series programs. Lancer Books offered the Lancer Suspense Library, bringing the works of British writers such as Michael Gilbert and Andrew Garve to the American reading public. Pyramid Books' Green Door Mysteries brought sixty classic mystery stories back to print. The early books featured a distinctive green spine that became part of the cover's door frame. The door itself had a small white skull for a knocker. The series featured Stout, Anthony Gilbert, Mabel Seely, Anthony *Boucher, and Ira Levin.

Publishers tried to differentiate paperbacks from hardcovers in many ways but succeeded chiefly through cover art. Most mystery paperbacks—especially the hard-boiled variety—sported sexy women on their covers. Robert McGinnis, whose work on Brett Halliday's Mike Shayne series for Dell and Australian Alan Geoffrey Yates's Carter *Brown series for Signet, is best known.

Paperback publishers learned that the crime and mystery readership is quite discerning, as when Canada's Harlequin tried to copy their enormous success in romance novels with a mystery series called Raven Books. The Ravens were packaged similarly, with golden yellow borders and photographic cover art. Some titles sold well; others didn't. Mystery fans bought books written by well-known writers such as William Campbell *Gault and Richard Moore but passed on books in the series written by lesser-known writers. Harlequin abandoned Raven Books after a couple years of uneven sales and sixty releases.

Paperbacks also created markets where there were no hardcover entries. For example, in the late 1960s Award Books offered a series about a spy reviving the name Nick Carter of dime novel fame, in books filled with action and adventure. A new publishing company, Pinnacle Books, multiplied the effort and launched a number of men's action-adventure series: Don Pendleton's Mack Bolan, who warred on the Mafia for more than thirty books; The Destroyer series, which became a cult favorite; The Butcher; The Death Merchant; The Penetrator; and Colonel Tobin's Private Army. Pinnacle Books' success in this new market forced other paperback publishers to offer their own action-adventure series: Dell had The Assassin; Lancer had The Enforcer; BT Books had The Marksman; and Berkley had the Lone Wolf series written by "Mike Barry" who was actually science fiction writer Barry Malzberg.

Paperbacks often gave writers a market they couldn't find with mainstream hardcover publishers. Rediscoveries in the 1990s of Jim *Thompson and Peter Rabe, whose major works were all published by paperback houses such as Lion Books and Fawcett's Gold Medal Books, are examples. Ed *McBain's Eighty-seventh Precinct series started out as Pocket Books paperback originals, as did Richard Stark's Parker series. MacDonald's Travis *McGee series and Donald Hamilton's Matt Helm spy series were both Fawcett paperback originals.

A measure of the paperback impact on the genre may be seen in the rediscovery and reprinting of authors like Thompson and Rabe, who are well-known not because of earlier hardback books but rather for classic volumes originally issued by paperback houses. To this day publishers and readers alike are willing to invest in the work of new authors printed in paperback.

• Piet Schreuders, *Paperbacks, U.S.A: A Graphic History 1939–1959* (1981). Thomas L. Bonn, *Under Cover: An Illustrated History of American Mass-Market Paperbacks* (1982). Allen Billy Crider, ed., *Mass Market Publishing in America* (1982). Kenneth C. Davis, *Two-Bit Culture: The Paperbacking of America* (1984). Walter Albert, *Detective and Mystery Fiction: An International Bibliography of Secondary Sources* (1985).
—George Kelley

PARETSKY, SARA (b. 1947), American writer of detective novels and short stories. Born in Ames, Iowa, Sara Paretsky was educated at the University of Kansas (B.A., 1967) and the University of Chicago (M.B.A. and Ph.D., 1977). From 1971 to 1985, she worked as a writer for several Chicago-area businesses.

Paretsky chose the mystery genre for her first attempt at fiction writing because she was a mystery fan and wanted to try a form she knew well. *Indemnity Only* (1982), with a complicated *plot informed by Paretsky's extensive knowledge of the insurance industry, introduced private investigator Victoria Iphi-

genia "V. I." *Warshawski. As signaled by the title's echo of James M. *Cain's *Double Indemnity,* Paretsky's novel both enters and begins to revise the hard-boiled detective genre. Paretsky has continued this revision with the next six Warshawski books: *Deadlock* (1984), *Killing Orders* (1985), *Bitter Medicine* (1987), *Blood Shot* (1988; *Toxic Shock,* 1988), which won the Silver Dagger Award from the Crime Writers Association, *Burn Marks* (1990), and *Guardian Angel* (1992).

In the tradition of hard-boiled detectives, Warshawski narrates the novels, but with results very different from the "bare style" of Paretsky's male predecessors. Paretsky's novels share other features with conventional hard-boiled fiction. For example, both give readers exhaustive catalogs of the flotsam and jetsam of daily life—meals cooked and eaten, clothing (Warshawski is partial to Bruno Magli pumps and silk blouses), baths, finances—along with intricate details about specific locales the detective knows well (in Warshawski's case, Chicago). Paretsky, however, introduces far more intimate explorations of her character's psychology than is usual in the genre. One staple of *hard-boiled fiction is the tough, loner hero. Paretsky's detective often questions the value of toughness and worries that her job diminishes human connection. Two of the most interesting continuing characters in the series—Lotte Herschel, a physician who is Warshawski's closest friend, and her neighbor Mr. Contreras, an elderly character who finds Warshawski's work exciting and wants to be part of it—often figure in the sleuth's ongoing struggle to balance independence and interconnection.

The plots of Paretsky's novels link specific crimes—usually *murders committed in order to preserve or consolidate power—with wider social problems. In *Bitter Medicine* Warshawski uncovers *corruption in the medical profession, for instance, while in *Blood Shot* her investigation leads her to both a child abuser and an environmental polluter. The other novels' plots turn on corruption in such areas as banking, shipping, and organized *religion. The position of women in society and the possible meanings of social *justice are important themes in all the novels, as is the question of *violence.

Paretsky has received more critical accolades and attracted more readers with each new book. She is one of the most popular contemporary feminist writers of detective fiction, and one of the most important figures in the current proliferation of female crime writing. A film based on her fiction, *V. I. Warshawski,* starring Kathleen Turner as the detective, was released in 1992; critics agree that Hollywood did not do justice to Paretsky's work. Her novels are intricately plotted but intensely character-driven, elegantly written, and thematically rich. Named a Woman of the Year by *Ms.* magazine in 1987, Paretsky is a founder and former president of the *Sisters in Crime organization.

[See also Females and Feminists; Hard-Boiled Sleuth; Loner, Sleuth as.]

• Kathleen Gregory Klein, *The Woman Detective* (1988). Maureen T. Reddy, *Sisters in Crime: Feminism and the Crime Novel* (1988). Sara Paretsky, ed., *Eye of a Woman* (1992).
—Maureen T. Reddy

PARKER, ROBERT B(ROWN), (b. 1932), American author, widely regarded as a leading contemporary writer of private-eye fiction. Parker was born 17 September 1932, in Springfield, Massachusetts, and educated at Colby College in Maine. Following graduation in 1954 and a two-year stint with the army in Korea, he worked at a variety of jobs (technical writer, co-owner of an advertising agency), earning his Ph.D. in English from Boston University in 1971. In 1968 he joined the faculty as an English professor at Boston's Northeastern University.

Parker's interest in detective fiction began at the age of fourteen when he first read Raymond *Chandler. Later, he wrote his Ph.D. dissertation on the novels of Chandler, Dashiell *Hammett, and Ross *Macdonald. At the age of thirty-nine, he decided to try his hand at a private-eye novel in the knight-errant tradition of Chandler. *The Godwulf Manuscript* (1973) introduced the character of *Spenser ("with an s, like the poet"), a Boston *private eye with the build of a prizefighter and the soul of a poet. Parker's admiration for Chandler eventually prompted him to write two "new" Philip *Marlowe novels: *Poodle Springs* (1989), a completion of Chandler's unfinished novel, and *Perchance to Dream* (1991), a sequel to *The Big Sleep* (1939).

Though originally modeled on Marlowe, Spenser differs from him in several respects. Most significantly, Parker abandoned the traditional model of the lone-wolf private eye. Spenser's long-term relationship with psychologist Susan Silverman comprises an eloquent celebration of enduring love that counters the uglier elements of his chosen profession. His African American sidekick, Hawk, a former adversary, is now a trusted ally, especially in dangerous situations. Unhampered by conscience, Hawk is also used to accentuate Spenser's efforts to develop a personal code of ethical behavior. Among the more compelling books in the series are *Mortal Stakes* (1975) and *Paper Doll* (1993), in which Spenser struggles to resolve the conflicting demands of his profession and his conscience and to balance his Arthurian fantasies of *heroism with the implacable demands of the real world.

Parker's novels are noted for their *humor (Spenser is master of the wisecrack and flippant one-liner) and polished style, with literary *allusions from the well-read Spenser liberally sprinkled throughout the series. Though he addresses a variety of topical issues, from feminist politics in *Looking for Rachel Wallace* (1980) to urban youth gangs in *Double Deuce* (1992), Parker's main theme is *family relationships, especially the damaging effects on children of parental failures at love. In *Early Autumn* (1981), Spenser even finds himself playing mentor and counselor to the emotionally damaged Paul Glacomin, who subsequently assumes the role of surrogate son in Spenser's extended family.

Critics agree that Parker's plots are occasionally thin and the exchanges between Spenser and Susan can become coy, but they also point out that Parker is consistently entertaining. And Spenser, a two-fisted hero with a tender heart, a man who can throw his weight around as deftly as he whips up gourmet meals or quotes poetry, has become the very model of the private eye for our time.

[*See also* Hard-Boiled Sleuth; Sidekicks and Sleuthing Teams; Voice: Wisecracking Voice.]

• David Geherin, *Sons of Sam Spade: The Private-Eye Novel in the 70s* (1980). John C. Carr, ed., *The Craft of Crime: Conversations with Crime Writers* (1983). Robert B. Parker, *The Private Eye in Hammett and Chandler* (1984). Robin W. Winks, ed., *Colloquium on Crime: Eleven Renowned Mystery Writers Discuss Their Work* (1986).   —David Geherin

PARTNERSHIPS, LITERARY. Collaborations between crime writers range from those absorbing both partners' creative energies over the long term to those occurring once in an author's lifetime. Some pairs share a joint *pseudonym; others identify each partner. Some literary collaborators are also married couples. The ultimate collaborator was perhaps Richard Wilson Webb, whose thirty novels over twenty years include two written with one coauthor, two with another, and twenty-five with a third. (L. T. Meade also had three collaborators, but she was more prolific without one.) Webb was the lynchpin of a complicated operation serving three pseudonyms: Q. Patrick with each coauthor in turn and Patrick Quentin and Jonathan Stagge with Hugh Wheeler. Though Wheeler kept the Quentin byline alive after breaking with his partner, Webb wrote nothing more. Evidently he was a natural collaborator. So, too, were Frederic Dannay and Manfred B. Lee, whose remarkable contribution to mystery fiction was made jointly, primarily as Ellery *Queen. They wrote only in collaboration, Dannay with other writers for some of the later titles in the Canon. Francis M. Nevine Jr. states that Dannay was largely responsible for "the conceptual work" of the books and Lee for "the detailed execution," including "the precise choice of words." Another commentator remarked on "the interlocking of their mental processes," making conversation with them "like talking to one man."

Francis Beeding also was the pseudonym of two men: Hilary St. George Saunders and John Palmer, friends with complementary literary gifts. Saunders is reported to have said: "Palmer can't be troubled with description and narrative and I'm no good at creating characters or dialogue." Manning Coles combined the talents of a man and a woman: Adelaide Manning and Cyril Coles, the latter with direct experience of British intelligence doubtless invaluable in the composition of *spy fiction. Emma *Lathen and R. B. Dominic were pseudonyms used together by Mary J. Latsis and Martha Henissart. They discussed each book before starting to write, "to get a fix on the characters." Then each wrote separate chapters, which were jointly checked for errors and omissions and dovetailed into the final narrative. Collaboration spared them "the hardest part of the author's lot, the loneliness": Each had "the knowledge that someone else is going to get a crack at it."

Barrie Hayne suggests the likely division of labor in the collaboration of Clemence Dane and Helen Simpson: Their actor detective, "one guesses, along with his theatrical background, is more Clemence

Dane's creation, the plotting of the mystery more Helen Simpson's." Bo Lundin confirms that Maj *Sjöwall and Per Wahlöö "wrote together, each writing alternate chapters after long research and detailed synopses."

G. D. H. *Cole wrote one detective novel solo and a further twenty-seven with his wife Margaret. In *Meet the Detective* (1935) she describes their taking turns to do "the main bit of the work" on each novel: "We settle on a plot . . . then one of us does a first draft and shows it to the other for criticism. Then the fun begins . . . And so it's altered and eventually turns up as a book, all in proper form." The Lockridges proceeded differently, Richard doing the writing from *plot outlines by Frances. Interestingly, after his wife's death, Richard Lockridge continued to produce crime novels for many years. The roles of planner and writer were reversed for John and Emery Bonett, whose Penguin biography records that "John, besides having imagination and plot-sense, has also grammar, spelling and a sense of humor and from the time they met he has done most of the spadework" on his wife's stories. The methods of Darwin and Hildegarde Teilhet were described by Douglas G. Greene in *The Armchair Detective*. Darwin invented characters and "devised the plots," which he and his wife then "vigorously" discussed. Since he was "less interested in plot details and development," Hildegarde often contributed "such points during discussion." Darwin then wrote the first draft and Hildegarde "rewrote and edited the manuscript." Even later novels signed individually are to some extent collaborations.

Some famous writers collaborated on occasion. John *Rhode wrote *Drop to His Death* (1939; *Fatal Descent*) with Carter Dickson, who, as John Dickson *Carr, cowrote certain *Exploits of Sherlock Holmes* (1954) and wholly wrote others. Dorothy L. *Sayers and Ngaio *Marsh both collaborated with doctors for medical accuracy. Stuart Palmer records that Craig *Rice's "real contribution" to *People vs. Withers and Malone* (1963), "apart from the unique character of Malone," was "in the gimmicks, the gadgets, the slant—a beginning or an ending or a line or two of dialogue." —B. A. Pike

PASSION, CRIMES OF. *See* Tragedy, Dramatic, Elements of in Crime and Mystery Writing.

PASSOVER. *See* Holiday Mysteries.

PASTICHE. In contrast to the comic intent of parody, pastiche is the serious imitation of another writer's style and characters. Given the prevalence of distinctly drawn series characters in crime and mystery fiction, the genre is particularly rich in pastiche.

The most frequent object of pastiche is Arthur Conan *Doyle's Sherlock *Holmes, paid notable homage in short story form in Vincent *Starrett's classic "The Unique Hamlet" (*The Misadventures of Sherlock Holmes* 1920); August Derleth's long series about Solar Pons; Adrian Conan Doyle and John Dickson *Carr's *The Exploits of Sherlock Holmes*

(1954); June Thomson's collections, beginning with *The Secret Files of Sherlock Holmes* (1990); and *The New Adventures of Sherlock Holmes* (1987), edited by Martin H. Greenberg and Carol-Lynn Rossel-Waugh, which includes Stephen King, John Lutz, Edward D. *Hoch, Dorothy B. Hughes, and Lillian de la Torre among its contributors.

The first notable novel-length Holmes pastiche, H. F. Heard's *A Taste for Honey* (1941), began a trilogy about Holmes's retirement under the alias Mr. Mycroft. The commercial success of Nicholas Meyer's *The Seven-per-Cent Solution* (1974) presaged a flood of ersatz Holmes novels, most involving interaction with other fictional characters, e.g., Loren D. Estleman's *Sherlock Holmes vs. Dracula; or, The Adventures of the Sanguinary Count* (1978) and *Dr. Jekyll and Mr. Holmes* (1979), Manly Wade Wellman and Wade Wellman's *Sherlock Holmes's War of the Worlds* (1975), Peter Rowland's *The Disappearance of Edwin Drood* (1991); attempted solutions to real-life mysteries, e.g., the Dreyfus case in Michael Hardwick's *Prisoner of the Devil* (1979), the Kennedy assassination in Edmund Aubrey's *Sherlock Holmes in Dallas* (1980), and the Jack the Ripper murders in several novels from Ellery *Queen's movie novelization *A Study in Terror* (1966) to Edward B. Hanna's *The Whitechapel Horror* (1992); or historical figures as characters, e.g., Sigmund Freud in *The Seven-per-Cent Solution*, George Bernard Shaw and Oscar Wilde in Meyer's *The West End Horror* (1976), Harry Houdini in Daniel Stashower's *The Adventure of the Ectoplasmic Man* (1985), and Theodore Roosevelt in H. Paul Jeffers's *The Adventure of the Stalwart Companions* (1978). Some of the most effective Holmes pastiches eschew such gimmicks, notably the novels of L. B. Greenwood, beginning with *Sherlock Holmes and the Case of the Raleigh Legacy* (1986).

Most non-Sherlockian examples of direct pastiche occur when series are taken over by another hand, usually after the death of the original creator, such as Barry Perowne's continuation of E. W. *Hornung's A. J. *Raffles; Gerard Fairlie's of Sapper's Bulldog *Drummond; Roderic Graeme's of his father Bruce Graeme's Blackshirt; John Gardner's of Ian *Fleming's James *Bond; Robert Goldsborough's of Rex *Stout's Nero *Wolfe; and Thomas Chastain's of Erle Stanley *Gardner's Perry *Mason.

In Byron Preiss's anthology *Raymond Chandler's Philip Marlowe: A Centennial Celebration* (1988), twenty-three writers, including Max Allan Collins, Sara *Paretsky, and Paco Ignacio Taibo II, contribute new Marlowe tales. Robert B. *Parker followed his completion of Chandler's unfinished *Poodle Springs* (1989) with *Perchance to Dream* (1991), a sequel to *The Big Sleep* (1939). Larry M. Harris paid homage to Craig *Rice with *The Pickled Poodles* (1960), while Terrence Lore Smith's *Reverend Randollph and Modern Miracles* (1988) added a final title to his late father Charles Merrill Smith's series. In *The Great Detectives* (1981), Julian *Symons imitates Doyle, Chandler, Stout, Queen, Agatha *Christie, and Georges *Simenon, while Norma Schier's *The Anagram Detectives* (1979) pays tribute to the sleuths of Doyle, Queen, Stout, Christie, Margery *Allingham, and Dorothy L. *Sayers. Though most of the stories in Jon L. Breen's *Hair of the Sleuthhound* (1982) are parodies, S. S. *Van Dine's Philo *Vance and Earl Derr *Biggers's Charlie *Chan appear in pastiches.

In the collaborative novel by *The Detection Club *Ask a Policeman* (1933), Helen Simpson writes about Gladys *Mitchell's Mrs. Beatrice Adela Lestrange *Bradley, Mitchell about Simpson and Clemence Dane's Sir John Saumarez, Sayers about Anthony *Berkeley's Roger Sheringham, and Berkeley about Sayers's Lord Peter *Wimsey. Another example of the group pastiche, Marion Mainwaring's *Murder in Pastiche* (1954), renames the characters, whose treatment may be nearer parody.

Some writers of pastiche do not directly adopt another writer's style and characters but rather borrow elements of them to write about similar characters and situations. Like many series of their period, Christie's early Hercule *Poirot short stories closely follow a Sherlockian pattern. In *A Three-Pipe Problem* (1975), Symons introduces a television actor playing Holmes who comes to take his role seriously, a situation used earlier by R. R. Irvine in the short story "Another Case of Identity" (1975).

Many owe a debt, usually freely acknowledged, to Stout and Wolfe: Rufus King's Cotton Moon in the one-shot *Holiday Homicide* (1940), Thomas B. Dewey's Singer Batts, William F. Love's Bishop Francis Regan, Chip Harrison's (Lawrence Block's) Leo Haig, Melodie Johnson Howe's Claire Conrad, and Monica Quill's (Ralph McInerny's) Sister Mary Teresa. A strong element of Chandler pastiche exists in Ross *Macdonald's early Lew *Archer novels, Howard Browne's novels about Paul Pine, initially signed John Evans, and Loren Estleman's Amos Walker series.

[*See also* Humor.]

• John Kennedy Melling, *Murder Done to Death* (1997).

—Jon L. Breen

PATHFINDER FICTION. The concept of the detective as literal hunter or tracker following the footprints of the criminal is an old one. It has also been used in a metaphorical sense. The prototype is found in James Fenimore Cooper's series, five-volume Leather-Stocking including *The Pathfinder* (1840), in which Natty Bumppo's skills as a tracker is displayed. In *The Last of the Mohicans* (1826), Hawkeye (the name used by Bumppo in the novel) describes the differences between moccasin tracks to Major Heyward in a manner that suggests a detective making logical deductions. The concept as expressed in nineteenth-century fiction does not end there. In William Leggett's short story "The Rifle" (*Tales and Sketches of a Country Schoolmaster*; 1829) the physical evidence leads to one conclusion until an early example of the science of ballistics indicates whose weapon actually fired the shot. Later writers such as Alexandre Dumas made passing, but significant, use of the ability of one character to explain the actions of another on the basis of physical evidence. In *Le Vicomte de Bragelonne* (1848) d'Artagnan makes astute deductions to the king about past events from the

horse hairs he finds on a tree as well as from footprints he sees.

The *dime novel detective fiction of the late nineteenth century continued to exhibit this concept as detectives were described as tracking the criminal or were referred to as "man trackers." In keeping with their real-life counterparts, the men and women of the Pinkerton Detective Agency, they were "on the trail" or "tracking down" the criminals. The metaphor became literal in the collection of detective stories by Hesketh Prichard, *November Joe: The Detective of the Woods* (1913). The detective is actually a backwoods tracker whose expertise at following trails in the Canadian woods is frequently called upon by the police.

The novels of James B. Hendryx often featured lawmen with the *Royal Canadian Mounted Police in roles that called upon them to use their tracking skills in the wilderness areas of North America. Hendryx's major character is Corporal Downey, who appears in his own series, but also as a character in the Halfaday Creek stories. The frontier wilderness settings make them difficult to classify, and some critics have considered them westerns rather than crime fiction.

Arthur W. Upfield's mixed-race aborigine detective, Napoleon *Bonaparte, carried the metaphor back to its literal roots. Many of the novels, including *The Sands of Windee* (1931), *The Bone is Pointed* (1938), and *Bushranger of the Skies* (1940; *No Footprints in the Bush*), take place in the Australian outback and afford Inspector Bonaparte (Bony) an opportunity to put his talents as a tracker to effective use.

In spite of the obvious possibilities for literal tracking in Tony *Hillerman's novels about Joe Leaphorn and Jim *Chee, the stories are more concerned with other aspects of Native American culture than following footprints through the desert.

• George Grella, "The Hard-Boiled Detective Novel," in *Detective Fiction A Collection of Critical Essays*, ed. Robin Winks, rev. ed. (1988). A. E. Murch, *The Development of the Detective Novel*, rev. ed. (1968). John Seelye, "Buckskin and Ballistics: William Leggett and the American Detective Story," *Journal of Popular Culture* 1 (summer 1967): 52–57.

—J. Randolph Cox

PATRIOT'S DAY. *See* Holiday Mysteries.

PENNY DREADFUL. The penny dreadful takes its name from the practice of publishing literature sold in parts selling for a penny each. Pierce Egan, author of a series of stories collectively entitled *Life in London* concerning Tom and Jerry on "rambles and sprees through the metropolis" (*ca.* 1820 ff.), is generally credited with producing the first notable examples of the penny writing that earned the scorn of middle-class critics who saw such works as dangerous to the morals of youth. John Dicks was a prominent publisher of such literature; his most prolific author may have been G. W. M. Reynolds (1814–79) who wrote *The Mysteries of London* (1847) and *Mysteries of the Court of London* (1849–56). The historian of popular literature Victor Neuberg counts forty-six weekly and monthly publications for the year 1885 selling fiction at a penny for a weekly, three shillings for the monthly issue containing a full novel. The works were not strictly crime or mystery in content, but their earned label of "dreadful" readily came to signify all sensational popular writing directed to a working-class audience and issued in cheap editions.

[See also Dime Novel; Newgate Novel; Sensation Novel.]

• Victor E. Neuberg, *Popular Literature: A History and Guide* (1977).
—John M. Reilly

PENTECOST, HUGH, pseudonym of Judson P(entecost) Philips (1930–1989), American writer of mystery novels, short fiction, screenplays, radio and television scripts, and 1973 *Mystery Writers of America Grand Master. Although he was first published while still in college, he took his pseudonym on winning the Dodd Mead "Red Badge" Prize Competition in 1939 with *Cancelled in Red*. He graduated from Columbia University in 1925, the same year he sold his first short stories to the *pulp magazines. In the 1930s and 1940s, he contributed short stories and novels to publications such as *Argosy*, *Flynn's*, and *Detective Fiction Weekly*. for which he created the Park Avenue Hunt Club series. He wrote stories with varied settings for the slicks, especially *American Magazine*. Pentecost enjoyed telling stories, and his own observations of people, his interests, and his research provided a rich background for his fiction. Critics praise his skillful *plots, well-defined *settings, and believable characters. His work as Pentecost is in the tradition of classic detection, while that written as Judson Philips offers increased thrills and suspense. Though Pentecost considered series characters restricting, most of his fiction involves continuing characters. His own favorites were written under the Pentecost pseudonym. They include John Jericho, a red-bearded Greenwich Village artist, and Uncle George Crowder, a former county attorney. Favorites with the public have been Pierre *Chambrun, who strives to keep things running smoothly even in the face of terrorism at New York's Hotel Beaumont; Julian Quist, a public relations man; and Peter Styles, a one-legged magazine columnist with a definite vendetta against the underworld.

[See also Hotel Milieu; Terrorism and the Terrorist Procedural.]

• Barnard A. Drew, "A Conversation with Judson Philips," *Armchair Detective* 13 (fall 1980): 325–30. Bill Pronzini and Marcia Muller, *1001 Midnights: The Aficionado's Guide to Mystery and Detective Fiction* (1986).
—J. Randolph Cox

PERIOD MYSTERY. The period mystery, a hybrid of the historical novel and crime fiction, may be distinguished from the *historical mystery, in which *historical figures, events, and crimes appear. This subgenre offers unique vantage points from which to comment on human behavior or contemporary life. For instance, Ray Harrison describes the problems of drugs in society in eerily modern terms in a story set in 1894 in *Tincture of Death* (1989), and Peter Lovesey

explores the unglamorous world of early moviemaking in *Keystone* (1983), set in 1915 California. For many writers, however, a period setting may be chosen primarily to give the reader a vivid experience of another time, such as H. R. F. *Keating's *The Murder of the Maharajah* (1980), which is set in 1930s India.

The key to persuasive writing in this subgenre depends upon the author's ability to provide a convincing *setting in a period other than the present. Because documentation for the twentieth century is abundant, should a writer choose to work in the more recent past, as Hiber Conteris has in his Chandler pastiche *El Diez por Ciento de Vida: El Test Chandler* (1985; *Ten Percent of Life*), or Stuart Kaminsky does in his Toby Peters series including *Murder on the Yellow Brick Road* (1978), setting is a comparatively easy element to create. Magazines, newspapers, films, radio recordings, even survivors from that period help the writer to achieve the semblance of authenticity necessary to reproduce the feel of the era.

Although there are now very few survivors of the Victorian era, the documentation is abundant enough to attract a growing number of contemporary writers to set stories in this period. Peter Lovesey has created two Victorian series: that employing Sergeant Cribb (including *Wobble to Death*, 1970) and that in which Edward Albert, Prince of Wales, is the (often hapless) investigator. Frances Selwyn has produced a series similar to that of Lovesey in her Sergeant Verity books (including *Sergeant Verity and the Imperial Diamond*, 1975), as has John Buxton Hilton, whose investigator is Inspector Brunt. Anne Perry has also created two series, that featuring Charlotte Ellison Pitt and her husband, Thomas, and a second in which Inspector Monk is the main character. Victorian America, and particularly Victorian New York, is the stage for Virgil Tillman, William Marshall's protagonist in his latest books (beginning with *The New York Detective*, 1989).

Fewer writers focus upon the decades before the Victorian era. Those who do must address the problem of telling a convincing tale of detection set in a period before the term "detective" was coined and before the creation of organized police forces. However, John Dickson *Carr in *The Demoniacs* (1962) and J. G. Jeffreys in *The Village of Rogues* (1972; *The Thief Taker*), employ the "Bow Street Runners," the forerunners of the modern police.

Beyond the eighteenth century, crime novels in English settings focus primarily upon two periods, the Elizabethan and the medieval. Leonard Tourney introduces Matthew Stock, a weaver, in *The Players' Boy Is Dead* (1980). Stock investigates cases as various as those involving crime against the state, in *Low Treason* (1983), and inheritance, in *Old Saxon Blood* (1988). Edward Marston centers his novels around an Elizabethan acting troupe.

Although P. C. Doherty has written several novels in which Hugh Corbett, clerk for Edward I late in the thirteenth century, solves mysteries, the best-known author to set her novels in the medieval period is Ellis *Peters. Her twelfth-century monk, Brother *Cadfael, exposes evildoers while surviving the spasmodic violence of the civil war that envelops western England.

Except for Margaret Doody's *Aristotle Detective?* (1978) and Agatha *Christie's *Death Comes as the End* (1944), set in the Egypt of the pharaohs, the farthest place in the past in which writers have chosen to set their mysteries is Rome, both of the Empire and Republic. Lindsey Davis's investigator, Marcus Didius Falco, is a *delator*, a public informer, just the sort who would be expected to look more deeply into crimes, if only for his own benefit, beginning with *The Silver Pigs* (1989). John Maddox Roberts employs a minor Roman city official who is also the black sheep of a famous family, the Metelli, thereby providing believable reasons for his involvement in investigations as informer, assistant to the defending attorney, official, and relative of the victim.

[*See also* Future, Use of the.]

—Carolyn Higbie *and* Timothy W. Boyd

PETERS, ELLIS, pseudonym of Edith Mary Pargeter (1913–1995), British author who is best known for her chronicles of Brother *Cadfael, mysteries set in Shrewsbury's Benedictine Abbey of Saint Peter and Saint Paul in the twelfth century. Born in Shropshire, England, on the Welsh border, Peters was educated at local schools and worked as a pharmacist's assistant before publishing her first novel at the age of twenty. She also translated Czechoslovakian literature. During World War II she served in the Women's Royal Naval Service and earned the British Empire medal. She returned to writing after the war and became known for historical novels written under her own name including *The Heaven Tree* trilogy (1960–63) and *A Bloody Field by Shrewsbury* (1972, *The Bloody Field*).

In 1959 she published her first *historical mystery under the Ellis Peters name about Shropshire Police Inspector George Felse. In 1977 she introduced the herbalist monk Cadfael in *A Morbid Taste for Bones*. He appears in some twenty novels. Peters has also produced *A Rare Benedictine* (1988) and *Shropshire*, (1992) which she wrote with Roy Morgan. Peters also produced two mysteries as Jolyon Carr and one as John Redfern early in her career. The popularity of Peter's Cadfael mysteries has inspired fans to contribute to the Abbey Restoration Project. Derek Jacobi appeared as Cadfael in a television series.

• Andrew M. Greeley, "Ellis Peters: Another Umberto Eco?" *Armchair Detective* (summer 1985): 238–45. Rosemary Herbert, "Ellis Peters: The Novelist-cum-Historian Has Written a New Mystery about Her Ever-Popular Sleuth, a Twelfth-Century Monk," *Publishers Weekly* 238, no. 36. (9 Aug. 1991): 40–41.

—Alzina Stone Dale

PLAGIARISM is defined as the false assumption of another's authorship, and although it can be notoriously difficult to prove in court, the offense has often been exposed simply by publishing the original and the theft side by side, in what William Dean Howells has called "the court of parallel columns" ("The Psychology of Plagiarism," *Literature*, 18 Aug. 1899).

The *Oxford English Dictionary* attests to English usage of the term—which derives from the Greek for "kidnapping"—from the early seventeenth century.

But in law, plagiarism has been subsumed under the general category of piracy, any unauthorized appropriation of a literary property. At first, the rights and responsibilities of publication were invested in booksellers and publishers through the Stationers' Company and the Stationers' Register. Authorial rights evolved only gradually in copyright law, from the Statute of Anne (1709–10), through nineteenth-century English parliamentary law and the international Berne Convention of 1886. Article I of the U.S. Constitution recognized "for limited terms to Authors and Inventors the exclusive Right to their respective Writings and Discoveries." Legislation in 1790, 1831, 1870, 1909, and 1976 codified American copyright law, and the United States became a signatory to the Berne Convention through the implementation Act of 1988.

But plagiarism per se has remained essentially a private grievance, controlled by professional guidelines, codes, and penalties, and by recourse by the injured party to civil court—or private redress. In crime and mystery fiction it is presented as a nasty personal violation, a kind of literary rape, but a crime that is hard to prove and even readily inverted and turned against an accuser. Its personal offensiveness lends itself to *blackmail, and its legal cumbersomeness to private *revenge, including *murder.

The conditions of modern scientific research and publication are conducive to abuses of authorial integrity. In *Unholy Dying* (1945) by Ruthven Campbell Todd writing as R. T. Campbell, the murder *victim is a senior scientist widely despised by junior colleagues because of his "magpie" habit of "stealing the credit for other people's ideas." Similarly, in James D. Doss's *The Shaman Sings* (1994), a graduate student who has made a significant breakthrough in superconductivity research is murdered by a senior professor who felt entitled to this intellectual property. In Aaron J. Elkins's *Icy Clutches* (1990), the leader of a botanical glacier expedition is murdered; among other things he had been accused of stealing his colleagues' ideas and the data of one of his graduate students.

A comic version occurs in Michael *Innes's *The Weight of the Evidence* (1943), in which the slain Professor Puckrose is universally perceived as an academic "nosy-parker" who, while not precisely a plagiarist, had an unseemly passion for raiding his colleagues' fields of specialization. Innes also constructs a whimsical form of "plagiarism" in *Stop Press* (1939; *The Spider Strikes*), *Appleby's End* (1945) and in *Appleby's Answer* (1973), in which an author's apparently original *plot ideas are staged or acted out in real life, even before publication, by someone who has mysteriously been able to appropriate them. Similarly, in Barbara Burnett Smith's *Writers of the Purple Sage* (1994) a judge is killed in the exact manner described by an aspiring writer in a novel in progress.

In *The Shakespeare Transcripts* (1993) by Mark P. Friedlander, Jr. and Robert W. Kenny, a deadwood English professor plots to plagiarize his student's doctoral dissertation and to permanently discredit the student by setting him on a fool's errand to trace and authenticate a Shakespeare divorce decree. The plot backfires when the student discovers an even more spectacular document: evidence of a plagiarism lawsuit brought by Francis Bacon against Shakespeare. In Martha Grimes's *The Horse You Came in On* (1993) the academic thievery is reversed, as a former graduate student plagiarizes the innovative "minimalist" style of her creative writing professor. Feminist issues are raised in *The Players Come Again* (1990) by Amanda *Cross. Kate *Fansler is commissioned to write the biography of the wife of a major modernist novelist whose masterpiece explored the psyche of a female protagonist. Doubts are raised about who actually wrote it; for that matter, "how many professors' wives have written their husbands' books"?

Exposing a plagiarist can be dangerous. In Jules Archer's "The Pagliacci Murders" (*National Forum* 67, 1987), a senior professor murders an untenured colleague who accused him of plagiarizing from an obscure journal. Making a claim can also prove deadly. In Rex *Stout's *Plot It Yourself* (1959; *Murder in Style*) Nero *Wolfe is hired by the Joint Committee on Plagiarism of the National Association of Artists and Dramatists to investigate five cases of accusation of plagiarism made by four different claimants, three of whom are subsequently slain. Wolfe conducts a stylistic analysis, based on distinctive word and phrase frequency and habits of punctuation and paragraphing. The false claims turn this into a case of "plagiarism upside-down." Wolfe's method resembles the "Theory of Stylometry" outlined in A. Q. Morton's *Literary Detection: How to Prove Authorship and Fraud in Literature and Documents* (1978).

Other plagiarism cases set in the professional literary world occur in novels by Jonathan Kellerman, Josephine Bell, Ngaio *Marsh, Susan Moody, and B. M. Gill. In Kellerman's *Self-Defense* (1995), a once prominent author suffering a terminal case of writer's block cuts a deal with a talented convict: The author will work for the convict's parole and arrange to have his prison diary published, but will, in exchange, publish the convict's poetry under his own name. In Bell's *A Swan-Song Betrayed* (1978; *Treachery in Type*), a local girl hired to type an elderly lady's Edwardian novel in progress, instead purloins the carbon copy of the manuscript, modernizes it, and publishes it. The fraud is exposed. But it is not always easy to combat a plagiarist, as author Barnaby Grant learns in Marsh's *When in Rome* (1971). Grant loses the manuscript of his new novel; it is returned three days later by a man who in that time not only generates his own plagiarized version of the plot but himself raises the charge of plagiarism against Grant, then successfully blackmails him for it.

Gill's *Seminar for Murder* (1985) brings the subject home to crime writing itself. At a mystery writers' meeting, the author who wins the club's award is accused of plagiarism by a fellow member and is defended by his son. Subsequently, both the accuser and the prize-winning author's son are murdered. In Moody's *Takeout Double* (1993) a woman is murdered who had accused the novelist Felicity Carridine of having stolen the plot of her most recent novel from the details of her own life, which she had confided to her at a writing workshop. Felicity's defense is that "All is grist to the novelist's mill," and that, anyway, "there are only seven plots in the entire universe. . . . Or is it thirty-six?"

[*See also* Crimes, Minor; Theft.]

• Maurice Salzman, *Plagiarism: The "Art" of Stealing Literary Material* (1931). Thomas Mallon, *Stolen Words: Forays into the Origins and Ravages of Plagiarism* (1989). Marcel C. LaFollette, *Stealing into Print: Fraud, Plagiarism, and Misconduct in Scientific Publishing* (1992).

—Peter V. Cenci *and* George L. Scheper

PLAINMAN SLEUTH. The portrayal of the *sleuth as a noticeably ordinary man or woman may have been done in reaction to the proliferation of *Great Detectives in fiction published around the turn of the nineteenth century. In contrast to the *superman sleuth endowed with an extraordinary intellect or professional access to the scene of the crime as official investigator, the plainman sleuth surprises readers by solving crimes via the application of ordinary powers of observation and commonsense reasoning.

As early as 1894, Arthur *Morrison introduced his "cheerful"-looking, average man, Martin Hewitt, in the pages of the *Strand*, the same magazine in which Arthur Conan *Doyle's omniscient Sherlock *Holmes was often featured. Hewitt insisted that he had "no system beyond the judicious use of ordinary faculties."

Samuel Hopkins Adams introduced a sleuth so average-looking that "he was, so to speak, a composite photograph of any thousand well-conditioned, clean-living Americans between the ages of twenty-five and thirty," and called him Average Jones. It turns out that Jones is commonplace in appearance only. His nickname is drawn from his initials, A. V. R. E., followed by the J. In fact, Adrian Van Reypen Egerton Jones is a man of grand financial expectations and strong deductive powers who pursues the "hobby" of setting himself up as the "Ad-visor" who helps clients who have been cheated by false advertising. The 1911 volume *Average Jones* features eleven stories about the Ad-visor.

Irish author M. McDonnell Bodkin created a more genuinely average man as sleuth in Paul Beck, who anticipated Margery *Allingham's *silly-ass sleuth Albert *Campion by sporting an expression of mild surprise that masked his intelligence. Beck is described as looking as innocuous as a milkman and giving the impression of being less than brilliant. Beck says, "I just go by the rule of thumb, and muddle and puzzle out my cases as best I can." Bodkin's anthology *Paul Beck, the Rule of Thumb Detective* was published in 1898. This was followed by the publication of *Dora Myrl, the Lady Detective* in 1900. While Myrl is too eccentrically genteel to qualify as a plainwoman sleuth, she marries Beck in *The Capture of Paul Beck* (1909). Plain attributes dominate in their offspring, who is introduced in *Young Beck, a Chip of the Old Block* (1911).

Closely related to the plainman sleuth is the obtuse sleuth, personified in the title character in *Philo Gubb: Correspondence School Detective* (1919). This comic creation of Ellis Parker Butler solves crimes despite his talent for interpreting clues incorrectly and his flair for sporting mail-order *disguises that inevitably fail to mask his purposes.

On a more serious note, a plain approach to the interpretation and even the discovery of *clues provides the truth about *guilt in Susan Glaspell's poignant story, "A Jury of Her Peers," first penned as a play and later published as a short story in 1917. Based on a case of spousal abuse that Glaspell had covered as a journalist, the perfectly titled story demonstrates how two housewives from the American heartland are able to discover the motive for *murder in their neighbor's sewing box, while the police blunder about upstairs, looking for more obvious clues.

These sleuths prove that ordinariness can be an asset in winning readers who may find it easier to identify with ordinary people than with super intellects, and who may enjoy feeling superior to the more comic of the plain sleuths. Average people as sleuths can demonstrate an advantage over professional or intellectually gifted detectives in possessing insight into the details of everyday existence. Similarly, the best *amateur detectives, *accidental sleuths, *nosy parker sleuths, and even inexperienced *private eyes, such as P. D. *James's Cordelia *Gray in An Unsuitable Job for a Woman (1972), find that it takes a commonsense approach and everyday experience to get to the truth of their cases.

[See also Humor; Reasoning, Types of.]

• Julian Symons, Bloody Murder: From the Detective Story to the Crime Novel; 3rd rev. ed. (1993). LeRoy Lad Panek, An Introduction to the Detective Story (1987).

—Rosemary Herbert

PLOT. The plot of any literary work is a map of what happens within it. In most classic crime and mystery fiction, plot is both chronological and linear. Events occur one after another, chronologically, with any flashback action clearly identified as out of the order of things. Linear plotting assures that events are connected in a logical sequence, conducive to the application of the science of reason.

A classic mystery plot has a clearly recognizable beginning, development section, climax, and resolution. At the start, a *puzzle is presented. This puzzle is centered around a significant act like *murder, which is worthy of the attention of the detective and will sustain *suspense for the reader. In the development section, information is gathered that enables the detective and the canny reader to solve the puzzle. The climax occurs when the solution is announced and all of the *clues are brought together. Finally, in the resolution the puzzle is solved, the solution explained, and the criminal is brought to *justice. The reader then leaves the novel satisfied: All questions have been answered, the puzzle has been solved in a plausible manner, and the world depicted in the novel is restored to order.

In such classic work, emphasis is placed on the solution to the puzzle rather than the psychological development of the characters caught up in one way or another by the fact of the crime. There is also little or no development of the aftereffects of the crime. Such long-term ramifications of crime as family grief, a business in ruins, or a terrible undermining of faith in the community are all beyond the scope of the well-plotted classic mystery whose ending is truly an ending, bringing the work to complete closure.

The plot of the classic mystery, with its chronological development, is a fine example of Aristotle's concept of unity of action. In a plot with such unity the arrangement of the incidents is crucial and everything within the work contributes to its resolution. There are no loose ends. In such a plot scheme, if one element were removed, the whole would be lacking.

One of the best examples of a classic mystery with a unified, Artistotelian plot is Agatha *Christie's The Murder of Roger Ackroyd (1926). Everything in the story, from physical items to visits by outsiders, contributes to the solution of the murder and at the conclusion readers are left with no unexplained clues or unanswered questions. This plot structure is sometimes inverted, most notably by R. Austin *Freeman in his collection of short stories, The Singing Bone (1912; The Adventures of Dr. Thorndyke). The *inverted detective story reveals the murder and its perpetrator at the opening and then follows, step by step, the process by which the detective solves the crime.

Although Aristotelian plot structure is commonly thought to be typical of the *cozy mysteries and *whodunits that flourished during the 1920s and 1930s, tidy solutions are also employed in some hard-boiled works, including Dashiell *Hammett's The Maltese Falcon (1930). At first, the plot of this novel seems anything but unified. To begin with, the reader is presented with the puzzle of a missing character, next with the puzzle of the whereabouts of a fabulous jeweled bird, the Maltese falcon of the title. Since much of the story deals with the falcon and its history, the reader's attention is diverted from the murder, but in the resolution, all the ends are neatly tied up. Any elements that may have seemed disparate turn out to be related to the solution of the murder, just as they are in a classic mystery.

However, as the crime and mystery genre has developed, there has been a move away from emphasis on pure puzzle to emphasis on character, and this often undermines the Aristotelian unity of plot. This shift in emphasis can be seen in the hard-boiled fiction of Raymond *Chandler. Because Chandler's novels are preoccupied with psychological motivation, his private eye is more concerned with reading people than with reading physical clues like footprints. Chandler's emphasis on psychological consistency and rich character development sometimes leads him to leave loose ends regarding physical clues. One example of this is found in The Long Goodbye (1953). Here readers are led to believe that an object left inside a white pigskin suitcase may be an important clue but, after a tantalizing mention, the object is never referred to again. To abandon a clue in this way would be unthinkable in a carefully crafted classic *whodunit.

In the contemporary mystery, the emphasis on character continues, with the concommitant move away from strict unity of plot. In this respect today's crime and mystery fiction mirrors developments in fiction as a whole, reflecting an everyday world in which there are more and more questions with fewer and fewer answers, and in which those answers are arrived at with decreasing certainty. An excellent example of a mystery with a plot structure built upon contemporary uncertainties and with themes informed by contemporary mores is Scott Turow's *legal procedural *Presumed Innocent* (1987). Here again, the puzzle centers upon a murder and the plot follows the steps that the detective takes to arrive at a solution. However, the conclusion of this novel leaves the reader with an element of doubt about the solution that is offered by the narrator-detective who is trying to clear his own name.

Readers of character-driven crime and mystery fiction leave each work with vivid recollections of the characters and the harm that has been done to them by the criminals. They may be less likely to recall the individual clues and steps taken to solve the case. This contrasts with puzzle-oriented plots in which the most memorable elements are those concerned with surprises and solutions.

Overall, as the mystery and detective genre has developed, there remains a mystery to be solved while the plot progresses along a chronological and linear path, but contemporary novels are more apt to close with a reader left more troubled by the fate of the characters than reassured by the solutions to puzzles.

[*See also* Formula: Plot; Resolution and Irresolution.]

• M. H. Abrams, *A Glossary of Literary Terms* (1957). John G. Cawelti, *Adventure, Mystery, and Romance* (1976). Elizabeth Dipple, *Plot* (1979). Frank MacShane, *Selected Letters of Raymond Chandler* (1981). Julian Symons, *Bloody Murder: From the Detective Story to the Crime Novel*, 3rd rev. ed. (1992).

—Joan G. Kotker

POE, EDGAR ALLAN (1809–1849), American short story writer, poet, and critic, widely considered as founding the genre of detective fiction. His seminal story, "The Murders in the Rue Morgue" (*Graham's Lady's and Gentleman's Magazine*, Apr. 1841), introduces the ratiocinative *sleuth The Chevalier C. Auguste *Dupin. Poe is also an early author of crime stories, for example "The Cask of Amontillado" (*Godey's Lady's Book*, Nov. 1846), in which he probes the psychology of crime.

Edgar Poe was born in Boston, Massachusetts, 19 January 1809, to Elizabeth Arnold Poe, a popular actress, and David Poe, a failed actor and alcoholic who soon deserted his wife and three children. Edgar's older brother and sister were placed with relatives in Baltimore, but Elizabeth kept Edgar with her as she toured with a theatrical company. Stranded in Richmond and ill with tuberculosis, she died a lingering death when Edgar was two. The boy was taken in by Frances Allan, the childless wife of a merchant who raised but never formally adopted him. They took Edgar with them when John Allan went on business to England from 1815 to 1820.

Edgar took Allan as his middle name. He was sent to the University of Virginia on a scant allowance. There, among sons of wealthy planters, he ran up tailor's and gambling debts Allan refused to pay. Allan,

who fully expected Poe to join his business, had no sympathy with his charge's literary ambitions. They parted with acrimony, and thereafter Poe signed his work "Edgar A. Poe," suppressing "Allan." Poe enlisted in the army, then enrolled at, and dropped out from, West Point. He went to live with his aunt, Maria Clemm, and her young daughter, Virginia. When the girl reached thirteen, Poe married her.

Poe's first work, *Tamerlane and Other Poems*, was published anonymously ("by a Bostonian") in 1827. He made a meager living as a magazine contributor and editor, writing scores of stories and sketches, some fifty poems, and more than three hundred book reviews. His "The Raven" (*The Raven and Other Poems*, 1845) was an immense success. He was a brilliant author and editor, but his occasional binge drinking led to his brief tenures at *The Southern Literary Messenger* (1835–36), *Burton's Gentleman's Magazine* (1839–40), *Graham's Lady's and Gentleman's Magazine* (1841–42), the *New York Evening Mirror* (1844–45), and the *Broadway Journal* (1845). Despite his literary successes, Poe had no regular income, and his wife, his aunt, and he himself were often near starvation. In the winter of 1847, his wife died of tuberculosis, as had his mother and Mrs. Allan before her.

After Virginia's death, Poe conducted agitated courtships of several literary ladies. Returning from a visit to one in Richmond, he stopped in Baltimore and was found insensible in the gutter. Taken to a hospital, he died on 7 October 1849. The circumstances of his death have never been satisfactorily explained.

Poe's preeminence as deviser of the modern detective story rests on four tales, "The Murders in the Rue Morgue," "The Mystery of Marie Roget" (*Snowden's Lady's Companion*, Nov. 1842), "The Gold Bug" (*Philadelphia Dollar Newspaper*, 21 June 1843), and "The Purloined Letter" (*The Gift*, 1845). Poe's depictions of detective work are remarkable, especially considering that he wrote at a time when few American cities had police departments and even *Scotland Yard had not yet established its Detective Department. According to *The Oxford English Dictionary*, the word "detective" first appeared in a British legal journal in 1843, two years after Poe wrote "The Murders in the Rue Morgue."

Poe is more concerned with detection than with crime. In "The Gold Bug," the crime occurred many years prior to the action, which centers on recovery of the pirate's treasure through decoding a set of directions written in a cipher. The proof of William Legrand's genius is his ability to read this code. The crime, or crimes—theft of the treasure, *murder of accomplices—are not solved at all. The tale concentrates on several of Poe's obsessive motifs: cracking the code as a metaphor for discovering hidden truths; embodiment of the ratiocinative principle, separated from the emotions by Poe's facultative psychology; and the contrivance of a tale in which every detail contributes to the desired effect.

Poe originated an astonishing number of conventions in detective fiction. The brilliant detective, the *locked room mystery, and the bungling of inept police are among the more obvious. The use of *sleight of hand—placing all *clues in sight while leading the reader to regard them from a point of view that will not reveal the truth—is another of Poe's inventions. His construction of the detective story has become classic. The most salient feature of Poe's detective tales is the introduction, as narrator, of an unnamed voice, the contrast with whose bland and obtuse normality dramatizes the genius of the detective. This unperceptive narrator is of course a surrogate for the reader, who shares his astonishment at the ingenious and intuitive processes by which the hero's mind leaps from the available facts to the hidden truths of the case.

Dupin and Legrand are reclusive heroes of mind and imagination, set apart from ordinary men by their erudite pursuits, arcane hobbies, special knowledge. Poe's unique achievement is to have recast as detective the Romantic hero of sensibility.

Poe's innovations have influenced many later writers, including Arthur Conan *Doyle, P. D. *James, and Colin *Dexter. Most later writers resemble Poe in having their detectives work outside the police bureaucracy. From this tension derive the private eye fictions of Raymond *Chandler, Dashiell *Hammett, and a host of others, in whose tales the elegance of Poe's milieus and characters are replaced by postnaturalistic tough guys and mean streets. Yet their descent from Poe's conceptions is nonetheless plain. Poe's genius is evident, too, in the psychological depths his tales reveal to the reader prepared to probe them. Preeminent among the few authors whose philosophical detective fictions extend Poe's influence are G. K. *Chesterton (The Man Who Was Thursday, 1908) and Jorge Luis Borges. Most crime and detective writers, however, have been more concerned with plot than with character. By their skillful manipulations of the conventions of these genres, many invented by Poe, the best of them have given us an ever growing literature of popular entertainment.

• John Evangelist Walsh, *Poe the Detective: The Curious Circumstances Behind "The Mystery of Marie Roget"* (1967). Daniel Hoffman, *Poe Poe Poe Poe Poe Poe Poe* (1972). John P. Muller and William J. Richardson, eds., *The Purloined Poe: Lacan, Derrida, and Psychological Reading* (1988). Kenneth Silverman, *Edgar A. Poe: Mournful and Never-Ending Remembrance* (1991). John T. Irwin, *The Mystery to a Solution: Poe, Borges, and the Analytical Detective Story* (1994).

—Daniel Hoffman

POETS AS CRIME WRITERS. From the time Edgar Allan *Poe wrote "The Murders in the Rue Morgue" (*Graham's Lady's and Gentleman's Magazine*, Apr. 1841), poets have also turned their hand to writing tales of mystery and imagination. Presumably, they are attracted to a literature that shares with much poetry the importance of form and structure. In *Ellery Queen's Poetic Justice, 23 Stories of Crime, Mystery, and Detection by World-Famous Poets from Geoffrey Chaucer to Dylan Thomas*, (1967) Ellery *Queen argues that poets, like detectives, seek to make order from chaos. Support for this thesis may be found in poet W. H. Auden's important essay, "The Guilty Vicarage" (*Harper's Magazine*, May 1948). Although Auden did not himself write crime fiction, he was an enthusiast of the genre who contended that

the most satisfying detective stories introduce crime into the "great good place" and then portray the restoration of order by the detective. Queen also points out that some poetry can be considered to fall within the crime and mystery genre, citing as examples Robert Frost's "The Witch of Coos" (*Poetry: A Magazine of Verse*, 22 Jan. 1922) and T. S. Eliot's "Macavity: The Mystery Cat" (*Old Possum's Book of Practical Cats*, 1939).

The mysteries written by poets do not fall into a single category. E. C. *Bentley, inventor of the clerihew (a verse form comprising two rhymed couplets) wrote the prototype for the Golden Age detective story, *Trent's Last Case* (1913; *The Woman in Black*). His contemporary Hilaire Belloc also wrote lighthearted detective fiction, but this has failed to stand the test of time. *The Big Clock* (1946; *No Way Out*) by Kenneth Fearing, a talented poet of the Depression era, is a masterpiece of suspense. In the 1980s and 1990s, Stephen Dobyns wrote a series of novels featuring the Saratoga private investigator Charlie Bradshaw, as well as several volumes of verse.

As a generalization, it seems that poets become crime writers rather than vice versa. Julian *Symons founded and edited the influential magazine *Twentieth Century Verse* and published collections of his own poetry before achieving distinction as an author and critic of mystery novels, while two of his friends and fellow poets, Ruthven Todd and Roy Fuller, flirted with the genre before abandoning it. Symons has related that Todd, writing as R. T. Campbell, wrote twelve detective novels in six months shortly after the Second World War, although only eight appear to have been published. Fuller's three mysteries appeared between 1948 and 1954; they include *The Second Curtain* (1953), which gives a bleak account of a writer's brush with violent crime. Agatha *Christie was one of many mystery novelists who dabbled with poetry before concentrating on prose. Reginald *Hill said he realized he was destined to write a crime novel after penning one poem that featured Death as a hitman and another taking the form of an interrogation of *suspects in a country house murder mystery. Others, like Dobyns, have continued to write both mysteries and poems. John Harvey, creator of the Nottingham policeman Charlie Resnick, not only writes poetry but also runs the small press that publishes it. No one, however, has worn the two hats of poet and crime writer more successfully than Cecil Day-Lewis. Under the pseudonym Nicholas *Blake, he created the detective Nigel Strangeways, a character based on W. H. Auden. Blake's finest novel is probably *The Beast Must Die* (1938), but he continued to write mystery novels until shortly before his death in 1972, despite his continuing commitment to poetry, which culminated in his appointment as Poet Laureate.

[See also Allusion, Literary; Nursery Rhyme.]

• Reginald Hill, "Looking for a Programme," in *Colloquium on Crime: Eleven Renowned Mystery Writers Discuss Their Work*, ed. Robin Winks (1986). Julian Symons, *Bloody Murder: From the Detective Story to the Crime Novel* 3rd rev. ed. (1992).

—Martin Edwards

POINT OF VIEW, NARRATIVE. Point of view, or the "angle" from which any story is told, involves both the identity of the narrator and the narrator's distinctive perspective. From its inception detective fiction has exploited point of view both for reader interest and for mystification.

Three distinct points of view stand out in crime fiction: the *sidekick narrator, the first-person hero-narrator, and the third-person omniscient narrator. Examples of first-person storytelling by a genius detective's sidekick include the unnamed friend of Edgar Allan *Poe's Chevalier C. Auguste *Dupin, Sherlock Holmes's Dr. John H. *Watson, created by Arthur Conan *Doyle, and Hercule *Poirot's Captain Hastings, created by Agatha *Christie. By contrast, *hard-boiled detectives, following Raymond *Chandler's Philip *Marlowe, narrate their own stories. Unlike both, the majority of detective fiction is narrated by a detached, omniscient author In these three conventional methods, point of view may affect perception and understanding. However hasty the sidekick, temporarily mistaken the detective, or wrong any or all of the players, there is ultimately available a view of the events that is wholly reliable. Perception itself is never called to the bar, nor any bias of the *sleuth that might prove to be entirely disabling.

The "Watson viewpoint," to use Dorothy L. *Sayers's phrase, has a number of virtues. Readers delight not only in Watson's story but also in his vitality, good humor, and lucid narrative style. Interplay with a sidekick often humanizes a cool genius like Holmes or Nero *Wolfe. In the detection itself, the limited Watson viewpoint helps both to mislead readers and to promote the reader's own deductions. Despite using the past tense, the sidekick represents events as at the moment of their happening; readers are presented with only the perspective that the sidekick had at that time. Yet, although readers may fall into the same hasty misjudgment as the sidekick, because the level of their understanding is likely to be slightly above his, readers feel a satisfying sense of superiority as they see the sidekick erring. Holmes's frequent comic undercutting of Watson—"You have seen but not understood"—promotes the conventional disjunction between Watson's ultra-reliable facts and his suspect hypotheses, and again reinforces readers' sense of intellectual superiority.

In *private eye novels the first-person narrator is as much the *adventurer as the reporter of events. The convention of representing the past as an unfolding present continues. Readers participate with Marlowe, Lew *Archer, or Kinsey *Milhone in their immediate experience. As with the classic detective story readers share the detective's understanding—or, most of it—but also share a confusion and uncertainty much greater than that found in any classic detective. The limited viewpoint again promotes *suspense and reader detection. Even more important, however, the private "I" of hard-boiled narratives presents the hard-boiled detective's distinctive voice and vision—the individualistic "tough" style and skeptical way of seeing the world.

The anonymous third-person narrative of many *detective novels and stories, particularly those of the *Golden Age, allows for a more flexible point of view than first-person narration. The narrating author can vary distance from the scene and move viewpoint around both inside and outside the detective's consciousness. The author can play with time and presentational sequence and present the reader with information that the detective does not yet know. Thus, the reader may at times be put in a better position for detecting than the detective. Christie's omniscient narrator novels—after the early 1930s she stopped using Captain Arthur Hastings—often have narrative "prologues" in which the reader learns much before Hercule *Poirot or Miss Jane *Marple comes on the scene. In Robert Robinson's *Landscape with Dead Dons* (1956), the omniscient author plays a wicked little game of viewpoint with the reader: the first page of the book if viewed the right way reveals *whodunit before the narration even begins.

As "point of view" obsessed modernist literary critics and twentieth-century novelists from Henry James to Donald Barthelme, so it concerned many a Golden Age writer, such as Sayers. In *The Omnibus of Crime* (1929) she argued that manipulation of point of view is a key element in the making of detective novels. Like E. C. *Bentley in *Trent's Last Case* (1913; *The Woman in Black*), the skillful writer alternates three viewpoints: representation of the situation, of what the detective sees, and of what the detective makes of what he sees. This alternation of viewpoints is merely a narrative device for mystifying the reader: the detective eventually—and the novelist always—views the truth.

The forerunner and frequent model for detective fiction's play of viewpoints is Wilkie *Collins's *The Moonstone* (1868). In it, successive narrators look at events differently depending on their role in the events and on their biases. The narrative contract forbids each "to tell more," as one narrator writes, "than I knew at the time," and enjoins each "to keep strictly within the limits of my own experience." Since *The Moonstone* there have been many notable *tours de force* in point of view, especially in "honest" first-person narratives, which are, perhaps not paradoxically, most vulnerable to misdirection or blindness. Christie's startling innovation in *The Murder of Roger Ackroyd* (1926) exploited the convention that the honesty of the Watson viewpoint need never be questioned. Honest good fellow Dr. James Sheppard, who seems only to narrate Poirot's detection, misleads Poirot by his schemes and the reader by telling less than "the whole truth and nothing but the truth." In novels like Helen Eustis's *The Horizontal Man* (1946) and Frank Palmer's *Unfit to Plead* (1992) where at times the viewpoint is that of the murderer, a principal deductive question may be who, or even of what *gender, is the narrator. From the inside readers see both the crime and the *criminal viewpoint; the narrator conceals but eventually betrays his or her own identity. In *The Horizontal Man* the murderer-narrator is made to appear female, but we learn eventually that that viewpoint may be multifaceted, as a powerful female self controls and at times bursts through the public male exterior.

Postmodernist detective fiction questions the premises of every narrative point of view. Jorge Luis Borges undermines the omniscient detective in "Death and the Compass" (*Ficciones*, 1941, 1962); and Peter *Dickinson the omniscient historian/novelist in *Hindsight* (1983). The first two volumes of Paul Auster's *New York Trilogy* (1985–86) foreground many issues of point of view: In each a hard-boiled detective, acting much like a classic detective, observes minutely the actions and personal effects of a "criminal." Yet neither the detectives nor detached narrators in the *New York Trilogy* can be sure that what their gazes fixate on may be read as *clues. In Sebastien Japrisot's *Trap for Cinderella* (1964), determinate personal identity, on which *a* point of view must depend, is undermined. A fire used to conceal a *murder kills one girl, while another survives with total amnesia. Who is the murderer-narrator and who the victim? It is not firmly established whether "Mi" or "Do" really tells the story, for each one's musical name suggests not so much a character with an individual viewpoint as a counter in a narrative structure. Not only is identity undermined, but also the promise of traditional detective fiction that the narrative will arrive at a point from which readers can see who truly "dunit." With Mi and Do we have come almost 180 degrees from such reliable points of view.

[*See also* Sidekicks and Sleuthing Teams; Voice: Overview.]

• Percy Lubbock, *The Craft of Fiction* (1921). Howard Haycraft, ed., *The Art of the Mystery Story: A Collection of Critical Essays* (1946). Susan Sniader Lanser, *The Narrative Act: Point of View in Prose Fiction* (1981). Peter Humm, "Camera Eye/Private Eye" in Brian Docherty, ed., *American Crime Fiction, Studies in the Genre* (1988).   —T. R. Steiner

Poirot, Hercule. Agatha *Christie's Belgian *sleuth was conceived as little more than a collection of foibles, yet today Hercule Poirot is acknowledged as second only to Sherlock *Holmes in the pantheon of *Great Detectives. His distinctive appearance, habits, and techniques established in Christie's first book, *The Mysterious Affair at Styles* (1920).

Short and dignified with an egg-shaped head and waxed mustache, Poirot has an obsession for neatness, order, and method. Formerly with the Belgian police, he retired and was smuggled out of France and into England during 1916 and soon renewed his acquaintance with Captain Arthur Hastings, whom he had previously met in his home country. Poirot's English is fractured and his use of idiom particularly eccentric, but the sharpness of his mind is undeniable. Comically immodest, he refers to his gift for detection as little more than the use of "the little grey cells" of his brain. After he solves a complex poisoning mystery at Styles court, he, though already into his sixties, embarks on a second career as a private inquiry agent in England.

In *The Mysterious Affair at Styles* and thirty-three later novels and five collections of short stories, Poirot is seen through the eyes of his friend Hastings. The relationship between the men resembles that of Holmes and Dr. John H. *Watson, and many other of Christie's touches in the early cases—including the pair's shared rooms at 14 Farraway Street in *London as well as several of the *puzzles themselves—echo the work of Arthur Conan *Doyle. As her skill and confidence developed, Christie recognized that Hastings was hardly capable of plausible growth and banished him, following marriage, to Argentina. Poirot moves to a large luxury flat, where he is assisted by an efficient secretary, Miss Felicity Lemon, and his manservant, George, whom Poirot addresses as Georges; his friends and acquaintances include police officers and the detective novelist Ariadne Oliver.

Christie came in time to tire of Poirot, but she did not make Doyle's mistake and seek to discard her most popular character; indeed, his flair for penetrating to the heart of a mystery continued to spark his creator's imagination, and he is the central figure in many of her best books, including *The Murder of Roger Ackroyd* (1926), *The ABC Murders* (1936; *The Alphabet Murders*), and *Cards on the Table* (1936), in which there are only four *suspects, yet the revelation of the truth still comes as a surprise. Because a conceited elderly bachelor such as Poirot had limited scope for development, Christie abandoned the Holmesian ambience and turned her detective's traits cleverly to advantage. In *Three Act Tragedy* (1935; *Murder in Three Acts*), Poirot acknowledges that speaking broken English is an enormous asset, since it tempts suspects to underestimate him and thus let their guard slip. Christie was not afraid to poke fun at him, but in his "bourgeois" disapproval of murder he reflects her attitudes. In *Hallow'en Party* (1969), Christie emphasizes that Poirot always thinks first of *justice and is suspicious of an excess of mercy. In *One, Two Buckle My Shoe* (1940; *The Patriotic Murders, An Overdose of Death*), he is prepared to see the downfall of a pillar of the establishment rather than allow the deaths of insignificant, and in some cases odious, individuals to go unavenged. He often speaks of the need to understand psychology, but his principal gift is for relentless logic. An acute observer of people, Poirot has a particular interest in the nature of murder *victims, explaining that without an understanding of the individual who has been killed, it is impossible to see the circumstances of a crime clearly. He develops a taste for fictional crime, and in *The Clocks* (1963) he treats his friend Colin Lamb to an entertaining discourse on the subject. He takes his last bow in *Curtain* (1975), a book written more than thirty years prior to its publication, when Christie's powers were at their peak. The *plot follows to its ultimate conclusion the belief that, in order to bring about justice, a Great Detective may need to act outside the law. "Murder is a drama," Poirot notes in one of his subtlest investigations, *Five Little Pigs* (1943; *Murder in Retrospect*), and no *sleuth ever left the stage with a more dramatic flourish.

[*See also* Reasoning, Types of; Whodunit.]

• Julian Symons, "The Life Of Hercule Poirot" in *The Great Detectives: Seven Original Investigations* (1981). Anne Hart, *The Life and Times of Hercule Poirot* (1990). Robert Barnard, *A Talent to Deceive: An Appreciation of Agatha Christie*, rev. ed. (1990).   —Martin Edwards

POISON PEN LETTERS, a popular device in crime fiction, vary in motivation, form, and the responses they evoke. The device offers ample opportunity for the mystery writer to speculate on the mind behind the missive and its effects on ordinary people.

The obvious purpose of a poison pen letter may be to destroy peace of mind, but individual motives are complex. In Agatha *Christie's *The Moving Finger* (1942; *The Case of the Moving Finger*), Jerry Burton imagines an empty life given purpose by "stabbing in the dark at people who are happy," and Mrs. Dane Calthrop considers "how lonely, how cut off from human kind" the writer must feel. In *The Deadly Joker* (1963) Nicholas *Blake concludes that the poison pen, to use W. H. Auden's phrase, has "no desire which he can call his own." In *Sleep of Death* (1982), Anne Morice uses biblical language to suggest that the poison pen writer presumes to speak with God's authority. Blake's *sleuth, Nigel *Strangeways, offers practical reasons such as the need "to damage a man's business or break up his home." In Colin *Watson's *Hopjoy Was Here* (1962), a "backroom vigilante" simply wants a neighboring house investigated. In Margaret *Millar's *The Murder of Miranda* (1979) the motive turns out to be sheer fun.

The poison pen letter builds tension by introducing an unseen hand acting in a seemingly arbitrary manner, thereby effectively setting the stage for *murder. In Philip *MacDonald's *R.I.P.* (1933; *Menace*), menacing letters arrive annually from points progressively nearer to the recipient, drawing a noose tighter and tighter around the victim; in his *Rope to Spare* (1932), elaborate "letters to a lady" threaten her life, while terser messages warn off sleuth Anthony *Gethryn. In Christie's *Murder on the Orient Express* (1934; *Murder in the Calais Coach*), anonymous threats prepare the way for murder.

The letters take numerous forms. Michael *Gilbert describes the "only really foolproof style of anonymous communication" in *Close Quarters* (1947): sticking words and letters cut from newspapers onto paper. In Leslie Ford's *The Simple Way of Poison* (1937) a "toy hand printing set" is used. Letters are stenciled onto greaseproof paper in Elizabeth Lemarchand's *Troubled Waters* (1982) or "oddly distorted" in green ink in MacDonald's *Rope to Spare* (1932). Slips of paper are glued to playing cards in Blake's *The Deadly Joker* (1963), and in W. J. Burley's *A Taste of Power* (1966) a teacher finds a message in yellow chalk on a blackboard flap.

Quotations from William *Shakespeare, Christopher Marlowe, or John Webster are used to threaten Clarissa Lisle in P. D. *James's *The Skull Beneath the Skin* (1982). In Timothy Robinson's *When Scholars Fall* (1961), the murderer leaves a pertinent poem with each victim. In *This Club Frowns on Murder* (1990) by Albert Borowitz women receive letters of condolence while their partners are still living. Four biblical quotations herald a woman's death in Burley's *Wycliffe and the Last Rites* (1992). All Blake's poison pens reveal a distinctive flair: a piquant sense of humor in *Thou Shell of Death* (1936; *Shell of Death*), a knack of adapting the style to the target in *The Dreadful Hollow* (1953), and a scurrilous wit in *The Deadly Joker* (1963). Albert *Campion receives perhaps the most charming anonymous letters, such as the invocation to "consider, o consider the lowly mole" in Margery Allingham's *The Case of the Late Pig* (1937).

The subject of poison pen letters invariably leads to an exploration of the *prejudices against aging women, for despite variety of composition, police and others almost uniformly attribute them to desiccated spinsters. In Christie's *The Moving Finger* (1942) the police expert pronounces categorically that a middle-aged woman, probably unmarried, is responsible; he is of course wrong, though even Miss Jane *Marple uses the female pronoun in discussing the writer. Sir Henry *Merrivale refuses to subscribe to the usual prejudices in Carter Dickson's *Night at the Mocking Widow* (1950), and Edmund *Crispin's sleuth Gervase *Fen dismisses such beliefs as "muddled, inaccurate" and "prurient" in *The Long Divorce* (1951; *A Noose for Her*).

The responses to such letters are usually the crux of the story. In rare cases recipients are unperturbed by their anonymous correspondence. Ronald Paston in *The Deadly Joker* (1963) files his. Mrs. Beatrice Adela Lestrange *Bradley studies hers "with an appreciative eye" and especially relishes being called an "undraped Thessalonian reconstruction" in Patricia *Wentworth's *Poison in the Pen* (1955). Miss Ginch in Christie's *The Moving Finger* (1942) is excited by hers, and Mr. Justice Barber in Cyril *Hare's *Tragedy at Law* (1942) is cheered by his. But most recipients are injured to some degree. Those who are especially vulnerable may be driven to suicide, as in Christie's *The Moving Finger* (1942), Dickson's *Night at the Mocking Widow* (1950), and Wentworth's *Poison in the Pen* (1955). No matter how the victim responds, it is clear that the writer of the poison pen letter works his or her cowardly cruelty to achieve injury at arm's length.

[*See also* Allusion, Literary; Letters and Written Messages.]　　　—Susan Oleksiw *and* Rosemary Herbert

POISONS AND POISONING. Many substances, in sufficiently high doses, potentially cause adverse effects to the body or destroy life, and yet such materials are not generally classified as poisons. Such a definition would be too all-encompassing and lack sufficient specificity to be meaningful. From a pharmacological and toxicological perspective, a poison is any substance that, when ingested, inhaled, absorbed or when applied to or injected into the body, in relatively small amounts, by its chemical action damages the body or disrupts its functioning.

In works of crime fiction chemicals, some of them poisons, are used to permanently dispose of the *victim; to control the victim, either physically or behaviorally; or as medicines that play an important role in the *plot development or denouement. Three types of poison-related questions appear in works of crime fiction: Was a poison given and, if so, what poison? How and when was the poison administered to the victim? By whom was the poison administered?

Poisons were so prolifically employed in detective fiction that Monseigneur Ronald A. *Knox drew up a rule regarding their fair use in his detective story decalogue (introduction to *The Best Detective Stories of 1928*, 1929). Knox stated that "no hitherto undiscovered poisons may be used." This rule helped to maintain a level playing field on which reader and author could compete.

Agatha *Christie, who had once served as a pharmacist's assistant, used poisons in more than half of her sixty-six novels and in many of her short stories. Although she employed a wider range of chemicals, poisons, and medicines in more creative ways than any other writer in her genre, Christie used several poisons with dependable frequency. These were generally colorless, tasteless, odorless, and readily dissolved in beverages. Chemicals that are poisonous at low doses and bring rapid results are indispensable assets to many mystery writers.

Poisons have been historically linked with female murderers because of women's control in the kitchen and the ease with which they can be surreptitiously added to the food or drink of the intended victim. Moreover, the physical attributes of the poisoner vis-à-vis the intended victim are immaterial where poisons are concerned. When the deceased is found poisoned, the common first impulse of a Christie criminal investigator is to consider suitable female suspects. Conversely, when the *corpse is the victim of a brutal injury, a male perpetrator seems more likely, as in *Towards Zero* (1941) and *Evil under the Sun* (1941). In Christie's works, female and male poisoners appear in approximately equal numbers, but, unlike males, females rarely resort to nonchemical approaches to murder.

[*See also* Poisons, Unusual; Weapons, Unusual Murder.]

• Peter R. Gwilt and John R. Gwilt, "The Use of Poison in Detective Fiction," *Clues* 1, no. 2 (1981): 8–17. Rodger J. Winn, "Poison Pharmacopoeia," in *Murder Ink* (1984). Serita Deborah Stevens with Anne Klarner, *Deadly Doses: A Writer's Guide to Poisons* (1990). Michael C. Gerald, *The Poisonous Pen of Agatha Christie* (1993).   —Michael C. Gerald

POISONS, UNUSUAL. Unusual poisons may be the most versatile of weapons in the mystery's writer's arsenal. They can have the attributes of being nearly undetectable both to the *victim before and during ingestion and to the authorities who investigate the poisoning. Poisons can also be used to simulate natural causes of death, and can be administered by the knowledgeable murderer so that they are ingested once he or she is away from the scene of the crime, conveniently establishing an *alibi. The use of unusual poisons may also demonstrate the *ingenuity, medical, and pharmacological expertise or outré knowledge of the author.

Poison is perhaps the easiest and most convenient means to commit *murder because the perpetrator need not be present when it is ingested. Moreover, poison can be derived from common objects, ordinary substances, or garden plants usually not considered lethal. In addition, it can be administered from or stored in handy containers. The villain in Margery *Allingham's *Death of a Ghost* (1934) has no difficulty obtaining a lethal dose of *Nicotiana tabacum* from a box of cigars. It can be extracted with very little knowledge and no special apparatus. The crafty killer adds this colorless, odorless solution to a bottle of whiskey before sending it to an alcoholic. Similarly, harmless over-the-counter remedies that are designed to be applied externally may have a toxic effect if swallowed. Antiseptic baby powder containing hexachlorophane to soothe diaper rash is substituted for icing sugar, whipped with cream, and served in cream cakes to dispatch a victim in Douglas Clark's *The Big Grouse* (1986).

Sometimes poison is administered in a way that simulates natural death, thus protecting the malefactor. For example, in John *Rhode's *The Claverton Mystery* (1933; *The Claverton Affair*) the postmortem examination on the recently deceased Sir John Claverton reveals that death resulted from perforation of the stomach due to ulceration. Tests on the stomach contents show an unusual quantity of harmless sodium salts, mainly in the form of the bicarbonate, but no trace of poison. The pathologist concludes that death ensued from natural causes and issues a death certificate accordingly. Actually, Claverton died when he swallowed a gelatine capsule containing ordinary metallic sodium that had been substituted for one of his usual pills for dyspepsia. Metallic sodium, when placed in warm water, burns the hydrogen contained in the water. When the gelatine capsule dissolved in the liquid contents of Sir John's stomach, the sodium combusted and burnt a hole in the stomach wall. The dissolved sodium combined with the chlorine of the gastric juices to form sodium chloride, or common salt, whose presence is normally found in autopsies; it therefore caused no comment.

Occasionally murder is committed by administering poison that exploits a victim's known dependency on or vulnerability to a common medicine usually regarded as harmless, such as digitalis, insulin, or aspirin. Agatha *Christie employs this technique in *Appointment with Death* (1938), when a petty tyrant with a thirst for power is given an injection of digitoxin in addition to the normal amount of digitalis she is already taking for heart disease. Death ensues very quickly due to tachycardia with the usual symptoms of cardiac arrest. Because digitalis is a cumulative drug, excess amounts detected in postmortem examination would be attributed to prolonged use. In *Sick to Death* (1971) by Clark, a young diabetic woman who relies on daily insulin injections to maintain the correct levels of sugar in her blood dies after the murderer heats her insulin supply, thus rendering it useless. The perpetrator in Amanda *Cross's *Poetic Justice* (1970) ends the life of a troublesome colleague by substituting aspirin for his normal headache medication, and thus produces a fatal allergic reaction.

Seemingly innocuous garden plants often have deadly potential. Clark's *Vicious Circle* (1983) is another case in which murder is disguised because death seems to result from an overdose of medicine prescribed for heart disease. Derivatives from two different garden plants are involved. A disagreeable old woman known for taking too much or too little of her digitoxin prescription dies after exhibiting symptoms of digitalis poisoning. Indeed, the autopsy reveals an overdose of cardiac glycosides. Because the deceased's drug supply had been carefully rationed and monitored by her physician, the question arises as to where the surplus digitoxin originated. Further tests disclose the presence of a second toxic cardiac glycoside, *Convallaria majalis*, or lily of the valley, masked by the first. After a simple extraction process, the resulting tincture was introduced into a strong chili-flavored condiment that the victim used to season her food. So, too, small brown spherical laburnum seeds are mistaken for pepper corns—with disastrous consequences—by an inexperienced cook preparing steak au poivre in *Golden Rain* (1980) by Clark. In Martha Grimes's *Jerusalem Inn* (1984) reference is made to the poisonous qualities of the root of the Christmas rose, but the villain actually attempts murder by substituting castor beans for coffee beans atop a glass of Sambuca.

In special cases, a substance may become lethal only in combination with another in the presence of a catalyst, whose existence sets up a toxic reaction among the substances or enhances their dangerous interaction. This occurs in Basil Copper's Solar Pons Sherlock *Holmes pastiche "The Adventure of the Singular Sandwich" (*The Recollections of Solar Pons*, 1996), wherein rye bread infected with ergot produces lysergic acid diethylamide, which induces a violent schizophrenic reaction in a man who murders his wife. The beer he drank while consuming the sandwich acted as a catalyst by circulating the poison more quickly.

Among the more original objects for concealing and conveying poison are the artificially produced caviar eggs containing ricin in Margaret Truman's *Murder on Embassy Row* (1984). The British Ambassador to Washington died suddenly while enjoying a late night snack in his library. Synthetically produced eggs have a firmer protein shell than ordinary sturgeon's eggs so that they do not break and leak their contents if the dish containing them is stirred or a dollop of caviar is scooped up. The poison is released only when the eggs are bitten or chewed. Therefore, the ricin in the serving of the ambassador's caviar does not register in lab tests. Equally ingenious is the villain's delicate dental bridge in Jane Haddam's *Feast of Murder* (1992), which is used to conceal strychnine. In this book a man wants to get rid of a business associate without being suspected of murder. The culprit, a skilled maker of intricate model ships, drills a tiny hole in a tooth near the gum line of his bridge, inserts poison, then reseales the hole. Later, while in prison, he breaks the bridge, extracts the poison, spreads another layer of glue onto the mucilage on an envelope flap and then sprinkles strychnine over it. The pre-addressed envelope accompanies important contracts that are delivered by the culprit's lawyers to the victim, who signs them and then posts the envelope after licking the flap. Of course, the murderer seems to have a perfect alibi, since he was behind bars when his opponent died and no one can identify the means by which the poison was transmitted.

[*See also* Clues: Poisons and Poisoning; Weapons, Unusual Murder; Whodunit.]

—B. J. Rahn

"POISON WOMEN." *See* Japan, Crime and Mystery Writing in.

POLICE DETECTIVE. A private detective may reject cases. An amateur detective might also, but the police detective must take every case presented. That fact underlies the *police procedural in its attempt to capture the daily routine of police professionals in which teamwork is all-important, even though it may be frustrated by political interference or the incessant demands of the official agency's caseload.

In fiction there are, of course, detectives who are police officers in name only. Seen more often with civilian sidekicks than at police headquarters, they address unusual and dramatic crimes. Anomalous cases, however, are the exception for the detective pictured as an integral part of the force charged with the public safety and security.

There seems to be no singular personality type on the force. Joyce *Porter's Inspector Wilfred *Dover stands out because he is childish, selfish, and physically disgusting. He backs into solutions others reach through painstaking footwork or agonizing thought. Others, like Martha Grimes's Inspector Richard Jury or P. D.*James's Commander Adam *Dalgliesh have uniquely distinctive personalities that develop from novel to novel, so that the reader will sympathetically follow their progress in earning professional approval or weathering personal disappointments. The most capable police detectives would not necessarily make sparkling dinner guests. While Michael *Innes's Sir John Appleby and Josephine *Tey's Inspector Alan Grant may move comfortably in all circles, many other police detectives are socially inept. Some, such as Joseph Wambaugh's uniformed officers, feel an isolation from the civilian world. What the best share is dedication to the job that helps them survive low pay, redundant paperwork, danger, and long hours.

The police detectives handle their career pressures differently. Some internalize their tensions until they develop stomach problems, like Maj *Sjöwall and Per Wahlöö's Martin *Beck, or depression, like his friend Lennart Kollberg. Some become workaholics, eschewing vacations, like Rex Burns's Gabriel Wager, or a social life, like Margaret Maron's Lieutenant Sigrid Harald. Many are shown by their authors losing out in personal relationships.

There are exceptions, for John *Creasey's Roger West is happily wed, as is Michael *Gilbert's Patrick Patrella. Dorothy Simpson's Detective Inspector Luke Thanet leaves stress behind when he goes home to his family. Ruth *Rendell's Chief Inspector Reginald *Wexford or Bartholomew Gill's inspector, later chief-superintendent, Peter McGarr may be helped on cases by their spouses, while Ngaio *Marsh's inspector (later superintendent) Roderick *Alleyn carries on a courtship while sleuthing.

Police detectives in fiction come from assorted backgrounds. K. C. Constantine's Mario Balzic is a product of the American immigrant working class, and Robert *Barnard's Inspector Perry Trethowan comes from an advantaged but quirky family, which

Trethowan, in one novel, must investigate. Sheila Radley's Inspector Douglas Quantrill dropped out of school at age fourteen, a fact about which he is very self-conscious, while Henry *Wade's Detective Inspector, later Chief Inspector, John Poole passed his bar exams and spent a year in chambers before joining the *CID. Although Leo *Bruce's Sergeant William *Beef is anything but a gentleman, Marsh's Alleyn is definitely to the manner born.

Often a better-educated officer will explain things to his subordinate, as Colin *Dexter's Inspector Endeavour *Morse explains Wagnerian opera to Sergeant Lewis, but some authors develop generational tension by reversing that order. Inspector Douglas Quantrill must contend with Sergeant Martin Tait, fresh from both college and the police academy, and Reginald *Hill's balding Andrew Dalziel may hold the rank of superintendent, but it is Sergeant Peter Pascoe who holds the degree.

Police detectives' methods of solving crimes range from the ratiocination similar to that exhibited by Golden Age detectives to the techniques from which the police procedural takes its name. The latter include using informants, tailing *suspects, staking out suspicious locations, interviewing *witnesses, combing the scene of the crime, and poring over forensic evidence. In addition, Alan Hunter's Inspector, later Superintendent, George Gently has long philosophical discussions with suspects; Freeman Wills *Crofts's Inspector Joseph *French breaks *alibis by concentrating on timetables; Arthur W. *Upfield's Inspector Napoleon *Bonaparte goes undercover to get the information he needs.

Edgar Allan *Poe's "Murders in the Rue Morgue" (in *Graham's Lady's and Gentleman's Magazine*, Apr. 1841), generally credited as the earliest detective story, presents a prefect of police, but he takes a backseat to the independent detective the Chevalier C. Auguste *Dupin. Charles *Dickens's Inspector Bucket was followed in the nineteenth century by Wilkie *Collins's Sergeant Richard Cuff and Émile Gaboriau's Monsieur Lecoq, but the detective as a member of a police force continued to be a minor figure until the twentieth century. Then, in 1910, A. E. W. *Mason's Inspector Hanaud of the Paris Sûreté, took center stage. Although Hanaud's striking powers of perception and observation are employed on behalf of the official order, they are applied like those of private *sleuths who flourish between the world wars in the country houses and watering holes of Europe. Inspector Jules *Maigret, creation of the prolific Georges *Simenon, comes on the scene in 1933 as an officer who works in many *milieus. Indeed, the bourgeois investigator solves his cases through gifted intuition and methodical immersion in the ambience of assorted crime scenes high and low.

For all the popularity of Maigret in France or of Alleyn or Appleby in England, American writers tended to avoid official detectives in favor of hardboiled private investigators until after World War II. Then in 1945, Lawrence *Treat's *V as in Victim* (1945) gave the world an American police procedural. Hillary *Waugh's *Last Seen Wearing* followed in 1952. Meanwhile, John Creasey had introduced Roger

West to England, following him up with Commander George Gideon in works written as J. J. Marric. Since then, the realistic depiction of police work has remained a strength of crime and mystery writing.

Despite attempts to wax poetic about Isola, a.k.a. New York, Ed *McBain typifies the procedural approach in language of clipped speech and concentration on "just the facts," a concept already proved popular by the television show *Dragnet*. To reinforce the cooperation necessary for police success, McBain presents his Eighty-seventh Precinct characters as a collective protagonist; once McBain even attempted to kill off Steve Carella when he became more popular than others in his cohort. McBain's example is reflected today in the work of the British author John Harvey. His jazz-loving Charlie Resnick is more fully developed than the rest of his squad, but the focus is on the group, and each member takes a turn in the spotlight.

Inevitably readers will see social themes in fiction devoted to detectives enrolled as professional agents of society. An early author to capitalize on this disposition was Earl Derr *Biggers, who deliberately created detective sergeant and inspector Charlie *Chan as an affirmative contrast to the Chinese villains of popular twenties fiction. The Martin Beck novels by Sjöwall and Wahlöö are highly critical of Sweden's welfare state. The preindependence South African setting of James *McClure's novels featuring Lieutenant Tromp *Kramer and Sergeant Mickey Zondi automatically demands social comments. Although this team of an Afrikaner and a Zulu works together well, the novels clearly reveal the injustices of apartheid. John *Ball's Virgil *Tibbs novels are written with a multicultural message, not only about the relationship between African Americans and Caucasians, but also about the Eastern cultures in which Ball is well versed.

For many years police detectives have been stalking international terrain. One can find Nicolas *Freeling's Inspector *Van der Valk in Amsterdam, H. R. F. *Keating's Inspector Ganesh Vinayak *Ghote in India, Bartholomew Gill's Inspector McGarr in the Irish Republic, and James Melville's Superintendent Tetsuo Otani in Japan. As might be expected, American tradition has begun to exhibit cultural and ethnic variety of police detectives. Chester *Himes's Coffin Ed *Johnson and Grave Digger Jones began working in Harlem in 1959, while Dell Shannon's Lieutenant Luis Mendoza hit the West Coast in 1960. Today Tony *Hillerman's Jim *Chee and Joe Leaphorn, Navajo detectives, bring details of Native American culture into police *plots.

*Gender diversity is newer. Joan Hess's Police Chief Arly Hanks is just assuming her job while she gets over a divorce. As the number of real women choosing police work as a profession is increasing, they are more frequent in fiction. Barbara Paul's Marian Larch seems to fit into her *New York department with little difficulty. Susan Dunlap's Sergeant Jill Smith, like Margaret Maron's Lieutenant Sigrid Harald, takes advantage of equal employment opportunities to move ahead despite resentment from older, male officers.

Some see the fictional detective as one who brings order to a disorderly world. In police detection, however, return to order is as elusive in the fictional plot as in the society it models. The most police detectives can do is effect temporary closure, one story at a time. For many readers, that is enough.

• George N. Dove, *The Police Procedural* (1982). Bernard Benstock, ed., *Art in Crime Writing: Essays on Detective Fiction* (1983). Howard Haycraft, *Murder for Pleasure* (1941; reprint, 1984). Earl F. Bargainnier and George N. Dove, eds., *Cops and Constables: American and British Fictional Policemen* (1986). Maxim Jakubowski, ed., *100 Great Detectives* (1991).   —Marcia J. Songer

POLICE HISTORY. *Readers of crime and mystery fiction gradually build up perceptions of various aspects of policing and police history. They also come across mentions of various agents of law and order, including the FBI and the Bow Street Runners. This entry, which is divided into two parts, puts these policing agencies in context of their times and outlines a general history of American policing in the first part, and of British policing in the second.*

History of American Policing
History of British Policing

For further information, please refer to Memoirs, Early Detective and Police; Police Detective; Police Procedural.

HISTORY OF AMERICAN POLICING

In the United States, as elsewhere, modern police departments appeared as metropolitan areas grew. In the colonial period, law enforcement was conducted by watchmen and constables in villages and sheriffs in rural areas. By the nineteenth century Boston had established independent day and night watches, but no American city had a unified police effort until 1845 when the New York State Legislature, responding to the sensational murder of Mary Rogers in 1841 (*see* Edgar Allan Poe) and other evidence of urban disorder authorized a department for *New York City based on the *London model.

Other cities—Chicago in 1851, Boston and Philadelphia in 1854—followed suit; however, the resemblance of American police departments to the centralized, paramilitary agency developed by Sir Robert Peel was limited because of popular resistance to interference in local affairs, the political appointment of officers, and dislike of a common uniform.

From the beginning, the American police possessed more discretion than their London counterparts in the use of force and a looser notion of appropriate duties. As a result, they were available to political power brokers for use in intimidating voters, quelling strikes, and harassing "undesirables." In the cities of the South they became essential to the maintenance of the racial caste system.

In the West, where law enforcement officers were too few to police the frontier, citizen vigilantes responded to crime by administering "rough justice." Since vigilante *justice sometimes claimed innocent victims, in time it created demands for genuine "law

and order" as it came to be enforced by men such as Wyatt Earp and Bat Masterson, who acquired reputations as "town tamers."

The Progressive Era of the late nineteenth and early twentieth centuries saw growing public concern to reform and professionalize urban police departments. Probably the best-known campaign occurred in New York City as Police Commissioner Theodore Roosevelt's reforms challenged the political machine for control of the police.

Greater long-term changes in American policing came through the efforts of career administrators such as Richard Sylvester, August Vollmer, and Orlando W. Wilson, who spearheaded the movement to turn policing into a profession. Sylvester, superintendent of the District of Columbia police department from 1898 to 1915, also served as first president of the International Association of Chiefs of Police. Vollmer, police chief in Berkeley, California from 1905 to 1932, was one of the first to recommend higher education for officers. One of his own students, Orlando Wilson, went on to serve as police chief in Wichita, Kansas and then as dean of the School of Criminology at the University of California. In 1960 Wilson moved to Chicago to serve there as superintendent.

After 1924, when he was appointed director of the Federal Bureau of Investigation in the Department of Justice, J. Edgar Hoover moved quickly to establish the reputation of the agency as the model of professionalism and the nation's premier crime-fighting unit. Because the *FBI thereafter made its academy training program and data-collection systems available to local and state police agencies, it became the organization to emulate.

However, while local police may think of themselves as crime fighters also, much of their work is routine patrol and public service. The contradiction between policing as it has been mythologized and as it is actually practiced has created one of the continuing tensions in American policing. A second tension, harking back to the origin of modern police departments, is that of maintaining public order in a culturally diverse urban setting. In communities of racial and ethnic minorities, charges of police discrimination and brutality have been commonplace, as when police conduct was questioned following the Los Angeles "Zoot Suit riots" of 1943, which involved violent encounters between uniformed military men and Mexican American civilians. Through the Civil Rights Era of the 1960s confrontations between police and demonstrators in the American South became routine media stories. Significantly, this was at the same time that federal civil rights legislation enabled women and minorities to begin entering law enforcement in more than a token way.

In 1970 police *corruption was again in the spotlight in New York City when Frank Serpico, a plainclothes detective, described widespread malfeasance in the NYPD and the failure of his superiors to act against it. Meanwhile, the United States Supreme Court had also turned its attention to policing. Between 1961 and 1966 the Court under Chief Justice Earl Warren in cases such as *Mapp* v. *Ohio* (1961),

Escobedo v. *Illinois* (1964), and *Miranda* v. *Arizona* (1966) affirmed the constitutional rights of suspects. Critics described these decisions as "handcuffing" the police, and by the 1970s films such as *Dirty Harry* (1971) and *The French Connection* (1971) had begun to feature vigilante police being forced to go outside the law to bring criminals to justice.

Official expressions of concern about "law and order" in the 1970s led to massive federal funding through the Law Enforcement Assistance Administration for recruitment, training, education, and criminal justice research. But despite the increased professionalism of police agencies, public security remains tenuous. On the one hand are demands that the police do whatever is necessary to bring crime under control; on the other, especially in inner-city communities where victimization from crime is greatest, distrust of the police is well entrenched.

In response to issues such as crime control versus due process under law and the inherent contradictions of "policing in a democratic society," two philosophies have emerged among police administrators: community-oriented policing and problem-oriented policing, each aiming to provide maximum control of crime but also responsiveness to community interests.

Since the 1940s police procedural writers have regularly provided fictionalized accounts of American policing. Writers such as Elizabeth *Linington, Joseph Wambaugh, John *Ball, and Ed *McBain are among the many authors who have made police officers their protagonists.

[*See also* Memoirs, Early Detective and Police; Police Detective; Police Procedural.]

• Thomas A. Reppetto, *The Blue Parade* (1978). Jack Kuykendall, "The Municipal Police Detective: An Historical Analysis," *Criminology* 24, no. 1 (1986): 175–201. Jerome H. Skolnick and James J. Fyfe, *Above the Law: Police and the Excessive Use of Force* (1993).   —Frankie Y. Bailey

HISTORY OF BRITISH POLICING

There has never been a centrally controlled British police force. From the days of the parish constable, control has always been local. While initially fairly successful, this system gradually fell into disrepute because wealthier or busier elected citizens tended to pay someone else to serve their year's term for them. Increasingly, these substitutes were drawn Dogberry, from the unemployable, corrupt, or just plain stupid, as exemplified by Verges, Dogberry, and the Sexton in William Shakespeare's *Much Ado About Nothing* (written 1598–99; first printed 1600).

By the mid-eighteenth century crime was rampant, particularly on the streets of *London. In response, the Bow Street magistrate and novelist, Henry Fielding, formed half a dozen of the best of the parish constables into a mobile, plainclothes, crime-fighting unit, the Bow Street Runners, who could be sent anywhere in the country in pursuit of criminals. Fielding, and later his blind half-brother, John Fielding, also initiated foot and horse patrols to combat the pickpockets and highwaymen who roamed the roads in and around London.

The Runners had considerable success but eventually deteriorated into a sometimes corrupt, for-hire police force. In *Oliver Twist* (1837) Charles *Dickens revealingly calls his two Bow Street men Blathers and Duff, reporting that they tended to leave a scene "as wise as they went." A more respectful record of their case work was left by one of the last of their kind, Henry Goddard, whose *Memoirs of a Bow Street Runner* was published in 1956.

Despite an increase in the Bow Street foot and horse patrols, more Runners being attached to other magistrates' courts, and the formation of a sixty-man river police, London remained ill-equipped to deal with ever increasing crime and civil disorder. Consequently, in 1829, the Metropolitan Police was formed. Its headquarters were at 4, Whitehall Court, with a rear entrance in *Scotland Yard.

The early difficult days of "The New Police" were not helped by the publication of the memoirs of Eugène François *Vidocq, a French criminal turned head of the *Sûreté by ratting on his former friends. A melodrama staged at the Surrey Theatre in 1829 entitled *Vidocq: The French Police Spy* depicted everything the British dreaded about the introduction of police. So great was the feeling against the Metropolitan Police that in several of their first *murder investigations the *victims were their own men.

Gradually the rest of the country (often reluctantly) followed the lead of London. The Metropolitan Police remained under the direct control of the Home Office while the various county and city forces were under the control of local watch committees, overseen by the Home Office, from which they received some of their funding.

Many forces had no detectives. Even Scotland Yard had very few, and scientific aids, transport, and communications were extremely limited. Small wonder that soon there were complaints that the fictional variety were more efficient. The situation improved a little in the Metropolitan Police in 1878 and some of the attention was drawn away from the Scotland Yard detectives by the appointment of local (or divisional) detective inspectors, some of whom proved very successful. Indeed, one colorful local inspector, Edmund Reid, appeared as Detective Dier in ten novels by Charles Gibbon. Dier, a local inspector in the area where the Jack the Ripper murders took place, was described in *By Mead and Stream*, (1884) as not having "the slightest touch of Scotland Yard about him," and also as being no Sherlock *Holmes. The latter was a common disclaimer uttered by police detectives themselves from the time of Holmes's appearance in the 1880s. Tensions between Yard and divisional detectives are illustrated in Leonard Gribble's Supt. Anthony Slade short story "The Case of Jacob Heylyn" (*Many Mysteries*, ed. E. Phillips Oppenheim, 1933).

Both Vidocq and the popular French crime novelist Émile *Gaboriau had made much of the value of *disguise, which most of the Yard detectives thought a nonsense. Holmes's success brought on a rash of "deduction" stories involving supermen *amateur detectives, which didn't impress Scotland Yard men either. In his autobiography *Detective Days: The Record* of *Forty-two Years' Service in the Criminal Investigation Department* (1931; *Forty Years of Scotland Yard*), the Yard's CID chief constable, Frederick Porter Wensley, declared that a discerning detective was always liable to make a coup in the Holmes manner, but that he himself had never been able miraculously to deduce the author of a crime from a piece of burnt matchstick. Hard work and good information was really what it was all about. Wensley could have been referring either to a spent match left behind deliberately to mislead the *Scotland Yard detective in *"The Lenton Croft Robberies" (Strand Magazine*, 1894) and which Arthur *Morrison's popular amateur investigator, Martin *Hewitt, sees for what it is, or to a burnt match *clue in a true-crime story quoted in Major Arthur Griffiths's influential, three-volume *Mysteries of Police and Crime* (1898).

During the First World War women police made their first tentative appearances and, in the 1920s, some of them gained limited entrance to the *CID in Lancashire, Birmingham, and the Metropolitan Police, where they were engaged chiefly in taking statements from the victims of sex crimes or catching shoplifters. Not until after the Second World War did they begin to make any real progress. They fared better in fiction. *Lady Molly of Scotland Yard*, created by Baroness Emmuska *Orczy, was the detective "Head of the Female Department" at the Yard as far back as 1910.

Police detectives who appeared in the increasingly popular amateur sleuth novels of the 1920s and 1930s tended to be scrupulously honest and honorable but inclined to be a trifle slow or even plain stupid. Some of those who managed to retain full charge of their cases took on the gentlemanly characteristics of the amateurs. For example, Edgar *Wallace's policeman, Socrates Smith, had a private income, and Ngaio *Marsh's Roderick *Alleyn was educated at Eton. Most others were solid, dependable, and a little dull. Some are allowed to make a virtue of their dullness. In the short story "The Almost Perfect Crime," (in *Fifty Famous Detectives of Fiction*, ed. anon., 1938) by Henry Holt, a humble "It's just routine; we keep plodding on" Yard detective, Inspector Jim Silver, is allowed to run apologetic rings around a haughty gentleman in a manner now familiar to fans of the American TV detective Columbo. It is also interesting to note that probably the only real aristocrat writing crime fiction at that time, Henry *Wade, pseudonym of Sir Henry Launcelot Aubrey-Fletcher, sixth Baronet, allowed a quietly intelligent Scotland Yard detective, Chief Inspector Poole, to solve the cases in seven of his novels and in the seven short stories in *Policeman's Lot* (1933).

Prominent among the first modern British *police procedurals was *Gideon's Day* by J. J. Marric (1955). It featured the introspective and honest Commander George Gideon of Scotland Yard. More down-to-earth police procedurals set in the north of England in that era are the works of two ex-policemen: Maurice Procter (e.g., *Man in Ambush*, 1958) and the prolific John Wainwright (e.g., *Death in a Sleeping City*, 1965). Both authors are much read by the police themselves.

A different note was struck in the first of what

crime writer Michael *Gilbert has dubbed "our police are not wonderful books." *My Name Is Michael Sibley* (1952) by John Bingham shows them as cold and ruthless when interrogating a *suspect who turns out to be innocent.

Many contemporary British crime novelists (e.g., P. D. *James, Ruth *Rendell, Colin *Dexter, June Thomson, and Reginald *Hill) place a police officer at the center of inquiries in at least some of their output, but they vary in the extent to which they keep up to date in police methods. Not only is this keeping-up difficult, but more realistic modern procedures such as a group investigation with the chief at the center directing operations, rather than wandering around with a sidekick, can dilute the drama.

Although there is still no centralized control of the British police, there has been increasing amalgamation into larger area forces, such as the West Midlands and Thames Valley. Further amalgamations are mooted. A National Criminal Intelligence Service and a National Crime Squad have been established.

The Royal Ulster Constabulary is unique in being the only British police force to carry firearms at all times. The law in Scotland (and therefore policing) is different from that of the rest of the United Kingdom. The modern, Scottish police procedural books of ex-crime reporter Bill Knox illustrate this well.

[*See also* Memoirs, Early Detective and Police; Police Detective.]

• J. M. Hart, *The British Police* (1951). T. A. Critchley, *A History of Police in England and Wales (*rev. ed. 1978). Joan Lock, *The British Policewoman. Her Story* (1979). Roger Graef, *Talking Blues. The Police in their Own Words* (1989). Paul Begg and Keith Skinner, *The Scotland Yard Files. 150 Years of the C.I.D. 1842–1992* (1992). Chris Ryder, *The RUC: A Force Under Fire*, rev. ed. (1992).   —Joan Lock

POLICE PROCEDURAL. *This entry is divided into four parts:*

Introduction
The American Police Procedural
The British Police Procedural
The International Police Procedural

INTRODUCTION

Police characters have been protagonists in crime and mystery writing since its beginnings. Émile *Gaboriau presented Monsieur Lecoq. Anna Katharine *Green employed Ebenezer Gryce. More recently Georges *Simenon's Inspector Jules *Maigret and Ngaio *Marsh's Chief Inspector, later Superintendent, Roderick *Alleyn have had serial appearances. Each of these figures is a singular individual employing distinctively personal methods of detection. By contrast, the police procedural features a collective, such as a homicide squad, as leading protagonists. Their detection methods derive from their real-life counterparts in organized police forces: routine interrogation, lots of legwork, digging into bureaucratic records, forensic technology, the use of informants, and trial and error. Unlike the fully imaginary detectives, procedural characters take cases as they come, rather than by choice.

Lawrence *Treat's *V as in Victim* (1945) is generally credited with introducing the procedural form to American readers. Maurice Procter brought it to Great Britain in *The Chief Inspector's Statement* (1951; *The Pennycross Murders*). Significant later practitioners include John *Creasey (writing as J. J. Marric), Elizabeth *Linington (under her own name and the pseudonyms Dell Shannon and Lesley Egan), and Ed *McBain. The familiar American dramatic production of *Dragnet*, appearing on radio in 1949 and on television after 1952, helped extend the taste for police procedurals to an enduring audience for its presentation in all media.

[*See also* Police Detective.]   —John M. Reilly

THE AMERICAN POLICE PROCEDURAL

Crime fiction is an ever-evolving genre, and one of the most fruitful recent developments has been the emergence of the police procedural. Originating in the 1940s in the United States, it soon spread to other countries, taking on the distinctive characteristics of each new culture.

Strictly speaking, the term should be reserved for the subgenre of crime fiction that attempts to portray the realities of police investigation and routine. The solution to the crime must depend upon police working as a team and using modern science to gather and interpret evidence. Matching fingerprints; analyzing chemical residues, bodily fluids, and other physical evidence; interpreting blood spatter patterns; scrutinizing public records; gathering computer data; using informants—these and other real-life components of crime solving, rather than individual intuitive brilliance, are at the heart of police procedurals. Typically, the fictional police in these stories have to write reports, keep superiors informed, follow rules of evidence, obey regulations, and avoid bureaucratic entanglements. In addition they must manage personal lives that influence their work. Like their real-life counterparts, fictional policemen and women rarely have the luxury of pursuing just one case at a time: Understaffed and overburdened, they must often divide their time and energy among several unrelated cases.

Lawrence *Treat's *V as in Victim* (1945) is usually cited as the first true example of the American police procedural. Treat followed this with eight additional novels, all utilizing true-to-life law enforcement routines and relying heavily on scientific evidence interpreted by Jub Freeman, the police scientist who figures importantly in all the novels.

Treat's innovations were extended by Hillary *Waugh, whose very popular *Last Seen Wearing . . .* (1952) led to his penning two series of procedurals. The first series is set in small-town Connecticut and centered around Chief Fred Fellows, who is introduced in *Sleep Long, My Love* (1959; *Jigsaw*). The second, featuring New York homicide detective Frank Sessions, is exemplified in *"30" Manhattan East* (1968).

It is also at this date that perhaps the best-known American police procedural writer, Ed *McBain, began his enormously popular, multibook Eighty-

seventh Precinct series. McBain's extensive research on police methodology resulted in accurate and detailed descriptions of police procedures, including such things as actual arrest report forms and lab reports. While the novels utilize a number of protagonists, the primary emphasis may change from one book to the next, offering the reader a variety of *characterization. Interspersed with the crime solving are ongoing developments in the personal and family relationships of the various detectives in this homicide squad. McBain's later novels reflect a change in actual police work by allotting increasing importance to the roles of women in the profession. McBain was an innovator in enlivening his books with the grimly realistic humor that policemen and policewomen use to balance their job's depressing realities.

McBain's novels are set in a thinly disguised *New York City. The grim procedurals of the black ex-convict turned writer Chester *Himes are set in Harlem and center around two black detectives, Grave Digger Jones and Coffin Ed *Johnson. Beginning with *For Love of Imabelle* (1957; *A Rage in Harlem*) and ending nine novels later with *Plan B* (1983), these books became bitter and cynical, marked by random *violence and brutality, as Jones and Johnson become increasingly hopeless about the future of black America. The novels contain a wealth of sociological comment and illustration, bringing to the procedural significant and powerful societal criticism.

In recent years, the realism in police procedurals has reflected the changes in actual police work. The increasing importance of women on the job is reflected in the pioneering work of Dorothy Uhnak, demonstrated in *The Bait* (1968) and Lillian O'Donnell in her *The Phone Calls* (1972). The increased complexity of big-city policing, including scientific advances, inter-and intra-agency rivalries, and political interference, is presented knowledgeably by authors who have served as high-ranking officers, such as Robert Daley (*To Kill a Cop*, 1976), ex-Deputy Police Commissioner, New York City; William J. Caunitz (*One Police Plaza*, 1984), retired New York City detective lieutenant; Joseph D. McNamara (*The First Directive*, 1984), San Jose, California, police chief; and Michael Grant (*Line of Duty*, 1991), twenty-three-year veteran of the NYPD.

Procedurals also reflect a trend in crime fiction: to set stories not only in large cities but in any place authors feel intimately acquainted with. Seattle is the locale for most of J. A. Jance's novels and for some of Ridley Pearson's (*Undercurrents*, 1988; *No Witness*, 1994). Robert Sims Reid, a Missoula officer, looks at law enforcement in a small Montana town (*Cupid*, 1991; *The Red Corvette*, 1992). Carsten Stroud has written about policing in New York City (*Close Pursuit*, 1987) as well as in Montana (*Lizardskin*, 1992), where Stroud's protagonist covers wide territory as a state trooper. Rex Burn's part Hispanic detective, Gabriel Wager, works in and around Denver, Colorado. John Sandford's Prey novels feature Lucas Davenport, a Minneapolis, Minnesota, detective. Tony *Hillerman's novels depict a very different kind of procedure used by his Navajo tribal police sergeants Jim *Chee and Joe Leaphorn.

As George Dove points out in his seminal study *The Police Procedural* (1982), novels referring to and then centering around police had been in existence long before the emergence of the procedural. One type, still very much in evidence, which he labels "The Great Policeman," focuses on a usually brilliant individual, a loner rather than part of a team, solving crimes through intuition rather than by systematic, scientific investigation involving all the resources available to the police.

A fairly recent offshoot, also not to be confused with the true procedural, is the police novel, which is primarily concerned with exploring the psychological effects and emotional stresses of police work, rather than the solving of crimes. Joseph Wambaugh's novels are prominent American examples, as are K. C. Constantine's Mario Balzic novels, set in southern Pennsylvania. Set in Scotland, William McIlvanney's Inspector Jack Laidlaw series provides similar psychic explorations in conjunction with crime solving.

Female police characters are also taking on importance. One of the best-known creators of police novels from the woman's point of view is Dorothy Uhnak, herself a fourteen-year veteran of the New York City Transit Police. Joan Hess brings humor into the police procedural in her series set in rural Maggody, Arkansas. The novels in Joe Gores's DKA series prove that the police procedural is influencing the larger genre. These books, about a team of auto repossessors who find themselves in fixes where they must track down murderers, portray men and women working as a team and using many of the same systematic techniques that the police do. Thus the police procedural seems to be showing every indication that its evolutionary course is not over.

[*See also* Mean Streets Milieu; Realism, Conventions of; Urban Milieu.]

• George N. Dove, *The Police Procedural* (1982).

—Donald C. Wall

THE BRITISH POLICE PROCEDURAL

The British police procedural did not fully develop as a separate genre until about the time of the Second World War. Earlier, the professional policeman, as exemplified by Arthur Conan *Doyle's bumbling Inspector Lestrade or Agatha *Christie's dogged Inspector Japp, was generally portrayed as a foil to the inspired amateur *sleuth who ruled the detecting game; this pattern continued right through the Golden Age of the 1920s and 1930s. While it is true that Ngaio *Marsh's Inspector Roderick *Alleyn made his first appearance as early as 1934 in *A Man Lay Dead*, Alleyn's *class (upper) and character (individualistic and confrontational) do not fit the police procedural mold and the same is true, for different reasons, of Christianna *Brand's idiosyncratic Inspector Cockrill, introduced in *Heads You Lose* (1941), or Michael *Innes's Sir John *Appleby, who first appeared in *Death at the President's Lodging* (1941; *Seven Suspects*).

The new appreciation of the professional policeman in detecting and solving serious crime probably can be dated to two successful series created by the prolific John *Creasey: his Detective Inspector Roger West sequence, begun in 1942 with *Inspector West Takes Charge*, and his George Gideon series, written under the pseudonym J. J. Marric, begun in 1955 with *Gideon's Day (Gideon of Scotland Yard)*. These characters are middle class in origin, intelligent and hardworking, strictly professional in outlook, and dedicated to protecting society against what might be broadly defined as a "criminal class." The Creasey/Marric crime novels combined fairly believable characters and thoroughly described procedural details with ingenious if mechanical plotting: a successful conclusion and solution is more or less guaranteed. Two other influential inventions also appeared in the mid-1950s: Alan Hunter's Inspector George Gently and Maurice Proctor's Detective Chief Inspector/Superintendent Martineau. The Gently series, running into the mid-1980s, introduced a policeman who does his detecting, usually alone, in a society that is often indifferent or even hostile to his stated mission of the discovery and the solution of crime, as, for example, in Hunter's early and emblematic *Gently Floating* (1963). Proctor's "Granchester" series moved its locale and personnel out of metropolitan *London, and brought to the genre a hard and gritty realism and a good sprinkling of well-drawn, believable secondary characters.

Broadly speaking, the normative police-procedural formula presents a *CID officer of the rank of detective inspector or higher, usually teamed with a detective sergeant in a more or less cordial or antagonistic but mutually forgiving working relationship. In a long series the main characters will be promoted to higher rank. The rest of the professional police apparatus—uniformed, and technical and support staff—may have a varying importance in the narrative, but a cynical though talented *forensic pathologist is often an important addition. The hierarchical superiors of this detective team can range from the inane or inept to the intelligent and supportive: Obviously the former makes for a tenser story line. The dominant fiction assumed in British police procedurals is that these teams of professional police officers are most often set to solve that statistically uncommon crime, a premeditated *murder committed among the British middle or upper classes. An example of such a team may be found in Dorothy Simpson's "Thames Valley" series, in which Detective Inspector Luke Thanet and Detective Sergeant Mike Lineham form a formidable detecting pair: Thanet is the intuitive and psychologically attuned adept at interrogation—skillful questioning usually "breaks" Thanet's cases, as in *Wake the Dead* (1992)—and Lineham is the more stolid and painstaking professional. The political-social ambiance is pre-Thatcherite Conservative, and a strong subtheme is that of familial tensions and pressures leading to deadly *violence.

If the foregoing is typical, the British police procedural is certainly neither static nor monolithic. Authors such as Peter Dickinson and Colin *Watson have inserted detective inspectors—Dickinson's Superintendent James (Jimmy) Pibble and Watson's Inspector Walter Purbright—into their inevitably ingenious and wildly convoluted *plots where, in Purbright's opinion, the stance of the police officer is that of an "umpire" who enjoys his job, "if only as an exercise in *ingenuity" (*Charity Ends at Home*, 1968). Another and opposite tendency stresses not intellect and ingenuity but the old, tried *virtues of the stubborn and single-minded thief-taker. An extreme and comic rendition of this type is seen in Joyce *Porter's Inspector Wilfred *Dover, a gross, predictable, and unpleasant caricature; Jack C. Scott created, in his Detective Inspector Alf Rosher (once reduced to sergeant for "conduct unbecoming") a more believable and enjoyable thief-taking copper, a hard man on the hunt who likes the physical side of police work. Rosher first appeared in *The Poor Old Lady's Dead* (1976). The type is still visible in the senior partner in Reginald *Hill's popular Superintendent Andrew Dalziel and Sergeant Peter Pascoe novels; the pachydermatous Dalziel often sets his experience and his "nose" for crime against the gentler, more cerebral skills of his university-educated junior, Pascoe. Another variation on this theme is seen in Douglas Clark's detective pair, Inspector/Superintendent Masters and Chief Inspector Green: Green is literally the "heavy" of the two, and seems to go in a kind of superstitious awe of Masters's intellect. Clark's plots are known for featuring some sort of murder by poison and range from the ingenious to the improbable and even the risible.

The fact that some writers in this genre have actually served as police officers produces no single or predictable thematic outlook: authors Jonathan Ross and John Wainwright both served on police forces, but Ross's fictional Inspector/Detective Superintendent George Rogers is presented as a more fully rounded detective fitting the police-procedural pattern, one who is very capable but also impatient and without illusions, whereas Wainwright's police (he has no completely dominant character) seem essentially to make up a fragile and failing barrier against an increasingly violent, desperate, and disordered criminal (or criminalized) world.

The current trends within the British police-procedural genre appear to follow two lines: the CID officer who investigates solo or at least dominates the detecting inquiry, some form of the "team" approach. P. D. *James's Adam Dalgliesh is a well-known exemplar of the first type: He seems to be more of an analyst than a detective in probing through James's psychologically charged plots to an often ambiguous ending. Ruth *Rendell's Detective Chief Inspector Reginald *Wexford operates with distinction and perseverance on the dark and bloody ground of Rendell's narratives, while for a more homely and distinctively regional example one may point to W. J. Burley's thoughtful Cornishman, Superintendent Charles Wycliffe, introduced in *The Three-Toed Pussy* (1968). The most complex fictional "team" now operating is that led by Detective Inspector Charlie Resnick and described by John Harvey in novels such as *Cutting Edge* (1991). Resnick, sympathetically disheveled and very human, leads a crew of fallible fellow officers in a Midlands city against a rising tide of often perverse crime. Another series, by Bill James, features Inspector/Superintendent Colin Harpur in violent confrontations with criminals where the police, or some of them, routinely use firearms and the central character himself is seriously flawed. A kind of existential coda is reached in Derek Raymond's acutely pessimistic novels featuring the forlorn-hope efforts of a nameless detective sergeant in the *London metropolitan police's "Department of Unexplained Deaths"; he first appeared in *He Died With His Eyes Open* (1984).

The British police procedural evidently gained its first popularity in a reaction against the escapist excesses of the Golden Age sleuths. The new genre presented a qualified realism and appreciated the presence of an organized counterforce set against the sense and the reality of social disintegration and anomie. As a genre, it may be marked by the most comfortable and predictable formulaic plotting, yet it also allows for the development of genuine, novelistic innovation and experiment. At base it posits the existence of an authority that is trusted, at least to a point, a detecting and protecting authority that may be temporarily frustrated but will see at last that *justice is done and seen to be done, at least by the satisfied reader.

[*See also* Mean Streets Milieu; Police Detective; Realism, Conventions of; Urban Milieu.]

• James McClure, *Spike Island: Portrait of a Police Division* (1980). George M. Dove, *The Police Procedural* (1985). Julian Symons, "Crime Novel and Police Novel" in *Bloody Murder: From the Detective Story to the Crime Novel*, 3rd. ed. (1992).

—Dean A. Miller

THE INTERNATIONAL POLICE PROCEDURAL

Although historians consider Lawrence *Treat's *V as in Victim* (1945) to be the first police procedural, Eugène François *Vidocq, a former convict become chief of the Paris police, or Sûreté, is usually credited with presenting in his *Mémoires* (1828–29) practical investigatory procedures. Vautrin in Honoré de Balzac's *Splendeurs et misères des courtisanes* (1838–47; Splendors and Miseries of Courtesans) and Monsieur Lecoq in Émile *Gaboriau's detective series (1866–1876), both former convicts as well, use surveillance and dossiers to thwart and unmask criminals.

Vautrin was a genius, and the "remarkable" Lecoq contributed to readers' admiration for policemen in literature, but later French-language detectives perform their competent work in a plodding, routine way, from Chief Inspector Wens in Stanislas-André Steeman's books to the professionals of Sébastien Japrisot and Dominique Roulet. Two exceptions are *Commissaire* San-Antonio in the Rabelaisian novels by Frédéric Dard, and Georges *Simenon's Inspector Jules *Maigret.

Created in 1931 in *Pietr-le-Letton* (The Strange Case of Peter the Lett; Maigret and the Enigmatic Lett), Maigret is without special greatness save an intuitive knowledge of human behavior, which gives him compassion for the guilty and prevents him from judging their actions. If he has a method, it consists of immersing himself in various environments in order to understand criminals' socio-psychological motivations. Seconded by assistants and the national police apparatus, he arrives at understanding *whydunit through his appreciation of the loneliness and tragic anguish of others' lives. Other writers, like Nicholas Freeling and the Dutch H. W. Haase, modeled their own insightful investigators after Maigret, as did to a lesser extent the Russian Julian Semyono (*Petrovka 38*, 1964) and the Pole Andrzej Piwowarczyk (*Królewna?!*, 1956), while J. J. Marric endowed Commander George Gideon of *Scotland Yard with a similar empathy for criminals. In Danish-born Poul Ørum's *Syndebuk* (1972; Scapegoat; The Whipping Boy) Detective Inspector Jonas Morck also seeks to solve crimes and understand the underlying reasons.

On the other hand, Janwillem *van de Wetering presents realistic and able Amsterdam detectives who often question the merits of their assignments. Far from being brutal and single-minded, they are considerate toward *suspects whose fragile humanity they appreciate. Quite different are the Swedish team Maj *Sjöwall and Per Wahlöö and their compatriots K. Arne Blom and Olle Hogstrand, the Swiss Friedrich *Dürrenmatt, and the Italian Carlo Fruttero and Franco Lucentini.

Martin *Beck, *Sjöwall and Wahlöö's gloomy anti-hero, first appeared in *Roseanna* (1965), where skillful and methodical work led to securing the criminal's conviction. In dealing with crime, Beck and his team criticize their welfare state and *justice system. Blom attacks police *violence in *Sanningens ögonblick* (1975; The Moment of Truth), and in *On the Prime Minister's Account* (1971) Hogstrand questions the relations of authority to the citizenry it governs by means of the dreaded Security Police. Dürrenmatt's Kommissar Hans Bärlach is an outspoken critic of bourgeois society, as is Fruttero and Lucentini's Commissario Santamaria.

Outside Europe and the United States, writers have also used police procedurals to comment on their individual countries. The South African James *McClure introduced Lieutenant Tromp *Kramer and Sergeant Micky Zondi in *The Steam Pig* (1971) and showed apartheid's injustice and ugliness. For his part, *Matsumoto Seichō is one of the first to write police procedurals depicting Japanese society realistically, as in *Suna no Utsuwa* (1961; Inspector Imanishi Investigates).

No author, however, has yet been able to rival Ed *McBain's 87th Precinct books, from *Cop Hater* (1956) on, for their authentic depiction of police routine and portrayal of believable, foible-ridden officers doing their job in mean streets and stressful situations made worse by constant dangers to themselves and their partners.

The genre offers a new exoticism through real or quasi-real information about police work and *milieus, since most readers know little of the systematic investigative methods by which detectives commonly acquire their power. Yet, in such fiction, unlike in mystery and detective novels, the social order is not re-established. And crime is not a defeated

aberration: it remains an inherent condition of the modern world.

[*See also* Mean Streets Milieu; Police Detective; Urban Milieu.]

• George N. Dove, *The Police Procedural* (1982). Bill Pronzini and Martin H. Greenberg, eds., *Police Procedurals* (1985).

—Pierre L. Horn

POLITICAL AND SOCIAL VIEWS, AUTHORS'.

Crime and detective fiction's social and political elements vary with the tastes and practices of individual writers, the times in which they write, and the development of the genre's self-conscious conventions. Although social concerns have been integral from the beginning, recent self-consciousness has driven the crime and detective genre in new sociopolitical directions.

Crime fiction's social concerns began with precursors such as Robert Greene's *The Art of Coney-Catching* (1591), which appealed to interest in the criminal underworld of "coney-catchers," or *con artists while attacking *greed, lechery, and Puritan hypocrisy. Another early practitioner, Charles *Dickens, integrated social and political commentary into his work, with, for example, *Oliver Twist* (1837–39) championing orphans and *Bleak House* (1853) showing the law courts at Chancery defeating *justice. Another early crime writer, Arthur *Morrison, the author of the Martin Hewitt stories published between 1894 and 1903, emphasized working-class *victims forced into crime.

In mainstream crime fiction, a few key writers established standards for sociopolitical concerns early. Writers such as Arthur Conan *Doyle, Wilkie *Collins, Agatha *Christie, and Dorothy L. *Sayers observed obvious social ills: late Victorian-Edwardian poverty, the memento mori under the benign surface of the English village, the constricting oppression of women. In these writers the status quo, not revolutionary sentiments, prevails, as both *plot and authorial commentary confirm the return to proper order and social stability. Disordering elements are eccentric exceptions; there is little overt social criticism or philosophy, and the politics remain in the Dickensian details, in closely described circumstances calling out for justice or change but only on their own behalf. For example, Collins's *The Woman in White* (1860) questions gender-biased laws giving unscrupulous husbands total dominance, *The Moonstone* (1868) deplores colonial *theft of sacred treasures, and *Blind Love* (1890) exposes Irish rebels with sinister plots, but in all three individual villainy overrides sociopolitical criticism. Likewise, in Sayers's *Gaudy Night* (1935), debate about women's rights, careers, and intellectual life, and the psychological idiosyncrasies of the ivory tower ultimately confirm the value of marriage and home, of rights tempered with responsibilities, of balance and order. In like manner, Christie's *A Murder is Announced* (1950) shows the English coping with hardships brought on by World War II—the breakup of the old manors and the servant *class, a topsy-turvy world with children reading the *Daily Worker*, black marketeering, and new technologies—and yet what dominates is the permanence of human fallibility, as Christie notes in *The Mirror Crack'd from Side to Side* (1962; *The Mirror Crack'd*): "The new world was the same as the old. The houses were different . . . the clothes were different, but the human beings were the same as they had always been."

Early on, American writers used detective fiction as a forum for discussion of social concerns. In 1917 Susan Glaspell addressed the taboo subject of spousal abuse in her short play and short story of the same title, "A Jury of Her Peers." The rough-and-ready nature of American culture and the revolutionary political and social turmoil of the 1930s and 1940s brought broader social criticism to the detective story. Raymond *Chandler and others called overt attention to social class conflicts. Dashiell *Hammett's hard-boiled detectives uncover not Christie's concern with secret gain and murderous advantage but rather wholesale corruption and degradation—the American mean streets rotten to the core. The corrupt city officials, cops on the take, striking miners, and rival mobsters of "Poisonville" in *Red Harvest* (1929) represent capitalism run amok, while *The Glass Key* (1931) delineates the more subtle intrigues of corrupt city politics.

Sociopolitical criticism in the late twentieth century has been most affected by the genre's increasing self-consciousness. Writers such as Ross *Macdonald, John D. *MacDonald, and Robert B. *Parker followed the Chandler model, but with distinctive signature themes and elements: the buried past, corruption in a tropical paradise, *racism, and delinquency. America's interest in its culturally diverse population produced ethnic detectives as spokesmen for minority points of view and agendas: John *Ball's Virgil *Tibbs, a black police officer dealing with racism firsthand in *In the Heat of the Night* (1985); E. V. Cunningham's Nisei detective, Sergeant Masao Masuto of Beverly Hills (*The Case of the One-Penny Orange*, 1977); Martin Cruz Smith's gypsy detective in *Gypsy in Amber* (1971); Elmore *Leonard's Raymond Cruz, a Chicano detective in *City Primeval: High Noon in Detroit* (1980); Tony *Hillerman's Navajo tribal policemen, Joe Leaphorn and Jim *Chee (1970–present); Jean Hager's Molly Bearpaw, an investigator for the Native American Advocacy League in Oklahoma (*Ravenmocker*, 1992); and Michael Collins's one-armed Polish New York private eye Dan Fortune, whose dealings with a multicultural population of African Americans, Indians, Latins, and Vietnamese verge on realistic sociological studies (1967–88). Each new ethnic detective has used new social and political perspectives on the genre, some decorative, some integral. In Hillerman's work, for example, solutions grow out of understanding the Navajo Way. In *The Ghostway* (1984), a reservation shootout leads to a grimy view of *Los Angeles: child prostitutes, callous convalescent home caretakers, greed, and street violence.

Another trend has been to focus directly on modern social concerns. Jonathan Kellerman's child psychologist Dr. Alex Delaware and Robert B. *Parker's guidance counselor-psychologist Susan Silverman in the *Spenser series both articulate the problems of youth, including juvenile delinquency and victimization. Lawrence Block's series character Matt Scudder, an ex-cop and alcoholic, provides psychological insights into alcoholism. Joseph *Hansen's Dave *Brandstetter and Jonathan Kellerman's police detective Milo Sturgis, both homosexuals, face homophobia and related issues.

Another trend has been to establish the historical origins of modern sociological preoccupations, particularly in Victorian England, as have Anne Perry, Peter Lovesey, Elizabeth Peters, Teona Tone, and Madeleine Brent. Such writers explore the cruel excesses behind outward shows of righteousness and the hardships of unjust laws, poverty, class divisions, and, most of all, patronizing attitudes toward women and the assumption of male superiority.

Just as ratiocination was an integral element of the early mysteries of Doyle and Christie, so social and political backdrop and commentary have become conventions of the modern crime story. Given the turbulence of the twentieth century, such a social backdrop is natural, given the crime novel's brief: the examination of forces disruptive to the smooth running of society. Yet like ratiocination, obligatory sociopolitical conventions risk conventionalism and even decadence of the genre, as detective heroes are chosen as if by affirmative action and political concerns react to the news of the day. Certainly, the new activism in crime fiction has reinvigorated a genre that was resting on logic and procedure; the danger is in social and political elements becoming ends in themselves, rather than elements of a lively genre of fiction.

[*See also* African-American Sleuth; Ethnic Sleuth; Ethnicity; Native American Sleuth; Prejudice.]

—Andrew *and* Gina Macdonald

PONTIFICATORS, THE. Authors whose works were instrumental in the growth, development, and consolidation of the genre of crime writing were inevitably soon followed by writers who wished to establish a framework within which such fiction should take place. Some of the latter were practitioners who also wrote in an advisory capacity for those who wished to follow in their footsteps; some wished only to explain how and why they themselves were influenced to write as they did.

Others who made important observations were purely critics although the noted Anthony *Boucher, whose memory is perpetuated by the annual "Bouchercon" for writers and readers, was both detective novelist and critic. Some—more often those who came later—were social commentators on detective fiction and how it mirrors society. Later still came the historians of the literature.

The most significant reference work on the subject as a whole is the collection of critical essays called *The Art of the Mystery Story: A Collection of Critical Essays* (1946) edited with commentary by Howard Haycraft. This followed his *Murder for Pleasure: The Life and Times of the Detective Story* (1941).

Among the earliest to write on the genre was G. K. *Chesterton, who was famous also as an essayist.

His "A Defence of Detective Stories" appeared in *The Defendant* (1901).

Authors who specified their own particular requirements include S. S. *Van Dine, who defined the detective story as both an intellectual game and a sporting event. His "Twenty Rules for Writing Detective Stories" appeared in *American Magazine* (Sept. 1928). The rules set a high standard for the would-be writer and included an attack on overworked themes.

Ronald A. *Knox also used the sporting analogy of fair play in likening the writing of a detective story to composing a crossword puzzle according to the rules of cricket. His famous decalogue Ten Commandments of Detection appeared in *The Best Detective Stories of the Year 1928* (1929; *The Best English Detective Stories of 1928*). They comprise prohibitions on the use of those contrived devices he deplored, the requirements he considered essential to a good story, and his view that all the emphasis be placed on the premise that the detective qua author should treat the reader fairly.

Even more exacting standards were laid down by Dorothy L. *Sayers in her introductions to the three volumes of the series *Great Short Stories of Detection Mystery and Horror* (1928; 1931; 1934; *The Omnibus of Crime*). In commending authors who avoided making official police procedure dull, she noted that the detective story had the advantage over every other kind of novel in "possessing the Aristotelian perfection of a beginning, middle and end." She also set out her academic credo of the importance of conscientious work at all times.

Others, for instance F. Tennyson Jesse, have provided information for fellow writers. In *Murder and its Motives* (1924) she laid down six classes of *motives for *murder in fiction, though leaving out one of the most common in real life—insanity. Raymond *Chandler, a proponent of realism, in his essay "The Simple Art of Murder" (in the *Atlantic Monthly*, Dec. 1944), described in detail his ideal detective as "a complete man and a common man and yet an unusual man."

Two other names famous in the genre also offered practical advice to would-be authors. R. Austin *Freeman, in his essay "The Art of the Detective Story," (in *Nineteenth Century And After*, May 1924), included strictures on maintaining standards. Freeman Wills *Crofts, in "The Writing of a Detective Novel" (in *The Authors Handbook*, 1935) is more concerned with how to get one written.

Not all critics are aficionados of the genre. Edmund Wilson, the eminent American novelist, wrote a series of three leading articles published in the *New Yorker* over the winter of 1944–45 entitled "Who Cares Who Killed Roger Ackroyd?" in which he derided both writers and readers of detective fiction.

In a celebrated essay entitled "Raffles and Miss Blandish" in *Horizon*, October 1944; later published in his *Critical Essays*, 1946), George Orwell favorably compared the gentlemanly activities of E. W. *Hornung's crook with the, to him, unattractive world of James Hadley Chase's tough *No Orchids for Miss Blandish* (1939; *The Villain and the Virgin*), which

takes for granted "the most complete corruption and self-seeking as the norm of human behaviour."

The English poet, W. H. Auden, in "The Guilty Vicarage" (*Harper's*, May 1948, later published in *The Dyer's Hand*, 1962), wrote of the magic formula that "is an innocence which is discovered to contain guilt." A. E. Murch, in her *The Development of the Detective Novel* (1958), felt that the primary interest "lies in the methodical discovery, by rational means, of the exact circumstances of a mysterious event or events."

A classic history of the detective-crime short story was written by Ellery *Queen (1951), who also published many random observations in *Ellery Queen's Mystery Magazine*.

Colin *Watson, himself a detective novelist, concluded in his study *Snobbery with Violence: Crime Stories and their Audience* (1971) that the predilection of other writers within the genre for using *settings in high life and the denizens therein as the chief protagonists constituted elitism. He was concerned especially with that aspect of mannered fictional crime writing he was the first to identify as the School of *Mayhem Parva.

In another standard reference work, the *Catalogue of Crime* (1971), Jacques Barzun and Wendell Hertig Taylor divided the detective story into five discrete categories. For Eric Routley in *The Puritan Pleasures of the Detective Story: A Personal Monograph* (1972), the satisfaction came from the methodical solution of mysterious events.

Most valuable for all who study the genre and probably the best working history is by Julian *Symons, critic, poet, crime writer, and, most importantly, social historian. His *Bloody Murder From the Detective Story to the Crime Novel: A History* (1972; *Mortal Consequences*) is an authoritative summation of most aspects of crime writing up to the time it was written.

—Catherine Aird

PORNOGRAPHY. Any definition of pornography is temporal and volatile. Personal taste appears to be a criterion in labeling something obscene. When a questionable work is brought before an adjudicating body, the "touchstone" position frequently becomes "I know it when I see it." Early usage, still occasionally applied to the term "pornographic," meant writing about prostitutes. The U.S. Supreme Court has categorized obscene materials as those that arouse prurient interests. Artists and psychologists have defined pornography as fantasy or wish fulfillment writing intended to provoke erotic response in the reader.

Over time, novels containing one or more of the following elements have been classified as pornographic: seduction, lascivious acts, sexual despoilment, flagellation, incest, homosexuality, and explicitly described sexual actions having no functional role in *plot or character development. Sexual *violence and cruelty have been defined as pornography since the 1970s.

Important distinctions exist between novels that have pornography as the motive for crime and those that are pornographic in style. Occasionally, a combination of the two appears in one work. A popular subject in the genre is pornographic photography and filmmaking. The plot of Raymond *Chandler's *private eye novel about *blackmail and *murder, *The Big Sleep* (1939), involves salacious pictures, nymphomania, and seduction. Pornographic movies are big business in Robert *Barnard's *Bodies* (1986), where the narcissistic world of bodybuilding is scrutinized. There is no obscenity in Barnard's descriptions, nor in Corinne Holt Sawyer's *The J. Alfred Prufrock Murders* (1988), where the *motive for murder is the blackmail of an elderly woman who once starred in a pornographic film. A Mafia-controlled pornography industry actuates the plot of Dorothy Salisbury *Davis's *Lullaby of Murder* (1984); the story line includes child molestation.

Mirroring cultural and social change, children as willing sexual partipants or *victims have become pornographic components of the modern mystery novel. Child molestation leads to murder in Edward Gorman's *The Night Remembers* (1991). Ted Wood's *police procedural *Corkscrew* (1987) concerns pornographic filmmaking and a sexually corrupt teenage boy. Very young girls not only engage in sexual activities but also discuss them graphically in Elizabeth George's *Missing Joseph* (1993), in which details of a savage rape are explicitly described.

As pornography has increased in violence, more novels have focused on gay and lesbian characters, both victims and detectives, subjected to brutality. In Barbara Wilson's *Sisters of the Road* (1986), a lesbian *amateur detective is raped by a murderer who runs a string of prostitutes; details about rape, prostitution, incest, and crude terminology for women abound. Rape, torture, and mutilation of women are not uncommon in modern mysteries. Julian *Symons's *The Players and the Game* (1972) describes sexual violation through bites, razor cuts, and insertion of foreign objects. Blood-painted genitalia decorate a crucifix on which women are tortured. Ed *McBain's *Puss in Boots* (1987) is even more horrific. Murder results from the making of a pornographic film. But it is the detailing of sexual actions, suggestive metaphoric language, barbarity, and sexual mutilation of a helpless, naked, starving woman that comes closest to current definitions of pornography.

[*See also* Child Abuse; Gay Characters and Perspectives; Lesbian Characters and Perspectives; Rape and Other Sex Crimes; Sex and Sexuality.]

• Andrea Dworkin, *Pornography: Men Possessing Women* (1984).
—Helen S. Garson

PORTER, JOYCE (1924–1990), British author of satiric detective novels and *spy fiction. Born in Cheshire and educated at King's College, *London, she served in the Women's Royal Air Force. Her British *police procedural series introduced the sixteen-stone antihero Detective Chief Inspector Wilfred *Dover (in *Dover One*, 1964), who manages to solve unsavory cases, some concerned with cannibalism and castrations in *Dover and the Unkindest Cut of All* (1967), while satisfying his considerable desire for

comfort. In the Honourable Constance Morrison-Burke series, beginning with *Rather a Common Sort of Crime* (1970), the insensitive Hon Con, an amateur, is warned off every crime scene by the police, but remains convinced of her importance to the investigation. With satiric jabs at sexism, elitism, and codes of honor, and with repulsive and unsavory characters, Porter creates an earthy world whose bleakness is tempered by *humor.

[*See also* Police Detective.]

• Joyce Porter, "Professional Jealousy: A Lesson in Patience," in *Murder Ink: The Mystery Reader's Companion* (1977).
—Georgia Rhoades

POST, MELVILLE DAVISSON (1869–1930), American author, lawyer, and political figure. Born and raised in West Virginia, Post obtained a law degree and practiced there for a dozen years, while emerging as a prominent figure in the state's Democratic Party politics. In 1896 he published *The Strange Schemes of Randolph Mason*, a collection of stories about an unscrupulous lawyer who exploits legal loopholes to the benefit of his clients. Another similar volume, *The Man of Last Resort; or, The Clients of Randolph Mason* appeared in 1897, followed by *The Corrector of Destinies* (1908), in which Mason does a turnabout and labors now on the side of justice.

Although he wrote scores of crime stories, his greatest success came with *Uncle Abner, Master of Mysteries* (1918), a collection in which Post drew on the rugged rural mountain setting he knew so well and created the righteous, Bible-quoting Uncle Abner, a country squire who roams the lawless Virginia backlands of the 1850s, a scourge of *evil, avenging crimes against God and man. The Uncle Abner tale in that volume, "The Doomdorf Mystery," is a classic regaded by critics as one of the most extraordinary locked room mysteries ever written.

[*See also* Lawyer: The American Lawyer-Sleuth; Rural Milieu.]

• Charles A. Norton, *Melville Davisson Post, Man of Many Mysteries* (1973). Allen J. Hubin, ed., introduction to *The Complete Uncle Abner* (1977).
—Donald A. Yates

POTBOILER. The potboiler is a piece of writing produced for money with little regard to quality; it developed in the mid-eighteenth century as the production of literature became increasingly commercial. The potboiler draws on two related aspects of literature, sensationalism and crime, and has been given various labels over the decades. For sixty years following the publication of Horace Walpole's *The Castle of Otranto* (1765), the *Gothic novel with its sensational *plots revolving around secrets flourished in England. These novels also contained a sense of mystery; Walpole's novel, for example, was mysteriously presented to the public as a translation of a genuine medieval manuscript. Both sensationalism and crime in literature were subject to considerable contemporary critical opprobrium. This combination of crime, sensationalism, and critical reproach has continued to the present day.

A series of fictional and semi-fictional works written for money in the nineteenth century played a crucial role in the development of the *crime novel; These include the autobiography of the first professional detective, *Mémoires de Vidocq* (1828–29; Memoirs of Vidocq); a description of a descent into the depths of a city, in Eugene Sue's *Les Mystères de Paris*, (1843–44; The Mysteries of Paris); and the work of Émile *Gaboriau, especially *Monsieur Lecoq* (1868). Yet these potboilers do not stand apart from a host of other nineteenth-century works of the same order by such writers as Mrs. Henry *Wood, M. E. *Braddon, and Joseph Sheridan Le Fanu who produced *sensation novels. The gap that was to separate the potboiler from other types of fiction opened up in the twentieth century.

As the figure of the *sleuth developed in the early twentieth century, the production of crime fiction as a simple money-making exercise became easier. The most famous magazine devoted to crime fiction, *Black Mask* (1920–51), took on the task of telling stories depicting crime similar to those that had drawn audiences to the *dime novel—for example, the stories featuring Nick *Carter. The editors of *Black Mask* discovered Dashiell *Hammett, served as midwife to the hard-boiled *private detective story, and introduced to the public the prolific Erle Stanley *Gardner, who produced more than 120 books. The magazine went on to establish a market for hard-boiled *private eye stories and later writers capitalized on this. In 1947 Mickey *Spillane initiated with *I, the Jury* an era of unprecedented bestsellerdom for his private eye hero, Mike *Hammer. The success of Spillane's novels was thought by many critics to be inversely proportional to their literary merit.

Once publishers understood the approach necessary for such commercial success they never looked back. The most significant advances in selling the potboiler came with the new publicity strategies of the 1970s, which are still prevalent. A number of novels are hyped by a publicity campaign that elevates them from potboilers to blockbusters, a process that began in earnest with Mario Puzo's story of a Mafia family, *The Godfather* (1969). Propelled by a hitherto uncountenanced publicity campaign centered mainly on the film version, the novel became one of the biggest sellers of the 1970s and the film broke box office records. Hot on its heels was William Peter Blatty's novel of demonic possession, *The Exorcist* (1971), which was sold using the same successful technique of tying it in with the film publicity. Like the next blockbuster in line, Peter Benchley's *Jaws* (1974), all of these potboilers had a crime and mystery subplot. Blockbuster hype became the order of the day for the potboiler and the strategy was applied to a host of crime and mystery stories in the 1980s and 1990s. Probably the most visible of these are the works of Michael Crichton; for example, the police novel *Rising Sun* (1992) and the *suspense *thriller *Disclosure* (1994).

[See also Suspense Novel.]

• R. F. Stewart, . . . *And Always a Detective: Chapters on the History of Detective Fiction* (1980).   —Paul Cobley

PREJUDICE. In crime and mystery writing, a literature well known to reflect popular culture, expressions of both conscious and unconscious prejudice abound. Sometimes questions of prejudice are central to *plot and theme. Often prejudices held by the author are revealed in dialogue or in an author's use of stereotyped characters. Fear of prejudice drives the plot in Arthur Conan *Doyle's "The Yellow Face" (in *The Memoirs of Sherlock Holmes*, 1894). In this Sherlock *Holmes tale, a British woman, whose first husband was an African American, feels compelled to hide her dark-complexioned child because she fears her new husband, a British gentleman, will be unable or unwilling to accept her daughter. In the Holmes story, prejudice involves the characters, but writers may also manipulate the perceived prejudices of readers, as does Dorothy B. Hughes in *The Expendable Man* (1963), when she does not reveal the race of her protagonist until after she has established him as an intelligent, compassionate, young middle-class professional.

Especially during the last three decades, *gender prejudice also has received inspired treatment. This is exemplified in the work of P. D. *James, who addresses the issue of biases against female police officers in *A Taste for Death* (1986). *Sexism also affects her *private eye, Cordelia *Gray, in *An Unsuitable Job for a Woman* (1972) and *The Skull Beneath the Skin* (1982). Across the Atlantic, in a small city in Illinois, African American police detective Marti McAlister, Eleanor Taylor Bland's *sleuth, deals with her male partner's outdated views of women as cops. Female private eyes such as Sara *Paretsky's V. I. *Warshawski and Sue *Grafton's Kinsey *Milhone respond to comments about the fact they are doing what was once considered a man's job with snappy, tongue-in-cheek retorts. But the point made by all these authors is that such attitudes continue to exist.

With regard to sexual orientation, writers such as Sandra Scoppettone, Nikki Baker, Ellen Hart, Richard Stevenson, and Joseph *Hansen have addressed the issue of prejudices against lesbians and gays. The authors focus on the dilemmas of choosing to be out of the closet or in, of choosing to speak out when disparaging remarks are made or to remain silent. And there is also the matter of AIDS, which carries its own stigma. However, writers such as Scoppettone and Hart depict their protoganists as well-adjusted members of a supportive group of family and friends.

As in real life, *religion spawns prejudice in mystery fiction. In Alan Scholefield's *Dirty Weekend* (1990), others wonder why Detective Sergeant Leopold Silver, a well-educated young Jew, would choose a career in policing when he could obviously do better. And Silver himself doubts he could ever explain the matter to his relatives' satisfaction, since they have their own prejudices about the police.

Racial prejudice may also determine whether or not the protagonist is considered suitable for a job. In James Patterson's *Along Came a Spider* (1993), African American Alex Cross is a homicide detective because, although he has a Ph.D. in psychology, patients were unwilling to consult him. Ironically, in *Blood Rights*

(1989) by Mike Phillips, a conservative politician turns to British journalist Samson Dean for help in finding his missing daughter because Dean is black and so is the daughter's male friend. And in Robert *Barnard's *Bodies* (1986), a young man who is doing some undercover work for the police is told he has an advantage as a model because he is black and advertisers are into affirmative action.

Writers have sometimes had minority sleuths use the preconceived notions of others to advantage. Veronica Parker Johns's African American detective Webster Flagg (*Murder by the Day*, 1953) is successful as a sleuth because as a manservant he is socially invisible. Detective Arthur Brown in Ed *McBain's Eighty-seventh Precinct series, a big black man who looks "bad," occasionally uses this to frighten *suspects into talking.

Beyond those prejudices held by people within the same society are those of the people of one nation toward those of another. This is dealt with gently in Simon Brett's *The Dead Side of the Mike* (1980), in which Charles Paris makes his first trip to America and discovers the country and the people are a bit different than he was led to believe from soap operas and police *thrillers. And in *Sayonara, Sweet Amaryllis* (1983), an entry in his Superintendent Tetsuo Otani series, James Melville touches on the prejudices of the Japanese toward ethnic minorities and on the ways in which the Eastern and Western characters perceive each other.

• Janet K. Swim and Charles Stangor, eds. *Prejudice: The Target's Perspective* (1998).   —Frankie Y. Bailey

PRIESTLEY, DR. LANCELOT, an *amateur detective sometimes called "the sage of Westbourne Terrace." Created by British author John Rhode, he appears in more than seventy novels and some short stories. Except for his early cases, Priestley works in the tradition of the *armchair detective, solving problems in cerebral splendor with a minimum of physical activity; relying largely on others to do the legwork and collect information.

Grim and virtually humorless, although a good host when discussing *murder, he is a mathematician of formidable intellect. His declining years (hardly an appropriate term) are spent in applying logic to crime *puzzles brought to him by friends from *Scotland Yard.

Following *The Paddington Mystery* (1925), which introduced Priestley and other recurring characters, the series extending to 1961 is known for its variety of ingenious murder methods. Perhaps the best is *The House on Tollard Ridge* (1929), concerning the death of a rich eccentric.

[*See also* Eccentrics: Ingenuity; Weapons, Unusual Murder.]   —Melvyn Barnes

PRIESTLEY, J. B. *See* Incidental Crime Writers.

PRISONS. *This entry is divided into two parts. The first section looks at the administration and conditions of British prisons over a longer history and cites examples of fiction in which British prisons figure impor-*

tantly. The second part notes the changing attitudes toward prisoners and the role of prisons in America and provides examples of crime and mystery writing in which American prisons are significant.

British Prisons
American Prisons

For further information, please refer to Memoirs, Early Detective and Police; Newgate Novel; Prison Writing; True Crime.

BRITISH PRISONS

Up until the nineteenth century in England prisoners served their sentences in a motley collection of often unsuitable buildings such as old castles, dungeons, manor houses, and gatehouses. Variously termed prisons, bridewells, or houses of correction, these were under the control either of the local magistrates or (for more serious offenders) the *Home Office. From 1717 the chronic overcrowding was alleviated by transportation of inmates to the colonies and by means of old ships, known as the hulks, moored on the Thames River and at Portsmouth. Further space was provided by the huge new Millbank Prison in London and by the dramatically isolated Dartmoor Prison, in Devon, built by the Napoleonic prisoners of war. As transportation ceased (1840–68) many more prisons were built, most operating some variant of the U.S. "separate system."

Since 1877 all British prisons have been under the control of the Home Office. They are divided, loosely, into four main types: local (remand and very short term), short-term, medium-term, and long-term, with some overlapping. The person in charge of a prison is known as the governor, and the uniformed staff, once warders, are now called prison officers. Some experimentation with privatization is taking place.

One of the first detective novels, *Things as They Are; or, The Adventures of Caleb Williams* (1794), spoke out on the filthy, tyrannically run prisons such as London's Newgate Prison. The author, William *Godwin, was influenced by *The State of the Prisons in England and Wales* (1777) by reformer John Howard and the *Annals of Newgate; or, Malefactors Register* (1776) by John Villette, which contains references to the prison escapes of highway robber Jack Sheppard. Charles *Dickens regularly visited prisons and wrote about them realistically. For example, the condemned cell inspected by Dickens for his "Visit to Newgate" (in *Sketches by Boz*, 1836–37) reappears, to be occupied by Fagin, in *Oliver Twist* (1837–38).

Newgate novels were popular in Dickens's day. Their plots are based on sensational criminal cases recorded in *The Newgate Calendar*, published about 1773 in five volumes, but their emphasis was on the crime rather than the imprisonment. Prison life rarely enters British detective fiction. Harriet *Vane may have spent a week in Holloway Prison in Dorothy L. *Sayers's *Strong Poison* (1930) but through Lord Peter *Wimsey's eyes we see little more than bare corridors, a long deal table, and "a couple of repellent chairs." Newfangled treatment ideas are pointed up briefly by Margery *Allingham in *The Tiger in the*

Smoke (1952) when a prisoner escapes by fooling a psychiatrist and then murdering him. In *Consider the Evidence* (1966), Jeffrey Ashford foretells the kind of treatment his policeman will receive inside, but in his *The Hands of Innocence* (1965), he provides a graphic account of the brutality afforded a terrified sex offender by other inmates. The author makes no mention of the possibility of segregation, always an option open to governors wishing to avoid trouble. Sex offender segregation is now common practice.

Novels in which prison life is more significant include Peter Lovesey's *Waxwork* (1978) and, to a lesser extent, Catherine Aird's *A Dead Liberty* (1986). In both, there is a return intermittently to an incarcerated heroine, who is behaving unusually (in the first she is unafraid, in the second she is mute). In *A Pin to See the Peepshow* (1934), F. Tennyson Jesse does not shirk the harrowing last moments in the condemned's cell. This novel is based on the real-life Thompson-Bywaters murder case.

The role of the chaplain is highlighted in Aird's *A Dead Liberty* and Ashford's *The Hands of Innocence*, and that of the voluntary prison visitor in Andrew *Garve's *Prisoner's Friend* (1962). The prison warder, tyrannical in *Things as They Are; or, The Adventures of Caleb Williams*, has become humanized enough in John *Mortimer's humorous short story "*Rumpole and the Reform of Joby Jonson" in *Rumpole on Trial* (1992) to believe that all the inmates need to keep them in order is "a bit of G. & S." (Gilbert and Sullivan). Nonetheless, Mortimer (who was a barrister and Queen's Counsel) felt strongly enough about modern prison conditions to edit, introduce, and contribute to *Great Law and Order Stories* (1990) on behalf of the Howard League for Penal Reform.

[*See also* Prison Writing.]

• Henry Mayhew and John Binny, *The Criminal Prisons of London* (1862; reprint 1986). Robert Hughes, *The Fatal Shore: A History of the Transportation of Convicts to Australia 1787–1868* (1987). J. A. Sharpe, *Judicial Punishment in England* (1990).   —Joan Lock

AMERICAN PRISONS

In the latter half of the nineteenth century and throughout the twentieth century, American prisons metamorphosed from being places of physical isolation and punishment intended for confinement and "correction." Thanks to the efforts of prison reformers, the focus gradually shifted from punishing prisoners through physical labor to attempting to understand the criminal mind. Regardless of prison reform, however, overcrowding leading to assaults among prisoners and uprisings against their keepers has often caused the inmate experience to remain grim. Popular literature, both fiction and nonfiction, has generally viewed the prisoner as an individual in opposition to the penal system.

Even before prison experience was incorporated into crime and mystery writing American prison literature, including autobiographical work, short stories, novels, plays, and poetry, evolved from third-person accounts of *true crime and from first-person confessions of condemned criminals published in the

United States and especially in England. A strong oral tradition related to the *nursery rhyme made memorable—and notorious—the exploits of those who captured the public imagination, such as Lizzie Borden and Bonnie and Clyde.

Prisons themselves are likely to be featured in didactic works, including everything from ditties sentamentalizing or villifying criminals to book-length contemporary critiques of the treatment of those who are incarcerated. In rare cases, the prison is portrayed more lightly, as in classic *puzzle-centered mysteries. One example is Jacques *Futrelle's story, "The Problem of Cell Thirteen" (*Boston American*, Oct. 1905), in which Professor S. F. X. *Van Dusen takes up the challenge to escape from a maximum security prison cell using nothing but his "shoes, stockings, trousers, and shirt" and, of course, his wits.

Other short stories tell of lawmen associated with prisons taking justice into their own hands. This is literally the case in Carter Dickson's "The Other Hangman" (*A Century of Detective Stories*, 1935).

The prison experience of some well-known writers is overshadowed by their later literary success. William Sidney Porter served almost four years in the state penitentiary at Columbus, Ohio where he began writing the short stories that would bring him fame under the name O. Henry. Chester *Himes began his writing career while serving seven years in Ohio State Prison. After his release he wrote several novels, including *Cast the First Stone* (1952), which is set in a prison. He went on to pen his well-known "Harlem domestic" *police procedurals.

Recent literature about prison life has been published mainly in the form of autobiographical books and novels by or about prisoners. Inmate authors, especially, tend to focus on the dehumanizing aspects of life in penal institutions. Some also offer portraits and critiques of the inmate subculture and the administrative structure of prisons. Such works often pinpoint the prisons in which they are set. Malcolm Braley's *On the Yard* (1967), set in California's San Quentin Prison and Nathan Heard's *House of Slammers* (1983), set in the New Jersey State Prison, provide brutally frank descriptions of life in those institutions.

Writers who have never been inmates have also used American prisons in their work, especially in *true crime accounts. The final scenes in Truman Capote's *In Cold Blood* (1965) are set in Kansas State Penitentiary, where two killers are awaiting execution. In Norman Mailer's *The Executioner's Song* (1979), Gary Gilmore spends his final days in Utah State Prison. *Dead Man Walking* (1993), written by Sister Helen Prejean, takes place in Angola State Prison in Louisiana.

[*See also* Prison Writing.]

• Robert Johnson, *Hard Time: Understanding and Reforming the Prison*, 2nd ed. (1996).   —Frankie Y. Bailey

PRISON WRITING. Writing by and about prisoners includes internal prison news reports, memoirs, and fiction. Literary quality may vary in this work, but verisimilitude to the prison *milieu and prisoners' experiences are often strengths. The first prison publication, *The Forlorn Hope*, was born in New York in the early 1800s and died within a few months, but it was followed by many more. Another early prison newspaper was founded by Cole Younger, who had been a guerrilla officer during the Civil War. Later, he and his brothers joined with Jesse James to form one of the most famous outlaw gangs in history. But when Cole and his brothers pooled their resources one summer day in 1887, they used the $50 not for crime but to help finance a newspaper. Today, *The Prison Mirror* is still published at the Minnesota State Prison, Stillwater, Minnesota and thousands of people both in and out of prison look forward to each issue.

Even though many have been discontinued, there are still more than 100 penal publications printed and distributed with some kind of regularity in the United States and Canada. Their format varies from one or two pages of mimeographed copy to slick stock magazines that rival professional publications. Their viewpoint varies almost as widely: many prison publications are nothing more than a means for the administration to circulate regulation changes and are rigidly controlled and censored. Others are produced with little censorship.

Originally, penal publications were permitted because they provided a means of keeping prisoners occupied. Few prison writers became professional authors. Those who did include Caryl Chessman, Los Angeles's infamous "Red Light Bandit," who began writing while he fought to have his death sentence commuted. The autobiographical *Cell 2455, Death Row* (1954) was an American best-seller. However, judging from *The Kid was a Killer* (1960), his last published work, which appeared as a paperback original, Chessman's earlier books were probably heavily edited.

Edgar Smith's *A Reasonable Doubt* (1970) is a novel that parallels his own case. And Jack Henry Abbott's *In the Belly of the Beast* (1981) is an epistolary account of life in prison addressed to Norman Mailer. Each man won his release from prison through the efforts of professional writers who had been impressed by their work, but neither stayed out for long. Smith tried to kidnap a woman from a parking lot in California—a carbon copy of his original crime—and Abbott killed a man in New York City.

E. Richard Johnson wrote *Silver Street* (1968; *The Silver Street Killer*) and other novels while incarcerated but focused on action in the mean streets rather than within prison walls. He won an Edgar Allan Poe Award from *Mystery Writers of America. But when released, Johnson too soon broke the law and was sent back to prison.

The late Malcolm Braly, who penned *Felony Tank* (1961) and *On the Yard* (1967), was one of the strongest of the prison crime writers. His success may rest upon the fact that he is not self-conscious in his autobiographical efforts.

G. Gordon Liddy, author of *Out of Control* (1979), and the other Watergate defendants who turned to writing can probably be considered prison writers although their prison experience was almost certainly different from that of the majority of inmates. E.

Howard Hunt had written many undistinguished thrillers before setting foot in prison.

A highly prolific prison inmate-crime writer is Donald MacKenzie, who penned *Occupation Thief* (1955) and the John Raven series of mystery novels. His books abound with realistically drawn ex-convicts and other shady characters.

The prison writer is uniquely qualified to write about the world in which he or she is literally an insider. The verisimilitude created by prison writers is generally far better than the writing itself. Prison writers are also able to portray the seductive thrill of crime, relying on first-hand experience.

[*See also* Prisons: American Prisons; Prisons: British Prisons.]
                                              —Albert F. Nussbaum

PRIVATE DETECTIVE. The private detective is one of the three main types of fictional detective, the others being the amateur *detective and the *police detective. Although characters who may be described as private detectives are occasionally to be met with in Victorian mystery fiction, they almost invariably play a peripheral role in the works in which they appear. An exception is *The Notting Hill Mystery* (1863), by Charles Felix, an author of whom little is known. This consists of reports and letters compiled by an insurance investigator, Ralph Henderson, to mount a case against a certain Baron R who is suspected of his wife's *murder. As an insurance investigator Henderson is not, strictly speaking, a private detective; in addition, he remains throughout the story a shadowy, disembodied figure. The first real private detective in fiction is therefore also the greatest and the best-known, Arthur Conan *Doyle's Sherlock *Holmes, who made his first appearance in *A Study in Scarlet* (1887). To create Holmes, Doyle borrowed characteristics from Edgar Allan *Poe's Chevalier C. Auguste *Dupin and Émile *Gaboriau's Monsieur Lecoq, giving him superhuman powers of ratiocination and making him a master of *disguise. From Poe he also took the relationship between the brilliant detective and the imperceptive, but admiring friend and narrator, humanizing both participants in the process: the Holmes-Watson paradigm was to be much imitated by later authors, commending itself chiefly as the fairest way of laying the *clues of a detective *puzzle before the reader.

The success of Holmes led to the appearance in the years preceding the First World War of a number of private detectives most of whom are now—perhaps deservedly—forgotten. Unlike Holmes, however, they are for the most part decidedly ordinary characters, lacking their predecessor's seemingly miraculous powers of deduction. As with Doyle, the format almost universally adopted was that of the magazine short story, collections of which were later published in book form. Among the first to follow Doyle was Arthur *Morrison, whose character Martin Hewitt, a former solicitor's clerk, runs a private detective agency near the Strand (*Martin Hewitt, Investigator*, 1894). More interesting, as one of the first female detectives, is George Sims's Dorcas Dene, "a professional lady detective," forced into the profession when her husband goes blind (*Dorcas Dene*,

Detective, 1897). Victor L. Whitechurch's Thorpe Hazell, a vegetarian, takes only cases concerned with the railways (*Thrilling Stories of the Railway*, 1912), while William Hope Hodgson's Carnacki occupies himself solely with the allegedly supernatural (*Carnacki the Ghost Finder*, 1913). An American example is the scholarly Fleming Stone, who appears in novels by Carolyn Wells (*The Clue*, 1909).

The interwar years, the Golden Age of the detective story and in which the novel regained its dominance, were ushered in by the appearance of the private detective who was almost to rival Holmes in popularity, Agatha *Christie's Hercule *Poirot (*The Mysterious Affair at Styles*, 1920). A. E. W. *Mason's Inspector Hanaud has been suggested as a model for Poirot; it seems also that Christie might have deliberately constructed her detective as an antipode to Holmes, since his characteristics are diametrically opposed to those of his predecessor. But she remains true to the original in making Poirot, like Holmes, a *superman sleuth, and in imitating the Holmes-Watson pattern of narration, using for this purpose Captain Arthur Hastings, Poirot's almost too obtuse friend. However, the majority of those writers—again, for the most part, now forgotten—who produced private detectives in the following decade favored a third-person over a first-person narrative, and broke further with the Holmes-Poirot tradition by abandoning the concept of the *sleuth with superhuman powers of ratiocination. Among the characters of this period are, in England, Lynn Brock's Colonel Wyckham Gore (*The Deductions of Colonel Gore*, 1924), Edgar *Wallace's Mr J. G. *Reeder (*The Mind of Mr J. G. Reeder*, 1925), J. S. Fletcher's Ronald Camberwell of the Chaney and Camberwell Detective Agency (*Murder at Wrides Park*, 1931) and R. A. J. Walling's Philip Tolefree (*The Fatal Five Minutes*, 1932); and, in America, Octavus Roy Cohen's Jim Hanvey of New York (*Jim Hanvey, Detective*, 1923) and Anthony *Boucher's Fergus O'Breen of Los Angeles (*The Case of the Crumpled Knave*, 1939). Two authors of this period, however, stand out above the rest: the English Nicholas *Blake and the American Rex *Stout. For his novels about the private detective Nigel Strangeways, which begin with *A Question of Proof* (1935), Blake chooses a third-person, occasionally omniscient narrator, and although he gives Strangeways, like Holmes, a number of eccentricities, he follows the contemporary trend by making him fallible and much less than superhuman. In creating Nero *Wolfe, who first appeared in *Fer-de-Lance* (1934), Stout takes the opposite path, returning to Poe and Doyle to produce another in the line of superman sleuths, and employing Archie *Goodwin, Wolfe's assistant, as a first-person narrator to continue the Holmes-Watson tradition.

Although Holmes and Poirot probably still form the popular image of the fictional detective, few other examples of this type—fewer, certainly, than in the case of the amateur or *police detective—can be placed by their side. In addition, Strangeways and Wolfe appear to mark the end of the tradition that began with Holmes. Although an occasional example can be found—P. D. *James's Cordelia *Gray (*An Un-suitable Job for a Woman*, 1972), for instance—in general the place of the private detective in fiction has been usurped by the *private eye: a process which began with the emergence of the private eye novel in America in the early 1920s. The typical private detective novel is thus a product of the classical period of detective fiction, and hence usually conforms strictly with the conventions then in force. That is, it presents a puzzle—most often the identification of a murderer among a closed group of *suspects—scrupulously makes available all the clues to which the detective has access, and challenges the reader to arrive at the solution before the detective.

[*See also* Great Detective, The; Private Eye.]

• Otto Penzler with Chris Steinbrunner and Marvin Lachman, eds., *Detectionary: A Biographical Dictionary of Leading Characters in Detective and Mystery Fiction* (1977). Jacques Barzun and Wendell Hertig Taylor, *A Catalogue of Crime*, 2nd ed. (1989). T. J. Binyon, *Murder Will Out. The Detective in Fiction* (1989).   —T. J. Binyon

PRIVATE EYE. The private eye, or private investigator (from whose initials the sobriquet derives), is the detective hero of a peculiarly American type of crime fiction that had its beginnings in the early 1920s. The gangsterism and *violence engendered by *Prohibition provided the subject, the popular *pulp magazines of the time—*Detective Story, Dime Detective*, and *Black Mask*, for example—constantly demanded new and exciting material, while the hero himself owes something to the hero—the lone individual—of the American Western. The first private eye story is generally taken to be Carroll John *Daly's "The False Burton Combs," published in *Black Mask* in 1922. Daly's hero in a long series of short stories and novels is the tough, fearless, and violent Race *Williams, who is capable of firing his two revolvers simultaneously yet making only one hole between the eyes of his *victims. There is an element of sadism in this hero's violence that, while in general foreign to the type and indeed unthinkable in most cases, was to resurface in the behavior of Mike *Hammer, Mickey *Spillane's private eye.

In 1923 Dashiell *Hammett produced the first of a number of stories about a short, tubby, forty-year-old known only as the *Continental Op, who works for the Continental Detective Agency in *San Francisco. In 1930 Hammett published *The Maltese Falcon*, believed by many to be the finest private eye novel of all, whose central character, Sam *Spade, provides an exemplar of the type. In 1939 Raymond *Chandler, who had written a number of short stories with a variety of heroes for pulp magazines, added a new dimension to the type with the creation, in *The Big Sleep*, of his private eye, Philip *Marlowe. In contrast to characters such as Spade, who have an eye for the main chance and pursue their own interests as ruthlessly as those of their client, Marlowe is a man of high moral principle, altruistic, always ready to sacrifice himself for his client, a blend of knight and father confessor, with touches of sainthood. Chandler made his intentions clear in "The Simple Art of Murder" (*Atlantic Monthly*, Dec. 1944), writing: "Down these mean streets a man must go who is not himself mean, who is neither tarnished nor afraid. . . . He must be . . . a man of honor . . . He must be the best man in his world and a good enough man for any world." This can be compared with Hammett's remark, in the introduction to a 1934 edition of *The Maltese Falcon*, that Spade is "a hard and shifty fellow, able to take care of himself in any situation, able to get the best of anybody he comes in contact with, whether criminal, innocent bystander or client."

The canonical formula had become firmly established by the 1940s: Occasionally working for an agency, sometimes with a partner, but more often alone, the private eye, who usually tells the story in the first person, is entrusted with a case that brings him into conflict with criminals or organized crime and frequently with the—usually corrupt—police; in the latter respect the narrative as a whole may often be read as an implicit or explicit commentary on American society and politics. Cynical and witty, with a keen and sometimes even poetic eye for his surroundings, he usually conceals a soft heart beneath a hard-boiled exterior. Regularly beaten up or shot at, and regularly replying in kind, he may also become sexually involved with his client or his secretary: characteristics that distinguish him from his more genteel counterpart, the English private detective.

The genre also introduced a new form, as well as a new character, into crime fiction. The detective story is closed and circular: It begins with a crime, most often murder, that is succeeded by the detective's investigation of a small group of subjects, and ends with a recapitulation of the opening crime. The private eye story, by contrast, is open and linear. The initial impetus is a client's problem; in investigating this the private eye moves from place to place, encountering a succession of new characters and uncovering a deeper intrigue. The resolution of this, rather than the original problem, provides the ending, and a murder or murders may occur at any point and are often ancillary to the main *plot. Ten years after Marlowe's first appearance, Ross *Macdonald published *The Moving Target* (1949), his first Lew *Archer novel written as John Macdonald. Though Archer shares many of Marlowe's characteristics, Macdonald's concern for the problems of the dysfunctional *family—the dominant theme in his novels—led him to give the character a psychotherapeutic bent; he becomes a surrogate father to the abandoned and lost children he encounters. Chandler's work and hero, however, were to provide the model for future authors; his influence on style and character creation has been immense, leading, at times, to almost parodic imitation, as in Robert B. *Parker's early novels about a Boston private eye, *Spenser.

Though the traditional setting—used by Hammett, Chandler, and Macdonald—for the private eye story is California, other real and fictional cities throughout the United States have been employed as the locale. Authors who have contributed to the genre include Jonathan Latimer, whose hero, Bill Crane, works in Chicago; Henry Kane, whose Peter Chambers works in *New York; William Campbell *Gault with Brock "The Rock" Callahan in *Los Angeles; Michael Z. Lewin, whose Albert Samson works in Indianapolis;

Michael Allegretto, whose Jacob Lomax works in Denver; Jonathan Valin with Harry Stoner in Cincinnati; Loren D. Estleman with Amos Walker in Detroit; Walter *Mosley's Ezekiel "Easy" *Rawlins in Los Angeles; and James Crumley, although his characters Milo Milodragovitch and C. W. Sughrue, both of Montana, are not, strictly speaking, private eyes.

The most recent development has been the emergence of the female private eye: Marcia *Muller's Sharon McCone, one-eighth Shoshone Indian, who works in San Francisco and appeared in *Edwin of the Iron Shoes* (1977), was the first, succeeded by Sue *Grafton's Kinsey *Milhone, also a Californian, Sara *Paretsky's V. I. *Warshawski of Chicago, and Linda Barnes's Boston detective, Carlotta Carlyle. To these can be added two British examples: Liza Cody's Anna Lee (*Dupe*, 1980) and Sarah Dunant's Hannah Wolfe (*Birth Marks*, 1991). Attempts to domicile the male private eye in Britain have been without success, however. While the traditional detective story, with a private or *amateur detective as its central character, now seems almost moribund, the private eye formula, by contrast, is full of life. The evidence for this lies not only in the continual emergence of new private eye novels, but also in the fact that the hallmarks of the genre—its style, its dialogue, its narrative method, and its central character—have been adapted to serve a wide variety of genres, from the *adventure story to the espionage novel.

[See also Chivalry, Code of; Hard-boiled Sleuth; Mean Streets Milieu.]

• William Ruehlmann, *Saint with a Gun: the Unlawful American Private Eye* (1974). Chris Steinbrunner and Otto Penzler, *Encyclopedia of Mystery and Detection* (1976). Brian Docherty, ed., *American Crime Fiction. Studies in the Genre* (1988). T. J. Binyon, *Murder Will Out. The Detective in Fiction* (1989).

—T. J. Binyon

PRIVATE EYE WRITERS OF AMERICA. The American author Robert J. Randisi founded Private Eye Writers of America in 1982 to promote and celebrate the achievements of writers of fiction centered around characters who are private investigators. The organization defines a *private eye as a person who is paid for investigative services but is not employed by a unit of the government. These standards apply to characters who have their own private eye agencies and include investigative news reporters and lawyers who do their own investigation.

Membership in the Private Eye Writers of America includes published American and international authors whose work falls into the private eye genre. Associate members include persons from related fields like publishing, and some fans. The organization presents Shamus awards on an annual basis for the best work in the field. With more than 300 members worldwide, Private Eye Writers of America works actively with other author groups such as *Mystery Writers of America and *Sisters in Crime to organize national and global mystery writers' conventions.

—Erica Noonan

PRODIGAL SON/DAUGHTER. It is easy to understand why the story of the prodigal's return has inspired succeeding generations of mystery writers. The arrival of a stranger in a small community often brings out into the open deep-rooted tensions. If that stranger happens to be a son or daughter who has come back to the heart of a family following a lengthy estrangement, old grudges are apt to be rekindled and long-concealed truths about ancient misdeeds may finally be brought to light. A prodigal is apt to disturb the comfortable certainties of those who stayed at home, particularly if he or she now lays unexpected and unwelcome claim to a handsome inheritance.

Elements of the Biblical tale appear in the work of many mystery writers, but few have made such effective use of it as Agatha *Christie. Harry Lee, the returning black sheep in *Hercule Poirot's Christmas* (1938; *Murder for Christmas, A Holiday for Murder*), makes repeated references to the parable. On first arriving at the family home for Christmas, he points out that in the original story, "the good brother" resented the prodigal's return and draws a direct analogy with the hostility of his own brother, Alfred. Later, explaining why he has come back after an absence of twenty years, he claims that he too had tired of the "husks that the swine do eat—or don't eat, I forget which." In *A Pocket Full of Rye* (1953), Inspector Neele is quick to characterize Lance Fortescue as the prodigal son and Lance readily accepts that description after returning home from Paris following the death of his tycoon father. Again, the stay-at-home elder brother Percival is dismayed by Lance's plan to rejoin the family business and another *murder occurs. Christie's use of the parable here is as explicit and ingenious as in the earlier novel. In contrast, in *Dead Man's Folly* (1956), her plot hinges upon the scheme of a returning prodigal, yet that is not apparent until the solution to a triple murder is revealed.

Josephine *Tey's celebrated novel of impersonation *Brat Farrar* (1949; *Come and Kill Me*) draws in a different way upon the Biblical precedent. The eponymous Brat is persuaded to masquerade as Patrick Ashby, a presumed *suicide who had disappeared eight years earlier and who would now have been about to come into his inheritance. When the family solicitor first meets Brat, he talks about the fatted calf while making it clear that this is more than just a simple matter of a prodigal's homecoming, since the ultimate destination of a fortune is at stake. Patrick's twin brother Simon also refers amiably to the parable, but his hostility toward Brat soon becomes apparent. In a final twist, it emerges that the prodigal in this case is not a son, but a nephew. The fraud in *Brat Farrar* is discussed and emulated by the conspirators in Mary Stewart's *The Ivy Tree* (1961), a novel of romantic suspense and Martha Grimes's *The Old Fox Deceiv'd* (1982) also has echoes of Tey's book, although the atmosphere is macabre and the mystery more elaborately contrived. Grimes's prodigal is a woman called Gemma Temple who claims to be Dillys March, the long-lost ward of Colonel Titus Crael.

The prodigal theme is found often in the books of writers working within the tradition of the classic *whodunit. In recent years they have included *Un-ruly Son* (1978; *Death of a Mystery Writer*) by Robert *Barnard, *Death of a God* (1987) by S. T. Haymon, Peter Robinson's *The Hanging Valley* (1989), and most notably Ruth *Rendell's *Put on by Cunning* (1981; *Death Notes*), which concerns a female prodigal whose claim to an inheritance raises questions about her true identity. Yet books with a harder edge may also derive some elements from the old story. *Blue City* (1947) by Kenneth Millar (who became better known by the pseudonym Ross *Macdonald) is an example in which an angry young man returns to his hometown and becomes involved in an attempt not only to solve the mystery of his father's murder but also to understand how his father contributed to the town's ethos of *corruption. For any writer fascinated, like Millar, by complex *family relationships, the tale of the returning prodigal provides many thought-provoking plot possibilities.

[See also Impersonation; Missing Persons.]

• Charles Osborne, *The Life and Crimes of Agatha Christie* (1982).   —Martin Edwards

PROFESSOR SLEUTH. *See* Academic Sleuth.

PROFILER. *See* Forensic Pathologist.

PROHIBITION. The Eighteenth Amendment to the United States Constitution was adopted in 1920 after a century-long campaign for reform of American drinking habits that had seen temperance associated in coalition with the anti-slavery movement, the struggle for women's rights, and other crusades to redeem the nation. The amendment expressly prohibited "the manufacture, sale, or transportation of intoxicating liquors" within the United States and its territories. Social historians differ about the effects of Prohibition, as the aim and enforcement of the law came to be termed: some say it did reduce the startling levels of alcohol consumption that had long amazed travelers to America, others aptly point out that popular displeasure with Prohibition engendered the conditions for successful criminal organization and a general disregard of law that undermined any moral improvement attributed to temperance. Literary historians, on the other hand, uniformly agree that precisely because it did foster lawlessness and criminal syndication, Prohibition bestowed a rich subject matter on detective fiction.

W. R. Burnett removed the romantic veneer from the outlaw hero in *Little Caesar* (1929) and recounted the rise and fall of Cesare "Rico" Bandello in one of Chicago's Mafia gangs, where liquor was an ordinary part of extraordinary experiences. Charles Francis Coe's *Hootch*, published in the same year, illuminated the pros and cons of Prohibition in a story of two police officers and *corruption.

In contrast to the direct treatment of the *underworld as the result of Prohibition are the novels that acknowledge Prohibition with subtlety. For instance, S. S. *Van Dine's *The Canary Murder Case* (1927) employs a nightclub *milieu where alcohol is available and refers to the criminal victim as "the toast of the town." Shortly before his death, the *victim in Ellery

*Queen's *The Roman Hat Mystery* (1929) is observed to be tipsy, smelling of booze, and eager to find a bottle of ginger ale, a common mixer. Dashiell *Hammett added glamour to violation of temperance laws in his portrayal of Nick and Nora *Charles in *The Thin Man* (1934) as jolly frequenters of speakeasies.

Detective short stories were more lurid. "Cassidy's War" by W. Wirt (*Detective Fiction Weekly*, Feb. 1929) presents corrupted police. An Erle Stanley *Gardner story in the same issue, "Just a Suspicion," tells of a gangster selling both liquor and protection services.

The "noble experiment" of Prohibition ended in 1933 with the adoption by the United States of the Twenty-First Amendment, repealing the Eighteenth; yet the brief life of Prohibition, when the power of the criminal underground dramatically surfaced in American life, remains a strongly viable context for crime literature. In five ingenious pages of Mario Puzo's *The Godfather* (1969), Vito Corleone grows from the ruthless owner of Genco Pura Oil Company into Don Corleone, head of a major crime family. George *Baxt's *New York City of 1926, portrayed in *The Dorothy Parker Murder Case* (1984) is awash in alcohol, especially for the rich and famous. Life was similarly intoxicating in Baxt's 1929 Hollywood as it is detailed in *The Talking Pictures Murder Case* (1990). Other Hollywood tales of illicit drink are those about Hollywood stuntman and private investigator Lucas Hallam in L. J. Washburn's *Dead-Stick* (1989) and *Dog Heavies* (1990). The historical adventures of undercover federal Prohibition officers receive treatment from Ed Mazzaro in his fictional accounts of the infiltration of the Al Capone mob in *One Death in the Red* (1976), *Bootleg Angel* (1977), and *Chicago Deadline* (1978).

Possibly the most comprehensive view of Prohibition and its effects on urban society is to be found in Loren Estleman's *Whiskey River* (1990), set in Detroit between 1928 and 1932. Estleman portrays a citizenry corrupted from top to bottom by the growth of illegal liquor distribution. At the other end of the spectrum of behavior are the "Iris Cooper" novels of K. K. Beck in which the proper upper classes indulge in genteel, although illegal, cocktails: *Death in a Deck Chair* (1984), *Murder in a Mummy Case* (1986), and *Peril Under the Palms* (1989).

Even as Repeal of Prohibition was imminent the grip of crime bosses on cities like Chicago remained firm. Max Allan Collins's *True Detective* (1983) employs these circumstances for a story about the assassination of Mayor A. J. Cermak, who may or may not have been the accidental victim of assassains who actually meant to kill Franklin Delano Roosevelt. FDR is also under fire from the mob in Elliot Roosevelt's *The President's Man* (1991), which presents the interesting theory that when candidate Roosevelt declared himself in favor of Repeal he became the major threat to the mob's revenues.

The visual media of film and television, as well as the publicity machine of the Federal Bureau of Investigation (*FBI) under J. Edgar Hoover, have immortalized Prohibition as a period of banditry akin to the brief glory days of the Wild West. The body of written literature on the time is comparatively smaller, but every newly published work about the influence of criminal syndicates, even those where the illegal substance is crack cocaine, owes a debt to the stalwart temperance reformers and the chronicles of bootleg criminals for creating the circumstances of a new type of fiction.

[*See also* Alcohol and Alcoholism; Underworld Figure; Urban Milieu.]

• Allen, Frederick Lewis, *Only Yesterday: An Informal History of the 1920s* (1931).   —Sue Feder

PROLIFIC WRITERS. *See* Industry Writers.

PSEUDONYMS are contrived substitutions for the names normally employed by people in everyday life. The synonym "pen name" captures the meaning perfectly: an instrument used for writing. The history of crime and mystery literature abounds in pseudonyms.

The motive for adopting a pseudonym may be commercial, as when the prolific author of fiction about Dr. Gideon Fell and other sleuths substituted Carter Dickson for John Dickson *Carr to identify his authorship of a distinct series of novels featuring Sir Henry Merrivale. *Disguise was hardly the point for Carr, just as it was not for Erle Stanley *Gardner when he wrote as A. A. Fair. A book in the series about Bertha Cool and Donald Lam was sometimes advertised by the publisher as "An A. A. Fair novel by Erle Stanley Gardner." John *Creasey may be the record holder for pseudonyms, since his industrial output required him to devise at least seventeen pen names.

Other authors have also adopted pen names to sort out their series novels when there is unlikely to have been any commercial demand for it from their publishers. Dennis Lynds, who writes non-criminal works, gained fame as Michael Collins, author of the Dan Fortune stories. Lynds, however, has also been William Arden, Mark Sadler, and John Crowe, each substitution allowing Lynds to establish authorial continuity for different series figures. The fact that Lynds has also written novels about The Shadow as Maxwell Grant and about Nick *Carter as, of course, Nick Carter reflects another purpose of pseudonyms related to publishing practices. Immensely popular long-running characters require many more writers than one over their life span, so publishers use writers for hire under "house names." The champion in this category must be Frederic Merrill Van Rensselaer Dey, who claimed to have written 1,000 Nick Carters. J. Randolph Cox says it was only 437, although it probably seemed like many more.

Sometimes a pseudonym is a means of disguise. Carolyn Gold Heilbrun became Amanda *Cross for her stories about the accidental detective Kate *Fansler in order to protect herself from possible charges by other academics that she was not a serious writer. Disguise can extend to questions of *gender, as with the famous Anthony Gilbert who was Lucy Beatrice Malleson away from her writing desk.

Take away the wish for concealment and plenty of reasons for using pseudonyms remain. J. I. M. Stewart, a noted literary historian, signed Michael *Innes to his detective works. Cecil Day-Lewis, the poet, became Nicholas Blake the detective author. Both cases indicate a wish to pursue distinct careers without the chance of confusion. This was also probably why the historical and satiric novelist Gore Vidal chose to be Edgar Box when he wrote three detective novels. Fulton Oursler, known for inspirational works, naturally enough needed a pseudonym when he wrote mysteries, but he showed special *ingenuity, or so it is reported, when he decided to be Anthony Abbot so that his books would be at the top of alphabetical listings.

Given the literary bent of the authors of detective fiction, it is not surprising to find subtle cross-references present in their use of pseudonyms. Robert Bruce Montgomery took the name Edmund *Crispin from a character created by J. I. M. Stewart when he was Michael *Innes. Doris Bell Collier Ball took for her detective writing the feminized version of Arthur Conan *Doyle's model for Sherlock *Holmes and became Josephine Bell.

The wish for simplification has led some authors to create substitute signatures out of their given names. Anthony Berkely left off the family name Cox when he wrote detective fiction. Ernest Bramah Smith chose to write as Ernest Bramah. On the other hand collaborations also create special variations on given names. Emma *Lathen, who is also R. B. Dominic, in real life is the writing partnership Mary J. Latis and Martha Henissart. The twin brothers Peter Shaffer and Anthony Shaffer write together as Peter Anthony. Kenneth Millar also had a family reason for using a pseudonym. His wife Margaret *Millar had already achieved note as a writer, so he became Ross *Macdonald.

The motives for adopting pseudonyms are many, but their prevalence among authors of detective fiction says as much about the repute of the genre as it does about its practitioners. Herman Melville did not alter the name on his title pages when he undertook different literary forms, nor did Charles *Dickens, because they were determined to make their (real) names as writers of the consensually approved kinds of literature. Writers of popular detective fiction, however, contend with the knowledge that their work maybe be classed in the second tier of literature because it is believed to be less profound. Fame and repute may therefore be fleeting. As a result the proprietary sense is less, the author more detached from his or her product and more likely, then, to entertain one of the many reasons for using a pseudonym.

[See also Allusion, Literary.]   —John M. Reilly

PSYCHIC SLEUTH. With the rise of modern Spiritualism after 1848, a new breed of *sleuths appeared in public life. They were not *police detectives empowered to uphold civil law and order; but scientists, philosophers, and professional magicians dedicated to proving or disproving psychic phenomena and the activities of mediums and occultists of the day. Moreover, these figures—as diverse as Sir William Crookes, William James, and Harry Houdini—became the models for a detective unique in literature, the psychic sleuth. Like the classical ratiocinators,

the psychic sleuths sought to separate fraud from fact and employed the traditional methods of observation and deduction; unlike them, they possessed special psi powers and a knowledge of occult practices. They embodied a new spirit of inquiry and speculation, functioning by turns as detectives, physicians, scientists, inventors, healers, and priests.

Although major novelists like Nathaniel Hawthorne, William Dean Howells, George Eliot, Edward Bulwer-Lytton, and Henry James had occasionally tackled occult subjects in their works, it was left to minor masters in the field to create the first full-fledged psychic sleuths. The prototype was Joseph Sheridan Le Fanu's Martin Hesselius, a self-styled "medical philosopher" who first appeared in 1864 in a classic ghost story, "Green Tea" (All the Year Round, 23 Oct. 1869). "I believe that the essential man is a spirit," Hesselius declared, "that the spirit is an organized substance, but as different in point of material from what we ordinarily understand by matter, as light or electricity is." Le Fanu may have molded him after two famous German ghost-hunters of the day, Justinius Kerner and Heinrich Jung-Stilling.

Subsequent works by other authors extend and develop Hesselius's example, including Algernon Blackwood's five John Silence stories, beginning in 1903; William Hope Hodgson's eight Carnacki the Ghost Finder tales, collected in 1913; Dion Fortune's eleven Dr. Taverner stories in The Secrets of Dr. Taverner (1926); Seabury Quinn's ninety-three Jules de Grandin stories, which began appearing in the *pulp magazine Weird Tales in 1925; Sax *Rohmer's Dream Detective stories (1920); Jack Mann's Gregory George Gordon "Gees" Green novels, including Gee's First Case (1936), Grey Shapes (1937), and The Glass Too Many (1940); Manley Wade Wellman's Silver John stories, collected in Who Fears the Devil? (1963); Randall Garrett's Lord Darcy stories, a science fantasy series collected in Too Many Magicians (1967); and Joseph Payne Brennan's twenty-five Lucius Leffing tales, collected in The Casebook of Lucius Leffing (1973), The Chronicles of Lucius Leffing (1977), and in The Adventures of Lucius Leffing (1990).

These unusual detectives demonstrate affinities with their more traditional brethren. Some, like Leffing and Carnacki, have no special psychic gifts of their own but employ, respectively, the dogged investigative methods characteristic of Ellery *Queen and a scientific technology like that used by Craig Kennedy. Among those sleuths with psychic gifts, the Dream Detective's aesthetic musings prefigure Philo *Vance's talky connoisseurship; Jules De Grandin's eccentric French mannerisms recall Hercule *Poirot's idiosyncrasies; Lord Darcy's bizarre cases are reminiscent of Gideon *Fell's more exotic investigations; and Silver John's backwoods milieu belongs to the world of Uncle *Abner.

Silver John also reminds us of another classic investigator, Father *Brown, in that his central concern is not the apprehension of a wrongdoer but the saving of a soul. This is no mere cops-and-robbers formula, but a cosmic struggle against hostile forces. In Le Fanu's words, "There does exist beyond this a spiritual world—a system whose workings are generally in mercy hidden from us—a system which may be, and which sometimes is, partially and terrible revealed. I am sure—I *know* . . . that there is a God—a dreadful God—and that retribution follows guilt, in ways the most mysterious and stupendous—by agencies the most inexplicable and terrific."

[*See also* Occult and Supernatural Literature.]

• Howard Kerr, *Mediums and Spirit-Rappers and Roaring Radicals: Spiritualism in American Literature, 1850–1900* (1972). Ronald Pearsall, *The Table-Rappers* (1972). Peter Haining, *Ghosts: An Illustrated History* (1975). Roy Stemman, *Spirits and Spirit Worlds* (1976). Ruth Brandon, *The Spiritualists: The Passion for the Occult in the Nineteenth and Twentieth Centuries* (1983). John C. Tibbets, "Phantom Fighters: 150 years of Occult Detection," *Armchair Detective* 29, no. 3 (Summer 1996): 340–45.   —John C. Tibbetts

PUBLISHING, HISTORY OF BOOK. The forms of popular genres, as much as their fortunes, have been determined by marketing decisions made by publishers. *The Moonstone* by Wilkie Collins began its effective life in 1868 as a serial publication in Charles Dickens's magazine *All the Year Round*. Before the year ended the complete novel was issued by the publisher, Tinsley, in a three-volume format containing the entire 900 pages. If readers today think *The Moonstone* unusually long for a mystery and wonder why writers back then were so prolix, the answer lies not entirely with Collins who, like any other author wrote with the expectation of having an audience, but with the preference of mid-century publishers for prose fiction in hefty triple-decker form.

The practice had been set by Archibald Constable, the publisher who in 1814 introduced Walter Scott to the public with the novel *Waverly* bound in inexpensive covers so as to attract a mass audience. While Constable set the standard three-volume form at for fiction, other publishers, such as Chapman and Hall who produced Charles Dickens's *The Pickwick Papers* (1836–37; *The Posthumous Papers of the Pickwick Club*), added to the business the techniques of advertising and intense distribution that characterize the modern book market. These techniques included the teasing use of serial publication before the appearance of bound books.

All this created a seemingly insatiable popular desire and was responsible for the acclaim and interest that greeted *The Newgate Calendar*, which had begun as a record of crime in 1773 but attained immense readership when it was issued in the years between 1824 and 1828 in four volumes, bound in a format of three. A considerable part of the audience for tales of crime and mystery obtained its reading matter through circulating libraries that offered books on loan for a fee. Because these libraries constituted a sure outlet for publishers, their preferences as to form and subject greatly affected publishing. The influence increased as entrepreneurs, such as Charles Edward Madie, bought up independent circulating libraries and linked them into a chain of distribution. According to John Feather in *A History of British Publishing* (1988), by 1875 Madie owned 125 branches throughout Great Britain and was capable of ordering new books from publishers in lots of

2,500. That Madie preferred the triple-decker format simply reinforced established publishing practice.

Again according to Feather, that changed with the growth of public libraries. For their own practical reasons, public librarians wanted to handle prose fiction in single volumes. In the face of the competition, the commercial circulating libraries also began to stock fiction complete in one volume when they could get it. Soon publishers adjusted to the change in public reading habits, and by 1897 the triple decker was gone and with it the leisurely paced experience of reading about crime and other topics of adventure in stories of multiplying *plots and expansive detail.

During this same period magazines associated with publishing houses by name and sometimes ownership sustained the publication of crime and mystery in short story form; thus, *Lippincott's Magazine* was responsible for issuing the early Sherlock *Holmes stories from an American press. Earlier, *Harper's New Monthly* had been the American outlet for the serial issue of Wilkie Collins. Yet another American magazine associated with a publishing house, *Scribner's Monthly*, shared responsibility for fostering the interest of an American audience in detective fiction by giving over some of its pages to stories by Julian Hawthorne, author of a series of romances fictionalizing the career of Inspector Thomas Byrnes, head of the *New York City Detectives from 1880 to 1894.

The years between the world wars, typically characterized in histories of popular literature as a period of consolidation of the detective and mystery genre into the elaborated formulas of the Golden Age, were also a time when publishing practices had a determining influence on the genre. National chains of circulating or lending libraries continued to be steady customers for large press runs of first issues of new novels. Public libraries directing their services to a nearly universally literate population, which included vast numbers of reading women toward whom authors of newer detective fiction had reason to appeal, were given new incentive to stock the popular genre. Meanwhile, Victor Gollancz, Stanley Unwin, and Allen Lane in Great Britain made special and innovative efforts to promote the best-selling authors. Agatha *Christie, whose career as a novelist began in 1920 with *The Mysterious Affair at Styles* was published by Lane. *Whose Body?* plus *Clouds of Witness*, the first two detective novels by Dorothy L. *Sayers, appeared under Unwin's imprint in 1923 and 1926, respectively. And Gollancz, who published the British editions of Ellery *Queen among other authors, adopted the use of uniformly colored book covers to signify a running series of fiction. In the United States Simon and Schuster, the first American publisher of Queen, and Scribner, the imprint of S. S. Van *Dine, played an important part in building the audience for the ratiocinative puzzles of Golden Age writing, just as Alfred A. Knopf did for hard-boiled writing when he boldly took the subgenre that originated in *pulp magazines and featured such masters as Dashiell *Hammett and Raymond *Chandler in hard cover.

As the audience grew, the market for detective fiction became too appealing for any single publisher to remain dominant. Soon competitors, for example, Collins in England and Doubleday in the United States, found that they, too, could profit by carrying the genre on their lists, particularly since they could tap prolific writers to market series detective stories, which became the latter-day equivalent of the serialized stories of the nineteenth century. Where readers had previously the pleasure of following the spinnings of a single plot, they now could enjoy becoming acquainted with a detective they followed through a cumulative compilation of fast-paced novels, a new adventure each time.

The example of novels published on the European continent in soft paper covers inspired the next revolution in English-language publishing. Allen Lane conceived the idea of printing uniform, small format books for distribution in chain stores such as Woolworth's and anywhere else books could be stocked in addition to the stores of established booksellers. The result was Penguin Books, which included Sayers among the authors of its first ten publications. In the United States Robert de Graaf quickly followed suit with Pocketbooks, which counted Erle Stanley *Gardner among its lead authors. Both Penguin and Pocketbooks produced their lists by purchasing the rights to their inexpensive editions from other publishers. Later companies served as the paperback outlets for single houses: Bantam, for example, initially carried only publications owned by Grosset and Dunlap and the Curtis Publishing Company. The more recent development, the "quality" paperback often consists of the pages printed for the hardback edition bound in soft covers.

The ubiquity of paperbacks greatly increased the audience for detective and mystery fiction simply by the principle of availability. During World War II that principle was extended for American readers by the publisher-sponsored organization Council on Books in Wartime. Charles A. Madison reported in *Book Publishing in America* (1966) that from an initial run of 50,000 copies for thirty-two titles, the council increased its production to runs of 150,000 for forty books a month. Eventually the council had issued 1,324 titles amounting in total to more than 123 million books, many detective stories among them; many new readers were won for the genre by this wartime publishing enterprise.

Many of those readers continued the habit of reading crime and mystery fiction by purchasing paperback original volumes. These were books that went directly from author to paperback publication, often for a set fee rather than royalties. Publishers estimated the demographics of the audience for paperback originals as predominantly male and eager more for tales of action than for intellectual *puzzles of detection. As a result, this niche of the book market, furnished with publications from Fawcett, Lion, Popular Library, Berkley, Bantam, and Pocketbooks, featured repeated variations on hard boiled fiction, as well as revivals of such older heroes as Nick *Carter.

Mystery Book Clubs have been similarly important for the distribution of detective and mystery fiction to the mass audience. The Detective Book Club, which specializes in a version of the triple decker by including three different novels in a single volume, has issued more than 500 titles since it began marketing to subscribers by mail in 1942. The Mystery Guild, which began in 1949, sends its subscribers single-title volumes twice a month. The distinguished historian and critic Howard Haycraft edited for the guild for many years.

A critical study of crime and mystery writing reveals that writers are endlessly inventive in the innovations they work upon the developed conventions of the genre. Taking into account the history of book publishing, however, it is clear that the possibilities available to book publishers for formatting and distributing their product time and again have influenced changes in narrative construction while broadening the audience. In a literary as much as a financial sense the actions of each are reciprocally enriching.

[*See also* Industry Writers; Serialization and Serial Publication.]

• Charles A. Madison, *Book Publishing in America* (1966). Victor E. Neuberg, *Popular Literature: A History and Guide from the Beginning of Printing to the Year 1897* (1977). Michael L. Cook, *Inside the Mystery Book Clubs*, rev. ed. (1983). John Feather, *A History of British Book Publishing* (1991).
                                              —John M. Reilly

PUBLISHING, HISTORY OF AMERICAN MAGAZINES. Ever since Edgar Allan Poe wrote "The Murders in the Rue Morgue" for the April 1841 issue of *Graham's Lady's and Gentleman's Magazine*, which he was editing at the time, crime and mystery fiction has been an important component of magazines. Detective fiction over the past century and a half has followed two distinct paths in magazines, appearing in both slick paper mass circulation family periodicals as well as in less respectable pulpwood publications.

The magazine in America began to flourish in the middle decades of the nineteenth century. The spread and growth was encouraged by the population's increasing literacy from the 1840s onward, improved methods of printing and distribution, favorable postal rates, and the growth of the newsstand. There is a common misconception that mystery stories were scorned by mainstream American magazines and relegated to the allegedly lowbrow pulp magazines. In reality, however, the slicks were almost all enthusiastic supporters of detective fiction and an enormous quantity of such material was published in them especially in the first half of the twentieth century.

Sherlock *Holmes, for example, was introduced to America when the slick paper *Lippincott's Monthly* published Arthur Conan *Doyle's *The Sign of the Four* in its February 1890 issue. The Great Detective's magazine career languished in the United States for more than a decade until *Collier's* brought him back to the newsstands in 1903, when it began running the stories that make up *The Return of Sherlock Holmes* (1905). These featured the memorable illustrations of Frederic Dorr Steele. The magazine followed the Holmes stories with a series about A. J. *Raffles the Amateur Cracksman written by E. W.

*Hornung, Doyle's brother-in-law. *Colliers* touted the event with the headline "Exit—Sherlock Holmes, Enter—'Raffles'."

Colliers, a nickel weekly offering a blend of fiction and nonfiction, began in 1888 and continued until 1957. In addition to Holmes and Raffles stories, the slick paper magazine presented a great deal of other mystery and detective fiction in its pages over the years. Edgar *Wallace was a regular contributor, as were Earl Derr *Biggers, E. Phillips *Oppenheim, Louis Joseph Vance, Mignon G. *Eberhart, Agatha *Christie, and Margery *Allingham. A long time contributor was Sax *Rohmer, whose serials about the insidious Dr. *Fu Manchu were a popular staple of *Collier's*. The magazine also made use of the works of such pulp graduates as Frederick Nebel, George F. Worts, and Dashiell *Hammett.

The chief rival of *Colliers* was the *Saturday Evening Post*. Detective fiction made up an important part of the *Post*'s lineup, too. The detectives found in the weekly included the Thinking Machine, Father *Brown, Randolph Mason, Charlie *Chan, Mr. I. O. *Moto, Nero *Wolfe, and Perry *Mason. By the 1920s both magazines were selling more than 2,000,000 copies a week. These figures climbed in the 1930s, despite the Great *Depression. The *Post* ended the decade with average sales of 3,000,000 each week and its rival tailed with 2,500,000. This guaranteed mystery fiction its largest audience anywhere.

The 1890s saw the rise of ten cent all-round monthly magazines, chief among them *McClure's*, *Cosmopolitan*, *Munsey's Magazine Hampton's Magazine*, and *Everybody's Magazine*. All of them used detective stories. In the early decades of the twentieth century, for instance, *McClure's* ran works by Mary Roberts *Rinehart, Robert Barr, and Harvey J. O'Higgins. The magazine also printed the adventures of G. K. *Chesterton's Father Brown and R. Austin *Freeman's Dr. John *Thorndyke.

On the cheap jack side an enormous amount of crime and mystery fiction was fed to the nineteenth-century public by way of the story papers. Looking more like newspapers than magazines in some cases, they began in the 1830s and lasted throughout the century, often with circulations in the hundreds of thousands. Among the numerous titles were the *Philadelphia Saturday Courier*, *Uncle Sam*, *New York Weekly*, *The Yankee*, and *The Flag of Our Union*. The fiction dealt with romance, *murder and, most important of all, sensation. Poe's tales appeared in the weeklies; Louisa May Alcott cranked out sensational stories for them under pen names; G. W. M. Reynolds's seemingly endless serial, *Mysteries of London*, was pirated by one of them. Detectives proliferated in the story papers in the 1880s and 1890s. Those years saw the advent of such publications as the *Old Sleuth Library*, *Secret Service*, *Old Cap. Collier Library*, and the *Nick Carter Weekly*. Carter, who made his debut in Street & Smith's *New York Weekly* in 1886, proved especially popular and was rewarded with publications of his own. He has remained, although undergoing many changes, a viable character until the present time.

The *pulp magazines, which eventually supplanted the fiction weeklies and *dime novels, owe their existence to publisher Frank A. Munsey. He introduced the *Golden Argosy* in 1882, initially an eight-page small-folio format weekly aimed at boys and girls. By the end of the century Munsey had shortened the title to *Argosy* and turned it into a fat all-fiction magazine printed on cheap pulpwood paper and appealing to a more grown-up audience. The circulation began to climb and in the early 1900s *Argosy* was selling 500,000 copies of each issue. It survived as a fiction magazine until the 1940s. The Munsey pulp frequently made room for detective stories in its mix of male-oriented adventure yarns. In addition to short stories, a great many novels ran as serials in the weekly pulp, especially in the 1920s and 1930s. The majority of these novels were never reprinted in any form. Among *Argosy*'s many mystery writers were Fred MacIsaac, one of the most prolific producers of serials, George F. Worts, Eustace L. Adams, Norbert Davis, and Erle Stanley *Gardner.

Other publishers followed Munsey's lead and pulps began to burgeon as the new century commenced. Street & Smith's *Popular Magazine* began in 1903, ended in 1931 and was a biweekly akin to *Argosy* in look and content. There was at least one mystery story in each issue and a goodly number of the complete novels were of the detective type. Other general fiction pulps that included detective stories were *Blue Book Magazine Adventure and Short Stories*.

Finally, in 1915, Street & Smith introduced the first pulp devoted exclusively to detective stories. Christened with the obvious title of *Detective Story Magazine*, this magazine, while undergoing various format and attitude changes, survived until 1949. A second series, *Black Mask*, followed from November 1952 and in September 1953 *Detective Fiction Weekly* was launched. These were followed by *Clues*, *Detective Tales*, *Dime Detective* and hundreds more, magazines offering every sort of detective from cerebral sleuth to hard-boiled dick.

The 1940s was a decade of digests. In the fall of 1941 *Ellery Queen's Mystery Magazine* was launched. Initially consisting primarily of reprints of stories by such writers as Hammett, Cornell *Woolrich, Freeman, Dorothy L. *Sayers, and Queen, it was published in the format made popular by *Reader's Digest*. The eventual success of *EQMM*, and the paper shortage engendered by World War II, prompted other publishers to think small. Street & Smith shrank its venerable *Detective Story* to digest size in 1943, along with *The Shadow* and *Doc Savage*. *Rex Stout Mystery Monthly*, *Craig Rice Mystery Digest*, and *The Saint's Choice* all began short-lived runs in 1945.

The following decade, during which pulp magazines departed, saw the coming of numerous new detective digests. The most successful was *Manhunt*, introduced in 1953 and featuring authors like Ross *Macdonald, Mickey *Spillane, Evan Hunter, David Goodis, Frank Kane, and Richard S. Prather. Numerous similar magazines followed, including *Verdict*, *Guilty*, *Trapped*, *Private Eye*, and *Offbeat Detective Stories*. Also brought forth in the 1950s were *Mike Shayne Mystery Magazine*, *Alfred Hitchcock's Mystery Magazine*, and *Saint Mystery Magazine*. More digests appeared in the 1960s, but then the expansion stopped. Today only a few titles remain on the newsstands. Since the major slicks are long gone as well, the amount of mystery and detective fiction to be found in magazines is lower today than ever before.

[See also Adventure Story; Industry Writers.]

• Frank Luther Mott, A History of American Magazines: 1865–1885 (1938). Howard Haycraft, Murder for Pleasure (1941). Mary Noel, Villains Galore (1954). Ron Goulart, Cheap Thrills (1972). Michael L. Cook, Mystery, Detective and Espionage Magazines (1983).   —Ron Goulart

PUBLISHING MILIEU. The publishing milieu has long been a rich environment in which to set crime and mystery fiction. It offers a variety of settings including book publishing and magazine publishing offices, the newsroom, and author conventions. Crimes specific to the milieu include plagiarism, manuscript theft, and financial misdeeds. Related issues like professional jealousy and the despair of scholars facing the pressure to "publish or perish" can provide motives for these crimes or more violent acts including *murder. The *milieu is also attractive to writers who have a flair for creating colorful, lively, and eccentric characters associated with literary creativity. Such characters may be contrasted with powerful editors and opinionated critics who have the ability to make or break literary careers. In addition, the milieu allows for the exploration of themes as varied as the banality of popular fiction and the folly of literary pretension.

Outstanding examples of novels set in the book publishing milieu are Nicholas *Blake's End of Chapter (1957), Margery *Allingham's Flowers for the Judge (1936; Legacy in Blood) and P. D. *James's Original Sin (1995). The first is set in a *London publishing house where the murderer is depicted as a tragic figure torn between strong moral principles and a desire for revenge. In Flowers for the Judge, Albert *Campion investigates the murder of a publisher found dead in his own strongroom. A similar murder is the focus of Original Sin, in which Commander Adam *Dalgliesh investigates the chairman of Peverell Press, a venerable London publishing firm. By means of focusing on family-run firms threatened with bankruptcy, the authors establish a parallel between high editorial standards and traditional social mores, linking deterioration of publishing ethics to the decay of *family and social values, resulting in betrayal, ruthlessness, *corruption, *greed, and finally, murder.

The business and politics of publishing is explored in Barbara Wilson's Murder in the Collective (1984) in which the protagonist, Pam Neilsen, is part-owner of a left-wing printing press. Wilson brings her experience as co-owner of Seal Press to this tale of murder during merger discussions between Neilson's press, for which men and women work, and a lesbian-run print collective that excludes men.

Novels focusing on the newsroom may look more at the activities of reporters on the beat than at the publishing dimension of the world of journailsm. But Lucille Kallen's series about C. B. Greenfield, the urbane publisher of Sloan's Ford Reporter and his part-time reporter, Maggie Rome, is rooted in detailed knowledge of the stresses of publishing a local newspaper filled with all-too-familiar local fare and the occasional revelation of graft, skulduggery, and incompetence.

Interesting for its eye-opening view into the lesser-known comic book publishing world is Max Allan Collins's Fly Paper (1981). Collins, who has written the Dick Tracy, Mike Mist, and Ms. Tree comic strips since the late 1970s draws on his insider's knowledge of that industry in this novel partly set during a comic books convention.

The publishing milieu has also attracted cutting edge approaches to the writing of detecive fiction. Anna Clarke, known for her incursions into metafiction, places her interest in the processes of mystery writing and publication at the center of her *plots. In her Plot Counter-Plot (1974) an established *suspense novelist engages in a love affair with an unsuccessful author about whom she is writing, and seems to fall into the plot of her own novel when her lover decides to steal her own manuscript and pass it off as his own. Clarke also looks at the the links between the academic and publishing worlds in Last Judgement (1985), in which two English professors battle to gain the sole rights to the literary property of a great novelist.

The publishing milieu has also been popular with authors with a parodic bent. Helen McCloy spoofs publishing practices and the literati in Two-Thirds of a Ghost (1956), a novel in which she also comments on the absence of plot in some modern fiction. Pamela Branch parodies the world of seedy magazine publishing in Murder's Little Lister (1958), in which the failed suicide attempt of an advice columnist is exploited by her failing magazine to boost circulation. Branch's broad satire draws humor our of the second-guessing, treachery, and ego-boosting banality of the magazine's staff, and from the various deaths and misadventures that result from the columnist's advice to readers. Robert *Barnard satirizes the writing life in Unruly Son (1978; Death of a Mystery Writer), Posthumous Papers (1979; Death of a Literary Widow), and Death in Purple Prose (1987; The Cherry Blossom Corpse). The last of these has detective Perry Trethowan attending a hilariously depicted convention of the World Association of Romantic Novelists (WARN). Likewise, Collins, in Kill Your Darlings (1984), satirizes the annual world mystery convention known as the Bouchercon. The existence of numerous parodies featuring the publishing milieu attests to the familiarity and importance of the setting throughout the development of mystery and detective fiction.

[See also Allusion, Literary; Journalist Sleuth.]
            —Lizabeth Paravisini-Gebert

PULP MAGAZINES, or pulps, derived their name from the cheap pulpwood paper they were printed on and, a dime or fifteen cents a copy, the pulps offered just about every category of popular fiction.

Sold at newsstands, cigar stores, and drug emporiums, there were pulp magazines love, aviation, the Wild West, *science fiction, and every conceivable kind of adventure.

The pulps flourished in the United States during the first half of this century, particularly in the decades between the two world wars. The first pulp magazine devoted exclusively to detective fiction appeared in 1915, and by the 1930s there were scores of mystery and detective titles on the stands. The hard-boiled *private eye was introduced in the rough, untrimmed pages of the pulps and such writers as Dashiell *Hammett, Raymond *Chandler, Erle Stanley *Gardner, and John D. *MacDonald did their earliest work in the mystery genre for the pulps.

Frank A. Munsey, a former telegraph operator from Maine, arrived in New York City in 1892. It was his ambition to publish a cheap fiction weekly of inspirational children's stories and call it *The Golden Argosy*. He was able to launch his magazine by the end of the year. While it did not thrive initially, Munsey hung on and kept modifying his faltering publication. He trimmed the title to *Argosy* and aimed it at older readers. In the 1890s he decided he could save even more money by using cheaper paper. The resulting magazine was a thick collection of popular fiction printed on pulpwood paper. Even though there was not a single illustration, the public took to the new format and its cheap price and the pulp magazine was born. Circulation climbed to eighty thousand an issue, and by the early 1900s *Argosy* was selling half a million copies a month. During World War I it became a weekly again and was offering fiction in all the popular categories, including the detective genre.

Street & Smith, a longtime publisher of fiction weeklies and *dime novels, followed Munsey into the pulps. They started *Popular Magazine* in 1903 and then *Top-Notch Magazine*, another all-category fiction magazine, in 1910. Five years later they introduced the first pulp featuring only detective fiction. The premiere issue of *Detective Story* carried the date 5 October 1915, on its bright red cover and sold for ten cents. It included an installment of a serial about the popular Nick *Carter and, for good measure, listed the master *sleuth as editor. A variety of mystery fiction appeared in the magazine in its early years. The *private detective stories of this period were set mostly in the past, in a gaslit Victorian world wherein detectives and villains alike were masters of *disguise and their methods and *motive had little to do with real life.

Black Mask, a pulp magazine that first appeared in 1920, changed the image of the private investigator. Initially this detective magazine was similar in content to its comparatively sedate competitor. Gradually, however, the outside world of the twenties began to intrude. Stories began to reflect the effects of *Prohibition, to talk of gangsters, hip flasks, and bootleg gin. In 1923 Carroll John Daly, a onetime movie theater manager and projectionist, introduced a character called Race Williams in *Black Mask*. Crude and raw, unintentionally funny in his tough talk, Williams was, nevertheless, the rough model for all the *hard-boiled sleuths that followed. "When you're hunting the top guy, you have to kick aside—or shoot aside—the gunmen he hires" is a typical Williams remark. Williams, who soon became the magazine's most popular character, once explained, "You can't make hamburger without grinding up a little meat."

Fortunately, writers more gifted than Daly began selling private detective stories to *Black Mask*. Chief among them was Hammett, a former Pinkerton investigator. In the early 1920s he created his tough, hefty operative for the Continental Detective Agency. The *Continental Op worked out of San Francisco, and his first-person adventures were narrated in a terse and believable vernacular style. At the end of the decade Hammett introduced Sam *Spade in *The Maltese Falcon*. (1930), serialized in *Black Mask*.

Several other hard-boiled writers graced the magazine's pages in the twenties and thirties, among them Gardner, Raoul Whitfield, Horace McCoy, Frederick Nebel, Norbert Davis, W. T. Ballard and Chandler. This was the period when *Black Mask*'s most influential editor, Joseph T. "Cap" Shaw, held the job. The publication survived until the early 1950s, specializing in series yarns about various private eyes and cops.

Black Mask's chief competitor was *Dime Detective*, launched in 1931 by Popular Publications. Publisher Henry Steeger was able to lure, by offering higher pay rates per word, several of *Black Mask*'s star authors to write for his magazine. He persuaded Nebel to do a long and impressive series about a tough operative named Cardigan. Gardner, Chandler, and Ballard also wrote for *Dime Detective*. Steeger even persuaded Daly to write Williams stories for his magazine. *Dime Detective* flourished during the Depression years, adding such writers as Norbert Davis, John K. Butler, and Fred MacIsaac. MacDonald was a frequent contributor in the years after World War II. By that time Steeger had long since bought out *Black Mask* and was publishing that, too.

All in all, more than two hundred different detective pulp titles appeared from the twenties to the fifties. These included *Detective Fiction Weekly*, *Detective Tales*, *Clues*, *Spicy Detective* (which introduced Dan Turner, Hollywood Detective), *Thrilling Detective*, *The Phantom Detective*, *Mystery*, *The Shadow*, *Private Detective Stories*, *Ten Detective Aces*, *Crime Busters*, and *Double Detective*.

Though the traditional British-style detective tale, with formal *clues, timetables, and pipe-smoking inspector, was now and then to be found in some of the detective pulps, it was the tough cops and the hard-boiled dicks who predominated. By the middle 1950s, unable to meet the competition of television or satisfy changing tastes, the pulps faded away and joined dime novels and other no longer fashionable formats.

[*See also* Adventure Story: Industry Writers, Juvenile Mystery: Boys' Juvenile Mystery; Publishing, History of Magazine: American Magazines; Western, The.].

• Robert Sampson, *Yesterday's Faces: A Study of Series Characters in the Early Pulp Magazines*, vol. 4 (1987). Michael L. Cook and Stephen T. Miller, *Mystery, Detective and Espionage Fiction: A Checklist of Fiction in U.S. Pulp Magazines, 1915–1974*, vol. 1 (1988). Ron Goulart, *The Dime Detectives* (1988).

—Ron Goulart.

PURSUIT. At base, all detective novels are pursuit narratives, being the pursuit of truth or knowledge. Most writers intellectualize the pursuit, as does Edgar Allan *Poe in his formative detective story, "The Purloined Letter" (*The Gift* 1845), where the identity of the criminal is known from the beginning, and the excitement and drama come from the detective, the Chevalier C. Auguste *Dupin, pitting his wits against those of the criminals. Just as the hunter identifies with the quarry, so, writes Poe in an earlier Dupin story, "The Murders in the Rue Morgue" (*Graham's Lady's and Gentleman's Magazine*, Apr. 1841) "the analyst throws himself into the spirit of his opponent, identifies himself therewith, and not unfrequently sees thus, at a glance, the sole methods (sometimes indeed absurdly simple ones) by which he may seduce into error or hurry into miscalculation."

Some of the most effective detective pursuit narratives direct the *plot into a questioning of social values; thus, in Dashiell *Hammett's *Red Harvest* (1929), the *Continental Op who pursues *corruption in the town of "Poisonville" is himself sucked into *violence and immorality, and the ending of the novel mocks rather than reinforces the restored social order. In this respect, Hammett's work suggests that the hard-boiled school's use of pursuit in narrative plot assumes the force of a presiding metaphor that stands for the perilous ethical condition of the individual in modern society. In contrast, while the ratiocinative pursuits of criminal solutions by Golden Age detectives such as Lord Peter *Wimsey, Hercule *Poirot, or Inspector/Superintendent Roderick Alleyn may involve incidental peril, the necessity of pursuit—hunting or, in turn, being hunted—appears as a temporary endeavor undertaken to reform the motionless society that is the conservative norm and ideal of the Golden Age. In this scenario, pursuit is the metaphor of a singular adventure.

Pursuit may also become the substance of detective narrative, its literal physical action forming the plot. Many of the novels by Dick *Francis display such use of pursuit for effect, as do many *police procedurals. In yet other instances of crime and adventure fiction, the use of pursuit as the basis for plot and narrative echoes the nineteenth century forest romances of James Fenimore Cooper, which Dorothy L. *Sayers maintained were the ancestors of modern detective stories. For example, there is Geoffrey Household's *Rogue Male* (1939; *Manhunt*). The English gentleman who conducts a "sporting" stalk of Adolph Hitler in this novel is caught just before readers find out whether or not he pulls the trigger. He escapes and is again hunted down before managing to destroy his pursuers. The novel ends with the gentleman setting off once more in pursuit of Hitler, leaving unanswered the question of whether the moral

justification for the hunt is actually an an excuse for an instinctive desire to kill.

In both *Rogue Male* and John *Buchan's *The Thirty-Nine Steps* (1915), another classic of pursuit, the narrative drive is maintained through constant shifts between pursuit and escape. The question of who is actually hunting whom at any particular point adds to the complexity and tension of the plot: in Buchan's novel, Richard Hannay is being wrongfully pursued by the police for murder, and is himself pursuing the real murderers, who in a further twist are pursuing Hannay. Alfred Hitchcock's film of the novel (1935) develops this triple structure quite beautifully—indeed, the film uses pursuit widely as both plot device and, as in John Ford's *The Searchers* (1956), part of the basic structure.

Ultimately the compulsive draw of pursuit in narrative, what locks readers into these modern tales of the hunt is psychological. Sometimes there may be little difference between hunter and hunted, but always the plot of pursuit simulates the minds of protagonists or villains in the face of challenge. The stress may yield satisfaction, as when the detective concludes a case successfully, or the account of pursuit may confirm the belief that there are no complete heroes, as in hard-boiled stories, yet in reaching either extreme, or finishing somewhere in between, narratives of pursuit embody the truth that the thrill of life lies in quest.

[*See also* Adventure Story; Suspense.]

—Nigel Rigby

PUZZLE. A puzzle novel or short story emphasizes the mystery and its solution, which is usually given at the climax of the story and often involves a challenge to the reader to unravel the mystery before the *sleuth has announced his or her solution. *Characterization and *setting, although significant, are of less importance than solving the puzzle. The emphasis on explaining a series of mysterious events developed in many *Gothic novels between the 1790s and the 1830s, especially those by Ann Radcliffe and William Child Green, who provided material solutions to ghostly doings. The Gothic novel, however, explained the events without investigation or detection. Nineteenth-century stories featuring detectives, on the other hand, tended to include few puzzles. Fictionalized police reminiscences, beginning in the 1850s with the short stories of Waters, emphasized police work rather than puzzles. Even Edgar Allan *Poe's detective stories, although they certainly have mysteries, place attention more on the character of the Chevalier C. Auguste *Dupin and on Poe's theories of genius than on the puzzle. There are exceptions to this pattern. For example, Anna Katharine *Green's *The Leavenworth Case* (1878) is an almost pure puzzle story, as are some of the works of B. L. Farjeon (1838–1903), especially *For the Defense* (1891), which challenged readers to send in their solutions.

Around the turn of the century the stories of Arthur Conan *Doyle and his followers, including Baroness Emmuska *Orczy and G. K. *Chesterton, much more consistently emphasize the puzzle, but they, too, focus on the *sleuth's character as much as the mystery.

Shortly before the First World War, *detective novels were more frequently constructed around the puzzle. R. Austin *Freeman's *The Eye of Osiris* (1911; *The Vanishing Man*), though replete with scientific minutiae, presents to readers all the *clues to solve the puzzle. Gaston Leroux's *Le Mystère de la chambre jaune* (1908; *The Mystery of the Yellow Room*) challenges the reader at the end of almost every chapter to solve the mystery. E. C. *Bentley's *Trent's Last Case* (1913; *The Woman in Black*) was not the first detective novel to adopt the gimmick of the false solution followed by the truth—or, in this instance, two false solutions before the truth is revealed—but it was the success of Bentley's book that led many writers of the 1920s and 1930s to adopt the device.

The Golden Age of the detective novel between the two World Wars was also the Golden Age of party games and other sorts of puzzles, including the crossword puzzle, various card games, Mah-Jongg, and board games like Monopoly. It was during these years that the most popular detective novelists developed their own gimmicks to fool the reader. Dorothy L. *Sayers emphasized arcane murder methods— hypodermics to inject air bubbles, arsenic administered by someone who had made him or herself immune to its effects, vibrations caused by church bells, and so on. Freeman Wills *Crofts challenged the reader to work out how to break an *alibi. John Dickson *Carr's specialty was the *locked room mystery or *impossible crime. His *corpses were found alone in rooms, all of whose doors and windows were locked, and sometimes sealed, on the inside, or in houses or sites surrounded by unmarked snow or sand. Carr's books also feature impossible disappearances: People walk into a room and vanish, or disappear from a swimming pool while being watched by others. Others authors also tried their hands at impossible crimes, for example, Anthony Wynne, Clayton Rawson, Anthony *Boucher, and Hake Talbot.

Agatha *Christie's main gimmick was the *least-likely suspect. The most famous example appeared in *The Murder of Roger Ackroyd* (1926), which demonstrated that everyone without exception must be considered a *suspect. Other puzzle devices included a double challenge in many of the books by Patrick Quentin. For instance, *A Puzzle for Fools* (1936) included not only the mystery of *whodunit but also of who will turn out to be the detective.

Ellery *Queen developed two gimmicks. One was his use of the *dying message—cryptic words scrawled in blood next to the corpse or whispered through dying lips. Another innovation was Queen's direct challenge to the reader. Many authors during the 1920s and 1930s challenged their readers by implication, and some, such as Carr, actually included footnotes to point out where the reader overlooked the clues. Queen went further by stopping the action with the statement that the reader now had all the clues necessary to solve the puzzle. Other authors, such as Rupert Penny and Hugh Austin, also included a page challenging the reader.

The years between the wars were dominated by the puzzle-masters and clue-sprinklers. Not only the writers already mentioned but also such writers as Darwin and Hildegarde Tolman Teilhet, Clyde B. Clason, Clifford Knight, Christopher Bush, John *Rhode, and Georgette *Heyer constructed their tales around the puzzle. Even the hard-boiled writers sometimes included puzzles. Dashiell *Hammett's *The Maltese Falcon* (1930) has several puzzling mysteries and is one of the first detective novels to have the detective know the solution almost from the outset but not reveal it till the climax.

Reviews during this period usually evaluated the plot and the puzzle rather than the believability of the characters or the interest of the settings. The membership oath taken by those who joined the *Detection Club, founded in 1930 by Anthony *Berkeley, demanded that they must play fair with the reader. Publishers teased readers with blurbs mentioning the bizarre clues in the book. And gimmicks abounded. In Patrick's *S. S. Murder* (1933) the publisher inserted a page printed on red paper to alert readers to an important clue. Knight's *The Affair of the Scarlet Crab* (1937) concluded with a sealed "clue index." Many books included charts, maps, plans, timetables, and lists of all sorts.

Eventually so heavy was the emphasis on the puzzle that other elements of story telling were avoided almost entirely. In 1928, the first important puzzle detective collection appeared, Lassiter Wren and Randle McKay's *The Baffle Book*, with thirty puzzle tales to use as contests at parties. There were at least seventeen volumes of puzzles published before the Second World War, with Austin Ripley's *Minute Mysteries* (1932) the most popular. Containing narrative was *Consider Your Verdict* (1937) by August Derleth, under the pseudonym Tally Mason.

Dennis Wheatley and others decided that everything but the clues could be dispensed with. Beginning in 1936, Wheatley introduced the *Crime Files*, which were made up of transcripts of interviews, telegrams and letters, copies of newspapers and photographs, glassine envelops holding face powder, burnt matches, stamps, and so on. At the end was a sealed section with the solution.

By the late 1930s, a shift began away from the puzzle as the dominant aspect of detective fiction. Writers like Margery *Allingham, Michael *Innes, and Ngaio *Marsh combined the puzzle with greater development of character and social observation. The solution to the mystery, however, remained important, and Marsh especially included bizarre *murder methods worthy of any of the purer puzzle-masters— guns hidden in pianos, poison darts at a pub, a *victim compressed in a bale of wool, and so on.

During and after the Second World War the emphasis was increasingly on characterization as well as clues. Nevertheless, some new writers carried on in the 1930s tradition. Edmund *Crispin with *The Case of the Gilded Fly* (1944; *Obsequies at Oxford*, 1945) and Christianna *Brand with *Green for Danger* (1944) proved themselves the equals of the earlier generation of clue-mongers, and some *private eye writers followed Hammett's lead in paying attention to the puzzle. In his reviews for *Ellery*

Queen's Mystery Magazine, during the 1960s, Carr pointed out that Ross *Macdonald always presented plenty of clues to the solution of his mysteries.

In the 1990s, the puzzle element remained important in detective fiction, although only with a few authors did it predominate as it had sixty years earlier. Beginning in 1955, for example, Edward D. *Hoch has written a steady series of stories, most of which are constructed around the puzzle, with clues and misdirection and surprise endings reminiscent of the past. In the private eye novel, Bill Pronzini—above all in *Labyrinth* (1980) and *Scattershot* (1982)—has his Nameless detective unravel clues and surprise the reader at the conclusion. Among British writers, Robert *Barnard has advocated keeping the puzzle the detective novel and Colin *Dexter has combined the modern interest in character and the seamy side of life with the 1930s interest in twists, turns, and bizarre clues: Dexter delights in crossword puzzles, anagrams, and elaborate word games. The fact that authors like Dexter continue to be among the most popular in the genre and to receive awards from their peers indicates that the puzzle continues to have a signifcant role in the detective novel and short story.

[*See also* Ingenuity; Truth, Quest For; Weapons, Unusual Murder; Whodunit.]

• Howard Haycraft, *Murder for Pleasure: The Life and Times of the Detective Story* (1941). LeRoy L. Panek, *Watteau's Shepherds: The Detective Novel in Britain 1914–1940* (1979). Robert Adey, *Locked Room Murders and Other Impossible Crimes* (1991). Douglas G. Green, "John Dickson Carr: Fairplay Foremost," *Armchair Detective* 28, no. 2 (spring 1995).

—Douglas G. Greene

Queen, Ellery. Because Frederic Dannay and Manfred B. Lee wisely used the same name, Ellery Queen, for their joint pseudonym and their detective, they created a name recognition that made Queen the best-known American detective during the 1930s and much of the 1940s. He appeared in a long series of novels and short stories, beginning in 1929 and continuing through 1971. Even radio scripts of the successful *The Adventures of Ellery Queen* (1939–48) program found their way into print.

Ellery Queen is introduced in *The Roman Hat Mystery* (1929), in which he is depicted as a handsome, aloof young man in the mold of Philo *Vance, then one of American fiction's most popular *sleuths. Queen is a dilettante who carries a walking stick, wears pince-nez, and drives a Duesenberg. In the character's first appearance, he is called away from a rare book buying expedition to a Broadway theater in which a *murder has taken place. He is a writer, but during his first decade as a fictional character he is also a willing unofficial consultant on difficult cases for his father, Inspector Richard Queen of the New York Police Department, with whom he shares a Manhattan brownstone.

Queen's most notable trait is his intelligence; and he is described as Sherlock *Holmes's logical successor. Using unassailable logic, he sifts through complex *clues, *motives, and *alibis to arrive at solutions. His forte is solving bizarre murders, as in *The Egyptian Cross Mystery* (1932), with its crucifixions. Later in his career, he becomes a highly proficient interpreter of *dying messages, obscure notes or objects left by murder *victims which, only if interpreted correctly, point to the killer.

By *The Devil to Pay* (1938), The Queen character is more serious about his writing, having been hired by a Hollywood studio as a screenwriter. However, he is not given assignments, and so relieves his frustration by solving murders. After a one-book stint (*The Dragon's Teeth*, 1939) as a paid *private detective, Ellery enters the most serious period of his career as writer and *amateur detective.

In *Calamity Town* (1942), to gain privacy to write a book, he goes to Wrightsville, a fictional New England village. While there, he becomes so deeply involved with Wrightsville's residents that he returns to the village throughout his career to help solve local crimes. He becomes more down to earth and less inclined to show off his mental prowess when explaining a solution. In *The Murderer Is a Fox* (1945) he helps a *war veteran who has been accused of murder. In *Ten Days' Wonder* (1948) and *Double, Double* (1950; *The Case of the Seven Murders*), he relies less on physical clues, now applying his wide reading of psychology and *religion.

In *New York City, he discovers a greater, if occasionally reluctant, involvement in social problems. In *Cat of Many Tails* (1949), the randomness with which a serial killer picks his victims brings the city to the brink of hysteria and *class warfare. Only at the request of the mayor does Ellery agree to find the killer. At about this time, Ellery solves a series of short cases dealing with current New York City problems, including juvenile delinquency.

His later cases refer to prior exploits. *The Finishing Stroke* (1958) is a flashback to 1929 when, as a newly published author, he attends a Christmas party and faces a case of murder among guests isolated by a snowstorm. *And on the Eighth Day* (1964) is set in 1944 when Queen, returning from Hollywood where he wrote war films for the government, is stranded in the desert community of a religious sect, which treats him as its possible messiah.

It is not only a name that Queen shares with his creator. Parallels, especially to Dannay, are many. Queen, the character, and Dannay were both bibliophiles, each amassing a valuable library of first editions. Dannay and Lee also both spent time in Hollywood, years of frustration in which they never received script credit. Following Dannay's near fatal automobile accident in 1940, the writers showed greater awareness of social issues, as did Ellery Queen, the detective.

• Francis M. Nevins, Jr., *Royal Bloodline: Ellery Queen, Author and Detective* (1974). Edward D. Hoch, "Ellery Queen's ELLERY QUEEN," in *100 Great Detectives*, ed. Maxim Jakubowski (1991). —Marvin Lachman

QUEEN, ELLERY. Joint pseudonym of Frederic Dannay (Daniel Nathan; 1905–1982) and Manfred B. Lee (Manford Lepofsky; 1905–1971), a team of American detective writers, magazine editors, anthologists, bibliographers, and chroniclers of the history of detective fiction. Dannay and Lee also employed the pseudonym "Barnaby Ross" for four detective novels in 1932–33 featuring Drury Lane, a deaf, ex-Shakespearean actor. (The true identity of Ross was not revealed until 1936.) To further complicate matters, the Queen name was used by other writers to fill out plots created by Dannay, and the name Ellery Queen, Jr. was appropriated by James Holding for a series of eleven juvenile novels featuring the

Queens' orphan-boy-of-all work, Djuna, written between 1941 and 1966.

Nathan and Lepofsky were first cousins, born nine months and five blocks apart, of immigrant Jewish stock in Brooklyn, New York. By the late 1920s Dannay was working as an advertising copywriter and Lee as a movie company publicist. Attracted by a $7,500 prize contest sponsored by *McClure's Magazine*, they submitted *The Roman Hat Mystery*, which employed the then-novel idea of giving both author and detective the same name, Ellery Queen. The magazine changed hands but the novel was published by Frederick A. Stokes in 1929. Success came quickly, and after the publication of the third "Queen" novel in 1931, *The Dutch Shoe Mystery*, the two collaborators gave up their jobs to write full time. Individually and together they toured on cross-country promotions, wearing masks while they autographed books and lectured on college campuses. When appearing together, they developed a platform routine impersonating "Ellery Queen" and "Barnaby Ross," challenging each other's skill as detectives. In Hollywood in the late 1930s they worked as scriptwriters for Columbia, Paramount, and M-G-M. Their frustrations as scenarists (they never received a screen credit) were reflected in their character's struggles in the movie industry in *The Devil to Pay* (1938; *The Perfect Crime*) and *The Four of Hearts* (1938). Back in New York by 1939, working out of a tiny office in the Fisk Building near Columbus Circle, they spent the next decade writing weekly scripts for *The Adventures of Ellery Queen* radio show on CBS (the first hour-long dramatic show in the history of radio), building up one of the world's finest private libraries of crime fiction, co-founding *Mystery Writers of America in 1945, and beginning a new magazine, *Ellery Queen's Mystery Magazine* (*EQMM*).

The pair's work as editors, anthologists, scholars, and bibliographers was more prolific than their output of fiction. Their first venture in editing was the legendary magazine *Mystery League*, which folded after only four issues, October 1933 through January 1934. Dannay and Lee assumed the entire work load. *EQMM* began in 1941 and, despite Dannay's death in 1982, continues to this day. Among the more than 100 outstanding anthologies also edited under the Queen byline were the annual *The Queen's Awards* (1946–59; continued as *Mystery Annuals*, 1958–62) and the seminal *101 Years' Entertainment: The Great Detective Stories of 1841–1941* (1941) and *The Female of the Species: The Great Women Detectives and Criminals* (1943; *Ladies in Crime; A Collection of Detective Stories by English and American Writers*). Nonfiction works about the mystery genre included *The Detective Short Story: A Bibliography* (1942) and *Queen's Quorum: A History of the Detective-Crime Short Story as Revealed by the 106 Most Important Books Published in This Field Since 1845* (1951). "Much though we may admire Queen the writer," said Anthony *Boucher, "it is Queen the editor who is unquestionably immortal."

In contrast to the lively activities of Queen the detective and Queen the man of letters, Dannay and Lee led relatively quiet lives. Lee lived in suburban Connecticut with his wife and eight children. When not working on his authorial duties, he pursued his various stamp, record, and medal collections. Dannay and his family settled in Larchmont, New York. Dannay's autobiography, *The Golden Summer* (1953), is a loving tribute to his childhood in Elmira, New York during the summer of 1915. The pair's last Ellery Queen novel, *A Fine and Private Place*, was published in 1971, shortly before Lee's death. For the remaining eleven years of his life, Dannay continued alone to edit *EQMM* and several crime fiction anthologies, including a multivolume series collectively entitled *Masterpieces of Mystery*.

Queen was voted a Grand Master of the mystery story in 1960 by *Mystery Writers of America. Other awards included five Edgars from the MWA and a TV Guide Award in 1950 for Best Mystery Show on Television.

The working relationship between Dannay and Lee was complex. Near the end of his life, Dannay described the process: "One of us does the plotting, the other does the writing, it doesn't matter which. We kind of try to top each other. It's a collaboration, but also a competition."

The diversity and quality of Queen the dective's activities reflect the entire range of modern crime fiction. No matter how varied the scholarly pursuits and the writing styles of the fiction—from the classic tradition of ratiocination to the more modern hardboiled and psychological schools—the Queen standard was always marked by wit, a literature style, dazzling *ingenuity, erudition, and respect for the reader (vide, the famous "Challenge to the Reader").

[*See also* Pseudonyms.]

• Anthony Boucher, *Ellery Queen: A Double Profile* (1951). Ellery Queen, "Who Shall Ever Forget?" in *The Mystery Writer's Arts*, ed. Francis M. Nevins (1970). Francis M. Nevins, *Royal Bloodline: Ellery Queen, Author and Detective* (1974). Julian Symons, *Great Detectives: Seven Original Investigations* (1981).   —John C. Tibbetts

RACISM. Popular fiction in general and detective fiction in particular, as literature consciously designed to appeal to a mass audience, naturally reflect the values of their readership. It is not surprising that popular culture is as infected by assumptions of racial superiority as have been national policies and political and social practices.

The most well-known examples of racism are British author Sax *Rohmer's *Fu Manchu novels in which the white heroes, Sir Denis Nayland Smith and Dr. Petrie, battle the Chinese arch fiend who personifies the "yellow peril." In these tales, Rohmer reflects the *prejudice common in both the United States and Great Britain that Asians are a race capable of industry, but are to be despised and feared for their presumed exotic and *evil perversions, including the opium habit.

In much of the crime and mystery fiction of the period, racism is also linked to *class prejudices. Thus in both Britain and the United States, the servants of Golden Age classic detective fiction are often from ethnic minorities. Whether Japanese, Irish, or African American, these characters are depicted as occupying a position appropriate to their place in *the social structure. Also reflective of existing prejudices, minorities tended to appear as *suspicious characters thugs, ruffians, and *underworld figures such as and murderers.

A well-known example of the acceptability of casual racism is found in the alternate titling of Agatha *Christie's *Ten Little Niggers* (1939), *And Then There Were None* (1940), and *Ten Little Indians* (1965).

In the United States, racism in the mystery can be traced back to Edgar Allan *Poe's antebellum portrayal of Jupiter, the ignorant, superstitious former slave in "The Gold-Bug" (*Philadelphia Dollar Newspaper*, 21 June 1843). By the 1920s, hard-boiled detective writers began dealing with race in an urban context. The responses of *private eyes such as the *Continental Op in Dashiell *Hammett's *The Dain Curse* (1929) or Philip *Marlowe in Raymond *Chandler's *Farewell, My Lovely* (1940) to the minorities they encounter is often blunt and crude. Nevertheless, such responses may speak less of the authors' racism than of their efforts to create characters who reflect a gritty reality.

As the twentieth century advanced, mystery writers began not only to reflect society's racism but to dissect it. Contemporary writers seem to be more sensitive than their predecessors to not only glaring acts of racism but to more subtle examples. In *Bootlegger's Daughter* (1992), Margaret Maron has her liberal characters observe and comment on examples of the racial etiquette that has historically governed relationships in the American South.

By contrast Walter *Mosley's novels about the stalwart accidental detective Ezekiel "Easy" *Rawlins, beginning with *Devil in a Blue Dress* (1990), use as their *milieu post–World War II Southern California, a locale whose pervasive racism makes ironic its touted significance as a land of opportunity. Likewise, Barbara Neely, in *Blanche on the Lam* (1992) reveals the disgrace masked by racist practice when she offers a pointed analysis of social mores that suppress recognition of the crime of rape because the victim is an African American domestic worker.

Writers such as Miriam Grace Monfredo have chosen to examine the roots of the American racial caste system. In *North Star Conspiracy* (1993), Monfredo's protagonist finds herself caught up in intrigue involving an escaped slave and the Underground Railroad. In this *historical mystery, Monfredo presents actual historical personages, including Frederick Douglass, the abolitionist.

Other mystery writers have made a race-related crime the key element in their *plots. In *The White Rook* (1990) J. Madison Davis sends his *private eye, Dub Calabrese, undercover to infiltrate a white-supremacist survivalist group. In *Rules of Evidence* (1992), Jay Brandon presents his African American lawyer, Raymond Boudro, with the task of defending a white *police detective accused of beating a black man to death. In *The Love That Kills* (1991) by Ronald Levitsky, Jewish civil rights lawyer Nate Rosen is in much the same predicament when he is called upon to defend a white bigot accused of the murder of a Vietnamese woman.

It is in their depiction of the everyday encounters of characters living in multicultural societies that writers continue to make their most telling statements about race. It is through the thoughts of the protagonist as he or she approaches, for example, a group of teenagers of another race that the writer comments on a world in which skin color continues to be relevant.

[*See also* Prejudice; Rape and Other Sex Crimes.]

• Christine Bolt, *Victorian Attitudes to Race* (1971). William F. Wu, *The Yellow Peril: Chinese Americans in American Fiction* (1982). Joseph Boskin, *Sambo: The Rise and Demise of an American Jester* (1986). Gary Hoppenstand, "Yellow Devil Doctors and Opium Dens: The Yellow Peril Stereotype in Mass Media Entertainment," in *Popular Culture*, ed. Jack Nachbar and Kevin Lausé (1992).

—Frankie Y. Bailey

RADIO. *The radio adaptations of works of crime and mystery writing and original writing in scripts written for radio broadcast have been a mainstay of dramatic radio. This two-part entry looks at the crime and mystery genre as it has been used in American and British radio programming.*

The Crime and Mystery Genre on American Radio
The Crime and Mystery Genre on British Radio

THE CRIME AND MYSTERY GENRE ON AMERICAN RADIO

The crime/mystery program held a unique niche during the heyday of American dramatic radio (1930–62). Encompassing both fiction and nonfiction, this genre consisted of four basic formats: The *private detective series, detailing the exploits of a major sleuth such as Sherlock *Holmes, Philip *Marlowe, Nick *Carter, or Sam *Spade; the civilian couple or individual who solves crimes as a hobby, the prime examples being Nick and Nora *Charles, Mr. and Mrs. North, or The Shadow; the law enforcement or law-related expert whose role is to bring miscreants to justice such as *The Man from Homicide, Gangbusters*, or *Dragnet*; and the anthology program, which often featured an omniscient or present host or narrator as in *Suspense, Inner Sanctum, The Whistler*, or *Crime Classics*.

Variations on the above also appeared as fifteen-minute soap operas such as *Mr. Keen, Tracer of Lost Persons*, and *Perry Mason*, and even children's serials such as *Little Orphan Annie*. The average full-length program usually filled a thirty-minute time slot, but some stretched to a full hour.

Writer-actress Edith Meiser (who wrote, produced, and directed the *Sherlock Holmes* program in 1930) set the pattern for transferring the printed word to broadcast drama. Plots were truncated, dialogue rewritten, and characters kept to a minimum number. Sound effects and music were used to enhance the mood and presentation of the story. New endings were frequently concocted to replace those that would not work in a sound medium. Early shows used full orchestras, but these were replaced by a single organ. With its subtle nuances, the organ fit the mood of mystery perfectly. Shows had their own individual themes, and listeners often found themselves humming their favorite detective's signature tune. By the late 1940s the hard-boiled shamus was a staple on the air. Few of the audio adventures of Spade or Marlowe were created in print by Dashiell *Hammett or Raymond *Chandler—instead radio writers devised a new world for these detectives. Spade dictated his case to his secretary, Effie, while Marlowe concluded his weekly exploit with a brief tag speech, usually about the hopelessness of the world and how people should cling to their dreams.

The Shadow, the longest-running of the nonprofessional detectives, began as an omniscient narrator, but soon evolved into a master crime-fighter in the pulp magazines, while transforming into an amateur sleuth on radio. In actuality, Lamont "The Shadow" Cranston possessed the power to "cloud men's minds" (through the use of a filter microphone, making him sound like a voice on the telephone). Assisted by his girlfriend, Margot Lane, The Shadow used his special ability to interrogate *suspects as well as rescue Lane and others from the clutches of a wide range of criminals. Setting the mold for "guy and gal" radio teams, *The Thin Man* (Nick and Nora Charles), *Mr. and Mrs. North*, and *The Abbotts* soon followed.

Fictional lawyers, police officials, and other civil servants also took their turns at the center of radio mysteries. The most successful led the listener through the maze of police procedure or the courts. *Dragnet* is still remembered for its hard-hitting, matter-of-fact style.

The anthology series offered the public a wider range of plots and possibilities. Ideal for presenting the great crime and mystery classics in abridged half-hour form, these shows tended to outlast the other crime programs. *Suspense*, the finest of all, remained on the air for twenty years (1942–62). It specialized in stream-of-consciousness narrations by an assortment of killers and degenerates. During its run, *Suspense* boasted many hosts, some omniscient and others very human, as well as a galaxy of famous stars in guest appearances. Most macabre of all the anthology hosts was the "gentle man" who welcomed the public into the *Inner Sanctum*. His "deadly puns" opened and closed the program accompanied by the sound of a creaking door (actually a swivel from an old chair). Famous for bashed-in heads in nearly every script, the *Inner Sanctum* sound effects team utilized any lettuce, cabbage, or melon they could get their hands on to smash. *The Whistler*, a formula anthology series, kept its many listeners entertained with its twist endings and whistled theme song.

[*See also* Adventure Story; Drama, Elements of.]

• Francis M. Nevins, Jr. and Ray Stanich, *The Sound of Detection* (1983). Jay Hickerson, *The Ultimate History of Network Radio Programming and Guide to All Circulating Shows* (rev. ed. 1993).
—William Nadel

THE CRIME AND MYSTERY GENRE ON BRITISH RADIO

Although the first original mystery drama was broadcast in 1925 (*The Mayfair Mystery*, by Frank H. Shaw), the radio life of the genre did not flourish in the United Kingdom until the 1930s, after attracting members of the recently formed *Detection Club, including Agatha *Christie (*Personal Call*, 1954), and later, members of *Crime Writers' Association, such as Elizabeth *Ferrars (*The Truthful Witness*, 1960) and Julian *Symons (*The Man Who Changed His Name*, 1960). From the 1930s to the 1960s, radio offered listeners a variety of shows based on the crime genre, including quizzes with celebrated authors (*Detective Quiz*, 1945 and *Guilty Party* 1954–57), talks about characters (*Meet the Detective*, 1935) or the business of writing in the genre (*Trials and Sorrows of a Mystery Writer* by Dorothy L. *Sayers, 1931 and *The Thoughts of a Detective Story Writer* by John *Rhode, 1935), and true crime (Christianna *Brand's *Members of the Jury*, 1951 and *No Further Questions?* 1993), as well as drama.

There was a time when it seemed almost every major writer in the genre in Britain had either written for radio or adapted work: examples range from Michael *Gilbert (*Crime Report*, 1956 and *Petrella*, 1976) and H. R. F. *Keating (*The Affair at No. 35*, 1972) to lesser lights from the Golden Age such as Sax *Rohmer (*Myself and Gaston Max*, 1942) and Anthony *Gilbert (*And Death Came Too*, 1962). But fewer did so after the 1960s and most drama is thereafter largely taken from published work.

Adaptations have always been popular, whether as single plays (Dorothy L. Sayers's *The Man with No Face*, 1943 and Agatha Christie's *The Pale Horse*, 1993, the first and fiftieth anniversary productions of *Saturday Night Theatre*) or as series (*Episodes from Dr. Fu Manchu*, Radio Luxembourg, 1936–38; *The Saint*, 1945–51; and *Father Brown Stories*, 1946–49). In the 1970s and 1980s, the range narrowed and, although the work of less well known names was occasionally broadcast (*Crime at Christmas*, 1987 and *The Christopher Marlowe Mysteries*, 1993), most adaptations were from firmly established writers. Such caution was presumably dictated by commercial considerations, and this seems still to be the principal consideration. However, there have been some notable exceptions. A series of Anglo-American adaptations of celebrated films noirs (*Saturday Night at the Movies*, 1993, including *Night of the Hunter* and James M. *Cain's *Double Indemnity*) showed that radio can present new perspectives on filmed work. Again, although Kathleen Turner's film portrayal of Sara *Paretsky's V. I. Warshawski was panned, her radio performance was widely praised (*Deadlock*, 1991).

With radio drama, the listener is a fellow traveller rather than a passive bystander, imaginatively and intimately involved in the transfer of characters, plots, and locations from the printed page or, with original material, in the act of creation itself. Yet while radio is arguably the most stimulating medium for the audience, it can be the hardest for the writer, especially in the crime and mystery genre where so much can depend on so little. However skillful the adaptation, the end product is always largely the responsibility of the production team and cast. Excellent scripts may be undermined. For example, in *The Adventures of Sherlock Holmes* (1991–97) the principals are almost indistinguishable, in contrast with *The Adventures of Sherlock Holmes* (1952–66) in which the acting, adaptations, and atmosphere reach a high standard, thus making these the definitive productions.

Radio drama is expensive. Pressures to economize at the B.B.C. in the 1990s, in order to accommodate a continuous news and sports service, forced a further cut in the amount of drama. If only for commercial reasons, the crime and mystery genre should continue to be well represented, but the choice might become increasingly conservative. A welcome move was the decision to follow the series of productions based on the work of Christie and Arthur Conan *Doyle with selections from the slightly less well-known Dr. Fell stories by John Dickson Carr (*The Hollow Man*, 1997) and Mgaio Marsh's Roderick *Alleyn mysteries.

[*See also* Adventure Story; Drama, Elements of in Crime and Mystery Writing.]

• Denis Gifford, *The Golden Age of Radio* (1985). Paul Donovan, *The Radio Companion* (1991).   —Tony Medawar

Raffles, A. J. is the upper class *gentleman thief and safecracker who appears in E. W. *Hornung's short stories first published between 1895 and 1923. Raffles appears to be the complete English gentleman of his day: public schoolboy turned into urbane bachelor of private means. In fact, Raffles cannot claim aristocratic birth. His social elevation derives from his celebrity as a cricketer and from his personal charm. These gain him entrée into the homes of the wealthy from whom he steals to support his posh lifestyle, including highly respectable *London digs in The Albany.

Raffles rationalizes some of his crime by redistributing wealth that he believes has fallen into the wrong hands. There are occasions when he acts with great aplomb, as when he celebrates the Diamond Jubilee of Queen Victoria by sending her a gold cup that he has stolen from the British Museum.

Pitted against the indefatigable Inspector Mackenzie, Raffles proves to be a master of *disguise and a trickster of great *ingenuity, but his social graces and amateur love of the game for its own sake make him more akin to the *gentleman adventurer than the loathsome *master criminal. As George Orwell described the stories in "Raffles and Miss Blandish" (in *Horizon*, Oct. 1944), "the main impression they leave behind is of boyishness." As his criminal career becomes increasingly fraught with danger, Raffles does the decent thing and goes off to fight in the Boer War. After a particularly heroic exploit during which he unmasks an enemy spy, he is killed at the front, an appropriately redemptive ending for such a morally ambiguous figure.

[*See also* Robin Hood Criminal; Theft.]

• Peter Haining, foreword to *The Complete Short Stories of Raffles—The Amateur Cracksman* (1984). Evan M. Wilson, "Sherlock Holmes and A. J. Raffles" in *Baker Street Journal*, 34, no. 3 (1984): 155–58.   —Ian Bell

RAILWAY MILIEU. Railways, which emerged as prime movers of goods and passengers in the 1830s, have long been a favored milieu for writers of detective fiction, due to the atmosphere use of timetables, and closed-world setting of the moving train. Both railways and detective fiction reached an apogee in the years between the two world wars when *puzzle mysteries were in vogue.

The earliest crime fiction featuring railways comes from the 1860s. There are examples by Andrew Forrester, Jr., Amelia B. Edwards, Mrs. Henry *Wood, Charles *Dickens, and Wilkie *Collins, whose *The Woman in White* (1860), *No Name* (1862), *Armadale* (1866), and *The Moonstone: A Romance* (1868) include references to "tidal trains" (boat-trains connecting with cross-Channel harbors open only at certain states of the tide) and other sidelights on early railways. Sherlock *Holmes and Dr. John H. *Watson were regular rail travellers; thirty-six of their sixty recorded cases describe or imply train journeys, some of which, due to Watson's inaccurate chronicling, seem decidedly eccentric. "The Adventure of the Bruce-Partington Plans" (*Strand*, Dec. 1908) and Arthur Conan *Doyle's apparently non-Holmes stories "The Story of the Lost Special" (*Strand*, Aug. 1898) and "The Story of the Man with the Watches" (*Strand*, July 1898) have specific railway interest. Some of Doyle's immediate successors, like Baroness *Orczy, M. McDonnell Bodkin, Mrs. L. T. Meade, and R. Austin *Freeman also used the railway milieu, mainly in short stories.

The first author to be particularly associated with the milieu is the clergyman Canon Victor L. Whitechurch, who began his railway writings around the turn of the twentieth century; his short story collection *Thrilling Stories of the Railway* was published in 1912. It reveals an intimate knowledge of railway workings; some tales are illustrated with diagrams and several feature the eccentric, hypochondriacal railway consultant Thorpe Hazell.

By the time of Whitechurch's death in 1933, Freeman Wills *Crofts, who was also a professional railway engineer, had emerged as one of the leading British detective novelists. Railways figure in his work not only as background but as important "actors" in the plot. Several novels, notably *The Cask* (1920), *The Ponson Case* (1921), and *Sir John Magill's Last Journey* (1930) see train timetables perused by criminals, and Inspector Joseph *French, hard on their trail, as vehicles for creating ingenious *alibis. In *The Pit Prop Syndicate* (1922) railways are cunningly used as a means of evading *pursuit. Two Crofts novels have a more specific railway setting: *Death of a Train* (1946), telling of attempted German sabotage of a munitions train; and *Death on the Way* (1932; *Double Death*), which has as its background a "widening" scheme in Dorset, the murders arising out of an attempt to "riddle" the contract.

Crofts's imitators include John *Rhode and J. J. Connington, whose *The Two Tickets Puzzle* (1930; *The Two Ticket Puzzle*) has a ticket forgery to back up a murderer's alibi, as does Dorothy L. *Sayers's *The Five Red Herrings* (1931; *Suspicious Characters*), whose railway alibi is as ingenious as any of those of Crofts, and is couched in writing more lively than his.

For other authors railways are the background to events, as in several of John *Buchan's thrillers and others by Manning Coles, Victor Canning, and Michael *Innes (*The Journeying Boy*, 1949). Many of Georges *Simenon's novels present the railways' seamier side and several works by Agatha *Christie, herself a railway enthusiast, employ the railway milieu: *The Mystery of the Blue Train* (1928), which recalls the luxury of travel to the Riviera in the twenties; *The ABC Murders* (1936; *The Alphabet Murders*); *4.50 from Paddington* (1957; *What Mrs. McGillicuddy Saw*), whose fascinating beginning is imperfectly sustained; several short stories; and *Murder on the Orient Express* (1934; *Murder in the Calais Coach*), supreme for its atmosphere. The charisma of the Orient Express attracted other crime writers: Maurice Dekobra, *The Madonna of the Sleeping Cars* (1927);

Graham *Greene, *Stamboul Train* (1932; *Orient Express*); Ethel Lina White, *The Wheel Spins* (1936; *The Lady Vanishes*); and Ian *Fleming, *From Russia with Love* (1957).

In Patricia *Highsmith's debut, *Strangers on a Train* (1950), the train is more than a source of background or well-timed alibis; hurtling through the countryside, divorced from its passengers' ordinary worlds, it becomes a place where two strangers—who would otherwise never have met—plot to eliminate for one another the bane of each other's existence.

The difficulties of English wartime train travel are described in novels by John Dickson *Carr and Edmund *Crispin and railway titles have continued to emerge since, including John Godey's *The Taking of Pelham One-Two-Three* (1973) and R. Wright Campbell's *Malloy's Subway* (1981), both featuring the *New York City Transit Authority Police, and Thomas Walsh's train cop novels *Nightmare in Manhattan* (1950) and *To Hide a Rogue* (1964), both also set in New York City.

A selection of postwar British titles, although not always about British railways, shows the astonishing variety of possible settings of place and period: J. J. Marric's *Gideon's Ride* (1963) and Barbara Vine's *King Solomon's Carpet* (1991) highlight the London Underground; H. R. F. *Keating's *Inspector Ghote Goes by Train* (1971) depicts Indian railways; Josephine *Tey's *The Singing Sands* (1952) features a Scottish sleeping-car express and demonstrates the ease with which one can commit murder on a train and leave unseen; Andrew Garve's *The Cuckoo Line Affair* (1953) is set on an Essex branch line; Jonathan Gash's *Spend Game* (1980) has Lovejoy tangling with old railway memorabilia; Christie's *At Bertram's Hotel* (1965) was inspired by the 1963 Great Train Robbery; Carr's *The Ghost's High Noon* (1969) is set partly in a 1912 Washington–New Orleans express; Margaret Hinxman's *The Corpse Now Arriving* (1983) refers to a southern region commuter train; Michael Crichton's *The Great Train Robbery*, (1975) reconstructs the 1855 bullion robbery on the South Eastern Railway; and the climax of Douglas Clark's *Doone Walk* (1982), on Devon's Lynton Cliff Railway, sees a police officer shoot out the water ballast in the descending car to foil the villains' escape in the ascending car, exemplifying the sense of speed, use of mechanical know-how, and elements of timing and *suspense that are indigenous to the railway milieu.

[See also Alibi, Unbreakable; "Time Is of the Essence."]

• J. Alan Rannie, "The Railway Journeys of Mr. Sherlock Holmes," *Railway Magazine* (1935): 316–21; reprinted in *Sherlock Holmes Railway Journal* 5 (1997): 5–19. Hugh Douglas, "Commuting: An Unscheduled Stop at an Isolated Junction," in *Murder Ink*, ed. Dilys Winn (1977). Philip L. Scowcroft, "Railways and Detective Fiction," *Journal of the Railway and Canal Historical Society* 23 (Nov. 1977): 87–93; 25 (Mar. 1979): 32–35; 27 (Nov. 1981): 16–18; 28 (July 1984): 67–68; 30 (Nov. 1990): 166–68; 32 (Mar. 1996): 41–44; (Nov. 1998): 655–66; "Transportation Themes in the Detective Fiction of F. W. Crofts," *CADS* 25 (Mar. 1995): 19–22; "Railway

Journeys of the Great Detectives" and "*Bradshaw* and Crime Fiction: A Few Observations," *Sherlock Holmes Railway Journal* 4 and 5, (1996): 48–54 and (1997): 47–49, respectively.

—Philip L. Scowcroft

RAILWAY TIMETABLES. *See* "Time Is of the Essence."

RAPE AND OTHER SEX CRIMES appear frequently in contemporary crime and mystery writing, mostly as first crimes, after which the rapists often turn to *murder to protect themselves from discovery, or those emotionally attached to the *victim commit murder as an act of *ravage. Rapes depicted in this genre are more commonly committed by a stranger or an acquaintance than by a relative or spouse, though depictions of incest do occur, as in Stanley Ellin's "You Can't Be a Little Girl All Your Life" (*Ellery Queen's Mystery Magazine*, May 1958). Serial rapes may also be described in this genre and they generally increase in *violence with each attack, often involving other sex crimes as well, as in Patricia Cornwell's *Postmortem* (1990).

Sex crimes other than rape include *stalking with threats of sexual violence, inflicting various forms of sexual torture, frequently involving bondage, forcing the victim to watch the perpetrator rape or torture others, and inflicting such postmortem injuries as piqueristic stab wounds and genital mutilation. In nineteenth-century and early-twentieth-century works, rape and other sex crimes are seldom described directly, more often serving as an unseen but palpable threat to women characters, as in Arthur Conan *Doyle's "The Adventure of the Copper Beeches" (*Strand*, June 1892). In later twentieth-century works, however, such crimes maybe described in graphic detail using the present tense, as in John Grisham's *A Time to Kill* (1989).

Rape and other sex crimes generally have two opposite functions in the *plot: either they propel the plot, their brutality and violation motivating detectives to solve the case quickly, or they retard it, their sexual nature leading victims and their families and friends to conceal information about the crimes. While a sexual assault by an outsider against a woman often motivates family members to enraged action, as in Margaret Maron's *Southern Discomfort* (1993), evidence that incest or another sex crime has been committed by a family member is often considered particularly shameful for the family and therefore a matter to hush up, as in Joan Hess's *Madness in Maggody* (1990).

Response to rape and other sex crimes becomes a way of characterizing both male and female detectives. Sympathetic male detectives respond with anger and sorrow and credit the victim's account of the crime, while unsympathetic *sleuths respond with indifference, or blame the victim particularly in cases of marital or homosexual abuse and rape, as in Katherine V. Forrest's *Murder by Tradition* (1991). Women detectives almost always consider that they, too, could easily have been victims of similar crimes, and their greater emotional involvement and identification with the victim sometimes influences their judgment and nearly always leads their male colleagues to consider their objectivity and investigative skill impaired.

As in contemporary politics and criminology, the debate continues in this genre over whether such crimes are the sexual expression of violence or a violent form of sexuality. As in life the vast majority of rape and other sex crimes in crime and mystery fiction are committed by men against women. These crimes almost always devastate their victims, and occasionally they motivate a survivor to redefine herself as a sexual being so that she need not consider herself permanently defined or redefined by the rape or other sex crime, as in Barbara Wilson's *Sisters of the Road* (1986). More often, however, they leave their victims humiliated and scarred, altering their character and behavior and thereby extending the perpetrators' control over the victims well beyond the crime itself. As a result, even if the perpetrators are caught, tried, and convicted, a sense remains that *justice has not and cannot be adequately served.

[*See also* Sex and Sexuality.]

• Barbara Lawrence, "Female Detectives: The Feminist—Anti-Feminist Debate," *Clues* 3, no. 1 (spring–summer 1982): 38–48. Carolyn Heilbrun, "Keynote Address: Gender and Detective Fiction" in *The Sleuth and the Scholar Origins, Evolution, and Current Trends in Detective Fiction*, ed. Barbara A. Rader and Howard G. Zettler (1988): 1–8. Art Taylor, "Blood Kin and Bloody Kin: Villainy and Family in the Works of Margaret Maron," *Armchair Detective* 27, no. 1 (winter 1994): 20–25.

—Ann K. Krook

RATIOCINATION. *See* Reasoning, Types of.

Rawlins, Ezekiel "Easy." The African American protagonist of Walter *Mosley's mysteries, Ezekiel "Easy" Rawlins narrates his own peripatetic adventures in a *wisecracking voice that evokes the time and place as surely as does the first-person narration of Raymond *Chandler's Philip *Marlowe. Mosley's post–World War II *Los Angeles, as described by Rawlins, is a place where *racism runs rampant and is mostly confronted sub rosa.

Rawlins engages in unlicensed private snooping that inevitably brings him into conflict with gangsters of both races, and with racist police officials. He enters each adventure reluctantly, and then only for self-preservation or in order to maintain for his children a tenuous grasp on security. Through the use of his native wit and courage, Rawlins achieves the stature of a folk hero who must face down brutal adversaries, despite his aversion to *violence. He is aided by Raymond "Mouse" Alexander, a childhood friend whom Rawlins both loves and fears. Like Hawk in Robert B. *Parker's Spenser series, Alexander is an amoral and conscienceless killer who commits acts of violence that would be impossible for Rawlins to execute.

[*See also* African American Sleuth; Prejudice.]

• D. J. R. Bruckner, "Mystery Stories Are Novelists Route to Moral Questions," *New York Times* (4 Sept. 1990): C13. Sara M. Lomax, "Double Agent Easy Rawlins," *American Visions*

32 (Apr.–May 1992). Gilbert H. Muller, "Double Agent: The Los Angeles Crime Cycle of Walter Mosley," in *Los Angeles in Fiction*, 2nd ed., ed. David Fine (1995).

—Robert E. Skinner

READERS, DISTINGUISHED. Distinguished men and women have been readers of the mystery almost as long as the genre has existed. Most historians date the detective story, as we know it, to Edgar Allan *Poe's "The Murders in the Rue Morgue" (*Graham's Lady's and Gentleman's Magazine*, Apr. 1841). According to an 1860 campaign biography, Abraham Lincoln was a great fan of Poe's mysteries and reread them yearly.

Lincoln was the first of many U.S. presidents who read mysteries to help them survive the stress of office. Theodore Roosevelt read Arthur B. *Reeve, who was once so popular that his detective, Craig Kennedy, was called "the American Sherlock Holmes."

In 1919, an alert White House reporter saw Woodrow Wilson reading J. S. Fletcher's *The Middle Temple Murder* (1919) and reported it, transforming a minor mystery into a popular book.

Franklin Delano Roosevelt's hobbies received considerable attention during his four terms in office. These included his enjoyment of mysteries. In 1935, during a White House supper, he told guests his idea for a story: A man disappears with five million dollars, without leaving a trace. One of FDR's guests was Fulton Oursler, who, under his pseudonym Anthony Abbot, was one of the nation's most popular mystery writers. Oursler and other writers wrote chapters for *The President's Mystery Story, Propounded by Franklin D. Roosevelt* (1935), which was serialized in *Liberty* and later became a book. Shortly before he died in 1945, Roosevelt had been reading *The Punch and Judy Murders* (1937; *The Magic Lantern Murders*), which John Dickson *Carr wrote pseudonymously as Carter Dickson.

In 1962, another alert reporter spotted John F. Kennedy carrying one of Ian *Fleming's James *Bond novels as he got off the presidential plane. After his report, sales of the Bond books rose dramatically in the United States.

During the 1992 presidential campaign, Bill Clinton's love of mysteries became common knowledge; he was often seen reading them on his campaign bus. His favorite authors include Patricia D. Cornwell, Tony *Hillerman, Elmore *Leonard, Robert B. *Parker, Sara *Paretsky, and especially Walter *Mosley. After Clinton took office, an enterprising bookstore owner presented Clinton with an advance copy of Michael Connelly's *The Concrete Blonde* (1994), a widely reported event that made that edition an instant collector's item.

Presidents are the most easily recognized mystery readers, and *Mystery Writers of America noted this, presenting Clinton with its Edgar for Mystery Reader of the Year in 1993. Franklin Delano Roosevelt died before MWA was formed, but in 1959 he was given the award posthumously; his widow, Eleanor Roosevelt, accepted for him. The list of recipients has been varied, including popular writer Phyllis McGinley, comedian Joey Adams, financial analyst Sylvia

Porter, and drama critic Richard Watts Jr. The award was also presented to two famous mainstream writers: Isaac Bashevis Singer and Eudora Welty. The latter's award recognized implicitly that her rave review, in the *New York Times Book Review*, of Ross *Macdonald's *The Underground Man* (1971) helped make it a best-seller.

Many American scholars and critics have been mystery readers. Jacques Barzun is perhaps the most famous of these. His *A Catalog of Crime*, with Wendell Hertig Taylor (1971; revised in 1989), is one of the best guides to the field. The reverse of the mystery-loving Barzun was Edmund Wilson, whose 1945 essay "Who Cares Who Killed Roger Ackroyd?" (*New Yorker*, 20 Jan. 1945) reflects his reluctant reading of mysteries. Wilson implied that paper, then scarce, might better be used for purposes other than publishing mysteries. Bernard De Voto, a noted historian of the American West, wrote mysteries as Jon August and occasionally wrote of them in his *Harper's Magazine* column.

During the early 1950s, *Ellery Queen's Mystery Magazine* advertised that among its readers were such famous people in the performing arts as Joan Crawford, Ethel Merman, Steve Allen, Beatrice Lillie, Arthur Murray, Helen Traubel, and Lauritz Melchior.

Reading mysteries is not limited to the elite of the United States. In France, André Gide trumpeted the work of Dashiell *Hammett and made him as popular in that country as in his native land. In England, famous writers T. S. Eliot, W. H. Auden, J. B. Priestley, Bertrand Russell, Anthony Burgess, and Elspeth Huxley were all distinguished readers of this genre who also put their views about detective fiction into print.

[*See also* Criticism Literary.]

• Marvin Lachman, "The President and the Mystery Story," *Mystery* (May 1981): 6–9.

—Marvin Lachman

REALISM, CONVENTIONS OF. No author sets out deliberately to write an unlikely story, because every author makes a tacit contract to gain readers' credence. If readers give my narrative attention, the writer implies, I will help them to believe that it works according to a sort of logic. This promise explains the prominence of verisimilitude, or the simulation of an actuality, in nearly all forms of literature, medieval romance and some lyric poetry, as well as prose fiction that has made verisimilitude in the description of character and place an indispensable technique. Verisimilitude, however, is not the same thing as realism. While the former term simply denominates a tactical way of writing, the use of the term realism always connotes the presence of a truth, not simply a facsimile.

William Dean Howells, the chief promoter of nineteenth-century American realism, persistently argued that realism is the basis of greatness in literature because it is faithful to the real experience of ordinary, actual people and because it insistently sticks to probability in its portraiture.

Realism arose in a time of rapid industrialization and great social transformation. Directed to a middle-class audience, it functioned to show the emergent values of pragmatic business in conflict with older moral codes and, thus, to pose questions about how new social conditions could best be understood. In other words, realism centered upon the new problems that grew out of new experiences. That is exactly what crime and mystery fiction arose to do also. Focused upon crime, which due to the economic conditions and social relations in industrial cities became a new, modern problem, the detective story, too, represented an effort to comprehend a problem that demanded new routes to understanding and control.

The common origin of detective fiction and the fiction of realism resulted in close technical similarity. Like the novel of realism, the narrative of detection carefully lays its story in a detailed and concrete *setting depending heavily upon reference to known or familiar events that suggest to readers that the fictional place is an accurate reproduction. When the locale is exotic, as the Stockholm setting for the Martin *Beck novels by Per Wahlöö and Maj *Sjöwall is likely to be for many English-language readers, the specificity of the physical description in combination with a knowledgeable tone in the *voice telling the story, testifies to its authenticity in the same fashion that Dr. John H. *Watson makes the site of Sherlock *Holmes's *London adventures seem quite real, or that Dorothy L. *Sayers convinces readers that the *Oxford in Gaudy Night (1935) equals the real Oxford. The treatment of *milieu in the novel of realism and the story of detection is similarly marked by specific and confirmable detail. High finance in Theodore Dreiser's The Financier (1912) is so accurately related that the reader learns much about the way capital deals are made. Likewise, the reader of novels by Ed *McBain, Lawrence *Treat, or Dell Shannon gains the feeling of having acquired new knowledge about the way the police conduct business.

In the beginning years of its history there were no authors of detective fiction making the programmatic claims to truth that William Dean Howells proclaimed. On the contrary, the critics who popularized the idea of the detective story as an intellectual *puzzle seemed to make an effort to dislodge plots of detection from gritty actuality. The same could be said of writers of the Golden Age tradition, who devised the convention of the closed world, often represented by the inhabitants of a country house, and the amused *sleuth conducting investigations with wit and panache. When E. C. *Bentley's Philip Trent and S. S. *Van Dine's Philo *Vance are restored to their historical period, however, it is clear that their mannered tales were posed as serious alternatives to the sensational treatment of crime found in pulp fiction. The Golden Age authors could not claim they were exploring the problem of crime as it occurs in everyday experience, but, like the realists who had set the tone for mainstream writing, they could argue that they meant to purge literature of the excesses of a decadent romanticism that made little effort to relate to the way the problem of crime might plausibly erupt.

In contrast to the priorities of the Golden Age, the agenda of hard-boiled writing gave a top spot to truth claims. Raymond *Chandler's famous essay "The Simple Art of Murder" (Atlantic Monthly, Dec. 1944)

took up the programmatic stance of earlier realists in claiming that the detective fiction of Dashiell *Hammett gave murder back to the people who commit it, for a reason. In an exercise of practical criticism that echoes Mark Twain's attack on James Fenimore Cooper's literary offenses, Chandler went on to indict the canonical Golden Age novel by A. A. Milne—The Red House Mystery (1922)—for high improbability and crimes against realism. In this way Chandler initiated the view that the appearance of thugs and universal *corruption in a narrative signified its fidelity to actuality. If by this point in the essay Chandler has staked a claim to truth for his preferred way of writing detective fiction, he proceeds to undercut this position with a concluding description of the hard-boiled detective as an ethical hero, which is a fully romanticized notion.

The evident ambiguity of Chandler's essay on realism has unintended merit due to its indirect confession that realism, after all, is a body of techniques or conventions for writing. Despite claims to the contrary made by Howells and those who followed his lead, realism is more a matter of seeming than being. The stories by George Harmon *Coxe about Flashgun Casey are full of information and lore about newspaper reporting, but the stories themselves are not reporting. Carroll John *Daly, generally acknowledged to be the first hard-boiled writer for his story "The False Burton Combs," which appeared in *Black Mask in 1922, introduced the paid adventurer who serves as prototype for the *private eye, but while his tales may symbolize a view of crime in the world, they do not render the entire truth about the banality of crime. In short, detective fiction has a patina of actuality overlaying its imaginative frame, which is just to say that realism is the sum of literary conventions.

Besides conventions associated with setting and *milieu, the repertory of detective fiction realism includes the practice of extensive exposition about criminal motive designed to convey plausibility. The exposition can extend from recall of the belief that since money is the root of all *evil, murder to gain an inheritance can be a likely explanation of crime, to exploration of the pathology of serial killers whose deeds are authenticated by textual references to clinical literature. Topicality also works to suggest relevance to actuality. In the period of *Prohibition stories about gangsters had a big play. Recently public concern about mistreatment of children has resulted in a spate of novels presenting the crime of *child abuse. When the gambling resort founded by mobsters in Las Vegas became a major tourist destination, the city also became a functional setting for detective writers desiring to project an image of a glitzy, tawdry reality that can readily serve as the background to tales of anomie.

The fact that realism amounts to a sum of conventions designed to authenticate the relevance of narratives to social reality helps to resolve a final paradox in crime and mystery writing. To make violence an object of contemplation, and its explanation a subject for admiration, requires that writers distance crime from their readers and center attention on the work of the detective. That is why murders so commonly occur before a story begins and why detective narratives give so much attention to detection methods. Distance can become too great, though. It can threaten the vital feeling that we are reading about experience. The conventions of realism are in conflict with the devices for distancing. They hold back the natural drift that would completely expose the artifice of a narrative and, by techniques that keep authenticating the setting, character, and milieu of the story sustain the readers' feeling that, however redundant they might be, every detective story has meaning.

[See also Conventions of the Genre: Overview.]

• Harold H. Kolb, Jr., *The Illusion of Life: American Realism as a Literary Form* (1969). P. Fisher, *Hard Facts: Setting and Form in the American Novel* (1987). Daniel N. Borus, *Writing Realism: Howells, Jones, and Norris in the Mass Market* (1989).
                                                              —John M. Reilly

REASONING, TYPES OF. Throughout its history detective fiction has celebrated the intellect. At some point most detective stories and novels present a detective reasoning. The process may be called "ratiocination," using the "little gray cells," or deduction, yet the role of reasoning remains central whether the detective is a methodical or intuitive amateur, a rough *private eye, or a professional policeman.

Edgar Allan *Poe made reasoning the subject as well as the action of detective fiction in his first story. "The Murders in the Rue Morgue" in *Graham's Lady's and Gentleman's Magazine*, April 1841). The opening pages analyze "analysis," a general logic that turns on experience of the world as well as method and therefore differs from the specialized logic of mathematical analysis. The analyst, the Chevalier Auguste C. *Dupin, reasons by inferences derived from his careful observations in order to construct the true story of a crime. Moreover, in order to understand the character and actions of the criminal adversary, the detective must apply, according to "The Purloined Letter" (in *The Gift* 1845), another distinctive "mode of reasoning"—the "identification of the reasoner's intellect with that of his opponent." The opponent's thinking is then understood from the inside, as it were. In practice, however, Poe's "identification" proves again to be observation and inference. In the detections of Arthur Conan *Doyle's Sherlock *Holmes, Dupin's reasoning is reprised and intensified. Nearly every story has both reasoning and a dazzling turn of inference through which Holmes proves to a startled Dr. John H. *Watson and the client his power of reasoning.

Deductive reasoning is neither the inductive generalization of experimental science nor the syllogistic deduction of formal logic. Rather, it proceeds through experienced understanding of human nature and action, tested maxims, and well-aged wisdom—through what cognitive scientists call knowledge schemas. This "Baker Street reasoning," as it has been named, is practical worldly reason. Fictional detectives almost always employ Baker Street reasoning, and claims that they detect using another mode do not hold up. Nevertheless, fictional *sleuths

fall into three broad categories according to how their method of detection is defined: logical/deductive; intuitive; and intuitive combined with a testing of insights. A small group of writers uses a true scientific method.

All of these forms of reasoning achieve similar goals. They enable the writer to explore the characters of *suspects, their *motivations and behaviors, and to draw discoveries or understandings to the readers' attention while misleading them about the true state of affairs. The various demonstrations of reasoning that are a *convention of the genre draw the reader to or away from meaning, as well as involving him or her in the story and the characters' lives.

The standards set by the logical and deductive approaches of Dupin and Holmes have remained popular over the decades. Wilkie *Collins's Sergeant Cuff plods methodically through the details of the crime of theft in *The Moonstone* (1868) until he reaches a satisfactory conclusion. Baroness *Orczy's Old Man in the Corner reasons to the solution on the basis of what he is told about the cirme and its participants in *The Old Man in the Corner* (1909), for example.

G. K. *Chesterton's Father *Brown is the most frequently cited representative of intuition, a priest who insists that he smells *evil and understands through an inspired insight. In such stories as "The Secret Garden" (in *The Storyteller*, Oct. 1910), the author's emphasis on the priest's intuition and holiness enables him to explore the concept of supernatural mysteries that transcend reason, as well as specific paradoxical questions. A detective with a different spiritual consciousness, Tony *Hillerman's Navajo policeman Joe *Leaphorn, searches for the "pattern . . . which the laws of natural harmony and reason" dictate. In *Skinwalkers* (1987) Leaphorn makes use of the insights of traditional Navajo ways as much the more obvious forms of evidence.

One of the most teasing combinations is intuition with a trial-and-error testing. Colin *Dexter's Inspector *Morse follows this pattern, working with a sergeant who epitomizes the *virtues of solid, practical investigative techniques as, for example, in *The Dead of Jericho* (1981). Jack Frost in Rodney D. Wingfield's *Frost at Christmas* (1984) charms the reader with his compassion and perception, and then surprises with his discovery of the criminal. Although Raymond Chandler's Philip Marlowe would deny that he is engaged in a reasoned approach to the problem of the missing Velma Valento in *Farewell, My Lovely* (1940), pointing to the *violence to which he seems to be arbitrarily subjected he is nevertheless pursuing an insight by testing it out in interrogations of the least receptive *suspects. Similar to the hard-boiled detectives who later followed, he prods and pries, and follows his instincts straight to the solution.

Two obvious exceptions to the Baker Street reasoning are to be found in the writings of Freeman Wills *Crofts and R. Austin *Freeman, an engineer and physician, respectively, who applied rigorous scientific training to fiction. In *The Sea Mystery* (1928), Crofts traces the path of a box found in an inlet to its source, relying on the calculation of tides, weather, and so on. Freeman is credited with introducing the first *scientific sleuth, Dr. John *Thorndyke, who rigorously applies the scientific approach to a crime scene and its evidence in his first case, *The Red Thumb Mark* (1907). Freeman's technical knowledge transfers the tension from discovery of the murderer to the construction of a convincing case against him.

This emphasis on reasoning has led to a predictable backlash—the modern mistrust of reason. In E. C. *Bentley's *Trent's Last Case* (1913; *The Woman in Black*), Philip Trent pursues strict Baker Street reasoning and ends up with the wrong solution more than once. Drunk private eyes like James Crumley's Milo Milodragovitch assert (somewhat invalidly) that they can't think straight. In Jorge Luis Borges's "La muerte y labrújala" in *Ficciones 1935–44* (1944) translated as "Death and the compass" in *Ficciones* (1962; Fictions) the detective Erik Lönnrot follows Baker Street reasoning with its observation and supersubtle inference to arrive at a bizarre solution—and a trap. Here again, detective logic is shown to be mere structure that can attain a formal goal but not the truth.

[*See also* Great Detective; Puzzle.]

• Howard Haycraft, *The Art of the Mystery Story: A Collection of Critical Essays* (1946). Leroy Lad Panek, *Watteau's Shepherds: The Detective Novel in Britain 1914–1940* (1979). Michael Holquist, "Whodunit and Other Questions" in Glenn W. Most and William W. Stowe, *The Poetics of Murder: Detective Fiction and Literary Theory* (1983). Stefano Tani, *The Doomed Detective: The Contribution of the Detective Novel to Postmodern American and Italian Fiction* (1984). Jeremy Campbell, "Baker Street Reasoning," in *The Improbable Machine: What the New Upheavels in Artificial Intelligence Research Reveal about How the Mind Really Works* (1989).
—T. R. Steiner

RED FLAGS. As the detective novel developed as an independent popular fiction genre in the 1920s, it acquired certain procedures that became commonplace (e.g., the bringing together of all the *suspects for the denouement) and certain taboos. The latter were wittily encapsulated by Ronald A. *Knox in his "Decalogue" of detection (though it must be said that most of the prohibitions were broken by Agatha *Christie at one time or another). As the detective novel became to a degree standardized and rulebound in this way, it also inevitably developed certain tricks which, used over and over again, warned the alert reader through their very familiarity.

The most obvious of these is the use of twins. Knox's last rule is that "twin brothers, and doubles generally, must not appear unless we have been duly prepared for them." This is reasonable, but it must be said that the mere mention of a twin, or a look-alike sibling, inevitably points forward to the solution. Twins were used memorably by Michael *Innes in *Lament for a Maker* (1938), by Christie in *A Murder Is Announced* (1950), and as late as 1986 by Dorothy Simpson in *Dead on Arrival*. In spite of Simpson's clever revival of the ploy it is difficult to see much mileage in twins nowadays, except as a *red herring—alerting the reader to something that is not in fact germane to the solution—and here there is a danger of anticlimax.

Another favorite device is the ambiguous name. Certain first names can be used for both men and women, though usually they are preponderate for one or the other. Thus in Britain Evelyn creates an expectation that the character will be a woman, Leslie that it will be a man. National variations enter into the matter here: in Australia and the United States, Robin or Robyn will usually be a woman, in Britain it will be a man. The ambiguity can be created also by the use of family names as first names (this ambiguity, incidentally, was aimed at by Charlotte Brontë in her novel *Shirley: A Tale* [1850] although it was lost when the novel led to Shirley becoming a popular girl's name). This is a device Christie uses frequently, notably in *Mrs. McGinty's Dead* (1952) and *A Murder Is Announced* (where, with typical Christie prodigality, she allies it with the twins ploy).

The new freedoms since the 1960s have liberated crime writers, and sexual ambiguities are creating a new set of red flags. In the Golden Age detective novel homosexuality is a near taboo subject; an exception is Dorothy L. Sayers's significantly titled *Unnatural Death* (1927). The taboo is no longer current, but there remains an *assumption* that a character is heterosexual, which several writers have used fruitfully as did Ruth *Rendell in her first crime novel *From Doon with Death* (1964). Sexual assumptions generally are a frequent piece of trickery: an older woman and a young man seen together may be assumed to be mother and son, but are not necessarily so; brother and sister may also be lovers as in Caroline Graham's *The Killings at Badger's Drift* (1987). The prevalence of (at least in newspaper headlines) sexual abuse within the *family has been seized on by several modern writers, so that the family unit is often not what it seems. Transvestism is as fruitful a source of confusion in the modern crime novel as it is in real life. Examples are Rendell's *A Sleeping Life* (1978) and Anthea Fraser's *Pretty Maids All in a Row* (1986), and potential ambiguity has been increased by the possibility of sex-change operations, as exemplified in Patricia Moyes's *Who Is Simon Warwick?* (1978).

The new freedom in sexual matters is too recent for any of the above ploys to have hardened into cliché. How common some *plot devices can become may be illustrated by a question to the inveterate crime reader: how often has the reader heard of a character "missing, believed killed in action," or missing without a body having been discovered, who remains missing for the rest of the book?

[*See also* Prodigal Son/Daughter; Sex and Sexuality.]

• Emma Lathen, "Cornwallis's Revenge," in *Agatha Christie: First Lady of Crime*, ed. H. R. F. Keating (1977).
—Robert Barnard

RED HERRING is a term used as early as 1420 to refer to fish that took on a red color during the process of being cured by smoke. By 1686, the notion of drawing a red herring across the track referred to an attempt to divert attention from the real matter. Often used in regard to political diversions, the image comes from the dragging of red herrings across the trail of a hunted fox to throw the pursuing hounds off the scent. In crime and mystery writing, the term has long been used to refer to false or misleading *clues and sometimes to *suspects. In this genre, the red herring may also appear in the form of a literary conceit.

The red herring was a staple of the *detective novel long before the term was commonly used by readers and commentators on the *conventions of the genre. Wilkie *Collins, for instance, used a red herring in *The Moonstone* (1861), when he encouraged readers to attach undue significance to the sudden change in Franklin Blake's smoking habits, while Sergeant Cuff is ultimately shown to sniff out the truth.

The traditional *detective novel, with its emphasis on the *puzzle element and its reliance on the *sleight of hand, was the natural spawning ground for the red herring. Agatha *Christie's first novel, *The Mysterious Affair at Styles* (1920) was laden with clues, including numerous red herrings, but she soon learned to use them judiciously. The device at the center of *The Murder of Roger Ackroyd* (1926) is essentially one brilliantly executed red herring.

The most famous example of the use of red herrings is in Dorothy L. *Sayers's aptly titled novel, *The Five Red Herrings* (1931; *Suspicious Characters*). Sayers takes Lord Peter *Wimsey to Scotland to investigate what the author called "a pure puzzle." Six *suspects, all of them artists, possessed *means, motive, and opportunity to kill, but five of them are red herrings. Sayers unmasks the villain after diverting readers to consider false *alibis linked to painting technique and railway timetables.

[See also Clues, Famous; Conventions of the Genre: Overview; Ingenuity: Mistaken Identity.]
—Edward Marston

Reeder, Mr. J(ohn) G., a character created by Edgar *Wallace, works for the Public Prosecutor's office, *Scotland Yard, and Banker's Trust. This Golden Age figure appears in short stories collected as *The Mind of Mr. J. G. Reeder* (1925; *The Murder Book of Mr. J. G. Reeder*), together with two other volumes of stories and the novels *Room 13* (1924) and *Terror Keep* (1927).

Middle-aged, outwardly meek, emotionless, and unassuming he is Victorian in appearance and manners. He wears side-whiskers, pince-nez, and an old-fashioned derby hat and carries an unfurled umbrella irrespective of weather or time of day. Such apparent eccentricities are deceptive, since the umbrella handle conceals a knife and he also carries a revolver. His apparently mild outward personality belies his ability to be fierce when the occasion demands.

Reeder is no weakling, despite his penchant for meditation, playing patience, and philosophizing. These attributes belie his tenacity and the danger he poses to wrongdoers. His skills at solving robberies, his expert eye for forgery, and his ability to identify with the "criminal mind" are used to great effect in solving both *locked room mysteries and other crimes.

[See also Eccentrics.]
—Melvyn Barnes

REEVE, ARTHUR B(ENJAMIN) (1880–1936), American writer of mystery novels, short stories, and screenplays, principally about Craig Kennedy, a character often referred to as "the American Sherlock *Holmes," a professor of chemistry at a New York university. Reeve graduated from Princeton in 1903 and attended New York Law School before choosing journalism as a career. His articles on science, politics, crime, and social conditions led him to write short stories about scientific crime detection. Reeve's success depended less on his characters than on the way he employed the latest scientific discoveries in a series of short stories and novels for the Hearst publications. From the first short stories anthologized in *The Silent Bullet* (1912) to the final novel, *The Stars Scream Murder* (1936), the detective depends more on lie detectors, ballistics, voiceprints, and wiretapping to solve crimes than observation and deduction. Most of the stories are narrated by his reporter friend, Walter Jameson, a Dr. John H. *Watson figure, in an appropriately journalistic style. Like Holmes, Kennedy kept files of information regarding paper types, inks, and other materials that he had studied. His creator's reputation for such fictional scientific sleuthing was noted by the U.S. government, which asked Reeve to create a scientific crime lab for anti-espionage purposes during World War I.

[See also Scientific Sleuth.]

• John Harwood, "Reeve, Arthur B (enjamin)" in *Twentieth-Century Crime and Mystery Writers*, ed. Lesley Henderson, 3rd. ed. (1991).
—J. Randolph Cox

REFERENCE WORKS devoted to crime and mystery fiction, now plentiful and varied, were once rare. The first full-length book about the genre was a manual for prospective writers, Carolyn Wells's *The Technique of the Mystery Story* (1913). Early histories of the form came in Willard Huntington Wright's introduction to *The Great Detective Stories: A Chronological Anthology* (1927) and Dorothy L. *Sayers's to *Great Short Stories of Detection, Mystery, and Horror* (1928–34; *The Omnibus of Crime*). The first book-length history in English was H. Douglas Thomson's *Masters of Mystery: A Study of the Detective Story* (1931), a useful and well-written volume with a pronounced British bias. Specialized bibliographies of the field were so lacking that for many years a dealer catalogue, John Carter's *Detective Fiction: A Collection of First and Rare Editions* (1934), was cited as a key source of information.

In the 1940s, the first standard titles in the form's history and scholarship were published: Howard Haycraft's *Murder for Pleasure: The Life and Times of the Detective Story* (1941), an extraordinarily thorough, accurate, and critically acute history of the field to that time; Ellery *Queen's *The Detective Short Story: A Bibliography* (1942), a similarly meticulous work, describing the first editions of single-author collections and anthologies of detective short stories; and Haycraft's *The Art of the Mystery Story: A Collection of Critical Essays* (1946), a large gathering of the best critical essays on the form. All three of these works have continued utility today.

The next twenty years saw scattered additions to the critical shelf. Some came in anthologies, such as James Sandoe's *Murder: Plain and Fanciful, with Some Milder Malefactions* (1948), with its "Criminal Clef" listing of fiction and drama based on real-life crime; Anthony *Boucher's *Four-&-Twenty Blood-hounds* (1950), a *Mystery Writers of America anthology that included who's-who biographies of several prominent fictional detectives, a concept used earlier by Kenneth MacGowan in *Sleuths; Twenty-three Great Detectives of Fiction and Their Best Stories* (1931); and the many anthologies edited by Ellery Queen (the Frederic Dannay half of the partnership) with their extensive, enthusiastic, and informative story notes, some reprinted from *Ellery Queen's Mystery Magazine*. Queen also produced *Queen's Quorum; A History of the Detective-Crime Short Story as Revealed by the 106 Most Important Books Published in this Field since 1845* (1951), an annotated listing of the most important short story collections by single authors. A. E. Murch's history, *The Development of the Detective Novel* (1958), was informative on the early roots of the form but marred by a plethora of errors.

The deluge of secondary sources of the last quarter of the twentieth century can be dated from the first appearance on the general mystery scene of fanzines, long a staple of the science fiction community and the Sherlockian wing of mystery fandom. Len and June Moffatt's *The JDM Bibliophile*, devoted to the works of John D. *MacDonald, first appeared in 1965. Two general fanzines, Allen J. Hubin's the *Armchair Detective* and Lianne Carlin's the *Mystery Lover's Newsletter* (later the *Mystery Reader's Newsletter*) first appeared within months of each other in 1967. The reader-contributors of these journals now had a place to share their checklists, critical opinions, notes, and queries and many of the reference works to come had their genesis here.

Although some specialized bibliographies had appeared, notably Dorothy Glover and Graham *Greene's *Victorian Detective Fiction; A Catalogue* (1966), the first attempt at bibliographic control of the entire genre was Ordean Hagen's *Who Done It?: A Guide to Detective, Mystery, and Suspense Fiction* (1969). This effort at a complete bibliography of books in the field was flawed by numerous errors and omissions, but Hubin took Hagen's model and built on it for his more complete and accurate compilation, *The Bibliography of Crime Fiction, 1749–1975* (1979). An updated version appeared in 1984 under the title *Crime Fiction 1749–1980: A Comprehensive Bibliography*, a supplement in 1988, and a new edition in 1994.

The standard bibliography of books and articles about the genre is Walter Albert's *Detective and Mystery Fiction: An International Bibliography of Secondary Sources* (1985). Michael L. Cook has produced several indexes that, although error-prone, are indispensable by virtue of their uniqueness: *Murder by Mail: Inside the Mystery Book Clubs, with Complete Checklist* (1979; rev. ed. 1983); *Monthly Murders: A Checklist and Chronological Listing of Fiction in the Digest-Size Mystery Magazines in the United States

and England (1982); *Mystery, Detective, and Espionage Fiction: A Checklist of Fiction in U.S. Pulp Magazines, 1915–1974* (1988, with Steven T. Miller); *Mystery, Detective, and Espionage Magazines* (1983); and *Mystery Fanfare: A Composite Annotated Index to Mystery and Related Fanzines 1963–1981* (1983). Another index of unique value is *Index to Crime and Mystery Anthologies* (1990) by William G. Contento with Martin H. Greenberg.

The first book to attempt a large-scale critical guide was Jacques Barzun and Wendell Hertig Taylor's *A Catalogue of Crime* (1971; rev. ed. 1989), which both delighted and infuriated mystery devotees with its forthright, often contrarian opinions and British, classical bias, and was as error-prone as Hagen's pioneering work. Later critical guides of note are Bill Pronzini and Marcia Muller's *1001 Midnights: The Aficionado's Guide to Mystery and Detective Fiction* (1986) and Art Bourgeau's *The Mystery Lover's Companion* (1986).

The first encyclopedic work on the form, still notable for its inclusiveness and accuracy, was Chris Steinbrunner and Otto Penzler's *Encyclopedia of Mystery and Detection* (1976), compiled with senior editors Marvin Lachman and Charles Shibuk. *Twentieth Century Crime and Mystery Writers* (1980; later editions 1985 and 1991), edited in its first two editions by John M. Reilly and in its third by Lesley Henderson, combines bibliography, biography, and critical summary in one of the most useful one-volume sources.

Julian *Symons's *Bloody Murder: From the Detective Story to the Crime Novel* (1972; *Mortal Consequences*, rev. eds. 1985 and 1992) was the first major history of the field since Haycraft and remains the most up-to-date one-volume summary of the genre. Other histories of note include R. F. Stewart's *. . . And Always a Detective: Chapters on the History of Detective Fiction* (1980), T. J. Binyon's *Murder Will Out: The Detective in Fiction* (1989), and LeRoy Lad Panek's *An Introduction to the Detective Story* (1987). Notable essay anthologies to follow Haycraft's *Art of the Mystery Story* include *The Mystery Writer's Art* (1970), edited by Francis M. Nevins Jr.; *The Mystery Story* (1976), edited by John Ball; *Dimensions of Detective Fiction* (1976), edited by Larry N. Landrum, Pat Browne, and Ray B. Browne; and *Detective Fiction: A Collection of Critical Essays* (1980), edited by Robin W. Winks.

Various attempts have been made at a subject index to crime fiction, all useful but none totally inclusive or reliable. The Hubin bibliographies include some indexing by locale. Specialized sources include Tasha Mackler's *Murder . . . by Category: A Subject Guide to Mystery Fiction* (1991), Albert J. Menendez's *The Subject Is Murder: A Selective Subject Guide to Mystery Fiction* (1986; supplement 1990), and Steven Olderr's *Mystery Index: Subjects, Settings, and Sleuths of 10,000 Titles* (1987).

Dilys Winn's *Murder Ink: The Mystery Reader's Companion* (1977), followed by *Murderess Ink: The Better Half of the Mystery* (1979) set the pattern for heavily illustrated, magazine-style coffee-table books about the form. Later examples include H. R. F.

*Keating's *Whodunit: A Guide to Crime, Suspense, and Spy Fiction* (1982) and *The Bedside Companion to Crime* (1989), and *The Fine Art of Murder* (1993), edited by Ed Gorman, Martin H. Greenberg, and Larry Segriff with Jon L. Breen.

Reference guides of more specialized interest include Robert C. S. Adey's *Locked Rooms and Impossible Crimes* (1979; revised as *Locked Room Murders and Other Impossible Crimes*, 1991); John E. Kramer Jr. and John E. Kramer III's *College Mystery Novels: An Annotated Bibliography, Including a Guide to Professorial Series-Character Sleuths* (1983); Jon L. Breen's *Novel Verdicts: A Guide to Courtroom Fiction* (1984); John Conquest's *Trouble Is Their Business: Private Eyes in Fiction, Film, and Television, 1927–1988* (1990); Victoria Nichols and Susan Thompson's *Silk Stalkings: When Women Write of Murder: A Survey of Series Characters Created by Women Authors in Crime and Mystery Fiction* (1988); Jean Swanson and Dean James's *By a Woman's Hand: A Guide to Mystery Fiction by Women* (1994); and Kathleen Gregory Klein's *Great Women Mystery Writers* (1994). Notable works especially directed to the book collector are Eric Quayle's *The Collector's Book of Detective Fiction* (1972) and John Cooper and B. A. Pike's *Detective Fiction: The Collector's Guide* (1988). Specialization has extended to books devoted to particular publishing imprints, notably Peter Foord and Richard Williams's *Collins Crime Club: A Checklist of the First Editions* (1987) and Ellen Nehr's *Doubleday Crime Club Compendium 1928–1991* (1992).

[*See also* Pontificators, The.]

• Jon L. Breen, *What About Murder: A Guide to Books About Mystery and Detective Fiction* (1981); *What About Murder (1981–1991) . . .* (1993).   —Jon L. Breen

REGESTER, SEELEY, pseudonym of Metta Victoria Fuller Victor (1831–1885), American author who wrote the first *detective novel in English. Born in Erie, Pennsylvania, she published her first book, *The Last Days of Tul: A Romance of the Lost Cities of Yucatan* (1846), while still in her teens. She also collaborated with her older sister, Frances Barritt Fuller, to produce a collection of poetry, *Poems of Sentiment and Imagination, with Dramatic and Descriptive Pieces* (1851). She married the publisher Orville James Victor, head of Beadle and Adams, who invented the *dime novel. Metta Victor was a versatile writer whose titles represent a wide variety of popular genres from sentimental, sensation, and adventure fiction to cookery and *humor. She also contributed to a great many periodicals such as the *Saturday Evening Post* and *Godey's Ladies Book*. In addition to her writing, she served as hostess at her husband's literary gatherings and was the mother of nine children.

The Dead Letter, the first American detective novel, was serialized in *Beadle's Monthly* in 1866 and published as a complete work by Beadle and Company in 1867. When Metta Victor wrote *The Dead Letter* using the nom de plume of Seeley Regester, the only models of detective fiction in English were Edgar Allan *Poe's short stories, Charles *Dickens's detective sub-

plot in *Bleak House* (1852–53), and Wilkie *Collins's *suspense novel, *The Woman in White* (1860). While revealing suggestive similarities to the work of Poe and Dickens, Regester's novel is original enough to dispel any charge that she merely imitated the work of widely admired male predecessors.

Regester's primary accomplishment lies in extending the puzzle plot of the detective short story to the longer narrative form of the novel. She contributed further to the development of the detective novel by enhancing the personality and the methods of the detective. She rejected the misanthropic bent of Poe's *sleuth in creating her investigator, Mr. Burton, whose character eschews the bizarre excesses of the reclusive, aristocratic Chevalier C. Auguste *Dupin as well as the working *class vulgarity of Dickens's Inspector Bucket. Mr. Burton is portrayed as an attractive, well-adjusted, and sociable person, A gentleman of private means, he leads a normal *family life and takes great delight in his children. Although Mr. Burton works with the police on a regular basis, he refuses to accept financial payment. Thus, he becomes the prototype for the gifted *amateur detective so popular in the early decades of the twentieth century.

Without sacrificing any of the rational skills of Dupin, Regester also augmented the talents of her sleuth. For example, Mr. Burton has an amazing ability to intuit character from samples of handwriting. His astonishing physical description of and insight into the character of the dead letter writer, expressed with arrogant egotism, are confirmed later in the narrative. This passage, now so reminiscent of the spectacular deductions of Sherlock *Holmes from a bit of cigar ash or a frayed coat sleeve, appeared twenty years before Arthur Conan *Doyle introduced his famous sleuth. It may be the first time this kind of inference appeared in print. Burton is also hypersensitive to *atmosphere and realizes when he is in the presence of *evil. His daughter is also clairvoyant.

Seeley Regester also enlarged the role of the assistant beyond that of Poe's anonymous "I." Richard Redfield contributes to the solution instead of merely recording events.

In meting out punishment to villains, Regester set a precedent that satisfied the demands of morality and literary decorum, without marring the happy ending by leaving the culprit to face capital punishment. To spare the feelings of his family, the villain of *The Dead Letter* is banished rather than turned over to the police, but his life in exile presents a bleak prospect.

It is quite possible that Regester's innovations influenced other contemporary authors, notably Anna Katharine *Green, whose *The Leavenworth Case* (1878) was cited as the first American detective novel before Regester's work was discovered by modern literary historians. Regester also wrote *Figure Eight; or, The Mystery of Meredith Place* (1869), which critics consider to be inferior in plot construction to *The Dead Letter*.

• Michele Slung, introduction to *The Dead Letter* by Seeley Regester (1979): v–ix. B. J. Rahn, "Seeley Register: America's First Detective Novelist" in *The Sleuth and the Scholar: Ori-*

gins, Evolution, and Current Trends in Detective Fiction, ed. Barbara A. Rader and Howard Zettler (1988).

—B. J. Rahn

REGIONALISM. Regionalism in literature is apparent in the character of a setting stemming from its geographical location and to the attitudes of the place. This two-part entry surveys the use of regional components in American and British works of crime and mystery writing.

American Regionalism
British Regionalism

For further information, please refer to Settings, Geographical; Rural Milieu; Urban Milieu.

AMERICAN REGIONALISM

For many years, *puzzle and *plot were foremost in American mysteries, and location only incidental. A high percentage of mysteries were set in wealthy mansions, often on the upper East Side of Manhattan or on Long Island. There were exceptions, notably Mary Roberts *Rinehart's The Case of Jennie Brice (1913), against the background of a Pittsburgh flood, and Melville Davisson *Post's Uncle *Abner tales, set in western Virginia in the early nineteenth century. Even Dashiell *Hammett, known for his *San Francisco scenes, was primarily a writer of dialogue and action, probably because he started his career in the *pulp magazines. The fog and hills of his city are conveyed mainly between his lines, not through detailed descriptions.

It is widely accepted that Raymond *Chandler, who made *Los Angeles an important "character" in his Philip *Marlowe stories, opened the eyes of critics and writers to the possibility of strong regional writing in the mystery. After Chandler, writers like Ross *Macdonald, William Campbell *Gault, and Margaret *Millar, consciously or unconsciously influenced by him, also wrote of Southern California. Thomas B. Dewey, John Evans, and Fredric *Brown wrote of Chicago, with the title of Brown's first book, The Fabulous Clipjoint (1947), becoming a widely accepted metaphor for that city. Ellery *Queen, whose Manhattan had once been merely a backdrop for novels of ratiocination, wrote Cat of Many Tails (1949), a superb portrait of urban panic in a *New York terrorized by a serial killer. Earlier, in Calamity Town (1942), Queen had created Wrightsville, a fictional New England town, and wove its history, geography, and social attitudes into a strong series of books over the next three decades.

As late as 1980, according to a study published in The *Armchair Detective, half of all American mystery novels were set either in New York or California. However, a trend soon developed, one that has resulted in almost every new American mystery novel having a strong regional component. Mysteries are now set in such diverse locations as Boston, Alaska, Philadelphia, Texas, Salt Lake City, and Key West.

Publishers encourage writers in this direction, especially when popular cities and areas are involved. At least six Santa Fe, New Mexico, mysteries were published between 1988 and 1993. Each of Philip R. Craig's mysteries with American settings is described on the cover as "A Martha's Vineyard Mystery." David Osborn's first three titles were Murder on Martha's Vineyard (1988), Murder on the Chesapeake (1992), and Murder in the Napa Valley (1993). For easy reader recognition, San Francisco mysteries usually show the Golden Gate Bridge on their covers, even when it is not germane to the plot.

Through regionalism, writers are able to create a sense of place and convey *atmosphere. Using regional material permits them to write of more varied crimes, including those endemic to specific areas, such as illegal immigration, drug running, violations of environmental law, political *corruption, and crimes related to gambling, even when it is legal. It also allows a far more varied cast of characters, including African Americans, Indians, Asian Americans, Hispanics, blue-collar workers, and others once very underrepresented in the mystery. Regional problems can even be used for *characterization. Marcia *Muller and Bill Pronzini have each subjected their San Francisco–based series characters to the stress of earthquakes. Cold Call (1993), the first mystery by Dianne G. Pugh, has scenes on the Los Angeles freeways in which driving habits and reaction to traffic delays are used to demonstrate character.

The most successful American mystery writers are often also the best regional writers. Ross *Macdonald became one of the first mystery writers to reach best-seller status, and critics lauded his limning of Southern California, especially depredations of its environment. For example, in The Underground Man (1971) and Sleeping Beauty (1973) he incorporated forest fires and oil spills endangering the hills and beaches of Santa Barbara.

Overdevelopment in Florida was long a concern of John D. *MacDonald. His Travis *McGee series, begun in 1964, gave him a consistent first-person voice for his opinions, and for every reader who noted that McGee's polemics occasionally slowed story development, there were hundreds who identified with his views.

Boston was a mystery *setting before Robert B. *Parker and George V. *Higgins, but early writers, such as Elliot Paul and Timothy Fuller, seldom went beyond mentioning locations. Their Boston generally was the home of aristocracy and prestigious universities. Parker and Higgins explore other aspects of Boston life, especially that of its criminals. Boston's Combat Zone, a former center of prostitution and pornography, is a favorite Parker setting. His private detective, *Spenser, is sensitive enough to appreciate cultural and historical Boston, but he is also tough enough to deal with pimps and gangsters.

Higgins is especially adept at reproducing the argot of Boston hoodlums. He has been compared to Elmore *Leonard, who, whether writing about Detroit, Florida, or Atlantic City, also captures local speech patterns and habits. Boston author Jeremiah Healy also captures the Boston accent of criminals and ordinary citizens alike in his series about *private eye John Francis Cuddy. Linda Barnes is particularly strong on Boston geography, with her cab-driving sleuth Carlotta Carlyle literally passing through every kind of neighborhood in Boston and environs.

James Lee Burke describes the drug trade and jazz clubs in New Orleans and also sends his Cajun detective Dave Robicheaux among the people of the nearby swamps, where his background helps him to get information.

For every mystery set in an American city, there is now often one exploring a rural or small-town setting. Sometimes, these produce regional writing laced with *humor, as in Joan Hess's Maggody series about a town in the Arkansas Ozarks. Sometimes, the purpose is more serious, as in K. C. Constantine's Mario Balzic books, about a town in western Pennsylvania where the closing of steel mills and coal mines has led to a long-term economic depression, which forms the background for crime.

Although readers remain interested in how mystery writers handle the places in which they live, they find another appeal of regional mysteries is the opportunity to "visit" new locales and learn about different cultures. For readers anxious to learn about Native Americans, the Navajo police series by Tony *Hillerman is the exemplar of the American regional mystery. Hillerman is especially perceptive in demonstrating how conflicts between Navajo ways and those of the predominant "Anglo" culture have led to social problems, including alcoholism.

To some mystery readers, American regionalism is a mixed blessing. While appreciating more interesting and realistic settings, they note a growing deemphasis on *clues, puzzles, and detection, but well-plotted mysteries describing crimes that grow out of the nature of specialized regional environments are among the most successful works in this genre today.

[See also Great Outdoors, The; Realism, Conventions of; Rural Milieu; Urban Milieu.]

• Susan Dunlap, "The Scene of the Crime," *Writers Connection* (Sept. 1989): 1, 6–7, 10. Michelle Bearden, "Death by Locale," *Publishers Weekly* (11 Oct. 1993): 60–64.

—Marvin Lachman

BRITISH REGIONALISM

Prior to the Second World War, the leading crime writers were almost invariably based in *London or the Home Counties; because they felt most at home in the south of England, it was natural for them to locate many of their mysteries either in London or those small market towns or villages that, in *Snobbery with Violence: Crime Stories and Their Audience* (1971), Colin *Watson famously dubbed *Mayhem Parva. Similarly, *Oxford men such as J. C. Masterman and Michael *Innes were apt to set their mysteries among Oxford's dreaming spires. When authors moved their settings farther afield within Britain, it was usually to pleasant holiday resorts in Devon or Cornwall, although Arthur Conan *Doyle's *The Hound of the Baskervilles* (1902) is memorable for its powerful evocation of Dartmoor and the sinister Grimpen Mire. Dorothy L. *Sayers's *Five Red Herrings* (1931; *Suspicious Characters*) portrays an artistic community in Galloway in southwest Scotland,

and her *The Nine Tailors* (1934) has an atmospheric Fenland setting. In the Golden Age, mystery novels with an urban backcloth were rare—even though the industrial cities of the north and midlands are much more plausible as scenes of crime than, say, peaceful spots such as Torquay or Truro.

The rise of regionalism in postwar British mystery fiction corresponds to the increasingly realistic tone of modern crime writing. Writers have begun to explore the possibilities of a wide variety of social and geographical *settings; among the earliest regularly to use regional settings were E. C. R. Lorac and Maurice Procter. Lorac was a Londoner, but she took her principal London metropolitan police detective, Inspector, later Superintendent, Robert MacDonald, to the Lake District and the Lune Valley in a number of successful detective stories. In *Fell Murder* (1944), *The Theft of the Iron Dogs* (1946; *Murderer's Mistake*), and *Crook O'Lune* (1953; *Shepherd's Crook*), the tranquil quality of the region in those days is superbly captured. Procter, a Lancashire-born policeman, set his procedural novels in tough, albeit fictionalized northern cities; the title of the book in which Detective Chief Inspector Harry Martineau made his first appearance, *Hell Is a City* (1954; *Somewhere in This City*, *Murder Somewhere in This City*), illustrates the difference in tone between his work and that of the Mayhem Parva school. From the 1960s onward, a growing number of writers from the provinces have been making effective use of their knowledge of areas that were once unfashionable in describing crime, its causes, and its consequences. Developing the Lorac tradition, Ellis *Peters set many of her books about the Felse family in the Welsh border country before going back in time to record, with extraordinary success, the exploits of a twelfth-century Benedictine monk, Brother *Cadfael, and his world in Shrewsbury and its environs. Procter has been followed by other northerners with experience on the police force, including the prolific John Wainwright and Peter N. Walker.

The many criminal possibilities of even an apparently quiet part of England, East Anglia, are evident in books as diverse as the police novels of Alan Hunter and the lively romps featuring the rascally antiques dealer Lovejoy written by Jonathan Gash. A sense of place is important to all the best writers, and in P. D. *James's *Devices and Desires* (1989), a complex *puzzle and sophisticated study of personalities under pressure is enhanced by the vivid backdrop, a lonely stretch of the north Norfolk coast dominated by the ruins of an old priory and the menacing bulk of a nuclear power station. The southwest's principal representative during the past quarter century has been W. J. Burley, whose long series about Superintendent Charles Wycliffe conveys the atmosphere of the author's native Cornwall with such power that his work has been likened to that of Georges *Simenon.

Peter Lovesey's *Rough Cider* (1986) and his books about the policeman Peter Diamond, such as *The Last Detective* (1991), are based in the west country, while in addition to his series about the Yorkshire policemen Superintendent Andrew Dalziel and Sergeant, later Chief Inspector, Pascoe, Peter Reginald

*Hill has written thrillers, including *Fell of Dark* (1971), with a Cumbrian setting. The title of Robert *Barnard's *A City of Strangers* (1990) is significant; although the mystery of the *murder of the obnoxious Jack Phelan is cunningly presented, Barnard is as interested in depicting the tensions between those who live in private homes cheek by jowl with council houses in Sleate, a grim fictional city that blends aspects of Leeds and Bradford. A group of younger British writers, heirs to Procter as well as Lorac, have set their series in real towns and cities: Glasgow (Peter Turnbull), Edinburgh (Ian Rankin), Newcastle (Chaz Brenchley), Liverpool (Martin Edwards), Manchester (Val McDermid), Nottingham (John Harvey), and Brighton (Alex Keegan). Their novels cover the spectrum of modern crime fiction, from cozy to psychopathy, and feature variously *police detectives, *amateur detectives, *private eyes, and serial killers. The establishment of regional chapters of the *Crime Writers Association has helped to foster a sense of identity among writers from many different parts of the country; a tangible result has been the publication of several anthologies of locally based stories by chapter members.

Regional mysteries add to the diversity of the genre in Britain today and contribute to its quality. Typically, the best regional work is strong on atmosphere, and writers such as Hill and Barnard have few equals in analyzing the mores of provincial society. On occasion, a regional setting can be crucial to the *plot. In Lorac's *Still Waters* (1949), the mystery depends on knowledge of a path across Morecambe Bay, while Eileen Dewhurst's Guernsey novel *Death in Candie Gardens* (1992) offers a murder *motive inspired by a unique feature of the island's laws.

[*See also* Great Outdoors, The; Realism, Conventions of; Rural Milieu; Urban Milieu.]

• Colin Watson, *Snobbery with Violence: Crime Stories and their Audience* (rev. ed. 1979). Martin Edwards, introduction to *Northern Blood* (1992). Robert Church and Martin Edwards, introduction to *Anglian Blood* (1995).

—Martin Edwards

RELIGION is a prominent theme in mystery fiction. Whether one recognizes the Old Testament or Greek myth as the source of the first detective stories, the preoccupation is with crime and sin, discovery, *guilt, and punishment. Writers often make religious characters, culture, and issues integral to their work and use myth, symbol, biblical allusions, and sacred objects incidentally, but widely observed conventions of detective fiction rule out supernatural interventions. Before 1939, the typical British detective work was grounded in orthodox Christian belief with a comforting if illusory morality. Early writers on both sides of the Atlantic such as G. K. *Chesterton, who published the first Father *Brown anthology in 1911, and Melville Davisson *Post, who published *Uncle Abner, Master of Mysteries* in 1918, wrote detective fiction full of allegory and biblical allusion with strong-minded religious detectives to convey the lesson that neither crime nor sin pays. Chesterton's work has the added object of depicting Catholicism as a reasonable and English belief system, not a *plot

of Rome. Religious connections of this period are further illustrated by clerics Ronald A. *Knox, Cyril Alington, and Victor L. Whitechurch, who wrote detective novels, and by the analyses of such fiction by Knox and Chesterton. W. H. Auden's imaginative essay "The Guilty Vicarage" (*Harper's Magazine*, May 1948), suggests that readers' enjoyment of *detective novels relates to their sense of guilt and a fantasy of being restored to an Edenic Great Good Place.

From the earliest works, the religious detective, often Catholic, has been popular, with Protestant, Jewish, and unorthodox figures less common. William David Spencer compiles examples in *Mysterium and Mystery* (1989). Like other professionals, clerical detectives bring the philosophy and practices of their primary calling to detecting. *The Rosary Murders* (1979) is typical of the Father Bob Koesler novels by William X. Kienzle in raising questions regarding the ability of the Catholic church to minister to the needs of contemporary communicants. Harry Kemelman's Rabbi David Small, a master of theological discourse and a shrewd analyst of human behavior, provides penetrating insights into Judaism against the backdrop of synagogue politics. Brother *Cadfael, in the Ellis *Peters series, sees twelfth-century monastic religion with a practical and ironic eye, and in *A Morbid Taste for Bones* (1977) he acts on his view of God's will and against the aspirations of his own order. Cloistered settings also lend themselves to the *locked room mystery. Women clerics such as the Reverand Claire Aldington in the Isabelle Holland novels investigate crime with a shrewd eye for *motive and relationships, while Sister Ursula, in works by Anthony *Boucher, and Sister Mary Helen, in works by Sister Carol Anne O'Marie, bring un-worldly wise perception from the convent to the crime scene.

Religion is highlighted as authors develop the potential of the theme in individual ways. In Dorothy L. *Sayers's *The Nine Tailors* (1934), allegory, allusions, floods, and providence heighten the effect as the baffled Lord Peter *Wimsey finally identifies himself as one of the guilty. Mr. Venables is a persuasive cleric, and the church bells play a decisive role. In Margery *Allingham's *The Tiger in the Smoke* (1952), a fourteenth-century statue of the virgin and child, whose "serenity flowed up naturally," shatters the confidence of the criminal, who expects a more negotiable treasure. Graphic contrasting of good and evil in Canon Avril and Jack Havoc displaces the detective in the novel's center. Even Ellery *Queen in *And on the Eighth Day* (1964) and P. D. *James in *A Taste for Death* (1986) utilize significant religious themes. In Umberto Eco's *Il Nome della Rosa* (1983; *The Name of the Rose*), William of Baskerville uses masterful cunning to discern the *plot and villain but fails to prevent the final crime of his blind adversary. The religious *motive in this work, to destroy laughter (in the form of Aristotle's treatise on comedy) before it destroys salvation, is a brilliant example of destructive zeal. In Kate Charles's "Book of Psalms" mysteries ecclesiastical architecture is a special interest, and Anglican parish intrigues motivate crime and focus on such issues as women priests and homosexual communicants.

Religious traditions other than the Judeo-Christian are not commonly used. Exceptions are Hinduism, portrayed by Wilkie *Collins in *The Moonstone*, wherein Brahmans forfeit their caste to recover the diamond of the moon god; Zen Buddhism, basic to the outlook of the detective Comissaris in Janwillem *van de Wetering's novels set in Amsterdam; and the Native American spiritual beliefs that permeate Tony *Hillerman's novels featuring policeman and apprentice shaman Jim Chee.

By the late 1920s, cynicism was a staple in hardboiled American novels, and sham religion represented social decay. In Dashiell *Hammett's *The Dain Curse* (1926), the Temple of the Holy Grain is a religious cult run by two former actors who find *San Francisco less competitive in the new-religion market than *Los Angeles. Jules Amthor, "a fakeloo artist, a hoopla spreader," in *Farewell, My Lovely* (1940), is Raymond *Chandler's contribution to the gallery of religious charlatans. Cultists and Satanists continue as sources of sensation in the mystery, with such "religions" often a cover for crime. Mormon and evangelical religions tend also to receive unfavorable representation.

In contemporary detective fiction, the religious are depicted with the full complement of human frailty and viciousness. Religious institutions and values of every culture are exposed to scrutiny and question, or given respectful attention. Knowledge, or partial knowledge, has replaced restoration of order by the detective. Such works, increasingly numerous, responded to readers' tastes in the 1990s as more reassuring fictions did in earlier times.

[See also Clerical Milieu: The American Clerical Milieu; Clerical Milieu: The British Clerical Milieu; Clerical Sleuth.]

• Catherine Aird, "The Devout: Benefit of Clergy" in *Murder Ink*, ed. Dilys Winn (1977). Jon L. Breen and Martin H. Greenberg, eds., *Synod of Sleuths, Essays on Judeo-Christian Detective Fiction* (1990). "Religious Mysteries," *Mystery Readers Journal* 8, no. 3 (fall 1992).   —Nancy Ellen Talburt

RENDELL, RUTH (b. 1930), also writes as Barbara Vine. British author of detective novels and psychological crime fiction. Born in *London on 17 February, the daughter of Arthur and Ebba (Kruse) Grasemann, Rendell attended Loughton High School in Essex, and worked on Essex newspapers from 1948 to 1952. In 1950 she married Donald Rendell, whom she divorced in 1975 and remarried two years later; they have one son and live in Polstead and London. Her first book, *From Doon with Death* (1964), introduced police Inspector Reginald *Wexford of Kingsmarkham in Sussex, the protagonist of what has become a popular series of *detective novels and stories. Wexford, a kindly father-figure, solves crimes by persistent examination of witnesses and talking through the cases with his assistant Mike Burden. Rendell emphasizes development of the detectives' characters as much as their crime solving: readers see the straitlaced Burden grow, particularly through the loss of his wife and near-loss of his career in *No More Dying Then* (1971), into a person more tolerant

of human frailty; they follow the sturdy but aging Wexford through bouts of ill health and self-doubt to where, in *Kissing the Gunner's Daughter* (1992), estrangement from a favorite daughter distracts him from obvious *clues to a killer's identity. In *Simisola* (1994), quiet Kingsmarkham is besieged by contemporary urban problems, from *racism to domestic enslavement; the depiction of a community rent by social ills from which no *class or *family is immune has caused this novel to be compared with George Eliot's *Middlemarch: A Study of Provincial Life* (1871–72) Between Wexford novels Rendell writes *crime novels without detectives, in which the absence of reason and moral order makes the *plots both more suspenseful and more disturbing: in *A Demon in My View* (1976), a psychology student organizing a children's game inadvertently sets off a neighborhood psychotic killer; *A Judgement in Stone* (1977) features a mentally disturbed housekeeper, *Heartstones* (1987), an anorexic teenager and a bloody *suicide. Many of Rendell's non-Wexford stories, in volumes such as *The Fallen Curtain and Other Stories* (1976) and *The Fever Tree and Other Stories of Suspense* (1982; reprinted in *Collected Stories*, 1988) also depict bizarre behavior, which Rendell makes both fascinating and repellent.

In the 1980s Rendell added to her other two categories of fiction a new kind of novel, for which she uses the pen name Barbara Vine. Feeling the need, she said, for "a softer voice speaking at a slower pace, more sensitive perhaps, and more intuitive," she has, in *A Dark-Adapted Eye* (1986), a woman recount her unnerving investigation into the family's role in the crime for which her aunt was executed thirty years earlier. In *The Brimstone Wedding* (1995), a young woman reveals her own guilty love affair to an elderly patient and learns, in turn, of the older woman's more appalling secret. The Vine novels show that even offenses deemed non-punishable by law may in fact be unpardonable. Rendell is not only prolific, with more than fifty books published, but also among the most highly acclaimed of mystery writers for her skill at plotting and psychological insight. She has received major British and American mystery awards, including Edgar Allan *Poe and Silver and Gold Dagger awards.

[See also Motivation, Psychological; Police Detective.]

• Jane S. Bakerman, "Ruth Rendell" in *Ten Women of Mystery*, ed. Earl F. Bargainnier (1981).

          —Mary Rose Sullivan

RESOLUTION AND IRRESOLUTION. The resolution section of a detective novel occurs just after the solution to a crime is revealed and the perpetrator is identified. The explanation of how *clues were interpreted to provide the solution is spelled out here. Resolution is also the primary gratification readers obtain from traditional mystery fiction. In real life, many crimes go unsolved even when investigation takes place, many are covered up and not even investigated, or a court case is dismissed on a technicality even when the identity of the criminal is known. But in the world of fictional homicide, justice prevails, the criminal is punished, order is restored. Poetic, not civic, justice rules. Because of this, readers experience the pleasure of narrative closure.

Certain conditions must be present in the mystery novel for resolution to be possible. These include a belief in rational, deductive powers to produce answers, the containment of crime for the purpose of limiting the cast of characters, the use of chronological time and a progressive narrative line, a belief in a strong connection between law and justice, a belief in the "objectivity" of the detective himself, and a conviction that it is always the correct and desirable course to expose the truth.

The detective story is the perfect model of a hermeneutic, or explanatory, interpretive tale: The process of the reading itself consists in detecting an enigma (literally, a gap, inconsistency, omission, loose end), searching for clues, forming many hypotheses, choosing among them, and finally constructing a solution. In detective fiction these features are so central and so crucial that they become the reading process itself.

Paradoxically, then, when all these conditions and states of mind are present, homicide as it is purveyed in the mystery story is a fiction of reassurance, of tidiness, of no loose ends, of the reestablishment of the hierarchy that was operative in the world-before-the-crime. Order implies hierarchy; as P. D. *James notes, this means people know their place in relation to others: No one is unrecognized or without value.

Although detective novels do reflect social problems, as is evident in the works of Robert *Barnard, Sue *Grafton, Reginald *Hill, Jonathan Gash, and Christianna *Brand, resolution within their covers is restricted to the solution of a particular crime, a single event, or related events, and does not extend to the achievement of social justice. To do so would be to leave the fiction open-ended, whereas, to the contrary, it still presumes a social, and therefore fictional, whole. Dorothy L. *Sayers, whose own work demonstrates resolution, concludes in her essay "Problem Picture" in The Mind of the Maker (1941) that the neatness of the problem and its solution in mystery fiction insure that large issues in the society, such as poverty, *war, and *racism, remain outside its purview.

Resolution consists in "bringing the criminal to justice" or, at the very least, identifying him or her and the circumstances, at first baffling, that surround the criminal event. A sense of propriety, as well as intellectual puzzlement, is satisfied.

This refers to conventional, traditional mystery fiction of the nineteenth century and some that is still being written today. However, departures from these conventions are many and on the increase, spurred by a modern or postmodern sensibility that questions the cherished formulas of detective fiction, its most basic tenets, denying, qualifying, ignoring each of the conditions necessary for resolution listed above.

An excellent bridge between resolution and irresolution is Joan Smith's mystery novel Why Aren't They Screaming? (1988). Smith maintains many stylistic *conventions of the genre, for example, the use of an

*amateur sleuth, relevant clues, chronological narrative time, and fair play, while at the same time subverting the ending by permitting the known criminal to flourish within the government.

Irresolution occurs in crime and mystery writing when the case is not neatly tied up at its close. This may happen in fiction where the balance between *plot and character changes, that is, the mystery story without resolution explores character more than it relies on archetypes. This distinction is expanded upon by Julian *Symons when he distinguishes between the *detective novel, which emphasizes plot, and *the crime novel, which is more interested in psychology, and hence, the individual in Bloody Murder: From the Detective Story to the Crime Novel: A History (1972; Mortal Consequences: A History: From the Detective Story to the Crime Novel).

Irresolution may also occur in fiction where *humor, including parody, is a strong ingredient. In the play Cap'n Simon Wheeler, the Amateur Detective: A Light Tragedy (Mark Twain's Satires and Burlesques, 1967), which he wrote but did not publish in 1877, Mark Twain parodies Pinkerton's famous detective agency and the *private eye. He demolishes the myth of the invincible, ratiocinative, and aristocratic detective hero who was the mainstay of the novel with resolution. E. C. *Bentley's Trent's Last Case (1913; The Woman in Black) is both an exposé of mystery fiction's stratagems and a spoof of the detective hero, who in this work reasons incorrectly and arrives at the wrong solutions. In fact, the incriminated *suspect turns out to be more clever than the hero. Bentley's work liberates the genre from the infallible sleuth and aims a telling blow at the persona of the hero.

Even without parody, the distinctions between the hero's character and capacities and those of the criminal can blur. When the criminal functions as a sort of author's alter ego, moral ambiguity and psychological complexity, rather than objectivity, exist within the detective as well as within the criminal. The psychosis in Robert Louis Stevenson's The Strange Case of Dr. Jekyll and Mr. Hyde (1886), the simultaneous indwelling of good and *evil impulses, has, in this psychologically informed age, been admitted to exist in a modified way in us all.

Irresolution also occurs when expectations of resolution are confounded. In Alain Robbe-Grillet's Les Gommes (1953; The Erasers) neither time nor space, invaluable guideposts for the reader of a traditional mystery novel, provides explanation of mysterious behavior and events. Here the spatial world consists of grids that never intersect, as in Jorge Luis Borges's "The Garden of Forking Paths" (EQMM, Aug. 1948), and the temporal world is not sequential. Rather, time is out of joint, an unresponsive and irresponsible element. Whereas conventional mystery novels use markers of time such as timetables of railroads and steamships, and verification of *alibis by witnesses to help the reader unravel the enigma, some modern masters such as Borges, Robbe-Grillet, and Thomas (Louis) Berger deny epic (heroic) coherence in their mystery novels.

If such external clues do not signify, neither does the power of ratiocination offer help. A detective such as Ross *Macdonald's Lew *Archer fights a losing battle with rationality. Rather, he expresses his author's sense that the single intelligence that can apply a simple and fixed moral law is no longer plausible in our world. The world of capitalism, suggests Macdonald, is a world that inevitably, for his detective Archer, produces *violence he cannot avert. For Archer, therefore, the return to the status quo is neither possible nor desirable. He is nostalgic for a bygone world, a world in which he could feel self-righteous. The hero, from being a man of action, has become inward-looking, an observer aware of psychological subtleties, not a *judge. Analysis that looks for motivation beneath the surface of the ordinary is part of contemporary Freudian understanding. And understanding is the key word here. Resolution does not signify understanding; resolution belongs to *plot, understanding to character.

Even right and wrong, not only good and evil, are no longer ultimately traceable. Can we validate a moral vision which idealizes heroes who trade off *violence for violence in a world where danger is theatricalized and therefore distanced? The law and justice are no longer synonymous. As Lew Archer observes in The Underground Man (1971), "The Law is illegal." Hence blame and judgment, administered by the mystery novel's poetic justice, become tentative. First, because society is so corrupt there is no bottom to sound; second, because much contemporary philosophy asserts the difficulty of knowing anything. Jacques Lacan describes the Great Psychoanalytic Task which can never end, an ongoing narrative with partial and slanted explanations, and this is the new outlook of the detective novel. With the suspension of judgment, resolution retreats.

• Frank Kermode, The Sense of an Ending: Studies in the Theory of Fiction (1968). Wolfgang Iser, The Implied Reader: Patterns of Communication in Fiction from Bunyan to Beckett (1978).
　　　　　　　　　　　　　　　　　　—Nadya Aisenberg

RETURN OF THE PRODIGAL. See Prodigal Son/Daughter.

REVENGE, or the act of harming another in return for an injury, real or imagined, has been an important component of crime and mystery fiction throughout the literary history of the genre. As a theme it allows for commentary on such topics as the nature of *evil and the limits of *justice, while as a *plot device it provides a basis for useful complication and mystification.

Edgar Allan *Poe made use of revenge as a *motive in his genre-establishing detective stories "Thou Art the Man" (Godey's Lady's Book, Nov. 1844), "Hopfrog" (Southern Literary Messenger, Apr. 1836), and "The Cask of Amontillado" (Godey's Lady's Book, Nov. 1846). Revenge may be one of the more mystifying of motives, since it is easy (and common) for a writer to create an odious *victim upon whom many characters wish to take revenge, as is the case in Nicholas *Blake's The Beast Must Die (1938) and Ruth *Rendell's To Fear a Painted Devil (1965). Revenge, therefore, can provide a host of *suspects,

whose particular reasons for revenge are mysterious and varied, including revenge for a crime (most commonly *murder or *blackmail) that the law cannot or did not punish, or punished inadequately, as is exemplified in Jonathan Gash's Firefly Gadroon and Arthur Conan *Doyle's "The Adventure of Charles Augustus Milverton" (Strand, Apr. 1904); betrayal in Sue *Grafton's "E" Is for Evidence (1988) and George V. *Higgins's The Friends of Eddie Coyle (1972); thwarted love in Ellis *Peters's The Confession of Brother Haluin (1989); or jealousy in Martha Grimes's The Five Bells and Bladebone (1987).

Motivating characters with revenge is advantageous to the writer of crime and mystery fiction, as multiple characters in each narrative may feel wronged by a single character who becomes the murder victim. Revenge, too, may sometimes be seen as a justifiable act. In some stories, revenge is represented as the only means of accomplishing justice in a world in which the legal and social systems are flawed. For example, the criminal in Doyle's first Sherlock Holmes tale, A Study in Scarlet (1887), is an avenger with whom the detective, the narrator, and presumably the reader strongly sympathize.

In addition to serving as a motive for crime, revenge may motivate the *sleuth to solve crimes, as is the case in P. M. Hubbard's Kill Claudio (1979). Figures such as John D. *MacDonald's Travis *McGee (The Deep Blue Goodbye, 1964), Robert B. *Parker's *Spenser (A Catskill Eagle, 1985), Robert Campbell's Jimmy Flannery (The Junkyard Dog, 1986), and James Lee Burke's Dave Robicheaux (A Morning for Flamingos, 1990) often operate as avengers rather than detectives. This is not to suggest that every detective figure is an avenger; many, however, are, and even among those many detectives who detect primarily for the praiseworthy purposes of exonerating the innocent and bringing the guilty to justice, it is by no means unusual to find detectives rejoicing either in their own ability to take revenge on the guilty or in the legal system's doing so—for example, Agatha *Christie's Miss Jane *Marple in The Body in the Library (1942) or in virtually any other of the Marple books.

Revenge also allows writers to manipulate mysterious complications. An avenger may wait many years before acting, as happens in Dorothy L. *Sayers's Whose Body? (1923). Vengeance may be taken by a group of characters, as in G. K. *Chesterton's "The Sign of the Broken Sword" (Storyteller, Feb. 1911); alternatively, revenge may be taken by one character on an offending group, as is the case in Christie's And Then There Were None (1939). Sayers's Gaudy Night (1935) and Barbara Paul's The Fourth Wall (1979) combine both of these types of revenge. Vengeance may even be arranged to be taken from beyond the grave, as shown in E. C. *Bentley's Trent's Last Case (1913) and Blake's Thou Shell of Death (1936). A criminal may conceal his or her true motive by leaving clues suggesting that the motive was revenge, as in Dashiell *Hammett's "The Tenth Clew" (Black Mask, 1 Jan. 1924) and Joseph *Hansen's Skinflick (1979); or take revenge by framing an innocent character, as happens in Christie's Sleeping Murder (1976) and Simon Brett's Star Trap (1977).

[*See also* Resolution and Irresolution.]

• Susan Jacoby, *Wild Justice: The Evolution of Revenge* (1983).   —L. M. Anderson

REVENGE TRAGEDY. See Tragedy, Dramatic, Elements of in Crime and Mystery Writing.

RHODE, JOHN, the punning pseudonym of Major Cecil John Charles Street (1884–1965), a prolific British detective novelist who also wrote as Miles Burton, the author of 144 mystery novels. He served in France during the First World War, and afterwards in Ireland, and was awarded the Military Cross. Under his own name he wrote widely on contemporary European history and politics.

As Rhode he produced sixty-nine novels, beginning with *The Paddington Mystery* (1925), with the mathematician Dr. Lancelot *Priestley as detective. At first an active investigator of crime, Priestley later confines himself to offering enigmatic advice to the police. Endowed with superior powers of reasoning, he follows the tradition of the *Great Detectives Sherlock *Holmes and Dr. John *Thorndyke, being especially close to the latter in his use of scientific evidence. Among Rhode's best novels are *The Davidson Case* (1929: *Murder at Bretton Grange*), *The Claverton Mystery* (1933; *The Claverton Affair*), and *Death in Harley Street* (1946).

As Miles Burton he wrote of the *amateur detective Desmond Merrion, who during the war becomes involved in counter-espionage in *The Secret of High Eldersham* (1930) and *Dead Stop* (1943).

Street's work sits squarely in the tradition of the British detective story of the interwar years; its merits are a constant *ingenuity and inventiveness in the devising of situations and details.
[*See also* Reasoning, Types of.]   —T. J. Binyon

RICE, CRAIG, the most favored pseudonym of Georgiana Ann Randolph Craig (1908–1957). Her other pen names included Daphne Sanders, Ruth Malone, and Michael Venning, but it was Craig Rice, that identified her authorship of *8 Faces at 3* (1939), the first of her twenty-two published novels and the one introducing her series characters the lawyer John J. Malone and his friends Jake and Helene Justus. Today's readers are likely to be startled at the quantities of alcohol the characters consume while they joke their serendipitous way through bars, versions of high and low society, and criminal cases. The alcohol, though, is a literary sign indicating to readers that they are in the stylized world of sophistication exploited by many writers during the 1930s and 1940s, while the mixed *milieu and the cast of reappearing supporting characters of police officers, *underworld figures, and saloon keepers place the Malone series in the American hard-boiled tradition, except that the mordancy of the *sleuth and the instability of the social order characteristic of hard-boiled writing is so exaggerated that the narratives take on the *atmosphere of the cinematic screwball comedy.

Rice also created a comic series featuring the accidental detectives Bingo Riggs and Handsome Kusak, who dream of making it big in movies. The subject was something Rice knew well from working in Hollywood as a screenwriter for films about The Falcon and as a publicist. Her skills in publicity may well have led her to the jobs she undertook as a ghostwriter, first for the burlesque personality Gypsy Rose Lee and then, with Cleve Cartmill, for the film star George Sanders. The Lee novels appeared as *The G-String Murders* (1941) and *Mother Finds a Body* (1942); the Sanders novel appeared as *Crime on My Hands* (1944).

Randolph also created under her favored pseudonym three collections of short stories, two of them in collaboration with Stuart Palmer and the last published after her death. Several Rice titles have returned to print in paperback, and for curators of some of the most distinctive writing of the 1940s and 1950s at least sixty-five uncollected short stories by Craig Rice and her alter ego Ruth Malone remain in archives of popular mystery magazines.
[*See also* Alcohol and Alcoholism; Couples: Secondary Characters: Humor.]

• Bill Pronzini and Marcia Muller, *1001 Midnights: The Aficianados Guide to Mystery and Detective Fiction* (1986).
                                          —John M. Reilly

RINEHART, MARY ROBERTS (1876–1958), American mystery and romance writer. She was born in Allegheny, Pennsylvania, in 1876. She trained as a nurse and married Dr. Stanley Rinehart in 1896. Although her health was poor and she had three small children at home, she began to write short stories in the first decade of the twentieth century and published her first full-length novel, *The Circular Staircase*, in 1908. It was a best-seller, and she remained a highly popular author for more than forty years. Although Rinehart is best remembered for her mysteries, she also wrote comic stories, romances, and plays, as well as editorials and feature articles.

Rinehart had a strong aversion to the realism of the 1920s; she found it offensive. However, she did not have an aversion to making her novels realistic, and she made a point of setting them in American places and using American *amateur detectives. She did create a quasi-professional detective in Hilda Adams, a nurse who is hired by the police department to go undercover in some of their more difficult investigations. Most of her mysteries take place in upper-class surroundings, although she occasionally and, not particularly successful, attempted to portray the working classes. Her mystery work bears most resemblance to some of the more cozy British writing of the period, but has no references to an aristocracy and contains a good deal more *violence, although Rinehart would never be mistaken for a hard-boiled novelist.

As befitted the wife of a physician, Rinehart often incorporated interesting medical problems into her work. She was also somewhat interested in spiritualism, although never fully convinced of its validity and the possibility of spirit communication is raised in *The Red Lamp* (1925). Rinehart was also interested in incorporating "true" situations into her novels: *The*

Case of Jennie Brice (1913) takes place during flooding in Pittsburgh, and *The Confession*, published with *Sight Unseen* in one volume in 1921, is based on the discovery of a written confession to an old *murder.

Rinehart is probably best known as the writer of *Had-I-But-Known fiction, which stereotypically includes a young woman narrator commenting on the story from a position of increased wisdom. However, Rinehart often used older women for her narrators, as well as men of all ages. For the most part, these narrators have had no previous experience with crime (even her lawyers have most of their experience in noncriminal law), and are sharing their stories because they are so unusual. Rinehart's best-known mystery novels include *The Circular Staircase* (1908) and *The Man in Lower Ten* (1909), her first two, but her popularity as a mystery writer continued unabated until the late 1940s. At this time, her sales began to decline, as the reading public was now more interested in a harsher realism than Rinehart was willing to produce. Her novels are still being reissued, attesting to her popular appeal more than forty years after her death.

Her work has been marketed differently in different periods. During the first half of the century, much of Rinehart's appeal lay in her humor, and her primary marketing tool was the short stories that appeared in magazines such as the *Saturday Evening Post*. Later, her work was reissued with covers more appropriate for *Gothic novels, and currently the blood in the cover designs has been emphasized. While her humor has certainly survived the test of time, critical judgment has tended to categorize her as a writer of romantic mysteries. Her mysteries have survived in part because of the comic bafflement of her narrator, however, who always seems to feel that he or she should have known better at the time.

[*See also* Females and Feminists; Menacing Characters; Suspense.]

• Jan Cohn, *Improbable Fiction: The Life of Mary Roberts Rinehart* (1980). Mary P. Freier, "The Decline of Hilda Adams" in *Women Times Three: Writers, Detectives, Readers*, ed. Kathleen Gregory Klein (1995).   —Mary P. Freier

ROBIN HOOD CRIMINAL is a phrase that provides a broad umbrella for a variety of criminal or semi-criminal types; it includes the lovable rogue, committing crimes for his own personal benefit, and those who prey on criminals or do crime for ultimate good, the latter perhaps deriving as much from Don Quixote as from Robin Hood. What all have in common is a morality which in some way does not cohere with that of authority.

Around the true Robin Hood type there exists a distinct aura of romance, although his (and it is almost invariably a he) morality is generally questionable and his code of conduct frequently bizarre. He is depicted as being more sophisticated than a mere criminal-as-hero; the morality of the latter (e.g. Richard Stark's Parker, *The Hunter*, 1962; *Point Blank*) is generally uncompromisingly straightforward and usually the reader is not asked to find him romantic or even particularly sympathetic.

The modern trend of the heroic criminal as opposed to the criminal-as-hero was begun by E. W. *Hornung's A. J. *Raffles, continued by Maurice *Leblanc's Arsène *Lupin, Leslie *Charteris's The *Saint, and John *Creasey's *The Toff and brought up to date by, among others, John D. *MacDonald's "salvage operator," Travis *McGee. Of all these it is Raffles, the acknowledged archetype, whose conduct is the most irredeemably unsavory. Whereas Lupin cooperates with the police and solves crimes, The Saint and The Toff work outside but alongside the law and McGee is acknowledged by his author to be a knight-errant, Raffles steals almost exclusively for personal gain (although he does occasionally right wrongs) and is always pitted against the law. In the century since Raffles, cricketer and "amateur cracksman" (i.e. thief), first appeared, social attitudes have undergone an immense change and the then noble sentiments of Raffles and his sidekick Bunny Manders now seem strange indeed. For example, Raffles will not steal from a house in which he is a guest, but makes an exception when he has been invited there solely on account of his cricket, as is the case in "Gentlemen and Players" (in *Cassell's*, Aug. 1898); in "The Gift of the Emperor" (in *Cassell's*, Nov. 1898), Bunny speculates that as stealing enables him not to run up bad debts, "the more downright dishonesty seemed to me less the ignoble." Far more acceptable in the light of current morality are The Toff and The Saint, who operate outside the law for no discernable reason other than love of adventure (The Toff), or to find a way of helping people when authority fails to do so (The Saint).

Other Robin Hood criminals and crooked characters include Frank Parrish's likable poacher, Dan Mallett in *Fire in the Barley* (1977), Bruce Graeme's Blackshirt, Gregory Mcdonald's investigative reporter Fletch, Arnold Bennett's millionaire thief Cecil Thorold in *The Loot of Cities* (1904), and Philip St. Ives, the character created by Ross Thomas writing as Oliver Bleeck (*The Highbinders*, 1974, etc.), who recovers stolen property by fair means or foul. A more minor character whose behavior is closer to the original Robin Hood is Susan Moody's Barnaby Midas, the lover of investigator Penny Wanawake; he is a professional jewel thief but much, if not all, of the proceeds of his thefts are used to help Third World countries. Of these individuals, some reveal characteristics that serve as metaphors for the whole genre: for example, Parrish's Mallett. The poacher is frequently a sympathetic character in fiction, skillfully stealing from those who can well afford it in order to supply his own basic physical needs—and thus the Robin Hood criminal, although here the needs are as often moral. Raffles's prowess as a cricketer is equally significant, not only symbolizing the sporting element in many of the Robin Hood criminal activities but also pointing a contrast between the most honorable of pastimes and a most dishonorable activity.

[*See also* Adventure Story; Adventurer and Adventuress; Gentleman Adventurer; Gentleman Thief.]

• George Orwell, "Raffles and Miss Blandish," *Horizon* (Oct. 1944): 232–44. Reprinted in George Orwell, *Decline of the English Murder and Other Essays* (1965).

—Judith Rhodes

ROHMER, SAX (1883–1959), British writer of mystery, fantasy, and supernatural novels, short fiction, plays, comic verse and music for the English music hall, and student of the occult. Born Arthur Henry (later Sarsfield) Ward in the Ladywood district of Birmingham, England, of Irish parents, he is best remembered as the creator of Dr. *Fu Manchu, would-be world conqueror protagonist of thirteen novels and four short stories.

Married to Rose Elizabeth Knox, Rohmer made his home in a succession of urban houses and country estates in England, as well as in White Plains, *New York. He counted illusionist Harry Houdini among his friends. He created his own image of a legendary, romantic figure to the outside world, but seldom revealed the real man behind the image. His appearance as a successful writer was part of the facade, because the money was spent almost as fast as he earned it. No business man, Rohmer was also defrauded by his literary agent. Besides writing prose fiction he wrote or edited many of the radio scripts based on his work.

Rohmer's lifelong interest in ancient Egypt and his travels to the Middle East gave him a supply of material for stories for magazines and books. He wrote mostly of places he had visited. His favorite *setting was Egypt and *Brood of the Witch-Queen* (1918) is considered by many to be his best work. Having adapted his journalist's knowledge of *London's Chinatown to his Fu Manchu stories, Rohmer continued the series when publishers offered him more money for it than for his other work.

Rohmer was an uneven writer. The best of his more than fifty books rely upon atmospheric *suspense or fantasy told in carefully crafted prose, while others are written to a formula. He balanced descriptions of the everyday world with references to unknown horrors, based upon his extensive reading and travels and tempered with a sardonic sense of humor. Included among his best works are *The Dream-Detective* (1920), *Tales of Chinatown* (1922), and *White Velvet* (1936).

[*See also* Ethnic Sleuth; Formula: Plot.]

• Robert E. Briney, "Sax Rohmer: An Informal Survey" in *The Mystery Writer's Art*, ed. Francis M. Nevins Jr. (1970). Cay Van Ash and Elizabeth Sax Rohmer, *Master of Villainy: A Biography of Sax Rohmer* (1972).   —J. Randolph Cox

ROMAN NOIR. *See* Fiction Noir; Roman Policier.

ROMAN POLICIER is the most widely used term for crime writing in France. Broadly used in the marketing of books to identify works across the crime and detection genre, the term *roman policier* may also be employed more specifically to refer to a subgenre of crime and mystery writing that evolved out of a realist and popular heritage. Like *fiction noir* and the cinematic *film noir*, the *roman policier* places importance on *milieu and *atmosphere, and on the mystery of the psyche.

Before any of these terms was used, Eugène François *Vidocq's chronicling of his own crime solving in *Mémoires de Vidocq* (1828–129; Memoirs of Vi-

docq; Vidocq the Police Spy) demonstrated his talent for *disguise and understanding of the criminal *underworld. Vidocq's combination of police procedure and emphasis on insight based on experience was to become very influential as the genre developed in France and in the work of other nationals who wrote in the French language, as exemplified by the work of the Belgian Georges *Simenon. In his many novels centered around the police work of Inspector Jules *Maigret, Simenon achieved a blend of the *roman problème* and the *roman policier* by centering his foci on psychological investigation of character and on milieu, rather than on reconstruction of crimes.

Others who fused the realist approach of the *roman noir* with the psychological intrigue of the *roman problème* include Pierre Boileau and Thomas Narcejac, whose *D'entre les morts* (1954; The Living and the Dead) is the angst-producing, psychologically driven *suspense novel that Alfred Hitchcock brought to the screen in *Vertigo*. An earlier exemplar is Camille Hedwige who created an anxiety-driven enigma in *L'Appel de la morte* (1935), a work that prefigures the work of Patricia *Highsmith. Hedwige's contemporary, Claude Aveline, is preoccupied with character and place in his imaginative *La Double mort de Frederic Belot: suivi d'une double note sur le roman policier* (1932; The Double Death of Frederic Belot), which, as the subtitle indicates, includes a discussion of the *roman policier*. Others who write in this vein include Catherine Arley, who focuses on the internal struggle accompanying a character's slide into crime, and Sebastien Japrisot and Madeleine Coudray.

Modeled on the heroes created by Dashiell *Hammett and Raymond *Chandler, Leo Malet created an early and highly popular French private investigator, Nestor Burma, in *120, Rue de la Gare* (1943) while moving the *roman policier* into the realm of the American-style hard-boiled school or *roman noir*. Also inspired by the work of James Hadley *Chase and Peter Cheney, the *roman noir* is characterized by its use of slang and the evocation of local milieus. This form is exemplified in the work of Mario Ropp and in John Amila's *Y'a pas de bon Dieu* (1950), which portrays the dark outlook of those living in post-war France, when a loss of idealism accompanied the growth of social criticism.

Later works also serve as social critiques as are the cases in the more militant leftist perspective in J. P. Manchette's *Nada* (1972), or in the violent underworld inhabited by Caroline Camara's fringe dwellers in *Le Desosseur* (1979). In works similar in tone to those of Ruth *Rendell, Laurence Oriole has been responsible for moving the *roman policier* toward an examination of social conventions, and laying bare some of society's most taboo topics, notably those dealing with race, sexual identity, and *gender, as exemplified in *Le Domaine du Prince* (1990).

Freceric Dard's Commissioner San Antoni novels exemplify a mix of subgenres and the use of psychological intrigue. Like much crime and mystery writing in France and in the French language, Dard's novels have an appeal that transcends social divisions, attracting intellectuals and working-class readers alike. The wide appeal of the *roman policier* has resulted in its influencing other literary genres, notably the *nouveau roman*, proving that the boundaries between the *roman policier* and other literary genres remain permeable.

[*See also* Police Procedural: Introduction; Realism, Conventions of.]

• Michel Lebrun, Michel and Jean-Paul Schweighaeuser, *Le Guide du polar: Histoire du roman policier français* (1987). Franz Blaha "Detective/Mystery/Spy Fiction," *Handbook of French Popular Culture*, ed. Pierre Horn (1991): 39–57. André Vanoncini, *Le Roman policier* (1993).

—Deborah E. Hamilton

ROMAN PROBLÈME. *See* Roman Policier.

ROYAL CANADIAN MOUNTED POLICE. The Royal Canadian Mounted Police may have the greatest reputation of any in the world for benevolence, handsome uniforms, and an ability to catch criminals. Founded in 1873 by Canada's first prime minister, Sir John A. Macdonald, the force, consisting of 300 men, was originally called the North West Mounted Rifles and was soon renamed the North West Mounted Police. Its headquarters were at Fort MacLeod in Alberta, from which the men set out to deal with traders from the United States who were stirring up unrest among the natives of the area by trading whiskey for buffalo hides. The "Mounties," as they were popularly known, used determination and tact to drive the traders home and to calm the natives. In addition, their assistance to waves of new settlers in the Canadian wilderness during the nineteenth century earned them more praise. Their scarlet jackets and broad-brimmed hats also made them among the world's most recognizable lawmen.

In 1904 the word "Royal" was added to the name and in 1920, when it became a federal force, the name was changed to the Royal Canadian Mounted Police. Today the acronym RCMP is almost as recognizable as the term "Mounties." After a newspaper account described the force as a group that "fetched their man every time," the phrase was reshaped by later writers to read, "they always get their man."

As early as 1893, in Gilbert Parker's *Pierre and His People*, the Mounties appeared in fiction. The first series of novels featuring a Mountie was by the Canadian author Luke Allan, who created Blue Pete, a reformed cattle rustler who became a North West Mounted Police agent. True exploits undertaken by the Mounties inspired many *Westerns and *adventure stories. The Mountie hero Sergeant Major Samuel B. Steele, who arrested moonshiners, skirmished with rebellious metis (people who are mixed White and Indian), pacified Canadian Pacific Railway workers, and stomped out lawlessness among gold rushers in the Yukon, is fictionalized in Harwood Steele's *The Marching Call* (1955) and Bill Pronzini's *Starvation Camp* (1984), to name only two novels.

Some generalizations hold true about Mountie characters as created by Canadians and other nationals. To Canadian authors, the Mountie is an arbitor, instituting civilized order and values for their own sake. British writers often depicted their Mountie heroes as men of the upper class who ventured to Canada for adventure, and brought justice to the settlers along with attitudes stemming from social standing. American writers often permitted logic and individual decisions about justice to override legal considerations in their Mounties, who often seem like transplanted Texas Rangers.

By the middle of the twentieth century, a steady stream of RCMP adventure stories and motion pictures made the force world famous. A television series, *Sergeant Preston of the Yukon*, won a huge juvenile audience; it depicted a strong and earnestly kind hero whose every case closed satisfactorily, usually after a dog-sled chase led by a huskie called King. The Mountie story became so over-popularized that it was not until the late 1970s that the Mountie hero was again treated seriously. Today these characters flourish in *cozy mysteries, *police procedurals, spy fiction, and even *horror fiction, largely written by Canadians. Examples include cozy mysteries by Alisa Craig featuring Inspector Madoc Rhys; Scott Young's depiction of an Inuk hero, Inspector Matthew "Mateesie" Kitologitak, who investigates the disappearance of a bush airplane in *Murder in a Cold Climate* (1988); and American L. R. Wright's suspense-crime novels about Staff Sergeant Karl Alberg of British Columbia, noteworthy for their intense psychological depictions.

[*See also* Canada, Crime and Mystery Writing in; Great Outdoors; Police Detective.]

—Bernard A. Drew

RULES OF THE GAME. The idea that the mystery story is a game in which the writer sets a *puzzle for the reader to solve was inherent in Edgar Allan *Poe's three stories about his detective, the Chevalier C. Auguste *Dupin, and in the problems solved by Sherlock *Holmes. It had not at that time, however, become a game with rules that made it necessary for the writer to provide *clues from which the reader might logically deduce correct answers. Poe's stories show Dupin's deductive skills but offer the reader no chance of emulating them, and Holmes's conclusions are often reached through knowledge that is kept from the reader. It was not until the twentieth century that critics found it necessary to draw up rules, generally called those of fair play, stating exactly in what ways it was legitimate for the writer to attempt deception, and what was impermissible.

One of the earliest suggestions that rules should be observed was made by G. K. *Chesterton, who insisted that "the detective story is only a game" that had nothing to do with reality. Hence any character in such a story "over and above any little crimes he may intend to indulge in . . . must have already some other justification as a character in a story and not only as a mere miserable material person in real life."

But it was not until the late 1920s that rules were numbered and codified in S. S. *Van Dine's "Twenty Rules for Writing Detective Stories" (1928), and the "Detective Story Decalogue" included by Ronald A. *Knox when introducing a collection of *Best Detective Stories of the Year 1928* (1929; *Best English Detective Stories of 1928*). Van Dine's rules went well beyond insisting on the prime basis of "fair play," which is that the reader should have access to all information available to the detective and all clues noticed by him. Van Dine also said there must be no love interest (a distraction), no secret societies or mafias, which "have no place in a detective story," and that there should be only one detective and one culprit, who must not be a professional criminal or a servant ("the culprit must be a decidedly worthwhile person"). The *motive must always be personal, and the final answer must never be in terms of accident or *suicide. Finally, Van Dine barred a number of devices as outworn, including forged fingerprints, ciphers, or code letters, and locked room murders committed after the police had entered the room. Knox, who might not have agreed with all Van Dine's proscriptions but repeated others in a slightly different form, added a ban on more than one secret room or passage, and a total prohibition of any Chinamen. He laid down that "the detective must not himself commit the crime," that the Watson figure's thoughts must not be concealed, and that twin brothers or doubles should not be used without the reader being adequately prepared for them.

These rules were set down with a twinkle in the eye, or tongue in cheek. Yet they were also meant to be taken seriously, and most of the best-known writers of the period conformed to them in spirit, if not always in fact. Dorothy L. *Sayers at first deplored love interest in the detective story, although later on she changed her mind, and members of Britain's *Detection Club swore on election to avoid mysterious poisons unknown to science, and to use "a seemly moderation" in relation to gangs, trapdoors, supercriminals, and lunatics. There were serious discussion about the legitimacy of what Knox called "some remarkable performances by Mrs Christie," particularly in *The Murder of Roger Ackroyd* (1926), although in the end they were approved. In the United States the first eight books by Ellery *Queen contained at a certain point a "Challenge to the Reader" saying all necessary clues for solving the mystery had now been provided, and that rightly interpreted they permitted only one possible answer.

Many stories by Christie, Queen, and others were marvels of *ingenuity, and so were John Dickson *Carr's many *locked room mysteries, which faithfully observed the rules of the game even though the solutions were sometimes extravagantly unlikely. Within their apparently severe limits, the rules allowed much variety of approach and expression, so that most detective story writers working in the Golden Age (roughly the years between World Wars I and II) moved comfortably within them.

Yet there were doubters, and even rebels. T. S. Eliot, in one of his occasional pronouncements on the detective story, wished that the writers would either concentrate on the detective interest or "take more trouble and space over the characters as human beings," and as early as 1930 Anthony *Berkeley suggested that the detective story of the future would hold readers "less by mathematics than by psychological ties." In the following year Berkeley, using the pseudonym Francis Iles, provided a masterly demonstration of this in *Malice Aforethought*, "the story of a commonplace crime," which contained no detection and ignored the rules rather than breaking them. And of course there were many books within the genre, *thrillers and spy stories, to which the rules did not apply. They were devised specifically to define and limit the detective story.

It would be hard to say just when the rules of the game fell into disuse. They were damaged by Raymond *Chandler's assault in "The Simple Art of Murder" (*Atlantic Monthly*, Dec. 1944), when he condemned those writers of detective stories who conducted "the same old futzing around with timetables and bits of charred paper and who trampled the jolly old flowering arbutus under the library window." Dashiell *Hammett and *Chandler replaced the rich *amateur detective at the heart of the rules-of-the-game approach by the private investigator who was a working stiff. Elsewhere Ngaio *Marsh made Chandler's point more gently when she said she liked to examine and probe into her characters, but found that the deeper she tried to dig into their psychological *motivation, the more she came in conflict with "the skulduggery [she was] obliged to produce in relation to the guilty party."

That was the technical limitation writers found in the rules of the game as they concentrated more on character, less on *plot. But there was a wider consideration. The rules presupposed an orderly world in which problems could be solved by logic, and a social hierarchy in which a servant was not a sufficiently interesting person to be the villain in a crime story. Much of World War II contradicted such comfortable assumptions. The triumph of the German blitzkrieg in France, saturation bombing of cities, the concentration camps, the chaos of postwar Europe, were all contradictions of the belief that social or other problems could be solved by logic. The writers of crime stories who emerged after World War II tried to create credible characters motivated by real reasons for murder, but were not aware of any rules they should observe.

Today all the leading practitioners of the rules of the game are dead, Christie, Sayers, Carr, Queen, and Van Dine, along with many lesser practitioners of their era. The Detection Club has changed its oath radically, omitting mention of trapdoors, supercriminals, and lunatics. Detectives today may be black or white, Jewish or Arab, gay or lesbian, honest or crooked. They are least likely to be the well-to-do amateurs who inhabit so many Golden Age detective novels, figures who, like the rules of the game, now belong to history.

[See also Conventions of the Genre: Traditional Conventions; Cozy Mystery; Pontificators, The].

• Howard Haycraft, ed., *The Art of the Mystery Story: A Collection of Critical Essays* (1946). Donald K. Adams, ed., *The Mystery and Detection Annual* (1973). Francis M. Nevins Jr., *Royal Bloodline: Ellery Queen, Author and Detective* (1974). Julian Symons, *Bloody Murder: From the Detective Story to the Crime Novel*, rev. ed. (1992). Michael Dibdin, ed., *The Picador Book of Crime Writing* (1993).   —Julian Symons

Rumpole, Horace, is the hero and first-person narrator of eleven collections of stories by John

*Mortimer Q. C., amiably satirizing the follies of the Bar, the judiciary, and the British Establishment in general. All have been made into successful television series.

Since his first appearance in *Rumpole of the Bailey* in 1978, Rumpole himself has changed little. While other members of his Chambers have aged and progressed, he has obstinately remained in his late sixties. Overweight, badly dressed, soup-stained, smoking the smallest cigars and drinking the cheapest claret, he does not look like a successful barrister, nor indeed is he: he is an "Old Bailey hack"—a barrister who has never attained the rank of Queen's Counsel, and whose practice deals almost entirely with crime rather than the more lucrative commercial cases. Defending perpetrators of petty crime is his forte. Although he encounters the occasional murderer, he is far more often to be found speaking out for a shoplifter or unsuccessful burglar.

At first sight, the stories and the central character seem mutually contradictory. Rumpole is represented as an effective advocate and skillful cross-examiner, and as quick as Sherlock *Holmes or Hercule *Poirot to observe the *clue that turns the case upside down and reveals the truth: usually, though not always, he wins his case. And yet, by most worldly standards—certainly by those of his wife Hilda, "She Who Must be Obeyed," and of the other members of his Chambers, who regularly conspire to persuade him into retirement—he is a failure.

The audience gradually see, however, that his *virtues, rather than his shortcomings, preclude success. As a lover of the language of William Shakespeare and William Wordsworth, he cannot become fluent in the latest fashionable jargon; as a lawyer who puts his duty to his client first, he cannot be expediently polite to prejudiced or overbearing *judges; as a man of humanity and imagination, who understands what life is like in prison, he cannot summon up the ambition to appear for the prosecution, still less to pass sentence. He attains heroic stature not despite failure, but because of it: success, for Mortimer, is always a trifle suspect.

[*See also* Courtroom Milieu; Lawyer: The British Lawyer-Sleuth; Lawyer: Lawyers as Secondary Characters; Legal Procedural.]

—Sarah Caudwell

RURAL MILIEU. As early as 1892, in "The Adventure of the Copper Breeches" (*Strand*, June 1892), Sherlock Holmes pointed out that the rural *milieu is a likely place for crime to occur. "It is my belief, Watson," he says, "founded upon my experience, that the lowest and vilest alleys in *London do not present a more dreadful record of sin than does the smiling and beautiful countryside." Ever since Holmes, there have been detectives who have used their special knowledge of the country outside the city to seek miscreants in rural localities and idyllic surroundings.

Prominent among those investigators who have worked in rustic areas is Melville Davisson *Post's Uncle *Abner. In a series of stories that were published beginning in 1911 (collected as *Uncle Abner, Master of Mysteries*, 1918), Post placed his fictional detective in the wild and lawless back country of western Virginia in the years around or just before the middle of the nineteenth century. The Uncle Abner stories are narrated by Abner's nephew, Martin, and Abner is often accompanied on his missions by Squire Randolph, a justice of the peace. Davisson's tales are told in a style heavily influenced by the King James translation of the Old Testament, and Abner carries his Bible with him as he executes the laws of God and those of humankind with evangelical zeal. Probably the best-known of the stories is "The Doomdorf Mystery" (*Saturday Evening Post*, 18 July 1914) with its "impossible crime" (a locked room shooting) that takes place at an isolated location where "the government of Virginia was remote and its arm short and feeble." Doomdorf's home-brewed liquor has caused wild disorder among the populace in the countryside surrounding his property, and though two people confess to Doomdorf's *murder, it is up to Abner to discover the man's true executioner.

Perhaps Uncle Abner's nearest fictional descendant is Gavin Stevens, who appears in a series of short stories by William Faulkner. The first of the Stevens tales, "Smoke," appeared in *Harpers* in April 1932, and the stories were eventually collected in the volume titled *Knight's Gambit* (1949). Like the Uncle Abner stories, these accounts are narrated by the detective's admiring nephew. Chick Mallison's complex, meditative style echoes that of other Faulkner narrators.

Faulkner's elaborately plotted "An Error in Chemistry" appeared in *Ellery Queen's Mystery Magazine* in 1946. Faulkner's *sleuth is a Harvard-educated attorney, but he knows the "broad, heat-miraged land" of Faulkner's Mississippi back-country as well as any of the characters who populate Yoknapatapha Country. In fact, in a story like "Hand upon the Waters" (*Saturday Evening Post*, 4 Nov. 1939) the solution to the crime turns on Stevens's knowledge of how a man fishes with a trot line.

Another detective who has flourished in remote regions is Arthur W. *Upfield's Napoleon *Bonaparte, who was named for a book of French history he chewed on while teething. Upfield's thirty-three mystery novels featuring the half-caste Bonaparte, beginning with *The Barrakee Mystery* (1928; *The Lure of the Bush*), are set in the Australian bush country, and Bonaparte (or Bony, as he insists that everyone call him) uses his special skills to solve crimes that are often half-forgotten before he arrives on the scene. From his Aboriginal mother, Bony inherited his ability in tracking, a skill that resulted in his rapid promotion in the Queensland Police, as well as his aptitude for reading the other pages of the "Book of the Bush." Bony specializes in crimes that occur in the remote places of Australia, providing the reader with fascinating accounts of such apparently measureless expanses as the bleak Nullabor Plain (*The Man of Two Tribes*, 1956), the Windee Station in New South Wales (*The Sands of Windee*, 1931), and the Land of Burning Water Bushranger of the Skies (1940, *No Footprints in the Bush*). The books are filled with characters with rural roots including swagmen, jackeroos, Aborigines, and pastoralists; Bony is at home among them all, and not infrequently goes out disguised as one of them. He is a good listener and a close observer, and the outcome of one case turns on something so simple as the behavior of an ant.

The Four Corners area of the United States, where New Mexico, Colorado, Utah, and Arizona join together, while not as enormous as the Australian outback, is also a remote area. There, the same skills that Bonaparte applies in his dealings with the Aborigines are needed by Tony *Hillerman's Joe Leaphorn and Jim *Chee when solving the crimes that occur within the 25,000 square mile confines of the Navajo reservation. Hillerman, who cites Upfield as an influence upon his development as a crime writer, creates heros who share Bony's patience, logical thought processes, and ability to function in the outdoors. The southwestern landscape is perhaps best depicted in *Listening Woman* (1978), though it is prominent in other books as well, including *The Blessing Way* (1970) and *The Dark Wind* (1982).

County sheriffs patrol an area much smaller than that allotted to the Navajo tribal police, but they sometimes encounter bizarre crimes, a fact that has made them quite popular in more recent mystery novels. A. B. Guthrie, Jr. won the Pulitzer Prize for *The Big Sky* (1947), a novel about the American West, but he is also a writer of mysteries, including a series about Sheriff Chick Charleston and Deputy Jason Beard, who operate in Midbury, Montana. Their duties are not confined to the town, however, and they frequently find themselves in the outlying areas when investigating things such as the apparent ritual slaughter of cattle in *No Second Wind* (1980). Simi-

larly, Bill Crider's Sheriff Dan Rhodes, of Blacklin County, Texas, often leaves the town limits when confronted with such outlandish circumstances as packages of neatly wrapped body parts that turn up in a pasture, in *Shotgun Saturday Night* (1987) or when a portable outhouse floating down a creek is found to contain a dead body in *Murder Most Fowl* (1994). And D. R. Meredith's Sheriff Charles Timothy Matthews of the Texas Panhandle's Crawford County has to deal with a woman stuffed into a barbecue pit and burned to death. Sharyn McCrumb has staked a claim to Appalachia with *If Ever I Return, Pretty Peggy-O* (1990), as Sheriff Spencer Atwood is confronted with slaughtered sheep, a hanged dog, and a nagging *suspicion that the past is never dead. Joan Hess uses small-town Maggody, Arkansas, as the scene of many crimes. The countryside provides no escape from crime when Amanda Hazard leaves Las Vegas for the supposed serenity of Vamoose, Oklahoma, in Connie Feddersen's *Dead in the Water* (1993). Amanda finds a farmer named William Farley drowned in his cattle trough, and she knows better than to believe that his death is accidental.

Clearly, population density has nothing to do with the murder rate, at least in fiction. There is no respite in the boondocks from murder and other crimes, and there is no shortage of sleuths to ferret out solutions to whatever nefarious deeds are done there.

• Tom and Enid Schantz, introduction to *The Methods of Uncle Abner* (1974).   —Bill Crider

Saint, The. Created by Leslie *Charteris, Simon Templar, or the Saint, is a rambunctious adventurer who believes in old-fashioned romantic ideals and is prepared to lay down his life for them. Using considerable wit and intelligence, the Saint often avenges innocent *victims.

The Saint became a British pop culture sensation in the early 1930s, his notoriety cutting across class lines. When Charteris adopted American citizenship in the 1940s, so did Simon Templar. During World War II, the Saint was an undercover agent for the U.S. government; after the war, Templar resumed his globetrotting escapades of benevolent outlawry.

Charteris introduced the Saint in *Meet the Tiger* (1928) and his character appeared in numerous novels, novelettes, and short stories, some published in the magazines named for him, including *The Saint Detective Magazine*, *The Saint Mystery Magazine*, and *The New Saint Magazine*. He also appeared in comic books, newspaper cartoon strips, motion pictures, and radio and television programs.

[*See also* Adventurer and Adventuress; Chivalry, Code of; Gentleman Adventurer.]   —Burl Barer

SAINT PATRICK'S DAY. *See* Holiday Mysteries.

SAN FRANCISCO, as a *setting, has been unusually generous to crime and mystery writers. Located in the moist, cool climate of northern California on a hilly peninsula at the entry to a major Pacific port, the city features steeply graded streets that run to the sea on three sides, offering splendid vistas of maritime commerce and the landmark Golden Gate Bridge in daylight hours, and layering the scene at nighttime with a chilly fog to blur the outlines of buildings and conceal the passage of foot traffic. Adding to the romance of the physical site, San Francisco's history—as a city founded by fevered adventurers in search of gold, and subsequently the home of such outsized heroes of industry as Leland Stanford—establishes the locale as a stage for the actions of men and women whose unbridled ambition has transformed their American Dreams into dramas of amoral desire.

Mark Twain, working as a newspaper writer in San Francisco, used the columns of a local paper and the lore of the city for one of his earliest tales of horror, "Kearny Street Ghost Story" (*Golden Era*, Jan. 1866). Ambrose Bierce, who also practiced the trade of journalism in San Francisco, chose to set his story "Beyond the Wall" (*Cosmopolitan*, Dec. 1907)—which echoes Edgar Allan *Poe in its use of a house that resembles the Ushers' and a character derived from the Chevalier C. Auguste *Dupin—in a lonely tower toward the ocean beach on the city's bay. San Francisco also served as a setting for Frank Norris and Jack London, authors of naturalist novels featuring the adventures of extraordinary individualists whose characters anticipate the existentialist *private eyes who later appeared in hard-boiled private eye stories. But although Norris and London explored themes of *violence and violation, they preferred to do so in fiction akin to the bildungsroman rather than the crime and mystery genre.

Probably Jack Boyle, author of *Boston Blackie* (1919), deserves to be remembered as the first author to employ San Francisco as a setting within the conventions of crime and mystery writing. Even as his title suggests, though, San Francisco was merely the starting place for the story. Fuller use of the city's suggestive potential awaited the pulp stories of Dashiell *Hammett. Tales such as "Fly Paper" (*Black Mask*, Aug. 1929), "The Gutting of Cuffignal" (*Black Mask*, Dec. 1925), and "The Big Knockover," (*The Big Knockover*, 1966; *The Dashiell Hammett Story Omnibus*) lead the *Continental Op among the neighborhoods and along the streets of San Francisco like a native aware of his physical terrain, if not comfortable in the moral realms he visits. It is *The Maltese Falcon* (1930), however, that elevates locale into character through a style that works sympathetic magic by which the singular *atmosphere of the city represents the obscure social relationships in the novel. San Francisco's fogs, dark streets, steep inclines, and drop-offs represent topographically the ambiguous relationships between characters like Brigid O'Shaughnessy and Sam *Spade. For example, O'Shaughnessy engages Spade in apparent love while she betrays him, and Spade states that he may love her but turns her in to the cops.

After Hammett, San Francisco was used by Lenore Glen Offord for romance mysteries such as the allusively titled *Murder on Russian Hill* (1938; *Murder Before Breakfast*) and by Frances Crane as the home base for her Pat and Jean Abbott series, which began with *The Turquoise Shop* (1941) and continued through twenty-four additional novels that play on color references in their titles.

The template for San Francisco as a setting was revived by Bill Pronzini, whose 1968 story "It's a Lousy World" (*Alfred Hitchcock's Mystery Magazine*, Jan. 1968) introduced his "Nameless Detective." In at least twenty novels and scores of short stories Pronzini has proceeded to map the city through regular use of place names, addresses, and businesses. The verisimilitude of the style by which Pronzini sets San Francisco as the scene is matched in the realism of the language spoken by his characters and by the plausibility with which he constructs his plots.

The possibilities that San Francisco offers to novelists of police stories can be observed in the series Collin Wilcox has written about Frank Hastings and Pete Friedman, homicide lieutenants on the city police force. Joe Gores displays yet further innovation in ways to use San Francisco for setting in his series of novels about Dan Kearny, who opened his skip-trace agency in *A Time of Predators* (1969). In testimony to the imaginative power that San Francisco holds for writers, Gores has also written *Hammett: A Novel* (1975), which reflexively directs the hard-boiled tradition to the production of a fictional memoir of the form's founding father.

The accomplishment of the male authors, who practically made San Francisco the birthplace of the hard-boiled private eye, has its counterpart in the creation by Marcia *Muller of the first major female private eye, Sharon McCone, who also resides and works in San Francisco. McCone debuted in *Edwin of the Iron Shoes* (1977), and in continuing the series Muller has extended her realist's eye to such distinguishing features of the city as its Victorian architecture, its historic forts, the famous bridge, which she informs us in the novellette "Deceptions" (*A Matter of Crime*, 1987) is not golden "but rust red, reminiscent of dried blood."

[*See also* Realism, Conventions of; Urban Milieu.]

—Frederick Isaac

SAPPER. *See* McNeile, H. C.

SATIRE has long been employed in all forms of literature to censure human conduct by mockery, sarcasm, ridicule, or irony. Crime fiction is attractive to satirists both as a medium in which to attack human frailties and as a target itself. A restrained use of satire complicates the background issues of the story, making characters and *plot less formulaic and one-dimensional. Satirizing the genre lays bare its pretensions and assumptions.

The *conventions of the genre lend themselves to satire, especially in the form of parody. One of the most popular targets has been the series character. E. C. *Bentley created an unforgettable detective in Philip Trent, the author's parody of the contemporary detective in *Trent's Last Case*; (1913; *The Woman in Black*) and initiated a new type of series character, the *silly-ass sleuth. Agatha *Christie happily mocked herself and her readers with her portrait of the mystery writer Mrs. Ariadne Oliver and her Finnish detective in *Cards on the Table* (1936). The Crimes Circle in Anthony *Berkeley's *The Poisoned Chocolates Case* (1929) pokes fun at the *London *Detection Club. The tradition of the old lady detective knitting is mocked by Gladys *Mitchell in *Dance to Your Daddy* (1969), where Mrs. Adela Beatrice Lestrange *Bradley works at "an indeterminate piece of knitting." Lawrence

*Block, writing as Chip Harrison, parodies Rex *Stout's Nero *Wolfe in *Make out with Murder* (1974; *The Five Little Rich Girls*). S. S. *Van Dine's Philo *Vance is similarly treated by Elliot Paul, whose *sleuth Homer Evans is more insufferable than his model in *Hugger-Mugger in the Louvre* (1940).

Leo *Bruce devotes *Case for Three Detectives* (1936) to mocking the conventions and mannerisms of the *amateur detective. His three sleuths, based on Lord Peter *Wimsey, Hercule *Poirot, and Father *Brown, are beaten to a correct solution of the crime by a stolid, seemingly stupid, village policeman, Sergeant *Beef. The three detectives describe complicated solutions to a *murder in a locked room, using the methods ascribed to them by their creators, but Beef finds the answer by using routine police work. He thus overturns the convention of the clever amateur succeeding where incompetent police officers have failed. On similar lines is Marion Mainwaring's *Murder in Pastiche* (1954), which parodies nine famous investigators from the United States and Britain.

Spoof-like treatment of beloved series characters such as Wimsey or admired writers such as Christie is not far from satire of the genre itself. Robert Louis Stevenson, writing with Lloyd Osbourne, mocked the detective novel in *The Wrong Box* (1889). Authors not normally associated with the genre have used it as a basis for satire. In "The Macbeth Murder Mystery" in *My World—And Welcome to It* (1942), James Thurber reflects on those who spend their time reading detective novels.

The classic detective story is easy to satirize, since its conventions and formulas require a tempting innocence. The hard-boiled novel poses a different challenge, for this writing is in some regards even more unrealistic than the traditional *detective novel. At the very least, satire is inherent in the self-mockery and sarcasm of the detective, and in the exaggerated villainy of such characters as Caspar Gutman in Dashiell *Hammett's *The Maltese Falcon* (1930) and Amthor in Raymond *Chandler's *Farewell, My Lovely* (1940). Satire of the hard-boiled genre as a whole often takes a form close to farce, as in L. A. Morse's *The Big Enchilada* (1982). Andrew Bergman manages to follow the investigations of Jack LeVine while mocking them, incorporating both humor and tension in *The Big Kiss-Off of 1944* (1974). Ed *McBain satirized hard-boiled attitudes and the form of the *police procedural in *Romance* (1995).

During the Golden Age many authors used crime fiction to deflate the pretensions of particular groups. Dorothy L. *Sayers deals with literary snobs in *The Unpleasantness at the Bellona Club* (1928). In *Death of a Ghost* (1934) Margery *Allingham wittily portrays the affectations of London's artistic community; Elliot Paul did the same for the artistic and literary coterie of the Left Bank in Paris in *The Mysterious Mickey Finn, or, Murder at the Café du Dôme.* (1939) Edmund *Crispin's *Buried for Pleasure* (1948) mixes politics and detection with entertaining irony. Robert *Barnard tilts at hypocrisy and smugness in many forms; *Death of an Old Goat* (1974) is a wicked portrayal of academic life in Australia, and *Death in Purple Prose* (1987; *The Cherry Blossom*

Corpse) satirizes a convention of romance writers. With gentler humor Simon Brett exposes the foibles in the world of show business in *Cast, in Order of Disappearance* (1975). Emma *Lathen often casts a sardonic eye on the world of Wall Street, laying bare the falsities of business men and women, as in *Banking on Death* (1961).

On both sides of the Atlantic writers have chosen small-town settings for the opportunities they afford to expose a broad range of human misconduct. Writers deride pompous or silly officials and citizens with inflated ideas of their own importance. Phoebe Atwood *Taylor satirizes New England life in her Asey *Mayo novels set on Cape Cod; in *Octagon House* (1937) local worthies are satirized in a mural. In England, Colin *Watson paints memorable, often bawdy portraits of the seemingly honest, upright inhabitants of Flaxborough. Only the series detective, Inspector Walter Purbright, is incorruptible and competent.

[*See also* Farceurs; Pastiche.]

—Christine R. Simpson

SAYERS, DOROTHY L[EIGH] (1893–1957), English author of detective fiction, the greatest and most widely read of the British Golden Age. Her aristocratic detective, Lord Peter *Wimsey, like Sherlock *Holmes, has become a household name.

The only child of the Reverend Henry and Helen Sayers, she was born in Oxford, where her father was headmaster of Christ Church Cathedral Choir School. When she was four years old, her father accepted a living in the fen country of East Anglia, a region she used as the *setting of one of her best-loved novels, *The Nine Tailors: Changes Rung on an Old Theme in Two Short Touches and Two Full Peals* (1934). Educated by governesses until she was fifteen and then at the Godolphin School, Salisbury, she won a scholarship to Somerville College, Oxford, where she achieved a first-class degree in French.

Her early love was poetry, which she continued writing most of her life. She was also a playwright, and her twelve radio plays on the life of Christ, *The Man Born to Be King: A Play-Cycle on the life of Our Lord and Savior, Jesus Christ* (broadcast 1941–42) made broadcast history. She was at work on a verse translation of Dante's *Divine Comedy* at the time of her death.

An admirer of Wilkie *Collins (of whom she began a biography) and of Arthur Conan *Doyle, she aimed at restoring detective fiction to the literary level from which it had lapsed since their time. She attached importance to the "fair play" rule (every clue to be as perceptible to the reader as to the detective), to the creation of character, and to the integration of theme and *plot. Her criteria are set out in her introduction to the first volume of *Great Short Stories of Detection, Mystery and Horror* (1928–34; *The Omnibus of Crime*) an authoritative selection of detective fiction, which was definitive in its day and remains a cornerstone anthology.

Among her contemporaries, those who influenced her most were G. K. *Chesterton and E. C. *Bentley. She regarded Chesterton's article "How to Write a Detective Story" (*G. K.'s Weekly*, 17 Oct. 1925) as the soundest advice on the subject. E. C. Bentley's detective, Philip Trent, was a forerunner of Wimsey, and her first novel, *Whose Body?* (1923), contains echoes of *Trent's Last Case*. Wimsey was also drawn from life. In appearance he was based on Maurice Roy Ridley, an Oxford graduate she had seen in 1913. For his sartorial elegance she drew on an old Etonian, Charles Crichton, whose manservant was the origin of Bunter. For his sophistication she drew also on a personal friend, Eric Whelpton. She admitted a resemblance to Bertie Wooster, although P. G. Wodehouse's character was scarcely known in 1923. Both Wooster and Wimsey reflect an actual lifestyle of the time: A well-known example was the writer Michael Arlen.

Wimsey's enduring vitality is mainly due, however, to his creator's own wit, exuberance, and intellectual energy. The same is true also of Sayers's character Harriet *Vane, a detective novelist with whom Lord Peter falls in love and whom he eventually marries. Sayers's achievement was not only the creation of a modern, independent woman—still a role model for many young women readers—but the perilous introduction of a love situation into detective fiction that becomes not only credible and moving but also an integral part of the plot. The relationship begins in *Strong Poison* (1930), continues in *Have His Carcase* (1932), and reaches betrothal in *Gaudy Night* (1935) and marriage in *Busman's Honeymoon* (1937, first written as a play).

Sayers's detective fiction (with the exception of some of the short stories) is drawn from the author's own life. She used *settings that were familiar to her—a fishing and painting community in Scotland in *The Five Red Herrings* (1931), an advertising agency in *Murder Must Advertise* (1933), the fen country in *The Nine Tailors*, and Oxford in *Gaudy Night*. Her characters read the books she read, quote the poets she knew, play and sing the music she herself enjoyed. They speak as she and her contemporaries spoke and comment similarly on current affairs. This provides what she (agreeing in this with Collins) considered an essential ingredient in detective fiction, namely "a vivid conviction of fact," on the basis of which the reader can be induced to accept the imaginary. Another consequence is that her novels are a vivid reflection of the social, economic, and cultural life of her time.

As a practicing Christian, Sayers was in no doubt as to the distinction between right and wrong, between free will and individual responsibility. In her day, the penalty for *murder was death by hanging. There is no sign that she was opposed to capital punishment, but she endows Wimsey with grave misgivings as to his right to bring about a criminal's undoing. Beneath his external frivolousness, a self-defensive *disguise, he is vulnerable. To readers who respond positively to him, this adds to his credibility as a human being. Others dislike him for his mannerisms, his aristocratic birth, and his wealth. The charge of snobbery has often been brought against his creator. Yet the society she depicts is mobile: Wimsey marries a commoner; his sister marries a chief inspector; his friend, the Honorable Freddy Arbuthnot, marries the daughter of a self-made Jewish financier, who is himself married to a Gentile.

The legacy of Sayers to present-day detective novelists has been acknowledged by P. D. *James, who sees her as an innovator of style rather than of form. Her murder methods are thought to have been too ingenious, and it is asserted that one or two of them would not work. Some critics consider her novels overwritten and too literary. In her day she was widely acclaimed, and her novels were translated into most European languages. Of all detective novelists, she is perhaps the most reread. This suggests that the murder method and the solving of the mystery are the least important elements in her work. The quality of her writing is the factor that ensures her continued importance.

• Trevor H. Hall, *Dorothy L. Sayers: Nine Literary Studies* (1980). Margaret P. Hannay, ed., *As Her Wimsey Took Her: Critical Essays on the Work of Dorothy L. Sayers* (1979). James Brabazon, *Dorothy L. Sayers: A Biography* (1981). David Coomes, *Dorothy L. Sayers: A Careless Rage for Life* (1992). Barbara Reynolds, *Dorothy L. Sayers: Her Life and Soul* (1993); *The Letters of Dorothy L. Sayers*, 4 vols. (from 1995).
—Barbara Reynolds

SCIENCE FICTION as a label exhibits some of the same mutable characteristics as the contents it affects to describe. For a brief period in the 1920s, the usage was "scientifiction." While "SF" is accepted as an affectionate label, "sci-fi" has also become common. And today, SF generally tends toward fantasy.

The genre is rather an *omnium-gatherum*, containing subgenres such as utopian and alternative world fiction, disaster novels, and so on. Its hallmark is an insistence on change and new things—inventions or freshly discovered worlds. Emphasis on space travel is less pronounced than in the past.

Just as Edgar Allan *Poe's detective stories were written before the term "detective" was used, so science fiction was written before the term "science" (or even the word "scientist") was coined. The two genres have in common the unravelling of a *mystery: Social conditions at the end of the eighteenth century were ripe for such things, as the world itself became increasingly susceptible to scientific inquiry. The criminal or pursuer is a solitary figure, typical of the romantic age.

According to Julian *Symons (*Bloody Murder*, 3rd rev. ed. 1992), *Things As They Are; or, The Adventures of Caleb Williams* (1794), by William *Godwin, is generally considered the first crime novel to deal centrally with a murder, its detection, and subsequent pursuit. The honor of writing the first true SF novel falls to Godwin's daughter, Mary Wollstonecraft Shelley. Her novel, *Frankenstein: Or, the Modern Prometheus* (1818), follows the pattern of her father's book in some of its details. There are murders, criminal elements, and false trails, but its central premise is startlingly new: that from the dead, by scientific means, new beings can be created. The scientist has seized new powers.

Both these novels, by father and daughter, are indebted to the *Gothic novel. Gothics invented *suspense and mystery, which keep the reader reading—even if the denouement proves banal. Crime and SF continue to flourish as genres long after the Church novel, for example, has died, because those who write them have perfected the techniques that keep readers turning the pages: stepping up tension, heightening revelation, and fine-tuning *ingenuity.

Hence many practitioners of one genre have performed well in the other. The creator of Sherlock *Holmes is also famous for *The Lost World* (1912) and other Professor Challenger stories. That prolific crime writer Edgar *Wallace also wrote the story behind one of the greatest SF movies, *King Kong* (1933).

The most celebrated writer of SF is H. G. Wells. Many of his novels include mystery and revelation. A brilliant example is *The War of the Worlds* (1898), which relies for its denouement on a cleverly concealed but well-signaled scientific *clue, bacterial action.

In its earlier days, popular SF existed only in magazine form. The era of the pulps produced the first magazine devoted entirely to SF, Hugo Gernsback's *Amazing Stories* (1926). Specialized genres did much to separate SF from crime fiction. SF novels proliferated with the paperback industry, often rounding off with a chase in imitation of gangster movies. Good examples are *The Joy Makers* (1961) and *The Immortals* (1958), both by James Gunn, who later became a distinguished historian in the field.

The celebrated crime novelist Anthony *Boucher was founding editor with J. Francis McComas of the *Magazine of Fantasy and Science Fiction*, which was launched in 1949 and is still flourishing. Fredric *Brown, author of *The Fabulous Clipjoint* (1947) and other crime novels, was also well known for his SF, in particular *What Mad Universe* (1949). Isaac Asimov's mysteries sold almost as well as his SF novels such as *The Foundation Trilogy* (assembled 1953). Asimov's *The Naked Sun* (1957) is a nicely constructed mystery novel with an android detective. The success of Asimov's *Foundation* trilogy perhaps began a trend, nowadays wearing thin, for novels sprawling over three or more volumes. SF/Fantasy can manage this feat with some ease. Whereas crime novels are most effective when set in known locations, SF and related heroic fantasy can explore invented worlds at greater length. L.A. we know about already; J. R. R. Tolkien's Middle Earth must be unveiled.

SF shows its vitality by spreading into other media, not unlike the crime story. While SF forms a predominant element in movies, arcade games, computer games, "shoot-'em-ups," and video, written SF has become more thoughtful and humanistic. Similar trends can be discerned in crime fiction. In such novels as P. D. *James's *The Children of Men* (1992), which takes up Brian Aldiss's theme of an England without children (*Greybeard*, 1964), the two genres come together once more.

As artificers of memorable modern icons, SF writers have been immensely successful. The spaceship, robot, and android, the matchless city, postnuclear landscape, and the alien world are powerful images embodying the anguish and excitement of our day. However, even the surreal "cyberpunk" novels of William Gibson, beginning with *Neuromancer* (1984), take as their blueprint the Chandleresque *thriller.

As the criminal is punished in detective fiction, so the Promethean idea of progress is frequently punished in SF. Whereas the world in detective fiction is usually restored to its customary state, in an SF text the world may be left in a profoundly changed condition for better or worse—generally for worse. The blame once attached to a malefactor has been shifted to an entire society.

[*See also* Future, Use of the.]

• Russel B. Nye, *The Unembarrassed Muse: The Popular Arts in America* (1970). John G. Cawelti, *Adventure, Mystery, and Romance: Formula Stories as Art and Popular Culture* (1976). Marshall B. Tymn and Mike Ashley, eds., *Science Fiction, Fantasy, and Weird Fiction Magazines* (1985). Brian W. Aldiss and David Wingrove, *Trillion Year Spree: The History of Science Fiction* (1986). Neil Barron, ed., *Anatomy of Wonder: A Critical Guide to Science Fiction* (4th ed. 1995). John Clute and Peter Nicholls, eds., *The Encyclopaedia of Science Fiction* (1993).   —Brian Aldiss

SCIENTIFIC SLEUTH. For its informing principle the genre of detective and mystery fiction owes an incalculable debt to science. Amid the disruptive changes in Europe and the Americas during the nineteenth century—the insecurity evoked by the shift of populations to the city where the miserable conditions of the poor starkly contrasted with the unprecedented personal wealth in the possession of people who were neither princes nor bishops, the alterations in modes of work that gave the machine precedence over its human operators, the anonymity consequent to migrations that eroded the foundations of traditional institutional and social relationships—amid the confusion of the journey to a new way of living impelled by vast economic and technological changes, intellectuals and others among the literate public found comfort in scientific optimism. The techniques of disciplined inquiry promised the means of comprehending a new order. The mind, it seemed, had power to give the world rationally apprehensible form, and, with the application of reason, the minds of men and women could address the mysteries of the physical world and thereby ameliorate the problems of the social world. Realism would single out such problems as crime; with the example of science before everyone, though, there was optimism to spur the will.

Such optimism readily entered popular literature. When the scientifically trained Dr. John H. *Watson meets the research scientist Sherlock *Holmes and bears witness to the inimitable series of inferences characterizing Holmes's way of greeting clients and the world at large, the consulting detective character emerges as the reader's Virgil, a guide through the latter-day inferno of modern life. The method of Holmes is innocent of theory. His studies of cigar ashes and soil samples are empirical and taxonomic, but they are sufficient to confirm Holmes as a champion of investigative reasoning.

Among the creators of rival *sleuths who sought to tap the popularity Holmes generated for the emergent genre of detective fiction, few tried to imitate the portrayal of a practicing scientist. Instead they took the optimism inspired by science as a given element of narration upon which to work their own variations. In the next generation of detective writers, however, R. Austin *Freeman selected the scientific vocation as the substance of investigation. As Ian Ousby has written in *Guilty Parties: A Mystery Lover's Companion* (1997), Doyle dealt with the principles of science "to convey its glamorous aura," but Freeman pursued the details of science, replacing the lodgings in Baker Street with the laboratory bench as the locale of criminal study. Freeman's sleuth, Dr. John *Thorndyke, is a forensic scientist who explains the intricacies of fingerprinting in *The Red Thumb Mark* (1907), zoology and marine science in other works. Edgar Allan *Poe had provided his detective, the Chevalier C. Auguste *Dupin, with full opportunity to discourse upon method, but where Dupin's disquisitions derived from *a priori* principles of logic, Thorndyke's scientific method was founded on contemporary research in physical science.

The character of the practical scientist reappeared in the United States in the works of Arthur B. *Reeve, whose detective, Professor Craig Kennedy, was once known as the American Sherlock Holmes. A professor of chemistry at Columbia University in New York City, Kennedy typically exhibited his method by the use of a new device or technique—blood sampling, the Dictaphone, the X ray, typewriter analysis, and so on—that he demonstrated before the assembly of *suspects and officials gathered for denouement in his laboratory. From 1911 when he issued his first collection of Kennedy short stories, *The Poisoned Pen*, until the appearance of *The Clutching Hand* (1934) and the novelettes about Kennedy adapted by Ashley Locke as *Enter Craig Kennedy* (1935), Reeve held a place in the top rank of genre writers, although his dependence upon apparatus that came to seem gimmicky makes his work dated in a way that the stories of Holmes have never become.

Doyle, Freeman, and Reeve had in common a conception of character that made science a wholly defining feature of character. Their sleuths were not just heroes, but scientific heroes. In the process of introducing greater complexity into *characterization, later writers have reduced the emphasis upon their characters' scientific profession; thus, Elizabeth Peters embeds Amelia Peabody's archaeological expertise among a range of engaging character traits, and Aaron Elkins's physical anthropologist, Gideon Oliver, employs his learning in the solution of crime, but engages as well in adventure requiring other attributes of strength and character besides. In that regard the inspiration of science that was once featured by some writers as the defining element of the detective hero has become a settled convention. All detectives, whether or not they display scientific method or learning, are now heirs to the imaging of mental powers once associated specifically with scientific learning.

Still, there are fashions and development in the representation of science. When John R. Feegel published *Autopsy* (1975), he suggested the possibilities for renewing interest in forensic science. Today Patricia D. Cornwell's series about Dr. Kay Scarpetta, medical examiner and resolute investigator, shows in its great popularity the continuing satisfaction that a scientist sleuth offers to readers who appreciate disciplined scientific technique as a source of entertainment and satisfaction.

[*See also* Forensic Pathologist; Medical Sleuth; Reasoning, Types of.]   —John M. Reilly

SCOTLAND YARD. New Scotland Yard is the headquarters of one of the world's largest forces, the London Metropolitan Police—and this force only. The original offices, in 1829, were situated in Whitehall Place just south of Trafalgar Square in *London. The rear entrance, used by lower ranking officers, opened onto Great Scotland Yard, and the rank and file began referring to their headquarters as Scotland Yard or simply "the Yard." In 1890 they moved to the purpose-built New Scotland Yard, the famous redbrick baronial building on the Thames Embankment. A further move was made in 1967 to a tall, modern block off Victoria Street. In keeping with tradition the name New Scotland Yard was retained.

Much of the Yard's fame stems from the fact that not only was the force's first detective branch based there but also that these detectives were loaned out to other forces to assist in difficult cases. Interest in these early *police detectives spawned several books purporting to be real-life memoirs, such as *Recollections of a Detective Police-Officer* (1856; *The Recollections of a Policeman; Diary of a Detective Police Officer*) by William Russell writing as Waters, and *The Detective's Notebook* (1860) and *Diary of an Ex-Detective* (1860) by Thomas Delf writing as Charles Martel. *The Casebook of a Victorian Detective* (1975)— a compilation from two similar "true life" memoirs, *Curiosities of Crime in Edinburgh* and *The Sliding Scale of Life; or Thirty Years' Observations of Falling Men and Women in Edinburgh* (1861)—is given more credence because the purported writer, James M'Levy, had been a detective in the Edinburgh Police.

The names of real Scotland Yard detectives soon became familiar to the public through the then fashionable extensive newspaper coverage of criminal proceedings. Charles *Dickens wrote about them very favorably in a number of articles in his magazine, *Household Words*, and there is little doubt that the ebullient and perspicacious Detective Inspector Charles Frederick Field was at least in part the model for Inspector Bucket in *Bleak House*, or that the extraordinary, real-life case of Constance Kent was used as a template for *The Moonstone* (1868) by Dickens's friend, Wilkie *Collins.

In 1881 a fictional detective was used as a stick to beat Howard Vincent, the new Director of the *CID at the yard. Soon after two detection disasters he was depicted in a *Punch* cartoon attempting to extract some tips from the popular crime novels of French writer Émile *Gaboriau, whose central character is a successful police detective named Lecoq. Some of the well-researched twentieth-century novels author Peter Lovesey set in Victorian times illustrate how Metropolitan Police detectives operated during this period (*Waxwork*, 1978). Covering a slightly later period is M. J. Trow's popular series of comic crime novels commencing with *The Adventures of Inspector Lestrade* (1985), which allow Sherlock *Holmes's scorned policeman to shine.

In 1907 a pool of six highly experienced Scotland Yard detectives was formed. Popularly known as the Murder Squad, they were ready to be called out on loan at short notice. Calling in the Yard has ceased in the United Kingdom, although Scotland Yard is still occasionally asked to help out abroad—chiefly in the smaller former colonies.

Early in the twentieth century, the Yard's reputation was enhanced by its introduction of the first practical fingerprint-sorting system. In his colorful book, *Queer People* (1922), Sir Basil Thomson claims that, on his appointment as Assistant Commissioner CID in 1913, he found his detectives lacking in imagination when keeping observation and searching premises, and their descriptions of wanted persons "colorless." Training improved matters, and in 1919 he was telling a committee that "gentleman detectives" (imagined by a public fed on a diet of aristocratic crime solvers who were inevitably far superior) had been tried and found wanting. (He was referring to those selected mainly for their language skills which were useful in extradition cases.) Thomson was also to satirize the superhuman *amateur detective in his stories featuring *Mr. Pepper, Investigator* (1925), one of whose mottoes was "look for the unlikely and preferably sensational explanation."

Fictional detectives, able to announce themselves with the magic words "from Scotland Yard," are legion and include Ngaio *Marsh's Chief Inspector Roderick *Alleyn, Freeman Wills *Croft's Inspector Joseph *French, and P. D. *James's Commander Adam *Dalgliesh.

[*See also* Police Detective; Police History: History of British Policing.]

• Douglas G. Browne, *The Rise of Scotland Yard: A History of the Metropolitan Police* (1956). Joan Lock, *Dreadful Deeds and Awful Murders, Scotland Yard's First Detectives 1829–1878* (1990). Paul Begg and Keith Skinner, *The Scotland Yard Files, 150 Years of the CID 1842–1992* (1992). Joan Lock, *Scotland Yard Casebook: The Making of the CID 1865–1935* (1993).   —Joan Lock

SECRET AGENT. Secret agents have been a fact of political life since ancient times, but the fictional secret agent appeared only in the nineteenth century, coinciding with the rise of nationalism. Indications of what was to come are found in James Fenimore Cooper's *The Spy* (1821), generally agreed to be the first modern spy novel, and George Chesney's *The Battle of Dorking* (*Blackwood's Magazine*, 1871), which began the practice of accurately predicting political developments. Beginning with his first novel, *Guilty Bonds* (1891), William Lequeux anticipated almost every development of the spy novel, including the nature of the secret agent, until the 1920s.

The early years of the twentieth century defined the world of the secret agent and laid out the main directions for the coming century. In Rudyard

Kipling's *Kim* (1901), espionage is a Great Game played out against an unforgettably evoked Indian backdrop; Kimball O'Hara, orphan and outsider, moves freely between two cultures. In *The Riddle of the Sands* (1903), Erskine *Childers introduces the amateur agent and predicts the coming war against the background of small-boat sailing along the German North Sea coast. Joseph Conrad introduced perhaps the first fictional double agent in *The Secret Agent* (1907), describing his sordid and dull life.

Childers's two yachtsmen are amateurs, even though one of them is a Foreign Office clerk, and for a considerable period of time the amateur agent held the field. John *Buchan's Sir Richard Hannay a one-time mining engineer in Rhodesia, becomes involved in the Great Game by accident when a professional agent is murdered in his flat in *The Thirty-Nine Steps* (1915). When war breaks out, Hannay is recruited to further the Allied cause abroad, appearing in two more wartime books, *Greenmantle* (1916) and *Mr. Standfast* (1919). In E. Phillips *Oppenheim's *A Maker of History* (1905), a young man comes upon a secret treaty between Germany and Russia and enters the domain of the secret agent out of a sense of duty.

After World War I, perhaps disillusioned by their experiences, writers chose to depict the life of a secret agent in realistic terms: boring, dangerous, sordid, even destabilizing. W. Somerset Maugham's *Ashenden, or the British Agent* (1928) reflects in large measure the author's experiences in the war; the agent, Ashenden, leads a boring life in Russia in 1917 and has no illusions about his ability to affect the course of events. Beginning with his first novel, *The Dark Frontier* (1936), Eric *Ambler sought to de-romanticize secret agents (both "ours" and "theirs"). Although his heroes come to espionage in the traditional way—an innocent young man gets caught up in events in Europe, for example—they face a more complex world that requires realistic assessment and mature judgment. In his second novel, *Uncommon Danger* (1937; *Background to Danger*), Desmond Kenton must choose between two Russian agents and the agents of a multinational corporation. Throughout his work, Ambler poses thought-provoking questions about political ideology and behavior, imbuing his work with leftist political sympathies.

The of World War II ultimately brought disillusionment and hopelessness as people surveyed the destruction of their lands and the growing Cold War; Graham *Greene vividly depicted this period in *The Third Man* (1950). The secret agent, a professional caught up in the brutal realities of a cruel, modern world, could not even dream of the success of his amateur predecessors. The stage was set for John *le Carré's *The Spy Who Came in from the Cold* (1963), in which the author explores the spiritual isolation demanded of those who would play the intelligence game; *friendship is impossible, as is any true intimacy with lover or family. With the fall of the Berlin Wall and the end of the Cold War, the theme suggested in le Carré's work, the role of an honorable man in a corrupt world, was taken up by other writers, such as Gavin Lyall in *The Secret Servant* (1980). A parallel development were the James *Bond stories

by Ian *Fleming, beginning with *Casino Royale* (1953), which restored to the professional agent something of the character of the early amateur while giving him the benefit of modern institutions and advanced technology. The Fleming novels have inspired numerous parodies, and led in part to the technothriller, such as Tom Clancy's *The Hunt for Red October* (1984), in which the hero is the technology rather than the agent who wields it.

[*See also* Heroism.]

• Janet Adam Smith, *John Buchan: A Biography* (1965). I. E. Clarke, *Voices Prophesying War 1763–1984* (1966); rev. ed. (1992): Ch. IV. Andrew Boyle, *The Riddle of Erskine Childers* (1977):108–14. Janet Adam Smith, *John Buchan and his World* (1979).
—Susan Oleksiw

SENSATION NOVEL. The sensation novel is a type of fiction intended to play on the emotions of the reader; it flourished in the last half of the nineteenth century. As an offshoot of the eighteenth-century novel of sensibility with elements of the *Gothic novel, the sensation novel retained the basic elements of the sufferings of the unfortunate, the persecuted, and the ill-fated with the intent of evoking a sympathetic response from the reader; it relied less on the Gothic trappings of crumbling castles in remote lands than on guilty secrets and implausible or ominous events in the middle or upper social *milieu. The guilty secrets typically concerned madness, *thefts, illegitimate births, incest, and loss of virginity. The machinations of the *plot often revolved around inheritance—a naive young man unaware of his rights, the forced *marriage of an innocent young woman to a villain who seeks control of her fortune, or a villain's deceits to secure ascendancy over a *family. It is notable that the harm is done by villains, not criminals. Again, ghosts and demons may be invoked but the diabolical exists mainly as suggestive and hyperbolic description. The police do not enter this closed world of gentility; any law enforcement that exists in the world of the sensation novel defers to patriarchy and wealth, standing on the doorstep with hat in hand. Major examples of the sensation novel are Wilkie *Collins's *Woman in White* (1860), Mrs. Henry *Wood's *East Lynne* (1861), and Mary Elizabeth *Braddon's *Lady Audley's Secret* (1862).

In *Bleak House* (1853), a sensation novel about a court battle over an inheritance, Charles *Dickens introduces Inspector Bucket, the first significant detective in English literature. This innovation was developed further by Collins in *The Moonstone* (1868). By following a crime and its detection, primarily through Sergeant Cuff of *Scotland Yard, Collins combined the features of the sensation novel with those of the fledgling *detective novel being developed by Émile *Gaboriau in France. Collins so successfully incorporated mystery and crime into his novels that in emulation Dickens started writing *The Mystery of Edwin Drood* (1870). Left unfinished at his death, the novel remains an enigma, its ending unknown and its form as a sensation novel or a detective novel or a combination of the two not fully defined.

The transition from the sensation to the detective novel brought about by Dickens and Collins was a logical one. The sensation reader encounters various sorts of mysteries; Wood's blockbuster novel *East Lynne* (1861) is packed with *murders, ingenious plots, and well-planted *clues. The sensation novel also draws the reader into questions about the character of the hero or the heroine as someone who is suspected of a crime, leading the reader to speculate on what might have happened.

Collins's deep concern with the delineation of the character and personality of women highlights a major feature of the sensation novel, which has a large female readership and was often written by women. This tendency to focus on the heightened thoughts and tragedies of women led to a romantic quality in some early mystery fiction. The American Anna Katharine *Green, acknowledged as the "mother of the detective novel," called *The Leavenworth Case: A Lawyer's Story* (1878) a criminal romance, though the book featured a police detective and was praised for its rational deduction. The same tone of romantic *suspense was maintained by Mary Roberts *Rinehart, whose *The Circular Staircase* (1908) initiated the *Had-I-But-Known-school. These and other novels carried on a strict morality and, in Julian *Symons's words, an "unbearable gentility." This nineteenth-century flavor was finally eliminated by Daphne *du Maurier, author of six romantic suspense novels, including *Rebecca* (1938). Mabel Seeley also took the Rinehart formula and combined it with carefully drawn suspense set in the ordinary places of the Midwest, beginning with *The Listening House* (1938).

Though *Golden Age critics dismissed the love interest and extensive characterization as distractions from the pure detective story, writers including Mignon G. *Eberhart, Phyllis A. *Whitney, and Barbara Michaels continued to turn out romantic suspense novels.

[*See also* Had-I-But-known; Terror: Villains and Villainy.]

• Louis I. Bredvold, *The Natural History of Sensibility* (1962). Mario Praz, introduction to *Three Gothic Novels* (1968). Lyn Pykett, *The 'Improper' Feminine: Women's Sensation Novels in the New Women's Writing* (1992).

—Joan Warthling Roberts

SERIAL KILLERS AND MASS MURDERERS. Those who take the lives of multiple *victims are referred to as either "mass murderers" or "serial killers." Serial killers are those who kill multiple victims over an extended period, usually one victim at a time; Peter Sutcliffe, the "Yorkshire Ripper," murdered at least thirteen women over about six years in England. "Mass murderer" is a term generally applied to those who kill several people at once; in 1984 James Huberty shot twenty-one people at a McDonald's restaurant in San Ysidio, California.

Much that has been written on the subject of killers of multiple victims is to be found in works by journalists and authors of nonfiction books in the *true crime genre. Newspaper and magazine articles tend to focus on the horrific nature of the crimes or the *innocence of the victims rather than the pathology of the killer and rely on mostly secondary sources. True crime books may involve more direct interview techniques. Psychiatric theories have been based on small and biased samples and have been limited by the high incidence of *suicide among the perpetrators, particularly mass murderers, resulting in a lack of availability of subjects for clinical study.

The characteristics of mass murder do not lend themselves readily to crime and mystery writing and are usually developed by those writers concentrating on the "thriller/horror" genre. The act is short-lived, explosive, and violent, and it is these aspects of it and the buildup to them that are available for development rather than mystery or intrigue.

Serial killings, on the other hand, are a staple of much crime and mystery writing. While the conventional *whodunit formula, as employed in the Golden Age, tended to feature additional killings only as necessary to protect a murderer who was motivated to perpetrate one central killing, the formula is used successfully to accommodate serial killings today by such authors as John Harvey and Patricia D. Cornwell. While these contemporary exemplars possess medical or forensic knowledge, it may be that limited scientific knowledge of this subject has facilitated the fantasy exploration by writers who have felt little restraint from realism in a field that is shadowy and unknown even to many experienced mental health and police professionals. The subject allows for full development of many aspects of the craft of crime, presenting unusual challenges to the skills and abilities of the detectives, the systematic seeding of *clues leading to denouement, and exotic, unlikely methods of perpetration. The psychopathology of the killer is often explored only by inference and is secondary to the development of an *atmosphere of horror and *evil.

A notable treatment of the topic is to be found in *Devices and Desires* (1989) by P. D. James. Here the serial killings are perpetrated in the environment of a nuclear reactor plant, allowing the author to explore current social and moral themes alongside the treatment of serial killing.

Authors vary in their depictions of serial killers. Cornwell consciously refrains from portraying the killers' sick pleasure, while Dean Koontz and others focus both on the victims' plight and the perpetrators' lust for *murder.

[*See also* Terror; Terrorism and the Terrorist Procedural.]

• Robert K. Ressler, Ann W. Burgess, and John E. Douglas, *Sexual Homicide Patterns and Motives* (1988). Colin Wilson and Donald Seaman, *The Serial Killers* (1990).

—Marion Swan

SERIALIZATION AND SERIES PUBLICATION. Serialization, or the publication of a unified work in installments, was an important means of publishing early crime and mystery fiction. Series publication, more important to this genre as the twentieth century progressed, entails the production of related works that also stand independently.

Precursors of the genre, including sensationalized accounts of true crime, were published in serial and series forms in newspapers, magazines, and *penny dreadfuls in the nineteenth century. During that century, the rise of the novel was linked with the accessibility of fiction to readers who could buy the works of favorite novelists serialized in popular magazines. Important sensation novelists and mystery novelists whose work reached the public this way include John Sheridan Le Fanu, Mrs. Henry *Wood, Mary Elizabeth *Braddon, and Charles *Dickens. Wilkie *Collins's *The Woman in White* was such a highly anticipated serial that when on 29 November 1859 the magazine *All the Year Round* launched its first installment in London, crowds waited on the publisher's doorstep to purchase copies. Later, Arthur Conan *Doyle's longer works were serialized too, while his individual short stories were published separately in series.

In America, Charles Brockton Brown's *Arthur Mervyn* was an early exemplar of a work with mystery elements to be published in serial form; it was issued in two parts in 1799 and 1800. One of the first generally accepted "modern mysteries," Edgar Allan *Poe's "The Mystery of Marie Roget," appeared in multiple parts in *Snowden's Lady's Companion* in 1842 and 1843. Later nineteenth-century American magazines contained serialized works, including mystery stories, by Samuel Clemens, Mary Noailles Murfee, and John Kendrick Bangs. During the first half of the twentieth century, the American *pulp magazines serialized an enormous amount of fiction to keep readers coming back for more. Writers as important as Dashiell *Hammett, Erle Stanley *Gardner, Carroll John *Daly, H. Bedford-Jones, Frank L. Packard, and Arthur B. *Reeve were serialized in such pulp publications as *Detective Story Magazine*, *Black Mask*, *Clues*, and *Detective Fiction Weekly*. As recently as 1996, Stephen King's novel with crime elements, *The Green Mile*, was serialized in fascicles, although that stands as an exception to the rule at a time when the vast majority of crime novels remain published as complete novels.

At its most basic level, the detective and mystery series utilizes the same character—and more rarely the same *setting. American *dime novels recycled characters, including Old Sleuth, Old King Brady, Old Broadbrim, and Nick *Carter into new situations ad infinitum. Typically the characters in these series did not carry away with them experiences from earlier cases that helped them to work better in their next cases. Such characters also recovered remarkably well from injuries received in altercations, hardly ever carrying a wound from one adventure to the next. Exceptions to this rule include some series characters developed in novels. Dorothy L. *Sayers's Lord Peter *Wimsey and Margery *Allingham's Albert *Campion are notable for character development over their series. Created as *silly-ass sleuths, both of these heroes became much more than that before their series were completed.

Series can also permit a writer to develop an idea or philosophy more fully than might be expected in a single work. Especially during the last third of the twentieth century, crime and mystery writing was used by some authors on a mission to accompany puzzling tales with ruminations on other matters. Exemplars are Lawrence *Block, whose sleuth Matt Scudder wrestles with recovery from alcoholism, and Amanda *Cross, whose series of mystery novels about Kate *Fansler also succeeds as a polemic on feminism. Writers may also choose the series form in order to educate readers over several books about periods of history, as Ellis *Peters does in her series about the twelfth-century monk Brother *Cadfael, or about the inner workings of a particular world, as Dick *Francis does in his books set in the *horse racing milieu, or about the experience of working in a particular profession, as does Jonathan Kellerman in his series about the child psychologist Alex Delaware. Publishers also find series attractive because they can market characters and sometimes settings as known quantities for which there are predictable audiences. In the last decades of the twentieth century, some talented writers who wish to try out new characters met with resistence from publishers who prefered to market the tried and true. Writers who do not wish to carry characters from one book to the next have sometimes found success in using a definite character type and general situation in book after book, as John Grisham does with his young lawyers who find themselves and their careers in jeopardy when they stumble across various secrets.

• Willeta Heising, *Detecting Men: A Reader's Guide and Checklist for Mystery Series Written by Men* (1998). Willeta Heising, *Detecting Women 2: A Reader's Guide and Checklist for Mystery Series Written by Women* (1996). Mary Jean DeMarr, ed., *In the Beginning: First Novels in Mystery Series* (1995). Michael Lund, *America's Continuing Story: An Introduction to Serial Fiction, 1850–1900* (1993). Robert Sampson, *Yesterday's Faces: A Study of Series Characters in the Early Pulp Magazines.* 6 vols. (1983–1993). —Richard Bleiler

SERIES MILIEU may be understood as the recurrent social or physical *setting for a significant part of an author's oeuvre. Contemporary examples include the *horse racing milieu depicted by Dick *Francis, the monastic milieu pictured by Ellis *Peters, and the acting world shown in Simon Brett's Charles Paris novels. But the series milieu is by no means a modern phenomenon, for the country house settings in the works of Agatha *Christie and the *mean streets milieu of Raymond *Chandler and Dashiell *Hammett are certainly series milieus, though so heavily exploited as to have become generic.

Initially the use of a *milieu may be governed simply by awareness that it will facilitate that variation of mood, tempo, and subject matter without which any novel palls. But employment in subsequent books indicates that it has been recognized as solving a number of technical problems on the author's behalf. In the Brother *Cadfael series by Peters, for example, the details of monastic life are interesting in themselves (series milieus are frequently historical for this reason) but also contrast effectively with the *violence and *evil that irrupt into a setting normally filled with peace and contemplation. Further, they can be used to highlight the tension and mystery of the main *plot, but also to postpone and thus accentuate their resolution. The milieu also provides a reason for Cadfael to become involved with suspicious death. The sophisticated reader balks at the amateur who continually stumbles over *murders; but a *medical milieu, be it in the twelfth century or the twentieth, plausibly solves this problem.

Equally important, the milieu provides a structure within which the mystery unfolds and its solution is pursued; and this is both physical (note how the monastic offices anchor the stories in time) and moral. The monastery is a world in microcosm. Offence against the code of the milieu disposes the reader to believe the offender guilty of murder. This may prove to be a *clue—or a *red herring.

All these properties apply to the milieu of any novel, but with increasing force and subtlety if it is developed through successive books. If series milieus are often born of the understandable desire to capitalize upon single-book success, a practical benefit is absolution from the tedious business of devising fresh settings for each new work. Frequently a glance at the author's biography confirms the source of the milieu. It may reflect his or her career, background, or technical expertise.

A series milieu is most often associated with the use of series characters, though this is less true of the "pure" thriller where, for example, a seafaring theme recurs in the works of Alistair MacLean, Hammond Innes, and Desmond Bagley because of the opportunities it offers for dramatic locations and encounters with the elements.

In crime and mystery writing the most notable exception to this generalization is Francis. In his work the horse-racing setting moves to the foreground to take the place of the series character as the ongoing focus of the reader's attention. Francis has an unusually thorough intimacy with his milieu that is matched by his understanding of its plotting possibilities; nevertheless, given the drawbacks and technical difficulties of maintaining the series character, it is surprising that this option has not been chosen more often. Despite the attractions of the shrewd halfway position adopted by Sarah Caudwell or Ed *McBain, themselves with casts of recurring characters with whom changes can be rung from book to book, it remains true that the series milieu almost always goes hand in hand with the series character.

—Stephen Murray

SETTING refers to the physical background against which a *plot occurs. A setting may be a specific geographic location, a general environment, or a particular historical period. Whether based on an actual place or an invented one, setting is an imaginative construction conveyed through selected significant details that may facilitate or limit plot elements, reflect or illuminate characters, and reinforce mood and theme.

The settings of mystery and crime fiction must meet additional formal plot requirements. A traditional *whodunit should have a limited number of *suspects; hence the frequency of rural or isolated settings. *Detective fiction, moreover, is not ordinarily set in countries subject to despotic rule, since ratiocination should prevail over brute power or author-

ity in the solution of the crime. Finally, the setting of private-eye fiction should be sufficiently sinister to account for the need for private investigators. Despite these limits, however, mystery and crime fiction has been set in virtually every country on earth—and some off it.

Howard Haycraft, in his pioneer study *Murder for Pleasure: The Life and Times of the Detective Story* (1941), regrets the tendency of writers to invent settings when real locations are so much more compelling. W. H. Auden's influential essay "The Guilty Vicarage" (*Harper's Magazine*, May 1948), argues that a *murder should be set in what he calls the Great Good Place: The more Eden-like the setting, the more shocking the *corpse when it appears. John G. Cawelti adds in *Adventure, Mystery, and Romance: Formula Stories as Art and Popular Culture* (1976) that the contrast between a comfortable, orderly environment and the disorderly crime scene heightens the symbolic distinction between order and chaos, rationality and *guilt.

When Dashiell *Hammett and Raymond Chandler moved detective fiction from the artificial, snobbish world of the vicarage garden to the mean streets of Prohibition-era America, they did more than change the *milieu. As Chandler recounts in *The Simple Art of Murder* (*Atlantic Monthly*, Dec. 1944), Hammett also changed the nature of the crime and the relationship of the detective to society. His settings are not orderly, nor can they be restored to *innocence, for in them crime is endemic and officialdom corrupt. The setting of the American hard-boiled novel, as Auden observes, is the Great Wrong Place.

The earliest detective writers used strongly realized home addresses to point out the eccentric natures of their detectives. Famous addresses such as No. 33, rue Dunot, Faubourg St. Germain in Paris, 221B Baker Street in London, and the brownstone on Manhattan's West Thirty-fifth Street became as real to readers as the sleuths who "lived" there: Edgar Allan *Poe's Chevalier C. Auguste *Dupin, Arthur Conan *Doyle's Sherlock *Holmes, and Rex *Stout's Nero *Wolfe, respectively.

Series detectives are also associated with locales. Sam *Spade's name evokes prewar *San Francisco just as Miss Jane *Marple's suggests cozy St. Mary Mead. Ross *Macdonald's Lew *Archer is unimaginable outside the landscape of Southern California, whereas Robert B. *Parker's *Spenser is identified with Boston. Howard Engel's soft-boiled *private eye Benny Cooperman walks the mean streets of Grantham, Ontario, while L. R. Wright's *Royal Canadian Mounted Police sergeant Karl Arlberg patrols British Columbia's "Sunshine Coast." Ruth *Rendell's Inspector *Wexford travels to California in *Put On by Cunning* (1981; *Death Notes*) and to China in *The Speaker of Mandarin* (1983), but his home is the fictional Kingsmarkham in Sussex. S. T. Haymon's Inspector Ben Jurnet belongs to the East Anglian cathedral town of Angleby as surely as Sara *Paretsky's feminist private eye V. I. *Warshawsky does to tough, working-class Chicago. These settings characterize and differentiate the detectives who inhabit them.

Setting also defines or limits specific social,

psychological, and technological realities, which in turn affect both the criminal's *motives and the detective's methods. In S. T. Haymon's *Ritual Murder* (1982), the anti-Semitic medieval history of Angleby proves relevant to a modern murder in the cathedral. H. R. F. *Keating's Inspector Ganesh *Ghote polices crowded Bombay and rural India, where crimes and cultural attitudes toward death differ profoundly from those that occupy Tony *Hillerman's Navajo tribal policemen Joe Leaphorn and Jim *Chee on their vast, sparsely populated reservation. Robert H. *van Gulik's Judge Dee, a magistrate in seventh-century China, and Ellis *Peters's Brother *Cadfael, a Benedictine monk in twelfth-century Shrewsbury Abbey, are subject to different laws from those of modern detectives and must solve their cases without benefit of fingerprints or databases. These historical and geographical settings clearly influence plots, *characterization, and themes.

The mystery and crime genre has always valued innovative settings that bring novelty to the formula. Golden Age writers favored isolated, hierarchical, apparently benign milieus such as the generic village, the ubiquitous country house, the university college, or the railway sleeping car, and they situated isolated communities of characters anywhere from Australia to Yugoslavia. Settings, however, were usually incidental to plot. For example, *Death Comes as the End* (1944), one of several Christie novels that take place in the Middle East, features a familiar country house-style murder set on the Nile River in ancient Egypt. Christie, however, claimed that any other time and place would have served as well. Robert *Barnard in *A Talent to Deceive: An Appreciation of Agatha Christie* (1980) suggests that Christie's usual settings are deliberately generic, allowing readers to fill in details from their own experience. Exotic settings rarely distract from the *puzzle central to fiction of the Golden Age.

Some writers create detailed new settings for each novel. Dick *Francis is noted for using meticulously researched settings such as Milan in *Flying Finish* (1966), South Africa in *Smokescreen* (1972), and a Canadian transcontinental train in *The Edge* (1988). His novels almost always involve a hero connected to the world of horse racing who proves himself against a sadistic villain, but the specifics of each setting allow him variety within what is essentially a *series milieu.

Peter Dickinson also uses settings as diverse as an Arabian desert kingdom in *The Poison Oracle* (1974) and colonial Nigeria in *Tefuga* (1986). For *King and Joker* (1976) and *Skeleton-in-Waiting* (1989), he even invents an alternate history in which King Victor II reigns in England. Dickinson also creates new characters and situations to fit each setting.

Setting frequently contributes to *atmosphere and mood. The eeriness and *suspense of Doyle's *The Hound of the Baskervilles* (1902) owes much to its Dartmoor landscape and the menace of the great Grimpen Mire, just as the wit and comedy of Reginald *Hill's novels featuring Superintendent Andrew Dalziel and Sergeant Peter Pascoe derive in large part from their Yorkshire characters and manners.

Setting can also reflect a novel's theme or a character's emotional state. In Chandler's hard-boiled private eye novels, the corrupt cities and suburbs of California become testing grounds for Philip *Marlowe who, like the questing knight of medieval allegory, must move with honor through a morally perilous landscape. Dorothy L. *Sayers's *The Nine Tailors* (1934) centers a tale of moral responsibility in the East Anglian fen country, while the village and parish church of Fenchurch St. Paul furnish a pastoral vision of redemptive community more powerful than any single character in the novel.

Although some critics feel that descriptions not essential to plot are distracting window dressings, a well-rendered setting can prove compelling in reinforcing the author's theme. P. D. *James's *Devices and Desires* (1989), for instance, is set on a remote Norfolk headland symbolically framed by a ruined Benedictine abbey and a twentieth-century nuclear power plant; a converted nineteenth-century mill belonging to CID commander Adam *Dalgliesh is also situated on the headland. Here religious faith, represented by the old abbey, is replaced by a Faustian view of science just as the old technology of waterpower, represented by the mill, is supplanted by the nuclear generator. James's bleak conclusion implies that settings can no longer be restored to the Great Good Place and proves that setting remains profoundly important to this genre.

[See also Addresses and Abodes, Famous; Closed-World Settings and Open-World Settings; Locked Room Mystery; Mayhem Parva; Milieu; Regionalism.]

• George Grella, "Murder and the Mean Streets," *Detective Fiction: Crime and Consequences*, ed. Dick Allen and David Chacko (1974). Deborah Bonetti, "Murder Can Happen Anywhere," *Armchair Detective* 14: 3 (summer 1981): 257–64. Leroy Lad Panek, *An Introduction to the Detective Story* (1987).
—Elaine Bander

SETTINGS, GEOGRAPHICAL. Much of the skill evident in the composition of crime and detective fiction derives from the authors' management of the necessities for a plausible narrative. The genre demands a crime and a *sleuth, narration requires the selection of a *voice, and the fictitious events comprising the story must occur in a believable locale. The latter obligation, that an author include details of a terrain or stage where the criminal events of the story and their solution will take place, originates in the tacit contract a writer makes with readers, promising them a semblance of reality, or verisimilitude, in return for their steady attention to the narration. Particularity, then, becomes the means of meeting the obligation to provide a satisfying *setting.

In his journalistic procedural novel *The Fly on the Wall* (1971) Tony *Hillerman places his *accidental sleuth in the employ of a daily newspaper's state capital bureau, leads him into the archives of public records in search of *clues, submits him to a harrowing chase through the corridors of the darkened state capitol, sends him as a fugitive into the mountains of New Mexico, and returns him to the home of a powerful political figure for a dramatic conclusion to a story of *corruption and *violence. Each step in the *plot proceeds on the solid ground of concrete detail. The names on the doors in the capitol and exhibits in the hallways are specified. The offices visited by the sleuth, his apartment, and the residences of his associates are located in the story as though on a map. The New Mexican wilderness, said to be distant from the detective's home base, is described with specificity about growth and hillside grade. Yet New Mexico is the only place named in the story that can be verified outside the text itself. The public buildings are sited in an unnamed capital city, in a state that is generically Midwestern. It could be Springfield, Illinois, but then it also could be Jefferson City, Missouri. The geography is accurate, but it is not actual.

The novel *Briarpatch* (1984) by Ross Thomas offers a similar example. The protagonist works in Washington, D.C. and has an apartment on N Street near Dupont Circle. When he is called home because his sister has been murdered, it seems like he goes to Baton Rouge. The city is a state capital. It is said to be Southern, but is not in Texas or the Southeast. Like Hillerman, Thomas meets the contractual obligation for verisimilitude by describing the setting for his detective's investigation of crime with concrete physical detail, treating it, therefore, as though it were real.

By including descriptions that particularize their unnamed cities, Hillerman and Thomas give substance to their fiction and, thus, grounds for readers to believe in the events they relate. On the other hand, by omitting ascription of the narrative events to an identifiable place in the readers' world, Hillerman and Thomas demonstrate that, after all, setting is a convention for fiction, not its referent. The tale works as well when its location cannot be found in an atlas as when it can. Named or not, all settings are fictitious, existing only in the imaginative world of narration.

Recognition of the invention involved in the presentation of setting allows for appreciation of authorial skill in exploiting its possibilities. Nevada Barr, whose avocational detective works for the National Parks Service, uses the settings of federal lands to create atmosphere. In *Track of the Cat* (1993) she pursues a case in the Guadalupe Mountains National Park of Texas, and in *A Superior Death* (1994) Isle Royale, Michigan becomes the site. While it seems on the face of it implausible that the ranger detective can conveniently gain assignment to a different park for each adventure, recalling that setting exists for the story and not for a logic external to the fictional events raises hope for a series that eventually will produce adventure in all the venues managed by the Parks Service.

Where the novelty in Barr's novels comes from her use of settings never before employed in crime or mystery writing, other authors can capitalize on the fact that their settings have an established place in fiction. This is the case for Robert Crais whose sleuth Elvis Cole speeds along the freeways of *Los Angeles. In a book like *Sunset Express* (1996) the immensity and suprahuman scale of Los Angeles County becomes the thematically suggestive ground upon which Crais deploys a story indicating that

the physical geography of the place is overlaid with an alternate geography of tenuous and temporary human relationships.

The scale of Jane Langton's settings markedly contrast with that of Robert Crais. Her crimes occur in the village of Concord, Massachusetts, sometimes within the boundaries of the *academic milieu of Cambridge, at others on the grounds of the small communities associated with museums. In *Dark Nantucket Noon* (1975) events transpire amidst the byways and hills of a well-known vacation spot, but a particular kind of vacation spot where signs of an older America remain and where a regional flavor of class is evident. So it is not scale alone that marks Langton's use of setting; her local color realism also produces resonances of a way of life. The same may be said of the novels by Frances and Richard *Lockridge, except that the local color conveyed in their stories of Mr. and Mrs. (Jerry and Pam) North emanates from images of sophisticated Manhattan.

In many cases physical setting achieves much more than utilitarian function. For example, Bartholomew Gill places his stories about Inspector McGarr in Dublin, but in a work like *McGarr and the Politician's Wife* (1977) the physical details of urban neighborhoods and elite homes also picture class relations in modern Ireland. Then, too, there is the sometimes exotic appeal of setting when readers are led into a different culture. Elspeth Huxley's *Murder at Government House* (1937) was no doubt enjoyed by many people who knew nothing first hand about its setting in West Africa and took Huxley's descriptions as equivalent to travel reportage. The same might be said of such novels by Matthew Head as *The Cabinda Affair* (1949) and *The Congo Venus* (1950). Readers of these novels could have known that settings for fiction are always inventions, but their acceptance of the verisimilitude of settings unknown to them in actuality gives testimony to the obvious importance that geographical setting can acquire in fiction. The invention of the fictional world when skillfully done becomes reality.

[See also Great Outdoors, The; Realism, Conventions of; Regionalism: American; Regionalism: British; Rural Milieu; Urban Milieu.]

• Allen J. Hubin, *Crime Fiction, 1749–1980: A Comprehensive Bibliography* (1984). Ralph Willett, *The Naked City: Urban Crime Fiction in the USA* (1996).   —John M. Reilly

SEX AND SEXUALITY. Since sexuality with its attendant processes of sexual display and competition for mates, mate selection, and mate guarding has such a determinative place in human life, it would seem just as natural for sexuality to become a central consideration for *plot and *characterization in the popular literary genre of crime, detection, and mystery. In works that were precursors of the genre, written before the middle of the nineteenth century, sexuality as a *motive for crime or a trait of character is notable by its absence except for slight allusion when bawdy houses are a *milieu, and that is very rare. Everyone knows that Sherlock *Holmes was captivated by Irene *Adler, presumably because of her sexual attractiveness, but the relationship provides an aura rather than a developed depiction of sexuality. A presumably sexual liaison between Adler and Holmes's client is at the center of "A Scandal in Bohemia" (*Strand*, July 1891), but sexuality is simply foundation for formula, just as it was in Edgar Allan *Poe's "The Purloined Letter" (*The Gift*, 1845).

Writing from the Golden Age of detection also avoids exploration of sexuality. Even though the typical crime of the Golden Age is a *murder within the *family circle, sexuality is generally displaced by a conception of society and character motivation dependent upon social *class and property. The resistance Dorothy L. *Sayers met from critics when she introduced the sexually active character of Harriet *Vane in *Strong Poison* (1930) serves to indicate how inappropriate sexuality seemed to be for exponents of the *Rules of the Game.

Hard-boiled writing drastically altered the treatment of sexuality, as can be seen by the eroticism of the best-known works of James M. *Cain, *The Postman Always Rings Twice* (1934) and *Double Indemnity* (1943). The ordinary people, not private investigators or other heroic types, to whom Cain gives his leading roles are stretched on the rack of sex, as one of the protagonists laments—consumed by sexual passions that drive them to crime and consequent destruction. Compared to Cain's treatment of sexuality as primary motivation, the handling of sexuality by other hard-boiled writers downplays sexuality and sex, because in their work sex is a characteristic of behavior but not its obsessive end. Dashiell *Hammett's Sam *Spade sleeps with Brigid O'Shaughnessy in *The Maltese Falcon* (1930) and, in the conclusion of the novel, is revealed to be still entranced by her, perhaps in love, even as he incoherently explains why he is turning her over to the police. Hammett's *The Thin Man* (1934) makes the relationship between Nick and Nora *Charles, the dual *sleuths, attractive in part because of the sexual play that informs their banter. Raymond Chandler's Philip Marlowe escapes physical seduction in *The Big Sleep* (1939), and although Chandler as well as Hammett is decidedly sexist in his portrayal of women as dangerously alluring characters, the *sexism of author and protagonist both grant sexual drives a prominent position among the nonrational forces that shape the hard-boiled world. What Hammett and Chandler began— treating sexuality as fundamental to living experience in their fiction—continues among their literary descendants. The entry of female authors such as Sue Grafton, Sara Paretsky, Marcia Muller, Linda Barnes, Lillian O'Donnell, and others into the tradition of hard-boiled writing has encouraged rejection of sexism, but that has more to do with a revised estimate of the socially produced patterns of *gender than it does with sexuality, which the hard-boiled authors, female and male, have made part of the fundamental matter of detective fiction.

Yet another important development in the genre's treatment of sexuality is to be found in the handling of sexual preference. With *Fadeout* (1972) Joseph *Hansen introduced Dave *Brandstetter, a homosexual sleuth whose personal life helps to characterize

him and whose familiarity with a homosexual milieu introduces him to clients and sources. The novelty of Hansen's novels about Brandstetter lies not in the introduction of a homosexual character: Joel Cairo had appeared in *The Maltese Falcon*, Terry Lennox in Chandler's *The Long Goodbye* (1954), and Mickey Spillane had defined his transvestite villain in *Vengeance Is Mine!* (1950) as homosexual. All of these characters, however, are stereotyped as narcissists who are obsessed with sex, "mistakes of nature," natural villains. Hansen, however, presents the homosexual as being very much like other people and as possessing insight that can be related to his character. Richard Stevenson, who began a series about the gay detective Donald Strachey with *Death Trick* (1981), builds upon Hansen's opening by making the gay scene of Albany, New York, a closely textured subject for fiction.

Women authors have been more prolific than the men in looking at the question sexual preference. *Detecting Women 2* (1996), a reference work compiled by Willetta L. Heising, lists at least twenty-five female detectives, professional and amateur, who are characterized by their creators as lesbian. For many of these characters, sexual preference is a trait that denominates their membership in the human race; they are just as influenced by the drives of sexuality and the interest in mates as others of the group. Examples include Ellen Hart's Jane Lawless and Sophie Greenway.

Crime writers have also turned out a growing number of works that direct psychological narration toward psychopaths who express themselves in sexual crime, as in *The Silence of the Lambs* (1989) by Thomas Harris, or the series of novels by Andrew Vachss that employ sexuality as a motive for child abuse.

[*See also* Females and Feminists; Gay Characters and Perspectives; Lesbian Characters and Perspectives; Males and the Male Image.]

• George Grella; "The Hard-Boiled Detective Novel," in *Detective Fiction: A Collection of Critical Essays*, ed. Robin W. Winks (1980). Bonnie Zimmerman, *The Sage Sea of Women: Lesbian Fiction, 1969–1989* (1990). Kathleen Gregory Klein; *The Woman Detective: Gender and Genre*, 2nd ed. (1995).

—John M. Reilly

SEXISM. As a form of literature intentionally designed to win a large audience, crime and mystery fiction is a good indicator of attitudes in society. One *prejudice that it reflects and addresses is sexism, discrimination based on *gender.

Some sexism is overt and, therefore, easy to identify. In *The Big Sleep* (1939), for instance, Raymond *Chandler's detective Philip *Marlowe comments, "I hate women," reinforcing his remark by slashing his bed after a woman has lain in it, with no implicit criticism from the author.

Far more of it, however, is implicit in some *conventions of the genre and in the social attitudes the genre often reflects. For instance, human traits were traditionally identified as masculine or feminine, with the traits (like reason) associated with masculinity almost always more highly prized than those associated with femininity (like intuition and emotion). From its beginnings, the crime and mystery genre has valued reason over emotion, even going so far as to scorn emotion and the femininity that is associated with it while creating male heroes like Sherlock *Holmes and Professor Augustus S. F. X. *Van Dusen who embody reason. This variety of sexism is one feature shared by such otherwise distinct subgenres as *Golden Age forms and *hard-boiled fiction, with the latter virtually celebrating the detective's independence from women and repudiation of intimacy as signs of strength.

Regardless of subgenre, crime novels for the most part have tended to validate traditionally masculine *virtues and to reinforce conservative social attitudes through their *plots, characters, and themes. A stock figure in mystery fiction is the sexually predatory, dangerous woman, or *femme fatale; almost as common is the mirror image, the meek, hapless female *victim. Yet early on stereotypes were consciously manipulated by creators of female sleuths. Agatha *Christie pioneered the use of sexist assumptions to advantage in the character of Miss Jane *Marple, whose image as an unthreatening elderly woman helped Marple to dupe the characters that she encountered.

Sexism has become less socially acceptable in recent years, a shift reflected in crime and mystery fiction. Several male writers including Robert B. *Parker, Jeremiah Healy, and Dick Cluster focus on male detectives who struggle to accommodate themselves to changing gender roles. These writers occasionally address sexism directly, generally through dialogue between the male hero and a female character.

In recent decades, women writers have created female sleuths whose very existence works as a challenge to sexism. The title of P. D. *James's novel featuring private investigator Cordelia *Gray, An Unsuitable Job for a Woman (1972), comments ironically both on widespread social attitudes and genre conventions.

With the entry of the female sleuth into the hardboiled and *police procedural subgenres, some of the genre's basic attitudes are questioned. As the heroines constantly prove themselves able to compete in traditionally male-dominated territory, their authors are creating a distinct counter-tradition in mystery fiction. Feminist authors are also questioning and revising the philosophical underpinnings of the genre, such as the knowability of truth and the possibility of *justice.

Sexism functions as both *plot and theme in some novels. For instance, Amanda *Cross's controversial Death in a Tenured Position (1981; A Death in the Faculty) takes the reader through a kind of consciousness-raising, with understanding of the solution dependent upon that raised consciousness about the effects of sexism. Similarly, Barbara Wilson's Sisters of the Road (1986) focuses on a continuum of *violence against women, including *child abuse, *rape and other sex crimes, and *murder, which it shows to be encouraged by sexism and homophobia.

Sexism also affects what gets published, the likelihood of being reviewed, and recognition and awards from mystery organizations. Several women writers, including Marcia *Muller and Sara *Paretsky, recounted their early experiences in a publishing industry that believed that mysteries featuring female sleuths where less marketable than those featuring male detectives. Their commercial success led publishers to welcome women detectives. Nevertheless, a review monitoring project begun in 1987 by the Sisters in Crime organization demonstrated that mystery novels by women were far less likely to be reviewed by major review media than were those by men, a situation that only began to change at the end of the twentieth century.

[See also Females and Feminists: Males and the Male Image.]

• Stephen Knight, Form and Ideology in Crime Fiction (1980). Geoffrey O'Brien, Hardboiled America: The Lurid Years of Paperbacks (1981). Kathleen Gregory Klein, The Woman Detective: Gender and Genre (1988). Maureen T. Reddy, Sisters in Crime: Feminism and the Crime Novel (1988). Ronald G. Walker and June M. Frazer, eds., The Cunning Craft (1990).

—Maureen T. Reddy

SEXUAL AMBIGUITY. See Red Flags.

Shadow, The. See Film; Radio: The Crime and Mystery Genre on American Radio.

SHADOWING. See Pursuit.

SHAKESPEARE, WILLIAM. The works of the Elizabethan poet and dramatist William Shakespeare (1564–1616) have long been sources of inspiration for crime and mystery writers who have turned to his plots, methods of murder, titles, and famous lines to enrich their own work. While Shakespeare is often viewed as the icon of high culture, it is also true that he epitomized the popular writer. As both master and transcender of formulas, he was able to see in the stylized conventions of Plautine comedy and Senecan tragedy the material to move and grip an audience. A master, too, of the bloody and sensational—Hamlet, for example, contains six corpses and a ghost—his *plots are full of violent passions: *revenge, jealousy, bigotry, lust, and ambition. Shakespeare himself used what he believed to be *true crime sources, particularly in his tragedies and histories.

Most crime and mystery writers who use Shakespeare as a source are Shakespeare aficionados rather than scholars, although one noted Shakespearean, Alfred Harbage, wrote mystery fiction using the name of the bard's contemporary, Thomas Kyd, for a pseudonym. Ngaio *Marsh knew Shakespeare's plays intimately, since she had acted and directed many productions of them. *Oxford don J. I. M. Stewart possessed scholarly expertise about Shakespeare and was adept at using Shakespearean *literary allusions in his *detective novels written as Michael *Innes.

Shakespeare's most obvious influence upon mystery and crime writing is evident in *titles borrowed from his texts. Scores of writers have used quotes from the plays to title their books, borrowing from comedies, as in P. M. Hubbard's *Kill Claudio* (1979) and Elizabeth Powers's *All That Glitters* (1981; *The Case of the Ice-Cold Diamond*), and tragedies, as in Agatha *Christie's *Sad Cypress* (1940) and Margaret *Millar's *How Like an Angel* (1962). Because titles are not protected by copyright, a Shakespearean phrase may be used as the title of more than one mystery: *A Dying Fall* was used by both Henry *Wade (1955) and Hildegarde Dolson (1973). Some writers make a play on the bard's words to produce titles like Craig *Rice's *My Kingdom for a Hearse* (1957) or Emma *Lathen's *Double, Double, Oil and Trouble* (1978). Since her 1962 *Bloody Instructions*, Sara Woods has used Shakespearean quotations to title all of her books.

Writers also turn to Shakespeare when inventing detectives. Ellery *Queen, writing as Barnaby Ross, created a detective who had been a Shakespearean actor, named Drury Lane after the *London theater. Forced to retire from the stage because of his deafness, Lane solves cases in four mystery novels published in 1932 and 1933. In *Drury Lane's Last Case* (1933), the crime is the theft of Shakespearean manuscripts. Phoebe Atwood *Taylor writing as Alice Tilton has eight comic novels featuring Leonidas Witherall, who is called Bill Shakespeare because he looks like the bust based on the Droeshout portrait of the bard. Shakespeare himself is the detective in Faye Kellerman's *The Quality of Mercy* (1989), in which Shakespeare finds the murderer of a friend while becoming involved in a doomed romance with a *conversa*, a Jewish woman posing as a Christian.

Ellery Queen's plot idea concerning missing or spurious Shakespeare manuscripts shows up in several other stories. In the Sherlock *Holmes *pastiche *The Unique Hamlet* (1920) by Vincent *Starrett, a client announces himself as "the greatest Shakespearean commentator in the world." A fellow collector has entrusted to him a unique copy of a 1602 *Hamlet* quarto, with additions in Shakespeare's own hand. Holmes solves the disappearance of this book and proves it a forgery. Chris Steinbrunner and Otto Penzler say this is "generally conceded to be the best Holmes pastiche ever written" in their *Encyclopedia of Mystery and Detection* (1976). In one of Lillian de la Torre's historical mysteries featuring Dr. Johnson and narrated by Boswell, *The Detections of Dr. Sam* (1960), Johnson detects the spuriousness of a "new" Shakespeare manuscript during the play's production by David Garrick.

Writers use Shakespearean plot situations to enliven their mysteries. The villain in *Foul Deeds* (1989) by Susan James admits to borrowing his modus operandi from the Vincent Price movie *Theatre of Blood* (1973). The Price character used Shakespearean methods to kill off the critics of his hammy performances, and in *Foul Deeds* one victim is hanged like Cordelia, another strangled like Desdemona, and so on.

Some mystery tales set out to correct or improve on the bard. In James Thurber's comic story "The Macbeth Murder Mystery" (*New Yorker*, 2 Oct. 1937), a woman who devours a mystery every night before going to sleep gets a paperback *Macbeth* by mistake.

She explains to the narrator how neither Macbeth nor his wife did it, but Macduff, and that Macduff is the Third Murderer as well. These revelations unnerve the narrator, who "solves" the *Macbeth* murder mystery in a different way and then determines to solve *Hamlet* also.

Josephine *Tey's *The Daughter of Time* (1951) is a more ambitious and serious attempt to rewrite Shakespeare's idea of *whodunit in a historical murder. Tey's detective, Inspector Alan Grant, bedridden after an injury, becomes interested in the historical case of the princes in the Tower when a portrait of Richard III convinces him that Shakespeare's "Crookback Dick" could not have been the murderer. Helped by an American researcher, Grant decides that the real culprit was the person who ultimately gained most by the crimes.

The most ambitious uses of Shakespeare in mysteries occur in books that describe productions of his plays. Invariably, such stories build toward a murder, either in rehearsal or in performance. Innes wrote one of the most famous of these books in *Hamlet, Revenge!* (1937), in which the lord chancellor of England, playing Polonius, is killed at an amateur production of *Hamlet*, performed by the duke of Horton's houseguests. Innes's Sir John *Appleby gets the case because he isn't intimidated by the suspects but also presumably because he can cap their frequent quotations. Thickening the plot are disturbing notes using lines from Shakespeare, a gardener familiar with arcane Shakespearean criticism, and a mystery writer who—like Innes—is also an Oxford don. The book ties mystery and play together: The production is a reading of *Hamlet* as a play of statecraft and the lord chancellor is engaged in international intrigue. The conclusion contains a witty allusion to *The Winter's Tale*. Innes turned his attention to *Othello, the Moor of Venice* a few years later in his short story "Tragedy of a Handkerchief" (*Appleby Talking*, 1954; *Dead Man's Shoes*). Appleby watches a touring company perform *Othello* in a provincial theater. When Desdemona is actually killed in the smothering scene, Appleby investigates, declaiming apt lines from the play as he does.

In Marvin Kaye's *Bullets for Macbeth* (1976), rehearsals for *Macbeth* in the Felt Forum at Madison Square Garden lead to murder. Publicity agent Hilary Quayle and her assistant Gene are present when Banquo is killed in dress rehearsal by the Third Murderer, a cloaked figure who then escapes from the theater. The director has kept secret the identity of the Third Murderer, and since the director is also playing Banquo, the secret dies with him. To solve the murder, Quayle and Gene must also solve the Shakespearean mystery about the identity of the Third Murderer, who shows up unexpectedly to help Macbeth's two henchmen kill Banquo and his son Fleance.

As the Innes and Kaye examples show, mysteries about Shakespearean productions often give interpretive readings of the plays, address problems of performance, and make use of theatrical traditions such as the bad luck attendant upon productions of *Macbeth*. In Ngaio Marsh's *Light Thickens* (1982), the recurrent subject is the superstition about *Macbeth*, whose title and lead characters are not to be named but called instead "the Scots play," "the Thane," and "the Lady." Marsh takes us through the rehearsals, opening nights, and beginning run of a production of *Macbeth* at the "Dolphin" theater in London. She has strong ideas, expressed through the director, about what is *not* Shakespeare's in the printed play, discusses other relevant matters about production such as how the convention of the soliloquy can be gracefully handled in modern productions, and provides much incidental appreciation. "Nobody else could write about the small empty hours as this man did," thinks the actor who plays Banquo.

John Dickson *Carr's Dr. Gideon *Fell solves a murder that occurs during a dress rehearsal of *Romeo and Juliet* in *Panic in Box C* (1966). More recent books using productions of Shakespeare include P. M. Carlson's 1985 *Audition for Murder*, about *Hamlet*, and James Yaffe's 1991 *Mom Doth Murder Sleep*, about *Macbeth*.

• Marshall McLuhan, "Footprints in the Sands of Crime," *Sewanee Review* 54 (Oct. 1946): 617–34. Brigid Brophy, "Detective Fiction: A Modern Myth of Violence?" *Hudson Review* 18 (spring 1965): 11–30. John G. Cawelti, *Adventure, Mystery, and Romance: Formula Stories as Art and Popular Culture* (1976). Charles A. Hallett, "The Retrospective Technique and Its Implications for Tragedy," *Comparative Drama* 12 (spring 1978): 3–22.   —Michael Cohen

Shaw, Joseph Thompson "Cap." *See* Black Mask; Black Mask School; Pulp Magazines.

Shayne, Michael (also Shane) was created in 1939 by Davis Dresser (1904–77) writing as Brett Halliday. Purportedly based on an acquaintance, Dresser's *private eye works out of Miami and sometimes New Orleans. His cases, however, take him to a variety of *settings. One of the longest-lived of series characters, Shayne has appeared in more than seventy novels so far, as well as hundreds of shorter tales. Since around 1958, his adventures have been ghostwritten, and ghostwriters continued the Mike Shayne stories until the demise of the *Mike Shayne Mystery Magazine* around 1986.

In the tradition of Dashiell *Hammett's and Raymond *Chandler's *characterization, Shayne is a loner whose pride and sense of *justice are paramount, though he's always interested in his fee. Described as "semi-hard-boiled," he tends to use his wits more than his fists to solve convoluted cases. Redheaded, big, and lanky, with an appetite for Martell's cognac and a ready appreciation for women, Shayne has remained essentially the same: a "hard-drinking, tough-minded guy on the wrong side of thirty."

[*See also* Loner, Sleuth as.]   —Rex Burns

SHERLOCKIAN SOCIETIES. Arthur Conan *Doyle's original stories featuring Sherlock *Holmes were being printed in the *Strand* and *Colliers* magazines when—to his creator's consternation—readers in both England and America began to talk and write about Holmes as if he were real. This began in 1902 when "The Hound of the Baskervilles" was published, but the Sherlock Holmes "industry" dates its real birth from 1912, when an elaborate approach to studying the Sherlockian *Canon was adumbrated by a precocious Oxford undergraduate, Ronald A. *Knox. His oft-repeated lecture "Studies in the Literature of Sherlock Holmes" was later published for the public at large in his *Essays in Satire* (1928), by which time Knox was on his way to becoming not only a leading prelate of England's Roman Catholic Church, but a popular mystery writer himself.

In June 1934, Knox, along with Dorothy L. *Sayers, A. G. Macdonell, and others, cofounded England's Sherlock Holmes Society. But it was in the United States that the Sherlock Holmes movement took shape most strongly in the years following Doyle's death in 1930. Boston archaeologist H. W. Bell published a book-length chronology of Holmes's cases in 1932, and in 1933 Chicago journalist and novelist Vincent *Starrett (later the *Mystery Writers of America's first Grand Master) published a biography of the detective. Then, in January 1934 New York writer Christopher Morley founded the Baker Street Irregulars, a club composed of writers and literary-minded professional men devoted to Holmes. They sought diversion in Holmes, but went about it in ways previously unseen in literary circles, insisting mock-seriously that Holmes was real and Doyle was merely Dr. John H. *Watson's literary agent. Their dedication to the cause of "perpetuating the myth that Sherlock Holmes is not a myth," as Morley put it, kept the BSI alive through depression, world war, and postwar nuclear anxiety, unto the present day.

England's Sherlock Holmes Society flickered out in 1937, but the BSI in America gathered strength early when its first annual dinner was attended by Bell, Starrett, actor William Gillette, who had personified Holmes on stage since 1899, Frederic Dorr Steele, the greatest American illustrator of the Holmes stories, and Alexander Woollcott, the Algonquin Round Table enfant terrible with a zest for celebrated murder cases. Its apotheosis came in 1940, when Denis Conan Doyle, one of Doyle's sons and trustee of his estate, spoke at the BSI dinner about "My Father's Friend, Sherlock Holmes." The following year, mystery writer Rex *Stout caused a widely reported uproar at the BSI dinner with his contention that "Watson Was a Woman"—setting a pattern of irreverent satire jousting with straight-faced exegesis that continues to this day, not only at the BSI's annual dinners, but in several hundred chapters ("scion societies") meeting across the United States. Other detective story writers the BSI has attracted include Frederic Dannay (half of the Ellery *Queen writing team), Anthony *Boucher, Edith Meiser (writer-producer of the Sherlock Holmes radio series of the 1930s and 1940s), Stuart Palmer, John Dickson *Carr (who also wrote a biography of Doyle and a series of Holmes *pastiches with Sir Arthur's younger son, Adrian), Robert L. Fish, Isaac Asimov, Loren D. Estleman, and John Gardner.

A new English society, the Sherlock Holmes Society of London, was founded in 1951, following enthusiastic public response to a re-creation of Holmes's Baker Street sitting room in the previous year's Festival of Britain. Today other Sherlock Holmes societies exist in Canada, Australia, Japan, France, Germany, Switzerland, Denmark, Russia, and elsewhere. The quantity of writings about Holmes by his devotees is staggering. Morley observed, in 1947 when the BSI's quarterly *Baker Street Journal* was still new, that "never has so much been written by so many for so few." This fervor has not always been approved of by others. Julian *Symons, for example, in his history of mystery and detection fiction *Bloody Murder: From the Detective Story to the Crime Novel: A History (1972; Mortal Consequences: From the Detective Story to the Crime Novel: A History)* called Sherlockian writings "the most tedious pieces of their kind ever written." (But he removed those remarks from the 1985 edition of his book.)

Doyle's status in the Sherlock Holmes movement has also changed over time. Although the English societies acknowledged him from the beginning, the BSI's attitude caused a feud with Doyle's sons. But in recent years even the BSI has made room for the creator as well as the creation. There is also an international Arthur Conan Doyle Society to which many Sherlockians belong.

The "few" of Morley's day have grown to a huge number, and the movement shows no signs of flagging even in the second century after Holmes's debut in *A Study in Scarlet* (1887). Though the concerns, values, and styles of the present are vastly different from those of the Victorian world of which Holmes was a part, he continues to possess near-universal appeal—attracting not only new legions of readers every year, but fresh recruits for the movement which, for over more than eighty years, has celebrated the life of a detective who, in Vincent Starrett's words, "never lived, and so shall never die."

[See also Fans and Fan Organizations.]

• Vincent Starrett, *The Private Life of Sherlock Holmes* (1933, rev. ed. 1960). William S. Baring-Gould, "A Singular Set of People, Watson" in *The Annotated Sherlock Holmes* (1967). Philip A. Shreffler, ed., *The Baker Street Reader* (1984). Cait Murphy, "The Game's Still Afoot," *Atlantic Monthly* (March 1987). Philip A. Shreffler, ed., *Sherlock Holmes by Gas-Lamp* (1989). Jon L. Lellenberg, *Irregular Memories of the 'Thirties* (1990); *Irregular Records of the Early 'Forties* (1991); *Irregular Proceedings of the Mid 'Forties* (1995); *Irregular Crises of the Late 'Forties* (1999).   —Jon Lellenberg

SHORT STORY. *This entry is divided into two parts. The first outlines the development of the mystery short story in the United States, citing examples of short stories featuring several types of sleuths, including detectives, private eyes, and medical experts. The second looks at the British crime short story, which includes works ranging from those that emphasize classic detection to stories that are strong on international intrigue.*

The American Crime Short Story
The British Crime Short Story

For further information, please refer to Golden Age Forms: The Golden Age Short Story; History of Crime and Mystery Writing.

THE AMERICAN CRIME SHORT STORY

The detective short story began with Edgar Allan *Poe, and it is generally considered to be an American innovation despite the great boost in popularity it received from the Arthur Conan Doyle's Sherlock *Holmes. Certainly just about every device of the modern mystery can be found in Poe's "The Murders in the Rue Morgue" (*Graham's Lady's and Gentleman's Magazine*, Apr. 1841) and his subsequent detective tales.

No other important practitioner of the American mystery short story appeared until Melville Davisson *Post and his criminal laywer Randolph *Mason in 1896. Today Post is best remembered for his highly atmospheric Uncle *Abner detective stories, which began appearing in 1911 and were first collected in *Uncle Abner, Master of Mysteries* (1918). The early 1900s also saw the appearance of Jacques *Futrelle's tales of Professor Augustus S. F. X. *Van Dunsen, notably "The Problem of Cell 13" (*Boston American*, 30 Oct. 1905), easily the most popular American mystery story of its period. Though he published forty-five stories about the detective known as the Thinking Machine, Futrelle's career was cut tragically short when he died on board the *Titanic* in 1912.

During 1925 and 1926 future Pulitzer Prize winner T. S. *Stribling published five stories about psychological sleuth Dr. Henry Poggioli, later collected as *Clues of the Caribbees* (1929). Though he tried to kill off his detective, Poggioli returned in two more series of adventures published during subsequent decades. By the mid-1920s, however, the growing influence of *Black Mask* magazine was beginning to be felt and the American mystery story would never be the same.

The hard-boiled *private eye tale, exemplified by the work of Dashiell *Hammett in the 1920s and Raymond *Chandler in the 1930s, paved the way for scores of other *Black Mask* writers, many of whom also became successful novelists. Hammett wrote some sixty-eight short stories in all, mostly for *Black Mask*. Chandler published only about twenty-five, nearly half of them for *Black Mask*. More than 200 pulp detective magazines were to appear in the United States between 1920 and 1950, enlarging upon a hard-boiled tradition that continues to the present day. For readers outside the United States, the term "American mystery story" is more likely to bring to mind Hammett, Chandler, and their followers than Ellery *Queen or Rex *Stout.

The 1930s, though, were also the golden age of the formal detective story. In addition to his novels, Ellery Queen produced nineteen masterful short stories and a short novel, collected in *The Adventures of Ellery Queen* (1934) and *The New Adventures of Ellery Queen* (1940). John Dickson *Carr, an American living in England, published *The Department of Queer Complaints* (1940) under his pseudonym Carter Dickson. Perhaps the first important book of mystery short stories by an American woman was Mignon G. *Eberhart's *The Cases of Susan Dare* (1934). One of the most imaginative volumes of short mysteries was *The Curious Mr. Tarrant* by C. Daly King, published in England in 1935 but not until 1977 in the author's native America.

One of the most memorable writers to appear in *Black Mask* and the other pulps during the late 1930s and early 1940s was Cornell *Woolrich, who also wrote under the name William Irish. He never created a hard-boiled private eye or any other series character, but his dark, brooding tales of *murder and *suspense became anthology favorites. Thirteen of his best stories are collected in *Rear Window and Other Stories* (1988). Others writers to emerge from the *pulp magazines included Fredric *Brown, Erle Stanley *Gardner, and John D. *MacDonald, all of whom became better known as novelists.

Beginning in the 1940s the careers of many short story writers were launched through the pages of *Ellery Queen's Mystery Magazine*. Notable among them was Stanley *Ellin, whose 1948 story "The Specialty of the House" became one of the most reprinted of all American mystery stories. Though he often produced only one new short story a year, Ellin published more than forty memorable tales, the first thirty-five of which are collected in *The Specialty of the House and Other Stories* (1979).

The 1950s and early 1960s saw frequent collections of Nero *Wolfe novelettes by Stout, originally written for magazine publication. In the tradition of Hammett and Chandler, Ross *Macdonald produced nine stories about his private eye *sleuth, collected as *Lew Archer, Private Investigator* (1977). Since that time Sue *Grafton has published over half a dozen stories about her female private eye Kinsey *Milhone. Other mystery novelists as varied as Lawrence *Block, Mary Higgins *Clark, Dorothy Salisbury *Davis, Marcia *Muller, Sara *Paretsky, Bill Pronzini, and Donald E. Westlake continue to produce regular short stories in addition to their books. Other writers like David Ely, Joyce Harrington, Edward D. *Hoch, Clark Howard, Jack Ritchie, and Henry Slesar have written mainly short stories, publishing only occasional mystery novels.

It is safe to say that from the time of Poe to the coming of novelists like Agatha *Christie and S. S. *Van Dine in the 1920s, the short story was the most popular form of the mystery genre. The growing popularity of novels and the decline of magazine fiction changed all that. Publishers discovered that mystery novels generally sold better than single-author collections of short mysteries. For their part, many writers were reluctant to devote much time to short stories in the face of dwindling magazine markets.

One answer to this has been the appearance of mystery anthologies using original stories rather than reprints. The stories are often written on assignment by writers the editor chooses, and sometimes they are built around a specific theme, like love or revenge. The *Sisters in Crime* series is devoted to stories by women mystery writers. Others are assembled by professional organizations like *Mystery Writers of America and *Private Eye Writers of America.

Although the *puzzle element remains strong in the work of many writers of mystery short stories,

others are structuring their tales to examine troubling social problems such as domestic violence and *child abuse. They are using their writing to break new ground, much as Poe did over a century and a half ago.

[*See also* Slicks.]

• Ellery Queen, *Queen's Quorum* (1969). William G. Contento and Martin H. Greenberg, *Index to Crime and Mystery Anthologies* (1991). Lesley-OCLC Henderson, ed., *Twentieth-Century Crime and Mystery Writers, 3rd. ed.* (1991). Bruce Cassiday, ed., *Modern Mystery, Fantasy and Science Fiction Writers: A Library of Literary Criticism* (1993).

—Edward D. Hoch

THE BRITISH CRIME SHORT STORY

The roots of the British crime short story are to be found in nonfiction. Presented as official memoir, early accounts proceeded systematically through crime, investigation, deduction, and explanation; *clues were rare, *red herrings nonexistent. Throughout the 1850s the stories were popular and cheap reading. The most enduring author in this area was William Russell, writing as Waters, or Thomas Waters, whose first volume was *Recollections of a Detective Police-Officer* (1856; *The Recollections of a Policeman; Diary of a Detective Police Officer*). His protagonist, typical of the breed, solved cases by a mixture of wit, cunning, subterfuge, and luck. More illustrious writers also produced short crime fiction including Wilkie *Collins in *After Dark* (1856), with its chilling "A Terribly Strange Bed," Charles *Dickens, and Robert Louis Stevenson. In July 1891, however, the crime story was changed forever when *The *Strand* published the first Sherlock *Holmes short story, "A Scandal in Bohemia." Neither the author, Arthur Conan *Doyle, nor his detective was unknown to the reading public, but Holmes was drawn with such clarity and detail, investigating and expounding with such deductive brilliance, that the detective story was never the same again. After two volumes of stories, *The Adventures of Sherlock Holmes* (1892) and *The Memoirs of Sherlock Holmes* (1894), Holmes was temporarily retired.

The *Strand* brought in Arthur *Morrison's Martin Hewitt, but he was a comparatively dull fellow. L. T. Meade coauthored with Clifford Halifax *Stories from the Diary of a Doctor* (1894), the first medico-detective stories. She then created a series of characters from the other side of the criminal equation, including Madame Sara in *The Sorceress of the Strand* (1903), and with Robert Eustace, Madam Koluchy, head of the sinister *Brotherhood of the Seven Kings* (1899). E. W. *Hornug, meanwhile, introduced his exuberant A. J. *Raffles, gentleman cracksman, cricketer, and socialite. In *The Amateur Cracksman* (1899; *Raffles, The Amateur Cracksman*), Raffles and his sidekick Bunny perpetrated a series of lighthearted burglaries, but by the volume's close Bunny was captured and Raffles possibly drowned. In *The Black Mask* (1901; *Raffles; Further Adventures of the Amateur Cracksman*), the mood was grimmer, and the book closed with Raffles's noble death for queen and country. Other *sleuths included M. McDonnell Bodkin's husband and wife team, Paul Beck and

Dora Myrl; George R. Sims's lady detective Dorcas Dene; Richard Marsh's Judith Lee, who read lips; and Catherine Louisa Pirkis's Loveday Brooke. M. P. Shiel created a mystical prince in *Prince Zaleski* (1895); in *Ghosts* (1899), by E. and H. Herons, Flaxman Low became the first investigator of supernatural. In 1902 came the earliest *armchair detective, Baroness *Orczy's *The Old Man in the Corner* (1909; *The Man in the Corner*), whose protagonist tied knots in string while unraveling police problems. Orczy also created a "new woman" detective in *Lady Molly of Scotland Yard* (1910).

The years before the First World War produced some of the most distinctive detectives. R. Austin *Freeman, physician and surgeon, bestowed medical and legal qualifications on his detective, Dr. John *Thorndyke. Freeman's writing, though lacking Doyle's atmospheric touch, was clear and concise, with dry humor and a keen eye for deductive detail. In his second volume, *The Singing Bone* (1912), Freeman came up with a new twist. Instead of starting with a crime committed offstage, he described the commission of the crime step by step. In the resulting *inverted detective story, the task was to discover how the detective would solve the crime, rather than to identify who perpetrated it.

G. K. *Chesterton introduced an intuitive and resourceful cleric in *The Innocence of Father Brown* (1911). Chesterton's tales are known for their brilliant *ingenuity, stunning use of paradox, and for satisfying solutions to some apparently supernatural crimes. Max Carrados, brainchild of Ernest Bramah, first appeared in 1914. Carrados was blind, yet possessed remarkable powers by which he could read newsprint, detect forgeries, even shoot straight. Since this seemed incredible, the author cited historical precedent in an explanatory introduction to *The Eyes of Max Carrados* (1923). Also during the twenties, H. C. *Bailey's Reggie *Fortune, indolent special adviser to *Scotland Yard, appeared in the first of twelve collections.

Other novelists also wrote short stories, but with varying success. Agatha *Christie's Hercule *Poirot, for instance, was a shadow of his fuller self; Miss Jane *Marple seemed better suited to the smaller canvas. Lord Peter *Wimsey positively sparkled in Dorothy L. *Sayers's *Lord Peter Views the Body* (1928), dealing with problems ranging from the bizarre to the bibliographical. Others writers covered crime without detection. Thomas Burke in *Limehouse Nights* (1916) penned beautiful, poignant pieces; "The Hands of Mr. Ottermole" in *The Pleasantries of Old Quong* (1931; *A Tea-Shop in Limehouse*), is deservedly one of the most anthologized stories. Edgar *Wallace wrote more often from the criminal's point of view; his protagonists included a jovial con man in *The Brigand* (1927), an unsuccessful and ungrammatical tipster in *Educated Evans* (1924), and a jewel thief in *Four Square Jane* (1929). Sapper's forte was the story with a twist in its tail, never better than in *Out of the Blue* (1925). Leslie *Charteris introduced Simon Templar (the *Saint), a figure in the Robin Hood mold whose amiable exploits spanned thirty years and are exemplified in *The Happy Highwayman* (1939). Espionage held its place from the turn of the century when the stories of William Lequeux and E. Phillips *Oppenheim bristled with international intrigue. The most accomplished in this arena was Somerset Maugham, a former spy himself, who recounted the activities of the Secret Service in *Ashenden* (1928). The stories, related with almost clinical detachment and devoid of dramatic action, are unsurpassed.

A diminishing postwar market did not prevent Roald Dahl from displaying a unique flair for combining shock and humor in *Someone Like You* (1954) and *Kiss, Kiss* (1960). Michael *Gilbert wrote about policeman Patrick Petrella, the legal profession in *Stay of Execution* (1971), and middle-aged spies in *Mr. Calder and Mr. Behrens* (1982). Pure *puzzle writers such as Christianna *Brand in *What Dread Hand?* (1968) and Edmund *Crispin in *Beware of the Trains* (1953) continued to entertain, but the trend was toward crime stories. New anthologies featured such writers as Julian *Symons, Ruth *Rendell, Peter Lovesey, and Simon Brett. Reginald *Hill, Colin *Dexter, and H. R. F. *Keating published collections about their popular *sleuths. Keating also devoted a volume to a charlady: *Mrs Craggs; Crimes Cleared Up* (1985). John *Mortimer's Horace *Rumpole, an *Old Bailey hack, first appeared on television but has since graced the pages of several books.

• Ellery Queen, *The Detective Short Story: A Bibliography* (1942). Ellery Queen, *Queen's Quorum: A History of the Detective-Crime Short Story as Revealed by the 106 Most Important Books Published in the Field since 1845* (rev. ed., 1969). E. H. Mundell, Jr., and F. Jay Rausch, *The Detective Short Story: A Bibliography and Index* (1974). Douglas G. Greene, "Additions to Queen's Quorum," in *Crime and Detective Stories* 14 (Aug. 1990). Douglas G. Greene, "Post-Queen's Quorum," in *Crime and Detective Stories* 15 (Nov. 1990). Douglas G. Green, "Queen's Quorum Extended," in *Crime and Detective Stories* 21 (Aug. 1993). —Robert C. S. Adey

SIDEKICKS AND SLEUTHING TEAMS. There are advantages for both detective and author when a "sidekick" or closely associated, subordinate partner is added to the cast of characters in a mystery. In those books where a trusted sidekick is utilized, he or she may become so crucial to the development of the detective as a character that the detective becomes paired in readers' minds with the helper.

Arthur Conan *Doyle let Sherlock *Holmes share a flat with Dr. John H. *Watson. Dorothy L. *Sayers gave Lord Peter *Wimsey the services of Bunter. Agatha *Christie's Hercule *Poirot and Rex *Stout's Nero *Wolfe could send Captain Arthur Hastings and Archie *Goodwin, respectively, to do the legwork on their cases. Even Ian *Fleming let James *Bond have a sidekick, Felix Leiter, to share the bullets, if not the girls and martinis.

A competent and trusted associate can expand the area of a detective's search. For example, Wimsey's upper-class status limits him in hunting for leads and gossip among working-class people, but a servant, Bunter, is able to investigate areas barred to the gentry, mingling with servants in the kitchen and locals in the pubs. An associate can also help provide balance for a detective's quirks. Because of his physical girth and the demands of tending his orchids, Wolfe seldom strays far from his overstuffed chair. This *armchair detective could not solve cases without Goodwin's legwork.

For the audience, these assistant detectives can provide comic relief or increase the tension. They may also direct attention toward or away from the truth, serving up all manner of *red herrings to confuse the reader. Sidekicks are also sounding boards, intimate friends with whom detectives can discuss cases in the presence of the reader, who is especially likely to identify with the sidekicks who serve as narrators. They stand in for the reader, asking the obvious questions and worrying after the fate of the usually eccentric, always cerebral hero.

While sidekicks are sometimes less brilliant than the Great Detectives they aid, their common sense can be necessary to solving crimes. This is often the case with Colin *Dexter's Inspector Endeavor *Morse and his Sergeant Lewis. The classic sidekick should also be in awe of the detective, demonstrating the esteem the writer hopes will transfer to the reader when the final twist is explained.

Watson is the classic sidekick: brave, capable, observant, and faithful. His very name is now generic: A detective's associate is universally known as his "Watson." But Watson was not the first of these very important characters. Like so many other aspects of mystery writing, the idea of an observing assistant came from Edgar Allan *Poe.

In Poe's "The Murders in the Rue Morgue" (*Graham's Lady's and Gentleman's Magazine*. Apr. 1841), the Chevalier C. Auguste *Dupin is introduced by his sidekick, an unnamed narrator so far from omniscient that his very thoughts are an open book to the detective. Poe's narrator serves three basic functions of the able assistant: He is first and foremost a friend, therefore also a confidant, to the detective; he is able to stand in for the reader, asking the questions or listening to the facts that move the story along; and, he admires Dupin.

In 1887, Doyle created Holmes, a detective so piercingly brilliant; that no reader could ever identify with him. Watson serves to tone down Holmes, to balance out the coldness with warmth. It is Watson with whom the reader identifies in the Holmes *Canon. Watson is the narrator and the one who tries, like the reader, to solve the mystery with Holmes. The reader sees only what Watson sees, after all. When Watson expresses care and concern for Holmes, he helps the reader to see the human side of the Great Detective.

Holmes is introduced in terms of his work in *A Study in Scarlet* (*Beeton's Christmas Annual*, 1887) as a "consulting detective" to the police, who bring their problems to him. Watson's presence increases Holmes's mobility, since Watson can remain at 221B Baker Street while Holmes disguises himself and stalks the darker recesses of *London. Watson can even face the horrific hound of the Baskervilles virtually on his own, while the absent Holmes sets himself up comfortably in the moor to spy on the *suspects.

The Holmes-Watson relationship suffers in motion picture versions, where Watson is usually treated as a character supplying only comic relief. When the late actor Jeremy Brett was offered the role of Holmes for a British television series, he accepted because he wanted to put the literature right, particularly the character of Watson. Brett referred to Watson as "—not a buffoon, but the *bestest* [sic] friend any man ever had," in a *Boston Herald* interview (14 Nov. 1991).

In the wake of Doyle's success, detective duos were rife in the early twentieth century. An exemplary pair are Margery Allingham's Albert Campion and his henchman Magersfontein Lugg.

Later, during the hard-boiled era of crime writing, detectives were cast as outsiders, virtually friendless loners. In *The Maltese Falcon* (1930), author Dashiell *Hammett gives Sam *Spade a partner, Miles Archer, whose only function in the *plot is to get himself killed immediately. Although Spade does have the help of a secretary, Effie Perrine, her role is minor. She does however exhibit all the strengths of a good sidekick: she is tough and reliable, and she loves the detective she serves.

From one associate to no associate, the historic trend eventually had to swing to multiple associates. The post–World War II *police procedurals pitted squads of detectives against the big city's killers. When Ed *McBain created his Eighty-Seventh Precinct detectives in *Cop Hater* (1956), Detective Steve Carella did not stand out as the group's leader. Carella became the luminary of the series, but importance is still given to Bert Kling, Meyer Meyer, and the rest of the squad.

The same is true in the police procedurals by the Swedish duo of Maj *Sjöwall and Per Wahlöö. Martin *Beck is the team leader, but the books are as much about the interaction among the other cops as they are about finding a criminal.

The police forces in contemporary British mysteries are less apt to indulge in squadroom camaraderie, however. Rank still matters and there is much still separating the poor sergeant from his or her higher-ranked inspector. In Dexter's Inspector Morse series, for example, Lewis is the classic beleaguered underling but plays a subordinate role by definition of his rank, not because the inspector does not trust him.

American writer Elizabeth George has created a British pair that functions despite being polar opposites of each other. Inspector Thomas Lynley comes from a higher station than does his sergeant, Barbara Havers, an inelegant commoner. While Havers does not like Lynley, and even admits it publicly, the two respect each other's abilities and so form a tentative, professional *friendship.

More than a century after Holmes and Watson, the sidekick became a full partner in the case. Teamwork became the hallmark of detecting duos of the 1990s.

Robert B. *Parker's poetry-quoting *Spenser originally began as loner, in the tradition of his immediate literary predecessor, Philip *Marlowe. Hawk was just a hired thug in *Promised Land* (1976), but his role grew over the course of the series and he became

Spenser's virtual partner in a relationship based on unwavering trust. The clients may hire Spenser, but he and Hawk work for each other.

Across the ocean, Dutch writer Janwillem *van de Wetterling's Adjutant Grijpstra and Sergeant DeGier also work as a team. Grijpstra is the senior officer, but they solve their cases as equal partners and are equally in awe of their Zen-master-like *Comissaris*.

Tony *Hillerman's Navajo detectives Joe Leaphorn and Jim *Chee began by working alone, each with his own series of books. Hillerman brought them together in *Skinwalkers* (1987) and created a new interpretation of detecting duos. Each detective works independently, sometimes not aware that the other is on the case. When they meet, having taken different routes to the same spot, it is a confirmation to both that the crime has been solved.

[*See also* Couples: Sleuth Couples.]

—Dana Bisbee

SILLY-ASS SLEUTH. The silly-ass *sleuth is primarily a creation of the British Golden Age mystery novelists. These *private detectives or amateur sleuths are distinguished by foppish demeanor and appearance. The most notable examples of the silly ass are Dorothy L. *Sayers's Lord Peter *Wimsey and Margery *Allingham's Albert *Campion. The closest American counterparts are S. S. *Van Dine's Philo *Vance, who affects British mannerisms, and the early Ellery *Queen with his various mannerisms and pince-nez. Upper-class detectives who are in fact police, such as Ngaio *Marsh's Roderick *Alleyn and Elizabeth George's Inspector Thomas Lynley, do not fit this character type.

The English silly-ass sleuths come from the British upper *class, adopting behavior that serves to *disguise their sleuthing. They rely on deception, covering up their real abilities and serious nature with silliness both of action and language. Their actions are designed to make others regard them as of no consequence, for being underestimated keeps their quarry off guard. The reader, who realizes the truth behind the misleading behavior, is both amused and at an advantage over characters who are confused by their casual, even flippant air.

Usually their relationships with the upper echelons of police are friendly because these elites recognize the abilities of the talent behind the fractious facades and tolerate the behavior of the silly-ass sleuth, usually welcoming his or her entry into the investigation, while sometimes the ordinary constables are skeptical of the sleuth's abilities but respectful of his or her class.

The silly-ass sleuths themselves are upper-class, even members of the nobility, who can afford to act the part of the overbred, perhaps effete, Oxbridge-educated dilettante. Their language often borders on the ridiculous, and they frequently act the part of the complete fool. For instance, in the opening scene of *Mystery Mile* (1930), Campion's almost childish insistence on sacrificing his mouse establishes his disguise as an absurdly juvenile figure, a pose reinforced by his business card, which declares "Coups neatly executed/ Nothing sordid, vulgar or plebeian." Like-

wise, Wimsey performs flamboyant acts, such as diving into the fountain in *Murder Must Advertise* (1933), all while speaking in affected Oxbridge slang. These sleuths, however, are taken seriously by some, for both Campion and Wimsey are entrusted with cases of great importance requiring not only their investigative skills but also their utmost discretion and loyalty to the Crown. It is interesting to note that both Campion and Wimsey outgrow their silliness as their series progress. The type virtually disappears from English mysteries with World War II, about the time that Wimsey and Campion discard their affectations.

The American silly-ass type shares the mannerisms and mannered language, but in a nominally classless society such qualities do not have the same impact. Philo Vance, educated at Harvard and Oxford, is an aesthete who can be intellectually insufferable, while the scholarly Queen, who spouts quotations from the classics, is an investigative aristocrat as the son of a police inspector. Queen, like Campion and Wimsey, develops over the course of a long series and does not remain the youthful silly ass of the early novels, while Vance remains essentially static in a much shorter series. Neither Vance nor Queen is, however, the comic equivalent of Campion or Wimsey, although those around them frequently regard them in much the same way that the British detectives are regarded by those surrounding them.

Silly-ass sleuths invariably have sidekicks who provide balance in their adventures by taking care of practicalities, behaving predictably, and having the ability to mingle among servants and villagers.

• Jon Tuska et al., *Philo Vance: The Life and Times of S. S. Van Dine* (1971). Francis M. Nevins Jr., *Royal Bloodline: Ellery Queen, Author and Detective* (1974). B. A. Pike, *Campion's Career: A Study of the Novels of Margery Allingham* (1987).

—Paula M. Woods

Silver, Miss Maud, is the principal series character in the *detective novels of Patricia *Wentworth. Although the mousey, nondescript former governess turned *spinster sleuth has a predilection for knitting, helping young lovers in distress, and underscoring her investigations with moral lectures complete with quotations from the poetry of Lord Tennyson, Miss Silver is a determinedly professional *private detective who relies on logic rather than mere intuition in her work. She uses her unthreatening outward appearance to considerable advantage in order to mislead *suspects, who frequently do not take her seriously while she employs acute powers of observation and thorough investigative techniques to solve her cases, usually set in the *English village milieu or *country house milieu or in *London, where she keeps a home office in her drawing room. With the support of *Scotland Yard's Detective Inspector Frank Abbott and Chief Detective Inspector Lamb, as well as her former pupil, Chief Constable Randal March, Silver uses her skills in the interests of truth and *innocence over the course of twenty-three *cozy novels, making her debut in *Grey Mask* (1928) and her final appearance in *The Girl in the Cellar* (1961).

—Barbara Sloan-Hendershott

SIMENON, GEORGES (1903–1989), Belgian novelist and short story writer, born in Liège of Flemish Catholic parents Désiré and Henriette Simenon. Georges Simenon was close to his father, but estranged from his mother for most of his life. Early accounts of his life contain inconsistencies because he told different versions of the same events to different interviewers. Even his twenty-seven volumes of autobiographical writings, including two novels, a diary, and a series of "intimate" memoirs, are unreliable sources.

Simenon left school at age fifteen, the same year his father suffered a heart attack. Eventually he became a crime reporter with the *Gazette de Liège*. He published his first novel, *Au Pont des Arches*, in 1921, the year his father died, and he became engaged to Régine Renchon. In 1923 he married and had one of his short stories accepted by Colette for *Le Matin*. He began writing pulp novels under the pen name "Georges Sim" and eventually published more than 100 pulp novels under several pen names.

In 1930, Simenon began to take his work more seriously and signed a contract with the publisher Fayard for a series of *detective novels about a Parisian policeman, Jules *Maigret. Most of the first nineteen books were written over the next three years, largely on board his boat, the *Ostrogoth*, moored near Delfzijl in the Netherlands. In later years, Simenon claimed never to have done any research on police procedure, and never to have set foot inside the Quai des Orfèvres, the main police station in Paris. In point of fact, he attended a series of lectures on forensics at the University of Liège in connection with some articles he wrote as a young reporter.

The Maigret books received good reviews, although some critics had reservations about the speed with which they had been written. Simenon and his publisher staged an elaborate party in 1931 to celebrate the publication of the first two titles, *M. Gallet, décède* (1931; *The Death of Monsieur Gallet*) and *Le pendu de St. Pholien* (1931; *The Crime of Inspector Maigret*). Author and publisher had reason to celebrate, as it had not been easy for the former to convince the latter that these unorthodox detective novels were worth publishing.

Three years later Simenon told Fayard he wanted to quit writing about Maigret to concentrate on serious fiction. To prove his point the nineteenth Maigret novel, *Maigret* (1934; *Maigret Returns*, 1941) depicts the detective in retirement. By the time it appeared, Simenon had broken with Fayard and signed a contract with Gallimard to write six novels a year.

Comfortably off, Simenon made a visit to Tahiti and returned to France to live in a succession of luxurious homes. When Germany invaded Belgium, Simenon was appointed commissioner for Belgian refugees at La Rochelle. He began work on a series of autobiographical writings and wrote his first Maigret novel in six years, *Cécile est morte* (1942; *Maigret and the Spinster*, 1977). There is no reference in it to the commissaire's retirement in 1934.

During the 1940s, Simenon wrote more than twenty novels, alternating the Maigrets with the dark, psychological novels, which he referred to as *romans durs, romans romans*, or *romans-tout-court*, Alication is the theme that predominates in his non-Maigret works. He left France with his family to settle in St. Luc Masson, Canada. It was there that he hired a French-Canadian, Denyse Ouimet, as his secretary. He renamed her Denise and she became his mistress.

Simenon and his family moved to the United States in 1946. In 1950 he divorced his wife, married Denise, and settled at Shadow Rock Farm, Lakeville, Connecticut where he lived for five years. He continued to write at a rapid rate and his sales reached 3 million a year. During this period he made a triumphant visit to Paris as a celebrity and was elected a member of the Belgian Académie Royale.

In 1955 Simenon moved back to France where he lived first at Cannes and later in a castle outside Lausanne in Switzerland. In 1963 he and his wife had a large house built to their own design at Epalinges. At about this time, Denise suffered a series of mental breakdowns and entered a psychiatric clinic. They separated a few years later.

In 1966, forty of Simenon's publishers staged a celebration of the creation of Maigret in the Netherlands, where a statue of the commissaire was unveiled at Delfzijl. In 1971 Simenon wrote his last psychological novel, *Les innocents* (1972; *The Innocents*, 1973), a few months later he finished the last Maigret, *Maigret et M. Charles* (1972; *Maigret and Monsieur Charles*, 1973). The rest of his writing life he devoted to his memoirs.

• Thomas Narcejac, *Le cas "Simenon"* (1950; *The Art of Simenon*, 1952). John Raymond, *Simenon in Court* (1968). Fenton S. Bresler, *The Mystery of Georges Simenon: A Biography* (1983). Patrick Marnham, *The Man Who Wasn't Maigret: A Portrait of Georges Simenon* (1992). Pierre Assouline, *Simenon: A Biography* (1997).　　　—J. Randolph Cox

SINGLETONS. Crime and mystery readers sometimes refer to authors who have written only one book in the genre as singletons. Whether such authors also have writing careers outside of the genre or are known for other careers and have simply written one book, they usually win the term "singleton" because their work in the crime and mystery field is singular in both number and memorability. Their books, too, may be called singleton mysteries. Some such novels arise out of the occupations of their writers, who use their expertise or experience to enrich a single *detective novel.

Between her terms in Parliament, Ellen Wilkinson wrote *The Division Bell Mystery* (1932), an *impossible crime story dependent on a point of ritual at the House of Commons. Eric Blom became "Sebastian Farr" for *Death on the Down Beat* (1941), drawing heavily on his musical learning for an epistolary tour de force much admired by Edmund *Crispin. *Exit Charlie* (1955), set in and around a provincial repertory theater, is the richer for Alex Atkinson's years of experience as an actor. Xantippe's familiarity with radio is everywhere apparent in *Death Catches Up with Mr. Kluck* (1935), in which a wireless engineer investigates the murder of a program sponsor.

The singleton novel may be an offshoot of an academic career. In *The Ariadne Clue* (1982), Carol

Clemeau made her detective a classics professor like herself. Philip Spencer set *Full Term* (1961) at Oxford, where he himself was a teacher. Cecil Jenkins's *Message from Sirius* (1961) was joint winner of the Crime Club's competition for dons in 1961. Margaret Doody's *Aristotle Detective* (1978) arose from amateur enthusiasm for the classics rather from than her professional discipline, which is literary criticism.

Certain mainstream writers have a single crime novel to their credit, such as James Hilton, who used the name "Glen Trevor" for *Murder at School* (1931; *Was It Murder?*); Somerset Maugham, whose *Ashenden; or, The British Agent* (1928) retains its reputation as a classic of spy fiction; H. F. M. Prescott, whose *Dead and Not Buried* (1938) stands apart from the biographies and historical novels with which she made her name; Charlotte Hough, a prolific children's writer, whose attractive detective novel, *The Bassington Murder* (1980), has had, regrettably, no sequel; and Forbes Bramble, who entered the field in 1985 with the admirable *Dead of Winter* but has not set foot in it since.

Sometimes the singleton is the launching pad to a different career. Penelope Fitzgerald won the Booker Prize in 1979 with her third novel, having begun as a fiction writer in 1977 with a distinctive crime story, *The Golden Child*. Timothy Robinson's *When Scholars Fall* (1961) was the only detective novel in Hutchinson's New Authors series. A donnish story of great charm and narrative ease, it appeared to herald a distinguished career—and perhaps did so, but not in crime writing. *Landscape with Dead Dons* (1956) is even more fetching, an Oxford novel in the high manic tradition with a notably audacious clue; but the author, Robert Robinson, became famous as a journalist and broadcaster rather than as a rival to Michael *Innes and Edmund Crispin.

The singleton mystery, inevitably, has less chance to establish itself than would a shelf of books from the same author, but a number have come to acquire something like classic status. Godfrey R. Benson's *Tracks in the Snow* (1906) and T. L. Davidson's *The Murder in the Laboratory* (1929) have the Jacques Barzun-Wendell Hertig Taylor seal of approval, as does *The Mummy Case* (1933; *The Mummy Case Mystery*), a diverting Oxford novel by Dermot Morrah, sometime editor of the *Times*. *The Face on the Cutting Room Floor* (1937) by Cameron McCabe is "dazzling" according to Julian *Symons in *Bloody Murder: From the Detective Story to the Crime Novel; A History* (1972; *Mortal Consequences*), but Barzun and Taylor qualify their praise. Whatever its merits, the book is clearly uniquely clever: Symons calls it "unrepeatable." Helen Eustis's *The Horizontal Man* (1947) is an undisputed classic, combining with immense aplomb the literary novel of detection and the psychological novel of *suspense and unease. (Her other book, *The Fool Killer*, 1954, is mainstream fiction). Frank Morley's *Dwelly Lane* (1952; *Death in Dwelly Lane*) appeared in 1952 to a chorus of praise from T. S. Eliot, Walter de la Mare, and Herbert Read, among others. Though deriving from Sherlock *Holmes, it does so obliquely, achieving its own identity with wit, imagination, and choice invention.

Other singletons deserve a wider fame: *She Died Without Light* by Nieves Mathews (1956), an intricate, sinister story set in a pension in Geneva; Clara Stone's *Death in Cranford* (1959), a decorous village mystery made memorable by a shrewd narrator with a waspish narrative manner; E. M. A. Allison's *Through the Valley of Death* (1983), a fourteenth-century mystery akin to Ellis *Peters's Brother *Cadfael chronicles and *II Name della Rosa* (*The Name of the Rose*; 1983) by Umberto Eco; and *The Random Factor* by Linda J. LaRosa and Barry Tannenbaum (1978), an intensely exciting novel set in *New York, concerning a series of *murders without apparent *motive.

—B. A. Pike

SISTERS IN CRIME. The organization Sisters in Crime was formed during the 1986 Bouchercon when a number of women who read, wrote, bought, or sold mysteries met for an impromptu breakfast to discuss mutual concerns, including their perception that women's books were taken less seriously than those written by men and were reviewed less often.

Sara *Paretsky was the driving force in organizing Sisters in Crime. In May 1987, the first steering committee was formed. Members were writers Paretsky, Charlotte MacLeod, Dorothy Salisbury Davis, Nancy Pickard, and Susan Dunlap; bookseller Kate Mattes; and mystery enthusiast Betty Francis.

The bylaws of Sisters in Crime define the purpose of the organization as follows: To combat discrimination against women in the mystery field, educate publishers and the general public as to the inequalities in the treatment of female authors, and raise the level of awareness of women's contribution to the field.

One of the group's first acts was to send a letter to the *New York Times* pointing out that in 1985, of the eighty-eight mysteries reviewed by that paper, only fourteen (16 percent) were written by women. This led to a survey of other major publications, which continues today. By 1992, the percentage of mysteries by women reviewed in the *New York Times* had risen to 30 percent.

Sisters in Crime is now an international organization of mystery readers and writers with more than 2,200 members in the United States and ten other countries. There are twenty chapters in the United States.

Sisters in Crime's outreach includes a twice yearly *Books in Print Catalog*, which goes to bookstores, libraries, and reviewers; a quarterly newsletter, which provides in-depth coverage of the American national mystery scene; a Speaker's Bureau, which connects libraries, schools, writing workshops, and booksellers with authors; and pamphlets containing information for beginning writers, authors, and booksellers planning book events and for authors interested in promotion.

—Carolyn G. Hart

SJÖWALL, MAJ (b. 1935) and **PER WAHLÖÖ** (1926–1975), Swedith husband and wife team who collaborated for a decade (1965–1975) to produce the remarkable series of ten novels featuring Superintendent Martin *Beck of Sweden's National Homicide

Squad. Planned in advance as a 300-chapter (297 in English translation) analytic portrait of Sweden's experiment in social democracy, the Beck novels may be judged as well-wrought entertainments in the *police procedural tradition, but also as a coherent ideological (leftist) indictment of social *justice in contemporary Sweden.

The immediate inspiration for the series came from Ed *McBain's Eighty-seventh Precinct novels, some of which Sjöwall and Wahlöö translated into Swedish in the 1960s. McBain offered a precedent for the close attention to realistic police procedure, for the exploitation of *humor and *sex and sexuality as added attractions, and, above all, for the focus upon a central cadre of investigators, each with his or her own personality. Beck is undoubtedly the hero of the series, but his colleagues, such as Lennart Kollberg and Gunvald Larsson, also make important contributions—both as investigators and as commentators upon the investigations.

The first five novels in the series from *Roseanna* (1965) to *Brandbilen som försvann* (1969; The Fire Engine that Disappeared), are fairly straightforward procedurals; signs of social malaise are evident, but not emphasized. The next two novels, *Polis polis Potatismos!* (1970; Murder at the Savoy) and *Den Vedervardige mannen fran Saffle* (1971; The Abominable Man) neatly balance the demands of the detective novel and social criticism: each serves to advance the other. The crime is fixed in a social matrix, and the detective must expose the more general veins of *corruption in the body politic as they excise the individual criminal. The final three novels tilt toward social criticism with a strong element of farce competing with the procedural realism.

Both Sjöwall and Wahlöö had worked as journalists and had been active in leftist politics. Wahlöö had published several political thrillers before coming to the collaboration; this background gave the Beck series its distinctive strengths: the careful embedding of Martin Beck's detective adventures in the historical realities of Sweden from 1965 to 1975 and the strong ideological perspective that the novels adopt toward the criminal matters they narrate. In the end, though he still engages in detecting individual murderers and assassins, Martin Beck shares his authors' view that the ultimate villain is the oppressive organization of the collapsing Welfare state.

[*See also* Police Detective.]

• George Dove, *The Police Procedural* (1982): 217–24. Bernard Benstock. "The Education of Martin Beck" in *Art in Crime Writing*, ed. Bernard Benstock (1983): 189–209. Nancy C. Mellerski and Robert P. Winston. "Sjöwall and Wahlöö's Brave New Sweden," *Clues* 7, no. 1 (1986): 1–17. J. K. Van Dover, *Polemical Pulps: The Martin Beck Novels* (1993).

—J. K. Van Dover

SLEIGHT OF HAND. The *whodunit writer's art is most often compared to that of the conjurer. The intention to deceive, the determination for audience to pay attention to the wrong thing, and the essentially theatrical nature of the storytelling make this an apt comparison as far as the process of planting *clues and producing a solution is concerned. The differ-

ence is that the reader of a whodunit finally understands how it has been done.

At its most artful sleight of hand is at work in those novels where the culprit is someone whom the reader has been persuaded not to view as a *suspect at all. Thus, most famously, the murderer in Agatha *Christie's *The Murder of Roger Ackroyd* (1926) is both narrator and *sidekick to Hercule *Poirot. The reader is inclined to trust the person telling the story, even though the convention of the unreliable narrator is well established in serious fiction. These two factors lead the reader to ignore the fact that Dr. Shepherd, by any account of the sequence of events, was with Roger Ackroyd shortly before his murder. Shepherd is (apparently) an observer-narrator. Christie worked a variation on the same trick in a late novel where it is a participant-narrator, one with whom the reader identifies emotionally, who turns out to be the criminal.

Variations on this trick come in novels in which a policeman, the *corpse itself, a child, or the series detective, is the murderer. Christie tried most of the possibilities more than once, and only in the last did she disappoint. *Curtain* published in (1975, but written in the late 1940s) is a perfunctory affair, as if she was beguiled by her own reputation for thinking the unthinkable into making Poirot the murderer, but could not come up with a satisfactory *plot, set of characters, or motivation to justify the solution.

Another trick is a collaboration between two or more of the suspects. The reader comes to a whodunit with the preconception that one of the suspects will be the murderer, but this need not be the case. Christie used this solution often (most flamboyantly in her 1934 novel *Murder on the Orient Express*), as did Ruth *Rendell in *Kissing the Gunner's Daughter* (1991). Some readers and writers (Christianna *Brand was one) feel this solution involves cheating, but it is not interdicted in Ronald A. *Knox's Decalogue of don'ts for crime writers.

In providing clues in a crime novel, the conjuring trick is to insert each *clue in such a way that the reader does not realize it is a clue: typically, while the detective discovers on the scene of the crime an object that seems immensely significant but will lead nowhere information that is the real clue to the solution is slyly and casually inserted. Alternatively the clue is brandished at the reader in the near certainty that it will be misunderstood. Christie places the handkerchief with the initial "H" on the floor of the aforementioned Orient Express confident that the reader will not remember there is one passenger on the train whose first language uses the Cyrillic alphabet. Much of the best clueing depends on the writer being assured that the reader will not make the necessary connection, for example the link between hemophilia and the Russian royal family in Dorothy L. Sayers's *Have His Carcase* (1932).

Often the placing of clues so as to deceive depends on the author's understanding of how a book, and in particular a work of popular fiction, is read. Christie knew that if a character says "Lottie" instead of "Lettie" from time to time readers either will not notice (reading what they expect to read) or will assume it is a misprint. Similarly, in the same book, *A Murder Is Announced* (1950), no one will notice that in two documents supposedly written by the same person, one writes "inquire" the other "enquire," proving them to be by different people since, as Christie rightly says, all educated people spell the word one or the other way, not interchangeably.

Recent writers also capitalize on the habits or preconceptions of their audience as readers. In *Dead Romantic* (1985) Simon Brett has one character ("he") arrive at his local railway station at the end of one chapter and begins the next chapter with a character ("he") leaving a *London terminus. He relies on the reader assuming that these are one and the same "he," though they are not. One of the finest pieces of modern reader-deception is the first page of Rendell's *Wolf to the Slaughter* (1967), where the sleight of hand depends not only on how the reader reads a book, but on the preconceptions he or she has about male and female sexual behavior.

Much of the above makes the writing of a whodunit sound like trivial trickery. But the craft of a mystery writer lies in his or her ability to combine the conjuring element with others (*atmosphere, *setting, *characterization, and so on) to create a satisfying whole. Writers will do this in different ways and produce different kinds of books. Christie's characterization, for example, is more conventionalized and surface-based than that of P. D. *James or Rendell. But it is precisely the different solutions to the problem of combining the conjuring element with normal fictional procedures that give the mystery novel its variety and wide appeal.

[*See also* Clues, Famous; Ingenuity; Stereotypes, Reversals of.]

• John G. Cawelti, *Adventure, Mystery and Romance* (1976). Robert, Barnard, *A Talent to Deceive* (1980).

—Robert Barnard

SLEUTH. A term dating from at least as early as 1194, "sleuth" first denoted a track or trail of a person or animal. By 1470, the word was used to refer to dogs used for tracking, as in sleuth-hound. In the United States the term became interchangeable with bloodhound, and by 1872 the noun form was a word for detective while the verb meant to track, investigate, or ferret out. During the twentieth century, the term has very commonly been used to refer to heroes who investigate and solve crimes in detective novels, stories, dramas, and films. A distinction that might be drawn between the crime novel and the detective novel is that, whereas the former may have no sleuth or may employ one only in a secondary role, in the latter the presence of a sleuth as the central figure is obligatory. Moreover, the detective novel, unlike perhaps any other genre, is, as its name suggests, character-led: Its history is the history of its central character. Though Dorothy L. *Sayers (*Great Short Stories of Detection, Mystery and Horror*, 1928) endeavored with some success to trace the science of deduction back to antiquity, she discovered no real sleuths in the remote past. The history of the character cannot be justifiably traced back beyond April 1841, when Edgar Allan *Poe's "The Murders in the Rue Morgue" (*Graham's Lady's and Gentleman's Magazine*) appeared, and the type sprang fully formed into existence in the shape of the Chevalier C. Auguste *Dupin.

Dupin provided a paradigm for future sleuths in two respects: first in the manner of operation—the minute examination of evidence, on which the sleuth's powerful ratiocinative abilities are brought to bear—and second in the manner of narration—in the first person by the sleuth's friend and companion, who describes the evidence but cannot interpret it and who constantly marvels at the sleuth's deductions. This method, later used by writers as varied as Arthur Conan *Doyle, R. Austin *Freeman, Agatha *Christie, S. S. *Van Dine, and Rex *Stout, is not only the most traditional but also undoubtedly the fairest way of presenting the mystery to the reader, and was to be characterized in the eighth of Ronald A. *Knox's ten commandments for the detective novelist: "The stupid friend of the detective, the Watson, must not conceal any thoughts which pass through his mind; his intelligence must be slightly, but very slightly, below that of the average reader" (introduction to *The Best Detective Stories of the Year 1928*, 1929; *The Best English Detective Stories: First Series*).

Dupin is not only the first real fictional sleuth but also the first *amateur detective. He is under no obligation to investigate mysteries but is motivated by curiosity, interest, and the desire to exercise his mind. This category, that of amateur sleuth, is one of the three into which, generally speaking, all sleuths may be divided. The others are the sleuth whose duty it is to investigate crime, and who is therefore usually a member of the police, and, lastly, the sleuth who is paid to investigate crime, usually a *private detective, sometimes a lawyer. Though the police sleuth has forerunners in the shape of characters such as Charles *Dickens's Inspector Bucket (*Bleak House*, (1852–3) and Wilkie *Collins's Sergeant *Cuff (*The Moonstone*, 1868), these are not central personages in the novels; the distinction of creating the first police sleuth lies with the French writer Émile *Gaboriau. His character, Monsieur Lecoq, plays only a subordinate role in the author's first novel, *L'Affaire Lerouge* (1866; The Widow Lerouge, 1873), but is the central figure in his best and most influential work, *Monsieur Lecoq* (1868; in English, 1880). The first private detective is, of course, Doyle's Sherlock *Holmes, introduced in *A Study in Scarlet* (*Beeton's Christmas Annual*, 1887), whose conception owed much both to Poe and Gaboriau.

The amateur sleuth may appear in any guise, ranging from the Roman Catholic priest—G. K. *Chesterton's Father *Brown (*The Innocence of Father Brown*, 1911)—to the elderly spinster—Christie's Miss Jane Marple (*The Murder at the Vicarage*, 1930). Academics are frequent—John Rhode's Dr. Lancelot *Priestley (*The Paddington Mystery*, 1925), Edmund *Crispin's Gervase *Fen (*The Case of the Gilded Fly*, 1944; *Obsequies at Oxford*) and Amanda *Cross's Kate *Fansler (*In the Last Analysis*, 1964)—but the character who perhaps most gives the tone to this category is that of the rich, young man-about-town, sometimes aristocratic, often a connoisseur of the arts, and usually facetious in speech: Sayers's Lord Peter *Wimsey (*Whose Body?*, 1923), *Van Dine's Philo *Vance (*The Benson Murder Case*, 1926), and Margery *Allingham's Albert *Campion (*The Crime at Black Dudley*, 1929; *The Black Dudley Murder*) are the best-known examples. Of the three categories that of amateur sleuth is naturally the least realistic, the most artificial, and the novels in which they feature often embody the same characteristics: settings may be outré, as in Allingham or Ellery *Queen (*The Roman Hat Mystery*, 1929), sleuths larger than life— John Dickson *Carr's Dr. Gideon *Fell (*Hag's Nook*, 1933)—and, most of all, *plots become intricate logical *puzzles with no pretensions to realism, which explicitly invite the reader, to whom all the evidence has been fairly presented, to arrive at the solution to the mystery before it is given by the sleuth: a type exemplified, above all, by Ellery *Queen and John Dickson Carr. The interwar years were the heyday of the amateur sleuth; since then, though the type has continued, and still continues, to appear, the incidence is less frequent, while the character has lost the dominance in the genre it earlier possessed. The most recent tendency is, perhaps, the attempt to draw this sleuth into a more realistic environment by giving him or her an occupation that is more likely to provide involvement with crime than that of the academic or idle aristocrat. An example is Jonathan Kellerman's California child psychologist, Alex Delaware (*When the Bough Breaks*, 1985; *Shrunken Heads*).

The history of the private sleuth who is a private detective is marked by the immense influence of Doyle. The detective, like Holmes, is characterized by a complex of eccentricities, and the relationship between detective and assistant echoes that between Holmes and Watson. Christie's Hercule *Poirot (*The Mysterious Affair at Styles*, 1920), whose cases are usually narrated by the imperceptive Captain Arthur Hastings, appears to have been conceived by negating Holmes's obvious characteristics: Holmes is English, tall, lean, clean-shaven, and surrounded by domestic disorder; Poirot is foreign, short, stout, mustached and obsessed by order. Stout's Nero *Wolfe (*Fer-de-Lance*, 1934; *Meet Nero Wolfe*), whose chronicler is his assistant, Archie *Goodwin, seems to be a Montenegrin reincarnation of Mycroft *Holmes, of whom Holmes remarks in "The Greek Interpreter" (*The Memoirs of Sherlock Holmes*, 1894): "If the art of detection began and ended in reasoning from an armchair, my brother would be the greatest criminal agent that ever lived." Nicholas *Blake's Nigel Strangeways (*A Question of Proof*, 1935) is an exception: Though possessing eccentricities, he derives many of these from the poet W. H. Auden, and does not otherwise fit the Holmesian pattern, while the narration is in the third person, not in the first by a Watson figure. In fact, though characters such as Holmes and Poirot provide the popular image of the fictional sleuth, private detectives have always been less numerous than amateur or police sleuths, and the type is now, to all intents and purposes, extinct. Its place has been usurped by the *private eye, a new type of sleuth who emerged in the United States in the early 1920s; the best-known examples are Dashiell *Hammett's Sam *Spade (*The Maltese Falcon*, 1930), Raymond *Chandler's Philip *Marlowe (*The Big Sleep*, 1939), and Ross *Macdonald's Lew *Archer (*The Moving Target*, 1949, as John Macdonald). Unlike the traditional sleuth, the private eye does not rely on the accumulation of evidence, nor is emphasis placed on the character's ratiocinative abilities. Instead the private eye, a far more active character, gains information generally through conversation and may arrive at the solution by chance. Further, whereas the traditional detective story is conservative and upholds the values of society, the private eye novel may be radical, subversive, or promote a cause: From Macdonald onwards ecological concerns are a recurrent theme.

The foremost example of the private sleuth who is a lawyer is Freeman's Dr. John *Thorndyke (*The Red Thumb Mark*, 1907). Though Freeman often adopts the Holmes-Watson pattern of narration in his novels and short stories, he consciously constructed the character as an antipode to Holmes: Thorndyke has no eccentricities, and his reasoning, unlike that of his contemporary, is distinguished by its rigorous logic—considered purely as a detective, he is perhaps the most impressive of all fictional sleuths. Later lawyers—Erle Stanley *Gardner's Perry *Mason (*The Case of the Velvet Claws*, 1933) is the best known—are closer to the private eye model than that of the private detective.

Despite Gaboriau's example, the *police detective took longer to become established than either the amateur or the private sleuth. The reason for this seems to have been twofold. On the one hand, the image of the policeman as incompetent and unimaginative, invariably drawing the wrong conclusions, and hindering or obstructing the sleuth in his investigations, which Doyle canonized in the figures of Lestrade and Holmes's other official rivals, militated against the use of the type as a central character. On the other, the social position of the policeman, inferior to that of the characters who at that time usually made up the dramatis personae of the detective story, presented another obstacle: While the police sleuth might be at no disadvantage when dealing with servants or retainers, he might—as indeed is the case with Lecoq in the conclusion to *Monsieur Lecoq*—be at a loss when confronted with their masters or mistresses. A. E. W. *Mason circumvents the difficulty with Inspector *Hanaud (*At the Villa Rose*, 1910), essentially by turning the character into another Holmes with a Watson in the form of Mr. Ricardo.

The first of the modern police sleuths, however, is Freeman Wills *Crofts's Inspector Burnley (*The Cask*, 1920), the prototype for the author's better-known detective, Joseph *French of *Scotland Yard (*Inspector French's Greatest Case*, 1925). In creating the type Crofts confronted both problems head-on and turned them into advantages. French is plodding and unimaginative, but instead of concealing his thoughts and narrating the story from the standpoint of a Watson, Crofts allows readers to follow every step in the construction of theory after theory until a solution is eventually reached. And in making French solidly bourgeois he conferred a certain degree of realism on the character. French was followed by a number of similar characters—Henry Wade's Chief Inspector Poole (*The Duke of York's Steps*, 1929), J. J. Connington's Superintendent Ross (*The Eye in the Museum*, 1929), Sir Basil Thomson's Scottish policeman Superintendent Richardson (*P. C. Richardson's First Case*, 1933)—and the type and method initiated by Crofts has maintained itself in British detective fiction up to the present. Recently, however, instead of attaching the police inspector to Scotland Yard, authors have preferred to base their characters in the provinces: Examples are Ruth *Rendell's Chief Inspector Wexford (*From Doon with Death*, 1964), who works in Sussex; Dorothy Simpson's Kent Policeman, Inspector Luke Thanet (*The Night She Died*, 1981); and Colin *Dexter's Inspector *Morse of Oxford (*Last Bus to Woodstock*, 1975). Georges *Simenon's Jules *Maigret of the Paris Police Judiciaire (*M. Gallet décédé*, 1931; *The Death of Monsieur Gallet*; *Maigret Stonewalled*) is, like French, quintessentially bourgeois, but this is the only trait he shares with this detective and his successors. Perhaps the best-known, and certainly the best, of all police detectives, his creation owes nothing to any of the progenitors of the genre; it is unique, both in the mode of detection and manner of narration, and those who have sought to imitate him have never succeeded in catching more than the most superficial traits of the character. While Crofts accepted the social status of the police sleuth as natural, other writers sought to solve the problem it posed by adapting the character of the gentlemanly amateur sleuth: Josephine *Tey's Inspector Alan Grant (*The Man in the Queue*, 1929; *Killer in the Crowd*), Ngaio *Marsh's Inspector/Superintendent Roderick *Alleyn (*A Man Lay Dead*, 1934), Michael *Innes's Sir John *Appleby (*Death at the President's Lodgings*, 1936; *Seven Suspects*), and even, surprisingly, P. D. *James's Adam *Dalgliesh (*Cover Her Face*, 1962) are all policeman, but are all recognizably descendants, to a greater or less degree, not of Lecoq and French but of Lord Peter *Wimsey. In America, Anna Katharine *Green produced an early example of the police sleuth in Ebenezer Gryce (*The Leavenworth Case: A Lawyer's Story*, 1878), but the character, and the novel itself, look back to Dickens and Collins rather than forward to Gaboriau; and over the next century American crime fiction conspicuously lacks the regular procession of police officers which, from 1920 onwards, is a feature of the British variant. Some isolated examples may be noted: Anthony Abbot's Thatcher Colt, the police commissioner of *New York, a blend of Wimsey and Philo *Vance (*About the Murder of Geraldine Foster*, 1930; *The Murder of a Man Afraid of Women*); Coffin Ed *Johnson and Grave Digger Jones, the police detectives in Chester *Himes's surreal, comic, and violent novels of black Harlem, originally published in French (*La reine des pommes*, 1958; *For Love of Imabelle*; *A Rage in Harlem*); and Tony *Hillerman's Navajo Indians Jim *Chee and Joe Leaphorn (*The Dark Wind*, 1982; *The Blessing Way*, 1970), who are more akin to the heroes of James Fenimore Cooper than to the traditional sleuth. As in Britain, the disinclination to the use the police sleuth is attributable to the conception of the character as incompetent, compared to the brilliance of the amateur or private sleuth, a view perpetuated, for example, both in the work of Van Dine and Stout; but a contributory factor must also have been the image of the police put forward, particularly in the private eye novel, as corrupt, and hence almost as much an enemy to the sleuth as the criminal. The situation changed in the 1950s with the emergence of the *police procedural novel. Up to this time the sleuth had always been an individual, sometimes with an assistant, engaged in the investigation of a single crime. In the police procedural the individual is replaced by a collective—a police squad—which is often engaged in the simultaneous investigation of several crimes. Ed *McBain (*Cop Hater*, 1956) is the bestknown in this genre, but its conventions have been adopted, to a greater or lesser extent, by most American writers who have taken the police as their subject.

The choice of sleuth indicates the author's general intention. To employ an amateur sleuth with no connection with crime, a private supersleuth, or a gentlemanly police officer implies that the work is primarily an entertaining puzzle, and that no social comment can be expected. As the short history above makes clear, the general tendency of the detective novel has been to move away from artificiality towards a certain degree of realism, often combined with social criticism, and the character of the sleuth has changed in consequence. The dilettante amateur has been largely replaced by the semiprofessional, the private detective by the private eye, and the individual police officer, gentlemanly or bourgeois, by the police squad. Though the older types may never die out completely, as the detective novel can never aspire to complete seriousness, it seems, however, likely that this tendency will continue, and that the days of the traditional sleuth are numbered.

[*See also* Academic Sleuth; Accidental Sleuth; Armchair Detective; Bluestocking Sleuth; Clerical Sleuth; Couples: Sleuth Couples; Elderly Sleuth; Ethnic Sleuth; Great Detective, The; Hard-Boiled Sleuth; Journalist Sleuth; Juvenile Sleuth: Boy Sleuth *and* Girl Sleuth; Lawyer: The American Lawyer-Sleuth *and* The British Lawyer-Sleuth; Medical Sleuth; Native American Sleuth; Plainman Sleuth; Psychic Sleuth; Scientific Sleuth; Silly-Ass Sleuth; Spinster Sleuth; Superman Sleuth; Surrogate Detective.]

• Howard Haycraft, *Murder for Pleasure: The Life and Times of the Detective Story*, 3rd ed. (1974). R. F. Stewart, . . . *And Always a Detective: Chapters on the History of Detective Fiction* (1980). Patricia Craig and Mary Cadogan, *The Lady Investigates: Women Detectives and Spies in Fiction* (1981). T. J. Binyon, *Murder Will Out. The Detective in Fiction* (1989).

—T. J. Binyon

SLICKS is an American slang term that refers to a magazine printed on paper with a glossy finish. Slick magazines were primarily general interest magazines containing a combination of fiction (short stories, novelettes, and serialized novels) and nonfiction. The style of writing in the slicks was geared to a family readership and differed from that found either in the earlier *dime novels or contemporaneously in the *pulp magazines. The reader of the slicks seldom chose a pulp magazine to read and may not have chosen a hardcover mystery book from the library. There were both prestige and greater financial rewards for the writer whose work was printed in the slick magazines. It was common for serial versions of mystery novels to appear in the slick magazines prior to book publication.

Some writers became identified with specific magazines. E. W. *Hornung's A. J. *Raffles stories appeared in Scribner's magazine and Arthur B. *Reeve's earliest Craig *Kennedy stories appeared in Cosmopolitan. Mary Roberts *Rinehart, Earl Derr *Biggers, and Erle Stanley *Gardner were regularly published in the Saturday Evening Post. Rinehart also published in the Slick magazines, Cosmopolitan, Ladies' Home Journal, and Good Housekeeping. Sax *Rohmer's work appeared regularly in Collier's Weekly and Liberty. S. S. *Van Dine was published in Scribner's magazine, The American magazine, and Cosmopolitan. Between 1934 and 1956 the American magazine published 237 short mystery novels, which regularly included stories by Leslie *Charteris, George Harmon *Coxe, Leslie Ford, Hugh *Pentecost, Phoebe Atwood *Taylor, and Rex *Stout. The majority of Stout's Nero *Wolfe novelettes first appeared in the American magazine. The large slick magazine market for mystery fiction ended during the 1950s.

• John William Tebbel, The American Magazine: A Compact History (1969). Jon L. Breen and Rita A. Breen, eds., American Murders: 11 Rediscovered Short Novels from the American Magazine, 1934–1954 (1986).   —J. Randolph Cox

SMALL, RABBI DAVID.

The first rabbi in the line of clerical sleuths that follows from G. K. *Chesterton's Father Brown, Harry Kemelman's Aabbi David Small makes an ideal detective both because of his vocation and his special place in the Yankee town of Barnard's Crossing, Massachusetts.

Unlike other clergymen, the traditional rabbi is not a spiritual leader or examplar of religious zeal but primarily a man of intellect, a lifelong student of the the Hebrew book of law, the Talmud. Small relies on the rabbinical art of pilpul, the "tracing of fine distinctions." His detection is promoted also by the intellectual openness asserted for Judaism, its "questioning of everything."

Kemelman frankly uses the detective fictions involving Small, his family, and his Conservative congregation to explore the social and religious situation of contemporary American Jewry. The rabbi usually is drawn into cases by his friend, Chief of Police Hugh Lanigan; however, the detection often helps to resolve a problem within his congregation or to defend someone in the Jewish community.

Like Brown, Small understands people through both a sacred book and wide experience. In his investigations of lawbreaking, the rabbi combines firm judgment (necessary to maintain any law, God's or humankind's) with a restraint and tolerance that are promoted "worldly" Judaism.

[See also Clerical Sleuth.]

• Harry Kemelman, preface to The Nine Mile Walk (1967); William David Spencer, Mysterium and Mystery: The Clerical Crime Novel (1989).   —T. R. Steiner

SMUGGLING, or conveying goods secretly to avoid payment of customs duties, is an age-old crime. In England it goes back at least to the Middle Ages, first of wool, whose export was officially forbidden, then of tea, spirits, brandy, silk, or lace on account of the high import duties they attracted. The century prior to about 1830 was the high point for the latter form of smuggling before more effective enforcement measures—notably the formation of the coast guard in 1831—coupled with reduced customs duties in the Victorian free-trade climate brought about a relative decline. Nowadays the major preoccupation of customs officials worldwide is drugs, the smuggling of which differs from that of earlier products because of the harmful nature of the goods. Smuggling is a problem for every country; for Great Britain and the United States it is accentuated by long coastlines and this is perhaps reflected in their literatures.

Smugglers have a romantic aura—they cheat governments, not individuals—yet *violence and *murder were, and are, often a part of their operations. This emerges in Daphne *du Maurier's Jamaica Inn (1936) set on Cornwall's often bleak Bodmin Moor during the nineteenth century. Many other English writers viewed smuggling with favor—Charles Lamb; R. H. Barham; Russell Thorndike, with his many Dr. Syn volumes; William Hope Hodgson, in Captain Gault (1917); even Frederick Marryat, though not Daniel Defoe or G. P. R. James.

Generally speaking, smuggling has only a minor role in classic *detective novels. Sometimes it merely flavors a novel's background, like the Smuggler Island (Devon) of Agatha *Christie's Evil Under the Sun (1941) or the locale of Margery *Allingham's Cargo of Eagles (1968). Smuggling drugs into Egypt is a three-chapter subplot in A. E. W. *Mason's The House in Lordship Lane (1946), which has little to do with the main murder investigation. Dorothy L. *Sayers's Murder Must Advertise (1933) contents itself with casual allusions to cocaine being imported by motorboat to the Essex coast. John *Rhode's A.S.F.: The Story of a Great Conspiracy (1924; The White Menace) tells of the cocaine traffic but is atypical, a *thriller with no mention of his series detective Dr. Lancelot *Priestley. There are exceptions: Douglas Clark's Dead Letter (1984) has drug smuggling in Dorset leading to murder, and in the Golden Age era, two books by Freeman Wills *Crofts's Anything to Declare? (1957) is a late, nonvintage Inspector Joseph *French essay but The Pit-Prop Syndicate (1922) is superb. The smuggling, of brandy from France, and its ingenious distribution are the book's main interest, as the murder, of one of the syndicate who threatens to jeopardize the others, is quickly solved by Inspector George Willis.

Smuggling of assorted contraband is a feature of many exciting thrillers: Drugs are smuggled in Andrew *Garve's The Riddle of Samson (1954), with its Scilly Isles backdrop, and John Christopher's A Scent of *White Poppies* (1959), set in rural Yorkshire. Microfilms are concealed in a circus panther's collar in Victor Canning's *Panther's Moon* (1948). Gunning occurs in Nicholas Monsarrat's short story "The Ship That Died of Shame" (*The Ship That Died of Shame, and Other Stories*, 1960). Baroness *Orczy's *The Scarlet Pimpernel* (1905) and its sequels are obvious examples; more recent ones come from Andrew Garve's *A Hero for Leanda* (1959) and *The Long Short Cut* (1968), and Edward Young's *The Fifth Passenger* (1963), set in a memorably evoked Brixham (South Devon). In many books the smuggling is portrayed as high jinks rather than crime. Examples are those written by Selwyn Jepson featuring the intrepid Eve Gill, who spends much time concealing her father's penchant for smuggling liquor, and Compton Mackenzie's *Whisky Galore* (1947).

America's smuggling problems are at least as great as Britain's. There have been several recent dope-running thrillers. Earlier essays include Thomas W. Knox's *New York short story "A Chemical Detective" (1893); a noteworthy fictional smuggling hero is Robert L. Fish's engaging Kek Huuygens of *The Hochmann Miniatures* (1967) and several short stories. Generally speaking, smuggling is, in the United States as in Britain, more at home in the thriller than in the classical detective story.

[*See also* Underworld, The.]

• John Douch, *Rough Rude Men: A History of Old-Time Kentish Smuggling* (1985). David Phillipson, *Smuggling: A History 1700–1970* (1973). Letitia Twyffert, "Smuggling Pitfalls," in *Murder Ink*, ed. Dilys Winn (1977). Philip L. Scowcroft, "Selwyn Jepson, Thriller Writer and Man of Action: A Short Tribute," *CADS* 21 (Aug. 1993): 23–24.

—Philip L. Scowcroft

SNOW, C. P. *See* Incidental Crime Writers.

Spade, Sam is the *private eye and main character in Dashiell *Hammett's novel *The Maltese Falcon* (1930). Although he also appears in three stories included in the volume edited by Ellery *Queen in 1944 as *The Adventures of Sam Spade and Other Stories* and assumed the lead in a series of 1940s radio dramas, Spade earned his place as the literary model of the *hard-boiled sleuth with Hammett's best-selling book and became an archetypal figure in the popular imagination through Humphrey Bogart's portrayal in the film version of *The Maltese Falcon*.

Sam Spade's most notable quality is his absolute adherence to a private code of ethics. Hammett's novel, written in the third person, offers little biographical background for Spade, but readers are apprised of the philosophical outlook he has drawn from his professional experience. In the midst of the novel, Spade tells the story of a missing person he pursued named Flitcraft. The man had left his home and business in Tacoma. When Mrs. Flitcraft employs Spade to find her husband, the detective turns him up in Spokane, living a life identical to the one he left behind, even to the extent of having a second wife similar to the one he abandoned. Flitcraft explains to Spade that a near fatal accident taught him that life is a set of chance events, but according to Spade, Flitcraft does not realize that he has settled back into determinative routine. What Spade likes about the story is that Flitcraft's philosophical inconsistency reveals the real premises of life to lie in immediate material situations.

The importance Spade sees in the Flitcraft tale helps explain Spade's existentialist consciousness. His terse speech shows him refusing the rituals of language he deems empty. His sexual affair with the wife of his partner and his resistance to the claims of affection that follow upon his relationship with Brigid O'Shaughnessy, the *femme fatale of the novel, indicate that Spade is forever seeking to retain control. For the same reason he mocks the personal relationship of the villain Gutman with his gunsel Wilmer, and refuses to cooperate with the police.

As a hard-boiled sleuth, Spade is a departure from the classical detective. Whereas the detectives of the Golden Age functioned as conservative agents of wealth and its preferred order, Sam Spade expresses Hammett's radical worldview. His mistrust of virtually all those around him; his cynicism about any code other than the one he has crafted—these are the traits necessary if one is to function successfully in a dangerous, threatening, and fundamentally corrupt world.

Hammett completed his effective formula for the hard-boiled sleuth by setting Spade to work in the nighttime streets of *San Francisco whose dark intensity limn a crime-ridden city where the thoughtful man could never find a home and might as well, then, become a freelance, if lonely, truth seeker.

[*See also* Chivalry; Mean Streets Milieu.]

• Peter Wolfe, "Sam Spade and Other Romantics," in *Beams Falling: The Art of Dashiell Hammett* (1980). Richard Layman, *Shadow Man: The Life of Dashiell Hammett* (1981). Dennis Dooley, *Dashiell Hammett* (1985). Jopi Nyman, *Hard-Boiled Fiction and Dark Romanticism* (1998).

—Bonnie C. Plummer

Spenser. The protagonist of Robert B. *Parker's series of *private eye novels, Spenser—who always goes by the single name only—is introduced in *The Godwulf Manuscript* (1973). A disenchanted former employee of the Suffolk County, Massachusetts district attorney's office, this existential hero is guided by a self-inscribed code of conduct modeled on that of Raymond *Chandler's Philip *Marlowe. Aided by his strongman sidekick, the enigmatic African American, Hawk, he is known for his wisecracks edged with sarcasm, often delivered as one-liners. While an imposing physical presence establishes him as a tough guy, when he was created he was remarkable for his sensitivity. Comfortable in physical confrontation, he also knows the importance of rapport in relationships. He is as believable jabbing and hooking at a punching bag as he is cooking up a gourmet meal to share with his psychologist-lover Susan Silverman, while drawing upon her professional insights for *clues to psychological *motivation.

[*See also* Hard-boiled Sleuth; Heroism; Sidekicks and Sleuthing Teams; Voice: Wisecracking Voice.]

• Gwendolyn Whitehead, *Hard-Boiled Heir: Robert B. Parker as Literary Descendent of Dashiell Hammett, Raymond Chandler, and Ross Macdonald* (1992).

—John M. Reilly

SPILLANE, MICKEY (Frank Morrison, b. 1918), American author of the *hard-boiled *private eye novel. Born in Brooklyn, New York, Spillane grew up in a rough Elizabeth, New Jersey neighborhood where his father was a bartender. Spillane was a born storyteller—particularly of ghost stories—and began to submit stories to the *pulp magazines as a teenager. After a brief stint at Kansas State College, he returned to New York and began writing short stories and scripts for comics books. In World War II he enlisted in the army and served as a fighter pilot instructor in Greenwood, Mississippi.

Spillane returned to writing after the war, publishing his first novel in 1947; he interrupted his career in 1952 after a religious conversion, and again in 1973 to become a Miller Lite beer spokesman. These decisions divide his career into three distinct periods: 1947–52; 1961–73; and 1980–89; but the periods do not reflect significant changes in his writing.

In 1946 Spillane created a comic book private eye called Mike Danger who became Mike *Hammer in the bestselling novel *I, the Jury* (1947). Hammer is a World War II veteran who sets out to avenge the death of a man who once saved his life, and vows to let nothing stand in his way, especially not the law. He is assisted by his loyal and sexy secretary, Velda. The novel is typical of Spillane's work, drawing together right-wing politics, unrestrained *violence, and strong, sexual women. Hammer executes his friend's killer but struggles thereafter to convince himself of the legitimacy of his act.

Subsequent stories adhere to the formula of vengeance, violence, and sex. The book titles are indicative: *I, the Jury* (1947), *My Gun Is Quick* (1950), *Vengeance Is Mine*: (1950), *The Big Kill* (1951), and *The Girl Hunters* (1962). Throughout the series Hammer ages but does not mellow, from the white-hot vigilante in *I, the Jury* to the older, more world-weary but still deadly Hammer of *The Killing Man* (1989) and *Black Alley* (1996). The series has been extremely popular; the sixth book, *Kiss Me Deadly* (1952), was the first mystery novel to appear on the *New York Times* best-seller list.

In the 1960s Spillane created Tiger Mann, an imitation of James *Bond who appeared in four novels and never achieved the stature of Hammer. Spillane also wrote nonseries books that continued his mix of conservative politics, violence, and sex.

One book stands out for its narrative purpose. In *One Lonely Night* (1951) Spillane offers an especially effective defense of his perspective to those who criticize him rather than analyzing his fiction. In the story Hammer challenges a liberal judge who condemns him and his actions. While Hammer is confronting the judge, Spillane is confronting his liberal critics. From Hammer's first appearance Spillane captured the psyche of America, from its loss of *innocence after World War II to the late 1980s loss of purpose and direction. His books offer a savagely lyrical depiction of the wounded American soul.

[See also Hard-Boiled Sleuth; Sex and Sexuality; Urban Milieu; Voice; Hard-Boiled Voice.]

• Max Allan Collins and James L. Traylor, *One Lonely Knight: Mickey Spillane's Mike Hammer* (1984).

—James L. Traylor *and* Max Allan Collins

SPINSTER SLEUTH. The term "spinster," originally appended to names to indicate the profession of spinner, has been used since the seventeenth century to denote a woman who is unmarried, especially a woman who is past the usual marrying age. In crime and mystery fiction, the spinster sleuth is usually an elderly woman with time on her hands and an observing eye. She may claim the advantage of detachment, and with scant personal life of her own, she may find the lives of others a consuming interest. Her low social profile, as a person both unmarried and elderly, may afford her natural camouflage. To quote Lord Peter *Wimsey in *Unnatural Death* (1927; *The Dawson Pedigree*), she can ask freely "questions which a young man could not put without a blush."

The prototype for the meddlesome old maid with time on her hands is Amelia Butterworth, who assists Ebenezer Gryce in two novels by Anna Katharine *Green, *That Affair Next Door* (1897) and *Lost Man's Lane* (1898). It seems agreed Butterworth had no immediate successors. Three decades later, Dorothy L. *Sayers refined the detecting potential of the "superfluous" woman when she introduced Miss Katharine Climpson in *Unnatural Death*. This redoubtable lady runs a typing pool, or secretarial agency, which has the dual purpose of providing occasional sleuthing assistance to Wimsey. Her exclamatory reports to Wimsey enhance the appeal of *Strong Poison* (1930), in which her investigations help to save Harriet *Vane from the gallows.

In 1928, Agatha *Christie introduced Miss Jane *Marple, an apparently unassuming elderly woman whose infallible insight into human affairs is based on her ability to make parallels about the *suspects she encounters with villagers whom she knows more intimately. During the same year Patricia *Wentworth created Miss Maud *Silver in *Grey Mask* (1928); a former governess turned *private detective to the gentry, who knits assiduously, inspires instant confidence, and, with thirty-two recorded cases, must be the busiest of all spinster detectives.

In 1931, Stuart Palmer's Miss Hildegarde *Withers took a class to the *New York zoo where she became an *accidental sleuth. She is exactly the assertive, prying spinster of caricature, complete with horse face, angular frame, pince-nez, and a "sharp, commanding voice" of "unmistakeable authority." Ethel Thomas who is also a New Yorker, is irresistibly drawn to investigate *murder, and figures in four novels by Courtland Fitzsimmons. D. B. Olsen's Rachel Murdock continually shocks her prim sister, Jennifer, with whom she lives in *Los Angeles. Her look of "a Dresden-china model with silky white curls" belies her adventurous spirit. Jane Amanda Edwards appears in a series by Charlotte Murray Russell, set in Rockport, Wisconsin. She boasts of her pedigree and confesses that she "sees all, hears some, and tells everything." Matilda Perks is the most disagreeable of spinster detectives. A fearsome old party with a mustache and a harsh, abrasive manner, "Miss Perks cared for nobody . . . and took no trouble to dissemble the fact." She figures in two of R. C. Woodthorpe's novels.

Julia Tyler is a retired Latin teacher in Rossville, Virginia, in Louisa Revell's novels. Her cases occur away from home, as far afield, even, as England and Italy. Despite her disciplined shrewdness, she tends to reach the wrong conclusion. Two British teachers turn professional in retirement. Austin Lee's Flora Hogg sets up in South Green, charging "two guineas a day and expenses" on her first case in 1955. Miss Emily Seeton taught art and has an eerie facility for psychic portraiture, invaluable to *Scotland Yard. She features in Heron Carvic's novels, operating more by instinct than judgment. Amanda and Lutie Beagle have professionalism thrust upon them when they inherit their brother's New York detective agency. Torrey Chanslor's two novels record their response to the challenge. Other spinsters encounter murder in the course of their working lives: the brave young governess, Harriet Unwin, in three novels by Evelyn Hervey; the nurses Sarah Keate and Hilda Adams, in books by Mignon G. *Eberhart and Mary Roberts *Rinehart, respectively; and the missionary pair in Matthew Head's African novels, Dr. Mary Finney, large, downright imperturbable, and untouched by fashion, and Emily Collins, small and wispy, "like a bundle of dried twigs tied up with a string."

Grace Severance is featured in four late novels by Margaret Scherf. A Chicago pathologist retired to Montana, she is clever and competent and dryly humorous about her new way of life, in which, predictably, her expertise continues to be called upon. Melinda Pink is Gwen Moffat's detective, well defined by the first title to feature her, *Lady with a Cool Eye* (1973). A seasoned naturalist and climber, she does most of her detecting in the open air.

The Honorable Constance Morrison-Burke is, like Joyce *Porter's male protagonists, a comic grotesque. A tomboy with a hockey stick, forty years on, she is a detective of the do-or-die school, lacking any sense of her own limitations, which are legion.

Some of the current spate of young women detectives are spinsters, though none would thank one for calling her so. They are unmarried by choice, either lesbian or resistant to conjugal ties. Antonia Fraser's Jemima Shore exemplifies their sexual freedom.

[See also Elderly Sleuth; Females and Feminists; Nosy Parker Sleuth; Stereotypes, Reversals of.]

• Michele Slung, ed., *Crime on Her Mind: Fifteen Stories of Female Sleuths from the Victorian Era to the Forties* (1975). Mary Cadogan and Patricia Craig, *The Lady Investigates: Women Detectives and Spies in Fiction* (1981).

—B. A. Pike

SPOOFS. See Farceurs; Pastiche; Spoof Scholarship.

SPOOF SCHOLARSHIP. The word "spoof" was first used in 1889 by a professional comedian; the *Oxford English Dictionary* defines it as "a game of hoaxing and nonsensical character." Its invention, therefore, postdates by only two years the first appearance of Sherlock *Holmes. The conjunction is appropriate, for no one in literature, except William *Shakespeare, has been spoofed as often as the *Great Detective of Baker Street. Spoof scholarship is an inverted kind of admiration: James Thurber's "How Many Children Had Lady Macbeth?" is the other side of bardolatry, but of a piece with it—so

with the many Baker Street Irregular articles that meticulously examine the almanacs for the year in which "the September equinoctial gales had set in with exceptional violence," or whether there was "a wild, tempestuous night towards the close of November" in 1894, as Watson states. All this extensive literature is both spoof and testimony of a deep and respectful curiosity.

It was Ronald A. *Knox who raised the studies in Sherlock to the level of art. In "Studies in the Literature of Sherlock Holmes" (*Essays in Satire*, 1928), he subjected the *Canon to the same rigorous, but tongue-in-cheek treatment that some of his fellow ecclesiastics had brought to the study of the Gospels. But unlike his followers, Knox had a double butt: scholarship itself, and the Holmes stories, for which, typically, he shows considerable respect and affection. "If there is anything pleasant in criticism," he writes, "it is finding out what we aren't meant to find out."

Thus was set the tone of Sherlockian spoof scholarship, which, critics agree, no subsequent writer has done better than Knox. There is a penetrating analysis of the role of Dr. John H. *Watson, his "Watsoninity," and rejection of the "deutero-Watson" theory. There is Knox's division of the typical story into eleven distinct parts, from Proomion to Epilogos, which without breaking the butterfly on the wheel does expose the structure of the typical tale. Knox's essay closes with a sense of his role as a pioneer: "You know my methods, Watson: apply them."

Among those following Knox's commission successfully is Rex *Stout, who owes no inconsiderable debt to the Holmes model for his creation of the eccentric *armchair detective Nero *Wolfe. In "Watson Was a Woman," a talk delivered on 31 January 1941 to a meeting of the Baker Street Irregulars, Stout replicated the scholarly process of thought that led him to his startling conclusion. His attention was caught by the absence in any of Watson's descriptions of domestic life at Baker Street of going to bed at night. Holmes is, however, seen eating breakfast, and the tone of those accounts, Stout reported, sounded to his ear much like that of a woman living with a man, a bit grouchy but indulgent. There's the hypothesis: Watson is a woman. To test the hypothesis, Stout sifted through dozens of additional domestic references, first to confirm his view that Watson wrote like a woman, and next to decide whether Watson is wife or mistress. Postulating that that no man would ignore his mistress as Holmes ignores Watson, Stout decided that Watson filled the role of wife. Stout next proceeded to show, through a complex acrostic formed by the titles of Holmes stories that Watson's true name is Irene Watson. Irene is elsewhere identified as "the woman" in Holmes's life. With one more turn of scholarly *ingenuity, Stout speculated that Irene *Adler was a simulation of Mrs. Holmes.

Of course, once applied to the greatest of the Great Detectives, spoof scholarship becomes available for sometimes wry, other times heavy-handed attachment to the genre of detective fiction itself. Stephen Leacock's "Murder at $2.50 a Crime" (*Here Are My Lectures and Stories*, 1938) falls into this category, appearing as advice to the writer that grapples particularly with the problem of bringing the story to a convincing end.

Perhaps the greatest piece of spoof scholarship is a spoof only in its tone—for in its scholarship it is deadly serious—Raymond *Chandler's "The Simple Art of Murder" (*Atlantic Monthly*, Dec. 1944). The serious thesis of Chandler's manifesto is that detective fiction must meet the same demands of realism as any other kind of fiction, rather than dealing with "how somebody stabbed Mrs. Pottington Postlethwaite III with the solid platinum poniard just as she flatted on the top note of the Bell Song from Lakme in the presence of fifteen ill-assorted guests." The derisive dismissal of classic mystery imports the note of spoof.

The final question about the spoof scholarship of detective fiction must be: why the prevalence of this kind of facetious, sometimes defensive, treatment of the genre? There is no body of criticism of Victorian fiction, say, which looks for errors in *Henry Esmond* and proceeds to explain them away as due to the deficiencies of the narrator. The answer must be found in the essentially comic nature of detective fiction. This type of fiction, Chandler says, "is written in a certain spirit of detachment; otherwise nobody but a psychopath would want to write it or read it." A genre that all too often doesn't take itself as seriously as it should may expect reactions of derision, but like Shakespeare himself, it may also attract shafts of envy.

[*See also* Humor.]

—Barrie Hayne

SPORTS MILIEU. With its *atmosphere of excitement and its structure, timing, and rules of play, the sports milieu, is useful to crime and mystery writers in providing a lively scene and readily available weaponry, as well as in determining an order of events and even predictability of playing areas that are useful to the crafting of crimes and their solutions. A character's participation in certain sports can be a clue to *class, while prowess at sports, being a good sport, or playing by the rules can also be used as means of defining character. In some cases, the desire to excel in sports or to win a sports match or race or game can provide the *motive for *murder or muddle an unrelated reason for murder that occurs within the sporting scene. Finally, the desire to clean up corruption in a favorite sport can motivate—and put at risk—*sleuths and other characters.

The elite games of the leisured class provide the *milieu for many memorable works of classic detective fiction. In these works, various well-defined playing areas serve as both indicators of class and grounds for the placement of clues in perplexing murders. An exemplar is John Dickson *Carr's *The Problem of the Wire Cage* (1939), an *impossible crime in which only one set of footprints leads to the *corpse on a wet tennis court—and the footprints are those of the *victim.

Cricket, England's national game from the eighteenth century, remains one of the more popular sports in the British Isles and countries which were once part of the former British Empire or common-wealth. Many British crime authors have featured it as an attractive background, particularly in stories set in schools or villages—Barbara Worsley-Gough's *Alibi Innings* (1954) is a pleasing example of the latter—but others like *Testkill* (1979) by Ted Dexter, former England captain and Test selector, and Clifford Makins and John *Creasey's *A Six for the Toff* (1955; *A Score for the Toff*) have first-class cricket as their milieu.

Not only is cricket used to provide background; it can contribute directly to the plot. In Dorothy L. *Sayers's *Murder Must Advertise* (1933), the ability of a murder suspect to throw down the wicket from the deep field is essential to the mystery. The nail-biting finish to a school match in Nicholas *Blake's *A Question of Proof* (1935) enables the killer to stab his unpopular headmaster and ingeniously dispose of the weapon while everyone is concentrating on the cricket. A cricket bat can be a weapon, as in *Murder at School* (1931; *Was It Murder?*) by Glen Trèvor and in *The Echoing Strangers* (1952) and the short story "Manor Park," both by Gladys *Mitchell.

Several investigators play cricket—Sayers's Lord Peter *Wimsey, Laurence Meynell's Hooky Heffernan, Robert Richardson's Augustus Maltravers, Tim Heald's Simon Bognor, and H. C. *McNeile's Ronald Standish—and this adds to their appeal. E. W. *Hornung's "gentleman-burglar" A. J. *Raffles is a cricketer, good enough to play for England, and this was surely a factor in the public's acceptance of a man who is after all a criminal.

While some sports scenes provide characters with weaponry designed to kill, as is the case in the stag hunt on Exmoor depicted in Cyril *Hare's *He Should Have Died Hereafter* (1958; *Untimely Death*), some sports equipment never intended for the purpose has been put to use as weaponry. The golf club, another accessory to the leisured life, plays this role in Agatha *Christie's *Towards Zero* (1944), although there it is a *red herring, Rex *Stout's *Fer-de-Lance* (1934; *Meet Nero Wolfe*), and in Anthony Wynne's *Death of a Golfer* (1937; *Murder in the Morning*), among other novels. Another piece of sports equipment, the oar to a rowboat, can also be used as a weapon, as in William Faulkner's "Hand upon the Waters" (*Knight's Gambit*, 1939).

Sports equipment can also provide a significant clue, as is the case with the culprit's spiked shoes, used for the practice of high jumping, in Arthur Conan ^Doyle's "The Adventure of the Three Students" (*Strand*, June 1904). Evidence of the playing of sports may be used to establish and break an *alibi, as occurs in George Allan England's "Ping-Pong" (*All-Story Weekly*, 28 Sept. 1918), a story in which a murderer plays table tennis with himself, holding a paddle in each hand, in order to create the sound of a game in progress to convince a housekeeper that two men were alive when one was already murdered.

Heroes of crime and mystery fiction are sometimes driven to clean up the games they revere while they also solve crimes set in those sporting worlds. Peter Lovesey's *period mystery *The Detective Wore Silk Drawers* (1971) looks at the horrors of bare-knuckled boxing in Victorian times. Robert B. *Parker has his sleuth *Spenser look at the corruption in professional basketball in *Playmates* (1989). The seamy side of female wrestling is the focus on Liza Cody's *Bucket Nut* (1992). *Murder on the Iditarod Trail* (1991) by Sue Henry shows the perils along the path of the famous dog-sled race across the Arctic wilderness.

Murder is often seen as the ultimate outrage against the concept of fair play that informs all sports. It can also be seen as the answer to assuring a win at sports, as is the case in David Winser's "The Boat Race Murder" (*Sporting Blood*, 1942), a story in which a member of the *Oxford crew, desperate to win the annual Boat Race, poisons a member of his own team who he believes will not lead the crew to victory. In an unusual twist, the coxswain willingly takes the blame for the murder so that the murderer, who is the strongest oar in the crew, can row in the race.

Some crime and mystery writers set their works in the context of major sporting events, displaying their affection for the games while attracting readers who share their enthusiasm for particular sports. The British Open golf championships form the background to Hugh McCutcheon's *Cover Her Face* (1954), Augus McVicar's *Murder at the Open* (1965), Janice Law's *Death under Par* (1981), and Keith Miles's *Bullet Hole* (1987), while the U.S. Open is the scene of John Logues's *Follow the Leader* (1979). The tennis tournament at Wimbledon is the setting of Nancy Spain's *Poison in Play* (1946), J. J. Marric's *Gideon's Sport* (1970), and Bernard Newman's *Death on the Centre Court* (1951). Murder occurs during the Boston Marathon in Linda Barnes's *Dead Heat* (1984). American football in the Super Bowl venue adds excitement to Thomas Harris's *Black Sunday* (1975), George La Fountaine's *Two Minute Warning* (1975), and Fran Tarkenton and Herb Resnicow's *Murder at the Super Bowl* (1986). Association football, known in America as soccer, culminates every four years in a contest for the World Cup. This event provides the scene for *The World Cup Murder* (1988), written by the Brazilian football great Pele with Resnicow.

The psychology of competition is explored on an intensely individual level in Josephine *Tey's *Miss Pym Disposes* (1946), set in a girls' physical training college, and in Lovesey's *Wobble to Death* (1970), which describes a pedestrian race held in a Victorian indoor arena, two books that epitomize the use of the sports milieu to set a scene, provide for the placement of clues, and define character.

[*See also* Clues; Great Outdoors, The; Horse Racing Milieu; Weapons, Unusual.]

• Marvin Lachman, "Tennis and the Mystery Story," in *World Tennis* 19, nos. 8 and 9 (Jan. and Feb. 1972): 58–60 and 52–56. Philip L. Scowcroft, "Murder Isn't Cricket: Some Notes on Cricket in Crime Fiction," in *Journal of the Cricket Society* 8, no. 3 (autumn 1977): 38–42 (with addenda in subsequent issues); "Golfing Mysteries," in *CADS 29* (Oct. 1996): 11–12.

—Edward Marston, Philip L. Scowcroft,
and Rosemary Herbert

SPY FICTION. Although spying in one form or another is recorded in various ancient texts, including Homer's *Iliad* and the Old Testament, it is only since the 1890s that a literary mode centrally concerned with espionage has emerged. The reason may lie in the perception of the spy during most of recorded history as contemptible. Judas Iscariot is the archetype of the double agent, and until relatively recently spies were generally seen as made in the image of Judas. In the world of Random House Webster's-realpolitik analyzed by Machiavelli, spies could be immensely useful to their employers, but they were necessary *evils inhabiting a world of darkness and secrecy. In William *Shakespeare's *Henry V*, the treason of the English nobles involved in the French plot to assassinate the king is attributed mainly to *greed for monetary gain. In real life as well, spies belonged with the lowest of the low. There was nothing romantic or glamorous about spying, little to invite literary exploration. James *Bond was inconceivable before the twentieth century.

The major revaluation of the spy as potential hero, serving a cause other than self-interest and acting out of patriotic or political duty, begins to occur in the late eighteenth century at the time of the American War of Independence and the French Revolution. What is arguably the earliest spy novel, James Fenimore Cooper's *The Spy* (1821), is about a heroic American double agent in the Revolutionary War. Nevertheless it is not until the later nineteenth century, during the intensely nationalistic competition between European countries for power and influence throughout the world, that this more positive conception of the spy gained ground. Because of the enormous advances in engineering technology, industrial, principally military, espionage became integral to national defense policies. By the outbreak of World War I in 1914, intelligence and counterintelligence were institutionalized and bureaucratized. The ideological spy, so familiar from the 1930s to the end of the Cold War, was born.

The fin de siècle author usually credited with doing most to develop the spy novel in the 1890s, by adding espionage to the usual ingredients of the Victorian melodramatic *suspense novel or *adventure story, was the immensely prolific William Le Queux, who mass-produced *potboilers until his death in 1927. Le Queux pioneered the *thriller, and this type of spy fiction was clearly distinguishable from the developing *crime novel or *mystery story in which the intellectual powers of the detective are paramount.

In the early years of the twentieth century, fiction dealing with spies reached a higher literary level in the hands of Erskine *Childers, whose seminal and well-written *The Riddle of the Sands* (1903), an adventure story about the discovery by two British amateurs of a top-secret German plan to invade England, raises questions about the morality of spying in relation to its political necessity that have pervaded good spy fiction ever since.

The next milestone was John *Buchan's *The Thirty-Nine Steps* (1915), which introduced his series character Richard Hannay in an exciting novel of *pursuit involving secret agents. Like several later writers of spy fiction, Buchan had firsthand experience of the intelligence world, having held high office during World War I. After 1914 spy novels were often vehicles for nationalist and right-wing attitudes, and remained so until Eric *Ambler's radical subversion of this kind of writing in the late 1930s. Buchan's Hannay novels, including *Greenmantle* (1916) and *Mr. Standfast* (1919), are comparatively sophisticated examples of this tendency. More representative are the once immensely popular Bulldog *Drummond novels by "Sapper," the pen name used by H. C. *McNeile, who published a string of titles between 1920 and his death in 1937. Crudely written, full of sadistic *violence, and jingoist, in tone, such fiction gave the thriller a terribly bad name, from which it took a long time to recover, and set back possible developments in spy fiction, while crime fiction, entering its Golden Age, was acquiring a degree of literary and intellectual respectability.

By far the brightest spot in the 1920s was provided by W. Somerset Maugham's collection of linked stories, *Ashenden; or, The British Agent* (1928), which are often seen as the precursor of realistic Cold War spy fiction. Maugham had worked for British intelligence, but only in these fine stories, a small fraction of his enormous oeuvre, did he draw on this experience. The cool, antiheroic realism of *Ashenden*, devoid of hothouse chauvinism and xenophobia, is a welcome relief from the lurid fantasies of Sapper and his ilk. Maugham refuses to romanticize the spy world, stressing instead its ordinariness in a way that anticipates John *le Carré.

In the 1930s both Eric *Ambler and Graham *Greene set out to redeem the thriller by reworking, even reversing, its formulas in innovative ways. While retaining the usual ingredients of adventure and pursuit, Ambler revolutionized spy fiction in the six novels he published between 1936 and 1940 by using it to explore the crisis in Europe caused by the triumphalism of Italian fascism and German Nazism. The first, *The Dark Frontier* (1936) is a parodic send-up of the standard secret-agent novel of the period, but the others are strongly rooted in contemporary political realities. Ambler's sympathies are with the *victims and opponents of fascism, and his left-wing stance is exemplified by his positive portrait of the same Soviet agent in two of these novels. Ambler's major achievement in these years is *The Mask of Dimitrios* (1939; *A Coffin for Dimitrios*), a determined attempt to bridge the gap between thriller and literary novel by use of a complex narrative structure. The spy world is much more marginal to Greene's parallel reclamation of the thriller for serious purposes in what he called his "Entertainment" of the 1930s and early 1940s, such as *The Confidential Agent* (1939). Yet his political concerns and his narratives of pursuit (hunter and hunted) involving borders and trains are similar to Ambler's. Greene's two main novels about the secret world date from after World War II: the comic *Our Man in Havana* (1958) and the tragic *The Human Factor* (1978), a book influenced by le Carré. Another outstanding book from the late 1930s is Geoffrey *Household's *Rogue Male* (1939; *Man Hunt*), only his second novel but usually considered his best. Household, who continued to publish until his death in 1988, was a distinguished writer of chase thrillers with a political dimension

rather than spy novels, but especially in *Rogue Male*, influenced by Buchan, the distinction is blurred.

The spy is a recurrent figure in words written during the 1930s including the poetry of W. H. Auden and his circle, and subsequently much was written about the real-life Cambridge spies of the period, notably Kim Philby. Indeed nonfiction books about espionage in the twentieth century found a substantial readership during the last fifty years, especially those dealing with the intelligence successes of the Allies in World War II, the extraordinary advances in gadgetry and technology culminating in spy satellites, and all the twists and turns, the bluffs and double-bluffs, of the Cold War. It was, of course, the Cold War that gave an enormous boost to spy fiction and led to its unprecedented popularity between the early 1950s and the late 1980s. As before the war, British writers were very much in the forefront.

With Ambler silent during the 1940s, this was not a distinguished decade for spy fiction, although the war encouraged crime novelists such as Margery *Allingham and Michael *Innes to incorporate elements of the spy and political thriller into their stories of detection. Ambler's return to fiction after eleven years was with a Cold War novel about Stalinist show trials, *Judgment on Deltchev* (1951), but after this he surprisingly changed direction, concentrating mainly on high-class political thrillers set outside Europe with little or no espionage. Even when, in *The Intercom Conspiracy* (1970), he returned to the intelligence arena in Europe, he did not write a Cold War spy novel but a story about a brilliant scam engineered by two disillusioned NATO intelligence officers against both the *CIA and the *KGB. If anything, *The Intercom Conspiracy* subverts the spy fiction of the time by treating Cold War espionage as a paranoid fantasy mutually indulged in by the opposing organizations.

With the first of his twelve James Bond novels, *Casino Royale* (1953), Ian *Fleming set the agenda for Cold War spy fiction until his death in 1964. His imitators were legion. As with the comparable cult of Sherlock *Holmes, Bond has taken on a life of his own virtually freed from his author, who is often barely mentioned in discussions about the character he created. In his cinematic existence Bond has certainly been protean, changing to suit the behavioral fashions of the times and being played by a number of actors. Fleming's novels are unabashed romances, often based on some legendary or folkloric archetype like Saint George and the Dragon, but the most effective of them, such as *From Russia, with Love* (1957), carry conviction as narratives of derring-do because of his attention to surface detail. Himself a one-time intelligence officer, Fleming makes the supremely individualistic Bond more credible than he would otherwise be by giving him a role within a professional organization. After Maugham, Ambler, and Greene, Fleming is bound to seem a literary throwback to Childers, Buchan, and Sapper, but the flag-waving nationalism, simple moral polarities ("goodies" and "baddies"), and cosmopolitan glamour had enormous appeal during the drab early years of the Cold War.

Spy fiction underwent a sea change in the 1960s

when a new generation of British writers, notably Len *Deighton and John *le Carré, reacted against Bond and the Bondians. They were soon followed in the 1970s by Anthony Price, Ted Allbeury, and Brian Freemantle. As le Carré has pointed out, the highly conspicuous and ostentatiously womanizing Bond would be the last person to be employed in real-life intelligence operations because he would not last a day. George *Smiley, the "invisible" series character le Carré introduced in his first novel, Call for the Dead (1961), a blend of spy and detective fiction, is the antithesis of Bond in every respect. The new writers set out to convey a much greater sense of authenticity and realism than did Fleming, and they consequently engaged with the moral dilemmas and ideological contradictions of the secret world. At their best they conveyed skepticism about the political rhetoric of the Cold War, challenging and interrogating received platitudes and stock responses.

The originality of Deighton's earliest and perhaps best novels, narrated by a wisecracking man-with-no-name, The Ipcress File (1962), Horse Under Water (1963), Funeral in Berlin (1964), and Billion-Dollar Brain (1966), was immediately recognized, but le Carré's third novel, The Spy Who Came in from the Cold (1963), had even more impact and enjoyed a huge international success. Like Ambler in the 1930s, le Carré revolutionized the spy novel by turning it inside out, creating a sympathetic Communist intelligence officer while dissecting the hypocrisy, Machiavellianism, and double standards of the British. Whereas much previous spy fiction concentrated on the adventures of individuals, the post-Fleming writers paid far more attention to the inner workings of *intelligence organizations as bureaucratic structures. Le Carré's "Circus" is the best-known of these fictional counterparts to *MI5 and *MI6. One consequence of this shift of emphasis is that detection often replaces adventure as a narrative basis, even though some form of pursuit with hunter and hunted remains de rigueur. Another consequence is that organizations like the Circus can be presented as microcosms of society as a whole. Le Carré, in particular, has made the spy novel a vehicle for exploring the condition of post-imperial England, a once-great world power in decline and collapsing in on itself. This has gradually led to the acceptance of le Carré as an important postwar novelist who has successfully bridged the gap between the literary novel and the spy thriller. A good example by a younger writer of the spy thriller's potential for provocative social and political analysis is Robert McCrum's In the Secret State (1980).

Changes in the Cold War were mirrored in spy fiction, especially during the period of glasnost and perestroika in the 1980s before the disintegration of the Soviet Union. Le Carré's The Russia House (1989) is the pre-eminent example, while Tim Sebastian is prominent among the younger British writers of the 1980s who adapted the genre to shifting historical circumstances. With the end of the Cold War the future direction of spy fiction became uncertain. Again le Carré suggested a way forward with The Night Manager (1993). Yet even during the Cold War a number of writers, even those most closely associated with it, escaped its grip. Le Carré tackled the Israeli-Palestinian conflict in The Little Drummer Girl (1983) while Deighton experimented with historical fantasy in SS-GB (1978). Price is the author who has most consistently and most successfully introduced historical dimension into his novels, such as Other Paths to Glory (1974) and War Game (1976), but others have followed his lead, including Julian Rathbone and Ken Follett. One of the few outstanding American contributors to spy fiction, Robert Littell, brilliantly interweaves historical material dating from the Revolutionary War with his contemporary narrative in The Once and Future Spy (1990). Littel has written historical fiction about the Soviet Union as well as conventional Cold War novels, but in The Sisters (1986), involving the CIA and the KGB, he engages with one of the subjects unique to American spy fiction, the assassination of President John F. Kennedy. The Vietnam War is another such subject. The action-packed suspense novels by two best-selling American authors, Robert Ludlum and Tom Clancy, sometimes involve espionage, as in Ludlum's The Osterman Weekend (1972) and Clancy's The Cardinal of the Kremlin (1988), but other than Littel the best received American spy novelist is Charles McCarry, whose first novel, The Miernik Dossier (1973), was lavishly praised for its sophistication. *McCarry also writes historical fiction, and in one of his best novels, The Last Supper (1983), he combines espionage with a family saga to produce a panoramic survey of the twentieth century, an epic of betrayal and treachery.

Although spy fiction sometimes employs the same conventions as crime fiction and is frequently linked with it, there is one highly conspicuous difference between the writers of the two modes. Whereas women excelled in crime writing throughout the twentieth century, men very largely monopolized the spy novel. To a lesser extent this gender distinction is reflected in the readership of the two kinds.

[See also Heroism; Pathfinder Fiction; Political and Social Views, Authors'.]

• Donald McCormick, Who's Who in Spy Fiction (1977). Bruce Merry, Anatomy of the Spy Thriller (1977). LeRoy L. Panek, The Special Branch: The British Spy Novel, 1890–1980 (1981). John Atkins, The British Spy Novel (1984). Lars Ole Sauerberg, Secret Agents in Fiction (1984). Richard L. Knudson, The Whole Spy Catalogue (1986). John G. Cawelti and Bruce A. Rosenburg, The Spy Story (1987). Michael Denning, Cover Stories: Narrative and Ideology in the British Spy Thriller (1987). Clive Bloom, ed., Spy Thrillers: From Buchan to le Carré (1990).
—Peter Lewis

STALKING is a crime in which a perpetrator, almost always male, follows a victim, almost always female, sometimes deliberately making the victim aware of the stalking, as in Elizabeth Peters's Crocodile on the Sandbank (1975), less often revealing his own identity as well. The stalker may intend simply to terrify the victim, often as revenge for the victim's having broken off a sexual relationship with the stalker. More frequently the stalker is trying to learn as much as possible about the victim in order to commit another crime, such as a burglary, sexual assault, or *murder. Stalking has traditionally included following the victim on foot and by car, tapping telephones, and searching mail; the crime now includes intruding on computer-based communication such as E-mail.

Stalking is a frequently used device in crime and mystery fiction, though it seldom stands on its own as the chief crime to be solved, more often preceding the main crime and revealing the personality of the stalker. When it appears near the opening of crime and mystery fiction, it displays the perpetrator's planning ability and previous emotional connections to the victim. Thus recounting the details of and the motivations for a stalking allows the author to develop the characters of perpetrator, victim, and detective, and the relationships between them. When it appears later in the *plot, stalking both allows development of the stalker's methods and identity and increases the narrative tension, as the detective by this time is ordinarily anticipating another attack. Introducing various electronic means of stalking enables perpetrators to remain physically absent from the crime scene while nonetheless continuing the stalking, thereby rendering the traditional helplessness, paranoia, and frustration of victims and detectives even more acute, as in Patricia Cornwell's *Postmortem* (1990).

Male detectives who pursue stalkers frequently reflect on the similarities between their roles and the actions of the stalkers they pursue. When the stalkers are male and their victims female, women detectives working on such cases often see themselves as attempting to redress the imbalance of power and fear used against women. In Evelyn E. Smith's *Miss Melville Regrets* (1986), the heroine is herself a stalker and assassin, a sympathetic figure in part because she attempts to redress a hopeless preponderance of injustice against weak, especially elderly women. Because stalking so frequently starts when one person ends a sexual relationship with another detectives often meditate on their sexual roles as they pursue a stalker, imagining how they would they do the job differently were they of the opposite *gender and wondering whether their gender matters at all. Like women detectives, women victims meditate on their frequently dual roles as hunted and hunter, particularly when the detective tries to induce the stalker to commit another crime, which is the most common method of catching the stalker.

[*See also* Deviance; Rape and Other Sex Crimes; Terror.]

• Maureen T. Reddy, "Loners and Hard-Boiled Women" In *Sisters in Crime: Feminism and the Crime Novel* (1988).
—Anne K. Krook

STARRETT, (CHARLES) VINCENT (EMERSON), 1886–1974. Vincent Starrett was born in Toronto but moved at an early age to Chicago, where he became a celebrated newspaperman and spent most of his life. He was a prolific essayist and was recognized as an outstanding bookman for his bibliographies and critical studies of a wide range of writers. Starrett was a

scholar of crime fiction, as well as a notable writer of mystery novels, and is credited with introducing Western readers to the pleasures of Chinese detective fiction through his seminal essay "Some Chinese Detective Stories" in his *Bookman's Holiday: The Private Satisfactions of an Incurable Collector* (1942). One of the grand old men of Sherlockianism, he was a cofounder of the Baker Street Irregulars. His remarkable *The Private Life of Sherlock Holmes* (1933) is the first biographical study of a fictional detective hero.

[*See also* Sherlockian Societies.]

• Vincent Starrett, *Born in a Bookshop* (1965).
—David Skene-Melvin

STATELY HOMES. *See* Country House Milieu.

STEREOTYPES, REVERSALS OF. Stereotypes, or characters cast from a predictable mold shaped by popular expectations, have a natural home in popular literature, which resounds with images and abbreviated thoughts that make up the common consciousness of a culture or one of its subdivisions. In crime and mystery fiction, the stereotyped character is especially useful in setting up expectations, particularly of trustworthiness or suspiciousness, in the mind of the reader. Writers in this genre have long realized that reversal of stereotypes is a reliable route to creating the element of surprise so prized by their readers.

Motivated by broad sympathy, genuine knowledge, or just the pressing need to create an original way of presenting their narratives, some writers have also found it especially fruitful to invert or reverse stereotypes with the consequences of not only surprising readers but providing them cause for reflection.

G. K. *Chesterton's use of the unlikely figure of the gentle cleric as his *Great Detective represents one of the earliest sorts of stereotype reversals. When Father *Brown came on the scene in *The Innocence of Father Brown* (1911), it is safe to assume that, at least outside of Roman Catholic parishes, a priest was taken to be either an unworldly character or a strict, hard-line papist. Father Brown maintains the quiet air and dull appearance thought to accompany detachment from secular doings, but the method he applies to the strange and dashing crimes he encounters shows the priest to be excellently equipped by theology and faith in redemption to address the problem of modern crime. Chesterton's successful inversion of the clerical stereotype has been followed by others. With *Friday the Rabbi Slept Late* (1964), Harry Kemelman launched a series about Rabbi David *Small, a modest, seemingly deferential student of the Torah whose learning enables him to become the *sleuth for crimes that beset his Jewish community in Massachusetts and the arbiter between tradition and modernity for his congregation. Ellis *Peters created a similarly unlikely detective when she initiated her series about the medieval monk Brother *Cadfael in *A Morbid Taste for Bones* (1977).

Elderly characters, particularly elderly females, have provided another productive opportunity for the reversal of stereotypes. Agatha *Christie's Miss Jane *Marple, who began her career in *The Murder at* the Vicarage (1930), stunned those who harbored stereotypes about old women by proving to be exceedingly capable of cracking crimes that baffle everybody else, and doing so in a manner as intuitive and eccentric as she is herself. Before Marple, however, there was Miss Maud *Silver, debuting in Grey Mask (1928), the creation of Patricia *Wentworth, who gives the stereotype a double turn by employing Silver as a professional detective who conducts her investigations with unimpeachable diligence. A contemporary author accepting the challenge of stereotypes about the elderly is Carolyn G. Hart, who introduced the journalist of Henrietta O'Dwyer Collins in Dead Man's Island (1993).

Stereotypes about physically handicapped people once assumed that they expected and deserved pity but never a starring role in life's events. Ernest Bramah upended that view with the introduction of crime and mystery fiction's first blind detective in the collection of short stories named after the sleuth Max Carrados (1914). In each of his cases Carrados displays the prowess he has developed because his other senses, in compensation for his sightlessness, have become superior to those possessed by the insensitive sighted people with whom he deals. Other blind sleuths are Baynard Kendrick war veteran Captain's Duncan Maclain and Clinton H. Stagg's Thornley Colton Ellery *Queen, the writing team, took up the handicap stereotype in four novels about Drury Lane, a deaf actor detective, that they published under the name of Barnaby Ross. The short-lived series began with The Tragedy of X (1932) and after proceeding through tragedies for Y and Z concluded in Drury Lane's Last Case (1933). In time, reversing stereotypes became a tradition of its own which represented handicapped people as "differently abled."

Although the first appearance of an African American detective was in Rudolph Fisher's The Conjure-Man Dies: A Mystery Tale of Dark Harlem (1932), concerted revision of stereotypes about African Americans in crime and mystery fiction did not get fully underway until Chester *Himes introduced Grave Digger *Jones and Coffin Ed Johnson, police officers featured in a cycle of novels opening with For Love of Imabelle (1957; A Rage in Harlem). The extent of the replacement of denigrating portrayals of African Americans in crime fiction can be measured by the abundance of recent works featuring capable, shrewd, and rounded characters who are black detectives. Barbara Neely performs a hat trick in reversing stereotypes with her presentation of Blanche White, a middle-aged, female domestic worker introduced in Blanche on the Lam (1992) Valerie Wilson Wesley created the capable Tamara Hayle a black, ex-cop who runs an agency in Newark. Hayle first appeared in When Death Comes Stealing (1994) Among male authors writing about male African American detectives, Walter *Mosley currently reigns as the leading writer with the series about Easy *Rawlins begun with Devil in a Blue Dress (1990), but Mosley is not alone. James Sallis is well along with a series about the New Orleans private eye Lew Griffin, and Robert Greer has recently introduced the Denver bail bondsman C. J. Floyd who comes naturally upon cases requiring investigation.

The other notable reversal of ethnic stereotypes in crime and mystery writing is to be seen in the novels of Tony *Hillerman about Joe *Leaphorn and Jim Chee, officers in the Navajo police. Hillerman introduced Leaphorn in The Blessing Way (1970) and Chee in People of Darkness (1980). As he has developed his detectives as vehicles for exploration of the cultural crisis fostered by the encounter of Native American traditions with modern Anglo life, Hillerman has joined his detectives together as a team, illustrating in that way the variety and range of character observable to readers who come to prefer knowledge to stereotype. Again the reversal of stereotypes promises to found a countertradition of fiction about Native Americans.

Mexican American characters have appeared from time to time in detective and mystery fiction set in California. For example, Margaret *Millar used a Hispanic lawyer named Tom Aragon in a brief series of novels she began with Ask for Me Tomorrow (1976). The promising prospect that occasional appearances will soon lead to a trend may be found in the entry of the distinguished mainstream novelist of Chicano life, Rudolfo Anaya, into the crime and mystery genre with stories about Sonny Baca, an Albuquerque private eye whose first case is told in Zia Summer (1995).

As deeply rooted as any stereotypes can be are those that label homosexuals and lesbians. These, too, however, have undergone reversal. Joseph *Hansen was not the first to give a homosexual the top position in detective fiction (George *Baxt's 1960s novels about the Pharoah Love are major contenders for the honor of priority), but Hansen's serious and frank treatment of Dave *Brandstetter, the gay investigator he introduced in Fadeout (1970), earns him special notice for deliberation. The craft of the stories makes it evident that Hansen is inspired by the conscious aim of reversing stereotype. The same must be said about many of the authors who have developed lesbian detectives. The reference book Detecting Women 2 by Willetta L. Heising (1996) provides evidence that more than twenty writers are currently publishing fiction in which gay women of all ages and social classes, of many occupations and diverse backgrounds, are recreating the character of the lesbian to make her a sometimes ordinary, sometimes special, but always complete human being.

[See also African American Sleuth; Characterization; Disability, Sleuth with a; Ethnic Sleuth; Ethnicity; Ethnic Sleuth; Formula: Characters; Gay Characters and Perspectives; Lesbian Characters and Perspectives; Native American Sleuth; Stock Characters.]

• William F. Wu, The Yellow Peril: Chinese Americans in American Fiction, 1850–1940 (1982). Terence D. Miethe, "Stereotypical Conceptions and Criminal Processing: The Case of the Victim-Offender Relationship," Justice Quarterly 4, no 4 (Dec. 1987): 511–93. Frankie Y. Bailey, Out of the Woodpile: Black Characters in Crime and Detective Fiction (1991). Frances A. DellaCava and Madeline H. Engel, Female Detectives in American Novels (1993).   —John M. Reilly

STEWART, MARY (FLORENCE ELINOR) (b. 1916), British author of romantic *suspense and historical novels and former lecturer in English at Durham University. Her novels, especially those set in the Arthurian world, are informed by her training in English literature.

Stewart's first ten novels, written during the 1950s and 1960s, are exemplars of romantic suspense in which the plucky heroine finds herself in an exotic locale where mysterious circumstances become increasingly sinister and an element of romance makes it difficult to separate the hero from the villain as the action develops. These novels bear some hallmarks of the *Gothic novel, especially in their maintenance of suspense by keeping the protagonist in constant peril. In *Touch Not the Cat* (1976) Stewart also used elements of the occult, in common with the Gothic tradition. Despite her romantic and perilous circumstances, the typical Stewart protagonist possesses some common sense which, when finally employed, rescues her from danger and causes her to consider the truth of the matter in a clear-headed manner. The story type that results has come to be known as *Had-I-But-Known.

[*See also* Females and Feminists; Menacing Characters.]
—Judith Rhodes

STOCK CHARACTERS are not to be confused with stereotyped characters. The latter are often pejorative renderings that elide individuality in order to present the character as a stand-in for a group denigrated by those with more social power, while stock characters form a repertory troupe of figures who have been repeatedly used in crime and mystery writing, because they serve functional purposes, most often related to creation of effect or to management of the narrative plot or of readers' expectations.

When Edgar Allan *Poe introduced a police official into "The Purloined Letter" (in *The Gift*, 1845) he found it a convenient way to indicate how Dupin's ratiocinative detection method exceeded the merely empirical power of the police authority. Since Poe's time, the contrasts between private investigator and government agent have served authors as an effective way to stress the superior ethical character of the outsider detective, as in the novels of Raymond *Chandler, and at other times to demonstrate how private efforts of detection by extraordinary investigators complement police procedures, as in the Golden Age novels by Dorothy L. *Sayers about Lord Peter *Wimsey and his brother-in-law Inspector Parker and Agatha *Christie's invention of a police friend Inspector Japp for Hercule *Poirot.

Arthur Conan *Doyle sought an effect similar to Poe's when he introduced Dr. John *Watson as sidekick to and chronicler of Sherlock *Holmes, for Watson's interrogation of the *Great Detective amply emphasizes Holmes's eccentric genius. Holmes's Watson, Poirot's Captain Arthur Hastings, Nero *Wolfe's Archie *Goodwin, and dozens of other detectives' aides-de-camp are, like Watson, developed into individuals by their creators. In origin and at root, though, they are stock figures whose first importance to the narrative rests in their functional value: They can be made privy to information about the detective that readers cannot gain directly from the *sleuth without violation of verisimilitude.

Two of the prominent schools of detective fiction—the Golden Age and the hard-boiled—employ stock characters expressive of their type's world view. Robert B. *Parker's Hawk evidently is a hireable gun, as is *Spenser's dependable accomplice; Raymond *Chandler's Philip *Marlowe tries to undo the damage done by dope doctors; characters redolent of organized crime drift in and out of other hard-boiled novels. Each of these figures making repeat performances in tough guy fiction helps to etch the image of a disorderly world where conventional morality is an illusion. Servants like Wimsey's valet Bunter and titled personages such as those in Elizabeth George's novels are predictable residents, and, therefore, stock figures illustrative of the ordered reality imagined by the conservative-minded authors of the Golden Age tradition and its latter-day appearance as *cozy mysteries.

Stock characters should also be distinguished from *archetypal characters, which are freighted with philosophical content. Hannibal Lecter in Thomas Harris's *The Silence of the Lambs* (1988) incarnates more *evil than is required by a narrative's "bad guy," while the killers and connivers in the fiction of Dick *Francis make their appearances not as icons, but as instrumental figures of plot. Like all stock characters, they are conventional and have been developed in the same way as other conventions: through writers' discovery of their repeated utility. Some, like coroners, doctors, and clerics may initially be seen as trustworthy characters, while others like attractive divorcées, second sons who stand to inherit family fortunes only after a sibling dies, and returning prodigals are *suspicious characters from the start. Inevitable material for authors, stock characters are the continuing players for the audience of crime and solution.

[*See also* Characterization; Formula: Character; Stereotypes, Reversals of.]
—John M. Reilly

STOUT, REX (TODHUNTER) (1886–1975), creator of Nero *Wolfe and Archie *Goodwin, perhaps the most successful detective team in American mystery fiction, was born in Noblesville, Indiana of parents who moved the family west to Kansas before he was a year old. He received early encouragement in reading from his mother and his teacher father, and had read all 1,126 books in his father's library by the time he was eleven. He went on to become the state's spelling champion at the age of thirteen.

One of nine children, Stout was prevented from entering the University of Kansas due to his family's lack of money. He joined the U.S. Navy at the age of eighteen and served as a yeoman on President Theodore Roosevelt's yacht for nearly two years. Some of his poems were published in *Smart Set* magazine, and he supported himself in a variety of jobs for four years after leaving the navy. For a time he returned to writing, publishing four serialized adventure novels in *All-Story Magazine* from 1913 to 1916, as well as more than thirty short stories in other magazines. Always a rapid calculator and bookkeeper, he achieved early success by founding the Educational Thrift Service with his brother Bob. Earnings from the school banking system enabled him to travel extensively in Europe with his first wife, Fay.

Stout returned to writing full time in 1927, leaving his job as president of Vanguard Press, a company he had helped found. In 1929 Vanguard published the first Stout novel to appear in book form, *How Like a God*. Though not usually listed with his crime and *detective novels, the book contains a fair amount of *suspense and culminates in a *murder.

Stout's personal life changed in 1932 with his divorce from his first wife and marriage to Pola Hoffman. He was publishing literary and romance novels at this time, but he still remembered the hundreds of detective stories he'd read since his boyhood. In October 1933, the same month his daughter was born, he created Wolfe and Goodwin, and began work on the first Wolfe novel, *Fer-de-Lance*. Nero Wolfe, weighing in at some 270 pounds, was a gourmet who loved orchids and beer. (His first recorded sentence, on the second page of *Fer-de-Lance*, is, "Where's the beer?") Like his creator he held firm, mainly liberal views on a variety of subjects. He rarely left his brownstone on *New York's West 35th Street. In short, he was something new in American detective fiction. His relationship with confidential assistant Goodwin, and its interplay of clever conversation and flashes of wit, was the most successful pairing since Sherlock *Holmes and Dr. John H. *Watson, and often compensated for some lapses in the plotting of later books.

There can be little doubt that four of the first six Wolfe novels are among the best of the series. *Fer-de-Lance* (1934; *Meet Nero Wolfe*), with its deadly golf club and titular serpent, set the stage for all that followed. The character of Wolfe had mellowed a bit by the second book, *The League of Frightened Men* (1935), but its *plot remains one of the strongest in the series. In the fifth and sixth books, *Too Many Cooks* and *Some Buried Caesar* (both 1938; *The Red Bull*), Wolfe makes two of his rare ventures outside New York City.

After 1941 Stout abandoned most of his other detective characters such as Tecumseh Fox and Alphabet Hicks to concentrate on Wolfe, turning out a total of thirty-three novels and forty-one novellas about the rotund sleuth. Following the early high spots in the saga, Wolfe probably hit his peak with the Zeck trilogy consisting of *And Be a Villain* (1948; *More Deaths Than One*), *The Second Confession* (1949), and *In the Best Families* (1950; *Even in the Best Families*). Each of the novels is complete and clever in itself, and together they tell of Wolfe's duel of wits with *master criminal Arnold Zeck, a man so powerful he finally drives Wolfe out of his home and into hiding.

Late in the series, Stout continued to communicate his social concerns. *A Right to Die* (1964) deals with the civil rights movement, while Wolfe battles the abuses of J. Edgar Hoover's *F.B.I. in *The Door-*

bell Rang (1965). The final Wolfe novel, *A Family Affair* (1975), was published shortly before Stout's death. Despite some plot weakness it is a fitting conclusion to the saga, dealing as it does with those closest to the master sleuth.

[*See also* Addresses and Abodes, Famous; Armchair Detective; Eccentrics; Friendship; Great Detective, The; Sidekicks and Sleuthing Teams.]

• John McAleer, *Rex Stout: A Biography* (1977). Guy M. Townsend, ed., *Rex Stout, an Annotated Primary and Secondary Bibliography* (1980). David R. Anderson, *Rex Stout* (1984). J. Kenneth Van Dover, *At Wolfe's Door: The Nero Wolfe Novels of Rex Stout* (1991).   —Edward D. Hoch

Strand [*Magazine, The*]. Launched in January 1891 and published by George Newnes, Ltd., the *Strand* contained an enticing mix of fiction, illustrated articles, popular politics, fine-art features, children's, jokes, puzzles and photographs sections, and interviews with the great and the good. Its formula seems banal enough today but was startlingly original, even avant-garde in its day. It was thus shamelessly imitated by periodical proprietors up and down *London's Fleet Street, though principally by Alfred Harmsworth (*London Magazine*), Arthur Pearson (*Royal Magazine*, *Pearson's Magazine*), Ernest Lock (*Windsor Magazine*), and W. W. Astor (*Pall Mall Magazine*).

It is arguable that, had Arthur Conan *Doyle not created Sherlock *Holmes and submitted two Holmes short stories to H. Greenhough Smith, editor of the new magazine, the monthly periodical would neither have risen—indeed rocketed—to the heights of circulation and reader popularity it subsequently achieved (sales of well over four hundred thousand copies at its zenith, with a probable readership of between two and three million) nor been the dramatic catalyst for change in the British magazine industry it conspicuously was.

It would be impossible to exaggerate not only the immense popularity of the Holmes short stories but also their profound influence on Doyle's contemporaries. Doyle achieved what Edgar Allan *Poe (with the Chevalier C. Auguste *Dupin) had not: a hero whose shadow was far greater than its substance. He also created a style of storytelling that precisely fitted in with Greenhough Smith's own ideals, and The *Strand* became a showcase not merely for investigators in the Holmes mold—Arthur *Morrison's Martin Hewitt, Grant Allen's spirited female sleuths, the many detectives created by L. T. Meade and her collaborators—but for storytellers purely in the Doyle mold.

That, however, was the downside of this extraordinary success story. While Smith retained control of The *Strand* (he only retired in 1930, aged seventy-five), deviants from the Doyle method, however brilliant, however creative, were unwelcome in the magazine's columns. G. K. *Chesterton fared particularly badly (a single, and poor, Father Brown story appeared there after Smith had died), the Baroness *Orczy, effectively creator of the *armchair detective subgenre, even worse (with nothing published in The *Strand*). Smith did not care much either for the *inverted detective story, as popularized by R. Austin *Freeman and Freeman Wills *Crofts, or *sleuths with disabilities such as Ernest Bramah's blind detective Max *Carrados. Ghost hunters and *psychic sleuths were virtually *anathematized*.

Criminous adventure yarns, however, were very much to Smith's taste—hence the interminable appearances of E. Phillips *Oppenheim's gaudy, though strictly two-dimensional, stories of intrigue in London's Mayfair and on the French Riviera, and tale after tale by H. C. *McNeile (better known to British readers by his military pseudonym Sapper) of rugged action at the Empire's outposts as well as rather unsubtle revenges in the English Home Countries. Smith also published, in 1921, Edgar *Wallace's new series of "Four Just Men" short stories, which not only later helped transform Wallace into one of the wealthiest writers of the day but also to all intents and purposes inaugurated the modern *thriller.

Smith's successor was Reeves Shaw, erstwhile editor of The *Humorist*, who brought an altogether lighter touch to the magazine, as well as more liberal tastes. He possessed a distinct bias towards writers of the younger generation who amused as well as thrilled—Agatha *Christie, Margery *Allingham, John Dickson *Carr, Dorothy L. *Sayers, Francis *Iles/Anthony Berkeley, the inexhaustibly ingenious Will Scott.

This "Golden Age" in the magazine's history was brutally cut short by the second world war, and the *Strand* itself was just as brutally downsized to "pocket-book" proportions due to falling sales and the paper shortage. Under Macdonald Hastings—who had taken over the editorship in 1946—it limped on through the late 1940s, the last of its breed, the odd classic crime story still surfacing occasionally. Its final issue appeared in March 1950, some months short of the magazine's sixtieth anniversary.

—Jack Adrian

STRIBLING, T(HOMAS) S(IGISMUND) (1881–1965) was born in Tennessee and in 1905 graduated from the University of Alabama's law school. He practiced law only briefly before becoming a professional writer. The first five of his thirty-six witty and ironic works appeared in the *pulp magazine *Adventure* in 1925 and 1926. They feature the *psychological sleuth Dr. Henry Poggioli, shown traveling through the Caribbean and Latin America. Variously identified as a professor of psychology, psychiatry, and criminology at The Ohio State University, Poggioli relies on his insights into human behavior more than upon the interpretation of physical clues to unravel baffling mysteries. In perhaps his best-known story, "Passage to Benares" (*Adventure*, 20 Feb. 1926) Poggioli is hanged for a murder that he has solved. But Stribling resurrected Poggioli in *Clues of the Caribbees* in 1929 and again in a final series of works published from 1945 to 1957. Stribling's detective fiction is notable for satirical asides that reveal a keen understanding of the paradoxes of human nature and a respect for racial and ethnic minorities. Although Stribling is today remembered best for his detective fiction, he also wrote mainstream novels,

winning the Pulitzer Prize for best novel with *The Store* (1932), the middle novel in a trilogy that began with *The Forge* (1931) and concluded with *Unfinished Cathedral* (1934).

[*See also* Reasoning; Types of.]

• "T. S. Stribling" in *The Oxford Book of American Detective Stories* ed. Tony Hillerman and Rosemary Herbert (1996).

—Richard Bleiler

SUICIDE and apparent suicide have long been used as complicating factors in detective fiction. Most *locked room mysteries, for example, use the implication of self-destruction to mislead the detective and the reader.

Suicide as part of a plot configuration is not new. Sherlock *Holmes encounters the suicide plot in "The Problem of Thor Bridge" (*Strand*, Feb. 1922), a story which twists the murder-masquerading-as-suicide into a suicide which appears to be *murder. The suicide *victim is regarded as the perpetrator of an horrendous crime.

Attitudes about suicide such as those found in Doyle's story have persisted into this century, and there have been few realistic treatments in detective fiction of the psychological problems which cause suicide. Perhaps this has been because the motives for suicide do not fit into the tidy plots typical of early detective fiction. The real reason for the "crime" of suicide is not verifiable since the perpetrator is no longer able to substantiate the *motive. In any case, motives are less clear in suicide than in murder, and therefore it is less suited to the formulas of detective fiction puzzles.

A twist to the suicide motif in detective fiction occurs in Rex Burns's *Suicide Season* (1987), in which the detective is seen first as a grieving son, angry and confused by his father's suicide. When he is confronted by a case in which his investigation may have caused the suspect's suicide, the detective is forced to examine his own attitudes about self-destruction. But in both of the apparent suicides in Burns's novel the outcome is similar to that of most detective novels: The suicides are actually murders in masquerade.

Few detective writers make use of actual suicide with its characteristically complicated motives of depression, aggression, and despair; However, one notable exception who does attempt to explore this fenlike territory is the British author P. D. *James, who in *An Unsuitable Job for a Woman* (1972) introduces Cordelia *Gray, a young woman who has "inherited" a detective agency after its previous owner, Bernie Pryde, has committed suicide. For her first case, Cordelia explores the possible reasons that another apparent suicide, Mark Callender, would hang himself. Motives become the focal point of the novel; and the young detective's intense empathy creates for the reader the same transference and dawning understanding of the destructive forces which surrounded the young man. A sense of uncertainty toward the act of suicide permeating the novel presents one of its primary themes.

Personal involvement and classical allusions are the key factors in the suicide of Anna Scott in Colin *Dexter's *The Dead of Jericho* (1981), in which a woman known to Inspector Morse apparently ends her own life. Not only is Morse at first considered as a possible *suspect; his involvement with the woman suggests how the emotional baggage accompanying suicide hinders the cool reasoning so prized by the Chevalier C. Auguste *Dupin and Holmes. No longer can modern detectives, Dexter seems to be saying, isolate themselves from social and emotional ties to the victims.

Dexter also uses the classical archetype of Jocasta's suicide to complicate the *plot. Dexter allows the suggestion that, as in the Greek tragedy, the suicide acts as atonement for past sins. Her supposed lover adds to the complexities, and to the allusion, by blinding himself. That the classical analogy is a conclusion jumped to by Morse, a *red herring rather than a *clue, expands Dexter's intent to show that perhaps atonement may not be possible in modern realistic detective fiction. Despite the red herrings, however, Anna Scott's suicide is actual, the pain revealed poignant—evidence of Dexter's admirable attempt to explore the actuality of suicide.

Police involvement and its entanglement with personal responsibility is central to Reginald *Hill's Bones and Silence (1990). The title, taken from Virginia Woolf, reflects Woolf's ambivalent attitude toward life and living. Ironically, Superintendent Andrew Dalziel is playing God in the local production of the Mysteries, and a series of suicide notes sent anonymously to Dalziel challenges him to solve that mystery before the writer of the notes attempts to solve the "Great Mystery." The successive seven letters leave clues as to the writer's identity, and finally reveal that the potential suicide is someone well known to Dalziel and his partner, Peter Pascoe. Proximity to the potential suicide complicates their efforts to stop it, while a debate between Pascoe and his sergeant illustrates the dilemma in which Pascoe realizes that the letter writer has no free choice, but is being driven to take her own life. Despite ambivalence regarding the detective's individual responsibility, Hill's novel represents a successful example of applying the deductive method to the motives of suicide. Yet, the policemen's failure to prevent the self-destruction illustrates the difficulty of imposing the puzzle pattern of detective fiction upon the complicated motives for suicide.

Reader responsibility is effectively challenged in Amanda *Cross's Death in a Tenured Position (1981), in which the author suggests that the male-only exclusivity of Harvard's English department, together with the victim's despair at her isolation, are the causes of Janet Mandelbaum's pathetic suicide. Cross suggests through her *amateur detective, Kate *Fansler, that Janet's despair and subsequent suicide are traceable in part to her attempting to fit into a niche created by and for men while at the same time refusing to ally herself with other women. Death in a Tenured Position becomes a searching examination of the realistic motivations for modern suicide set against a backdrop of feminism in prejudicious academia.

Traditionally detective fiction has treated suicide as a plot configuration only, with little scrutiny of the realistic motives behind actual suicide. However, as the genre engenders a more realistic presentation of crime, both by those authors who examine the psychology of crime as well as those writers who treat the social issues which surround it, we should expect more in-depth presentations and analyses of suicide in detective fiction.

• Barbara T. Gates, "Wilkie Collins's Suicides: 'Truth as It Is in Nature,'" Dickens Studies Annual: Essays on Victorian Fiction 12 (1983): 303–18. Barbara T. Gates, "Not Choosing to Be: Victorian Literary Responses to Suicide," Literature and Medicine 6 (1987): 77–91. Barbara T. Gates, Victorian Suicide: Mad Crimes and Sad Histories (1988). Diane Maginn, "Suicide Disguised as Murder: A Munchausen-Related Event at Thor Bridge," Baker Street Journal: An Irregular Quarterly of Sherlockiana 39, no. 1 (March 1989): 13–15. Beate Carle, "Homicide and Suicide: Deadlock Conflict Resolutions as Part of Literary Concepts," Tenggara 29 (1990): 19–29. Marty S. Knepper, "Who Killed Janet Mandelbaum and India Wonder? A Look at the Suicides of the Token Women in Amanda Cross's Death in a Tenured Position and Dorothy Bryant's Killing Wonder," Clues: A Journal of Detection 13, no. 1 (spring–summer 1992): 45–58.   —Louise Conley Jones

SUPERMAN SLEUTH. Edgar Allan *Poe, who founded modern detective fiction with "The Murders in the Rue Morgue" (Graham's Lady's and Gentleman's Magazine, Apr. 1841), in the same story gave the genre its first superman sleuth: the Chevalier C. Auguste *Dupin. Dupin bears the characteristics that were to become the hallmark of the type: He is an *eccentric genius who possesses what Poe describes as "a peculiar analytic ability" that enables him, through observation, to follow another's train of thought or to deduce, after the examination of evidence, the solution to a crime that has baffled the police. Poe also bequeathed to his successors a narrative format: The tales are told by a loyal, admiring, but imperceptive and uncomprehending friend whose astonishment at Dupin's powers gives added refulgence to the latter's brilliant feats of deduction.

Émile *Gaboriau added one more to the characteristics established by Poe: His detective, Lecoq, in Le Crime d'Orcival (1867; The Mystery of Orcival), is a master of *disguise—so much so that his real appearance is known only to a few. Finally, to produce the definitive superman detective—Sherlock *Holmes—Arthur Conan *Doyle merged the qualities of Dupin and Lecoq, supplementing them with traits that became integral to the type. Insensible to normal human emotions, and conscious of his own superiority, indeed conceited, Holmes is impatient with police obtuseness, but aids Inspector Lestrade and others, allowing them to take the credit for success. Yet Holmes is above the law and at times takes *justice into his own hands, as in "The Adventure of Charles Augustus Milverton" (Strand, Apr. 1904). Holmes also has a store of recondite knowledge that can be brought to bear on the interpretation of evidence; he has written, for example, "a little monograph on the ashes of 140 different varieties of pipe, cigar, and cigarette tobacco," as noted in "The Boscombe Valley Mystery." (Strand, Apr. 1891). And in Dr. John H. *Watson Doyle rounded out the figure of Poe's anonymous narrator, creating the archetype of the detective's friend and assistant. Ronald A. *Knox, in the ninth of his ten commandments for the detective novelist (*The Best Detective Stories of the Year 1928*, 1928), codified the type, writing: "the stupid friend of the detective, the Watson, must not conceal any thoughts which pass through his mind; his intelligence must be slightly, but very slightly, below that of the average reader." At the same time, in Mycroft *Holmes, even superior in reasoning power to his brother, Doyle devised another superman, who was in addition the prototype of the *armchair detective. R. Austin *Freeman's Dr. John *Thorndyke in *The Red Thumb Mark* (1907) was obviously conceived as an antipode to Holmes; while possessing some of the characteristics of the superman—intellectual power, depth of knowledge, and a Watson-like narrator—he lacks the type's defining characteristics of inhumanity and eccentricity. However, Jacques *Futrelle's Professor Augustus S. F. X *Van Dusen, a scientist known as the Thinking Machine who first appeared in *The Thinking Machine* (1907), is undoubtedly a superman. So is John *Rhode's mathematician Dr. Lancelot *Priestley, introduced in *The Paddington Mystery* (1925). A. E. W. *Mason varied the formula by making his superman a French policeman, Inspector *Hanaud, whose Watson is Julius Ricardo in *At the Villa Rose* (1910), and was imitated by Agatha *Christie with the Belgian Hercule *Poirot and Captain Arthur Hastings in *The Mysterious Affair at Styles* (1920) and later novels. S. S. Van *Dine returned to Doyle's formula, though replacing conceit with intellectual arrogance, in his Philo *Vance novels beginning with *The Benson Murder Case* (1926). *Stout, taking Mycroft, rather than Sherlock, as his model, but preserving all other characteristics of the type, in *Fer-de-Lance* (1934; *Meet Nero Wolfe*) introduced Nero *Wolfe and Archie *Goodwin, undoubtedly the most successful attempt to replicate the Holmes Watson relationship. Of female detectives, only Gladys *Mitchell's Mrs. Beatrice Adela Lestrange *Bradley, introduced in *Speedy Death* (1929), has claims to belong to the type: She is eccentric and intellectually far above those around her, although she is not accompanied by a Watson figure. The same is true of John Dickson *Carr's Dr. Gideon *Fell, created in *Hag's Nook* (1933), who perhaps just scrapes into this category, rather than that of *Great Detective. The categories are not congruent: that of superman or superwoman is a subset of that of the Great Detective, and the characteristic that distinguishes him or her is inhumanity. E. C. *Bentley, in *Those Days: An Autobiography* (1940), wrote that he wanted to make his detective, Philip Trent who first appears in *Trent's Last Case* (1913; *The Woman in Black*), "recognisable as a human being." Once this aim was generally accepted, the type was doomed: allowed to experience emotion and even to fall in love, the detective could no longer be pure animated reason, a "thinking machine."

[*See also* Reasoning, Types of; Scientific Sleuth.]

—T. J. Binyon

SUPERNATURAL LITERATURE. *See* Occult and Supernatural Literature.

SÛRETÉ is the term often used to designate the French police in detective novels. To understand its meaning, it is necessary to trace the beginnings of police services in France.

In 1666 King Louis XIV created the office of *lieutenant de police*, entrusted with all general policing prerogatives for the area of Paris. His responsibilities were varied: to maintain public order; to check registers; to police commerce, traffic, and food supply; to keep a watch over beggars and vagrants. Soon he was helped in this task by *commissaires de police de quartier*, and from 1708 on by the body of *inspecteurs de police*. The Parisian model was such a success that posts of *lieutenants généraux* de police were created in many provincial towns.

The 1789 revolution abolished the system of *lieutenants généraux*. Then the 1792 Convention created a Comité de Sûreté Générale in charge of "all that is connected to persons, and general and interior police."

In 1796, a Ministère de la Police Générale was created; at its head for several periods between 1799 and 1815 was Joseph Fouché, the initiator of the modern police in France. The second department of his ministry was called Sûreté Générale et Police Secrète. Headed by policeman P. M. Desmarest, it was in charge of state police, commissioned in particular to track any plot against the Constitution and government. Fouché extended the system of the *commissaires de police* to the provinces, and appointed a *préfet de police* for the capital. Eugène François *Vidocq was at that time in charge of organizing the town's *brigade de Sûreté*. A former convict turned policeman, he served as a model for characters created by several novelists: Balzac's Vautrin, Hugo's Javert, and Dumas's Jackal are based on him, as is Émile *Gaboriau's Lecoq, introduced in *L'Affaire Lerouge* (1866; The Widow Lerouge).

The Restauration after the end of Napoleon's empire abolished the Ministère de la Police Générale, which was converted into the Direction Générale de la Sûreté Publique and made part of the ministry of the interior.

In 1876, with the return of the Republic, the dualism of the French police was reinforced: On one side was the Préfecture de Police, concerned only with the Seine department; on the other side was the Direction de la Sûreté Générale at the ministry of the interior, heading all other police services in the territory.

The first scientific police services were developed at the Préfecture de Police de Paris, including Alphonse Bertillon's invention of *bertillonage* in 1882, a method of identification of second offenders; the creation of the technical police laboratory in 1888; and the creation of *identité judiciaire* in 1893.

In 1907, in reaction to new forms of criminality and the compartmentalization of police services, the *brigades mobiles*, which specialized in the search for criminals, were created under Georges Clemenceau. In 1908 a law placing police services under the authority of the prefects instead of the mayors completed the takeover of the police by the state.

In 1934, the Direction de la Sûreté Générale became the Direction Générale de la Sûreté Nationale and tasks were progressively organized into four main areas: Renseignements Généraux, Sécurité Publique, Surveillance du Territoire, and Police Judiciare. This last department was in charge of the repression of crime.

The most famous policeman in French literature, Georges *Simenon's Inspector *Maigret, works for the Brigade Criminale. Several English authors used characters working for la Sûreté, such as Agatha *Christie with M. Giraud in *Murder on the Links* (1923) and Richard Grayson in the series of novels featuring Inspector Jean-Paul Gautier, introduced in *The Murders at Impasse Louvain* (1978).

[*See also* Police Detective.]

• Henry Buisson, *La police, son histoire* (1949). Philip John Stead, *The Police of France* (1983).   —Jacques Bandou

SURROGATE DETECTIVE. The term "surrogate detective" is applied to characters who solve crimes yet who are neither amateur nor professional detectives. Like the *accidental sleuth, the surrogate *sleuth may simply have stumbled upon the crime scene, but whereas the accidental sleuth acts out of pluckiness or sometimes self-defense in order to prove who committed the crime, the surrogate sleuth feels compelled to act by applying expertise that he or she brings to the situation. Areas of expertise that surrogate sleuths find useful to crime solving include the scientific as is the case with R. Austin *Freeman's Dr. John *Thorndyke, the psychological as exemplified in the work of Jonathan Kellerman's character Alex Delaware, and a professional eye for domestic detail as displayed by Barbara Neely's domestic worker, Blanche White. The surrogate sleuth's profession often provides entrée to the scene of the crime at the start of the narrative and helps to keep doors open for the sleuth throughout the story. The prime example of the surrogate sleuth is the *journalist sleuth, who is able to gain access to a murder scene and to remain in contact with suspects whom the character interviews with practiced professionalism.   —Rosemary Herbert

SUSPECTS. When an unsolved crime is the problem, logic indicates that there will be a roster of possible commissioners of the deed, one, or sometimes more, of whom will be demonstrably responsible. In real crime, the irrefutability of logic may lay *suspicion heavily upon one party (with the *murder of a spouse, experience shows it to be wise to start the investigation with the partner), or, as in the case of a random killing, suspicion will be directed toward persons that experience again suggests are the likely perpetrators: known criminals, people seen in the vicinity of the crime scene, and so on. Authors of fictitious crimes repeat this logic of real-life crime in their narratives because, of course, it becomes a source of verisimilitude, or the appearance of reality, for their tales.

The introduction of suspects into detective and mystery fiction, however, allows for more than a simulation of reality. In her famed novel *Murder on the Orient Express* (1934; *Murder in the Calais Coach*), Agatha *Christie confounds the probability deriving from police experience with suspects, namely, the likelihood that conspirators to murder will be economical about the number of participants they involve, in order to develop a murder *plot involving everyone on the scene. Earlier, in her equally famed story *The Murder of Roger Ackroyd* (1926), Christie had transgressed a presumptive logic that categorically separates investigators from suspects by revealing that the narrator of the tale, and investigator manqué, was the killer. What Christie demonstrates in these two examples is the field of possibility opened to an inventive writer by the axiom that, until it is solved, a crime leaves a wake of suspicion touching innocent and guilty alike.

Most commonly the inevitability of a crime producing suspects engenders plot for writers of fiction, not only the criminal plot that is to be illuminated when detectives complete their work, but the plot of investigation itself. Although the term "plot" ordinarily refers to the crime and its solution or *whodunit, the narrative plot of detective fiction is almost invariably the progress of an investigation, which can include mistaken estimations of the *guilt of suspects and the *pursuit of sterile lines of reasoning in the attempt to prove the guilt of a likely suspect and finally the satisfaction of a conclusive demonstration effectively converting one or more suspects into guilty perpetrators. Many novels illustrate the utility of suspects for engendering investigative plots, but *The Case Has Altered* (1997) by Martha Grimes represents the general principle. In this Richard Jury mystery Grimes relates the story of two killings in the Lincolnshire fens. The local police, led by Chief Inspector Arthur Bannen, have fixed upon Lady Jenny Kennington as the single viable suspect. She had the opportunity and, it seems, a *motive she sought to conceal. Even the means for committing the crime are speculatively plausible. All that is needed to prove the case is a way of corroborating the circumstantial evidence. Because Richard Jury of *Scotland Yard *CID has a deep fondness for Kennington and wishes to be her lover, he intuits her *innocence and sets his good friend Melrose Plant to the task of checking details, while he pursues his own investigation. Capitalizing on the identity and affections of the prime suspect, Grimes constructs a complex narration. This includes the investigation by Jury that runs parallel to Bannen's, and the inquiries by Plant that present a third line of investigation. It also permits the introduction by Grimes of half a dozen more characters who serve Jury, if not Bannen, as alternative suspects, and Grimes uses the suspicious behavior of Kennington not only to establish her as a suspect but also as a catalyst for an exploration of the fated personal relationship between Jury and Jenny. In other words, characterization of the suspect generates ways of deliberately violating linear order and elongating the rendering of events for the pleasure of it all. In regard to crime and mystery writing, the pleasure includes the *puzzle of an unsolved crime and focus on the workings of the detection method. In regard to all narrative, the crime and mystery genre included, the experience of character and character relationships as they may be dramatically related provides the satisfaction of finding that fiction resembles life. The necessity to have suspects when there is an unsolved crime helps to generate the structure of narration. There is more to the use of suspects than logic. There is creative opportunity too.

Because of the creative possibilities for fiction inherent in the character of suspects, Golden Age commentators indicated that writers ought to select suspects with care to avoid sensation and secondary suggestions. Ronald A. *Knox expressed this view in the racist language too often characteristic of the European literary elite when he stated as rule number five in his Decalogue for crime writing, published in 1929, that "no Chinaman must figure in the story." Presumably this rule was meant to curtail the introduction of ethnic or political conspiracy into a form that Knox and others wished to purify into neat and logical *puzzles. Out of the same desire to confine the detection story within the conventional possibilities of an intellectual puzzle, Knox advanced the idea in rule number one that "the criminal must be mentioned in the early part of the story, but must not be anyone whose thoughts the reader has been allowed to follow." To reinforce the implied censure Agatha Christie and other writers tempted to work a too innovative change in the treatment of suspects, Knox also gave rule number seven: "The detective himself must not commit the crime."

Fortunately, able writers have ignored any attempts to impose rules on their use of suspects, preferring to let the genre itself dictate the possibilities for their handling. That those possibilities are nearly limitless was illustrated when E. C. *Bentley gave his detective in *Trent's Last Case* (1913; *The Woman in Black*) the wit to devise three different solutions to the murder of Sigsbee Manderson. The first analysis is overturned when testimony using the same facts results in a different conclusion and points to a different culprit. The second proposed solution is also overturned when the murderer confesses and thus allows for another reinterpretation of the original facts. The confession certifies the third solution as correct and the final suspect as guilty, but because the story is fiction, the last result cannot be said to be actually truer. Instead, the progress of resolutions demonstrates the literariness of the fictional story of crime and, with that, the considerable chance for accomplished invention as authors fiddle with suspects. It is this opportunity for invention that distances the treatment of suspect characters in fiction from the logic with which they are examined in real-life crime.

[See also Alibi; Alibis, Unbreakable; Characterization: Stereotypes, Reversals of; Suspicious Characters.]

—John M. Reilly

SUSPENSE, or the the state of mental uncertainty accompanied by expectation, apprehension, or anxiety, is an element that is used in literature to cause readers to eagerly continue to follow the action in a story or drama. In *suspense novels, this element is paramount, but suspense is also very important to varying degrees across the crime and mystery writing genre.

An important aspect of suspense is the state of expectant waiting that it arouses. A competent writer knows that human beings generally become impatient with waiting, and that they will seek to escape from the waiting state. Depending on the writer's intent, suspense can be manipulated to build anxiety, expectation, or puzzlement that will only be relieved when the narrative closes. In suspense novels, the state of waiting is filled with threat and anxiety that is heightened as the reader increasingly identifies with the character in jeopardy and is often provided with more information than the character possesses about the impending nature of the the threat. In the *Had-I-But-Known novel, which often features a plucky female protagonist who happens across a crime, the use of suspense is similar.

In *detective novels, *private eye fiction, and *police procedurals, which employ lead characters who are seen as accomplished professional *sleuths, the suspense may be more dependent upon building the reader's puzzlement and attendant expectations of surprise in discovery of an explanation for the crime. When *amateur detectives are used, some suspense may lie in the question of whether or not they are as capable as the pros. If the amateur is inexperienced, as is the case in P. D. *James's *An Unsuitable Job for a Woman* (1972), readers may also experience suspense because they are led to identify with the character. In the *inverted detective story, in which the reader knows from the start who perpetrated the crime, the suspense rests in keeping the reader wondering how the criminal will either get away with the crime or be caught.

—Rosemary Herbert

SUSPENSE NOVEL. *Suspense exists in all narratives; audiences want to know what happens next and are willing to tolerate a pleasurable state of anxious uncertainty until the story is resolved. If the classic mystery *plot concerns finding out what happened and who the villain is, the suspense novel often concerns an innocent drawn into a threatening situation; in both the reader watches events unfold. Suspense is generated by seeing how the protagonist deals with the results of the villain's conspiracies and plots, or by seeing how an ordinary person is drawn into commiting a crime.

The suspense novel began in the nineteenth century in works by Edgar Allan *Poe, Wilkie *Collins, Bram Stoker, and Charles *Dickens. These writers are associated with the transition from the fantastic to the realistic in literature; the transition was accompanied by a shift in the origins of *terror, from supernatural to everyday events, and by a new, middle-class perspective, by which criminals were viewed as threats rather than heroes fighting an oppressive social order. One of the earliest suspense novels is Wilkie Collins's *The Woman in White* (serialized in *All the Year Round*, 1849–51, and published as a book in 1860). In this work, Laura Fairlie marries a man she doesn't love who is deeply in debt; soon afterward a woman escapes from an asylum claiming that she can ruin Sir Percival. There is no doubt that Laura is in danger from her husband's machinations to gain her inheritance, and the suspense revolves around the identity of the escaped woman and Laura's increasingly precarious future. The creation of suspense around a single character or unknown act of that character became popular and was used to inform the *sensation novel and other genres; *Lady Audley's Secret* (1862) by M. E. *Braddon identified in its title the chief cause of suspense: the secret. Henry James's *The Turn of the Screw* (1898) is for many readers an exploration of the *evil that can arise in anyone faced with an uncertain world. In the twentieth century the suspense novel led to the development of several distinct genres, including *spy fiction, the *adventure story, and the *thriller.

Suspense novels generally follow the fate of an innocent, male or female, and are set primarily, but not exclusively, in the private spaces traditionally assigned to women. These may be the home, village or countryside, or even cities, but whatever the location, the plot and character development tend to be based on everyday life and psychology. In Agatha *Christie's *They Came to Baghdad* (1951) young Victoria Jones is smitten with a young man in *London and follows him to Baghdad when she needs a job; her *innocence and curiosity get her into serious trouble, and also get her out of it. Patricia *Highsmith concentrates on psychology and creates a universe where anyone has the ability to commit an evil act; her major focus is on the criminal's mind and emotions. In *The Talented Mr. Ripley* (1955) two young men travel to Italy for a vacation, but one has been commissioned by the father of the other to persuade his son to return to the United States; the reader must come to understand the young men before realizing the turn of events that will come about.

Ruth *Rendell explores character and what drives people to kill; she is skillful at turning the ordinary things of life into disturbing warnings that all is not well. In *A Judgment in Stone* (1977), the narrator reveals at the outset that Eunice Parchmain, a housekeeper, kills the family she works for because she is illiterate. The suspense lies in the reader's fascination with the concatenation of small incidents—minor turns of phrase or actions that are forgotten by most people—that press the illiterate woman to kill. In her novels as Barbara *Vine, Rendell explores the consequences of an accidental crime; and these are as chilling as the consequences of an act of willful murder.

Typical of the contemporary suspense novel is the work of Mary Higgins *Clark, whose successful formula allows her to explore related issues. In the typical Clark novel, a strong female protagonist, usually young, is menaced when she innocently raises a question or gains information that threatens another; a child, her own or another's, may be menaced by the villain in his or her attempt to reach the heroine, and the protagonist must take steps to save herself and the child because the police cannot or will not do so. In *I'll Be Seeing You* (1993) Meghan Collins, a television news reporter, is threatened by someone who kills another woman by mistake; as problems escalate, the identity of the villain becomes less and less clear. Collins is a nice young woman with a widowed mother facing financial difficulties; there is nothing exotic or spectacular in her life, yet she is the object of a gathering storm of evil. It is this quality of life reeling out of control that underlies the suspense novel.

Daphne *du Maurier created the subgenre of romantic suspense with *Rebecca* (1938). Du Maurier was particularly concerned with the issue of mobility for women in a *class system that defined women by their husband's status and in a society that defined a woman's identity by her husband's. Within this frame du Maurier explored the moral issues of good and evil, how individuals can distinguish them, the ambivalence of criminal acts, and the ability of the state to deal with them.

[*See also* Gothic Novel; Had-I-But-Known; Menacing Characters: Terror.]

• Francois Truffaut, *Hitchcock* (1967). Jerry Palmer, "Thrillers" *Popular Fiction and Social Change*. Christopher Pawling, ed. (1984). Art Bourgeau *The Mystery Lover's Companion* (1986). Clive Bloom Briam Docherty, Jane Gibb and Keith Shand, eds., *Nineteenth-Century Suspense: From Poe to Conan Doyle* (1988). George N. Dove, *Suspense in the Formula Story* (1989).   —Robin Anne Reid

SUSPICION is a state or act of conjecture concerning the as yet unproved existence of evil, guilt, or fault in a person or circumstance. Suspicion is used in crime and mystery fiction to hide the real criminal and obscure relationships, establish a detective's credibility, explore the tenuous nature of human relationships, and develop other themes. In the *whodunit *puzzle, which requires a cast of characters with plausible motives for *murder, suspicion falls on each character in turn, keeping the detective and the reader off balance and thus advancing the *plot. The detective exhibits his or her ability to see beyond appearances and discern deeper truths about the characters at the same time that the element of suspicion effectively opens questions about human relationships and attitudes toward society.

Whodunit puzzles come in a variety of formats. They present the reader with a limited set of characters linked to the crime. These characters share opportunity, potential motives, and varying degrees of *innocence. The English Country House tradition presents this plot structure at its most refined. As typified by Nicholas *Blake's *Thou Shell of Death* (1936; *Shell of Death*), Michael *Innes's *Hamlet, Revenge!* (1937), Agatha *Christie's classic *Three Blind Mice* (1950; *The Mousetrap*), Elizabeth Peters's *The Murders of Richard III* (1974), and Elizabeth George's *Payment in Blood* (1989), characters gather in isolated *settings and are confronted with a murder in their midst. Casual acquaintances and longtime friends find themselves caught in what Michael Innes termed "a poison in the air," a growing sense of fear and distrust. Relationships are strained and old secrets revealed. The most extreme effects of suspicion appear in Christie's novel *Ten Little Niggers* (1939; *And Then There Were None*), where an intense *atmosphere of suspicion created by the murderer drives the other characters to murder and *suicide. The elements of this tradition have been recast in a number of settings: luxury cruises, as in K. K. Beck's *Death in a Deck Chair* (1984) and Carol Higgins Clark's *Decked* (1992); holiday tours, as in Christianna *Brand's *Tour de Force* (1955); college campuses, as in Dorothy L. *Sayers's *Gaudy Night* (1935) and Amanda *Cross's *Death in a Tenured Position* (1981; *A Death in the Faculty*); and fan conventions, as in Sharyn McCrumb's *Zombies of the Gene Pool* (1992). All provide relatively confined locales, close contact among the characters, and adequate room for suspicion to fall upon ordinary souls. It is this ordinariness that heightens the power of suspicion; it reveals an extraordinary potential for criminal activity in the most ordinary of citizens.

Suspicion may be shown as a critical element in the makeup of detectives, whether *amateur or professional. To succeed in the revelation of criminals, the detective must be able to view the world and his or her fellow citizens with a degree of distrust. Several detectives have also had to face the question of suspicion from the perspective of the suspect. In John *Creasey's *Inspector West Alone* (1975), the inspector is caught in a nightmare, held under the power of a criminal and suspected by *Scotland Yard. The dislocating power of suspicion, isolating the detective from friends and coworkers, is also explored in E. C. *Bentley's *Trent's Own Case* (1936) and Martha Grimes's *The Old Contemptibles* (1991).

Suspicion comes most naturally to *private detectives. The introduction of Dashiell *Hammett's Sam *Spade and Raymond *Chandler's Philip *Marlowe brought out the dark side of detection. *Private eyes operate in dangerous worlds, where *greed and *violence are more real than trust and honesty, and their survival depends on an ability to see through appearances. Their distrust is ingrained, acquired through experience and reinforced with each case, often pushing them to extreme isolation. A similar sense of isolation and mistrust appears in the *spy fiction of John *le Carré, Eric *Ambler, and Anthony Price, whose protagonists must operate with a continual sense of distrust toward their own agencies and coworkers. Beyond the threat of betrayal by double agents is the constant awareness of the duplicity of politicians and prime ministers.

The female *hard-boiled sleuths created by Sara *Paretsky, Sue *Grafton, and Marcia *Muller bring variation to the theme of suspicion and the detectives V. I. *Warshawski, Kinsey *Milhone, and especially Sharon McCone operate in worlds where *friendships are not only possible but desirable. Survival requires the ability to trust and to risk betrayal. Suspicion is directed at those who cannot sustain relationships or who use people to further their own ends.

*Amateur detectives also need suspicious natures. For Agatha Christie's Miss Jane *Marple, the microcosm of St. Mary Mead provides a lesson in human nature and the untrustworthiness of appearances. In the tradition of the *cozy mystery, the amateur either learns to become suspicious through involvement with a crime or has to be provided with an appropriate background. Diane Mott Davidson's Goldy Bear is a victim of domestic violence; Nancy Pickard's Jenny

Cain carries memories of her family's betrayal. In other amateur characters, the detective's career provides training in questioning appearances. Robert Campbell's Jimmy Flannery is embedded in Chicago politics; Sara Woods's Antony Maitland and Ed *McBain's Matthew Hope are lawyers; G. K. *Chesterton's Father *Brown and Harry Kemelman's Rabbi David *Small are theologically prepared to acknowledge *evil.

The successful detective, whether amateur or professional, possesses a difficult gift: the ability to perceive and understand the human capacity for violence and evil. The best detectives, amateur or professional, reflect the tension of the balance between suspicion and trust. Their success in resolving a crime includes the ability to restore social equilibrium.

The suspicion the detective feels toward the other characters is complemented by the questioning about the larger society. Chandler's California mean streets of the 1940s and Muller's 1990 San Francisco are commentaries on social conditions: Critical questions are raised about the types of people suspicion falls upon. Are particular *classes or ethnic or social groupings more acceptable as criminals? What qualities inspire suspicion—money, profession, age, *gender, politics, religion? The increasing variety of mystery and detective fiction offers a rich field for analysis and reflection. In the tradition of women detectives, for example, several striking themes are apparent: the price of independence for a woman, the divisive effects of suspicion upon communities, and the value of those communities. Sayers's *Gaudy Night* (1935) is as much about the suspicions directed toward women who choose the academic life as it is about the crime that forces that community into fear and distrust.

The theme of community is equally important in P. D. *James's *An Unsuitable Job for a Woman* (1972). Cordelia *Gray's suspicions of *Scotland Yard in general and Adam *Dalgliesh in particular place her at risk and keep her from forming new relationships. For Amanda *Cross's Kate *Fansler, the relationships she develops while solving mysteries keep her on the job when the clues do not fit together and suspicions threaten to destroy families and friendships. These detectives are constantly aware of the shattering effects of suspicion as they pursue their investigations. For them justice is embedded in communities; the resolution of crimes must include the restoring of trust broken by suspicion.

• Jacques Barzun and Wendell Hertig Taylor, *A Catalogue of Crime* (1971). John Cawelti, *Adventure, Mystery, and Romance: Formula Stories as Art and Popular Culture* (1976). Julian Symons, *Bloody Murder: From the Detective Story to the Crime Novel: A History*, rev. ed. (1985). S. E. Sweeney, "Locked Rooms: Detective Fiction, Narrative Theory, and Self-Reflexivity" in *Cunning Craft: Original Essays on Detective Fiction and Contemporary Literary Theory*, ed. Ronald G. Walker and June M. Frazer (1990). Carolyn G. Heilbrun, *Hamlet's Mother and Other Women* (1990).

—Jan Blodgett

SUSPICIOUS CHARACTERS. Given the human predilection to assign blame, the presence in a novel of individuals who, because of their race, religion, ethnic identity, "shady" occupation, sexual preference, and so on, have been relegated to the fringes of society, makes them the obvious focus for *suspicion when a crime occurs. The use of characters who can be safely suspect, because they are "other" than designed by dominant norms and social power, affords the writer room to maneuver *plot and to manipulate the reader who is likely to be taken in by false suspicion cast upon this character type.

The stranger is a prime example of the suspicious character due to his or her lack of ties to the community. With no family to dismay, no employer to displease, the vagabond is generally viewed with suspicion as is the case when one is suggested to Inspector Thomas Pitt as a likely killer in Anne Perry's Victorian thriller *Highgate Rise* (1991).

Outsiders have played an important role throughout the history of the novel, although the exact identity of these characters changes as society's attitudes change. Jews, Gypsies, Arabs, Asians, homosexuals, servants, fascists, socialists, as well as a variety of shady characters such as *con artists, card sharks, and gamblers have all been included on the list. Cultural xenophobia can account for the hostility that is directed toward people and ideas that are different and therefore looked upon as threatening, but so can ideologically elaborated forms of bigotry, such as *racism and *sexism, generate the hostility in its vicious or genteel forms.

As writers use society's attitudes to strengthen plot and to establish verisimilitude, they may well reveal their own attitudes as well as the fears and *prejudices of their own culture and time. In the best times, the "other" is dealt with variously. In times of crisis, such a character becomes almost exclusively the focus of suspicion.

In Wilkie Collins's *The Moonstone: A Romance* (1868), considered the first English *detective novel, Indian characters are cast as suspects. This established a tradition. If exotic characters were observed in the area at or near the time a crime took place, they immediately became suspect. Their presence, at least briefly, allays the thought that someone close, familiar, or "respectable" might be responsible.

Over the span of fifty-six years, the works of Agatha *Christie for display society's changing vogues as to the groups considered to be the suspicious "other." For instance, the sleek good looks of a character in her 1934 novel *Murder in Three Acts* (1934; *Three Act Tragedy*) are first noted as "un-English," then as "foreign," and finally as "Jew," all three conclusions delivered with a suggestion of distrust.

Other novels written during the same time reflect a similar attitude, for the *Golden Age world did not look upon *anti-Semitism with particular censure, especially in Britain. Writers such as Dorothy L. *Sayers and G. K. *Chesterton allowed many anti-Semitic characterizations to find their way into their writing. In later years, Christie and others expressed similar bias against prodigals returning from British colonies, visitors from Central Europe, and dissident youth. Xenophobia in the detective novel especially focused on Asians, exemplified in Sax *Rohmer's de-

piction of the fictional Dr. Fu Manchu as a sinister, inscrutable "Oriental."

A version of sex discrimination also directed suspicion toward homosexuals. For instance, Sayers in *Unnatural Death* (1927; *The Dawson Pedigree*) described the relationship between two murder suspects as "Rather Unnatural." Gay and lesbian characters, however, have come a long way from being described euphemistically as people shadowed with a problem to serving as heroes of novels written during the last three decades of the twentieth century.

Less serious in its implications for the survival of a civil society is the use of the dubious occupation or activity to generate suspicion about a character. Card sharks, gamblers, and heavy drinkers, because they live outside the borders of respectability, become convenient targets of suspicion. Yet even these examples of "otherness" affirm that in the mystery genre the underside of the plot that restores order and security by solution of a crime is a compulsive conformity that can be socially prejudiced as well as socially protective.

• Solomon Hastings, "Homosexuals in the Mystery," in *Murder Ink: The Mystery Reader's Companion*, ed. Dilys Winn (1977).   —Barbara Sloan-Hendershott

SWIFT, TOM. *See* Juvenile Sleuths: Boy Sleuth.

SYMBOLISM. Literary symbolism occurs when something described in words represents something other than the literal meaning of the words. The detective story was born in an age of literary symbolism. As an organizing principle in the West, literary symbolism moved from Germany through England in the latter eighteenth century and to the United States two generations later, where it came into increasing competition with a growing literary realism. Edgar Allan *Poe, Herman Melville, and Nathaniel Hawthorne all struggled with the seemingly opposite contentions of "natural" and "rational" or "scientific" symbolization, as had Samuel Taylor Coleridge, William Wordsworth, Mary Shelley, and others before them. Such stories as Hawthorne's "The Artist of the Beautiful" and "The Birthmark" (both published in *Mosses from an Old Manse*, 1846) Melville's "The Apple-Tree Table" and Poe's handful of tales of ratiocination portray (*Harper's Magazine*, *Putnam's*, 1850–56); ambivalence about nature and science as a conflict between natural and conventional symbols— the spiritual versus the scientific, or Gothic impulses versus rational thought. As subsets of literature, crime and mystery fiction share the literary conflict between an organic nature (symbolism of passion, spirit, and instinct) and the exclusively rationalizing tendencies of the industrial revolution of the mid-nineteenth century. In crime and mystery fiction destructive actions are most often those that subvert reason to the service of passions such as *greed, jealousy, and *revenge. In this respect the detective reestablishes the primacy of reason and since reason is increasingly claimed by institutions, those institutions are reaffirmed as well.

Poe's stories of ratiocination and horror, the city

exposé fiction of Eugène Sue, George William MacArthur Reynolds, and George Lippard, along with domestic romances, murder broadsides, newspapers and later magazines devoted to crime reporting all provided tropes for crime and mystery writers. Other social changes specific to symbolism in crime and mystery fiction include the birth of the prison and modern police forces, which may have precipitated the invention of the *amateur detective in competition with police; the eclipse of the outlaw hero; and the growth of popular science. In a sense these kinds of literary and institutional effects are inscribed on all aspects of the crime story—the choice of *settings, the action, the who, why, how, and what of crime, and the figure of the detective.

Setting, for example, has often been given figurative treatment in crime and mystery fiction, sometimes in the construction of the story itself as in G. K. *Chesterton's "The Sins of Prince Saradine," (Cassell's, May 1911) where mirror imagery reflects the illusions a man uses to entrap his brother, but more often by drawing current public imagery into the narrative. The city exposé novels of Sue, Reynolds, Lippard, and others contained explosive *class imagery, and the instant popularity of these exposés in the 1840s seems clearly related to class exploitation in the heyday of the industrial revolution. But this kind of social representation tends to be concealed in the detective tradition of Poe. When it resurfaces in *hard-boiled fiction from the late 1920s and in the *police procedural from the mid-1940s, it tends to confirm the isolation of the detective, as in Raymond *Chandler's famous mean streets speech, or reflect the institutional opposition of the police to the overwhelming *violence and *corruption of the city, as in the self-consciously symbolic Fort Apache, the Bronx by Heywood Gould, 1981.

City symbolism may be created largely from the figures of a worldview, as in Fredric *Brown's Chicago in The Fabulous Clipjoint (1947), or simply borrowed from popular iconology. When it is borrowed it is often because the city has connotations suitable to romance, intrigue, corruption, *suspense—Cairo, Casablanca, *London, Istanbul, Paris, Moscow, Madrid. This borrowing of conventional symbolization extends to any place that is included in current international tourist itineraries—Niagara Falls, the Zambezi, the Nile, the Thames. Much light mystery fiction in the Agatha *Christie tradition includes combinations of larger romantic locales and more restricted or isolated places—castles, resorts, beaches, hotels, restaurants—or forms of public transportation that allow internal movement, such as trains, ships, and caravans of various sorts chosen for their evocative features. Cities are also collapsed into their components—ethnic areas such as the Chinatown of Dashiell *Hammett or the Harlem of Chester *Himes, or streets, individual as well as mean, and precincts such as Ed *McBain's Eighty-Seventh.

Poe combines symbols of Gothic and Romantic autonomy to isolate and elevate his archetypal detective, the Chevalier C. Auguste *Dupin. But Dupin also exemplifies the quality produced by science and technology that Jacques Ellul called technic, the internal-ization of systematic method. In the course of a few short stories, Poe managed to keep these two divergent features in dynamic tension and Arthur Conan *Doyle reaffirms them in Sherlock *Holmes, but over time "criminal justice" institutions displace this detective, first to the figure of the *aristocratic dandy and *gentleman Sleuth then to the *private detective and realistic policeman, and finally to the police officer disguised as anyone—the pervasive undercover cop. These developments move the story from contemplation to action, from the independent figure who reluctantly agrees to investigate, to a complicit figure who struggles for autonomy. For Poe, and for much crime and mystery fiction that followed, the crime and its solution were locked into the bestial symbology of motive and the technic of recovering it.

The reputation of crime and mystery fiction as lacking literary qualities is usually based on the leanness of its figuration, due mainly to authors being coerced by *formula to stay within a relatively hermetic form or to expand into broad adventure. The exhaustion of the permutations and combinations of the *least likely suspect in the classic story during the *Golden Age helped open the possibility of telling crime and mystery stories in a way that could disperse motive into the social fabric. Writers not confined to the classic form could be much more flexible in exploiting existing social symbolism. In Little Caesar (1929) and Asphalt Jungle (1949) for example, W. R. Burnett invested criminal activities with the bourgeois values of success and efficiency, giving rise to symbols that evoke complex social questions. Even the classic formula may be deepened through the intensification of social imagery. P. D. *James's use of institutions in A Mind to Murder (1963) and Shroud for a Nightingale (1971), for example, or Emma *Lathen's corporate and financial novels become symbolic as they circle around sites that illustrate the collapse of competitive constraint. In what might be called the realistic gesture, writers have begun to take the form more seriously, to begin to construct a more vital symbology. In Sara *Paretsky's Guardian Angel (1992) V. I. *Warshawski develops an intimate relationship with a black policeman in the midst of the casual and earnest racism around them while investigating a pension scam and battling continuous sexism. It is this kind of story that lays the groundwork for a fiction that finds as much *evil beneath the urbane facades of corporate rationality as it does in modern-day orangutans wearing skin suits.

• W. Y. Tindall, The Literary Symbol (1955). Maurice Beebe, Literary Symbolism (1960). Monroe C. Beardsley, Aesthetics: Problems in the Philosophy of Criticism (1981). Glenn W. Most and William W. Stowe, eds., The Poetics of Murder: Detective Fiction and Literary Theory (1983). Raymond Williams, Keywords: A Vocabulary of Culture and Society, rev. ed. (1985). Hugh Holman and William Harmon, A Handbook to Literature (1986). Tzvetan Todorov, Theories of the Symbol, trans. Catherine Porter. (1986).   —Larry N. Landrum

SYMONS, JULIAN (GUSTAVE) (1912–1994), established a high reputation in the crime and mystery field resting on his work as a crime novelist and literary historian of the genre and biographer of Edgar

Allan *Poe and Arthur Conan *Doyle. Symons also penned poetry, literary criticism, military history, and biographies of other figures. Symons was born in *London, the youngest child in a talented, tightly knit, and strangely isolated family. He received no encouragement from a severe Victorian father whose fortunes rose and fell like those of Charles *Dickens's Mr. Micawber. After demonstrating an early ability to recite poetry, Symons developed a stammer so severe that he was sent to a school for backward children. His mother and siblings were supportive, and he soon formed friendships with everyone from neighborhood cricket and snooker players to intellectuals, writers, and poets. As a youth, Symons plunged into self-education with a passion. By his own estimation, he succeeded as a "minor poet," and edited the small but influential journal, *Twentieth Century Verse*, an enterprise that he supported by means of a tedious job as secretary at the slightly seedy company, Victoria Lighting and Dynamo.

Symons married Kathleen Clark, served in World War II, and worked as an advertising copywriter at the London firm of Humble, Crowther, and Nicholas until 1947, when he became a full-time writer. From the start, he turned his talents in multiple directions. One of his earliest book manuscripts, *The Immaterial Murder Case*, was penned in 1939. Symons's wife discovered this parody of the classic detective novel in the back of a drawer and urged him to publish it, which he finally did in 1945. This novel introduced Inspector Bland and the *amateur detective Teake Wood. Bland appeared again, but Symons soon launched into work that illustrated his belief, expressed in his tract *The Detective Story in Britain* (1962), that post–World War II writers could no longer take the view that human affairs were ruled by reason and that "virtue, generally identified with the order of society, must prevail in the end." Symons felt that modern crime writers were more concerned with character and *motive than with *puzzle elements, and more inclined to be preoccupied with the question of *whydunit than *whodunit. In his own work, he did incorporate puzzles and surprises, but was more absorbed with finding psychological explanations for the *violence behind respectable faces than with step-by-step detection leading to identification of perpetrators of crimes.

In 1972 Symons published his study of the crime and mystery writing genre, titled *Bloody Murder: From the Detective Story to the Crime Novel: A History* in the English edition and *Mortal Consequences* in the first American printing. Two later revisions were given the original title in all editions. This seminal work stands as an important literary history of the genre and a persuasive argument for Symons's notion that the psychologically centered *crime novel represents a step forward from the classic detective story. Along with outlining developments in the crime and mystery genre, this book did much to win support within academic circles for crime fiction as a literary genre worthy of study. Symons's work as a literary critic for the *London Sunday Times* was as important as Anthony *Boucher's reviewing for the *New York Times Book Review* in winning critical regard for this popular fiction.

[*See also* Criticism, Literary.]

• Julian Symons, *Notes from Another Country* (1972). Julian Symons, *The Modern Crime Story* (1980). Rosemary Herbert, *The Fatal Art of Entertainment; Interviews with Mystery Writers* (1994).
—Rosemary Herbert

SYNDICATE AUTHORS. Nineteenth-century publishers of popular fiction quickly adopted the practices of commodity manufacture. Like their counterparts who produced soap or clothing or foodstuffs for a mass market, makers of magazines and books realized that high-volume distribution of uniformly patterned items under a distinctive trade name could lead to commercial success. The repeated use of an author's name for an extended series of tales was a common way to achieve the uniformity that would assure readers of a predictable quality. Prolific authors such as William Adams, who wrote more than twenty serials for *Golden Argosy* and *Golden Days* under the name Oliver Optic from 1853 to 1897, or Horatio Alger, whose approximately 100 didactic tales of luck and pluck starting with *Ragged Dick* (1867) achieved reported sales of over twenty million were especially valuable resources of both labor and raw material to be marketed in this way. When a single writer could not maintain that high level of output, though, publishers had recourse to the use of house names; thus Street & Smith used Nicholas Carter as the author's name on the three serials written by John Russell Coryell, the more than four hundred written by Frederic Van Rennselaer Dey, the twenty-two written by Edward Stratemeyer, and all of the adventures about Carter written by thirty-five or forty staff writers.

While Dey claimed, incorrectly, to have written more than 1,000 Nick Carter stories, it was actually Stratemeyer whose prolific output accelerated production of commodity fiction in the crime and mystery genre. Deirdre Johnson maintains that Stratemeyer employed eighty-three pen names, but more significantly he employed many other writers in a new means of organizing production that he termed a "literary syndicate." Stratemeyer learned the publishing business with Street & Smith, the firm that published his work in a boys' weekly known as *Good News*, Merriam who issued his Richard Dare stories, and Frank J. Earll's *Young People of America*. His innovation began with his hiring writers to fill in the outlines of *plots he devised. He then contracted directly with a publisher to provide the finished products that could be marketed under a common name. These books centered on sleuths such as the Rover Boys, Tom Swift, or Nancy *Drew. Effectively Stratemeyer the entrepreneur carried forward the process of dividing the levels of book production. He took on the business of creating intellectual property, leaving to Grosset & Dunlap, his favored publisher, the physical production and distribution of books.

For many years very little about the Stratemeyer Syndicate authors was known to the public. In order to protect the image of Carolyn Keene (the name on the Nancy Drew stories) and others, the identities of the actual writers were concealed and they were not permitted to claim authorship or a share in royalties. Howard Garis, one of the first writers hired by Stratemeyer's Syndicate after its founding in 1904, was paid $75 for the first Tom Swift book.

Syndicate authors, in general, were competent writers, not hacks. Because the income from Syndicate writing was steady, Stratemeyer had little trouble attracting writers to do the piece work of fleshing out plots and casts of characters. There was evidently opportunity for the hired writers to place their stamp on the work. Mildred Wirt Benson's initial interpretation of Nancy Drew's character had much to do with that series' success. Similarly, Leslie McFarlane, who wrote the first eleven Hardy Boys stories, set the tone for those books. Other important employees of the syndicate were Lillian Garis, St. George Rathbone, W. Bert Foster, and James Duncan Lawrence (author of most of the Tom Swift, Jr. books). Several of these authors also wrote and published books under their own names, and these publications have no connection to the syndicate.

Even though the Stratemeyer productions are among the most famous, and most researched, serial publications, they represent a modest percentage of the total product issued by publishers of adventure and mystery stories for young readers. According to Johnson's findings, there were 115 series in circulation by 1909, and between 1910 and 1930 more than 480 series were being published.

In addition to what syndicate writing shows about the development of the mass market for books, the products also illustrate literary changes. Many of the older stories released under house names stressed more or less traditional *virtues while changing protagonists from tale to tale. The Horatio Alger stories illustrate this. Syndicate productions, however, stressed the appearance of recurring heroes and, in a very significant development, introduced new milieus such as aviation and the motion pictures that endorsed modern technological progress. Moreover, the syndicated protagonists, detective and other, became increasingly detached from a fixed home community so that their adventures came to provide readers in an increasingly mobile society the added interest of changing settings.

The relationship of these literary developments in the syndicated work for young readers to mainstream detective fiction for adult readers may be seen in the modern offerings of two syndicate-style series. Davis Dresser began his Michael Shayne stories in 1939 under the name Brett Halliday, but all of the novels written after 1958 about Shayne were written by authors employed by Dresser, as were all the short novels signed Brett Halliday that appeared in *Mike Shayne Mystery Magazine* (1956–90). The cousins Frederic Dannay and Manfred B. Lee began their memorable writing as Ellery *Queen in 1929, but between 1961 and 1972 a series of twenty-eight paperback originals signed by Ellery Queen were reportedly written by other writers under contract to Dannay and Lee.

[See also Juvenile Mystery: Boys' Juvenile Mysteries; Juvenile Mystery: Girls' Juvenile Mysteries; Juvenile Sleuth: Boy Sleuth; Juvenile Sleuth: Girl Sleuth.]

• Roger Garis, *My Father Was Uncle Wiggily* (1966). Leslie McFarlane, *Ghost of the Hardy Boys* (1976). Deidre Johnson, *Stratemeyer Pseudonyms and Series Books* (1982). John T. Dizer, *Tom Swift and Company: "Boys' Books" by Stratemeyer and Others* (1982). Deidre Johnson, *Edward Stratemeyer and the Stratemeyer Syndicate* (1993).   —John T. Dizer

TAKING OF LIFE is by far the most important crime committed in crime and mystery fiction, not only because of its sheer numerical predominance, but also because of its importance in initiating and advancing *plot and revealing character. The crime itself can be premeditated, like a planned *murder or political assassination, unpremeditated but intentional, like a killing motivated by sudden rage or fear, or accidental, as in a case where one character shakes another by the shoulders and accidentally breaks his neck (Ellis *Peters, *A Morbid Taste for Bones*, 1977). The extraordinary range of methods used includes administering poisons, household and exotic; committing *assault, with every conceivable weapon, including the hands; causing what appear to be accidents, such as pushing the *victims in front of a car or subway; depriving victims of or altering necessary medications or causing severe allergic reactions; and inflicting emotional torment that drives the victim to *suicide. When the taking of life is not premeditated, weapons are those ready to hand: the bare hands used to strangle or to smother or the proverbial blunt instrument, which can be any heavy object at the scene of the crime, such as a poker, a crowbar, or a heavy vase. Famous methods by which life has been taken include the sound and vibration from the bells of a church (Dorothy L. *Sayers, *The Nine Tailors*, 1934), an enclosed motorcycle sidecar in which a known claustrophobe is transported (P. D. *James, *Unnatural Causes*, 1967), and a large vicious dog with phosphorescent paint on its muzzle (Arthur Conan *Doyle, *The Hound of the Baskervilles*, 1902).

More than any other crime, the taking of life initiates the plot in crime and mystery fiction, drawing detectives to it and away from investigating other crimes not only by virtue of its frequently shocking, grotesque *violence but by virtue of its finality. Central motivations for solving the crime are not only ensuring public safety and searching for truth, usually represented as discovering the identity of the criminal, but also seeking to punish the criminal on the victim's behalf. Detectives stymied or weary in their investigations often remind themselves that they act for victims who cannot do for themselves. In Katherine V. Forrest's procedural *Murder by Tradition*, the detective focuses her concentration on the witness stand by reminding herself to do the best she can for the victim: "You're all he has." Relatives and friends of victims often use the same plea to detectives, especially in asking them to investigate crimes committed long since (Agatha *Christie, *Nemesis*, 1971) or those the detective is personally disinclined to pursue.

As well as initiating the plot, the taking of life occurs toward the end of crime and mystery fiction, where it serves several narrative purposes: providing the detective with further *clues to the criminal's identity, increasing the sense of urgency in seeking the solution, and complicating the detective's relation to the criminal. Particularly if the investigation has been long, criminals, feeling suspected or endangered after a long period of considering themselves safe, kill to protect themselves, increasing fear that they will kill yet again but also thereby providing detectives with further clues. In this way the author can create sympathy for the criminal by revealing his or her panic or remorse. This sympathy is more likely to arise if the criminal has not originally committed murder; in such cases, if the criminal afterward kills in fear of being captured, the extreme emotional reaction he or she reveals upon realizing that a life has been taken often causes the murderer to confess or break down so badly as to give him or herself away (Sayers, *Murder Must Advertise*, 1933).

Detectives sometimes take life in the act of solving the crime, particularly in actually apprehending the criminal, when either the criminal or an innocent bystander often dies. Thus taking a life often leads detectives to reflect on the nature of their profession (or sideline, if they are not private investigators or regular law-enforcement professionals) and their resemblance to criminals. When detectives reflect on the taking of life caused by their own capacities for violence and therefore on their resemblances to criminals (Sue *Grafton, *A Is for Alibi*, 1982), they also often reflect on the relative value of discovering who committed a crime, particularly if the discovery frightens the criminal into further killing that might otherwise not have happened. The search for the criminal's identity, generally appearing early in the plot as an absolute good, most often comes to seem a relative good, which the detective must weigh against the harm caused by the life lost and other damage done in searching for and finally unmasking the criminal, meditation that has characterized the denouement of violent crime since Sophocles's *Oedipus Rex*. Such reflection characterizes and debilitates some detectives, such as Sayers's Lord Peter *Wimsey in *Busman's Honeymoon* (1937). In a woman detective, this meditation on resemblances between pursued and pursuers as revealed by her own fatal violence often leads to reflection on general questions of *gender roles and their relation to individual identity. Women detectives, less accustomed than men to exercising sheer physical control and more often operating outside conventional law-enforcement channels and alienated within them because of their gender, often are forced to ask themselves whether by exercising control over human life they have come not only to resemble (most often male) criminals but to adopt aspects of physical dominance and violence they may wish to reject.

Taking of life is also manifested in the acts of some terrorists and spies whose killing is politically motivated, in prison environments in the course of uprisings or by means of brutality perpetrated by wardens, and in the deviant behavior of psychopaths who may commit serial killings and mass murders. Fiction focusing on these crimes is usually less tidily resolved than are stories involving a limited number of murders. Murders that occur in the *military milieu, too, may be a mix of killings sanctioned as acts of *war and straightforward murders.

[See also Truth, Quest for.]

• Stephen Knight, Form and Ideology in Crime Fiction (1980). Maureen T. Reddy, Sisters in Crime: Feminism and the Crime Novel (1988). Patricia Craig and Mary Cadogan, "A Curious Career for a Woman?," in The Lady Investigates (1981). Kathleen Gregory Klein, The Woman Detective: Gender and Genre (1988). Robin Winks, ed., Detective Fiction: A Collection of Critical Essays, rev. and expanded ed. (1988).

—Anne K. Krook

TAYLOR, PHOEBE ATWOOD (1909–1976), who also wrote as Alice Tilton, Freeman Dana, American author of detective novels. In The Cape Cod Mystery (1931), Taylor introduced Yankee detective Asey *Mayo, the prototype for the shrewd, homespun detective who uses his wits and knowledge of the locale and inhabitants to solve crimes. Writing as Alice Tilton, Taylor also created Leonidas Witherall, a professor in a private boys' school who loses his job during the Depression. Witherall, who cultivates a beard to exploit his resemblance to William *Shakespeare, first appears in "The Murder in Volume Four" (1933) in Mystery League magazine, edited by Ellery *Queen. Murder at the New York World's Fair (1938) by Freeman Dana, based on an earlier Tilton novel, was commissioned by Bennett Cerf to predate that 1939 event.

All Taylor's books explore the details of contemporary life on Cape Cod or around Boston, such as unmodernized boardinghouses, local legends, and natives profiting from tourists. Her emphasis is on *humor and character rather than *plot, and her sense of *atmosphere and locale is superb. Especially well delineated is the effect of World War II on the civilian population on a sea coast with rationing, threat of sabotage, and possible invasion of German spies.

[See also Academic Sleuth.]

—Ellen A. Nehr

TECHNICAL BACKGROUNDS. A technical background to *setting or theme in a novel is a detailed presentation of a subject on a level more advanced than that normally found within the scope of fiction. The technical background is distinguished from geographical setting primarily by a focus on acquired knowledge and skills, though the intricacies of geographical settings themselves can sometimes constitute a form of expertise, as in the work of H. R. F. *Keating and Tony *Hillerman. The quintessential example of a mainstream novel that succeeds largely because of the richness of the technical material is Moby-Dick (1851), based on Herman Melville's years aboard a whaling ship. Experience is not the main requirement in creating an authentic background, however; Stephen Crane's The Red Badge of Courage (1895) is another mainstream novel based on research and underscores the importance of the writer's being able to imagine the world of the story. In detective fiction, Dorothy L. *Sayers's The Nine Tailors (1934), with its details about campanology and evocative descriptions of England's fen country, is drawn from research on the former and childhood knowledge of the countryside. The effectiveness of a technical background does not depend on whether it stems from experience or research, but on whether it is handled skillfully and persuasively enough to allow the reader to enter into the spirit of an unknown world.

The technical background may advance the *plot, provide color, raise tension, disclose character, counterpoint the main action, satisfy the reader's taste for detail, and provide an alternative ethical framework. Given factual accuracy and technical skill, the technical background will be organically absorbed into the very texture of the book, substantially increasing the reader's satisfaction. Writers have employed a wide variety of technical backgrounds in crime and mystery writing, and many are identified with specific books rich in material. Erskine *Childers uses coastal navigation in The Riddle of the Sands (1903), and Peter Dickinson uses linguistics in The Poison Oracle (1974). Sayers writes of advertising in Murder Must Advertise (1933) and of academe in Gaudy Night (1935). In these books, the technical background affects the way characters think and interact, thereby determining the shape of the crime and its solution.

Technical backgrounds may serve structural ends of considerable complexity. One of the contemporary masters of the technical background, Dick *Francis, customarily employs two in each book: a horse-racing setting, which amounts to a *series milieu and is born of experience, and a secondary area of expertise researched for one book only. In Reflex (1980), for example, the secondary background is photography. The degree and selection of detail is fascinating in itself, but the photographic background also provides a self-contained subplot with its own highpoints of *suspense and romantic interest. As the subplot unfolds, it simultaneously advances the main story as the discovery of photographic clues progressively reveals the solution to the central mystery. Finally, the technical background provides a subsidiary ethical framework for the revelation of character—a subtle, often overlooked virtue that may be put to good use by the skillful writer.

Francis exemplifies one approach to presenting a technical background; he uses both research and experience to create a convincing verisimilitude. Gwen Moffat also relies on research and experience. In addition to a thorough knowledge of rock climbing and hiking evident in all her books, she describes the grizzly bear and its habits in *Grizzly Trail* (1984). Other writers may attain the same goal of verisimilitude by the judicious insertion of mere snippets of information. Gladys *Mitchell interjects interesting information on pigs in *Spotted Hemlock* (1958) without removing the story from an essentially closed, academic setting. In either case the aim is credibility, which will reinforce the reader's willingness to accept other, perhaps more fanciful aspects of the story.

The multilayered novel has made increased use of technical background at the same time that many areas of traditional expertise have become dominated by technology and hardware. Indeed, a category of fiction has arisen in which the technical background becomes the foreground, a technological showcase of such dazzling sophistication that plot and character play a subsidiary role. This is the realm of such works as Thomas Harris's *Black Sunday* (1975) and Tom Clancy's *The Hunt for Red October* (1984); its origins may be traced in *spy fiction as far back as the James *Bond books of Ian *Fleming.

[See also Academic Milieu; Academic Sleuth; Coroner; Forensic Pathologist; Horse Racing Milieu; Journalist Sleuth; Publishing Milieu.]

—Stephen Murray

TELEVISION. *Crime and mystery plots have long figured in television programming in the United States and Britain. This two-part entry surveys crime and mystery elements in American and British television programming, cites important individual programs and some long-running series, and notes that the dramatic elements and vicarious voyeurism engendered by suspenseful plots was useful in winning broad audiences of viewers.*

The Crime and Mystery Genre on American
    Television
The Crime and Mystery Genre on British Television

THE CRIME AND MYSTERY GENRE ON AMERICAN TELEVISION

Crime and detection programs have been, along with variety shows, soap operas, situation comedies, and westerns, important staples of television programming in America. However, during the medium's formative years, 1947–52, the new networks—DuMont, NBC, CBS—had little access to the product of the major motion picture studios. Out of fear of competition, the studios withheld their movies and talent from the rival medium. As a result, new telefilm companies and independent film companies sprang up to produce live broadcasts and filmed programs with relatively little-known actors and production staffs. Among the earliest and most popular half-hour weekly television series were the detective programs that began in 1949–50—*Martin Kane, Private Eye*, with William Gargan; *Man Against Crime*, with Ralph Bellamy; and *Rocky King, Inside Detective*, with

Roscoe Karns. Because all three were live broadcasts, they labored under severe technical restrictions, crowded studio space, low budgets, brief shooting schedules, and crude story formulas. Compared to motion pictures, they had a cramped and primitive look. Sponsor pressures had a particularly annoying effect on these programs. For example, cigarette advertisements were a prominent part of *Martin Kane*, which had much of its action set in a tobacconist's shop.

Courtroom dramas worked especially well within the constraints of early television production. An early entry was *Mr. District Attorney* (1951–52), with Jay Jostyn. When production values improved in the mid-1950s, television was ready for its most popular attorney, *Perry Mason* (1957–66), starring Raymond Burr. Other notable examples were Macdonald Carey in *Lock Up* (1959–61) and E. G. Marshall and Robert Reed in *The Defenders* (1961–65).

At one time or another most of the established sleuths of fiction, radio, and the movies have appeared on television. Foremost in longevity has been Ellery *Queen, who first appeared in *The Adventures of Ellery Queen* in 1950 with Richard Hart in the role; over the next twenty-six years the character was played by Lee Bowman, George Nader, Lee Philips, and Jim Hutton. The latter series restored the famous Queen "Challenge," giving the viewer an opportunity to guess the culprit. Other investigators included Philip Carey playing the title character in *Philip Marlowe* (1959–60), Richard Denning as the lead in *Michael Shane* (1960–61), Darren McGavin as *Mickey Spillane's Mike Hammer* (1957–59), J. Carroll Naish as sleuth in *The New Adventures of Charlie Chan* (1957), David Janssen as *Richard Diamond Private Detective*, (1957–60), Roger Moore as the *Saint (1967–69), Richard Denning and Barbara Britton as Mr. and Mrs. *North (1952–54), and Peter Lawford and Phyllis Kirk as Nick and Nora *Charles in *The Thin Man* (1957–59), and William Conrad in *Nero Wolfe* (1981). Even famous fictional villains were featured on television, including *Fu Manchu* (1956), played by Glen Gordon. Mike Hammer was later played by Stacy Keach from 1984 to 1987. Ian Ogilvy played the Saint in 1978.

Among the new investigators created especially for television were Blake Edward's hip and jazzy *Peter Gunn* (1958–61) as portrayed by Craig Stevens; this became the prototype for a quick succession of imitators—John Cassavetes playing *Johnny Staccato* (1959–60), Mike Connors as *Mannix* (1967–75), and Efrem Zimbalist, Jr., and Roger Smith portraying the detective team of *77 Sunset Strip* (1958–64). An anthology series, *The NBC Mystery Movie* (1971–77), presented in rotation the exploits of Peter Falk's *Columbo*, Rock Hudson's *MacMillan and Wife*, and Dennis Weaver's *McCloud*. There have also been several female investigators—*The Snoop Sisters* (1973–74), played by Helen Hayes and Mildred Natwick; sexy Sergeant Pepper Anderson in *Police Woman* (1974–78), starring Angie Dickinson; and author Jessica Fletcher in the long-running *Murder, She Wrote* (1984–96), played by Angela Lansbury.

*Police procedural dramas also date back to com-

mercial television's beginnings. *Dragnet* (1952–59, 1967–70) and *Racket Squad* (1951–53) set the pattern with their terse, clipped dialogue, narration, and documentary-like structure. Later came *Highway Patrol* (1955–59), starring Broderick Crawford; *M Squad* (1957–60), featuring Lee Marvin; *The Untouchables* (1959–1963), led by Robert Stack; *The Detectives* (1959–62), headed by Robert Taylor; *Naked City* (1958–63), investigated by John McIntire and Horace McMahon; and *87th Precinct* (1961–62), starring Robert Lansing. During the next two decades other long-running police series included *Hawaii Five-O* (1968–80), with Jack Lord; *Adam 12* (1968–75), with Martin Milner; *The Mod Squad* (1968–73); and *The F.B.I.* (1965–74), with Efrem Zimbalist, Jr. Satirizing all the above was the delicious but short-lived *Police Squad* (1982), in which Leslie Nielsen's Detective Frank Drebin and his team wrought havoc during the course of their investigations.

The paranoia of the early 1950s—stemming in part from Cold War nerves and anti-Communist witch hunts—inspired many television newsroom dramas and spy intrigues. Prototypes in the former category included *Big Town* (1950–56) and *Foreign Intrigue* (1951–55), which was the first major American television series to be filmed abroad; in the latter category were *I Led Three Lives* (1953–56), in which Richard Carlson portrayed real-life undercover agent Herbert Philbrick. The most ambitious of later popular newsroom dramas was the ninety-minute *The Name of the Game* (1968–71), which weekly alternated among the adventures of Robert Stack, Tony Franciosa, and Gene Barry; the most popular espionage series included *The Man from U.N.C.L.E.* (1964–68), starring Robert Vaughn and David McCallum as Napoleon Solo and Illya Kuryakin; *I Spy* (1965–68), with Robert Culp and Bill Cosby; and *Mission: Impossible* (1966–73, 1988–90), starring Peter Graves.

The *violence, sex, and occasional gore inherent in crime and detection dramas have always tested the limits of the network censors, not to mention the patience of the United States Congress, the Federal Communications Commission, and citizens' pressure groups. As early as 1949 Arch Oboler's *Lights Out* and the DuMont network's *Hands of Murder*, both live-broadcast anthology shows produced on minimal budgets, startled home viewers with relatively gruesome stories enacted by stellar guest stars like Boris Karloff and Basil Rathbone. "Mr. Raymond" (Paul McGrath) introduced weekly stories of madness and Grand Guignol horror on *Inner Sanctum* (1954), derived from the radio series, and Alfred Hitchcock introduced episodes on his series (1955–65), which featured numerous adaptations of the stories of Charles Beaumont, Henry Slesar, John Collier, Roald Dahl, and others. Many of the episodes, notably Dahl's "Man from the South" and "The Landlady," were controversial—although the sponsors demanded tacked-on endings that resolved the dilemmas and punished the wrongdoers. In response to charges of questionable morality and excessive violence, the television industry adopted its first agenda of standards and practices in the mid-1950s, the Television Code.

Nonetheless, the violence and gruesomeness has continued unabated. Two acclaimed police procedural series, *Kojak* (1973–78), starring Telly Savalas, and *Bronk* (1975–76), starring Jack Palance, were embroiled in controversies in the mid-1970s that saw the Federal Communications Commission threatening to intervene in network programming. The situation repeated itself in the 1990s when the nudity and violence of the police procedural *NYPD Blue* (beginning 1993) aroused congressional protest, resulting in the first adoption of a "disclaimer" by a network.

[*See also* Chan, Charlie; Mason, Perry; Police Detective; Radio: The Crime and Mystery Genre on American Radio; Theater: The Crime and Mystery Genre in the American Theater.]

• Erik Barnouw, *Tube of Plenty: The Evolution of American Television* (1975). Geoffrey Cowan, *See No Evil: The Backstage Battle over Sex and Violence on Television* (1980). John E. O'Connor, ed., *American History/American Television* (1983). William Boddy, *Fifties Television: The Industry and Its Critics* (1990, 1993). Tim Brooks and Earle Marsh, eds., *The Complete Directory to Prime Time Network TV Shows, 1946–Present* (1979).   —John C. Tibbetts

THE CRIME AND MYSTERY GENRE ON BRITISH TELEVISION

The crime and mystery genre is now firmly established as the heart of much British television drama. The enduring popularity of crime's mystery in this medium can most obviously be traced to vicarious voyeurism, allowing the viewer to play the game of detection from a comfortable distance: to experience crime, detection, the excitement of the chase, and punishment from the perspective of the *victim, the criminal, or the investigator.

Legal procedurals and courtroom dramas are popular television fare exemplified by *Crown Court* (1972–84), which presented fictional criminal and civil cases in the form of a trial before a jury whose verdict was unscripted. Its format attracted several celebrated writers, including Ngaio *Marsh, and, by portraying accurately and realistically the handling of such cases, this series and others, like *Boyd Q. C.* (1956–64) and *Kavanagh Q. C.* (1995–99), have compensated for the fact that actual trials are not televised in Britain. John *Mortimer's *Rumpole of the Bailey* (1978–95) also featured trials but encompassed the wider community of barristers, solicitors, and the judiciary, leavening serious issues with broad humor and genial warmth.

The most famous *police procedural program is probably *Dixon of Dock Green* (1955–76), which sustained the wartime image of benevolent local law enforcement while others, such as *Tales of Soho/Big Guns* (1956–58) and *Murder Bag/Crime Sheet/No Hiding Place* (1957–67), covered investigations, often drawing on actual cases. But it was not until *Z Cars* (1962–78) that the reality of less glamorous police-work was presented and *New Scotland Yard* (1971–74) was among the first series to deal with less palatable issues such as police *corruption, racist attitudes, and the perversion of *justice. In *The Sweeney* (1975–78) and the infamous *Law and Order* (1978), the wheel turned full circle—the police were depicted as little better than criminals—but the situation has become more balanced with current series covering all aspects, good and bad. Notable among domestic series are *Juliet Bravo* (1980–85) and *The Bill* (1984–99), the latter particularly for the occasional use of hand-held cameras, which involve the viewer more closely. More substantial series include *Strangers/Bulman* (1978–87), *Taggart* (1983–99), and the much-praised *Prime Suspect* (1991–96), which has set major investigations into serial *murder and vice against the background of internal police politics. Against the background of the European Community, there was a resurgence of series dealing with the work of other European police forces, among them *Derrick* (1987–91), *Eurocops* (1988–91), and the Russia-based *Grushko* (1994). According to the respected scriptwriter Alan Plater, it is difficult to get funding except for series dealing with the police.

Many police procedurals have been developed from popular novels, including J. J. Marric's *Gideon's Way* (1965–66) and, more recently, the dramatization of Ruth Rendell's Wexford series, *Ruth *Rendell Mysteries* (1987–99), and *P. D. *James* (1983–98), capitalizing on the success of the original novels and, symbiotically, increased sales.

Like the work of Rendell and James, the hugely popular *Inspector *Morse* (1987–98)—based largely on Colin *Dexter's novels—combines the police procedural with the *puzzle mysteries of the *Golden Age. Although much of Dexter's cerebral "crossword" clueing could never work on television, *Morse* has generally been in keeping with the novels, notwithstanding some poor scripts by writers who have saddled the detective with a surfeit of neuroses and bad luck. Nevertheless, John Thaw's superb performance in the series has even influenced Dexter's writing—Morse's gray eyes have become blue, his Lancia has been replaced by a Jaguar, and Sergeant Lewis has become curiously ageless, avoiding the problem that he is portrayed by an actor in his thirties but was a grandfather in the first novel. *Cribb* (1980–81) posed similar problems for Peter Lovesey, who abandoned the character once unable to picture him except as Alan Dobie, who played the part in the series.

On television, as in crime and mystery fiction, detectives on the fringes of police work have generally been less plausible than the police. *Shoestring* (1979–80) was a radio private eye, while *Zero One* (1962–64) concerned an airline detective (whose cases must have deterred all but the most foolhardy passengers), and *Zodiac* (1974) and the slightly better *Moon and Son* (1992) combined crime and astrology. Presented with little credibility but a straight face, *The Professionals* (1977–83) and *Dempsey and Makepeace* (1985–86) alternated between criminal investigations and unraveling political intrigue, but were criticized as glamorizing violence. More successfully, the magician detective Jonathan Creek (1997–98) brought *locked room puzzles into the 1990s to great acclaim.

British television has always drawn heavily on classic crime and mystery fiction with series such as *Cluff* (1964–65), *The *Saint* (1966–69), and *Father *Brown* (1974). The ambitious *Detective* (1964–69) trawled the Golden Age while *The Rivals of Sherlock *Holmes* (1971–73) featured stories by William Hope Hodgson, Jacques *Futrelle and R. Austin *Freeman in excellent and atmospheric productions. Perhaps recognizing that viewers will often have a strong idea of the relevant period and appearance of the characters, productions of classic mysteries have tended to stick closely to the original creations, as in *Dorothy L. *Sayers's Mysteries* (1987), which accordingly lacked the spirited charm and amiability of *Lord Peter Wimsey* (1972–75). However, the balance between *plot and period has sometimes swung too far. *Campion* (1989–91) looked tremendous but Margery *Allingham's novels had been bleached of their humor and color, while *Maigret* (1992–93) lacked the humanity of Rupert Davies's series (1960–63).

Arthur Conan *Doyle's immortal detective has probably appeared in more programs than any other character from the genre, with three series entitled *Sherlock Holmes* (1951, 1965, and 1967) and *Young Sherlock* (1982). But it was not until *The Adventures of Sherlock Holmes* (1984–94) that a concerted effort was made to re-create Holmes's world as accurately as possible. Jeremy Brett embodied Holmes and David Burke, latterly Edward Hardwicke, restored Watson's dignity and credibility. Despite a risible finale, the series stands head and shoulders above all other adaptations.

The other stalwart of British television is the work of Agatha *Christie, with series such as *The Agatha Christie Hour* (1982) and *Partners in Crime* (1983–84) as well as adaptations of radio and stage plays, including *The Wasp's Nest* (1937) and *Three Blind Mice* (1947). *Poirot* (1989–97) and *Miss Marple* (1984–92) feature definitive central performances from David Suchet and Joan Hickson with strong supporting casts, excellent period detail, and high production values. All of the Miss *Marple novels have been filmed and, wisely, none of the short stories for *Poirot* has demonstrated that condensed novels are generally more effective than expanded short stories.

The appeal of such established characters to television companies is obvious, not least because tie-in editions of the books effectively place advertisements throughout the country and, at least initially, an army of loyal readers will watch. But, while standing by "safe" adaptations from the work of the most well-known writers in the genre, British television makers are still prepared to take chances on newer names, too, with adaptations from the work of Robert Goddard (*Into the Blue*, 1997), Minette Walters (*The Echo*, 1999), and a range of others. There is also a welcome, if slow, stream of original mysteries, such as *Forgotten* (1999). On television, as alas in real life, crime shows no signs of waning in popularity. .

[*See also* Police Detective; Radio: The Crime and Mystery Genre on British Radio; Theater: The Crime and Mystery Genre in the British Theater.]

• Leslie Halliwell with Philip Purser, *Halliwell's Television Companion* (1986). Dave Rogers, *The ITV Encyclopaedia of Adventure* (1988). Mark Sanderson, *The Making of Inspector Morse* (1991). Geoff Tibballs, *The Boxtree Encyclopaedia of TV Detectives* (1992).

—Tony Medawar

Templar, Simon. *See* Saint, The.

TENNIS MILIEU. *See* Sports Milieu.

TERROR. The evocation of terror in the *Gothic novel and its further development in the *sensation novel whetted readers' appetites for an *atmosphere of fear and dread and introduced *suspense into the novel. Crime and mystery fiction has drawn on this and sometimes reversed it, using terror both as a suspenseful element to drive the *plot or deploying the detective figure as a force of reason in a more rational world.

Current scholarship holds that the disorderly worlds of the Gothic and sensation novels represent a number of social changes and their resultant anxieties that occurred during the eighteenth and nineteenth centuries, centering primarily on changing *gender roles, *family structure, and expressions of sexuality. Blurred gender identities are apparent in characters like Wilkie *Collins's Marian Halcombe (*The Woman in White*, 1860), whose unusual strength of will is underlined by her mustachioed appearance, and M. E. *Braddon's Lady Audley (*Lady Audley's Secret*, 1862), who appears to be the gentle and virtuous Victorian "angel of the house" but is in fact a calculating murderess.

If closure of the sensation novel seeks to calm these fears in a final domestic tableau, it often fails to overcome the prevailing dread the novel produces. Detective fiction, too, regards the element of closure, or *resolution, as vital. After the author establishes disorder and suspense with the event of the crime, the detective is brought in. The *sleuth's status as an outsider allows him or her to translate chaos into rational order. For example, Edgar Allan *Poe's "The Murders in the Rue Morgue" (*Graham's Lady's and Gentleman's Magazine*, April 1841) depicts two female *victims—one decapitated with a razor and the other strangled and stuffed up a chimney—in a scene that initially inspires genuine terror until the detective demonstrates that the bizarre and horrific details, if viewed in a rational manner, actually provide the solution to the case.

In "The Adventure of the Speckled Band" (*Strand*, Feb. 1892), while Sherlock *Holmes and Dr. John H. *Watson work in concert, the atmosphere of fear and dread is heightened by the fact that Holmes leaves Watson (and the reader) in the dark regarding the threat from a highly poisonous snake. In this and the other more terrifying stories in the Holmes *Canon, female clients are the targets of physical, often sexually charged, violence. Their jeopardy is used to manipulate the reader's emotions and their circumstances are tied in with Doyle's use of the Married Women's Act, a piece of newly released legislation in Doyle's day. At least in the world of mystery fiction, women's increased financial power actually endangered them.

Terror is also a hallmark of the later *Had-I-But-Known school of writing, in which there is a distinct echo of the role of female characters in the Gothic and sensation novels. In the Had-I-But-Known female characters are typically threatened while the suspense is sustained by the professional sleuth taking control only at the last minute. In *Rebecca* (1938),

by Daphne *du Maurier, the character is unable to realize the power that she might assume as the new wife of a wealthy man because she is confined by her limited point of view and overawed by the Gothic environment in which she is placed.

In much *hard-boiled fiction the sleuth is the individual in jeopardy working in a world in which order is no longer guaranteed. *Private eyes literally laugh in the face of fear, using witty cynicism to help them function in a dangerous world. It is the private eye's ability to make wisecracks rather than an acuity for logical deductions that makes him or her immune from terror.

In the world of P. D. *James's private eye, Cordelia *Gray, questions of sexuality and power remain essential elements of terror. In *The Skull Beneath the Skin* (1982), allusions to Victorian melodrama and Jacobean tragedy highlight the novel's ambiguous attitude toward the murder motivated by a stepson's revulsion at his stepmother's aggressive sexuality. In *An Unsuitable Job for a Woman* (1972), the true motives of the murderer are masked by misleading clues to do with sexuality. The intentionally ambiguous title underlines the fact that Gray's determination to take power as a detective also places her in jeopardy. This title, voiced as a refrain throughout the novel and challenged by Gray at every mention, is all the more telling, since Gray was an early female character to assume the traditionally male role of private investigator.

[*See also* Horror Fiction; Menacing Characters; Sex and Sexuality.]

• William Patrick Day, *In the Circles of Fear and Desire: A Study of Gothic Fantasy* (1985). Beth Kalikoff, *Murder and Moral Decay in Victorian Fiction* (1986). Jenny Bourne Taylor, *In the Secret Theatre of Home: Wilkie Collins, Sensation Narrative, and Nineteenth-Century Psychology* (1988). Thomas Boyle, *Black Swine in the Sewers of Hampstead: Beneath the Surface of Victorian Sensationalism* (1989).

—Jasmine Yong Hall

TERRORISM AND THE TERRORIST PROCEDURAL. Terrorism is the application of political power through intimidation and *violence. While there are some examples of detectives preventing or halting terrorist plots-in-progress in classic detective fiction, contemporary fiction with *plot driven by the depiction of terrorist activities is a subgenre of its own. Golden Age writers may have looked at terrorism as something to be quashed so that the social order might be restored; increasingly writers regard it as the essence of plot in novels so focused on step-by-step terrorism that their books can be termed terrorist procedurals.

Early examples of terrorism controlled by classic *sleuths include G. K. *Chesterton's prevention of anarchy in *The Man Who Was Thursday* (1908) and Nigel *Strangeways's exposure of a criminal gang with terrorist designs on Albert Hall in Nicholas *Blake's *The Whisper in the Gloom* (1954; *Catch and Kill*).

Later, terrorism in literature was promoted by such fanciful criminal organizations as SPECTRE in Ian *Fleming's James *Bond books or THRUSH in *The Man from U.N.C.L.E.* television series. The plot of Fleming's *Goldfinger* (1959) to steal all the gold in Fort Knox seems quaint today, because the fanciful has been supplanted by designs drawn from headline coverage of international politics, as in Tom Clancy's *Patriot Games* (1987), where Irish terrorists attempt to assassinate the Prince and Princess of Wales and their young son.

Reeva Simon dates topical portrayals of terrorism in fiction from after the 1967 Arab-Israeli War, when terrorists went international with plane hijackings, assassinations, kidnappings, and bombings. Media coverage of such actual events coupled with the oil shocks of the 1970s provided an ideal combination of *suspense elements for fictional *thriller plots.

One best-selling terrorist procedural was Thomas Harris's *Black Sunday* (1975), in which U.S. and MOSSAD agents race to stop a conspiracy to drop a bomb from the Goodyear Blimp during the Super Bowl in order to kill its chief fan, the president of the United States. Alistair MacLean was hugely successful in *Goodbye California* (1977) with a portrayal of Muslim terrorists threatening to set off atomic bombs to produce a massive earthquake that would send California sliding into the Pacific Ocean. Another best-seller was John *le Carré's *The Little Drummer Girl* (1983), which relates the efforts of a British actress who works for an antiterrorist Israeli organization to infiltrate an Arab terrorist group.

The challenge of innovation in the plot of the terrorist procedural yields such works as Richard Jessup's *Threat* (1981), involving a Vietnam veteran skilled in demolition who sets a number of dummy bombs in a luxury skyscraper and then demands $4 million in ransom to prevent his setting off an actual bomb. Christopher Hyde's *Maxwell's Train* (1985) follows the actions of an Amtrak maintenance man who plans to steal a $35 million shipment of Federal Reserve cash being shipped from Washington, D.C. to Boston via rail. Unknown to Maxwell, the shipment is also targeted by a group of terrorists led by Annalise Shenker.

Further use of terrorism in conjunction with other crimes can be found in Steve Sohmer's *Favorite Son* (1987). Senator Terry Fallon becomes the favored candidate for the next election after he is nearly assassinated on live television along with the leader of the Nicaraguan Contras. But FBI agent Joe Mancuso investigates the inconsistencies of the attack and uncovers a plot to manipulate the American electorate.

Innovation in plotting, portrayal of adversaries racing against time, and the depiction of specific terrorist activities in a high-stakes contest make the terrorist procedural one of the most compelling subgenres of crime and mystery and espionage fiction to be produced.

[*See also* Menacing Characters; Spy Fiction; "Time is of the Essence."]

• Reeva S. Simon, *The Middle East in Crime Fiction* (1989).

—George Kelley

TEY, JOSEPHINE, is the better-known pseudonym of Scottish author and playwright Elizabeth Mackintosh (1896–1952). She kept her personal life private,

refusing interviews and preferring to be listed as Gordon Daviot (another pseudonym) in *Who's Who* and even in her death notice, which appeared on page one of the *Times* (London), and characteristically specified "no flowers." Born at Inverness, Scotland, she completed her education at Anstey Physical Training College near Birmingham in 1918 and taught in Liverpool, Oban, Eastbourne, and Tunbridge Wells schools until 1926, when she resigned to keep house for her widowed father. A product of the Golden Age of detective fiction, she soon developed a popularity that overshadowed her fame as a playwright, psychological novelist, and biographer.

Tey's prestige as a mystery writer rests on eight novels she dismissed as "her 'yearly knitting,'" according to John Gielgud's foreword to *Plays, by Gordon Daviot* (1953–54). Of these, the best-known and most critically debated is *The Daughter of Time* (1951), in which Inspector Alan Grant investigates, from his hospital bed, the fifteenth-century murders of Richard III's two nephews in the Tower of London, for which the king was vilified by William *Shakespeare and others. While contemporary critic Anthony Boucher praised it as "re-creating the intense excitement of scholarly research" (in the *New York Times Book Review*, 24 Feb. 1952), some 1970s historians saw Tey's acquittal of Richard III as a "sophomoric" slap at their profession, according to Guy M. Townsend in the *Armchair Detective* 10 (summer 1977).

Tey began her characteristic defense of the wrongly accused with *The Man in the Queue* (1929; republished posthumously under the Tey pseudonym as *Killer in the Crowd*, 1954), published under the Gordon Daviot name, which she later reserved for what she regarded as more serious works. This classically plotted mystery introduces Inspector Grant and establishes his reputation for "flair," a combination of intelligence, intuition, integrity, and Scottish tenacity. Letting misconceptions cloud his judgment, Grant nearly drowns his innocent suspect before intuition leads him to the murderer, who goes unpunished. Tey repeated this successful formula in *A Shilling for Candles* (1936), revealing her scorn of greedy poseurs and the mass media. In *Miss Pym Disposes* (1946) she examined the consequences of favoritism in a school like Anstey, proving popular psychology no guarantee against fallibility. *The Franchise Affair* (1948), her fourth crime novel, was a murderless *locked room mystery based on the Elizabeth Canning case of 1754 and set in a walled English country house inhabited by two uncongenial females whom a mendacious teenager denounces as kidnappers. It was quickly followed by *Brat Farrar* (1949; *Come and Kill Me*), a novel featuring a sympathetic impostor. Here Tey ponders the identification between a charming drifter who strikingly resembles Patrick Ashby, whose murder by his selfish twin Brat uncovers while posing as Patrick. Her sixth, *To Love and Be Wise* (1950), a murderless mystery, asks Grant to solve the disappearance of a charismatic photographer. Tey's eighth and last crime novel, *The Singing Sands* (1952), a work with nuances of Brat Farrar, leads Grant from a cryptic poem to the riddle of

Shangri-La. All these novels remain in print, suggesting a loyal following.

The author's fame as Gordon Daviot rests on six plays—*Richard of Bordeaux* (1932), *The Laughing woman* (1934), *Queen of Scots* (1934), *The Stars Bow Down* (1939), *Leith Sands* (1946), *The Little Dry Thorn* (1947); three novels—*Kif; An Unvarnished History* (1929), *The Expensive Halo* (1931), *The Privateer* (1952); and a biography—*Claverhouse* (1937).

[*See also* Impersonation; Kidnapping.]

• Sandra Roy, *Josephine Tey* (1980). Nancy Ellen Talburt, "Josephine Tey," in *Ten Women of Mystery*, ed. Earl F. Bargainnier (1981). Kathleen Gregory Klein, "Tey, Josephine," in *Twentieth Century Crime and Mystery Writers*, ed. Lesley Henderson, 3rd ed. (1991).   —Jean A. Coakley

Thatcher, John Putnam, the *amateur detective created by Mary Jane Latsis and Martha Henissart, who wrote together under the pseudonym Emma *Lathen, is vice president of the Sloan Guaranty Trust Bank of New York City. He is a silver-haired widower in his sixties. As a detective Thatcher uses his acute powers of observation, but also calls upon long experience in banking, which has left him knowledgeable about the U.S. financial system and properly cynical about human nature. Because of his financial expertise, he is a prime example of the *surrogate detective.

In his first case, *Banking on Death* (1961), Thatcher searches for a missing heir. Thatcher often travels to a Sloan-financed company to investigate its financial soundness and stays to solve a *murder that threatens the bank's investment. In *Murder Makes the Wheels Go Round* (1966), Michigan Motors unveils a new luxury car as part of a comeback attempt. When the car door is opened, a body tumbles out. Even on vacation, Thatcher comes upon murder; in *Pick Up Sticks* (1970), he finds a body while hiking. Thatcher's cases reflect the detailed financial knowledge of his creators, an economist and a lawyer.

[*See also* Banking and Financial Milieu.]

• Jeanne F. Bedell, "Emma Lathen," in *Ten Women of Mystery*, Earl F. Bargainnier, ed. (1981). William A. S. Sarjeant, "Crime on Wall Street," *Armchair Detective*, 21, no. 2 (spring 1988): 128–45.   —Marvin Lachman

THEATER, THE CRIME AND MYSTERY GENRE IN. *This entry is divided into two parts, noting very early exemplars of dramatic works in which the discovery of a murderer was central, looking at the traditions including those of Gothic melodramas and bandit plays, and outlining the use of elements of crime and mystery in late-nineteenth-century and twentieth-century British and American theater.*

British Theater
American Theater

For further information, please refer to Tragedy, Dramatic Elements of in Crime and Mystery Writing.

BRITISH THEATER

*Murder, mystery, and *suspense have been staples of drama ever since the plays of ancient Greece; indeed two of the most famous plays in the Western tradition, William *Shakespeare's *Hamlet* and Sophocles' *Oedipus Rex*, are each centrally concerned with discovering and exposing the perpetrator of an unsolved murder. The immediate background for the modern mystery drama, however, clearly lies in the tradition of the popular melodrama of the nineteenth century. Many of the atmospheric elements and devices for creating tension and suspense in the modern English detective novel or *thriller can be traced directly back to the early-nineteenth-century English Gothic melodramas, while the specific attention to the mechanics of the crime itself owes much to the sensational plays based on real-life murders, such as Maria Marten's death in the infamous Red Barn or the exploits of the "demon barber" Sweeney Todd which enjoyed great popularity in the London melodrama houses during the 1820s and 1830s. The crime melodramas of the early nineteenth century had little mystery about them, and so had no need of anyone to "solve" the mystery. Representatives of the law usually were minor figures, often appearing only at the end to apprehend the villain (like the Bowery Street Runner who arrests William Corder in *Maria Marten; or, The Murder in the Red Barn* (1827).

Around the middle of the century, however, several popular dramatists began placing detectives in much more important roles. Tom Taylor was the leader of these, offering a variety of plainclothes officers and detectives in his dramas of the 1850s and 1860s and creating one of the first and most famous stage detectives, Hawkshaw, in his extremely successful *The Ticket of Leave Man* (1863). Taylor's plays were as popular in America as in England, as were the melodramas of his leading rivals such as Dion Boucicault and Watts Phillips, both of whom contributed importantly to the growing body of detective drama. Phillips's *Maude's Peril: A Drama in Four Acts* (1867) featured what was probably the first of an endless series of stage Scotland Yard officers. Boucicault's spectacular *After Dark: A Drama of London Life in 1868, in Four Acts* (1868) offered a panorama of Lonon's underworld, roamed by Captain Gordon Chumley and Policeman Pointer early "hard-boiled" figures whose tough descendants often appeared in the popular crime dramas of the 1880s and 1890s. Popular novels of mystery and detection, headed by those of Wilkie *Collins and Charles *Dickens, also found their way onto the late-nineteenth-century stage.

Throughout the nineteenth century, the American theater enthusiastically but rather passively accepted these British dramas, but at the end of the century, with the international success of William Gillette's *Sherlock Holmes* (1899), it took the clear lead in detective drama, and for the next quarter of a century it was the British stage that imported its major new mystery plays from America. During the 1920s, however, the success of American mysteries on the London stage, along with the growing popularity of the mystery novel thanks to authors like G. K. *Chesterton and Agatha *Christie, stimulated an interest in such work among British dramatists. A. E. W. *Mason's Inspector *Hanaud appeared on stage in *At the

Villa Rose in 1920 and H. C. *McNeile's *Bulldog Drummond* in 1921. Edgar *Wallace was the first major British thriller dramatist of the century, beginning with *The Gaunt Stranger* (1925) and *The Terror* (1929). Michael Morton's *Alibi* (1929), based on *The Murder of Roger Ackroyd*, was the first dramatization of Agatha Christie, who would become the most successful of all stage mystery authors. Plays like A. A. Milne's *The Fourth Wall* (1929; *The Perfect Alibi*) and Patrick Hamilton's *Rope* (1929; *Rope's End*) were international successes. *Rope* was subsequently the basis for one of Alfred Hitchcock's most admired films, and Hitchcock continued to draw on British detective plays for subsequent films, such as *Dial "M" for Murder* (1954), based on a television and stage play (1952) by Frederick Knott.

During the 1930s and 1940s the classic detective story reached its apogee in the works of such authors as Christie, Dorothy L. *Sayers, John Dickson *Carr, and Ellery *Queen. During these same years the detective drama, dominated by Wallace and Christie, was also becoming a standard feature of the English-language stage, though its real blossoming came somewhat later, in the 1940s and 1950s. Sayers collaborated on *Busman's Holiday* for the stage in 1937, but Christie soon became queen of the genre, offering at least one new play in eleven of the fifteen seasons between 1944 and 1960 and often having several plays running concurrently. Although an average of five or six new thrillers appeared each season on the London stage from 1952 onward, no other dramatist in this genre approached Christie either in quantity or popularity. Her works included both "scene of the crime" dramas like *The Mousetrap* (1952) and courtroom dramas like *Witness for the Prosecution* (1953). The former enjoys the longest run in the history of the British theater, is often imitated, and inspired Tom Stoppard's witty parody of the genre, *The Real Inspector Hound* (1968).

The genre maintained its popularity through the 1960s with the plays of Philip Mackie, Michael *Gilbert, William Fairchild, and a host of others, then took a surprising turn with Anthony Shaffer's innovative *Sleuth* (1970), the first and one of the most popular of the modern "trick" mysteries or comedy thrillers, such as Shaffer's own *Murderer* (1975), Simon Gray's *Stage Struck* (1979), Gerald Moon's *Corpse!* (1985), and Edward Taylor's *Murder by Misadventure* (1992). Mystery and murder are common to these plays, but the emphasis is upon surprising the audience, and the problem-solving detective is thus often missing. More traditional mystery dramas have, however, continued to flourish alongside the comedy thrillers, most notably in the series of successes by Francis Durbridge, who has carried on the Wallace and Christie tradition in the popular radio and TV adventures of detective Paul Temple and in a series of stage plays beginning with *Suddenly at Home* (1973) and including *Deadly Nightcap* (1986) and *A Touch of Danger* (1989).

[See also Drama, Elements of; Theater: The Crime and Mystery Genre in the American Theater.]

• H. Chance Newton, *Crime and the Drama; or, Dark Deeds Dramatized* (1927). Michael R. Booth, *English Melodrama* (1965). Maurice Willson Disher, *Blood and Thunder* (1974). Marvin Carlson, *Deathtraps: The Postmodern Comedy Thriller* (1993).
                                                              —Marvin Carlson

AMERICAN THEATER

Bandit and crime plays, often highly sensationalized versions of actual notorious cases, were very popular in the early-nineteenth-century American theater, as they were in England. Indeed they were very often the same plays, since the popular English theater was the major source for such entertainments. This close relationship continued through most of the century, so that when the detective as an important character began to appear in England in the plays of such dramatists as Tom Taylor, Dion Boucicault, and Watts Phillips, American productions of these same plays soon introduced him to this country as well.

After the imported British detectives flourished on the American stage in the 1860s (and more of these appeared in following decades), American dramatists began in the 1870s to create local versions. From the *dime novel tradition came such heroes as J. J. McCloskey's Daring Dick, the Brooklyn Detective (1870), Butts, the Boy Detective, and Harlan Page Halsey's Old Sleuth. Halsey, a prolific novelist and dramatist, was the first to use the term *sleuth for a detective, and tried, unsuccessfully, to copyright its use. The center for such dramatizations was New York's Bowery Theatre, one of the great homes of nineteenth-century melodrama. Detectives appeared in other plays, but they were often distinctly secondary characters with a rough comic edge, in the vein of the plainclothes officer Gimlet in Tom Taylor's popular imported drawing-room melodrama *Still Waters Run Deep* (1855). By the final decade of the century, however, detective plays were scoring major successes in the Broadway theater. William Gillette's *Sherlock Holmes*, using Doyle's popular characters in a romantic plot that owes almost nothing to Doyle, opened in 1899 and was a great hit, frequently revived in America and England for years. In 1894 Frank Mayo wrote and starred in a popular stage version of Mark Twain's *Pudd'nhead Wilson* with its early use of fingerprinting to solve a crime. Anna Katharine *Green, the Brooklyn author who created detective Ebenezer Gryce in 1878, nearly a decade before the creation of Sherlock *Holmes, offered a stage version of her popular novel *The Leavenworth Case* in 1892.

Although these nineteenth-century works provided the standard characters and situations of detective drama, the form of the modern *murder mystery play was developed on Broadway more or less during the period of World War I, and primarily by two popular and prolific masters of the genre, Owen Davis and Bayard Veiller. They evolved a more concentrated type of mystery drama, one in which a murder is committed at or before the beginning of the play and *suspicion falls upon a number of characters before the detective, usually not a policeman, reveals the true murderer at the end of the action, often through some psychological entrapment. There is usually a single *setting, either the scene of the crime, as in Veiller's *The Thirteenth Chair* (1916), or a courtroom, as in Veiller's *The Trial of Mary Dugan*

(1917). Elmer Rice ingeniously combined these in courtroom drama with film-inspired flashbacks in *On Trial* (1914) and *For the Defense* (1922). Complex and elaborate plotting also marked this genre, and was utilized for comic ends in such "mystery farces" as Augustin McHugh's *Officer 666* (1912) and George M. Cohan's *Seven Keys to Baldplate* (1913), based on Earl Derr *Biggers's 1913 novel of the same title, in which the entire elaborate plot is ultimately revealed as taking place in a mystery writer's mind. A popular variation of the genre was the "mystery melodrama," launched by *The Thirteenth Chair*, adding thrills with an almost always fraudulent occult element—ghosts, spiritualists, and countless haunted houses, theaters, even ships.

New detectives (Miss Van Gorder in Mary Roberts Rinehart's popular *The Bat*, 1920), new locations for mysteries (*Subway Express*, by Martha Madison, 1929), and new murder tricks (a revolver hidden in a radio in Albert C. Fuller and Clyde North's *Remote Control*, 1929) were explored during the next decade, and American crime plays steadily grew in popularity in London. By the 1930s, however, a strong school of British crime drama had begun to develop, and authors such as A. A. Milne, Patrick Hamilton, and, later, Agatha *Christie began to be imported to Broadway, gradually coming to dominate it despite such American successes as Basil Mitchell's *The Holmeses of Baker Street* (1933), which provided a crime-solving daughter for the famous detective, Owen Davis's *Mr. and Mrs. North* (1941), and Vera Caspary's stage version of her *Laura* (1947). Then the appearance of Ira Levin with *Interlock* (1958) and of Alec Coppel with *The Joshua Tree* (1958) and *The Gazebo* (1959), as well as the immigration of Frederick Knott, who brought to Broadway *Write Me a Murder* (1961) and *Wait until Dark* (1966), heralded a new generation of American contributors to this genre.

Anthony Shaffer's *Sleuth* (1970), with its playful subversion of generic expectations, was as great a success in America as in England, and was perhaps even more influential in America. Ira Levin's *Deathtrap* (1979) is probably the best known of the subsequent "comedy thrillers" in either country, and John Pielmeier's *Sleight of Hand* (1988) and Rupert Holmes's *Accomplice* (1989) and *Solitary Confinement* (1992) continued to develop this subgenre in striking new directions.

Despite the appearance of many new mystery writers in America during this generation, no major author of traditional crime drama, like Francis Durbridge in England, appeared, nor were such dramas imported from *London. With very few exceptions, such as Warren Manzi's *The Perfect Crime* (1988), which enjoyed a long run off-Broadway, recent American mystery plays have been either unconventional comedy thrillers, or, rather surprisingly, musicals. A major musical treatment of the Norths, *Nick and Nora*, was a costly failure in 1992, but a much more modest parody of *private eye films by Eric Overmyer, *In a Pig's Valise*, gained success in 1989, as did Larry Gelbart's *City of Angels*, a large Broadway musical. All three of these works, interestingly, relied heavily on filmic references and effects.

[*See also* Drama, Elements of; Theater: The Crime and Mystery Genre in the British Theater.]

• H. Chance Newton, *Crime and the Drama; or, Dark Deeds Dramatized* (1927). Frank Rahill, *The World of Melodrama* (1967). David Grimsted, *Melodrama Unveiled: American Theatre and Culture, 1800–1850* (1968). Marvin Carlson, *Deathtraps: The Postmodern Comedy Thriller* (1993).

—Marvin Carlson

THEATRICAL MILIEU. *This entry surveying crime and mystery writing set in the theatrical milieu is divided into three parts, the first viewing the milieus pertinent to the Legitimate Theater, Amateur Theater and Touring Companies; the second focusing on the Motion Picture Industry milieu; and the third treating the Radio and Television Industry as a milieu.*

Legitimate Theater, Amateur Theater, and Touring
    Companies
Motion Picture Industry
Radio and Television Industry

For further information, please refer to Radio; Television.

LEGITIMATE THEATER, AMATEUR THEATER, AND TOURING COMPANIES

Throughout the literary history of crime and mystery writing, the theater has been a popular *milieu in which to set novels and stories. The theater world, which is populated by flamboyant characters skilled at delivering lines that may or may not be truthful, and who are prone to professional jealousy, is useful to the writer in creating characters. In addition, the trappings of the stage are often excellent places to set *clues, and the progress of productions can be significant to nailing down timing in cases whose solutions are dependent on this. The themes of plays that are being rehearsed or performed in some novels can also be used to underline the actions and themes that the mystery writer is exploring in his or her work.

Michael *Innes's *Hamlet Revenge* (1937) is an exemplar of the classic detective novel set in the theatrical milieu. A performance of *Hamlet* in a country house is the occasion for *murder by stabbing through a curtain at the very moment that William *Shakespeare's stage directions call for the same action. The theme of *revenge is vital in both the stage drama and in the mystery, and the solution to the latter is dependent upon understanding the movement of the actors on and offstage throughout the progress of the production.

An actor is also murdered before an audience in Ngaio *Marsh's *Enter a Murderer* (1935), one of several detective novels set in the theater by this author who was also a celebrated director. In her mysteries, Marsh convincingly set the stages of several different types of acting worlds. In *Vintage Murder* (1937), she focuses on the murderous activities of the Carolyn Dacres Comedy Company, a touring group. In *Overture to Death* (1939), she looks at a play staged by parishioners for their church. In *Opening Night* (1951), Marsh uses a professional acting group. And in *Light Thickens* (1982), she plays with the superstitions around the production of Shakespeare's *Macbeth*, when criminal activities at first look like unlucky disasters associated with the Scottish play. In *Killer Dolphin* (1966; *Death at the Dolphin*), the focus is the restoration of an old theater and a new play intended to be performed there.

Robert Bruce Montgomery, a composer, wrote two novels as Edmund *Crispin that used the theatrical milieu. *The Case of the Gilded Fly* (1944; *Obsequies at Oxford*) is a *locked room mystery set among a group of actors whose professional and personal conflicts lead to the murder of one of them in *Oxford. *Swan Song* (1947; *Dead and Dumb*) takes place in the backstage world of opera.

Anne Morice, who was raised in a family of actors, used the theater world in some of her novels featuring the actress-sleuth Tessa Crichton. *Murder in Mimicry* (1977) is focused on a seasoned cast beginning an American run of a play in Washington, D.C. *Death in the Round* (1980) shows a theater patron who finds it difficult to believe that a teenaged orphan whom she has befriended may have betrayed her. *Sleep of Death* (1982) looks at the faltering production of a play about to open in *London's West End.

Edward Marston's *historical mysteries are set in the Elizabethan Age and concern a group of touring actors known as Lord Westfield's Men. The sleuth in the company is Nicholas Bracewell, who is the bookholder, or stage manager, for the troupe. Marston's series begins with *The Queen's Head* (1989), a volume that establishes the author's flair for writing that is accessible to any reader while offering greater rewards to those who recognize the literary *allusions to work of Elizabethan dramatists.

In another historical mystery, *Abracadaver* (1972), Peter Lovesey depicts the flamboyance of late-nineteenth-century music hall life. Practical jokes like spreading mustard on a sword-swallower's sword become increasingly dangerous as the action progresses, and Sergeant Cribb is charged with identifying the perpetrator of the life-threatening pranks.

In his series of novels centered on the English actor Charles Paris, Simon Brett, himself a television writer and producer, uses a variety of theatrical milieus, including the worlds of radio and television. The variety of his stage-oriented settings is exemplified in *So Much Blood* (1976), in which his hero is asked to perform a one-man show about Thomas Hood; *Star Trap* (1977), concerning an ill-fated production of the musical comedy *She Stoops to Conquer; An Amateur Corpse* (1978), which concerns an amateur dramatic society; *A Comedian Dies* (1979), which depicts acting in a seaside resort; and in *Dead Room Farce* (1998), in which Paris plays a leading role in bedroom farces on and offstage. In Brett's fiction, the progress of the crime is accompanied by the ongoing saga of the life of a less than successful actor. Linda Barnes, in her series about Michael Spraggue beginning with *Blood Will Have Blood* (1982), also depicts the ups and downs of the acting life.

In *Romance* (1995), Ed *McBain proves that a relatively hard-boiled approach can be taken to the depiction of the acting life. In a *police procedural that balances three story lines, McBain has the lovelorn detective Bert Kling investigate the murder of an actress who is stabbed to death in a manner that mirrors the murder scene she has been rehearsing on stage.

—Rosemary Herbert

MOTION PICTURE INDUSTRY

The rise of film in the 1890s coincides with the ascendancy of the *Great Detective. No visit by Sherlock *Holmes to the cinema is recorded, but the man often called the American Sherlock Holmes, Craig Kennedy, investigated, in *The Film Mystery* (1921), what seems to be the first crime committed during the making of a motion picture. Kennedy's creator, Arthur B. *Reeve, had an intimate knowledge of the fledgling film industry, having written a number of scripts, including that for *The Exploits of Elaine* (1914). He turned this knowledge to account in this story of the murder of the company's leading lady during filming, with much description of the process of filming and editing, and the final unmasking is produced through the creative use of the negative of the *murder scene.

At the end of the silent film era, Carolyn Wells, one of the most prolific writers in the genre, most of whose eighty-two volumes feature the detective Fleming Stone, introduced in three novels Kenneth Carlisle, a matinee idol who has given up the screen for the magnifying glass. But there is little about the film industry here; Carlisle merely uses his acting abilities to entrap his criminal quarries. At about the same time, Helen Simpson and Clemence Dance wrote three detective novels starring the great actor-manager Sir John Saumarez.

With the coming of sound, film was more directly tied to scripts, and more and more writers came to Hollywood to write them. One of the most notable groupings of detective fictions arising out of the authors' stints in Hollywood are the three novels written by Ellery *Queen: two in the thirties (*The Devil to Pay*, 1938, and *The Four of Hearts*, 1938), and one later (*The Origin of Evil*, 1951). In the first two, Ellery is a screenwriter at Magna Studios solving murders committed in what is presented as a trivial, even absurd, *milieu. In *The Origin of Evil*, Ellery returns to a Hollywood endangered by both McCarthyism and television, but the book is finally more about the Cold War and Korea than about Tinseltown. An earlier novel that underscores the glamour of filmmaking, but also its emptiness, is Earl Derr *Biggers's *The Black Camel* (1929), dealing with the murder of a famous screen actress.

Of the 1930s, but sui generis, is Cameron McCabe's *The Face on the Cutting-Room Floor* (1937). Like Queen, McCabe is both a *pseudonym and the name of the narrator. The author professed to be steeped in Marcel Proust, James Joyce, and others, but claimed as well that he drew on his own experiences in Douglas Fairbanks's office. The result is a weird house of literary mirrors reflects which much of the authentic Hollywood of the 1930s.

It may be that in the 1940s and the two decades that followed, more writers were writing for Hollywood than about it. Two major, representative figures, Jonathan Latimer and Horace McCoy, wrote more film scripts than novels. Raymond *Chandler, who also served his turn in Hollywood, wrote *The Little Sister* (1949) out of his experience. Of all Hollywood novels, this gives us the film capital at its most corrupt, but it is finally less about Hollywood than about that more general strip of southern *California that Chandler made his own. He was succeeded as its topographer by Ross *Macdonald, who set three novels in Hollywood, of which the best is *The Moving Target* (1949), originally written under the name John Macdonald; but no more than Chandler does he deal with the process of filmmaking, or even much with the world of film itself. More directly concerned with that world is Robert B. *Parker's *A Savage Place* (1981), which takes *Spenser out of Boston to the world, well captured, of moguls, directors, actors, and agents.

The 1970s brought, along with the many pastiches of Holmes, another kind of nostalgia—for the Hollywood of the Golden Age. Andrew Bergman, a film scholar, wrote in *Hollywood and LeVine* (1975) a brilliant evocation of the film industry under the siege of McCarthyism, but in this novel and in *The Big Kiss-Off of 1944* (1974) we are more widely in the world of historical fiction, of Thomas E. Dewey and a youthful Richard M. Nixon, than in the world of actors.

Stuart Kaminsky, starting with *Bullet for a Star* (1977) and *Murder on the Yellow Brick Road* (1978), has carried this tendency to the nth degree, but more facetiously. And Peter Lovesey has employed the careful research he usually reserves for his Victorian England, in *Keystone* (1983). Here he penetrates the famous silent comedy studio, with its Kops and bathing beauties; its leading characters, Mabel Normand and Mack Sennett, are painted as credible people, doing things we know they did. Other novels, more clearly *romans à clef*, are Evan Field's *What Nigel Knew* (1981) and Samuel A. Peoples's *The Man Who Died Twice* (1976), based on the William Desmond Taylor murder of the 1920s, still not officially solved. Actors who have written detective novels are not many, but George Kennedy placed a series of plausible murders on the set in *Murder on Location* (1983).

Hollywood is not the only place where films are made. Two of the best film novels written on the other side of the Atlantic—Reginald *Hill's *A Pinch of Snuff* (1978) and Colin *Watson's *Blue Murder* (1979)—deal with pornographic film. James Anderson's *The Affair of the Mutilated Mink Coat* (1981) is truer to type, presenting a zany aristocratic household of the thirties with a Hollywood mogul pursuing the mansion as a film set. Even Agatha *Christie, whose characters trod in every walk of life, depicted a number of stage players, but only in *The Mirror Crack'd* (1962; *The Mirror Crack'd from Side to Side*) does she give us a glimpse of the film world.

Filmmaking settings are prevalent in detective fiction. The film world provides the closed circle of aspects favored by detective writers. But it is a closed circle with a difference, encompassing vain, immature, excitable people whose infantile jealousies and fragmented personalities often spill over into murder.

- Albert J. Menendez, *The Subject Is Murder: A Selective Guide to Mystery Fiction* (1986).   —Barrie Hayne

RADIO AND TELEVISION INDUSTRY

Several factors give broadcasting backgrounds a special attractiveness among the theatrical and entertainment *settings so well suited to crime fiction: the increased size of the audience for *murder during a performance, the importance of specialized technology to the process, the public curiosity about a medium that comes into virtually every potential reader's home, and the perceived cutthroat nature of the business. The first writers to make memorable use of a broadcasting background were Val Gielgud, dramatic director of the British Broadcasting Corporation, and Eric Maschwitz writing pseudonomysly as in *Death at Broadcasting House* (1934; *London Calling*), which concerned the murder of an actor during a live broadcast and included many authentic details of the period's elaborate and meticulous production methods. In *The First Television Murder* (1940), the same team pioneered the use of a television background. Writing alone, Gielgud returned even more memorably to a television setting in *The Goggle-Box Affair* (1963; *Through a Glass Darkly*), which looks at the commercial side of the medium in Britain. British radio of the 1930s is the backdrop for John Sherwood's *A Shot in the Arm* (1982; *Death at the B.B.C.*), while Antonia Fraser uses a background of contemporary television in her series about investigative reporter Jemima Shore. Simon Brett's actor-detective Charles Paris works in television in several of his adventures, a comedy series in *Situation Tragedy* (1981), a game show in *Dead Giveaway* (1985), a Golden Age mystery program in *A Series of Murders* (1989), and a crime "reality" program in *A Reconstructed Corpse* (1993).

An early use of an American radio background came in the satirical *Death Catches Up with Mr. Kluck* (1935), written by Edith Meiser, the author of many Sherlock *Holmes radio scripts, under the name Xantippe. Carolyn Wells depicted the on-the-air death of a big game hunter in *The Radio Studio Murder* (1937). In *And Be a Villain* (1948), Nero *Wolfe investigates the murder of a radio talk-show guest, a situation somewhat recalling author Rex *Stout's experience as a panelist on the program during which Alexander Woollcott was fatally stricken. George Harmon *Coxe explores the world of radio soap opera in *The Fifth Key* (1947), with a plot gimmick that would still be valid in today's television equivalent. H. Paul Jeffers looks back on radio days of the 1930s in *Murder on Mike* (1984), while the talk-show hosts of present-day radio figure in Stuart M. Kaminsky's *When the Dark Man Calls* (1983) and Sharyn McCrumb's *She Walks These Hills* (1994). Hugh *Pentecost collaborated with Virginia Faulkner on the novelette "Murder on the Fred Allen Program" (1944), featuring a real-life radio comedian of the time, and later used a background of early live television in "Death in Studio 2," which appeared on a CBS television series coincident with its appearance in the *American* magazine (June 1951).

The dramatic possibilities of live television as an occasion for murder were explored by Patricia McGerr in *Death in a Million Living Rooms* (1951;

Die Laughing) and by Ed *McBain in *Eighty Million Eyes* (1966), which was published when live television entertainment programs were no longer common. Harry Olesker's *Now, Will You Try for Murder?* (1958) concerns big money quiz shows. The leading American *sleuth to specialize in television industry mysteries is William L. DeAndrea's Matt Cobb, in several novels, beginning with *Killed in the Ratings* (1978). Television talk shows are used as a backdrop by one of the form's pioneers in Steve Allen's *The Talk Show Murders* (1982) and *Murder on the Glitter Box* (1989), while Eileen Fulton uses a television soap background for her series beginning with *Take One for Murder* (1988). Soap operas also figure in John Lutz's *Shadowtown* (1988), Judi Miller's *Phantom of the Soap Opera* (1988), and Henry Slesar's *Murder at Heartbreak Hospital* (1988).

The American television news business has been surprisingly little exploited in crime fiction. R. R. Irvine featured field reporter Bob Christopher in *Jump Cut* (1974) and three subsequent novels, and returned to a television news background in *Barking Dogs* (1994). A television reporter stars in Mike Lupica's *Dead Air* (1986), and Edward Gorman's *Murder Straight Up* (1986) concerns the murder of a local news anchorman.

[*See also* Drama, Elements of in Crime and Mystery Writing.]

—Jon L. Breen

THEFT—the dishonest taking of another's property—is used in crime and mystery writing as an incidental or central criminal act that must be solved by a detective, or as an action or *caper engaged in by a character type like the *gentleman thief or the *Robin Hood figure. As incidental activity, theft may be used to complicate, confuse, or motivate other crimes such as *murder. In fiction as in real life, a *murder scene where theft has occurred presents a double challenge to the detective.

Theft as a central crime to be solved is often featured in short stories. In novels, thieving may lead characters like Jonathan Gash's Lovejoy and Lawrence Block's Bernie Rhodenbarr into crime scenes where murder has occurred. Donald Westlake's Parker novels also fit this pattern. In all of these authors' works the thrill of illicit activity is celebrated and tips are given as to burglary techniques or how to identify property of value.

Gentlemen thieves and Robin Hood figures are central characters who are themselves thieves. Their thievery is portrayed as high jinx perpetrated by sympathetic characters. Upper-crust characters like E. W. *Hornung's A. J. *Raffles are portrayed as stylish rogues who use their entrees into high society homes to burgle their hosts and posh guests.

Sometimes called the French equivalent of Raffles, Arsène *Lupin, created by Maurice *Leblanc, becomes a gentleman burglar. Although his father died in prison and his mother was maid to a countess, Lupin identifies with the aristocracy against the bourgeoisie. Employing quick wits and his talent for disguise, he outwits the plodding police with his complex robberies, for example in his first adventure, *The Hollow Needle* (1909). Later in his career, Lupin, who has always abhorred violent crime, aids the police and is presented more fully as a detective.

Canadian-British writer Grant Allen, created perhaps the first short-story thief in detective fiction, Colonel Clay, also a master of *disguise, who delights in robbing the title character of *An African Millionaire* (1897), Sir Charles Vandrift. Colonel Clay is a confidence man and thief who robs the more villainous capitalist, who has already preyed on society.

Figures who also seem to reflect the Raffles prototype include Romney Pringle, created by R. Austin *Freeman and Dr. John James Pitcairn, writing as Clifford Ashdown. Pringle's exploits are chronicled in *The Adventures of Romney Pringle* (1902). Frederick Irving Anderson's "the Infallible Godahl," a genius and scientific thief who has been called the American Raffles, amazes his *victims in short stories beginning in 1914. The Lone Wolf is a safecracker and master criminal, created by Louis Joseph Vance, a thief antagonistic to gangs who try to make him join them. The character first appeared in *The Lone Wolf* (1914) and reappeared in *crime novels for the next twenty years. Fidelity Dove is an unusual female burglar who heads a gang of male thieves. She is featured in *The Exploits of Fidelity Dove* (1924), written by David Durham, a pseudonym of Roy Vickers.

Many detectives, such as Margery *Allingham's Albert *Campion and Anthony Morton's Baron, have criminal pasts. Campion, whose detective cases run from 1929 to 1969, was first a *con artist who lived by his wits, and his valet, Magersfontein Lugg, was a convicted cat burglar. Novels written by John *Creasey feature the Baron, also known as John Mannering, who was first a jewel thief and later a legitimate antiques dealer and consultant to *Scotland Yard. The rogue pasts of these detectives help explain their knowledge of criminal behavior, set them off as law-abiding individuals by choice rather than conformity, and sharpen the opposition between them and the more unimaginative police who believe that criminals and the greedy are a race apart.

Leslie *Charteris's Simon Templar, known as the *Saint, is a notorious jewel thief turned adventurer who takes the law into his own hands throughout his career (in forty-five novels several films, and a television series). The Saint, who has been seen as a precursor of James *Bond, is also seen as a successor of Raffles, a romantic figure whose crimes, like those of Raffles, are expunged as he is turned into a patriot late in his career.

The Parker novels written by Donald E. Westlake as Richard Stark, starting with *The Hunter* (1962), center on the adventures of Parker, a ruthless and brilliant thief. The adventures in the hard-boiled mode fit the form that John Cawelti describes as the *caper, the planning and execution of a difficult and complex feat. Although Parker, the narrator, is brilliant, his larcenous capers almost always fail because of the cupidity and incompetence of the other gang members or because he is betrayed by the criminal organization that employs him. Parker's stoic victory is in remaining alive and in sometimes wreaking vengeance on his betrayers.

Bernie Rhodenbarr is the protagonist of Lawrence *Block's Burglar series, begun in 1977. Written in a light tone, a central theme of the novels is the skill of the professional, who may impart a certain amount of lore about breaking and entering, as in *Burglars Can't Be Choosers* (1977). In the standard plot, corrupt people try to force Bernie to use his skills for their benefit or to make him a scapegoat for their iniquities. To extricate himself, Bernie has to solve a case, usually of murder. He has to manufacture evidence or at least point the police in a direction of his choosing to achieve a kind of rough *justice. Although Bernie is trying to attain the good life for himself, he usually acts with restraint.

Westlake has also created a distinct form, the comic caper—for example, *The Hot Rock* (1970); *How to Steal a Diamond in Four Uneasy Lessons*—in which the intricate plotting of a heist is foiled when one of the complex details goes wrong or some absurd coincidence or other arbitrary factor intervenes before the gang achieves its score. John Dortmunder, the protagonist, is often lured into crime by Andy Kelp, a car thief. Stan Murch, a getaway driver, is another regular member of the gang. The aim of the caper, to attain wealth and power, always slips away from the hapless group.

The chronicles of the thieves run the gambit in tone from light-hearted to almost despairing. Although the emphasis is usually on adventure, included are the melodramatic rise and fall of the gangster, the comic caper in which the gang's plans unravel, the detective-caper in which the burglar succeeds, the depiction of the amazing thief like the super-detective, the thief who presents himself as a knight rescuing maidens, the lone individual who will not be absorbed into a bureaucratic society, and other variations. All of the fictions of theft assert some value other than property, whether it be life or justice or the *pursuit of happiness or the intelligence and skill wielded by the thief. In a bourgeois society, thieves both rebel against and reflect the capitalist obsession with wealth and power.

[*See also* Adventurer and Adventuress; Farceurs.]

• John T. Cawelti, *Adventure, Mystery, and Romance: Formula Stories as Art and Popular Culture* (1976).   —Kate Begnal

THEORY. *Once it became a field of academic study, crime and mystery writing also became the provenance of literary theorists. This entry is divided into two parts, the first focusing on descriptive theory, which looks at the origins and development of the genre and its subgenres, and the second explicating prescriptive theory, which lays down prescribed rules for writers who work in the genre.*

Descriptive Theory
Prescriptive Theory

For further information, please refer to Craft of Crime and Mystery Writing, The; Golden Age Forms; Pontificators, The; Rules of the Game.

DESCRIPTIVE THEORY

Through the early years of crime and mystery writing commentary on the form followed the predictable route usually followed in a period of literary genre formation. Critics, many of them practicing authors, sought to establish the distinctiveness of the type by recovering its origins in earlier literature and by contrasting its technical requirements and characteristics with those of mainstream short fiction and the novel. Meanwhile, reviewers of the growing output of detective and mystery fiction in the late years of the nineteenth century, and especially in the first decades of the twentieth, joined in genre formation by rendering praise when works fit expected formal patterns and by the repeated reference to declared masters of the form that results in the creation of a *Canon.

With consensus more or less complete about the nature of its genre, the abundant productions of detective and mystery writing have gained a broadened critical audience. A significant result of the attention directed toward the form by professional critics and scholars of literature in the late twentieth century has been the appearance of a body of descriptive theory as fecund as the prescriptive *theory that dominated commentary in early years. W. H. Auden's "The Guilty Vicarage" (*Harper's Magazine*, May 1948) states directly what the author prescribes for inclusion in detective fiction; it also describes stories about criminal solution as secular reenactments of a core myth granting readers a glimpse of spiritual redemption. The criticism of Roger Caillois in "*Le Roman policier: ou, comment l'intelligence se retire du monde pour se consacrer a ses yeux et comment la société introduit ses problèmes dans ceux-ci*" (1941) also adapts the interests of earlier prescriptive theory, in his case the emphasis upon determinative *rules of the game, but Caillois's intent is not to state requirements for writing mysteries but rather to examine the subtle ways that *puzzles are embodied in narrative and, then, to conclude from these observations that the genre of crime and mystery writing supplants the subject of human nature, which is to be found in mainstream novels, with an almost completely formal pattern of narrative construction.

In "Narrative Structures in Fleming" (*Il Caso Bond*, 1965; trans. in *The Role of the Reader*, 1979) Umberto Eco produces a taxonomy for five levels of narration in the James *Bond stories, including character oppositions, games, Manichean ideology, literary techniques, and literary collage, which he then further subdivides for analysis. Robert Champigny's *What Will Have Happened; A Philosophical and Technical Essay on Mystery Stories* (1977), as its provocative title indicates, addresses the treatment of narrative time in selected works of detection fiction. John G. Cawelti focuses his structural approach in *Adventure, Mystery, and Romance: Formula Stories as Art and Popular Culture* (1976) on the archetypes that generate and inform the narrative formulas for several types of popular literature, and Dennis Porter in *The Pursuit of Crime: Art and Ideology in Detective Fiction* (1981) attends to the creation of *suspense in detection literature.

The essays of George Grella look at the relationships to other established literary types; thus, Grella's "Murder and Manners: *The Formal Detective Novel*" (*Novel*, Fall 1970) describes the classic detective story as a latter-day version of the Comedy of Manners and his "Murder and the Mean Streets" (1974) identifies elements of romance in hard-boiled detection stories.

In contrast, some socially inspired criticism elaborates the theme of crime and detection literature as a product of capitalist culture. Steven Marcus in his 1974 edition of the *Continental Op stories of Dashiell *Hammett identifies duplicity and *corruption as fundamental traits of capitalism. Ernst Kaemmel writing about "Literature under the Table: The Detective Novel and Its Social Mission" (*Poetics of Murder*, 1983) explains that the typical crimes against property in detection narratives are often beyond the abilities of government agencies to solve and that, therefore, an outsider must assume the job. Ernest Mandel, another Marxist critic, devotes his social history of the crime story entitled *Delightful Murder: A Social History of the Crime Story* (1984) to establishing that a bourgeois ideology is the foundation of plots that work on behalf of established power. A similar but non-Marxist exploration of the ideological functions of crime writing occurs as a central argument in David Grossvogel's *Mystery and Its Fictions : From Oedipus to Agatha Christie* (1979), while a consummate treatment of crime fiction as a social product is detailed in Stephen Knight's *Form and Ideology in Crime Fiction* (1980).

Yet another variety of descriptive theory runs through criticism that may be termed epistemological. Frederick Jameson writing "On Raymond Chandler" (*Poetics of Murder*, 1983) analyzes the hard-boiled writer's style as a method of probing American social reality. Michael Holquist in "Whodunit and Other Questions" (*New Literary History*, Autumn 1971) discerns the recent appearance of the metaphysical detective story that dedicates its craft to representing the process of knowing reality, and Glenn Most, whose essay on the "The Hippocratic Smile," which is published in the collection of theory he edited with William W. Stowe entitled *The Poetics of Murder* (1983), argues that the fictional detective stands in for the reader in constructing the conclusive narrative explaining the fictitious crime.

Finally, a significant variety of descriptive theory appears in psychoanalytic literature. The most frequently cited instance of the sort is "Detective Stories and the Primal Scene" (*Pscychoanalytic Quarterly*, 1949) by Geraldine Pederson-Krag who asserts that the secret wrongdoing in detective fiction, the perceptive detective, and above all the intense curiosity aroused in readers of the genre derives from their repressed memory of the scene that creates the Oedipal relationships between a child and her or his parents. The famed predecessor in this line of analysis, aside from Sigmund Freud himself, was Marie Bonaparte whose *Edgar Allan Poe: Etude Psychanalytique* (1933) pursued the primal scene as the genesis of the short stories written by the accepted father of the literary genre. As Freudian theory has become detached from the practice of therapy, so too has its application to

detective fiction, as can be seen in the "Seminar on 'The Purloined Letter'" (*Yale French Studies*, 1972) by Jacques Lacan, which uses the *Poe story as the occasion for a linguistic investigation of the significance of "letter."

Beyond the intrinsic interest the growing body of descriptive theory holds for the study of crime and mystery literature, it provides a sign that the work of genre formation is complete and that a new stage of definition has arrived that takes the writing about crime as an entire literature.

[*See also* Theory: Prescriptive Theory.]

—John M. Reilly

PRESCRIPTIVE THEORY

A library or database search of popular literary criticism will scarcely turn up an advisory word about the proper construction of a *Gothic novel, the romance, or the *Western story, but for the *detective novel there is an abundance of commentary on acceptable ingredients in the recipe for fiction about crime. An early illustration of the disposition to set rules appears in R. Austin *Freeman's "The Art of the Detective Story" (*Nineteenth Century and After 95*, 1924), which founds its prescription for the genre on the observation that "a completely executed detective story is a very difficult and technical work." Noting that the form has earned contempt among the "professedly literary," Freeman declares that they have allowed the sensationalism and melodrama of poor detective fiction to represent what the distinctive quality of the genre should be, namely, an artistic rendering of the work of ratiocination offering readers intellectual satisfaction. For Freeman, it follows, therefore, that the indispensable elements of a detective story are, first, complete presentation of data, and, second, freedom from fallacies of reasoning. Adherence to the prescription will lead to the dramatically effective emergence of "the only possible conclusion" to the criminal problem and its demonstrable proof by the detective.

Freeman's attempt to distill the ideal essence of the genre reveals his eventual aim in the essay to be legitimation of detective fiction as proper reading for an audience of intellect and culture. The same paradoxical interest in establishing hierarchy within the loose, and ever-changing boundaries of popular literature underlies E. M. Wrong's inferring general rules for portraying detectives and detection from the historical survey of the genre's emergence he provides as an introduction to the anthology *Crime and Detection* (1926). Similarly, Willard Huntington Wright, who presented the detective cases of Philo *Vance under the pseudonym S. S. *Van Dine, inscribed the indispensable characteristics he demanded of the genre in an introduction to *The Great Detective Stories* (1927). "There is no more exciting adventure than that of the intellect," he writes, and the artful engagement of readers in the intellectual problem of criminal detection results in a singular genre that "has practically reversed the principles on which the ordinary popular novel is based." For example, the setting of a detective story requires detailed realism, but *atmosphere has no place in the narrative. The *plot must seem to be an actual record of events, whereas *characterization needs to be no more than plausible, and the material of the plot should be commonplace. The style of writing must be "unencumbered," involving no authorial *sleight of hand. For the most part Wright's prescription, like Wrong's, derives from examination of the practice of worthy authors, but there is a suggestion of something else besides when Wright asserts that "there is a strict ethical course of conduct imposed upon the author" demanding that "the truth must at all times be in the printed word." No deception is allowed, no false *clues, no withheld information.

Wright continued his translation of literary tactics into ethical behavior with his writing, as Van Dine, of "Twenty Rules for Writing Detective Stories" (*American Magazine*, Sept. 1928), which he introduced as a credo prompted in part by his writer's conscience. Rules such as the necessity for a *corpse in a *detective novel speak to his preference for a certain type of detection problem. The rule that there be no love interest in the story indicates an intellectual purism, as does the rule that the method of *murder and its detection must be rational and scientific. The final rule, in which Van Dine lists devices he contemns, clarifies the tone of this ethical prescription finally as seriocomic. The same tone pertains in the introduction to *The Best Detective Stories of The Year 1928* (1929), which its author Ronald A. *Knox titled "A Detective Story Decalogue." The commandments he hands down rule out supernatural agencies in a story, the use of more than one secret passage, unannounced introduction of twin brothers into the story, and sinister Asians.

The lightening of tone as earnest apology for detective fiction underwent a partial reversal with the appearance in the 1940s of two classically inspired essays. "Aristotle on Detective Fiction" (*English*, 1 Jan. 1936) by Dorothy L. *Sayers (1946) reads the Greek critic's *Poetics* as a guide to writing detective fiction. With liberal use of invention in citing Aristotle's words, Sayers finds him recommending the detective story to young readers, because it makes *virtue more interesting than vice; helpfully reminding writers that a plot must have a beginning, a middle, and an end; advising that unity of plot may be achieved through selective narrating; and distinguishing the types of discovery that will constitute the denouement of a story. The second notable work of 1940s theory came from the hand of W. H. Auden, whose essay "The Guilty Vicarage" (*Harper's Magazine*, May 1948) seeks to account for the "magical function" of the kind of detective story he enjoyed. At the heart of Auden's study lies the idea that the society, which is the site of the crime in the story, exists, or because of its closed nature appears to exist, in a state of innocent grace. The job of the detective is to restore the state of grace when it has been disrupted by murder, the only crime that is both an offense against God and an offense against society. Following upon this prescriptive proposition are the structural specifics that the murderer must be a demonic rebel and the detective ought to be either an official agent of the ethical or an exceptional person who is in a state of grace, a person such as Sherlock *Holmes.

Explicitly, then, the detective story is, and ought to be by Auden's advice and preference, a fantasy of restoration to a state of *innocence driven by readers' real feelings of a *guilt of unknown origins.

Today critics lack the temerity, and the sense of necessity, to sift the enormous production of crime and mystery literature to infer a single recipe for success for presentation in a didactic essay. Prescriptive theory endures, however, as a subtext for weekly book reviewers. It may be unexpressed, but whenever authors are chided for implausibility in their plots or for misleading their readers, prescriptive theory has its vestigial effect.

[*See also* Formula: Character *and* Plot; Theory: Descriptive Theory.]

—John M. Reilly

"Thinking Machine, The." *See* Van Dusen, Professor Augustus S. F. X.

THOMPSON, JIM (James Myers) (1906–1977). Born in Oklahoma, the recipient of a B.A. from the University of Nebraska, Thompson held jobs as both a blue-collar oil well worker—providing realistic cultural detail for his fiction—and a more-or-less white-collar position in the Federal Writers Project in Oklahoma during the 1930s. After this apprenticeship he became a prolific author of paperback original novels, beginning with *Now and on Earth* (1942).

Thompson shows the darkest side of *fiction noir by using unreliable narrators and protagonists whose mental state constantly verges toward and often enters psychosis. *The Killer Inside Me* (1952) is deservedly his most famous dark descent. Deputy Lou Ford, the psychopathic narrator, pretends to be a simpleminded hick but is actually a cunning killer responsible for the *murders he is supposedly investigating. Through masterful craft the narration deludes the reader, just as Ford's character fools the townspeople of Central City.

The presentation of madness as the norm is characteristic of Thompson's best works. These include *Pop. 1280* (1964), a humorous reversal of *The Killer Inside Me*; *The Grifters* (1963), which shows the training of a young *con artist by a "loving" mother; and *After Dark, My Sweet* (1955). The cumulative effect of the view of reality Thompson proffers in these works is portrayal of a world of "sickness."

Nowhere is the overwhelming sickness more prevalent than in *Savage Night* (1953), the story of a diminutive hit man Charlie "Little" Bigger who falls in love with the woman sent to spy on him by the man who hired him. Isolated in a secluded house, the would-be lovers become increasingly mad. Bigger hides in the basement where Ruthie attacks and chops him up with an ax. The dismembered Bigger crawls about the basement and meets Death, who "smelled good."

Thompson's works have undergone varying treatments in the films that have added to his reputation. *The Getaway* (1959) has had its roughness smoothed twice for the screen, while *After Dark, My Sweet*, *The Grifters*, and *Pop. 1280* have been stylishly handled on film. Thompson himself worked briefly in films, receiving screen credit on Stanley Kubrick's *Paths of Glory*.

[*See also* Deviance; Violence.]

—James L. Traylor *and* Max Allan Collins

Thorndyke, Dr. John, the creation of R. Austin *Freeman, surveys crimes and criminals from his residence at 5A King's Bench Walk in London's Inner Temple, with a detached, analytical eye. A man of many talents—lawyer, forensic scientist, authority in subjects as diverse as Egyptology, archaeology, ophthalmology, criminal jurisprudence, and botany—Thorndyke is commonly acknowledged as the first and greatest medicolegal deective of all time. His intrepid assistants are aide and chronicler Christopher Jervis and butler and jack-of-all-trades Nathaniel Polton.

Of Thorndyke's past and personal life Freeman offers us relatively little, save that he was born on 4 July 1870, educated at the medical school of St. Margaret's Hospital, *London, where he later became professor of medical jurisprudence, and remained a bachelor all his life. Freeman noted that the character's professional pursuits had a real-life inspiration, Dr. Alfred Swaine Taylor, considered to be the father of medical jurisprudence. His first case was *The Mystery of 31, New Inn*, depicted in a novel written around 1905 but not published until 1912. His first appearance in print was *The Red Thumb Mark* (1907), a mystery novel whose solution revolved around the possibilities of fingerprint fabrication, a *plot device that Freeman used subsequently in "The Old Lag" (*The Singing Bone*, 1912) and the novel *The Cat's Eye* (1923). English stories appeared in rapid succession in *Pearson's* magazine in 1908–9 and were collected in book form in *John Thorndyke's Cases* in 1909.

It was about this time that Thorndyke's "The Case of Oscar Brodski" (*Pearson's*, 1910) introduced an entirely new form of detective story, in which the reader is aware from the start of the secret of the crime. "Here, the usual conditions are reversed," explained author Freeman; "the reader knows everything, and the detective knows nothing, and the interest focuses on the unexpected significance of trivial circumstances." In Freeman's *inverted detective story, the first part is typically narrated in the third person and the second is related by Jervis. Additional inverted tales appeared in the seminal collection *The Singing Bone* (1912). The novels *The Shadow of the Wolf* (1925) and *Mr. Pottermack's Oversight* (1930) are also in this form.

Throughout the 1920s Thorndyke stories appeared in, successively, *Dr. Thorndyke's Case Book* (1923; *The Blue Scarab*), *The Puzzle Lock* (1925), and *The Magic Casket* (1927). In 1929 an omnibus volume of thirty-seven stories was published in England, *The Famous Cases of Dr. Thorndyke*. The American edition, entitled *The Dr. Thorndyke Omnibus* (1932), contained one more story. For the remainder of his life Freeman produced no more Thorndyke short stories but featured him in several more novels, including *Mr. Pottermack's Oversight* (1930), *Dr. Thorndyke Intervenes* (1933), *The Penrose Mystery* (1936), *The Stoneware Monkey* (1938), and *The Jacob Street Mystery*

(1942; *The Unconscious Witness*), his last case. In all, the good doctor appeared in twenty-one novels and forty short stories.

[*See also* Forensic Pathologist, Medical Milieu; Medical Sleuth; Scientific Sleuth.]

• R. Austin Freeman, "The Art of the Detective Story," in *The Art of the Mystery Story: A Collection of Critical Essays*, ed. Howard Haycraft (1946). Norman Donaldson, *In Search of Dr. Thorndyke* (1971). E. F. Bleiler, introduction to *The Stoneware Monkey and The Penrose Mystery* (1973).

—John C. Tibbetts

THREATENING CHARACTERS. *See* Menacing Characters.

THRILLER. *This entry is divided into three parts.*

Introduction
Action Thriller
Psychological Thriller

INTRODUCTION

"Thriller" entered British usage in the final quarter of the nineteenth century in reference to stories of heroic adventure set in criminal situations. In their *plots of contest, thrillers bore a relationship to *heroic romance, their rendition of sinister villains and *atmosphere indicated their kinship to the *Gothic novel, and their use of criminal matter and lowlife detail classed them with the popular police memoirs of the time. The type of writing "thriller" denominates has American membership through authors such as Mickey *Spillane and Michael *Shayne, as well as famed British practitioners such as John *Buchan, Ian *Fleming, Len *Deighton, Dick *Francis, and John *le Carré. There is more looseness than definitiveness with the application of "thriller," so that at times it seems to include intriguing tales of singular detectives along with narratives about espionage, terrorism, and corporate scheming. Nevertheless, the term has value for distinguishing a durable subtype of crime and mystery writing. In *Thrillers: Genesis and Structure of a Popular Genre* (1978) Jerry Palmer describes this subtype as a structure dominated by the presence of a competitively individualistic protagonist engaged in suspenseful struggle against a conspiracy, a pattern Palmer explains as derivative from the field of ideology that has prevailed in Great Britain and the United States since the rise of industrialism. For Ralph Harper, in *The World of the Thriller* (1969), it is a literature of crisis and departure from normality that engages its audience because the hunt and chase of the plot, with their attendant fear of peril and relief in escaping it, correspond to life situations. By the reckoning of both critics the requisites for a thriller are both an overt plot of action and a latent representation of common psychology.

The origin of the modern thriller lies in the world of pulp fiction. Known in Great Britain variously as bloods, shockers, and *penny dreadfuls, the action stories mass produced for an adolescent male audience featured accounts of highwaymen, pirates, adventurers, and such champions of right against criminal wrong as Sexton Blake. In the United States, where similar publications were known as *dime novels and, later, simply as pulps, the mass market for boys and young men could draw from legends of the frontier, the Wild West, and the active pursuit of crime by dauntless figures such as Nick *Carter.

The nature of narratives in its pulp sources indicates that the thriller is rooted in a variety of magical of fantasy resolutions. When stories of action and triumph in a Manichaean world of good and bad are transformed into narratives for grown-up audiences, they direct their magic against the anxieties that beset their time; thus, fears of anarchy are contained in such works by Edgar *Wallace as *The Four Just Men* (1905), and a buildup of the German naval forces is reflected in Erskine *Childers's *The Riddle of the Sands* (1903). Although they claim to be memoirs, the writings attributed to Allan Pinkerton, founder of the famed detective agency, are the American counterparts to British thrillers about domestic unrest. The application of thriller magic may be seen continuing in the abundance of fiction about the Cold War written by *Fleming, Deighton, Charles McCarry and others. For continuation of the tradition now that the Cold War has concluded, one may turn to the novels of John *le Carré, who has turned the attention of the thriller to the dangers facing the new world order from arms smuggling and small-scale nationalist insurrections.

[See also Adventure Story: Heroism; Terrorism and the Terrorist Procedural; Villains and Villainy.]

—John M. Reilly *and* Clive Bloom

ACTION THRILLER

The thriller may be said to share many of its features with other action genres such as the western novel, which so influenced Arthur Conan *Doyle's "A Study in Scarlet" (*Beeton's Christmas Annual*, 1887); the historical romance-adventures of Baroness *Orczy, P. C. Wren, and A. E. W. *Mason; and the crime novelettes, or American dime adventures, that influenced John *Buchan. Such writing emphasized episodic narrative (good for serialization), teleological and purposive movement (the unveiling of secrets and the unmasking of villains), outward appearance and the avoidance of psychology (character is expressed only in action), elevation of the central character over *plot, heightened realism in which the possible replaces the probable. The action thriller per se adds to these elements the confluence of criminality and espionage, a recurring theme from Edgar *Wallace's *The Four Just Men* to Frederick Forsyth's opening chapters in *The Fourth Protocol* (1983).

Criminality and espionage differentiate the action thriller from the novel of action. In the former genre the individual is pitted against criminal or governmental forces beyond his or her understanding or control, and the central figure has to prove credibile in a world where trust is impossible. Such a universe is deeply and structurally paranoid and is predicated on doubt. Unlike the detective genre, whose elements are adapted in thrillers, such stories rarely end with the expulsion of the culprit once and for all and very often have a "detective" figure who is himself the hunted. In action thrillers the individual, as citizen, is called into being specifically by his or her culpability in a world dominated by conspiracy. It is not surprising that the twentieth century is both the age of mass democracy and the age of secrecy, nor that the genre that deals with this political contradiction takes as its subject matter such organizations as *MI5 and MI6; the *CIA and *FBI; SMERSH, BOSS, and MOSSAD; the Triads; the Mafia and the Mob; and the fictional SPECTRE nor that from this stems the excitement of reading about the clandestine, code breaking, political assassination, unholy alliances, drug barons, spymasters, exotic locations, and the corridors of political power. Such subject matter is ironically both escapist and realist.

Most typical of all action thrillers remains the spy thriller, which takes as its raison d'être the conspiratorial alliance between politics and crime, and which has mirrored and exaggerated the contemporary worlds of both diplomacy and domestic political tension. Some, such as Ian *Fleming's *Dr No* (1958), take their cue from the imperial adventure; others, such as Robert Harling's *The Enormous Shadow* (1955) and Frederick Forsyth's *The Fourth Protocol*, from political journalism and current affairs. With the end of the Cold War, writers have turned to "possible" scenarios—events that could have occurred, as in Robert Harris's *Fatherland* (1992), which allies the political thriller with Nazi conspiracy thrillers such as Ira Levin's *The Boys from Brazil* (1976). Thus the thriller takes a new direction.

[See also Adventure Story: Escapism; Heroism; Menacing Characters; Spy Fiction.]

—John M. Reilly

PSYCHOLOGICAL THRILLER

Since its inception with the writings of Freud in the 1900s it has been axiomatic of psychoanalytic criticism that fiction must be studied in terms of characters' psychology. In fact, the influence of psychoanalysis in the twentieth century is such that it is difficult to discuss the bulk of thrillers without recourse to psychological observations even when they are not strictly speaking psychoanalytic, that is, beholden to Freud's theories. What makes the thriller and crime genre so suitable for psychology as it might be seen in many schools of thought is that constantly deals with people embroiled in conspiracies or extreme situations. If an extreme situation such as *pursuit is central to many psychological thrillers, then it could be argued—as it is in Stephen Knight's *Form and Ideology in Crime Fiction* (1980)—that the first thriller is a psychological one, William *Godwin's *Things as They Are; or the Adventures of Caleb Williams* (1794). Equally, the traditional view of Edgar Allan *Poe's paternity of detective fiction might hold for a theory of the origins of the psychological thriller: Here ratiocination is the process that probes the vagaries of a disrupted world, often involving attempts to understand the *motives and reasoning of criminals. Clearly, the latter applies to a great many succeeding mystery writers through Arthur Conan *Doyle and Agatha *Christie; however, the psychological thriller is characterized by the foregrounding of psychology.

A subgenre associated with psychology is the spy thriller. The chases that occur in the novels of John *Buchan, particularly *The Thirty-nine Steps* (1915), and in the "entertainments" of Graham *Greene, keep the hero in peril. However, as the spy thriller developed through the Cold War, adventure and pursuit were not necessarily integral to the depiction of psychological states.

Another subgenre that allows for psychological complexity is the hard-boiled story, which, for Raymond *Chandler and others, emphasized motive in mystery fiction. Even a British imitator of the hard-boiled style, James Hadley *Chase, could cause a furor with his ersatz psychological *No Orchids for Miss Blandish* (1939; *The Villain and the Virgin*), a study of sadism that was actually a thinly veiled reworking of William Faulker's *Sanctuary* (1931). By far the most eminent practitioner of hard-boiled conventions who also embraced an acute understanding of psychology was Ross *Macdonald. In his Lew *Archer novels, beginning with *The Moving Target* (1949), he examines the role of family constellations in human destiny, presenting characters motivated by uncertain parentage in *The Drowning Pool* (1950), the trauma of a father's death in *The Barbarous Coast* (1956), an oedipal configuration in *The Chill* (1964), and an Electra complex in *The Zebra-Striped Hearse* (1962).

In virtually all of Macdonald's novels the psychological dynamic is a result of the past coming home to roost in the present. This is also true in the fiction of one of the most successful recent exponents of the psychological thriller, Ruth *Rendell, who has even described the vicissitudes of characters caught up in circumstances where no crime has been committed, as is the case in *Vanity Dies Hard* (1966; *In Sickness and in Health*). When Rendell has written as Barbara Vine, she has concentrated almost exclusively on psychology, rather than detection. If Vine's *A Dark Adapted Eye* (1986) is to be thought of as a *whydunit, then *Asta's Book* (1993) can only be considered a "what happened?" In the latter, a complex tale told through Asta's diary from 1905 to 1967 and Anne Eastbrook's present-day narrative reveals a crime that takes place in a sequence parallel to the diary events of 1905, but retold some years later in the account of a famous trial. The traditional *clues of detective fiction are subtly placed at various junctures in the narrative as a whole in such a way as to require a symptomatic reading of both the diary and the characters before the crime can be revealed.

One special area of character where psychology is paramount is in the depiction of *antiheroes. Patricia *Highsmith's first novel, *Strangers on a Train* (1950) inaugurated an oeuvre characterized by its acute observation of human motives. Since then, Highsmith has gained recognition for a series of novels that coolly examine the mind of a murderer, Tom Ripley. In this way, perhaps, there is a link between her fiction and what some consider the pinnacle of psychological thrillers in the last ten years, the serial killer subgenre. The detailed depictions of the crimes and motivations of characters such as Dr. Hannibal Lecter in Thomas Harris's *Red Dragon* (1981; *Manhunter*) and *The Silence of the Lambs* (1988) represent one logical extension of the antihero into abnormal psychology, but this takes place only insofar as the knowledge of professionals (for example, profilers) is crucial to the resolution of an extreme or threatening situation. By far the most skillful examples of such plotting—even while they call for a considerable suspension of disbelief—are to be found in the fiction of Patricia D. Cornwell. In her first three novels, a serial killer finally meets his nemesis after targetting the chief medical examiner, Dr. Kay Scarpetta. These are no less powerful than her fourth novel, *Cruel and Unusual* (1993), in which this does not happen; instead, there is a search for a killer who has assumed the identity of a recently executed murderer. The central threatening situation consists of the way in which, rather than attempting to straightforwardly murder her, the participants in the conspiracy that conceals the identity of the serial killer seek to thoroughly discredit and ultimately eradicate Scarpetta. Cornwell's novels are therefore particularly distinguished by the way they depict the effect that an abnormal psychology has on the (relatively) normal psychologies involved in the investigation.

In general, the convoluted dynamics of character found throughout the history of the psychological thriller serve as a powerful antidote to portrayals of the crime and mystery genre as mere *puzzle solving.

[*See also* Had-I-But-Known; Menacing Characters; Terror.]

—Paul Cobley

Tibbs, Virgil. Author John Dudley Ball created African American detective Virgil Tibbs in 1965's *In the Heat of the Night*, the first of a Tibbs series. The violent-crimes specialist at the Pasadena, California, police department, Tibbs is about thirty years old throughout the series. He is a slender and extremely well dressed, well read, and physically fit, an expert in karate and other martial arts.

The Tibbs novels are *whodunits rather than typical *police procedurals, since they emphasize the thinking rather than the procedure of the hero. His deductions are based on observation of minute detail and small slips of speech. His approach is therefore Sherlockian, and the *Great Detective is often referred to in the series.

His race can create antagonism in *suspects and *witnesses, particularly in his debut book. While he can turn this to his advantage in interrogation, he mostly confronts *racism with a prodigious patience. It is his politeness and correctness that win the trust of witnesses.

In 1967, *In the Heat of the Night* was adapted into an Academy Award-winning film starring Sidney Poitier as a Tibbs with an angrier edge. The real film is mentioned in succeeding novels, and the fictional Tibbs is embarrassed by it. In *The Eyes of Buddha* (1976), Tibbs is told that he does not look like Sidney Poitier, the film *In the Heat of the Night* is mentioned as a missing woman's favorite, and, when undercover, Tibbs's identity is compromised because people have seen the film. His formidable patience almost withers at these times.

[*See also* African American Sleuth; Prejudice.]

—Dana Bisbee

TIME. *See* Alibi; Alibi, Unbreakable; "Time Is of the Essence."

"TIME IS OF THE ESSENCE." A preoccupation with time is at the heart of detective fiction, much of which is a kind of contest between author and reader. For the contest to be worthwhile, an explanation of the mystery must be supplied at or near the end, covering *means, motive, and opportunity, and this explanation must be clearly shown to work. *Ingenuity in *motive and means has distinguished much crime fiction, but all culprits must have the opportunity to commit their crimes or, in other words, have the time to do them, while their authors have to attempt to disguise that opportunity. Hence the importance in crime fiction of references to time. The most important use of time is to construct an *alibi.

Characters frequently attempt to use mechanical devices to create the appearance that the *victim is still alive at a crucial period. The simplest device is to alter a clock whose time an investigator (and the reader) treats as standard, as in Anthony Armstrong's 1933 play, *Ten Minute Alibi*, adapted as a novel by Armstrong with Herbert Shaw a year later. If the clock has chimes, the exercise must be carried out with care or the ruse is revealed, as was the case in Armstrong's play and novel. A dictaphone is used in Agatha *Christie's *The Murder of Roger Ackroyd* (1926) to create an alibi; a gramophone is used in S. S. *Van Dine's *The Canary Murder Case* (1927). Unfortunately, the dictaphone/gramophone trick can only be used a few times before it becomes outworn; as early as 1931 Dorothy L. *Sayers advised that the gramophone be given a rest.

Another way of altering time is to manipulate the means of transportation to or from the scene of the crime. The past master of this is Freeman Wills *Crofts, a former railway engineer who used railway timetables in his first two novels, *The Cask* (1920) and *The Ponson Case* (1921). Other authors followed suit, especially Sayers in *The Five Red Herrings* (1931; *Suspicious Characters*), who backs up the railway misdirection with an ingenious ticket forgery derived from J. J. Connington's *The Two Tickets Puzzle* (1930). In *Mystery in the Channel* (1931; *Mystery in the English Channel*) Crofts fashions an alibi by finding a way in which a motorboat can exceed its (established) designed speed. In *Sir John Magill's Last Journey* (1930) he combines railways and a motorboat, whereas in *Fatal Venture* (1939; *Tragedy in the Hollow*) a number of camera snapshots that appear to show a *suspect to be miles away at the critical time are proved to be clever fakes. In some instances *impersonation of the victim either conceals a crime or confuses the facts of the crime by changing the apparent time of the *murder. A young secretary dresses as his employee and irritates his voice to conceal his death for at least a few hours in E. C. *Bentley's *Trent's Last Case* (1913; *The Woman in Black*). An old woman appears to live on as an invalid under the care of her niece and her husband in Barbara Neely's *Blanche on the Lam* (1992).

The author may persuade the reader that the murder was committed at an earlier or later time than is apparent and generally accepted. Many of John Dickson *Carr/Carter Dickson's *locked room mysteries or *impossible crimes have their basis in this technique, including *The Three Coffins* (1935; *The Hollow Man*) and *The Crooked Hinge* (1938). An early French example, much admired by Carr, is Gaston Leroux's *The Mystery of the Yellow Room* (1908). This trick does not need a locked room or impossible situation, as Christie showed in *Evil Under the Sun* (1941) and *Appointment with Death* (1938) and Ngaio *Marsh demonstrated in *Death at the Bar* (1940). An unexpected complication may produce an "accidental" alibi. In Sayers's *Have His Carcase* (1932), a bleeding body is discovered on a beach; the time of the murder is placed immediately before the discovery. All suspects have an alibi for that time and are thus eliminated until the victim is proved to be a hemophiliac. In A. E. W. *Mason's *The House of the Arrow* (1924), a witness does not realize she is looking at a clock through a mirror and unwittingly gives the police, and the reader, the wrong time for a murder.

In the most common type of alibi a confederate swears untruthfully that a suspect was elsewhere at the material time, as in Sayers's *Unnatural Death* (1927; *The Dawson Pedigree*), which can lead to a second murder.

The emphasis on the timing of the murder has lead to an overall emphasis on time. Detectives work up timetables of events surrounding the crime, the postmark on a letter is carefully noted, and the hour of retiring for the evening is an essential detail. When Sherlock *Holmes invites Dr. John H. *Watson to join him in "The Boscombe Valley Mystery" (*Strand*, Oct. 1891) advising him to "leave Paddington by the 11:15," he is setting in motion a type of story in which the ordinary details of daily life acquire significance while giving texture to the narrative.

[*See also* Alibi, Unbreakable; Clues, Famous; Craft of Crime and Mystery Writing, The; Railway Milieu; Red Herrings; Sleight of Hand.]

• John Dickson Carr, *The Three Coffins* (1935; *The Hollow Man*), especially Chapter 17. H. R. F. Keating, "Freeman Wills Crofts" in *CADS* 3 (Apr. 1986): 3–5. Philip L. Scowcroft, "Transportation Themes in the Detective Fiction of Freeman Wills Crofts in *CADS* 25 (Mar. 1995): 19–22.

—Philip Scowcroft

TIMETABLES. *See* Alibi; Alibi, Unbreakable; Railway Milieu; "Time Is of the Essence."

TITLES AND TITLING. In broad terms, the nineteenth-century novel in English encompassed the history of a life or a locale, which its title reflected. In the late nineteenth century titles become more symbolic, and in the 1920s, more literary. Detective fiction has tended to follow this descriptive-symbolic-allusive progression. Edgar Allan *Poe's "The Murders in the Rue Morgue" (*Graham's Lady's and Gentleman's Magazine*, Apr. 1841) and Émile *Gaboriau's *Monsieur Lecoq* (1880) are followed by Arthur Conan *Doyle's *A Study in Scarlet* (*Beeton's Christmas Annual*, 1887), though Doyle's titles are more often traditionally descriptive, like Poe's. With the 1920s, allusive titles become predominant (H. C. *McNeile's *The Female of* *the Species*, 1928; Agatha *Christie's *Evil Under the Sun*, 1941). Contemporary writers make extensive use of quotations: Amanda *Cross's *A Trap for Fools* (1989), Robert B. *Parker's *Mortal Stakes* (1975), and P. D. *James's *A Taste for Death* (1986) provide examples. Elizabethan and Jacobean drama have supplied myriad titles: From William *Shakespeare's *Hamlet* come Rex *Stout's *Some Buried Caesar* (1939) and Margery *Allingham's *Look to the Lady* (1931; *The Gyrth Chalice Mystery*); from Shakespeare's *Macbeth*, Ellery *Queen's *Double, Double* (1950; *The Case of the Seven Murders*) and Ruth *Rendell's *To Fear a Painted Devil* (1965). Other titles refer to more recent works. Raymond *Chandler's *The Lady in the Lake* (1943) pits the romanticism of Sir Walter Scott's ballad against Philip *Marlowe's decadent California, underscored by the substitution of "in" for "of." Peter *Lovesey's *Swing, Swing, Together* (1976) also sets an idealistic past, connoted by the Eton boating song, against a sordid present.

There is much that is hackneyed about mystery titles; Allen Hubin's *The Bibliography of Crime Fiction 1749–1980* (1984) lists nearly two thousand titles beginning with the word "death," and more than two thousand with the word "murder," making them instantly identifiable to mystery readers browsing in bookstores. Of unknown number are clichés that have been wittily altered: Craig *Rice's *Having Wonderful Crime* (1943) or J. R. Macdonald's *The Way Some People Die* (1951). Or the clichés are left as they are, with the context casting a sinister tone, such as Christianna *Brand's *Suddenly at His Residence* (1947; *The Crooked Wreath*) and John Dickson *Carr's *Till Death Do Us Part* (1944). Another fruitful source for titles is the *nursery rhyme. Christie's titles include several examples, such as *Five Little Pigs* (1943; *Murder in Retrospect*). Perhaps the most challenging device for a title is a significant *clue, as in Christie's *Why Didn't They Ask Evans?* (1934; *The Boomerang Clue*) and Miriam Allen De Ford's "Something to Do with Figures" (*EQMM*, Mar. 1945).

One of the most popular features of detective fiction is the reassuring presence of a reliable, highly intelligent, usually likable protagonist—the series character; a serial title offers the reader a similar security. The obvious disadvantage in this form is its artificiality, and the obvious advantage, its audience appeal. One of the most famous as well as one of the earliest serial titles is that used for the Philo *Vance series by S. S. *Van Dine, a dozen titles (with one exception) following the pattern "The (six-letter word) Murder Case," beginning with *The Benson Murder Case* (1926). Queen followed suit with nine in a similar vein: "The (adjective) (noun) Case," beginning with *The Roman Hat Mystery* (1929). Fulton Oursler, determined to lead, at least alphabetically, adopted the pseudonym of Anthony Abbot and wrote six novels beginning with the phrase "About the Murder of," beginning with *About the Murder of Geraldine Foster* (*1930*; *The Murder of Geraldine Foster*). Patrick Quentin wrote six novels using the phrase "A Puzzle for," the last being *A Puzzle for Pilgrims* (1947; *The Fate of the Immodest Blonde*). Sue *Grafton has titled a series alphabetically, beginning with with *A Is for Alibi* (1982). In this endeavor she was preceded by Lawrence *Treat, who wrote in the 1940s—without regard to alphabetical order and including two with the letter *H*—ten novels following the pattern of *B as in Banshee* (1940; *Wail for the Corpses*). Harry Kemelman, with more modest goals, began a series with *Friday the Rabbi Slept Late* (1964). Grafton's father, C. W. Grafton, made a modest step in the direction of the serial title with *The Rat Began to Gnaw the Rope* (1943) and *The Rope Began to Hang the Butcher* (1944). Lillian Jackson Braun's series, beginning with *The Cat Who Could Read Backwards* (1966), theoretically has no limit. Other authors signal the serial nature of their works through motifs, the commonest of which may be color, as in John D. *MacDonald's Travis *McGee novels, beginning with *A Flash of Green* (1962), or Cornell *Woolrich's six novels with "black" in their titles, beginning with *The Bride Wore Black* (1940; *Beware the Lady*). Some writers provide continuity by using the series character's name in the titles. G. K. *Chesterton published five such collections of stories, starting with *The Innocence of Father Brown* (1911). A striking example is Joyce *Porter's Wilfred *Dover series, beginning with *Dover One* (1964) and consisting of eleven novels and three patterns for the titles.

Mystery novels are subject to a distinctive problem: title changes. Most of the changes are from East to West, perhaps because the British public, long exposed to Hollywood, seldom needs an explanation of American idiom. Thus Cyril *Hare's *That Yew Tree's Shade* (1954) becomes *Death Walks the Woods* in the United States, and Christie's *The Mirror Crack'd from Side to Side* (1962) is shortened to *The Mirror Crack'd*. American publishers seem to have assumed that their readers were unfamiliar with Thomas Gray's "Elegy Written in a Country Church-Yard" and Alfred Tennyson's "The Lady of Shalott." On the other hand, Brand's *London Particular* (1952) called for a literal translation in America to *Fog of Doubt*. Going the other way, Bruno Fischer's *The Bleeding Scissors* (1948) was changed because of its mild profanity (in 1950) to *The Scarlet Scissors*. The title of Quentin's last book, *A Puzzle for Pilgrims* (1947), was changed to *The Fate of the Immodest Blonde* three years later for a mass, and perhaps less modest, market. Though some of the changes are inexplicable, and the practice has become less frequent in recent years, there is no mystery about Christie's *Ten Little Niggers* (1939), changed to *Ten Little Indians* and *And Then There Were None*.

[See also Allusion, Literary.]

• Sutherland Scott, "Titles, Settings and Locales," in *Blood in Their Ink: The March of the Modern Mystery Novel* (1953).

—Barrie Hayne

"Toff, The." *See* Adventurer and Adventuress.

TOWER OF LONDON, THE. Begun by William the Conqueror soon after the Norman Conquest of 1066 as a fortress to dominate the city of *London, the central keep or stone tower, which gives the building its name, was constructed inside a corner of the city wall but not completed until some time after 1086. Successive medieval monarchs strengthened the defenses by adding further towers, an inner and outer wall, and a moat to make the tower the chief stronghold of the kingdom. Over the centuries the Tower of London has been by turn a royal residence housing the royal armories, the mint, the public records, the menagerie, the observatory, and the crown jewels, which are still there today. Its reputation as a place of punishment, *murder, and execution continues to fascinate the public.

In the tower chapel of St. Peter ad Vincula lie the bodies of some of those executed by beheading within the privacy of the tower, or on nearby Tower Hill. At least seventy-five persons are known by name to have been beheaded there. Lord Lovat (1747) was the last person to be executed by beheading in England. The tower was once again used as a place of execution in World War I (1914–18), when eleven German spies were executed by firing squad in the outer ward by the Martin Tower. William *Shakespeare's tetralogy of plays the three parts of *Henry VI* and *Richard III*, which completes the cycle, although a recitative of horrible deaths, is a dramatization of historical fact. The conventional image of the tower as a place of detention or execution has carried over into literature including crime and mystery writing; the convention was firmly established by nineteenth-century novelists such as William Harrison Ainsworth in *The Tower of London: A Historical Romance* (1840). In John Dickson *Carr's *The Devil in Velvet*, (1951) set in seventeenth-century Restoration England, the imprisonment brings about the resolution. In Jack Higgins's World War II thriller, *The Eagle Has Flown* (1991), the imprisonment and how to rescue the German is the focus of the story. The novel echoes the real-life detention in 1941 of Rudolf Hess, Hitler's deputy, after his flight to England, when he was temporarily imprisoned in the tower. Unlike the fictional hero, he did not escape.

[*See also* Prisons: British Prisons.]

• John Marriott, *English History in English Fiction* (1940). Keith Hollingsworth, *The Newgate Novels: 1830–1847: Bulwer, Ainsworth, Dickens and Thackeray* (1963). Ben Weinreb and Christopher Hibbert, eds., *The London Encyclopedia* (1983). —Donald Rumbelow

TRAGEDY, DRAMATIC, ELEMENTS OF IN CRIME AND MYSTERY WRITING. The tragedy, a dramatic work that moves with a sense of inevitability toward a disastrous conclusion, has influenced crime and mystery writers, and particularly practitioners of the classic *detective novel, throughout the literary history of the genre. Tragedies written during the Elizabethan and Jacobean periods, especially revenge tragedies and domestic dramas, have been sources for crime writers for everything from *plots and themes to playfully chosen *pseudonyms and titles rich in literary *allusion.

The link between tragic drama and the detective novel is apparent in the confluence of themes and actions that run through both: *family conflicts over money and/or contested *wills, adultery leading to

crimes of passion, the perpetration of acts of *revenge to settle old grievances; revelation of shameful secrets, and exposure by officials and private citizens of those to whom reputation is paramount. Plot devices favored by tragedians and detective novelists may also be similar: Compromising letters and/or *poison pen letters are often used to complicate the plots, poisons and bladed weapons are popular, and the play-within-a-play advances the action. In detective fiction, the play-within-a-play may be literal, as is the case in Michael *Innes's *Hamlet, Revenge!* (1937), in which *murder occurs during a staging of William *Shakespeare's *Hamlet*. The play-within-a-play idea is also frequently employed when the *sleuth stages a reenactment of the crime for dramatic effect that may produce a revelation through its repetition of the circumstances of the crime or inspire a confession from a culprit in the company of *suspects.

Shakespearean scholar Alfred Harbage exemplified the use of elements of drama in his detective novel *Blood Is a Beggar* (1946). He chose the pseudonym Thomas Kyd, taken from the name of the author of *The Spanish Tragedy* (*ca.* 1592), a drama that is considered to be the prototype for subsequent Elizabethan revenge tragedy, of which Christopher Marlowe's *The Jew of Malta* (written *ca.* 1589; published 1633) and Shakespeare's *Titus Andronicus* (1594) and *Hamlet* (*ca.* 1601) are notable examples. Generally set in royal courts, such plays dramatize the conflicts among members of the nobility. Behind facades of normality, intrigue and *corruption flourish, spurred by sibling or political rivalry and the desire for social or financial advancement. Protagonists in such dramas may hold ambiguous positions in society, sometimes due to circumstances of birth. Alienated from society, such characters may execute acts of revenge, often over old grievances. In classic detective fiction, too, the focus is on people leading lives of privilege in *settings like the *country house milieu. Sometimes prodigals return from Australia or other British colonies. Such characters may be black sheep of the family or adventurers; in any case, they are outsiders of questionable social status whose return to the fold is not greeted warmly. These characters can enact vengeance, and sometimes echo the role of classical avenging ghost that has its origins in ancient Roman tragedies by Seneca, and was a staple of early revenge tragedies.

Detective novelists also use elements that were common to Elizabethan domestic tragedy, exemplified in Thomas Heywood's *A Woman Killed with Kindness* (1603) and the anonymously authored *Arden of Feversham* (*ca.* 1590) and *A Yorkshire Tragedy* (1608). Such works looked at the crimes and passions of the English middle *class and employed plots based on actual events often familiar to the audience, concerning adultery and monetary gain as reasons for murder. Their sensational, even titillating, subject matter notwithstanding, these plays conclude not only with exposure and punishment of the guilty, but also with penitence and requests for divine mercy.

Madness, real or feigned, is another issue dealt with in both Elizabethan tragedy and detective fiction. In the latter, in which all must be ultimately explained rationally, apparent madness may figure as a state to be explained, as is the case in many detective novels in which apparent *suicide must be verified or accounted for as *homicide.

Elizabethan drama has been a particularly rich source for titles used by twentieth-century crime writers. P. D. *James uses a statement from John Webster's *The Duchess of Malfi* (*ca.* 1612–14) as the title of her novel *Cover Her Face* (1962), and another of her titles, *The Skull Beneath the Skin* (1982), comes from T. S. Eliot's comment about Webster's achievement in *The Duchess of Malfi*. In *The Skull Beneath the Skin*, James's dialogue is enriched with literary allusions to Christopher Marlowe, Shakespeare, and Webster. Both Ruth Fenisong and Colin *Dexter have books, published in 1953 and 1989, respectively, called *The Wench is Dead*, words originally spoken by Barabas in Marlowe's *The Jew of Malta*. The title of Nicholas *Blake's 1936 novel, *Thou Shell of Death*, is also a phrase spoken by the revenger in Cyril Tourneur's *The Revenger's Tragedy* (1606–7) while looking at a skull. The title of Anne Morice's 1974 novel about *amateur detective-actress Tessa Crichton, *Killing with Kindness*, recall's Heywood's domestic tragedy. A character in Julian *Symons's *Death's Darkest Face* (1990) describes himself as being keen on Elizabethan drama, "Especially when it was really bloodthirsty," and he plays Beduaer in Thomas Otway's Restoration tragedy *Venice Preserv'd* (1682); another character tours in Shakespeare. Symons's title is from *Vortigern and Rowena* (1795), a tragedy by the forger William Henry Ireland, who claimed it was authored by Shakespeare.

The Elizabethan period is also a popular time in which to set *historical mysteries. Crime novels by the pseudonymous Edward Marston, whose name derives from that of the Elizabethan playwright John Marston, are set in that period. For example, in *The Merry Devils* (1990), a production by a *London theater company of *The Merry Devils* (which recalls the 1608 comedy *The Merry Devils of Edmonton*, sometimes attributed to Michael Drayton) is interrupted by a murder that stage manager Nick Bracewell then solves. Leonard Tourney's Matthew Stock books are also Elizabethan mysteries; *The Players' Boy is Dead* (1980) is about a group of itinerant actors.

[See also Resolution and Irresolution.]

• Fredson Bowers, *Elizabethan Revenge Tragedy 1587–1642* (1940). Irving Ribner, *Jacobean Tragedy: The Quest for Moral Order* (1962). Charles A. Hallett and Elaine S. Hallett, *The Revenger's Madness: A Study of Revenge Tragedy Motifs* (1980). Wendy Griswold, *Renaissance Revivals: City Comedy and Revenge Tragedy in the London Theatre, 1576–1980* (1986). Alexander Leggatt, *English Drama: Shakespeare to the Restoration, 1590–1660* (1988). David Lehman, *The Perfect Murder: A Study in Detection* (1989).

—Gerald H. Strauss

TRAINS. See Railway Milieu.

TRANSPORTATION, MODES OF. Ever since Sherlock *Holmes and Dr. John H. *Watson leapt into a hansom cab or onto a train, the trappings of transportation have played a significant role in crime and mystery writing. The genre offers a significant sampling of modes of transportation, from the hansom cabs and trains of the earlier stories, through the cruise ships and motor cars of the Golden Age, to the airplanes and even spaceships in contemporary stories that cross over into *science fiction.

Perhaps no vehicle has so indelibly left its stamp on the genre as the hansom cab, its availability and privacy making it suitable not only for flight and pursuit, but for purposes ranging from discreet conversation, through romance and seduction, to abduction and *murder—as in Fergus Hume's Melbourne-based novel, *The Mystery of a Hansom Cab* (1886).

The hansom cab, named for the English architect Joseph Aloysius Hansom, who in 1834 patented the "Patent Safety Cab," is most memorably associated with the Holmes stories. Holmes and Watson commandeer hansom cabs in many stories, but "The Man with the Twisted Lip" (*The Adventures of Sherlock Holmes*, 1892) contains one of the most detailed descriptions of a cab ride, through a succession of *London streets and three English counties.

Frequently, Holmes's cab conveys him to Waterloo, Charing Cross, Paddington, or Victoria stations, where he is just in time to catch the train he had looked up in his *Bradshaw*. Usually, Holmes and Watson are ensconced in the privacy of a first-class compartment, a fine setting for rumination or discussion of a case, as in "The Boscombe Valley Mystery" (*Strand*, Oct. 1891), "The Adventure of the Copper Beeches" (*Strand*, June 1892), or "Silver Blaze" (*Strand*, Dec. 1892). Holmes tries to keep a step ahead of Professor James Moriarty in a complicated cab, train, and boat-train pursuit to the Continent in "The Final Problem" (*Strand*, Dec. 1893), whereas a suburban commuter line is featured in "The Adventure of the Norwood Builder" (*The Return of Sherlock Holmes*, 1905). The London underground appears in several stories, notably "The Adventure of the Bruce-Partington Plans" (*Strand*, Dec. 1908), where the exact disposition of tracks, points, and tunnel provides clues to the mystery. Another turn-of-the-century icon, the bicycle, commonly used by village constables, appears in a number of Holmes stories, and "His Last Bow" (*Strand*, Dec. 1917) prominently features the motor car.

Trains, and especially those private first-class compartments, continue as prominent settings throughout the history of the genre (See Railway Milieu), as in Arthur Griffiths's *The Rome Express* (1896), a period piece with a great deal of fin de siècle Parisian ambience, or H. F. Wood's *The Passenger from Scotland Yard* (1888; *The Night Mail*).

Between the wars, transatlantic luxury liners, cruise ships, yachts, and sailing vessels all became favored venues of the well-to-do, and not surprisingly became favored vehicles for Golden Age mysteries. The isolation and physically complex layout of a great ocean liner made it a floating counterpart of the great country house as a setting for a closed-society mystery, and for some writers, such as Freeman Wills *Crofts and Andrew *Garve, the nautical mystery became something of a specialty. R. Austin *Freeman's "The Fugitive" (chapter 1 of *A Certain Dr.

Thorndyke, 1927) involves intrigue on a Conradesque steamer off the west coast of Africa. Agatha *Christie's uses include *Death on the Nile* (1937; the play version, without Hercule *Poirot, was published as *Murder on the Nile,* 1948); *The Secret Adversary* (1922), concerning the *Lusitania;* and *The Man in the Brown Suit* (1924), set on board a liner bound for South Africa. Crofts presents nautical atmosphere and works in technical details about boating in *Mystery in the Channel* (1931; *Mystery in the English Channel*) and *Found Floating* (1937), in which he offers a detailed description of the cruise ship itself, down to the engine room, and carefully explains the use of landing cards to keep track of who is on and off ship. The *nautical milieu as explored by writers of short stories is showcased in *Murder on Deck: Shipboard and Shoreline Mysteries* (1998), edited by Rosemary Herbert.

After the turn of the century, the motor car became a prominent fixture, notably in the series of stories narrated by the chauffeur of Count Bindo di Farraris, *The Count's Chauffeur* (1907), by William Le Queux, himself a great motoring enthusiast. Cars and car chases subsequently became a staple of *police procedurals. Notable on the British scene has been the Wolseley 6/80, used by the force in the 1950s, while fictional detectives such as Lord Peter *Wimsey, Sir John *Appleby, Gervase *Fen, and Albert *Campion often used tonier cars such as Daimlers, Bentleys, and Lagondas.

Airplanes and airports are prominent in such stories as Crofts's *The 12:30 from Croydon* (1934; *Wilful and Premeditated*), and Christie's *Death in the Clouds* (1935; *Death in the Air*), *Destination Unknown* (1954; *So Many Steps to Death*), and *Passenger to Frankfurt* (1970), but what they effectively convey is the *lack* of *atmosphere and romance of airports and plane travel.

More unusual transportation vehicles are sometimes pivotal, and thrillers featuring elaborate chases may involve the participants in an extraordinary sequence of vehicles of conveyance, as in Michael *Innes's *Operation Pax* (1951; *The Paper Thunderbolt*) or *Appleby Plays Chicken* (1957; *Death on a Quiet Day*), or Christie's *Destination Unknown* (1954; *So Many Steps to Death*). More outré vehicles have included submarines, as in George Alec Effinger's "The Musgrave Version," or spaceships, as in Mark Aronson's "The Adventure of the Second Scarf," a pair of Holmes pastiches in *Sherlock Holmes in Orbit,* edited by Mike Resnick and Martin H. Greenberg (1995).

[*See also* Railway Milieu.]

• Hugh Douglas, "Commuting: An Unscheduled Stop at an Isolated Junction," in *Murder Ink,* ed. Dilys Winn (rev. ed. 1984). Albert J. Menendez, "Murder on the High Seas" and "Murder Rides the Rails," in *The Subject Is Murder/ A Selective Subject Guide to Mystery Fiction* (1986). Philip L. Scowcroft, "Railways and Detective Fiction," *Mystery Readers of America Journal* 2 (June/July 1986): 20–30. Philip L. Scowcroft, "Murder on the Water," *CADS* 5 (Feb. 1987): 30–32. H. R. F. Keating, "Presence of Body," in *The Bedside Companion to Crime* (1991).

—Peter V. Cenci *and* George L. Scheper

TRAVEL MILIEU. The travel milieu offers obvious advantages to the mystery writer: a variety of *settings, with opportunities for descriptive local color; locales that may be disorienting in topography or language; and situations in which the principals are surrounded by strangers. As Agatha *Christie's Miss Jane *Marple observes in *A Caribbean Mystery* (1964), "One really knows so little about the people one meets when one is travelling. . . . I mean—how shall I put it—One only knows, doesn't one, what they choose to tell you about themselves." There's no Somerset House to check up on their stories. Or, as a character puts it in Christianna *Brand's *Tour de Force* (1955), "[O]n holiday, nothing's quite what it seems. People aren't what they seem. . . . Surrounded by people who don't know one. No give-away relatives, no childhood friends, no birth certificantes, no diplomas, no marriage lines. . . ." And, "No police records," adds the inspector.

Thus, "the English abroad" provide a persistent theme for fun and mystification: In adventurous, foreign environments, the English community in the traditional mystery, constitutes a closed society in which foreign elements are always suspect. The postcolonial "simmering stock-pot of the Middle East" provides the backdrop for M. M. Kaye's *Death Walked in Cyprus* (1956), in which a Colonel Blimp type offers his unabashed and unflattering views about foreign places. This "Orientalist" atmosphere is classically purveyed in Christie's *Death on the Nile,* filled with humorous vignettes of the various species of tourist and their different reactions to the artifacts of the Pharoahs; Hercule *Poirot just manages to endure all this, as well as the local vendors and "riffraff" who buzz around the tourists.

Sometimes Christie's device is the "busman's holiday," the detective on vacation, inevitably drawn into solving yet another murder, as happens to Marple in *A Caribbean Mystery,* where life seems all sunshine, sea, and social pleasures but where travelers soon learn that they "cannot be careful enough while abroad." Poirot, too, takes a couple of busman's holidays, although he does not share his creator's love of travel and is a frequent victim of mal de mer. In *Appointment with Death* (1938; also converted into a Poirot-less play of the same title in 1956), set in the Near East, characters testify to "the nervous and mental strain" of travel conditions. Poirot is vacationing at a resort island off the Cornish coast in a novel with a title that serves as a warning, *Evil Under the Sun* (1941).

Notable among the many busman's holiday stories is Dorothy L. *Sayers's *Busman's Honeymoon: A Love Story with Detective Interruptions* (1937; a three-act play of the same title was published the same year), in which the honeymoon of Lord Peter *Wimsey and Harriet *Vane is interrupted by the discovery of a body in the basement of their quaint farmhouse. Another example is Aaron J. Elkins's *Murder in the Queen's Armes* (1985), with anthropologist Gideon Oliver on honeymoon in England. Vastly different in atmosphere is Ellery *Queen's *The Siamese Twin Mystery* (1933), in which Inspector Queen and his son Ellery are vacationing in Tomahawk Valley; it's in the

United States but about as foreign-feeling as Transylvania to the two easterners.

Brand's *Tour de Force* puts the vacationing Inspector Cockrill on the more conventionally high-culture tour of Italy, which eventually leads the usual motley group of tourists to a threateningly piratical island off the coast. Also using the device of the cultural tour in Italy is Ngaio *Marsh's *When in Rome* (1971). Josephine *Tey's contribution to the busman's holiday story is *The Singing Sands* (1952), which begins with an evocative description of the *London night mail train to Scotland; Inspector Alan Grant is on board when a body is discovered in a compartment on his sleeper.

Another travel category involves vacation/holiday mysteries set at resorts or spas, which can range from the ultraposh to the seamier working-class resorts for day-trippers. In the former category is St. Loo, "the Queen of Watering Places" on the Cornish coast, in Christie's *Peril at End House* (1932), where Poirot needs a bit of persuasion to come out of retirement and get involved in the case that comes his way. A seaside hotel replete with a hired gigolo furnishes the setting for Sayers's *Have His Carcase* (1932). At the lower end of the social scale is Breston, the gaudy and tacky setting for *Crime on the Coast* (1954), one of a series of collaborations by members of The *Detection Club (John Dickson *Carr and others), in which a body replaces a wax figure in a Fun Fair haunted house. A similar atmosphere pervades George Bellairs's *The Corpse at the Carnival* (1958), an Inspector Thomas Littlejohn novel set on the Isle of Man and filled with local color descriptions with a Manx accent, from the garish seafront, boardwalk, and nighttime illuminations, to the ruined crofts and homesteads of the interior, and groves and rivers haunted by Manx fairies.

A distinctly American version of the holiday resort setting is Rex *Stout's *Death of a Dude* (1969), in which Nero *Wolfe bestirs his bulk to a Montana ranch. Despite being out of his element, Wolfe successfully adapts his methods and proves to be not at all a "gump." A spoof on the health spa motif is Simon Brett's *Mrs. Pargeter's Pound of Flesh* (1992), in which the widow of a master criminal finds herself at a fat farm run by former criminal associates of her late husband, where, amid such faddish regimens as Dead Sea mud baths, illegal and fatal experiments are being carried out.

Plots based on murder-mystery tours and murder-mystery weekends allow the author to tap into the history of real crime. Two titles by Sharyn McCrumb use the device of a murder-mystery tour. In *Paying the Piper* (1988), a contemporary crime committed in the course of an Edinburgh murder tour becomes the occasion for the murder of two amateur criminologists. *Missing Susan* (1991) devotes the whole plot line to a murder tour of England, ending back at London for a Jack the Ripper segment; at each locale the group and the reader are regaled with true-crime lore, amid a series of unsuccessful attempts to murder one of the participants. A Ripper tour in the centennial anniversary year of the crimes (1988) is the device of Albert Borowitz's *The Jack the Ripper Walking Tour Murder* (1986), as an amateur criminologist on vacation observes a real murder attempt during the tour.

At a further remove from travel associated with the mystery tour and the mystery weekend are the futurist themes of space travel and time travel. Space travel and instantaneous transport through hyperspace provide the galactic setting for Janet Asimov's *Murder at the Galactic Writers' Society* (1995; second in the Isaac's Universe series). Here, supplementing the rules of fair play that govern more conventional mystery novels, are the Laws of Robotics, as laid down originally by Isaac Asimov in his Robot series (including the space mystery *The Caves of Steel*, 1954), and developed in such android thrillers as Philip K. Dick's *Do Androids Dream of Electric Sheep?* (1968), upon which the film *Blade Runner* is based. A policewoman is aboard an intergalactic catamaran in Ian Wallace's *Deathstar Voyage* (1969), yet amid all the futuristic technology her methods are those of conventional detection.

More radical deconstruction of the conventions of the mystery story occur in tales of time travel, such as Douglas Adam's *Dirk Gently's Holistic Detective Agency* (1987), Thomas F. Monteleone's *The Time Connection* (1976), or Jack Finney's cult classic *Time and Again* (1970), listed by *Murder Ink* as one of the five best mysteries of all time. Among the time travel stories in the anthology *Sherlock Holmes in Orbit* (1995), edited by Mike Resnick and Martin K. Greenberg, all the stories in part 3, "Holmes in the Future," involve time travel.

• Simon Reeve, *The Middle East in Crime Fiction: Mysteries, Spy Novels and Thrillers from 1916 to the 1980's* (1989). Eugene Schleh, *Mysteries of Africa* (1991). Richard Maxwell, *The Mysteries of Paris and London* (1992). Nina King, *Crimes of the Scene: a Mystery Novel Guide for the International Traveller* (1997).

—Peter V. Cenci *and* George L. Scheper

TREAT, LAWRENCE, pseudonym of Lawrence Arthur Goldstone (1903–1998). The writer who was to become best known as the author of *police procedurals and *puzzle books under the pseudonym Lawrence Treat was born in *New York City and educated at Dartmouth College and Columbia University. He began his writing career with the novel *Run Far, Run Fast* (1937), penned under the Goldstone name, before using the Treat pseudonym to launch his first four-book series featuring the intuitive criminologist Carl Wayward in 1940. He followed these with a series of police procedurals featuring Lieutenant Bill Decker, Detective Jub Freeman, and Detective (later Lieutenant still later Police Officer) Mitch Taylor. The capable Decker administers the NYPD's Homicide Department, Freeman is a technical wizard, and Taylor is a fallible character whose developing greed and involvement in graft lead to his being demoted and removed from the NYPD in *The Big Shot* (1951). Long before Sue *Grafton used the device to advantage, Treat was known for titling his works after alphabet letters. Many of these were short stories. His "H as in Homicide" (*Ellery Queen's Mystery Magazine*, 1964), for example, won an Edgar Award for best short story of the year. Treat's puzzle books for adults and children include *Crime and Puzzlement: Twenty-Four Solve-Them-Yourself Mysteries* (1981–88) and *You're the Detective!* (1983).

—Richard Bleiler

TRUE CRIME. The true crime literary genre generally takes the form of nonfiction accounts of the dark and often deadly deeds perpetrated by human beings upon their fellows. While it often deals with the horrific and sensational, it may also explore such aspects of crime as forensics, investigations, and trials. Like crime fiction, true crime offers a mirror of society's values and shifting public attitudes toward crime and criminals. The same characteristic that distinguishes true crime from the crime and mystery genres renders it more compelling: Truth is stranger than fiction and, therefore, more shocking. But a good true crime novel reads like fiction, structured to be a dramatic page-turner, even when the outcome is known.

Considered by some a subgenre of crime and mystery writing, true crime actually predates the invention of the detective novel. As Alex Ross observed in "The Shock of the True" (*New Yorker*, vol. 72, 1996), true crime's roots may date back to Daniel Defoe's 1725 publication of *A True and Genuine Account of the Life and Actions of the Late Jonathan Wild . . .* , a novel that detailed the exploits of a *London criminal genius. The public's appetite for lurid details of criminal mayhem was further whetted by accounts of crime in newspapers, periodicals, and sixpence pamphlets, such as those published by John Fairburn in 1811 describing the horrific Ratcliffe Highway murders. Eugène François *Vidocq's *Memoires de Vidocq* (1828–29; Memoirs of Vidocq; Vidocq the Police Spy) is also cited by many as an early influential work in the true crime genre.

The creation of the modern police force early in the Victorian era introduced the detective character in both real life and literature. The sensational press provided an abundance of gory crime detail ranging from grisly accounts of *murders committed by *London's Jack the Ripper and Chicago's H. H. Holmes in police gazettes and detective magazines at the end of the century to police and detective memoirs fusing fact and fiction by Ned Buntline, Allen Pinkerton, and Thomas F. Byrne. Of their influence on the crime and mystery genre there is ample evidence, beginning with Edgar Allan *Poe who based "The Mystery of Marie Roget" (*Snowden's Lady's Companion*, Nov. 1842) on the mysterious death of an actual *New York tobacconist, Mary Rogers, and his character the Chevalier C. Auguste *Dupin on real-life detective George Lippard; Similarly, Julian Hawthorne based his detective creations on the exploits of ace *New York detective Thomas F. Byrne.

True crime continued to provide inspiration for such writers of crime and mystery fiction as Wilkie *Collins, who based *The Moonstone* (1868) on the Constance Kent murder case (1860); Dorothy L. *Sayers, who wrote "The Murder of Julia Wallace" (*London Evening Standard*, 6 Nov. 1934) based on the actual 1931 crime; Erle Stanley *Gardner, whose *The Court of Last Resort* (1952) investigated true cases of convicted murderers; Hillary *Waugh, whose *The* *Missing Man* (1964) was based on the Mary Bennett murder at Yarmouth in 1900; and Raymond *Chandler, whose *The Blue Dahlia* (1976) was based on the famous 1940s murder case. John Dixon Mann's *Forensic Medicine and Toxicology* (1893) proved useful to crime fiction writers in the early Golden Age. And writers found no need to invent monsters when real life provided such appalling specimens as Wisconsin's Edward Gein, on whom Robert Bloch based *Psycho* (1959).

In the grimly fascinating narrative of the Ratcliffe Highway murders in the postscript to his brilliant "On Murder Considered as One of the Fine Arts" (*Selecting Grave and Gay from Writings Published and Unpublished by Thomas De Quincey*, 1854), essayist Thomas De Quincey established the main characteristics of the true crime literary form. The ominous introduction of *evil in the unmasked persona of the vicious murderer into the unsuspecting *innocence of his *victims and their everyday world and his use of real-time narrative make the reader a witness to the actual unseen act.

Truman Capote's 1965 best-seller *In Cold Blood* provides another model. In this work, the victims are made palpably real by means of detailing the minutiae of their life and dreams. The action begins with the unexpected intrusion of violent evil into their everyday world via the villains, whose true nature is concealed by a mask of normalcy. Capote starkly contrasts the ordinariness of everyday life with the horrific nature of the deed as signified in the grim scene of the crime. He also established a best-selling formula focusing on the dramatic reenactment of events moving slowly yet inexorably toward the conclusion; an examination of the criminal psyche, promising to reveal the inner workings of the aberrant mind; and finally, the courtroom spectacle, through which good triumphs over evil, *justice is meted out, and society's moral standards are reasserted. One more hallmark of modern true crime best-sellers is the use of dramatic, ominous, and often alliterative words in their titles: deadly, death, fatal, poison, evil, murder, madness, dreams.

Landmark works include Vincent Bugliosi's *Helter Skelter: A True Story of the Manson Murders* (1974), Ann Rule's *The Stranger Beside Me* (1980), Joseph Wambaugh's *The Onion Field* (1973) and *The Blooding* (1989), Peter Maas's *The Valachi Papers* (1968), Colin Wilson's *A Casebook of Murder* (1969), William Bolitho's *Murder for Profit* (1926), John Dickson Carr's *The Murder of Sir Edmund Godfrey* (1936), Jonathan Goodman's *The Burning of Evelyn Foster* (1977), and *Classic Crimes: A Selection from the Works of William Roughead* (1951).

• LeRoy Lad Panek, *Probable Cause: Crime Fiction in America* (1990). Alex Ross, "The Shock of the True," *New Yorker* 72 (19 Aug. 1996): 70–77. —Patricia Anderson-Boerger

TRUSTED FIGURE AS CRIMINAL. Most long-established societies have within them figures in whom trust and authority is vested by virtue of the positions these persons hold.

Many of the situations around which crime fiction

is centered, particularly in works set in the Golden Age of detective fiction, feature characters who would appear to be utterly reliable. They are often holders of minor public office, the clerically ordained, and members of the judiciary, the police force, and the professions. These are callings once greatly esteemed by the general public. Nearly always male and middle-aged, these incumbents are usually seen to have much to gain by their criminal activities or, conversely, a great deal to lose by being exposed.

Within the framework of both real life and much detective fiction is the unwritten social convention, implicit in the nature of their occupations, that such people are thoroughly trustworthy in every respect. The improbability of having one of these trusted figures as the murderer offers the added advantage to the writer of disarming the early suspicions of the reader. A memorable and utterly unexpected fall from grace by a member of the staff of the British Inland Revenue Service, an occupation notably free from perfidy, takes the reader by surprise in Michael *Gilbert's short story "Mr Portway's Practice" (EQMM, May 1958).

It also follows that the more important or improbable the fictional villain, the more profound will be the shock at the unveiling of his or her lapse from the accepted mores of the society in which the book is set. The murderer in Whose Body (1923) by Dorothy L. *Sayers, a man greatly elevated both professionally and socially, is a good example of this, while the perpetrator of the crime in The Murder of Roger Ackroyd (1926) by Agatha *Christie is similarly a surprise but in two quite different and separate respects. The identity of the murderer in the *medical milieu of The Attending Physician (1980) by R. B. Dominic is carefully concealed by the double entendre of the title.

Few vocations have proved immune in fiction from having murderers within their ranks. Certainly not the Church, which numbers several surprising clerical criminals among the shepherds of its various flocks in The Vicar's Experiments by Anthony Rolls (1932; Clerical Errors) and Julian Callender's A Corpse Too Many (1965).

That of *judge is an even more unexpected role in which to find the culprit but Christie uses this in Ten Little Niggers (1939; Ten Little Indians; And Then There Were None).

Also taking an oath of allegiance and ordinarily not expected to depart from the straight and narrow are policemen. Guilty ones may be found at the high levels of chief constable in The Noose (1930), by Philip *MacDonald, and chief of police in G. K. *Chesterton's "The Secret Garden" in The Innocence of Father Brown (1911), and in a lowly constable in A Blunt Instrument (1938) by Georgette *Heyer. A corrupt policeman appears in Death of a Favorite Girl (1980; The Killing of Katie Steelstock) by Gilbert.

An unusual and graver extension of this breach of the accepted norm is where there is a failure in fealty and the criminal is found to be tied by bonds of *friendship to the *victim. Here, too, natural suspicions are at first disarmed by the sheer unlikelihood of the breaking of this ancient and primitive taboo by

the murderer, as in Slay-Ride (1970) by Dick *Francis. Emma *Lathen combines something of this with an unlikely candidate for crime who is both in a position of trust and not quite friendship in Going for GOLD (1981; Going for the Gold).

The use of the trusted figure as criminal in crime fiction not only changed parameters and added to the uncertainties within the genre but also implied a more subtle approach by the writer, manifested in the progressive moving away from the stereotyped allocation of villainy to a stock character with all the assigned traits associated with culpability.

The seeming probity of the professions has also been used in a different and doubly disconcerting way. These are the cases where the device has been extended still further by the use of the respectability of the suspect's occupation to allay suspicion, only for the reader to find later rather than sooner that the murderer is an impostor. Trusted by virtue of their assumed positions and a medical and religious aura have been criminals in Dr Goodwood's Locum (1951; The Affair of the Substitute Doctor) by John Rhode and Hag's Nook (1933) by John Dickson *Carr.

More recently this "professional indemnity" has become a less useful artifice. The possession of clay feet by some members of most professions has been drawn to the attention of readers in real life, and a more radical view has gathered strength in an altogether less trustful climate.

[See also Stereotypes, Reversals of; Villains and Villainy.]

—Catherine Aird

TRUTH, QUEST FOR. In the first of Edgar Allan *Poe's three detective tales, "The Murders in the Rue Morgue" (Graham's Lady's and Gentlman's Magazine, Apr. 1841), the Chevalier C. Auguste *Dupin finds the culprit of the brutal killing of Mme. l'Espanaye and her daughter, but his interest in the slaughter as an act of loyalty to his acquaintance Adolphe le Bon, unjustly accused, remains a mere narrative expedient to call him into the case. Eventually the assassin turns out to be an ape, an animal, and as such, below any moral judgment. Thus the first detective tale asserts that the genre is not interested in any moral assessment, that its "quest for truth" is limited to the reconstruction of what happened and the perfunctory apprehension of the criminal. Truth matters even less in "The Purloined Letter" (1845; Tales), a battle of wits between very similar characters, Dupin and the Minister D., in which the identity of the letter's thief is known from the very beginning. In "The Mystery of Marie Roget" Snowden's Lady's Companion, Nov. 1842) truth is never proved, as Marie's killer remains a rational assumption, a ghost evoked by Dupin, who identifies truth with solving a puzzling mystery, even at a merely theoretical level. Dupin does not ascribe to the solution, and to the triumph of truth as a consequence of a successful solution. Truth as "good" is elusive because it implies an ethical and speculative level that goes far beyond the entertaining purpose that detective fiction, as Poe conceived it, pursues. This is one of the reasons why detective fiction has been considered a form of escapist (nonmoral and low-brow) fiction.

After Poe, two basic currents can be distinguished in the development of mystery writing, each one with its own specific traits and attitudes toward truth. One is typified by British writers in the traditional form: Rational and intellectual, it is well exemplified by authors such as Arthur Conan *Doyle, R. Austin *Freeman, G. K. *Chesterton, Ronald A. *Knox, Agatha *Christie, and Dorothy L. *Sayers. Like Poe, these and other practitioners believe that truth overlaps with solution, and that finding a solution amounts to reconstructing what happened and to restoring the order broken by the criminal, who is most likely one *evil person acting in a Victorian or post-Victorian Positivistic society that is otherwise healthy and law-abiding.

The other current is the *hard-boiled fiction of the American writers of the 1930s and 1940s: Nonintellectual, adventurous, and popular, it is set not in the idyllic countryside of many British mysteries but in the violent American urban wastelands. The *hard-boiled sleuths created by Dashiell *Hammett and Raymond *Chandler confront evil as an elusive force, deep-rooted in a crass, corrupt society; evil is not an isolated individual but a powerful organization, numbering among its members apparently honest citizens. The shift is from the old-fashioned Positivistic world of the British formula to a modern and realistic one, ridden by uneasiness and relativism. Evil is ambiguous and pervasive, and truth becomes problematic: It can no longer be reduced to a simplistic solution based on a factual reconstruction.

The hard-boiled detective becomes a more human, emotional, and vulnerable character; he is not a genius like Dupin and cannot maintain Dupin's machinelike detachment, but rather fumbles and suffers through the detecting process. In his classic essay "The Simple Art of Murder" (*Atlantic Monthly*, Dec. 1944) Chandler writes: "He must be a complete man and a common man and yet an unusual man. He must be, to use a rather weathered phrase, a man of honor . . . The story is this man's adventure in search of a hidden truth." Honor, adventure, and finally truth are the key to understanding this new kind of detective who, in a lawless and often irrational world, clings to a personal moral code and is willing to risk his life in order not to betray it. Under a cynical mask, he hides a loyal and generous personality; although represented in a realistic, tough environment, the hard-boiled detective thus becomes, again, an ideal character. He cares more about human emotions than laws, about how it could happen than what happened, and is willing to forgive a crime if the desperate criminal had noble reasons for committing it, for example, Moose Malloy in Chandler's *Farewell, My Lovely* (1940). Since he acts and judges according to his own code of conduct, truth and good become closer concepts, but the hidden truth he eventually reconstructs hardly fits with the official police report, for it finds its reasons in the murky, tormented side of the human heart. The investigation turns into an existential process, if not a metaphysical quest reminiscent of Arthurian chivalry's legendary *pursuit of the Holy Grail. The outcome of such a quest is uncertain and often "unsatisfactory," as found in the last line of Hammett's *The Thin Man* (1934), but it is selfless pursuit against all odds and stoic acceptance of possible defeat that turns the hard-boiled detective, as it did the knight, into a romantic hero.

In the recent postmodern mutations of the detective novel by writers such as Jorge Luis Borges, Carlo Emilio Gadda, Alain Robbe-Grillet, Leonardo Sciascia, Patrick Modiano, Umberto Eco, Thomas Pynchon, and Antonio Tabucchi, the metaphysical side of quest for truth has been further emphasized, since these fictions end with either a solution undermining the *rules of the game or no solution at all. Not only can't the facts of "what happened" be reconstructed, but the very quest for truth is often abruptly truncated by an inconclusive final page, leaving all possibilities open. In such works the reader's last image of the detective is that of a vulnerable human being still striving for comprehension: The formulaic genre invented by Poe no longer epitomizes a fictitious triumph of rationality but has been transformed into allusive literature dramatizing the problematic search for knowledge and wisdom.

• Michael Holquist, "Whodunit and Other Questions: Metaphysical Detective Stories in Post-War Fiction," *New Literary History* 3, no. 1 (autumn 1971): 135–56. Steven Marcus, introduction to *The Continental Op* by Dashiell Hammett (1974). Edward Margolies, "The American Detective Thriller and the Idea of Society," in *Dimensions of Detective Fiction*, ed. Larry N. Landrum, Pat Browne, and Ray B. Browne (1976). Stefano Tani, *The Doomed Detective: The Contribution of the Detective Novel to Postmodern American and Italian Fiction* (1984).   —Stefano Tani

TWINS. *See* Red Flags.

221B BAKER STREET. *See* Addresses and Abodes, Famous; Holmes, Sherlock; Watson, Dr. John H.

UNBREAKABLE ALIBI. *See* Alibi, Unbreakable.

UNDERWORLD is a term that refers to organized crime, a world in which crime is a business. In the underworld, *murder is perpetrated for profit, rather than as a result of emotion. The introduction of the underworld into mystery writing is largely a twentieth-century phenomenon, but it has its roots in the novels of Daniel Defoe, exemplified in *The Fortunes and Misfortunes of the Famous Moll Flanders* (1722), in Charles Dickens's *Oliver Twist* (1838), and in some of Arthur Conan *Doyle's Sherlock *Holmes adventures, including *The Valley of Fear* (1915).

The underworld also has roots in the legends of Robin Hood figures such as Jesse James and Billy the Kid, outlaws who foreshadowed the gangsters of modern fiction. *Prohibition (1919–33), which accounted for the phenomenal rise of organized crime in the United States, produced the "bad gangster," best represented in Frank Packard *The Big Shot* (1925) and W. R. Burnett's *Little Caesar (1929)*. At the same time, unskilled immigrant workers banded together in gangs led by "good gangsters" who had their own way of achieving the American dream. Mario Puzo's *The Godfather* (1969) is the best-known example of a good gangster underworld fiction.

With the advent of the "tough tale" in the 1930s, characters based on real racketeers such as Al Capone and John Dillinger made underworld fiction more realistic. Mobsters like these assumed the status of folk heroes, rebels who mocked the *corruption of the system by breaking its laws. Writers also began to draw on real-life events such as the St. Valentine Day's Massacre in Chicago in 1929 and the great train robbery in England in 1963. Later, writers capitalized on rumors of underworld involvement in such events as the Bay of Pigs invasion of Cuba, the assassination of President John F. Kennedy, and the disappearance of Jimmy Hoffa.

The *Great Depression of the 1930s only reinforced the image of the gangster as rebel hero. Underworld stories were served up in such *pulp magazines as *The Feds, Ace G-Man Stories, Public Enemy, G-Men Detective,* and *True Detective Magazine* and its radio spin-off, *True Detective Mysteries.* Radio did its part to draw in the war between the police and their underworld adversaries. In addition to *True Detective,* which dramatized stories from *True Detective Magazine,* there were enormously popular programs such as *Gangbusters* and *The F.B.I. in Peace and War.*

Underworld fiction thrived during the 1930's and 1940's in the works of novelists such as Dashiell *Hammett, Raymond *Chandler, Horace McCoy, W. R. Burnett, and Frank Packard. Hammett, for example, wrote about urban corruption, showing how big business and gangsters were mutually involved in running cities for profit. Both Hammett and Chandler had a great influence on Hollywood at a time when movies like *Little Caesar, Scarface,* and *Public Enemy,* featuring dynamic performances by Edward G. Robinson, Paul Muni, and James Cagney, had audiences cheering the villains instead of the good guys.

In the 1970s, the popularity of *The Godfather* reflected a renewed interest in the antihero gangster and in underworld fiction in general. Like its predecessors in the 1930s, *The Godfather* is both a parody of the free-enterprise system and a tribute to it. Martin Scorsese's 1990 film *GoodFellas* (based on Nicholas Pileggi's *Wiseguy,* 1987, the life of mobster Henry Hill) is indebted to both Burnett and Puzo. Here again, there is a sense that as the fabric of society unravels, family values such as loyalty, honor, and trust can be found only in the disciplined world of organized crime and, most particularly, the Mafia.

In British crime fiction, the underworld is not a major element, although William McIlvanney in *Laidlaw* (1977) owes a debt to Hammett and Chandler in his taste for *hard-boiled sleuths pitted against ruthless underworld forces. For most British writers, however, the use of underworld elements is the exception; for example, Piers Paul Read in *The Train Robbers* (1979) or Jack Higgins in *On Dangerous Ground* (1994). However, it was Ian *Fleming, in his James *Bond *thrillers, who elevated the underworld kingpin to world-class bogeyman. His Blofelds and Goldfingers and Mr. Bigg are the ultimate gangsters, while Bond, a law unto himself, satisfies the taste for a rebel-hero who does whatever it takes to win.

Underworld elements have popped up in the novels of American writers who don't ordinarily deal in such material; for example, Stuart Woods' *L.A. Times* (1993) Sidney Sheldon's *Rage of Angles* (1980), Robin Cook's *Blindsight* (1992), and James Lee Burke's *In the Electric Mist with the Confederate Dead* (1993). There are also underworld elements in John Grisham's *The Firm* (1991) and *The Client* (1993). In fact, the underworld as an element in mystery fiction is in danger of losing its credibility the more it is used to take up the slack in a weak plot.

[*See also* Heroism; Loyalty and Betrayal; Master Criminal; Organized Crime; Villains and Villainy.]

• Michael L. Cook, *Mystery, Detective, and Espionage Magazines* (1983). Gary C. Hoppenstand, *In Search of the Paper Tiger* (1987). Brian Docherty, ed., *American Crime Fiction: Studies in the Genre* (1988). Ian A. Bell and Graham Daldry, eds., *Watching the Detectives: Essays on Crime Fiction* (1990). LeRoy Lad Panek, *Probable Cause: Crime Fiction in America* (1990).
—Thomas Whissen

UNDERWORLD FIGURE. The underworld figure has long provided writers a means of characterizing the environment of crime. The anonymous author of *Richmond; or, Scenes from the Life of a Bow Street Runner* (1827) introduces a sequence of criminal types into the narrative of the picaresque hero's adventures in order to illustrate his aptitude for containing the forces of an *evil *underworld. The vignettes of gang members, burglars, bunco men, and other criminal types in Benjamin P. Eldridge and William B. Watts's *Our Rival—The Rascal, a Faithful Portrayal of the Conflict Between the Criminals of the Age and the Defenders of Society—the Police* (1897) serve to establish a theme of eternal conflict between forces of evil and agents of domestic protection. As tales of crime control migrated from memoirs into the fictional forms of short story and novel, however, underworld figures lost their prominence because the treatment of detection shifted dramatic focus to the methodology for solving crimes and the character of the *sleuth. Since the point of detection stories, notably in the Golden Age versions, was to introduce the *puzzles of crime into the orderly precincts of established society, the image of a vast underworld network was no longer desirable. Underworld figures were eclipsed by criminals of apparently higher repute.

The sea change in crime and mystery writing represented by the appearance of hard-boiled writing provided the opportunity for authors to reinsert underworld figures into their criminal dramas. The radical hard-boiled view of a world fundamentally corrupted by capitalism and its attendant materialistic values naturalized the underworld character as a representative of that world. American *pulp magazine stories such as those featured in *Black Mask* and *Dime Detective* during the 1920s and 1930s often came populated with underworld figures demanding tough responses from the detectives. The underworld figures in these works helped to register their claim to realism. *Prohibition had alerted the public to the existence of organized criminal syndicates engaged in hijacking, *smuggling, *extortion, and bloody turf wars; consequently, the appearance of underworld figures in fiction staked its claim to recording the way crime actually took place.

The greater their power, the grander the aura of glamour surrounding the underworld figure becomes. Not surprisingly, then, the gangster became a hero as well as a villain for fiction. W. R. Burnett's *Little Caesar* (1929) made the underworld figure representative of his time. Burnett's invention of the gangster protagonist, extended by countless repetition of the type in films, eventually turned into grounds for a controlling myth in crime and mystery writing, the myth of the omnipotent Mafia. Mario Puzo's treatment in *The Godfather* (1969) of a family of underworld figures who conduct their business in the manner of a corporation took the myth to its acme. Once again the cinema joined in spreading the image until it became a general impression in popular consciousness.

As the underworld organizations once known simply as "the Mob" became particularized in the Mafia, or one of its related names such as Cosa Nostra, and as its agents—soldiers, counselers, and hit men—became familiar to the public, writers found in them a convenient shorthand for introducing into narrative resonances of social disorder and peril. The appearance of an underworld figure requires little elaboration any longer. His entry into a story becomes sufficient to remind an audience that the specific crime they are reading about has larger implications. In addition, the reputation of organized crime lends immediate credibility to the use of an underworld figure as the expediter of crime. There is no need to plumb for his *motive. He just makes crime happen.

Recent fiction most commonly places its underworld figures in drug traffic. Robert B. Parker's *Double Deuce* (1992) effectively exploits the prevailing image of underworld figures in presenting an entire housing project governed by drug lords. Like other contemporary authors of the urban detective story, such as Carl Hiassen, James Lee Burke, and Richard Hoyt, Parker also uses his underworld characters to explore a relationship to "respectable" society and show generalized complicity in crime.

The works of George V. *Higgins illustrate another use for underworld figures in fiction. In Higgins's novels underworld figures are not heroic. More often than not they are only small-time bunco artists and low-level hirelings. Nor are they used by Higgins as symptoms of social illness. Rather he employs them for the color they give to his mannered comedies by their speech and personality quirks. In that regard the underworld figures for Higgins are subjects for latter-day local color writing.

The existence of an underworld of diverse criminal types may have been news for some nineteenth-century readers of detective memoirs, and the audience for Golden Age and cozy detective fiction may rarely meet characters from the underworld, but audiences of the remaining types of crime and mystery writing recognize underworld figures as part of the genre's stock company, so capable of variation and so valuable to *plot that they are indispensable.

[See also Antihero; Heroism; Master Criminal; Realism, Conventions of.]

• George Grella, "The Gangster Novel: The Urban Pastoral," in *Tough Guy Writers of the Thirties*, ed. David Madden (1968). Dwight C. Smith, Jr., *The Mafia Mystique* (1975).
—John M. Reilly

UNUSUAL MURDER WEAPONS. *See* Weapons, Unusual Murder.

UPFIELD, ARTHUR W(ILLIAM) (1888–1964), Australian author of detective novels. Born in Gosport, Hampshire, England, Upfield was the eldest of five sons of a prosperous draper. Apprenticed at sixteen to a firm of estate agents, he failed the qualifying examination and his father shipped him off to Australia.

Upfield was fascinated by the wildness of the country and by the colorful characters he met. During the next ten years, he worked as bullock-wagon driver, boundary rider, and drover; he prospected for opals; but most of all, he roamed Australia's vastness. When war came, he joined the Australian Imperial Force and survived campaigns in Flanders and Gallipoli. His marriage to a nurse, Anne Douglas, produced a son, Arthur James. When the marriage failed he returned to Australia.

All of Upfield's books are set in Australia and draw heavily upon his experience. Although he wrote four serious novels from 1928 to 1932, none sold well. Instead, it was his crime novels that brought success. These feature the half-aboriginal detective Inspector Napoleon *Bonaparte, a character based upon Leon Wood, a tracker employed by the Queensland Police and introduced in *The Barrakee Mystery* (1929). While trying to think out a device for the disposal of the body for his second novel, *The Sands of Windee* (1931; *The Lure of the Bush*), Upfield discussed his problem with a group that included a drifter, "Snowy" Rowles, who promptly used the method in three slayings.

Upfield's mysteries appealed to a considerable public outside Australia and sold well, but they attracted harsh criticism. He was never admitted to the Australian literary establishment, upon which he took an oblique revenge in *An Author Bites the Dust* (1948).

His writings are made especially memorable by their evocations of Australia's natural environment—of bright skies and sunshine, dust storms and sand clouds, bush fires, drought and rabbit plagues, sudden rains and the reflooding of long-dry lakes. The *characterization of Napoleon Bonaparte, perpetually torn between the different worlds of his paternal and maternal inheritance and with a perilous vanity that can endure no defeats, is central. The rich array of other characters, formidably diverse but almost always depicted with sympathy, is an important adjunct. Upfield was good at depicting tough females—huge Mary Answerth and her *evil sister in *Venom House* (1952) and policewoman Alice McGorr in *Murder Must Wait* (1953) and *The Battling Prophet* (1956)—but much less successful with gentler women, who tend to be idealized and unmemorable. His sympathetic characterization of the aborigines and clear appreciation, both of their abilities and their problems in a white-dominated world, gives his novels a particular appeal at a time when attitudes to indigenous peoples are being so vigorously reassessed.

[See also Hillerman, Tony.]

• Jessica Hawke, *Follow My Dust: A Biography of Arthur Upfield* (1957). William A. S. Sarjeant, "The Great Australian Detective," *Armchair Detective* 12, no. 2 (spring 1979) (99–105) and no. 4 (fall 1979): 358–59. Ray B. Browne, *The Spirit of Australia: The Crime Fiction of Arthur W. Upfield* (1988).
—William A. S. Sarjeant

URBANISM, or the character of life in the city, is most significant to two subgenres of twentieth-century crime and mystery writing: the *police procedural and *private eye fiction. Many police procedurals have been produced in the United States, Great Britain, Scandinavia, and Europe that highlight the intertwining of the work of police officers and the city. In such works, police officers are seen as encountering and evaluating the connection between urban life and crime. For example, the ten-novel series of police procedurals by Maj *Sjöwall and Per Wahlöö often demonstrate that social problems leading to crime have been engendered by the alienation experienced by city dwellers. Because they are people of the city themselves, police characters are able to understand the urban pressures that exacerbate crime. Moreover, while they experience those pressures themselves, they are also agents working to counteract them. In the work of Ed *McBain, the nature of the city is so central that the city functions like a character, complete with a mood and personality of its own.

In private eye fiction, as in police procedurals, the detective functions as commentator on society. Private eyes, like policemen, are both city insiders and outsiders. These denizens of the mean streets also possess a wisecracking cynicism that gives them the distance needed to observe and comment on the *corruption they see. The *hard-boiled fiction of Dashiell *Hammett suggests that cities transform their inhabitants, as is the case with the *missing person whose odyssey through the city is recorded in *The Maltese Falcon* (1930).

[See also Mean Streets Milieu; Urban Milieu; Voice: Wisecracking Voice.]

• Robert Paul Winston and Nancy C. Mellerski, *The Public Eye: Ideology and the Police Procedural* (1992).
—Helaine Razovsky

URBAN MILIEU. The anonymity and peril of the city are attractive to writers who concentrate on the reality of crime. While cozy *settings of country houses and the cathedral close abound in stylized versions of criminous stories, the basic matter of crime arises as a subject in literature together with the social and cultural complexity of the modern city. Whereas the cozy milieus may serve as closed-world settings in which to place physical *clues such as the proverbial footprints in the perennial border, the fluid environment of the city's social conflicts, economic activities, and movement of people in spaces is integral to crime.

Historically cities have been places of both hope and despair. Because of this duality, they are places where tensions abound. These tensions make cities places of uncertain order. Writers of *police procedurals use representatives of the law to impose order. *Private eye writers are less certain about the validity of written law and rely on personal codes of honor to guide them through the mean streets.

Disorder abounds in the urban milieu. In Ed *McBain's *Mischief* (1993), a character known as the Deaf Man orchestrates a race riot during a spring rap music concert in the park. McBain shows how disorder arises when neighborhoods are racially and ethnically segregated in *Another Part of the City* (1985), in which uptown and downtown are two different worlds, one rich, one poor.

As early as the 1930s, Raymond *Chandler charted the "ethnic succession" occurring in *Los Angeles when neighborhoods underwent changes of color, culture, and *class. The movement of populations produced streets with "mixed blocks" such as the one in *Farewell, My Lovely* (1940) where private eye Philip *Marlowe encounters Moose Malloy, who is looking for his lost love.

Chandler's city is seen as exerting physical and psychological tensions upon its population. An evening of blustering Santa Ana winds can draw tight the nerves of city dwellers. As Marlowe observes in *Red Wind* (1946), those citizens may entertain lethal thoughts. In Chandler's novels, the city of *Los Angeles assumes the status of a character with whom the protagonist interacts.

In Sara *Paretsky's novels the personal history of her protagonist, V. I. *Warshawski is interwoven with the history of the city of Chicago. In *Guardian Angel* (1992), during a train ride downtown, Warshawski recalls childhood rides with her mother, but the scenery has changed. The small animals that once were visible in the scrub along the track are gone. Now all she can see from the window of the train are pigeons and broken bottles on rooftops.

The city, as seen through the eyes of a small-towner, can effectively add a sense of threat or danger to any story. Nancy Pickard uses this to her advantage in *But I Wouldn't Want to Die There* (1993) when she takes her small-town *sleuth, Jenny Cain, to *New York City.

Dorothy Salisbury *Davis portrays the city as a place of danger and death in her 1976 novel *A Death in the Life*. "The life" is that of prostitutes as observed by Julie Hayes, an upper-class portagonist who finds herself at odds with a pimp.

The drug trade is depicted as a deadly business by Robert B. *Parker in *Double Deuce* (1992) in which *Spenser and Hawk investigate the drive-by shooting of a fourteen-year-old girl and her infant daughter. The *victims lived in a Boston housing project known as the Double Deuce, an example of failed urban planning. In this slum, drug dealers pervert the American dream of success when they use *murder to defend their "turf."

The ugly underbelly of the city is exposed in Parker's *Ceremony* (1982), when Spenser looks for a missing teenage girl in Boston's Combat Zone. Along this strip there is a 24-hour sex trade, run by literally perverted enterpreneurs.

Stephen Greenleaf looks at the death of idealism in *Beyond Blame* (1986), in which parkland that was once the object of political and ideological conflicts is now neglected, almost forgotten. The weed-tangled and littered turf here is used effectively as a symbol of lost hope. In *Death Bed* (1980), Greenleaf's sleuth, John Marshall Tanner, notes that Broadway, a street that once symbolized adventure and sexual freedom has become another cheap vice district. He focuses on the Tenderloin section of *San Francisco an area of cheap real estate and broken lives, in *Blood Type* (1992).

In Loren D. Estleman's Detroit, the 1960s resulted in an affirmative action program that brought more women and minorities into the police force. But in the aftermath of failed social and economic programs, Detroit, like other cities, is a place of languishing industry and urban blight. Estleman's protoganist Amos Walker must make some personal decisions about how he responds to the city. In *Downriver* (1988), he returns to find that someone has tried to break into his house. In spite of this attempted burglary, he remains firm in his decision to live without bars on his windows. This is in contrast to the paranoia of the liquor store clerk who waits on him with one hand out of sight under the counter (presumably holding a gun).

But cities are places in which at least some paranoia is appropriate. In Elmore *Leonard's *Glitz* (1985), a Miami police lieutenant is shot by a mugger he encounters while walking from his car to his apartment building with his arms full of grocery bags. A young woman that the lieutenant meets while he is recuperating in Puerto Rico goes off to Atlantic City to become a "hostess" in a casino. Her dreams of a glamorous life come to an end when she is thrown from an eighteenth-story balcony.

In *Glitz* and his other novels, Leonard presents characters of diverse ethnic and cultural backgrounds who are pursuing the opportunities—criminal and otherwise—that the city offers. In this urban setting, Leonard's characters engage in a series of moves and countermoves. In *Stick* (1983), Ernest Stickley, ex-con, tries to work out a semilegitimate racket while staying one step ahead of a wealthy commodities dealer who likes to play street games, a Hispanic drug dealer who plays hoodoo games, and a drug-addicted middleman who is playing games inside his own head. After years in prison, Stick must learn how to function in the open society of an urban environment.

A similar type of adjustment is necessary for the rookie police officers in Joseph Wambaugh's *The New Centurions* (1970), set in Los Angeles in the early 1960s. In his police novels, such as *The Blue Knight* (1972) and *The Choirboys* (1975), Wambaugh depicts not only the urban milieu but the impact of that environment on the men and women who are "the thin blue line" between order and chaos.

[*See also* Urbanism; Violence.]

• Gunther Barth, *City People: The Rise of Modern City Culture in Nineteenth-Century America* (1980). Ralph Willett, "Introduction: Urban Discourse," in *The Naked City: Urban Crime Fiction in the U.S.A.* (1996). Randall Bartlett, *The Crisis of America's Cities* (1998).

—Frankie Y. Bailey

VALENTINE'S DAY, SAINT. *See* Holiday Mysteries.

Vance, Philo, created by American author S. S. *Van Dine (pseudonym of Huntington Willard Wright) in 1926, is one of many *gentleman sleuths of mystery writing's Golden Age. He might also be the biggest snob among them. In *The Bedside Companion to Crime* (1989), H. R. F. *Keating writes that Manfred Bennington Lee, cocreator of Ellery *Queen, once called Vance "the biggest prig that ever came down the pike."

Beginning with *The Benson Murder Case* (1926), Vance appears in eleven novels over twelve years, concluding with the self-satirizing *The Gracie Allen Murder Case* (1938; *The Smell of Murder*). As first-person narrator and putative author, Van Dine is more Boswell than Watson. Vance's sidekick is District Attorney John F. X. Markham, who asks Vance to help solve the more perplexing cases that come up in the *New York City of the Roaring Twenties.

Working in *Prohibition-era New York, Vance, with his aristocratic airs, stands out against workaday cops. His laconic, bemused, and drowsy eyes; imperious demeanor; bored speech patterns; and upper-class pretensions (art collecting, for example) all contribute to his perceived priggishness.

In his second book, the locked room classic *The Canary Murder Case* (1927), Van Dine came to his sleuth's defense: "His manner was cynical and aloof; and those who met him only casually, set him down as a snob. . . . I knew that his cynicism and aloofness, far from being a pose, sprang instinctively from a nature that was at once sensitive and solitary."

Like Sherlock *Holmes and Hercule *Poirot, Vance has a cerebral technique. Mistrusting the complexity of *clues that may lead nowhere or may even be deliberately placed *red herrings, Vance observes the scene and characters and gets at the truth through a psychological study of the crime. Often, he sits in on police interrogations of *witnesses and, at the end, tosses off some question in an indolent drawl, usually clipping off syllables and even calling Markham "my dear," perhaps an attempt by Van Dine to give his character a British accent. The whole packaging, though, looks facetious to modern readers and recalls a phrase used by the late U.S. vice president Spiro Agnew: "effete intellectual snob."

[*See also* Class; Voice: Genteel Voice.]

• John Loughery, *Alias S. S. Van Dine* (1992).

—Dana Bisbee

Van der Valk, Inspector. the Amsterdam police officer who departs from the common convention governing detective and sidekicks by discovering his best professional support lies in his wife Arlette, was the creation of the British writer and cooking specialist Nicolas *Freeling. Piet Van der Valk first appeared in *Love in Amsterdam* (1962; *Death in Amsterdam*), a novel that critics adjudge to be derived from the author's own experience with false arrest and imprisonment. The successful debut of the Dutch inspector in that tale led to a series of twelve *police procedural novels and at least a dozen more short stories published in *Ellery Queen's Mystery Magazine* between 1969 and 1976.

Freeling has averred dislike for the tendency of series stories to become mechanical. Accordingly in *A Long Silence* (1972; *Aupres de Ma Blonde*) he dispatched Van der Valk, leaving Arlette to complete the criminal tale and to undertake yet other adventures on her own in *The Widow* (1979) and *One Damn Thing after Another* (1981; *Arlette*). Devotees of the inspector, who became a commissioner before his death, had one more opportunity to enjoy his work when Freeling "recovered" a story from Van der Valk's career for a reprise entitled *Sand Castles* (1989).

• Norman Jeffares, "Nicolas Freeling," in *Twentieth-Century Crime and Mystery Writers*, 3rd ed., ed. Lesley Henderson (1991).

—John M. Reilly

VAN DE WETERING, JAN WILLEM (b. 1931) is best known as the author of a *police procedural series featuring Adjutant Henk Grijpstra and Sergeant Rinus De Gier of the homicide squad of the Amsterdam Municipal Police.

The Dutch author began his writing career with two autobiographical books. *Der Lege Spiegel* (1971; *The Empty Mirror: Experiences in a Japanese Monastery*) was an account of more than a year he spent as a disciple in a Zen Buddhist monastery in Kyoto, Japan. *A Glimpse of Nothingness: Experiences in an American Zen Community* (1975) detailed his further Zen study in the United States. Van de Wetering has also authored a series of short stories about Inspector Saito, a Japanese cop whose deductions are aided by an ancient Chinese crime manual. He has also written children's books.

The son of a prosperous financier, van de Wetering was born in Rotterdam. When he was a child, his homeland was occupied by the Nazis. He fled Holland at nineteen to live in South Africa, England, and

Japan. Returning to Amsterdam, he worked for seven years as a reserve police officer to discharge his military obligation. He moved to South America, where he married. He then worked briefly in Australia before settling on the coast of Maine in the United States.

His police experience and his Zen training are seen in *Outsider in Amsterdam* (1975), the first in a series of police procedurals featuring the overweight Grijpstra, the handsome De Gier, and their wise Commissaris, the elderly commissioner of Amsterdam's "murder brigade."

Different from police procedurals by Ed *McBain or Maj *Sjöwall and Per Wahlöö, van de Wetering's works show his *sleuths to be as likely to meditate over cups of coffee as to gumshoe around the dikes looking for *clues. The Commissaris, very much like van de Wetering's Zen master, encourages politeness, gentleness, and thought over action.

—Dana Bisbee

VAN DINE, S. S., pseudonym of Willard Huntington Wright (1887–1939), American author who created the Philo *Vance series of detective novels. Wright was already well established as an important literary editor and art critic, when he began his first *detective novel at the age of thirty-seven. A member of a circle that included H. L. Mencken, Theodore Dreiser, and Alfred Stieglitz, he had seen himself as helping make the world ready for modern art and the new realist fiction. His standards and aspirations were high, and his tolerance for popular success in the arts was limited. Indeed, as book critic for the *Los Angeles Times* in 1908, Wright had dismissed detective novels as a notoriously low order of literature appealing to small minds.

By 1924, however, Wright's time as a well-known member of the avant-garde was over. He was broke, ravaged by a drug addiction that had lasted for several years, and eager to remake himself in a form that would be both dramatic and lucrative. Aware that Americans in the postwar years were paying more attention than ever to British detective fiction, he devoted himself to an exhaustive study of the genre and approached Max Perkins, a renowned editor at Scribner's, with a plan for a series of detective novels that would feature an American *sleuth as memorable as Sherlock *Holmes, a Manhattan flavor, and a style of detection that was more concerned with creating a psychological portrait of the murderer than with any mere deciphering of physical *clues.

The result was a publishing phenomenon in the United States. The Philo Vance novels of S. S. Van Dine sold more than a million copies by 1930, demonstrating that there existed a vast market for American detective fiction. In *The Benson Murder Case* (1926), *The Canary Murder Case* (1927), and *The Greene Murder Case* (1928), readers were introduced to a self-consciously sophisticated, cynical, and verbose *amateur detective, a Nietzschean intellectual with a private income and a healthy ego. His presence in the ten novels Scribner's published between 1926 and 1939 is the distinctive feature of all the Van

Dine books; *plot, dialogue, relationships, plausibility—everything is secondary to Vance's flamboyant persona and the charm of his *New York in the last years of the Jazz Age.

The changes in detective fiction that came with the *Great Depression had a predictable impact on Van Dine's career. He was unable to adapt to the new interest in hard-boiled detectives, grimy urban *settings, and terse dialogue and descriptions. By the mid-1930s Philo Vance seemed more than ever a period figure, a holdover from the day of the speakeasy and the flapper. When Vance does engage in stakeouts and car chases, as in *The Kidnap Murder Case* (1936), the result is a stilted, formulaic novel obviously written with the new market in mind. Van Dine died in 1939, a bitter and angry man, well aware that his audience had abandoned him for the rowdier style of crime fiction he disdained.

[*See also* Gentleman Sleuth.]

• John Loughery, *Alias S. S. Van Dine.* (1992).

—John Loughery

Van Dusen, Professor Augustus S. F. X., Ph.D., LL.D., F.R.S., M.D., MD.S., also known as "the Thinking Machine," detective-protagonist of one novel and forty-six known short stories by Jacques *Futrelle. A professor in an unnamed American university, he first appears as, a small man aged fifty, with a scholar's squint and a disproportionately large skull. He believes the human mind can master any problem. His cases have won him fame; it is newspaper reporters who have given him his nickname. One reporter, Hutchinson Hatch, gathers information for him in a manner later developed further by Rex *Stout in his Nero *Wolfe/Archie *Goodwin stories.

The Thinking Machine first appears in "The Problem of Cell 13," still the best-known story, serialized in the *Boston American* beginning 30 October 1905. On a bet, the Thinking Machine vows to escape from the death cell of a penitentiary, equipped only with polished shoes, tooth powder, and $25. The story appeared in six parts; readers were offered $100 for the best solution. Stories that followed similarly feature a *locked room mystery or *impossible crime. All cases yield to the detective's logic, emphasized at the expense of character development, *plot, or *setting; subtle *humor ensures readability. About half the stories were collected in *The Thinking Machine* (1907; *The Problem of Cell 13*) and *The Thinking Machine on the Case* (1908; *The Professor on the Case*). The detective also appears in *The Chase of the Golden Plate*, written before "The Problem of Cell 13" but not published until 1906. Other stories remain uncollected.

[*See also* Great Detective; Reasoning, Types of.]

• E. F. Bleiler, introduction to *Best "Thinking Machine" Detective Stories* by Jacques Futrelle (1973).

—Betty Richardson

Vane, Harriet. A fictional character created by Dorothy L. *Sayers, Harriet Vane is one of the best-known female *amateur detectives in the genre. When Sayers introduced Vane as a person on trial for the *murder of her lover in *Strong Poison* (1930), the author's intent was to have Wimsey marry Vane and thereby end the Wimsey series of novels. At the time, the *sleuth as loner predominated in detective fiction, and romance was seen as incompatible with the ratiocincation central to stories of detection. Sayers soon found, however, that it would not be in character for Vane, a feminist and intellectual, to accept Wimsey without further development of the latter's character. Sayers may also have kept the pair in three more novels and two short stories because in Vane she had an alter ego through whom she could write about issues that concerned her, including character, integrity, the academic life, and thwarted love. Vane is, like Sayers, a detective novelist who has suffered an unhappy, illicit love affair.

Sayers delays marrying Wimsey to Vane by having the female sleuth refuse his many proposals in *Have His Carcase* (1932), a novel in which Vane investigates a murder at a seaside resort. In *Gaudy Night* (1937), set in the fictional Shrewsbury College of Oxford University, Vane finally consents to marry Wimsey, but only when he proposes to her in Latin, in a moment of dialogue that has caused countless critics to celebrate Wimsey's meeting Vane as an equal on her own terms. While Wimsey is instrumental in helping the case to come to a conclusion, *Gaudy Night* is remembered for its detailed depiction of the lives of female academics in a world mostly closed to men. Vane is considered to be the ideal detective to investigate a case involving poison pen missives, because she is a woman who has experience of the academic life. Much of Vane's character development occurs in this book, in which she acts largely on her own to understand the pressures experienced by other women who are leading the academic life.

Busman's Honeymoon (1925) shows the married duo solving a case that they come across during their honeymoon. A sequel, called *Thrones, Dominations*, was left uncompleted at Sayers's death. It describes the Wimseys' early married life. The manuscript was finished by Jill Paton Walsh and published to good reviews in 1998. Vane also appears in the short stories "Haunted Policeman" (*Harper's Bazaar*, Feb. 1938) and "Talboys" (written in 1942 and published in *Lord Peter* in 1972), which concerns the Wimsey children, Bredon, Roger, and Paul.

As a viewpoint character whom Wimsey seeks to impress and win as a wife, Vane seems to have served as in inspiration for further development of the Wimsey character. Vane provides a prototype for the female, intellectual, feminist sleuth whose personal life is often as challenging as the detection that she undertakes.
                                                    —Rosemary Herbert

VAN GULIK, ROBERT H(ANS) (1910–1967), Dutch diplomat, linguist, and scholar who translated and then authored tales featuring Judge Dee, a character based on the seventh-century Chinese judge Dee Jendjieh. Born in the Netherlands, van Gulik spent his childhood largely in the then Dutch colony of Java where his father served as a military doctor, and where his own talent for languages was awakened.

When he returned to the Netherlands at age twelve, he studied Sanskrit, Chinese, and the language of North America's Blackfeet Indians, later studying additional languages at the University of Leyden. Upon completing his university work, van Gulik entered the Dutch foreign service in 1935. In 1940, he came across an anonymous eighteenth-century manuscript, *Wu tse t'ien ssu ta ch'i an*, which he translated into English as *Dee Goong An: Three Murder Cases Solved by Judge Dee* (1949). He subsequently composed his own stories centered around Dee, working his Asian expertise into them and illustrating them with his own woodcuts. Van Gulik also wrote nonfiction on a wide variety of subjects, including the Chinese flute, erotic art, and sexual practices in ancient China. In 1956 he published an English translation of a thirteenth-century Chinese casebook, *T'ang-yin pi-shih*.

• Donald F. Lach, introduction to *The Chinese Bell Murders* by Robert van Gulik (1977). Janwillem van de Wetering, *Robert van Gulik: His Life, His Work* (1987).
                                                    —Rosemary Herbert

VERNACULAR. *See* Voice.

VICTIM. Every murder mystery requires a victim, but until recently writers devoted far more attention to *suspects and culprits. During the Golden Age of crime and mystery writing, the victim was usually a cipher and the discovery of a body, whether in a country house library or elsewhere, was simply a signal for a battle of wits to begin between murderer and *sleuth and, often, between author and reader. Even when authors began to explore psychology, their main interest lay in the *motivation of killers rather than in the circumstances of the slain. In this, the genre mirrored life: Everyone has heard of Jack the Ripper, but few recall the names of his victims.

The traditional *whodunit demanded a closed circle of suspects, each possessing a credible *motive for murder. Most victims were odious or very rich, characteristics highlighted by the parodist E. V. Knox in his story "The Murder at the Towers" (*This Other Eden*, 1929), while the second victim in a book tended to be a witness to the first crime or a blackmailer. In a different way, victims in *hard-boiled fiction, however well written, were also apt to be two-dimensional; in books like Dashiell *Hammett's *Red Harvest* (1929), it is easy to lose count of the number of bodies. Yet eventually, the most skillful writers began to play games with readers' expectations. In *The Face on the Cutting Room Floor* (1937), Cameron McCabe combines the roles of narrator and murderer with that of victim. More commonly, in multiple murder cases, an unexpected common link might connect victims seemingly chosen at random, as is the case in *The ABC Murders* (1936; *The Alphabet Murders*), *Peril at End House* (1932), *One, Two, Buckle My Shoe* (1940; *The Patriotic Murders*; *An Overdose Of Death*), and *By the Pricking of My Thumbs* (1968), all by Agatha *Christie. In Richard Hull's *The Murder of My Aunt* (1934), an intended victim turns the tables on her would-be murderer; a killer also gets his comeuppance in *Little Victims* (1983; *School for Murder*) by Robert *Barnard. In *The Disposal of the Living* (1985), Barnard describes the activities of an apparently obvious "murderee," but when death strikes, the victim is someone entirely unforeseen.

Francis *Iles's *Before the Fact* (1932) was ahead of its time in providing a compelling psychological study of a born victim, but from the 1940s on more writers began to draw victims in depth. In *Laura* (1943) by Vera Caspary, the detective falls in love with a portrait of a supposed victim, thus giving a carefully crafted mystery an extra dimension. Patricia McGerr's *Pick Your Victim* (1946) inaugurated the *who-was-dun-in, and in *The Widow of Bath* (1952) by Margot Bennett, the character of the victim, a stern and legalistic *judge, is the key to the explanation for his death. Today, the victims of murder are usually rather more than a mere excuse for a mystery; even in comic novels, they are now seldom treated as figures of fun. Sometimes they may be seen as having brought their fate upon themselves, as in Margaret Yorke's *Dangerous to Know* (1993), but they are equally apt to be portrayed as deserving of pity, as in *A Helping Hand* (1966) by Celia Dale and *The Secret House of Death* (1968) by Ruth *Rendell. Such books reflect the genre's move away from fantasy and toward a realistic depiction of those destroyed by crime as well as of those who commit it.

[*See also* Characterization; Corpse; Formula: Character; Taking of Life.]

• Tony Hilfer, *The Crime Novel: A Deviant Genre* (1990).

—Martin Edwards

VIDOCQ, EUGÈNE FRANÇOIS (1775–1857), founder of the first official and *private detective agencies and hero of the first *police procedurals. Born in Arras, France, and educated by Franciscans, Vidocq fought in the royal army during the 1789 revolution, attaining officer rank but deserting to live as a gambler and vagabond. His frequent arrests and escapes became legend, but, late in 1798, he faced slave labor in the naval yards when convicted of forging release papers for a fellow prisoner. The sentence was lengthened thanks to his repeatedly escaping and being recaptured; then, in 1809, apparently to win a pardon, he volunteered his services to the police, convincing officials that plainclothes agents, especially those who themselves had been criminals, would be more effective than uniformed officers in curbing the high crime rate.

By 1811, Vidocq was training new agents and, in 1812, he was given command of the Brigade de la Sûreté or security police. By 1814, Vidocq was a deputy prefect; by 1824, he was in charge of tens of detectives. He instituted a detailed record system of criminals and criminal activity, held patents on tamperproof paper and ink that reduced counterfeiting and forgery, and may have been the first to recognize the importance of fingerprinting, ballistics, and blood testing in criminal investigation.

After political intrigue forced his resignation in 1827, he published his four-volume—and certainly partly fictional—*Mémoires de Vidocq* (1828–29; *Memoirs of Vidocq*; *Vidocq, the Police Spy*), 50,000 copies of which were sold within a year. By 1832, after the July Revolution brought Louis-Philippe to the throne, Vidocq had resumed his duties as chief of the *Sûreté. He was dismissed in 1833 and established the first-known private detective agency, the Bureau des Renseignements. Problems with the official police led to his final retirement after he was exonerated from criminal charges in 1842. He then wrote, or had ghostwritten, *Les vrais mystères de Paris* (1844), *Quelques mots sur une question à l'ordre du jour* (1844), and *Les chauffeurs du nord* (1845–46). Other works are attributed to him as well.

Edgar Allan *Poe acknowledged his debt to Vidocq, and Honoré de Balzac used him as the basis for the character Vautrin in the multivolume *La comédie humaine* (1842–48; *Comedy of Human Life*, 1887–96); he appears as well in stories collected as *Crimes célébres* (1841; *Celebrated Crimes*, 1843) by Alexandre Dumas *père*. Vidocq's theories of criminal reform influenced Victor Hugo in *Les misérables* (1862) and Eugène Sue in *Les mystères de Paris* (1842–43); *Mysteries of Paris*, 1843).

[*See also* Fingerprints and Footprints; Memoirs; Early Detective and Police.]

• Samuel Edwards, *The Vidocq Dossier* (1977).

—Betty Richardson

VILLAINS AND VILLAINY. The contest between good and *evil is a constant theme of mystery writing, but as the certainties of the Victorian era have given way to the moral ambiguities of modern times, the genre's villains, or wrongdoers, and their ignominious acts, or villainy, have moved from exemplars of evil to relatively sympathetic characters and behavior and back to ignominious again. When Wilkie *Collins was constructing *The Woman in White* (1860), he regarded the *ingenuity necessary to the central crime as beyond any Englishman and thus created in Count Fosco an Italian villain who seemed all the more sinister because of his gross physical appearance, his habit of allowing pet mice to frolic over his waistcoat, and his superficial charm. Equally formidable was Joseph Sheridan Le Fanu's Silas Ruthyn, whose *plot to murder his heiress niece was abetted by a wicked French governess, Madame de la Rouguierre. The book was originally to be called *Maud Ruthyn*, but Le Fanu soon recognized that the dominating presence was the villain's and changed the title to *Uncle Silas* (1864; *Uncle Silas: A Tale of Bartram-Haugh*).

Less subtle successors also made use of foreign villains, not so much from a desire to make their clever crimes credible but rather from a dislike and distrust of anything un-English. Especially popular in the early years of the twentieth century were Sax *Rohmer's books about *Fu Manchu—the classic Oriental villain—and the series in which H. C. *McNeile, or Sapper, pitted his clean-cut clubland hero Hugh "Bulldog" *Drummond against the archfiend Carl Peterson. English-born villains were often portrayed as members of the upper social *class. Professor James *Moriarty, Arthur Conan

*Doyle's "Napoleon of crime" was of good birth and excellent education, as was his sometime chief of staff, Colonel Sebastian Moran. Equally cultivated were *gentlemen thieves such as Grant Allen's Colonel Clay and E. W. *Hornung's amateur cracksman, A. J. *Raffles. Doyle expressed disquiet about the way in which his brother-in-law Hornung celebrated Raffles's villainy, but writers from far afield took their cue from the exploits of the man who played cricket at the highest level by day and burgled wealthy families by night. Maurice *Leblanc's Arsène *Lupin was notable as a master of *disguise, but more sophisticated were the stories about the unscrupulous American lawyer Randolph Mason created by Melville Davisson *Post. *The Strange Schemes of Randolph Mason* (1896; *Randolph Mason: The Strange Schemes*) was intended to show how knowledge of legal loopholes could enable the thwarting of *justice. Yet it is difficult to write a series about any character, however villanous, without endowing him with some *virtues: Raffles, Lupin, and Mason, as well as G. K. *Chesterton's daring colossus of crime Flambeau, all eventually decided to put their talents to the cause of justice—although in moving away from the windy side of the law, they sacrificed much of their original appeal.

Supercriminals have never fallen altogether out of fashion. Rex *Stout matched Nero *Wolfe with Arnold Zeck and more recently Ed *McBain's cops of the Eighty-seventh Precinct have been confronted time and again by the Deaf Man. In the postwar era, British writers—notably Ian *Fleming, creator of *master criminals Auric Goldfinger and Ernst Stavro Blofeld as well as James *Bond—have on occasion succumbed to the temptation to equate foreignness with exotic villainy. In hard-boiled American novels, W. R. Burnett's Cesare Bandello, alias Rico or "Little Caesar," and Caspar Gutman, whom Dashiell *Hammett immortalized in *The Maltese Falcon* (1930) and whose sinister obesity is reminiscent of Fosco's, were made all the more menacing by their obsessive single-mindedness. In contrast, the tone of books by British-based authors such as Leslie *Charteris and John *Creasey about those "durable desperadoes" Simon Templar (the Saint) and Richard Rollison (The Toff), both characters firmly within the Robin Hood tradition, are much lighter.

Another strand of writing concentrates more upon explanation of the personality traits that give rise to villainous behavior than upon the physical effects of that behavior. Many readers will sympathize with the predicaments of Andrew Taylor's William Dougal even when, as in *Odd Man Out* (1993) he kills an acquaintance, while in Walter Satterthwait's *Miss Lizzie* (1989), the supposed ax murderer Lizzie Borden turns detective a generation after the killing of her own parents. Patrick Hamilton's Ernest Ralph Gorse, who first appeared in *The West Pier* (1951), was an early example of the cold-blooded and amoral charmer. Patricia *Highsmith is widely hailed as a writer who has created distinctive and memorable modern villains, starting with Bruno, who proposes an "exchange of murders" to the respectable Guy Haines in *Strangers on a Train* (1950). Her most celebrated criminal protagonist is Tom Ripley, but although he has appeared in five novels over a period of more than thirty years, *The Talented Mr. Ripley* (1955), in which he made his debut, remains the most successful. Ruth *Rendell's insight into the criminal mind is equally acute and *A Fatal Inversion* (1987), written under the pseudonym of Barbara Vine, is but one of her compelling novels, which, while never condoning *evil deeds, makes them explicable.

Today mystery readers have come to appreciate that villainy is not the prerogative of those who come from other countries or different social classes—any person may, in certain circumstances, be capable of it. As Julian *Symons put it, writers are apt to be concerned and "fascinated by the violence behind respectable faces" and the random nature of crime. While some writers continue to make the psyches of criminals understandable and their crimes sometimes, therefore, pardonable, others portray monstrous villains in the form of serial killers who personify deviance and dementedness. Patricia D. Cornwell and Thomas Harris are exemplars of authors who have brought a new frisson to readers' views of villainy.

[*See also* Antihero; Robin Hood Criminal.]

• Ellery Queen, ed., *Rogue's Gallery: The Great Criminals of Modern Fiction* (1945). William Vivian Butler, *The Durable Desperadoes* (1973). Colin Watson, *Snobbery with Violence: Crime Stories and Their Audience*, rev. ed. (1979). H. R. F. Keating, *The Bedside Companion to Crime* (1989).

—Martin Edwards

VIOLENCE is the infliction of physical of emotional force so as to damage a person or property. Writers of crime and mystery fiction portray violence in many forms. In traditional detective fiction, *murder was indispensable because this capital crime is serious enough to deserve the efforts of a Great Detective to explain it. Lesser crimes were matters for the police. Despite this emphasis on the destruction of human life, and despite the endless *ingenuity of murderers, the inherent violence of the act held little more than minor interest for the Golden Age authors. More often than not the killing around which tales of detection were centered occurred before the story began, or took place beyond the narrator's eye with the effect that the narratives could concentrate on the detective confronting an intellectual *puzzle and solving it with wit. In this respect the classic stories worked in a way entirely opposite to the sensational writing from which the genre grew, as well as differently from tabloid journalism, which sometimes supplied ideas to authors of detective fiction. Whereas news accounts of actual crimes tend to draw violence close to readers, making them feel a sense of vulnerability, the ratiocinative detective stories abstracted murder from its violent circumstances.

Hard-boiled detective writing is less demanding about the crimes that will satisfy the necessity of impelling a story forward, but it brings violence into the accounts of detective adventure. The *hard-boiled sleuth witnesses violence, sometimes receives it, and is never loath to administer it by gun or fist. This has been the case since the days of the *Black Mask *pulp magazine stories that consistently wove violence into the texture of narratives. Yet, even so, the violence of *hard-boiled fiction can be stylized and, for that reason, also distanced from the reader. In hard-boiled writing, violence characterizes a realm symbolizing the corrupt underside of its readers' mundane social reality, but the fabric of the symbolic realm differs from the known world because the narrative methods create the opportunity for *voyeurism. When Raymond *Chandler's Philip *Marlowe, Bill Pronzini's Nameless detective, or Robert B. *Parker's *Spenser come before readers, they are guides to a different land.

With the advent of the *crime novel, that variety of literature defined by Julian *Symons as writing that centers upon the commission of crimes, violence edges its way into the center of narration. Stories of serial killings, *child abuse, and *underworld activity employ violence as the characteristic expression of central characters. As a consequence, the distance between the reader and violence is drastically reduced so that a frisson of *terror becomes an important outcome of the story. Still, it must be noted that the violence of the crime novel functions like the special effects of disaster films, drawing attention to its rendition at the same time that it terrifies.

The implication of violence in all of crime and mystery writing, however distanced or close it may be to readers, indicates the curious fact that on its deep structural level the genre offers the satisfactions of control and security. Violence provides not just the occasion and instigation for story, as surely it does for authors of any of the varieties of crime and mystery fiction, but since the plots of any type of crime or mystery story comprise explanations of violence through revelation of its *motivation and methods, the literature subjects violence to reason, showing that it can be understood. If violence can be known, it can be controlled. There is consolation in that.

[See also Assault; Rape and Other Sex Crimes; Taking of Life.]

• Thomas De Quincey, "On Murder Considered as One of the Fine Arts," in The Collected Writings of Thomas De Quincey 13, ed. David Musson (1889–90).   —John M. Reilly

VIOLENT ENTERTAINMENT, THE PARADOX OF. Centered as it is upon puzzles surrounding violent crime, crime and mystery fiction is a literature particularly concerned with the paradox of violent entertainment or the question of reconciling the painful effects of actual *violence with the fact that readers may derive pleasure or entertainment from reading about it. Atavism may account for this: some say that everyone wants to mangle, mutilate, or murder someone. In Thomas Harris's The Silence of the Lambs (1988), the novel's hero, Clarice Starling, relates the game of detection to the fact of violence. After she's figured out who the murderer is—and just shortly before she kills him—she thinks, "Problem-solving is hunting; it is savage pleasure and we are born to it."

From the beginning, some mysteries have used atavism to suggest the subhuman depths of the psyche where crime has its origins; sounding such depths may be inferred as a process readers reproduce within themselves. The brutal violence of Edgar Allan *Poe's "The Murders in the Rue Morgue" (Graham's Lady's and Gentleman's Magazine, Apr. 1841) is the act of an orangutan, and Arthur Conan *Doyle introduces, in "The Adventure of the Creeping Man" (Strand, Mar. 1923), a professor who takes monkey gland injections to recover his youth but who turns into a throwback, illustrating Sherlock *Holmes's observation that "the highest type of man may revert to the animal" if he tries to thwart nature. Authors employ atavism when they invent unstoppable, hyperviolent monsters as antagonists: T. H. White's Professor Mauleverer in Darkness at Pemberley (1932), Margery *Allingham's even more aptly named Jack Havoc in The Tiger in the Smoke (1952), or John D. MacDonald's Max Cady in The Executioners (1958; Cape Fear). These stories also use atavism as the model for manipulating readers to identify with the terrorized protagonists and therefore agree with their decision to kill the monster that preys upon them.

Atavism does not explain the relatively bloodless homicides in the mysteries often labeled cozies, where the murder eliminates a character deliberately constructed as hateful and where the violence, brief and invisible, scarcely delays the next country house tea service or interrupts the vicar's evensong. Yet Agatha *Christie's Miss Jane *Marple argues that one is as likely to find primitive passions in her own village of Saint Mary Mead as in the meanest streets of *London.

Catharsis is another explanation of the paradox of violence's appeal. Aristotle argued in the Poetics that tragic drama raised the emotions of pity and fear and then purged them. In Modus Operandi: An Excursion into Detective Fiction (1982), Robin Winks argues that readers seek in mysteries a similar evocation and then quieting of their deepest fears. Fears of the unknown, of rioting nature, and of threats beyond nature are raised and then quieted when Holmes explains away the footprints of a gigantic hound, a mother raising her bloodstained mouth from the wound in her baby's throat, and a snake coiled like a speckled band around a dead man's forehead. Fear of death is the main terror aroused by stories of violent crime, and the fear of death probably explains why most mysteries are *murder mysteries. Such stories acknowledge that death exists by depicting a murder, but by finally eliminating that one deadly agent, the murderer, they seem to eliminate the threat of death itself.

Violence may also appeal because it is an accurate imitation of the real world. Aristotle speculates, also in the Poetics, that instinctual drives lead us to imitate and to enjoy imitation. Raymond *Chandler writes in "The Simple Art of Murder" (Atlantic Monthly, Dec. 1944) that the brutal and ferocious world shown in some crime fiction "is not a very fragrant world, but it is the world you live in."

American fiction appears to confirm this mimetic hypothesis. America is a violent place, and American crime writers mastered violence early and made it their province. Nothing in Doyle, for example, matches the random, crazy violence of the women with their heads almost severed, stuffed up the chimney in "The Murders in the Rue Morgue." Hard-boiled crime fiction, whose hallmark is violence, is an American invention, from the "blood simple" gunplay of Dashiell *Hammett's Continental Detective Agency "operative" in *Red Harvest* (1929) to Mickey *Spillane's enormously popular detective, Mike *Hammer, who reserves the right to maim and kill anyone he judges morally or politically wrong. American writers also developed, from the 1940s onward, a fiction in which abnormal psychology, sexual stress, and the tensions of urban life combine in what might be called psychocultural violence. H. R. F. *Keating, in *Crime and Mystery: The 100 Best Books* (1987), has called such writing a "willingness to go down the mean streets of the mind," adapting a phrase made famous by Raymond Chandler that was earlier used by Arthur *Morrison in his *Tales of the Mean Streets* (1894). Examples are Helen Eustis's *The Horizontal Man* (1946), John Franklin Bardin's *Devil Take the Blue-Tail Fly* (1948), Jim Thompson's *The Killer Inside Me* (1952), Margaret *Millar's *Beast in View* (1955), and Stanley Ellin's *Mirror, Mirror on the Wall* (1972). The exploration of violent psychological transference or paranoid schizophrenia in these books may go beyond the attempt to exorcise private psychic demons and reflect a wish to understand and thus neutralize some of society's ills.

A still darker explanation for the pleasure to be had in violent entertainment is sadomasochism. Recent writers seem to have less trouble than those of the past in acknowledging that readers simply enjoy the pain of others. Robert Bloch's *Psycho* (1959) took great pains to explain the sickness of Norman Bates, while the much grislier outrages of Bret Easton Ellis's narrator, Patrick Bateman, in *American Psycho: A Novel* (1991) are graphically recorded without comment and without resolution. Ellis identifies the bleak materialism of latter-day American urban culture with a violence that has hardly ever been so graphically described in fiction.

There may be no more satisfactory answer to the paradox of violent entertainment than Thomas De Quincey offered two centuries ago in "Murder Considered as One of the Fine Arts" (*Blackwood's Magazine*, 1827): If violence is "managed with art, and covered with mystery," it transcends the pain of its origins and becomes art itself, so "let us treat it aesthetically, and see if it will turn to account in that way."

[*See also* Taking of Life.]

—Michael Cohen

VIRTUE in detective fiction means, in Aristotelian terms, right reason applied to the achieving of *justice. Although detectives may occasionally pursue *truth for its own sake, their usual purpose in solving crimes is restoration of social order.

Implicit in this definition is the assumption that *victims' right to redress for violation of their person or property does not depend on their moral standing. For Edgar Allan *Poe, the victim may serve as little more than object of irrational violence, as exempli-fied by "The Murders in the Rue Morgue" (*Graham's Lady's and Gentleman's Magazine*, Apr. 1841) and "The Tell-Tale Heart" (*Pioneer*, Jan. 1843); for other writers, a victim's passivity or indiscretion may invite criminality (Wilkie *Collins's *The Woman in White*, 1860), even to the point of complicity (Georges *Simenon's *Ami Maigret*, 1949; *The Methods of Maigret*). For still others, an absence of virtue in the victim is an opportunity to present multiple *suspects and *motives and to focus on the "how" of the crime, as in Agatha *Christie's *Murder on the Orient Express* (1934; *Murder in the Calais Coach*). The point is that, guilty or not, crime victims are entitled in justice to some reparation by society.

The one crime that is fundamentally irreparable—*murder—thus becomes a prime element in detective fiction, with the detective assuming the symbolic role of society's agent of justice. The murder victim may be beyond help—as the taunting killer in Charles *Dickens's *Bleak House* (1853) reminds Inspector Bucket—but the detective can still "speak for the dead," by uncovering the murder when it has been hidden or misread as accident or suicide, exculpating the falsely accused, and, most importantly, bringing the murderer to justice.

Invested by society with extraordinary prerogatives—to track, expose, and judge suspects—the detective, whether official or private, had inevitably become, by the end of the nineteenth century, the primary locus of virtue in detective fiction. Poe was more interested in intellectual than moral virtues in his detective the Chevalier C. Auguste *Dupin, who brilliantly employed right reason but out of dubious motives such as ego satisfaction and revenge, and Dickens, reflecting Victorian ambivalence about the police, gave Bucket admirable qualities such as perseverance and pluck yet showed him resorting to questionable techniques such as bribery and bullying. As Dennis Porter notes, detection's "voyeurism" can be sanctioned only by making it "goal-oriented and morally necessary"; hence, only when the moral justification for detection was generally accepted could the *Great Detective appear on the scene. Such traits as arrogance and irascibility were not only excusable but came to be viewed, in a Sherlock *Holmes or Professor Augustus S. F. X. *Van Dusen, as natural accompaniments to professional competence. Even in his high-handedness with legalities—letting a criminal go free in "The "The Adventure of the Blue Carbuncle" (*Strand*, Jan. 1892), housebreaking in "The Adventure of Charles Augustus Milverton" (*Strand*, Apr. 1904)—Holmes remained above reproach. Like Holmes, later detectives, from Dashiell *Hammett's Sam *Spade in the 1920s to Sue *Grafton's Kinsey *Milhone in the 1990s, pride themselves on their skill at lying and outwitting the authorities. G. K. *Chesterton's Father *Brown is a rarity in eschewing deception and putting duty to the criminal—helping him save his soul—over duty to society, as in "The Invisible Man" (*Cassell's*, Feb. 1911).

When the emergence of the *Black Mask school of fiction challenged the detective's image of probity, Raymond *Chandler proposed, in "The Simple Art of Murder" (*Atlantic Monthly*, Dec. 1944), a new kind of detective—"a man of honor," who could walk mean streets without himself becoming mean. Chandler's Philip *Marlowe exemplifies the knight-errant struggling to maintain an ethical code in a corrupting world, but the Chandler ideal is perhaps best personified in Hammett's Spade. In *The Maltese Falcon* (1930) right reason leads Spade to identify instantaneously his partner's killer and foil the gang of thieves. With few illusions, and immune to Marlovian acedia, he exercises in his confrontation with the criminals all the cardinal virtues: prudence, in shrewdly setting them against one another; fortitude, in holding out against their threats and the *suspicions of the police; temperance, in mastering his baser instincts of *greed and lust; and, above all, justice, in turning in the principal culprit, who happens to be the woman he loves. Spade embodies the Aristotelian man of virtue who, despite natural frailties, brings criminality to light and to the bar of justice.

Writers' views of what constitutes virtue are inevitably reshaped as social mores change. As yesterday's villains, from society fortune-hunters to big-city gangsters, have given way to today's more complex schemers, with their political machinations and corporate fraud, women writers have led the trend toward emphasizing communal rather than individual rights as objects of criminal attacks. Virtue lies in uncovering crimes of environmental spoliation in Jane Langton's *Natural Enemy* (1982) and institutional malpractice in Sara *Paretsky's *Bitter Medicine* (1987). Women writers, beginning with Dorothy L. *Sayers's *Gaudy Night* (1935), have also broadened the definition of right reason in detection to include an ethic of caring. Grafton's Milhone, for example, replaces professional detachment with compassion, identifying with victim and suspect in *"D" Is for Deadbeat* (1987), and P. D. *James's Cordelia *Gray goes even further in contextualizing morality, lying under oath to protect a murderer she feels was justified in *An Unsuitable Job for a Woman* (1972). These writers consider themselves to be reformulating, not abandoning, the traditional view of moral virtue. What has not changed in detective fiction, clearly, is a basic faith in the power of human intelligence and perseverance to achieve, however imperfectly, the goal of justice for all.

[*See also* Chivalry, Code of; Loyalty and Betrayal; Truth, Quest for; Villains and Villainy.]

• Raymond Chandler, "The Simple Art of Murder" in *The Simple Art of Murder* (1950). Dennis Porter, *The Pursuit of Crime: Art and Ideology in Detective Fiction* (1981). Barbara A. Rader and Howard G. Zettler, *The Sleuth and the Scholar: Origins, Evolution, and Current Trends in Detective Fiction* (1988).

—Mary Rose Sullivan

VISITORS ABROAD. Much crime and mystery fiction is set in *milieus that represent home to the authors of the work. Some writers, however, have worked in, resided in, or visited places that were, at least initially, foreign to them, and have gone on to realize them in their crime and mystery fiction. Such writers have found a large audience of readers who enjoy the experience of being not only *armchair detectives but armchair travelers. Writers of works set in lands where they were not born are sometimes referred to as visitors abroad.

Some of the most well-remembered introductions of international locales into the genre resulted from the use of archaeological sites as *settings. Agatha *Christie's *Murder in Mesopotamia* (1936), a work that reflected her experiences with her husband in excavations in Egypt and the Near East, opened new avenues for the introduction of foreign elements. Ancient curses, exotic poisons, bizarre methods of *murder, threatening landscapes, and inscrutable foreigners enter mystery fiction when murder moves to Mesopotamia. Christie began a tradition that continues in the works of writers like Margot Arnold, whose Penelope Spring/Tobias Glendower series makes full use of her archaeological and anthropological background. Novels centered on archaeological settings are usually lightly sprinkled with arcane facts about civilizations both ancient and modern and interesting sidelights on cultures as diverse as those of ancient Greece, Rome, England, and Hawaii, and feature methods of murder normally inspired by the culture in question.

Foreign settings allow authors a freer hand with the traditional elements of mystery fiction. They often unsettle the process of detection, placing the detective in unfamiliar surroundings where his or her skills are tested to the utmost. In various books set outside the United Kingdom, Dick *Francis places his detectives in dangers springing from unfamiliar languages, geographies, and cultures. In *Slay-Ride* (1970), which opens in the deep and freezing waters of Norway, Francis places the forbidding climate at the center of the plot; in *Trial Run* (1987) Francis uses Russian culture and the unfamiliar political system to create the novel's menacing atmosphere. Similar elements are explored in Robert *Barnard's *Death in a Cold Climate* (1980), which conveys the dreary and dispiriting quality of a Scandinavian winter while allowing the reader entry into unfamiliar patterns of logic rooted in a different culture. The novels of Desmond *Bagley are international in setting and have been acclaimed for their success in conjuring the feel of places as various and remote as the Mexican jungle in *The Vivero Letter* (1968), the peaks of the Andes in *High Citadel* (1965), the Icelandic wastes in *Running Blind* (1970), and the Kenyan savannah in *Windfall* (1982). Bagley's novels have been praised for their painstaking reproduction of geographical and cultural milieus.

Various American and British authors have developed series set in foreign locales. H. R. F. *Keating's Inspector Ganesh Ghote series—featuring the henpecked and bullied homicide expert of the Bombay Criminal Investigation Department—has been hailed for its vivid evocations of the Indian landscape, climate, and culture and for its depiction of the non-Western mind at work. In *Inspector Ghote Goes by Train* (1971), for example, the reader is treated to a wealth of descriptive detail in the course of a trip, from Bombay to Calcutta and back. Likewise, in *Death of a Dissident* (1981; *Rostnikov's Corpse*) an entry in Stuart M. Kaminsky's Inspector Porfiry

Rostnikov's series, Soviet police work is depicted as tainted by political control, and life in the Soviet Union emerges in all its dullness and shabbiness. In *Red Chameleon* (1985) he ponders the prospects of the average Soviet citizen, especially one in the lower ranks of the harassed bureaucracy.

The Caribbean setting in works like Donald McNutt Douglass's *Rebecca's Pride* (1956), Christie's *A Caribbean Mystery* (1964), Peter Dickinson's *Walking Dead* (1977), Elmore *Leonard's *Cat Chaser* (1982), and Norman Lewis's *Cuban Passage* (1982) focuses on elements that traditionally have had no legitimacy in detective fiction: the use of means other than reason for the solution of the mystery; the immersion of the heroes in psychological adventures possible only in a place foreign to their natural surroundings; the rendering of characters and situations as the embodiment of the phantasms that haunt the Western subconscious. As with the Caribbean setting, mysteries set in Asia depend for their effect on geographical, psychological, or political elements that are peculiar to the locale and not easily transferable. John P. Marquand's Mr. *Moto series, for example, emphasized colonial relations, and rested on the illusion of cordial cooperation between Japanese and Western characters, the latter mostly figuring as diplomatic personnel negotiating the intricacies of potential economic and political quagmires. John le Carré's *The Honourable Schoolboy* (1977), with its vivid descriptions of Hong Kong, succeeds marvelously at re-creating the atmosphere of colonial relationships. Mark Derby's series of thrillers set in Malaysia, including *Malayan Rose* (1951; *Afraid in the Dark*), *Out of Asia Alive* (1954; *The Bad Step*), and *Sun in the Hunter's Eyes* (1958), epitomizes another type of Asian mystery focusing on Western loners pitted against diabolic Asian villains aided by the harsh local climate and topography. With his Curt Stone series—*The Cave of the Chinese Skeletons* (1964), *Assignment: Find Cherry* (1969), *The Chinese Pleasure Girl* (1969)—Jack Seward transferred the familiar elements of the thriller to Japan and presented a wealth of obscure facts about Japanese culture in the process. Oswald Wynd's excellent Paul Harris series—written under the pen name of Gavin Black and including titles like *Suddenly, at Singapore . . .* (1961), *The Eyes Around Me* (1964), and *Night Run from Java* (1979)—is unmatched in the accuracy of its geographical, cultural, and historical detail. In his series featuring Superintendent Tetsuo Otani of the Hyogo (Japan) Prefectural Police, James Melville offers a fine example of the police procedural with emphasis on the cultural clashes between Japanese concepts of crime and punishment and Western passions and psychology.

[*See also* Settings, Geographical.]

• Deborah Bonetti, "Murder Can Happen Anywhere," *Armchair Detective* 14, no. 3 (1981): 257–64. Greg Goode, "The Oriental in Mystery Fiction I: The Sinister Oriental," *Armchair Detective* 15, no. 3 (1982):196–202; "The Oriental in Mystery Fiction II: The Orient," *Armchair Detective* 15, no. 4 (1982): 306–13. Mark Schreiber, "The Unanswered Questions about Asia: Mysteries in the Far East," *Armchair Detective* 18, no. 2 (1985):164–66. Lizabeth Paravisini, "Murder in the Caribbean: In Search of Difference," *Clues* 9, no. 1 (1988): 1–9.   —Lizabeth Paravisini-Gebert

VISUALLY IMPAIRED DETECTIVE. *See* Disability, Sleuth with a.

VOCALLY IMPAIRED DETECTIVE. *See* Disability, Sleuth with a.

VOICE. *This entry consists of four articles.*

> Overview
> Genteel Voice
> Hard-Boiled Voice
> Wisecracking Voice

OVERVIEW

Selecting a storytelling perspective or voice can be the most determining decision of craft an author makes. Inherent in each author's decision about who is telling the story may be *clues to the worldview, moral orientation, personal and social values, and cultural legacy of the writer. At the opening of a text, the chosen narrative voice distinguishes the genre of the story to come and specifies the point of view that will preside over the events related. Although a printed text is silent, it may be identified by the animate term of voice because it carries the traces of personality and outlook conveyed in the tone and manner of an oral speaker, traces that permit the writer to influence audience reception of the printed narrative.

The preferred voice for most crime and mystery writing remains that of a storyteller distinct from any of the characters in the tale; for that reason, it is called third person. The attraction of the third person voice is that the writer can use it to set scenes from a general perspective, introduce exposition necessary to establish *milieu, and follow the actions of an unlimited number of characters. The third person voice suggests objectivity and detachment and thus is likely to build trust among readers. It seems to command the world on the page and to offer nothing but the unvarnished truth of that world.

Sometimes the third person voice assumes a transparent quality, like a window on the world. Tony *Hillerman sets the scene of *Listening Woman* (1978) by writing, "The southwest wind picked up turbulence around the San Francisco Peaks, howled across the emptiness of the Moenkopi plateau, and made a thousand strange sounds in windows of the old Hopi villages at Shongopovi and Second Mesa." The text suggests the perspective of a map, the product of cartographic measurement and disciplined observation, but then the wind "howls" and makes "a thousand strange sounds," descriptions indicating a subjective interpretation of mood. This third person voice is never identified with a character, yet it effortlessly projects through the window of narrative a humanized interpretation of the nonhuman natural occurrence. It is not at all transparent.

P. D. *James tells her readers in *Original Sin*

(1994), "For a temporary shorthand-typist to be present at the discovery of a corpse on the first day of a new assignment, if not unique, is sufficiently rare to prevent its being regarded as an occupational hazard." In this way the third person voice of the novel specifically announces that the genre of the story will be crime and mystery and illustrates the trace of personality in the wry tone taken by the voice at the intrusion of a *corpse on the humdrum affairs of a business office. That is not all, for a few lines later James states that Mandy Price, the temporary employee, had "set out on the morning of Tuesday 14 September for her interview at the Peverell Press with no more apprehension than she usually felt at the start of a new job. . . ." There are the objective details of place and date, but this third person voice has an intimate knowledge exceeding objectivity. The voice is omnisciently aware of Price's state of mind and is therefore able to fill the story to come with the private responses and thoughts of other characters.

Eager as they are to endow the third person voice with omniscience, writers of mystery fiction must place some limits on it. Rudolph Fisher in *The Conjure Man Dies* (1932) can personify a midwinter night in Harlem as growing warm and friendly on the "mid-realm of rhythm and laughter" on Seventh Avenue, but he dares not extend the observing and interpretative powers of the third person voice to a point where it is privy to all of the behavior of the *victim and killer. That would destroy the mystery at the heart of the novel and make it impossible for Fisher to work the reversal that makes the solution to the crime a surprise.

The most common alternative to the customary third person voice of crime and mystery fiction is to employ the voice of one of the characters in the story. In using an admiring aide to the chief detective to this end, Edgar Allan *Poe, Arthur Conan *Doyle, and Rex *Stout were able to enhance the stature of the *sleuth and to direct attention to the detection method. By providing the *Great Detective with a sidekick who displays faultless memory yet merely normal intelligence, the author throws into relief the detective's superior powers of ratiocination. Sidekicks have their limits, however, for they cannot directly convey the moods and values of the story's lead character—only the detective in person can do that.

In addition to elevating the *private eye to the status of popular hero, hard-boiled writing has been responsible for exploring the unique thematic possibilities of first person narration. Assuming the voice of the *Continental Op, Dashiell *Hammett projected into the tough world of American crime a character as hard and philosophically existentialist as the environment demands. Raymond *Chandler revealed by his use of Philip *Marlowe as narrator that the private eye may be a damaged and melancholy individual whose wariness communicates disillusion with the American dream. And Sue *Grafton's Kinsey *Milhone, in such a novel as *"J" Is for Judgment* (1993), illustrates how the subjective viewpoint of a first person voice can be used to create dual narratives, one recording the investigation of a crime, the second inquiring into the detective's own life.

The audience expectation's naive that the narrative voice will be a reliable witness has been capitalized upon by Agatha *Christie in *The Murder of Roger Ackroyd* (1926), where the narrator ultimately proves to be concealing the real murderer, and by Margaret *Millar in *Beast in View* (1955), where voice is employed to compel the reader to overlook a split personality. Such experiments have been few, however, not only because they do not survive repetition but, more importantly, because the range of voices in conventional use already offers writers nearly unlimited room to maneuver.

[See also Point of View, Narrative.]

• J. L. Austin, *How to Do Things with Words* (1962). Wolfgang Iser, *The Implied Reader* (1974). J. A. Cuddon, "Narrator," "Persona," and "Viewpoint," in *Dictionary of Literary Terms,* 3rd ed. (1991).   —John M. Reilly

GENTEEL VOICE

The concept of the genteel voice, or one that speaks with a cultured or superior air, is an elusive one, recognizable when encountered but difficult to define. Its literary roots go back to Jane Austen, who shared a certain quality of observation as well as a rigorous moral judgment and a sort of mental toughness with her successor Mrs. Elizabeth Cleghorn Gaskell. In the twentieth century they were followed by Barbara Pym, whose trenchant comedies of manners were set in a world of prim, well-bred spinsters and proper clergymen. In each of these writers there exists a subversive element, an irony, an underlying recognition that gentility is only skin deep.

In the mystery genre, the genteel voice is chiefly identified with *Golden Age forms. It is partly a matter of *setting: The *country house milieu is often used in books of the period, as is clear from the list by location in Susan Oleksiw's *A Reader's Guide to the Classic British Mystery* (1988). This world is peopled by those of "superior station." Social *class is significant: Dorothy L. *Sayers, Margery *Allingham, and Ngaio *Marsh all created detective characters of high birth, capable of holding their own in the rarefied circles in which they were required to exercise their detecting skills. But the preeminent practitioner of the genteel voice in the Golden Age was Agatha *Christie. She wrote of this world without irony; it was the world in which she lived, and whose attitudes she exemplified. Her Miss Jane *Marple is the quintessential genteel sleuth, moving through the worlds of the vicarage, English village, and comfortable hotels to solve crimes.

There is a large element of snobbery, unattractive to the modern reader, in books of this period. At their worst, they elevate respectability to a stature usually reserved for morality. But in Christie's work, in particular, this is unself-conscious and should be accepted as such.

This sort of sensibility is not so easy to find in contemporary crime writing—just as country houses are now out of fashion. Modern equivalents are set in clerical and *academic milieus. One current practitioner of the genteel voice is Hazel Holt, Pym's literary executor and biographer, who has created a Pymlike *amateur detective in Sheila Mallory. *The Cruellest Month* (1991) is replete with the trappings of academic gentility: *Oxford's dreaming spires, tea with cream cakes, William Morris wallpaper, and cricket on the green. The first-person narrative reinforces the genteel tone. But another example serves to demonstrate that it is not setting alone that defines the genteel voice. Veronica Stallwood's *Oxford Exit* (1994) is a book with, on the surface, an uncannily similar *plot to Holt's: a nosy Bodleian librarian is murdered, and her death is investigated by an amateur detective, a woman writer. But Stallwood's authorial voice, as well as the voice of her character Kate Ivory, is anything but genteel.

Margaret Yorke writes books in which, typically, an ordinary person, usually an upper-middle-class woman, finds the peace of her own sheltered life shattered by the intrusion of some sort of *evil, exposing the emptiness at the heart of her respectable world. This is part of the strength of the genteel voice: The eruption of *violence and *murder into a serene world is far more powerful and disturbing than that same violence and murder would be on the mean streets of some urban crime center—it does not belong there, just as the young blonde's body does not belong on the hearthrug in Colonel Bantry's library in Christie's *The Body in the Library* (1942). As Mrs. Bantry says to Marple, "It's not *nice* to have a body in one's house." The contrast between the idyllic, if unreal, world of the genteel voice and the brutality of murder creates enormous possibilities for the writer.

[*See also* Genteel Woman Sleuth.]

• Heron Carvic, "Little Old Ladies," in *Murder Ink: The Mystery Reader's Companion* (1977), ed. Dilys Winn. Dilys Winn, "Golden Age Legacy: The House Party," in *Murderess Ink: The Better Half of the Mystery* (1979). H. R. F. Keating, *Whodunit?: A Guide to Crime, Suspense and Spy Fiction* (1982). John M. Reilly, ed., *Twentieth Century Crime and Mystery Writers*, 3rd ed. (1991). Julian Symons, *Bloody Murder: From the Detective Story to the Crime Novel*, 3rd. rev. ed. (1992). Jean Swanson and Dean James, *By a Woman's Hand: A Guide to Mystery Fiction by Women.* (1994).

—Kate Charles *and* Lucy Walker

HARD-BOILED VOICE

In determining their choices for narrative voice, hard-boiled writers have followed the lead of Carroll John *Daly, whose prototypical "The False Burton Combs" (*Black Mask*, Dec. 1922) set the tough guy to speaking: "I ain't a crook; just a gentleman adventurer and make my living working against the law breakers. Not that I work with the police—no, not me. I'm no knight errant either. It just came to me that the simplest people in the world are crooks." With exceptions so rare as to be startling, as when readers realize that *The Maltese Falcon* (1930) is not a story uttered by Sam *Spade, hard-boiled writers have continued the practice begun by Daly of privileging the protagonist to give the account of crime and detection.

It makes good narrative sense to do so. Since alienation is the primary condition of the hard-boiled world and hostility pervades it, the detective must be a loner who keeps thoughts and personal feelings well guarded behind a dead pan and a sometimes cynical manner that are meant to deflect approaches from anyone probing for weak spots in the detective's emotional armor. Such a stance before society can be described by an omniscient third person, but it is conveyed most economically by means of a voice enacting the role of the *hard-boiled sleuth.

Everything necessary to be said about a crime comes by way of the hard-boiled voice, as when Paul Cain's tough narrator in "Trouble-Chaser" (*Black Mask*, Apr. 1934) relates a prelude to murder: "Then one of Tony's arms went around her white throat and his other arm went smoothly, swiftly out along her arm, his hand grasped her hand and the revolver. They moved like one thing. It was like watching the complex, terribly efficient working of a deadly machine; Tony twisted her arm back slowly, steadily, his arm tightened around her throat slowly. Her eyes widened, the white transparent skin of her face grew dark." The killing, completed when Tony puts a gun to the woman's temple, is brutal, but the voice is nonjudgmental. The focus is action, the view of it behaviorist.

Still, a consciousness is evident in the voice of hard-boiled narrative. As a tactic before the world, the detective assumes detachment but not disengagement. In fact, the drama of hard-boiled fiction is much less about detecting solutions to crimes than it is about the protagonist's response to events, the interaction of the hard-boiled consciousness and personality with others. In "So Pale, So Cold, So Fair" (*Argosy*, 1957) Leigh Brackett's *sleuth discovers the sleeping form of his former fiancée on the porch of his rented cabin; he touches her bare shoulder, feels her throat for a pulse. "She was not sleeping. She was dead. I stood there, hanging onto the porch rail, feeling sick as the whiskey turned in me and the glow went out. . . . The night and world rocked around me, and then, when they steadied down again, I began to feel another emotion. Alarm."

The vitality of the hard-boiled voice derives from its basis in the spoken American vernacular. Its slang and syntax suggest hard-won acceptance of life's underside. Benjamin Appel makes rare use of the stylized third person voice in *Dock Walloper* (1953): "Johnny Blue Jaw Gibbons offered Willy Toth the chance to get himself connected right on the waterfront—and not the first time either that opportunity has come knocking on a prison door. Those two could have become buddies only in a clink, for they were about as different as a pearl-handled .38 is from a piece of lead pipe."

Thanks to the resilience and resonance of the vernacular, hard-boiled dialogue helps to reinforce the dominant tone set by the narrative voice of the fiction. Gruff as it seems at times, signifying detachment as it does at other times, the hard-boiled voice is nonetheless as subtle an instrument as any in narrative art. Through timbre and tone it means more than it directly says.

[See also Gentleman Adventurer; Point of View, Narrative.]

• Stephen Knight, *Form and Ideology in Crime Fiction* (1980). Dennis Porter, *The Pursuit of Crime: Art and Ideology in Detective Fiction* (1981).   —John M. Reilly

WISECRACKING VOICE

The wisecrack—an ironic, cynical, and surprising remark that often succeeds as dry humor—became an art form in pulp *private eye fiction during the 1920s and 1930s. Associated at first with the American male voices of detectives like Dashiell *Hammett's Sam *Spade and Raymond *Chandler's Philip *Marlowe, wisecracks were often wry observations or conversational comebacks that advertised the male protagonist's intellectual dexterity and suggested his physical and emotional toughness. Closely related to the simile and metaphor, wisecracks could be used to reflect skepticism, antiauthoritarianism, irreverence, and an I-don't-give-a-damn attitude. The hard-boiled detective typically directs wisecracks at the establishment (especially as personified by the police) and adversaries. In the hands of more recent writers, the wisecracks is often a part of exchanges with sidekicks, lovers, and innocent bystanders. In the work of Sue *Grafton, wisecracks even appear in internal monologues.

The wisecrack defines the hard-boiled detective and is part of his or her intellectual syntax. Spade's wisecracks, for example, are as instinctive and edgy as his temper and sexuality, as in this exchange in *The Maltese Falcon* (1930).

> Cairo hesitated, said dubiously: "You have always, I must say, a smooth explanation ready."
> Spade scowled. "What do you want me to do? Learn to stutter?"

The wisecrack is to the modern, hard-boiled, streetwise detective what the aphorism was to Charlie *Chan or "elementary" was to Sherlock *Holmes. In *pulp magazines like *Dime Detective* and *Black Mask* and novels of the 1930s and beyond, the wisecrack is the voice of male experience meant to reflect realism and a true American vernacular. Spade in *The Maltese Falcon* is archetypal. The terse, wry comments suggest a virile, sardonic, disillusioned male who takes risks and who sees the world as being as ambiguous and fraudulent as Brigid O'Shaughnessy or the falcon itself. Language, values, and behavior are melded together so that they become inseparable. Wisecracking speech both reveals and makes the protagonist.

The wisecrack must be seen in context. It is a response to another character's comments or action, and it is not unusual for the target to respond by acknowledging the protagonist's wisecrack or (particularly in the case of sidekicks and romantic interests) responding in kind. In Chandler's *Farewell, My Lovely* (1940), Marlowe has an exchange with the police detective assigned to the case.

> "Was he wearing a fancy hat and white golf balls on his jacket?"
> Nulty frowned and twisted his hands on his kneecaps. "No, a blue suit. Maybe brown."

> "Sure it wasn't a sarong?"
> "Huh? Oh yeah, funny. Remind me to laugh on my day off."

The wisecrack reflects the protagonist's detachment. He or she is an outsider and wants to remain that way. The wisecrack is a way of distancing oneself from the surrounding *corruption and deception and thus reflects a strategy for moral (if not physical) survival. It often has a mocking, derisive quality to it. With the exception of repartee with lovers or friends, the wisecrack is often for the protagonist's own benefit. Lacking a fawning biographer or sidekick, the wisecracking detective creates sources of self-gratification.

The wisecrack and the accompanying dialogue typically take a form close to free verse. The comments are terse and improvisational, with an e.e. cummings-type of cadence that suggests the throwing off of convention. The wisecracking voice is itself a type of action. When the corporate executive Timmons asks Spenser "Who are you?" Robert B. *Parker's *Looking for Rachel Wallace* (1980), there is an elemental quality to Spenser's response—"the tooth fairy . . . I loosen teeth"—that is not much different from the short, quick jab to the solar plexus that he delivered earlier to the right-winger Square Jaw.

The wisecrack serves as verbal legerdemain: It misleads the reader (supporting Dorothy Parker's observation that wit contains truth while wisecracks are "simply calisthenics with words") or gives the author an opportunity to heighten the tension that surrounds it. But despite its lightness, the wisecrack itself is often unsettling. The private eye takes chances with wisecracks, demonstrating the fact that it is risk that gives much of the meaning to the detective's life.

[See also Humor; Narrative Theory; Point of View, Narrative.]

• David Geherin, *Sons of Sam Spade* (1980). Dennis Porter, *The Pursuit of Crime* (1981). Bernard Benstock, ed., *Essays on Detective Fiction* (1983).   —David N. Smith

VOYEURISM, or the act of secret and often illicit observation, is often used as a *plot device in crime writing. Voyeurism underscores the mystery's air of pervasive menace or serves as a comment on the fragility of privacy and personal safety. Beyond this, voyeurism applies to readers of the genre who gain satisfaction by observing the victimization of some characters. The uneasy complicity between reader and writer in voyeuristic examination of crime is a large part of the experience of reading Cornell *Woolrich's "It Had to Be Murder" (in *Dime Detective*, 1942), a story later made famous as the Alfred Hitchcock film *Rear Window* and later republished in prose form under that title.

Several prominent strains in modern mystery fiction have played on that same knot of culpability, granting the wish to learn the forbidden even as they criminalize that impulse. The hard-boiled novelists' promise to strip the lies from society and lay bare what lies underneath plays off related urges, as do the psychosexual tableaux presented in Mickey *Spillane novels such as *One Lonely Night* (1951) (which concludes with a horde of slavering Commies shipping Mike *Hammer's nude secretary, which Hammer stops to watch before killing them all), or—albeit more guardedly and with a greater degree of self-awareness—the brutalities writers like Andrew Vachss simultaneously indulge in and condemn. James *Ellroy deserves special mention for the density of his involvement with this theme: All of his novels, most explicitly *The Black Dahlia* (1987), present in great detail and then obsessively revisit scenes of grotesque violation; his characters are often voyeurs themselves who are fascinated by the spectacle of violation; and his *My Dark Places: An L.A. Crime Memoir* (1996) traces his own pursuit of dead women back to his mother's unsolved murder. The rash of best-selling true-crime accounts and serial-killer novels in the 1990s, stuffed with lovingly detailed fetishes and perversions, gratifies a similar impulse; David Lindsey's novel *Mercy* (1990), for example, opens with a thorough description of an S&M scene's escalation into *murder.

Voyeurism has served more often as a crime to be investigated by police than by *gentleman detectives. Inspector *Morse looks into a case involving a Peeping Tom in Colin *Dexter's *The Dead of Jericho* (1981). The voyeur ends up dead, but his death has more to do with the novel's real crimes, neglect and selfishness, than with spying on his attractive neighbor. Male voyeurs seeking sexual satisfaction through obsessive observation of women sometimes also entrap their prey, as is the case in John Fowles's *The Collector*, or ensnare, assault, and kill several victims, as is the case in any number of books focusing on serial killers.

[*See also* Deviance; Menacing Characters; Serial Killers and Mass Murderers.]

—Jesse Berrett

WADE, HENRY, pseudonym of Sir Henry Lancelot Aubrey-Fletcher (1887–1969), British crime writer active between 1927 and 1954. Wade was an influential figure in his day, chiefly in England, where all of his works were published, in contrast with the United States, where only some of his fiction saw publication. He has been compared with Freeman Wills *Crofts, R. A. J. Walling, J. S. Fletcher, and G. D. H. and Margaret *Cole as a member of what Julian *Symons called the "Humdrum" school of comfortable and systematic police mysteries.

Wade was born in Surrey and educated at Eton and at New College, Oxford. A decorated veteran of World War I, he succeeded to the baronetcy in 1937. He served as a justice of the peace and county alderman and high sheriff in Buckinghamshire.

Wade's earliest novels, *The Verdict of You All* (1926) and *The Missing Partners* (1928), deal with possible miscarriages of *justice, their *plots revolving around precisely handled factual detail. *The Duke of York's Steps* (1929) introduced the series character Chief Inspector Poole, who also appeared in *No Friendly Drop* (1931), *Constable, Guard Thyself!* (1934), *Bury Him Darkly* (1936), and a number of less successful later novels. Wade continued to write into the 1950s, when his work seemed rather old-fashioned and antiquated. Nonetheless, *Too Soon to Die* (1953) and *A Dying Fall* (1955) are highly accomplished and interesting classical tales, and some signs of Wade's influence linger on in the work of P. D. *James.

[*See also* Police Detective.]

—Ian Bell

WALLACE, (RICHARD HORATIO) EDGAR (1875–1932), British author, dramatist, and journalist who wrote in many genres but is best remembered as the "King of Thrillers." The illegitimate son of an actor, he was born in Greenwich (London) and adopted in infancy by a Deptford fish porter. After leaving school at the age of twelve, he took numerous jobs, and later served with the Royal West Kent Regiment and the Medical Staff Corps in South Africa. A subsequent period with Reuters during the Boer War launched him on a lifelong career in journalism—as reporter, racing editor, and proprietor of newspapers and racing journals.

Wallace's commercial approach to writing was evident from the outset, when he founded the Tallis Press and published *The Four Just Men* (1905), an incomplete *locked room mystery containing a tear-out slip offering £500 to readers furnishing the solution.

This proved to be financially disastrous, but it was to become his best-known book and was followed by several sequels.

In the crime fiction field alone, Wallace produced some ninety novels and numerous short stories and plays. He often worked simultaneously on several books, and reputedly dictated *The Coat of Arms* (1931; *The Arranways Mystery*) in one weekend and his play *On the Spot* (1930) in just four days. The latter is nevertheless regarded as his best drama, showing his skill in *plot construction and gift for writing dialogue. These indeed were the hallmarks of his success, together with his ability to build *suspense, to combine comedy and *terror, and to cling steadfastly to the triumph of good over *evil. He also made excellent use of his humble background when portraying small-time crooks and chirpy cockneys, his knowledge of Africa in the series beginning with *Sanders of the River* (1911), and his luckless love of the turf in tales such as *Educated Evans* (1924).

While his writing could be slapdash, his situations predictable, and his characters wooden, Wallace knew what his public wanted and gave it to them—in novels of gangland such as *When the Gangs Came to London* (1932), in such clever detective *puzzles as *The Crimson Circle* (1922) and *The Clue of the New Pin* (1923), and in a host of pure *thrillers. His economy of style made him a master of the short story, most notably those collected in *The Mind of Mr. J. G. Reeder* (1925; *The Murder Book of J. G. Reeder*).

[*See also* Formula.]

• Margaret Lane, *Edgar Wallace: The Biography of a Phenomenon*, rev. ed. (1964).

—Melvyn Barnes

WAR in fiction, Diana Trilling pointed out in 1944, is too often like a storm, something noisy going on outside the house. It is hard to bring it into the house in detective stories because in the classic form killing violates a peaceful order and is committed in secret for personal reasons. E. C. R. Lorac's *Murder by Matchlight* (1945) turns the trick literally by having a German incendiary bomb crash through a *London roof and psychologically by having the murderer's *motive be inextricably linked to the war.

Before the Second World War even the best spy novels, such as Erskine *Childers's *The Riddle of the Sands* (1903), John *Buchan's *The Thirty-Nine Steps* (1915), and the 1930s novels of Eric *Ambler—all of which used the premise of innocent middle-class men being plunged into foreign intrigue—treated war as a coming probability, not a present reality.

Richard Hannay, however, in Buchan's *Greenmantle* (1916) and *Mr. Standfast* (1919), did go into combat as an officer, fighting in a historical battle (Erzerum) and declaring himself a devotee of war as "the only task for a man." But the *puzzle element, intriguingly present in Childers, is increasingly overwhelmed in his successors by melodramatic adventure. An interesting exception is Graham *Greene's *The Ministry of Fear* (1943) because its hero, who is "fond of investigation," feels himself more at home in "an old-fashioned world of detective inspectors" than in the *London of the Blitz, which seems to have been "remade by William Le Queux," prolific writer of sensational spy stories.

Some British writers, with a foot in both genres, have found original ways of integrating war and detection. Michael *Gilbert's *Death in Captivity* (1952; *The Danger Within*), for example, finds a classic closed community in an Italian prison camp, engaged in organizing a mass escape. The puzzle involves a captive found dead at the face of a hidden tunnel, and an English prisoner who by detection gradually discovers the surprising reality beneath the appearances. Len Deighton audaciously solved the problem of integration in a pseudohistorical novel, *SS-GB* (1978), in which England surrenders in 1941 to its German occupiers. Even so, an educated detective superintendent carries on traditional police procedure in solving a homicide, but finds himself inexorably drawn into the complex politics of the Resistance.

A more common solution is to use war as a historical past that is uncovered in the present. Gilbert's *Death Has Deep Roots* (1951), premised on the trial in England of a Frenchwoman for allegedly stabbing an English officer, proves in court that "everything that happened in England depended on what had happened five years before in France." The wartime past is crucial also for Patricia Moyes's *Johnny Under Ground* (1965). An abandoned former Royal Air Force Station links all the characters and is the site for the entrapment of a murderer, threatened by a female detective's biography of a missing airman. Robert *Barnard's *Out of the Blackout* (1985), the moving story of a man's search for his childhood identity, uses the historical evacuation of children in 1941 from London to the West Country. Evoking the *urban milieu of Oswald Mosley's Blackshirts, Barnard finds a method for hiding a murder *victim during an air raid that is as ingeniously simple as the trick in Poe's purloined letter. In Robert Goddard's complex *Hand in Glove* (1992), two amateur inquirers uncover literary and political secrets which link a present crime with one committed during the Spanish Civil War.

The modern English master of blending military history with fictional mystery is Anthony Price. His best intricately plotted novels combine a knowledge of British military history with a modern cast of Buchan's patriotic gentlemen and women. The protagonists vary, but each novel shows Price's feeling for the resonance of the present with the past, whether it be England's Roman Wall, a German victory over Roman legions, the English Civil War, a British frigate lost in the Napoleonic Wars, or the Battle of the Somme, its British dead "the cream of the nation, irreplaceable as men," the German dead, "the cream of the army, irreplaceable as soldiers" (*Other Paths to Glory*, 1974). This novel, with its characteristic lore about guns, ammunition, and tactics of an earlier war, engrossingly shows how two historians of the Hindenburg Line are threatened by their study of it.

[*See also* missing Persons; Violence.]

• Cyril Hare, "The Classic Form," in *Crime in Good Company: Essays on Criminals and Crime Writing*, ed. Michael Francis Gilbert (1959). John M. Reilly, ed., *Twentieth Century Crime and Mystery Writers*, 3rd ed. (1991). William Reynolds, "The Labyrinth Maker: The Espionage Fiction of Anthony Price," *Armchair Detective* 19, no. 4 (1986), 350–58.

—Cushing Strout

Warshawski, V(ictoria) I(phigenia), Sara Paretsky's feminist American hard-boiled private eye, appearing first in *Indemnity Only* (1982). Warshawski, who insists on using her initials to avoid being patronized, has left behind the Chicago public defender's office, a brief marriage, and her initial naïveté to take on the culturally privileged social institutions whose power and authority are used to protect the guilty. Challenging the insurance industry and labor unions in *Indemnity Only*, the Catholic Church and organized crime in *Killing Orders*, (1985), the medical establishment in *Bitter Medicine* (1987), and even the police department, Warshawski uncovers the *corruption which accompanies unchecked power. Unlike Raymond *Chandler's Philip *Marlowe, who takes on similarly corrupt criminals, Paretsky's feminist detective clearly articulates patriarchal privilege as the site of sanctioned oppression. Warshawski's clients include women and girls, the elderly, the poor, and Hispanics in unequal battles against the wealthy, powerful Chicago establishment.

Warshawski's private life differs as much as her professional one from those of the conventional male *hard-boiled sleuth of Chandler, Dashiell *Hammett, and Ross *Macdonald. Despite being orphaned and divorced, she is no isolated loner. Instead, Paretsky has woven together an improbable "family of choice" for Warshawski; although the most important is Dr. Charlotte "Lotty" Herschel, a Holocaust survivor, Warshawski also values her intrusive neighbor, Mr. Contreras, and his enthusiastic golden retriever, Peppy, as well as her father's old friend, police lieutenant Bobby Mallory. And, in each novel, beginning with *Deadlock* (1984), Paretsky weaves Warshawski's professional and personal lives together so that her friends and family also become her clients.

As a first-person narrator, Warshawski directly engages readers in her life: her messy apartment, her fascination with the Chicago Cubs, and her precious, inherited Venetian wine glasses are as well articulated as her passion for causes like abortion rights or affirmative action and against sexual harassment or racial discrimination. She is intensely self-aware; recognizing her own limitations, motives, and ambivalence, Warshawski follows neither the formula of the hard-boiled private eye nor the polemics of the separatist feminist. In Warshawski, Paretsky has created a "heroic" character, carving out new territory for both women and detectives.

[*See also* Females and Feminists; Urban Milieu.]

• Jane S. Bakerman, "Living 'Openly and with Dignity': Sara Paretsky's New Boiled Feminist Fiction," *Midamerica* (1985): 120–35. Priscilla Walton, "Paretsky's V. I. as P. I. Revising the Script and Recasting the Dick," *Literature Interpretation Theory* 4 (1993): 203–13.   —Kathleen Gregory Klein

"WATERS." *See* History of Crime and Mystery Writing: Formation of the Genre.

WATSON, COLIN (1920–1982), author of thirteen comic mystery novels satirizing the world of the classic village mystery as well as of a scathing study of *prejudice and sentimentality in crime fiction (*Snobbery with Violence: Crime Stories and Their Audience*, 1971). He was born and educated in Croydon, Surrey, and worked in advertising and print and television/radio journalism.

The harbor town of Flaxborough and its environs in Lincolnshire is home to a bawdy population forever engaged in erotic behavior, criminal and otherwise. Introduced in *Coffin, Scarcely Used* (1958), Watson's series character Inspector Purbright is patient, astute, and down to earth while he tracks down criminals who run sideways and widows who disappear into unexpected occupations. Watson mocks the middle-class devotion to good works in *Charity Ends at Home* (1968) and the lust hidden beneath apparent intellectual activities in *Broomsticks over Flaxborough* (1972; *Kissing Covens*). His books are invariably funny with ribald humor and vivid secondary characters, such as Lucilla Teatime, a genteel criminal who appears in *Lonelyheart 4122* (1967).

—Susan Oleksiw

Watson, Dr. John H. When Arthur Conan *Doyle created Sherlock *Holmes, he simultaneously created Dr. John H. Watson, a companion and intellectual foil who is so essential to the optimum deployment of Holmes's art that, to most readers, the two men have become firmly linked. As he recorded the character and a few titillating biographical details of Watson, Doyle could never have anticipated that every scrap of information would be so meticulously analyzed by subsequent Holmesian devotees. Doyle remains consistent as to the outlines of Watson's biography, but there are important inconsistencies in details. The bullet wound he suffered while upon military service in Afghanistan wanders from his leg to his shoulder, he has been married at least twice, yet Holmes on occasion refers to Watson's last marriage as his first. Even his name raises problems. He is usually, and often definitively, Dr. John H. Watson, yet his wife calls him James, perhaps the *H* standing for Hamish, the Scottish form of James, as was suggested by Dorothy L. *Sayers.

Although the immediate intimacy of the Holmes/Watson association varies greatly during their time together, principally depending upon Watson's marital state—one year goes by with Watson being involved in only three cases—the basic terms of the as-

sociation change little. Except in the final story, "His Last Bow" (*Strand*, Sept. 1917), neither Holmes nor Watson matures or ages significantly during the more than thirty years of their recorded collaboration. Watson marries, becomes a widower, and is remarried. He changes the location of his practice at least three times during the course of his civilian medical career, but he remains his same solid self. Today's public sometimes believes Watson to have been dense, if not positively stupid; but, in fact, Doyle implies this only to the minimal extent that is necessary to show off Holmes's brilliance. As Watson says in "The Adventure of the Creeping Man" (*Strand*, Mar. 1923), "I was a whetstone for his mind; I stimulated him; he liked to think aloud in my presence."

Watson fulfills many distinct functions for Holmes (and Doyle), more, in fact, than most other characters cast in similar roles. As well as being his trusted confidant, Watson is a friend whose commitment is profound. He refers to Holmes as "the man whom above all others I revere" in "The Problem of the Thor Bridge" (*Strand*, Feb. 1922) and "the best and wisest man whom I have ever known" in "The Final Problem" (*Strand*, Dec. 1893). The emotional depths of the association are rarely plumbed. Once only, when Watson is wounded in "The Adventure of the Three Garridebs" (*Collier's*, 25 Oct. 1924), does Holmes's anxiety reveal, if only for an instant, "the great heart within." Watson is the usual narrator of the stories. When he is not—as in "The Adventure of the Blanched Soldier" (*Liberty Magazine*, 16 Oct. 1926)—he is sorely missed.

Watson is the counterbalance to Holmes's misanthropic tendencies, especially with respect to women, Holmes being essentially immune to the "gentler passions," while Watson enjoys a reputation as a ladies' man.

Watson always provides a wondering, astonished, and loyally admiring audience for Holmes's explanations of his deductions, however incompletely convincing the certainty of his reasoning may be. "Elementary, my dear Watson" reflects this aspect of Watson, even though it is not a true canonical quotation.

[*See also* Friendship; Sidekicks and Sleuthing Teams.]   —John D. Constable

WAUGH, HILLARY (BALDWIN), (b. 1920). A pioneer in the development of the American *police procedural, Hillary Waugh had published three promising novels in the late 1940s before producing his best-known book, *Last Seen Wearing—* (1952). Told in a deliberately unsensational style with an uncluttered *plot line and a killer who remains just off-stage, Waugh's novel was coolly received by some critics. It was not until Raymond *Chandler praised it and Julian *Symons included it on a list of the hundred best crime stories that readers began to recognize it as a true classic.

Chief Frank Ford, the detective in the New England college town that is the setting for *Last Seen Wearing—*, never reappeared in Waugh's work, but Waugh created a similar *sleuth, Chief Fred Fellows, who worked in another New England town. Fellows appeared in eleven novels, notably *The Missing Man* (1964) and *The Con Game* (1968), before Waugh moved on to a big-city detective, Frank Sessions, introduced in *"30" Manhattan East* (1968).

Born in New Haven, Connecticut, Waugh received a bachelor's degree from Yale University in 1942, where he later taught mystery writing. He also worked as a cartoonist, newspaper editor, and high school teacher.

Waugh has written nearly fifty novels, some under the pseudonym Elissa Grandower, and served as president of the *Mystery Writers of America. The organization honored him with its Grand Master award in 1989.

• George N. Dove, introduction to *Last Seen Wearing* — Mystery Library ed. (1978).   —Edward D. Hoch

WEAPONS, UNUSUAL MURDER.

Unusual murder weapons are a well-established tradition in crime and mystery fiction. Since the early days of the genre, many authors have striven to demonstrate their *ingenuity by creating unique weapons to do away with hapless *victims. In the classical *detective novel murderers employ such weapons to obfuscate the circumstances of the crime. From the perpetrator's viewpoint, the perfect *murder weapon is one which will not link him to the crime, either because it cannot be identified or because it is destroyed. After all, if the police cannot show how a crime was committed, they cannot build a chain of evidence proving *means, motive, and opportunity; therefore, they will not have a case strong enough to take to court. Innovative weapons include mundane objects which have some ordinary harmless function and are not commonly considered lethal instruments as well as purposely designed ingenious contrivances, both mechanical and nonmechanical. At times even innocent nature has been pressed into service by desperate miscreants.

The ideal murder weapon is one which disappears after being used. One of the best examples is the frozen leg of lamb in Roald Dahl's "Lamb to the Slaughter" (*Harper's*, Sept. 1953) which is employed as a bludgeon to kill an errant husband and then roasted by his wife and fed to the investigating officers. Other killers have resorted to bullets made of ice or icicles to stab their victim. This device first appeared in Anna Katharine *Green's *Initials Only* (1911), in which a young woman is felled by a small icicle shot from a pistol. The master criminal in Edgar *Wallace's *The Three Just Men* (1925) improves upon this idea by freezing deadly snake venom into the shape of tiny darts and using a fake cigarette holder with an insulated chamber as a blowpipe. The film *Charlie Chan's Secret* (1936) presents a variation on the device when the villain dispatches his quarry during a séance by firing an ice bullet from a cigar case fitted with a trigger mechanism.

Almost as good is the lethal instrument which is so innocuous as never to be associated with murder. Among innocent household objects converted to deadly weapons, perhaps the most unlikely is the common bed. In Ronald A. *Knox's "Solved by Inspection" (*My Best Detective Story*, 1931), a rich man with a fear of heights is starved to death when his bed is raised by ropes to the ceiling of his private gymnasium and he cannot get down to a buffet laden with food without falling to a certain death. In Agatha *Christie's *Towards Zero* (1944), the killer fashions an effective bludgeon by screwing a round steel knob from a fireplace fender onto the handle of a tennis racquet after removing the stringed oval frame from it. He subsequently replaces the stringed frame, disguising the join with adhesive tape, and hides the racquet among several others in a cupboard where it should attract no special notice. In a similar vein, the murderer in Catherine Aird's *The Religious Body* (1966) creates a blunt instrument by clutching the shaft which connects the heavy round wooden ball serving as a finial to an oaken newel post of a staircase and striking his victim a swinging blow. He then returns it to its normal position where it is ignored as police search for the murder weapon.

A more modern and more sophisticated household appliance is featured in P. M. Carlson's *Murder in the Dog Days* (1991), wherein an ill man goes into convulsions and dies of heatstroke when the temperature of his study reaches an intolerable level. His death is contrived by means of a hallway thermostat whose setting is raised outside his room early in the day and then readjusted before the body is discovered. With the door bolted on the inside, the crime scene appears to be a perfect locked room murder.

Lethal mechanical contrivances span a large range. R. Austin *Freeman's short story "The Aluminium Dagger" (*John Thorndyke's Cases*, 1909) presents a locked room *puzzle in which a man has been stabbed in the back; the sitting room door is locked and bolted from the inside, and the windows, although open, are forty feet from the ground with no vines or drainpipes nearby to offer a handhold for climbing up. The Freeman's Dr. Thorndyke ultimately deduces that the dagger in question was fired from a chassepôt rifle through a window in another building thirty yards away. Another sophisticated device appears in Dorothy L. *Sayers's "The Poisoned Dow '08" (*Hangman's Holiday*, 1933), in which a corkscrew has been altered so that poison stored in the hollow handle is released by pressing the plunger. The advantage of this mechanism lies in concealing that the poison is added to the wine by the server after the bottle has been sealed rather than during the vinting and bottling process. Designed to be operated by the victim rather than the villain, the devilishly clever murder weapon in Rex *Stout's *Fer-de-Lance* (1934; *Meet Nero Wolfe*) drew attention to him the author at the beginning of his career; here the head of an ordinary golf club has been modified so that when a ball is struck, a trigger is released and a poisoned needle is shot out of the handle into the golfer's abdomen.

Death has often been arranged by means of mechanical or nonmechanical booby traps rigged to look like bizarre accidents. In Ngaio *Marsh's *Vintage Murder* (1937), a jeroboam of champagne that is supposed to descend slowly from on high to rest on a banquet table in front of the guest of honor instead plummets upon release. Its counterweight having been removed, the skull of the stunt's creator is crushed. More recently, in Ruth Dudley Edwards's *Matricide at St. Martha's* (1995), a Cambridge don propells herself to her death when she mounts a library ladder and gives a strong push to slide the ladder along its grooves to the other end of a wall of books. The ladder gathers speed, and because the brakes at the end of the rails has been removed, both don and ladder are catapult out of a window. In Reginald *Hill's *Deadheads* (1983), highly toxic insecticides and weed killers are tipped into an attic cistern used to supply a shower below, ultimately drenching the intended victim.

Unusual murder weapons have sometimes been drawn from nature. Animals and insects have been recruited as agents of destruction. In Arthur Conan *Doyle's "The Adventure of the Speckled Band" (*Strand*, Feb. 1892), an Indian swamp adder has been deliberately trained to strike at an intended victim. A rattlesnake has been used by Kathryn Lasky Knight in *Trace Elements* (1986), a coral snake by Aaron J. Elkins in *Curses!* (1989). In Ruth *Rendell's *To Fear a Painted Devil* (1965), a man dies of allergic reaction when a bee is induced to sting him. The aid of natural phenomena is occasionally enlisted to arrange what looks like accidental death. For example, the victim in Marsh's *Colour Scheme* (1943) is boiled to death when he is pushed into a seething mud pool at a thermal springs resort.

Perhaps the most bizarre instrument of death, but not of murder, appears in Sayers's *The Nine Tailors* (1934) when a man locked in a church belfry dies of no visible cause. It is later determined that he was so stunned by the volume of sound produced by the ringing bells that he expired from the pressure of the sound waves. And perhaps the most amusing device occurs in Lindsey Davis's *Venus in Copper* (1991), in which a woman is held responsible when her husband dies by choking on one of the suppositories he had been using to treat his piles. The circumstances were extremely suspicious because he had not had a cough, and as an apothecary he would not have mistaken a suppository for a cough lozenge.

—B. J. Rahn

WENTWORTH, PATRICIA (1878–1961), British author of detective novels. Born Dora Amy Elles in Musoorie, India, Wentworth was educated privately and at the Blackheath High School for Girls in London. She married twice and had one daughter with her second husband, Lt. Col. George Oliver Turnbull, who assisted her in preparing her manuscripts for publication. After 1920, Wentworth lived in Surrey, and beginning in 1923, produced novels at a steady rate. Thirty-two of Wentworth's seventy-one novels feature governess-turned-detective Miss Maud *Silver, who first appeared in *Grey Mask* (1928). Wentworth excelled in creating the world of the *cozy mystery novel in which Silver, with her knowledge of human nature, chatted with *suspects and discreetly gossiped until she found the truth. Tidy plots, a con-

ventional world, and an unassuming, genteel detective make Wentworth's novels appealing seven decades after the series began. Among the most highly regarded is *The Benevent Treasure* (1956).

[*See also* Elderly Sleuth; English Village Milieu; Genteel Woman Sleuth; Spinster Sleuth.]

• Nancy Blue Wynne, "Patricia Wentworth Revisited," *Armchair Detective* 14, no. 1 (1981): 90–92. Virginia S. Hale, "Patricia Wentworth," in *Great Women Mystery Writers*, ed. Kathleen Gregory Klein (1994).   —Dean James

WESTERN, THE. The first western hero in American fiction was James Fenimore Cooper's Natty Bumppo, who D. H. Lawrence believed was the archetypal American. Cooper's characterization of Bumppo led Lawrence to write in his *Studies in Classic American Literature* (1923) that "the essential American soul is hard, isolate, stoic, and a killer," or as Richard Brookhiser put it in his essay "Deerslayer Helped Define us All" (*Time*, 9 Nov. 1992), "Down those mean forest paths Natty must walk alone, except for his Indian comrade, Chingachgook." Brookhiser's allusion to Raymond *Chandler makes clear the connection between crime fiction and western fiction; the two genres developed practically side by side in the United States, and it is easy to see that the distance between Natty Bumppo/Chingachgook and *Spenser/Hawk is not as wide as it might at first appear.

The western hero after Cooper was developed primarily by the the authors of the *dime novel of the nineteenth century, which, according to Henry Nash Smith in *Virgin Land*, "by the 1890s . . . had come to hinge almost entirely upon conflicts between detectives and bands of robbers." Two of the most famous western heroes of the dime novel era were Deadwood Dick and the fictional (as opposed to the actual) Buffalo Bill, both of whom, Smith says, often functioned as detectives in the stories about them.

The dime novels eventually evolved into the *pulp magazines of the early twentieth century, and western fiction was a prominent feature in many of them. *Black Mask*, which was to become the most famous detective pulp of them all, printed a great deal of western fiction until well into the 1930s, at which time Carroll John *Daly's hard, stoic killers, Race *Williams and Three Gun Terry Mack, led the way for the hard-boiled *private eyes who came to dominate the publication.

Later pulp writers included Louis L'Amour, now best known for his western fiction. L'Amour, however, wrote all kinds of stories, including crime and mystery fiction, for the pulps before establishing himself as a western writer in the paperback market (the natural descendant of the pulps) in the 1950s.

In the paperback field, a number of writers known mostly for crime and mystery fiction wrote western fiction as well. While their names might not be familiar to today's readers, William R. Cox, Richard Wormser, Harry Whittington, Richard Jessup, and Jack Ehrlich, among others, all wrote entertaining novels in both genres for various paperback publishers. Donald Hamilton, author of the popular Matt

Helm series of spy novels, wrote several distinguished westerns, including *The Big Country* (1957), before creating the Helm character. Elmore *Leonard, who went on to reach best-seller lists with his crime novels, started his career as a western writer just as the pulps were fading and moved into the paperback western market when he began publishing novels. Two of his early successes were *Hombre* (1961) and *Valdez Is Coming* (1969), both of which were filmed (in 1967 and 1971, respectively) before the publication of Leonard's first successful crime novel in 1974.

Today, there are a number of writers working in both the western and crime fields. Among them are Loren Estleman, L. J. Washburn, James M. Reasoner, Edward Gorman, Bill Pronzini, and Bill Crider. The westerns of all these writers are often built around criminous story lines, and some of their novels, such as Crider's *A Time for Hanging* (1989), have straight mystery *plots, though the books are set in the Old West. Ed D. *Hoch's short stories about western detective Ben Snow appear with some regularity in *Ellery Queen's Mystery Magazine*, while stories by Clark Howard, Pronzini, and Jeremiah Healy, known primarily for their crime fiction, have appeared in *Louis L'Amour Western Magazine*.

Obviously the frontier tale and stories of crime and detection are closely connected in the history of American popular literature. The link between the two has existed almost from their beginnings or even before their beginnings, since it can be argued that America's fictional frontiersmen and the private eyes so popular in crime fiction have a common ancestor: the questing knights of Arthurian romance. Considering their parallel development and common ancestry, it is not surprising that the two fields have shared writers who work with equal facility in both.

[*See also* Chivalry, Code of; Great Outdoors; Heroism; Pathfinder Fiction.]

—Bill Crider

WEXFORD, INSPECTOR. Chief Inspector Reginald Wexford is the central character in a series of novels by Ruth *Rendell. He made his initial appearance in Rendell's first novel, *From Doon with Death* (1964), and has featured in over fifteen novels since. (The character also served as the the basis for a popular British television series of the early 1990s.) Throughout the sequence, Wexford remains as a senior police officer in Kingsmarkham, a fictional mid-Sussex town. He is in his fifties, of a pragmatic temperament, but no mere follower of standard procedures, and capable of sudden intuitive insights. He forms a contrast with his subordinate associate, Inspector Mike Burden, an altogether more severe figure, much less sympathetic to the modern world, and much more traditional in his attitudes. The interaction of these characters can be compared to the relationship of the policemen Andrew Dalziel and Peter Pascoe in the work of Reginald *Hill, and there are many other parallel cases in British crime writing. Although the character of Burden is carefully developed—in *No More Dying Then* (1971) he has to handle a complex case while mourning the death of his wife—it is the senior officer whose personality dominates the books. Alongside the difficulties of policing, Wexford has to deal with domestic problems involving his wife Dora and his daughters, one of whom (Sheila) becomes a successful actress with the Royal Shakespeare Company. He also undergoes a stressful middle age, culminating in his suffering a stroke in *Murder Being Once Done* (1972). The Wexfords have a wide circle of friends and acquaintances in Kingsmarkham, as well as a taste for dinner parties, so that the police work is always situated within a recognizable middle-class social context. The cases investigated by Wexford often deal with extreme psychological conditions and sudden outbreaks of catastrophic *violence. While police procedure is important in the Wexford novels, more central is the portrayal of a fundamentally decent and talented man confronting a world in which mayhem may break out at any time. As he investigates cases of internecine strife or sexual frustration or *child abuse (Rendell's recurrent themes), Wexford strives to act dispassionately and struggles to maintain the security of his *family. Again and again, the central character has to reappraise his own life and that of his wife and daughters in the light of the sordid revelations arising from the cases he investigates. While Wexford is never given a full poetical veneer, he is nonetheless a cultivated man of sensitivity and humanity, and the brutality he encounters in his work often disturbs him. In the best Wexford novels—*Some Lie and Some Die* (1973), *Shake Hands Forever* (1975), and *A Sleeping Life* (1978)—the intricacies of the plot combine with the familiarity of the central figure to produce complex and satisfying tales of the madness of modern life.

[*See also* Police Detective; Police Procedural.]

• T. J. Binyon, *Murder Will Out: The Detective in Fiction* (1989). Ian A. Bell, "'He Do the Police in Different Voices': Representations of the Police in Contemporary British Crime Fiction," in *The Art of Murder*, ed. H. Gustav Klaus and Stephen Knight (1998).

—Ian A. Bell

WHITE-COLLAR CRIME. If fiction actually were the reflection of common reality that common sense encourages us to believe it is, and if crime and mystery writing literally did comment on the world where most of its readers reside, as some expect it to do, then most narratives about crime and its detection would relate those nonviolent deceptions, *thefts, and frauds known as white-collar crimes. After all, people in clerical jobs, management positions, skilled technical and professional work—typical readers of the genre—are more likely to have knowledge of falsified documents or testimony, misrepresentation in business, even conspiracies to cheat the unwitting, than they are to know about actual *murders. And the same may be said of writers themselves. Yet when it comes to constructing narratives, writers will defer to the demands of narrative form. Descriptions of action offer them the shortest route to dramatic conflict. Violent death seems the worthiest subject for expenditure of a fictional detective's energy and the best source of elegant *puzzles. As a result, the violations of practices of business abounding in the real white-collar world are the material of specialists in the fictitious realms of fiction.

A notable example of such specialization during the Golden Age is to be found in the works of Freeman Wills *Crofts, who is at his best when describing young clerks in offices, on their way up from a working-class background or down from a professional one, tempted by hopes of easy profit into schemes ranging from the shady to the clearly illegal. In *Fatal Venture* (1939; *Tragedy in the Hollow*) for example, he describes a chain of thefts of a business idea with the same painstaking attention to detail that his stolid, unglamorous hero, Inspector Joseph *French, devotes to detective work.

Some of the most sophisticated forms of fraud, in fiction as in life, are aimed at would-be investors in shares or bonds who are hoodwinked into believing their money is going into secure articles when in fact it is being siphoned off into covert accounts. Modern frauds are not just cons with *class—their operations are underpinned by meticulous paperwork. As fraud has grown more complex, so has the law relating to it. Jeffrey Archer's *Not a Penny More, Not a Penny Less* (1976) takes account of the evolution of fraudulent practice and law to present a scheme meant to lure innocent investors into excessive payment for shares of stock. Paul E. Erdman, himself experienced in banking, has written about rich and unscrupulous dealers manipulating the precious metals and commodity markets. Overall, however, it was the pair of authors writing under the pseudonyms Emma *Lathen and R. B. Dominic who did the most to show the increasing diversity of financial crime and the laws designed to counter it.

[See also Banking and Financial Milieu; Bribery; Con Artist; Extortion; Murderless Mystery.]
—Sarah Caudwell *and* Jenny Grove

WHITNEY, PHYLLIS A(YAME) (b. 1903), prolific author of highly popular novels of romantic *suspense and of suspenseful mysteries for the juvenile market. An American born in Yokohama, Japan, Whitney has lived in Japan, China, the Philippines, and the United States and has set novels for both of her audiences, adult and juvenile, in these countries and in other exotic *settings that she investigated during research trips.

Whitney's work is preoccupied with showing female protagonists in the process of discovering themselves through finding the solutions to old *family secrets and crimes. Predictably, there is danger, or the distinct threat of it, along the way, with the villain often turning out to be one of the protagonist's own relatives while the initially frightening *suspicious character may be the person to whom the heroine turns for rescue in the end. Usually, romantic tension accompanies danger in Whitney's novels, with the two resolved together at the close.

Whitney has worked as a dance instructor, children's book editor for two newspapers, and instructor in children's book writing. She is also known for writing about the art of writing and sharing her "how-to" tips with aspiring authors.

[See also Had-I-But-Known; Menacing Characters.]

• Phyllis A. Whitney, "Writing the Gothic Novel," *Writer* 80 (Feb. 1967). Phyllis A. Whitney, "Springboard to Fiction," *Writer* 89 (Oct. 1976). —Rosemary Herbert

WHODUNIT. The term "whodunit"—as in "Who done it?" "Who committed the murder?"—was coined in 1930 by D. Jordan in *American News of Books*. It refers to the form of writing invented by Edgar Allan *Poe in "The Murders in the Rue Morgue" (1841), one governed by a set of conventions requiring fair play in the telling of the *murder and presentation of *clues and the withholding of the identity of the murderer until the end. Because of the completeness of Poe's invention in its first appearance and the strictness with which writers obeyed the *conventions of the genre, several writers have catalogued the main features of the form. In "A Ghost Haunting America" (*In the Queen's Parlor*, 1957), Ellery *Queen listed the features of Poe's story that instantly became conventional; the eccentric detective, the confidant, the false trail, the *double bluff, the *least likely suspect as murderer, and others. Not every one need be used in every whodunit, but an inventory of Poe's story continues to be the best guide to the form. In her preface to *The Mysterious Mr. Campion* (1963), Margery *Allingham singled out a smaller group of essential features: "a Killing, a Mystery, an Enquiry and a Conclusion with an Element of Satisfaction in it."

The emphasis in the whodunit is on identifying the murderer; this means an emphasis on observing behavior and events, an emphasis on *plot. The murder usually happens offstage after the main characters, who are future *suspects, have been introduced, as in Jane Haddam's *Act of Darkness* (1991), but the reader may also witness the murder without realizing it, as in Ngaio *Marsh's *Swing, Brother, Swing* (1949; *A Wreath for Rivera*) or her *Death in Ecstasy* (1936). Again, the detectives may simply discover a body without any clue to its identity: this was common in the Mr. and Mrs. *North series by Frances and Richard Lockridge. The Norths find a body in a bathtub in an empty apartment in *The Norths Meet Murder* (1940).

The art of the whodunit comes in the *pursuit of the identity of the murderer through the skillful presentation of clues. The writer is expected to adhere to the standard of fair play; that is, the writer must present to the reader all clues essential to the solution of the crime. This does not mean, however, that the writer must reveal the significance of the clues. Indeed, the writer's task is to deceive the reader whenever possible. Dorothy L. *Sayers wrote of "The Art of Framing Lies" and Gwendoline Butler pointed out that the writer is telling one story while appearing to tell another. Queen emphasized this point when he chose a quotation from Mark Twain as an epigraph for *In the Queen's Parlor*; " . . . he told the truth, mainly." Misdirection is central to the whodunit, allowing the writer to convey information without conveying its significance—Agatha *Christie was a genius at this. The writer misleads the reader in several ways: by making false or erroneous suggestions about the significance of certain evidence, by diminishing the value of certain information, by offering an erroneous interpretation of a clue, by ignoring a piece of evidence.

Their skill at misdirection emboldened some writers to offer a formal challenge to the reader. This is a natural outgrowth of the intellectual competition between reader and writer implicit in this form. In the early novels, Queen issued a challenge to the reader after all the evidence necessary for a logical solution had been presented, a common feature of *Golden Age forms. Ronald A. *Knox provided page references for the clues in Still Dead (1934) and C. Daly King appended a comprehensive index of clues to Obelists Fly High (1935). This emphasis on clues accounts for the form's being characterized as a game in its earliest examples. E. C. *Bentley's Philip Trent chides the police inspector for not playing the game in Trent's Last Case (1913; The Woman in Black), and John Dickson *Carr called the form "The Grandest Game in the World." The whodunit has also been compared to a jigsaw *puzzle, and this game has supplied numerous metaphors for writers in the genre.

The pacing of the presentation of the clues determines in part the success of a whodunit. The writer maintains *suspense by revealing clues gradually, one at a time, building up a complex picture of what might have happened. At every step the reader is evaluating the writer's presentation and interpretation. This intellectual engagement is one of the main appeals of this fiction. The reader is not only interested in figuring out who perpetrated the crime but also in attending to how the writer is trying not to tell the truth directly.

The writer is striving for surprise and satisfaction at the final unveiling of the murderer's identity. Some writers put this off as long as possible; others prefer to have a longer period, or resolution, after the pronouncement to explain the details of the crime. In At the Villa Rose (1910), A. E. W. *Mason's Inspector *Hanaud unmasks the murderer two-thirds of the way through the narrative, whereas Rufus King names the killer on the final page of Murder on the Yacht (1932), just before dispatching him with a last equivocal comment. Anthony *Berkeley reveals the murderer only in the closing sentence of Jumping Jenny (1933; Dead Mrs. Stratton). Clifford Witting appears to identify the killers quite early but ultimately surprises the reader at the end with a further revelation in The Case of the Michaelmas Goose (1938). For many decades the dominant convention was to identify the murderer in the penultimate chapter and close with a thorough discussion of the evidence. In more recent years, writers have developed a new convention of allowing the murderer's identity to emerge gradually so that the surprise is muted at the end.

The emphasis on plot, on identifying one person through the intellectual examination of evidence, has the consequence of diminishing other features of fiction, in particular, *characterization. The whodunit never focuses on the inner life of its characters, relying instead on the stock figures of the time: the rich industrialist, the arrogant government official, the bumbling diplomat, the socialite, the young schoolteacher. Anyone can be reduced to his or her occupation, sex, or *class in order to play a role in the game.

The emphasis on plot and the deemphasis on character can lead to caricature and farce, but the whodunit is not by definition humorous. It can range in style from the fey novels of Edmund *Crispin featuring Gervase *Fen to the more solemn work of S. T. Haymon. Recent authors have eschewed the upper-class *milieu of early examples. Joan Hess's Roll Over and Play Dead (1991) is set on a working ranch and Gwen Moffat's Snare (1987) takes place in a bleak village in Scotland. Combined with this broadening of milieus is a greater awareness of social issues, which now appear as background. Although many readers do not recognize the social commentary implicit in Bentley's villain in Trent's Last Case, Haymon's feelings on the ethics of terrorists are plain in A Beautiful Death (1994). The trend to more or less social background is secondary to the close attention paid to the details of the murder. This is not a denial of the importance of these social issues but only an affirmation of a different sort of pleasure to be gained from the whodunit.

• Erik Routley, The Puritan Pleasures of the Detective Story (1972). LeRoy Panek, Watteau's Shepherds: the Detective Novel in Britain, 1914–1940 (1979).   —Susan Oleksin

WHO-GETS-AWAY-WITH-IT. Although crime fiction on the whole endorses the precept that crime should not pay, there are three situations in classical crime fiction in which an individual gets away with committing a crime. In the first, the criminal outwits or evades the forces of the law. In the second, the detective decides not to press charges for some reason. In a third group of stories the malefactor emerges scot-free by exploiting inadequacies, technicalities, or loopholes in the law.

Villain-centered stories fall into the categories of studies of criminal mentality and accounts of ingenious scams. The concerns of the former exclude them from consideration here because they focus on internal psychological states rather than external reality. In the second type of story, the reader may sympathize with the protagonist's dishonest scheme—usually *theft or fraud but sometimes *murder.

For example, the malefactor may right a previous wrong, as when an unrepentant Montresor tells the tale of his undetected and unpunished *revenge killing in Edgar Allan *Poe's "The Cask of Amontillado" (Godey's Lady's Book, Nov. 1846). Or perhaps the unfortunate villain tries to compensate for his unfair social disadvantages. Zachary Stone's The Modigliani Scandal (1976) exposes the *greed, snobbery, and incompetence of the *London art establishment and concurrently reveals the plight of struggling young painters. Occasionally, elaborate philosophical and moral rationalizations are introduced to justify the breaking of the law. In Martin Page's *The Man Who Stole the Mona Lisa* (1984; *Set a Thief*), the main character concocts a complex plan to steal the Mona Lisa from the Louvre in Paris because he objects to the practice of locking up great art where most people have no access to it. In some books the protagonist is merely a clever rogue who is so ingenious that he wins the reader's support. E. W. *Hornung's A. J. *Raffles, who appears in *The Amateur Cracksman* (1899; *Raffles, the Amateur Cracksman*), is a member of this fraternity, as is Bernie Rhodenbarr in Lawrence *Block's *Burglars Can't Be Choosers* (1977). Sometimes a positive good results from the crime. A Robin Hood motif occurs in Leslie *Charteris's series featuring Simon Templar, gentleman outlaw and knight-errant.

Of course, getting away with murder, as opposed to robbery, is a much more serious matter. When the crime is excused in investigator-centered fiction, it is usually because of extenuating circumstances. For example, the deed was an accident but it cannot be proved. Poe set the precedent in this regard in "The Murders in the Rue Morgue" (*Graham's Lady's and Gentleman's Magazine*, Apr. 1841) when The Chevalier C. Auguste *Dupin decides not to prosecute the owner of the violent orangutan because there was no criminal intent in the grotesque deaths of Madame L'Espanaye and her daughter.

The *sleuth may keep silent because the perpetrator was provoked and struck out in self-defense, as in Arthur Conan *Doyle's "The Adventure of the Abbey Grange" (*Strand*, Sept. 1903). Sherlock *Holmes allows Captain Crocker to rejoin his ship because the man he accidentally killed—an alcoholic wife-abuser—attacked him first in a maniacal rage.

Other grounds for "justifiable homicide" include murders in which the *victim is a moral leper beyond the reach of the law. Holmes holds his tongue in cases where the victim is himself a murderer or has injured others, as in "The Adventure of Charles Augustus Milverton" in *The Return of Sherlock Holmes* (1905), "The Adventure of the Red Circle," and "The Adventure of the Devil's Foot" (*His Last Bow*, 1917).

Sometimes the release of the villain averts the suffering of other people. In America's first detective novel, Seeley *Regester's *The Dead Letter* (1867), the detective Mr. Burton allows both the killer and his accomplice to go free in order to avoid emotional distress for his clients.

In other cases, the culprit may already have paid for his crime. In R. Austin *Freeman's *Mr. Pottermack's Oversight* (1931), Dr. John *Thorndyke decides not to expose a killer because he was previously framed by his victim for a crime he didn't commit and imprisoned. Dr. Thorndyke's decision is not lightly taken, and Freeman includes a long discussion of the ethical considerations in the case.

Youth and old age are also factors in determining whether the detective will press charges. In a few stories Holmes keeps his own counsel in order to give a young person a second chance ("The Adventure of the Three Students" and "The Adventure of the Priory School" in *The Return of Sherlock Holmes*, 1905). In Ellery *Queen's *The Finishing Stroke* (1958),

*Queen solves two related murders twenty-seven years after they happened and confronts the perpetrator, who admits his guilt. Because he lacks hard evidence and because the malefactor is ninety-two years old, Queen decides to let the matter drop.

Occasionally, political considerations intervene. In Rex *Stout's novella *Immune to Murder* (in *Three for the Chair*, 1955), private murder motivated by sexual jealousy goes unpunished because the villain is protected from prosecution by diplomatic immunity.

In some instances, the criminal outwits or evades the sleuth. Perhaps the most famous episode of the detective outsmarted occurs in Doyle's "A Scandal in Bohemia" (*Strand*, July 1891) when Irene *Adler wins Holmes's admiration and respect by penetrating both his *disguise and the false fire alarm designed to trick her into revealing the hiding place of the compromising photograph of the king of Bohemia.

Alternatively, the detective may be unable to marshal proof sufficient for an arrest, as happens in Anthony Berkeley Cox's *The Poisoned Chocolates Case* (1929). Very rarely, the culprit escapes arrest because the detective is emotionally involved with him/her as in George *Baxt's *A Queer Kind of Death* (1966).

Sometimes an author attempts to justify a villain's crimes but the rationalizations are inadequate and reveal instead the author's own hostility to authority or latent anarchic tendencies. Baroness Emmuska *Orczy's tales of Bill Owen in *The Old Man in the Corner* (1909) disclose this attitude.

The third group of tales reveals problems inherent in the law or the judicial system. With the publication of *The Strange Schemes of Randolph Mason* (1896; *Randolph Mason: The Strange Schemes*) followed by *The Man of Last Resort* (1897; *The Clients of Randolph Mason; Randolph Mason: The Clients*), Melville Davisson *Post introduced a new type of crime story in which the cantankerous attorney Randolph Mason exploited loopholes in the law to benefit his clients. In "Corpus Delicti" (in *The Strange Schemes of Randolph Mason*), for example, Mason advises a client how to commit murder and escape punishment on a legal technicality. Other inadequacies of the law treated in this subgenre include the fallibility of the principle of double jeopardy (Agatha *Christie's "Witness for the Prosecution," collected in *The Witness for the Prosecution*, 1948) as well as the overreliance on circumstantial evidence and the limitations of the McNaghten rules (Julian *Symons, *The Colour of Murder*, 1957). Procedural flaws including the unreliability of witnesses or jurors are examined in Edward Lustgarten's *A Case to Answer*, (1947; *One More Unfortunate*) and Raymond Postgate's *Verdict of Twelve* (1940), while the incompetence of investigating officers or the deliberately obstructive actions of attorneys and judges are addressed in Richard Hull's *Excellent Intentions* (1938; *Beyond a Reasonable Doubt*). The recent spate of mysteries with legal backgrounds written by lawyers, such as Scott Turow's *Presumed Innocent* (1987), offers interesting departures from earlier approaches by providing examples of victim-centered narratives.

[*See also* Villains and Villainy.]   —B. J. Rahn

WHO-WAS-DUN-IN refers to a category of detective fiction in which the central interest lies in discovering the true identity of the *victim. Although the term did not appear until 1971 with the publication of Jacques Barzun and Wendell Hertig Taylor's *A Catalogue of Crime*, credit for originating the who-was-dun-in rightly belongs to the American novelist Patricia McGerr, whose *Pick Your Victim* (1946) was immediately recognized as having broken new ground. (Earlier novels in which an unidentified body is found—*Whose Body?*, Dorothy L. *Sayers's novel of 1923, is, as its title indicates, an example—had fallen broadly within the existing conventions.) In McGerr's novel, a group of Marines discover a torn newspaper clipping which reveals that Paul Stetson has admitted killing a colleague; however, the name of his victim is missing. One member of the group had worked with Stetson, and the bored men while away time by listening to his account of the personalities involved and trying to guess whom Stetson strangled. The mystery is solved through psychological understanding: Stetson was a potential murderer only because one particular co-worker was a potential victim. McGerr adopted a similar approach in *The Seven Deadly Sisters* (1947), but included a mystery about the identity of the killer as well as of the victim. In her fifth novel, *Follow, as the Night* (1950; *Your Loving Victim*), she again returned to the who-was-dun-in.

As interest has increased in the *motive that can drive one human being to murder another, the possibilities of this type of novel have become apparent, but so have its drawbacks. Typically, the book will begin with a description of a victim's death or the discovery of a *corpse and a flashback will follow in which the events leading up to the crime are described in detail before the final disclosure (which may or may not occur as a result of shrewd detective work) of the victim's identity and often also that of the culprit. The danger is that the pace may flag, and thus writers employ a range of plotting techniques in order to maintain reader interest.

The Man Who Didn't Fly (1955) by Margot Bennett is a clever variation on the basic theme. Four men are due to board an airplane, yet only three do so; when the plane crashes into the sea and the bodies cannot be recovered, the police must establish who the fourth man is and why he did not fly. Bennett intersperses with the flashbacks short chapters set in the present and thereby manages to keep the central mysteries clear in the reader's mind without sacrificing momentum. Writing as Barbara Vine, Ruth *Rendell has shown the flexibility of the who-was-dun-in in providing a structural framework for novels of unquestioned literary excellence. *A Fatal Inversion* (1987) starts with the discovery of a human skeleton in an animal graveyard; blending scenes from past and present, Vine creates almost unbearable tension. Julian *Symons's *Something like a Love Affair* (1992) begins when an old man reports the discovery of a body without identifying its sex. Symons then combines a perceptive study of the disintegration of a woman's life with brief references to the continuing police inquiries, before revealing culprit, victim, and

motive in a startling climax. The continuing popularity of the who-was-dun-in is shown by Robert Richardson's *The Hand of Strange Children* (1993). His method is to interweave extracts from news agency reports detailing the discovery of two bodies with flashbacks told in both the first and third person. Again the careful judgment of time-shifts contributes to the building of *suspense. By treating the apparent limitations of the who-was-dun-in as a challenge, writers have transformed it into one of the most effective of all forms of mystery fiction.

[*See also* Taking of Life; Whodunit; Whydunit.]

• Jacques Barzun and Wendell Hertig Taylor, *A Catalogue of Crime*, rev. ed. (1989). James R. McCahery, "Patricia McGerr," in *St. James Guide to Crime and Mystery Writers*, 4th ed., ed. Jay P. Pederson (1996).   —Martin Edwards

WHYDUNIT. In contrast with the *whodunit, which is concerned with establishing the identity of a criminal, the whydunit has the mission to answer the question of why a crime has been committed. While the detective in the whodunit seeks to establish material *motive for the crime, the *sleuth in the whydunit explores the psychological *motivation that drives a person to perpetrate a crime. Whydunits can proceed in linear time as do most classic detective stories, but they are much more likely than whodunits to move differently through time and to reveal more points of view, utilizing flashbacks and the inner thoughts of a variety of characters.

Some whydunits are *inverted detective stories, in which the perpetration of the crime and the identity of the criminal are revealed at the start; the rest of the work is concerned with elucidating why the criminal committed the crime while keeping the reader wondering if the criminal will be caught. When whydunits do not reveal the identity of the perpetrator early on, much focus is placed on the investigator's work at creating a psychological profile of the criminal, with the result of establishing a profoundly drawn psychological identity rather than simply identifying the fact of who committed the crime. The whydunit is therefore the most character-driven subgenre in crime and mystery writing.

*Crime novels, mystery stories, *thrillers, and *Had-I-But-Known fiction, which keep characters and readers in the dark while threatening situations are slowly resolved, are likely to incorporate elements of the whydunit. *Menacing characters including *serial killers and mass murderers are frequently used types in this subgenre, since understanding their psyches is often necessary to anticipating their next crimes and apprehending them. Patricia D. Cornwell's works exemplify the use of the criminal profiler, a professional who uses psychological training to interpret forensic evidence. Enigmatic characters such as the title figure in Daphne *du Maurier's *Rebecca* (1938) are also ideal types for the whydunit, since becoming acquainted with the motivations of the deceased character is essential to resolving a mystery.

Comedic characters, too, can be central to much

more lighthearted whydunits. Such is the case in Nigel Williams's *The Wimbledon Poisoner* (1990), which explores the mental makeup of a would-be wife murderer; in Ellis Parker Butler's "Our First Burglar" (*Everybody's Magazine*, 1909; "The Silver Protector"), which illuminates the paranoia of a man who does in an intruder with a Rube Goldbergian burglar trap of his own invention; and in Catherine Aird's "The Man Who Rowed for the Shore" (*Injury Time*, 1994), which depicts the predicament of a wife killer who tries to dispose of the victim's ashes at sea in the company of her bereaved and increasingly suspicious relatives.

Sometimes the result of character-driven whydunits is an ambivalent view of crime. When the actions of a criminal become psychologically explicable, they can also become understandable and even rather pardonable. While this is rarely, if ever, the case in fiction featuring serial killers, readers may find themselves feeling sympathetic to perpetrators of lesser crimes portrayed in mystery fiction. An example is Josephine *Tey's *Brat Farrar* (1949; *Come and Kill Me*), in which a highly personable young man is talked into impersonating the heir to a fortune. Readers may also hope that crimes are not pinned on characters who are less likable. In Ruth *Rendell's novel *Going Wrong* (1990), the narrator is a conniving manipulator whose actions lead the police to wrongly suspect him of the crime. Readers, knowing that the protagonist is innocent, may empathize with the character's predicament even if they cannot condone his behavior.

[*See also* Howdunit.]

—Louise Conley Jones

Williams, Race. Although Carroll John *Daly created the prototype of the *private eye in his short story "The False Burton Combs" (*Black Mask*, Dec. 1922), the protagonist in that story, possibly because he remained unnamed and was not a series character, did not gain the fame of Daly's character Race Williams, who has gone down in the pages of literary history as the prime exemplar of the hard-boiled dick. The tough-talking Williams toted two forty-fives to back up his heroic courage in the face of the *underworld figures and corrupt politicians that he encountered in eight novels and numerous short stories, many of which were published in *Black Mask* and the *pulp magazines. A selection of the short stories is collected in *The Adventures of Race Williams* (1987). The Williams character helped to establish the hard-boiled traditions of working according to a personal code of honor and of viewing most women with *suspicion or indifference. Williams is pursued by a red-haired siren known as "The Flame."

[*See also* Black Mask School; Hard-Boiled Sleuth; Mean Streets Milieu; Urban Milieu; Violence.]

—Rosemary Herbert

WILLS. Ever since the Victorian age, the will, or legal statement of a person's wishes for the disposal of property after death, has played an important part in mystery fiction. Moreover, the technical legal rules on wills and settlements have proved a fertile source of *plot ideas and the prospect of inheritance has served as a timeless *motive for *murder.

Nineteenth-century authors were quick to see that the law on wills and inheritance could provide the framework for an elaborate mystery. Wilkie *Collins, who had trained as a barrister, was fascinated by the way in which the law might be exploited for criminal gain. A key point in *The Woman in White* (1860) is that if Laura Fairlie dies childless before her husband, he inherits £20,000, a sum she cannot bequeath to any other beneficiary. In "Mr. Bovey's Unexpected Will" by L. T. Meade and Robert Eustace (*The Third Bedside Book of Great Detective Stories*, 1978), inheritance under a miser's will depends on the claimant's body weight, whereas Arthur Conan *Doyle's "The Adventure of the Three Garridebs" (*Collier's*, 25 Oct. 1924) concerns "the queerest will that has ever been filed in the State of Kansas." Later writers showed even more *ingenuity; for example, in *The Eye Of Osiris* (1911; *The Vanishing Man*), R. Austin *Freeman's Dr. John *Thorndyke solves with the aid of X rays a *puzzle based upon a will that contains curious provisions about where the testator should be buried.

Ingenious use of the will as a plot device was made by many Golden Age writers, including Agatha *Christie, whose "Motive v. Opportunity" (*Miss Marple*, 1985) concerns a bequest written in disappearing ink, and Dorothy L. *Sayers, whose "The Fascinating Problem of Uncle Meleager's Will" (*Lord Peter*, 1972) offers crossword puzzle clues to a fortune. In novels, the terms of a will often provide the inspiration for a complex puzzle; examples can be found in books as diverse as Sayers's *Unnatural Death* (1927; *The Dawson Pedigree*) and the *Detection Club's *The Floating Admiral* (1931), which boasts an appendix containing a counsel's opinion on the legal implications of the Fitzgerald will.

The very title of Christie's *Why Didn't They Ask Evans?* (1934; *The Boomerang Clue*) is an allusion to the witnessing of a rich man's will. Ellery *Queen's *The Greek Coffin Mystery* (1932) involves the search for a missing will; Harry Stephen Keeler made frequent and inventive (sometimes bizarre) use of wills as a means of developing his spider web plots in novels such as *The Spectacles of Mr. Cagliostro* (1929; *The Blue Spectacles*). Many short stories turn upon a single point of law, such as Cyril *Hare's "Where There's a Will" (*The Best Detective Stories of Cyril Hare*, 1959), which highlights a limitation on the general rule that marriage invalidates a will, and Michael *Gilbert's "Xinia Florata" (*Stay of Execution*, 1971), which is based on the principle that a will that observes the legal requirements may take any form.

In the past half century, writers working within the tradition of the classic *whodunit have continued to explore the possibilities of wills. They include American authors such as Erle Stanley *Gardner, Rex *Stout, and the less well-known Michael A. Kahn, in whose *The Canaan Legacy* (1988; *Grave Desire*) a will establishes a fund to maintain the grave of a pet that the testator never owned. Hare, a barrister, wrote several novels in which legal points are significant elements. In *That Yew Tree's Shade* (1954; *Death Walks the Woods*), Francis Pettigrew's recollection of a dispute over Dr. Hawley Harley Crippen's estate furnishes a crucial clue to the puzzle. The opportunity that a solicitor may have to forge a will forms the basis of Elizabeth Lemarchand's *Buried in the Past* (1974), and the plot elements of Catherine Aird's *A Going Concern* (1993) include a will, a codicil, a precatory trust, and the testator's request for a police presence at her funeral. Julian *Symons's *The Belting Inheritance* (1965) is unusual in that the terms of the vital bequest are only revealed at the end of the book. Such novels may be regarded as *cozy mysteries, but Reginald *Hill's *Child's Play* (1987), in which an eccentric old woman leaves a fortune to be split between an animal rights organization, a services benevolent fund, and a fascist front, has a harder edge.

Short stories centering upon wills in recent years have come from many writers. In P. D. *James's "Great Aunt Allie's Fly-Papers" (*Verdict of Thirteen*, edited by Julian Symons), for example, a legatee's conscience prompts Adam *Dalgliesh to look into an old case, and Sarah Caudwell's "An Acquaintance with Mr. Collins" (*A Suit of Diamonds*, 1990) makes telling reference to one of the inaugurators of this branch of mystery fiction, the eponymous Wilkie Collins.

[*See also* Legal Procedural.]

• Jon L. Breen, *Novel Verdicts: A Critical Guide to Courtroom Fiction* (1984).

—Martin Edwards

Wimsey, Lord Peter. Created by Dorothy L. *Sayers as her major series character, Lord Peter Wimsey surely the best-remembered *aristocratic sleuth. The second son of the fifteenth duke of Denver, Peter Death Bredon Wimsey was introduced in *Whose Body?* (1923) and appeared in ten subsequent novels and twenty-one short stories. Sayers claimed she did not "remember inventing Lord Peter," that he "walked in complete with spats" into her imagination. This may be true, but she toyed with him as a character in an unpublished detective story for children and an unfinished play before he appeared in print. His last appearance in a novel is in *Busman's Honeymoon* (1937), though he figures in two later short stories, some wartime propaganda articles in the *Spectator* (1939–1940), and a 1954 radio feature on Sherlock *Holmes.

Various sources of inspiration have been suggested with more or less justification as influencing Sayers in her creation of Wimsey, but a literary derivation seems most plausible, from Philip Trent, the protagonist of E. C. *Bentley's *Trent's Last Case* (1913; *The Woman in Black*). Wimsey and Trent share many attributes, including their "amateur" attitude toward investigation; in earlier books Wimsey also resembles P. G. Wodehouse's Bertie Wooster, a likeness heightened by the Jeevesian qualities of his manservant Mervyn Bunter. Sayers's desire to raise the artistic standing of the detective story to that of a *novel of manners meant humanizing Wimsey to make him a three-dimensional hero and a plausible marriage partner. The result is a rounder, mellower character, more vulnerable than the majority of fictional detectives, at least those of the *Golden Age, and one of the few that matures with the passage of time.

Wimsey is given a varied career. Born in 1890, educated at Eton and Balliol, he took a first-class honors degree in history and was decorated for his service in World War I. His first love affair ended during the war. After the war he resides with Bunter at 110A Piccadilly. In keeping with his education, he is knowledgeable about art, a musician of "some skill and more understanding," and a book collector with a wide literary appreciation. Thanks to his skill with words, he fares nicely as a temporary advertising copywriter in *Murder Must Advertise* (1933). Wimsey is also a gourmet with an encyclopedic knowledge of wine; he is skilled in campanology, espionage, and cracking codes; a renowned cricketer; and adept in the arts of self-defense. These qualities, except perhaps the music, assist him in his cases, as do his wealth, generosity, and way with women. He is a kind of ideal Englishman, like Holmes before him, but only up to a point, for he has his faults. He is not racist by the standards of his time or even, as some commentators have asserted, snobbish, but his arrogance is sometimes resented and his rudeness to an admittedly tiresome houseguest in *Talboys* (1942) is embarrassing. His quick-witted intelligence is not generally in doubt, but one feels he is slow to tumble to the truth in *Have His Carcase* (1932) and *The Nine Tailors* (1934).

Sayers surrounds her *sleuth with a diverse group of relatives and associates, who constitute much of the attraction of her novels. Bunter, who was Wimsey's sergeant during World War I, later serves as photographer, valet, cook, and factotum. Wimsey is also assisted by Alexandra Katherine Climpson, who runs a typing pool. Wimsey's older brother is charged with *murder in *Clouds of Witness* (1926), and his sister falls in love with and marries an inspector from *Scotland Yard. The defining moment of Wimsey's career and his life, however, comes when he meets Harriet *Vane, with whom he falls in love in *Strong Poison* (1930), when she is on trial for murder. Harriet, because of her experiences, is slow to succumb but Wimsey finds strength and fulfillment in his courtship with her in *Gaudy Night* (1935) and their marriage in *Busman's Honeymoon*; they eventually have three sons. In every story Sayers carefully depicts the English social background of the interwar years in which Wimsey operates. So deeply did she imagine Wimsey that eventually she produced a volume entitled *Papers Relating to the Family of Wimsey*, which was published privately in 1936. It is hardly surprising that his creator said that his affairs were more real to her than her own.

[*See also* Gentleman Sleuth; Great Detective; Sidekicks and Sleuthing Teams.]

• Dorothy L. Sayers, "How I Came to Invent the Character of Lord Peter," *Harcourt Brace News*, 15 July 1936. Dorothy L. Sayers, "Gaudy Night," in *Titles to Fame*, ed. D. K. Roberts (1937). Philip L. Scowcroft et al., *Sidelights on Sayers*, vols. 1–47 (beginning in (1981). Kathleen Slack, *The Character of*

Lord Peter Wimsey (1981). Catherine Kenney, *The Remarkable Case of Dorothy L. Sayers* (1990). Barbara Reynolds, *Dorothy L. Sayers: Her Life and Soul* (1993).

—Philip L. Scowcroft

WISECRACK. *See* Voice: Wisecracking Voice.

Withers, Miss, angular of frame and equine of face, is the creation of Stuart Palmer and appears in fourteen novels and more than two dozen short stories published between 1931 and 1969. A spinster schoolteacher (rarely observed at her profession), Hildegarde Withers wears elaborate hats, carries a cotton umbrella and an oversized handbag, and is accompanied by an apricot poodle, Talleyrand. Miss Withers solves crimes with her good friend and cigar-smoking foil, Inspector Oscar Piper of the *New York Police Department. She is sometimes referred to as being on leave from her duties at Jefferson Grammar School or P. S. 38, or in the later books recently retired, to explain how she has time to detect. In retirement, she moves to *Los Angeles, occasionally returning to New York to bedevil Piper. She is sharp of eye and wit, noticing the small things others overlook and solving mysteries by intuition. In print, she is more a figure of eccentricity than the broad caricature portrayed in films. Miss Withers keeps regular hours and picks a lock with ease, but is no mistress of *disguise. On occasion, she has been known to solve criminous *puzzles in the company of Craig *Rice's John J. Malone.

[*See also* Spinster Sleuth.]   —J. Randolph Cox

WITNESS. An essential character in virtually all crime and mystery fiction, the witness may be defined as one who has observed an activity, remark, or other piece of information that is germane to understanding the case in question. Such observations may be accomplished visually, auditorily, or by means of various technologies, including by means of sophisticated surveillance. Even more sophisticated means of witnessing include the application of special knowledge like art or antiques expertise, archaeological skills, or cultural awareness that permits one to see from a special perspective what others see in a less informed and therefore less revealing manner.

Witnessing not only involves being in the right place at the right time to observe an action but also entails giving evidence to a detective or, more formally, doing so in a courtroom. In the first case, the delivery of information may occur in the proverbial library or any one of a variety of isolated *settings, or in the police interrogation room. Since such witnesses usually are not overheard by other witnesses, the reader may feel at an advantage in evaluating their accounts of the crime. A courtroom witness, however, must deliver his or her testimony in public or in front of other characters who may then alter their own testimony with the knowledge of what has been said by the earlier witness. Writers, like the lawyers that they portray, often enjoy pitting one witness against another, thereby increasing courtroom drama and manipulating the reader.

Vitally useful to the author, the truthful or reliable witness can substantiate or negate the truth at many stages of a criminal investigation or courtroom drama. The unreliable witness can conveniently confuse the *sleuth—and reader—along the path to a solution to the crime or throughout the courtroom action. Most crime and mystery novels employ a number of witnesses and, because the writer does not identify which are trustworthy and which are not, it is essential for the reader to evaluate the reliability of each. Sorting out the often conflicting accounts or testimonies of witnesses often becomes a central action in crime and mystery fiction, both for the detective and the reader. Doubt about the reliability of each assures that those who play the roles of witnesses must also be viewed as *suspects until the case is finally solved.

Witnesses may also be used to advantage by the author to enhance *suspense, increase emotional drama, and provide points of view beyond simple observation of criminal activity. Frequently, suspense is sustained when a witness becomes vulnerable to the criminal. If the witness is also a child or in some manner helpless, suspense is further heightened. Examples are the boy Bert Hall in Nicholas Blake's *The Whisper in the Gloom* (1954) and the wheelchair-bound Hal Jeffries in Cornell Woolrich's "Rear Window" (*Dime Detective*, Feb. 1942), both of whom put themselves in jeopardy when they play at crime solving.

Witnessing need not be limited to observing an action. One of the most memorable witnesses in detective fiction is the dog that failed to bark in the night in Arthur Conan *Doyle's "Silver Blaze" (*Strand*, Aug. 1908), whose silence testified to the animal's familiarity with a person on the premises. This story also proves that one need not be human to be an effective witness.

[*See also* Truth, Quest for.]   —Rosemary Herbert

Wolfe, Nero, perhaps the best-known private investigator in mystery fiction after Sherlock *Holmes and Hercule *Poirot. Weighing approximately "one-seventh of a ton," Rex *Stout's great man changes almost not at all (he remains in his mid-fifties) in the series of 33 novels beginning with *Fer-de-Lance* (1935) and 38 novelettes. Wolfe is a man of fixed routine and multiple eccentricities. His enormous size is maintained by the superb cuisine provided by his chef, the incomparable Fritz Brenner, by his daily consumption of a good amount of beer, and by his sedentary life; he is memorable for an aversion to leaving his brownstone on *New York City's West Thirty-fifth Street and for a horror of riding in mechanized vehicles; his irascibility is well known, as is his insistence on a daily regimen and the "rules" of the house (*e.g.*, no smoking and no business conversation during meals). A voracious reader of intellectually challenging books, Wolfe can remember their content down to the page number, and he spends four hours a day in his fourth-floor plant rooms, where he and his gardener, Theodore Horstmann, cultivate some 10,000 priceless orchids. His ratiocinative detection is internationally famous, as is his behavior toward his clients, which is condescending at best and often downright rude. His unapologetic misogyny and pedantic attitude toward grammar stand in stark contrast to his sensual delight in dining.

Since Wolfe is immobile and, according to Archie *Goodwin, so lazy, it is imperative that he have an active partner for legwork—and in Goodwin he has found the perfect man. Goodwin also serves as Wolfe's amanuensis and conversational foil, the person who goads him into taking cases when the bank account is low, and, ultimately, as his friend.

Wolfe's *modus operandi* is to ponder the information Goodwin gathers; to interview clients and others involved in the case; to plan strategies for tripping up nervous *suspects; and, while seldom giving even Goodwin a hint about what he is thinking, to narrow the list of suspects while never varying his daily personal routine. His signature device is to summon all those involved to his office in order to announce his conclusion and how he arrived at it. Since it is not Wolfe's job to arrest the criminal, usually Inspector Cramer of the New York Police Homicide Division, with whom Wolfe has a distinctly adversarial relationship, is present at these sessions, which Cramer calls Wolfe's "charades."

Like that of many heroes in literature and myth, Wolfe's personal background is mysterious and ambiguous. At one point he claims to have been born in the United States in the early 1890s; at another, that he is a naturalized citizen, having been born in Montenegro. There is even speculation that Sherlock Holmes was his father (accounting genetically for his deductive powers) and that Irene *Adler, the opera star created by Arthur Conan *Doyle, was his mother. The years 1913–16 are identified as a time when Wolfe served in Austro-Hungarian intelligence and the Montenegrin army; in 1917–18 he walked 600 miles to join the American Expeditionary Force and killed 200 Germans; from 1918 to 1921 he "moved around" and returned to the Balkans, where he adopted a daughter; 1922–28 are his "lost years"; and in 1930 he bought the brownstone, hired Goodwin, and began his career as *private detective. Meanwhile, his purported twin brother, Marko Vukcic, is mentioned frequently and eventually becomes the owner of Rusterman's restaurant in New York—one of the few places at which Wolfe will eat outside his own house.

A unique character, Wolfe remains unchallenged in the field of American deductive investigators. From his yellow pajamas to his folded hands over his immense girth, from his grumpy disposition to his brilliant mind, this notoriously taciturn character stands as one of fiction's most memorable *Great Detectives.

Since Stout's death in 1975, Robert Goldsborough, has continued the Wolfe saga, with the blessing of Stout's heirs and with modest success, starting with *Murder in E Minor* (1986) and adding a new novel almost every year thereafter.

[*See also* Armchair Detective; Eccentrics; Sidekicks and Sleuthing Teams.]

• William S. Baring-Gould, *Nero Wolfe of West Thirty-Fifth Street; The Life and Times of America's Largest Private Detective* (1969).
—Landon Burns

"Woman, The." *See* Adler, Irene.

WOOD, MRS. HENRY (1814–1887), born Ellen Price, English novelist and short-story writer whose work frequently included an element of crime. She is best known for the novel *East Lynne* (1861), which was successful both in print and as adapted to the Victorian stage. Suspected *murder figures in the novel *Trevlyn Hold; or, Squire Trevlyn's Heir* (1864), actual murder in *The Red Court Farm* (1865). It is the twelve volumes of *Johnny Ludlow* short stories (1874–99), however, which most closely resemble detective fiction.

According to E. F. Bleiler (*Twentieth Century Crime and Mystery Writers*, 2nd ed., 1985), Mrs. Wood is interested not so much in crime itself as in its impact on the social fabric and on the personalities of suspects. In this regard she can be counted among those whose explorations of "the problem of crime" contributed to the rise of the modern crime and detective genre.
—John M. Reilly

WOOLRICH, CORNELL (George Hopley) (1903–1968), popular and prolific American author of novels and stories in the noir manner. Woolrich published dozens of stories in the 1930s in such magazines as *Argosy*, *Black Mask*, and *Dime Detective*. The first of his *suspense novels was *The Bride Wore Black* (1940; *Beware the Lady*), followed by the rest of his "black" series: *The Black Curtain* (1941), *Black Alibi* (1942), *The Black Angel* (1943), *The Black Path of Fear* (1944), and *Rendezvous in Black* (1948). Under his pseudonym William Irish, he wrote *Phantom Lady* (1942), *Deadline at Dawn* (1944), *I Married a Dead Man* (1948), and *Strangler's Serenade* (1951). Under the name George Hopley, he penned *Night Has a Thousand Eyes* (1945). His fiction has been the basis of many films, radio plays, and television productions. Among the best-known are the films *Phantom Lady* (1944), *Rear Window* (1954, directed by Alfred Hitchcock, based on the story "It Had to Be Murder" in *Dime Detective*, Feb. 1942; "Rear Window"), and *Le mariée etait en noire* (1968, directed by François Truffaut, based on *The Bride Wore Black*).

By all accounts a lonely and tormented man, homosexual in an intolerant era, Woolrich was brought up in Latin America and New York by his ill-matched parents, a civil engineer and a socialite. He studied writing at Columbia University, wrote two romantic novels, and worked in Hollywood as a scriptwriter. His own marriage dissolved in a matter of weeks, after which he lived in a series of New York hotels with his mother until her death and then on his own as a virtual recluse. He found the ideal outlet for the bitterness and isolation of his own life in fiction noir melodrama. The most common themes of his novels are *mistaken identity, *revenge, and lost love; his most frequently used *plot device is the desperate race against time, usually concluding with an improbable victory for the protagonist. Critics in his own day judged Woolrich's plotting often awkward and unconvincing, his style tending to overwrought, and his characters one-dimensional. But against this must be weighed the fertility of Woolrich's imagination and the sheer power of his dark visions. In the "black" series in particular, he is remarkably adept at depicting the anxiety of the hunter and the hunted, usually in a darkly atmospheric urban setting. His stark vision of life, however, is somewhat vitiated by Woolrich's wish to satisfy his audience's presumed desire for romantic idealization and conventional *resolution. As recent interest in his work shows, Woolrich's suspenseful novels and stories continue to strike a responsive chord in readers.

[*See also* Deviance; Fiction Noir; Voyeurism.]

• Francis M. Nevins Jr., *Cornell Woolrich: First You Dream, Then You Die* (1988). Mark T. Bassett, ed., *Blues of a Lifetime: The Autobiography of Cornell Woolrich* (1991).

—Richard Steiger

YATES, DORNFORD, pseudonym of Maj. Cecil William Mercer (1885–1960), British author and barrister who assisted in the prosecution of Hawley Harley Crippen and served in both world wars. As well as humorous light romances, some of which have a detective element—like *Adele and Co.* (1931) and *The House That Berry Built* (1945)—Yates wrote a number of *adventure stories, set for the most part in Austria or southern France, in which the hero—usually Richard Chandos—often confronts the same gang of crooks. The standard motifs include booby-trapped treasure—as in *Blind Corner* (1927) and *Safe Custody* (1932)—and mass murder—as in *She Fell Among Thieves* (1935). Though the books were best-sellers during Yates's lifetime, his reactionary political views and *anti-Semitism, together with his lush style, now obscure their merits. Along with H. C. *McNeile and John *Buchan, Yates is one of three major *thriller writers of the 1920s and 1930s.

[*See also* Adventure Story; Conservative vs. Radical Worldview: Conservative Worldview; Political and Social Views, Authors'.]

• A. J. Smithers, *Dornford Yates: A Biography* (1982). Richard Usborne, *Clubland Heroes: A Nostalgic Study of Some Recurrent Characters in the Romantic Fiction of Dornford Yates, John Buchan and Sapper* (1983).   —T. J. Binyon

YOM KIPPUR. *See* Holiday Mysteries.

ZANGWILL, ISRAEL (1864–1926), British novelist, short story writer, essayist, playwright, poet, and translator. Born to immigrant parents in *London's Whitechapel ghetto, Zangwill was best known for his fictional portrayals of Anglo-Jewish life in London's East End and as a spokesperson for Jewish nationalism and other political and social causes. Although Zangwill's only major contribution to crime and mystery writing was *The Big Bow Mystery* (1892), this single novelette, serialized in 1891 in the London *Star*, exemplifies three conventions of the genre—the *locked room mystery, the perfect crime, and the *least likely suspect. Set in the working-class *milieu of London's East End, the novelette interweaves satiric views of detection and detectives and of the aesthetic movement of the 1880s. *The Big Bow Mystery* shares with Zangwill's other fiction not only its witty, ironic tone but also its use of newspaper accounts to build the narrative, the mark of Zangwill's own work as a journalist. Thematically, the novelette shares the concern with multiple identities that recurs throughout the author's fiction, including the short story "Cheating the Gallows" (*The King of Schnorrers: Grotesques and Fantasies*, 1893), the only other of Zangwill's works that approaches *Big Bow*'s focus on crime and mystery. Three films have been based on *The Big Bow Mystery*: *The Perfect Crime* (1928), *Crime Doctor* (1934), and *The Verdict* (1946).

• Maurice Wohlgelernter, *Israel Zangwill: A Study* (1964). Elsie Bonita Adams, *Israel Zangwill* (1971). Joseph H. Udelson, *Dreamer of the Ghetto: The Life and Works of Israel Zangwill* (1990). —Martha Stoddard Holmes

Glossary

Baker Street Irregulars   *n.* **1.** street urchins employed by Sherlock Holmes to gather information or follow up clues **2.** an organization of fans of Sherlock Holmes.

bobby   *n.* in Britain, a policeman; *pl.* bobbies, nickname for members of London's Metropolitan Police founded by Sir Robert Peel.

bodice-ripper   *n.* a sexually explicit or titillating novel or drama, especially one in which the heroine is seduced.

caper   *n.* a work of detective fiction characterized by playful antics on the part of the characters, who may perpetrate lesser crimes, such as burglary, rather than graver offenses, such as murder.

con   *n. abbrev.* convict. *v.* to trick, to hustle.

con artist   *n.* a person who gains the confidence of trust of another in order to swindle or cheat; a hustler.

cop, copper   *n.* a policeman. *v.* to capture, arrest.

cozy   *n.* a work of detective fiction in which violence generally occurs out of sight, the atmosphere is civilized, and social and household routines are celebrated.

crook   *n.* a professional criminal.

crooked   *adj.* dishonest, illegal, unscrupulous.

deep throat   *n.* an anonymous informer; from Carl Bernstein and Bob Woodward's famous Watergate source.

detective   *n.* a person who investigates crimes.

dick   *n.* a detective, from a shortening and altering of the word detective.

dime novel   *n.* a cheap popular novel.

Fed   *n.* any federal government agent, especially in law enforcement or taxation, often used plural, "the Feds."

femme fatale	*n.* a seductively attractive woman; a dangerous female.
gangster	*n.* a member of a gang of violent criminals.
gaudy	*n.* an annual feast, gathering, or entertainment, especially a college dinner for alumni.
gumshoe	*n.* a detective, after the soft-soled shoes worn for stealthy enterprises.
gun moll	*n.* **1.** an armed female **2.** a female thief.
HIBK	*n. abbrev.* Had-I-But-Known, a mystery novel in which a heroine is thrust into threatening circumstances with little knowledge of the criminal context in which she has been placed.
hard dick	*n.* a tough or recalcitrant male.
hard-boiled	*adj.* **1.** of a person: a tough character who is little affected by sentiment or fear **2.** of fiction: crime writing, especially private eye fiction or the police procedural, in which the prose is generally terse, the dialogue laconic and likely to be enlivened with wisecracks, and the action fast-paced and physical.
hard case	*n.* **1.** a tough, hard-bitten person, especially a criminal **2.** an intractable witness **3.** a delinquent or recalcitrant youth.
heavy	*n.* **1.** a person who commits crimes of violence, especially a thug **2.** a person who plays the role of villain in a drama or fiction.
high tea	*n.* a later-afternoon or evening meal, usually consisting of several dishes served with tea.
highbrow	*n.* an intellectual or a person who has pretensions of intellectual, cultural, or artistic superiority; a snob. *adj.* intellectual, cultured.
hit list	*n.* a list of persons targeted to be murdered or assassinated.
hit man/woman	*n.* a man/woman who is a hired killer.
hold up	*v.* to rob a person or institution by threatening the victim with a weapon. *n.* an armed robbery.
hood	*n. colloq. abbrev.* **1.** a hoodlum **2.** a neighborhood, especially within a city.
hoodlum	*n.* a loafer, street ruffian, thug, gangster.

hotfoot	*n.* a policeman, from the action of a policeman slapping a vagrant's feet to make him move; *v.* to take prompt action, run, flee.
howdunit	*n.* **1.** a work of detective fiction or crime writing primarily concerned with discovering a criminal's modus operandi **2.** a work of detective fiction in which a crime appears astonishing, difficult, or impossible to have been carried out, and in which the reader is eager to discover the manner in which the crime was perpetrated.
impossible crime	*n.* a crime that apparently could not have been accomplished by human hands, especially a locked-room murder.
ingenue	*n.* an innocent or unsophisticated young woman, or one who plays such a role.
inverted detective story	*n.* a crime novel or story in which the identity of the criminal, especially a murderer, is made known at the start and the action is centered around issues other than discovering whodunit.
kiss off	*v.* to murder.
knockover	*n.* an armed robbery or burglary.
locked room murder	*n.* a homicide that has occurred in a sealed chamber from which there is apparently no egress for the perpetrator who, nonetheless, has exited the scene of the crime.
lowbrow	*adj.* unintellectual, vulgar.
MO	*n., abbrev.* modus operandi, a criminal's method of procedure or usual pattern.
Mountie	*n.* nickname for a member of the Royal Canadian Mounted Police.
nick	*n.* **1.** police station **2.** prison. *v.* **1.** to steal **2.** to arrest.
op	*n. abbrev.* an operative, or private detective who works for an agency.
P.I.	*n., abbrev.* private investigator.
Peeler	*n.* **1.** in Britain, policeman **2.** a nickname for a member of London's Metropolitan Police, after the organization's founder, Sir Robert Peel.

penny dreadful *n.* a cheaply printed publication of sensational literature.

perfect crime *n.* a crime so cleverly done that it appears to have resulted from natural or accidental causes.

perfect murder *n.* a crime in which the murderer is not suspected.

private eye *n.* **1.** a private investigator **2.** a detective for hire. Allan Pinkerton, who used a human eye as the logo for his Pinkerton detective agency, is credited with the origin of the expression.

pulp fiction *n.* sensational writing printed on cheap paper.

senior common room *n.* a room used by senior members of a college.

serial *n.* a story presented in a series of installments.

serial killer *n.* a murderer who kills more than once.

series character *n.* a fictional character who appears in a number of stories, novels, or dramas.

shadow *n.* a detective; *v.* to follow.

shamus *n.* **1.** a policeman **2.** a private detective, after the Irish name Seamus.

shark *n.* a person who exploits others.

sidekick *n.* **1.** a close associate **2.** a detective's confidante, fellow adventurer, helpmeet.

sleuth *n.* a detective. *v.* to track, investigate, or ferret out (from the Old Norse slōth, track trail).

SOCO *n. abbrev.* scene of the crime officer.

third degree *n.* prolonged interrogation, usually by the authorities (including the police, military, or intelligence organizations), often accompanied by physical violence or the threat thereof.

thriller *n.* a novel in which suspenseful action is paramount.

thug *n.* **1.** a cutthroat, ruffian **2.** a heavy (from the Hindi for a professional robber and murderer who strangled the victim).

Watson; Watson figure *n.* **1.** a character who is sidekick to a sleuth, especially one who narrates accounts of the detective's activities, as Dr. John H. Watson recounted the adventures of Sherlock Holmes **2.** a character who is a helpmeet as well as sidekick to the sleuth, as is Bunter to Lord Peter Wimsey **3.** a detective's confidante.

whodunit   *n.* a work of detective fiction in which the action is centered around identifying the perpetrator of the crime.

whydunit   *n.* **1.** a work of crime writing in which the plot is centered around discovering the reason that the crime occurred **2.** a work of crime writing preoccupied with portraying a criminal's reasoning or psychological state.

Yard, The   *n.* New Scotland Yard, headquarters of London's Metropolitan Police.

Editors

Rosemary Herbert writes a mystery book review column for the *Boston Herald* and hosts the cable television program *Rosemary Herbert Investigates* on C3TV in Cape Cod, Massachusetts. Her articles and book reviews about crime and mystery writing have appeared in *The New York Times Book Review*, *The Paris Review*, *Publishers Weekly*, and elsewhere. She is the author of Anthony Award nominee *The Fatal Art of Entertainment: Interviews with Mystery Writers* (1994), for which she was dubbed "first lady of crime-writer interrogators." Herbert is the editor of *Murder on Deck! Shipboard and Shoreline Mystery Stories* (1998), which *The Wall Street Journal* described as "the most satisfactory anthology of the year." She has also edited *Twelve American Crime Stories* (1998) and, with Tony Hillerman, *The Oxford Book of American Detective Stories* (1996). She created a course in detective fiction at Tufts University and served as a reference librarian at Harvard University's Harry Elkins Widener Memorial Library.

Catherine Aird, who is a former chairman of the United Kingdom Crime Writers Association, is the author of more than sixteen detective novels and a volume of short stories. She has edited and published works on local history in Kent, England, where she lives. Aird was awarded the M.B.E. for her services to the United Kingdom Guide Association. She was given an honorary degree by the University of Kent at Canterbury in 1986 and was the first recipient of the CWA's Golden Handcuffs Award.

John M. Reilly is Professor of English and Director of the Graduate Program at Howard University. In 1980 he won an Edgar from the Mystery Writers of America for the best critical work of the year, *Twentieth Century Crime and Mystery Writers*. Subsequently he has served that organization as a judge for the Best First Mystery of the Year and the Best Biographical-Critical Work of the Year. Among his other prizes are the George Dove Award from the Detective and Mystery Literature section of the Popular Culture Association and a citation for distinguished study of popular and other ethnic literature from the Society for the Study of the Multi-Ethnic Literature of the U.S. His critical studies of mystery writing have appeared in many scholarly journals, and his books include *Richard Wright: The Critical Reception, Tony Hillerman: A Critical Companion*, and *Larry McMurtry*.

Index